LAST DAY

LAST DAY

A novel

Domenica Ruta

SPIEGEL & GRAU · NEW YORK

Published in the United States by Spiegel & Grau, an imprint of Random House, a division of Penguin Random House LLC, New York.

SPIEGEL & GRAU and colophon is a registered trademark of Penguin Random House LLC.

LIBRARY OF CONGRESS CATALOGING-IN-PUBLICATION DATA
Names: Ruta, Domenica, author.
Title: Last day: a novel / by Domenica Ruta.
Description: First edition. | New York: Spiegel & Grau, 2019.
Identifiers: LCCN 2018051202 | ISBN 9780525510819 (hardback) |
ISBN 9780525510826 (ebook) | ISBN 9781984855879 (international)
Subjects: | BISAC: FICTION / Literary. | FICTION / Coming of Age.
Classification: LCC PS3618.U776 L37 2019 | DDC 813/.6—dc23
LC record available at https://lccn.loc.gov/2018051202

Printed in the United States of America on acid-free paper

spiegelandgrau.com
randomhousebooks.com

9 8 7 6 5 4 3 2 1

First Edition

Book design by Jo Anne Metsch

For Will Stanton

Planet Earth is blue and there's nothing I can do

LAST DAY

"THERE SHE IS," he whispered to himself, as if a little surprised to still see her twinkling in the darkness.

It was universally agreed, Earth was always *she*. The astronauts needed to latch onto this umbilical pronoun, a reminder, while they were as far from home as one could be, that they were still human.

The form she took was different for everyone. Some astronauts saw an eye, others thought of her as a jewel. Just today Bear saw something new: the blue head of a baby, slathered in a caul made of clouds, crowning from out of a black womb. Bear remembered his own daughters being born, and the happy terror of that first, sickening glimpse.

It was the twenty-sixth of May. He had completed six months of his mission on the ISS and was already preparing for his exit, still six more months away. He was a three-hour ride from home, and though it was technically possible to make an early departure, no one in the short history of the International Space Station had ever deorbited before they were scheduled. What would it take, Bear wondered now, to justify an early exit? A medical emergency, or a family tragedy? What kind of calamity could he in good conscience withstand?

Bear stopped himself. This kind of future-tripping was dangerous. He knew that. He'd advised other astronauts at Johnson Space Center against the countdown mentality when preparing them for their missions. You can't stop the demons of isolation from knocking on your door, he'd say, but you can stop inviting them in for coffee.

He decided to take his own advice and redirect this morbid longing into something more productive: drafting notes for the things he would say about this mission after landing. There would be a barrage of interviews, both in-house and for publicity, and Bear put a lot of pressure on himself to say something no one had ever said before about the experience of space flight. This womb-birth analogy was quotable, with potential to go viral in the media, just the kind of thing he needed to preserve. He reached for the pad and pencil attached by cords to his sleeve, catching the pad but missing the pencil. He reached again and missed it, again and then again. Entwined with the floating pad, it eluded his grasp like a tiny pet playing tag.

"Got you," he said at last. He scribbled down his notes about the earth looking like a birth in progress, then immediately crossed them out. It was a stupid metaphor. He watched the sun rise over the earth for the eleventh time that day. The clouds unthreaded for a moment and he saw the staggering blue that could only be the shallow waters of the Caribbean.

No, he decided, taking one last look at the earth before heading back to work. What he saw through the windows of the Cupola was so much more than any single human birth, more than any man could pin down with words.

He pressed his hand against the thick glass. "There you are."

She was the biggest thing in the galaxy from this perspective, though really just a pebble. Less than a pebble. But a pretty one, Bear thought, prettier than any other; he wasn't afraid to admit this most basic chauvinism—to think of his home planet as better than all other bodies in space. She was his, after all. Or he was hers. He'd felt that on his first mission over a decade ago, and now on his second mission he felt it even more, a sense of humility so precious it dangled wildly on the edge of tragedy.

His watch vibrated with a reminder that his break in the Cupola was up. He'd spent as many minutes as he could possibly spare in this Earth-sick reverie. It was time to go.

SARAH MOSS HATED her name. It was a mistake, a fundamental one, with possibly catastrophic results for the rest of her life. Her last name, Moss, was okay, she guessed. Monosyllabic, rhizomatic, and green, *Moss* was actually pretty cool. *Sarah* was not and never would be.

But did she really *hate* her name? Hate had lust at its core, a dark quicksand of desire, which was a little dramatic, even for Sarah. And besides, how could she bring herself to hate something that was essentially a gift from her parents? The second gift they'd ever given her, life itself being the first. Even though her parents were the most annoying people she knew, they were eternally well intentioned, so it felt wrong to hate in any official way the name they had chosen for her. She was their first and only child. They must have been fumbling in a postnatal stupor when they'd picked out the name Sarah—she had to believe this. Something as boring as *Sarah* could not have been premeditated. They were probably tired. What could she expect of people in that state? They didn't even know her yet.

When Sarah was three and a half, she requested that her parents start calling her Buckle. Those two smiling syllables, like a drink of sweetened milk, never mind what they denoted. But her parents laughed at her—an eternally well-intentioned laugh—because it was funny, this tiny girl with big owl eyes and toy-sized glasses, asking to be called Buckle, and Sarah had burst into tears.

Science was a later pseudonym, the brainchild of her seven-year-old self. Science was her favorite subject at school, so adopting it as her name seemed like the next logical step. She confessed this wish only to her babysitter. Her parents had laughed at her once; she would not allow them to do it again.

"Human beings can't have names like *Science*," her babysitter snorted. She was an elderly next-door neighbor with black wiry hairs sprouting from her chin that she paid young Sarah a dime per hair to pluck out with rusty tweezers. "Especially not little girls," Mrs. Whiskers had said as a final judgment. Older now, Sarah knew this was a sexist and small-minded thing to say. It was pathological how much resentment she still harbored toward that lady and her chin hairs.

She asked her friends at school to call her Claudia when she was eleven. It sounded elegant and strong, as a girl approaching adolescence should be. But everyone kept forgetting, so Sarah let it go. Just last year, she'd made a case for elective name-changing at school, trying to piggyback onto the burgeoning transgender rights movement. "It's transnominalism," she'd said to Dr. Vasquez-McQueen, her guidance counselor. It didn't go over well. Sarah was a freshman in high school by then. It wasn't cute to think like this anymore. She understood that completely. She'd actually understood it the same day she tried (and failed) to pull off the Claudia conversion. It had been embarrassing and lame four years earlier, and now even more so.

There were over 1.6 million Sarahs in the world (she'd looked it up), and eight of them were at her high school—eight!—out of a student body of only fifty-two students. Plus at least a dozen more Sarahs in the lower school, and probably close to a hundred in her town's overcrowded public school system.

Famous Sarahs throughout history failed to inspire her. Even supposedly cool historical Sarahs couldn't be trusted, because who knew what was real and what was fiction when it came to famous people.

Of the not-famous Sarahs that Sarah Moss knew personally, all of them were seriously lacking. Sarah Wilmington, for example, was a senior at the Phoenix School who collected pewter figurines of dragons and unicorns, wore a variety of hand-stitched velvet capes, and wrote sad, sensual poetry, especially discomfiting, Sarah Moss felt, because everyone knew that Sarah Wilmington was a virgin. Sarah W. often hijacked the weekly all-school meetings to read her poetry out loud in that lispy voice of hers. "Juicy mangoes" and "sweat-studded skin." It was enough to make you puke. No one at school could really look each other in the eye after a few couplets from Sarah Wilmington.

Sarah Burke was a sophomore like Sarah Moss. She'd come to the school in the middle of freshman year, a transplant from some suburb in Connecticut that sounded identical to Edgewater, Massachusetts, their home now, though Sarah Burke loved to insist it was so different there. This Sarah had a nose so large it cast a shadow across her face, a feature Sarah Moss would have completely overlooked if Sarah Burke had been at all nice, but, and perhaps because of her nose, Sarah Burke had a cruel hatred of the world. The opposite of Sarah Wilmington, Sarah Burke had lots of sex. Sarah B. bragged that she blew random guys she met on the commuter rail to Boston. It was obvious to everybody but Sarah Burke that sex was a weapon she wielded with zero mastery, only hurting herself. She was often found crying in the girls' bathroom as she texted novella-length screeds to her uncaring lovers. Poor Sarah Burke. Except—no, she'd once made fun of Sarah Moss's dirty sneakers, so screw her.

Sarah Curtis and Sarah Mitzenberg had been best friends since fifth grade. They had a secret sign language and were totally insufferable. Sarah Hunt was way too proud of all the antidepressants she was taking. Sarah Jones picked her nose in public, then examined whatever she'd excavated on her fingertips for a long time. Up close. She had Asperger's, or something like that, it was reported, which made her easier to forgive, but the sight of her, even when not engaged in her oblivious grotesqueries, made Sarah Moss cringe.

And then there was Sara-without-an-H Toomey. A junior, this stream-lined Sara wasn't so bad. But she wasn't so good, either. She represented a perfect mediocrity, equally as far from being cool as being awful. Five minutes alone in conversation with this Sara left one longing for any-thing that evoked deep feeling—even failure, cruelty, pain!

These were her closest namesakes, this pseudo-sorority of Sarahs. It was dispiriting, and maybe even a portent of the coming end. The signs were everywhere. Genetic diversity was in decline—not too long ago there were thousands of species of apples grown in North America alone. Now? A few dozen. There were too many people in the world, and not enough resources to sustain them, not even enough names to go around. This was what was really troubling, Sarah thought—the growing lack of creativity. How many movies were exactly like other movies? How many times could people tell the same story? The world was running out of ideas. If there was any death knell for humanity, it was not peak oil or global warming or beehive collapse but the superfluity of Sarahs.

And her parents' response to all this?

"Stressosaurus Rex! Lighten up!"

The kitchen was warm and filled with the scent of butter and sugar. Light streamed in from the east and north, easing any sharp edges in its glow. The radio was set as ever to the local public classical station, to which the Mosses contributed annually, amassing an absurd number of tote bags. The first low notes of a Wagnerian prelude lapped over each other like currents in a great river.

"You're just a kid, Sarah. You should be worrying about boys."

"Or girls? We don't care. We love you unconditionally, no matter what."

"Have a brownie, kiddo. They're perfectly undercooked, just like you like them."

Their abundant love was an unwavering beam of light in Sarah's adolescent universe of doubt and dread. And it hurt more than anything else in the world that this did nothing to comfort her.

CHRISTIAN FUNDAMENTALISTS EAGER for Armageddon were always relatively calm on Last Day. Their Lord and Savior Jesus Christ would never pick some heathen festival for His rapture. No way in hell.

And yet these faithful lovers of Christ's promised end times were mistakenly lumped in with another faction known as Doomsdayers. A loose confederacy of pagan fundamentalists, Doomsdayers subscribed wholesale to all apocalyptic prophecies, regardless of contradiction: the almanacs of Nostradamus, the Book of Revelations, the Mayan calendar, the underwhelming turn of the millennium, the coming of Bahá'u'lláh, the prophecy in the Book of Daniel, the Frashokereti, and many more humble, homely tales spun out of that comforting nightmare that everything comes to an end.

Like alcoholics passing for normal amid the debauchery of St. Patrick's Day, during Last Day these apocalyptic lovers found a yearly pass to come out of their gloomy, conspiratorial hovels and party. They would take to the streets, littering city parks with their encampments, scaring away tourists with their sloppy bivouacs and homemade signs. Their children were pulled out of school, all normalcy and basic hygiene jettisoned, so that they could band together in a public display and wait for the inevitable nothing.

What they did after, when the world did not end, was almost sweet in its resilience. It never actually mattered to these people that the prophecy failed to fulfill. Their love for the end was everlasting. And so as the month of May ended, the Doomsdayers would slowly dismantle their camps, pour sand on the fire pits, fold up the tarps, pack up their vans (they were a van-driving folk), and return to whatever temporary place—in the worldly sense—they called home. They went back to normal, to *their* normal, in which fear and righteousness attended the mundane business of living. Standing over a sink of dirty dishes, a battered mother of three could look with tenderness toward the coming end. All those unmade beds, the children with ringworm, the bills in arrears, would eventually be obliterated. The abuse and betrayals, the longings and resentments, all the little and big failures, would be irrelevant. They simply had to wait for the next sign, the next opportunity, to give it all up again.

It was a miracle that none of these sects had yet to absorb the likes of Karen Donovan. She certainly met the criteria for a militant Doomsdayer: her passions were scattered all over the occult; she held fast to wild misinterpretations of life's most basic systems; she was all too willing to believe any message whose messenger burned with intensity, stoking her own easily inflamed heart; and finally, as she'd been excluded from every social group in her life so far, including the most basic unit of family, she was so hungry just to belong.

But you had to be willing to rough it to be a member of a doomsday cult, carry your share of canned goods, weaponry, and bedding, and Karen hated walking almost as much as she hated carrying. She would rather wait forty-five minutes for the bus than walk the five blocks from her house to the local library. And though her mental landscape was scorched with traumas, both real and grotesquely imagined, the end of the world didn't register high on her litany of fears.

Karen belonged to a different caste of crazy. Heavily medicated and monitored by a slew of social workers her whole, well-documented life, she had a talent for causing trouble for herself even within narrow parameters, restricted to her job at the YMCA, the Boston public library system, the counseling center where her long-suffering psychiatrist, Nora, saw her pro bono, and a group home where she was currently on very thin ice. At twenty, Karen was too old to qualify for many of the social services that had sustained her as a child, and the current administration's refusal to fund what few programs were out there for people at strange intersections of lunacy and competency limited Karen's options to only four group homes in the state, three of which she'd already been booted from.

Her most recent infraction had occurred at the Copley branch of the Boston Public Library, where she'd frightened little children with her totally earnest though still elementary attempts at augury. Sitting in on the library's story hour, the only adult without a child, she noticed a little boy's aura glowing wan and misshapen around his head and shoulders. After the story was over, she informed the child that although she wasn't totally sure, there was a good chance he had been raped, or if not, would be soon.

"It's okay, you can tell me. I have signed a safety contract with Nora to be always vigilant and aware of inappropriate touching," she'd explained to the boy, who ran to ask his unsuspecting mother, "Mummy, what's rape?" Phone calls were made, though not many. The trail back to Karen was straightforward and short. Nora was able to pull some strings and arrange for yet another relocation to her current group home at Heart House, as well as stop the library system from completely banning Karen, if she promised to switch branches and never enter the children's section again. Nora tinkered with Karen's regimen of antipsychotics and mood stabilizers and begged her, please, absolutely no more caffeine.

"Even Diet Coke?" Karen cried.

"Diet Coke has caffeine," Nora sighed, tugging on the gauzy scarf knotted around her throat as if to strangle herself.

"Okay. But what about Diet Pepsi?"

Together Nora and Karen wrote another social contract, which Karen signed and dated. Karen was quickly sobered by bureaucracy. Paperwork elicited in her a solemn deference, a tool Nora utilized in their ongoing therapy. Karen promised in writing that she would no longer talk to strangers about death, monsters (even in an allegorical sense), rape, natural disasters, or anything that took place in a bathroom.

So there was no way she was going to tell anyone about the voices.

They were old, familiar. She almost welcomed their return after such a long silence. Whispers tangled into her hair, making a nest. Only at night. They sounded like lizards, and hummingbirds, and sometimes mice, speaking a heavily accented English, their patois fractured and inconsistent. No instructions so far, Karen noticed with relief. Just a pleasant hypnogogic phenomenon, they disappeared once she fell asleep.

But after a few weeks the voices began filtering into her morning, then gradually persisted throughout the day. Karen attempted to greet them cheerfully, as Nora instructed her to do with difficult people in the realm of the real, to let them pass before her without engaging in a fight.

Then, on the evening of May 26, Karen heard a ghastly scene taking place under her bed: a snake was suckling the udder of a cow. She was alone in her room, waiting for her sleeping meds to kick down the door of her consciousness and carry her fireman-style over the threshold of dreams. But the sucking and slurping! It was so loud her eyes, dry and open, scarcely blinked in their vigilance. She didn't want to report this to Nora, who would furrow her brow in such deep, empathic pain. The two of them sometimes got caught in a regressive loop of empathy, Nora tearing up at Karen's stories of abandonment and degradation, Karen weeping at the sight of Nora's tears, a dolorous, tissue-strewn stalemate from which there was no productive conclusion, only release when the clicking of Nora's clock at last signaled that Karen's fifty-minute session was over. Besides, Nora was on vacation in Mykonos for Last Day, and why should Karen be the one to ruin her trip?

She couldn't tell the counselors at Heart House. They'd make her go to the hospital, which was what had happened the last time she'd started hallucinating. Once she was gone, they'd give her room away to someone else on the miles-long wait list. Then where would she live? Where would she go?

And besides, maybe these voices weren't so bad. For a few years now, Karen had been trying to heighten the sensory acuity of her soul. She studied everything she could at the library: the zodiac, divination, reincarnation, Tibetan demonology, the hierarchy of Christian angels. The floor of her bedroom was stacked with spiral-bound notebooks filled with arcana. Deep inside her, Karen believed, extraordinary gifts were about to come flying out, if she could just cultivate the right conditions. It involved deeper perception, but so far, only blur and jumble led the way. Perhaps these voices were just part of the path.

Then, before the sun rose on the morning of May 27, the snake slurping ended abruptly, and in the silence that followed she heard a voice say, "Dennis."

She got out of bed and yawned loudly. The wood floor groaned beneath her feet. She'd gained so much weight on her new meds. She stomped loudly, hoping to scare the voice away.

"Dennis," the voice said again. The clarity of it rang like a high church bell on a cloudless day.

"Yeah, but why now?" she asked.

There was no answer. She called her friend Rosette, the only civilian outside of Karen's company of professional help whose phone number Karen knew.

"Rose," Karen said when her call went straight to voicemail, "does the God of your understanding concern him/her/itself with details, or just big-picture stuff? Examples off the top of my head: the exact size of a tumor, the eye color of your soulmate, the sequence of songs on a random shuffle. Because that seems like a lot, even for an omnipotent—"
She was cut off.

Fine.

Karen knelt before her closet and pulled out the only shoes that had laces, a pair of generic-brand sneakers bought from a discount store. She unthreaded the lace of the right shoe and slurped it down like a noodle. It burned her throat and esophagus, but a moment afterward she felt strangely peaceful: it was gone. Done.

And, Karen thought brightly, she now had an excuse to wear her good shoes today, her party shoes, those little strappy leather sandals with the kitten heels! This afforded another fun opportunity—to build a whole outfit from the bottom up! She chose her pistachio-green Easter dress, not that there were many other options that still fit her, and her tan purse, not her backpack.

More would be revealed. It always was.

Walking the two unrelenting, uphill blocks from the group home to the bus stop, her feet were already protesting. Karen had to stop midway to catch her breath. She bent down and inspected a bed of spring flowers. "Look at living things and imagine them already dead," was one of the dictums of her extrasensory training. She gazed at the tulips and daffodils, their petals splayed open, their anthers naked and stigmas caked with powdery residue.

"Sexuality is sacred!" she yelled at the tulips, whose petals had curled so wide open that the rounded edges now tapered blade-like to points. But, no. No. Try not to view these flowers moralistically, Karen thought a moment later, squeezing her thighs together as she sat down on the bench at the bus stop. After all, who was *she* to pass judgment on perennials? In the not-too-distant past, Karen had rented her mouth to a homeless man in exchange for a swig of cough syrup with codeine.

Karen was not crazy to notice the profligacy of plants that spring. Pollen counts for May had already broken records. At night the silent sex of angiosperms left a golden sheath of pollen so thick it choked the grass beneath it. People were scraping it off their windshields like ice in winter, Karen noticed as she trudged the last block of her trip from the bus stop to the YMCA. In the parking lot, someone had traced the word *asshole* into the yellow film on the back window of a minivan. Karen wiped it away with her hands. Negative thoughts were like twigs floating by in a tiny babbling brook, Nora had told her. Even less than twigs — like ripples in the water. You weren't supposed to get attached. Just let them pass, Karen reminded herself. But it was hard. She licked the yellow dust off her fingers, her eyes watered with the urge to vomit, then this, too, passed.

Karen was opening the YMCA by herself for the first time that morning. Her boss, Roberto, had given her a set of keys earlier in the week, entrusting *her*, Karen Donovan, to captain the ship in his absence. To be chosen, to be seen and selected as special enough to perform this job — it was a sign that things were moving in the right direction. The keys glittered in the morning light. Her hands shook a little with their eminence.

As soon as Karen unlocked the doors, she spotted two women waddling arm in arm from the parking lot up the front steps. Myra and Marlene. They lived at the luxury retirement condos down the street, Morning Pines, a name that made no sense at all, because the building was not even adjacent to a single conifer and what did morning have to do with it? If anything, Marlene and Myra were in the twilight of their lives. They were devoted to fitness, though in their eighties, their bodies were getting worse, not better. It was their cells, Karen wanted to explain to them. All the yoga and aquacise and squats in the world could not stop cellular decay. Keeping your muscles strong was pretty much useless. But there was no arguing with these two. Marlene was a Taurus and Myra a Scorpio, Karen had discerned from their account files, where their birthdays were listed. She smiled at them as they entered. They sang hello to Karen, grabbed their towels from the pyramid Karen had stacked so neatly on the front desk the night before, and waddled with impressive speed toward the women's locker room.

"You have to wait, I haven't booted up the computer yet. . . ."

Three more members glided past her as she hurried behind the reception desk. Where the hell was Rosette? Karen picked up the phone to call her, then remembered that Rosette had put her on restriction. She was only allowed to call her friend's cellphone once a day, exclud-

ing emergencies, which Rosette had defined as events that involved police, fire, or ambulance personnel. If Rosette did not call her back, Karen
was supposed to pray for acceptance. Those were Rosette's rules. Karen
had an eighty percent success rate in obeying them, which both women
regarded as a real victory.

Karen wiped her fingers clean on the towel at the top of the pile and
rearranged the remaining towels in a pyramid. A woman she'd never met
before walked in. Strapped to her stomach was a large sack printed with
little turtles. Karen tried to make conversation but the woman was no-
nonsense, tapping some haiku of love or hate into her phone with one
hand, her membership card at the ready in the other. She had brown
curly hair graying at the roots, which gave her whole face a kind of silvery aura. She didn't look at Karen, nor at the perfect pyramid of towels.
Instead she grabbed one recklessly, sending the whole structure tumbling to the floor. Karen knelt to rescue them, her knees aching. By the
time Karen got up, the woman had disappeared inside.

An hour passed and no word from Rosette. Karen microwaved two
French bread pizzas and read the classified ads in the newspaper. She
remembered there being so much free stuff in the classifieds when she
was a little girl. Hardly anyone gave stuff away for free anymore. Not
even kittens. Something that comes in dozens and totally by accident
now cost a truckload of money, and anyway, Nora told her she had to
start saving. In "Lost and Found" someone in Arlington was looking for
her wedding ring. The ad offered a five-hundred-dollar reward. It was a
long shot, but Karen decided to check the lost-and-found box in the ladies' locker room. All kinds of stuff turned up there. Five hundred dollars would buy a really good kitten. Maybe a Persian or an Egyptian
Mau.

Myra and Marlene were standing near the water fountain in the ladies' locker room, wearing nothing but flip-flops. Myra lifted her arm,
exposing the prickly skin underneath where a surgical incision had
healed into a long purple stripe. Marlene examined the scar coolly and
nodded.

"How're your knees doing, Karen?" Myra asked. "Are you having that surgery? What did your ortho say?"

Before she had a chance to answer, the brisk, silvery woman walked in carrying a baby.

"Where did that baby come from?" Karen yelped.

"From my uterus," the woman sniffed.

"Oh," Karen said. The specificity of *uterus* threw a stick in her spokes. She sat on a bench and fished around her pockets until she found a paper clip; swiftly, furtively, she swallowed it like a pill.

Myra and Marlene exchanged looks. Did Karen-from-the-Y, as she was named by them, not know how babies were made? It was plausible that she didn't, given the other insane things they'd heard her say. Both women filed the conversation away, to be discussed later, over Chardonnay on the patio of their retirement condo. The more compassionate YMCA members learned how to steer around Karen, restoring the gym banter back to its rightful domain of injuries, fitness goals, and weather.

"How old is she?" Myra asked the new mother.

"Two and a half months," the mother answered.

"Oh! Brand-new!" Myra wrapped a towel beneath her wrinkly arms and tickled the baby's foot.

"Welcome to the world, little one," Marlene cooed.

The mother held the baby and twisted her hips from side to side. Karen stayed planted on her bench but leaned in for a closer look. The baby's face was hidden somewhere inside the soft yellow folds of blanket, behind the mother and the two elderly, half-naked women whispering gentle, knowledgeable things among themselves. Motherhood was a coven Karen had forfeited when a faith-based group home convinced her to get a hysterectomy at age eighteen. She had always been indifferent to her body's reproductive powers, and at the time had thought, *What the hell, at least now I can swim whenever I want and never worry about menstruation.* She did not regret this decision now.

When Myra and Marlene headed off to the showers, Karen was alone with the woman and her baby. This made her nervous. She didn't want to stay or leave, so she rummaged in the lost-and-found box and pulled out a comb. She raked it through her long, tangled hair.

"Would you mind doing me a quick favor?" the woman asked Karen. "Would you hold her for just a second?"

If you pick up a fallen hatchling and return him to his nest, his mother will smell your touch and be repulsed, Karen remembered learning. One whiff of you on its downy little feathers and the baby bird's mother will say, *You are not mine, not anymore.* She will shun the entire nest you'd tainted with your smelly hands, leaving her babies there to starve, and it would be all your fault.

"Oh God," Karen whispered, "oh God."

The mother stood on the scale while holding her baby, then stepped off and walked toward Karen. "I just want to see how much weight she's gained," she said, handing the bundle over like an offering. Karen took the baby confidently in her arms. *How did I know how to do that?* she wondered. Then she remembered that one of her foster families had had a baby—the redheaded family in Somerville. They were all so covered in freckles it looked as if they needed to wash their faces even when they were clean, and when Karen had pointed that out, the father pulled down her pants in the middle of the kitchen and spanked her with a spatula.

Karen looked at the baby, at her small, flushed face, her short almost translucent fringe of eyelashes. Babies knew everything. Their eyes quivered with the opaque knowledge of the world. That's why they cried so much. They were trying to tell us, and no one believed them.

"You might have come just in time for the end," Karen whispered to her.

The mother weighed herself and frowned.

"Well, I'm not losing any weight but my baby has gained one pound."

"We grow imperceptibly every minute of every day."

"That's a nice thought," the mother said, taking her baby back from Karen.

Rosette stormed into the locker room. She'd had her hair done that morning, Karen could tell right away, the mystery of her lateness explained. Rosette was a pious Christian, but vanity was her weakness. Her hair was a gleaming auburn color with a few purple and magenta feathers tightly woven in. Her bangs cut a crisp line across her brow. Karen could see that Rosette had also hit the tanning salon recently, as the pale outline of eye goggles betrayed.

"Stay, Mr. Cox," Rosette shouted through the open door. "Sit there, I tell you, and don't you move."

"Rose, did you read that article I sent you? About the pod of dolphins who killed themselves all together on that beach in England?"

Rosette looked at herself in the mirror, squared her shoulders, and turned her head from side to side. "Too terrible! I was shocked. Even the animals now are sinning against God who made them."

"Rosie, my stomach hurts. Can I have one of Mr. Cox's pills?"

"Hush your mouth," Rosette scolded. She was wearing cosmetic contact lenses that made her dark brown eyes appear a shattered, reptilian blue. She nodded at the woman with the baby and rolled her eyes, the YMCA's universal code for *You know crazy Karen. Can't believe a word she says. . . .* Rosette laid her hands on Karen's shoulders and gave them a deep, penetrating squeeze. "You're too fat, babygirl. That's the problem. You're not doing your exercises."

"I am. Sometimes. Sometimes I forget."

"You have to do them every day. That's how you change yourself."

"A guy in India grew his muscles just by thinking about lifting weights."

"Lord, help us all today. She's making up stories again," Rosette said to the mother, who packed her gym bag silently, avoiding eye contact. The woman, tired from the demands of new motherhood, felt entitled to withdraw from polite civilization. She was in no mood to connect with the human periphery, the Rosettes and Karens of the world. Not even on hallowed Last Day.

"It's true," Karen cried. But as usual she couldn't prove it, the source of the story long lost in the unmapped city of her mind. The part about the guy being from India she'd made up. But it was probably true. India was one of those places where elemental shape-shifting was still possible. Karen attributed this to all the wild animals roaming the streets. She had never been there, but she'd seen pictures. What mattered most was intention. Sometimes, things are true simply because they are supposed to be.

A CREW OF megalomaniacs would not survive very long in the cramped white tunnels of a space station, and so, while astronauts cannot be classified among mere mortals—their expertise in so many areas is too extraordinary—they are distinguished less by their talents as by a level of humility unusual among the rest of us who live and work our entire lives on Earth.

So there are mortals, and there are astronauts, and then there are astronauts selected to go to space, and an even smaller pool of astronauts called back for a second mission; and even among this elite group, Thomas "Bear" Clark was known as the human avatar of humility. According to a biography of him slated for release in the next year, his ex-wife attributed Bear's humility to the fact of his growing up as the middle child of two sisters, one taller than him (he'd inherited their mother's good looks as well as her small frame) and one born with Down syndrome.

"No, that's not quite it," his mother had reported to the biographer, not long before she died. "They are how they are from their very first day," she'd said, insisting to the author that Bear had been a cooperative, mild-mannered soul from his infancy, long before he was aware of the compensations he would have to make as a brother or a son. His deep sense of humility was simply part and parcel with all his other gifts.

If function followed form, Bear should have been a quarterback, with his square jaw and steep cheekbones. He was so good-looking as a child, old women in the grocery store used to give him money just because. Bear would save these quarters and dimes in a piggy bank, then buy presents for his younger sister, his mother had told the biographer.

He'd grown up in San Diego, in a ranch house identical in size and shape to all the other ranch houses in their neighborhood, in a WASP family that could trace its roots back to the crew of the *Mayflower*. As a boy, Bear aspired to become one of the sandy-haired surfers who eked by on hobo jobs. There was a purity to that kind of life, lived in obeisance to the ocean, that Bear admired. He loved surfing and all it encompassed: studying the waves, asking permission to walk on their backs, waiting with sublime patience for their consent. He could have made those vows and been just as happy as a beach bum as he was now on the International Space Station. But when his father was killed by a drunk driver, the most sensible response to that stunning pain was for Bear to distract himself, his grieving mother, and his sisters with his achievements. He turned his attention away from the sea and toward his studies, where he excelled in math and science, and was encouraged rather glibly by a high school physics teacher to pursue a career in astronautics.

"Sounds neat," young Bear had said.

He was the blue-eyed only son of a nice family in Southern California, a place where the climate and culture are suffused by an optimism that stands in utter defiance to geological reality, as though dangling on the edge of a chthonic fault line could be made A-OK if you believe in goodness, in your ability to manufacture safety and hope, and in that erratic human covenant that promises anything is possible if you only put your mind to it.

Which is exactly what Bear did, and like a curse in reverse, everything he touched turned to gold. He joined the Air Force, studied at Stanford, was accepted into the NASA training program, and flew his first mission while still in his thirties, on the now-retired Space Shuttle. His crew then was rescuing a wayward satellite that had failed to reach its optimal orbital height, offering Bear the opportunity for an Extravehicular Activity, the golden ring of all astronauts. Floating outside the shuttle, he had seen asteroids streak the black sky beneath his feet. "If this is the only chance I get, if I never get called up for another mission, I will still die the happiest man on Earth," he told his wife then.

With the same combination of humility and hard work that had gotten him into space, he devoted himself to a grounded life mentoring other astronauts, working in Mission Control for other flights, being the best team player he could be. When this current mission came up—one year on the ISS, the opportunity of a lifetime—his dominant feeling was not pride but gratitude.

From a distance his whole life glittered with the charm of the elect. Which is why his dark mood, and the accompanying dark thoughts of calamity, were so alarming to him.

He made the mistake of confessing this in an email to his ex-wife. *The only thing worse than being with your family on the holidays is not being with your family on the holidays,* she replied. *But that has always been your MO—to make yourself busy when there's something you want to avoid, hiding behind "work." I tried to explain to the girls that that is just your love-language—you're a provider, so you feel the need to work hard to provide. But they could use less providing and more of your time.*

He hated that she talked to him like this now. She took the familiarity between them too far, exploiting their post-divorce friendship as license to casually criticize him. But in that same castigating email, she had also included very helpful links to the things their daughters wanted for their Last Day presents, a considerate gesture that would make shopping from space easier.

Thanks was all he wrote back to her.

Bear worked with his customary efficiency that day, despite a persistent headache, and was able to recoup eleven minutes of R&R before dinner. He used the time to do a three-minute meditation exercise in the privacy of his crew quarters, part of a thirty-day challenge he was partaking in alongside a group of high school kids on Earth, and then tackle his holiday shopping. His younger daughter, Kayley, both needed and wanted a new phone. For Elyse he got a little silver dove for her charm bracelet. For his ex-wife's birthday, which fell on Last Day, he found a specially designed foam roller—she had been complaining about leg cramps during her marathon training. He placed all the items into his virtual cart at the mega online retailer Jungle.com and clicked "Purchase."

A minutes-long delay was followed by an automatic return to the Jungle home page. His shopping attempt had failed. He would have to search and select the items all over again. These precious minutes had been wasted. Bear punched the quilted walls of his CQ.

Immediately he blamed Donna: it was her gift that had crashed the order. It was irrational, he knew, but he resented that he felt guilty if he didn't buy her a birthday gift. Being the amicable ex-husband was Who He Was. It was part of the reason he had been selected for this second mission in space. Lots of astronauts were permanently grounded after a divorce. It was an unspoken practice of NASA, with roots in the military component of the program—if you couldn't keep the peace in your own household, how could they trust you on board the $2.9 billion operation in space? But not Bear. He was agreeable. He was good. He followed the rules even when he broke his marriage vows.

His daughters hated Jungle.com anyway. It was a corporate overlord, or some such fulmination they'd picked up in college. They always made smart comments about it. And Last Day was not really a gift-giving holiday. This shopping was a gesture reaching out of Bear's guilt for being away from them for so long.

Was it even possible, Bear thought, for a good man to do the right thing anymore?

Perhaps it was the excess CO_2 in the station that was making him so sloppy and morose. The second CDRA was broken—again—leaving just one operating air scrubber for the six people on board. But that was changing tonight. Three of the six members were leaving first thing in the morning. Even if Mission Control would not grant Bear permission to try and fix the CDRA, halving the population of the station would lighten the load of the one that still worked, and the air would be a little cleaner.

Bear floated into the Russian module, where the mission captain, Mikhail Mikhailovich Svec, was cementing a crown in his own molar.

"I could have done that for you, comrade," Bear offered.

Svec snorted. "Hyouston never allow extra time for you Americans in schedule. I can do myself. No problem."

Svec was something of a legend in the international space community. Among many more obvious triumphs of physicality (mountaineering, dead-lifting) he had inured his mucus membranes to withstand pepper spray. It was a trick that got a lot of applause at bars across the globe. He never soiled his space diaper, not even during launch. "Well-trained dog can hold bowels for twelve hours. So can I," Svec declared. His record for holding his breath underwater was six minutes and three seconds, and he was a skilled practitioner of tantric sex.

He also claimed to have willed the color of his eyes to change from brown to blue. As there were no color photographs of a young Svec extant, this claim could only have been substantiated by his now long-deceased mother, an infamous alcoholic in a city where binge drinking was hardly noteworthy.

The mythology Svec perpetuated was that on his thirteenth birthday his mother had confessed to him the identity of his father. Before that day, the only thing Svec knew about this man was his shoe size—forty-three—the worn number on the sole of the boots his father had left behind one night when Svec was still a baby. These boots remained by the back door of their apartment for years, an eerie, truncated effigy to the man who'd left and never come back. His mother would sob whenever Svec asked her about them—the disembodied *them,* never *him,* never the man the boots represented. Svec knew his patronymic was a sham, that it was derived from his maternal grandfather, and that these things—

his name, those boots—were a source of deep pain he must not aggravate if he wanted his mother to sleep at night.

But on his thirteenth birthday Mama Svec sat him down at their kitchen table, sliced some sour pickles and pumpernickel bread, poured a shot of vodka for each of them, and told him the whole story. It was a short story in the end, a disappointingly common one at odds with young Svec's already burgeoning notion of himself as a heroic figure with mythic origins. His dad was a high-ranking Roscosmos administrator who had another family, a legitimate one, that prevented him from acknowledging the alcoholic waitress he had impregnated, other than the occasional envelopes of cash he left her, usually enough to buy a week's worth of groceries but never more than that.

From that day on, Svec despised his father. He was obviously a coward. So close to the ships that could reach the skies yet he chose to become an administrator? He cursed this man and the short limbs and brown eyes he had passed down to Svec. He and his mother took turns refilling the glasses of vodka until the bottle was empty, and moments before throwing up, Svec vowed to grow taller than six feet, to change the color of his eyes from his father's cow-dung brown to his mother's forget-me-not blue, and to become one of the few men to touch the void of outer space. He failed at only one of these, and could not entirely forgive himself.

It was Svec's honor and duty as captain to give the goodbye speech and toast to the departing astronauts, an American whom Bear knew from the Air Force, a Swiss particle physicist, and a Canadian industrial engineer. It could not be a real toast, Svec felt, without alcohol, but the Westerners were strict about the ban on alcohol in space and so he did his best to incant the drinking spirit into their sad little pouches of reconstituted apple juice.

". . . and so I say to you, our comrades Linda, Deitiker, and Sanjay, fly straight home. No wandering. Do not go like arrogant bird of our Russian fairy tale and fly directly into sun. . . ."

The other astronauts, including Bear and a billionaire Japanese space tourist, Yui, listened patiently while microwaving their individual dinners as quietly as they could. Svec did not let their eating stop him.

"... *Budem zdorovy*—to our health. *Na pososhok*—safe travels ..."

The crew hovered awkwardly around the table bolted into the wall. Bear wolfed down his barbecue beef and used his leftover tortilla to hold a polite sample of the caviar Svec offered each crew member to commemorate the occasion. The smell of it, mixed with Yui's crabmeat and the odor of Deitiker's irradiated sausage, was making Bear's stomach turn.

He gulped his nausea stoically and told the group, "I also want to say a little farewell, but I'm not as good at toasts as our Commander Svec. So if you don't mind, I've been practicing this for weeks. ..."

Svec watched with a bemused smile as the American pulled a harmonica out of his zippered pocket. It was the captain's job to oversee special functions, and Bear was second seat.

"I hope I'm not overstepping," Bear said.

"*Nekogda*," Svec said, nodding.

Bear played a jazzy rendition of "Mercy Mercy Mercy" that he had been practicing for this night's farewell. He chose it because it was a bit more upbeat than the standard blues and gospel tunes in his songbook. As he played, one by one the other astronauts drifted away to their CQs to watch TV on their personal laptops.

Only Svec remained, and Bear was touched by this show of solidarity. The Russian commander was almost stereotypically macho, and came off to Bear as downright cold at times, but like many other Russians Bear had known, Svec was a sentimental man with a tenderness for ritual, tradition, and symbolic gesture. Bear took Svec's quiet attention as a cue to keep playing, so he tried a more modern pop song he was just beginning to learn. He fumbled a bit through the chord transitions, but Svec was a respectful and sympathetic audience, listening in perfect silence. Bear had begun the second verse when he heard the rattle, then the rasp, followed by a snore.

Those legendary eyes that could withstand pepper spray and allegedly change pigmentation could also remain open during sleep, it appeared now, as Svec snored. Drool gathered on Svec's slack lower lip and remained there, weightless, shining like a pearl. Bear dabbed Svec's face with a tissue—stray particles of water, even tiny ones, were dangerous for the ship—and woke him. Svec snorted again, and floated off without so much as a goodbye.

L AST DAY WAS an oddity on the calendar. Slightly more than one day, but not quite two, it began at some point on May 27 and ended on May 28. Whether encircled by sunrise, sunset, midnight, or quitting time, the parameters of the day were entirely personal. This lack of clear boundary was just one of the many reasons Sarah Moss hated the holiday. As a child she would cry and cry for the duration of Last Day, refusing to fall asleep all night, making May 28 cranky and miserable for both her and her parents. Everyone assured her she would grow out of it. When that didn't happen, she affected a teenage air of disavowal. The perfect mask for her shuddering fear.

The fear was totally irrational, she knew. Despite what felt like a never-ending fountain of oil spills, carbon emissions, and toxic waste, the planet had yet to smolder into one big ashtray. Life marched on. It always did. It probably always would, at least in her lifetime and for many thousands of lifetimes after hers. No big deal. It was a dramatic holiday of self-inflicted upheaval drawn out into a public performance. Collective catharsis and all that. Right?

Sarah had researched the many apocryphal histories of Last Day for various school projects. The earliest antecedent supposedly took place during the Babylonian era, on the last full moon of the vernal equinox of 2807 BCE, when a meteor struck the Indian Ocean during a total lunar eclipse. Terrified, the Babylonians scurried to propitiate whichever god they had offended, slaughtering prized animals, building pyres, bathing in sacred waters, giving gifts to loved ones and strangers alike, and this crisis narrowly averted gave rise to a tradition of yearly reckoning.

Later, astrologers of the Ayyubid empire predicted the end of the world for May 28, 1186. The sultan Saladin, in flagrant mockery of his superstitious advisers and his primitive father-in-law they still loyally served, held an open-air candlelit party for all the nonbelievers the night before. They danced and ate and drank themselves into an orgy that would make a Dionysian blush. The lines between man and woman, ruler and servant, pain and pleasure shattered.

In illuminated manuscripts of the fourteenth century, later proven to be forgeries made by Romany peddlers of the seventeenth century, was the story of a Florentine village that had lost more than half of its citizens to the plague. The story went that a Franciscan monk took a vow of silence after the last of his brothers had died. Alone in his monastery, he meditated day and night, hoping to understand the wisdom in his God's seemingly sadistic plan. He spent weeks in this trance, sipping only water steeped weakly with nettles, fasting in solitude. Then, in a very Italian mix of Christian and pagan devotion, he emerged from his monastery naked as a baby, trundling a small cart full of linens. He built a fire in the town's piazza and urged passersby to add their garments, their bedclothes, the shirts on their backs, right then and there, into the fire. At last the whole village stood naked in the chill spring air, their bodies warmed by the enormous fire, and on that day ever after, not another soul was touched by the Black Death.

All of these stories could not be more obvious bullshit, Sarah thought, and yet the broader her knowledge of Last Day mythology grew, the deeper her fear took root. Sometimes people will things into being, so what possible good could a couple thousand years of end-time fetishizing bring?

For her school's chapter of Mock Trial, from which she had defected earlier that year (high levels of theater-kid solipsism and disenfranchised-nerd neediness—an insufferable combo), she could wax philosophical on the mythopoetic function of Last Day, its vitality and necessity in today's techno-dependent, isolating world. But every word she'd uttered in those debates had been insincere, a homily delivered for a teacher's approval. And she was ultimately annoyed that she'd brought her team to victory in the debate. The opposing team should have won. Their argument was much better—that Last Day was a perpetuation of an intensely self-centered lie: the world could not go on without us.

"A product," her best friend Terrence pronounced, "of our pattern-making brains, that so crave completion they cannot hear *tick tick* without the inevitable *tock.*"

Now, that was a good point. But when being judged by a committee, especially of high school teachers, sentimentality was going to take the prize over bleak truth.

Almost sixteen now, Sarah realized for the first time that Last Day was completely racist. Its seeming ubiquity was actually, like so much else, a consequence of Western hegemony. "And! It ignores, like, the whole *continent* of Africa, which is made of, like, so many different ethnic groups that don't know or care about it. And Native Americans— they have totally different creation and apocalypse myths. It's a stupid, largely Western, *white* invention."

"Oh, you're such a Scrooge," her mother said, which made Sarah wither. For one, as a literary allusion it didn't even make sense. Sarah had read Dickens, and that novel was about a character suffering from a general spiritual bankruptcy that transcended culture and calendar, thank you very much, and besides that, Sarah really liked Christmas. Christmas was about a little baby and farm animals and hope. Her dad's Judaism was pretty much phoned in. He'd taught her to light candles on

Chanukah but he didn't know any prayers, so the blessing he recited was a gibberish they pretended was Hebrew. On Yom Kippur they flushed a crust of rye toast down the toilet, a tradition she'd always looked forward to. She liked the renewal of New Year's, and at least it made sense on the calendar. Halloween was always fun. The Mexican Día de los Muertos was even better. Easter was the coolest, a mash-up of seasonal changes and diluted paganism and Christianity and zombies. Easter was about surrealism and chocolate. What was not to love there?

Maybe she just needed to ignore the holiday and focus on school-work. She had a paper to write that weekend on *Lear*. She was toying with a thesis about impotence, but broader, like the ultimate human impotence in the face of Nature. Or Time. Or something like that. She regretted not having written a draft by now. Deadlines scraped away at her already fragile nervous system, and she hated herself a little for let-ting this one creep up on her.

It was hard to make plans for a day that you secretly considered to be your last. How could anyone enjoy herself under that kind of pressure? It made every idea feel holy and totally wrong at the same time. She knew some kids from school were dropping acid on Crane Beach, and while it was fun to watch her friends' pupils dilate and to listen to their mad prose-poems of insight, eventually Sarah, as always the only sober person there, would get bored and want a coherent dialogue, which she realized made her a total loser.

Her parents were having their annual pizza party but they said she could skip it this year if she wanted. Last year she'd met the love of her life at her parents' party. It was, she realized now, the one-year anniver-sary of their *whatever*.

He was her mother's colleague's plus-one, the unwitting boyfriend dragged to a lame work party where he knew no one else. Sarah's mother taught women's history at a small, private Christian college. She invited only the select few faculty members who shared her liberal politics, and last year she'd used the holiday to win over some more support for her personal campaign to repaint a dated, early-seventies-era Eve-shaming mural of the Book of Genesis in the student union. (In the mural, Adam looked like a hapless dork, shrugging his shoulders in a sitcom pose of "Take my wife . . . please!" Eve was narrow-eyed and ugly, with a darker complexion than Adam, a blatantly racist choice. The mural had to go, Dr. Moss insisted.) One of the invitees to the Mosses' Last Day pizza party was Emily, a young creative-writing adjunct, a newly minted MFA with two minor publications to her name. She'd been particularly vocal in support of repainting the mural at a faculty meeting. Dr. Moss was eager to get to know her better.

The man Emily brought as her date to the Mosses' Last Day pizza party was hungover and gray. He was tattooed everywhere you could see, his arms sleeved in ghouls and skeletons, a storm amassing above his collar shooting lightning up his throat.

"Kurt is a visual artist," Emily announced several times after her boyfriend mumbled his hellos and nice-to-meet-yous to the other guests.

"I'm a tattooer," Kurt said to Sarah, who discovered the nauseous-looking man skulking in her most favorite place to skulk, down the hill from her house. They'd both found themselves sitting on the stones that encircled the Last Day fire pit, watching silently as the flames fizzled down to black and white embers. "This artist shit is about her, not me. She keeps telling people I'm working on a graphic novel. I mentioned to her once that I had half an idea for a comic book, but she knows as well as I do that I work and drink too much to ever get it started, let alone finished."

"Women will say absolutely anything to justify their sexual selections," Sarah replied in a matter-of-fact tone. She felt equipped to judge because her paper on *Madame Bovary* had gotten an A. "It would be so cool if people could just say, 'His pheromones smell like safety' or 'She successfully distracts me from thoughts of death.' And then we could all nod and be like, 'Yeah, mazel tov,' and move on to more important stuff."

"Huh." Kurt inhaled his cigarette and held the smoke for a long time in his mouth, like an actor in a movie. "Yeah, I guess you're right."

"Self-deception is the greatest crime," Sarah said, then wondered if she believed this was true or was just saying it to sound cool. Surely there were worse crimes. Like rape, and anything involving children. Her companion looked at her with his squinted, bloodshot eyes and nodded in agreement, which made her feel, in the dumbest possible way, so good.

Up the hill, Emily teetered across the yard, continually sinking then extracting the heels of her muddy sandals out of the soft, moist lawn. A hard rain had fallen the night before and relented suddenly, as though bidden to do so, just before dawn. Sarah had listened to every drop fall with an impatient, hopeful heart. She was panicked as usual, waiting for the end, or not the end, and had refused to take even one tiny milligram of the Valium her mother saved for long airplane flights and Sarah's Last Day panic attacks. Though she changed her mind about everything every single day, exasperating her parents with her constantly relapsing vegetarianism, she knew one thing for sure—if the end was coming, she wanted to be fully awake to see it.

"I'm still here," she had wept silently in her bed once the rain had stopped and the sun rose. "We must be okay."

This long, anxious night had made for a groggy, exhausting day, but sitting next to this man now, she felt she was falling into a deep, transformative sleep and waking up from it at the same time.

"She shouldn't have worn heels," Sarah observed of Emily.

"Are you a student at the college?" Kurt asked.

"Yes," Sarah said. The pistons of her heart quickened, fueling the audacity she needed to lie. "My name's . . . Sarah."

"I'm Kurt," the man said.

"One question." Sarah touched his shoulder, an action that surprised her. She was not a hugger. This was often remarked upon at her very emotive private school. "If you did write a graphic novel, what would it be? I don't care if you ever do it or not. I'm just curious."

"It's from a dream I had once a long time ago. About a little boy who swallows a butterfly, then one day coughs up an egg that hatches into a lizard who becomes his best friend. Their adventures and stuff. I don't really like writing. So it would be mostly pictures."

"Like a fable."

"Yeah, but not a fairy tale. Not for kids. They would get into real danger. Ghosts and hurricanes and serial killers would come after them. Did you ever see *M* by Fritz Lang?"

She had not. She had seen the movie poster for *Metropolis*. Her friend Terrence's parents had a large vintage print framed in their upstairs hallway.

"Totally," she answered. "That would look awesome. Like, as your aesthetic."

"Here's the prototype." Kurt pulled up his T-shirt. His torso was largely untouched by ink, which made the few images tattooed there even more vivid. He twisted to show her a tattoo on the left side of his rib cage. A blue-and-yellow lizard munched on a turquoise butterfly. The attention to detail was remarkable. The butterfly's tiny face was etched with infinitesimal agony. Crumbs of its iridescent wings fell from the lizard's smiling mouth. There was a quality of light to the tattoo that Sarah thought miraculous. Even flat against Kurt's pale, dry skin, the lizard and its prey seemed to glitter.

Again she reached over and touched him, this time letting her fingers run over his skin for what felt like a long time, as though deciphering a code written in the rise and fall of his ribs. She looked at the tattoo on the other side of his ribs, the happy lizard's evil twin—a scorpion that was inked too dark and was now fading, looking more like a badly healed scar than a picture of anything. She looked at Kurt's thick waist, his softly protruding beer belly, the way the hair sprouted erratically over his abdomen, then gathered darkly, with purpose, at a central point below his navel. She imagined where his spleen was hidden. She thought about his kidneys, the ruffled scarf of his intestines, how fragile and alive he was, all the secrets he was keeping beneath his skin.

What?

This was something new. Sarah was a sworn asexual. It was a well-explored part of her identity. Ninth grade at the Phoenix School meant completing Dr. Heather Vasquez-McQueen's practicum in human sexuality. Dr. Heather made her class read selections from the Kinsey report and Freud and the newest edition of *Our Bodies, Ourselves*, which the boys in the practicum protested. What about *their* bodies, *themselves*, hmmm? Dr. Heather was a lesbian married to a transgender man and she had no time for parity, what with eons of subjugation to counterattack in one semester, one abbreviated semester, as the practicum was supposed to be finished before Thanksgiving break. In just ten weeks they had to cover STDs, rape culture, masturbation, gender identity, the whole sexuality-is-a-continuum-not-a-fixed-point thing, and still drive home all the practicalities of how to put on and properly dispose of condoms as well as other safe-sex options and watch at least one documentary on *Roe v. Wade*.

Their final project was to "map your sexuality" in a four- to five-thousand-word essay. It was optional to read this essay out loud, though highly encouraged by Dr. Heather, who said it was a critical strike in the war against repression. The Sarahs Wilmington and Burke naturally jumped at the chance, but that year a surprising number of other kids did, too. Even Terrence. He wrote about the time his mother walked in on him jerking off and the shame that followed, which got a lot of sympathetic head nodding from Dr. Heather. Sean Fusco talked about knowing he was gay when he was a little boy watching soap operas with his grandmother, how he'd wished the men would kiss each other. Lindsey LaSalle wrote an essay on pansexuality that had Dr. Heather practically weeping with pride.

Sarah Moss wrote her essay about the parallels between the energetic attraction of subatomic particles in the first microseconds following the Big Bang and the attraction of humans, and how attraction plus collision makes new matter, whether that matter is a universe or a baby. The connection was flimsy and kind of sentimental, she knew, but the story of baryons was rife with meaning, worthy of a B+ at least, though she'd hoped for more.

"The energy of creation is attractive but it is not sexual. It's narcissistic projection to label it as sexual when these forces of attraction and creation began before there was carbon-based life," Sarah read.

Dr. Vasquez-McQueen smiled a smile that made her face look like a rag being wrung out to dry. After class Lindsey told Sarah that she should get tested for autism.

"Don't worry, kiddo. They think everyone is autistic these days," Sarah's father consoled her later. "The noise of the world is deafening. People shut down."

"And besides, you're not autistic, pumpkin," her mother added. "You're just a late bloomer."

Or maybe she was not made to bloom at all. Never in her life had Sarah been sexually attracted to another person, male or female. She'd never had a boyfriend or a girlfriend, and had never wanted one. It was rumored that Terrence had a crush on her, but he was shy and waiting for her to make the first move, which was perfect—it meant she could stall him forever, or at least until graduation, without losing his friendship.

That fall Sarah had kissed a freshman named Marcus Stroman at the school Halloween dance. He'd pushed himself on her but she was able to shove him away. He was drunk and arrogant and smoked unfiltered Camels. Sarah could taste the cigarettes on his teeth, and the acrid residue of his spit lingered on her tongue for a while after they stopped kissing, like the gentle pain of a tiny animal's bite. She'd kissed Lindsey LaSalle one day two summers earlier. Lindsey had talked a lot about consent beforehand, so much so that Sarah finally blurted, "Yeah, fine, let's kiss or whatever," just to shut her up. Lindsey's mouth was soft and a little sandy because they were on the beach. Both times, Sarah had opened her mouth, and there the experience had lived and died. Besides a tiny splash of fear that had quickly turned to tedium, clock-watching, when-will-this-be-over, she felt nothing anywhere in her body. Not even a tingle. But she couldn't write an essay about that. It was the most shameful thing anyone could possibly admit in Dr. Heather's class, that she was fifteen and asexual. It was worse than getting aroused by mascot animal costumes or period-staining your skirt or getting caught jerking off in the living room. Sarah was the biggest freak of them all.

A phase, her parents said calmly, a rebellion in reverse. They'd raised her in such a loving, accepting, shame-free milieu that she was forced to reject basic biology to be different.

"You're just afraid of getting hurt," Terrence suggested.

But what if they were all wrong? What if she was born this way, part of a growing number of genetically unproductive people, evolved because the world had reached its limit and humanity was coming to its end?

In her sunny backyard with Kurt that day almost precisely one year ago, Sarah had been able to forget all about the end of time. They had talked for two hours in a breathless, exhilarating way about music and movies and forgivably embarrassing things they had once done. Full disclosure was still out of reach; both had wanted to impress even as they'd pretended to disarm. For example, Sarah did not tell the story of the time she'd pissed her pants during a cross-country track race. Kurt did not reveal how much debt he was still in ten years after opening his tattoo studio. They'd told innocent tales of pratfalls and mistaken identity instead, pretending to be more mortified than they actually were.

They'd discovered that they both loved a graphic novelist named Val Corwin, a reclusive artist and writer whose controversial work was published sporadically, always to mixed reviews, and about whom not much was known personally, not even the gender of the author. The biggest commercial and critical hit was Corwin's fully illustrated version of Kafka's *Metamorphosis*. While many other graphic novelists had taken a stab at this story, Corwin's edition centered on Gregor Samsa's sister, casting the ordinarily tragic beetle as an ugly antagonist. The book was hailed as a feminist masterpiece, but the graphic novel that followed it, about a lecherous Hollywood screenwriter and his chronic impotence, was both lauded and reviled for its grotesque precision. An entire chapter was devoted to the protagonist's botched penis-enlargement surgery, one that many readers, even devoted fans, found hard to take. Like most of Corwin's work, it was an uncomfortable mixture of the sacred and the profane that left readers uneasy.

Corwin's work, in different ways, had carried both Sarah and Kurt in their darkest hours. The newest book, release date unknown, was rumored to be an illustrated anthropology of the Last Day holiday. Sarah had gushed that it was her greatest fantasy to meet Corwin in person. Kurt confessed that when he was a teenager he had staked out an address in Boston he had heard belonged to the artist. He'd stood outside in the rain like a creep until the owner of the house invited him inside for a cup of tea. She was an elderly woman adorned head to toe with silver and turquoise jewelry and a caftan, under which she wore no bra. The woman claimed she didn't know who Val Corwin was, though she had the charcoal-stained fingertips of an artist at work.

"All Corwin's work is black-and-white!" Sarah swooned.

"I know. I can never prove it, but I swear it was her."

"I always hoped Corwin was a woman."

"Me, too."

Sarah and Kurt sat on the low stones around the fire pit, close enough to feel the discrete energy of each other's bodies without touching. The heavy rain had prevented a proper fire, but Sarah's father had stayed up all night like the good patriarch that he was, and once the storm had subsided, around four in the morning, he'd built a small, sputtering flame in the pit. Now the ashes had turned smoldering and white but were still radiating heat. The sun shone on the glittering grass.

Up the hill, Kurt's girlfriend, Emily, had finally extracted herself from an awkward conversation with a theology professor. She was beckoning Kurt with a wave. It was time for him to go.

Kurt got up and gave Sarah a long hug.

"Keep in touch," Kurt said, and handed her his business card.

Sarah opened a new email account, pretending to be the fictional college student Kurt thought she was, and wrote to him the very next day. *We made it. The end is not for us, not this time*, she said.

Over the course of the past year, Sarah had revealed herself in a way she had never done before with another human being, all the while remaining perfectly hidden behind a screen and the false identity of a Christian college student. Sarah was good about spacing out her correspondences—she didn't want to appear needy or deranged—and Kurt responded, when he responded, either with long, stream-of-consciousness tracts or incomplete sentences that made him sound drunk. For the most part his messages were funny, cryptic, and a little sad. He refused to use first-person pronouns, giving his voice a foreign, disembodied timber.

crazy busy indulging artless drunks their shamrocks and roses and yin yangs. possibly ruining lives. wicked cool. you??

Later that fall when Sarah had planted a strategic line about Emily in her email, Kurt reported that they had broken up.

disappointed her to death, he wrote. *only way to get her to leave. otherwise you stay stuck forever. she doesn't even realize it wasnt me who disappointed her—her imagination of me did.*

Bummer, Sarah wrote back, a word she would never use in real life. Cool, slightly archaic, self-consciously retro, totally blasé. She took this opportunity to copy and paste the final draft of her essay for Dr. Vasquez-McQueen's sexuality practicum (peppered with strategic spelling and grammar mistakes, to make it appear like her own spontaneous, stream-of-consciousness rant). It was a test—to see if he would get weird and/or dismiss her. Also, he'd once told her, apropos of nothing, that the TVs he'd grown up with, when disconnected from their antennae, had produced a flurry of black and white dots (a snowstorm effect Sarah had only ever seen replicated on the digital screens of her lifetime) and that this static contained one percent of the big bang. He had not clarified what that meant—*contained 1% of the Big Bang*—but he had honored the birth of the universe with a rare use of capitalization, which made Sarah's heart thump so loudly she could hear it.

Kurt did not respond for three months, almost four. In that time Sarah sustained a mood of bridled alarm; his response times usually ranged between two days to two months. Not that she was measuring. She didn't need to. She had looked at his emails so often and for so long that they were burned into her memory. All she had to do was close her eyes and the beaming white screens appeared on the backs of her lids, where she could see with perfect clarity the always blank subject lines and the dates of his pithy, precious missives.

So she panicked, waited another day, and then another, until she couldn't stand it any longer and wrote to him in late March, just two months ago now, deploying a calculated terseness, a deliberate absence of capitalization, so he would know just how cool and fine she was, what a not-big deal it was, this silence, his silence.

how's tricks, stranger?

She considered, even wrote a draft, without punctuation, but couldn't bear to send it.

The next day he responded. *sara my dear you are too good for this world.*

Who said things like that? No one, Sarah was sure. Kurt was the most fascinating creature she'd ever met. He'd spelled her name wrong but she didn't care. Reading this one sentence over and over, she'd never been so sure that she was doomed, that everyone, the whole world, was inescapably, officially doomed, and coming from Kurt, this eulogy was glorious.

AFTER THE DAILY inspection, Bear microwaved some coffee for Svec and himself and prepared Yui's pouch of matcha so that all three beverages would be hot and ready to drink by the time they gathered in the galley for their debriefing with Mission Control. His strange mood of the last few weeks was now infecting his dreams, a fact he would have ordinarily ignored if he had not been assigned the task of recording his dreams for a NASA psychologist who was doing heavens-knew-what with the information. Just before waking, he'd had a nightmare that was following him through his morning now. In the dream, he was at summer camp, on a bunk bed thousands of miles above the earth. Trapped in a cycle of paralytic analysis, he wondered, *Am I an adult or a child? Should I climb down or stay here and radio for help?* He ran through a series of disaster inventories and decision trees—his dreams could not relieve him of this responsibility to rational thought; he was an astronaut even while unconscious. He determined, at last, in the credulity of dreams, that he was suspended in a middle-gravity zone where the rules shifted often and without warning and that everything he knew, everything he'd studied, was no longer relevant.

Bear thought the dream was psychologically significant, illuminating his fears about what *might* happen with the subtle power dynamic that had emerged, leaving Svec, Yui, and him alone. But Svec had put a moratorium on the discussion of dreams.

"*Nekogda.* We will die of boredom."

"I had a dream," Yui announced as he floated over to them later that morning. "I rented the special observatory deck in the Tokyo Tower," he went on, ignoring Svec's thick brows pinching toward the center of his forehead. "The floor is covered by people. All naked. Lying like tatami mats. Covering the entire floor. I do not have to yell at them because they know they are under my command. I go down on my hands and knees and do a somersault. Then another and another until I cross the whole floor like this. When I get up, I bow, wave my hands, and say, 'Thank you very much. I am finished now.' The people say nothing. They will not move until I leave. I know this because it is my dream."

Svec gazed out of a porthole, watching the sun being snuffed out behind the earth like the ember of a cigar. "Dreams are garbage of human mind," he pronounced.

"I am not telling you another part of the dream. I cannot."

"Good," said Svec, wiping his mouth and hands.

"It is too dangerous for me to tell you. You would not be able to sleep or eat or think or work if I told you."

"Today's agenda is ridiculously packed," Bear said. "We'd better get to it."

"Our countries could go to war." Yui chewed thoughtfully on strips of dehydrated salmon. "If I told you."

"He reminds me of my son," Svec said, not without a tinge of affection. "Relentless."

"No, I will not tell you. I must not. I care about peace," Yui declared, and somersaulted the whole way to the exercise station.

Bear saw on his schedule that he had finally gotten the okay from Mission Control to fix what they referred to as the "extra" CDRA. Both CDRAs were necessary at all times; excess CO_2 in the air affected mood as well as mental acuity, Bear had argued, but NASA contended that the effects were "negligible" and that the levels were acceptable.

Technically, this was a victory for Bear, who'd been lobbying for permission to service the machine for over two months, but the feeling of triumph was short-lived and he quickly slipped into a state of quiet resentment. He worked alone for hours, dismantling the large machine one piece at a time, taking care to seal each tiny part in a series of ziplock bags tethered nearby or affix them to a large magnetic board. The station had a habit of swallowing small objects, and once lost, there was no sensible way to search for them in the floating chaos of microgravity. The sounds of the ISS, grating and constant, were somewhere between a factory and a hospital in terms of ambience. The idea struck Bear that some music would be soothing while he worked, then a moment later he forgot about the music and kept working in silence, only for the thought to resurface after another hour.

Again he counted the weeks he had left in this mission, breaking them into days, hours, and then individual tasks he had left to complete. How many more urine samples would he collect from now until departure? How many more hours would he log on the treadmill? It was a depressing arithmetic.

Another hour passed like this, in a silence scraped by groaning filters and fans. When he reached a benchmark in the repair process nine minutes earlier than planned, Bear felt a surge of dopey joy. He did some quadriceps stretches and tried again to do the three-minute breathing exercise he had learned in his meditation challenge that was supposedly so therapeutic. But the good feeling evaporated as quickly as it arrived, and Bear felt worse than ever.

Bear liked to describe himself as easygoing, rarely angry. He believed he was among a minority of humans organically hardwired toward contentment, and that the unhappiness of others was a maladaptive trait inherited from primitive ancestors—to hold on to bad memories at the expense of the good ones. And yet he had woken up this morning—at that artificially contrived moment they called morning—with such rage at his surroundings it felt like a fever, an angry longing for Earth consuming him with a quality of light, aching, and burning, both particle and wave.

At last Bear discovered the faulty valve in the CDRA and was pleased it was something simple enough that he could make a new one in the 3D printer right away. He sent his design for the part to the printer, then again found himself imagining a catastrophe that would require him to deorbit immediately. A medicine-resistant bacteria, one that significantly impacted his ability to function—that would do the trick. What symptoms would he be willing to endure for this to happen? Hyperemesis? He hated puking so much. Maybe an upper respiratory infection would be enough, if accompanied by severe chest pain. Ideally it would be quick, acute, and a manageable amount of pain soldiered by him alone. He didn't want anything to happen to the station—no fires or breakdowns of essential systems. The success of the ISS was too important to mankind, this was one of his core beliefs. The only other option besides personal illness was the death of an immediate family member on Earth. . . .

"Your face," Svec remarked, sounding a little unnerved at the sour expression on the ever-smiling American. "Your health? No good today?"

"Perhaps our Bear-o might be constipated," Yui suggested. He was upside down from the position Svec and now Bear had chosen to orient themselves, a thick hardcover comic book in his hands. "Perhaps our friendo might need to reach inside anus to—"

"Nope. Regular as always, Yui."

Svec was making what felt like an endless series of tiny plastic coils on the 3D printer. "You almost done with that, comrade?" Bear asked him. Bear felt that because his work today on the CDRA would improve the CO_2 levels for the whole ship, benefiting them all, his job should have priority on the printer. "I only have one small part to print. How many do you have left, Svec?"

"Thirty, maybe thirty-five more."

"I am concerned about our American friendo," Yui said. He closed his book and held it against his heart. "I look at you and I wonder, *Why he is so sad?*"

"I think we'll all feel a lot better once I get this second CDRA up and running, friendo. And I only need to print this one part to finish up. . . ."

Bear stifled a yawn while waiting for Yui to search his vast, largely libidinous vocabulary bank for the right words. Yui's fluency in English, while advanced by any metric, still lagged behind the lightning field of his mind. He refused to make a mistake or be misunderstood when he spoke, so sentences issued from his mouth with impeccable care, the delivery painstakingly slow.

"No, I don't think that is it," Yui replied. A series of lewd hypotheses cycled rapidly through Yui's brain. When at last he spoke, he looked at Svec, not Bear: "Commander, perhaps you did not remember to brush your teeth before you kissed your little Bear good night?"

"*Nyet.*" Svec shook his head. "Am thoughtful lover. Is known across globe."

Svec sipped kvas from a plastic pouch and waited patiently as the printer issued coil after coil. He looked to Bear like a coffee shop folk singer, with his thinning gray hair plaited in a French braid that floated off his neck.

"Not now, boys," Bear said, his voice wilting. He was in no mood for the locker room antics that Yui spewed so automatically it seemed a reflex, and that Svec, as commander, did nothing but indulge. Svec derived no pleasure from policing grown men, and so saw no benefit to censuring Yui, who was not an astronaut. This trip on the ISS was an expensive research vacation for the crude savant, one he had paid forty million dollars and trained for six months to attend.

An almost perfectly circular break in the white clouds opened over the coast of New England. Bear spotted the battered, imbecile forehead of Maine and, a click below, the palsied arm of Massachusetts.

"You guys ever been to Boston?" Bear asked.

"Ah, yes, Boston," Svec said, a memory returning suddenly. "I go once. Very pretty city. Spoke at conference at Garvard. Big lobsters, big as my arm. Ate three for dinner. Met beautiful woman. She own dry-cleaning business. She and I had fun for night. All pubs have televisions. This I did not like."

"Harvard is in Cambridge, not Boston."

"True," Svec said.

"Cambridge isn't so bad. The way the necrotic tissue surrounding a tumor is not as bad as the tumor."

"Very interesting," Svec said. "The sunshine American astronaut has dark spot after all?"

He did. If there was a nucleus for all of Bear's pain as an adult, it was in Boston. His older sister had moved there after college, gotten married, had two daughters, then drank herself into near psychosis after her younger daughter died. Once their mother died, this same elder sister moved their disabled younger sister from their childhood ranch house in San Diego to a group home nearby in Boston, ostensibly so she could visit more easily. Bear had disagreed with this move, and he doubted very much that his older sister ever made good on her intention to visit their younger sister, but he could not bring himself to confront her. They'd been through too much already. It was better to swallow his opinions and anxieties and quietly foot the bill for it all.

"It's too cold there," Bear said.

Svec sneered. "You cannot say to native Russian."

Yui said, "Boston is the home city of my favorite writer and illustrator. Val Corwin."

"Never heard of him," Bear said.

"Here." Yui thrust his book into Bear's hands. It was a galley copy, bound in a plain white cover free of ornamentation. Yui's assistant had secured an advance copy just before the launch. The type was in Japanese, but Yui explained that it had been translated from the original English edition. "I cannot believe you do not know who he is. He is one of the most popular in Japan."

Bear and Svec looked at the pictures. A pregnant woman watched in horror as the lower half of her body liquefied. Each panel moved closer to her agony as her body and that of her fetus became a dangling tendril of mucus. It was, Bear thought, unnecessarily grotesque.

"Ha-ha," Svec laughed. "This comic book? For children? Can't be. Picture very—how do we say? Corrupt and bizarre?"

"No, definitely not for children," Yui said.

"Well, I'm heading back to the CDRA. I'll print this missing part later, I guess. Hopefully we will all be feeling a lot better soon."

"Have not been feeling bad, comrade." Russians were loath to complain, as Roscosmos docked them pay for ingratitude. So maybe he was lying. It couldn't be Bear alone who was feeling off. Bear looked to Yui for the truth.

"How about you, friendo? You been experiencing any headaches lately?"

"I feel . . ." Yui thought a long time. "Extraordinary. Ten years younger. We are weightless, friendos. Nothing can keep us down. Now I will go and play with the two-headed mouse."

"Don't be crass. Please," Bear said. Without some reining in, Yui could quickly become a hazard on the station. If Svec wouldn't take this duty seriously as commander and nip his behavior in the bud, Bear was not afraid to step up and be the adult.

"I promise that I am not joking, Bear-u."

"Yes. True," Svec said. "Mutation. Born this morning. Your NASA very excited. You don't know?"

"I've been busy," Bear said.

"Perhaps you should work a little less, friendo," Yui said, bowing to him. "You would see more."

Through the porthole Bear saw clouds swirling over North America, their long white skeins pointing like the thin spectral fingers of a ghost casting spells.

HISTORICALLY, LAST DAY was celebrated with a community pyre. It is legend that in Egypt stray dogs were corralled for the sacrifice, and in parts of southeastern Europe, a stillborn baby was included in the pyre to prevent dark spirits from repopulating the newly evacuated earth. On top of these embers townsfolk would toss their most beloved article of clothing, a perfectly useful, well-conditioned saddle, a warm, clean quilt. The offering was not a bargain to forestall death but rather a tiptoeing into the greater sacrifice possibly awaiting, to prepare the living for the coming of the end.

Now, for most Americans, throwing some hot dogs on the grill was considered an adequate homage to the pyres of antiquity, and piñatas stood in for live animal sacrifice. What was once a communal celebration, Last Day became more personal and private, confined to one's own backyard. But some cities were making a return to large public observances, such as the Brooklyn Do or Dye. On May 27 volunteers built a series of stations throughout Prospect Park in which New Yorkers could screenprint a T-shirt with a confession to be worn all day on May 28:

I pray that my good friends fail
Hey, Bill: EAT SHIT AND DIE
The condom broke
He hits me
I told my best friend I had an abortion to get her sympathy
It doesn't get better
Will you please hug me please

A macabre swap meet was held annually at the Drake Hotel in Chicago, where people brought a cherished object—"the one thing you would take to the grave," the invitation commanded—and left it on a table for a perfect stranger to claim. Someone's childhood teddy bear might be traded randomly and anonymously for another's illicit love letter. The wait list to be included in this somber gala event was over two years long, and the price of admission was five hundred dollars and a quart of blood donated at a designated blood bank one week prior to the event.

Minneapolis had an annual Zombie Parade, a ritual adhering to the discomfiting fiction that, somehow, some people would survive the end of the world (never a tenet in any culture's interpretation of the day) and that those survivors, for inexplicable reasons, would be transmogrified into movie monsters. The parade ended with a twelve-hour dance-off-cum-fundraiser for the homeless, which had raised over three million dollars to date.

In Boston, a city subject to wild vicissitudes of weather well into the month of May, a city where joy not earned by a measure of pain was not to be trusted, there existed a singular Last Day celebration. Each year for more or less twenty-four hours, from whatever time they felt like opening on May 27 to whatever time they closed on May 28, the staff at Redemption Tattoo inked free of charge anyone willing to wait in line. The catch was that you could not choose your tattoo. You were at another man's mercy, and the men who worked at Redemption were notorious drunkards even on non-holidays.

Kurt, Tom, Jake, and Ringo. That was the Redemption crew. Kurt was the owner of Redemption. He was in his forties, short and muscular with a growing beer belly, often mistaken as languid, even serene, until he rolled up his shirtsleeves and revealed the black and gray ghosts screaming in violent despair down his arms. He had made a living saying yes to whatever asinine idea his customers proposed, tailoring his at times ingenious craft to meet their vulgar needs. He created this Last Day tradition simply so that for twenty-four hours he got to do whatever he wanted at work.

"Is it hopeless?"

The customer who first sat in Kurt's chair had a jolly face. His hair was strawberry blond and curly, his eyes a bright, easy blue. "I started it this morning," he said, sipping beer from a red plastic cup. "But, fuck, man, I can't finish it."

Kurt probed the man's bloody sternum with his gloved hand. "You do time, man?"

"Old Colony Correctional. You?"

"South Middlesex. That's where you learned to tattoo?" Kurt asked him.

"Yeah. And I give myself a new one every year on Last Day since I got out. But this time, I don't know, this time it *hurts*. I couldn't finish."

"What's it supposed to be?" There was a mess of sloppy tattoos on the man's chest. Celtic knots, mostly.

"It's the letters CEC. For *Cecilia*."

Kurt took the man's plastic cup and handed it to Ringo. "Refill this, man, will ya?" He looked at the brick wall and was quiet. Ringo passed the fresh beer back to Kurt, who handed it to the man.

"Okay," he said. "I'm not fixing what you've done and I'm not finishing it, either. Instead I want to do a hanged man whose foot is just barely touching the petal of a huge fucking flower. A daisy, but a nuclear mutation of a daisy. Enormous. Bigger than the man. Meaning that the petals are firm enough to stand on, to support some but not all of the hanged man's weight."

"Where you going to put it?"

"Your left arm. The hanged man takes up the whole outer biceps. The spot where the dangling foot makes contact with the petal will be here, inside your elbow. The daisy or whatever will go down the underside of your forearm."

The man's face softened. He had never, in his entire life, felt so seen. He drained the beer and crushed the empty cup in his fist. "Okay," he finally said. His eyes welled up in a slippery, wobbling membrane he would not allow to break.

On the morning of May 27 the line outside Redemption stretched a mile down Commonwealth Avenue. The next person to appear before Kurt was a woman in an artfully ripped-up T-shirt, attended by a coterie of less attractive girlfriends. A woman, Kurt could tell just by looking at her, who vacationed in the realm of darkness but had never actually lived there.

Kurt bent over his notebook so that she couldn't see what he was drawing. "Okay, check this out." He handed her his notebook, then sat back and sipped his beer.

She and her attendants peered at the drawing.

"What is it?"

"Are those twigs?"

"It just looks like a bunch of lines."

"I don't get it," the pretty woman finally declared.

"It spells *wrong number*. I'll do it vertically down your spine. Gotta warn you—people say the spine hurts a lot. It's my personal experience that that's horseshit. It all fuckin' hurts. But this is what people, mostly girls, tell me. So I'm telling you. You've been warned."

"Can you do it around my ankle instead?"

"No."

"Can you do it in a prettier font?"

"If you make one more demand, you have to get out of my studio," Kurt said, his tone so gentle it sounded like a concession. He took another slug of his beer. He'd been nursing this cup slowly for the last hour.

It was warm and delicious. A line of bubbles collected on his upper lip and he made no move to wipe them off.

"I don't know . . . ," the lady whined. She was not a regular, no one Kurt recognized anyway. Many first-timers like her waited in line on Last Day, then chickened out at the last minute.

"You can go back to the end of the line, try again with another artist," he said.

"Nope," Jake shouted over the din of the crowd. "She'll never get another chance." He was delighted by this prospect. Jake had red hair and small, beady eyes that also appeared red. Exclusivity jazzed the hell out of him.

The woman bit her lip. She squinted, closed her eyes, took a deep breath, paused, then took another. It was a pantomime, this deliberation; she was riding a three-mimosa buzz and not in the mood to give much thought to anything today.

"Okay," she exhaled. "I'll do it!"

Her gaggle of friends woo-hooed and high-fived. They'd brought with them a shopping bag full of holiday-themed party favors and started handing out strands of purple and gold beads, fake engagement rings, and novelty condoms to all the people in line behind them.

She was lucky she hadn't gotten stuck with Jake. By that point in the morning he was so swirly, woozy, rope-a-dope drunk that every single tattoo he gave for the rest of the day and night was the single word: *RE-DEMPTION.*

"It's an exercise in formalism, eh, man?" said a hipster with a goatee and a Mao Zedong T-shirt.

"Shut your whore mouth," Jake drooled as he needled *REDEMP-TION* in sloppy cursive across the man's left calf.

It was like this every year, and yet people still waited for their turn. They waited for hours in all kinds of weather, happy to sign the waiver releasing all rights to any expanse of skin claimed by the artist as his canvas. People brought beach chairs and blankets and picnic baskets to the line. Outside the studio, strangers were sharing sandwiches and beers. This year it was seventy-nine degrees out, the smog-blue sky covered in a gauzy heat. Magnolia, forsythia, and cherry blossoms were past bloom, carpeting the sidewalk with a confetti of browning petals.

"Nothing like last year," someone said far down the line, slurping the dregs of her iced coffee.

"Our basement flooded," a fellow line-waiter chimed in. "And our insurance had lapsed. We got black mold. I'm still paying for that storm."

"What a nightmare that storm was," another man said, spitting brown tobacco juice into an empty seltzer can.

"You kids don't even know. Before you were even born we had the Last Day nor'easter. The bums in Public Works were all shitfaced. Good for nothing. I had to drive around with a chainsaw to break up the fallen trees blocking the roads."

"Yeah, 1985. I remember. We lost power for two friggin' weeks."

"Remember the year that asshole set off fireworks inside North Station?"

"To be honest, I thought that was kind of awesome."

"A lady got burned. Like, bad. Her ear was maimed for life."

"It's just an ear. It could be worse."

Back at Redemption, Tom was inking those exact words, *it could be worse*, onto a customer's rib cage. Tom was the looker of this quartet. The women always gravitated toward him. The other guys joked that Tom laced the ink with aphrodisiacs, though it was the much simpler combination of good looks, confidence, and implicit willingness. He had large brown eyes and a handsome face you knew without any picture of proof was the mirror image of a very pretty mother. He kept his dark hair combed back in a neat pompadour and wore T-shirts and jeans that showed off his muscular body without appearing to try too hard. When dressed in long sleeves and a tie, Tom could pass for a respectable family man with a white-collar job, but in reality it was a miracle that he had maintained employment at Redemption for as long as he had. Color was not Tom's strong suit—Kurt was the master of color—but his black and gray shading was impeccable, the best in New England.

Tom had started celebrating the night before and had woken up that morning already feeling tired. He wanted to call it quits, but one look of disappointment from Kurt would set off a slew of latent emotions he did not have time to drink away today. So he'd decided to forgo his typical Gothic images, and taking a page from drunk Jake's playbook, he began tattooing simple words. Lettering was easy—all you had to worry about was proportion. It was like taking a break without taking a break, if only the man on his table now would stop squirming. The man was probably in his late thirties but had the scrawny build of a twelve-year-old who happened to hit the gym and hit it hard. His rib cage was delicate and narrow, like the hull of a toy canoe. The man mentioned that he was a lawyer. Tom pulled the gun away.

"You signed the waiver, right? It's airtight. You can't sue me later."

"It is absolutely not airtight but, no, I'm not going to sue you. Jesus."

"I have nothing," Tom replied. "I live in the back room of my friends' apartment. We call it a room but it's actually a porch. Beautiful this time of year but fucking freezing in the winter, and you know what? I will stay there until those guys kick me out, because I spend all my money as soon as I make it on bars and restaurants and grass and girls. Sometimes coke, but mostly I let people buy coke for me, which is easy, because cokeheads never want to get high alone. I own nothing and have zero dollars in savings. If I ever get sick, with, like, cancer or something, I will invite that shit to multiply all it wants because I will never, ever be able to afford treatment. See these boots?" Tom lifted his foot up so that the man lying prone and shirtless in his chair could see it. "These boots were three hundred dollars and I will wear them until they fall off my fuckin' feet. The boots I had before these ones I wore for eight years and not until I started feeling the pavement through the soles did I buy these replacements. If you sued me, these steel-toed bad boys would be the best thing you would get."

"The legal system doesn't work like that, asshole. And don't worry. I don't want your boots."

"I don't want the headache of showing up at court, either. I'd rather be flogged than sit around and wait. Hit me in the face with a brick. Pry out my toenails. I'd take that any day over waiting for the judge to call me."

"Just finish my tattoo, all right? I got a party to go to later tonight."

"I know all about you lawyers," Tom said.

"You're right, okay? Lawyers are bastards. I'm a bastard. She fucking left me because I was a coldhearted bastard. . . ."

RINGO WAS BOTH the youngest and the newest artist at Redemption. His real name was Patrick. The other guys had christened him Ringo as a joke, and after a while it stuck. Ringo was a good sport about things, and he had a long, beak-like nose, so the name seemed to suit him. He was twenty-three and wide-eyed, a tall skinny boy whose specialty was flowers. Ringo had been raised by his widowed grandmother, a gardener who'd taught him the name of everything green that grew. As a young boy he liked to draw pictures of flowers, filled whole notebooks with them; then, with a twist of pride and shame, he hid the notebooks under his pillow, knowing that his grandmother made his bed every morning after he left for school. The old woman would look at his drawings, then place the notebook in the same position as she'd found it under the pillow, never saying a word.

Ringo's first customer on Last Day was a man with broken yellow teeth who asked for a derringer pointing down his calf. Ringo gave him a lilac cluster shaped like a gun. This man was followed by a college kid who asked for Jesus on his back. Ringo gave him a skull blooming daisies out of the eye sockets. One lady asked for the dates of her daughter's birth and death inscribed inside a heart. The kid was not even three years old when she died. Ringo thought long and hard about that one. He gave her a piñata burro exploding with every kind of flower he could fit on her shoulder.

Kurt had taken a break to check his text messages, coming to terms with yet another promise he had made in a drunken state that he was now regretting. Staring at his phone, he overheard the young mother crying softly to Ringo, who made an effort to touch her body with care, even as he made permanent scars in her skin.

"You are too good for this world," Kurt said, shaking his head.

"Who is?" Ringo asked. He had just been thinking the opposite— that he had such an easy life and he'd done nothing to deserve it, while other people, like the grieving mother in his chair, had to live with a reality that was unbearable. It felt cruel and unfair, even if such things were beyond fairness. "Not me," Ringo said, dabbing at the red trickle bleeding from the rose he'd just finished.

"We all are," Kurt said, already looking exhausted.

By POPULAR VOTE, the local classical station was piped into the weight room at the YMCA. That day the entire fifteen hours of Wagner's *Ring* cycle was being broadcast without interruption in honor of the holiday. At that point in the morning, mortals and gods were still wrestling for control, as if they had a chance.

"Rosette, do you ever feel like your shoes might hurt just as much as your feet do?"

"My shoes take me where I need to go," Rosette answered, "and that's all they need to do."

Rosette was watching with great admiration her own body as she did squats in front of the giant mirror. Her charge, Mr. Cox, sat on the floor snoozing against a stack of yoga blankets. He was sixty-three, physically healthy enough to live another twenty active years, except for the plaque in his brain, gumming up the pathway of his thoughts, even simple thoughts like *Red means stop, Don't drink the Windex, My name is George Dean Cox.* For twenty bucks an hour under the table, Rosette picked him up at Morning Pines and took him with her to do whatever she wanted to do that day. "A program of enrichment," she billed it to his adult daughters, who were happy to pay any price not to worry about him.

"How do you know when you, specifically, are doing what your God wants you to do? I mean, anything can be an augury of anything. Like, a leaf on the sidewalk shiny side down could mean yes as well as no, depending on your interpretation."

"No leaves, Karen baby. God trying to tell you to follow Him and you looking at the ground."

"Yeah but follow *where*?"

"If what you want is so hard to get, if you have to stop all the time and red lights are everywhere, and no no no is all you hear, and you still do it, and then you feel terrible after, that was because you not on God's path. If God is making a way for you, it's always easy."

"But bad things are so easy."

"Because sometimes what we think meant evil for us meant good for God's plan. Sometimes God uses us to make pain because then that can make others do good. Jesus would never have died if Judas didn't betray him."

"Oh." It hadn't occurred to Karen, in all her studies, that she could use her powers for evil. Or that she ought to. She picked a corner off a pockmarked old yoga block. Rolling the purple foam between her fingers, she heard a twitter. *Do it*. Karen plopped the bit of foam into her mouth and swallowed it.

"Mr. Cox!" Rosette slapped her hands together, trying to wake the old man. He had slid off the pile of blankets and was lying awkwardly on the floor. "Help me get him up, Karen. Now. Before he gets stuck like this."

"I want some candy. Can I borrow some money for the vending machine?"

"No. You can eat lunch when it is lunchtime."

"I didn't bring a lunch," Karen said. A lie. She'd eaten both of her frozen pizzas in the first hour of her shift.

"I always bring extra for you, my friend," Rosette said. She had made fried pork chops, a fact she kept to herself for now, or the girl would be begging like a stray dog until it was time to eat.

Karen both was and was not a girl, Rosette felt. Bulk collected around her hips like a mother of ten, but her voice fluttered and shrieked like a toddler's. Her breasts were enormous and scored by the lines of an ill-fitting bra. Her blond hair curled in girlish ringlets and her big blue eyes protruded with the never-ending alacrity of a curious, slightly stunned child. Rosette didn't know Karen's whole story, but she could tell the girl had been raped at least once, probably more. Karen bore the unmistakable stain of sexual trauma. There was the way she walked, a broken, yelping gait, not quite mannish but definitely not feminine. And she was obviously protecting herself from fleshly danger through many extra pounds of fat. That much was obvious. Rosette didn't need to ask, nor did she want to. The fountain of Karen's crazy was hard to shut off once it started, she'd learned regretfully after giving Karen her phone number.

All Rosette knew for sure was that Karen had no family, no one to teach her right from wrong. Such a pity, though unsurprising in this godforsaken country. Rosette had been in the U.S. for twenty years, long enough to know it was a beautiful land tilled for doom. Her island in the Azores had its problems, yes, but was superior to her new home in most ways. Though of course superiority did not guarantee admittance to the afterlife. You had to work because it was good to work, to sacrifice and be glad about it. In time Rosette knew she could make Karen understand. As insufferable as the girl could be, she had a good heart, and Rosette wanted to prepare her for the possibility of deliverance. Why else had God put this annoying woman into her life?

First Karen would need to lose weight. She was big as a hippo. It would be rude to arrive in Paradise with all that fat, like showing up as a guest in someone's house carrying more luggage than could fit in your room. Also, Karen's mind jumped around like a grasshopper. She needed the focus of the one true God. More than once Rosette had had to reprimand Karen for reading YMCA members' palms. "The Devil's sideshow!" Rosette had screamed, and had given a reproving tug, short but sharp, on Karen's bouncy ponytail. But even these palm readings she did with good intentions, Rosette had to admit. Karen just wanted to be liked, and she was willing to learn, especially when Rosette offered to feed her.

Rosette was no angel, she was the first to admit. But all had been forgiven when she'd turned her life over to the Jehovah's Witnesses. The main reason Rosette had joined was because she liked the idea that the unfaithful would be destroyed in a violent cosmic comeuppance, as this surely included her ex-husband, the most unfaithful human being to walk this rotting earth.

For a time she'd wondered if she had brought this misery on herself, if her ex-husband had been sent by God to punish her for the wantonness of her youth. But this theory didn't hold up to scrutiny. All Rosette's childhood friends had been rapacious sluts—it was something about the plaid jumpers of their Catholic school, so ugly and itchy. It wasn't enough to take them off after a long day; you wanted to rip such a skirt off your body in a violent passion and throw it in the face of a man panting with lust. And all of these Catholic school friends were in blessedly boring marriages now.

When she was only thirteen, Rosette had seduced a seventeen-year-old neighbor, a boy who later flung himself off a fishing boat in a storm when he learned that Rosette had also taken his cousin as her lover. There were plenty of other boys to follow. São Miguel had become too small for her by the age of twenty. She decided to hunt for bigger game in the States. Once she had saved enough money for airfare and tuition, she'd enrolled in a nurse's aide program in Boston, where there were enough other Azoreans to ensure that she could still find her native food and music and laughter. She told her friends and family she would come back as a millionaire's wife.

She knew her life was unfolding according to plan when she met Joey Mazzone in the Italian restaurant he claimed to own. He bought her gold necklaces, silver bracelets, and emerald earrings. He gave her the keys to his car and his golden American Express and said, "Don't come home, sweetheart, until you've spent at least a grand."

After they'd exchanged vows at City Hall, she learned that Joey was in staggering debt to multiple credit card accounts. And he was the manager, not the owner, of Enoteca. He didn't own anything, in fact, not even his car, a Lincoln Continental that belonged to his mother, who let him drive it whenever he wanted as she had become legally blind.

They'd been married two years when, one miserable Saturday night, Joey was "out" again, and Rosette, quaking with rage at her kitchen table, couldn't stop imagining a violent collision. And while Joey was out riding the Vespa he had bought with Rosette's paycheck, impressing some harlot—which harlot Rosette no longer cared, there were too many to count—he hit a pothole and their two bodies went flying. Joey smashed into the overarching beam of a streetlamp, snapping his neck instantly. The harlot skidded across the pavement, crushed and skinned like a rabbit.

Rosette believed she had made this happen with her mind. Guilt and pride swirled in a sour mixture in her mouth. If Rosette had given it a little more thought, she would have tempered the violence. Have Joey choke to death in his sleep, or develop spontaneous nut allergies and die of anaphylaxis. Yes, a good old-fashioned poisoning by natural causes, that would have been a peaceful end to him and his passions. But in her grief and rage that night, she'd had no control over her imagination.

As a widow, Rosette was angrier than ever. She'd remained sitting at her kitchen table for days after the funeral, her thick black hair growing into a dark shroud around her face, her eyes swollen with powerlessness and mania. All day she nursed a coffee mug full of rum, occasionally, in the middle of her sobs, stopping to blow on the rim of her cup, as if there were really hot coffee in there that needed cooling. She didn't want God to see her carrying on. She'd feared Him all her life, even when she'd blocked Him out.

So it seemed like a message from the Divine when two teenage boys in short-sleeve shirts and skinny black ties knocked on her door, bearing the good news.

"He float, he float, he float. This woman, that woman. But he always float back to me. I ask the Lord let me never ask him where he goes. And one day I did. Joey say it was because he was Italian. It was his nature, his God-given duty, to please as many women as he could. But it was my fault he ran off with harlots," Rosette wept. She catalogued her flaws for the two boys—big feet, sagging breasts, excessive pride, and a very promiscuous past. "My mother tell me when I was a little girl, 'Men love a wild woman for fun, but they only marry a boring one.' I wanted to get married. So I pretended to be boring. Now look at me!"

Her head collapsed onto the table and she sobbed into a pool of rum spilled from her overturned mug. One boy got up and found a rag to wipe it up with; the other began sorting through her mail, stacking neatly all her unread newspapers and magazines, throwing out the coupon circulars that were now out-of-date. They did her dishes and made her some toast. After she had nibbled a little of the crust, she said, "So, what do I do now?"

The two young men were immigrants like Rosette. Their parents had brought them from Haiti to give them a better life in the States, even as they sought to protect them from so much of that new life. As Jehovahs they were not allowed to go to college, making this door-to-door ministry an important outlet for their youthful energy and ingenuity. They made sweet attempts to connect their ultimate message to Rosette's story of betrayal and grief. It was Satan's rule on Earth, they explained. It really wasn't anybody's fault. Lots of innocent people and nearly all politicians were under Satan's spell and couldn't help it. They told her about the End of Days, which she welcomed. The Catholics of her childhood had preached that all would be one in heaven. Hell no, Rosette thought now. Heaven on Earth, as the Jehovahs promised, was much more selective. It was a place that definitely excluded her dead husband, meaning she would never have to see that man's bloated, stubbly face again. All that was required was her belief.

Karen had shown some interest in Rosette's church, but to her it was more like a cabinet of wonders. She was fascinated by their arcana, their chosen symbols and songs. She'd read that the Jehovah's Witnesses were not allowed to participate in any war, that they hated flags and were terrified of blood. Even if Rosette was dying, she was not allowed to accept a transfusion.

"What if you were unconscious and the doctor went ahead and gave you a transfusion anyway, then what?" Karen asked.

"Your mind jump on all the wrong things," Rosette responded.

Karen's head was resting on Rosette's thigh. Rosette pulled one of her blond curls straight, then released it. Karen had traded Rosette a couple of her tranquilizers for one of Mr. Cox's painkillers. The three of them lay beneath the lifeguard's chair in a listless calm, watching diamonds of sunlight rupture the surface of the pool.

TERRENCE HAD CALLED the night before to say that someone had dropped out of the Habitat for Humanity Club's camping trip and there was an open spot. Did Sarah want to come? Sarah had no gear, but Terrence assured her he had plenty for the two of them. Sarah allowed an awkward pause to speak for her.

"B-besides," Terrence stuttered, "these guys know how to build houses. They can make a shelter out of wet leaves and a shoelace. If there's anyone you want to be with at the end of the world, it's the Habitat for Humanity Club."

She said she'd let him know after her morning run.

"Meet us at the train depot. We have a charter bus. Leaves at 11 A.M."

Sarah double-knotted her sneakers and hit the road. Even Terrence was so goddamn glib about the world ending. She was furious at him. He of all people should know better: this whole stupid holiday was nothing more than a political distraction from the real destruction and cruelty happening worldwide; everyone was celebrating an imaginary apocalypse while schools filled with children were bombed by dictators and pipelines leaked millions of tons of crude oil into the sea. It was so obvious it was stupid, and Sarah hated herself for being sucked into the myth, for being so afraid.

She ran until her legs seemed to disappear. She stopped finally at the Edgewater causeway to catch her breath, a good eight miles from home, not remembering the preceding hour of her life. Two egrets stood on either side of the channel, their legs so lissome and still as to appear invisible at that distance, making their round white rumps seem to levitate above the marsh. The water was mute and silver, flowing eastward into the sea. Sarah listened to the wind, her soft panting breath, and the sound of the water. One of the egrets took three steps on its spindly legs, then stopped, plunged its nose into the tall grass, nibbled on something brackish and small, then stood erect and still once more. The other egret did not move at all.

"I know the world is shit, but I still don't want to lose it," she said, gazing now at the birds. She felt tears welling up. A hollowness in her chest rose to her throat and pushed hard on the walls of her soul. The membrane between her mind and the atmosphere was burning away. She felt like she was being lifted out of her sneakers, off the pavement, about to be hurtled into the endless sky.

This is it, she thought, *this is what the end is.*

Then the feeling passed, her feet were on the ground, it was still morning. She began to run again, hitting a 7:30 mile on the way home, a personal best.

Her parents were in the kitchen still, twirling globs of dough into pizza crusts for their party. Sarah breezed past them, took the quickest shower of her life, then stuffed a backpack with clothes, her journal, and a sleeping bag.

"Where are you going?" her mother asked her. She was wearing a frilly pink-and-red apron that Sarah's father had bought as a joke for Valentine's Day. They'd been married nineteen years and were the two happiest people she had ever met in her life.

"I'm going camping," Sarah answered.

"Where? With whom?" Her father taught in the physics department at the college, on the floor above her mom.

"Don't say 'whom,' Ari. You sound like a pedant."

"Which friends, Saralita?"

"The Habitat for Humanity Club."

"Oh, good. You'll be in good hands."

"Do you need any money?"

"No," Sarah answered. "I mean, yes."

Her parents exchanged looks. Her dad wiped his hands on his wife's apron and looked around the kitchen for his wallet. Sarah inspected the toppings. Eggplant and mango.

"Purple and gold," her mother explained. Sarah's pulse fluttered in a bitter, stringy rhythm. "You've got to try this marinated chicken. We used pineapple juice! Your dad and I are geniuses. We're going to quit academia and sell this stuff full-time at farmers' markets. You won't mind going to a state college, right, honey?"

"Very funny, Mom. I'm in a hurry. I've got a bus to catch."

"Here you go, kiddo." Her dad handed her two damp twenty-dollar bills. "We'll save you a couple slices for when you get back, okay?"

"I'm not eating meat, remember?"

"That's right," her mother said. "Oh, that's too bad. These are going to be so good."

"We can just make one without chicken," her dad suggested.

"Of course! That's what we'll do. Sorry, I'm frazzled. You know how I get on the holiday."

"You guys, I really have to go."

Did she kiss them goodbye? she would wonder later. Did they say they loved her? It was an utterance so common in their happy house that the sounds of those words had lost all resonance over the years. It had become a reflex of the mouth, a hum as constant and forgettable as the refrigerator's motor, audible but seldom heard.

ANOTHER OF BEAR'S directives was to maintain a social media presence for the ISS, curating images and short videos that people on Earth would find interesting, in the hope that it would stoke an electorate with a dispiriting apathy toward science to vote for more government-funded space projects. This doubled as an excuse for Bear to hang out in the Cupola, as it provided the best optics, where he liked to take what he'd come to think of as a nice cool drink of Earth.

Just looking at her made Bear's mouth water, as though at a cellular level his body was aware of the artificial environment he was in, where the only water existed in plastic sacks. He attached his camera to the end of a selfie stick and positioned himself so that a glimpse of Earth was behind him in the shot. He was recording a laymen's guide to the weather research NASA was conducting at the moment, but his spiel, which he'd written out beforehand on index cards, kept losing focus when he tried to go off script. He could see in the camera's screen that they were flying over Africa now. The Nile River appeared as a crack in a thin shard of clay.

"Look," Bear heard someone say, and he turned his head away from the camera and past his feet where he saw Yui floating toward him, his hands cupped against his chest.

"They are so cute. Too cute. I cannot believe how cute," Yui said. As he got closer he showed Bear what he was holding so delicately in his hands. It was the infamous newborn mouse pup, about the size of a cashew nut, scrawny and gray with one white belly, four tiny paws, and two heads curled into each other as though taking refuge.

"No way," Bear said. He quickly hit "Pause" on the recording and swatted at Yui like an errant child. "Get that thing back to the lab before it—"

"Too late."

A string of gold liquid issued from the mouse pair and re-formed into a ball. Yui let go of the mouse, whose legs paddled against the air as its ball of urine floated aimlessly away from its body.

"Awww, even their urine is so cute," Yui said. He cupped his hands around the wriggly animal again and gave a gentle kiss to each of its heads. Bear wrapped his hand in his T-shirt to catch the floating globule of piss before it hit the sides of the ship.

"You absolutely cannot do this, Yui."

"I may not, but I can. A surprise for you. To cheer you up. You looked so lonely this morning. You are very welcome, friendo," Yui said.

Yui was a man who had never been asked to grow up. He and his twin brother, Tadeshi, were born into oceans of family money, wealth so vast and deep and regenerative it strained the imagination to picture a future when it would be depleted. Their father had inherited a fortune from his own father, a Tokyo real estate mogul, and increased this fortune exponentially by starting what became the largest, most successful video game company in the world. Their mother was a child model-actress who had married their father at nineteen and committed suicide eight years later. Yui and his brother did not mourn her for very long; they were raised by a staff of doting, indulgent nannies who insulated the twins from every blunt strike the world might fling in their direction. Their father was distant and impossible to impress, and their mother, while alive, had been a very pretty ghost, striking a vision in the hallways as she glided in and out of rooms in her bright silk dresses that, lacking the creativity to do anything else, she changed several times a day. A creature of alien and alienating beauty, she was less like a parent than a tropical bird whose clipped wings prevented her from going anywhere beyond their lavish compound in Roppongi.

Yui began sketching ideas for his company's newest virtual reality game, a strangulating dreamscape of outer space in which the first-person player-protagonist is confronted by the myriad buttons, dials, and instruments of a space station without any knowledge of what function each instrument performs. He was populating the game with monsters, real and unreal: vanishing air pressure, missiles from warring nations, mendacious aliens, synthesizing the horror of banality—*I can't breathe! I'm trapped!*—with the elaborate terrors of the mind. It was to be his magnum opus.

And as he drew and dreamed on this thesis now, his mother stole out of his unconscious for the first time in years, appearing on his tablet as a sketch of a bird of paradise flitting improbably across the black velvet void of space.

Yui had awakened to the alarm at 6 A.M. Greenwich Mean Time along with his other two crewmates, then retreated back to his sleeping pod to masturbate, reread his favorite graphic novel, and nap. Napping was an essential step in his creative process. He believed it re-created the bleary color splash between sleep and consciousness that fueled his imagination. As he hammered away at his game now, another vision emerged—that one day he and his brother would open the first brothel in space. He smiled to himself, already proud. Yui was the idea man; Tadeshi made things happen. Because of this, there was perfect harmony in the world.

Yui closed his eyes and swallowed three times, a fraternal ritual encoded in childhood for sending thoughts back and forth between the twins without speaking. It worked at least half the time. Yui would call his brother later to ask him if he'd received the transmission. He hurried to scribble down the last few notes about the game before he forgot them: the protagonist of the game would have to decide whether or not to follow this bird of paradise, to determine as one of his many possible obstacles if she was real or not, trustworthy or not, as the player swam in his unwieldy spacesuit between the unblinking stars in search of help.

Along with his work on the VR game, Yui was supposed to be aiding the other astronauts with their ongoing scientific experiments and representing the nation of Japan in the spirit of cooperation and brotherly love. So far he had used his time perfecting the art of peeing upside down.

"Not so perfect," Bear pointed out as he flew out of the bathroom with a wad of paper towels and slammed them into the trash receptacle. Yui did manage to take many of his duties on this mission seriously, but cleaning up after himself as diligently as was required in these cramped quarters was not one of them.

"To be fair, he's probably not used to cleaning up after himself," Bear said to Svec, after reporting the mouse incident to him. Much had been written about Yui and Tadeshi, the CEO counterpart of their video-gaming dynasty. In his attempt to be more empathetic to his annoying crewmate, Bear had taken the time to read a ridiculous, panegyric eight-thousand-word *New Yorker* profile of him that only succeeded in deepening the mystery. Both Yui and his twin were married to women, both fathers now, yet the two brothers maintained a shared apartment separate from their wives, and this flat, small even by Tokyo standards, had only one bedroom. The article painted them as post-modern Castor and Pollux. *Strange ducks indeed*, Bear thought.

He had to be politic, to convince Svec of the severity of the situation without seeming to be culturally insensitive. The problem, he argued with Svec, was not that Yui was careless or willfully destructive, but that he simply didn't see the messes he left behind, let alone the ramifications for the station, because living with servants had meant that such messes, for all intents and purposes, had erased themselves from his vision.

"I'm trying to think of it as a kind of handicap, really," Bear said.

He and Svec had both ended up in the American lab at the same time, a rare occurrence on this ship where daily work was carried out in the seclusion of each national's module. Yui, they assumed, was still in the Kibo laboratory, drawing in staggering detail portraits of the monotony that surrounded them—the white tunnels they'd come to think of as rooms, the arrows and instructions in various languages printed everywhere like cheerless, obsessive graffiti.

Bear pricked his finger with a lancet and watched the blood bubble onto his skin. He flicked it gently, allowing the orb to float like a tiny red gem in the air before catching it on the plastic slide he inserted into the cholesterol meter. "Developmental delays as a symptom of ultra-wealth."

"Bullshit," Svec answered. He scratched his thick beard, his fingers disappearing inside a wiry bib of black hair. This was his third six-month term on the ISS. He could not have gotten to this stage in his career if he had not known how to play well with others, but he brooked no tolerance for Bear's particularly American tendency to wrap piss-poor excuses in a ribbon of unflagging cheer.

"Serfs played tricks like this. They pretended to be stupid, to be lazy. But really this was their way to say 'fuck you' to masters."

"You might want to speak to him about it, Captain. Before it gets out of hand." Bear sealed his blood smear in a plastic container, reset the meter, and handed it to Svec.

"You can be his master if you want. I don't want."

"Perhaps a report to JAXA could do the work for us. Coming from his home space agency, a reproval might inspire more respect in him. Keep him in line. "

Svec lanced his own finger and squeezed blood to the surface. His face creased in what might have been a smile. Bear could never decipher Svec's moods from his facial expressions. The smirk he saw now could just as easily be derision or affection. "He is only here for six more weeks."

"You will cry when I am gone," Yui said, floating noiselessly into the module. He waited while the two men squirmed in their mutual embarrassment. After a long silence, Yui bowed to them.

"This is the day that could be our last," he said when he lifted his head. "I give you my deepest forgiveness."

"You mean apologies."

"No, friendo. *Mou ii yo. Kin is shinade*. All is forgiven."

KAREN KNELT ON the floor and pulled the trigger on a bottle of glass cleaner. The liquid looked like fireworks smashing against the window. She had thrown up from Mr. Cox's painkillers, as she usually did, just a little. Rosette had, too. But now they were better. She watched the blasts of liquid start to run, their wild rays dripping into tentacles.

"There's no point in cleaning," Karen mumbled. She let the blue cleaner stream down the window in pale streaks and walked hunchbacked to the front desk.

"Hmmm," Rosette replied, simultaneously texting and peeling the black reptilian skin of an avocado.

Cleaning was the stupidest thing about life. First, with the pollen outside, she could clean and clean all day and the windows would still look dirty. The world was golden and hopeless out there. Second, Karen was not a good cleaner. She got demerits all the time at Heart House because her room was such a disaster. The staff said it was a fire hazard with all her library books and journals and newspapers stacked up everywhere, but the house was run by Lutherans, or used to be once upon a time, so there might have been a strain of puritanism in all the insistence on cleanliness.

"And third, it's Last Day. These are possibly the last moments on Earth. I mean, I don't really believe this year is the year. Plus there are so many other astral conflicts with today's position in the zodiac. It's a day for planting, not reaping, technically. But who even cares?"

Rosette shot her a stern look. She dragged a spoon across the soft green flesh of the avocado and fed it to Mr. Cox. "This attitude is poor. You need to be grateful. We gonna make a list. This will help."

Rosette gave the spoon to Mr. Cox to hold. He was very tall with broad stooped shoulders. His hair was thin and gray, pasted by sweat against his brown-spotted scalp. It was getting a little too long in the back. Rosette charged his daughters extra to bring him to a barber, then cut it herself and pocketed the cash. Mr. Cox stood up, clenched the spoon in his fist, and examined it. "Princeton," he said.

"That's right, Mr. Cox. Now sit down like a good boy."

"Princeton!" he said again, the veins on his forehead swelling blue.

Rosette waved her hand in his face as though shooing a mosquito, and Mr. Cox sat down. She rummaged through her purse and slapped a pad of paper down on the front desk. "The lady on TV say this is the key to happiness. They studied the brain. People who do this every day don't get depressed. Write down a list of everything you grateful for. I'll make one, too. You'll see. No matter what happens, you can't do nothing to change it. But you can face it all with a grateful heart."

"How many things should I list?" Karen asked.

"As many—" Rosette began, then thought better of it. "Five."

The two women bent over their papers and wrote their lists.

"So fun! Now let's exchange," Karen suggested. She took Rosette's paper and read:

> Lord, I am so grateful to You for all that You have blessed me with,
> but today most of all for—
> Your kingdom, in Heaven and on Earth
> Pastor Alfred
> Freedom from lust

Not being born Italian
My mother's cozido

"Your handwriting is so straight and tall. Like you," Karen exclaimed. "Mine is so loopy."

"Ha-ha! Like you!" She read from Karen's list:

Things Karen (me) is grateful for:
Candy
Tigers
Kittens
Swimming
Rosette

"That's sweet of you, baby. I am grateful for you, too. Sometimes."

"Rose, do you think, when the end comes, that we will melt or explode or crumble or what? What does your new church think will happen to those of us who aren't saved?"

"I think every bad thing will happen all at once. Fires and floods, earthquakes and volcanoes, freezing nights and boiling days. But I am ready, so I don't worry about it no more."

"Yeah, me, too," Karen said. Her stomach twisted hard around the remaining objects she had swallowed but not thrown up that day. She knew in this case, as many times before, that more was not better. She called upon the voice of Nora in her head and Nora agreed. She looked at Rosette roughly wiping the avocado off Mr. Cox's face and knew that if she asked her counsel, Rosette would say the same thing: *No more.* But there was another voice, hungry and hoarse and whining like a baby. *One more. One more and you'll be done. Just one more.* Karen broke the eraser off Rosette's pencil and swallowed it. Again it burned and then she felt nothing at all.

THE CHARTER BUS grumbled in the parking lot of the Edgewater train station. Terrence stood outside it tapping on his phone. In her pocket Sarah felt her phone vibrating with his message.

U coming? We're waiting 4 u

Sarah hid behind the pillars that supported the depot platform. The ground beneath her feet began to rattle. In the distance she heard the train's approaching horn.

I can't. Sorry, she texted back. She watched as he received the message, slid his phone into his front jeans pocket, and knocked on the door of the bus. With a great gaseous sigh, the door opened and Terrence disappeared inside.

What was wrong with her? Why couldn't she just fall in love with Terrence and climb into a sleeping bag with him under the stars? That was romantic, normal, and probably fun. Sarah Burke would have killed for Terrence's attention. Sarah Burke had even tried to seduce him over spring break, but Terrence had refused. He was saving himself for love, for Sarah. And what was she doing? Obsessing over a strange man she'd met only once, a grandiose imaginary friend.

"Train to Boston. Train to Boston. Last Day, no fare. All aboard. Train to Boston," the conductor sang.

Maybe she didn't have to know the answer. Maybe she just had to show up and see what happened. That was the Last Day spirit, wasn't it? Sarah hopped onto the train just as it began to depart from the platform. It was already so full that she had to take a seat among a group of teenage boys, all of them wearing dirty white baseball caps. They were passing around a pint bottle of liquor wrapped in a brown paper bag. They laughed and jostled each other in a way Sarah found cute, sociologically speaking.

One of the boys noticed her watching them and offered her a sip from his bottle.

"No thank you," Sarah said.

"You're beautiful. You know that?" the boy slurred. He was a bit older than she was. His cheeks were rosy in a way that suggested skin disease. "Sweetheart," the boy said, leaning so close to Sarah she could smell the cheapness of the booze on his breath. "You gotta boyfriend?"

"I do." Sarah smiled. *Sort of.*

"Lucky man," the boy replied. "You tell him I said so."

He turned back to face his friends, who were covering their faces, laughing into their shirts, so ashamed for and of him.

"Don't laugh," the rosacea-faced guy told his buddies. "At least I take risks. That's what today is all about." He lit the wrong end of his cigarette, then flipped it around and burned his lips with the ember.

"Relax, dude. She's a seven."

"Not even. She's a six, max."

"A blond six is a seven, bro."

"Guys, it's *Last Day*," Sarah's former suitor insisted. "We should strive for eights. Eights or higher."

"Good call."

"Even O'Keefe can score a drunk-enough eight tonight."

"I don't care. We're on the road. A two is a ten on the road."

As the boys evaluated her worth and laughed, Sarah looked for an escape route. So many more people had gotten on at the succeeding stops that there was not even room to stand in the aisle anymore. She was stuck with these boys, who were so much easier to confront in the abstract, in her journal or in her opinion essays at school. In real life, boys like this made her feel nervous and depressed. She looked out the window of the train as it glided over a marsh—thick green grass studded by pools of water that reflected the broken blue of the sky. She didn't want any of this to end. It was too beautiful. Even if it meant sharing the world with snot-nosed sexists in Patriots hats.

Maybe, Sarah thought, she could create a cosmic reversal. Maybe, if she made the day *memorable,* it would beget a future from which she could stand and look back and remember. There would be another new day, and then another and another. For a few seconds this possibility felt real.

But.

What if today, with its too-nice weather and too-pretty sky, was too ordinary to be anything but profoundly, ironically doomed?

Maybe her parents were right. Maybe she should try going on medication.

When she got off the train, she marched into a convenience store and asked the cashier for cigarettes. "Pack of Reds," she blurted, not entirely sure that was a thing people actually said. She could feel her entire body shaking under her clothes. "And this." She slapped an issue of that week's *The Economist* on the counter. The cover was an illustration of a dead dove, belly-up, a stock market ticker tape streaming from its beak. Outside, Sarah inhaled three drags of her first ever cigarette and promptly threw up.

"What am I going to do?" she said.

Sarah's psyche was in its chrysalis, a place where all the inventions of her childhood, her desires and opinions and perceived truths, were being dismantled, then liquefied into a putrid ooze out of which her adult character would eventually take shape. But before she could emerge from that glorious unfiltered roux of teenage narcissism, she would have to spend hours that added up to days of very sincere, very insane, unattractive but psychologically necessary navel-gazing. All sorts of thoughts sprang delightfully from this moody introspection. Some of them—for example, that algebra was pointless for all but computer programmers and should be cut from the school curriculum—she had believed passionately, then dismissed later. Others cycled more quickly through the inchoate intellectual mill in less than a day, such as *I will never be the kind of girl who gets pedicures*. (Until she did, and loved it.) There were ideas she cherished and would have nurtured for the rest of her life, like the realization that she was wanted into existence by two people in love, wanted even before she was born. And then there were overzealous opinions that would later embarrass her: that Kerouac was the Blake of the twentieth century. The unifying thread in all her meditations was the seriousness she applied to them.

So when a reckless mix of fables, myths, movies, and self-importance presented her with one particular idea at around noon of Last Day, Sarah felt deeply and instantaneously that this was right and true: *if I have sex with Kurt tonight, the world will not end.*

It made a comforting kind of sense—how about supplanting a fear of the apocalypse with a new set of more tangible anxieties? Like, would he even want to have sex with her? How would she broach the subject? What was she expected to do? Were there prescriptive movements and sounds she should perform? Would it hurt? Would she hemorrhage like courtly maidens on their wedding nights? Was she pretty enough to pull this off? What if Kurt wasn't there? What if he had made other plans? What if she got pregnant, or herpes, or both? Wasn't it tradition not to use a condom on Last Day? What if at this very moment he was in Buenos Aires? What would she do then?

She closed her eyes and saw a vision of Kurt beside her on the beach, a pink sun emerging from the ocean. Watching the sunrise was cheesy, she knew. There were so many nauseating movies and TV shows and commercials about Last Day set against the backdrop of a shy but inde-

fatigable rising sun. It was the universal symbol of the holiday, representing the hope that life would go on. (Duh.) It wasn't the sun's fault that
sunrises had become a cliché. Natural phenomena were always getting
co-opted as symbols for causes that had nothing to do with them. It happened to rainbows and lightning and shooting stars. So why not, Sarah
reasoned, do the thing that everyone else said was so special and watch
the sun rise on May 28? Maybe doing this was so trite that it actually
doubled back to being cool. And Sarah had never watched the sun rise
over Last Day, and never having done something before seemed as good
a reason as any to do it.

Y UI GRABBED THE cholesterol meter from Svec and took his own reading. "Who will be master of all men now?" he said, his eyebrows arched.

Yui had inaugurated an ersatz Olympics with a game of space darts the moment the previous crew had departed. With a woman on board, the atmosphere had been less competitive. Bear had known and respected Linda for many years, but he had to admit that she wafted a relentlessly feminine air of consensus-building and kinship throughout the ship. As soon as she and the other two astronauts were gone, Yui burst out of what little shell was restraining him and the games began.

It was hard to prove one's prowess with nothing weighted to lift. There could be none of the push-up contests both Bear and Svec had grown to love in the military. So the three men relied on vision tests, space darts, chess matches, and even cholesterol readings in their not-quite-kidding quest to assert personal and national dominance over each other.

Yui frowned at his daily cholesterol reading. "Typically, Japanese people have very low cholesterol," Yui said. He rubbed his soft, protruding belly. "I am not typical Japanese."

"You are not typical nothing," Svec replied.

Bear wrote down their results in the notebook where all their competitions were recorded. Instead of their names, Yui had drawn penises in the colors of each man's flags (the white and red penis of Japan was pornographically large and erect while those of the U.S. and Russia were flaccid and small). Svec was in the lead almost across the board, though Yui was a formidable threat in chess; cholesterol was the one category where Bear had the other two squarely beat. He stuck the notebook back to the Velcro strip on the wall.

"Sixty-nine HDL, Yui. Not too bad," he said, trying not to gloat.

Svec and Yui were already absorbed in a game of speed chess they played with Velcro chess pieces on the galley table.

"Got to go do that video conference," Bear said to them as he exited.

"Check." Svec slapped the timer, and Yui let out a belch before replying with his own move and subsequent slap.

"Check, friendo."

Bear rigged up his laptop in the Cupola and set up the connection with the high school in Pasadena. There was an annoying delay, more than the usual one- to two-second pauses that punctuated conversations with Earth. Bear tried to explain this to the teacher, a young woman in a bright green cardigan with whom he'd been corresponding for over a month now. She had convinced him to do the meditation challenge alongside her class and then discuss the results, her goal being to bridge the gap between science and spirituality.

"Happy Last Day from the International Space Station, kids!" Bear said brightly. "I have to say I am impressed that a bunch of teenagers would come into school on a Saturday, a holiday no less, to talk to me."

"Oh, we don't recognize that holiday at Pasadena Christian Academy," said the teacher. Bear was embarrassed. He could have sworn that the teacher, who had reached out to him over social media, and whom he'd found attractive, had been very flirtatious in her emails with him, and never once did she mention her school's religious affiliation.

"Well, any day that I can connect with people on Earth is a good one for me, and I am happy to talk about what I have learned from this meditation, but I'm more interested in hearing from you guys."

In varying degrees of elegance, bravado, and embarrassment, the teenagers spoke about finding clearer focus after meditation, about the way time seemed to expand, the short sessions of sitting and breath somehow generating even more space inside the day. What had begun as an assignment, all of them reported, became something they greatly looked forward to.

"Since I started meditating, I can hear, like, literally *hear* the fear in my dad's voice when he criticizes us. He's, like, just a man, a person. And he's afraid."

"I wasn't feeling anything. But I kept doing it, at least when I had to in class. Then one day I was sitting at home and closed my eyes—not to meditate but to rest—when I felt a big *whoosh* and I saw a white light. It turned out to be a lightning bug, but how did only one lightning bug get into my bedroom in the middle of the day when all the doors and windows are shut in my house?"

"This is so dumb," one girl said, her voice lisping through the heavy-duty mouth guard holding back her wayward teeth. "I had this thought, listening to all of us breathing, and shifting in our seats, and, like, sniffling and stuff, that we are actually just different parts of one body, and that one body is trying to get comfortable, which is hard with all us different parts thinking we're in charge of it."

The kids laughed nervously at that last one, and their laughter, after a second's delay, made Bear laugh. He was slightly jealous—he had not experienced any of what they described; most of his meditations were consumed by a chastising inner monologue about not being better at meditation—but he was also moved to see these kids, with their plump faces and muddy pores, engaging with the world on a level so beyond him.

His eyes moistened a little as he listened to one boy say, "It's like I found another room hidden inside my own house, where I've been living my whole life, a room I never knew was here."

"I see so much destruction up here," Bear replied. "From my vantage point, I can see the visual evidence of pollution, global warming, deforestation, like a doctor sees disease in a microscope, and it gets very depressing," he confessed. "Sorry, not depressing. Discouraging. But listening to you, I have so much faith in your generation, in the good you are capable of—"

"Who is the master of all men now?" Yui cried, thrusting the scorebook in Bear's face.

"Ha-ha, sorry, folks, that is just another of our crew members here on the station, Yui Yamamoto, of the famous Yamamoto brand, doing some research for—"

"Sir?" The teacher looked into the camera. Her face was disconcertingly close, her hands shielding the rest of the space in the frame. With a sting of shame, Bear realized that the screen image he was projecting back to the classroom on Earth had frozen on Yui's graphic depiction of Japanese, Russian, and American flag penises in their record of contests.

Bear heard his last faltering attempt at diplomacy finally reaching the class, a disconcerting echo repeating every syllable of his apology. He saw his own blinking eyes freeze, then release in the small square at the bottom of his screen. Then, after what felt like the longest delay yet, he watched with a feeling of suffocation as the video feed to the kids on Earth disconnected.

RECORDS OF LAST Day good deeds and acts of chivalry dated back to medieval Europe. In the seventeenth century a tradition of the settling of all debts arose, evolving at last to the present custom, borrowed from the self-help movement of the twentieth century: that of making amends to all those you have harmed before the sun sets on May 28.

There were as many different practices as there were people practicing this secular sacrament. Some were very public apologies on television, radio, and social networking sites. For $200,000 you could buy a whole page in *The New York Times* to print such cryptic poems of contrition as:

Evan, I'm so sorry I stole from you. I've made a donation in your name to Save the Pandas. Sincerely, Nick

There was a retainer wall in Cleveland Heights, Ohio, where someone once spray-painted a florid apology, and decades later the trend exploded until it became the Wailing Wall of the Buckeye State. The city eventually started whitewashing it every April in preparation for the yearly onslaught of apologetic graffiti.

Some folks chose one person every year to seek out and apologize to; others made long, exhaustive lists of people and tried to contact each one in twenty-four hours, going "on tour," sometimes traveling great distances over the holiday just to make face-to-face apologies. It was considered good form to make appointments ahead of time, many etiquette columnists wrote, so that the former victims of whatever moral crime you had committed could be prepared for the inevitably awkward conversation.

Karen's plan was backward. She started with a list of things she had stolen: underwear; a cheese grater; an expensive pair of scissors; Pop-Tarts; a very pretty spoon—tiny, as for a baby, with a soft white rubber coating the lip and a snail embossed on the handle; countless hairbrushes; a box of oranges—the whole box.

"This is what is holding me back—my past," Karen said to herself. She wondered, At what age did one's past transgressions start requiring Last Day amends? At eighteen? Twenty-one? Everyone's conscience emerged at a different moment. How were such things measured by the people of this world?

Rosette was gone now, so Karen would have to look up the answer herself. Except she was forbidden to use the internet at work. She'd gotten into trouble twice already and nearly fired both times, close calls, as consistent employment was one of the conditions of her stay at Heart House. The first infraction was when Karen tried to play matchmaker. Looking up members' confidential information, finding out who was not married, assembling romantic profiles according to astrological sign and address, she would try to bait unsuspecting parties with the details she'd unearthed from her research. People were understandably creeped out, and Karen got a month of custodial work as her punishment. The second infraction concerned a more sinister element. She'd become obsessed with registered sex offenders. There were over thirty in the same zip code as the Huntington branch of the YMCA, a fact she was happy to publicize while people did their circuit training, accosting members in the middle of their lat-pulls to report the names and addresses and descriptions of these local pedophiles.

"In case they were lurking in the parking lot," Karen later defended herself. Karen's abstention from the office internet was on the honor system—her boss, Roberto, never monitored her usage; he didn't even know how to. Since her second strike, Karen had only caved in one time, after listening to some members describe a video of a kitten that had gone viral. She simply could not wait until the end of the day to watch the video at the library. With heart pounding, Karen logged on to the front desk computer to find it. Two kittens crawled around the inside of a grand piano. Their legs kept slipping between the strings and they cried a lot. It was supposed to be cute, but Karen was disgusted. Their paws were too delicate for this! Then someone offscreen started playing chords, and the kittens tumbled over headfirst, their faces the very portrait of terror.

After watching the video eight times, Karen burned with the desire to discuss each and every layer of her outrage. For her there was only now; waiting until tomorrow, when she could pretend to have seen the video at the library on her own time, was simply impossible. It was just the punishment she needed—to have something so important to talk about, and for it to be verboten because of her own treachery. This was her definition of torture. She vowed never to go on the internet at work again.

But now it was Last Day. Surely these were extenuating circumstances. Rosette's gratitude list had inspired her, and after she and Mr. Cox had left, Karen made an exhaustive inventory of everyone she had ever harmed. It was, like so many millions of other Last Day inventories, a dishonest and manipulative tactic, a way to reach the collection of people she just wanted to touch again, to feel the static spark of drama, even if only over the phone.

Karen broke up her inventory into three columns: foster families she'd stayed with for under six months (they could wait, as she hadn't been with them long enough to cause any real harm); then families who'd fostered her for a year or more; and a third category labeled *Before*. It had only one name listed under it: *Dennis*. She was saving him for last.

She opened up a search site and started plugging in names. This meant, of course, that now she would need to add her boss, Roberto, to this very list, for this very infraction. But that could wait until next year.

Memories flew at her in clusters, the younger memories dark and globed while the older ones were translucent and pointy. So many families, so many houses, each one she remembered by its bathroom. Though the first few she totally forgot. That was in the very beginning, when the apartment was raided by the FBI, and their real parents went to jail. Dennis was still with her then. After that was the lady with the black hair. That lady straightened it out with the same iron she used on their clothes, which Karen, nearly eight years old, thought was novel. She had filthy wall-to-wall carpeting throughout the apartment, even in the bathroom. It was gray with a low loop pile. Karen remembered getting out of the shower and making wet footprints on the already soggy fibers.

Her list grew, first names, fewer last names, towns, and the occasional zip code—all of it ejected from her memory bank with a vile, emetic force. Like the Colsons. Where were they? Karen remembered at least six of them in the real family, all with the same carrot-colored hair. They were so proud of this fact that they found a way to work it into every conversation. "Do you know," Mrs. Colson liked to say, "that only one percent of the human population has true red hair?" Long, curly strands of their hair were always sticking to the porcelain of the bathtub, writing secret notes in a loose, lazy cursive only redheads could decipher. Karen was so angry when they said they were not adopting her that she broke a coffee cup on Mrs. Colson's gingery head. She wasn't sorry at first, and then she was never not sorry, because they had an in-ground swimming pool in their backyard. She'd slept with Mrs. Colson's hairbrush in her arms like a baby doll for months after she'd left them.

Karen wrote down *The Colsons* on the YMCA stationery pad. Then there was that woman who called herself Auntie. Auntie what? What was her real name? Her boyfriend was named Roger and he had inappropriate boundaries, Nora helped her to learn later. There was no column for such people, Karen decided. Let the stars in their pitiless wisdom handle Auntie and her pervert paramour.

The Giraud family was fun for a while. They fostered lots of kids, it was a career for them, their house a kind of outsourced orphanage. Mrs. Giraud made pancakes every single morning on a big griddle that covered half of her stovetop. Other kids got sick of pancakes and complained after a while, but not Karen. For her, there was no upper threshold when it came to breakfast sweets. She simply wasn't born that way. It was sad when she had to leave the Giraud house. Mr. Giraud was adventurous and he was usually hanging around the house, unlike most foster fathers. He worked from home, he used to say, but didn't say what work he did.

One day a huge cardboard box appeared at their house full of scratch tickets, and Mr. Giraud put all the foster kids to work scratching them. Karen wanted to be in charge of collecting the winners and tallying the earnings, but Mr. Giraud said only Barry could do that. It was because Barry was a boy, Karen thought then, and it wasn't fair. She complained about this to her social worker, who launched an investigation and later busted up the whole house.

After that Karen went to live with the old spinster in Dorchester who made her wear braids to school every single day. Karen was in high school by then. It was embarrassing. The old lady's name was Miss Catherine May and she had a short, thick tuft of gray hair. Miss May hung framed pictures of herself in her youth all over her apartment. There were never any friends or family in the pictures — just Miss May on the deck of a boat, Miss May on a horse, Miss May drinking from a coconut. At breakfast she would push Karen down into a chair and brush her blond curls until they were straight and frizzy, then braid her hair so tightly that Karen felt her eyes squinting. If she squirmed, Miss May would whack her several times with the brush. If Karen was more than three minutes late for curfew at 7 P.M., Miss May would lock all the doors and make Karen sleep on the wicker couch on the screened-in porch. Karen spent a lot of nights on that porch. Like cleanliness, punctuality had never been her strong suit.

What would Karen say if she got ahold of these people? *I'm sorry, I love you, Happy Last Day, goodbye?* She didn't know which of those things she actually meant, only that the need to say them was dire.

The internet was not the magical portal of solutions she had hoped for. It was as fickle and confused as any other augury. After searching all the names she could remember, the only phone number Karen was able to track down was for Deborah Giraud, the Girauds' one real daughter. Karen imagined this girl was still seventeen, beautiful, and glamorous, wearing high heels and ankle socks even when it was snowing.

"Did you guys end up winning a lot of money off those scratch tickets?" Karen asked her on the phone now.

"I don't remember much after the stroke, honey," Deborah replied. It sounded nothing like Deborah. Not that Karen remembered. But the woman on the other end of the phone did not sound pretty at all. Pretty was something you could hear, and this woman didn't have it.

"How's your mom's cat? Tabitha was her name. I remember her fondly."

"Tabs? Tabs was a trooper. Tabs will outlive us all." Deborah pulled her face away from the phone and coughed a very liquid, tumultuous cough.

"Did your parents ever talk about me?" Karen asked. "Did they miss me after I left?"

"They missed the checks, that's for sure. Mom had to get a job as a nurse's aide. She hated it. But then some rich old fuck left her a bunch of money, so she and Pop moved to Florida. They sell hot dogs and Popsicles out of a truck at the beaches down there. Happy as pigs in shit, those two."

"Can I have their number?" Karen asked.

"I don't even have their number. Couldn't come up with a lousy five grand for my wedding? Come on! I'm through with cheap people. Life's too short."

"Okay," Karen said, her eyes welling up. "Happy Last Day! I love you!"

"Good night, honey," Deborah said. She cleared her throat loudly before hanging up. It was quarter past noon.

S PRING WAS SHY that year, emerging slowly, raw, soggy, and pale like a newly healed limb coming out of a cast. There'd been a feeling of apprehension lingering in the air, a feeling of being run aground. Then the end of May brought a flamboyant display of sunshine. Overnight, flowering plants exploded, their pollen and petals scattering everywhere. By the twenty-seventh of May people were peeling off layers of clothing, letting the sun touch their skin for the first time. Sitting on the sidewalk of Commonwealth Avenue, waiting for their free tattoos, their skin began to burn. No one cared. The sky was nothing to them but a fresh swell of blue.

They sat and stood, flitted and danced, eating each other's snacks and drinking each other's booze on the sidewalk in front of Redemption. Suddenly a dog darted into the street and a car came to a screeching stop from hitting it. The dog, a stocky pit bull the color of baked yams, bounced off the front fender. The driver leaned on the horn. The dog shook his head, then his back, then his rump until the near-death experience had wriggled out of him; he bounded across the street and into the line of people waiting on the sidewalk for their tattoos. He smelled chicken somewhere and nothing could stop him, not even his owner, who was pounding her fist on the hood of the stopped car.

The dog at last plunged his nose into the purse of a woman sitting in line and chomped down on her half-eaten burrito.

"Hey," the woman said, laughing. "Let me peel the foil off for you first, boy."

Sarah had arrived just in time to see all this. The dog ate the burrito in three bites, then swallowed it foil and all. Laughter erupted among the few people who had looked up from their phone screens to see it. A couple tried to pat the dog, who sniffed their reaching hands and licked them profusely. When the dog trotted into the tattoo studio through the open door, Sarah saw an opportunity, and followed quickly behind.

"What the fuck?" A redheaded lady with thin penciled eyebrows stood up on her chair. "Jake, help me!"

"I'm busy, Janine," Jake yelled across the fray.

"For Chrissakes! We're being attacked by a wild dog."

"Kurt's paying you to handle this shit today. So handle it."

Janine was bossy and feckless and always hanging around Redemption, keeping a codependent eye on her boyfriend, so Jake had suggested to Kurt that she work a shift that day, helping sort out the holiday chaos, hopefully keeping busy and saving Jake from death by nagging. Kurt was happy to oblige. He loved Jake like a war buddy; theirs was a steadfast friendship free from scrutiny of any kind. For Kurt it was platonic love at first sight. He'd poached Jake from a rival studio after the two men had met at a tattoo convention in Providence over a decade earlier. Jake was the drunkest, meanest guy in the bar. Short and barrel-chested, he'd been trying to bait everyone, including Kurt, into a fistfight. He had a long wiry red beard forever studded with food crumbs and glistening beer foam, and his shaved head was branched with scars. The kid was a mess, and Kurt, who was a bit older and already softened by life's many defeats, saw Jake instantly as just that—a messy kid searching for direction. Kurt had met a lot of guys like Jake in prison, and it felt like a calling to take him under his wing.

That first night in Providence, Jake had flung every taunt and trap he could at Kurt, who blasted back with unconditional respect and affection. If Jake made a surly claim that the song playing on the stereo was shit, Kurt twisted a lyric of the song into a dirty joke Jake couldn't help laughing at. When Jake tried to punch the ironic mustache off a scrawny hipster's face, Kurt convinced him that the same guy had been talking about what amazing work Jake had demonstrated during the convention. And finally, in a last surge of primitive, almost comical jungle dominance, as Kurt helped a stumbling Jake into a cab, Jake accused him of potential faggotry, to which Kurt responded, "Nah, man. I had cancer of the prick a couple years back."

It was a response that made no logical sense at all, except to the Jakes of the world, drunken Irish pugilists who were eternally chastened by male confessions of cancer. "My uncle had that," Jake said, his face suddenly lamb-like in the glow of the streetlight. "Great fuckin' guy, though. Athletic, the whole thing."

"Good for him," Kurt said, and Jake slammed his fist into the roof of the cab twice like a judge's gavel.

Kurt had just signed a lease on the space on Commonwealth Avenue and saw in Jake skills of both muscle and artistry. (He was right; in addition to inking tattoos, Jake had experience in construction, light plumbing and electric, and bar security.) He knew that if he just let Jake be exactly who he was without trying to change him, he would have a friend for life. And as drunk as Jake got every single night, as fucked up on whatever cocktail of chemicals he packed into his bloodstream, the man was never late for work at Redemption. He puked outside in the bushes like a dog, he tortured the other artists, many of whom quit after a couple of months because of Jake's truculence, he raged about the customers as soon as they had paid and gone, but he never said no to Kurt, who in turn never needed to ask for anything, because Jake always volunteered.

He was thirty-five years old and ate acid, mushrooms, or mescaline almost every weekend. His ears were loaded with metal studs and bolts, and his lobes wrapped around black wooden discs the size of Communion wafers. He wanted to get horns implanted in his skull but his girlfriend, Janine, wouldn't let him. They were always on the verge of a breakup over this shit; Jake was always threatening to dump her, once and for all, but Janine was so damn shrill and Jake was just too high to argue.

Sarah grabbed the drooling pit bull by his collar as Janine continued to whine from her perch. The dog's fur was so thin in places that Sarah could see his pink skin scabbing already with sunburn. The muscles beneath his fur stretched and bundled as he prepared to leap over the desk and lick the screaming woman standing on a chair. He wanted her! Her breath had a whiff of bacon and eggs left over from breakfast! He wanted the stapler on the desk! He wanted the red plastic cups sweet with beer! He wanted everything in this new fascinating place! His owner finally made it into the studio and punched the dog's skull with a closed fist.

"Sit, Marshall. Sit! I said sit, goddammit!" She latched his leash back onto his collar, and Marshall jumped up, placed his paws on her shoulders, and licked her angry face.

"Get that thing out of here," Janine cried, still standing on her chair.

"My pleasure, you Visigoth slag," the dog owner yelled. She yanked her happy pup by the throat back onto the street and slammed the door behind her.

"Janine! Are you handling this or what?"

"Jesus," moaned Janine. "Who's next?"

"I am," Sarah said.

"Sign this." She handed Sarah a waiver. "Whatever the artist wants. No exceptions. Not invalidated by intoxication. Et cetera, et cetera."

Sarah signed quickly without looking. "I'm only here for Kurt," Sarah said.

"You get who you get," Janine snapped back. "Jake, who's next?" she screamed over the fray.

"How the hell do I know?" Jake answered.

Jake leaned over the body squirming in his chair and continued working. On the back of Jake's shaved skull was a tattoo of a hand flipping the middle finger. A terrifying man, Sarah thought. In the next stall a man who looked like a movie star Sarah couldn't remember was inking the chest of another man lying supine on the table, the two of them locked in a state of silent concentration. Sitting in the chair beyond them was a tiny woman with soft, almond-shaped eyes. She watched eagerly as the young tattooer in her stall washed his hands in the sink. He had a nose like an eagle and a goofy smile that seemed kind. Why hadn't Kurt ever written to her about the characters who worked for him? These were the people he saw every day, with whom he spent the majority of his time. There was so much more she needed to know about him.

"Okay, your wish is being granted today. Kurt's next," Janine said, pointing. "All the way in the back." She placed Sarah's waiver on the top of a messy stack of papers. "What are you standing there for?" Her skin was very white in the places not covered by tattoos. Sarah saw a vein throbbing minutely at the woman's temple.

"Don't worry, honey," Janine said. "It only hurts like hell."

T HE GENTLE OPIATE high of Mr. Cox's pills was waning in direct proportion to Karen's waxing spiritual angst. She held her fingertips to her collarbone and closed her eyes, trying to manifest an early dismissal from her work shift. Not long after, her wish was granted when a surly, self-absorbed member refused to return Karen's "Happy Last Day" wishes, and she snapped and called the man a cunt. She did this in full view of her manager, Roberto, who had recently arrived. Roberto gaped at her from a stool behind the entrance desk, a glistening slice of pizza resting on his lap.

"Did you just call that guy a cunt?" he cried.

"It was a term of distinction and honor in the Middle Ages," she said, trying to cover.

Roberto took a big, joyless bite of his pizza. "You're fired. I mean *done. Finito.* Life's too short for me to deal with this crap."

Karen began to sob. After the library debacle, she had been given one more chance at Heart House. She had tried to bargain for three strikes, but Nora had had to explain, "Not in this economy."

Karen gathered her meager belongings from her locker and headed to the door. She cried big shuddering sobs all the way to the bus stop.

The bus was crowded, and Karen, with her tears, expected someone to give up a seat for her, but no one budged. Last Day was supposed to be a holiday of grand and selfless gestures, but her fellow bus riders refused to acknowledge her, their mouths sealed in acceptance of this grim world. It was what made cities so lonely. So many people to talk to and not a word, not even a *hi* exchanged with the person who sat so close that her arm skin was sticking to yours.

Karen's stomach hurt badly. She'd been down this road before. There was a lot of tearing inside her viscera. She did visualization exercises every night to mend them, but it wasn't enough. The last time she was in the hospital, the doctors had warned her.

"You could die," one had said, a gastroenterologist. "Do you understand what that means?"

It means a lot of things, she wanted to say to him, *depending on your spiritual belief system,* but her mind was frothy with all the meds she was on. "Yeah," was what came out of her mouth.

"I saved your life!" the gastroenterologist cried. He was shorter than she was and had very cold, silky hands.

Another doctor had started her on a new antipsychotic that made her brain feel like it was blistering under her scalp. She had trouble reading. It was hell. These side effects subsided eventually but she was not willing to go through another adjustment of her meds. Her stomach hurt a lot now, but she was sure she would pass everything and prayed to be relieved of her worst compulsions.

HEART HOUSE WAS a large gray Victorian set back from the main road on top of a high hill. It offered a striking view of the city—the Prudential Building was visible from the window of the third-floor bathroom—though few of the residents had the faculties to appreciate it. A lovely building with ugly, utilitarian modifications for its new purpose as a group home, Heart House was surrounded by a neat, uncultivated yard where awkwardly placed benches green with mold slowly rotted in the damp air. The residents of Heart House were hopeless cases—schizophrenics and mentally disabled adults, unemployable men and women who watched reruns of game shows on a continuous loop all day in the common room. Narrative programming put the residents to sleep, which made them stay up all night, a hassle for the staff. Music triggered all kinds of agitation, fists flying, inconsolable tears, the occasional masturbatory spree. So the staff had compiled a library of game shows. Low stakes and solvable puzzles: it put the residents' minds at ease.

Karen never watched TV. The light gave her headaches, which she self-diagnosed as an allergy to gamma rays. She had a library card and stacks of books teetering on the sill of her bay window. She loved best thick, hard-covered romance novels with gold lettering embossed on their jackets. All those stories of damaged men and women in love. She had several slim volumes of Rudolf Steiner's sorcery that she saved for nights when she ran out of sleeping pills. And she had collected most of an incomplete set of outdated children's encyclopedias culled from the free box at the library. As the only high-functioning resident of Heart House, Karen had certain privileges. The library card and the biggest room with the bay window were two of them, she liked to believe, though the staff said the room was the luck of the lottery, nothing more. But she was certainly the only resident who was allowed a mini-fridge in her room. If she had had family, she would have been allowed to go visit them on her own, without asking for permission, for an entire day if she liked, as long as she was back by 8 P.M. She was not allowed to have a phone, none of the residents were, but she was confident that in time she would find a crack in that prohibitory wall and erode it with her insistent carping.

Buddy and Jon-Jon were hanging streamers in the front lobby when Karen got home from the YMCA. Lexi was frosting a vanilla sheet cake very slowly, her tongue pushed out of the corner of her mouth in deep concentration. Same as last year, Karen thought, almost exactly, this tableau. Lauren, the counselor on duty, sat at the front desk, her face resting on her fist, while the other hand punched out perforated cardboard crowns from a Last Day activity booklet published for institutionalized adults. Lauren was a pretty girl around Karen's age with a partially shaved head and a tongue ring. She liked to read Christian romance novels, which piqued Karen's interest: she was curious what nuances Lauren's savior allowed when it came to things like blowjobs. Karen's secular romance novels were teeming with them, and she was honestly curious how Christians handled it. For that query Karen had lost library privileges for a week, and Lauren never really forgave her.

"Why is the icing blue?" Karen asked her now. "It's not appropriate."

"Didn't stop you from digging your grimy fingers into the jar. Jeesh." Lauren took the tub of frosting away from her.

"Purple is the traditional Last Day color. This might very well be the last time we ever make a celebratory sheet cake. It might be the last sheet cake on Earth. We should try to get it right."

"There wasn't any purple frosting left at the store. I looked."

"We could make our own," Karen suggested, "by mixing blue and red."

"I don't get paid enough for that," was Lauren's reply. Karen frowned. She liked to think of the Heart House staff as distant cousins whose presence in the house was inspired by love or, in the case of curmudgeons like Lauren, familial loyalty. The fact that they got paid, and were unhappy with their pay, made the whole operation feel mercenary and gross.

Karen picked up the communal phone and ordered herself a large cheese pizza, her voice low so that Lauren couldn't hear her. She was supposed to get permission before ordering delivery, but Lauren loved to say no without reason. A vice principal in disguise, she always shushed the Heart House residents when they talked in the hallways, as though there were a religious ceremony or standardized test taking place somewhere else in the building. "Come to the back door," Karen whispered into the phone. The man taking her order said to expect at least a two-hour wait.

Karen went to her room and retrieved her safe from where she hid it under her laundry bag. Inside she discovered there was not enough money for even one slice of pizza. She'd saved over a hundred dollars since Christmas, but she'd forgotten that she'd spent it all on her donation to Save the Tigers. She had been promised a plush toy Bengal as a thank-you gift, but it turned out to be one of those cheap carnival versions, stuffed with Styrofoam beads that spilled out from rips in the stitching when she hugged it too hard.

How long would it take before Heart House found out she'd been fired and made her leave? At least a week, she figured. What would happen then? Nora's sphere of influence had been maxed out, and she had many times explained to Karen the boundary between therapist and client, that she would not be able to adopt her or even house her for one night.

That's okay, Karen thought. That was not her destiny.

"I have choices!" Karen said to the stuffed animals resting beneath the covers of her unmade bed. She packed a plastic grocery bag with essentials, filled her pockets with all the loose change she could find strewn about the floor, and left this lovely bedroom for the last time.

In the foyer of Heart House was a thick, leather-bound logbook where residents and their nonexistent guests were supposed to sign in and out. It sat regally on a podium, lit by an imitation Tiffany lamp, giving the whole Heart House operation the impression of a quaint New England bed-and-breakfast. Karen's name was the only one listed in the logbook. Line after line, page after page, her loopy script detailed every trip she had taken to work and the library for the calendar year so far. The constancy of her own life struck her as both gratifying and pointless. Surely she must have been other places, Karen thought as she flipped through the pages. She could only remember an apple-picking excursion with Nora, but that was last fall, recorded in last year's logbook.

Today she wrote out in her fat, bubbly cursive:

May 27 — Karen Donovan — 3:20 P.M. — Library
(Allston Branch) — Home by 8 P.M.

In the TV lounge the cheers of a once-live studio audience intensified and the voice of a game-show host strained amiably to rise above it. Sadie sat on the pillows of the bay window seat, pressing her hand up against the glass, then removing it. "Hello, brother bear," she said to the sky.

One story up was Karen's room, empty of her. Sometimes, when she entered her room after a prolonged absence, like when she'd had a long workday followed by a therapy session, she heard a sudden hush before entering, as though her clothes and stuffed animals and library books were leading a fantastic life that all jolted to a collective halt as soon as she unlocked the door.

What would happen to them, to all her things?

Lauren was scolding Gregory in the kitchen for eating an extra pudding cup. They were *his* pudding cups, Karen wanted to argue; Gregory's social worker bought them for him as a special treat. If he wanted to eat an extra one, who was Lauren to tell him no? But if she didn't leave right now, Karen knew, she never would, and with uncharacteristic quiet, she slipped out the door.

THE MORE KURT thought about the day ahead, the more he felt trapped. This feeling—even if it was an illusion, a recognizable haunting from his months in prison—was now worse than any possible outcome. But understanding things and believing they were true were not the work of the same organ, and so every attempt Kurt made to console himself only impounded him more.

He needed to stop mixing prescription sleeping pills with beer. That had for the last twelve years been both the solution and the source of pretty much all his problems. He loved the feeling—as if someone had pulled the plug on his consciousness—but he would wake up just refreshed enough to puzzle over what the hell he might have done during the previous night's blackout. In the past he had ordered and paid for an antique trumpet as well as four different books on falconry, made reservations at a bed-and-breakfast in Spain (impressive, he admitted to himself, as Kurt did not speak a word of Spanish), and, more than once, eaten a whole pizza and possibly some of its box. He drank every night, so if he didn't take pills when he was drinking, he couldn't take them at all. Maybe he should hide his computer earlier in the evening to prevent these fugue-state sprees. Or just disable his email account. If he could commit to that last option alone, it would cut his usual trouble down by about a third. But how many times before had he come to this precise realization and continued to do the same thing?

He drank one beer very quickly and another slowly. The idea for his next tattoo swam to him as if in a dream—an image of classical octopus *hentai*. When Kurt's next customer said he was a stripper, it seemed an example of what Kurt's old Irish grandma used to call *providence*. An encouraging step away from the ghosts of dread and guilt taking jabs at his peace of mind. Kurt rerouted his nervousness about the afternoon into the stripper's tattoo, the curves of the tentacles, the detailed suckers each with a tiny hook inside it. The squid's human lover arched her back; her long hair spilled down the calf of the man in Kurt's tattoo chair. Kurt was pleased with the finished product, and the customer loved it. For a moment Kurt relaxed.

He was washing his hands when a girl with long legs and dull blond hair hopped onto his empty chair. Dressed in magenta athletic shorts and a baggy blue T-shirt, she was obviously very young, though he couldn't tell how young. Her forehead bore deep age lines of wonder or distress, but her mouth, her cheeks, the delicate skin around her eyes were baby smooth. A neon-pink Band-Aid protected a nick on her shin, and a tiny spot of blood seeped through the plastic. Her sneakers were filthy. The most disgusting sneakers he'd ever seen. They smelled awful.

"Hello, I'm Kurt." He offered her a handshake.

Sarah Moss stared into his eyes. "It's me," she said. "Sarah." She sank her straight, slightly gapped top teeth into her lip.

He remembered the name but the face not at all. That girl from the barbecue? When was that? Fourth of July? Did he sleep with her? He was ninety-nine percent sure he hadn't. Yes, it was coming back to him, slowly: it had all been completely chaste, so chaste, in fact, he'd only jerked off to her twice, and one of those times by accident—in the pantheon of angels his subconscious had presented to him one night, these same long legs so pale and pure had randomly appeared in the fray. Kurt was relieved. As long as he hadn't slept with her, he didn't owe her anything.

"Kidding. How could I forget you?" Kurt said, and shuffled through the memories of so many mornings waking up with his laptop next to him on the bed, the screen wide open against the pillow like a lover with her mouth agape. Most likely he'd emailed this girl Sarah in a blackout, as was his wont. But he could have sworn she was in college. Young, but not *this* young. Though that was a piece of fiction he had told himself about many other girls many times before, with his faculties relatively awake and alert.

"You're a sight for sore eyes, Sarah. What can I do for you?"

"Oh, good," she said, recovering. "Okay. I've been thinking about this for a while actually. Since I met you." She searched his face for the light of love and thought she saw it, a tiny glimmer, in the gold flecks of his brown eyes. "I know I can't choose my tattoo, and I'm totally okay with whatever you give me. I trust you completely. Like, totally. But I want you to know what I would choose, so it can be, like, our common vocabulary for the moment. Right?"

"Go on."

"So, I've been obsessively watching birds my whole life. For as long as I can remember. My first memory is not of my mom or my dad but this time at the park when a swan bit my hand as I was trying to feed it my French fries. When I was little, as soon as I could walk, I was chasing birds across our lawn. I wanted more than anything to see them up close. As up close as possible. And obviously they never let me. Birds fly away. It's what they do. I love that about birds. Admire, love, and envy—like, there should be a word for those three things mixed into one."

"You want those words."

"Oh, no. No no no. I don't want any words on my body. I read too much as it is. I don't want to read my own skin."

"Good," Kurt said.

"Right? You get it. I knew you would."

Sarah was thunderstruck with self-consciousness. It was weird how you could totally forget you had a body, then suddenly remember and think of nothing else. She pawed anxiously at her bangs. It was an awkward fringe of hair she was trying to train into a swoop across her forehead. So far unsuccessfully. The rest of her hair was limp. It just hung there, as though it grew only as much as it wanted to and then gave up. She pulled it into a messy ponytail and prayed her armpits were not visibly damp.

"It was frustrating," she went on. "There's only so much you can learn from books. Field research is key. My dad bought me these amazing binoculars. Made by NASA. But I hate using them. I get seasick easily, and tracking a bird from tree to tree at such a close magnification makes me really dizzy."

Sarah could hear herself prattling on. I sound like such a *girl*, she thought, but felt powerless to stop herself. She talked even faster now.

"Then one day, I figured out that if I scattered birdseed on my windowsill, the birds would come and perch there, and hang out for a while, and let me watch them through the glass. Instead of chasing them, I could invite them closer to me. Which is, like, a metaphor. Right? I started scattering seeds on my lawn and other places in town. And as long as I sat still, and was patient, they would always come. Not quite close enough, but closer than before. And I know, it's obvious. But it was kind of a big breakthrough for me."

She lifted the fabric of her T-shirt off her belly in a weird flutter that horrified her as she was doing it. *Stop it*, she told herself. *Be normal. Just BE. NORMAL.*

"So for a tattoo," she said slowly, deliberately, until her voice did not sound real, "if I could choose, and I know I can't—you have your tradition and everything, which I think is amazing—but just for an exercise, this is what I'd want: a hand reaching out, palm open, all the lines and stuff, a real hand. And seeds falling in a light spray, and some collecting on the ground, though I don't want an actual line to demarcate *ground*.

And some birds eating away at those seeds. But cool, realistic birds. Nothing cartoonish."

"Like what?"

"Maybe a lark. Or is that cheesy?"

"The heart wants what it wants."

"You're right." Sarah smiled. "Thank you for saying that. I really like larks."

"Nothing wrong with that."

"So?"

"Yeah." Kurt scratched his neck. "I would love to do that tattoo."

"You would?"

"When you turn eighteen."

"I am."

"What year were you born?"

Quick arithmetic was not one of Sarah's gifts.

"Exactly," Kurt said.

"Come on!"

"I don't have many rules here. Especially today, as you can see. It's drunken pandemonium. But that is one rule I must abide by."

"Your ads promise free tattoos for everyone. Everyone is everyone. Including me."

"Drunks. Pregnant women. The criminally insane. Anything goes today, as long as you are the age of consent."

"I promise I will never sue you."

"Your parents might."

"You've met my parents. They would never do that. Not in a million years."

"I've heard that before."

"But I'm telling you the truth."

"And I've heard *that* before, too."

"You won't even consider it?"

Kurt ran his hands over his face like he was washing it. "I did consider it. I would be honored to do that tattoo. And I promise I will, free of charge, but next year. You'll be eighteen next year, right?"

Fat tears sprang from Sarah's eyes.

"Take a deep breath. You're way too emotional about this. You on your period?"

"Excuse me?"

"It's okay. I have sisters."

Sarah couldn't believe that the man she had decided to love could say such a thing. It was sexist and reductive and uncreative and *untrue*! If anything, she was closest to the ovulation phase of her cycle, a time of peak anxiety, she theorized, because of her asexuality. It was as if a part of her primitive biology despaired all those lost little eggs going to waste. The time of her period, on the other hand, was usually relaxing and productive.

She jumped off the chair and heaved her backpack over her shoulder. "Don't you get it? In the calendar of the cosmos, we're living—right now—at December 31, 11:59 P.M. It's the end. Every decision matters. I thought you—you of all people in the whole doomed world—would understand. . . ."

It was fascinating, disorienting, and unspeakably sad, Kurt thought, how still her face remained as she sobbed. It was like watching an animal cry. And yet, the sight of an attractive female in tears had always given him an erection—a phenomenon too shameful for him to explore. It was Kurt's sexual kryptonite and it had caused him nothing but pain.

As if to cement this point, another crying woman flung open the door of Redemption and scanned the studio with bleary, blackened eyes.

It was Megan Brown, aspiring model-actress and onetime fling Kurt had quickly regretted when she'd claimed a week later that he had gotten her pregnant. "I don't think that's possible," Kurt had said to her then, and her tears at that point turned to rage. "Don't worry—I had it *taken care of*!" she screamed loud enough for the whole tattoo studio to hear. A year later Megan returned on Last Day to drop another grenade: "I just wanted you to know that I am a lesbian and I am moving to New

York. You'll never hear from me again!" Kurt could not hide his relief, which enraged her all the more, so she swept her hand across his tray of inks and sent them clattering to the floor. A year after that she came to Redemption again on Last Day, this time to make amends. "I'm sorry. I made that whole story up. I was never pregnant. I never had an abortion. I was just—I don't know—I guess I wanted your attention." She offered Kurt a wad of twenty-dollar bills for the spilled ink but he refused to accept it. "It's all good," he assured her then, believing this was the last he would ever see of Megan Brown.

"Oh Christ. Not again . . . ," Janine growled. "Kurt!"

"I'm sorry, Sarah. Please forgive me. I'm just—really hungry. I don't know about you, but I start talking some nonsense when I'm hungry. You hungry? Let's get burritos. On me." Kurt wrapped his arm around Sarah's shoulders and ushered her toward the back door.

"I'm starving," Sarah admitted, her pulse bolting at his touch.

WHILE KURT WAITED at the counter for their food, he reviewed their correspondence on his phone. He'd gotten pretty intimate with this girl, telling her things he hadn't admitted to anyone else, not even to himself in the sober light of day. In her emails she went on and on, as most women did, but she seemed to really pay attention to him, and pick up on things intuitively. She might be young, but she knew what she was talking about.

"You're smart," Kurt said, taking a seat across from her. He placed the tray between them and started in on the nachos.

"That's so misogynistic," Sarah shot back.

"What? Why?"

"You say it like it's a surprise."

"I—I . . ."

"I'm choosing to take it as a compliment, because men are only surprised by intelligence in women they also find pretty. So, thank you. But also, you're welcome."

"Ok. Whoa. That's not at all where I was going."

"Then where were you going?"

"I was going to say, for someone as smart as you, did it ever occur to you that the calendar of the cosmos is just getting ready to turn another page? Everything looks like the end when you're moving forward."

"I wish it were that simple." She folded her paper napkin into a tight square that she squeezed in the palm of her hand.

"I know how you feel. And it's okay. It's normal. The end of the world is the scariest thing when you're young. Then you grow old and realize that dealing with a world of shit that never ends is even scarier."

"I saw a bumper sticker on the way here. It said, *Cat-titude*. That's it. Fucking *cat-titude*, with a picture of a cat apparently copping an attitude. And I was like, yup, we're done. Our reign here is over."

Kurt laughed a big expulsive laugh, with bits of rice flying out of his mouth, culminating in a choking cough; Sarah swore she could feel the serotonin surge in her own brain.

"And I know you're probably right. But I still can't get rid of the feeling that this year is different. This year is really the end. But then again, I feel like this every year. I don't know. My generation or whatever, which includes you, too, by the way—I mean epochal generation, not what-TV-shows-did-you-grow-up-with generation. We're all so— *derivative*."

She paused to scan his face for evidence that she was using the word correctly. He was handsome at the edges but not at the core, she noted with some disappointment, a diffused beauty that scattered and fled. His jaw was sharp and the shadow of his thick, short beard cast the lines of his cheeks and nose in a shifty light. His eyes were too small, too far apart, too determined. His nose looked like it had been broken and roughly slapped back together several times. His forehead was waxy with huge pores.

"Yeah," he said.

"Like, when was the last time someone thought of something new? I mean really new. Not an improvement on something that already exists.

And don't get me started on pollution. . . . This planet wants to scratch us off like fleas."

Kurt took two wolfish bites of his burrito. "What's the matter?" he asked her. "I mean really. The thing that scares you is never the thing that gets you. It's the thing hiding behind the thing. So the end of the world means, what? Your parents are getting divorced?"

"My parents are the most happily married people in the world. They're soulmates."

"That's cool. That's rare. My parents had an Irish divorce," Kurt said.

"What does that mean?"

"Sometime, when I was nine or ten years old, my dad started sleeping on the couch. Every morning he'd fold up his sheets and blankets and pillows and stuff them in the space between the couch and the front window. Like it didn't happen. Except we all knew it did. He did this every night until my little sister finally moved out. Then he repainted her room and moved in there. He died a couple years ago. They were still married, he and my mother, forty-two years. Still in the same house, they just never spoke to each other."

Women were always pressing Kurt for personal information, their blatant attempt to force some kind of emotional dependency. The longer he kept silent, the easier it was to stall. But with Sarah he kept blurting out these dark little tales. There was something about her that elicited his trust. It was more than the Ambien, more than the safety of near-anonymous email. It had to be, because he was doing it again here, sitting across from her.

"You going to any bonfires today?"

"I hate today," she said. "Everyone acts like it's a big joke. Or a big party. No one thinks about what it really means. What if we really lost the whole world? The whole world!" Her eyes started to well up again and she wiped them with the backs of her hands, smearing a bit of guacamole on her forehead. "And don't get me started on our lame-ass rituals. Beer and bonfires? What about a blood rite?" she said, composed again.

Kurt reached across the table and wiped the green off her brow. "My whole business is a blood rite."

"Yeah," Sarah said. "That's why I wanted to get a tattoo."

"You're still pissed about that, huh?"

"I'm ninety percent over it." Sarah sighed. "Fatigue makes everyone more forgiving."

"That's a good one. Who said that?"

It was the one gem of wisdom bestowed by her former therapist. "Free-floating anxiety is so bourgeois," Sarah had said to the old woman her parents' insurance policy had assigned to treat her. This practitioner, who was neither a PhD nor a shaman—which irked Sarah; she'd been hoping for a little of both, but Jungians, her parents explained, seldom accepted COBRA—had only the blandest anodynes, the saltines of psychiatric advice. "You judge yourself too harshly," this silver-haired woman would say. "The future is a mystery, so focus on the present." The moment their work together ventured into Sarah's fear of Last Day, she quit going and refused to return.

"I said it," Sarah lied, for what felt like the millionth time that day. It was getting too easy.

Kurt thought he was long past the age when teenagers would find him attractive. On occasion, a very drunk twenty-something would present herself as an option, if he hung around the bar late enough. Boston's blue laws were the biggest impediment, or lifesaver, depending on the night, the girl. Those drunk twenty-somethings had been offering diminishing returns lately. They fell into two categories: the ones who woke up, looked at Kurt and his pale naked body sliding off his tired bones like loose meat, and cringed with regret, tiptoeing out of his house while he pretended to sleep, the only remnant of the previous night a makeup-smeared pillow on his bed like a hideous Shroud of Turin; or the crazy-as-shithouse-rats girls with serious daddy issues who refused to leave the next morning. The former were ego-crushing, the latter ballbusting, which is why, in his forties, Kurt was wont to go home early and abstain from both. Sometimes things worked out all right. Another satisfied customer. Other times—*Jesus*. He didn't like to think about it too much.

"So you really have nothing planned for today?"

"Nothing," she blurted. "I mean, I have a bunch of parties I could go to, but I'm not committed to any of them."

"Right," he laughed. "We always have our parties. But how about we do something different?"

IN MOROCCO GRANDMOTHERS make a spicy root vegetable stew on Last Day, and the greater the number of mouths they can feed that one night, the longer it will take for the end of the world to come. There are conflicting algorithms in this calculus: some believe each mouth fed is equivalent to one hundred years, others one thousand years. Throughout Morocco and parts of Algeria it is considered impolite to refuse the food of any married woman on the night of May 27, a tradition expanded over time so that it has become standard to say yes to any offer made by a married Morrocan woman on Last Day.

In Laos and some parts of Vietnam, people don't speak after the stroke of midnight on May 27. Except for those necessary to sustain life, all noise-making machines are shut down. No televisions, no radios. The night is a pool of inky silence. The following day no one speaks except to assist children, and even these directions are whispered. Doors are shut with such softness, footfalls are slow and gentle. As a prank, children will try to startle their relatives into shouting by jumping out of a dark corner or placing a sharp pin on their chair. If you are caught in such a trap, you have to pay the cunning child a small amount of money. It is very bad luck to be born on Last Day unless your mother can claim she birthed you without screaming and that you took your first breaths without a cry.

Western Europe, like North America, has its bonfires. Italians burn their old bed linens. During the Great Wars, when nothing could be wasted, they used Last Day to cut up their old linens into bandages. Nowadays most Italians burn a sacrificial dishrag. The holiday is marked by special sales in the home-goods sections of department stores. Italians believe that sleeping in a bed whose sheets have not been changed over Last Day will result in a year of impotence.

Hungarians burn broomsticks. The Dutch burn all the candles in their houses down to the nubs on May 27 and walk through their neighborhoods on May 28 gifting brand-new candles to their neighbors. Women in Iceland throw one piece of jewelry into the sea, lake, or river. The English wash their windows, eyeglasses, and computer screens on May 28. The Irish drink.

Certain Nordic tribes considered trees to be earthbound angels who silently, dutifully interceded between Earth and heaven, and so sometime later, even after Christianity was introduced, people left their homes on the night of May 27 to sleep in the forest. In coastal communities, villagers would gather on beaches and wade together into the sea at midnight, where they shivered before a dawn that might never come.

Before Communism, the Chinese lit fireworks. To better illuminate the sky, fires were snuffed out and electric lights unplugged or else black drapes were hung over windows to hide the light. If not, neighbors would nail pictures of clocks on the negligent occupants' front door, reminding them that their days were numbered.

Orthodox Jews do not acknowledge the holiday. Conservative Jews recognize it as a kind of Rosh Hashanah–cum–Yom Kippur for gentiles. Secular Jews do what secular Christians, Muslims, and nondenominational folks do throughout the U.S., and that is order pizza.

Last Day was a late arrival to Japan, forced in with so much other Western culture, in the mid-nineteenth century. Today the Japanese celebrate with wild, extravagant spending sprees. Small family-run boutiques and huge big-box stores alike offer seemingly endless kegs of beer for their shoppers. Fueled by alcohol and nihilism, many Japanese households have plunged into financial ruin on this one night, causing many prudent wives to order holds on their husbands' credit and bank accounts for that day alone.

Consumption had little appeal for Yui, so he had to find creative ways to observe the holiday, which he was incredulous to discover was not deemed significant enough to be celebrated on the International Space Station. All day he ignored directives from Mission Control in protest. He tied his ankle to a toe bar in the Japanese laboratory, where he napped on and off. He watched the mutant baby mouse and marveled as the two heads took turns breastfeeding from their mother while floating in their plexiglass cage. After lunch and another nap, he flew, arms extended Superman-style, down to the American lab in the Destiny module and began drawing pictures on the walls in black Magic Marker.

"What the heck, Yui?" Bear gasped. In one image, lightning ignited a great fire teeming with the arms and legs of humans. A lizard's tail, bicycle wheels, ice cream cones, a startlingly precise handgun, all of it danced chaotically between the licking tongues of the blaze. Bear grabbed the marker out of Yui's hands. Without reacting, without even pausing, Yui unclipped another marker from his belt and continued limning his ghastly mural.

"*Mokushi hi*," he replied. "The day of silent revelation. It is my Last Day present. I am drawing it for you, friendo."

"Thanks . . . but you can't . . ."

"I can."

"You're not supposed to." Bear hated how whiny he sounded when reproving Yui, like a high school hall monitor, a pedant and a fool.

Yui clung to the wall with his feet. His toenails were as long as talons. He must not have cut them in weeks, Bear realized. He wondered if it was part of an experiment. It was hard to tell with Yui which choices were recalcitrant defects of character also present on Earth, which had crystallized in the pressure cooker of space, and which were in the name of science.

Yui stopped drawing, placed the marker in his mouth, and gave himself a long scratch deep in his pants. A solemn look had sunk into his face. This mural was no act of rebellion. Or it was, but only in part. He had been struck all of a sudden with a bout of anxiety. He missed the comforts of home, his hydroponic persimmon tree, his skateboard ramp, his chauffeur, Asami, an elderly fetishist who regaled Yui with stories about the extramarital affairs he had with drag queens. He missed his brother, Tadeshi, so painfully he could not speak about it.

"I am sad, friendo," he pouted. He was now drawing a volcano spewing thick rivers of oozing, erotic lava. Bear squinted at the fine print on the marker, to see if it was washable or not. Yui embellished the streams of lava so that figures engaged in lurid sex acts appeared in the swooping arcs of its flow. Bear couldn't be sure, but it looked like there was some bestiality going on.

"In Japan, today is the day we celebrate the man who was born before man. He was born dead. What is the word in English?"

"Stillborn?"

"Yes. Stillborn. The gods had to start over. They went through many drafts. They failed. Sometimes man failed. Mostly man failed, but the gods were joking sometimes. They built man's asshole over his heart. They made a man with two penises — one in front and one in back. They made a man who was too dark to see at night. These men kept getting lost every new moon, falling off mountains, breaking their necks. Then they made a man who was so light he caught fire at sunrise and burned away. All these men wanted to live, like we want to live, but they had to die. That's why we celebrate today."

"That's cool, Yui. I never knew that about Japanese Last Day."

"It is not exactly true. Your American friendo Val Corwin wrote it. It might be true. Perhaps." He held the book in his arms like a teddy bear.

"Kitsch holiday," Svec said, appearing suddenly. Despite his thick fire hydrant of a body, he navigated the ship like a water snake.

"We believe what has meaning for us. Or what has meaning we believe. I change my mind. But, because I am confused, I know it is true." Yui smiled wanly.

"JAXA has been trying to reach you," Svec said with a tenderness that caught the other two men off guard.

"I know," Yui said, his gaze fastened to his mural. He was about to destroy its perfection with too many lines. He was aware of this yet he continued to draw fast, tumultuous waves undulating in the rock, in the lava, in the scorched earth bereft of man.

"Don't make me tell you," Svec said.

Yui capped the marker and let it float in the air. He pushed off the toe bar and glided toward the Kibo lab as if backstroking on the surface of water.

"What's wrong?" Bear asked once Yui was out of sight.

"His brother died," Svec said.

"What? How?"

"Don't know. Didn't ask."

"Whoa," Bear said, tracing his fingers over the mural. "Poor guy."

"Very sad," Svec agreed. They floated in silence for a moment. The only sound was the whir of the air ventilation system and the erratic ping of meteoroids striking the ship.

"Everything changes," Svec declared at last, "nothing disappears."

He squirted cleaner into a paper towel and with fast circling swipes erased Yui's dream song of the end of the world.

THE LIBRARY WAS a modern, one-story building made of caramel-colored bricks. It wasn't the best-stocked branch of Boston's library system, though the staff there tried to make up for this by programming elaborate community events. Karen had grown fond of the librarians, who either didn't know about her past troubles at the main branch or had decided to allow her a fresh start. Either way, she was grateful and on her best behavior.

For Last Day the librarians had transformed the main hall into an exotic street bazaar. A banner in purple and gold announced their bleak and whimsical intentions: OH, THE PLACES YOU'LL GO—NOW OR NEVER! Large swaths of metallic cloth hung from the ceilings and draped over bookcases, creating darkened channels of mystery between the stacks. Stalls were set up throughout the lobby, each representing a different place, both real and imaginary, which library patrons were able to visit for the first and/or last time. As expected, the stalls were set up in alphabetical order. Algeria, Alice's Wonderland, Bethlehem, and China were all disassembling their stations by the time Karen arrived at quarter to four. Two dads and their geriatric-looking toddler walked toward the Jurassic Age, where a live iguana sat on top of a card table, placidly waiting to be adored.

Somewhere between Mexico and Mount Olympus, Karen found Joyce, her favorite librarian, wearing a sombrero. Joyce was passing out samples of mangoes with lime salt to children. She waited until their faces puckered, then snapped a picture of them with a Polaroid. Near her, a slim Chinese man in overalls sat barefooted on the floor playing the erhu. A little girl offered the musician her already-bitten slice of mango, but the man shook his head.

"He's fasting," Joyce explained to the girl.

"What's fasting?" The girl was around six or seven years old. She had been deposited there by a nanny, who was now napping in one of the leather armchairs by the front entrance, an Avon catalogue spread over her snoring face.

"It means he won't eat or drink anything."

"Why not?"

"To empty himself, starting with his belly, then his heart, and finally his mind, so that he can make room for the new world that might or might not come tomorrow."

A bolt of lightning made of sequins was stitched on the front of the girl's T-shirt and she picked at it avidly, flicking the tiny discs of silver and scattering them across the floor like seeds.

"I will eat macaroni and cheese for my last supper," she said. "My mom will eat Pinot Grigio. Daddy doesn't live with us anymore. He can eat shit, Mommy said."

"Even rage deserves a place at the table," Joyce said, patting the little girl's head.

Joyce was not foster-mother material, Karen knew, but she was on Karen's short list of people who would probably host her for a week or two in the near future while she found a more permanent home. But there was time for all that later. The celebration was winding down. Crumb-strewn platters were piled high with crumpled napkins and lipstick-stained cups, the paper corpses of a once bountiful feast. Mexico had one churro left and Karen shoved it into her mouth before anyone else could get it.

A row of potted Ficus trees marked the entrance to Xanadu. It was rigged up like a tent, or an elaborate blanket fort, constructed out of white bedsheets and hat racks. The entire Coleridge poem was silk-screened onto one of the tent walls. Several cones of pungent incense were burning on an altar. In the very center of the tent a chocolate fondu fountain bubbled, surrounded by skewers of fresh fruit for dipping. *This is what Rosette means when she says the Devil is always tempting her,* Karen thought. She wanted to dip her lips into the chocolate fountain and drink forever, but she needed to get onto the internet and time was running out. The system automatically logged you off after thirty minutes and made you wait ninety minutes more before allowing you the chance to go on again. The library would be closed by then.

"I have to look something up," Karen said, her mouth full of bananas, to Pam, her second favorite librarian, after Joyce.

"Be careful, sweetie," Pam warned. She was wearing a scarlet kimono, her black and gray hair swept up in a topknot. "We've been so busy creating this *spiritus mundi* that no one's had time to police the computer room. It could look like *Caligula* in there for all I know."

Karen did not know what *Caligula* was but she could guess.

The library's computer room, a way station for homeless men locked out of their shelters for the day, was not decorated at all. A brightly lit purgatory, it reeked of mouthwash, which the men guzzled in place of real booze, and the minty urine that soaked their pants afterward. Karen found all the usual patrons, bearded men slumped like statues of slowly melting wax, rapt in listless concentration as thick cocks thrust in and out of the raw, pink bodies on their various screens. Fluorescent lights buzzed reproachfully above them. The extreme wattage was meant to discourage these men, freeing the computers up for more civic-minded research. It didn't work. The exploding sun could not keep them from their porn.

Karen selected the sharpest mini-pencil from the box provided, both a writing instrument and a weapon in a place like this, and sat next to a man with a hole in his cheek. Each time he swallowed, his teeth flashed for a second behind the rotted hole. He either didn't notice or didn't care when Karen gaped at him; another moment of devilish temptation — Rosette would be proud that she had recognized it. Karen wanted so badly to ask this man a million questions, squandering the few minutes she had left. How did he eat? Was the hole self-inflicted? A piercing gone gangrenous? Oooh, maybe it was part of a scarification ritual. But, no, she had to focus.

Dennis.

She couldn't remember his last name, and so she began a search with her own name, quickly finding newspaper articles from the time of their rescue. Front page of the *Herald*, fifth page of the *Globe*. Those were the days of the early internet and much had been made of the innovations it brought to a very old form of evil. She saw her mother's name and felt a string being plucked inside her, ringing through the center of her body. Her hands shook, clumsy on the keyboard. Karen crumpled a wad of tissue and sucked on it until it was soft enough to swallow. She saw Dennis's father's name and her body clanged again. But this was no time for a seizure. She searched for Dennis Conhaile — his father's last name — and boom, there he was.

In a few moments more she had located his address and jotted it down on a piece of scrap paper. He lived just minutes away, according to the map. He had been so close to her all this time.

The man sitting next to her began to rub the outside of his pants as though vigorously wiping out a stain. Karen plotted the bus route as quickly as she could, and staggered back into the festival.

Most of the people were gone now. Tables were flattened and stacked next to a pile of drapery. Joyce was directing Pam with great, sweeping arm movements, and Pam ignored her, showing the remaining patrons a picture on her phone. Karen explored the last stalls in search of more food. Between the drinking fountain and the bathrooms was a station still standing, draped all in white. Lace and chiffon and satins were pleated together in thick, voluptuous folds. It looked to Karen like an enormous wedding dress. There was nothing else except for a white plastic chair.

"This one is Nowhere. It was my idea," Joyce said, appearing suddenly at Karen's side. "I wanted to capture the negative space that makes reality real. The *wa* in *konnichiwa*. I thought about making it completely empty, but we have too many elderly patrons who might collapse if they don't have a place to sit down." She folded up the chair and held it under her arm.

"It's really pretty," Karen said. Joyce frowned. Her face had a clayey texture that furrowed deeply, almost comically, with emotion. Joyce had been trained as a rare-books librarian but had a laundry list of gripes against her colleagues in that field, and a longer list still of vengeful machinations she'd plotted against them, only some of which she had gotten away with. She'd been exiled to this quiet outpost of the city library system as a result. It was her Elba.

"I didn't want Nowhere to be pretty," Joyce confessed. "That was all Pam. I wanted it to be stark, to inspire contemplation. To push people past the anxiety and fear, the grasping and desire, and into a place of sublime acceptance at the end of the world. But then someone donated all this lace. It is really pretty, though. You're right." She rubbed it between her fingers a little resentfully.

Pam waddled into the tent and unloosed her obi, where her phone was hidden. "Hey, Karen, did I show you the new love of my life?" Pam pulled up a photo of a miniature potbellied pig. It had black and white spots like a Holstein cow. Pam had driven to Vermont to buy her from a breeder. "She fits into the palm of my hand!" Pam squealed.

"Not for long," Joyce said. "There's a reason gluttony is represented by a pig."

"Joyce's just afraid she might feel something so base as to resemble affection," Pam said, and skipped through dozens of shots of her pig until she found one of Joyce cradling the animal like a baby, feeding her a bottle, a beatific smile on her face. "Ha! See?" she said, thrusting the phone in Karen's face.

Pam would be an ideal foster mother. And her home came with an alternative-mammal pet! If tonight didn't go well, Pam was a contender for plan B.

"We're ordering pizza and watching movies tonight while we try to house-train Pam's pig, if you want to join us," Joyce said.

Karen wanted all of those things very, very much.

"I can't," she heard herself stammer. "I have—a date."

"Ooh-la-la," Pam whistled. "Do you want a little color?"

Before Karen could ask what that meant, Joyce had unfolded the plastic chair and Pam was pushing her into it. Both women took a tactile inventory of Karen's face. Their fingertips were cool and smooth, as though softened by turning the pages of so many books.

"She has great bone structure. Very Nordic."

"What does *Nordic* mean?"

There were huge gaps in Karen's education. Though adequately intelligent—more than adequately, according to some tests—she had been relegated to special education classes her whole academic life because of disturbing, intractable emotional difficulties (tantrums, talking out of turn, obsessive attachment to inanimate objects in the classroom, inappropriate physical boundaries with fellow students, truancy). She could name the entire pantheon of Greek gods as well as list their salient character traits, but she could not locate Greece on a map. She knew what the word *perihelion* meant, thirsted for any opportunity to use it in conversation, but had only realized a few years ago that animals that lay eggs, such as birds, cannot also give birth in the mammalian way. For years she'd reasoned that chickens laid eggs for eating and then gestated baby chicks for progeny inside their stomachs. Karen's quest for knowledge was largely self-directed, and her interests were celestial, not terrestrial. She attributed this to having been born under a Libra sun.

"Your foremothers milked reindeer in the Laplands," Joyce said.

"They knew the direction of the wind according to the pitch of its howl, and could smell an approaching bear. When they smiled, these marvelous cheekbones of yours had the power to stop Vikings dead in their tracks."

"I like that story," Karen said. "Tell me more."

"We don't know that she's Lapp, Joyce. She looks Irish to me."

"Jesus, Pam. You think everyone's Irish."

Pam didn't argue the point. She rooted around her cavernous pocketbook and removed a pair of patent leather tap shoes, a flashlight, and the collected works of Philip Larkin, until at last she found a tube of hot-pink lipstick. She applied layer after layer on Karen's bow-tie lips, making her blot them on a tissue she procured from inside another of her hidden pockets. When Pam was satisfied, she dashed blush across each of Karen's ethnically contested, though highly esteemed, cheekbones. "You look hale," Joyce admitted.

"Go get him, tiger," Pam said, smiling.

THE SUN WAS blinding. The highway appeared to crumble atomically in its relentless light. Even with sunglasses, Kurt squinted to see, relying on reflexes to pull off the highway in the right spot. They passed a mini-golf course terraced into the hill that overlooked the highway. A long line of people waited to be admitted for eighteen holes of fabricated whimsy. Sarah could not contain her disgust.

"Who the hell would want to spend Last Day playing mini-golf?"

"Takes all kinds to make a world."

Kurt lived in a trailer park behind the mini-golf course. It was a shame to his proud, hardworking family, who subscribed wholesale to the American dream of ever-upward mobility, that their only son would elect such a conspicuous downshift.

"Fiberglass is for Gypsies," his mother had muttered over her steaming cup of tea when Kurt showed her the brochure for the home he'd bought for himself. "Your father is rolling in his grave."

His father had been a shipbuilder, a member of the guild, as had his father and grandfather before him. Kurt's two sisters, one older, one younger, had both gone to college and gotten jobs their parents could be proud of. The elder sister was a middle school math teacher and the younger managed all the food vendors at Fenway Park. Kurt was the name bearer, and what had he done with that name? Dropped out of art school after one year, then foundered for a spell as a gas station attendant before the accident and the stint in jail. He'd assumed his family would be happy when he was released early, but his homecoming had been treated as a silent disgrace.

Kurt was proud of his double-wide. He owned it. Bought it with money he'd earned himself. And he liked his trailer park neighbors, only a small fraction of whom identified as Romany Gypsies. There was a self-reliant economy here in which many outside needs were conveniently provided. Pot, plumbing, rat extermination, childcare, elder care, pirated internet, discount Indian reservation cigarettes, taxidermy, and tattoos were all bartered with a fluidity and friendliness that Kurt knew his self-reliance-loving family would respect if they could relax their classist hypocrisy. That hypocrisy was exactly what Kurt had been fleeing when he'd made the decision to buy his double-wide.

The bike motored up a short steep hill into the neighborhood. People were gathered in clusters around smoky grills, ambling in and out of each other's homes, celebrating the holiday. His neighbors waved and nodded when Kurt passed by on his bike, the men cocking an eyebrow at the helmeted young lady behind him. A pack of small boys were practicing bike jumps off a homemade ramp. When they saw Kurt approaching, they got serious and rode faster, popping wheelies. Kurt revved his engine in approval and the boys with their squinted eyes and sideways smiles raced off.

Sarah had never been on a motorcycle before. She'd never been to a trailer park, either. This day was taking an unusual shape, and though she was desperate to know Kurt's plan for them, she was playing it cool.

"They look like regular houses," she remarked, noticing the shutters on the windows and the hedges out front. She was expecting something bedouin, a vast network of corrugated metal huts and merchants on the road selling beaded jewelry and stolen cellphones. Most of the double-wides looked new. Their white siding was laced with a yellow fringe, the same buildup of pollen that plagued the wooden shingles of Sarah's house. It seemed like a requirement to fly a flag from the front door. The faded colors of many sports teams and veterans' groups and the good old red, white, and blue hung motionless in the thickening air. A couple of people had even hung Last Day flags, the tacky gold flame encircled by white doves set against a lavender background.

"They *are* regular houses," Kurt said. They'd pulled up into his driveway. He also had a flagpole extending obliquely from the front of his house, but no flag was hanging. A giant spider web connecting the naked, outstretched pole to the side of the house sparkled in the early afternoon sun.

"Wow, that's the biggest spider web I've ever seen," Sarah said as she removed her helmet and got off the bike.

"It's a beaut, isn't it? Been there for weeks." He got off the bike with a little hop and started walking across the street. "I'll be right back," Kurt told her. "Go on in. Door's unlocked."

Sarah crouched in for a closer look at the web. Nothing, not even a gnat, was ensnared in the twinkling, translucent fibers. She flicked her fingers against the thickest spot and a spray of moisture flew into her face. A boy ambled toward her. He was barefoot and chubby, around eight years old, Sarah estimated. His hair was a curly mess. He looked at Sarah as though assaying her worth.

"Hello," Sarah said, creeped out by his silent stare.

The boy clicked his tongue in a soft, patient rhythm. *"Tich, tich, tich."*

Sarah wondered if the child was a special-needs case, though admittedly, she'd never been very good with children. Not even when she'd been a child herself. Suddenly the green underbrush sprouting around Kurt's front steps shivered and a small brown rabbit hopped out. *"Tich, tich, tich,"* the boy continued, and after a moment of consideration, the rabbit hopped straight into the boy's arms.

"Arturo the Fourth! He's still among the living?" Kurt said, returned now from wherever he'd gone.

"Arturo da Fift," the child lisped.

"Sorry. Arturo the Fifth. Josh's mother keeps getting these rabbits for him, but they always escape their cages and get smooshed by cars. Josh isn't standing for it, though. He went on a campaign, didn't you, *kimo sabe*?"

The boy pressed his face into the rabbit's fur and inhaled deeply. "I made signs."

"Posted them everywhere." Kurt pointed out the white scabs of paper still clinging to a few trees and lampposts. "Arturo the Fifth is an agent of change. He helps keep the speed limit down in this neighborhood."

The rabbit leapt from Josh's arm and disappeared into the shrubbery behind Kurt's trailer.

"Can I please have a cigarette for my mom, Kurt?"

Kurt tapped one out of his pack and tossed it. Josh caught it midair and ran away. The bottoms of his feet were pitch black except for the arches.

"He'd be a good runner if someone trained him," Sarah observed.

"Not a chance," Kurt said. "He's going to smoke that cigarette himself once he's out of sight."

"How can you let him do that?"

"You can't raise other people's kids."

He gave Sarah a little tour of his home. The kitchen was wood-paneled and underused. The living room was a dumping ground of pizza boxes and beer bottles. Clothes were strewn all around the floor of the bedroom. There was a damp, skunky smell that Sarah connected to the joint Kurt was rolling for himself and not to the cleanliness of his home, which was about average, she guessed, for a man like him. Though she had no idea what a man's home ought to look like, let alone smell like. Terrence's bedroom was the only categorically male space she'd spent any time in, and he suffered from the most tragic, strangling OCD she'd ever seen. Pens and pencils were stored in separate identical

Lucite boxes that Terrence cleaned once a month with Q-tips and rubbing alcohol, and all the venetian blinds on his windows were calibrated to hover at the same fraction of an inch above the sills. If there was an odor to his room, Terrence masked it with the earthy-smelling cones of burning incense that he arranged on a porcelain Japanese dish with painstaking, ritualistic care.

Poor Terrence. She wished that he were here with her now. It was such an odd longing, when confronted with a new romantic possibility—to want to retreat to an older, more familiar (though unfulfilled) one. Terrence was so safe. She never felt awkward when she disappointed him, because she could trust he would always forgive her when conflicts came up. His face would twitch and he wouldn't look at her, but within an hour he'd relax and everything would be okay again. It had happened like that a million times with Terrence. She could count on it. Not so with Kurt. She was so uneasy in his presence. He made her want to plumb unfamiliar parts of herself and present them to him as offerings. "Here is my secret fear of children," she might say, "here are my self-important prophecies, my latent, possibly nonexistent, sexuality. Have them. Have them all. . . ."

"It's way bigger than I expected" is what came out of her instead.

Kurt chuckled. "What were you expecting?"

"I guess an Airstream. Something you hitch up to a truck and go camping in." She tucked herself into the small bench behind the kitchen table, glad that half of her weird, spastic body was hidden for the moment.

"People live here. Permanently."

"So weird not to have a cellar." Was this a classist thing to say? Was *she* classist? It had never occurred to her before that she could have blind spots in her ultra-embracing worldview. She tried to recover. "But then again, cellars are, like, all about symbolic fears and rats. They're totally overrated."

She hoped this sounded supportive. She was taking this man as her lover, her first and maybe only lover, and though the trailer park was underwhelming, it was definitely *memorable*, which was a relief. In fact, this whole experience was already imbued with iniquity and enchantment. She would not screw this up.

"So here's the plan." Kurt pulled out a kitchen chair and leaned over his lap to face Sarah. It was something Dr. Vasquez-McQueen did during office hours and smacked of condescension. "I'm going to shave and change my clothes and collect some things for this amends I need to make. I would offer you a beer or a joint, but since you're underage, that is illegal for me to do. However, if you help yourself while I'm not looking, that's fine with me. You catch my drift?"

"I hate that phrase, but yeah. And I don't smoke or drink. Not, like, puritanically, I just, real life is weird enough, you know?"

"You're amazing, sweetheart." Kurt lifted her hand and kissed her knuckles, then hopped out of his guidance counselor posture and headed into the bathroom. Sarah sat at the table a moment, the fingers of her left hand still ablaze from his touch.

Kurt had rinsed and lathered his face when Sarah knocked on the bathroom door. "Can I watch?"

"Uhhh, sure."

She lowered the seat and the lid of his toilet, which was so disgusting she only allowed her eyes to skim the surface before sitting down. She watched in a happy trance as Kurt plowed away paths of speckled white to reveal the smooth pink skin underneath. She envied the way men could bear such totally different faces to the world in a matter of weeks. Kurt had an impressive scar on his chin, a deep diagonal line that glowed a little pinker from the brief attention of the razor.

"That's a cool scar." Sarah pointed.

"Hockey game."

"Actors always talk about having a good and bad side of their face, and I always thought that was stupid, but you actually have two distinct sides of your face. Like you're two different people."

"I am a Gemini," Kurt told her.

Sarah suppressed a groan. If she were a guy, her penis would totally deflate right now. She didn't know what the female equivalent of that was, but her brain was certainly losing its boner. Astrology was so, so unforgivably dumb. And ten times dumber when straight guys talked about it.

Kurt wiped his face clean, a new man. He patted Sarah on the head and went into his bedroom. She followed him, feeling bolder. Standing there as he sorted through the piles on the floor, she took off her sneakers, then crawled onto his bed.

Kurt ignored this and continued rummaging around the mess. Time for that later, he thought, if *that* was going to happen at all—she was just a kid, after all. He was still on the fence, still hoping that after his impending confrontation, where this girl would act as his buffer/guardian angel, something much better would work out for both of them independently later on in the night, and they'd part ways happily. And if they did end up in bed together, then, well, disappointments were better faced in the dark.

Sarah continued to lie in Kurt's bed, her anxiety growing by the minute. Was it her job to seduce Kurt, she wondered, or was she supposed to wait for him to move toward her? The rules of all this were confusing at best, unfair at worst. She lay there, trying to look cool. A full retreat, such as jumping off his bed, would give this moment a case of whiplash. Besides, her socks reeked and she needed to hide them under his blankets. She angled her body in what she hoped looked like a sexy pose and pretended to take a nap. There were more clothes tangled in his sheets. Errant socks and a pair of boxers she avoided touching.

It wasn't supposed to feel like this, Sarah thought; or maybe this was exactly how it was supposed to feel?

"Hey, I could use your help a minute," Kurt said.

He had gotten a hammer to take down an Indian tapestry nailed to the windowsill. The elephant god Ganesha sat on a golden throne in the middle of a woodland scene, proffering his own broken tusk in one of his many hands.

"I don't want it to get all ripped or frayed if I can help it."

Sarah climbed out of the bed. She caught the cloth as it fell and shook out the dust.

"Why are you taking this down?"

"I need to return it today."

"You've had it for a long time." She shaded her eyes against the light from outside.

"Yeah."

Her ponytail had gotten limp and a lock of hair fell into her face. Kurt reached over and smoothed it behind her ear.

"Okay," Sarah said, an answer to a question he didn't ask, her voice feathery and strange.

Kurt made a pile on his bed of things that he was collecting for his amends. The tapestry. A field guide to North American mushrooms, its pages waterlogged and crispy. A coffee tin that he sealed with a plastic bag and rubber bands.

"Are those—ashes?" Sarah asked.

"Some of it, yeah," Kurt answered.

Sarah was about to ask whose ashes they were when something stopped her. She heard a thump overhead and gazed up at the skylight. A mass of pollen and dirt had whorled together, looking kind of like the Milky Way. A cat scurried over the roof. The bottoms of its paws pressed into the window, leaving behind tracks in the thick yellow film.

Kurt moved his bed away from the wall and reached behind it to pull out a small painting mounted in a cheap gilt frame. It was a pinwheel of blue and green wings flying away from the center point, an ersatz mandala. Sarah judged it to be the work of a precocious but untalented teenager, someone her age but not as smart. She was hoping that was the answer. The signature at the bottom said *Mary*. Maybe a long-lost niece?

"My old girlfriend," Kurt corrected.

"Oh," Sarah said. "Did she die tragically?" She couldn't believe how much she wanted this to be true.

"Everyone's death is tragic."

MARY HAD BEEN the one bright spot in Kurt's life after he'd dropped out of art school. Kurt was nineteen when he met her and Mary was a sophomore in high school. She was a gorgeous earth child with large brown eyes and dark, gleaming hair, the kind of girl who wore sandals with wool socks in the dead of winter, who smoked like a chimney but wouldn't touch a plate with meat on it. She thought Kurt's illustrations of dragons and heroes were genius and she loved his family as much as her own. She hailed from a long dynasty of semi-important Americans — the last of whom was her uncle Bear, an astronaut — WASPs clutching desperately to relevance as their storied past collected more and more dust in the annals of local libraries.

"We were switched before birth," she liked to joke about Kurt. She fit in so much better with his German-Irish Catholic family, and in a parallel world, Kurt would have been much happier in hers. Mary's vague ambition to one day run a daycare center out of her home was applauded by Kurt's parents, while his artistic impulses — mostly ignored, at times derided by his folks — would have been nurtured to the fullest if he had been born into her clan instead. Mary was the first member of her family not to go to Choate. She said she'd bombed the entrance exam on purpose. But she would have done poorly regardless of her effort. She wasn't stupid, just simple, content with whatever knowledge landed in her lap, curious about her world, but only to a point. She felt no need to waste time reading that the woods were lovely, dark, and deep when she could just go there and see for herself. She was looking forward to marrying Kurt as soon as she was eighteen and wanted nothing more than to start a family.

"Her parents hated me long before the accident," Kurt told Sarah. "I don't blame them. I'd bring her home drunk or stoned, she'd have twigs and pine needles and sap in her hair. Those expensive sweaters they bought her would be all ripped. They'd say, 'What were you doing, Mary? Rolling around in the forest?' And she was so goddamn sweet she couldn't lie. To anyone. She'd look at them with her full-moon eyes and just say, 'Yes.'"

Kurt cleaned the dust off another picture frame he pulled out from under his bed and handed it to Sarah. It was a badly scanned photograph of Mary, printed at a drugstore, but Sarah could see, even in this slightly pixilated, desaturated form, how beautiful and unself-conscious the girl was. It was a picture of her smiling face, a scrap of shadow creeping up under her chin, suggesting Kurt, her photographer, hovering above her, probably in some delightful springtime field. She was so heartbreakingly pretty. Even the bump on the bridge of her nose was pretty, as though her beauty was so powerful it cracked under its own weight, becoming greater from the resulting flaw.

About two years into their relationship, Kurt had crashed Mary's car into a tree. They had just left Kurt's parents' house. He was drunk but she was drunker and so he reasoned it was better for him to drive. Rain pelted the metal roof like gunfire and the windshield wipers swung hysterically to keep up, offering brief, vanishing glimpses of the road.

He woke up in a hospital and was quickly transferred to South Middlesex Correctional. Mary had survived the accident, he would learn from his parents. He had no idea what kind of condition she was in, only that she was alive. After he'd served his time, her parents forbade him from seeing her. "You ruined her!" her father raged, his breath so saturated with scotch it could catch fire.

"What happened to her—it would have been better if she had died," Kurt said to Sarah, who was still holding Mary's picture in her lap. "A couple months after I got out of jail, her mother wrote me a weird letter. Said she'd had a 'spiritual awakening'—her words, not mine—and wanted me over to their house for lunch on Last Day. I didn't know what to expect."

Mary's mother had greeted him at the door with a vodka tonic, as if

Kurt were her husband coming home from work. Her actual husband, Mary's father, had left the country. "He's taken his grief into exile," Mary's mother explained, offering no more on the subject. They sat around drinking in the sunroom while the Azorean woman they'd hired to take care of Mary got her dressed and ready upstairs. Mary's mother offered Kurt a Librium, and when he refused, she told him, "I was afraid for so long that you were going to ruin her life. I hated you for that. And now that you have, and the worst has happened, I can't hate you anymore."

"Please, just let me see her."

"Get ready, young man," her mother warned.

What finally emerged from the upstairs bedrooms was a wild animal in the shape of Mary. A scar ran up the back of her skull and onto her forehead, a satin strip where the hair refused to grow back. Half of her face sagged and her eyebrows had grown bushy and uneven. Even her eyes had changed. It was as though the human light in them had been snuffed out.

"She started screaming when she saw me. Brayed, like a donkey. She hit herself in the face and wouldn't stop. The CNA had to force some liquid tranquilizer down her throat to get her to stop. Then we all sat in their goddamn sunroom and had lunch together. It was awful. Her mother drank and this nurse's aide pretended the spoon was an airplane and pushed tuna salad into Mary's mouth. She'd chew and then drool half of it back out. When she swallowed, the aide clapped for her. I wished that she had died. Or that I had died. That we could have died together. Then right when I thought things could not be worse, Mary shit her pants at the table. While her mother and the nurse were changing her diaper upstairs, I just got up and left and never looked back."

Sarah handed the framed photo back to him. Kurt placed it in a backpack along with the other effects.

"So we're going to see her again?" Sarah asked.

"She died, finally, two years later. Pneumonia. Her immune system was wrecked after the accident."

"Then where are we going with all this stuff?"

"To her sister. This belongs to her, not me. I should have done this years ago." Kurt folded his hands over his stomach for a moment. He looked scared. He rearranged the contents of the backpack so that everything fit and belted it shut. What Sarah thought were tassels dangling from the top flap turned out to be long strands of hair.

"It's a cool backpack."

"She made it. She's an artist," Kurt said, swishing the strands around with his fingers. "Her sister, I mean, not Mary. It's Mary's hair, but that could be a lie. Her sister is—look, Sarah, I don't want to go there alone, but I don't want to force you into something you can't handle. If you want, I'll drive you home right now, or anywhere else you want to go. It's been nice to have someone listen to me, someone who's smart. Not some drunk girl who's gonna end up causing trouble. Not someone who thinks she's cute and deserves a free tattoo."

He lifted up his motorcycle helmet and offered it to her.

"I mean it. No pressure. If you want to go home, I have a plan B."

"What's that?"

"Go down to one of the bonfires. Burn this stuff. Go to a bar and get drunk."

"I don't want you to do that," she said. "I'll go with you to make amends to this sister. But afterward, we're going to watch the sunset on the beach."

LONG BEFORE THERE was sleep, there was night, Earth rolling away from the sun as a lover in a bed. But now such darkness is an old dream. The light of cities, of towns, and the highways connecting them, rupture the black hemisphere, bleeding through the membrane of night. Tokyo appeared to Yui as a great hemorrhage of electricity, and somewhere inside it his brother lay dead. Weeks of looking through these windows had taught Yui to recognize the particular patterns of Tokyo on sight, a homing mechanism that failed to soothe him as he floated now alone in the dark. He wished all the lights of Tokyo would shut off, then all the lights in Asia, so that the world could disappear into the black space surrounding it.

Right now the monk was sitting with Tadeshi's body. Yui had seen to that right away. His sister-in-law was too hysterical and had to be medicated. Yui had called upon Chiyo, his company's COO, to handle the details in his stead. The cremation could proceed but interment of his brother's ashes, Yui had instructed Chiyo, would wait until he returned. He'd given his sister-in-law permission to pick the bones out of Tadeshi's ashes along with an uncle neither Yui nor his brother had felt any special emotion toward, but who could serve as a representative of the generation that preceded the brothers, a link to their father, who had died a few years back. His nephews were too young and spoiled to be trusted with this task, and his own wife and children had always been resentful of Tadeshi, who was closer to Yui than they could ever hope to be.

Because of multiple failures in their connection, these arrangements had taken hours to discuss, with voices stilted and screens stalled, cutting off in the middle of a sob. At one point Yui had to confront the immobile face of his wife frozen mid-yawn on the screen of his laptop. He hated her for yawning, for feeling anything, for being so near his brother when he was not.

But it was all settled now. There was nothing left for him to do but float in the Cupola and look at the world spinning below. Mission Control had offered their sincere, uneasy condolences. They'd granted the three men a work dispensation for the next day. Yui was getting his Last Day holiday after all.

KAREN REMEMBERED THE day she met Dennis better than she remembered anything else that happened before or after.

"Pack for a trip," her mother had told her, thrusting a plastic shopping bag into her hand. Karen packed a sweatshirt, a bathing suit, a stuffed rabbit, an old cigarette carton filled with remarkable-looking rocks, a handful of crayons bound by a rubber band, and a pad of paper. She fell asleep in the car, so there was no way of determining how long or how far they'd driven. She woke up when her mother was pulling her out of the car to lead her up the stairs to an apartment above a convenience store. It was summer. She was done with school and eager to go back. The length of a summer was for her an immeasurable gulf, and *when* was an impossible question always dangling off the precipice of her mind—when could she go back to school, when was it time to go home, when would she be able to drive, when was Christmas, when was supper.

"When I say so," her mother always responded, and if Karen argued, she got pinched until a bruise appeared.

The air inside the apartment was hot and still. Dennis was there with his father, or the man Karen assumed was his father. She never actually knew, until this day, if that was true. His father was smoking a cigarette out of the corner of his mouth, blowing smoke out of his nostrils, grunting as he tried to heave an air conditioner onto the windowsill.

"Be careful, you moron, or you'll kill someone on the sidewalk," her mother said to this man. Like they'd known each other for a long time and she had earned her right to be annoyed by him ages ago.

The man said nothing. Neither did Dennis. He was sitting on a white leather couch, his eyes lowered, already ashamed.

Years later she would try to describe Dennis to people, but she never could. Sometimes when she lay awake at night, she would try to remember his face and falter. He had two eyes, a nose, a mouth. He had ears and hair, a chin. A way of walking all his own. A voice. She could picture these things in her heart but not in her mind, as though Dennis were a ghost that could be felt but not seen. He was Dennis. He looked exactly like Dennis. What more could she say?

That summer day so long ago, Karen had run around the empty little apartment with a last gust of energy, and for once her mother did not yell at her to stop or slow down. In the bathroom hung a set of new towels with the tags still on them. On the tank of the toilet sat an Easter basket Karen recognized as hers from earlier in the year, full of tiny motel soaps, strands of green plastic grass still tangled into the basket's weave. In the kitchen, there was a large gap in the counter where a stove should have been and a hole in the wall sprouting a few pointless wires. In the living room was just the white couch where Dennis sat.

There was nothing else, except the bedroom, which is where she and Dennis would remain for the next year. Some of the people who came brought them presents of candy or Halloween costumes and took lots of pictures. Others hated them for no reason Karen could ever discern. One man liked to cover their entire heads with a dark wool hat and call them by different names. Another spanked them, then afterward held them and cried. Their own parents seemed indifferent. But there were some visitors who said they came for love.

"I drove for miles just to see you," one man said. "After I saw your pictures, I got in a car and didn't stop once. I peed in a bottle. All the way from Ohio. Do you know how far that is?"

Dennis did and Karen didn't. Karen was seven, lagging behind in school because of so much absence, just beginning to master her letters. A was still a tepee in her mind, housing wild Indians intoning the vowel in a long, unbroken chant. Aaaaaaaaaaaaaah. B was a yellowjacket denuded of its stinger as it flew away from a painful welt. C was a cookie only partially eaten. K was a stick figure of Karen herself, but only half of her. Where was the other half?

Dennis was nine years old. He told her that he hated school, and offered no explanation.

After the apartment was raided, a foster family had kept Dennis and Karen together. It had seemed like the right thing to do, until it became clear that it wasn't. Karen was always sneaking into Dennis's bed at night. To stop her from kissing everyone with an open mouth, her foster mother, a Catholic, put red pepper flakes on her tongue and made her sit in the corner with her hands on her head to stop the little girl from touching herself so much. When it was time to start first grade, Karen was transferred to a new house. She hadn't seen Dennis since.

*R*EDEMPTION AS AN armband for the stocky war veteran who stubbornly, angrily, refused a free beer. *REDEMPTION*, one letter per knuckle, on the hands of the actor who'd recently given up on Los Angeles and moved back home to Boston. *REDEMPTION* written vertically down the side of the rib cage and onto the hip of the pretty young brunette who couldn't stop crying about someone named Hailee.

"I just miss her so much," she said. "I can't stand it. I don't want to live without her."

"Sweetheart, I've been there," Jake said to her. "Everyone in this shop has been there. Even the ugly old miserable bastards you can't imagine anyone touching, let alone fucking, have been there."

She blinked at him, the tears for one moment suspended, her sadness quivering in her eyes like the last dream to bring you from sleep into morning.

"Just tell me it's going to be okay," she said to Jake.

"It will probably get worse. But then it will be okay."

DEATH AND DISEASE didn't scare Kurt, but Mary's sister did. Whenever he'd spent holidays with Mary and her family, her sister had spoken to him in the same brisk tone her parents used, if she talked to him at all. Far worse was when she would walk away from Kurt and Mary in the middle of a conversation and not return. "What the hell?" Kurt asked Mary once. "Oh, she gets bored easily," was Mary's placid answer.

So it came as a shock when this witchy sister spent Mary's share of their trust fund, which had transferred to her, on Kurt's outstanding legal fees. Stranger still when she picked him up and took him home to her bed the night he was released from prison. He had always assumed she hated him before the accident. He would learn in the manic six months that followed that night that hate and love were indistinguishable passions for her, and that the expression of either was always for her a form of punishment.

She was the exact opposite of Mary, who was guileless and sweet, almost mentally disabled by optimism. What the sisters had in common was that they both recognized Kurt's talent, though the elder sister was less starstruck.

"You're a hand, not an eye," she told Kurt.

"What does that mean?"

"You've got skills but not talent. You're a craftsman, not an artist."

There was malice in her assessment, but a brutal honesty, too, which brought Kurt a tremendous sense of relief: he could finally accept his limitations and build from there. He'd never be in a gallery or a museum but he was good enough to start a tattoo business, and that was good enough for him. It was Mary's sister who had come up with the name Redemption Tattoo, and fronted him ten thousand dollars to start out, only to disappear a few days before the grand opening, hopping a flight to Guatemala without so much as a goodbye.

Every time Kurt had started to feel stable, the demons of his past muted to a low murmur he could mostly ignore, a message in his inbox would appear like clockwork from MorningStar76, Mary's sister, re-minding him of all the things he had done and would never do, what he was and what he wasn't, how different, interesting, and real his life could be if he had never left her, as though the fact was not that she had left him. She'd haunted him with the unwanted details of her hateful sex life, tales of the poverty and squalor she elected to live in, the shanty-towns in Africa, the South American slums, the weird cult-like ashrams in India where she was ritualistically molested by purported gurus. And always, at the end of each letter, she would urge Kurt to drop everything, to give everything up, and come to her.

Kurt refused to respond to these emails, though he read each one carefully, chewed on them until his jaws actually ached during many sleepless nights (the sleeping pills he took now more or less resolved this). But her most recent message had been different. It was terse and gentle, saying that she was in town for the Last Day holiday and that she'd love a visitor. Here was her address, if he wanted to stop by. He had sat on this prospect like an egg, waiting for the answer to hatch beneath him, freeing him from the true mammalian labor of birthing a decision himself. It was only this morning, in the fugue of nihilistic and ethereal hope that was the Last Day, that Kurt had been moved to write her back. He regretted it now.

The sun fired at the earth in invisible rays, striking the pavement so that it glittered like a large elusive fish swimming in and out of a net of shadows. Every traffic light on the way to her address winked green at his approach, and he wondered if her sorcery was responsible for this, as mindfuckery was her typical foreplay. He hoped Sarah would protest or offer up a new plan, a bunch of high school kids getting stoned in the woods somewhere, something, anything but this. But Sarah was agreeable, though a little tense, wanting only to follow him wherever he went.

"I haven't seen her in years," Kurt explained to Sarah as they parked in front of a convenience store. Kurt and Sarah searched the empty shelves of the store for a decent bottle of wine. They could only find beer, which he knew would disappoint her. As if on cue, the Last Day standard "I Just Called to Say I'm Sorry" by Winston Wonderful began playing on the radio from crackly speakers in the store. Kurt took Sarah's hand and squeezed it. He wasn't going to waste his whole day on a scavenger hunt, so he grabbed a six-pack of the most expensive beer in the store and got in line to pay.

The old woman in front of them was trying to pay for her cigarettes with loose change. Her hands shook violently as she separated the pennies, nickels, and dimes on the counter. Her hair was short, thick, and white, half of it a poof of curls, the other half flattened from sleeping.

"Let me buy those for you," Kurt said, slapping a twenty-dollar bill down on the counter. "A Last Day good deed."

"I want a lottery ticket, too," the old woman demanded. Her face was blotchy and bruised and her breath smelled like mold.

"And a lotto ticket for my friend here," Kurt said to the clerk.

"A quick pick," the lady added. "I don't have no luck with my own numbers."

"She didn't even say thank you," Sarah said after the woman left.

"It was sadder to watch her count coins." He paid the clerk, who was watching TV behind a plexiglass barrier.

They walked back outside to his motorcycle. Kurt stuffed the beer into the backpack he was returning. "I'm glad you're coming with me," he said, and slung the backpack over his stomach. "Once we get rid of all this stuff, we'll pick something up for dinner. And eat it on the beach."

The girl beamed back at him a dizzy smile. The bright-eyed elixir of teenage adoration made him feel smarter and more confident. Maybe a better man could do without all that, but not Kurt, not today. He had learned through much trial and error that it didn't matter what happened in the end, so he might as well surrender to his own idiocy. He took Sarah's chin in his hand and kissed her.

It wasn't Sarah's first kiss, but she decided right there to rewrite history so that from now on it would be. *We were standing on the sidewalk in front of this convenience store, it was Last Day.* . . . His lips were warm and very dry and did not linger long. A carbonated tingling erupted behind Sarah's kneecaps. Her wrists fell numb, useless.

MARY'S SISTER HAD just returned from another one of her pilgrimages. She was gaunt inside her pale gray T-shirt, and her jeans looked like a sack her body had rolled into. Kurt held her for a long time when he saw her. Neither one of them spoke, until Kurt pulled away, a sad look on his face, and said, "Jesus, Sarah. When was the last time you ate something?"

"I have some plums. They're mealy and taste like paper. It's not their season yet. I shouldn't have bought them."

Kurt shook his head. "This is Sarah. It's a day full of Sarahs, I guess. . . ."

"Sarah with an *H*?" Sarah Moss blurted out.

"It's the least interesting fact about me," her namesake answered. She took the younger girl's hand and squeezed it as hard as her bony fingers were able.

The only feature she shared with her sister, Mary, Sarah thought, comparing the figure in front of her to the photograph she had seen earlier, was their nose, though on the elder sister it looked ugly. This other Sarah had unnerving blue eyes set far apart on her face, giving her the vigilant look of an animal.

"Could I have a glass of water?" Sarah Moss asked.

"Of course," the woman answered and walked as though in great pain toward the kitchen. Her black hair reached down to her waist and was streaked with white strands.

The apartment she had sublet was unfurnished except for a long wooden picnic table on which she had arranged a series of photographs.

"So you were in Asia this time?" Kurt lifted a photograph from the table and winced at what he saw. Sarah inched closer to him and looked over his shoulder. All the photos were portraits of people peering directly into the camera. The one Kurt held was full of little children squatting in a darkened doorway. Their mouths were ringed with erupting pustules, and tears streamed clean tracks down the filth of their faces.

"That one's called *The Impetigos*. Isn't the light perfect?" the other Sarah called from the kitchen sink.

Kurt returned it to the table and picked up another: a man with a mangled half of an arm held a chicken by the throat with his other, intact hand.

The other Sarah handed Sarah Moss a mason jar of lukewarm water teeming with particles. Sarah Moss sipped it warily as she watched the older woman stack the photos to make room for her guests at the table. "That man lost his arm as a teenager. He chased a soccer ball into a thicket where an unexploded ordnance was waiting for him. There are thousands of them left over from the Vietnam War."

"You work for an NGO?" Sarah Moss asked.

"No, I don't believe in activism. The idea that people's lives are supposed to get infinitely better is the very barrier holding our species back from true fulfillment."

"Sarah's got a trust fund," Kurt quipped. "So she can afford to be radical."

"Not anymore." She lowered herself to the floor and folded her long, willowy legs into a tight lotus. "I spent the last of it this year. I bought this girl out of sexual slavery." She reached up for the cigarette Kurt had just lit for himself, and without looking or even thinking about it he gave it to her.

"She was sixteen and had a severely lazy eye. I mean, the thing looked like it was going to roll out of her face at any moment. That one lazy eyeball had seen more in its sixteen years than most of us see with both eyes in a lifetime. It had had enough, was ready to abandon ship. 'Let the other guy do the witnessing,' is what that eye was saying. I liked her lazy eye. I liked her, too. I took some amazing photographs of her, then erased the data from my camera. I wanted to stipulate that this prostitute never wear sunglasses again, but my Thai is fluent only to a four-year-old, and you can't make stipulations when bargaining over human lives. I paid a gigantic sum to her pimp. Emptied my trust fund."

"That's a kind of activism," Sarah said.

"I just wanted to see what would happen. I wasn't trying to save her."

"No one would accuse you of that," Kurt said, lighting another cigarette he kept partially cupped in his hand, as though hiding it from her.

"What happened?" Sarah Moss asked.

"She went back to her pimp. Not even a week later. But it was my goal to get my bank balance down to zero, so I succeeded."

"Sweetheart," Kurt began, but the conclusion of that thought was too sad for him to finish. He excused himself to the bathroom.

What was the attraction? Sarah wondered. This elder Sarah was frightening and came off as even more asexual than she was. Then, as if she'd read the question gleaming in Sarah Moss's eyes, the woman offered this:

"It might not appear so, but I do love that man. In my own way. And he loves me, though he can't admit it. Not anymore. It's like the darkness within him recognizes the darkness within me. A negative *namaste*."

Sarah wanted to run out the door that very moment, to leave this witch forever, but she would not let this woman win Kurt's love. Not today. She picked up a photograph and asked about it, trying to change the subject. "What's going on in this one?" It was a picture of a dead tiger hog-tied to a stick being carried by two slight, stern-faced men.

"That was in Indonesia. That tiger killed a little girl in the village. The villagers took it really personally, which I found fascinating. We see natural disasters as blameless, senseless tragedies. Typhoons and earthquakes are emotionally fraught but simple at the same time. Not like the bulk of life's traumas, caused by some human being's fear. But these villagers regard the realm of nature on the same level as any other human endeavor. So when nature strikes, they first propitiate the gods they offended and then seek vengeance. They stalked that tiger for a month before they caught and killed him. I was there the day they took his corpse on a parade for everyone to see."

"How did they know which tiger did it?"

"I wondered the same thing. Animal faces are as distinguishable as human faces to them. They're all neighbors. They were confident it was him."

"I feel bad for him. If it was a him," Sarah Moss said. "The tiger."

"The only thing left of the girl was her arm. The tiger left it at the edge of the village as a kind of offering. Like a house cat leaves a dead mouse on the doorstep. It was a hell of a parade."

"I bet." Sarah Moss wanted to cry. It was taking all her strength to maintain this posture of cool immunity.

Kurt returned from the bathroom and it was obvious right away to both women that he had been crying. "What do you say, Sarah? Should we order a pizza? My treat."

"Thank you," the woman said, gazing up at him. "No."

"You got to eat something. You're disappearing."

"I know." She unfolded her legs and gathered them into herself. She rose slowly from the floor and walked her imperious, exhausted body over to the window, where she sat again and stared. For a long time no one said anything. Sarah Moss began flipping over the photographs so that she and Kurt wouldn't have to see them anymore. When she was done, she looked at Kurt and tapped an imaginary watch on her wrist, telling him that she was done with this adventure. He smiled at her. That's what he had brought her there to do, to let him know when it was time to leave. Without her, he would have stayed all night, trapped in this abyss.

"So," Kurt said. "I wanted to return these to you." He unlatched the fringed top of the backpack and took out the can of Mary's ashes.

"Don't," Sarah said from the window.

"They don't belong to me." Kurt pulled out the items one by one. "It wasn't right for me to keep them."

"Guilt is a waste of time," she started to argue. "It's a—"

"Yeah, yeah, I know your intellectual arguments very well and I don't need to hear them again. I feel bad and have felt bad for years now because she made this painting for you, and I didn't think you deserved it. I didn't want you to have it. I didn't even want you to have her fucking ashes. So I took it all from you. Even though I couldn't look at it, either. It was under my bed, for Christ's sake."

"It doesn't matter—" she groaned.

"Yes it does. She loved you. She made this for you. I was spiteful and selfish and I'm sorry. That's why I'm returning it to you."

He placed the painting on the floor and slid it across the room to where she stood by the window. Sarah Moss was scared that the woman would do something horrible, like throw the painting out the window or drop her pants and pee on it. But she didn't do anything; she didn't even look at it. She continued to stare at the sky.

Sarah Moss looked out the same window. The uppermost branches of a tree were wiggling a little in the wind. Beyond them, nothing.

"Happy Last Day. Until night falls." Kurt took Sarah Moss by the hand. "Come on. We're leaving."

"Wait." The other Sarah pulled herself out of her reverie and walked up to Kurt. She put her hand on his cheek, and kissed him. It was a long, slow kiss that Sarah Moss could see involved tongue.

"Thank you, Kurt," she said at last. "I'm grateful that you took such good care of these things. I've moved around so much over the years. I've acquired and lost so many possessions, some of them, I'm loath to admit, quite meaningful to me. There's no way I could have been a good steward of her ashes and effects. But you were. And I'm truly grateful."

"Jesus Christ," Kurt whispered, his eyes tearing up again. "You're too good for this world, sweetheart."

"We all are, Kurt." She opened the door for them. "Goodbye."

The door shut behind them with a bang followed by the clatter of multiple locks.

The air outside had cooled quite a lot. The sun was not ready to set but its light was thinner, almost watery, as it prepared to swim away.

"Thank you for coming with me," Kurt said, wiping his eyes with the backs of his hands. "She was always weird before, but not like that, not so—"

"Sadistic?"

"Maybe." Kurt remembered the last time he'd slept with her. She'd said things he shuddered to recall now.

Sarah fished her sweatshirt out of her bag and wrapped it tightly around her body. She looked up at the wan blue of the sky. A thick tower of cloud was disintegrating fast like something on fire. If there was proof of anything mystical—answers, explanations—she couldn't think of a dumber place to look for it than the sky.

"IT'S FUNNY," BEAR said, "she doesn't look all that far away."

"I am surprised every time I come here and see that she is so close."

The green tangled veils of the aurora borealis rippled over the North Pole. The ISS made another lap around the world.

"He was supposed to be here," Yui said, following Bear to the galley.

"I read that."

Yui and Tadeshi had both trained to become guests in space. Their ultimate goal was to go together. Tadeshi, who was six minutes older, had offered ridiculous sums to JAXA, NASA, and Roscosmos to allow for the first time not one but two non-astronauts concurrently on the mission. Even the desperately underfunded European Space Agency had refused their offer. The Yamamoto twins had never been separated like this before. They were a study in cooperation. They had been since they were born, and probably before then. Yui would not drink from his mother's breast until his brother latched onto the other. When the boys started their schooling, their tutors learned early on to give them identical grades, an easy indulgence as their test scores often *were* identical, or near enough. The woman who became Tadeshi's wife had first approached Yui for a date. She'd been a silent stalker of his at university, claiming that she alone could tell the twins apart from across the street, a boast that was probably true given the amount of time she spent staring at them. Yui had spent their only date combing through her friends' online profiles to find a girl he could claim was prettier, confabulating a story that he liked her friend instead, so that she would like Tadeshi better. In a standoff of kindness, each of the two brothers, both engaged, stalled his wedding plans so that the other could have the honor of marrying first and offering his bride their mother's wedding ring. In their company, they assumed separate roles—Yui was the artist and Tadeshi the businessman—but drew the same salary. They were competitive only in their ability to surrender and sacrifice for the other. When Tadeshi won the first seat on ISS Mission 47-48, his brother was overjoyed that he would not have the burden of taking it from him. Then, two weeks before they were to fly to Moscow, Tadeshi tore his Achilles tendon getting out of a Jacuzzi.

"I demanded to see the MRI. I thought Tadeshi was faking, to give me the trip. He was not faking. But the injury was intentional. Definitely. I know."

Svec had smuggled several pints of vodka on board, which he now offered to Yui. He had been saving them for his last night on the ship—this would be his last mission in space, he was planning to announce his retirement once he landed—but the death of a twin certainly called for drinks, no matter what that punctilious American said. The vodka was hidden among all the other beverages in soft plastic pouches, suggesting some outside cooperation with the team that had packed the Soyuz that had brought them here.

"It might not—" Bear stammered when he smelled the alcohol on the other men's breath. "I mean, I suppose it's okay, on Last Day. But don't you think drinking, and whatnot, will interfere with our mineral balance tests?"

Svec swigged without apology. "This one here"—he pointed at Bear—"was not supposed to be on mission, either. Greg Koehler was my left-seat man. He got sinus infection before launch."

"That's true," Bear admitted. "Greg's a good man. A great astronaut. I feel sorry for him, missing out on this."

"Greg is like brother to me," Svec said.

"Do you have a brother?" Yui asked Bear.

"Two sisters," Bear said.

Yui sobbed, but without gravity his tears could not fall, forcing him to blink like a maniac in a grand mal seizure and blot his face constantly with a towel.

"My older sister lives in Boston. My younger sister just moved into a group home there recently. She's special needs."

"What does she need?" Yui asked.

"She has Down syndrome."

"My son," Svec began, then stopped. A meniscus of water pooled over his eyes. It took very little—the opening bars of "Ochi Chernye," a single line of Pushkin—added to a few milliliters of vodka to make Svec cry. He threw the remainder of the empty carcass of his liquefied dinner in the trash and pulled a laminated index card out from under his shirt. It was held in place by two clamps attached to a chain of tiny metal beads around his neck, like a Christian scapular. "He made," Svec said, smirking again in that expression Bear now realized was involuntary, not ironic. On the paper, printed in messy Cyrillic scrawl, was the name and birth date of every single man and woman who had ever orbited the earth in space, Svec explained. "Maxim cannot be in school. He is not normal. But loves astronauts. Knows everything. More than me! He can recite this list without looking. Like machine."

"Oh." Bear held the plastic sheet in his hand and smiled. "He's autistic."

"He is good boy!" Svec slapped his hand hard on the table.

"Tadeshi choked to death."

"Terrible. Terrible."

"He was alone. Eating at his desk. I suppose, eating too fast. Why was he rushing? I wonder."

"Best not to think about it."

"He had a mole. On his left buttocks. I do not have this mole."

"Okay, Yui. It's going to be okay—"

"If the crack in the buttocks is the equator, Tadeshi's mole would be somewhere near Madagascar."

"Which orientation are you using?" Svec asked.

"All right, fellas, let's be careful with this stuff." Bear took the vodka pouch from Yui and saw that it too was already empty. Yui and Svec laughed and opened another pouch that they passed back and forth to each other. Ripples of laughter flowed into rushes and within minutes they were out of control.

"Svec, you have girls, too. Daughters, am I right?" Bear needed to take control and steer this ship in a different direction.

"Whores," Svec said, his eyes squeezed shut, trying either to hold their image in his mind or prevent it from entering. "Like their mothers."

"I love whores," Yui sighed. The very thought calmed him immensely.

"Oldest daughter is dancer. Not real dancer. How do we say? Strip dancer. Whore dancer. Her mother is, too. I tried. I send her to good school. I give her good advice. Always give her mother money. They don't care. They like to take their clothes off. Her grandmother was whore, too. Mother's mother. It's in their blood. Nothing can be done about it. Second daughter, from second wife, she is lesbian. She has hair like you." He pointed to Bear. "And ring in nose like bull. She hates me."

"Tadeshi has a gay son. Masami. His mother wanted a girl and gave him a girl's name and now he is fully gay. This is how it happened."

"It doesn't work that way," Bear said.

"My sons are little assholes," Yui said, then doubled over laughing until he was spinning in place.

"Kids can be tough," Bear offered. "I know I certainly had a hard time with my girls. And once they hit the teen years? Phew, it was tense. Everybody about to burst into tears or rage at any second. My wife, my ex-wife, she was a mess about it. Crying and screaming right alongside the girls. I was so glad to go to work every day back then, I'm telling you. Pack it on, I told my project manager. Anything to get me away from their mood swings. But now they're both in college, my girls. One's in graduate school, for special education therapy. The other is studying economics at UCLA. They're great girls. I really feel like they are my buddies now. Like, if I met them in some other context, if they were my interns, I'd be really impressed by them, and interested in what they had to say. But man oh man, the road here was a rough one."

"My sons were born little assholes. It is their destiny."

"But you love them, right?"

Yui sucked the vodka out of the pouch until the package crinkled and folded in on itself. "Yes, of course. I love them. But I love Tadeshi more. No one can compare."

"I understand," Svec said, opening another pouch. "I feel same about Greg Koehler. He is my truest friend. Like brother. I would die for him."

"I would die for my brother," Yui said. "I feel one emotion right now. Just one. I am furious Tadeshi did not let me die first."

Bear wasn't sure how long he could babysit his colleagues as they drank. The porthole window offered a glimpse of Australia, a fat, stunned rhinoceros marooned in the middle of the sea. A meteoroid sailed into the atmosphere and burned up like a cigarette tossed out the window of a moving car.

"I should send a few emails out before I hit the hay," he told the men, but they were not listening to him.

After settling into his CQ, Bear opened his laptop and began typing in his journal. He used to think he would die for his wife, that she was his partner in every sense, that his success depended on her nurturance, and that without her, there was no point in succeeding. Then she left him for a pharmaceutical exec from Boston. And his daughters? Would he die for them? They were self-sufficient, resourceful, tough. He'd raised them that way, and so never, not even in their childhood, had he loved them with the vertiginous pity so many parents feel toward their helpless young. His daughters could survive anything; they didn't need their dad's even hypothetical, metaphorical pledge to give up his life for them. And besides, they had chosen their mother in the divorce, had followed her across the country to Boston, treating Bear like a beloved uncle they patronized with visits not more than twice a year. He loved his sisters, but he would never give his life up for them.

Bear wrote in his journal that if he died tomorrow, there would be no lingering resentments. No unfinished business. He had been a good husband, and then a compassionate ex-husband, a great son and brother, a loving father, a dependable friend. But there was no one he would die for, like Yui's Tadeshi or Svec's Greg. *Is this a fundamental failing of mine?* he wrote, his neck perspiring. *There is no one, not even my children, whose life I value above my own.*

"Hotel of Bad Dreams. That is where we are. That is the name I will give my new game. Because that is the name of this place," Bear heard Yui saying to Svec outside his CQ. A long silence followed, floating like matter, carrying weight and dimension. What were they doing? Bear wondered. Then at last he heard each of the men crawl into their crew quarters.

"Name of this world," Svec answered.

THE BUS STOP nearest Dennis's address was at the bottom of a hill in a neighborhood Karen had only ever heard of on the news, and never for a good reason. Trash cans were lined up on and around the sidewalk, standing expectantly, like children waiting for the school bus. In the distance, at the top of another, even taller hill, sat a power plant surrounded by a few straggly trees. The sun sank behind it, streaking the sky like a chemical explosion slowly burning off its rainbow of gases.

She continued down the long street. It looked like all the other streets in the neighborhood. Rows and rows of triple-decker apartments, each building a different shade of Easter egg pastel, with wooden front porches that sagged in the middle, on the verge of collapse. Karen came upon a lean woman in a conical straw hat picking bottles and cans out of the trash. The woman wore a surgical mask and purple rubber gloves that spanned almost the entire length of her slim arms. She reached intrepidly into the barrel, practically disappearing inside, then resurfaced with a bottle that she shook empty and stowed in one of the many plastic bags tied to her grocery carriage. It was an elaborate system, Karen could see, separating items by material and size.

"Get out of my trash!" a man yelled from his porch. His hair had been shaved off and was growing back in patches over his white skull. No one, certainly no immigrant, which this trash picker probably was, had a right to touch his private property, even if it was private property he didn't want. He yelled at the woman more and she yelled back in her language, some kind of Chinese-sounding tongue whose very tone infuriated him.

"It's a friggin' holiday. Even God took a day off." He nodded at Karen, as though they were in agreement.

Could this be Dennis? Karen wondered. She double-checked the address she had written down at the library. No, Dennis lived ten houses down, she was relieved to see. The man took a last drag of his cigarette, wincing as though it hurt him to smoke it, then flicked the still-burning ember into a bucket of murky, brown water standing on the small front lawn. He looked at Karen with a knowing leer, and she froze in that old, old way, grinning back at him like a scared animal. Sometimes men could just tell. They knew all about her just by looking at her, and before she knew it, they were unbuttoning their pants. She had to be careful. She and Nora were working on boundaries. "You have choices," Nora was always saying.

"I have choices," Karen repeated to the man, her voice quavering like a pool of water disturbed by a tiny leaf. She prayed the house would reabsorb this man, suck him back into its hideous belly. She held her breath. "Go away," she whispered. The man rose and returned inside, letting the screen door slam behind him.

Of course that was not Dennis. Karen rebuked herself for even thinking it might be. Dennis was her brother. Well, this wasn't really true, but it seemed *spiritually* true. They'd shared a kind of womb together. A terrible one.

In the distance Karen heard the train approaching. The tension of its arrival rattled the ground. Pulses of silver, splashed with graffiti, swam fast behind the houses like a school of fish. She was glad Dennis lived near a train. It would make traveling to and from this place easier for her. She imagined a whole future in which she lived here with him, in this neighborhood, in the house she had yet to reach, a house she was fast furnishing with the frills of her own imagination. The thoughts were unspooling too quickly. Rip by rip she ate a brown paper napkin her fingers found at the bottom of her purse.

Would she marry him? Yes, she would. She would ask Rosette to be the maid of honor at her wedding. Dennis would stroke her hair every night until her eyes closed. He would get cancer and she would have to nurse him to health, but it would never be the same. Such is life. They would survive until the end. Just the two of them, sitting on the cement foundation of a house that had been burned down along with everything else in the great undoing of a Last Day far in the future.

She kept walking, the numbers on the houses ascending. By now, a deep blue darkness had gathered above the great pillowy clouds, a siphoning point where night was slowly being released. And then she was there at Dennis's house, number 60. There was no front porch, only a cement step without a railing. Three names were listed next to the buzzers, but not one of them was Dennis's. A strip of duct tape covered the doorbells but Karen pressed them anyway. The tape felt sticky and the buttons inert. When no one responded, she opened the front door, which, she discovered, was unlocked.

Loud Spanish music rattled through the first-floor apartment. She heard voices on the other side of the door, talking and laughing. The door opened and a man emerged holding a tray of uncooked hamburgers. He said something to Karen in Spanish. It sounded busy and congratulatory. Karen peered behind him. A Last Day party was in full bloom: a bouquet of gold and purple balloons tied to a chair, a toddler bouncing on the hip of a woman in a purple dress. The woman leaned over a table of food to kiss a man who was uncorking a bottle of wine. It was a nice little scene, and Karen was distantly satisfied to see that no matter what happened to the earth tomorrow, these people were leaving it in joy. The man in the hallway finished whatever he had to say to Karen, then headed down the hall to the back deck. Karen climbed the stairs to the second floor.

The door to this apartment was open only as far as the chain that locked it would allow. A woman appeared in its frame at the sound of Karen's heavy feet on the landing. She was an erecter set of bones bound in pale yellowing skin, wearing a loose gray T-shirt. Two bare feet protruded from beneath the thickly folded cuffs of her jeans.

"You're not the delivery service, are you?" she asked Karen, in a grainy, colorless voice.

"No. I'm sorry," Karen said.

"Don't apologize. Colloquially, people attach the words *I'm sorry* to the word *no*, when a simple 'no' is enough. It cheapens the whole English language when you toss an apology into a conversation where it doesn't belong."

"I'm sorry," Karen repeated, feeling sweaty and uneasy in her green dress.

"Fine," the woman allowed. She leaned against the doorframe and rolled herself a cigarette. She picked bits of tobacco off her lips and tongue and tucked the cigarette behind her ear. Her hair was long and black, with silvery white strands. Karen remembered her fifth-grade teacher telling her that all human hair longer than one and a half inches was just a string of dead cells swinging uselessly off our heads, and that if aliens ever landed on Earth and met us, they would think our habits disgusting.

Karen lingered on the stairs, transfixed by this opinionated ghost of a woman. "Today was a really pretty day. A good one to go out on," Karen offered.

"I haven't left this apartment since—I can't remember. Thursday?"

"Oh. Do you have one of those ankle bracelets that go off at the police station when you leave?"

"No."

Karen wanted to know whether the woman behind the door was pretty or not, but she could only see one narrow slice of her at a time. Almost every face in the whole world was gorgeous if you looked at only one small piece of it, especially if that piece was an eye. All put together was where most people's beauty fell apart.

"I'm testing myself. It's an exercise," the woman said. She waved the smoke away from her face, stirring the white tendrils into a messy cloud.

"Like, for losing weight?"

"How much can we live without? At what point does isolation force us into connection? At what point does something become everything?"

"Yeah." Karen had no idea what she meant. "Does Dennis live here?"

"I think there is a guy who lives upstairs with that hog and her piglets. I'm just subletting. I don't really keep track."

"I'm going to see him now," Karen explained.

"I am ready for it to end," the woman said. Her voice came from a well, not a fountain, Karen decided.

"Okay." She was getting anxious now. And hungry. She hoped Dennis was friends with the Spanish-speaking family downstairs and would want to go join them for hamburgers.

"Could you do me one last favor?" the woman asked.

A last one? Karen was scared that she had inadvertently agreed to do a first favor and had already forgotten it and failed.

"If you pass by a bonfire tonight, could you toss this in?"

She held up a backpack, and before Karen could assent the woman was cramming her bundle through the four-inch space her chain lock allowed. It took a lot of finagling. Whatever the bag contained, it must have been a collection of things small enough to rearrange themselves into an agreeable shape with one large thing that wanted to cause trouble. Karen immediately pictured a human skull, a man's. The woman pushed with her weak, malnourished arms and Karen pulled. The bag popped through at last. It was made of tan canvas and the top flap had been threaded with what looked like long strands of human hair.

"It's heavy," Karen observed. "But not too heavy."

"Good."

"What's in it?"

"It's bad luck to ask."

"I'm sorry."

"I forgive you," the woman said. Karen couldn't be sure, but she thought she saw the woman wink at her.

SHE HEARD THE sound of a baby wailing as she reached the landing of the third floor. This was something she had not considered—that Dennis might already be married, that he would have gone and started a family without her.

She knocked on the door. At first no one answered, so Karen knocked harder. A scurry of feet and sulky moans and the continued cries of a baby were the only response. A low-pitched "Get it" blasted through the noise and at last the door opened. The little boy who opened it immediately ran away from her, his job done. He wore underpants decorated with cowboy hats and guns, and a pair of thick glasses that magnified his eyes. He leapt onto the couch where a young girl, presumably his sister, also sporting thick, goggle-looking glasses, was reading a magazine. The boy grabbed the magazine from her and threw it behind the couch onto the floor. The little boy was around seven, Karen guessed, and his sister a bit older but not much. The baby she'd heard crying was nowhere to be seen.

Karen entered the apartment, closing the door behind her. "Here you go," Karen said, picking the magazine off the floor and returning it to the girl, who did not look up or thank her. It was a back issue of *Famous, Etc.*, a weekly periodical reporting on famous people doing banal things and banal people doing extraordinary things. This issue, which Karen had read in Nora's office months ago, featured a TV actress talking about her lactose intolerance and a teenage girl who had given birth to a baby in the middle of her school's field trip to the Bronx Zoo. The teenager had washed the baby in a bathroom sink, cut the umbilical cord with a plastic cafeteria knife, and left her son swaddled in her jeans jacket at the entrance to the reptile exhibit. Later she changed her mind and wanted the baby back, and through a surprising amount of legal mercy, she was now reunited with her baby, who was doing fine, the article said. The TV actress talked about her battle with gas and bloating, a hereditary response to milk, but admitted that she indulged in goat cheese every once in a while. The magazine in the girl's hands had the address square ripped out of the cover, a telltale sign of a doctor's office magazine.

"My therapist is named Nora. Who's your therapist?" Karen asked the girl.

"Hillaria," the girl answered, still not lifting her enlarged, bespectacled eyes from the glossy photos of infant abandonment.

"Do you like her?"

"She sucks."

"Oh. I'm sor—" Karen began, "I mean, that's too bad. Where's your dad?"

"I don't know. Probably jail. You can ask Ma when she gets home from work. But be careful. Sometimes, just mentioning my dad puts her in a bad mood."

"Jail?" Karen's heart rattled inside her chest. "Is your dad named Dennis?"

"Dennis is in the bedroom," she said, and pointed with her chin to a dark hallway behind the kitchen.

The boy was busy building a fort out of towels and blankets that stretched from the kitchen table to the couch where his sister read. He yanked a cushion from behind her head and she swatted him like a puppy with the magazine. The front window of the apartment was blocked almost entirely by a large television, the big boxy kind Karen thought of as old-fashioned. At Heart House they had a flat-screen TV. One of the rich absentee relatives of a catatonic named Aimee had bought it to make herself feel better about never visiting. Karen felt a little bad for these kids, living with such an unwieldy, obsolete piece of machinery. On the TV a cartoon mouse was traversing the vast landscape of a dining room table laid out for a banquet. Karen remembered watching this same show when she was a child.

The crying baby emerged from beneath the draped blankets of the fort. He was not the same race as the other two children, Karen observed. The older kids were white, pasty even, and the baby looked African American, but maybe not, as Rosette was always assumed to be Spanish or Brazilian when she was in fact from the Azores. Rosette felt these distinctions mattered a lot but Karen had read that race wasn't even real so who cares. This baby was cute, for sure, with round mournful eyes and a loaded diaper about to fall off his little hips.

"He fucking smells. Change him," the middle brother instructed his older sister, who groaned as she hauled the baby into her arms and carried him down the hall.

"Dennis is in there," the girl said to Karen as she went, kicking at the second door of the hallway with her foot.

Karen followed the girl down the hallway and tapped at the bedroom door. "Hello?" she said softly, and turned the knob. Another giant television—this one flat and new—occluded the only window in the room, and towels and black trash bags were tacked to the sill, covering what little light might sneak in from the edges. A video game stood idle, the crosshairs of a gun's scope trained on a blank expanse of desert. The sand shimmered like the great sea that had once covered it. Karen recognized the game immediately. Jared, the Sunday overnight counselor, liked to play it. Karen knew the game's pause music all too well. It was intense, like a beating heart over an electrical storm of guitars. The volume was up so loud and Dennis—her Dennis—was fast asleep in the bed. He lay on top of the blankets, a jumble of pink comforter and sheets, the joystick a few inches from his inert hand. He had a large round belly lopping over his boxer shorts, his face covered by a bunched-up sheet. Karen remembered, when they were together in the apartment as kids, Dennis would hide his face inside his shirt when he cried. Even when they were alone. If he wasn't wearing a shirt, he would pull a pillowcase over his head. Once he'd used a paper bag. If she touched him in these moments, he would slap her, but that had never stopped her from doing it again. She hated when Dennis cried. It hurt more than when she cried.

"Dennis?" Karen whispered.

With the controller she turned the volume of the TV down to just one bar. She knelt by the side of the bed and peeked under the sheet. His breath was hot and smelled polluted. It was too dark to get a good look at his face. Karen stroked his ear with her fingernails. Dennis did not move. He was breathing, his swollen belly expanding and contracting in an even rhythm, but he did not wake up.

Under the bed was a pile of magazines. Pornographic and amateurish, full of poorly reproduced snapshots of young, not very pretty women. The sheer number of magazines was staggering to Karen; there were maybe as many as a hundred.

"You can't help it," Karen said to her sleeping love. "You've been so lost for so long. So have I. But it's okay now. I'm back. I'm here."

She decided to let him sleep and get to know his children a little better. They would be her children soon, in some way or another. She would be their stepmother. Or step-aunt? She kept tossing herself back and forth between the two roles, hoping one would choose her rather than the other way around.

Karen closed the bedroom door quietly and took a seat on the living room couch. The boy was staring at the TV now, his eyes lulled by a violent fight between cat and mouse. Their scrambling bodies rolled into a cloud that bounced across the screen.

"Excuse me," Karen said to him, and he jumped into alertness. "What is your name?"

"Miles," he answered.

"I'm Karen."

"Okay," he said.

"Do you know what today is?"

"It's Last Day," Miles said proudly.

"That's right. Do you know what that means?"

"God doesn't love us anymore. He's sick of our bullshit. He said we can either act better and not hit each other and not say swears or he will get rid of us all and start over with new people."

"What?" Karen cried.

"He goes to kindergarten at Catholic Charities," Miles's sister chimed in. She was leading her baby brother by the hand, his diaper changed. "I go to Centerville. Because I'm gifted."

"No, Tianna. Sit on the floor." Miles swung his legs out over the empty cushion beside him so that his siblings could not share the couch with Karen and him. It was a transparent display of dominance that thrilled Karen more than she was comfortable admitting.

"Do you know the story of the Selfless Knight?" Karen asked.

Tianna picked up her stolen magazine and began copying pictures of famous people in a thick spiral notebook. "*I* know it." She licked her palms and tried to smooth down her thin, straight hair. A very white, disciplined part was combed down the middle of her scalp, bisecting her head with astonishing precision. "But you can tell the story to Miles. I don't care. Hopefully it will shut him up for five friggin' seconds, so I can get some work done for once." She slumped down on the floor at Karen's feet and shaded in the jawline of the actor slated to play Zeus in the newest mythological blockbuster franchise.

The girl *was* gifted, Karen admitted with a jealous pique. The likeness of her portrait was incredible. The baby, whom no one bothered to call by name, found a dusty remote control under the couch and began gnawing on it.

"Once upon a time . . . ," Karen began, skipping over the pre-Gregorian-calendar history of the tale, in part because she only knew the broad strokes of that history: that once upon a time, Last Day was a populist response to the second Sacking of Rome and the barbarian belief that the old gods of antiquity took better care of their people than the one true Christian God, and that the tradition had blossomed and spread for a thousand years, surviving suppressive orders from the time of Augustine to the Knights Templar, the latter being the involuntary sire of the tale's protagonist; but mostly because she loved the invocation of those words—*once upon a time*—and the way it lulled children into a spell. ". . . there was a selfless knight who lived in a kingdom far away."

Miles inched closer to Karen and began sucking his thumb.

"The knight was in love with his king's only daughter, but she was betrothed to another prince in a kingdom very far away. Do you know what *betrothed* means?" Karen asked.

"It means get married," Tianna said.

"Oooh," Miles squealed. "She's going to show him her penis and boobs."

"Don't be an idiot." His sister rolled her eyes. "Girls don't have penises."

"Yes they do!" He stood up on the couch and lifted his T-shirt up to his neck, slapped the rippling bones of his chest, then yanked his shirt back down, sat back on the couch, and hid his face in Karen's arm. She could feel his eyelashes fluttering against her skin.

Karen decided not to address the outburst, which triggered too many of her core issues contained in several social contracts drafted by Nora, so she continued as though nothing had happened.

"The princess was going to get married and go so far away that it would be impossible for her to ever come back home again. They had no technology back then."

"That's not true," Tianna piped up. "Technology doesn't mean computers and stuff. A wheelbarrow is technology."

"Yeah, but in olden times, once you went away, you went away for good. Right?"

The girl rubbed her eyes. She sighed. "Yeah. Fine."

"So, the morning of the Last Day, the princess fell ill and everyone thought that she would die. The Selfless Knight loved his princess so much that he rode for miles and miles to a sorcerer at the edge of the forest to ask for help. At first the sorcerer argued with the knight. He said, 'Once she is married and gone, she will be as good as dead anyway, so there is no point in saving her. And if the sun does not rise again tomorrow, there will be no one left, not even you, Selfless Knight, to mourn her. Go, my son, go back to your parents and eat one last meal at their table, drink with your brothers, enjoy these precious hours that you will never have again.' But the knight insisted. Do you know what *insisted* means?"

"I don't care!" Miles said, his owlish eyes delighted.

"Okay." Karen smiled a toothy, subservient grin. "But the knight cared a lot. That's what *insisted* means. He cared so much that he said he would rather spend his last day on Earth in service to his princess. If she died because of his selfishness, he did not want to live anyway, he told the sorcerer. And if he was able to save her, and the world turned again tomorrow, then he would be happy knowing she was alive in it, even if she was betrothed to another prince in another kingdom out of his sight. The sorcerer was so touched, he shed a single tear that he wiped with a handkerchief. Then he dropped the handkerchief into a boiling pot of soup. Sparks of purple and gold light flew out—"

"That part is from the movies, the purple and gold," Tianna interrupted. "It's a modern part that we only just started including. In the olden days, the colors didn't matter."

"I like purple and gold," Karen said.

Tianna rolled her eyes and noisily flipped the pages of her magazine. She was finished with Zeus. A pop star who had recently gone to rehab was her next subject. She was a bleach blonde with dramatic, black eyebrows and a fake mole above her lip. The actress was feeling better than ever, her picture's caption asserted.

"But I guess you're right," Karen conceded. "It doesn't matter."

"And it's a cauldron of magic potions. Not a pot of soup."

"I know that," Karen said. "I just wanted to help Miles understand."

"I hate soup!" Miles cheered. "I hate doctors and soup and doo-doo diapers and my sister. I like you, though."

He took a fold of Karen's Easter dress into his hands and stroked it lovingly.

"I love you, too!" Karen wasn't supposed to say that to strangers. It was a direct violation of Nora's provisions in another of their personal and emotional safety contracts. But it was a holiday, possibly the last holiday ever, a day that stood outside of the temporal world and so should not count under contractual agreements.

"Tell him what happened next," Tianna said. "They don't get to learn this stuff at his Catholic school. They don't learn anything over there."

Tianna sat up on her heels and gently removed Miles's glasses from his face, which she cleaned with spit and the hem of her purple T-shirt. When she was finished, she cleaned her own glasses. Her eyes were tiny and dark without them, the color of burnt wood, and her sockets were ringed with addled, exhausted shadows.

"The sorcerer agreed to help the knight but said that first the knight must fetch him three important things. 'Anything you ask,' said the Selfless Knight. 'Bring me a flame from the fire at the top of Mount Elder,' instructed the sorcerer, 'a leaping frog from the Lake of Days, and a stone from the Great Wall of Dreams.'"

"Those things change in other countries' versions of the story," Tianna said. "Sometimes it's the feather of a special wild chicken. Or a fish or a mushroom protected by an ogre. It just shows what's important to people in different places. Like farming or mining or forests or fishing."

This girl was a lot older than Karen had guessed. Or maybe not. She was staring at Karen with her ancient-looking eyes. *How old are you?* Karen wanted to ask, but she was afraid of the glare cutting through those thick glasses. What came out of her mouth instead was, "How many freckles do you have?"

"That's a stupid question," Tianna answered.

"I have a freckle on my bum," Miles said.

"Don't," Tianna said with a quiet ferocity that hushed the boy, body and soul.

"Okay." Karen laughed nervously. "Where was I?" Her stomach hurt badly. She'd noticed an array of pill bottles on top of the bureau in Dennis's bedroom. Maybe he had something good. "The knight went to fetch these things for the sorcerer. He learned a lot of lessons along the way. To keep the flame from Mount Elder alive, he had to ride slowly on his horse, because if he went too fast it would blow out. To collect the stone from the Wall of Dreams, he had to wait for gravity to release one. If he pulled one out himself, the whole wall would come tumbling down and crush the village of elves living beneath it. The frog could only be lured from the Lake of Days, because the water was so cold that if he touched it, his hand would freeze and fall off. So the Selfless Knight sat on the banks and sang frog songs until a frog hopped out and joined him."

"It's about patience," Tianna added.

"Yes, thank you." The child's intellectual gifts were starting to annoy Karen. "The knight delivered all these things to the sorcerer, who had fallen asleep. When he woke up, he'd forgotten who the knight was, and what the whole task was about."

"This is my favorite part in the movie," Tianna said, sitting up tall. "The live-action one. Not the cartoon version. The cartoon version is stupid."

"I like the cartoon version," Karen said. It was older than she was and illustrated in a palette of Day-Glo colors popular in the era of its production. Watching the animated *Selfless Knight* always made her wish she had been born sooner.

"I like the cartoon version better, too," Miles said.

"He's never seen either." Tianna shrank back down and twisted little curls in her glossy hair, which unwound immediately. "His attention span is too short for movies."

The story itself bent time in a way that was allegorical, as it would be impossible for the knight to complete even one of those tasks, on horseback, in the span of one day. It begged questions of time and relativity, calendars and clocks, a leitmotif of a holiday that compressed the whole spectrum of human emotion into an amorphous span of hours, not quite one day, not quite two, a fact of the tale that Karen and the children took for granted.

"What happens next is funny," Karen told them. "The sorcerer tells the knight, 'Look, I don't know who you are or what you're doing with this rock and frog and flame, but if your princess is sick, feed her a bowl of porridge made with cold milk that is one day old.' 'That's it?' cries the knight. 'Are you crazy? I could have done that ages ago! I thought you were going to use all these things I got you as ingredients in your magic potion.' He was furious. That means very angry."

"I know what *furious* means," Miles said.

"Of course you do, sweet boy."

"Get to the end!"

"Sorry," Karen said, meaning it more than ever now. "'My son,' said the sorcerer. 'You can yell at me all you want, but the sun is rising on the Last Day and the world may end at any moment, and you yourself said you wanted to spend your last hours in service to the princess.'"

"And the knight says, 'So you *do* remember!'" Tianna yelped. "Sorry. I can't help it. It's my favorite part."

"It's everyone's favorite part," Karen said. "The sorcerer smiled and poured himself a drink from a certain bottle into a certain cup and said, 'I always drink wine from this bottle in this cup at the dawn of Last Day.' He offered the knight a drink, but the knight refused. Instead, he dashed for the door, hopped on his horse, and rode like lightning back to the palace. It just so happened that the handmaid of the princess was a friend of the knight's from childhood, and he told her how to fix the porridge that would save the princess. The handmaid made the porridge and spooned it into the blue lips of the princess, who was very near death. The princess got out of her bed, vomited, and stood up tall. She was all better. The castle rejoiced. The king put out a banquet for the whole kingdom. Everyone ate and drank and danced all day and into the night. The next day, the sun rose again, as it has done every day and every year up until now. The world did not end, but the princess set sail for her fiancé's new land soon after. The Selfless Knight, along with everyone else in the kingdom, went to the port to watch her ship set sail. The princess waved from the bow, crying and smiling. A gust of wind blew the handkerchief wet with her tears out of her hand and into the air. It landed in the knight's hands. As he walked home that day he saw an old hag squatting beside a fire, struggling to keep it burning. The knight dropped the princess's handkerchief into the fire. He was sad to see his princess go, but knew she would always be a part of him, that he didn't need her handkerchief to remember her. He also wanted to help the old hag keep her fire burning. He was, after all, a selfless knight. Just then, purple and gold sparks flew out of the fire and it grew warm and strong. The hag turned into the princess, his princess, and they kissed at last before the beautiful setting sun. The end."

"Wow!" Miles leapt into the air and fell into Karen's lap, his forehead banging hard into hers. "Wow wow wow!" he said.

"You don't even understand what it's about," Tianna scolded.

"Yes, I do!" He turned his face into Karen's stomach and screamed, "You're a motherfucker, Tianna. And a meanie!"

He began crying and kicked the sofa with his dirty feet.

"I'm sorry, Miles," Tianna said, offering her hand to her brother, letting him slap it repeatedly in penance. "Want to make cookies? I'll let you lick the spoon."

Miles considered this for a length of time Karen found to be astonishing. Why wasn't he screaming *Yes, yes, yes*? The boy was deeply hurt and could not seem to shut off the flow of his rage.

"I want to make cookies by myself," he said with a pout.

"You can't do that," Tianna said, with what Karen sensed was a little frisson of power. "Only I am allowed to use the oven. You need me to help."

"This lady can help. She's big."

The baby, who had been napping peacefully on the carpet, woke up with a vague whimper.

"That notebook is exactly the kind of thing you should burn in the bonfire tonight," Karen told Tianna.

"But I love this notebook. And it's not finished yet." She fanned through the many white, lined pages, showcasing its potential.

"That makes it even more perfect."

"No, I should burn something bad I want to get rid of. To make room for something good."

"Not in the olden days. Back then people burned all kinds of things. Good things and bad things and things they'd had forever and things that were brand-new. Just to make a point."

"Like what?" Tianna was clutching her notebook against her chest. The lights of the TV twinkled in her glasses.

"Like baby horses and ball gowns and gold necklaces and all kinds of things. Anything you can think of."

"That's stupid," Tianna said. "Gold wouldn't even burn in a regular fire."

Karen wasn't sure if this was right and reproached herself for not knowing. She'd studied the symbols for alchemy, had made flash cards and everything. The one for gold looked like the left eyeball of a subtly powerful bird. But melting gold, what that involved, she had no idea.

"Why would they burn a baby horse?" Miles's voice cracked. His lips trembled as he tried bravely to contain this question and its inscrutable answer, but within seconds he was in tears. Karen had miscalculated. That parable was meant to shame Tianna for her snobbery and prideful attachment, but Miles was the one who was wounded. The sacrificial horse Karen had spoken of was something she had seen in a medieval triptych by a German painter. It was called *Last Day Offering*. In the painting, a whole procession of barnyard animals waited to be torched. Red lightning cracked the flat black sky so that it looked like a broken plate. The humans had stern faces and foreshortened limbs.

"Now that I think of it, the horse might have been a pony, not a baby."

"A foal," Tianna corrected.

"Stop it!" Miles cried. "You're lying." He was inconsolable, recoiling now from any gesture of affection.

Telling the whole truth had clearly been the worst idea in this situation. But how could you tell only half the truth? Wouldn't that make things more confusing, like offering someone half a story?

The sound of jangling keys pulled the attention of all three children toward the door with a magnetic force. Their mother was home. She was very tall for a woman, and also very fat, which lent her overall presence a distinct power. Her feet fell like cement bricks across the floor. She was wearing purple hospital scrubs. A pair of white, sparkly sunglasses pushed back her burgundy hair. Her face was freckled like Tianna's, though much tanner, and her cheeks sagged as though her prettiness had been pawed off her face by her children.

"Are you going to just sit there, Tianna? Jesus . . ." The woman dropped half a dozen rustling plastic shopping bags at the threshold of the door and stepped over them.

The baby rose to his feet and toddled warily toward his mother. "There he is," his mother sang, her voice, her whole body, softening as soon as the baby was in her arms. "No one gave you a bath today? Like I asked them to?"

Tianna was struggling to lift every single grocery bag at once and carry them en masse to the kitchen. She got as far as the living room couch, where she implored Karen to help her. "She loves Avonte the most because he's the baby," Tianna observed. "He isn't any cuter than Miles was. He's just the newest."

Their mother, who had yet to acknowledge Karen, a stranger in her home, carried Avonte into the kitchen, where she opened and slammed shut a succession of cabinet doors.

"Why is Miles crying?" she bellowed.

"She told us a scary story," Tianna yelled back.

"I'm Karen. I'm Dennis's old friend. We used to be in foster care together." This, Karen decided, was the best explanation of herself, under the circumstances.

"Is he even up?" their mother asked Tianna. She couldn't have been less interested in Karen. But the feeling was mutual. This woman would be a distant memory soon. Miles could come with them if he wanted, wherever she and Dennis decided to go, but Tianna would probably stay behind. They would have her every other weekend and holidays, but not all of them, she hoped. The baby looked like too much work. And it was best to leave a baby with its biological mother anyway.

"He's been out cold all day," Tianna answered in a tone that belied her pleasure in this report. "I made breakfast and lunch."

"Figures."

Their mother disappeared with the baby into the bedroom where Dennis was still asleep. No, they would not be staying here at all, Karen decided. It was a nice enough building, adjacent to the train, friendly neighbors, good natural light if they moved the televisions to different spots, but she and Dennis needed a fresh start. They couldn't go back to Heart House. Overnight guests were not allowed and it was only a matter of days before Karen herself was kicked out. They would have to stay in a motel. The very thought sent shivers up and down her legs.

"Tianna!" the mother bellowed from the bedroom. "Get your brother dressed."

"Are we going to the bonfire?" the girl asked. She eyed her notebook lying on the floor and shot Karen a look so caustic it could peel paint.

"Yeah, after I drop you off at your grandmother's. She's gonna take you."

"Is Miles coming with me?" Tianna explained to Karen, "We have different grandmothers. Mine lives in Dorchester. His lives in Roslindale. Avonte's grandmother lives in Maryland. Our mom's mom is dead."

"Just do what I ask and stop badgering me. I don't have the stomach for it today."

Tianna took her brother to their bedroom in the back, leaving Karen alone. She flipped through Tianna's notebook of celebrity portraits. The girl had an accurate but light hand, her pencil strokes a faint whisper over the pages. Among the faces were lists of words in alphabetical order, spelling lists, obviously, and they too were printed as though by a ghost who could not manipulate the pencil close enough to the page to make real lines.

"It's you."

Karen looked up from the notebook and saw Dennis standing before her. He was awake, barely. His eyes were small and sunk deep in their sockets. His lips were pale. There was a yellowish tint to him. A yellow aura was not good, Karen remembered dimly. Her mind had drained its vast catalogue of information and she could think of nothing to say. So she repeated him.

"It's you."

Dennis sat down in the armchair diagonal from her. His gaze was loose and slow to catch focus. He looked at Karen, but only for a moment, then languidly turned his attention to the TV, or the window behind it.

"Is it cold out?"

"I don't know," Karen said. "It was nice out today. It was getting cooler as the sun set, but not cold."

"It's Saturday?"

"Yes, it's Saturday. It's Last Day. That's why I'm here."

"Forecast was good for this weekend, I think."

"Dennis, I have so much to tell you. I had a good job. At the YMCA. But then they fired me. And I have to move. I'm scared, but also really feel that this is all part of a bigger plan. What about you?"

Dennis mumbled a response. In volume it was the most he had said to her so far, though she couldn't understand a word of it. The phrase *disability benefits* came through.

"I get disability, too," Karen said. "And social security. I have a lot of friends."

"Good," Dennis said. "Good."

She wanted to touch him. Her hand lifted to reach the arm of his chair, then stopped midway and returned to her lap. She felt that her body was not her own anymore, that it would act out of turn, that even though she felt no urge to pee, at any moment she might wet her pants.

"Are you happy here, Dennis? Do you ever miss me?"

"Karen," he said with a troubled certainty. "It's really you."

"That's right. I'm here."

"The one and only . . ." His voice trailed off again.

"I've missed you so much, Dennis. I think about you all the time. A lot more lately. I don't know why."

"Do you have a job someplace? Where do you live?"

"I just told you, I had a job at the Y but I got fired. I live at a group home in Allston."

"Ooof. The Green Line. Rough. Worst transit line in the city. Walking is faster."

"Are you married? Is that woman your wife? Are those your children?"

"We're engaged." Dennis smiled and lowered his eyelids until they were nearly shut. "Engaged to be engaged." He laughed but did not explain the joke. The laughter sputtered out like a tiny mechanical toy whose battery was nearly spent. His head dropped suddenly and he fell asleep.

How could Dennis, her Dennis, have ended up here engaged to this woman? Karen had never been in a romantic relationship, outside her imagination, that is, and could not imagine the workings of such a utilitarian partnership: that the children's mother, Amanda, had a steady job with decent healthcare coverage, and Dennis offered disability benefits, food stamps, and free, if not quality, childcare; between the two of them they had enough connections in the world of pills to keep each other high and living comfortably, something neither of them could achieve alone.

"Dennis," Karen hissed. "Dennis, come with me. Let's get out of here. Let's go."

"Oh, yeah?" he answered, his head still slack, his eyes closed.

"Don't you want to come with me?"

"Okay."

"Okay," Karen whispered. "Okay, then. You'll tell them? Or should I?"

"Let me rest a minute." He reached over to pat her knee but missed and nearly fell over. Karen caught him, felt the weight of his shoulder against her hands. He was so heavy, like a bag of wet cement. His shirt had no sleeves and his arms were covered with a rash of pink pimples. There was a tattoo on his biceps, a Chinese symbol, each stroke like a sword balanced to build a complicated, unstable house.

"Aw, shit. Did he fall?" Dennis's fiancée shouted from the kitchen. "He's on all new meds. He'll probably just stay in tonight. You're welcome to hang out here with him, but I'm leaving. The kids are going to their grandmother. I have the night off for once and I'm not wasting it laying around at home."

"Can I use your restroom?" Karen asked.

"We call it the bathroom. And sure. Be my guest," she said in mock grandeur.

Karen propped Dennis up with a pillow until she was reasonably sure he was stable, then she excused herself to the bathroom. There was no window in the bathroom, but the door locked, which put Karen at ease. She splashed water on her face, then washed her hands. This fiancée had what Karen considered to be an alarming number of perfumes. They crowded the dingy, gold-flecked Formica counter. Further proof, Karen saw, that this woman was cuckolding Dennis, her purported life partner, covering the stench of her betrayals and lies with so much cherry-vanilla body spray.

Dennis had to know that he was not the father of any of those kids. He deserved better than this. He probably had diminished self-esteem, after being traumatized the way they were as kids, and then who knows what had happened to him afterward in his spate of foster homes. Karen was lucky. She'd been seeing Nora for years, and that had helped her self-esteem a lot. She wanted Dennis to start seeing Nora. She wanted all the best things for him. But first they had to leave this place.

When Karen emerged from the bathroom, Tianna and Miles were dressed and ready to go, waiting by the door, while their mother consulted her reflection in the microwave's door to apply mascara.

"Oh, good. Finally," she said, foisting the baby into Tianna's arms and taking her makeup bag into the bathroom.

"I'm going to burn Viscount Darkdoom," Miles said, holding up a plastic figurine of a homely, well-dressed man from some cartoon show or movie Karen had only vaguely heard of. "He's a bad guy," Miles explained.

"He's starting to get it," Tianna said proudly. "I talked him into it." She had put on a purple ruffled dress and a pair of cowgirl boots. Her face was clean and Karen detected a layer of gloss on her lips. "I'm going to burn my old bunny," she told Karen. The toy in question was a limp carcass of blue plush fur stained on the ears with an awful, crunchy brown matter. "Avonte puked on it and the smell won't come out, even though I washed it."

"You'll have a nice time," Karen said weakly. "Bonfires are fun."

"This one has face painting," Tianna informed her. "Too bad you're not coming."

"Come with us!" Miles said.

"Maybe Dennis and I will meet up with you later."

Both children shot her a dubious glare. Dennis had slumped over his knees in the recliner, his palm extended as though to receive alms.

Karen had the backpack that the woman downstairs had given to her by the front door. She picked it up and handed it to Tianna. "Can you do me a favor and burn this?" Tiana hoisted the bag onto her shoulder.

"It's heavy," she sighed, and adjusted the straps. Her own overnight backpack she slung across her chest.

"Okay, let's go," their mother shouted. She had done a lot to herself in a short amount of time. A purple leather skirt and chunky black heels exposed her legs, which were long and nicely shaped. A green shamrock tattoo floated above her ankle. Black, spidery lashes fringed her eyes, which were watering from the purple contact lenses she'd put in.

"Hey, Prince Charming, I'm going out," she shouted at the recliner. Dennis made no reply. "If you end up leaving him here," Amanda told Karen, "make sure the door's locked." She took the baby from Tianna and herded her brood out the door and down the stairs.

"Dennis." Karen took his empty hand in hers and squeezed it. "You don't have to stay here. Maybe you feel guilty. I don't know, but I think they'll be fine without you."

Dennis rubbed his eyes. "What time is it?"

Karen scanned the room for a working clock. "I don't know. It's getting late."

Dennis sat back and pulled his phone out of his jeans pocket.

"Six fifty-seven," he said. He found a crumpled pack of cigarettes in another of his pockets and lit one.

"You look like your dad when you do that," Karen said.

"I don't remember what he looked like."

"He smoked. I remember that." She sneezed three times in a row and Dennis said nothing. "Let's go, Dennis. I don't want to stay here anymore."

"Okay." He reached over again to touch her knee and this time his hand made contact. Karen felt a jolt like a rubber band snapping against her skin. He was looking into her eyes now, his cheeks sunken and his eyes glazed.

"Want to watch a movie?" he asked. He was looking right through her, at something behind her. She turned around to see what it was.

"Yeah, that's right," he said. "Back there. In my bedroom."

He got up from the chair and Karen rose to follow him.

He was barely undressed when his penis sprang out of his underwear all pink and flushed as though surprised. He pushed Karen backward onto his unmade bed. Dennis squeezed his eyes shut the whole time. Was he shy or ashamed? She couldn't tell. He didn't want to talk, which was all Karen wanted to do. She didn't even realize how much she was talking until he put his hand over her mouth. "Dennis, I can't breathe," she tried to say, but only thick, low notes escaped her. Finally he groaned and collapsed next to her.

"Dennis," she whispered. The sheets were wet and sticky and quickly getting cold. "Dennis?" she said again, and when he didn't answer, she shouted.

"What."

"I want to go now," she said, crying. "Please say you're coming with me."

"I'll meet you there," he said, drifting off, away from her.

"But where? I don't even know where we're going. I was hoping you would know. That you'd have an idea, at least."

"Okay." He patted her thigh.

"Dennis?"

She found her dress bunched up between the mattress and the bed-side table. Her underwear was on the floor near the foot of the bed. She dressed in the dark of Dennis's bedroom, a red orb glowing on the bottom corner of the TV pulsing slowly, too slowly, like an alarm that knew it was already too late.

The top of Dennis's bureau was covered with pill bottles. Tall ones. Fat ones. Orange with white tops. White with no tops. Most had labels but only some were labeled for Dennis. If the occult could have been Karen's college major, psychopharmacology would have been her minor. She was practically fluent in medical Greek. Anything ending in -done, like its sound suggested, rang her soul's deepest gong and produced an almost immediate sense of calm and well-being. It was false, Karen knew. She did not like to abuse drugs. They interfered with her intuition. But her stomach was twisted hard inside her, a legitimate pain. And eighty milligrams equaled eighty dollars: who was she to turn away from a tiny pot of gold so clearly delivered by the universe? Karen selected three half-full bottles and put them in her purse. Then she found Dennis's phone and dialed the only number that made sense at the moment.

"Rosette? It's me, Karen. I need you. It's a real emergency this time. I'm dying."

M ANY PEOPLE SUBSCRIBED to the once-a-decade Last Day apology, including Kurt's own father, who believed that anything more than that was excessive and prideful. Though Kurt's father also thought painting the family's last name on their mailbox was excessive and prideful. Kurt remembered going on a Last Day drive with his father when he was still a boy so that his dad could make amends to a former colleague. The old friend lived in his mother's basement, Kurt's father explained, and without a word more Kurt understood that this was a shameful state of being.

"I've owed him this money for ten years," his dad said on the drive down, "but I didn't think it mattered. He'd just blow it at the tracks. I thought I was sparing him the trouble a wad of cash would cause. But fair is fair, and when you owe someone money, you pay it back, no matter what a son of a bitch that person is."

It was a rare moment of mercy in an otherwise relentless life. Kurt wondered whether, if his father had lived longer, the old man would have made amends to his son one day, too. Kurt was the spitting image of his father, a genetic jackpot closer to a psychic spittoon, as Kurt was the target of all his father's bile. They had the same square face, the same light brown eyes, the same sour stomach. Their little league stats were a weapon of comparison, which his father trotted out often, almost daily, as though meaningful. Kurt had been a decent outfielder but the old man's pitching bested the son's squarely. That Kurt's batting average was slightly higher was a point seldom made, not after Kurt realized that making it caused the whole family, especially his mother, to suffer come the first drink at nightfall.

But gravity is one of the great miracle workers, softening even the most obdurate in old age, and perhaps, Kurt speculated, his old man's persistent scrutiny and unforgiving appraisal of everyone, especially his son, would have broken down over time as his body did. In time, if he had lived, Kurt's old man might have mellowed into a tolerable guy. It used to bother Kurt, all the acid his dad spat so expertly into his eyes; then one night while still in prison, after suffering the requisite abuse of the day with the stoicism that was another of his father's genetic gifts, he figured it out—*Dad hates me because he thinks I am him*—and he never took the old man's vitriol personally again.

Kurt kept his distance from then on, noticing from afar that once his father had lost his son as a punching bag, he began to push away first Kurt's older sister, then the younger, the baby of the family, who had always been Daddy's girl. When the first grandchild was expected, the old man had a last surge of bitterness. Kurt's older sister had married a Pakistani man, a Hindu, a religion their father could not differentiate from Islam, which he could not defuse from a primatological alarm system that sounded "Threat!" despite all logical arguments to the contrary. He refused to allow his wife to host the baby shower at their house and he grumbled unintelligibly when friends congratulated him on the new grandchild. It looked like things were beginning to relent as the grand-baby, a boy, grew up and showed an interest in backyard baseball. Then his father dropped dead at fifty-seven of an aortic aneurysm, and there was nothing left to say.

At forty-two, Kurt had never made amends to anyone in his life. From every angle, the tradition appeared to him as supremely selfish, a conversation that dredged up a painful or forgotten or wished-to-be-forgotten past in the hope of relieving the perpetrator of the burden of guilt at the expense of the victim. The few amends he'd received had followed this pattern. Megan Brown's amends had been more like a one-woman show without a stage. Another former girlfriend had written to him apologizing for the way she'd used her affair with Kurt to get revenge on her husband. Kurt hadn't even known that she was married at the time. Not that he would have cared. It was just a pebble of information he could have done without. Another woman had approached him at a crowded Indian restaurant hosting an early morning all-you-can-eat Last Day buffet. She was drunk and spilling her plate of chicken saag on the floor. He didn't recognize her at first until she announced in her inebriated, too-loud, South Boston bray (that voice he could not forget), "I made your, uh, your *dysfunctions* all about me. It's clearly the cancer, or stuff that happened in prison, or whatever. Not your fault, not mine. But I'm sorry." Kurt bought her a beer and sent her back to her table of delusional, supportive female friends, all of them hungover or still drunk from the night before.

Kurt was freely able to admit that he'd been a bastard to certain women he'd slept with, but he was an honest bastard, and so any hurt they still felt was their morbid toy to play with. With his male friends he was quick to back away from a fight before it even started. His sisters loved him in their distant, emotionally convenient way, and he loved them back when circumstance (their father's funeral) or calendar (Thanksgiving dinner) demanded it. To force anything more out of these relationships would be dishonest, as all the past harms—that time he knowingly left the gas tank on empty when his sister had a soccer tournament to get to, the broken promise to pay back that now trivial sum of money—had been ironed out of time by many more small acts of unspoken kindness. It was not his family's way to talk critically about their actions, let alone their feelings, and to foist such a conversation onto his sisters, merely because of a kitschy holiday, would be unfair. His mother was in Florida now with her new husband. She was enjoying a warmth of climate and companionship she had never gotten in the first half of her life, and the best amends Kurt could make to her was to be happy for her.

His entire relationship with Sarah Clark-Davenport had been a perverted amends to Mary; further proof, he thought years after he'd extricated himself from *that* shitshow, that the whole institution of reparations was faulty at its core. And yet, now that Mary's ashes and everything else attached to her were no longer under his bed, he felt freer than he had ever known possible.

"I've never made amends on Last Day," Kurt said to Sarah Moss as they pushed a grocery cart around a supermarket. "I mean, ever. In my life." Clouds of mist sprayed intermittently on the slanted stacks of apples. "It's incredible. There's like a runner's high, or something, that comes along with it. I finally get why people do this. Do you have any amends you want to make?"

"No," Sarah said.

"I'll drive you anywhere. I'm serious. I want you to have this experience." He wrapped an arm around her shoulder and guided the direction of the cart she was pushing. "What am I saying? You're too young to have hurt anyone. Too sweet." He gave her shoulder a little squeeze, then bounded across the aisle to grab some oranges.

It was a long ride to the beach. The sky was a vapid shade of blue full of lumpy metastasizing clouds. Behind them the sun was setting in all its tacky grandiosity. Sarah refused to look at it. She hated that she had to hold Kurt's body now, that she had to synchronize with his every lean and sway. Motorcycles were stupid. Dead Mary was stupid. Sarah, sister of dead Mary, was stupid. The idea that Kurt had had sexual intercourse with other people ignited nothing inside her, but that he could love someone as clearly as he loved this evil harpy Sarah was the absolute stupidest thing in the world.

"What's wrong?" Kurt asked her after they parked at the beach. She pulled off her helmet and revealed a scowl.

"Nothing."

Nothing. That little two-syllable word coming from the lips of a silent, brooding woman was the grenade of all pronouns. Kurt had heard its lethal frequency a thousand times before. It didn't matter how old or young or pretty or ugly or proud or insecure they were. Women always wanted to fight. He assumed they were born that way.

A vendor in the parking lot was selling cords of firewood at a criminal markup, five dollars extra for cords of driftwood, for the Last Day bonfires. Kurt bought two bundles and trudged over the dunes toward the beach.

A long row of shoes had been left at the entrance to the boardwalk by dozens of other holiday revelers. It was considered good luck to walk barefoot on the beach on May 27, and many people left their shoes behind in a show of solidarity. If the world did not end, Sarah knew, her shoes would still be there tomorrow. Yet she couldn't help feeling apprehensive about this tradition. She'd had this particular pair of sneakers for years, they'd been through a lot together, and here they were, getting abandoned moments before the world ended. Maybe she should burn them? But then what if things turned out fine? She'd have to ride Kurt's motorcycle with bare feet.

She held her sneakers close against her chest and followed Kurt's path in the sand.

"If it were possible to divorce myself, I would," Sarah grumbled.

A woman with a magnificent Afro overheard this and laughed. She was crafting a photograph of all the shoes with a very large professional-looking camera. She was dressed in a lot of wheat-colored linen separates cut on a bias. She asked Kurt and Sarah if she could take their picture, too. She was writing an article for a national travel magazine, she said. This beach had become a popular spot for Last Day.

Kurt put his arm around Sarah's shoulders, felt her stiffen at his touch, and arranged the tender, unsmiling face he always used for pictures. The photographer looked at the image she'd captured and winced.

"Great. Thanks. Do you want me to send it to you?"

"I'm fine," Sarah snapped. "I don't need to document every single moment in my life with pictures and post them online for digital applause, thanks."

"Sure," Kurt said. "You can send it to me."

He and the photographer exchanged cards and Sarah rolled her eyes.

"Until night falls," the woman said. Sarah watched Kurt watch the photographer walk away.

They trudged onward in silence over the high dunes. The sand was cool and uncooperative, and each step was difficult, sapping the wind from their lungs so that even if they'd wanted to talk, they were too out of breath. Then, all at once, there it was: the ocean, beautiful and indifferent.

They walked by a teenage boy vomiting into a rusty trash barrel. Sarah recognized him immediately as one of the boys on the train ride from Edgewater that morning, though he was too ill to recognize her. He held on to his dirty white baseball cap in one hand and with the other gripped the barrel.

"I'm so wasted, man," he said to Kurt. He did not remember how he had ended up at the beach. It was a bush-league move, to get so wasted before midnight. "But I am not a bush-league drinker," he insisted.

Kurt took the boy's hat, gave it a hard shake. Sand issued from inside the empty dome and slapped against the barrel with a pleasant sound. Kurt replaced the hat on the boy's head so that it wouldn't fall off.

"I puked out of my nose. My nostril. How does that happen?"

"You don't want to know the answer to that right now," Kurt said to him.

"I . . . am a phe-nom-enom."

"We all are, brother."

Sarah could just as easily choose to be happy. Or at least accepting. But she didn't want to. The simplicity of anger was its most attractive feature right now, a slash-and-burn approach to all the problems this night was presenting. It made her feel better for the moment. She chewed on the inside of her cheek until she tasted the metallic tang of her blood.

"Look at them all," she said, still chewing, nodding in the direction of the crowds setting up camp for the night. "The way they're all clumped together in one spot. It looks like a microscopic slide of bacteria. That's the human race. A sophisticated disease."

"You're too young to be this cynical."

"I'm an old soul, apparently. My guidance counselor told me. She claims she can read auras. I hate her."

Kurt handed her a can of soda from the bag. After a few sips Kurt offered her a splash of whiskey, which she accepted. Why not, she decided, it can't make things worse. The whiskey tasted like a punishment. There was no way she could finish the can, but she didn't need to. Very quickly there was a sensation that the screws holding together her cranial apparatus were now just a little bit looser. So this was the draw of alcohol, Sarah thought. It was kind of nice.

Kurt walked in front of Sarah, his path hugging the shore. The sand gleamed like a sheet of melting ice. She watched his tracks imprint, then vanish. She could not lift her gaze above the ground. Kurt, his stooped shoulders, the last light of day glimmering on the water—it was all too much to take in. The tide crept closer and the water sent a chill up from the soles of her feet to her knees. The sound of voices began to fade behind them. The shore was studded with seashells, some of them really stellar specimens, a perfect whelk, a razor clam with both valves still attached, its opalescent inner chamber flashing in the slanted light of dusk. Sarah wanted so badly to collect them all in her pockets, but what could be more pointless than hoarding seashells at the end of the world? She was about to cry when Kurt's voice snapped up her attention.

"Look," he said.

The sun was scattering its colored light all across the sky. Deep shades of pink stained the scalloped underbelly of the clouds. Gold clasped unevenly to the edges of a dark, stormy-looking mass. The blue sky was a mess, with white blooms and streaks, clouds growing tall as buildings, clouds stretched thin as old, threadbare rags, clouds like the tracks of animals dotting the horizon.

"Wow," Sarah admitted.

"Beautiful."

"That one cloud there looks stormy."

"It's blowing out to sea."

"How can you tell?"

"Look at the birds."

Seagulls were flapping their wings against the wind, holding fast in the air as though frozen. Sarah looked at Kurt. He was powerless and kind and nothing he did or said to her would make the world end or keep it going. In fact, it was a lot of pressure to put on one man, and it wasn't fair. She wanted to apologize for this, but also to punch him, and maybe kiss again? She looked back down at the wet sand. Pink and gold light spilled into the puddles made by the anxious digging of her feet.

"You said I was too good for this world. But you said it to her, too."

"I don't have a defense against that, and I don't think I should have to. If you're so mad, I can bring you home now. I thought we'd have a nice night together. But we don't have to be nice and we don't have to be together."

"Did you love her? Sarah, sister of your dead girlfriend Mary?"

"Christ, I almost married her," Kurt said, realizing his mistake a moment too late. He meant it as a declaration of gratitude for a bullet dodged, but this young girl was a coiled viper right now.

"You almost married that horrible woman?"

"You don't know her—it's complicated. She had a really messed-up life. You don't want to know the half of it," Kurt tried to explain.

"You're right. I don't. I don't care about her tragic life. It doesn't make her special."

"Why do all girls do this? Hate each other for no reason. It must be exhausting. Hopefully you'll outgrow it."

"Nope!" Sarah said. She drank as much of the whiskey and Coke as she could stomach, slugged it dramatically, as she'd seen actors do in movies, and when she felt she was about to gag she poured the rest in the sand, drowning a collection of barnacles floating in the sugary foam.

"Do you feel better now?" he asked her.

"A little, yes. Thank you."

"Let's build a fire."

He dropped the cords of driftwood into the sand and began arranging them in a cone. Sarah wanted to argue about the dioxin released from burning driftwood but she kept her mouth shut, instead ripping up her issue of *The Economist* and the unused pages of her journal for kindling.

"Why did you love her?"

"She was beautiful and smart and mean. She took care of me when I had no one."

"Did you love Mary more?"

"Maybe?" He blew onto the flames, urging the ropes of blue fire to latch onto the wood. "Probably. I was a kid. She was a kid. Who knows. We might have grown out of each other. I felt like such a loser, like everything I touched turned to shit, including Mary. Sarah seemed to reverse that. For a time. She was a sociopath, but she was brilliant, and she believed in me. In a really basic way. She believed I would kick cancer when I was sure I would die, and she was right. She believed I could make a career as a tattoo artist when it seemed like a pipe dream. When I got well again, when I was stable, she dumped me. Even that was a gift because then I was free."

The fire burned a pale lavender color that neither of them had expected to be so pretty, so enchanting. When Kurt was satisfied that it would burn without his coaxing, he sat on the sleeping bag Sarah had laid out and together they watched the waves cross each other in wide, endless X's, watched until even these subtle hatches were rubbed away by the night and the waves were nothing but sound. The bluish-purple fire crackled softly in the dark.

"There's no moon tonight."

"It's a new moon."

"I hate how no moon is called a new moon. It's a fucked-up name."

"You're hungry. Time to eat."

So they ate. They ate every single thing they'd bought at the store.

Two packages of chicken sausage, an entire bag of marshmallows, an extra-large bag of barbecue potato chips, two slightly sour oranges. Kurt swigged his pint of whiskey straight, saving the last sip for Sarah, who drank it, shuddered, then fell into his arms. Kurt turned his face toward hers like she was the last thing left to eat. He chewed on her neck, her earlobe, the sides of her face. The actual coitus part did not hurt the way Sarah thought it would. From Lindsey's accounts, the first time was supposed to be so painful you almost died, and if the pain didn't kill you, the hemorrhaging would. There was none of the fabled bleeding. The only thing that hurt was her face from kissing. Kurt's beard had clearly started to grow back a couple of hours after he'd shaved (*Oh!* she thought, *that's where the phrase* five-o'clock shadow *comes from*), and the stubble abraded her skin. His teeth kept clanking into hers, a collision more uncomfortable than painful. Kurt's penis felt like a sweaty hand that had fallen asleep against her upper inner thigh. He struggled to get inside her, and once he did he didn't stay there long before slipping out again. Some people walked by—they could hear the voices approaching in the dark. Kurt pulled the corner of the sleeping bag over them and covered Sarah's face with his. When the people had passed, he kissed her on the forehead and tried again to work his way inside. Finally he made a sound like choking and she felt the warm trickle of his semen on her stomach.

"Huh," Sarah said when it was all over.

"Yeah," Kurt sighed.

"Is it always like that?"

"Sometimes." He pulled his jeans back on and rolled himself a cigarette. "You don't shave at all?"

"Only in the summer."

Kurt crouched by the fire and fed more logs into its snapping flames. Sarah's underwear was knotted up around one ankle. She pulled them on and let the cool air chill her body. She still didn't know what to feel. Was she repulsed, piqued, or suddenly insatiable? No. But she felt fine. With or without orgasm, the mere concentration of sex, its focused physicality, had a calming effect. At least for the moment. She gazed at the black sea shimmering beneath the opaque black of the sky and was so grateful to have had this experience at this exact location, at this time, with this person. It was nothing to write poetry about, but it was nice being so close to someone, trusting him to care for her body and knowing he trusted her to care for his. If he asked her for more, she would probably consent, but if they never did it again, that would be fine, too. As long as he wanted to lie next to her and hold her, protecting her again like he had when those strangers passed by.

"There are no stars, either," she said. "Are you sure there isn't a storm coming?"

Kurt looked at the dark folding over the sky.

"It's okay. It will blow over."

She wiped her stomach off and put on her shorts.

"We should burn something. Each of us. Here." She handed Kurt her journal, her scattershot dissertation on names, birds, time, sex, and the cosmos, all the hopes and anxieties of her life so far. "There's some pretty important stuff in there," she added, as though he had contested the worth of her offering. "Stuff I won't be able to remember or repeat."

"Sounds good," he said. He took a check out of his wallet. It was for $350, from a customer getting a full-back piece that he was paying for in installments. It was a toss-up whether or not the check would even clear. Kurt threw it into the fire.

"It's cozy over here," Sarah said. She shook the sand off the sleeping bag and smoothed it with her hand. "Come back."

"In a minute. Got to keep this going." He poked at the burning logs.

"In love," Sarah's mother had once said, "there is always the one who offers the kiss, and the one who offers the cheek." She had never elaborated on this. Sarah wondered which thing her mother offered, which her father did. Sitting here now, she couldn't even venture a guess. Sarah had had several major epiphanies so far in the protracted crossover from childhood to adulthood: that her parents were once kids with dreams of being something different from what they actually became; that she had lived with them for a decade and a half and that there were things she would never know about them, nor they about her; that all people were fundamentally unknowable; that her body had pretty much reached the size and shape it would always be for the rest of her life as long as she took care of it; that if she was lucky, she would be with her parents when they died, and if she was unlucky, they would outlive her. Intellectually, she'd figured it out a long time ago, or most of it—what it meant to be an adult, to grow up. But there was still so much she didn't know. She had imagined that sex would be a portal to more answers, but it was only another question.

"Come over here," she said again. Kurt continued rearranging the burning logs, reaching into the flames. "Be careful."

"Don't worry."

She considered her parents again. They definitely loved each other. Perhaps they loved each other more than they loved her. Growing up, she'd never felt a lack or a longing. Being with them, sitting at the dinner table, all three of them content, paying attention, making jokes—it was good. But she was a discrete object outside of the force field created by their composite energies. Not left out, just outside. There was a standing invitation for her to join them, but it was her choice, and for reasons she was just beginning to understand, she chose not to. She didn't want to live inside their love, because it was theirs, and she wanted her own love. Was this it? This feeling for the man tending the fire that kept her warm on the last night of the living world? Was this love?

Maybe it was not about a biological balance of immunities, but about one body of knowledge compensating for another. What he knew, what she understood, his observations, her readings, the way two of them together annealed each other's mental weaknesses, leaving them with a greater wisdom.

"Do you remember the email I sent you? About the formation of the universe?"

"Yeah." Kurt tossed his cigarette into the fire. "But remind me. I forgot some of it."

"That's okay. Because I want to tell you about the part I cut out. It was too long already, and it seemed irrelevant, but it was actually the most relevant part of the story. In the first microsecond of the universe, as all the gases were cooling and expanding, the intensity of heat and radiation formed quarks, which bundled together according to mutual attraction. The positively charged bundles are called baryons, and the negatively charged baryons are antibaryons. They existed at a precise ratio of one billion negative to one billion and one positive. If they had been perfectly balanced, their respective charges would have nullified each other, ending in total annihilation, which would have produced such expansive, diluted radiation that no new particles could be formed. Instead, because of this imbalance, we got atoms, which later became matter, which became the universe as we know it. Isn't that amazing?"

"Pretty cool."

The fire was roaring now. Kurt returned to the sleeping bag. He collapsed next to her, wrinkling the blanket she had so carefully smoothed out, and making rivulets of sand pour in again.

"Come closer," she said. "I'm cold."

Kurt lay next to Sarah and held her in an uneasy spoon pose. Then he rolled away and she remained, their backs facing each other and radiating heat. The stars were still absent from the sky, a fact neither one of them wanted to point out. They dropped in and out of sleep, their bodies softening, giving up, then jolting back from the accidental touch of the other's arm or a foot.

"Look. They're back."

"What's back?"

"The stars."

A few of them, at least.

The sound of the waves softened and they fell deeper.

"They're gone now."

Which one of them said this? Sarah didn't know.

"I love you," she said, unsure if these were her last conscious words or the first ones uttered in her dream.

THE NEXT MORNING, they let Yui sleep. Svec gladly conceded to Bear first dibs on the treadmill, though he was otherwise unbothered by his hangover.

"I'm amazed," Bear said to him.

"We train for this," Svec said, his typing like rapid gunfire on his laptop. "How to drink in microgravity. No Russian has ever thrown up in space."

"Really?" Bear adjusted the harnesses and belts strapping him into the treadmill, then increased the speed and lengthened his stride.

"No," Svec said, smirking again. "Joke."

It was seven o'clock in the morning for the astronauts, eleven in Star City, and 2 A.M. in Houston. Mission Control never slept, and if there had been raucous partying in any of the command centers (there had been), the crew on the ISS was shielded from it. That morning they downloaded the customary schedule, broken down in certain places to five-minute increments. Bear spent the morning taking pictures of colloidal particles in the Destiny module, and Svec added to the database of bioproductive ocean areas. They worked alone, in silence, with the contentment of men doing what they were put on Earth to do, in their case, to study her from afar.

Bear finished earlier than Mission Control had predicted and decided to spend his surplus eleven minutes of leisure time eating a Last Day snack, a bag of pizza-flavored corn puffs. Svec had also hit a major benchmark in his work and was treating himself to some jelly beans as a reward.

"You know what, comrade," Bear said, "these puffs have both the ideal structural integrity and volume for—"

"I know what you will say," Svec interrupted. "But some of us actually prefer to be challenged."

Bear was already constructing lariats out of dental floss, one each for him and Svec, who examined his, then threw it in the trash. "Will make my own," he said.

"Practicing your dribbling with a tennis ball can improve overall handling in basketball," Bear submitted. "Popcorn rodeo is good for the rookies. To get them warmed up. But I'm talking about the big leagues here."

He tossed a corn puff into the air and flicked it gently, giving it spin. Using their floss lassos, he and Svec took turns trying to harness the burnt orange morsel and return it to their mouths. Svec made contact on his first try but tugged a little too hard and lost the puff five inches in front of his face. Bear failed several times to lasso the corn puff, but once he did manage to get it, he drew it to within two inches of his mouth.

"I win," Bear said.

"Nyet. We both fail."

"Jesus." Bear chomped the air until the puff was in his mouth, his top and bottom teeth clanging too hard against each other.

"We should wake him up."

"I don't want to go near his pod. It smells."

"Loser must get him to lunch," Svec said, setting a new corn puff in motion. Mission Control murmured into their headsets and both men ignored it. Svec hung his floss lariat gingerly onto the puff and pulled it in a slow, downward motion to his open mouth.

"Do not forget to tell Yui to record my victory in notebook," Svec offered.

Yui's crew quarters smelled brackish on a normal day, but Bear was assaulted by a much more noxious scent as he now approached it. Grief, he decided, remembering the particular stench of his clothes as he'd undressed every day that he'd visited his teenage niece in hospice years ago. It was a pituitary nightmare, pain sneaking out through his pores in total defiance of the stolid, supportive presence he was hoping to provide to his sister and brother-in-law during that time. Hygiene was no picnic on the station and forgiveness was critical, but this was something else. Yui would need to do a thorough wipe-down and fast. Maybe even dispose of the clothes he'd been wearing that night. Broaching this would be a psychological challenge, one Bear was not looking forward to, but he rationalized that it would yield interpersonal insights he could use later when debriefing new astronauts before their missions.

"Hey, friendo." He rapped on the plastic sliding door of Yui's CQ. There was no answer, only the horrible smell. "I know, friendo," Bear confessed. "You want to go home, and barring that, you want to stay in bed and dream about it. I want to do that, too, sometimes. We all do. But you need to get up, have something to eat, and, um, clean up."

He was holding his nose now. The smell was overpowering.

"Did you get sick last night, friendo?" There was no answer. "I'm going to open this door now. Okay?"

Yui floated in a sleeping bag strapped to the wall, with his arms crossed over his chest. It was how he always slept, how Tadeshi slept, too, though Bear could not have known that. His skin looked like a mixture of ash and milk, and his eyes, wide open, were not moving. Only his hair floating on end around his still face gave the impression that he had once been alive.

"He's dead," Bear told Svec.

The permanent striations of Svec's mimetic muscles twitched.

"I don't know when. Or how. Or—"

"None of that matters. NORAD reports that debris from meteor storm is coming toward us. We need to maneuver station out of way."

"Roger that. Yui's body can wait."

"He will be patient."

"Yes, he will. Poor guy."

Svec made the executive decision to handle one crisis at a time, and postpone telling Mission Control about the onboard fatality. The two men got to work and in short order had shifted the orbit of the massive station out of harm's way. Once the station was reoriented, the internet shut down and the satellite connection was lost. This happened from time to time, and while disruptive, it was no crisis. Svec told Bear to connect to CAPCOM via the ham radio.

"No response."

"Try again in ten minutes."

He did. Nothing.

They were cruising over the shadow line now, an orbital path where the sun seemed to drift in a restless circle alongside the earth, neither rising nor setting. Bear had always been curious what this orientation looked like, and now that his wish was granted, he felt uneasy. They tried again to reach Mission Control and again they could not connect on any platform. They had never experienced a break in communication this long before. Svec decided to use the time to exercise. He loaded his music player into the sound system and blasted his favorite heavy metal album, *Chornoye Utro*.

"Self-titled album. Very best one. After 1990 they were shit. Freedom ruins heavy metal. Need iron fist—bad father, bad dictator—to make true metal." He panted and smirked, sweat beading up on his skin like crystal dewdrops as he pushed his feet down on the treadmill.

"I don't know what they're saying," Bear sighed, biting his tongue to keep from adding *and I don't care*.

"This song is about woman. Bigger breasts, bigger problems. It is true."

"I'm taking some R&R in the Cupola."

The sound of disconnection hummed low and steady in their headsets. It threatened to seep into the crimped tunnels of their brains, implanting the tiny, psychic seeds of madness such isolation can wreak. Watching the sun as it slowly circled, never crossing before or behind the earth, refusing to offer that one supreme metaphor of renewal—this was madness. Strapping oneself into a treadmill, running toward nothing—this, too, was madness.

Duᴜʀɪɴɢ ᴀ ʜᴇᴀᴛ wave last year, a man at Rosette's Kingdom Hall of the Jehovah's Witnesses claimed to have received a vision from God. Alfred Guy was a Haitian émigré who worked for an HVAC company, a man as sober and staid as his job, too boring to be selected by God for spiritual ascendancy. But God did come to Alfred, he reported, in the dark of early morning last August, in the form of a man cloaked in blinding light.

"Burn everything you believe," the monsieur spoke without moving his lips, his face as explosive and formless as time. With his long arm like a ray of the sun, this deific stand-in set fire to Alfred's Bible just by pointing at it.

Alfred produced the scorched *New World Translation of the Holy Scriptures* as evidence to the elders at the Jehovah's Witness Kingdom Hall in Cambridge, where Rosette was a faithful sister. The leather cover was black and crispy.

The elders told Alfred to go home and get some sleep.

Alfred tried again before a larger audience the following Sunday. They were reading about Peter on the Sea of Galilee, his boat so full of fish it would sink. Alfred leapt to the dais and cried before the other Witnesses, "It's coming. We are not ready." His lips were wide and dry from smiling. "It's time to give up."

Within minutes the elders were escorting Alfred out the door. Rosette remembered the hush, the feeling of shame that unfurled across the hall, causing many to bow their heads. But a few people could not bow their heads and Rosette was among them. Paralyzed for a moment, she was incapable of looking away from Alfred, a tall handsome man whom she had somehow never noticed before.

One by one, folks left the Jehovahs and joined Alfred, who had spent his own money to rent a space above a Cambridge strip mall between an office-supply chain store and a discount sports clothier. He declared himself Pastor of the Last Kingdom on Earth, which is to say he sat in a left-behind office chair and talked about his vision for the coming end to anyone who came in through his open door.

There was nothing to fear, he promised. The end would be brief, total, and complete, a heartbeat in time, almost merciful in its efficiency. There would be no pain for the wicked; they would die instantly. Then it would all be over.

"And then what?" they asked.

"I don't know," Alfred replied.

"But, but, but . . ."

"Don't try too hard to know," he implored them instead. "If you can help it."

His lessons were short, often monosyllabic. Sometimes, when plied with existential puzzles, Alfred would offer no more than a sigh. His congregants, however, made up for his silence. That was the point of the Last Kingdom — to fill the last days of this world with a joyful noise. They batted around their stories all at once, talking to and at and over and through each other. The dominant story at Last Kingdom was that there would be a blast that would scorch the earth to ashes, and after everything cooled off, new plants and animals would emerge, hardier and more beautiful than before.

"Or not," Alfred offered, inspiring a frenzy of discussion, babble, and song, all at once.

"That actually makes a lot of sense," Karen said when Rosette tried to explain all this to her in the car. "Forest fires are wicked good for the soil. It's because of the sulfur."

"Never mind the sulfur," Rosette said, leaning hard on the horn. "Aye! *Puta!* I'll fry your ass in a rusty pan!" She slammed on the brakes and flung her arm across Karen's chest as though this alone would prevent her large body from hurtling through the windshield. It was the most maternal of gestures. The seat belt could barely contain the wild beating of Karen's heart.

"People in this city are crazy. They think we can read minds. Turn left whenever you want but don't signal to the other drivers. Lord have mercy . . ."

"I'm hungry, Rose." Karen had said this three times already. They had been her first words when Rosette had arrived in Mr. Cox's big silver Lincoln Town Car at Dennis's address. Mr. Cox was asleep in the back seat. "We could stop at McDonald's but I'll have to pay you back," Karen suggested.

"You can eat at Last Kingdom," Rosette said. "I made my mother's octopus stew. The best in the world."

They arrived at the shopping center around nine o'clock at night. All the stores were closed for the holiday, their windows papered with purple and gold banners advertising their grim sales. BUY NOW—BEFORE IT'S TOO LATE! Rosette unlocked a glass door that led to a staircase filled with a plasticky, chemical scent. The walls were a pale gray bearing perfect squares of a clean, lighter shade of paint where pictures had once hung, the ghostly reminders of vacated businesses. Even those that had remained in these sad office suites were halfhearted operations—a party rental company that was in actuality a front for Mafia interests; the headquarters of a nearly bankrupt, poorly attended French Canadian film festival; and the Last Kingdom on Earth Parish.

The music of Last Kingdom could be heard all the way down the hall. It was an office space like all the others, furnished only with what the previous occupants had left behind, half a dozen high-backed, rolling office chairs and a conference table pushed against the far wall, lined with aluminum foil trays of food. Only the elderly were seated. They rocked back and forth in the wobbly chairs as the music washed over their subdued faces. Everyone else was standing barefoot. Rosette removed Mr. Cox's and her shoes at the entrance and Karen did the same.

"We stand a long time. Hours and hours," Rosette explained. "It's hard on the feet. No shoes is better. Let the body balance the way it is designed to." She plopped Mr. Cox down in a chair but he immediately stood up, his chest full and proud.

"I'll be fine sitting on the floor," Karen said.

"No. We are greeting our Maker standing."

Karen angled toward the food table, but it was blocked by three guitarists blasting a long, improvisational song. The faithful numbered close to thirty people, exiles from the Jehovah's Witnesses and the stragglers they'd collected along the way. The music was loud and electric and seemed to have no beginning and no end.

Everyone was talking at the same time.

". . . I am so grate-ful! I am so grate-ful! I am so . . ."

". . . and you knew. You knew exactly what you were doing. You left me alone with wolves. I was a child—a friggin' child . . ."

". . . *pleine de grâce. Le Seigneur est avec vous . . .*"

". . . *hold me, hold me, never let me go until you've told me, told me . . .*"

". . . and a dishwasher and a mudroom and a fireplace and central air . . ."

". . . two three four five six seven eight nine ten one two three four five . . ."

". . . Doug can burn in a fire. Amber can explode. Shep—actually Shep's whole family—they should be eaten alive by lions. No, by maggots . . ."

". . . that's an insult to wolves. Wolves are ten thousand times kinder than the monsters you . . ."

Whatever came to their minds, whatever moved their spirits. Theirs was a faith uncluttered by mytho-historical characters and poorly translated verse. It left a lot to the imagination. It got very personal. The true language of God was spontaneous and perishable, they believed; recitations by rote were another faulty life-preserver in the floods of deception. Or so they assumed. Alfred had never actually told them any of this, but he'd implied it.

"Can anyone hear each other?" Karen asked Rosette.

For no reason she could discern, a man at the center of the rabble lifted his arms up in supplication. His long fingers reached all the way to the drop ceiling.

"Yes or no, *oui ou non, sí o no, sim ou não . . .*"

The lead guitarist ripped a lawless, boiling lick, nodding his head as if in response.

"Pastor Alfred," Rosette said, nudging Karen. The supplicating man was almost as broad as he was tall. For years he'd tried to make himself fit into the small enclave of Haitian immigrants in Boston, a place that felt no more his rightful home than Haiti had, and so, he'd decided, home must be a notion that simply did not exist in this world. What he'd found instead was a people so battered by weather and addiction, fear and pride, that the sheer pragmatism of Armageddon made perfect sense. Exhaustion was the best motivator, and so they all decided to stand until they dropped.

It was a tenet of this new church that the drama of the coming apocalypse not overshadow its message of surrender. Alfred tried, in his passive, lazy way, to discourage discussions of fire and nuclear winter, horsemen and demons. They were beside the point. Passion needed to be conserved for the awe and splendor of whatever was coming, and though Alfred did not purport to know anything for sure, he mused aloud that histrionics would probably irritate the Supreme Being burdened with such a brutally complete task of search and destroy.

"Chill," he urged his parishioners when they lapsed again and again into talk of blood-black rivers and fire in the skies.

They came every Monday and Wednesday night for lectures, stream-of-consciousness rants from Alfred that expounded on the finer points of his utilitarian hopelessness. He had few concrete ideas himself, which allowed his congregants to come up with the details, approved by a simple majority vote. Thursday nights were for meditation, a practice in which members stood in two rows facing each other and stared, eyes wide open, into the eyes opposite them for a full ten minutes, then they switched, square-dance style, to a new partner, until everyone in the fold had been "seen" by everyone else. Friday nights were for cooking and resting in preparation for Saturday, when, at sundown, their weekly vigil for the end began. It was a twenty-four-hour ritual, with members coming and going, though most stayed for the entire saga, joint pain be damned.

Karen watched the whole circus in amazement. While not in their Sunday best, most folks looked as if they'd put thought into their clothing. They stood and swayed, hollering their prayers to and at each other and whatever God they hoped was listening. There were no Bibles at the Last Kingdom. No hymnals or pamphlets. The word of God could not be trusted coming from man, Alfred had warned them repeatedly. That this included him was a fact he fully acknowledged.

"This happens to be where I am waiting for deliverance," he said, as though he had heard Karen's thoughts and was responding in kind. "Don't mean you have to wait here, too."

A pretty young Korean woman in a floral, grandmotherly dress started jumping up and down. "I am so grate-ful! I am so grate-ful. I am so gra-a-a-a-te-FUL!" she sang in an almost petulant, schoolyard tune. "How can I say thanks for all that you have done for me? All this life we don't deserve! Lord, take it away from me!"

"It was never ours to begin with," the pastor said in a natural tone of voice. Sweat pooled in the thick folds of skin at the back of his neck. Despite the heat, Alfred wore a brown wool suit. A white man with hairy knuckles removed a handkerchief from his suit pocket and dabbed the pastor's neck with it.

"Thanks, brother," Alfred said.

"Don't mention it, Al," the hairy man brayed.

It was an unusually diverse crowd for Boston. There were a decent number of nations represented, considering the size of the sample. The lead and rhythm guitarists were brothers, Adiel and Anildo, Cape Verdean high school students wearing thin neckties and crisp, collared shirts tucked into their sagging jeans. They would have joined Last Kingdom even if their parents hadn't belonged, such was their sweet fatalistic fervor. They liked the idea that nothing mattered but God, as the majority of stuff in their life—their grades, their skin, their sex prospects—was so unruly and frustrating, the source of all their pain. The message they gleaned from this new religion—forget it all!—met the paradoxical needs of their adolescence: to feel both totally powerful and completely taken care of at the same time.

The pastor rewarded their commitment by giving them free musical rein on Saturdays. Their bassist, Nate, was a white boy with shoulder-length hair and a nose that looked broken too long ago to be fixed. After nineteen years, his life felt long enough. The maintenance manager of this office complex, he lived in a squalid apartment with two disrespectful roommates he'd met online, and he worked long hours to pay for this tiny scrap of undignified freedom. Until he'd befriended Adiel and Anildo and joined the fold, he had been on the verge of suicide.

The three of them stood together at the edge of the crowd, playing shifting melodies that swelled with feeling, then drew back.

"I really friggin' hope God sees us, sees our love and devotion," shouted Moira, a deliriously smiling white lady. In her early fifties, she was decked out in black jeans and a black sweatshirt that had been cropped at the waist and the neck, exposing the tanned, very wrinkled skin of her shoulder, where a wobbly, amateurish shamrock had been tattooed a long time ago. Moira held her hands over the eyes of a small girl, Shayla, standing by her side. Shayla had dressed herself in boyish hand-me-down gym shorts and white athletic socks that were scrunched up at her slim ankles. New breasts pushed disconcertingly into the billowing, man-sized T-shirt she'd chosen to hide them in. Moira guarded her fiercely.

"Can God see us?" Moira was crying now. "We are giving Him friggin' everything."

Alfred folded his hands over his stomach. At heart he was an antinomian. Good works, he believed, were just another currency in the bankrupt economies of human faith, a way for man to barter his way into salvation. The greatest sin, the only sin, Alfred believed, was trying to make a mystery make sense. But he didn't want to be dogmatic about any of this. If his followers got the finer points, great. If those parts were lost on them, well, that's just how things go. They liked to take his words letter by letter. It was what they were used to doing and he had no delusion about breaking their habits in this lifetime, not with the deadline of a looming apocalypse ahead. That's why he tried to say as little as he could get away with. It was easier to let them make their own meaning. And anyway, half the time he couldn't remember what he preached from one day to the next. There were wild inconsistencies in his sermons, he was sure, which worked toward the ultimate good. It gave everyone less to hold on to.

But they wanted an answer and they wanted it now. He'd already forgotten the question.

It hurts to love you so much, he wanted to tell them.

"It's a shot in the dark," he said.

Rosette grabbed Karen's hand, kissed it, and held it enjoined with hers in the air.

They went on like this for hours, straight through the midnight hour, when the Great Hush of Last Day unfurled across the Eastern Standard Time zone. House lights switched off, restaurants got dark. Voices everywhere reduced to a whisper, uttering only the sibilant command, "Shhhhh, shut that off, shut up, shhhhhh." Light withdrew in stutters and voices darkened to shadows. People mouthed their last words, voiceless confessions offered up for the sky to swallow. They muted their kisses, softened their breaths, paused the music and the dancing, ceased their chewing, drinking, urinating, lovemaking.

> *"Lacrimosa dies illa*
> *Qua resurget ex favi—"*

At Symphony Hall, the conductor dropped his arms and all the musicians and singers stopped. They sat and waited.

Up and down the eastern seaboard, radio frequencies did not so much mute as morph into an otherworldly buzz, the hiss of cosmic inhalation, a slow, deliberate breath measured one time zone at a time. TVs still blared their regularly scheduled commercials, though a few stations offered a quiet, though not entirely silent, thirty-second spot of holiday greeting at the midnight hour. In New York's Grand Central Station, only the four clocks, hidden behind its garish holiday flags, could be heard ticking. Even the vagrants, the ones who were awake, knew to hold their tongue.

The sound of cars on highways swam in their ceaseless current. In just a moment, the lights would stutter back on. Voices would return to their normal levels. Some would scream their way out of the silence, howling and whistling like a victory had been won. In São Paulo, Atlanta, Brooklyn, and Belize, men on rooftops would shoot guns into the air. Throngs in Times Square would cheer and throw their hats, their cups, their lighters, whatever they had in their hands, into the blind, invisible sky.

But not yet. For this moment, all was quiet, dark, and still.

Time twitched and the bottomless stars grew brighter.

Outside the window of the Last Kingdom office parish, the lights of the parking lot went on a timed hiatus. The wind pushed trash across the pavement. For sixty seconds all was dim. Inside, however, the band played on. Last Kingdom did not recognize holidays, Christian or secular, and so at the stroke of midnight on the Last Day the congregants continued to hold forth and wail at and with each other. Then it was over. The lights of the parking lot came back on.

Karen had many times tried to witness the Great Hush of Last Day but was foiled year after year by her meds, which knocked her out into an almost vegetative state not long after dinner. Now her eyes strained to see what, if anything, was happening around her that was different or special. In the ceiling just above the window a stain like spilled coffee flowered outward from the corner of the room. Karen's eyes, tired from straining, lost focus, until she saw in the perforated drop ceiling a face emerge. Smiling and blotchy, it pushed itself out of the ceiling stain, taking shape in three dimensions, until Karen saw—she swore she was seeing, swore on her heart, on Nora's heart, on the hearts of all the kittens in the world—the tiny, hovering face of an angel.

"Do you see her?" Karen asked Rosette, who was still holding Karen's upraised hand in hers. "She looks like Glinda the Good Witch. Do you remember her?" Karen pointed at the ceiling.

"Oh, my sweet girl. Sweet, sweet, crazy, crazy girl."

"No. Look, Rose. There she is. Tell me you don't see her."

Rosette shook her head. "It's time to eat," she called out, and Pastor Alfred threw his arms in the air and shouted, "Amen!"

The musicians unplugged their instruments and sat on the carpet along with everyone else. An assembly line of women formed to plate and deliver food to each parishioner. A bowl of stew was put in Karen's hands. She ate it so fast she cracked a tooth on a chunk of bone floating in the thick broth.

"Mmmm," she said, pretending to wipe her mouth with a napkin so she could spit out fragments of her tooth. "What kind of meat is this?"

"Goat," an old woman answered.

"I've never had goat before. It's delicious. Did anyone else see that angel?"

The angel had disappeared. Squinting at the ceiling stain, Karen could almost make out a two-dimensional likeness of the face, but she wasn't pushing it. You couldn't force astral communion, or else everyone would be doing it all the time, and then who would there be to drive the buses and check the chemicals in the pool and perform vital surgeries?

"No such thing as angels here, hon," Moira said, picking her teeth with a plastic fork. "The real God don't need all those accessories."

"Rose? You saw her, didn't you?"

Rosette held her hand up to Karen's face. She was listening to the messages on her phone. When she was finished, she fixed Karen in a flinty stare. "Babygirl, is there something you are not telling me?"

Karen could only blink at her. Where to begin?

"Your home called me. Asking if I had seen you. You are a missing woman tonight. . . ."

"I've finally found a faith that works, Rosie. I'm ready to join your church. You can't make me go back. Not yet, anyway."

Everyone was looking at them now. What a moment! This was the drama Karen had longed for. She sensed serious potential for applause. If only Rosette were not the antagonist in the scene. She considered Rosette a kindred spirit, a big sister. No matter who Karen got to foster her, and there were plenty of new options here at this church, Rosette would always be family. Karen had always imagined that in a past life, once upon a time, she and Rosette had been crushed under the same heavy stones for the same crimes of witchcraft/generally disruptive female power, that their spirits were forever entwined as they followed each other into successive lifetimes.

"I can make a major contribution."

"I don't believe anything you say."

"No, really. Look."

Karen produced one of the three bottles she had taken from Dennis. She shook it like a little maraca. "Like last time, Rose. Except this time you can give my half of the money to the church. As my initiation fee, or whatever."

"Crazy girl!" Rosette said under her breath. She snatched the bottle from Karen and hid it in her pocket. "You are crazy in the head. Half intelligent, half stupid. How can you be so stupid?"

"You always say the meanest things in whispers," Karen replied. "Just because it's quiet doesn't make it hurt less."

"What's the problem, Karen?" Moira asked. She had never liked Rosette. Didn't trust her.

"I want to join!" Karen cried. "I want to be in your church."

The congregation gathered around Karen and Rosette. Someone said, "Let's ask her the Central Questions," and everyone murmured in agreement.

"Sister Karen, do you believe in one all-powerful God?"

"Do you accept His will totally and completely, even if it means you are going to die in the fiery hell of Armageddon?"

"Even if you are not among those elected to be saved?"

"Are you willing to give up everything? To give it all to Him?"

"And admit that no matter what you do, no matter how good you are, how hard you try, it might not amount to a hill of beans?"

"Do you promise to die trying?"

Karen was not at all willing to agree to any of these terms. She could not accept a world in which she was not a co-creator alongside the Divine. She had seen too much—portals to unknown worlds in every puddle of water, winking omens in the highway lights, dented cans baring to her their souls. There wasn't just one God who took everything away greedily; there was a web of intersecting lines like spider's silk connecting the souls of all things living, dead, and inanimate in a giant inescapable whole. It was never-ending, and she definitely had the power to affect it by her thoughts and energies and actions. And it wasn't fair that some people got to go to Rosette's God's party in the sky and some people didn't. She looked at the faces staring at her now, these variegated masks of humanity, all wanting her, all offering her this covenant.

"Yes!" she cried, and everyone cheered.

Shayla ran up to Karen and hugged her hip. She reached into her pocket where she had been saving a single package of cherry fruit leather. She ripped off the wrapper and tore it in two, offering Karen half.

"Cherry is the best flavor," Karen said.

"It's the only one for me," the girl agreed.

"Don't just stand there, girl. You think because everyone is clapping for you, you are some princess now. Hmmph. Clean out those coffee-pots," Rosette said to Karen.

Everyone was collecting the plastic bowls and spoons to be wiped clean for another use. How nice, Karen thought, that despite the end of the world, these folks were still recycling.

It was just before dawn when the parish of Last Kingdom arrived at the YMCA. The sky was a flimsy dark tinged by a veil of green. They parked their cars in the handicapped spots, the members-only spots, the fire lane. It was Last Day—who was going to stop them? But Karen urged them and they agreed to file in quietly. There was no need for stealth. Everything they were doing was being recorded on a closed-loop surveillance system. For all her powers and ambitions of vision, Karen had never noticed the cameras installed outside and inside the Y.

Today she was going swimming with her thirty new best friends! A super-secret pool party at the YMCA. It was a fantasy she had spent hours describing to Nora as they tried to construct a psychic safe place where Karen could retreat to when disturbing memories were triggered. Nora had given her full poetic license in this fabrication, suggesting trip wire and laser guns to keep out bad guys, for comfort a basket of kittens who never ever peed, the visibility and vantage point of a high mountain lair surrounded by a moat teeming with loyal alligators. But for once Karen's mental landscape remained firmly rooted in reality: the place she always returned to in these therapeutic exercises was the YMCA swimming pool with its high, echoing walls, its pistachio-green tiles, the milky light pouring in from the frosted glass of the windows; and presiding over everything, sitting way up high in the lifeguard chair, solid as a caryatid in an ancient temple, inviolable, loving, and stern, was Rosette.

Nothing ever hurt in the pool. Here she was neither fat nor clumsy. She was never cold, never hot, and hours could pass before she realized she hadn't eaten. It was a place where all her limitations and needs dissolved. She looked at her green dress rippling like an anemone around her legs. This dress had been through so much today, and now it was being bathed in chlorine. She would wash it in perfume and fabric softener when she got to her new home, wherever that would be.

"Pick a song everyone knows," someone instructed Karen.

"Everyone?" she cried. "I can't—"

"Don't think about it. Just sing."

"*Happy birthday to you*," Karen began, and everyone else joined in. This was her baptism! The acoustic effect of the whole congregation in the pool was stunning. Karen felt her blood thicken and slow, the rush-hour pumping of her heart ease, the water surrounding them flatten under the command of their chorus. Musically they harmonized about as well as a flock of shorebirds at sunset, but it was a powerful invocation. As a welcoming ceremony, Karen had to admit, it was working. Maybe the God they believed in was capricious and snobby, but their encouragement was sincere.

"What do I do now?"

"Go," Rosette said, splashing her. "Go swim under and come back up."

Karen dove headfirst under the water and swam as deep as she could. She opened her eyes and saw a million fractured beams of light flashing everywhere, like a star had fallen from the sky, broken open, and scattered too fast to dissolve in the water. She felt the pressure around her building, trying to lift her to the surface. She flapped her arms, fighting to stay underwater. She thought about Dennis. Just his name. She thought about her mother and how she had floated anxiously like this inside her once, wanting to be born but waiting for her mother to push her out.

Dennis was never going to be okay, and neither was she. No one was. This moment was as good as it was ever going to get. If the world ended right now, Karen thought, it would be okay, but it needed to happen quickly. Right now. *I don't want to be here anymore. Come take me. Us.*

Come, she said in her head, until it was no longer a word. Her eyes were burning. The pressure was building inside her lungs. *Come right now. Right now.*

"Baaaaah," Karen screamed as she surged to the surface.

"Sister Karen," an old Haitian man shouted. *"Byenveni lakay ou."*

"Look at her."

"Did you feel it?" Rosette asked.

Karen, gasping for air, dog-paddled weakly to the side of the pool. She threw her arms over the edge and held the concrete side like a favorite pillow in the aftermath of a nightmare. She didn't know what was real anymore. Everything she believed in this life had drained out of her body, been siphoned through the pool's filter, disinfected, and pumped back out invisible as water.

"I'm still here," she said, unsure if even this was true.

IN FRENCH, LAST Day is called *le jour d'infini rien* or, more simply, *le jour rien*. In Italian, *giorno di nient'altro*. In Spanish, *el día de la entrega*. In Japanese, *mokushi hi*. In Slavic tongues, some variation of *the gate of no dawn*. In Nordic cultures, *the day time takes a nap*. Tom tried his best to spell these words right, to angle the strokes of the kanji appropriately, but he was very drunk and very tired and even letters in English looked alien as he scraped them into people's skin.

THAT NIGHT SARAH dreamed she had a baby with no body. It was a large smiling head she kept swaddled in a yellow blanket. She was ashamed of her genderless little imp but filled with love for it, too. A mutant and a mistake, it had her eyes and nose and mouth, and it was so happy, its smile inextinguishable. "Cantaloupe," she named the baby. "You can't name a baby Cantaloupe," Kurt said to her; he was ostensibly, in the logic of the dream, her baby's father. "Please?" she said, but he was walking away from her and into the vaporous corridor of her unconscious. "Please?" she kept shouting in the empty hallway, until the sound of her own voice woke her up.

She was on the beach. The sun was a muted white light behind a screen of clouds. The ocean was churning, the color of dull utensils. It was day, and she was still alive. But Kurt was gone. She peered into the horizon, as if he had walked on water and would be waiting for her at the edge of the sea. She shook herself more awake, stood up, scanned the length of the beach left and right. In the far-off distance, she saw the abandoned campfires of last night releasing strings of smoke into the morning air. Kurt's helmet was gone. A fresh pile of sand had been poured onto their fire.

THE FIRST RAYS of morning seeped through the cloudy glass.

"We used to baptize everyone at Carson Beach," the hairy-knuckled man explained to Karen. "This is much better. You think we can use this pool from now on?"

"Definitely," Karen promised. Carson Beach was home to used tampons, syringes, and plastic bags containing the occasional mobster body part. Even the seagulls who fed there looked disgusted and ashamed.

She practiced her butterfly stroke for a few laps, then decided to join Moira and her grandchild Shayla in the shallow end, where they were pretending it was the Olympics.

"Rate my handstands," Shayla begged Karen. "But take it serious. Grandma is bullshitting me because I'm a kid. I'm not playing around here. I need a real friggin' judge. *Capiche?*"

Each time Shayla's head plunged underwater, Moira fired at Karen rapid disjointed installments of her life story. There were three ex-husbands, a dead son, a daughter in assisted living because she'd overdosed so many times she'd lost her gross motor skills. Shayla was not even her biological granddaughter. Moira had inherited the child from—

"How was that one? Were you even paying attention?" the child cried, eyes burning red with chlorine.

"Good, Shay. Do another one."

"Eight point five," Karen said, an honest assessment, which the child took as a personal challenge to try harder. She dove under again.

"So, that was the last time I bailed his sorry you-know-what out of jail," Moira went on. She was a petite muscular woman with long blondish-white hair and a gold hoop in her left nostril. Her skin was inscribed all over with shamrocks and mermaids, clipper ships and anchors. One tattoo inked onto her shoulder was a lot brighter than the others: the image of a sapling, spindly and leafless, embracing with two branch-like arms a two-by-four board of knotty pine bearing the yellow price tag of a hardware store.

"Got that one for free nine years ago," Moira explained. "Couldn't choose the picture, just had to accept what I got. Never met the artist before in my life. Hardly said two words to him, but he sure knew me all right." She kissed her fingertips and pressed them against the little sapling on her shoulder.

"Oh," Karen said. She had so much to say but couldn't find her voice. It had slid down her throat and was curled up and hiding somewhere beneath her stomach. Tears fell down her dripping wet face but for once she couldn't make a sound.

"Come here, sweetheart," the old woman said, and pulled Karen into her for a long, weightless hug. Karen felt her feet slipping down at the drop-off point where the deep end began. She held on to Moira.

"I never had a real mother," she whimpered.

"I know, baby," Moira said. "Neither did I. A lot of us here didn't."

If Dennis died, which she knew he would, probably soon, would she feel his soul leaving the earth, or would it get lost in all the garbage floating around, the lies people told and the hateful things they said? Even the spiritual realm was vulnerable to pollution, and it was getting worse every day.

"Rose," Karen called, her voice smacking against the walls and bouncing off. She spotted Rosette and Alfred pulling a stiff and soaking Mr. Cox out of the pool. They laid him on the floor beneath the lifeguard's chair. There were so many voices caroming off the tile, colliding into each other, expanding in air. "Rosette!" Karen shouted. Karen tried to run to her, to run across the shallow end of the pool. Her legs dragged behind her. She'd had dreams like this. Was this one of them? Rosette was crying, wringing her hands, and Alfred was whispering to her. He knelt down by Mr. Cox and pumped his chest. Through the windows Karen saw a blue flashing light. Then red. She heard the single chirp of a siren, turned on and then just as suddenly turned off, as though by mistake.

"I KNOW THE ham is working," Bear said when he returned, "but I'm not getting anything back. They can hear us, we just can't hear them."

"We should not wait for CAPCOM. Need to handle his body."

"Agreed."

"The MELFI locker is cold. He will fit in there."

"We'd lose all our samples. That's a lot of data."

"Could jettison his body. What I would want if I died in space."

"But we don't know that is what he would want. We have his family to consider. And JAXA. It would be an international disaster."

"Even in cold locker, we will have smell."

"The new crew is coming in two weeks. We could preserve him in a spacesuit, tether him outside, until we can send him back with the return capsule."

"Like bad dog? On leash?"

"Heck, I don't know."

"Okay. For now we wait," Svec said.

He wiped the sweat from his body and took off his shirt. Over his heart was tattooed in blocky Cyrillic *MAXIM*.

"Never knew you had a tattoo."

"You like?"

"That smirk, man. I know you don't mean it, but it just looks like you're making fun of me."

"Never. Here, comrade." Svec handed Bear a plastic pouch of vodka.

"How many of these do you have?"

"Enough."

"I don't drink. I told you that months ago."

"Today is exception. Today is too much for any man. Even you."

"You don't understand," Bear said. "My father died in a drunk-driving accident."

"My father, too." Svec sucked on the nozzle of the drink pouch, tempering the ridiculous indignity of the apparatus by his audacious sense of comfort and ease with it. "Crashed car into brick wall."

"Well, my father *wasn't* drunk. Someone's selfish drinking took his life. I won't mess with this stuff."

"Think of it like medicine." Svec held the pouch out to Bear. "To Yui. Our fallen friendo."

Madness, Bear thought, and took the drink.

"Yowww!"

"Now you feel fire. Good. Fire burns all rubbish. Make you new."

The men drank their way through one pouch and opened another. It was a mutiny, Bear thought, vomiting into his favorite baseball cap. There would be hell to pay once they got linked up again to the ground.

It was still possible, Svec countered, to put in a half-decent day's work, and Mission Control would be none the wiser. He fiddled with a spectrometer for a few minutes and began to laugh. "I don't know what we are measuring with this thing. Probably trying to make new weapon. To destroy U.S.A. To kill your whole family! Ha-ha!"

"I don't know what half of our experiments are doing, either. They told me it was intentional, so I don't fudge the data. But we're probably trying to kill you guys, too." He grabbed the pouch of vodka out of Svec's hand and pulled hard. "I like the beginning of drinking, when I feel like all the screws in my brain just got blasted with WD-40. I do not like the end of drinking, when I—" He wretched some more, shuddering in the hollow places of his body, heaving from what felt like the bones of his feet.

"If you drink often enough, it is never beginning or end," Svec explained. "But is harder up here. Vestibular system already confused. Me, I do not vomit in test flights. Not in parabolic flight. Not in high-G training. Okay, comrade. I will help to clean you now."

Bear was pawing at the bullets of floating bile he had managed to produce. His eyes were the color of ripe strawberries and brimming with unmoving tears. Svec dabbed Bear's face with a soft towel. He captured the wayward stomach matter and disposed of it, made his friend a batch of weak reconstituted grapefruit juice, and instructed him to sip slowly.

"I'm going to the Cupola," Bear said. "I always feel better in the Cupola. Just saying the word *cupola* makes me feel better."

"Okay, comrade. You go. I will clean some more."

Svec wiped down all the places where Bear's vomit might have splattered. He wondered about his life in retirement. He'd spent so much time striving toward one goal or another. What would he do now? Of course he would always be a representative of Roscosmos, talking to people about space, delivering speeches and lectures, cutting ribbons, shaking hands with men who envied him. But beyond that? There was nothing. Only life, which, as far as Svec could see, boiled down to eating. You chewed on the thread of life until you met your end. He could spend his days hunting big game. There would always be a tiger or a bear to stalk and kill. But then what? Stuff it? Hang the dead thing above a fireplace? It was disrespectful to turn an animal like that into a decoration or a toy. He could chase young women. It would not be so different from the bears and tigers after a while. His mentor, Gregori Borisovitch, had died three months into his retirement. Without a mission to prepare for, his heart had grown weak and stopped beating in his sleep. *This is what will happen to me*, Svec said to himself. *I will go home and be dead in three months.*

"Come quick, Svec. You got to see this."

"Your face is white."

"Just look."

Bear grabbed Svec's hand and tugged him along like a child pulling a parent to the site of his latest accident. Svec tried to free himself but Bear would not let go. They entered the Cupola one at a time and there beheld the earth they had been unable to reach for several hours. Flimsy clouds swirled in tatters over Central America.

"What?" Svec asked.

"Just look."

The clouds disintegrated and blew apart, revealing what looked like another layer of clouds beneath them, brown ones, piling up and spreading in liquid spurts over the horn of Brazil. All of North and South America, every square mile of it, was covered with brown suppurating sores. They oozed and dribbled in thick brown rivers, swirled in brown eddies, spilled into the sea.

"There's no rain forest. We used to be able to see the rain forest."

"Maybe there was fire?"

"Over the whole continent?"

"It is everywhere."

They checked the photos captured earlier in the day. At 13:41 P.M. GMT the brown clouds had begun mushrooming all over the earth. If there was a point of origin, Bear and Svec could not find it.

HARDLY ANYONE WAS looking at the sky when it happened. That posture of curiosity and awe was reserved symbolically for the night before, May 27, when heads tilted upward in waves across the globe as darkness descended one meridian at a time in the Great Hush. It was a reenactment, conscious or not, of the moment those terrified Babylonians had watched the sky in the aftermath of the eclipse that they were sure was ushering the end. May 28 was devoted to more timid celebration. Pouring water on the ashes of last night's fires, cleaning the syrup of spilled drinks, munching on cold pizza, nursing hangovers, running a commemorative 5K.

But An Chu was staring at the sky. It was evening in Hong Kong, past her bedtime. She knew that today was special but she did not know why. She was exhausted by the past two days of celebration, vacillating between elation and rage. The sugar in her blood had spiked and fallen in rapid cycles from all the candy she'd been allowed to eat. When the doorbell began ringing with another round of holiday guests, she slapped her nanny across the face. An was done with them, and her nanny kept insisting, as her mother had instructed, that she give each guest eight kisses for good luck.

An Chu's nanny, Dai, hated An Chu. She hated the child's flat-faced mother and her ubiquitous string of fat black pearls. The father was a grumbling suit who did not strain his eyes even to glance in the nanny's direction. Dai was saving up to get her teeth fixed. They were crooked and irregularly sized, as though Dai's mouth had been assembled with spare parts. Her top right incisor sprang out with the alacrity of a diving board. That night, waiting for An to fall asleep, Dai calculated how much longer it would take, in terms of hours, days, months, before she would have enough money to get her teeth fixed. The thought so depressed her that she lay down beside An on the bed, and as the din of the party outside rose to a clamor, she cried herself to sleep.

An watched her nanny's face soften, listened for the delicate gurgle of sleep to take over, then climbed over Dai to the floor. She put on her shoes without buckling them—buckles were still beyond her—and stepped awkwardly into the fray outside.

"Until night falls," she repeated, not knowing why everyone laughed in response. It had been the refrain of last night, so why not tonight? The adults touched her head and face, tugged on her pigtails, and told her she was pretty. She'd heard this so often—how pretty she was—that the sentence felt like a long surname. *Hello, my name is An Chu the-Prettiest-Girl-in-the-World.*

She skated across the polished wood floor in her shiny unbuckled shoes, navigating the crowd of giants, not finding her parents among them.

The sliding glass door that led to the deck was open. An knew as well as she knew anything else in her flowering, inchoate mind that she was not allowed to go onto the deck alone, but she was doing it anyway, a cerebral explosion between impulse and thoughtful decision-making inching her closer to autonomy.

A strong wind lifted the strands of hair that had fallen out of the elastics Dai had wound so tightly just a few hours earlier. Her cheeks were pink and warm. The sky was a cloudy black stained blue at the horizon where day smoldered on the other side of the world. The moon was a filament of light outside of An's line of vision. She watched, instead, the billboard across the street blinking purple and gold. It was a sign for a parking lot and was made of twisted neon bulbs, an antiquated spectacle in the largely digital lumisphere of the city.

The light blinked on and off from the top stroke of the first character to the bottom, pausing at dead bulbs where the neon had burned out, a flickering that transfixed the child. She noticed how the purple and gold light reflected on the glass of her building, and kicked her foot in a confounding ache to be closer to the pretty sparkles reflected on the window below. Her shoe flew off her foot and tumbled from the balcony, falling thirty-seven stories to the ground below. An looked down in terror, then back at the parking lot sign as if its mysteries would now be revealed. She looked behind her into her apartment. A man grabbed a woman by the hips and pulled her close; the woman pulled away from him, arching her torso like a wind-bent reed. An Chu looked out again, down at the ground, then up at the sky.

NICOLE JOHNSON MET the man of her dreams at a bar with a broken neon sign. Six years later she married that man, Luke, and two years after that he left her for another woman. Luke had been walking their dog, a chocolate labradoodle named Tallulah, when a car on their street got rear-ended, spun out of control, and crashed into a retainer wall. The car immediately burst into flames and Luke, letting go of Tallulah's leash, dashed into oncoming traffic to pull the driver out to safety. He rode in the ambulance with her to the hospital, Tallulah long gone, never to be seen again, and after the woman had been stabilized Luke continued to call the ICU to check on her.

Nicole watched her husband fall in love with this woman over the next six months, like another car accident happening, this time in slow motion. She'd told herself she was paranoid, she was insecure, she should have a baby, she should not have a baby, she should be sexier, she should focus on her career, she should be empathetic, she should trust.

Nine months after the accident Luke had moved out and filed for divorce.

Now Luke and this woman were getting married in Palm Springs, on Last Day, Nicole had learned from a bout of social media stalking. Of all the clichés.

She drove around for hours that night, making herself sick. Even her car was now tainted. She had bought it with Luke when a much less dramatic accident had totaled her old car. They'd brought Tallulah home from the breeder in that car. They'd made love in the back seat once when Luke's parents were visiting from Ohio and they had nowhere private to go. It still smelled faintly of Tallulah's fur, like a mixture of corn chips and rainwater.

Nicole had to get rid of it. Now.

She pulled off at a dealership called Hugo's that every year hosted a famous Last Day sale, plastering the city with ominous billboards, signs, flyers, and airplane banners, always a bleak biblical nightmarescape of the end and the words IT'S NOW OR NEVER AT HUGO'S. Nicole traded her Honda in for an even older Toyota, plus two hundred dollars in cash. Worth it, she felt, her heart clanging against the bones of her chest like a prisoner with an empty tin cup. This new car smelled like Lysol, fake cherries, and ash, someone else's ghosts.

She drove past all the Last Day parties she'd been invited to, past all those pitying, insistent friends who'd vied to be the one to hold her together right now. None of them understood that she didn't want to be held—she wanted to disintegrate, she wanted everyone and everything to break apart. Thinking about it did not depress her at all. The Last Day holiday had never made more sense.

She stopped to refill her tank, get a Diet Coke, pee, then hit the road for another two hours. If she ran into traffic on the highway, she got off at the very next exit without caring where it led. She traced asymmetries all over Los Angeles, following a tangle of invisible lines.

At one point she thought she saw Tallulah being walked by a fat teenager juggling the dog's leash and a slice of pizza.

"That girl is me," Nicole gasped, wondering if her life was being lived in a multiverse and if her body, in this car driving around in unfinished circles, was its nucleus. She'd seen something like that in a creepy documentary Luke had made her watch years ago, about time and space and particles and intentions. There had been a bit about jars of water expressing sadness and rage in the arrangement of their molecules, and earnest talk of the possibility that every living moment of your life was occurring simultaneously on different planes of existence. It had given her nightmares, she remembered, and Luke had had to rub her back so she could fall asleep. Right now she wished it were all true, that on some plane of existence she was in bed, dreaming this last year and a half, and that she would wake up and Luke would still be there holding her. If she only kept driving she might find the portal back to him and then, back home.

And where was she when this realization dawned? Right smack in front of the bar where she'd first met Luke. She parked her car in front, the same broken pink of the neon sign glowing in the window. It was around six o'clock in the morning. The world had not ended. The bar was still open. She sat at the same stool she'd sat at years ago.

"Do you have anything to eat?" she asked the bartender.

He was reading on his phone and refused to look up, pointing with his elbow toward a stack of pizza boxes on a side table. Nicole opened each box and found only chewed-up bits of crust until she reached the very last box at the bottom of the pile, where a single slice was left. Pineapple and chicken, her favorite.

"I just don't know what I did wrong," Nicole said to the bartender. He wasn't the same man who had tended bar the day she'd met Luke. Even though no one else was there, she had to ask him twice for a glass of water. The bartender all those years ago had been old and bearded, not terribly big but saddled with a fat, round belly, a tired, dispirited Santa Claus sort of man. This kid was barely old enough to drink. His hair was shaved to a pale golden-white fuzz except for a long swoop of bangs that fell into his eyes.

"Luke is half-white and half-Korean and I'm half-black and half-Mexican, and that both matters a lot and doesn't matter at all in our breakup."

At hearing the word *breakup*, the boy looked up and flung his bangs out of his face with a sudden jerk of his neck. His eyes were light and colorless and Nicole was febrile and exhausted.

"She's white. The other woman. Just white. And not as pretty as me, but younger. Though only five years younger, which isn't *that* significant, right?"

His bangs had returned to his face, shielding his impassive, unearthly eyes once again.

"I was a good wife. I stayed in shape. I kept things interesting in bed. I looked up exotic recipes for dinner. I cooked, for God's sake! I said yes to sex even when I was exhausted. I did that thing with the scrunchie all the women's magazines say will 'drive him wild'. . . ."

"What's a scrunchie?"

"It's a glorified rubber band." It amazed her that she was talking about all this in complete sobriety and not a single tear was in production. Maybe she'd finally cried out her life's allotment of tears and now there were none left. She felt chalky inside, as if her bones could be rinsed away by a light rain. Her head clanked. Maybe she'd spent her life's allotment of love and there was none of that left, either.

"Sometimes I wonder if I am being punished for something, and I have to make it right, which I'd do, gladly, if only I could remember what it was I did wrong."

The bartender stabbed the ice in his drink with a straw, his face solemn and intent. She couldn't tell if he was even listening. He harpooned a maraschino cherry at last and slowly, patiently dragged it to the lip of the glass. He balanced the cherry on the straw and brought it to his mouth without dipping his head to meet it.

"The universe doesn't care enough about any one being to punish it," he said after he'd swallowed. "You need to think bigger."

"Yeah, but—" she began.

• • •

IT WAS NOT Last Day on the island of Bali. Last Day had never been celebrated there. It was simply the evening of May 28, time to set out the last *canang sari* offering of the day. A woman shook the branches of a Japon tree and collected the fallen blossoms in her shirt. She added them to the folded-coconut-leaf dishes full of betel, lime, cigarettes, and gambier, decorated with plumeria and marigolds, and laid them before her doorstep and on the dashboard of her husband's parked car. The smell of incense drifted through the air, mixing with the smell of burning trash. A stray dog ambled down the street. He lifted his leg to pee on the *canang sari* that had just been laid out. A little boy watched him and laughed. A black butterfly took flight.

IT WAS MIDAFTERNOON in Addis Ababa. Zelalem Jember slumped over his piano with his head in his hands, scratching an itch that did not exist. Somewhere beneath his hair, the dermis of his scalp, and his obdurate skull, the music wriggled between his synapses, little electric eels of melody stinging him with one note, then vanishing, leaving him bereft, in that simultaneous longing and dread known to all artists in the middle of difficult work.

"You have no idea what it's like to compose an opera with the sound of giants pounding behind you!" he had screamed at his wife before she'd left for the day.

She couldn't stand him when he was like this. "You do this all the time. Why don't you try relaxing?" she'd suggested as she tied the lacings of her shoes. "Listen to some Kebede. Take a nap."

Zela did exactly as she'd said, in part to spite her, to prove that she was wrong and her advice inane and futile. The great Kebede scowled at him through the speakers of their stereo. *You simpleton*, his bust of Bach mocked him, *oaf*. Yared's framed portrait simply shook his head, his face wrinkled with disappointment. Specters of the great composers hovered around him as he lay writhing on his bed. He had won a sizable international grant to write an opera about genocide. It was to be his magnum opus. Now the prize money and the unfinished second act conspired to strangle him. For the past month he'd refused all social engagements, eaten too little, slept like the dying, clinging to his sandy-eyed insomnia as though the skeins of life itself were unraveling before him, and he had no choice but to bear witness.

But he was not dying. He was just a disgruntled fifty-nine-year-old man slamming up against the limitations he'd created out of fear. This nap was not helping. The masters were not inspiring. He couldn't wait until his wife returned, so that he could tell her that she was wrong.

It was the opera, Zela decided. Who wouldn't be angry, miserable, hopeless, spending hours a day amid the hell of humanity? And yet he loved this opera so much, even its slow, painful birth. How could he love something so elusive, so violent, so heartbreaking and out of control? A sweet breeze lifted the dark curtains in his bedroom window, and the sizzling light of day flashed for a moment like a young girl offering a glimpse of the thighs beneath her skirt.

Zela yanked himself out of bed and trudged to the kitchen, where he stood slack-jawed for a long moment. He opened a tin of cookies and shoved them into his mouth two at a time. He wasn't hungry, he just wanted to feel something churning in his stomach besides envy, despair, and fear. "You're too dramatic," his wife said all the time. Instead of replying, "You're right," which he knew she was, he said, "Then you were a fool to marry me."

He ate two more cookies, hardly tasting them. In the apartment next door a baby was shrieking. Zela chewed and listened to the pulsating wail. *Whatever it is, baby, it will pass and then return*, he thought. *Pass and return.* He reached for another cookie but just held it in his hand. "Feed that baby a lullaby," he whispered to the desperate parents on the other side of the wall. *Pass and return.* He hummed to himself and walked to his piano. He would not work on his opera today, Zela decided. He would write a lullaby instead. A lullaby for the world. He began pressing chords into the keys. But the fear returned, the despair, the futility. No, not for the world, he sighed. Just for a baby, that baby on the other side of the wall. The song was flowing through him.

VAL CORWIN HAD a satisfying, almost mystical sense of her work as an artist: stories and pictures came to her from worlds unknown and she set them free on the populace just as soon as she was able, urging them, like children of a certain age, to live a life of their own, apart from her. While there were plenty of accolades, there was just as much censure, some of it nasty and personally damning. To keep working was her only goal, that and enough money to pay her half of the bills, and this was best accomplished by insulating herself from certain social scenes. But she was by no means reclusive. She was on her third husband—the one, she joked, who just might stick around—and they had lived together for forty years in an apartment on Manhattan's Upper West Side. She had two grown sons and a network of stepchildren, former and present, who had given her five biological grandchildren and sixteen more she doted on without any legal or biological reason. She and her husband traveled several months of the year, visiting family and friends across the country and abroad, and attended about one-third of the parties they were invited to, depending on their energy that day.

There were so many rumors surrounding the reclusive author, including the mythology of reclusiveness, that when Val Corwin was awakened that morning by a phone call from her agent, her first instinct was to ignore it. "Did you know you are a man?" her agent had said, laughing, many years ago. "Breaking news, Val: you are actually a gay man," he informed her years later. She was a Communist, a Canadian, a Trappist monk, and a fugitive. It was mostly funny, but in her eighties now, Val was tired and wanted to sleep in. When she didn't answer the phone, her agent called back immediately, something he never did, so Val, her mind up and running already, answered him at last.

"Val, they're giving you a Pulitzer."

"La-di-da," Val said, and hung up.

THE CONGREGANTS OF Last Kingdom dripped large puddles all over the beautiful parquet floor of the YMCA lobby. Her boss, Roberto, was going to be so mad about that, Karen thought. He was obsessed with these floors. He tended them like an orchid, blocked off the lobby and its entrance every winter in order to protect these floors from the salty, sandy trudging of shoes.

"I really need to wipe this up," Karen said to the police officers buzzing around. "Can I go get some towels? I'll come right back. Promise."

No one answered her.

The parishioners had been instructed to remain quiet while the interrogations proceeded, but it was as if none of them spoke English, Officer Stone said. "It's like the Tower of Fucking Babel in here, am I right?" he sneered.

"I think they speak English just fine, they're pretending not to," Officer McCarron replied after he'd radioed the precinct for a couple of interpreters. "They're all out of their gourds is what they are," he concluded.

Karen saw a police officer handcuffing Rosette and leading her to the door.

"Rose!" she yelled, her heart throwing itself again and again against the cage of her chest.

Rosette's foot slipped in an invisible puddle of pool water that had collected near the front entrance. Karen rushed toward her and caught Rosette by the shoulders before she could fall. "Today is a day that's never been before, babygirl," Rosette said to Karen as the police pulled her away.

THE OCEAN WAS a dull mirror of the sky, the tide sweeping sideways across the sand. A flock of noisy shorebirds milled around its wake. Laughing gulls and herring gulls waddled together in the shallow water; oystercatchers ran on their absurd legs and startled each other into flight. Perched on a stone, a cormorant spread its wings to dry in the sun. Cormorants were Sarah's favorite shorebird. They were impressive hunters, and their turquoise eyes were proof that there existed a breach in the world of magic and fairy tales into this one. But Sarah was not looking at any of it. She was staring directly at the sun, holding it in her gaze as long she could stand it, hoping to go blind.

How long would it take before that actually happened? she wondered. It was one of life's precepts—*don't stare at the sun*—and like many others, it was something that assumed understanding while the nuances were never fully explained.

Sarah stared at the sun a while longer, then blinked away the glare and looked at the birds. *Whatever*, she thought, blindness was only cool if you were musically gifted, and Sarah hadn't been able to get through six weeks of guitar lessons—the strings had hurt her fingers. Now she was giving up on blindness, too.

She trudged back toward the entrance of the beach. The sea was an unvarnished sheet of silver pocked by nodes of white light. Wind pushed paper trash and empty cans from the night before in crab-like patterns across the sand. Here and there, extinguished fires had scarred the sand black. She'd had sex for the first time; she'd been dumped for the first time: now she was alone and full of feelings that were at once ancient, almost inherent, and also brand-new. She didn't know what to do next.

As she walked a long path to the entrance of the beach, Sarah tried on a sunny little delusion for size—maybe Kurt was coming back? Maybe he had simply gone for coffee and would return any minute now with a steaming cup for her, black with three sugars, which he didn't know she liked but he would guess it about her and be right. But that was exactly the delusion that had gotten her into this situation. He'd packed up all his things when he left. He was gone.

The only thing worse than being dumped was being dumped via the biggest cliché in the world. Young girl gives virginity to older man who hightails it out before she wakes up the next morning. I mean, come on! That was supposed to happen to those other ordinary Sarahs, she thought, the kind who wore high heels and different varieties of underwear and burst into song when they drove around in cars together. Those girls were well equipped for this moment. Sarah had expected a lot of disasters, but not this. The worst-case scenario she could come up with before this was that Kurt's heart would seize up in the night, the completion of love having an arresting effect on him, and he would die in her arms; the next morning she would light his body on fire, and later face the police brave as Electra, answering to a higher law. Or they would fall more deeply in love than she could even imagine and live a long, interesting life together, their intimacy so powerful they would feel each other's illnesses and hunger and stubbed toes from the next room; they would be childless and grow old, a sculpture garden they built together their legacy after death. That and some swans. They would raise swans.

It pleased her mildly that her storm prediction was right, and annoyed her still that Kurt had doubted her and wasn't here to acknowledge it. The sun tucked itself behind a wispy gray cloud that was fast erasing color from the sky. The temperature had dropped since she'd woken up. In the distance Sarah saw a very fat man in a black wetsuit followed by two golden retrievers lumber over the dunes and into the water. He was as big as a walrus, with short, sausagey arms and a small bald head settled into the deep folds of his neck skin. He had a thick black mustache and a rubbery smile, the kind seen only on the faces of the very religious, the mentally slow, or those recently returned from a brush with death. The man tossed a ball into the ocean and the dogs darted over the sand and raced into the waves to fetch it. He waded in after them, lobbing the ball again and again as he swam deeper, his dogs paddling nearby.

The spangled surface of the water flattened suddenly, as though hushed, and the first raindrops fell, cool pricks against the skin, stippling the dirty-looking sand. Sarah dropped her backpack and walked into the water.

It was cold. Bolts of ice shot up from her ankles to her knees. She was a strong swimmer but her clothes and sneakers were weighing her down. Numbness was working its way up her body, starting with her toes, then her legs. She wanted to swim as far as she could and let herself be held by the ocean until she slipped out of its grip and just drowned. A watery, Shakespearean end to this psychosexual tragedy, a clichéd coda to the clichéd climax of her clichéd life.

Sarah had dog-paddled a little deeper into the water when the selfishness and absurdity of her suicide sank in. Who was she kidding? She didn't want to die. She loved her parents. Had she remembered to tell them that before she'd left the house? She wanted to know what grade she'd gotten on her politics paper. And the water was too damn cold. So she turned around and began to swim back to shore.

The current had carried her out much farther than she'd thought. It pulled her deeper, tugging her body with such force it felt personal. She realized her feet couldn't touch the bottom and a shock of fear ripped through her. Reaching with her toes, she couldn't even sense how far down the bottom might be. The fat man and his dogs were still bobbing in the water, tiny dots very far away now. Rain pelted the back of her head. She took off her sneakers and let them drop, hoping the lost weight would help her. She swam hard against the current, not seeming to move any closer to the shore. In the sky the clouds broke over the beach and the faintest rainbow leaked through the haze.

KURT HEARD THE rain slapping his helmet. The gray sky was thickening like a scab over the weak light of morning. He hoped he could make it home before it really started raining. He hoped the girl, Sarah, made it home okay. He'd left her sixty dollars, all the cash he had left in his wallet, and a note. *What did I tell you? The world isn't done with us yet. Fun night. Take care.*

What was he supposed to do? Hang around? She was smart and tough and clearly got off on little adventures like this. She'd be fine.

He needed gas but he was almost home and he needed a shower and his bed more. Nice rainy day to sleep and watch movies in bed. There was cold pizza left over in his fridge. He was looking forward to it. Basic needs, so easily met. Before him an almost empty highway and a peaceful day full of nothing. A song caromed around his head, an isolated line in pursuit of its full verse, *I can't keep track of each fallen robin.* How did the rest of it go? he wondered.

SARAH CLARK-DAVENPORT WAS willing to do the hard work of dying. She had not eaten much in weeks. She sipped water but did not drink it. The attrition of her cardiovascular muscle tissue was quickening. Her pulse was slackening. The air that flowed in and out of her body was slow and unwelcome.

Had she slept? She couldn't remember. She sat on the floor and gazed out the window. She had been in this spot for a long time, since before sunset. Now it was morning and she was still there. A robin landed on the windowsill. Sarah thought of Emily Dickinson. That bitch. She could never look at a robin and not think of Dickinson, and she hated her for that. She could not look at a robin without thinking of her sister, either: Mary, with her perennial gasps of awe at the sight of a simple bird.

"Please—" Sarah said to the robin, tears falling from her eyes without her permission. She lifted her hand to tap the glass.

NORA HAD JUST woken up from an afternoon nap. She'd left her window open and a cool breeze carried the scent of the sea into her room. How vulnerable it felt to sleep without a window screen. She brought her long white fingers to her fluttering heart. A line from Dickinson shot through her like a tranquilizer.

"Merry, and Nought, and gay, and numb—"

After the morning excursion to Delos, their tour guide had left the rest of the afternoon open for wandering, with a wine tasting and five-course meal scheduled for 8 P.M. What to do in the meantime? Nora had meditated already. She'd read her Buddhist self-help books and written in her journal. What she needed to do now and for the next four hours was to *embrace the moment*. Enjoy its spaciousness. It was so much harder than she felt it should be. Nora was used to time being broken into very specific fifty-minute blocks, each client a different shade of crazy coloring in the open spaces of her day. It was a problem of privilege, but a problem all the same, that relaxing into this vacation was so much bloody work for her.

She decided on coffee downstairs in the hotel café and then a walk through the village. She put on a white linen dress that showed off her lovely collarbone and a lavender silk scarf to cover it back up. For today it was enough that she was willing to walk and not run, to dress nicely and not hide in yoga pants.

In the lobby of the hotel sat the Italian widower from her tour group, drinking a cup of coffee and reading the local Mykonos newspaper. He folded it immediately when he saw Nora, a brightness in his eyes that Nora wanted to dismiss but couldn't. She ordered her coffee and took the seat next to him, as his gallant wave of hand bid her.

"I'm so impressed," Nora said, lifting his newspaper and refolding it more neatly. "Do all Europeans speak so many languages or just you? We Americans are so dumb in comparison. We only speak English and barely that."

"Oh, no. I look only at the pictures. It's all a-Greek to me." He smiled. He had several gold fillings in his molars that winked in the sunlight.

It took Nora a moment to get the joke, and the Italian widower waited for her, holding his breath until she did, then they laughed together hard and loud. Nora's scarf came unloosed from her neck and fell to the floor. He bent over to pick it up. He held it in his hand, not yet ready to return it.

BREAKFAST WAS OVER at Heart House. Two staff members, morbidly hungover, scraped spongy unfinished pancakes off plates, then stacked them in the dishwasher. Lauren herded the residents one by one into the living room, where they watched a sensationalist documentary on the possible alien origins of Stonehenge. They were supposed to be doing arts and crafts, but the missing-Karen controversy had screwed up the whole schedule.

"Here you go," Lauren said as she walked Sadie over to the window seat, surrendering at last to the chaos of the day. She laid some extra pillows on the bench for the woman, who looked both older and younger than she actually was. Lauren ran her fingers through Sadie's silvery hair, recently trimmed and seeming to sparkle in the morning light that streamed through the bay window. Lauren fluffed the pillows some more. "Nice and comfy," she said. It felt good to do this one thing right.

"Do you see him up there?" she asked Sadie, whose fingers were already pressed up against the glass.

"Hello, brother Bear," Sadie said to the sky.

TIANNA WAS USED to blaming her brothers for her troubles, but this time she couldn't. She and Miles and Avonte had not made it to the bonfire last night, but it wasn't their fault. It wasn't anyone's fault, really, that her grandmother's car had a busted alternator, and without a scapegoat to contain her disappointment, Tianna's world began to unravel.

"Why can't you get it fixed?" Tianna had wailed, her face dripping with tears and snot as she beseeched her grandmother, a woman she had until now assumed was all-powerful because she was fifty-six. This fiction was just beginning to dismantle itself and Tianna could not handle it.

"We can't just sit here," Tianna cried.

"I can't afford to pay attention," Maeve answered, "let alone what they charge at that crooked auto shop. They're swindlers! All of them!"

Tianna suggested asking Dorothy, Maryann, Beryl, Lucy—every name her grandmother had ever mentioned in her long tirades against the women in her social circle.

"It's none of their business what's going on under the hood of my car!" Maeve crushed a cigarette into a pristine glass ashtray.

"What about the bus?"

To this Maeve rolled her eyes and waved her hand in a way that let Tianna know the whole idea of going out was hopeless. Her mother was useless, her father nonexistent, her mother's boyfriends, Dennis especially, a burden, her teachers disgruntled, indifferent, and mean. Maeve was a decent woman—she never treated Miles or Avonte differently even though they were not her blood, a kindness not extended by Miles's grandmother whenever the three children stayed with her. Maeve's house was clean and well stocked with both real food and junk food. But last night her grandmother, the one official grown-up who cared enough to try, at least a little, proved to be as impotent as the rest of the adults in her life.

"We're on our own," Tianna told Miles. He was falling asleep on the pullout couch, his eyelids fluttering as he clutched Maeve's tablet in his arms like a teddy bear, the animated *Selfless Knight* playing too loudly on the screen.

Tianna could not go to school Monday and say she had done nothing on Last Day, so she would take matters into her own hands. She woke Miles early the next morning with the promise of breakfast ice cream ("Grandma told me we could have it. No, we don't have to wake her up and ask first. . . ."), then led her brother into the kitchen. She had already set up an offering—a big saucepot, a box of matches, yesterday's crumpled newspaper, the backpack Dennis's weird friend had given her, and a big mixing bowl of water.

"I need your help carrying this to the backyard," she told Miles.

Miles was sleepy and agreeable. He took the empty pot, paper, and matches while Tianna transported the backpack and bowl of water, careful not to spill it.

They went through nearly the whole box of matches before they were able to make one ignite. Minutes later they had a roaring fire going in the pot that they fed with ripped-up newspaper.

"Okay, go get your doll," Tianna told Miles.

"He's not a doll. He's Viscount Darkdoom."

"Whatever. It's time to burn him."

"I don't want to anymore."

"You have to—" she began, when a leaf of burning newspaper floated up out of the fire and collided with the dry, stiff bedsheets that Maeve had left too long on the clothesline.

"Oh shit," Miles said.

"Get the bowl!" Tianna cried, then pushed him out of the way as she scrambled to get it herself. She tripped on her way to the now-ignited sheet and spilled the water into the grass. The fire leapt from sheet to towel, working its way through Maeve's clean laundry. Tianna tried the garden hose but the spigot was so rusty she couldn't turn the knob.

"Mom's going to kill us," Miles said, reading his sister's mind. The children watched, stunned, while flames leapt up and up, as though yearning to grab the low branches of a tree.

TERRENCE LOOKED AT the white feathery remnants of the previous night's fire and heard her voice. He knew exactly what she would say: that his need to ejaculate onto recently vacated areas was a function of male privilege. It was the same cowardly assertion of dominance that had fueled the Columbian conquest of the indigenous lands now known patriarchically as the Americas. Marking his territory like a tyrant. Co-opting spaces as his own genetic field through a passive-aggressive violation of an empty—read vaginal, read feminine—space.

But it wasn't! It really, really wasn't, Terrence argued with her in his head. He was all for nonbinary gender egalitarianism. Like one hundred percent. This had nothing to do with that. It was just an itch, and when he saw the clean living room rug after everyone had gone upstairs to bed, or right now, this empty campsite—he had to scratch it, or it would nag at him until he couldn't calm down or concentrate on anything else. It relaxed him and it was so quick, averaging three minutes. It was a function of his OCD. Not his fault.

Oh yeah, and rape culture is not anyone's fault? Next you'll tell me mental illness is an excuse for racism and genocide? Her imaginary censure aroused him even more. Why did he love her so much? She was a forty-seven-year-old woman with flagrant displays of body hair, a lesbian happily married to a transgender man. She was a teacher at his goddamn school. Dr. Vasquez-McQueen could not be more out of his league; he had never wanted anything more.

Terrence kicked some dirt over the pearlescent dribble of his semen and buttoned his pants. He took a deep, relaxing breath. He looked toward the path where the others had set out on their morning hike. If he ran, he could catch up to them.

ARI AND ALISON Moss were fast asleep, their bodies pressed close as spoons, their minds awash in delta waves, pitching them toward the next round of dreams.

IN A QUEEN-SIZED bed on the fourth floor of Morning Pines, Myra and Marlene were, too.

JOSH LIKED TO leave the cage open, kindling the hope that his rabbit might hop into bed with him at night and snuggle. Just because it had never happened didn't mean it never would, Josh had told his mother, who smiled and let it be.

But when Josh woke up that morning, Arturo the Fifth was not in his bed or his cage. He looked in all of Arturo's favorite spots, under his bed, at the bottom of his closet, until at last he found the rabbit in the laundry basket in the bathroom, surrounded by seven newborn bunnies. Josh brought his mother in to confirm.

"Yep, seven of them. Arturo's a girl!" She waved the smoke twirling out of her cigarette away from the little nest in her dirty laundry basket, away from her son, and thought about what to do. The house was a mess and now the laundry stank like a barn on a day when the Laundromat would be closed. Her car needed gas and she was waiting for a check to clear before using her debit card, which was so maxed out she feared sparks might fly from the ATM if she inserted it. Josh looked at her with wonder and fear, with perfect trust. It was the same face he had shown her in his first minutes of life, as if he had known her from long ago, before either one of them had been born, when a perfect version of everyone still existed.

His mother ran the bathroom tap to extinguish her cigarette. "Go outside and pick some grass and weeds and stuff." She filled a hot water bottle and wrapped it in the now-ruined T-shirt from the top of the laundry basket. She put the water bottle in a shoebox and let Josh arrange the greenery on top of it, including several dandelions he had picked along with the grass, which his mother assured him was a nice touch.

"What are you doing?" Josh asked, as his mother probed each baby rabbit with her fingers.

"Making sure their hearts are strong and their bellies are full."

"Are they?"

"Uh-huh. Their mommy must have just fed them before we woke up."

"They're kinda ugly."

"Most things are in the beginning."

RINGO HAD JUST woken up from his nap on the floor of his workspace and immediately took the next customer in line, a stately old drag queen named Taboo.

"Do you mind if I just do an apple?" Ringo asked her. "My brain is fried. I can't think of another flower."

"Honey, you do whatever you want," Taboo said.

Jake had passed out leaning over the toilet, a safe enough position as he could not aspirate on his vomit, Janine decided, after checking on him one last time. She'd woken up from her own disco nap with a strong feeling of *fuck it*. For over two decades she'd been watching the boys make their art. All her boyfriends, even before Jake, had been tattoo artists. She'd lived her entire adult life like a stupid fucking groupie, and not even for a rich rock band. Not even for a broke punk band. But for tattoo artists. What was the point? "Fuck it," she said, and called the next customer into Jake's chair.

This was a big no-no. She was not licensed. She hadn't even been to school — Jake had discouraged her, for selfish and sexist reasons he didn't bother to deny. And Janine, if she was being honest, had allowed his barking to stop her, secretly glad of it, so that she didn't have to face the fear of actually trying. What if she wasn't as good as Jake? What if she was much better? How would it change their perfectly dysfunctional codependency?

With that she began inking the letters *REDEMPTION* on a man's biceps.

Tom was inscribing a double helix on the thigh of a woman a little older than he was. Maybe she was the one he would go home with. He'd been waiting all night and all morning for the signal, that it was time to stop. He wiped away her blood and looked into her eyes.

"You're pretty hot for your age," he said.

"Stop talking," the woman replied, shifting a little closer to him in the chair, "and this day might work out beautifully for both of us."

Tom mimed the zipping of his lips, pretended to lock them, then tossed the key behind his shoulder. The woman laughed without making a sound.

In the early light of May 28, the buzzing of needles continued, but all conversation stopped. A calm energy had taken over, quiet and diffused with light. Ringo's breathing began to synchronize with his customer's, as did Tom's and Janine's, until all of them, even Jake asleep on the floor, were inhaling, exhaling, together, without knowing.

IF WE ARE going to die, Bear and Svec decided, we die at home. They were in perfect harmony on this. Even if there is no one left there to mourn us. Home was where they belonged. And so with no assistance from Mission Control, Bear and Svec began the first steps of protocol for an emergency exit. They had calculated a landing in Kazakhstan during daylight hours, hoping a crew would be there to help them out. Now the only thing left was wonder, and it was terrible.

The rage of the past century had finally been released. The stuff of dystopian novels and movies, one nuclear bomb launching after another until everything was fried. Gone. "War. Big. Bigger than before. Biggest in all time," Svec said.

"Maybe." But maybe a few survivors? Bear wondered. He wanted to water the plants, to quickly design and rig a system to keep the mice appropriately fed for as long as possible, just in case.

"Comrade, no one is coming back here."

"Eventually . . ."

"Look." Svec took Bear by the hand and sailed him into the Cupola. The once blue gem was a whorling, frothy brown. The distinction between land and sea was so blurred it was hard to discern by sight exactly where on Earth they were looking.

"If we survive, if we find others who survive, coming back to station will not be priority for many, many years. In that time, station's orbit will decay. She will fall back to Earth with Yui inside her. All this will be destroyed."

"We have to hold on to some hope, Svec. I can't just nosedive into an empty pool so fast. We don't know what is going on right now. That is the truth. We do not know."

"You're right. But what can be done about it?"

PULLING THEMSELVES INTO the Soyuz, the two men shared a common nightmare—the very real possibility that no ground team would be there to pull them out after landing. There might not be a living soul for hundreds of miles. After six months in microgravity, they would have the leg power of arthritic, bedridden eighty-year-olds. Both men agreed that they were equipped to survive this. What they would not admit to each other: they might be the last humans alive.

"God bless Yui," Svec said.

"What?"

Svec heaved himself close to Bear, until he was close enough to hold him in his arms. "Night before Yui died, he held me like this." Svec thrust his hand behind Bear's skull and held it. "He kissed me. After, he went to bed and died. Was kiss of death. Goodbye. Can you see?"

Bear smelled vodka on Svec's breath and it enraged him. "Let's get this show on the road," he said. Svec was still holding Bear in an embrace. Bear tried to pry himself away but Svec held on. He pulled Bear's head closer and kissed him on the mouth. Then he slapped Bear's face three times, kissed him again on both cheeks, and let go.

Strapped into their seats, they hurtled toward Earth at five hundred miles per hour. "*Zhatka, zhatka, ya zhdu tebya,*" Svec whispered. A prayer, Bear guessed, wishing that he too had a prescribed set of words he could recite. It seemed comforting, even if it was imaginary, to incant the hopes of another time, something older if not bigger than himself. Bear had learned a prayer or two in his life, but nothing that had stuck. A few sentences, a few words even, would suffice. He settled instead for a list:

Rain, falling in sheets, falling in drops, collecting in gutters, streaming down drainpipes, slamming against the windshield of a car, swished away by wipers, returning a half second later like a report of gunfire, then swish, ratatatat, swish; bathtubs his girls used to splash in until their fingertips wrinkled and their teeth chattered; the obnoxious plop of a leaky faucet; a still pond troubled by a frog plunking below the surface; the spray of a car driving through a large puddle; the rhythmic gurgle and swoosh of a washing machine alternating the direction of its toss; the sound of his childhood dog lapping water from her bowl; the sound of gulping several long sips in a row on a hot day, ice tinkling against the glass.

THEY WERE DYING. They could feel it as surely as the sweat on their skin, as the ship rumbling all around them. Dreaming the same dream, dying the same death. *If nothing else,* Svec thought, *I am grateful to you, comrade, to hold the other half of this fear. If nothing else,* Bear thought, *we are home, we are—*

AS THEY BREACHED the atmosphere over Central Africa, the ship's parachutes opened. A silvery-brown matter sloshes out of the seats that once held them.

A POD OF eleven dolphins swim in the Bay of Bengal. Six juveniles, not all of them related, a mother and her newborn calf, two adult females, and a badly injured male who'd escaped a shameful battle with a male from another pod. The wounded dolphin keeps sinking too deep to catch his breath. The adult females take turns pushing him up to the surface for air. The nursing mother communicates to the group to swim slower, and they do. Darting through the warmer, shallow waters near the coast, they feast on a school of mackerel. One of the youngsters, a female with a uniquely low whistle, decides it is time to jump. Her body shatters the tensile skin of the water as she leaps into the air. A spray like a thousand diamonds rolls off her back. An act of joy and an invitation to play, there is no other reason for it. Her schoolmates follow her in scattered succession, jumping in and out of the water. The sun burns low in the sky, golden and overripe as a peach. Three of them are midair, the other eight underwater, when all of them melt from the inside out, leaving slimy, limp tendrils of their old form in the wake.

THERE ARE DEEP rich pools of sludge where the Amazon rain forest once breathed. The greenery now wafts a scent never smelled before, the reek of all life and all manner of death combined, like burnt hair, low tide, afterbirth, and sick. That river, now nameless, pushes its snake-like pattern into the earth, slowed down by the sedimentary weight of all its dead.

A TINY DUTCH garden enclosed by a stone wall steams like a hot bowl of brown stew. Stone-carved angels kneel in the dry granite fountain at the garden's center, the shadows of them stretching over the viscous roux, against the wall in dark, elongated repose.

THE SITES OF three different genocide campaigns on three different continents congeal into an even bigger pool of the dead.

A FLOATING RADIOACTIVE island made of fishing nets and plastic bags, almost a mile in diameter, rides the waves as ever off the coast of Fukushima.

THE GOLD DOME of a mosque in Brunei glitters in the setting sun, its white stone still pristine at the top, as though purified by the approaching sky, its foundation laced with the brown accretion of matter lapping like a tide on its shore.

A U.S. NAVY aircraft carrier, named for a president credited with once forestalling the end of the world, floats across the roiling brown sea. Steam rolls off the surface of the ocean, all the life released now in a surge of heat. Enough heat to melt the thick plastic of the computers inside the ship, which slowly, then quickly begins to sink.

TREES BUCKLE AND collapse like grieving women, reduced now to a hot brown sap. Sunlight stabs the atrium of a cave, piercing the waves that splash against its glittering minerals, the remnants of stars.

Rays of light gleam against the brown water, where blooming clouds of dead fish, dead flora, dead plankton, and things even smaller rise and fall in eddies of brown foam.

The sea grows hot with death, the energy released boils even the most frigid water, until the oceans are seething with brown foam, and the steam rolls off the surface in clouds so thick they block out the sky.

Hills are blistered and brown. Grasses melt into slime, along with the millions of insects tunneling beneath them: the trillions of microbes, cell by cell, reduce and recombine into brown sludge. The sludge oozes everywhere. Dripping down fjords in Norway, smearing the faces of Mount Rushmore, bleeding beneath the fast-melting snows of Kilimanjaro. What were herds of antelope, oryx, buffalo, are now dark smears on the plains. The brown ooze of human communities dries up in the hot sun, leaving stains on the cement of the cities they built.

For a while the lights stay on. In Tokyo, London, Times Square, screens still flash images of beautiful women twirling their skirts, lying on the beach, rubbing lotion into their skin. Generators continue to burn unmanned for several hours until the systems governing the power plants across the globe start beeping and shut down. Pumps that keep running water in its place shut down, too, flooding the streets of the dead.

AIRPLANES, WHOSE PILOTS have liquefied to puddles in their cockpits, whose passengers are now seeping into the upholstery of their seats, fall by the thousands out of the sky. Trains skid off their tracks, knifing long wounds into the earth that soon will be sealed with the liniment of sludge. Across the globe, highways are littered with smashed cars, embolisms of gleaming metal on corridors east and west, north and south. Oil fields burn black smoke. Gas plants explode. Nuclear reactors, scrupulously programmed, remain intact for a while longer, until they, too, combust.

TIME PASSES. ATOMS of carbon dance in perfect terror. Ocean waves beat the shore.

AND HIGH ABOVE it all, a message in a bottle. Before launch, Bear and Svec had sent a small craft through the airlock, hurtling via timed thrusters they had programmed manually to travel as far from the earth as its fuel would take it, then sailing forever after on its own trajectory into deep space. Among the data installed, all their findings from decades of research, all the records of their time on the ISS and their observations of their home below, and three objects they hoped one day, if never fully understood, would be loved as relics from another world: Svec's son's handwritten list of astronauts, Bear's harmonica, Yui's favorite Val Corwin book.

.   .   .

ALL WAS WATER and waste, heat and odor. Cell membranes puckered and shrank, nuclei collapsed, all the constituent parts of life recombined into one plasmic ooze.

What was lost? Mitochondria, proteins, reproductive organs, bones, gymnosperms, voices, music, faces, hunger, dreams, flowers, fields, ferns, snakes, crabs, snails, algae, bacteria, stories, traffic, apologies, wolves, holidays, rage, anthills, rhizomes, gratitude, pain . . .

What remained? Clouds. Great big clouds. Shadows. And wind. And beauty remained. It had existed before, and always would, whether or not it could be borne.

IT WAS OVER almost as soon as it began. The sun continued to rise and set, moving across the galaxy, a distinct but ordinary flame in the deep. Planets continued orbiting in their ellipses. And it would be like this for a very, very long time, before the first thing happened, then another, a cause, and then its effect, and then the new story that would begin.

ACKNOWLEDGMENTS

This book was not easily born. Cindy Spiegel was a wise, patient, and trustworthy editor. I won't embarrass you with the superlative ("the wisest . . .") though I know this is true. I am so fortunate to work with you twice. Thank you, Cindy. This story is immeasurably better because of you.

Big thanks to Jim Rutman, whose extemporaneous emails are more lucid and thoughtful than my best rewritten prose. You were a wonderful support, truly going above and beyond, long before there was anything substantial to support. It's an honor to work with you.

A whole team of talented people at Penguin Random House have again worked to make the difficult progression from draft to book appear easy: Mengfei Chen, Kelly Chian, and copy editor Deborah Dwyer did with grace and skill.

I would not have put up with this book beyond its very ugly first draft if not for the intelligent and kind appraisal of Ariel Colletti, who gave the first read. Thank you forever.

Stephen Taylor, you are the smartest, most well-rounded and well-read person I know. I wanted above all to write something you would like. I'm glad I got to meet you again.

Paul Citroni, Elyse Citroni, and Kayley LeFrancois, I am so lucky to call you family.

I wrote a good chunk of this book in a postpartum fugue state. There were times I didn't think I'd survive, let alone make art again, once I became a solo mother. Marika Lindholm, you were a guide and an inspiration; your generosity kept me going, along with our ESME.com dream team Cheryl Dumesnil, Katie Shonk, and Heidi Kronenberg.

For love, support, good advice, and the occasional invaluable hour of childcare (in order of appearance on my phone contact list): Adam Gardener, Cassie Bachovchin, Cathy Casey, Chelsee Shiels, Debra Crist, Joan Pelletier, Kathleen Cunningham, Dave Andalman, Dawn Mordowski, Lauren DeLeon, Donika Kelly PhD, Emily Einhorn, Enoka Strait, Melissa Febos, Halley Feiffer, Jumana Grassi, Katie Freeman, Lauren Gello, Michelle Gomez, Beckie Hickok, Kenny Hillman-Love, Jenny Hobbs, Lynne Jay, John Cusack, Gabrielle Kerson, Greg Koehler, Megan Krebs, Leina Boncar, Linda Gnat-Mullin, Christine Love-Hillman, Lynn Buckley, Amy Meyer, Molly Oswacks, Jamie Panagoplos, Diantha Parker, Patti McDannell, Sharon Pinsker, Kate Rath, Robert Atchinson, Lucy Rorech, Onnesha Roychoudhouri, Amy Stewart, Brian Avers, Emily Stone, Joanne Swanson, Victoria Morey, Teddy Wayne, Mark Wright, Pam, Michael & Cece, Midday, my family, and Z.

ABOUT THE AUTHOR

DOMENICA RUTA grew up in a working-class, unforgiving town north of Boston. Her mother, Kathi, was a notorious drug addict and sometime dealer whose life swung between welfare and riches, and whose highbrow taste was at odds with her hardscrabble life. Ruta is a graduate of Oberlin College and holds an MFA from the Michener Center for Writers at the University of Texas at Austin. Her stories have appeared in the *Boston Review,* the *Indiana Review,* and *Epoch,* and she has been awarded residencies at Yaddo, MacDowell Colony, Blue Mountain Center, Jentel, and Hedgebrook. The author of *The New York Times* bestselling memoir *With or Without You,* a darkly hilarious mother-daughter story and chronicle of a misfit nineties youth, Ruta lives in New York City.

domenicaruta.com
Twitter: @DomenicaMary

ABOUT THE TYPE

This book was set in Bembo, a typeface designed for the Monotype by W. A. Dwiggins. The typeface was based on drawings by G. Griffo (c. 1495). Bembo is a roman typeface, avoiding the coldness of Didot and the quaintness of the earlier humanist faces of the fifteenth century.

Specific Usability Features of
Technical Communication, Eleventh Edition

*"Usability is not just a conceptual term. In writing this book,
my intent has always been to create a usable document for readers
—so that users of this book can 'read to do.'"*

John M. Lannon, From the Preface,
Technical Communication 11th Edition

CASE: Delivering the Essential Information

Sarah Burnes was hired two months ago as a chemical engineer for Millisun, a leading maker of cameras, multipurpose film, and photographic equipment. Sarah's first major assignment is to evaluate the plant's incoming and outgoing water. (Waterborne contaminants can taint film during production, and the production process itself can pollute outgoing water.) Management wants an answer to this question: How often should we change water filters? The filters are expensive and hard to change, halting production for up to a day at a time. The company wants as much "mileage" as possible from these filters, without in—————————es or tainting its film production.
————————ss printouts of chemical analysis, review current re-———————egulations, do some testing of her own, and consult ———————n she finally decides on what all the data mean, Sarah

CASE STUDIES

Situations that call for decision-making based on material you are learning

---

ON THE JOB

Honest, authentic comments from communicators about the role that writing plays— sometimes unexpectedly— in the jobs they do

---

ON THE JOB... Audiences

■ *"Audience makes all the difference. I write for students, small groups of scholars, and general readers. I pitch grant proposals to larger groups of scholars, either nationally (as for the National Endowment for the Humanities) or locally (among colleagues throughout the disciplines at my university). I assume my audiences are happy enough to listen to me at first, but that to keep them reading I need to supply varying degrees of background and explanation pitched to their background and fo———————ith th———————matter.*

■ *"I write for elected officials, public decision-making groups (commissions, boards of directors, etc.), commu-———————————— foundation staff and dir———————*

■ *"I'm writing for psychiatrists, nurses, psychologists, and other staff on the unit. Since we use a 'medical model,' I use standard 'jargon' and abbreviations for medical staff."*

—Emma Bryant,
Social Worker

☑ Checklist: Proofreading

(Numbers in parentheses refer to the first page of discussion.)

Sentences

☐ Are all sentences complete (no unacceptable fragments)? (000)
☐ Is the document free of comma splices and run-on sentences? (000)
☐ Does each verb agree with its subject? (000)
☐ Does each pronoun refer to and agre———————————specific noun? (000)
☐ Are ideas of equal importance c————————
☐ Are ideas of lesser importance ————————
☐ Is each pronoun in the correct c————————

CHECKLISTS

Key questions to help you focus on user needs as you review and revise your documents

---

Consider This Ethical Standards Are Good for Business

To earn public trust, companies increasingly are hiring "professional ethical advisors" to help them "sort out right from wrong when it comes to developing, marketing, and talking about new technology" (Brower 25). Here are instances of good standards that pay off.

By Telling Investors the Truth, a Company Can Increase Its Stock Value

Publicly traded companies that tell the truth about profits and losses are tracked by m————————
analysts than companies that ————————
smoke screens" to hide bad eco————————
it takes is the inferential leap t————————
touti————————

• *Lies (including "legal lies") to colleagues or customers are grounds for being fired.*
• *Gossip or backbiting are penalized.*

From a $50,000 start-up budget and 45 people who shared this ethical philosophy in 1978, the company has grown to 480 employees and $160 million in yearly sales and $16 million in profit—and continues growing at 25 percent annually (Burger 200–01).

CONSIDER THIS...

Summaries of recent research and insight into current topics—today's scholarship at a glance

---

Guidelines for Persuasion

Later chapters offer specific guidelines for various persuasive documents. But beyond attending to specific requirements of a particular document, remember this principle:

No matter how brilliant, any argument rejected by its audience is a failed argument.

If readers find cause to dislike you or conclude that your argument has no meaning for them personally, they usually reject *anything* you say. Connecting with an audience means being able to see thi————————————wing guidelines can help you make that ————————

Analyze the Situation

• **Assess the political climate.** Who————————ll

GUIDELINES

Direct, practical advice and accessible strategies, summarizing chapter content in an authoritative, handy format

W9-BNU-437

Why Do You Need this New Edition?

If you're wondering why you should buy this new edition of *Technical Communication,* here are 10 good reasons!

1. A new introductory chapter focuses for the first time on technical communicators as **information managers,** using new media technologies to create and distribute information in multiple formats for multiple audiences. This realistic portrayal of today's workplace will get you ready for the career you choose.

2. **Case Studies**—a new feature in this edition—appear throughout the book, putting you into authentic situations and helping you understand how information managers make decisions in critical situations.

3. New and expanded **Checklists**—the most popular feature in this book—offer clear summaries of essential topics like proofreading, style, using email, writing resumes and application letters, and creating proposals and analytical reports.

4. New and expanded **Guidelines** provide step-by-step strategies for running a meeting, researching online, evaluating Web sources, interpreting information, using questionnaires and interviews, summarizing information, delivering bad news, and many, many more.

5. A brand new section on **conducting meetings** (Ch. 6) reflects a role often played by technical communicators.

6. A new, dedicated chapter on **employment correspondence** (Ch. 18) focuses on what you really need to know to find—and win—your first job.

7. A new section on **corporate blogs and wikis** (Ch. 16) reflects the realities of today's workplace communication and information delivery, including coverage of corporate internal blogs and policies, and information on RSS feeds and formatting.

8. The **Quick Guides**—to **Documentation** and to **Grammar, Usage, and Mechanics**— offer brief, accessible reference guides for two essential (and often troublesome) areas.

9. The expanded **Casebook: The Writing Process Illustrated** now provides new templates and sample documents, including personal statements for law and medical school, as well as more on the rhetorical considerations you need to keep in mind when composing documents.

10. And now—use *Technical Communication* alongside Pearson's unique **MyTechComm-Lab** and find a world of resources developed specifically for you!

ELEVENTH EDITION

Technical Communication

John M. Lannon

University of Massachusetts, Dartmouth

PEARSON

Longman

New York   San Francisco   Boston
London   Toronto   Sydney   Tokyo   Singapore   Madrid
Mexico City   Munich   Paris   Cape Town   Hong Kong   Montreal

Senior Sponsoring Editor: Virginia L. Blanford
Senior Development Editor: Michael Greer
Marketing Manager: Thomas DeMarco
Senior Supplements Editor: Donna Campion
Assistant Editor: Rebecca Gilpin
Production Manager: Ellen MacElree
Project Coordination, Text Design, and Electronic Page Makeup: Nesbitt Graphics, Inc.
Cover Designer/Manager: John Callahan
Cover and Part Opener Photo: David Mark Soulsby/Arcaid/Corbis
Photo Researcher: Rona Tuccillo
Manufacturing Buyer: Roy Pickering
Printer and Binder: Quebecor World/Taunton
Cover: Phoenix Color Corp./Hagerstown

For permission to use copyrighted material, grateful acknowledgment is made to the copyright holders on pp. 737–53, which are hereby made part of this copyright page.

Between the time Web site information is gathered and published, some sites may have closed. Also, the transcription of URLs can result in typographical errors. The publisher would appreciate notification where these occur so that they may be corrected in subsequent editions.

Many of the designations used by manufacturers and sellers to distinguish their products are claimed as trademarks. Where these designations appear in this book, and Pearson Education was aware of a trademark claim, the designations have been printed in initial caps.

Library of Congress Cataloging-in-Publication Data

Lannon, John M.
   Technical communication / John M. Lannon. -- Eleventh ed.
     p. cm.
   Includes bibliographical references and index.
   ISBN 13: 978-0-205-55957-2
   ISBN 10:   0-205-55957-3
  1. Technical writing. 2. Communication of technical information. I. Title.
   T11.L24 2007
   808'.0666--dc22

                2008037562

Please visit us at http://www.ablongman.com/lannon

ISBN 13: 978-0-205-55957-2
ISBN 10:   0-205-55957-3

2 3 4 5 6 7 8 9 10—WCT—10 09 08

Brief Contents

Detailed Contents   *vii*
List of Sample Documents   *xix*
Preface   *xxi*

CHAPTER 1   Introduction to Technical Communication 1

PART I   **Communicating in the Workplace**   **13**

CHAPTER 2   Preparing an Effective Technical Document   14
CHAPTER 3   Delivering Usable Information   25
CHAPTER 4   Being Persuasive   48
CHAPTER 5   Weighing the Ethical Issues   75
CHAPTER 6   Working in Teams   96

PART II   **The Research Process**   **113**

CHAPTER 7   Thinking Critically about the Research Process   114
CHAPTER 8   Exploring Electronic and Hard Copy Sources   122
CHAPTER 9   Exploring Primary Sources   137
CHAPTER 10   Evaluating and Interpreting Information   149
CHAPTER 11   Summarizing and Abstracting Information   173

PART III   **Structure, Style, Graphics and Page Design**   **193**

CHAPTER 12   Organizing for Users   194
CHAPTER 13   Editing for Readable Style   215
CHAPTER 14   Designing Visual Information   252
CHAPTER 15   Designing Pages and Documents   297

P A R T I V   **Specific Documents and Applications   325**

CHAPTER 16   Memo Reports and Electronic Correspondence   326

CHAPTER 17   Workplace Letters   359

CHAPTER 18   Employment Correspondence   388

CHAPTER 19   Web Pages   425

CHAPTER 20   Technical Definitions   439

CHAPTER 21   Technical Descriptions and Specifications   462

CHAPTER 22   Instructions and Procedures   490

CHAPTER 23   Proposals   522

CHAPTER 24   Formal Analytical Reports   560

CHAPTER 25   Front Matter and End Matter in Long Documents   597

CHAPTER 26   Oral Presentations   608

P A R T V   **Resources for Writers   633**

A Quick Guide to Documentation   634

A Quick Guide to Grammar, Usage, and Mechanics   670

A Casebook: The Writing Process Illustrated   698

Is It Plagiarism? *Test Yourself on In-Text (Parenthetical) References*   735

Works Cited   737

Index   755

Detailed Contents

List of Sample Documents   *xix*

Preface   xxi

CHAPTER 1

Introduction to Technical Communication   1

Technical Communication Is User Centered   *2*

Technical Communication Is Accessible   *2*

Technical Communication Comes in All Shapes and Sizes   *5*

Technical Communicators Rely on Many Skills   *7*

Technical Communication Is Part of Most Careers   *7*

Communication Has Both an Electronic and a Human Side   *8*

Communication Reaches a Diverse Audience   *9*

Consider This Twenty-First Century Jobs Require Portable Skills   *10*

On the Job . . . Types of Writing   *11*

EXERCISES   *12*

COLLABORATIVE PROJECT   *12*

SERVICE-LEARNING PROJECT   *12*

PART I

Communicating in the Workplace   13

CHAPTER 2

Preparing an Effective Technical Document   14

Complete the Key Tasks   *15*

Rely on Creative and Critical Thinking   *18*

Make Proofreading Your Final Step   *21*

Guidelines for Proofreading   *21*

Checklist: Proofreading   *22*

Consider This Workplace Settings Are Increasingly "Virtual"   *23*

EXERCISES   *23*

COLLABORATIVE PROJECT   *24*

SERVICE-LEARNING PROJECT   *24*

CHAPTER 3

Delivering Usable Information   25

Know What Different Audiences Expect   *26*

Assess the Audience's Information Needs   *27*

Identify Levels of Technicality   *28*

The Highly Technical Document   28

The Semitechnical Document   29

The Nontechnical Document   30

Primary and Secondary Audiences   31

Web-Based Documents for Multiple Audiences   33

Develop an Audience and Use Profile   *34*

Audience Characteristics   34

Purpose of the Document   34

Intended Use of the Document   34

Audience's Technical Background   36

Audience's Cultural Background   36

Performance Objectives for This Document   36

Setting   37

Possible Hazards or Sources of Error   38

Appropriate Details and Page Design   38

Due Date and Timing   38

Create a Design Plan for the Document   38

Write, Test, and Revise Your Document   42

Checklist: Usability   43

Consider This Communication Failure Can Have Drastic Consequences   44

On the Job . . . Audiences   45

EXERCISES   46

COLLABORATIVE PROJECT   46

SERVICE-LEARNING PROJECT   47

CHAPTER 4

Being Persuasive   48

Identify Your Specific Goal   50

Try to Predict Audience Reaction   51

Expect Audience Resistance   51

Know How to Connect with the Audience   53

Allow for Give-and-Take   55

Ask for a Specific Response   56

Never Ask for Too Much   56

Recognize All Constraints   56

Organizational Constraints   56

Legal Constraints   57

Ethical Constraints   58

Time Constraints   58

Social and Psychological Constraints   58

Consider This People Often React Emotionally to Persuasive Appeals   59

Support Your Claims Convincingly   60

Offer Convincing Evidence   61

Appeal to Common Goals and Values   62

Consider the Cultural Context   63

Guidelines for Persuasion   65

Shaping Your Argument   67

Checklist: Persuasion   71

On the Job . . . Persuasive Challenges   72

EXERCISES   73

COLLABORATIVE PROJECT   74

SERVICE-LEARNING PROJECT   74

CHAPTER 5

Weighing the Ethical Issues   75

Recognize Unethical Communication in the Workplace   76

Know the Major Causes of Unethical Communication   77

Yielding to Social Pressure   77

Mistaking Groupthink for Teamwork   78

Understand the Potential for Communication Abuse   79

Suppressing Knowledge the Public Needs   79

Hiding Conflicts of Interest   80

Exaggerating Claims about Technology   80

Falsifying or Fabricating Data   80

Using Visual Images That Conceal the Truth   80

Stealing or Divulging Proprietary Information   80

Misusing Electronic Information   81

Withholding Information People Need for Their Jobs   81

Exploiting Cultural Differences   81

Rely on Critical Thinking for Ethical Decisions   82

Reasonable Criteria for Ethical Judgment   82

Ethical Dilemmas   83

Anticipate Some Hard Choices   84

Never Depend Only on Legal Guidelines   85

Learn to Recognize Plagiarism   87

Consider This Ethical Standards Are Good for Business   88

Decide Where and How to Draw the Line   88

Checklist: Ethical Communication   90

Guidelines for Ethical Communication   92

On the Job . . . Ethical Issues   *93*

EXERCISES   *94*

COLLABORATIVE PROJECT   *94*

SERVICE-LEARNING PROJECT   *95*

CHAPTER 6

Working in Teams   96

Teamwork and Project Management   *97*

Guidelines for Managing a Collaborative
Project   *97*

Conducting Meetings   *98*

Guidelines for Running a Meeting   *101*

Sources of Conflict in Collaborative
Groups   *101*

Interpersonal Differences   101

Gender and Cultural Differences   102

Managing Group Conflict   *103*

Overcoming Differences by Active
Listening   *103*

Guidelines for Active Listening   *104*

Thinking Creatively   *105*

Brainstorming   105

Brainwriting   106

Mind-Mapping   106

Storyboarding   106

Reviewing and Editing Others' Work   *107*

Guidelines for Peer Reviewing and Editing   *107*

Face-to-Face Versus Electronically Mediated
Collaboration   *108*

Ethical Abuses in Workplace Collaboration   *109*

Intimidating One's Peers   109

Claiming Credit for Others' Work   109

Hoarding Information   109

On the Job . . . Collaborative Writing   *110*

EXERCISES   *111*

COLLABORATIVE PROJECTS   *111*

SERVICE-LEARNING PROJECT   *111*

PART II

The Research Process   113

CHAPTER 7

Thinking Critically about the Research Process   114

Asking the Right Questions   *115*

Exploring a Balance of Views   *117*

Achieving Adequate Depth in Your Search   *117*

Evaluating Your Findings   *119*

Interpreting Your Findings   *119*

Consider This Expert Opinion Is Not Always
Reliable   *119*

Guidelines for Evaluating Expert Opinion   *120*

EXERCISE   *121*

CHAPTER 8

Exploring Electronic and Hard Copy Sources   122

Internet Sources   *123*

Online News and Magazines   123

Government Sites   124

*Community Discussion Groups and
Bulletin Boards   124*

Blogs and Wikis   124

Email Lists   125

Library Chatrooms   125

Library Databases Searchable via the Internet   125

Other Types of Web Sites   126

Guidelines for Researching on the Internet   *126*

Intranets and Extranets   *127*

Other Electronic Sources   *127*

Compact Discs   127

Online Retrieval Services   127

Hard Copy Sources   *128*

Reference Works   128

Card Catalog   129

Guides to Literature   129

Indexes   129

Abstracts   131

Access Tools for U.S. Government Publications   131

Microforms   132

Consider This Frequently Asked Questions about Copyright of Hard Copy Information   132

Consider This Information in Electronic Form Is Copyright Protected   134

On the Job . . . The Role of Research   135

EXERCISE   136

COLLABORATIVE PROJECTS   136

SERVICE-LEARNING PROJECT   136

CHAPTER 9

Exploring Primary Sources   137

Informative Interviews   138

Guidelines for Informative Interviews   138

Surveys and Questionnaires   140

Defining the Survey's Purpose and Target Population   140

Identifying the Sample Group   140

Defining the Survey Method   140

Guidelines for Developing a Questionnaire   142

A Sample Questionnaire   143

Inquiry Letters, Phone Calls, and Email Inquiries   143

Public Records and Organizational Publications   146

Personal Observation and Experiments   146

EXERCISES   147

COLLABORATIVE PROJECT   147

SERVICE-LEARNING PROJECT   147

CHAPTER 10

Evaluating and Interpreting Information   149

Evaluate the Sources   150

Guidelines for Evaluating Sources on the Web   153

Evaluate the Evidence   154

Interpret Your Findings   155

Identify Your Level of Certainty   156

Examine the Underlying Assumptions   156

Be Alert for Personal Bias   157

Consider Other Possible Interpretations   157

Consider This Standards of Proof Vary for Different Audiences and Cultural Settings   158

Avoid Errors in Reasoning   158

Faulty Generalization   159

Faulty Causal Reasoning   159

Faulty Statistical Reasoning   162

Acknowledge the Limits of Research   166

Obstacles to Validity and Reliability   166

Flaws in Research Studies   166

Measurement Errors   167

Deceptive Reporting   167

Guidelines for Evaluating and Interpreting Information   168

Checklist: The Research Process   170

EXERCISES   171

COLLABORATIVE PROJECTS   172

SERVICE-LEARNING PROJECT   172

CHAPTER 11

Summarizing and Abstracting Information   173

Purpose of Summaries   174

What Users Expect from a Summary   175

Guidelines for Summarizing Information   175

A Situation Requiring a Summary   176

Forms of Summarized Information   182

Closing Summary   183

Informative Abstract ("Summary")   183

Descriptive Abstract ("Abstract")   184

Executive Abstract   184

Ethical Considerations in Summarizing Information   186

Checklist: Usability of Summaries   187

On the Job . . . The Importance of Summaries   188

EXERCISES   *189*

COLLABORATIVE PROJECT   *189*

SERVICE-LEARNING PROJECT   *189*

PART III

Structure, Style, Graphics, and Page Design   193

CHAPTER 12

Organizing for Users   *194*

Partitioning and Classifying   *195*

Outlining   *196*

A Document's Basic Shape   *196*

The Formal Outline   *196*

Organizing for Cross-Cultural Audiences   *200*

The Report Design Worksheet   *200*

Storyboarding   *200*

Paragraphing   *204*

The Support Paragraph   *204*

The Topic Sentence   *205*

Paragraph Unity   *205*

Paragraph Coherence   *206*

Paragraph Length   *207*

Sequencing   *207*

Spatial Sequence   *207*

Chronological Sequence   *208*

Effect-to-Cause Sequence   *208*

Cause-to-Effect Sequence   *209*

Emphatic Sequence   *209*

Problem-Causes-Solution Sequence   *209*

Comparison-Contrast Sequence   *210*

Chunking   *211*

Creating an Overview   *212*

EXERCISES   *213*

COLLABORATIVE PROJECT   *213*

CHAPTER 13

Editing for Readable Style   215

Editing for Clarity   *217*

Avoid Ambiguous Pronoun References   *217*

Avoid Ambiguous Modifiers   *217*

Unstack Modifying Nouns   *218*

Arrange Word Order for Coherence and Emphasis   *218*

Use Active Voice Whenever Possible   *219*

Use Passive Voice Selectively   *221*

Avoid Overstuffed Sentences   *222*

Editing for Conciseness   *223*

Avoid Wordy Phrases   *223*

Eliminate Redundancy   *223*

Avoid Needless Repetition   *223*

Avoid There Sentence Openers   *224*

Avoid Some It Sentence Openers   *224*

Delete Needless Prefaces   *224*

Avoid Weak Verbs   *225*

Avoid Excessive Prepositions   *226*

Fight Noun Addiction   *226*

Make Negatives Positive   *227*

Clean Out Clutter Words   *228*

Delete Needless Qualifiers   *228*

Editing for Fluency   *229*

Combine Related Ideas   *229*

Vary Sentence Construction and Length   *231*

Use Short Sentences for Special Emphasis   *232*

Finding the Exact Words   *232*

Prefer Simple and Familiar Wording   *232*

Avoid Useless Jargon   *233*

Use Acronyms Selectively   *234*

Avoid Triteness   *234*

Avoid Misleading Euphemisms   *235*

Avoid Overstatement   *235*

Avoid Imprecise Wording   *236*

Be Specific and Concrete   *238*

Adjusting Your Tone   *238*

Guidelines for Deciding about Tone   *240*

Consider Using an Occasional Contraction   *240*

Address Readers Directly 240

Use I *and* We *When Appropriate* 241

Prefer the Active Voice 241

Emphasize the Positive 242

Avoid an Overly Informal Tone 242

Avoid Personal Bias 242

Avoid Sexist Usage 243

Guidelines for Nonsexist Usage 243

Avoid Offensive Usage of All Types 244

Guidelines for Inoffensive Usage 244

Considering the Cultural Context 245

**Legal and Ethical Implications
of Word Choice** 246

Using Automated Editing Tools Effectively 247

Checklist: Style 248

On the Job . . . Revising a Document 249

EXERCISES 250

COLLABORATIVE PROJECT 251

CHAPTER 14

Designing Visual Information 252

Why Visuals Matter 253

When to Use Visuals 254

Types of Visuals to Consider 255

How to Select Visuals 257

Tables 257

Graphs 260

Bar Graphs 260

Guidelines for Displaying a Bar Graph 265

Line Graphs 266

Guidelines for Displaying a Line Graph 269

Charts 269

Pie Charts 269

Guidelines for Displaying a Pie Chart 271

Organization Charts 271

Flowcharts 271

Tree Charts 271

Gantt and PERT Charts 272

Pictograms 274

Graphic Illustrations 275

Diagrams 276

Maps 278

Photographs 279

Guidelines for Using Photographs 280

Software and Downloadable Images 282

Using the Software 282

Using Symbols and Icons 282

Using Web Sites for Graphics Support 283

Using Color 283

Guidelines for Incorporating Color 288

Ethical Considerations 288

Present the Real Picture 288

Present the Complete Picture 289

Don't Mistake Distortion for Emphasis 290

Cultural Considerations 290

Guidelines for Fitting Visuals with Text 292

Checklist: Usability of Visuals 293

EXERCISES 294

COLLABORATIVE PROJECTS 296

CHAPTER 15

Designing Pages and Documents 297

Page Design in Workplace Documents 298

**How Page Design Transforms
a Document** 298

**Design Skills Needed in Today's
Workplace** 301

Desktop Publishing 301

Electronic Publishing 301

*Using Style Sheets and Company Style
Guides* 301

Creating a Usable Design 302

Shaping the Page 303

Using Typography Effectively 308

Guidelines for Highlighting for Emphasis   *311*

Using Headings for Access and Orientation   312

Guidelines for Using Headings   *315*

Audience Considerations in Page Design   *317*

Designing On-Screen Documents   *318*

Web Pages   318

Guidelines for Designing a Web Page   *318*

Online Help   320

Adobe Acrobat™ and PDF Files   320

CDs and Other Media   320

Checklist: Usability of Page Design   *321*

On the Job . . . Designing Documents   *322*

EXERCISES   *323*

COLLABORATIVE PROJECT   *323*

PART IV

Specific Documents and Applications   325

CHAPTER 16

Memo Reports and Electronic Correspondence   326

Documents in Hard-Copy Versus Digital Format   *327*

Informational Versus Analytical Reports   *327*

Formal Versus Informal Reports   *327*

Purpose of Memo Reports   *328*

Elements of a Usable Memo   *328*

Interpersonal Considerations in Writing a Memo   *328*

Direct Versus Indirect Organizing Patterns   *330*

Informational Reports in Memo Form   *331*

Progress Reports   331

Periodic Activity Reports   335

Meeting Minutes   337

Analytical Reports in Memo Form   *338*

Feasibility Reports   338

Recommendation Reports   341

Justification Reports   341

Checklist: Usability of Memo Reports   *345*

Electronic Mail   *346*

Email Benefits   347

Email Copyright Issues   348

Email Privacy Issues   348

Guidelines for Using Electronic Mail   *349*

Guidelines for Choosing Email Versus Paper, Telephone, or Fax   *350*

Checklist: Email   *351*

Instant Messaging   *351*

Corporate Blogs and Wikis   *352*

Internal Blogs   352

External Blogs   353

RSS Feeds   353

Ethical, Legal, and Privacy Issues   353

EXERCISES   *356*

COLLABORATIVE PROJECTS   *357*

CHAPTER 17

Workplace Letters   359

Elements of Usable Letters   *360*

Standard Parts of Letters   360

Specialized Parts of Letters   364

Design Features   365

Interpersonal Considerations in Workplace Letters   *369*

Focus on Your Recipient's Interests: The "You" Perspective   369

Use Plain English   370

Focus on the Human Connection   370

Anticipate the Recipient's Reaction   371

Decide on a Direct or Indirect Organizing Pattern   371

Conveying Bad or Unwelcome News   *372*

Guidelines for Conveying Bad News   *372*

Inquiry Letters   *373*

Guidelines for Writing an Inquiry   *373*

Telephone and Email Inquiries   377

Claim Letters   *377*

   Routine Claims   *377*

Guidelines for Routine Claim Letters   *378*

   Arguable Claims   *379*

Guidelines for Arguable Claim Letters   *379*

Adjustment Letters   *381*

   Granting Adjustments   *382*

Guidelines for Granting Adjustments   *382*

   Refusing Adjustments   *383*

Guidelines for Refusing Adjustments   383

Checklist: Usability of Letters   *385*

EXERCISES   *386*

COLLABORATIVE PROJECT   *386*

CHAPTER 18

Employment Correspondence   388

Employment Outlook in the Twenty-First Century   *389*

Prospecting for Jobs   *389*

   Assess Your Skills and Aptitudes   *389*

   Research the Job Market   *390*

   Search Online   *390*

   Learn to Network   *392*

Preparing Your Résumé   *393*

   Typical Components of a Résumé   *393*

   Organizing Your Résumé   *397*

   Sample Résumés for Different Situations   *397*

Guidelines for Résumés   *401*

Preparing Your Job Application Letter   *402*

   The Solicited Application Letter   *402*

   The Unsolicited Application Letter   *406*

Guidelines for Job Application Letters   *408*

Consider This How Applicants Are Screened for Personal Qualities   *409*

Submitting Electronic Résumés   *409*

   How Scanning Works   *410*

Guidelines for Preparing a Scannable Résumé   *410*

   Types of Electronic Résumés   *411*

   Protecting Privacy and Security When You Post a Résumé Online   *414*

   Protecting Your Good Name Online   *414*

Support for the Application   *415*

   Your Dossier   *415*

   Your Professional Portfolio   *415*

Guidelines for Preparing a Portfolio   *416*

Employment Interviews   *416*

Guidelines for Surviving a Job Interview   *418*

   The Follow-Up Letter   *420*

   Letters of Acceptance or Refusal   *421*

Checklist: Résumés   *421*

Checklist: Job Application Letters   *422*

EXERCISES   *423*

COLLABORATIVE PROJECTS   *423*

CHAPTER 19

Web Pages   425

HTML: Hypertext Markup Language   *426*

Elements of a Usable Web Site   *427*

Guidelines for Creating a Web Site   *432*

Privacy Issues in Online Communication   *435*

Checklist: Usability of Web Sites   *436*

INDIVIDUAL OR COLLABORATIVE PROJECTS   *438*

SERVICE-LEARNING PROJECT   *438*

CHAPTER 20

Technical Definitions   439

Purpose of Technical Definitions   *440*

Levels of Detail in a Definition   *441*

   Parenthetical Definition   *441*

   Sentence Definition   *442*

   Expanded Definition   *442*

Expansion Methods   *444*

   Etymology   444

   History and Background   445

   Negation   445

   Operating Principle   445

   Analysis of Parts   446

   Visuals   447

   Comparison and Contrast   447

   Required Materials or Conditions   448

   Example   448

Situations Requiring Definitions   *449*

Placement of Definitions   *454*

Guidelines for Defining Clearly and Precisely   *456*

Checklist: Usability of Definitions   *457*

EXERCISES   *458*

COLLABORATIVE PROJECTS   *460*

SERVICE-LEARNING PROJECT   *460*

CHAPTER 21

**Technical Descriptions and
Specifications**   *462*

Purposes and Types of Technical Description   *463*

Objectivity in Technical Description   *463*

Elements of a Usable Description   *466*

   Clear and Limiting Title   466

   Appropriate Level of Detail and Technicality   466

   Visuals   467

   Clearest Descriptive Sequence   467

An Outline and Model for Product Description   *469*

   Introduction: General Description   470

   Description and Function of Parts   471

   Summary and Operating Description   472

A Situation Requiring Product Description   *472*

An Outline for Process Description   *475*

A Situation Requiring Process Description   *476*

Specifications   *479*

Technical Marketing Literature   *482*

Checklist: Usability of Technical Descriptions   *485*

EXERCISES   *486*

COLLABORATIVE PROJECTS   *486*

CHAPTER 22

Instructions and Procedures   490

Purpose of Instructional Documents   *491*

Formats for Instructional Documents   *491*

Faulty Instructions and Legal Liability   *492*

Elements of Usable Instructions   *495*

   Clear and Limiting Title   495

   Informed Content   495

   Visuals   496

   *Appropriate Level of Detail and
    Technicality   496*

Guidelines for Providing Appropriate Detail   *501*

   Logically Ordered Steps   502

   Notes and Hazard Notices   502

   Readability   503

   Effective Design   505

Guidelines for Designing Instructions   *505*

An Outline for Instructions   *507*

   Introduction   507

   Body: Required Steps   508

   Conclusion   508

A Situation Requiring Instructions   *508*

Online Documentation   *510*

Testing the Usability of Your Document   *512*

   How Usability Testing Is Done   512

   Usability Testing in the Classroom   514

Procedures   *514*

Checklist: Usability of Instructions   *517*

EXERCISES   *518*

COLLABORATIVE PROJECTS   *520*

SERVICE-LEARNING PROJECT   *520*

CHAPTER 23

Proposals   522

How Proposals and Reports Differ in Purpose   *523*

The Proposal Audience   *523*

The Proposal Process   *524*

Proposal Types   *526*

Planning Proposal   *528*

Research Proposal   *530*

Sales Proposal   *532*

Elements of a Persuasive Proposal   *534*

A Forecasting Title   *534*

Clear Understanding of the Audience's Needs   *534*

A Clear Focus on Benefits   *535*

Honest and Supportable Claims   *535*

Appropriate Detail   *536*

Readability   *537*

Convincing Language   *537*

Visuals   *537*

Accessible Page Design   *538*

Supplements Tailored for a Diverse Audience   *538*

Proper Citation of Sources and Contributors   *538*

An Outline and Model for Proposals   *539*

Introduction   *539*

Body   *541*

Conclusion   *543*

A Situation Requiring a Proposal   *544*

Checklist: Usability of Proposals   *555*

EXERCISES   *557*

SERVICE-LEARNING PROJECT   *557*

CHAPTER 24

Formal Analytical Reports   560

Purpose of Analysis   *561*

Typical Analytical Problems   *562*

Causal Analysis: "Why Does X Happen?"   *562*

Comparative Analysis: "Is X or Y Better for Our Purpose?"   *562*

Feasibility Analysis: "Is This a Good Idea?"   *563*

Combining Types of Analysis   *564*

Elements of a Usable Analysis   *564*

Clearly Identified Problem or Goal   *564*

Adequate but Not Excessive Data   *564*

Accurate and Balanced Data   *565*

Fully Interpreted Data   *567*

Subordination of Personal Bias   *567*

Appropriate Visuals   *567*

Valid Conclusions and Recommendations   *567*

Self-Assessment   *569*

An Outline and Model for Analytical Reports   *571*

Introduction   *572*

Body   *573*

Conclusion   *581*

Supplements   *583*

A Situation Requiring an Analytical Report   *583*

Guidelines for Reasoning through an Analytical Problem   *592*

Checklist: Usability of Analytical Reports   *594*

EXERCISE   *595*

COLLABORATIVE PROJECTS   *596*

CHAPTER 25

Front Matter and End Matter in Long Documents   597

Cover   *598*

Title Page   *598*

Letter of Transmittal   *598*

Table of Contents   *601*

List of Tables and Figures   *603*

Abstract or Executive Summary   *603*

Glossary   *604*

Appendices   *605*

Documentation   *606*

EXERCISES   *607*

CHAPTER 26

Oral Presentations *608*

Advantages and Drawbacks of Oral
  Reports *609*

Avoiding Presentation Pitfalls *609*

Planning Your Presentation *610*

  Analyze Your Listeners *610*

  Work from an Explicit Purpose
    Statement *610*

  Analyze Your Speaking Situation *611*

  Select a Delivery Method *611*

Preparing Your Presentation *612*

  Research Your Topic *612*

  Aim for Simplicity and Conciseness *613*

  Anticipate Audience Questions *613*

  Outline Your Presentation *613*

  Plan Your Visuals *615*

  Prepare Your Visuals *617*

Guidelines for Readable Visuals *617*

Guidelines for Understandable Visuals *618*

  Consider the Available Technology *618*

  Use PowerPoint or Other Software
    Wisely *618*

Guidelines for Using Presentation
  Software *623*

  Rehearse Your Delivery *624*

Delivering Your Presentation *624*

  Cultivate the Human Landscape *625*

  Keep Your Listeners Oriented *625*

  Manage Your Visuals *626*

Guidelines for Presenting Visuals *627*

  Manage Your Presentation Style *627*

  Manage Your Speaking Situation *628*

Guidelines for Managing Listener
  Questions *628*

Consider This Cross-Cultural Audiences May Have
  Specific Expectations *629*

EXERCISES *630*

PART V

Resources for Writers *633*

A Quick Guide to Documentation *634*

  Taking Notes *635*

  Guidelines for Recording Research Findings *635*

  Quoting the Work of Others *636*

  Guidelines for Quoting the Work of Others *636*

  Paraphrasing the Work of Others *638*

  Guidelines for Paraphrasing *638*

  What You Should Document *638*

  How You Should Document *639*

  MLA Documentation Style *640*

    MLA Parenthetical References *640*

    MLA Works Cited Entries *641*

    MLA Sample Works Cited Pages *652*

  APA Documentation Style *653*

    APA Parenthetical References *653*

    APA Reference List Entries *657*

    APA Sample Reference List *664*

  CSE and Other Numbered Documentation
    Styles *665*

    CSE Numbered Citations *667*

    References *667*

    CSE Reference List Entries *667*

A Quick Guide to Grammar, Usage, and
Mechanics *670*

  Common Sentence Errors *671*

    Sentence Fragment *671*

    Acceptable Fragments *672*

    Comma Splice *673*

    Run-On Sentence *673*

    Faulty Agreement—Subject and Verb *674*

    Faulty Agreement—Pronoun and Referent *675*

    Faulty Coordination *675*

Faulty Subordination   676

Faulty Pronoun Case   677

Faulty Modification   678

Faulty Parallelism   679

Sentence Shifts   680

Effective Punctuation   *681*

End Punctuation   681

Semicolon   682

Colon   683

Comma   683

Apostrophe   687

Quotation Marks   688

Ellipses   689

Italics   690

Parentheses   690

Brackets   690

Dashes   691

Avoiding Ambiguous Punctuation   691

Lists   *691*

Embedded Lists   691

Vertical Lists   692

Transitions Within and Between Paragraphs   *693*

Mechanics   *694*

Abbreviations   694

Hyphenation   695

Capitalization   695

Use of Numbers   696

Spelling   697

A Casebook: The Writing Process Illustrated   698

Critical Thinking in the Writing Process   *699*

Case 1: An Everyday Writing Situation: The Evolution of a Short Report   *700*

Working with the Information   701

Planning the Document   702

Drafting the Document   704

Revising the Document   705

Case 2: Preparing a Personal Statement: For Internship, Medical School, or Law School Applications   *709*

Audience Expectations in a Personal Statement   709

Discussion of Mike's First Draft   710

Discussion of Mike's Final Draft   713

Two Additional Examples for Analysis and Discussion   713

Case 3: Documents for the Course Project: A Sequence Culminating in the Final Report   *716*

The Project Documents   718

The Proposal Stage   718

The Progress Report Stage   718

The Final Report Stage   721

Is It Plagiarism? *Test Yourself on In-Text (Parenthetical) References*   **735**

Works Cited   737

Index   755

List of Sample Documents

Fig. 1.1   An Accessible Technical
            Document   *3*

Figs.   Technical, Semitechnical, and
  3.3–3.5   Nontechnical Versions of an
            Emergency Treatment
            Report   *29, 30, 31*

Fig. 3.9   Design Plan for a Lawnmower
            Manual   *39*

Fig. 4.4   Persuasive Letter: Supporting a
            Claim with Good Reasons   *68*

Fig. 9.1   Text of an Informative
            Interview   *141*

Fig. 9.2   Questionnaire Cover Letter   *142*

Fig. 9.3   Sample Questionnaire   *145*

Figs.   Article to Be Summarized,
  11.1–11.3 Summary, More Compressed
            Summary   *177, 181, 182*

Fig. 11.5   Executive Abstract   *185*

Fig. 12.4   One Module from a
            Storyboard   *203*

Fig. 14.39 Web Page that Uses Color
            Effectively   *286*

Fig. 15.1   Ineffective Page Design   *299*

Fig. 15.2   Effective Page Design   *300*

Fig. 16.2   On-the-Job Progress Report   *332*

Fig. 16.3   Term Project Progress Report   *334*

Fig. 16.4   Periodic Activity Report   *336*

Fig. 16.5   Sample Set of Meeting
            Minutes   *337*

Fig. 16.6   Feasibility Analysis   *339*

Fig. 16.7   Recommendation Memo   *342*

Fig. 16.8   Justification Report   *344*

Fig. 16.9   Elements of a Typical Email
            Message   *347*

Fig. 17.1   Standard Design for a Workplace
            Letter   *361*

Fig. 17.5   Unsolicited Inquiry   *374*

Fig. 17.6   Request for an Informative
            Interview   *376*

Fig. 17.7   Routine Claim Letter   *378*

Fig. 17.8   Arguable Claim Letter   *380*

Fig. 17.9   Letter Granting Adjustment   *382*

Fig. 17.10 Letter Refusing Adjustment   *384*

Fig. 18.2   Request for Employment
            Reference   *396*

Fig. 18.3   Reverse Chronological
            Résumé   *399*

Fig. 18.4   Functional Résumé   *400*

Fig. 18.5   Résumé with Combined
            Organization   *401*

Fig. 18.6   Solicited Job Application
            Letter   *404*

Fig. 18.7   Solicited Internship Application
            Letter   *405*

Fig. 18.8   Unsolicited Job Application
            Letter   *407*

Fig. 18.9   Computer-Scannable Résumé   *412*

Fig. 18.10 Searchable (Hyperlinked)
            Résumé   *413*

Fig. 19.3   Award-Winning Web Page   *430*

Fig. 19.4   A Simplified Web-Page
            Design   *431*

Fig. 20.1   Expanded Definition   *443*

Fig. 20.3   Expanded Definition for Semitechnical Readers   *449*

Fig. 20.4   Expanded Definition for Nontechnical Readers   *452*

Fig. 20.5   Hyperlinked Glossary Page   *454*

Fig. 20.6   Hyperlinked Expanded Definition   *455*

Fig. 20.7   Expanded Definition in a Technical Brochure   *459*

Fig. 20.8   Expanded Definition in FAQ List Format   *460*

Fig. 20.9   Definition for Laypersons in a Two-Column Brochure   *461*

Fig. 21.1   Product Description   *464*

Fig. 21.2   Process Description   *465*

Fig. 21.3   Process Description in Visual Format   *468*

Fig. 21.4   Mechanism Description for Nontechnical Readers   *473*

Fig. 21.5   Process Description for Nontechnical Readers   *476*

Fig. 21.6   Specifications for Building Project   *480*

Fig. 21.9   Technical Marketing Brochure   *483*

Fig. 21.10   Technical Marketing Web Page   *484*

Fig. 21.11   Technical Marketing Fact Sheet   *487*

Fig. 22.1   Fold-out Instructional Brochure   *492*

Fig. 22.2   Opening Page from a Manual   *493*

Fig. 22.3   Brief Reference Card   *493*

Fig. 22.4   Web-Based Instructions   *494*

Fig. 22.6   Instructions with Adequate Detail for Laypersons   *500*

Fig. 22.8   Instructions for Nontechnical Readers   *509*

Fig. 22.10   Basic Usability Survey   *513*

Fig. 22.11   Manual with Standard Operating Procedures   *515*

Fig. 22.12   Safety Procedures   *516*

Fig. 22.13   Instructions for Testing Grill   *519*

Fig. 22.14   Procedure for Caring for Contact Lenses   *521*

Fig. 23.1   Request for Proposal   *526*

Fig. 23.2   Planning Proposal   *529*

Fig. 23.3   Research Proposal   *531*

Fig. 23.4   Sales Proposal   *533*

Fig. 23.5   Funding Proposal   *546*

Fig. 24.1   Summary Description: Feasibility Study   *566*

Fig. 24.4   Formal Analytical Report   *585*

Figs. 25.1–2   Title Page, Letter of Transmittal: Formal Report   *599, 600*

Figs. 25.3–4   Table of Contents, List of Tables and Figures: Formal Report   *602, 603*

Fig. 25.5   Informative Abstract: Formal Report   *604*

Fig. 25.6   Glossary: Formal Report   *605*

The Casebook (page 698) includes a series of drafts, revised drafts, and final versions of memos, personal statements, proposals, and reports.

Preface

Whether handwritten, electronically mediated, or face-to-face, workplace communication is more than a value-neutral exercise in "information transfer"; it is a complex social transaction. Every rhetorical situation—from submitting a report or proposal to applying for a job to giving an oral presentation—has its own specific interpersonal, ethical, legal, and cultural demands. Moreover, today's professional is not only a fluent communicator, but also a discriminating consumer of information, skilled in the methods of inquiry, retrieval, evaluation, and interpretation essential to informed decision making.

Designed in response to these issues, *Technical Communication*, Eleventh Edition, addresses a wide range of interests for classes in which students from a variety of majors are enrolled. The text explains, illustrates, and applies rhetorical principles to an array of assignments, from brief memos and summaries to formal reports and proposals. To help students develop awareness of audience and accountability, exercises incorporate the problem-solving demands typical in college and on the job. Self-contained chapters allow for various course plans and customized assignments.

What's New in This Edition?

Students will benefit from a variety of new content and features in this edition, including:

- An entirely rewritten first chapter that reflects the full range of technology available now to technical communicators, and their role as *information managers.*
- A new dedicated chapter (Chapter 18) on employment correspondence.
- An array of new and expanded Checklists and Guidelines, which many students feel are the most useful elements in the book.
- New content on avoiding plagiarism at the end of the book.
- Authentic workplace situations, identified now as Case Studies, that allow students to see real decision-making at work.
- Many new annotated sample documents throughout.

How This Book Is Organized

Technical Communication is designed to allow instructors maximum flexibility. Each chapter is self-contained, and each part focuses on a critical piece of the communication process. A brief overview and introduction is followed by five major sections:

- **Part I: Communicating in the Workplace** treats job-related communication as a problem-solving process. Students learn to think critically about the informative, persuasive, and ethical dimensions of their communications. They also learn how to adapt to the interpersonal challenges of collaborative work, and to the various needs and expectations of global audiences.
- **Part II: The Research Process** treats research as a deliberate inquiry process. Students learn to formulate significant research questions; to explore primary and secondary sources in hard copy and electronic form; to evaluate and interpret their findings; and to summarize for economy, accuracy, and emphasis.
- **Part III: Structure, Style, Graphics, and Page Design** offers strategies for organizing, composing, and designing messages that users can follow and understand. Students learn to control their material and develop a readable style. They also learn about the rhetorical implications of graphics and page design—specifically, how to enhance a document's access, appeal, and visual impact for audiences who need to locate, understand, and use the information successfully.
- **Part IV: Specific Documents and Applications** applies earlier concepts and strategies to the preparation of print and electronic documents and oral presentations. Various letters, memos, reports, and proposals offer a balance of examples from the workplace and from student writing. Each sample document has been chosen so that students can emulate it easily.
- **Part V: Resources for Writers** offers resource sections on critically important areas, and—bringing everything together—a Casebook on writing shows the process from beginning to end.

  - **A Quick Guide to Documentation** includes general guidance as well as specific style guides and citation models for MLA, APA, and CSE.
  - **A Quick Guide to Grammar, Usage, Style, and Mechanics** provides a handy resource for answering questions about the the basic building blocks of writing.
  - **A Casebook: The Writing Process Illustrated** follows three cases—step by step—from inception to final product.
  - **Is it Plagiarism?** *Test Yourself on In-Text (Parenthetical) References* offers a brief tutorial.

Hallmarks of the Eleventh Edition

Technical Communication, Eleventh Edition, retains—and enhances or expands—the features that have made it a best-selling text for technical communication over ten editions. These include the following:

- **A focus on applications beyond the classroom.** Clear ties to the workplace have always been a primary feature of this book, and this edition includes more examples from everyday business situations and more sample documents, including on-the-job and internship documents written by students, expanded sections on career paths in Chapter 1, and on design skills for today's workplace in Chapter 15. Discussion about actual jobs held by technical communicators and about communication in various fields is supplemented by day-in-the-life observations in the expanded *On the Job* features at the end of many chapters.

- **Emphasis on the humanistic aspects of technical communication.** Technical communication is ultimately a humanistic endeavor, with broad societal impact—not just a set of job-related transcription tasks. To underscore this fact, situations and sample documents in this edition address complex technical and societal issues such as global warming, population growth, trans fats, nanotechnology, and the implications of genomic research.

- **Updated technology coverage.** Content throughout the book—but particularly the chapters on Web design, document design, and electronic correspondence—reflects changes in technology and the increasing use of Web-based documents and platforms. Updated information on communicating electronically includes more on submitting online résumés, expanded guidelines for creating a Web site, and new information on corporate blogs and wikis. Fully integrated computing advice is supplemented by "Consider This" discussions of technology and interpersonal issues that are shaping workplace communication.

- **Coverage of international and global workplace issues.** This edition includes numerous samples, cases, and exercises premised on a multinational intercultural workplace, foregrounding issues of cultural and social style differences, all identified by marginal globe icons. Many end-of-chapter exercises call for research into cultural differences in communication practices.

- **A service-learning component.** Many chapters include projects specifically intended for use in service-learning courses. A focus on nonprofit organizations supplements the corporate culture examples.

- **Expanded chapter on collaboration.** With new coverage of cross-cultural collaboration and an emphasis on computer-mediated and Internet collaboration, collaborative projects are featured throughout the text as well as in Chapter 6, Working in Teams. A new section on meetings includes guidelines for running a meeting.

- **Strong coverage of information literacy.** Information-literate people are those who "know how knowledge is organized, how to find information, and how to use information in such a way that others can learn from them."[*] Critical thinking—the basis of information literacy—is covered intensively in Part II and integrated throughout the text.

- **Enhanced coverage of usability.** Documents are only effective if they can be used effectively. Usability receives consistent and explicit emphasis throughout

---

[*]*American Library Association Presidential Committee on Information Literacy: Final Report.* Chicago: ALA, 1989.

this edition of *Technical Communication*, highlighted by an illustrated introduction to planning and designing a usable document and a generic usability checklist in Chapter 3. Usability checklists for specific documents and components appear at the end of appropriate chapters in Parts III and IV, and Chapter 22 includes a section on testing a document's usability.

- **Expanded treatment of ethical and legal issues.** Woven into the fabric of the communication process are legal and ethical considerations in word choice, product descriptions, instructions, and other forms of hard copy and electronic communication. Chapter 5, Weighing the Ethical Issues, also includes new information on recognizing unethical communication, including the misuse of electronic information. Chapters on collaboration and design also include extended discussion of ethical communication in the workplace.

Specific Usability Features of the Eleventh Edition

"Usability" is not just a conceptual term. In writing this book, my intent has always been to create a usable document for readers—so that users of this book can "read to do." *Technical Communication*, Eleventh Edition, includes the following features designed to help students become effective practitioners:

- **Cases** throughout the text illustrate situations both in the workplace and in academia, and encourage students to make appropriate choices as they analyze their audience and purpose and then compose their document.
- **Sample documents** respond to each case and also model various kinds of technical writing, illustrating for students what *they* need to do. Captions, labels, and marginal comments identify key features in most sample documents.
- **Guidelines** help students prepare specific documents by applying and synthesizing the information in most chapters, including practical suggestions for real workplace situations.
- **Checklists** promote careful editing, revision, and collaboration. Students polish their writing by reviewing key criteria for the document and by referring to cross-referenced pages in the text for more information on each point.
- **Consider This** features provide interesting and topical applications of the important issues discussed in various chapters, such as collaboration, technology, and ethics.
- **Exercises, Collaborative Projects, and Service-Learning Projects** at the end of chapters help students apply what they've learned in individual, team, and community contexts.
- **On the Job** boxes at the end of many chapters offer authentic comments focusing on how the skills and strategies learned from this book are needed in real-world careers of all kinds.

- **Notes** clarify up-to-the-minute business and technological advances and underscore important advice.
- **Globe icons** point out important information about communicating across cultures—a critical piece of today's technical communication.
- **Weblink icons** lead students to a wealth of additional resources in both *MyTechCommLab*, available packaged with this book, and the Companion Website for *Technical Communication*, Eleventh Edition. See below for details!

Instructional Supplements

Accompanying *Technical Communication,* Eleventh Edition, is a wide array of supplements for both instructors and students, most of which are available packaged with this book at no additional cost.

- ***MyTechCommLab* with ebook.** Instructors who package *MyTechCommLab* with *Technical Communication,* Eleventh Edition, provide their students not only with the full text of *Technical Communication* as an ebook, but also with a comprehensive resource that offers the very best multimedia support for technical writing, and an array of book-specific assets, in one integrated, easy-to-use site. Gradable chapter review quizzes provide targeted study guides for classroom tests. Marginal Weblink icons in this book and in the ebook lead students to *MyTechCommLab* online resources, including a wealth of interactive sample documents, tutorials in writing and research, exercises for grammar, writing, and research, an online reference library, and Pearson's unique Research Navigator and Avoiding Plagiarism programs. *MyTechCommLab* is available packaged with this text at no additional cost, or for purchase at <www.mytechcommlab.com>.

  MyTechCommLab for *Technical Communication,* Eleventh Edition, also offers course management tools, project-based individual and collaborative exercises, additional forms and document templates, and many sample Web and print documents for student response and class discussion.
- An open-access **Companion Website,** offers an array of tools and resources for students and instructors, including chapter review quizzes, Weblinks, teaching tips and sample syllabi, PowerPoint presentations, interactive model documents, and much more. Go to <www.ablongman.com/lannon>.
- ***Resources for Technical Communication.*** This print supplement includes over forty sample documents in a variety of categories, as well as more than half a dozen case studies with exercises, and can be ordered at no additional cost packaged with this book.
- ***The Instructor's Resource Manual.*** Available both in print and online, the IRM for *Technical Communication,* Eleventh Edition, supports both traditional and Web-based instruction. The manual includes general suggestions and ideas for teaching technical communication, sample syllabi, transparency

masters, and an annotated bibliography of resources for teaching tech comm. In addition, the IRM includes detailed strategies for incorporating Web resources and technology with the book; an extensive set of annotated links to resources in grammar and writing, technical communication organizations, and online journals and publications; chapter overviews and teaching notes; additional exercises; and downloadable *PowerPoint* slides for classroom use.

Acknowledgments

Many of the refinements in this and earlier editions were inspired by generous and insightful suggestions from the following reviewers:

Mary Beth Bamforth
    Wake Technical Community College
Marian G. Barchilon
    Arizona State University East
Christiana Birchak
    University of Houston Downtown
Susan L. Booker
    Hampden-Sydney College
Gene Booth
    Albuquerque Technical Vocational Institute
Alma Bryant
    University of South Florida
Beth Camp
    Linn-Benton Community College
Joanna B. Chrzanowski
    Jefferson Community College
Jim Collier
    Virginia Tech
Daryl Davis
    Northern Michigan University
Charlie Dawkins
    Virginia Polytechnical Institute
    and State University
Pat Dorazio
    SUNY Institute of Technology
Julia Ferganchick-Neufang
    University of Arkansas
Madelyn Flammia
    University of Central Florida

Clint Gardner
    Salt Lake Community College
Mary Frances Gibbons
    Richland College
Lucy Graca
    Arapahoe Community College
Roger Graves
    DePaul University
Baotong Gu
    Eastern Washington University
Gil Haroian-Guerin
    Syracuse University
Susan Guzman-Trevino
    Temple College
Wade Harrell
    Howard University
Linda Harris
    University of Maryland, Baltimore
    County
Michael Joseph Hassett
    Brigham Young University
Cecilia Hawkins
    Texas A & M University
Robert A. Henderson
    Southeastern Oklahoma State University
TyAnna K. Herrington
    Georgia Institute of Technology
Mary Hocks
    Georgia State University

Robert Hogge
  Weber State University
Glenda A. Hudson
  California State University-Bakersfield
Gloria Jaffe
  University of Central Florida
Bruce L. Janoff
  University of Pittsburgh
Mitchell H. Jarosz
  Delta College
Jeanette Jeneault
  Syracuse University
Jack Jobst
  Michigan Technical University
Christopher Keller
  University of Hawaii at Hilo
Kathleen Kincade
  Stephen F. Austin State University
Susan E. Kincaid
  Lakeland Community College
JoAnn Kubala
  Southwest Texas State University
Karen Kuralt
  Louisiana Tech University
Thomas LaJeunesse
  University of Minnesota Duluth
Elizabeth A. Latshaw
  University of South Florida
Lindsay Lewan
  Arapahoe Community College
Sherry Little
  San Diego State University
Linda Loehr
  Northeastern University
Tom Long
  Thomas Nelson Community College
Lisa J. McClure
  Southern Illinois University-Carbondale
Michael McCord
  Minnesota State University, Moorhead
Devonee McDonald
  Kirkwood Community College

James L. McKenna
  San Jacinto College
Lisa McNair
  Georgia Institute of Technology
Troy Meyers
  California State University
Long Beach
  Mohsen Mirshafiei, California State
  University, Fullerton
Roxanne Munch
  Joliet Junior College
Thomas Murphy
  Mansfield University
Thomas A. Murray
  SUNY Institute of Technology
Shirley Nelson
  Chattanooga State Technical Community
  College
Gerald Nix
  San Juan College
Megan O'Neill
  Creighton University
Celia Patterson
  Pittsburgh State University
Don Pierstorff
  Orange Coast College
Peter Porosky
  Johns Hopkins University
Carol Clark Powell
  University of Texas at El Paso
Mark Rollins
  Ohio University, Athens
Beverly Sauer
  Carnegie Mellon University
Jan Schlegel
  Tri-State University
Lauren Sewell Ingraham
  University of Tennessee at Chattanooga
Carol M. H. Shehadeh
  Florida Institute of Technology
Sharla Shine
  Terra Community College

Rick Simmons
  Louisiana Technical University
Susan Simon
  City College of the City University
  of New York
Tom Stuckert
  University of Findlay
Terry Tannacito
  Frostburg State University
Anne Thomas
  San Jacinto College
Maxine Turner
  Georgia Institute of Technology
Mary Beth VanNess
  University of Toledo

Jeff Wedge
  Embry-Riddle University
Christian Weisser
  Florida Atlantic U. Honors College
Kristin Woolever
  Northeastern University
Carolyn Young
  University of Wyoming
Stephanee Zerkel
  Westark College
Beverly Zimmerman
  Brigham Young University
Don Zimmerman
  Colorado State University

For this edition, I am grateful for the comments of the following reviewers:

Cindy Allen
  James Madison University
Dana Anderson
  Indiana University
John Carlberg
  University of Wisconsin-Whitewater
Lynn Hublou
  South Dakota State University
Phillip Jacowitz
  Embry-Riddle Aeronautical University
Kevin LaGrandeur
  New York Institute of Technology
Rose Marie Mastricola
  Northeast Wisconsin Technical College

Dirk Remley
  Kent State University
Don Rhyne
  San Joaquin Valley College
Kenneth Risdon
  University of Minnesota
Elizabeth Robinson
  Texas A&M University
Judy Sneller
  South Dakota School of Mines & Technology
Clay Kinchen Smith
  Santa Fe Community College
Nicole Wilson
  Bowie State University

I thank my UMASS colleagues, graduate students, teaching assistants, and alumni for their invaluable and ongoing suggestions. As always, my students continue to provide feedback and inspiration.

This edition is the product of exceptional guidance and support from Ginny Blanford, Michael Greer, Joe Opiela, Ellen MacElree, Rebecca Gilpin, and Janet Nuciforo, and benefits from the design talents of Jerilyn Bockorick. Thank you once again for sharing your talents so generously.

Special thanks to those who help me keep going: Chega, Daniel, Sarah, Patrick, and Zorro.

John M. Lannon

CHAPTER 1

Introduction to Technical Communication

Technical Communication Is User Centered

Technical Communication Is Accessible

Technical Communication Comes in All Shapes and Sizes

Technical Communicators Rely on Many Skills

Technical Communication Is Part of Most Careers

Communication Has Both an Electronic and a Human Side

Communication Reaches a Diverse Audience

   Consider This Twenty-First Century Jobs Require
      Portable Skills

On the Job . . . Types of Writing

More and more of our everyday actions and decisions depend on complex but usable technical information. When we purchase a cell phone, for instance, we immediately turn to the instruction manual. When we install any new device, from a microwave oven to a new printer, it's the setup information that we look for as soon as we open the box. Before we opt for the latest high-tech medical treatment, we learn all we can about its benefits and risks. From banking systems to online courses to business negotiations, countless aspects of daily life are affected by technology. To interact with technology in so many ways, we all rely on usable technical information.

Technical communication conveys information that serves the needs of various people in various settings. People might need this information to complete a task, answer a question, solve a problem, or make a decision. In the workplace, we are not only *consumers* of technical communication, but *producers* as well. Any document or presentation we prepare (memo, letter, report, Web page, Power-Point) must advance the goals of our readers, viewers, or listeners.

Technical communication defined

Technical Communication Is User Centered

Unlike poetry or fiction or essays, a technical document rarely focuses on the writer's personal thoughts and feelings. This doesn't mean that your document should have no personality (or *voice*), but that the needs of your audience come first. Users typically are interested in "who you are" only to the extent that they want to know *what you have done, what you recommend,* or *how you speak for your company*. While a user-centered document never makes the writer "disappear," it does focus on what the audience considers important.

What users expect

Technical Communication Is Accessible

Professors read to *test* our knowledge, but colleagues, customers, and supervisors read to *use* our knowledge. In fact, much of your own technical communication may involve translating specialized information for nontechnical audiences, as Figure 1.1 illustrates.

How workplace and school writing differ

In the United States especially, people using a technical document often go back and forth: instead of reading from beginning to end, they look up the information they need at that moment. For users to find the information and to understand it, a document has to be easy to navigate and straightforward.

 NOTE *For any type of global communication, keep in mind that many cultures consider a direct, straightforward communication style offensive. For more detail, see page 10.*

Information is accessible if people can actually get to it and understand it. An accessible technical document is carefully designed to include features such as those displayed in Figure 1.1 and listed on page 5.

The topic and sponsoring agency are clearly identified

United States
Environmental Protection
Agency

Office of Solid Waste and
Emergency Response
(5102G)

EPA 542-F-01-001
April 2001
www.epa.gov/superfund/sites
www.cluin.org

♻EPA | A Citizen's Guide to Bioremediation

The introduction offers a clear preview

The Citizen's Guide Series

EPA uses many methods to clean up pollution at Superfund and other sites. Some, like bioremediation, are considered new or innovative. Such methods can be quicker and cheaper than more common methods. If you live, work, or go to school near a Superfund site, you may want to learn more about cleanup methods. Perhaps they are being used or are proposed for use at your site. How do they work? Are they safe? This Citizen's Guide is one in a series to help answer your questions.

Headings aid navigation and are phrased as typical questions users would need answered

What is bioremediation?

Bioremediation allows natural processes to clean up harmful chemicals in the environment. Microscopic "bugs" or microbes that live in soil and groundwater like to eat certain harmful chemicals, such as those found in gasoline and oil spills. When microbes completely digest these chemicals, they change them into water and harmless gases such as carbon dioxide.

The illustration provides a clear visual referent for nonspecialists

Microbe eats oil

Microbe digests oil and changes
it to water and harmless gases

Microbe releases water and
harmless gases into soil or ground

How does it work?

Clear, direct writing explains a complex concept in terms geared to a general audience

In order for microbes to clean up harmful chemicals, the right temperature, nutrients (fertilizers), and amount of oxygen must be present in the soil and groundwater. These conditions allow the microbes to grow and multiply—and eat more chemicals. When conditions are not right, microbes grow too slowly or die. Or they can create more harmful chemicals. If conditions are not right at a site, EPA works to improve them. One way they improve conditions is to pump air, nutrients, or other substances (such as molasses) underground. Sometimes microbes are added if enough aren't already there.

The right conditions for bioremediation cannot always be achieved underground. At some sites, the weather is too cold or the soil is too dense. At such sites, EPA might dig up the soil to clean it above ground where heaters and soil mixing help improve conditions. After the soil is dug up, the proper nutrients are added. Oxygen also may be added by stirring the mixture or by forcing air through it. However, some microbes work better without oxygen. With the right temperature and amount of oxygen and nutrients, microbes can do their work to "bioremediate" the harmful chemicals.

FIGURE 1.1 An Accessible Technical Document The text, organization, and design of this brief guide work together to make technical information accessible to a general audience.

Source: U.S. Environmental Protection Agency, April 2001. Information available at <www.epa.gov/superfund/sites> or <www.cluin.org>.

The material follows an overall sequence that would make sense to users

Overall content is sufficient–but not excessive –for the stipulated audience

A question of special importance to the audience is set off in its own box

This box points to more specific information sources

The note spells out the specific purpose, audience, and legal constraints of this document

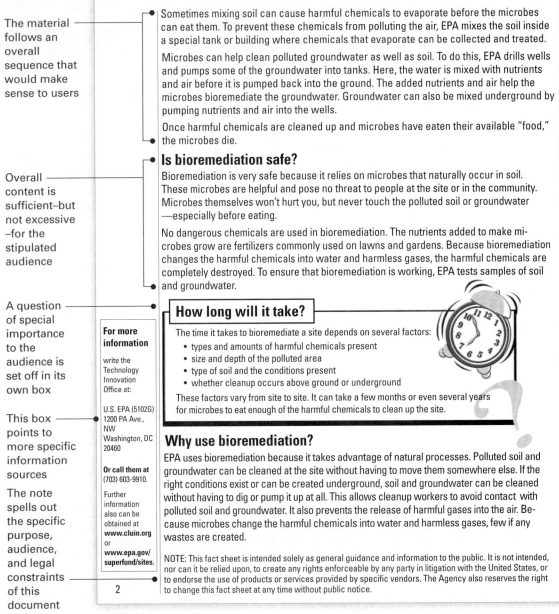

Sometimes mixing soil can cause harmful chemicals to evaporate before the microbes can eat them. To prevent these chemicals from polluting the air, EPA mixes the soil inside a special tank or building where chemicals that evaporate can be collected and treated.

Microbes can help clean polluted groundwater as well as soil. To do this, EPA drills wells and pumps some of the groundwater into tanks. Here, the water is mixed with nutrients and air before it is pumped back into the ground. The added nutrients and air help the microbes bioremediate the groundwater. Groundwater can also be mixed underground by pumping nutrients and air into the wells.

Once harmful chemicals are cleaned up and microbes have eaten their available "food," the microbes die.

Is bioremediation safe?

Bioremediation is very safe because it relies on microbes that naturally occur in soil. These microbes are helpful and pose no threat to people at the site or in the community. Microbes themselves won't hurt you, but never touch the polluted soil or groundwater —especially before eating.

No dangerous chemicals are used in bioremediation. The nutrients added to make microbes grow are fertilizers commonly used on lawns and gardens. Because bioremediation changes the harmful chemicals into water and harmless gases, the harmful chemicals are completely destroyed. To ensure that bioremediation is working, EPA tests samples of soil and groundwater.

How long will it take?

The time it takes to bioremediate a site depends on several factors:
- types and amounts of harmful chemicals present
- size and depth of the polluted area
- type of soil and the conditions present
- whether cleanup occurs above ground or underground

These factors vary from site to site. It can take a few months or even several years for microbes to eat enough of the harmful chemicals to clean up the site.

Why use bioremediation?

EPA uses bioremediation because it takes advantage of natural processes. Polluted soil and groundwater can be cleaned at the site without having to move them somewhere else. If the right conditions exist or can be created underground, soil and groundwater can be cleaned without having to dig or pump it up at all. This allows cleanup workers to avoid contact with polluted soil and groundwater. It also prevents the release of harmful gases into the air. Because microbes change the harmful chemicals into water and harmless gases, few if any wastes are created.

NOTE: This fact sheet is intended solely as general guidance and information to the public. It is not intended, nor can it be relied upon, to create any rights enforceable by any party in litigation with the United States, or to endorse the use of products or services provided by specific vendors. The Agency also reserves the right to change this fact sheet at any time without public notice.

For more information

write the Technology Innovation Office at:

U.S. EPA (5102G) 1200 PA Ave., NW Washington, DC 20460

Or call them at (703) 603-9910.

Further information also can be obtained at **www.cluin.org** or **www.epa.gov/ superfund/sites.**

2

FIGURE 1.1 *(Continued)*

Features of accessible documents

- **worthwhile content**—includes all (and only) the information users need
- **sensible organization**—guides the user and emphasizes important material
- **readable style**—promotes fluid reading and accurate understanding
- **effective visuals**—clarify concepts and relationships, and substitute for words whenever possible
- **effective page design**—provides heads, lists, type styles, white space, and other aids to navigation
- **supplements** (abstract, appendix, glossary, linked pages, and so on)—allow each user to focus on the specific parts of a long document that are relevant

A communicator's legal accountability

User-centered and accessible communication is no mere abstract notion: In the event of a lawsuit, faulty writing is treated like any other faulty product. If your inaccurate, unclear, or incomplete information leads to injury, damage, or loss, you and your company or organization can be held responsible.

NOTE   *Make sure your message is clear and straightforward—but don't oversimplify. Information designer Nathan Shedroff reminds us that, while **clarity** makes information easier to understand, **simplicity** is "often responsible for the 'dumbing down' of information rather than the illumination of it" (280). The "sound bytes" that often masquerade as network news reports serve as a good case in point.*

Technical Communication Comes in All Shapes and Sizes

Common types of technical communication

Here is a sampling of the kinds of technical communication you might encounter or prepare, either on the job or in the community.

- **Letters.** Letters are the most "personal" form of technical communication, but they also provide written records and often serve as contracts. As a student you might write to request research data or to apply for a summer internship. On the job, you might write to persuade a client to invest in a new technology venture or to explain the delay in a construction project. See Chapter 17.
- **Memos.** Organizations use memos (and their email versions) as the primary means of internal written communication. Unlike a conversation, a memo leaves a "paper trail." Memos are usually brief, with a format that includes a header ("To," "From," "Date," "Subject") and a page or two of body text. An employee might write to her manager requesting a pay raise; a team of students might write to their instructor explaining their progress on a term project. See Chapter 16.
- **Email.** Basically a memo in electronic form, email is now more common than paper memos. People are more inclined to forward email messages, and to write more informally and hastily than they would with paper memos. See Chapter 16.

- **Brochures, Pamphlets, and Fact Sheets.** These brief documents are often designed for public consumption. To market goods or services, companies produce brochures. Professional organizations, such as the American Medical Association, produce brochures and pamphlets defining various medical conditions, explaining the causes, and describing available treatments. Government agencies provide online fact sheets (as in Figure 1.1) that offer technical definitions and descriptions on topics ranging from mad cow disease to stem cells to bioterrorism. See Chapters 20 and 21.
- **Instructional Material.** Instructions explain the steps or course of action for completing a specific task, such as how to program a DVD player or how to install system software. Instructions come in various formats: Brief *reference cards* often fit on a single page; *brochures* can be mailed or handed out; book-length *manuals* accompany complex products; *online help* is built right into the computer application; *hyperlinked pages* offer various levels and layers of information. See Chapter 22.
- **Reports.** Reports, both short and long, are generally based on the study of a specific problem or issue. Some reports are strictly informative ("Why Laptop Computer Batteries Can Explode"); other reports recommend solutions to urgent problems ("Recommended Security Measures for Airline Safety"); still others have an overtly persuasive goal, advocating a particular course of action ("Why Voters Should Reject the Nuclear Waste Storage Facility Proposed for Our County"). See Chapters 16 and 24.
- **Proposals.** A proposal presents a specific strategy for solving a particular problem. A proposal's purpose is usually to persuade readers to improve conditions, accept a service or product, provide research funding, or otherwise support a plan of action. Proposals are sometimes written in response to requests for proposals (RFPs). For example, a community may seek to expand its middle school or the Defense Department may wish to develop an intensive training program for airport baggage screeners. These organizations would issue RFPs, and each interested vendor would prepare a proposal that examines the problem, presents a solution, and stipulates a fee for completing the project. See Chapter 23.

The preceding listing is by no means exhaustive. Each profession has its own specific formats for communicating, and many organizations use prepared forms for much of their internal communication.

Other Media for Technical Communications.   Most versions of paper-based communication can be formatted and packaged in other media such as CDs, DVDs, Web pages, email attachments, ebooks, podcasts, and the like. These technologies are known as the *new media* because they blend features of many traditional media types. For example, podcasts offer news but are different from print newspapers. CDs or online help systems offer instructions but are distinct from printed manuals. Yet the trend today is toward *convergence,* meaning that distinctions between these forms of communication are becoming blurred. For example, online news-feeds (see page 353) blur the distinctions between a newspaper, an email network, and a Web site. As more and more of this convergence occurs, technical communicators face information design issues unique to the new media.

NOTE
Despite stunning advances in electronic communication, paper is by no means disappearing from today's workplace. According to research firm IDC, the 1.49 trillion printed pages in 2002 increased to 1.84 trillion pages in 2006 (Grimes).

Technical Communicators Rely on Many Skills

What technical
communicators do

"Full-time" technical communicators serve many roles.[1] Trade and professional organizations employ technical communicators to produce newsletters, pamphlets, journals, and public relations material. Many work in business and industry, preparing instructional material, reports, proposals, and scripts for industrial films. They also prepare sales literature, publicity releases, handbooks, catalogs, brochures, Web pages, intranet content, articles, speeches, and oral and multimedia presentations.

To reduce costs and to speed production, technical communicators use software such as *InDesign* or *Quark* to design and produce documents for distribution in multiple formats. For instance, a technical writer at a software company may be asked not only to research and write the material for a printed user's guide—but also to design this information for a Web site or an online help screen. In many organizations, these tasks are performed by different communication specialists. Some employees may focus solely on writing, others on Web design. Even so, each technical communicator must know the principles involved in designing for various media.

Related career
paths

Technical communicators also do other work: For example, they edit reports for punctuation, grammar, style, and logical organization; they oversee publishing projects, coordinating the efforts of writers, visual artists, graphic designers, content experts, and lawyers to produce a complex manual or proposal. Given their broad range of skills, technical communicators often enter related fields such as publishing, magazine editing, Web site management, television, and college teaching.

Technical Communication Is Part of Most Careers

Whatever your job description, expect to be evaluated, at least in part, on your communication skills. At one IBM subsidiary, for example, 25 percent of an employee's evaluation is based on how effectively that person shares information

---

[1] My thanks to Pamela Herbert for this overview.

(Davenport 99). Even if you don't anticipate a "writing" career, expect to be a "part-time" technical communicator, who will routinely face situations like these:

How various
professionals serve
as part-time
technical
communicators

- As a medical professional, psychologist, social worker, or accountant, you will keep precise records that are, increasingly, a basis for legal action.
- As a scientist, you will report on your research and explain its significance.
- As a manager, you will write memos, personnel evaluations, inspection reports, and give oral presentations.
- As a lab or service technician, you will keep daily activity records and help train coworkers in using, installing, or servicing equipment.
- As an attorney, you will research and interpret the law for clients.
- As an engineer or architect, you will collaborate with colleagues as well as experts in related fields before presenting a proposal to your client. (For example, an architect's plans are reviewed by a structural engineer who certifies that the design is sound.)

The more you advance in your field, the more you will share information and establish human contacts. Managers and executives spend much of their time negotiating, setting policies, and promoting their ideas—often among diverse cultures around the globe. In short, the higher your career goals, the more effectively you need to communicate.

NOTE   *Instead of joining corporate ranks, you might work in the nonprofit sector, say, for an environmental group such as the Sierra Club or a community service agency such as the United Way or Head Start, the preschool program for disadvantaged children. Or you might be an intern or volunteer in these organizations. Whatever the setting, your writing will serve the community—say, in a brochure for public outreach, or a grant request for state funding, or a handbook for clients. In short, technical communication is not merely an instrument for financial gain. It can also serve the good of society. To explore this societal dimension, see the Service-Learning Project at the end of most chapters.*

Electronic
collaboration

Communication Has Both an Electronic and a Human Side

The rise of
information
technology

Limitations of
information
technology

Electronic mail, instant messaging, blogs, fax, teleconferencing, videoconferencing, Internet chat rooms, hypertext, multimedia—resources collectively known as *information technology* (IT)—enhance the speed, volume, and ways of transmitting information. Despite the tremendous advantages IT gives today's communicators, much of their information still needs to be *written*. Also, only humans can give *meaning* to all the information they convey and receive. Information technology, in short, is a tool, not a substitute for human interaction. People make information meaningful by addressing questions no computer can answer. These include the following:

Questions only humans can answer

- Which information is most relevant to this situation?
- Can I verify the accuracy of this source?
- What does this information mean?
- What action does it suggest?
- How does this information affect me or my colleagues?
- With whom should I share it?
- How might others interpret this information?

With so much information required, and so much available, no one can afford to "let the data speak for themselves." In this context, technical communicators serve a vital role as information managers who help others access and understand all the information available to them.

More on global communication

Communication Reaches a Diverse Audience

Electronically linked, our global community shares social, political, and financial interests. Corporations are increasingly multinational. Research crosses national boundaries, and people transact across cultures with documents like these (Weymouth 143):

Documents that address global audiences

- scientific reports and articles on AIDS, influenza, and other diseases
- studies of global pollution and industrial emissions
- specifications for hydroelectric dams and other engineering projects
- operating instructions for appliances and electronic equipment
- catalogs, promotional literature, and repair manuals
- contracts and business agreements

To connect diverse communities, any document needs to connect with everyone involved. Also, the message must embody respect not only for language differences, but also for cultural differences:

How cultures shape communication styles

> Our accumulated knowledge and experiences, beliefs and values, attitudes and roles—in other words, our cultures—shape us as individuals and differentiate us as a people. Our cultures, inbred through family life, religious training, and educational and work experiences . . . manifest themselves . . . in our thoughts and feelings, our actions and reactions, and our views of the world.
>
> Most important for communicators, our cultures manifest themselves in our information needs and our styles of communication . . . our expectations as to how information should be organized, what should be included in its content, and how it should be expressed. (Hein 125)

 Cross-cultural communication

Cultures differ over which behaviors seem appropriate for social interaction, business relationships, contract negotiation, and communication practices. An effective communication style in one culture may be offensive elsewhere. One survey of top international executives reveals the following attitudes toward U.S. communication style (Wandycz 22–23):

How various cultures view U.S. communication style

- Latin America: "Americans are too straightforward, too direct."
- Eastern Europe: "An imperial tone . . . It's always about how [Americans] know best."
- Southeast Asia: "To get my respect, American business [people] should know something about [our culture]. But they don't."
- Western Europe: "Americans miss the small points."
- Central Europe: "Americans tend to oversell themselves."

In addition to being broadly accessible, any document prepared for a global audience must reflect sensitivity to cultural differences. For more on cross-cultural communication, see pages 36, 63, 81, 245.

CONSIDER This Twenty-First Century Jobs Require Portable Skills

In today's workplace nothing lasts forever. High-tech and dotcom companies emerge and vanish overnight. Even large, established companies expanding at one moment may be "downsizing" at the next.

More and more jobs are temporary: for contract workers, part-timers, consultants, and the like (Jones 51). Instead of joining a company, climbing through the ranks, and retiring with a comfortable pension, today's college graduate can look forward to a series of employers—and careers.

UC–San Francisco researchers Yelin and Trupin found that only 33 percent of the California workforce held "traditional," permanent, full-time jobs, only 22 percent of them having held these jobs for three years or more (cited in Koretz 32). As of early 2006, workers nationwide had been with their current employer an average of 4 years, according to the Bureau of Labor Statistics.

Your job security in the twenty-first century will depend on skills you can carry from one employer to another—no matter what the job (Peters 172; Task Force 19):

- *Can you write and speak effectively?*
- *Can you research information, verify its accuracy, figure out what it means, and shape it for the user's specific purposes?*
- *Can you work on a team, with people from diverse backgrounds?*
- *Can you get along with, listen to, and motivate others?*
- *Are you flexible enough to adapt to rapid changes in business conditions and technology?*
- *Can you market yourself and your ideas persuasively?*
- *Are you ready to pursue lifelong learning and constant improvement?*

These are among the *portable skills* employers seek in today's college graduates—skills all related to communication.

ON THE **JOB**... Types of Writing

■ *"Writing is essential to my work. Everything we do [at my company] results in a written product of some kind—a formal technical report, a summary of key findings, recommendations and submissions to academic journals or professional associations. We also write proposals to help secure new engagements. Writing is the most important skill we seek in potential employees and nurture and reward in current employees. It is very hard to find people with strong writing skills, regardless of their academic background."*

—Paul Harder,
President,
mid-sized consulting firm

■ *"I do 'Social History' assessments on all new patients who are admitted to the unit. This includes my written assessment (based on an interview of the patient) of why the patient has been admitted, a brief psychosocial history of the patient (previous hospitalizations, family history of mental illness or substance abuse, any history of physical or sexual abuse, and the family and cultural dynamics), a description of the patient's educational background, and a final evaluation of what issues I feel need to be treated or focused upon during the patient's stay (usually including aftercare plans, discharge planning, individual and group therapy)."*

—Emma Bryant,
Social Worker

■ *"I generate emails continually. These include status reports, replies to queries, requests for missing information or outstanding materials due, jokes, etc. I sometimes have to write up instructions for media projects. I have to write bids. I write up invoices. I sometimes have to write for returns for equipment that isn't up to expectations. I sometimes have to write introductory messages to try to get new sales. Sometimes I have to write copy for Web sites."*

—Lorraine Patsco,
Director of Prepress
and multimedia production

■ *"Writing is probably 30 to 40 percent of my job, with editing taking up another 50 percent, and training and tutoring accounting for the remainder. I oversee semi-technical reports from my managers to upper managers and to our military sponsors—usually progress reports ranging from one to twenty pages; I also edit some sections of highly technical, engineer-to-engineer reports. The engineers and scientists write the body, and I handle the abstract, introduction, executive summary, acknowledgments, conclusion, and list of references, and I sometimes add figures and tables. I also write general reports—things like articles for the company newsletter—and training materials for engineers. I'm currently writing materials on grammar, audience analysis, and techniques for oral presentation."*

—Bill Trippe,
Communications Specialist
with military contract company

Exercises

 Exercises

1. Research the kinds of communicating you will do in your career. (Begin with the *Dictionary of Occupational Titles* in your library or on the Web.) Interview a member of your chosen profession or a technical communicator in a related field or industry. What kinds of documents and presentations can you expect to produce on the job, and for what audiences and purposes? What types of global audiences can you expect? How much of your writing will be transmitted in electronic forms (Web sites, intranets, and so on)? Summarize your findings in a memo to your instructor or in a brief oral report to your class. (See pages 327, 329 for memo elements and format.)

2. Write a memo to your boss, justifying reimbursement for this course. Explain how the course will help you become more effective on the job. (See pages 327, 329 for memo elements and format.)

3. Locate a Web site for a company or organization that hires graduates in your major. In addition to technical knowledge, what skills does this company seek in its job candidates? Discuss your findings in class. Also, trace the sequence of links you followed to reach your topic.

Collaborative Project

Introducing a Classmate

Class members will work together often this semester. So that everyone becomes acquainted, your task is to introduce to the class the person seated next to you. (That person, in turn, will introduce you.) Follow this procedure:

a. Exchange with your neighbor whatever personal information you think the class needs: background, major, career plans, communication needs of your intended profession, and so on. Each person gets five minutes to tell her or his story.

b. Take careful notes; ask questions if you need to.

c. Take your notes home and select only what you think the class will find useful.

d. Prepare a one-page memo telling your classmates who this person is. (See pages 327, 329 for memo elements and format.)

e. Ask your neighbor to review the memo for accuracy; revise as needed.

f. Present the class with a two-minute oral paraphrase of your memo, and submit a copy of the memo to your instructor.

Service-Learning Project

Identify a community service agency in your area that needs to have one or more documents prepared. Start by looking in the yellow pages under "Social and Human Services" or "Environmental Organizations." Or look through your campus directory for campus service agencies such as the Writing and Reading Center, Health Services, International Student Services, Women's Resource Center, or Career Resources Center. Then narrow your list to one or two agencies that interest you. Explore the kinds of documents and publications that agency produces and then write a one-page memo (pages 327, 329) reporting your findings to your classmates.

Communicating in the Workplace

CHAPTER 2
Preparing an Effective Technical Document   14

CHAPTER 3
Delivering Usable Information   25

CHAPTER 4
Being Persuasive   48

CHAPTER 5
Weighing the Ethical Issues   75

CHAPTER 6
Working in Teams   96

Preparing an Effective Technical Document

Complete the Key Tasks

Rely on Creative and Critical Thinking

Make Proofreading Your Final Step

Guidelines for Proofreading

Checklist: Proofreading

Consider This Workplace Settings Are Increasingly "Virtual"

All professionals specialize in solving problems (how to repair equipment, how to improve a product, how to diagnose an ailment). But whatever your specialty, when you communicate on the job, your main problem is this: "How do I prepare the right document for this situation?"

Complete the Key Tasks

To produce an effective document in the workplace, you typically need to complete four basic tasks (Figure 2.1):

What workplace communicators need to do

- **Deliver the essential information**—because different people in different situations have different information needs.
- **Make a persuasive case**—because people often disagree about what the information means and what action should be taken.
- **Weigh the ethical issues**—because the interests of your employer may conflict with the interests of other people involved.
- **Work in teams**—because this is how roughly 90 percent of U.S. workers spend some part of their day ("People" 57).

The cases that follow illustrate how a typical professional confronts these tasks in her own day-to-day communication on the job.

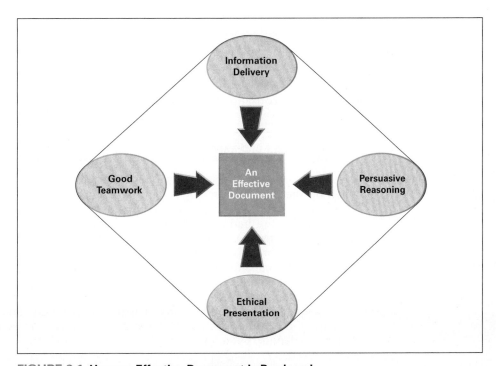

FIGURE 2.1 How an Effective Document Is Produced

CASE: Delivering the Essential Information

"Can I provide exactly what users need?"

Sarah Burnes was hired two months ago as a chemical engineer for Millisun, a leading maker of cameras, multipurpose film, and photographic equipment. Sarah's first major assignment is to evaluate the plant's incoming and outgoing water. (Waterborne contaminants can taint film during production, and the production process itself can pollute outgoing water.) Management wants an answer to this question: How often should we change water filters? The filters are expensive and hard to change, halting production for up to a day at a time. The company wants as much "mileage" as possible from these filters, without incurring government fines or tainting its film production.

Sarah will study endless printouts of chemical analysis, review current research and government regulations, do some testing of her own, and consult with her colleagues. When she finally decides on what all the data mean, Sarah will prepare a recommendation report for her bosses.

Later, she will collaborate with the company training manager and the maintenance supervisor to prepare a manual, instructing employees how to check and change the filters. To cut publishing costs, the company has asked Sarah to design and produce this manual using its desktop publishing system.

Sarah's report, above all, needs to be accurate; otherwise, the company gets fined or lowers production. Once she has processed all the information, she faces the problem of giving users what they need: *How much explaining should I do? How will I organize? Do I need visuals?* And so on.

In other situations, Sarah will face a persuasion problem as well: for example, when decisions must be made or actions taken on the basis of incomplete or inconclusive facts or conflicting interpretations (Hauser 72). In these instances, Sarah will seek consensus for *her* view.

CASE: Being Persuasive

"Can I influence people to see things my way?"

Millisun and other electronics producers are located on the shores of a small harbor, the port for a major fishing fleet. For twenty years, these companies have discharged effluents containing metal compounds, PCBs, and other toxins directly into the harbor. Sarah is on a multicompany team, assigned to work with the Environmental Protection Agency to clean up the harbor. Much of the team's collaboration occurs via email.

Enraged local citizens are demanding immediate action, and the companies themselves are anxious to end this public relations nightmare. But the team's analysis reveals that any type of cleanup would stir up harbor sediment, possibly dispersing the solution into surrounding waters and the atmosphere. (Many of the contaminants can be airborne.) Premature action might actually *increase* danger, but team members disagree on the degree of risk and on how to proceed.

Sarah's communication here takes on a persuasive dimension: she and her team members first have to resolve their own disagreements and produce an environmental impact report that reflects the team's consensus. If the report recommends further study, Sarah will have to justify the delays to her bosses and the public relations office. She will have to make people understand the dangers as well as she understands them.

In the above situation, the facts are neither complete nor conclusive, and views differ about what these facts mean. Sarah will have to balance the various political pressures and make a case for *her* interpretation. Also, as company spokesperson, Sarah will be expected to protect her company's interests. Some elements of Sarah's persuasion problem: *Are other interpretations possible? Is there a better way? Can I expect political or legal fallout?*

Sarah also will have to reckon with the ethical implications of her writing, with the question of "doing the right thing." For instance, Sarah might feel pressured to overlook or sugarcoat or suppress facts that would be costly or embarrassing to her company.

CASE: Weighing the Ethical Issues

"Can I be honest and still keep my job?"

To ensure compliance with OSHA[1] standards for worker safety, Sarah is assigned to test the air purification system in Millisun's chemical division. After finding the filters hopelessly clogged, she decides to test the air quality and discovers dangerous levels of benzene (a potent carcinogen). She reports these findings in a memo to the production manager, with an urgent recommendation that all employees be tested for benzene poisoning. The manager phones and tells Sarah to "have the filters replaced," but says nothing at all about her recommendation to test for benzene poisoning. Now Sarah has to decide what to do about this lack of response: Assume the test is being handled, and bury the memo in some file cabinet? Raise the issue again, and risk alienating her boss? Send copies of her original memo to someone else who might take action?

 Ethics in technical communication

Situations that compromise truth and fairness present the hardest choices of all: Remain silent and look the other way or speak out and risk being fired. Some elements of Sarah's ethics problem: *Is this fair? Who might benefit or suffer? What other consequences could this have?*

In addition to solving these various problems, Sarah has to work in a team setting: Much of her writing will be produced in collaboration with others (editors, managers, graphic artists), and her audience will extend beyond her own culture.

---

[1] Occupational Safety and Health Administration.

CASE: Working on a Team

"Can I connect with all these different colleagues?"

Recent mergers have transformed Millisun into a multinational corporation with branches in eleven countries, all connected by an intranet. Sarah can expect to collaborate with coworkers from diverse cultures on research and development and with government agencies of the host countries on safety issues, patents and licensing rights, product liability laws, and environmental concerns.

In order to standardize the sensitive management of the toxic, volatile, and even explosive chemicals used in film production, Millisun is developing automated procedures for quality control, troubleshooting, and emergency response to chemical leakage. Sarah has been assigned to a team that is preparing computer-based training packages and instructional videos for all personnel involved in Millisun's chemical management worldwide.

As a further complication, Sarah will have to develop working relationships with people she has never met face-to-face, people from other cultures, people she knows only via an electronic medium.

For Sarah Burnes, or any of us, writing is a process of *discovering* what we want to say, "a way to end up thinking something [we] couldn't have started out thinking" (Elbow 15). Throughout this process in the workplace, we rarely work alone, but instead collaborate with others for information, help in writing, and feedback (Grice, "Document" 29–30). We must satisfy not only our audience, but also our employer, whose goals and values ultimately shape the document (Selzer 46–47). Almost any document for people outside our organization will be *reviewed* for accuracy, appropriateness, usefulness, and legality before it is finally approved (Kleimann 521).

Rely on Creative and Critical Thinking

In *creative thinking*, we explore new ideas; we build on information; we devise better ways of doing things. (For example, "How do we get as much mileage as possible from our water filters?")

In *critical thinking*, we test the strength of our ideas or the quality of our information. Instead of accepting an idea at face value, we examine, evaluate, verify, analyze, weigh alternatives, and consider consequences—at every stage of that idea's development. We use critical thinking to examine our evidence and our reasoning, to discover new connections and new possibilities, and to test the effectiveness and the limits of our solutions.

We apply creative and critical thinking throughout the four stages in the *writing process*:

Stages in the writing process

1. Gather and evaluate ideas and information.
2. Plan the document.

3. Draft the document.

4. Revise the document.

One engineering professional describes how creative and critical thinking enrich every stage of the writing process:

Writing sharpens thinking

> Good writing is a process of thinking, writing, revising, thinking, and revising, until the idea is fully developed. An engineer can develop better perspectives and even new technical concepts when writing a report of a project. Many an engineer, at the completion of a laboratory project, senses a new interpretation or sees a defect in the results and goes back to the laboratory for additional data, a more thorough analysis, or a modified design (Franke 13).

As the arrows in Figure 2.2 indicate, no single stage of the writing process is complete until all stages are complete. Figure 2.3 lists the kinds of questions we answer at various stages. On the job, we must often complete these stages under deadline pressure. Like the exposed tip of an iceberg, the finished document provides the only visible evidence of our labor in preparing it.

For illustrations of the writing process in actual workplace settings, see A Casebook: The Writing Process, page 698.

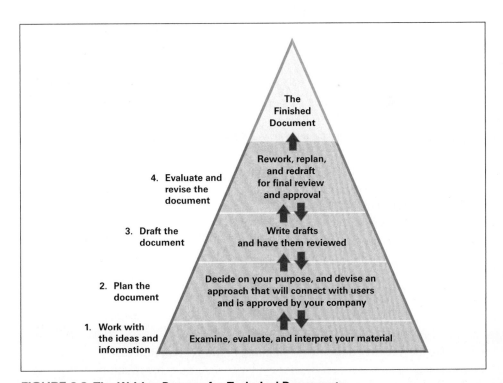

FIGURE 2.2 The Writing Process for Technical Documents

1. Work with the ideas and information:
- Have I defined the problem accurately?
- Is the information complete, accurate, reliable, and unbiased?
- Can it be verified?
- How much of it is useful?
- Do I need more information?
- What do these facts mean?
- What connections seem to emerge?
- Do the facts conflict?
- Are other interpretations or conclusions possible?
- Is a balance of viewpoints represented?
- What, if anything, should be done?
- Is the information honest and fair?
- Is there a better way?
- What are the risks and benefits?
- What other consequences might this have?
- Should I reconsider?

2. Plan the document:
- When is it due?
- What do I want it to do?
- Who is my audience, and why will they use it?
- What do they need to know?
- What are the "political realities" (feelings, egos, cultural differences, and so on)?
- How will I organize?
- What format and visuals should I use?
- Whose help will I need?

3. Draft the document:
- How do I begin, and what comes next?
- How much is enough?
- What can I leave out?
- Am I forgetting anything?
- How will I end?
- Who needs to review my drafts?

4. Evaluate and revise the document:
- Is the draft usable?
- Does it do what I want it to do?
- Is the content worthwhile?
- Is the organization sensible?
- Is the style readable?
- Is everything easy to find?
- Is the format appealing?
- Is everything accurate, complete, appropriate, and correct?
- Who needs to review and approve the final version?
- Does it advance my organization's goals?
- Does it advance my audience's goals?

FIGURE 2.3 **Creative and Critical Thinking in the Writing Process**

NOTE   *Revising a draft doesn't always guarantee that you will improve it. Save each draft and then compare them to select the best material from each one.*

Make Proofreading Your Final Step

No matter how engaging and informative the document, basic errors distract the reader and make the writer look bad (including on various drafts being reviewed by colleagues). Proofreading detects easily correctable errors such as these:

Errors we look for during proofreading

- **Sentence errors,** such as fragments, comma splices, or run-ons
- **Punctuation errors,** such as missing apostrophes or excessive commas
- **Usage errors,** such as "it's" for "its," "lay" for "lie," or "their" for "there"
- **Mechanical errors,** such as misspelled words, inaccurate dates, or incorrect abbreviations
- **Format errors,** such as missing page numbers, inconsistent spacing, or incorrect form of documenting sources
- **Typographical errors** (typos), such as repeated or missing words or letters, missing word endings (say, *-s* or *-ed* or *-ing*), or a left-out quotation mark.

Guidelines for Proofreading

- **Save it for the final draft.** Proofreading earlier drafts might cause writer's block and distract you from the document's "rhetorical features" (content, organization, style, and design).
- **Take a break before proofreading your final document.**
- **Work from hard copy.** Research indicates that people read more perceptively (and with less fatigue) from a printed page than from a computer screen.
- **Keep it slow.** Read each word—don't skim. Slide a ruler under each line or move backward through the document, sentence by sentence. For a long document, read only small chunks at one time.
- **Be especially alert for problem areas in your writing.** Do you have trouble spelling? Do you get commas confused with semicolons? Do you make a lot of typos? Make one final pass to check on any problem areas.
- **Proofread more than once.** The more often you do it, the better.
- **Never rely only on computerized writing aids.** A synonym found in an electronic thesaurus may distort your meaning. The spell checker cannot diffentiate among correctly spelled words such as "their," "they're," and "there" or "it's" versus "its." In the end, nothing can replace your own careful proofreading. (Page 247 summarizes the limitations of computerized aids.)

☑ Checklist: Proofreading

(Numbers in parentheses refer to the first page of discussion.)

Sentences

- ☐ Are all sentences complete (no unacceptable fragments)? (671)
- ☐ Is the document free of comma splices and run-on sentences? (673)
- ☐ Does each verb agree with its subject? (674)
- ☐ Does each pronoun refer to and agree with a specific noun? (675)
- ☐ Are ideas of equal importance coordinated? (675)
- ☐ Are ideas of lesser importance subordinated? (676)
- ☐ Is each pronoun in the correct case (nominative, objective, possessive)? (677)
- ☐ Is each modifier positioned to reflect the intended meaning? (678)
- ☐ Are items of equal importance expressed in equal (parallel) grammatical form? (679)
- ☐ Is the document free of shifts in person, voice, tense, or mood? (680)

Punctuation

- ☐ Does each sentence conclude with appropriate end punctuation? (681)
- ☐ Are semicolons and colons used correctly as a *break* between items? (682)
- ☐ Are commas used correctly as a *pause* between items? (683)
- ☐ Do apostrophes signal possessives, contractions, and certain plurals? (687)
- ☐ Do quotation marks set off direct quotes and certain titles? (688)
- ☐ Is each quotation punctuated correctly? (689)
- ☐ Do ellipses indicate material omitted from a quotation? (689)
- ☐ Do italics indicate certain titles or names, or emphasis or special use of a word? (690)
- ☐ Are brackets, parentheses, and dashes used correctly and as needed? (690)

Mechanics

- ☐ Are abbreviations used correctly and without confusing the reader? (694)
- ☐ Are hyphens used correctly? (695)
- ☐ Are words capitalized correctly? (695)
- ☐ Are numbers written out or expressed as numerals as needed? (696)
- ☐ Has electronic spell checking been supplemented by actual proofreading for words spelled correctly but used incorrectly (as in *there* for *their*)? (247)

Format and Keyboarding

- ☐ Are pages numbered correctly? (303)
- ☐ Are sources cited in a standard form of documentation? (639)
- ☐ Have typographical errors been corrected?

Consider This Workplace Settings Are Increasingly "Virtual"

- Instead of being housed in one location, the virtual company may have branches across the state, the nation, or the world, to which many employees "commute" electronically. These telecommuters include freelance workers who are employed by other companies as well.
- Workplace discussions and document sharing occur via email, instant messaging, blogs, or videoconferencing. Networked employees worldwide collaborate and converse in real time. Email newsfeeds announce daily developments such as price and inventory lists, changes or updates in policies or procedures, and press releases.
- Employees work and write collaboratively (as in developing a proposal or a marketing

plan). Drafts circulated electronically allow colleagues to add comments directly on the manuscript. Multimedia systems present text, graphics, sound, and animated material retrieved from a computer file. Colleagues in any location work on the electronic document and comment on one another's "work in progress."
- Instead of relying on secretaries, managers compose their own letters and memoranda for distribution across the building or across the globe via email or email attachments.
- On desktop publishing (DTP) networks, the composition, layout, graphic design, typesetting, and printing of external documents and Web pages can be done in-house.

Exercises

 Exercises
WEBLINK

1. Locate a Web site that describes some form of multinational collaboration to address an environmental threat such as global warming, nuclear accident, deforestation, or species depletion. In a one-page memo, summarize how various cultures are working together to address the problem. (For example, to learn about international cooperation to save fish populations, go to the National Marine Fisheries site at <www.nmfs.noaa.gov>.) Trace the sequence of links you followed to reach your material, and cite each source.

2. As you respond to the following scenario,[2] carefully consider the information, persuasion, and ethical problems involved (and be prepared to discuss them in class).

You are Manager of Product Development at High-Tech Toys, Inc. You need to send a memo to the Vice President of Information Services, explaining the following:

 a. The laser printer in your department is often out of order.
 b. The laser printer is seldom repaired satisfactorily.
 c. Either the machine is faulty or the repairperson is incompetent (but this person always appears promptly and cheerfully when summoned from Corporate Maintenance—and is a single parent raising three young children).
 d. It is difficult to get things done in your department without being able to use the laser printer.
 e. The members of your department share ideas and plans daily.
 f. You want the problem solved—but without getting the repairperson fired.

In your memo, recommend a solution, and briefly justify your recommendation. (See pages 327, 329 for details on memo format.)

---

[2] My thanks to Teresa Pawelcyzk for the original version of this exercise.

Collaborative Project

An Issue of Ethics

Working in small groups, analyze Sarah Burnes's ethical decisions (page 17). What could happen if Sarah follows her boss's orders? What could happen if she takes no further action? After discussing the issues involved and the possible consequences, try to reach a consensus about what action Sarah should take in this situation. Appoint one member to present your group's conclusion to the class.

Service-Learning Project

Social service agencies work toward varied goals. As you scan the list of United Way agencies and others researched by your classmates, can you identify agencies whose goals or values conflict with yours or your family's? If your instructor assigned you to work for one of these agencies, how might you respond?

In a one-page memo to your instructor, summarize the key values and goals of the agency you have researched, and explain how you would or would not make a good "fit" in working with that agency.

CHAPTER 3

Delivering Usable Information

Know What Different Audiences Expect

Assess the Audience's Information Needs

Identify Levels of Technicality

Develop an Audience and Use Profile

Create a Design Plan for the Document

Write, Test, and Revise Your Document

Consider This Communication Failure Can Have Drastic Consequences

On the Job . . . Audiences

Usability defined

A document's *usability* is a measure of how well that document fulfills the information needs of its audience. Whatever their specific goals and concerns in using a particular document, people must be able to do at least three things (Coe, *Human Factors* 193; Spencer 74):

What a usable document enables readers to do

- easily locate the information they need
- understand the information immediately
- use the information successfully

To assess the usability of a manual that comes with your new lawnmower, for instance, you would ask: "How well do these instructions enable me or anyone else to assemble, operate, and maintain the mower safely and effectively?" Preparing usable information requires systematic analysis of your audience and the ways in which they will use your document (Figure 3.1).

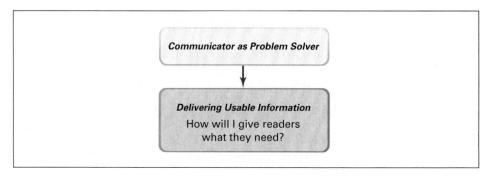

FIGURE 3.1 Communicators Begin by Considering Their Audience

Know What Different Audiences Expect

 Understanding workplace cultures

Following are typical audiences you will encounter in the workplace. Granted, these audience categories overlap to a certain extent, and it's impossible to speak of "all scientists" or "all engineers" without stereotyping. But a specific type of audience generally shares specific concerns, interests, and information needs (Gurak and Lannon 29).

Different audiences have different information needs and interests

- *Scientists* search for knowledge to "understand the world as it is" (Petroski 2). Scientists look for at least 95 percent probability that chance played no role in a particular outcome. They want to know how well a study was designed and conducted and whether its findings can be replicated. Their research is never "final," but open-ended and ongoing: What seems probable today may well be rendered improbable by tomorrow's research.
- *Engineers* rearrange "the materials and forces of nature" to improve the way things work (Petroski 1). Engineers solve problems: how to erect a suspension

bridge that withstands high winds, how to design a lighter airplane or a smaller pacemaker, how to boost rocket thrust on a space shuttle. The engineer's concern is usually with practical applications, with structures and materials that are tested for safety and dependability.

- *Executives* focus on decision making. In a global business climate of overnight developments (world markets, political strife, military conflicts, natural disasters) executives must often react on the spur of the moment. In such cases they rely on the best information immediately available—even when this information is incomplete or unverified (Seglin 54).
- *Managers* oversee day-to-day operations, focusing on problems like these: how to motivate employees, how to increase production, how to save money, how to avoid workplace accidents. They collaborate with colleagues and supervise various projects. To keep things running smoothly, managers rely on memos, reports, and other forms of information sharing.
- *Lawyers* focus on protecting the corporation from liability or corporate sabotage by answering questions like these: Do these instructions contain adequate warnings and cautions? Is there anything about this product or document that could generate a lawsuit? Have any of our trade secrets been revealed? Lawyers carefully review documents before approving their distribution outside the company.
- *The public* focuses on the big picture—on what pertains to them directly: What does this mean to me? How can I use this product safely and effectively? Why should I even read this? They rely on information for some immediate practical purpose: to complete a task (What do I do next?), to learn more about something (What are the facts and what do they mean?), to make a judgment (Is this good enough?).

Because audiences' basic purposes vary, every audience expects a message tailored to its own specific interests, social conventions, ways of understanding problems, and information needs.

Assess the Audience's Information Needs

Usable information connects with an audience by recognizing its unique background, needs, and preferences. The same basic message can be conveyed in different ways for different audiences. For instance, an article describing a new cancer treatment might appear in a medical journal for doctors and nurses. A less technical version might appear in a textbook for medical and nursing students. A more simplified version might appear in *Reader's Digest*. All three versions treat the same topic, but each meets the needs of a different audience.

Because your audience knows less than you, it will have questions. These might include the following.

Typical audience
questions about a
document

- What is the purpose of this document?
- Why should I read it?
- What information can I expect to find here?
- What happened, and why?
- How should I perform this task?
- What action should be taken?
- How much will it cost?
- What are the risks?
- Do I need to respond to this document? If so, how?

Identify Levels of Technicality

When you write for a close acquaintance (coworker, engineering colleague, chemistry professor who reads your lab reports, or supervisor), you adapt your report to that person's knowledge, interests, and needs. But some audiences are larger and less defined (say, for a journal article, a computer manual, a set of first-aid procedures, or an accident report). When you have only a general notion about your audience's background, decide whether your document should be *highly technical,* *semitechnical,* or *nontechnical,* as depicted in Figure 3.2.

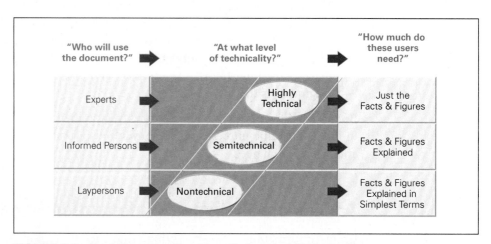

FIGURE 3.2   **Deciding on a Document's Level of Technicality**

The languages
and cultures of
expertise

The Highly Technical Document

Users at a specialized level expect the facts and figures they need—without long explanations. In the document in Figure 3.3, an emergency-room physician reports to the patient's doctor, who needs an exact record of symptoms, treatment, and results.

Expert users need just the facts and figures, which they can interpret for themselves

The patient was brought to the ER by ambulance at 1:00 A.M., September 27, 2007. The patient complained of severe chest pains, dyspnea, and vertigo. Auscultation and EKG revealed a massive cardiac infarction and pulmonary edema marked by pronounced cyanosis. Vital signs: blood pressure, 80/40; pulse, 140/min; respiration, 35/min. Lab: wbc, 20,000; elevated serum transaminase; urea nitrogen, 60 mg%. Urinalysis showed 4+ protein and 4+ granular casts/field, indicating acute renal failure secondary to the hypotension.

The patient received 10 mg of morphine stat, subcutaneously, followed by nasal oxygen and 5% D & W intravenously. At 1:25 A.M. the cardiac monitor recorded an irregular sinus rhythm, indicating left ventricular fibrillation. The patient was defibrillated stat and given a 50 mg bolus of Xylocaine intravenously. A Xylocaine drip was started, and sodium bicarbonate administered until a normal heartbeat was established. By 3:00 A.M., the oscilloscope was recording a normal sinus rhythm.

As the heartbeat stabilized and cyanosis diminished, the patient received 5 cc of Heparin intravenously, to be repeated every six hours. By 5:00 A.M. the BUN had fallen to 20 mg% and vital signs had stabilized: blood pressure, 110/60; pulse, 105/min; respiration, 22/min. The patient was now conscious and responsive.

FIGURE 3.3 A Technical Version of an Emergency Treatment Report

For her expert colleague, this physician defines no technical terms (*pulmonary edema, sinus rhythm*). Nor does she interpret lab findings (*4+ protein, elevated serum transaminase*). She uses abbreviations that her colleague clearly understands (*wbc, BUN, 5% D & W*). Because her colleague knows all about specific treatments and medications (*defibrillation, Xylocaine drip*), she does not explain their scientific bases. Her report answers concisely the main questions she can anticipate from this particular reader: *What was the problem? What was the treatment? What were the results?*

The Semitechnical Document

One broad class of users has some technical background, but less than the experts. For instance, first-year medical students have specialized knowledge, but less than advanced students. Yet all medical students could be considered semitechnical. Therefore, when you write for a semitechnical audience, identify the *lowest* level of

Informed but nonexpert users need enough explanation to understand what the data mean

Examination by stethoscope and electrocardiogram revealed a massive failure of the heart muscle along with fluid buildup in the lungs, which produced a cyanotic **discoloration of the lips and fingertips from lack of oxygen.**

The patient's blood pressure at 80 mm Hg (systolic)/40 mm Hg (diastolic) was **dangerously below its normal measure of 130/70.** A pulse rate of 140/minute was **almost twice the normal rate of 60–80.** Respiration at 35/minute was more than **twice the normal rate of 12–16.**

Laboratory blood tests yielded a white blood cell count of 20,000/cu mm (normal value: 5,000–10,000), **indicating a severe inflammatory response by the heart muscle.** The elevated serum transaminase enzymes (**produced in quantity only when the heart muscle fails**) confirmed the earlier diagnosis. A blood urea nitrogen level of 60 mg% (normal value: 12–16 mg%) **indicated that the kidneys had ceased to filter out metabolic waste products.** The 4+ protein and casts reported from the urinalysis (normal value: 0) **revealed that the kidney tubules were degenerating as a result of the lowered blood pressure.**

The patient immediately received **morphine to ease the chest pain,** followed by **oxygen to relieve strain on the cardiopulmonary system,** and an intravenous solution of **dextrose and water to prevent shock.**

FIGURE 3.4 A Semitechnical Version of an Emergency Treatment Report

understanding in the group, and write to that level. Too much explanation is better than too little.

The partial version of the medical report in Figure 3.4 might appear in a textbook for medical or nursing students, in a report for a medical social worker, or in a monthly report for the hospital administration.

This version explains the raw data (in boldface). Exact dosages are omitted because no one in this audience actually will be treating this patient. Normal values of lab tests and vital signs, however, help readers interpret. (Experts know these values.) Knowing what medications the patient received would be especially important to answering this audience's central question: *How is a typical heart attack treated?*

Techniques for writing to a general audience

The Nontechnical Document

People with no training look for the big picture instead of complex details. They expect technical data to be translated into words most people understand. Laypersons

Heart sounds and electrical impulses were both abnormal, **indicating a massive heart attack caused by failure of a large part of the heart muscle**. The lungs were swollen with fluid and the lips and fingertips showed **a bluish discoloration from lack of oxygen**.

Blood pressure was **dangerously low, creating the risk of shock.** Pulse and respiration were **almost twice the normal rate, indicating that the heart and lungs were being overworked** in keeping oxygenated blood circulating freely.

Blood tests confirmed the heart attack diagnosis and **indicated that waste products usually filtered out by the kidneys were building up in the bloodstream. Urine tests showed that the kidneys were failing as a result of the lowered blood pressure.**

The patient was given **medication to ease the chest pain, oxygen to ease the strain on the heart and lungs, and intravenous solution to prevent the blood vessels from collapsing and causing irreversible shock.**

FIGURE 3.5 A Nontechnical Version of an Emergency Treatment Report

Laypersons need everything translated into terms they understand

are impatient with abstract theories but they want enough background to help them make the right decision or take the right action. They are bored or confused by excessive detail, but frustrated by raw facts left unexplained or uninterpreted. They expect to understand the document after reading it only once.

The nontechnical version of the medical report shown in Figure 3.5 might be written for the patient's spouse who is overseas on business, or as part of a script for a documentary about emergency room treatment. Nearly all interpretation (in boldface), this version mentions no specific medications, lab tests, or normal values. It merely summarizes events and briefly explains what they mean and why these particular treatments were given.

In a different situation, however (say, a malpractice trial), the layperson jury would require detailed technical information about medication and treatment. Such a report would naturally be much longer—a short course in emergency coronary treatment.

Primary and Secondary Audiences

Whenever you prepare a single document for multiple users, classify your audience as *primary* or *secondary*. Generally, primary users are decision makers who requested the document. Secondary users are those who will carry out the project, who will advise the decision makers, or who will be affected by this decision in some way.

Primary and secondary audiences often differ in technical background. When you must write for audiences at different levels, follow these guidelines:

How to tailor a
single document
for multiple users

- If the document is short (a letter, memo, or anything less than two pages), rewrite it at various levels.
- If the document exceeds two pages, address the primary users. Then provide appendices for secondary users. Transmittal letters, informative abstracts, and glossaries can also help nonexperts understand a highly technical report. (See Chapter 25 for use and preparation of appendices and other supplements.)

The document in this next scenario must be tailored for both primary and secondary users.

CASE: Tailoring a Single Document for Different Users

Different users
have different
information
needs

You are a metallurgical engineer in an automotive consulting firm. Your supervisor has asked you to test the fractured rear axle of a 2006 Delphi pickup truck recently involved in a fatal accident. Your assignment is to determine whether the fractured axle *caused* or *resulted from* the accident.

After testing the hardness and chemical composition of the metal and examining microscopic photographs of the fractured surfaces (fractographs), you conclude that the fracture resulted from stress that developed *during* the accident. Now you must report your procedure and your findings to a variety of readers.

"What do these
findings mean?"

Because your report may serve as courtroom evidence, you must explain your findings in meticulous detail. But your primary users (the decision makers) will be nonspecialists (the attorneys who have requested the report, insurance representatives, possibly a judge and a jury), so you must translate your report, explaining the principles behind the various tests, defining specialized terms such as "chevron marks," "shrinkage cavities," and "dimpled core," and showing the significance of these features as evidence.

"How did you
arrive at these
conclusions?"

Secondary users will include your supervisor and outside consulting engineers who will be evaluating your test procedures and assessing the validity of your findings. Consultants will be focusing on various parts of your report, to verify that your procedure has been exact and faultless. For this group, you will have to include appendices spelling out the technical details of your analysis: *how* hardness testing of the axle's case and core indicated that the axle had been properly carburized; *how* chemical analysis ruled out the possibility that the manufacturer had used inferior alloys; *how* light-microscopic fractographs revealed that the origin of the fracture, its direction of propagation, and the point of final rupture indicated a ductile fast fracture, not one caused by torsional fatigue.

In the previous situation, primary users need to know *what your findings mean*, whereas secondary users need to know *how you arrived at your conclusions*. Unless it serves the needs of each group independently, your information will be worthless.

Web-Based Documents for Multiple Audiences

Web pages are ideal for packaging and linking various levels of information. Figure 3.6 accommodates different levels of interest and expertise.

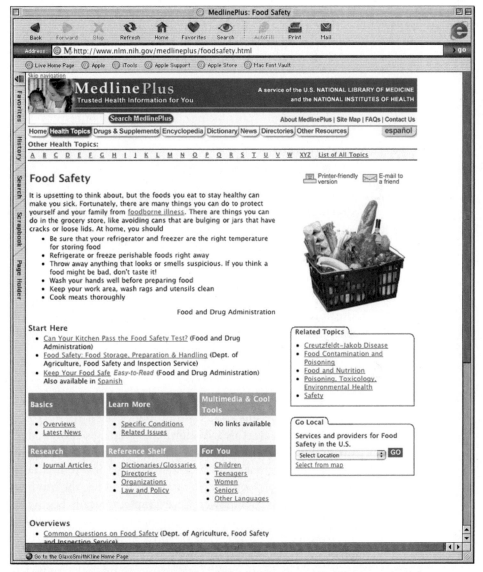

FIGURE 3.6 A Web Page Linked to Various User Needs and Interests At its top layer, this page addresses diverse groups of laypersons including non-English speakers (links listed under **For You**). For medical professionals and other specialized users, links include *Journal Articles* and *Law and Policy*.
Source: National Library of Medicine <www.nlm.nih.gov/medlineplus/foodsafety.html>.

Develop an Audience and Use Profile

To deliver usable information, learn all you can about *who* will use your document, *why* they will use it, and *how* they will use it. Ask these questions:

Questions about a document's audience and use

- Who wants the document? Who else will read it
- What is the purpose of the document?
- Why do people want the document? How will they use it?
- What is the primary audience's technical background? The secondary audience's?
- How might cultural differences create misunderstanding?
- What tasks must users accomplish successfully?
- In what setting will the document be used?
- Are there any possible hazards or sources of error?
- What exactly does the audience need to know, and in what format? How much is enough?
- When is the document due?

Answer these questions by considering the suggestions that follow, and by using a version of the Audience and Use Profile Sheet shown in Figure 3.7 for all your writing.

Audience Characteristics

Are your primary readers superiors, colleagues, or subordinates? Are they inside or outside your organization? What do they already know about this topic? How much do they care? Are they likely to welcome or reject your information? How might cultural differences play a role? Who else might be interested or affected?

Purpose of the Document

All forms of technical communication are intended for specific *purposes*. If the purpose is to *persuade*, this will influence the form of communication. If the purpose is to *instruct*, this will affect the language, format, and other features. Many documents have multiple purposes. For example, the primary purpose in most instruction manuals is to teach an audience how to use the product. But for ethical and legal reasons, companies want people to use the product safely. A manual for a power tool or a lawnmower, for example, typically begins with a page of safety instructions. In planning your document, work from a clear statement of purpose (as shown on page 47). "The purpose of my document is to [describe using verbs: persuade, instruct, describe, propose, etc.]."

Intended Use of the Document

Learn why people want this information and how they will use it. Do they simply want to learn facts or understand concepts? Will they use your information in

Audience Identity and Needs

Primary audience: _____ *(name, title)*

Secondary audience: _____

Relationship: _____ *(client, employer, other)*

Purpose of the document: _____ *(instruct, persuade, other)*

Intended use of document: _____ *(perform a task, solve a problem, other)*

Technical background: _____ *(layperson, expert, other)*

Prior knowledge about this topic: _____ *(knows nothing, a few details, other)*

Additional information needed: _____ *(background, only bare facts, other)*

Probable questions: _____ *?*

_____ *?*

_____ *?*

_____ *?*

Audience's Probable Attitude and Personality

Attitude toward topic: _____ *(indifferent, skeptical, other)*

Probable objections: _____ *(cost, time, none, other)*

Probable attitude toward this writer: _____ *(intimidated, hostile, receptive, other)*

Organizational climate: _____

Persons most affected by this document: _____

Temperament: _____ *(cautious, impatient, other)*

Probable reaction to document: _____ *(resistance, approval, anger, guilt, other)*

Risk of alienating anyone: _____

Audience Expectations about the Document

Reason document originated: _____ *(audience request, my idea, other)*

Acceptable length: _____ *(comprehensive, concise, other)*

Material important to this audience: _____ *(interpretations, costs, other)*

Most useful arrangement: _____ *(problem-causes-solutions, other)*

Tone: _____ *(businesslike, apologetic, enthusiastic, other)*

Cultural considerations: _____ *(level of detail or directness, other)*

Intended effect on this audience: _____ *(win support, change behavior, other)*

Due date: _____

FIGURE 3.7 Audience and Use Profile Sheet For a completed profile in an actual writing situation, see Figure 4.5.

making some decision? Will people act immediately on the information? Do they need step-by-step instructions? In your audience's view, what is most important about this document? Try asking them directly.

Audience's Technical Background

Colleagues who speak your technical language will understand raw data. Managers who have limited technical knowledge expect interpretations and explanations. Clients with little or no technical background want to know what this information means to them, personally (to their health, pocketbook, finances). However, none of these generalizations might apply to your situation. When in doubt, aim for low technicality.

Audience's Cultural Background

Some information needs are culturally determined. German audiences, for example, often value thoroughness and complexity, with detail included and explained in a businesslike tone. Japanese audiences generally prefer multiple perspectives on the material, lots of graphics, and a friendly, encouraging tone (Hein 125–26). Anglo-American business culture generally values plain talk that gets right to the point, but Asian cultures consider this rude, preferring indirect, more ambiguous messages, which leave interpretation up to the reader (Leki 151; Martin and Chaney 276–77). Consider how cultural differences might create misunderstanding in your situation.

Performance Objectives for This Document

Spell out the *performance objectives*, the precise tasks that users must accomplish successfully (or the precise knowledge they must acquire) (Carliner, "Physical" 564; Zibell 13). These tasks are most apparent when the document is a set of instructions, say, for installing software or for using a new piece of medical equipment. But other forms of communication, such as reports and memos, also involve user tasks. For instance, a project manager might read daily progress reports to keep track of a team's work activities and to plan future activities; or the manager might study an accident report to learn all the facts before drafting a proposal for stricter safety procedures. A potential investor might need to understand the concept of gene therapy before deciding to invest in a biomedical company. In short, people read the document because they want to use this knowledge to *do* something.

For defining the tasks or topics your document will cover, develop an outline of steps and substeps (or of major points and supporting points). In preparing an instruction manual to accompany a lawnmower, for example, you might specify the performance objectives outlined in Figure 3.8.

Performance Objectives for Using the Model 76 Boban Lawnmower

1. Assemble the lawnmower
   a. Remove the unit from the carton.
   b. Assemble the handle.
   c. Assemble the cover plate.
   d. Connect the spark plug wire.
2. Operate the lawnmower
   a. Add oil and fuel.
   b. Adjust the cutting height.
   c. Adjust the engine control.
   d. Start the engine.
   e. Mow the grass.
   f. Stop the engine.
3. Maintain the lawnmower
   a. Clean the mower after each use.
   b. Keep oil level full and key parts lubricated.
   c. Replace the air filter as needed.
   d. Keep the blade sharpened.

FIGURE 3.8 A Task Outline You can determine these tasks by interviewing the lawnmower's designers and by watching "model" users perform the actions.
Source: Adapted from Gurak and Lannon, p. 36.

Many of the substeps in Figure 3.8 can be divided further: For example, "Press primer bulb" and "Hold down control handle" are part of starting the engine.

Setting

Identify the conditions under which this document will be used. Will distractions or interruptions make it hard to pay attention? Will users always have the document in front of them? Will they be scanning the document, studying it, or memorizing it? Will they read page by page or consult the document only randomly?

Possible Hazards or Sources of Error

How might the document be misinterpreted or misunderstood (Boiarsky 100)? Are there any potential "trouble spots" (material too complex for these users, too hard too follow, or too loaded with information)? In planning the lawn-mower instruction manual, for example, learn all you can about the typical users (age, education, and so on). You might observe first-time operators coping with a manual for an earlier model and then ask for their feedback. Find out how most lawnmower injuries occur. Check company records for customer complaints. Get feedback from dealers. Ask your legal department about prior injury claims by customers.

Appropriate Details and Page Design

How much is enough? This depends on what you can learn about your audience's needs. Were you asked to "keep it short" or to "be comprehensive"? Are people more interested in conclusions and recommendations, or do they want everything spelled out? Do they expect a letter, a memo, a short report, or a long, formal report with supplements (title page, table of contents, appendixes, and so)? Can visuals and page layout (charts, graphs, drawings, headings, lists) make the material more accessible?

NOTE   *Although a detailed analysis can tell you a great deal, rarely is it possible to pin down an audience with absolute certainty—especially when the audience is large and diverse. Before submitting a final document, examine every aspect, trying to anticipate specific audience questions or objections. Better yet, ask selected readers for feedback on early drafts.*

Due Date and Timing

Does your document have a deadline? Workplace documents almost always do. Is there a best time to submit it? Due dates and timing are vital for competing effectively (as in submitting bids for a project) or for documenting a new product (as in the Boban Lawnmower "Production Schedule," in Figure 3.9).

Create a Design Plan for the Document

Once you have a clear picture of the audience, purpose, setting, and performance objectives for your document, you can specify what the document should contain and how it should look.

Your *design plan* is your blueprint for meeting the performance objectives you spelled out earlier (Kostur, cited in Carliner, "Physical" 564). A design plan is especially important in collaborative work, so that everyone can coordinate their efforts throughout the document's production. In preparing the instruction manual to accompany the Boban Lawnmower, for example, you might submit the design plan shown in Figure 3.9.

Boban Lawnmowers, Inc.

7/5/07

To: Manual Design Team
From: Jessica Brown and Fred Bowen, team leaders
Subject: Audience/Use Profile and Design Plan for the Model 76 User
           Manual

Based on the following analysis, we offer a design plan for the Model 76 user manual, which will provide safe and accurate instructions for assembling, operating, and maintaining the lawnmower.

PART ONE: AUDIENCE AND USE PROFILE

Audience

The audience for this manual is extremely diverse, ranging from early teens to retirees. Some may be using a walk-behind power mower for the first time; others may be highly experienced. Some are mechanically minded; others are not. Some will approach the mowing task with reasonable caution; others will not.

Setting and Hazards

The 76 mower will be used in the broadest possible variety of settings and conditions, ranging from manicured lawns to wet grass or rough terrain littered with branches, stones, and even small tree stumps—often obscured by weeds and tall grass. Also, the operator will need to handle gasoline on a regular basis.

Our research indicates that most user injuries fall into three categories, in descending order of frequency: foreign objects thrown into the eyes, accidental contact with the rotating blade, and fire or explosion from gasoline.

Our research also suggests that most users read a lawnmower instruction manual (with varying degrees of attention) before initially using the mower, and they consult it later only when the mower malfunctions. Therefore, our manual needs to highlight safety issues as early as the cover page.

FIGURE 3.9 **Design Plan for the Lawnmower Manual** Here you incorporate your analysis of the tasks, users, and setting along with a specific proposal for the content, shape, style, and layout of your document. Depending on its complexity, some other type of document (say, a memo) would call for a design plan that is far more simple—perhaps merely a rough outline; a long proposal, on the other hand, would call for a far more intricate plan.

Source: Adapted from Gurak and Lannon, p. 38.

Purpose

This manual has three purposes:

1. Instruct the user in assembling, operating, and maintaining the lawnmower.

2. Provide adequate safety instructions to protect the user and to comply with legal requirements.

3. Provide a phone number, Web address, and other contact information for users who have questions or who need replacement parts.

Performance Objectives

This manual will address three main tasks:

1. **How to assemble the lawnmower.** This task is fairly straightforward, involving four simple steps—but they have to be done correctly to avoid damage to the unit and to ensure smooth operation.

2. **How to operate the lawnmower.** This task requires accurate measurements and adjustments and constant vigilance. Because this is the part of the procedure during which the vast proportion of injuries occur, we need to stress safety at all times.

3. **How to maintain the lawnmower.** To keep the mower in good operating condition, users need to attend to these steps regularly and to be especially careful to wear eye protection if they sharpen their own blade.

PART TWO: DESIGN PLAN

For a manual that is inviting, readable, and easily accessible, we recommend the following plan:

Tentative Outline

- Size, page layout, and color: $8\frac{1}{2} \times 11$ trim size; two-column pages; black ink on white paper.

- *Cover page:* Includes a drawing of the 76 mower and a highlighted reference to safety instructions throughout the manual.

- *Safety considerations:* Cautions and warnings displayed prominently before a given step.

FIGURE 3.9 *(Continued)*

- *Visuals:* Drawings and/or diagrams to accompany each step as needed.
- *Inside front cover:* Table of contents, and customer contact information.
- *Introduction:* A complete listing of all safety warnings that appear at various points in the manual.
- *Section One:* A numbered list of steps for assembling the mower.
- *Section Two:* A numbered list of steps for operating the mower.
- *Section Three:* A bulleted list of tasks required for maintaining the mower, with diagrams and cautions, and warnings as needed.

Production Schedule

The first units of our Model 76 are scheduled for shipment May 4, 2007, and completed manuals are to be included in that shipment. To meet this deadline, we propose the following production schedule:

> **January 15:** First draft, including artwork, is completed and usability tested on sample users.
>
> **February 15:** Manual is revised based on results of usability test.
>
> **March 15:** After copyediting, proofreading, and final changes, manual goes to the compositor.
>
> **April 10:** Page proofs and art proofs are reviewed and corrected.
>
> **April 17:** Corrected proofs go to the printer.
>
> **April 30:** Finished manual returns from printer and is packaged for May 4 shipment.

FIGURE 3.9 *(Continued)*

Write, Test, and Revise Your Document

When your analysis and planning are completed, you can write, test, and revise the document. For a lawnmower manual, you would write the instructions, design the graphics, and select a medium (print, CD, Web—or some combination) for distributing the information.

Once you have a workable draft, test the document on potential users, if possible. Ask people what they find useful and what they find confusing. Or watch people use the material and measure their performance. If someone trying to assemble a lawnmower, for instance, could not locate a part because of unclear instructions, knowing this would be valuable as you revise your material.

How to get user feedback

Ask respondents to identify specific difficulties they encountered in reading the instructions and in performing the task (Hart 53–57; Daugherty 17–18):

- **Content:** Too much or too little information? Inaccuracies?
- **Organization:** Anything out of order, or hard to find or follow?
- **Style:** Anything hard to understand, imprecise, too complex or wordy?
- **Page Design:** Any confusing headings? Too many or too few? Excessively long paragraphs, lists, or steps? Overly complex or misleading visuals? Anything that could be clarified by a visual? Anything cramped and hard to read?
- **Ethical, legal, and cultural considerations:** Any distortion of the facts? Possible legal or cross-cultural problems?

(For more on usability testing, see page 512.)

Based on user feedback, revise your plan and your draft document. To guide your revision, consult the following Usability Checklist. This checklist identifies broad usability standards that apply to virtually any document. In addition, specific elements (visuals, page layout) and specific document types (proposals, memos, instructions) have their own standards. These standards are detailed in the individual checklists for usability throughout this book. In revising the lawnmower instruction manual, for example, you would consult the Checklist for Usability of Instructions (page 517).

☑Checklist: Usability

(Numbers in parentheses refer to the first page of discussion)

Content

☐ Is all material relevant to this user for this task? (36)

☐ Is all material technically accurate? (16)

☐ Is the level of technicality appropriate for this audience? (28)

☐ Are warnings and cautions inserted where needed? (502)

☐ Are claims, conclusions, and recommendations supported by evidence? (60)

☐ Is the material free of gaps, foggy areas, or needless details? (38)

☐ Are all key terms clearly defined? (440)

☐ Are all data sources documented? (634)

Organization

☐ Is the structure of the document visible at a glance? (196)

☐ Is there a clear line of reasoning that emphasizes what is most important? (197)

☐ Is material organized in the sequence users are expected to follow? (207)

☐ Is everything easy to locate? (195)

☐ Is the material "chunked" into easily digestable parts? (211)

Style

☐ Is each sentence understandable the first time it is read? (217)

☐ Is rich information expressed in the fewest words possible? (223)

☐ Are sentences put together with enough variety? (229)

☐ Are words chosen for exactness, and not for camouflage? (232)

☐ Is the tone appropriate for the situation and audience? (238)

Page Design

☐ Is page design inviting, accessible, and appropriate for the user's needs? (298)

☐ Are there adequate aids to navigation (heads, lists, type styles)? (300)

☐ Are adequate visuals used to clarify, emphasize, or summarize? (253)

☐ Do supplements accommodate the needs of a diverse audience? (32)

Ethical, Legal, and Cultural Considerations

☐ Does the document reflect sound ethical judgment? (76)

☐ Does the document comply with copyright law and other legal standards? (85)

☐ Does the document respect users' cultural diversity? (63)

Consider This Communication Failure Can Have Drastic Consequences

Accidents that make headlines often result from human errors such as these:

- *The information is delivered "in the wrong form, at the wrong time, . . . to the wrong person" (Devlin 22).*
- *The information's complexity overwhelms the person receiving it (Wickens 2).*
- *The people involved aren't being attentive or assertive enough.*

Below is a sampling of "honest mistakes" in communication caused by human limitations.

Neglecting to Convey Vital Information

November 1973: The Vermont Yankee Nuclear Power Plant experienced near-meltdown "after day workers installing a closed-circuit television cut off power to a primary safety system and failed to inform the night shift" (Monmonier 209–10).

Not Being Assertive about Vital Information

January 1982: A Boeing 737 crashes on takeoff from Washington National Airport, killing 78 people. "The copilot had warned the captain of possible trouble several times—icy conditions were causing false readings on an engine-thrust gauge—but the copilot had not spoken forcefully enough, and the pilot ignored him" (Pool 44).

Downplaying Vital Information

September 11, 2001: Undetected by airport security, terrorists seize and crash four passenger planes, killing thousands. Investigators later find that, although it had no definite intelligence about suicide hijackings, the Federal Aviation Administration had considered such a possibility as early as 1998. But in its briefings and terrorism alerts to airlines, the FAA either discounted this possibility or failed to mention it at all, focusing instead on the threat of explosives inside of baggage (Yen 7).

Conveying the Wrong Information

December 1998: Nine months after launching, the spacecraft *Mars Climate Orbiter* disappeared just before reaching its orbit around the planet. This $2 billion loss was traced to the fact that metric units of measurement had been used by one NASA ground control team and English units by the other (e.g., meters versus yards). As a result, the confusing instructions to the spacecraft caused it to miss its orbit and burn up in the Martian atmosphere (M. Martin 3).

Underestimating Vital Information

December 1941: "Some people within the U.S. Army knew that a large group of airplanes was headed toward Pearl Harbor; others knew that six Japanese aircraft carriers weren't where they were supposed to be; yet nobody acted on that information" (Davenport 7).

Overlooking Vital Mistakes

August 1996: A 2-month-old boy with a heart defect is admitted to a major hospital in apparent heart failure. He is treated with the drug Digoxin and expected to recover fully. Within hours, his heart stops. All revival efforts fail.

A medical resident had mistakenly ordered a dose of 0.9 milligram—instead of the correct .09 mg. The mistake was then overlooked by the attending doctor, the pharmacy technician who filled the order, and a second resident physician who was asked by a nurse to check the dosage. Because of this error of one decimal point, the patient received 10 times the correct dose of Digoxin (Belkin 28+).

ON THE JOB... Audiences

■ *"Audience makes all the difference. I write for students, small groups of scholars, and general readers. I pitch grant proposals to larger groups of scholars, either nationally (as for the National Endowment for the Humanities) or locally (among colleagues throughout the disciplines at my university). I assume my audiences are happy enough to listen to me at first, but that to keep them reading I need to supply varying degrees of background and explanation pitched to their background and familiarity with the subject matter."*

—John Bryant,
Professor of English

■ *"I write procedures for technicians who install and service our company's photocopiers and other business machines. When the company comes out with a new machine or a better way of installing or servicing our equipment, all district offices get the technical information, the specifications, and a set of procedures written by the engineers who designed the equipment. I then rewrite the procedures to make them easier for technicians to follow. I also give follow-up training sessions to provide our technicians with hands-on experience."*

—Leslie Jacobs,
Service Representative
and former technician

■ *"I'm writing for psychiatrists, nurses, psychologists, and other staff on the unit. Since we use a 'medical model,' I use standard 'jargon' and abbreviations for medical staff."*

—Emma Bryant,
Social Worker

■ *"I write for elected officials, public decision-making groups (commissions, boards of directors, etc.), community organizations, foundation staff and directors, and the general public. The audience makes a very important difference in the writing. We adjust the writing style and the content according to the interests of the audience, their technical knowledge, and the amount of detail needed to make a convincing case. Writing over the head of your audience (sometimes known as 'talking down') is a big risk and a big mistake. We take a lot of time to understand our audiences before we start any writing assignment."*

—Paul Harder,
President,
mid-sized consulting company

Exercises

 Exercises

1. Find a short article from your field (or part of a long article or a selection from your textbook for an advanced course). Choose a piece written at the highest level of technicality you can understand and then translate the piece for a layperson, as in the example on page 31. Exchange translations with a classmate from a different major. Read your neighbor's translation and write a paragraph evaluating its level of technicality. Submit to your instructor a copy of the original, your translated version, and your evaluation of your neighbor's translation.

2. Assume that a new employee is taking over your job because you have been promoted. Identify a specific problem in the job that could cause difficulty for the new employee. Write instructions for the employee for avoiding or dealing with the problem. Before writing, create an audience and use profile by answering (on paper) the questions on page 34.

3. The U.S. Immigration and Naturalization Service's Web site, at <www.ins.gov>, is designed for a truly global audience. After visiting the site, answer these questions:

   • Would this site be easy for virtually any English speaker to navigate? List the features that accommodate users from diverse areas of the globe.
   • Could improvements be made in the site's usability? What improvements would you recommend?

Print out relevant site pages, and be prepared to discuss your conclusions in class.

4. Locate a Web site that accommodates various users at various levels of technicality. Sites for government agencies such as those listed below are good sources of both general and specialized information.

   • Environmental Protection Agency (EPA) <www.epa.gov>
   • Nuclear Regulatory Commission (NRC) <www.nrc.gov>
   • National Institutes of Health (NIH) <www.nih.gov>
   • Food and Drug Administration (FDA) <www.fda.gov>

Examine one of these sites and find one example of (a) material aimed at a general audience, and (b) material on the same topic aimed at a specialized or expert audience. First, list the specific features that enabled you to identify each piece's level of technicality. Next, using the Audience and Use Profile Sheet, record the assumptions about the audience made by the author of the nontechnical version. Finally, evaluate how well that piece addresses a nontechnical user's information needs. (*Hint:* Check out, for instance, the MEDLINE link at the NIH site.)

Print out the site's home page as well as key linking pages, and be prepared to discuss your evaluation in class.

Collaborative Project

Form teams of 3–6 people. If possible, teammates should be of the same or similar majors (electrical engineering, biology, graphic design, etc.). Address the following situation: An increasing number of first-year students are dropping out of the major because of low grades, stress, or inability to keep up with the work. Your task is to prepare a "Survival Guide" for incoming students, to be posted on your department's Web site. The posting should focus on the challenges and pitfalls of the first year in this major. It should include a brief motivational section along with whatever else team members decide readers need. But before you can prepare the guide, you need to do a thorough analysis of its audience and purpose.

Perform your audience and use analysis using the worksheet on page 35 or a modified version of this worksheet. On the basis of your analysis, draft an audience and purpose statement for your online Survival Guide. For example:

The purpose of this document is to explain to new students the challenges and pitfalls of the first year in our major. We will show how dropouts have increased, discuss what seems to go wrong, give advice on avoiding some common mistakes, and emphasize the benefits of remaining in the program.

Brainstorm (page 105) for content (for this exercise, make up some reasons for the dropout rate if you need to). Do any research that may be needed. Prepare a task outline (Figure 3.5) and Part One of your design plan (Figure 3.6). Write a workable draft, and revise until it represents your team's best work.

Appoint a team member to present the finished document (along with a complete audience and use analysis) for class evaluation, comparison, and response.

Service-Learning Project

Create a one-page summary of the purpose, programs, and history of the agency you are planning to work with. Design your summary as an information flyer/fact sheet or as a brochure (page 482) to be distributed to first-time visitors to the agency, or to be included in grant applications or other mailings to request support.

CHAPTER 4

Being Persuasive

Identify Your Specific Goal

Try to Predict Audience Reaction

Expect Audience Resistance

Know How to Connect with the Audience

Allow for Give-and-Take

Ask for a Specific Response

Never Ask for Too Much

Recognize All Constraints

> *Consider This* People Often React Emotionally to Persuasive Appeals

Support Your Claims Convincingly

Consider the Cultural Context

> *Guidelines* for Persuasion

Shaping Your Argument

> *Checklist:* Persuasion

On the Job . . . Persuasive Challenges

Persuasion means trying to influence someone's actions, opinions, or decisions (Figure 4.1). In the workplace, we rely on persuasion daily: to win coworker support, to attract clients and customers, to request funding. But changing someone's mind is never easy, and sometimes impossible. Your success will depend on who you are trying to persuade, what you are requesting, and how entrenched they are in their own views.

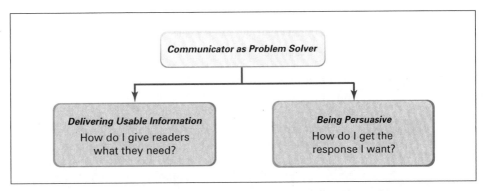

FIGURE 4.1 Informing and Persuading Both Require Audience Awareness

Persuasion is required whenever you tackle an issue about which people disagree. Assume, for example, that you are Manager of Employee Relations at Softbyte, a software developer whose recent sales have plunged. To avoid layoffs, the company is trying to persuade employees to accept a temporary cut in salary. As you plan your various memos and presentations on this volatile issue, you identify your major *claims*. (A claim is a statement of the point you are trying to prove.) For instance, you might want employees to recognize facts they've ignored:

A claim about what the facts are

> Because of the global recession, our software sales in two recent quarters have fallen nearly 30 percent, and earnings should remain flat all year.

Even when a fact is obvious, people often disagree about what it means or what should be done about it. And so you might want to influence their interpretation of the facts:

A claim about what the facts mean

> Reduced earnings mean temporary layoffs for roughly 25 percent of our staff. But we could avoid layoffs entirely if each of us at Softbyte would accept a 10-percent salary cut until the market improves.

And eventually you might want to ask for direct action:

A claim about what should be done

> Our labor contract stipulates that such an across-the-board salary cut would require a two-thirds majority vote. Once you've had time to examine the facts, we hope you'll vote "yes" on next Tuesday's secret ballot.

Whenever people disagree about what the facts are or what the facts mean or what should be done, you need to make the best case for your own view.

On the job, your memos, letters, reports, and proposals advance claims like these (Gilsdorf, "Executives' and Academics' Perception" 59–62):

Claims require
support

> • We can't possibly meet this production deadline without sacrificing quality.
> • We're doing all we can to correct your software problem.
> • This hiring policy is discriminatory.
> • Our equipment is exactly what you need.
> • I deserve a raise.

Such claims, of course, are likely to be rejected—unless they are backed up by a convincing argument.

NOTE   *"Argument," in this context, means "a process of careful reasoning in support of a par-ticular claim"—it does not mean "a quarrel or dispute." People who "argue skillfully" are able to connect with others in a rational, sensible way, without causing animosity. But people who are merely "argumentative," on the other hand, simply make others defensive.*

Identify Your Specific Goal

What do you want people to be doing or thinking? Arguments differ considerably in the level of involvement they ask from people.

- **Arguing to influence people's opinions**. Some arguments ask for minimal audience involvement. Maybe you want people to agree that the benefits of bio-engineered foods outweigh the risks, or that your company's monitoring of employee email is hurting morale. The goal here is merely to move readers to change their thinking, to say "I agree."
- **Arguing to enlist people's support**. Some arguments ask people to take a definite stand. Maybe you want readers to support a referendum that would restrict cloning experiments, or to lobby for a daycare center where you work. The goal is to get people actively involved, to get them to ask "How can I help?"
- **Submitting a proposal.** Proposals offer specific plans for solving technical problems. The proposals we examine in Chapter 23 typically ask audiences to take—or to approve—some form of direct action (say, a plan for improving your firm's computer security or a Web-based orientation program for new employees). Your proposal goal is achieved when people say "Okay, let's do this project."
- **Arguing to change people's behavior**. Getting people to change their behavior is a huge challenge. Maybe you want a coworker to stop dominating your staff meetings, or to be more open about sharing information that you need to do

your job. People naturally take such arguments personally. And the more personal the issue, the greater people's resistance. After all, you're trying to get them to admit, "I was wrong. From now on, I'll do it differently."

The above categories can—and often do—overlap, depending on the situation. But never launch an argument without a clear view of exactly what you want to see happen.

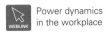 Power dynamics in the workplace

Try to Predict Audience Reaction

Any document can evoke different reactions depending on a user's temperament, interests, fears, biases, ambitions, or assumptions. Whenever peoples' views are challenged, they react with defensive questions such as these:

Audience questions about attempts to persuade

- Says who?
- So what?
- Why should I?
- Why rock the boat?
- What's in this for me?
- What will it cost?

- What are the risks?
- What are you up to?
- What's in it for you?
- What does this really mean?
- Will it mean more work for me?
- Will it make me look bad?

People read between the lines. Some might be impressed and pleased by your suggestions for increasing productivity or cutting expenses; some might feel offended or threatened. Some might suspect you of trying to undermine your boss. Such are the "political realities" in any organization (Hays 19).

No one wants bad news; some people prefer to ignore it. If you know something is wrong, that a product or project is unsafe, inefficient, or worthless, you have to decide whether "to try to change company plans, to keep silent, to 'blow the whistle,' or to quit" (19). Does your organization encourage outspokenness and constructive criticism? Is bad news allowed to travel upward, from subordinates to superiors (say, senior management), and if so, is the news likely to be accepted or suppressed? Can the decision makers be persuaded to respond in positive ways? Find out—preferably before you take the job. For more on conveying bad-news messages, see pages 331, 372–73.

Expect Audience Resistance

People who haven't made up their minds about what to do or think are more likely to be receptive to persuasive influence.

We rely on persuasion to help us make up our minds

We need others' arguments and evidence. We're busy. We can't and don't want to discover and reason out everything for ourselves. We look for help, for short cuts, in making up our minds. (Gilsdorf, "Write Me" 12)

People who *have* decided what to think, however, naturally assume they're right, and they often refuse to budge. Whenever you question people's stance on an issue or try to change their behavior, expect resistance:

> By its nature, informing "works" more often than persuading does. While most people do not mind taking in some new facts, many people do resist efforts to change their opinions, attitudes, or behaviors. (Gilsdorf, "Executives' and Academics' Perception" 61)

Getting people to admit you might be right means getting them to admit they might be wrong. The more strongly they identify with their position, the more resistance you can expect.

When people do yield to persuasion, they may respond grudgingly, willingly, or enthusiastically (Figure 4.2). Researchers categorize these responses as compliance, identification, or internalization (Kelman 51–60):

- **Compliance:** "I'm yielding to your demand in order to get a reward or to avoid punishment. I really don't accept it, but I feel pressured, and so I'll go along to get along."
- **Identification:** "I'm going along with your appeal because I like and believe you, I want you to like me, and I feel we have something in common."
- **Internalization:** "I'm yielding because what you're saying makes good sense and it fits my goals and values."

Although compliance is sometimes necessary (as in military orders or workplace safety regulations), nobody likes to be coerced. If readers merely comply because they feel they have no choice, you probably have lost their loyalty and goodwill—and as soon as the threat or reward disappears, you will lose their compliance as well.

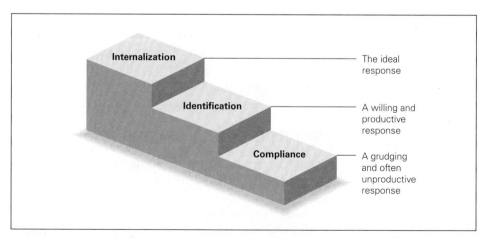

FIGURE 4.2 The Levels of Response to Persuasion

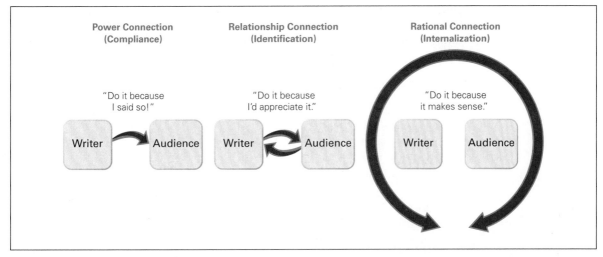

FIGURE 4.3 **Three Strategies for Connecting with an Audience**   Instead of intimidating people, try to appeal to the relationship or—better yet—appeal to people's intelligence as well.

Know How to Connect with the Audience

Persuasive people know when to simply declare what they want, when to reach out and create a relationship, when to appeal to reason and common sense—or when to employ some combination of these strategies (Kipnis and Schmidt 40–46). These three strategies, respectively, can be labeled the *power connection*, the *relationship connection*, and the *rational connection* (Figure 4.3). For an illustration of these different connections, picture the following scenario.

CASE: Connecting with the Audience

Your Company, XYZ Engineering, has just developed a fitness program, based on findings that healthy employees work better, take fewer sick days, and cost less to insure. This program offers clinics for smoking, stress reduction, and weight loss, along with group exercise. In your second month on the job you read this notice in your email:

TO: Employees at XYZ.com
FROM: GMaximus@XYZ.com
DATE: June 6, 20xx
SUBJECT: Physical Fitness

Power connection: Orders readers to show up

On Monday, June 10, all employees will report to the company gymnasium at 8:00 a.m. for the purpose of choosing a walking or jogging group. Each group will meet for 30 minutes three times weekly during lunch time.

How would you react? Despite the reference to "choosing," people are given no real choice but simply ordered to show up. Typically used by bosses and other authority figures, this type of *power connection* does get people to comply but it almost always alienates them as well!

Suppose, instead, that you receive this next version of our memo. How would you react in this instance?

TO: Employees at XYZ.com
FROM: GMaximus@XYZ.com
DATE: June 6, 20xx
SUBJECT: An Invitation to Physical Fitness

I realize most of you spend lunch hour playing cards, reading, or just enjoying a bit of well-earned relaxation in the middle of a hectic day. But I'd like to invite you to join our lunchtime walking/jogging club.

We're starting this club in hopes that it will be a great way for us all to feel better. Why not give it a try?

Relationship connection: Invites readers to participate

Leaves the choice to the reader

This second version conveys the sense that "we're all in this together." Instead of being commanded, readers are invited—offered a real choice by someone who seems likable and considerate.

Often the biggest factor in persuasion is the reader's perception of the writer. Readers are more open to people they like and trust. The *relationship connection* is especially vital in cross-cultural communication—as long as it does not sound too "chummy" and informal to carry any real authority. For more on tone, see pages 238–45).

Of course, you would be unethical in appealing to—or faking—the relationship merely to hide the fact that you have no evidence to support your claim (R. Ross 28). People need to find the claim believable ("Exercise will help me feel better") and relevant ("I personally need this kind of exercise").

Here is a third version of the memo. As you read, think about the ways in which it makes a persuasive argument.

 The politics of memo writing

TO: Employees at XYZ.com
FROM: GMaximus@XYZ.com
DATE: June 6, 20xx
SUBJECT: Invitation to Join One of Our Jogging or Walking Groups

I want to share a recent study from the *New England Journal of Medicine,* which reports that adults who walk two miles a day could increase their life expectancy by three years.

Other research shows that 30 minutes of moderate aerobic exercise, at least three times weekly, has a significant and long-term effect in reducing stress, lowering blood pressure, and improving job performance.

Rational connection: Presents authoritative evidence

Offers alternatives

As a first step in our exercise program, XYZ Engineering is offering a variety of daily jogging groups: The One-Milers, Three-Milers, and Five-Milers. All groups will meet at designated times on our brand new, quarter-mile, rubberized clay track.

For beginners or skeptics, we're offering daily two-mile walking groups. For the truly resistant, we offer the option of a Monday–Wednesday–Friday two-mile walk.

Offers a compromise

Coffee and lunch breaks can be rearranged to accommodate whichever group you select.

Leaves the choice to the reader

Offers incentives

Why not take advantage of our hot new track? As small incentives, XYZ will reimburse anyone who signs up as much as $100 for running or walking shoes, and will even throw in an extra fifteen minutes for lunch breaks. And with a consistent turnout of 90 percent or better, our company insurer may be able to eliminate everyone's $200 yearly deductible in medical costs.

This *rational connection* conveys respect for the reader's intelligence *and* for the relationship. With any reasonable audience, the rational connection stands the best chance of succeeding.

NOTE

Keep in mind that no cookbook formula exists, and in many situations, even the best persuasive attempts may be rejected.

Allow for Give-and-Take

Reasonable people expect a balanced argument, with both sides of the issue considered evenly and fairly. Persuasion requires flexibility on your part. Instead of merely pushing your own case forward, consider other viewpoints. In advocating your position, for example, you need to do these things:

How to promote your view

- explain the reasoning and evidence behind it
- invite people to find weak spots in your case, and to improve on it
- invite people to challenge your ideas (say, with alternative reasoning or data)

When others offer an opposing view, you need to do these things:

How to respond to opposing views

- try to see things their way, instead of insisting on your way
- rephrase an opposing position in your own words, to be sure you understand it accurately
- try reaching agreement on what to do next, to resolve any insurmountable differences
- explore possible compromises others might accept

Perhaps some XYZ employees, for example, have better ideas for making the exercise program work for everyone.

Ask for a Specific Response

Unless you are giving an order, diplomacy is essential in persuasion. But don't be afraid to ask for what you want:

Spell out what you want

> The moment of decision is made easier for people when we show them what the desired action is, rather than leaving it up to them. . . . No one likes to make decisions: there is always a risk involved. But if the writer asks for the action, and makes it look easy and urgent, the decision itself looks less risky. (Cross 3)

Let people know what you want them to do or think.

 NOTE   *Keep in mind that overly direct communication can offend audiences from other cultures. Don't mistake bluntness for clarity.*

Never Ask for Too Much

Stick with what is achievable

People never accept anything they consider unreasonable. And the definition of "reasonable" varies with the individual. Employees at XYZ, for example, differ as to which walking/jogging option they might accept. To the runner writing the memo, a daily five-mile jog might seem perfectly reasonable, but to most people this would seem outrageous. XYZ's program, therefore, has to offer something most of its audience (except, say, couch potatoes and those in poor health) accept as reasonable.

Any request that exceeds its audience's "latitude of acceptance" (Sherif 39–59) is doomed.

Recognize All Constraints

Constraints are limits or restrictions imposed by the situation:

Communication constraints in the workplace

- What can I say around here, to whom, and how?
- Should I say it in person, by phone, in print, online?
- Could I be creating any ethical or legal problems?
- Is this the best time to say it?
- What is my relationship with the audience?
- Who are the personalities involved?
- Is there any peer pressure to overcome?
- How big an issue is this?

Organizational Constraints

Organizations announce their own official constraints: deadlines; budgets; guidelines for organizing, formatting, and distributing documents; and so on. But communicators also face *unofficial* constraints:

Decide carefully when to say what to whom

Most organizations have clear rules for interpreting and acting on statements made by colleagues. Even if the rules are unstated, we know who can initiate interaction, who can be approached, who can propose a delay, what topics can or cannot be discussed, who can interrupt or be interrupted, who can order or be ordered, who can terminate interaction, and how long interaction should last. (Littlejohn and Jabusch 143)

The exact rules vary among organizations, but anyone who ignores those rules (say, by going over a supervisor's head with a complaint or suggestion) invites disaster.

Airing even a legitimate gripe in the wrong way through the wrong medium to the wrong person can be fatal to your work relationships. The following email, for instance, is likely to be interpreted by the executive officer as petty and whining behavior, and by the maintenance director as a public attack.

Wrong way to the wrong person

> TO: CEO@XYZ.com
> CC: MaintenanceDirector@XYZ.com
> FROM: Middle Manager@XYZ.com
> DATE: May 13, 20xx
> RE: Trash Problem
>
> Please ask the Maintenance Director to get his people to do their job for a change. I realize we're all understaffed, but I've gotten dozens of complaints this week about the filthy restrooms and overflowing wastebaskets in my department. If he wants us to empty our own wastebaskets, why doesn't he let us know?

Instead, why not address the message directly to the key person—or better yet, phone the person?

A better way to the right person

> TO: MaintenanceDirector@XYZ.com
> FROM: MiddleManager@XYZ.com
> DATE: May 13, 20xx
> RE: Staffing Shortage
>
> I wonder if we could meet to exchange some ideas about how our departments might be able to help one another during these staff shortages.

Can you identify the unspoken rules in companies where you have worked? What happens when such rules are ignored?

Legal Constraints

What you are allowed to say may be limited by contract or by laws protecting confidentiality or customers' rights or laws affecting product liability:

Major legal
constraints on
communication

- In a collection letter for nonpayment, you can threaten to take legal action, but you cannot threaten to publicize the refusal to pay, nor pretend to be an attorney (Varner and Varner 31–40).
- If someone requests information on one of your employees, you can "respond only to specific requests that have been approved by the employee. Further, your comments should relate only to job performance which is documented" (Harcourt 64).
- When writing sales literature or manuals, you and your company are liable for faulty information that leads to injury or damage.

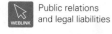 Public relations and legal liabilities

Whenever you prepare a document, be aware of possible legal problems. For instance, suppose an employee of XYZ Engineering (case on page 54) is injured or dies during the new exercise program you've marketed so persuasively. Could you and your company be liable? Should you require physical exams and stress tests (at company expense) for participants? When in doubt, always consult an attorney.

Ethical Constraints

While legal constraints are defined by federal and state law, ethical constraints are defined by honesty and fair play. For example, it may be perfectly legal to promote a new pesticide by emphasizing its effectiveness, while downplaying its carcinogenic effects; whether such action is *ethical*, however, is another issue entirely. To earn people's trust, you will find that "saying the right thing" involves more than legal considerations. (See Chapter 5 for more on ethics.)

NOTE   *Persuasive skills carry tremendous potential for abuse. "Presenting your best case" does not mean deceiving others—even if the dishonest answer is the one people want to hear.*

Time Constraints

Persuasion often depends on good timing. Should you wait for an opening, release the message immediately, or what? Let's assume that you're trying to "bring out the vote" among members of your professional society on some hotly debated issue, say, whether to refuse to work on any project related to biological warfare. You might prefer to wait until you have all the information you need or until you've analyzed the situation and planned a strategy. But if you delay, rumors or paranoia could cause people to harden their positions—and their resistance.

Social and Psychological Constraints

Too often, what we say can be misunderstood or misinterpreted because of constraints such as these:

"What is our relationship?"

- **Relationship with the audience:** Is your reader a superior, a subordinate, a peer? (Try not to dictate to subordinates nor to shield superiors from bad news.) How well do you know each other? Can you joke around or should you be serious? Do you get along or have a history of conflict or mistrust? What you say and how you say it—and how it is interpreted—will be influenced by the relationship.

"How receptive is this audience?"

- **Audience's personality:** Willingness to be persuaded depends largely on personality (Stonecipher 188–89). Does this person tend to be more open- or closed-minded, more skeptical or trusting, more bold or cautious, more of a conformist or a rugged individual? The less persuadable your audience, the harder you have to work. For a totally resistant audience, you may want to back off—or give up altogether.

"How unified is this audience?"

- **Audience's sense of identity and affiliation as a group:** Does the group have a strong sense of identity (union members, conservationists, engineers)? Will group loyalty or pressure to conform prevent certain appeals from working? Address the group's collective concerns.

"Where are people coming from on this?"

- **Perceived size and urgency of the issue:** Does the audience see this as a cause for fear or for hope? Is trouble looming or has a great opportunity emerged? Has the issue been understated or overstated? Big problems often cause people to exaggerate their fears, loyalties, and resistance to change—or to seek quick solutions. Assess the problem realistically. Don't downplay a serious problem, but don't cause panic, either.

Consider This   People Often React Emotionally to Persuasive Appeals

We've all been on the receiving end of attempts to influence our thinking:

- *You need this product!*
- *This candidate is the one to vote for!*
- *Try doing things this way!*

How do we decide which appeals to accept or reject? One way is by evaluating the argument itself, by asking *Does it make good sense? Is it balanced and fair?* But arguments rarely succeed or fail merely on their own merits. Emotions play a major role.

Why We Say No

Management expert Edgar Schein outlines various fears that prevent people from trying or learning something new (34–39):

- **Fear of the unknown:** *Why rock the boat?* (Change can be scary, and so we cling to old, familiar ways of doing things, even when those ways aren't working.)
- **Fear of disruption:** *Who needs these headaches?* (We resist change if it seems too complicated or troublesome.)
- **Fear of failure:** *Suppose I screw up?* (We worry about the shame or punishment that might result from making errors.)

To overcome these basic fears, Schein explains, people need to feel "psychologically safe":

> . . . they have to see a manageable path forward, a direction that will not be catastrophic. They

(continues)

Consider This (continued)

have to feel that a change will not jeopardize their current sense of identity and wholeness. They must feel that . . . they can . . . try out new things without fear of punishment. (59)

Why We Say Yes

Social psychologist Robert Cialdini pinpoints six subjective criteria that move people to accept a persuasive appeal (76–81):

- **Reciprocation:** *Do I owe this person a favor?* (We feel obligated—and we look for the chance—to reciprocate, or return, a good deed.)
- **Consistency:** *Have I made an earlier commitment along these lines?* (We like to see ourselves as behaving consistently. People who have declared even minor support for a particular position [say by signing a petition], will tend to accept requests for major support of that position [say, a financial contribution].)
- **Social validation:** *Are other people agreeing or disagreeing?* (We often feel reassured by going along with our peers.)
- **Liking:** *Do I like the person making the argument?* (We are far more receptive to people we like—and often more willing to accept a bad argument from a likable person than a good one from an unlikable person!)
- **Authority:** *How knowledgeable does this person seem about the issue?* (We place confidence in experts and authorities.)

- **Scarcity:** *Does this person know (or have) something that others don't?* (The scarcer something seems, the more we value it [say, a hot tip about the stock market].)

A typical sales pitch, for example, might include a "free sample of our most popular brand, which is nearly sold out" offered by a chummy salesperson full of "expert" details about the item itself.

Cross-Cultural Differences

Different cultures can weigh these criteria differently: Cialdini cites a survey of Citibank employees in four countries by researchers Morris, Podolny, and Ariel. When asked by a coworker for help with a task, U.S. bank employees felt obligated to comply, or reciprocate, if they owed that person a favor. Chinese employees were influenced mostly by the requester's status, or authority, while Spanish employees based their decision mainly on liking and friendship, regardless of the requester's status. German employees were motivated mainly by a sense of consistency in following the bank's official rules: If the rules stipulated they should help coworkers, they felt compelled to do so (81).

To avoid seeming impolite, certain audiences hesitate to ask for clarification or additional information. In Asian cultures even disagreement or refusal might be expressed as "We will do our best" or "This is very difficult," instead of "No"—to avoid offending and to preserve harmony (D. Rowland 47).

Support Your Claims Convincingly

The most persuasive argument will be the one that presents the strongest case—from its audience's perspective:

Persuasive claims are backed up by reasons that have meaning for the audience

When we seek a project extension, argue for a raise, interview for a job . . . we are involved in acts that require good reasons. Good reasons allow our audience and ourselves to find a shared basis for cooperating. . . . [Y]ou can use marvelous language, tell great stories, provide exciting metaphors, speak in enthralling tones, and even use your reputation to advantage, but what it comes down to is that you must speak to your audience with reasons they understand. (Hauser 71)

Imagine yourself in the following situation: As documentation manager for Bemis Software, a rapidly growing company, you supervise preparation and production of all user manuals. The present system for producing manuals is inefficient because three respective departments are involved in (1) assembling the material, (2) word processing and designing, and (3) publishing the manuals. Much time and energy are wasted as a manual goes back and forth among software specialists, communication specialists, and the art and printing department. After studying the problem and calling in a consultant, you decide that greater efficiency would result if desktop publishing software were installed on all computers. This way, all employees involved could contribute to all three phases of the process. To sell this plan to supervisors and coworkers you will need good reasons, in the form of *evidence* and *appeals to readers' needs and values* (Rottenberg 104–06).

Offer Convincing Evidence

Evidence (factual support from an outside source) is a powerful persuader—as long as it measures up to readers' standards. Discerning readers evaluate evidence by using these criteria (Perloff 157–58):

Criteria for worthwhile evidence

- **The evidence has quality.** Instead of sheer quantity, people expect evidence that is strong, specific, new, different, and verifiable (provable).
- **The sources are credible.** People want to know where the evidence comes from, how it was collected, and who collected it.
- **The evidence is considered reasonable.** It falls within the audience's "latitude of acceptance" (discussed on page 56).

Common types of evidence include factual statements, statistics, examples, and expert testimony.

Factual Statements.   A *fact* is something that can be demonstrated by observation, experience, research, or measurement—and that your audience is willing to recognize.

Offer the facts

| Most of our competitors already have desktop publishing networks in place.

Be selective. Decide which facts best support your case.

Statistics.   Numbers can be highly convincing. Many readers focus on the "bottom line": costs, savings, losses, profits.

Cite the numbers

| After a cost/benefit analysis, our accounting office estimates that an integrated desktop publishing network will save Bemis 30 percent in production costs and 25 percent in production time—savings that will enable the system to pay for itself within one year.

But numbers can mislead. Your statistics must be accurate, trustworthy, and easy to understand and verify (see pages 162–65). Always cite your source.

Examples.   Examples help people visualize and remember the point. For example, the best way to explain what you mean by "inefficiency" in your company is to show "inefficiency" occurring:

Show what you mean

The figure illustrates the inefficiency of Bemis's present system for producing manuals:

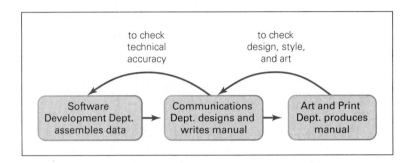

A manual typically goes back and forth through this cycle three or four times, wasting time and effort in all three departments.

Always explain how each example fits the point it is designed to illustrate.

Expert Testimony.   Expert opinion—if it is unbiased and if people recognize the expert—lends authority and credibility to any claim.

Cite the experts

Ron Catabia, nationally recognized networking consultant, has studied our needs and strongly recommends we move ahead with the integrated network.

See page 119 for the limits of expert testimony.

NOTE   *Finding evidence to support a claim often requires that we go beyond our own experience by doing some type of research. (See Part II.)*

Appeal to Common Goals and Values

Evidence alone may not be enough to change a person's mind. At Bemis, for example, the bottom line might be very persuasive for company executives but managers and employees will be asking: Does this threaten my authority? Will I have to work harder? Will I fall behind? Is my job in danger? These readers will have to perceive some benefit beyond company profit.

"What makes these people tick?"

If you hope to create any kind of consensus, you have to identify at least one goal you and your audience have in common: "What do we all want most?" Bemis employees, like most people, share these goals: job security and control over their jobs and destinies. Any persuasive recommendation will have to take these goals into account:

Appeal to shared goals

> I'd like to show how desktop publishing skills, instead of threatening anyone's job, would only increase career mobility for all of us.

People's goals are shaped by their values (qualities they believe in, ideals they stand for): friendship, loyalty, honesty, equality, fairness, and so on (Rokeach 57–58).

At Bemis, you might appeal to the commitment to quality and achievement shared by the company and individual employees:

Appeal to shared values

> None of us needs reminding of the fierce competition in the software industry. The improved collaboration among networking departments will result in better manuals, keeping us on the front line of quality and achievement.

Give your audience reasons that have real meaning for *them* personally. For example, in a recent study of teenage attitudes about the hazards of smoking, respondents listed these reasons for not smoking: bad breath, difficulty concentrating, loss of friends, and trouble with adults. No respondents listed dying of cancer—presumably because this last reason carries little meaning for young people personally (Baumann et al. 510–30).

NOTE *We are often tempted to emphasize anything that advances our case and to ignore anything that impedes it. But any message that prevents readers from making their best decision is unethical, as discussed in Chapter 5.*

 ## Consider the Cultural Context

How cultural differences govern a persuasive situation

 Global communication

Reaction to persuasive appeals can be influenced by a culture's customs and values[1]: Cultures might differ in their willingness to debate, criticize, or express disagreement or emotion. They might differ in their definitions of "convincing support," or they might observe special formalities in communicating. Expressions of feelings and concern for one's family might be valued more than logic, fact, statistics, research findings, or expert testimony. Some cultures consider the *source* of a message as important as its content, or they trust oral more than written communication. Establishing rapport and building a relationship might weigh more heavily than proof and might be an essential prelude to getting down to business. Some cultures take indirect, roundabout approaches to an issue—viewing it from all angles before declaring a position.

Cultures differ in their attitudes toward big business, technology, competition, or women in the workplace. They might value delayed gratification more than

---

[1] Adapted from Beamer 293–95; Gesteland 24; Hulbert, "Overcoming" 42; Jameson 9–11; Kohl et al. 65; Martin and Chaney 271–77; Nydell 61; Thatcher 193–94; Thrush 276–77; Victor 159–66.

immediate reward, stability more than progress, time more than profit, politeness more than candor, age more than youth. Cultures respond differently to different emotional pressures, such as feeling obliged to return favors or following the lead of their peers. (See Consider This, page 60.)

Face saving is every person's bottom line

One key value in all cultures is the primacy of *face saving:* "the act of preserving one's prestige or outward dignity" (Victor 159–61). People lose face in situations like the following:

How people lose face

- **When they are offended or embarrassed by blatant criticism:** A U.S. businessperson in China decides to "tell it like it is," and proceeds to criticize the Tiananmen Square massacre and China's illegal contributions to American political parties (Stepanek 4).
- **When their customs are ignored:** An American female arrives to negotiate with older, Japanese males; Silicon Valley businesspeople show up in T-shirts and baseball caps to meet with hosts wearing suits.
- **When their values are trivialized:** An American in Paris greets his French host as "Pierre," slaps him on the back, and jokes that the "rich French food" on the flight had him "throwing up all the way over" (Isaacs 43).

 Ethnocentrism and cultural difference

Whenever people feel insulted, meaningful interaction is over

Roughly 60 percent of business ventures between the United States and other countries fail (Isaacs 43), often, arguably, because of cultural differences.

Show respect for a culture's heritage by learning all you can about its history, landmarks, famous people, and especially its customs and values (Isaacs 43). The following questions can get you started.

Questions for analyzing cultural differences

What is accepted behavior?

- Preferred form for greetings or introductions (first or family names, titles)
- Casual versus formal interaction
- Directness and plain talk versus indirectness and ambiguity
- Rapid decision making versus extensive analysis and discussion
- Willingness to request clarification
- Willingness to argue, criticize, or disagree
- Willingness to be contradicted
- Willingness to express emotion

What are the values and attitudes?

- Big business, competition, and U.S. culture
- Youth versus age
- Rugged individualism versus group loyalty
- Status of women in the workplace
- Feelings versus logic
- Candor versus face saving
- Progress and risk taking versus stability
- Importance of trust and relationship building
- Importance of time ("Time is money!" or "Never rush!")
- Preference for oral versus written communication

Take the time to know your audience, to appreciate their frame of reference, and to establish common ground.

NOTE
Violating a person's cultural frame of reference is offensive, but so is reducing individual complexity to a laundry list of cultural stereotypes. Any generalization about any group presents a limited picture and in no way accurately characterizes any or all members of the group.

Guidelines for Persuasion

Later chapters offer specific guidelines for various persuasive documents. But beyond attending to specific requirements of a particular document, remember this principle:

No matter how brilliant, any argument rejected by its audience is a failed argument.

If readers find cause to dislike you or conclude that your argument has no meaning for them personally, they usually reject *anything* you say. Connecting with an audience means being able to see things from their perspective. The following guidelines can help you make that connection.

Analyze the Situation

- **Assess the political climate.** Who will be affected by your document? How will they react? How will they interpret your motives? Can you be outspoken? Could the argument cause legal problems? The better you assess readers' political feelings, the less likely your document will backfire. Do what you can to earn confidence and goodwill:

  - Be aware of your status in the organization; don't overstep.
  - Do not expect anyone to be perfect—including yourself.
  - Never overstate your certainty or make promises you cannot keep.
  - Be diplomatic; don't make anyone look bad or lose face.
  - Ask directly for support: "Is this idea worthy of your commitment?" (Senge 7).
  - Ask your intended readers to review early drafts.

  When reporting company negligence, dishonesty, incompetence, or anything else that others do not want to hear, expect fallout. Decide beforehand whether you want to keep your job (or status) or your dignity (more in Chapter 5).

- **Learn the unspoken rules.** Know the constraints on what you can say, to whom you can say it, and how and when you can say it. Consider the cultural context.

- **Decide on a connection (or combination of connections).** Does the situation call for you to merely declare your position, appeal to the relationship, or appeal to common sense and reason?

- **Anticipate your audience's reaction.** Will people be surprised, annoyed, angry? Try to address their biggest objections beforehand. Express your judgments ("We could do better") without making people defensive ("It's all your fault").

(continues)

Guidelines (continued)

Develop a Clear and Credible Plan

- **Define your precise goal.** Develop the clearest possible view of what you want to see happen.

- **Do your homework.** Be sure your facts are straight, your figures are accurate, and that the evidence supports your claim.

- **Think your idea through.** Are there holes in this argument? Will it stand up under scrutiny?

- **Never make a claim or ask for something that people will reject outright.** Consider how much is *achievable* in this situation by asking what people are thinking. Invite them to share in decision making. Offer real choices.

Prepare Your Argument

- **Be clear about what you want.** Diplomacy is always important, but people won't like having to guess about your purpose.

- **Avoid an extreme persona.** Persona is the image or impression of the writer's personality suggested by the document's tone. Resist the urge to "sound off" no matter how strongly you feel, because audiences tune out aggressive people, no matter how sensible the argument. Admit the imperfections in your case. Invite people to respond. A little humility never hurts. Don't hesitate to offer praise when it's deserved.

- **Find points of agreement with your audience.** "What do we *all* want?" Focus early on a shared value, goal, or experience. Emphasize your similarities.

- **Never distort the opponent's position.** A sure way to alienate people is to cast the opponent in a more negative light than the facts warrant.

- **Try to concede something to the opponent.** Reasonable people respect an argument that is fair and balanced. Admit the merits of the opposing case before arguing for your own. Show empathy and willingness to compromise. Encourage people to air their own views.

- **Do not merely criticize.** If you're arguing that something is wrong, be sure you can offer realistic suggestions for making it right.

- **Stick to claims you can support.** Show people what's in it for them—but never distort the facts just to please the audience. Be honest about the risks.

- **Stick to your best material.** Not all points are equal. Decide which material—from your audience's view—best advances your case.

Present Your Argument

- **Before releasing the document, seek a second opinion.** Ask someone you trust and who has no stake in the issue at hand. If possible, have your company's legal department review the document.

Guidelines (continued)

- **Get the timing right.** When will your case most likely fly—or crash and burn? What else is going on that could influence people's reactions? Look for a good opening.

- **Decide on the appropriate medium.** Given the specific issue and audience, should you communicate in person, in print, by phone, email, fax, newsletter, bulletin board? (See also page 57.) Should all recipients receive your message via the same medium? If your document is likely to surprise readers, try to warn them.

- **Be sure everyone involved receives a copy.** People hate being left out of the loop—especially when any change that affects them is being discussed.

- **Invite responses.** After people have had a chance to consider your argument, gauge their reactions by asking them directly.

- **Do not be defensive about negative reactions.** Admit mistakes, invite people to improve on your ideas, and try to build support (Bashein and Marcus 43).

- **Know when to back off.** If you seem to be "hitting the wall," don't push. Try again later or drop the whole effort. People who feel they have been bullied or deceived will likely become your enemies.

NOTE

Trying to change someone's opinion can be hard—but can also make a huge difference. For example, consider this study by the Rand Institute: Health insurers and HMOs often refuse to pay for costly medical treatment or additional services. Among patients who are denied benefits, only 3 or 4 per thousand ever make an appeal to the company, yet 42 percent of such appeals are successful (Fischman 50).

Shaping Your Argument

To understand how our guidelines are employed in an actual persuasive situation, see Figure 4.4. The letter is from a company that distributes systems for generating electrical power from recycled steam (cogeneration). President Tom Ewing writes a persuasive answer to a potential customer's question: "Why should I invest in the system you are proposing for my plant?" As you read the letter, notice the kinds of evidence and appeals that support the opening claim. Notice also how the writer focuses on reasons important to the reader.

Figure 4.5 shows the audience and use profile for the writing situation in Figure 4.4.

NOTE

People rarely change their minds quickly or without good reason. A truly resistant audience will dismiss even the best arguments and may end up feeling threatened and resentful. Even with a receptive audience, attempts at persuasion can fail. Often, the best you can do is avoid disaster and give people the chance to ponder the merits of the argument.

EWING
POWER SYSTEMS
5 North Street   South Deerfield MA 01373

July 20, 20XX

Mr. Richard White, President
Southern Wood Products
Box 84
Memphis, TN 37162

Dear Mr. White:

The writer states his claim

In our meeting last week, you asked me to explain why we have such confidence in the project we are proposing. Let me outline what I think are excellent reasons.

Offers first reason

Gives examples

First, you and Don Smith have given us a clear idea of your needs, and our recent discussions confirm that we fully understand these needs. For instance, our proposal specifies an air-cooled condenser rather than a water-cooled condenser for your project because water in Memphis is expensive. And besides saving money, an air-cooled condenser will be easier to operate and maintain.

Offers second reason

Appeals to shared value (quality)

Gives example

Further examples

Appeals to reader's goal (security)

Second, we have confidence in our component suppliers and they have confidence in this project. We don't manufacture the equipment; instead, we integrate and package cogeneration systems by selecting for each application the best components from leading manufacturers. For example, Alias Engineering, the turbine manufacturer, is the world's leading producer of single-stage turbines, having built more than 40,000 turbines in 70 years. Likewise, each component manufacturer leads the field and has a proven track record. We have reviewed your project with each major component supplier, and each guarantees the equipment. This guarantee is of course transferable to you and is supplemented by our own performance guarantee.

Phone: (413)555-1767   Fax: (413)555-8791   Email: eps@valcom.com

FIGURE 4.4 Supporting a Claim with Good Reasons Give your audience a clear and logical path.
Source: Used with permission of Turbosteam Corporation, Turners Falls, MA.

Richard White, July 20, 20XX, page 2

Offers third reason

Third, we have confidence in the system design. We developed the CX Series specifically for applications like yours, in which there is a need for both a condensing and a backpressure turbine. In our last meeting, I pointed out the cost, maintenance, and performance benefits of the CX Series. And although the CX Series is an innovative design, all components are fully proven in many other applications, and our suppliers fully endorse this design.

Cites experts

Closes with best reason

Appeals to shared value (trust) and shared goal (success)

Finally, and perhaps most important, you should have confidence in this project because we will stand behind it. As you know, we are eager to establish ourselves in Memphis-area industries. If we plan to succeed, this project must succeed. We have a tremendous amount at stake in keeping you happy.

If I can answer any questions, please phone me. We look forward to working with you.

Sincerely,

Tom Ewing

Thomas S. Ewing
President
EWING POWER SYSTEMS, INC.

FIGURE 4.4 *(Continued)*

Audience Identity and Needs

Primary audience: _Richard White, President of Southern Wood Products_

Secondary audience: _Don Smith, Plant Engineer; several plant managers_

Relationship: _A possible customer for a customized cogeneration system_

Purpose of the document: _To make a major sale_

Intended use of document: _To provide information for a purchasing decision_

Technical background: _From high to moderate (for entire audience)_

Prior knowledge about this topic: _Has compared various power-generation systems_

Additional information needed: _Seems to doubt the reliability of our system_

Probable questions: _How much money will your proposed system really save?_

How reliable is the equipment?

Can we depend on the innovative design you are proposing?

What quality of service can we expect?

Audience's Probable Attitude and Personality

Attitude toward topic: _Highly interested, but somewhat skeptical_

Probable objections: _This technology is too recent to have a solid track record_

Probable attitude toward this writer: _Receptive but cautious_

Organizational climate: _Open and flexible; lots of collaboration_

Persons most affected by this document: _White and other decision makers_

Temperament: _White takes a deliberate and conservative approach to decision making_

Probable reaction to document: _Readers should feel somewhat reassured_

Risk of alienating anyone: _No apparent risks_

Audience Expectations about the Document

Reason document originated: _Response to management concerns about reliability_

Cultural considerations: _None in particular_

Acceptable length: _Average business letter that gets right to the point_

Material important to this audience: _Solid evidence to back up our claim of "confidence" in this project_

Most useful arrangement: _A convincing list of reasons and appeals_

Tone: _Encouraging, friendly, and confident_

Intended effect on this audience: _To pave the way for a decision to purchase_

Due date: _ASAP—to illustrate our responsiveness to customer concerns_

FIGURE 4.5 Audience and Use Profile Sheet for Figure 4.4

☑ Checklist: Persuasion

(Numbers in parentheses refer to the first page of discussion.)

Planning and Preparing Your Document

☐ Have I identified my precise goal in this situation? (50)

☐ Am I accounting for the political realities involved? (51)

☐ Can I elicit more than mere audience compliance in this situation? (52)

☐ Have I chosen the approach most likely to connect with this audience? (53)

☐ Am I constructing a balanced and reasonable argument? (55)

☐ Have I spelled out what I want this audience to do or think? (56)

☐ Am I seeking an outcome that is achievable in this situation? (56)

☐ Have I considered the various constraints in this situation? (56)

☐ Do I provide convincing evidence to support my claims? (60)

☐ Will my appeals have personal meaning for this audience? (62)

☐ Overall, do I argue skillfully without being "argumentative"? (50)

Cultural Considerations*

☐ Does the document enable everyone to save face? (64)

☐ Is the document sensitive to the culture's customs and values? (63)

☐ Does the document conform to the country's safety and regulatory standards? (86)

☐ Does the document provide the expected level of detail? (36)

☐ Does the document avoid possible misinterpretation? (36)

☐ Is the document organized in a way that readers will consider appropriate? (200)

☐ Does the document observe accepted interpersonal conventions? (63)

☐ Does the tone reflect the appropriate level of formality or casualness? (64)

☐ Is the document's style appropriately direct or indirect? (63)

☐ Is the document's format consistent with the culture's expectations? (317)

☐ Does the document embody universal standards for ethical communication? (81)

☐ Should the document be supplemented by a more personal medium? (67)

Source: Adapted from Caswell-Coward 265; Weymouth 144; Beamer 293–95; Martin and Chaney 271–77; Thatcher 193–94; Victor 159–61.

ON THE JOB... **Persuasive Challenges**

■ *"Everyone is busy and you must be very clear about why they need to read your communication and, if appropriate, act on it. You are constantly competing to get the 'mindshare' of your readers."*

—Mary Hoffmann, Marketing Communications Manager for a major computer company

■ *"Argument and persuasion are crucial or you will never get done working."*

—Lorraine Patsco, Director of Prepress and Multimedia Production

■ *"My work is all about persuasion. I mainly write for panels or committees reviewing grant proposals to decide whether to fund them: for example, corporate officers making a decision on a corporate gift, trustees of private foundations deciding on a foundation gift, along with private donors. If someone's been generous for years, I can't just write back and say 'Thank you for your check.' Instead, I acknowledge their commitment: 'Once again, you've proven yourself a friend to us at a time when we really needed assistance.'"*

—Ellen Catabia, Grant Writer for a major museum

■ *"I spend much of my time trying to persuade people that the information we offer can help them. Managers have to be persuaded that your recommendations are worthwhile and the best way to go. Clerical staff want to know, 'Will this help me keep my job?'"*

—Blair Cordasco, Training Specialist for an international bank

■ *"For me, persuasion is mostly about getting along with coworkers. What I didn't understand when I started working after college is the whole idea of organizational behavior. I assumed that, as long as I worked hard and did a good job, I would get my raises and promotions. But it's not that simple. I had to leave my first job because I didn't learn soon enough how people react in certain situations, for instance, that 'constructive' suggestions from the new person are not always appreciated.*

My advice: Learn about the people you're working for and with. Spend a lot of time observing, listening, and asking questions about how the organization works at the person-to-person level."

—Ryan Donavan, Programmer

Exercises

 Exercises

1. You work for a technical marketing firm proud of its reputation for honesty and fair dealing. A handbook being prepared for new personnel includes a section titled "How to Avoid Abusing Your Persuasive Skills." All employees have been asked to contribute to this section by preparing a written response to the following:

   > Share a personal experience in which you or a friend were the victim of persuasive abuse in a business transaction. In a one- or two-page memo, describe the situation and explain exactly how the intimidation, manipulation, or deception occurred.

   Write the memo and be prepared to discuss it in class. (See pages 327, 329 for memo format.)

2. Recall an experience in which you accepted or rejected a persuasive appeal that involved some major decision (selecting a college, buying your first car, supporting a political cause, joining the military, or the like). After reviewing pages 59–60, identify the influences that caused you to say "yes" or "no." Be prepared to discuss your experience and its persuasion dynamics in class.

3. Find an example of an effective persuasive letter. In a memo (pages 327, 329) to your instructor, explain why and how the message succeeds. Base your evaluation on the persuasion guidelines, pages 65–67. Attach a copy of the letter to your memo. Be prepared to discuss your evaluation in class.

   Now, evaluate an ineffective document, explaining how and why it fails.

4. Think about some change you would like to see on your campus or at work. Perhaps you would like to promote something new, such as a campus-wide policy on plagiarism, changes in course offerings or requirements, an off-campus shuttle service, or a daycare center. Or perhaps you would like to improve something, such as the grading system, campus lighting, the system for student evaluation of teachers, or the promotion system at work. Or perhaps you would like to stop something from happening, such as noise in the library or conflict at work.

   Decide whom you want to persuade and write a memo (pages 327, 329) to that audience. Anticipate your audience's questions, such as:

   - Do we really have a problem or need?
   - If so, should we care enough about it to do anything?
   - Can the problem be solved?
   - What are some possible solutions?
   - What benefits can we anticipate? What liabilities?

   Can you think of additional audience questions? Do an audience and use analysis based on the profile sheet, page 70.

   Don't think of this memo as the final word but as a consciousness-raising introduction that gets the reader to acknowledge that the issue deserves attention. At this early stage, highly specific recommendations would be premature and inappropriate.

5. Challenge an attitude or viewpoint that is widely held by your audience. Maybe you want to persuade your classmates that the time required to earn a bachelor's degree should be extended to five years or that grade inflation is watering down your school's reputation. Maybe you want to claim that the campus police should (or should not) wear guns. Or maybe you want to ask students to support a 10 percent tuition increase in order to build a new campus center.

   Do an audience and use analysis based on the profile sheet, page 70. Write specific answers to the following questions:

   - What are the political realities?
   - What kind of resistance could you anticipate?
   - How would you connect with readers?
   - What about their latitude of acceptance?
   - Any other constraints?
   - What reasons could you offer to support your claim?

   In a memo (pages 327, 329) to your instructor, submit your plan for presenting your case. Be prepared to discuss your plan in class.

6. Assess the political climate of an organization where you have worked—as an employee, a volunteer, an intern, a member of the military, or a member of a campus group (say, the school newspaper or the student senate). Analyze the decision-making culture of that organization:

- Who are the key decision makers? How are decisions made?
- How are policies primarily communicated (via power connection, relationship connection, rational connection)?
- How much resistance occurs? How much give-and-take occurs?
- What major constraints govern communication?
- How would these considerations affect the way you would construct a persuasive case on an issue of importance to this organization?
- How could the organizational structure be improved to encourage the sharing of new and constructive ideas?

Prepare a memo reporting your findings and recommendations, addressed to a stipulated audience, and based on a thorough audience and use profile. (See pages 341, 342 for more on recommendation reports.)

NOTE: This assignment might serve as the basis for the major term project (the formal proposal or analytical report, Chapters 23 and 24).

 7. Use the questions on page 64 as a basis for interviewing a student from another country. Be prepared to share your findings with the class.

Collaborative Project

Assume the following scenario: Members of your environmental consulting firm travel in teams worldwide on short notice to manage various environmental emergencies (toxic spills, chemical fires, and the like). Because of the rapid response required for these assignments and the international array of clients being served, team members have little or no time to research the particular cultural values of each client. Members typically find themselves having to establish immediate rapport and achieve agreement as they collaborate with clients during highly stressful situations.

Too often, however, ignorance of cultural differences leads to misunderstanding and needless delays in critical situations. Clients can lose face when they feel they are being overtly criticized and when their customs or values are ignored. When people feel insulted, or offended by inappropriate behavior, communication breaks down.

To avoid such problems, your boss has asked you to prepare a set of brief, general instructions titled "How to Avoid Offending International Clients." For immediate access, the instructions should fit on a pocket-sized quick reference card (see page 493).

Working in groups, do the research and design the reference card. You might begin your research at the Library of Congress Country Studies Web site, at <http://lcweb2.locgov/frd/cs/cshome.html>.

Service-Learning Project

Just as the cultures of other nations have different values, so too do subcultures within the United States. Write a letter inviting neighborhood residents to an open house at a Latino community center in a predominantly Hispanic neighborhood. What factors influence how you shape and write your invitation? What language(s) would you use? Explain how your persuasive writing is influenced by cultural and linguistic differences.

CHAPTER 5

Weighing the Ethical Issues

Recognize Unethical Communication in the Workplace

Know the Major Causes of Unethical Communication

Understand the Potential for Communication Abuse

Rely on Critical Thinking for Ethical Decisions

Anticipate Some Hard Choices

Never Depend Only on Legal Guidelines

Learn to Recognize Plagiarism

Consider This Ethical Standards Are Good for Business

Decide Where and How to Draw the Line

Checklist: Ethical Communication

Guidelines for Ethical Communication

On the Job . . . Ethical Issues

Arguments can "win" without being ethical if they "win" at any cost. For instance, advertisers effectively win customers with an implied argument that "our product is just what you need!" Some of their more specific claims can be: "Our artificial sweetener is composed of proteins that occur naturally in the human body [amino acids]" or "Our Krunchy Cookies contain no cholesterol!" Such claims are technically accurate but misleading: amino acids in certain sweeteners can alter body chemistry to cause headaches, seizures, and possibly brain tumors; processed food snacks often contain saturated fat and trans fats—from which the liver produces cholesterol.

We are often tempted to emphasize anything that advances our case and to ignore anything that impedes it. But communication is unethical if it leaves recipients at a disadvantage or prevents them from making their best decision (Figure 5.1). To help insure that your writing is ethical, keep it accurate, honest, and fair (Johannesen 1).

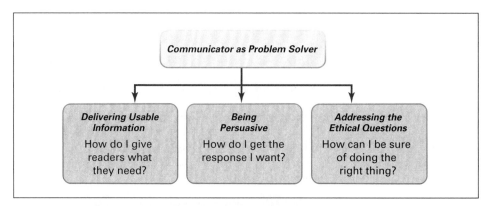

FIGURE 5.1 Three Problems Confronted by Communicators

Recognize Unethical Communication in the Workplace

Recent financial scandals reveal a growing list of corporations accused of boosting the value of company stock by overstating profits and understating debt. As inevitable bankruptcy loomed, executives hid behind deceptive accounting practices; company officers quietly unloaded personal shares of inflated stock while employees and investors were kept in the dark and ended up losing billions. Small wonder that "opinion polls now place business people in lower esteem than politicians" (Merritt, "For MBAs" 64).

NOTE   *Among the 84 percent of college students surveyed who claim to be "disturbed" by corporate dishonesty, "59 percent admit to cheating on a test . . . and only 19 percent say they would report a classmate who cheated" (Merritt, "You Mean" 8).*

Corporate scandals make for dramatic headlines, but more routine examples of deliberate miscommunication rarely are publicized:

Routine instances
of unethical
communication

- A person lands a great job by exaggerating his credentials, experience, or expertise
- A marketing specialist for a chemical company negotiates a huge bulk sale of its powerful new pesticide by downplaying its carcinogenic hazards
- A manager writes a strong recommendation to get a friend promoted, while overlooking someone more deserving

BusinessWeek reports that 20 percent of employees surveyed claim to have witnessed fraud on the job. Common abuses range from falsifying expense accounts to overstating hours worked ("Crime Spree" 8).

Other instances of unethical communication, however, are less black and white. Here is one engineer's description of the gray area in which issues of product safety and quality often are decided:

Ethical decisions
are not always
"black and white"

> The company must be able to produce its products at a cost low enough to be competitive. . . . To design a product that is of the highest quality and consequently has a high and uncompetitive price may mean that the company will not be able to remain profitable, and be forced out of business. (Burghardt 92)

Do you emphasize to a customer the need for extra careful maintenance of a highly sensitive computer—and risk losing the sale? Or do you downplay maintenance requirements, focusing instead on the computer's positive features? The decisions we make in these situations are often influenced by the pressures we feel.

Know the Major Causes of Unethical Communication

Well over 50 percent of managers surveyed nationwide feel "pressure to compromise personal ethics for company goals" (Golen et al. 75). To save face, escape blame, or get ahead, anyone might be tempted to say what people want to hear or to suppress or downplay bad news. But normally honest people usually break the rules only when compelled by an employer, coworkers, or their own bad judgment. Figure 5.2 depicts how workplace pressures to "succeed at any cost" can influence ethical values.

Yielding to Social Pressure

Sometimes, you may have to choose between doing what you know is right and doing what your employer or organization expects, as in this next example:

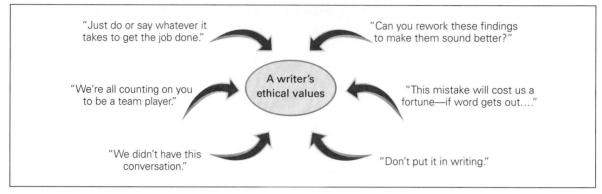

FIGURE 5.2 How Workplace Pressures Can Influence Ethical Values A decision that is more efficient, profitable, or better for the company might overshadow a person's sense of what is right.

An example of pressure to "look the other way"

Just as your automobile company is about to unveil its new pickup truck, your safety engineering team discovers that the reserve gas tanks (installed beneath the truck but outside the frame) may, in rare circumstances, explode on impact from a side collision. You know that this information should be included in the owner's manual or, at a minimum, in a letter to the truck dealers, but the company has spent a fortune building this truck and does not want to hear about this problem.

 Group dynamics and collaboration

Companies often face the contradictory goals of *production* (producing a product and making money on it) and *safety* (producing a product but spending money to avoid accidents that may or may not happen). When production receives first priority, safety concerns may suffer (Wickens 434–36). In these circumstances, you need to rely on your own ethical standards. In the case of the reserve gas tanks, if you decide to publicize the problem, expect to be fired for taking on the company.

Mistaking Groupthink for Teamwork

Organizations rely on teamwork and collaboration to get a job done; technical communicators often work as part of a larger team of writers, editors, designers, engineers, and production specialists. Teamwork is important in these situations, but teamwork should not be confused with *groupthink*, which occurs when group pressure prevents individuals from questioning, criticizing, reporting bad news, or "making waves" (Janis 9). Group members may feel a need to be accepted by the team, often at the expense of making the right decision. Anyone who has ever given in to adolescent peer pressure has experienced a version of groupthink.

"I was only following orders!"

Groupthink also can provide a handy excuse for individuals to deny responsibility (see Figure 5.3). For example, because countless people work on a complex project (say, a new airplane), identifying those responsible for an error is often impossible—especially in errors of omission, that is, of overlooking something that should have been done (Unger 137).

People commit unethical acts inside corporations that they never would commit as individuals representing only themselves. (Bryan 86)

Once their assigned task has been completed, employees might mistakenly assume that their responsibility has been fulfilled.

FIGURE 5.3 Hiding behind Groupthink
(*Source:* Judith Kaufman)

Understand the Potential for Communication Abuse

On the job, you write in the service of your employer. Your effectiveness is judged by how well your documents speak for the company and advance its interests and agendas (Ornatowski 100–01). You walk the proverbial line between telling the truth and doing what your employer expects (Dombrowski 79).

Workplace communication influences the thinking, actions, and welfare of numerous people: customers, investors, coworkers, the public, policymakers—to name a few. These people are victims of communication abuse whenever we give them information that is less than the truth as we know it, as in the following situations.

Suppressing Knowledge the Public Needs

Pressures to downplay the dangers of technology can result in censorship:

Examples of suppressed information

- The biotech industry continues to resist any food labeling that would identify genetically modified ingredients (Raeburn 78).
- Some prestigious science journals have refused to publish studies linking chlorine and fluoride in drinking water with cancer risk, and fluorescent lights with childhood leukemia (Begley, "Is Science" 63).
- MIT's Arnold Barnett has found that information about airline safety lapses and near-accidents is often suppressed by air traffic controllers because of "a natural tendency not to call attention to events in which their own performance was not exemplary" or their hesitation to "squeal" about pilot error (qtd. in Ball 13).

Hiding Conflicts of Interest

Can scientists and other experts who have a financial stake in a particular issue or experiment provide fair and impartial information about the topic?

Hidden conflicts of interest

- In one analysis of 800 scientific papers, Tufts University's Sheldon Krimsky found that 34 percent of authors had "research-related financial ties," but none had been disclosed (King B1).
- *Los Angeles Times* medical writer Terence Monmaney recently investigated 36 drug review pieces in a prestigious medical journal and found "eight articles by researchers with undisclosed financial links to drug companies that market treatments evaluated in the articles" (qtd. in Rosman 100).
- Analysts on a popular TV financial program have recommended certain company stocks (thus potentially inflating the price of that stock) without disclosing that their investment firms hold stock in these companies (Oxfeld 105).

Recent conflicts of interest in medical research

Exaggerating Claims about Technology

Organizations that have a stake in a particular technology (say, bioengineered foods) may be especially tempted to exaggerate its benefits, potential, or safety and to downplay the technology's risks. If your organization depends on outside funding (as in the defense or space industry), you might find yourself pressured to make unrealistic promises.

Falsifying or Fabricating Data

Research data might be manipulated or invented to support specific agendas (say, by a scientist seeking grant money). Sometimes it's a matter of timing; developments in fields such as biotechnology often occur too rapidly to allow for adequate peer review of articles before they are published ("Misconduct Scandal" 2).

Distorted visuals and exaggerated claims

Using Visual Images That Conceal the Truth

Pictures are generally more powerful than words and can easily distort the real meaning of a message. For example, as required by law, TV commercials for prescription medications must identify a drug's side effects—which can often be serious. But the typical drug commercial lists the side effects while showing images of smiling, healthy people. The happy images eclipse the sobering verbal message.

A sample nondisclosure agreement

Stealing or Divulging Proprietary Information

Information that originates in a specific company is the exclusive intellectual property of that company. Proprietary information includes company records, product formulas, test and experiment results, surveys financed by clients, market research, plans, specifications, and minutes of meetings (Lavin 5). In theory, such information is legally protected, but it remains vulnerable to sabotage, theft, or leaks to the press. Fierce competition among rival companies for the very latest intelligence gives rise to measures like these:

Examples of corporate espionage

> Companies have been known to use business school students to garner information on competitors under the guise of conducting "research." Even more commonplace is interviewing employees for slots that don't exist and wringing them dry about their current employer. (Gilbert 24)

Misusing Electronic Information

Ever-increasing amounts of personal information are stored in databases (by schools, governments, credit card companies, insurance companies, pharmacies) and of course all employers keep data about their employees. So how we combine, use, and share that information raises questions about privacy (Finkelstein 471). Also, a database is easy to alter; one simple command can change the facts or wipe them out. Private or inaccurate information can be sent from one database to countless others.

Web-based communication abuses

The proliferation of Web transactions creates broad opportunities for communication abuse, as in these examples:

- Plagiarizing or republishing electronic sources without giving proper credit or obtaining permission
- Copying digital files—music CDs, for example—without consent of the copyright holders
- Failing to safeguard the privacy of personal information about a Web site visitor's health, finances, buying habits, or affiliations
- Publishing anonymous attacks, or smear campaigns, against people, products, or organizations
- Selling prescription medications online without adequate patient screening or physician consultation
- Offering inaccurate medical advice or information

Withholding Information People Need for Their Jobs

Nowhere is the adage that "information is power" more true than among coworkers. One sure way to sabotage a colleague is to deprive that person of information about the task at hand. Studies show that employees withhold information for more benign reasons as well, such as fear that someone else might take credit for their work or might "shoot them down" (Davenport 90). See also page 109.

 ## Exploiting Cultural Differences

Based on its level of business experience or its particular social values or financial need, a given culture might be especially vulnerable to manipulation or deception.

Some countries, for example, place greater reliance on interpersonal trust than on lawyers or legal wording, and a handshake can be worth more than the fine print of a legal contract. Other countries may tolerate abuse or destruction of their natural resources in order to generate much-needed income. If you know something about a culture's habits or business practices and if you use this information unfairly to get a sale or make a profit, you are behaving unethically.

Consider this recent attempt to use cultural differences as a basis for violating personal privacy: In a program of library surveillance, the FBI asked librarians to compile lists of materials being read by any "foreign national patron" or anyone with a "foreign sounding name." The librarians refused (Crumpton 8).

Rely on Critical Thinking for Ethical Decisions

Because of their effects on people and on your career, ethical decisions challenge your critical thinking skills:

Ethical decisions require critical thinking

- How can I know the "right action" in this situation?
- What are my obligations, and to whom, in this situation?
- What values or ideals do I want to stand for in this situation?
- What is likely to happen if I do X—or Y?

Ethical issues resist simple formulas, but the following criteria offer some guidance.

Reasonable Criteria for Ethical Judgment

Reasonable criteria (standards that most people consider acceptable) take the form of *obligations, ideals,* and *consequences* (Ruggiero, 3rd ed. 33–34; Christians et al. 17–18). *Obligations* are the responsibilities you have to everyone involved:

Our obligations are varied and often conflicting

- **Obligation to yourself,** to act in your own self-interest and according to good conscience
- **Obligation to clients and customers,** to stand by the people to whom you are bound by contract—and who pay the bills
- **Obligation to your company,** to advance its goals, respect its policies, protect confidential information, and expose misconduct that would harm the organization
- **Obligation to coworkers,** to promote their safety and well-being
- **Obligation to the community,** to preserve the local economy, welfare, and quality of life
- **Obligation to society,** to consider the national and global impact of your actions

When the interests of these parties conflict—as they often do—you have to decide where your primary obligations lie.

Ideals are the values that you believe in or stand for: loyalty, friendship, compassion, dignity, fairness, and whatever qualities make you who you are. *Consequences* are the beneficial or harmful results of your actions. Consequences may be immediate or delayed, intentional or unintentional, obvious or subtle. Some consequences are easy to predict; some are difficult; some are impossible. Figure 5.4 depicts the relations among these three criteria.

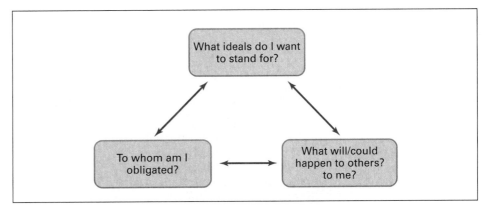

FIGURE 5.4 Reasonable Criteria for Ethical Judgment

The preceding criteria help us understand why even good intentions can produce bad judgments, as in the following situation.

What seems like the "right action" might be the wrong one

> Someone observes . . . that waste from the local mill is seeping into the water table and polluting the water supply. This is a serious situation and requires a remedy. But before one can be found, extremists condemn the mill for lack of conscience and for exploiting the community. People get upset and clamor for the mill to be shut down and its management tried on criminal charges. The next thing you know, the plant does close, 500 workers are without jobs, and no solution has been found for the pollution problem. (Hauser 96)

Because of their zealous dedication to the *ideal* of a pollution-free environment, the extremist protestors failed to anticipate the *consequences* of their protest or to respect their *obligation* to the community's economic welfare.

Ethical Dilemmas

Ethical questions often resist easy answers

Ethics decisions are especially frustrating when no single choice seems acceptable (Ruggiero, 3rd ed. 35). In private and public ways, such dilemmas are inescapable. For example, the proclaimed goal of "welfare reform" is to free people from lifelong economic dependence. One could argue that dedication to this *consequence* would violate our *obligations* (to the poor and the sick) and our *ideals* (of compassion or fairness). On the basis of our three criteria, how else might the welfare-reform issue be considered?

Anticipate Some Hard Choices

Communicators' ethical choices basically are concerned with honesty in choosing to reveal or conceal information:

- What exactly do I report and to whom?
- How much do I reveal or conceal?
- How do I say what I have to say?
- Could misplaced obligation to one party be causing me to deceive others?

The following scenario illustrates a hard choice at a workplace.

CASE: A Hard Choice

You are an assistant structural engineer working on the construction of a nuclear power plant in a developing country. After years of construction delays and cost overruns, the plant finally has received its limited operating license from the country's Nuclear Regulatory Commission (NRC).

During your final inspection of the nuclear core containment unit, on February 15, you discover a ten-foot-long hairline crack in a section of the reinforced concrete floor, within 20 feet of the area where the cooling pipes enter the containment unit. (The especially cold and snowless winter likely has caused a frost heave under a small part of the foundation.) The crack has either just appeared or was overlooked by NRC inspectors on February 10.

The crack could be perfectly harmless, caused by normal settling of the structure; and this is, after all, a "redundant" containment system (a shell within a shell). But, then again, the crack might also signal some kind of serious stress on the entire containment unit, which ultimately could damage the entry and exit cooling pipes or other vital structures.

You phone your boss, who is just about to leave on vacation, and who tells you, "Forget it; no problem," and hangs up.

You know that if the crack is reported, the whole start-up process scheduled for February 16 will be delayed indefinitely. More money will be lost; excavation, reinforcement, and further testing will be required—and many people with a stake in this project (from company executives to construction officials to shareholders) will be furious—especially if your report turns out to be a false alarm. All segments of plant management are geared up for the final big moment. Media coverage will be widespread. As the bearer of bad news—and bad publicity—you suspect that, even if you turn out to be right, your own career could be damaged by your apparent overreaction.

On the other hand, ignoring the crack could compromise the system's safety, with unforeseeable consequences. Of course, no one would ever be able to implicate you. The NRC has already inspected and approved the containment unit—leaving you, your boss, and your company in the clear. You have very little time to decide. Start-up is scheduled for tomorrow, at which time the containment system will become intensely radioactive.

What would you do? Justify your decision on the basis of the obligations, ideals, and consequences involved.

You may have to choose between the goals of your organization and what you know is right

Working professionals commonly face similar choices, which they must often make alone or on the spur of the moment, without the luxury of meditation or consultation.

Never Depend Only on Legal Guidelines

Communication can be legal without being ethical

Can the law tell you how to communicate ethically? Sometimes. If you stay within the law, are you being ethical? Not always—as illustrated in this chapter's earlier section on communication abuses. In fact, even threatening statements made on the Web are considered legal by the Supreme Court as long as they are not likely to cause "imminent lawless action" (Gibbs, "Speech" 34).

Legal standards "sometimes do no more than delineate minimally acceptable behavior." In contrast, ethical standards "often attempt to describe ideal behavior, to define the best possible practices for corporations" (Porter 183).

Except for the instances listed below, lying is rarely illegal. Common types of legal lies are depicted in Figure 5.5. Later chapters cover other kinds of legal lying, such as page design that distorts the real emphasis or words that are deliberately unclear, misleading, or ambiguous.

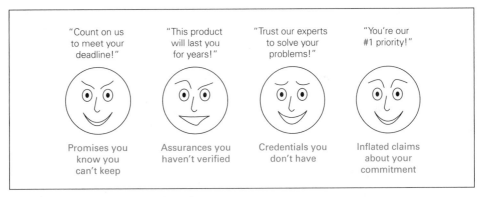

FIGURE 5.5 **Lies That Are Legal**

What, then, are a communicator's legal guidelines? Workplace communication is regulated by the types of laws described below.

Laws that govern workplace communication

- **Laws against deception** prohibit lying under oath, lying to a federal agent, lying about a product so as to cause injury, or breaking a contractual promise.
- **Laws against libel** prohibit any false written statement that attacks or ridicules anyone. A statement is considered libelous when it damages someone's reputation, character, career, or livelihood or when it causes humiliation or mental suffering. Material that is damaging but *truthful* would not be considered libelous unless it

were used intentionally to cause harm. In the event of a libel suit, a writer's ignorance is no defense; even when the damaging material has been obtained from a source presumed reliable, the writer (and publisher) are accountable.[1]

- **Laws protecting employee privacy** impose strict limits on information employers are allowed to give out about an employee. (See page 246 for more on this topic.)
- **Copyright laws** (pages 132–34) protect the ownership rights of authors—or of their employers, in cases where the writing was done as part of their employment.
- **Law against software theft** prohibits unauthorized duplication of copyrighted software. A first offense carries up to five years in prison and fines up to $250,000. Piracy is estimated to cost the software industry more than $2 billion yearly ("On Line" A29).
- **Law against electronic theft** prohibits unauthorized distribution of copyrighted material via the Internet as well as possession of ten or more electronic copies of any material worth $2,500 or more (Evans, "Legal Briefs" 22).
- **Laws against stealing or revealing trade secrets.** The FBI estimates that roughly $25 billion of proprietary information (trade secrets and other intellectual property) is stolen yearly. The 1996 Economic Espionage Act makes such theft a federal crime; this law classifies as "trade secret" not only items such as computer source code or the recipe for our favorite cola, but even a listing of clients and contacts brought from a previous employer (Farnham 114, 116).
- **Laws against deceptive or fraudulent advertising** prohibit false claims or suggestions, say, that a product or treatment will cure disease, or representation of a used product as new. Fraud is defined as lying that causes another person monetary damage (Harcourt 64). Even a factual statement such as "our cigarettes have fewer additives" is considered deceptive because it implies that a cigarette with fewer additives is safer than other cigarettes (Savan 63).
- **Liability laws** define the responsibilities of authors, editors, and publishers for damages resulting from incomplete, unclear, misleading, or otherwise defective information. The misinformation might be about a product (such as failure to warn about the toxic fumes from a spray-on oven cleaner) or a procedure (such as misleading instructions in an owner's manual for using a tire jack). Even if misinformation is given out of ignorance, the writer is liable (Walter and Marsteller 164–65).

Legal standards for product literature vary from country to country. A document must satisfy the legal standards for safety, health, accuracy, or language for the country in which it will be distributed. For example, instructions for any product requiring assembly or operation have to carry warnings as stipulated by the country in which the product will be sold. Inadequate documentation, as judged by that country's standards, can result in a lawsuit (Caswell-Coward 264–66; Weymouth 145).

---

[1] Thanks to my colleague Peter Owens for the material on libel.

NOTE *Large companies have legal departments to consult about various documents. Most professions have ethics guidelines (as on page 91). If your field has its own formal code, obtain a copy.*

Learn to Recognize Plagiarism

Ethical communication includes giving proper credit to the work of others. In both workplace and academic settings, plagiarism (representing the words, ideas, or perspectives of others as your own) is a serious breach of ethics. Even when your use of a source may be perfectly legal, you may still be violating ethical standards if you do not cite the information source.

Examples of plagiarism

Blatant cases of plagiarism occur when a writer consciously lifts passages from another work (print or online) and incorporates them into his or her own work without quoting or documenting the original source. As most students know, this can result in a failing grade and potential disciplinary action. More often, writers will simply fail to cite a source being quoted or paraphrased, often because they misplaced the original source and publication information, or forgot to note it during their research (Anson and Schwegler 633–36). Whereas this more subtle, sometimes unconscious, form of misrepresentation is less blatant, it still constitutes plagiarism and can undermine the offender's credibility, or worse. Whether the infraction is intentional or unintentional, people accused of plagiarism can lose their reputation and be sued or fired.

Plagiarism and the Internet

The rapid development of Internet resources has spawned a wild array of misconceptions about plagiarism. Some people mistakenly assume that because material posted on a Web site is free, it can be paraphrased or copied without citation. Despite the ease of cutting and pasting from Web sites, the fact remains: Any time you borrow someone else's words, ideas, perspectives, or images—regardless of the medium used in the original source—you need to document the original source accurately.

 Plagiarism and corporate document "reuse"

Whatever your career plans, learning to gather, incorporate, and document authoritative source material is an absolutely essential job skill. By properly citing a range of sources in your work, you bolster your own credibility and demonstrate your skills as a researcher and a writer. (For more on incorporating and documenting sources, see A Quick Guide to Documentation, page 634. For more on recognizing plagiarism, go to <www.indiana.edu/~wts/pamphlets/plagiarism.shtml>.)

NOTE *Plagiarism and copyright infringement are not the same. You can plagiarize someone else's work without actually infringing copyright. These two issues are frequently confused, but plagiarism is primarily an ethical issue, whereas copyright infringement is a legal and economic issue. (For more on copyright and related legal issues, see Chapter 8.)*

Consider This   Ethical Standards Are Good for Business

To earn public trust, companies increasingly are hiring "professional ethical advisors" to help them "sort out right from wrong when it comes to developing, marketing, and talking about new technology" (Brower 25). Here are instances of good standards that pay off.

By Telling Investors the Truth, a Company Can Increase Its Stock Value

Publicly traded companies that tell the truth about profits and losses are tracked by more securities analysts than companies that use "accounting smoke screens" to hide bad economic news. "All it takes is the inferential leap that more analysts touting your stock means a higher stock price" (Fox 303).

High Standards Earn Customer Trust

Wetherill Associates, Inc., a car parts supply company, was founded on the principle of honesty and "taking the right action." Among Wetherill's policies:

- *Employees are given no sales quotas, so that no one will be tempted to camouflage disappointing sales figures.*
- *Employees are required to be honest in all business practices.*

- *Lies (including "legal lies") to colleagues or customers are grounds for being fired.*
- *Gossip or backbiting are penalized.*

From a $50,000 start-up budget and 45 people who shared this ethical philosophy in 1978, the company has grown to 480 employees and $160 million in yearly sales and $16 million in profit—and continues growing at 25 percent annually (Burger 200–01).

Sharing Information with Coworkers Leads to a Huge Invention

Information expert Keith Devlin describes how one company's "strong culture of sharing ideas paid a handsome dividend":

> The invention of Post-it Notes by 3M's Art Fry came about as a result of a memo from another 3M scientist who described the new glue he had developed. The new glue had the unusual property of providing firm but very temporary adhesion. As a traditional bonding agent, it was a failure. But Fry was able to see a novel use for it, and within a short time, Post-it Notes could be seen adorning every refrigerator door in the land. (179–80)

For more on the problem of information hoarding among employees, see page 109.

Decide Where and How to Draw the Line

Suppose your employer asks you to cover up fraudulent Medicare charges or a violation of federal pollution standards. If you decide to resist, your choices seem limited: resign or go public (i.e., blow the whistle).

Walking away from a job isn't easy, and whistle-blowing can spell career disaster. Many organizations refuse to hire anyone blacklisted as a whistle-blower. Even if you do not end up being fired, expect your job to become hellish. Consider, for example, the Research Triangle Institute's study of consequences for whistle-blowers in 68 different instances; following is an excerpt:

Consequences of whistle-blowing

"More than two-thirds of all whistle-blowers reported experiencing at least one negative outcome. . . . " Those most likely to experience adverse consequences were "lower ranking [personnel]." Negative consequences included pressure to drop their allegations, [ostracism] by colleagues, reduced research support, and threatened or actual legal action. Interestingly, . . . three-fourths of these whistle-blowers experiencing "severe negative consequences" said they would definitely or probably blow the whistle again. (qtd. in "Consequences of Whistle Blowing" 2)

Despite the retaliation they suffered, few people surveyed regretted their decision to go public.

Employers are generally immune from lawsuits by employees who have been dismissed unfairly but who have no contract or union agreement specifying length of employment (Unger 94). Current law, however, offers some protection for whistle-blowers.

Limited legal protections for whistle-blowers

- The Federal False Claims Act allows an employee to sue, in the government's name, a contractor who defrauds the government (say, by overcharging for military parts). The employee receives up to 25 percent of money recovered by the suit. Also, this law allows employees of government contractors to sue when they are punished for whistle-blowing (Stevenson A7).
- Anyone punished for reporting employer violations to a regulatory agency (Federal Aviation Administration, Nuclear Regulatory Commission, Occupational Health and Safety Administration, and so on) can request a Labor Department investigation. A claim ruled valid leads to reinstatement and reimbursement for back pay and legal expenses.[2]
- Laws in several states protect employees who report discrimination or harassment on the basis of sexual orientation (Fisher, "Can I Stop" 205).
- Beyond requiring greater accuracy and clarity in the financial reports of publicly traded companies, The Sarbanes-Oxley Act of 2002 imposes criminal penalties for executives who retaliate against employees who blow the whistle on corporate misconduct. This legislation also requires companies to establish confidential hotlines for reporting ethical violations.
- One Web-based service, Ethicspoint.com, allows employees to file their reports anonymously and then forwards this information to the company's ethics committee.

Ethical codes for various professions

Even with such protections, an employee who takes on a company without the backing of a labor union or other powerful group can expect lengthy court battles, high legal fees (which may or may not be recouped), and disruption of life and career.

Before accepting a job offer, do some discreet research about the company's reputation. (Of course you can learn only so much before actually working there.)

---

[2] Although employees are legally entitled to speak confidentially with OSHA inspectors about health and safety violations, one survey reveals that inspectors themselves believe such laws offer little protection against company retribution (Kraft 5).

Learn whether the company has *ombudspersons*, who help employees file complaints, or hotlines for advice on ethics problems or for reporting misconduct. Ask whether the company or organization has a formal code for personal and organizational behavior (Figure 5.6). Finally, assume that no employer, no matter how ethical, will tolerate any public statement that makes the company look bad.

NOTE *Sometimes the right choice is obvious, but often it is not. No one has any sure way of always knowing what to do. This chapter is only an introduction to the inevitable hard choices that, throughout your career, will be yours to make and to live with. For further guidance and case examples, go to The Online Ethics Center for Engineering and Science at <www.onlineethics.org>.*

✔ Checklist: Ethical Communication

Use this checklist for any document you prepare or for which you are responsible. (Numbers in parentheses refer to the first page of discussion.)

Accuracy

☐ Have I explored all sides of the issue and all possible alternatives? (117)

☐ Do I provide enough information and interpretation for recipients to understand the facts as I know them? (92)

☐ Do I avoid exaggeration, understatement, sugarcoating, or any distortion or omission that would leave readers at a disadvantage? (80)

☐ Do I state the case clearly instead of hiding behind jargon and euphemism? (233)

Honesty

☐ Do I make a clear distinction between "certainty" and "probability"? (156)

☐ Are my information sources valid, reliable, and relatively unbiased? (150)

☐ Do I actually believe what I'm saying, instead of being a mouthpiece for groupthink or advancing some hidden agenda? (78)

☐ Would I still advocate this position if I were held publicly accountable for it? (78)

☐ Do I inform people of all the consequences or risks (as I am able to predict) of what I am advocating? (77)

☐ Do I give candid feedback or criticism, if it is warranted? (78)

Fairness

☐ Am I reasonably sure this document will harm no innocent persons or damage their reputations? (85)

☐ Am I respecting all legitimate rights to privacy and confidentiality? (80)

☐ Am I distributing copies of this document to every person who has the right to know about it? (81)

☐ Do I credit all contributors and sources of ideas and information? (87)

Source: Adapted from Brownell and Fitzgerald 18; Bryan 87; Johannesen 21–22; Larson 39; Unger 39–46; Yoos 50–55.

IEEE CODE OF ETHICS

WE, THE MEMBERS OF THE IEEE, in recognition of the importance of our technologies in affecting the quality of life throughout the world and in accepting a personal obligation to our profession, its members and the communities we serve, do hereby commit ourselves to the highest ethical and professional conduct and agree:

1. to accept responsibility in making decisions consistent with the safety, health and welfare of the public, and to disclose promptly factors that might endanger the public or the environment;

2. to avoid real or perceived conflicts of interest whenever possible, and to disclose them to affected parties when they do exist;

3. to be honest and realistic in stating claims or estimates based on available data;

4. to reject bribery in all its forms;

5. to improve the understanding of technology, its appropriate application, and potential consequences;

6. to maintain and improve our technical competence and to undertake technological tasks for others only if qualified by training or experience, or after full disclosure of pertinent limitations;

7. to seek, accept, and offer honest criticism of technical work, to acknowledge and correct errors, and to credit properly the contributions of others;

8. to treat fairly all persons regardless of such factors as race, religion, gender, disability, age, or national origin;

9. to avoid injuring others, their property, reputation, or employment by false or malicious action;

10. to assist colleagues and co-workers in their professional development and to support them in following this code of ethics.

Approved by the IEEE Board of Directors | February 2006

FIGURE 5.6 A Sample Code of Ethics Notice the many references to ethical communication in this engineering association's code of professional conduct.

Source: The Institute of Electrical and Electronics Engineers, Inc., <www.ieee.org>. Copyright © 2007 IEEE. Reprinted with permission of the IEEE.

Guidelines for Ethical Communication

How do we balance self-interest with the interests of others—our employers, the public, our customers? Listed below are guidelines:

Satisfying the Audience's Information Needs

1. **Give the audience everything it needs to know.** To see things as accurately as you do, people need more than just a partial view. Don't bury readers in needless details, but do make sure they get all of the facts and get them straight. If you're at fault, admit it and apologize immediately.

2. **Give people a clear understanding of what the information means.** Even when all the facts are known, they can be misinterpreted. Do all you can to ensure that your readers understand the facts as you do. If you're not certain about your own understanding, say so.

Taking a Stand versus the Company

1. **Get your facts straight, and get them on paper.** Don't blow matters out of proportion, but do keep a paper (and digital) trail in case of possible legal proceedings.

2. **Appeal your case in terms of the company's interests.** Instead of being pious and judgmental ("This is a racist and sexist policy, and you'd better get your act together"), focus on what the company stands to gain or lose ("Promoting too few women and minorities makes us vulnerable to legal action").

3. **Aim your appeal toward the right person.** If you have to go to the top, find someone who knows enough to appreciate the problem and who has enough clout to make something happen.

4. **Get legal advice.** Contact a lawyer and your professional society.

Leaving the Job

1. **Make no waves before departure.** Discuss your departure only with people "who need to know." Say nothing negative about your employer to clients, coworkers, or anyone else.

2. **Leave all proprietary information behind.** Take no hard copy documents or computer disks prepared on the job—except for those records tracing the process of your resignation or termination.

The ethics checklist (page 90) incorporates additional guidelines from other chapters. For additional advice, go to "Online Science Ethics Resources" at <www.chem.vt.edu/ethics/vinny/ethxonline.html>.

Source: Adapted from G. Clark 194; Unger 127–30; Lenzer and Shook 102.

ON THE JOB... Ethical Issues

■ *"You want to present your information in the most compelling way without being misleading. It's easy to go over the edge in your effort to make your case. That's why the company requires a legal review for most customer communications."*

—Mary Hoffmann,
Marketing Communications Manager
for a major computer company

■ *"I have to be EXTREMELY careful of cultural bias. I also have to be conscious of as many related issues as possible when assessing the patient so as not to skew the evaluation. This documentation may also be seen by state agencies and case workers and if for some reason this child brings the hospital to court or vice versa, the document may be used in court."*

—Emma Bryant,
Social Worker

■ *"No one will fault you for promoting your product, as long as the product is legitimate and your claims are honest. The reputation of your company ultimately is your best means of persuading consumers to buy—and buy again. If customers can't depend on you to give them reliable products and service, they will end up going elsewhere."*

—Roger Cayer, Sales Manager
for an electronics retailer

■ *"Most of my writing is for clients who will make investment decisions based on their understanding of complex financial data, presented in a concise, nontechnical way. These people are not in any way experts . They want to know, 'What do I do next?' While I can never guarantee the certainty of any stock or mutual fund investment, my advice has to be based on an accurate and honest assessment of all the facts involved."*

—Roger Fernandez,
Certified Financial Planner

■ *"Organizations that rely on funding from grants and donations are especially conscious of ethical requirements. For example, we submit periodic reports to museum trustees, so they can verify that we're doing what we are supposed to be doing. Also, granting agencies read our reports to make sure everything was done according to rules and regulations and according to the way the grant proposal was originally outlined. In short, maintaining trust and credibility is essential to our survival."*

—Ellen Catabia, Grant Writer
for a major museum

Exercises

 Exercises

1. Visit a Web site for a professional association in your field (American Psychological Association, Society for Technical Communication, American Nursing Association) and locate its code of ethics. How often are communication-related issues mentioned? Print a copy of the code for a class discussion of the role of ethical communication in different fields.

2. Prepare a brief presentation for classmates or coworkers in which you answer these questions: *What is plagiarism? How do I avoid it?* Start by exploring the following sites:

   • *Plagiarism: What It Is and How to Recognize and Avoid It,* from Writing Tutorial Services at <http://www.indiana.edu/~wts/pamphlets/plagiarism.html>

   • *Avoiding Plagiarism,* from the Writing Lab at <http://www.gervaseprograms.georgetown.edu/hc/plagiarism.html>

   Find at least one additional Web source.

   In one page or less, summarize a practical, working definition of plagiarism, and a list of strategies for avoiding it. (See page 175 for guidelines for summarizing.) Attach a copy of relevant Web pages to your presentation. Be sure to credit each source of information (page 638).

3. Examine Web sites that make competing claims about a controversial topic such as bioengineered foods and crops, nuclear power, or alternative medicine. For example, compare claims about nuclear energy from the Nuclear Energy Institute <www.nei.org> with claims from the Sierra Club <www.sierraclub.org>, the American Council on Science and Health <www.acsh.org>, and the Nuclear Regulatory Commission <www.nrc. gov>. Do you find possible examples of unethical communication, such as conflicts of interest or exaggerated claims? Refer to pages 79–82 and the Checklist for Ethical Communication (page 90) as a basis for evaluating the various claims. Report your findings in a memo (pages 327, 329) to your instructor and classmates.

4. Assume that you are a training manager for ABC Corporation, which is in the process of overhauling its policies on company ethics. Developing the company's official Code of Ethics will require months of research and collaboration with attorneys, ethics consultants, editors, and the like. Meanwhile, your boss has asked you to develop a brief but practical set of "Guidelines for Ethical Communication," as a quick and easy reference for all employees until the official code is finalized. Using the material in this chapter, prepare a two-page memo (pages 327, 329) for employees, explaining how to avoid ethical pitfalls in corporate communication.

Collaborative Project

In groups, complete this assignment: You belong to the Forestry Management Division in a state whose year-round economy depends almost totally on forest products (lumber, paper, etc.) but whose summer economy is greatly enriched by tourism, especially from fishing, canoeing, and other outdoor activities. The state's poorest area is also its most scenic, largely because of the virgin stands of hardwoods. Your division faces growing political pressure from this area to allow logging companies to harvest the trees. Logging here would have positive and negative consequences: for the foreseeable future, the area's economy would benefit greatly from the jobs created; but traditional logging practices would erode the soil, pollute waterways, and decimate wildlife, including several endangered species—besides posing a serious threat to the area's tourist industry. Logging, in short, would give a desperately needed boost to the area's standard of living, but would put an end to many tourist-oriented businesses and would change the landscape forever.

Your group has been assigned to weigh the economic and environmental effects of logging, and prepare recommendations (to log or not to log) for your bosses, who will use your report in making their final decision. To whom do you owe the most loyalty here: the unemployed or underemployed residents, the tourist businesses (mostly owned by residents), the wildlife, the land, future generations? In a memo (pages 327, 329) to your supervisor, tell what action you would recommend and explain why. Defend your group's ethical choice in class on the basis of the obligations, ideals, and consequences (page 82) involved.

 Service-Learning Project

Identify a service agency or advocacy group whose goals and values you support: for example, an environmental group or one that opposes the use of animals in laboratory experiments. What is the main ethical argument advanced by this group? What are two or three major objections that opponents offer to justify a different position? After reviewing Chapter 4, prepare a one- or two-page memo (pages 327, 329) responding to these objections for distribution to group members as "Arguing Points."

CHAPTER 6

Working in Teams

Teamwork and Project Management

Guidelines for Managing a Collaborative Project

Conducting Meetings

Guidelines for Running a Meeting

Sources of Conflict in Collaborative Groups

Managing Group Conflict

Overcoming Differences by Active Listening

Guidelines for Active Listening

Thinking Creatively

Reviewing and Editing Others' Work

Guidelines for Peer Reviewing and Editing

Face-to-Face Versus Electronically Mediated Collaboration

Ethical Abuses in Workplace Collaboration

On the Job . . . Collaborative Writing

Technical writers often collaborate

How a collaborative document is produced

Complex documents (especially long reports, proposals, and manuals) rarely are produced by one person working alone. A software manual, for instance, is typically produced by a team of writers, engineers, graphic artists, editors, reviewers, marketing personnel, and lawyers (Debs, "Recent Research" 477). Other team members might research, edit, proofread, or test the document's *usability* (Chapter 3).

Traditionally composed of people from one location, teams are increasingly distributed across different job sites, time zones, and countries. The Internet—via email, streamed video, instant messaging, blogs, and other communication tools— offers the primary means for distributed (or virtual) teams to interact. In addition, tools such as computer-supported cooperative work (CSCW) software and project management software such as Microsoft Project allow distributed teams to collaborate. But whether the team is on-site or distributed, members have to find ways of expressing their views persuasively, of accepting constructive criticism, and of getting along and reaching agreement with others who hold different views.

Teamwork and Project Management

Teamwork is successful only when there is strong cooperation, a recognized team structure, and clear communication. The following guidelines explain how to manage a team project in a systematic way.

Using project-planning software and tools

Guidelines for Managing a Collaborative Project

- **Appoint a group manager.** The manager assigns tasks, enforces deadlines, conducts meetings, consults with supervisors, and "runs the show."
- **Define a clear and definite goal.** Compose a purpose statement (page 47) that spells out the project's goal and the plan for achieving the goal. Be sure each member understands the goal.
- **Identify the type of document required.** Is this a report, a proposal, a manual, a brochure? Are visuals and supplements (abstract, appendices, and so on) needed? Will the document be in hard copy or digital form or both?
- **Divide the tasks.** Who will be responsible for which parts of the document or which phases of the project? Who is best at doing what (writing, editing, layout and graphics, oral presentation)? Which tasks will be done individually and which collectively?

NOTE *Spell out—in writing—clear expectations for each team member. Also keep in mind that the final version should display one consistent style throughout, as if written by one person only.*

(continues)

Guidelines (continued)

- **Establish a timetable.** Gantt and PERT charts (see pages 272–74) help the team visualize the whole project as well as each part, along with start-up and completion dates for each phase.
- **Decide on a meeting schedule.** How often will the group meet, and where and for how long?
- **Establish a procedure for responding to the work of other members.** Will reviewing and editing be done in writing, face-to-face, as a group, one-on-one, or online?
- **Develop a file-naming system for various drafts.** It's too easy to save over a previous version and lose something important.
- **Establish procedures for dealing with interpersonal problems.** How will gripes and disputes be aired and resolved (by vote, by the manager, or by some other means)? How will irrelevant discussion be curtailed?
- **Select a group decision-making style.** Will decisions be made alone by the group manager, or by group input or majority vote?
- **Decide how to evaluate each member's contribution.** Will the manager assess each member's performance and in turn be evaluated by each member? Will members evaluate each other? What are the criteria? Figure 6.1 shows one possible form for a manager's evaluation of members. Members might keep a journal of personal observations for overall evaluation of the project.
- **Prepare a project management plan.** Figure 6.2 shows a sample planning form. Distribute completed copies to members.
- **Submit regular progress reports.** These reports (page 331) track activities, problems, and rate of progress.

Source: Adapted from Debs, "Collaborative Writing" 38–41; Hill-Duin 45–50; Hulbert, "Developing" 53–54; McGuire 467–68; Morgan 540–41.

Conducting Meetings

Despite our many digital tools for collaboration (see page 108), face-to-face meetings are still a fact of life because they provide vital *personal contact*. Meetings are usually scheduled for two purposes: to convey or exchange information, or to make decisions. Informational meetings tend to run smoothly because there is less cause for disagreement. But decision-making meetings often fail to reach clear resolution. Such meetings often end in frustration because the leader fails to take charge.

Taking charge doesn't mean imposing one's views or stifling opposing views. Taking charge *does* mean keeping the discussion moving and keeping it centered on the issue, as explained in the guidelines on page 101.

Performance Appraisal for _J. Fishkill_ _____
(Rate each element as [superior], [acceptable], or [unacceptable] and use
the "Comment" section to explain each rating briefly.)
_____

• _Cooperation:_ [_____superior_____]
    Comment: _works extremely well with others; always willing to
                 help out; responds positively to constructive criticism_
_____

• _Dependability:_ [_____acceptable_____]
    Comment: _arrives on time for meetings; completes all assigned
                 work_
_____

• _Effort:_ [_____acceptable_____]
    Comment: _does fair share of work; needs no prodding_
_____

• _Quality of work produced:_ [_____superior_____]
    Comment: _produces work that is carefully researched, well
                 documented, and clearly written_
_____

• _Ability to meet deadlines:_ [_____superior_____]
    Comment: _delivers all assigned work on or before the deadline;
                 helps other team members with last-minute tasks_
_____

                                 R.P. Ketchum _____
                                   Project manager's signature

FIGURE 6.1 Form for Evaluating Team Members Any evaluation of strengths and weaknesses should be backed up by comments that explain the ratings. A group needs to decide beforehand what constitutes "effort," "cooperation," and so on. Equivalent criteria for evaluating the manager might include open-mindedness, ability to organize the team, fairness in assigning tasks, and ability to resolve conflicts and to motivate.

Project Planning Form

Project title:

Audience:

Project manager:

Team members:

Purpose of the project:

Type of document required:

Specific Assignments	**Due Dates**
Research:	Research due:
Planning:	Plan and outline due:
Drafting:	First draft due:
Revising:	Reviews due:
Preparing final document:	Revision due:
Presenting oral briefing:	Progress report(s) due:
	Final document due:

Work Schedule

Team meetings:	*Date*	*Place*	*Time*	*Note taker*
#1				
#2				
#3				
etc.				

Mtgs. w/instructor

#1

#2

etc.

Miscellaneous

How will disputes and grievances be resolved?

How will performances be evaluated?

Other matters (Internet searches, email routing, computer conferences, etc.)?

FIGURE 6.2 Project Planning Form for Managing a Collaborative Project To manage a team project you need to (a) spell out the project goal, (b) break the entire task down into manageable steps, (c) create a climate in which people work well together, and (d) keep each phase of the project under control.

Guidelines for Running a Meeting

- **Set an agenda.** Distribute copies to members beforehand: "Our 10 A.M. Monday meeting will cover the following items: . . ." Spell out each item and set a strict time limit for discussion, and stick to this plan.
- **Ask each person to prepare as needed.** A meeting works best when each member prepares a specific contribution. Appoint someone to take notes or minutes (see page 337).
- **Appoint a different "observer" for each meeting.** At Charles Schwab & Co., the designated observer keeps a list of what worked well during the meeting and what didn't. The list is added to that meeting's minutes (Matson, "The Seven Sins" 31).
- **Begin by summarizing the minutes of the last meeting.**
- **Give all members a chance to speak.** Don't allow anyone to monopolize.
- **Stick to the issue.** Curb irrelevant discussion. Politely nudge members back on track.
- **Keep things moving.** Don't get hung up on a single issue; work toward a consensus by highlighting points of agreement; push for a resolution.
- **Observe, guide, and listen.** Don't lecture or dictate.
- **Summarize major points before calling for a vote.**
- **End the meeting on schedule.** This is not a hard-and-fast rule. If you feel the issue is about to be resolved, continue.

NOTE *For detailed advice on motions, debate, and voting, consult* Robert's Rules of Order, *the classic guide to meetings, at <www.robertsrules.org>.*

Sources of Conflict in Collaborative Groups

Workplace surveys show that people view meetings as "their biggest waste of time" (Schrage 232). This fact alone accounts for the boredom, impatience, or irritability that might crop up in any meeting. But even the most dynamic group setting can produce conflict because of differences like the following.

Interpersonal Differences

A team assessment controversy at Microsoft

People might clash because of differences in personality, working style, commitment, standards, or ability to take criticism. Some might disagree about exactly what or how much the group should accomplish, who should do what, or who should have the final say. Some might feel intimidated or hesitant to speak out.[1]

---

[1] Adapted from Bogert and Butt 51; Burnett 533–34; Debs, "Collaborative Writing" 38; Hill-Duin 45–46; Nelson and Smith 61.

These interpersonal conflicts can actually worsen when the group interacts exclusively online: lack of personal contact makes it hard for trust to develop.

Gender and workplace culture

Gender and Cultural Differences

Collaboration involves working with peers—those of equal status, rank, and expertise. But gender and cultural differences can create perceptions of inequality.

Gender Codes and Communication Style.   Research on ways women and men communicate in meetings indicates a definite gender gap. Communication specialist Kathleen Kelley-Reardon offers this assessment:

How gender
codes influence
communication

> Women and men operate according to communication rules for their gender, what experts call "gender codes." They learn, for example, to show gratitude, ask for help, take control, and express emotion, deference, and commitment in different ways. (88–89)

Kelley-Reardon explains how women tend to communicate during meetings: Women are more likely to take as much time as needed to explore an issue, build consensus and relationship among members, use tact in expressing views, use care in choosing their words, consider the listener's feelings, speak softly, allow interruptions, make requests instead of giving commands (*Could I have the report by Friday?* versus *Have this ready by Friday.*), and preface assertions in ways that avoid offending (*I don't want to seem disagreeable here, but . . .*).

One study of mixed-gender interaction among peers indicates that women tend to be agreeable, solicit and admit the merits of other opinions, ask questions, and admit uncertainty (say, with qualifiers such as *maybe, probably, it seems as if*) more often than men (Wojahn 747).

None of these traits, of course, is gender specific. People of either gender can be soft-spoken and reflective. But such traits most often are attributed to the "feminine" stereotype.

Any woman who breaches the gender code, say, by being assertive, may be seen as "too controlling" (Kelley-Reardon 6). In fact, studies suggest that women have less freedom than male peers to alter their communication strategies: Less assertive males often are still considered persuasive, whereas more assertive females often are not (Perloff 273).

Cultural Codes and Communication Style.   International business expert David A. Victor describes cultural codes that influence interaction in group settings: Some cultures value silence more than speech, intuition and ambiguity more than hard evidence or data, politeness and personal relationships more than business relationships. Cultures differ in their perceptions of time. Some are "all business" and in a big rush; others take as long as needed to weigh the issues, engage in small talk and digressions, chat about family, health, and other personal matters (233).

How cultural codes
influence
communication

 Current information on cultures around the world

Cultures differ in willingness to express disagreement, question or be questioned, leave things unstated, touch, shake hands, kiss, hug, or backslap. Direct eye contact is not always a good indicator of listening. In some cultures it is offensive. Other eye movements, such as squinting, closing the eyes, staring away, staring at legs or other body parts, are acceptable in some cultures but insulting in others (206).

Managing Group Conflict

No team will agree about everything. Before any group can reach final agreement, conflicts must be addressed openly. Management expert David House has this advice for overcoming personal differences (Warshaw 48):

How to manage group conflict

- Give everyone a chance to be heard.
- Take everyone's feelings and opinions seriously.
- Don't be afraid to disagree.
- Offer and accept constructive criticism.
- Find points of agreement with others who hold different views.
- When the group does make a decision, support it fully.

Business etiquette expert Ann Marie Sabath offers these suggestions for reducing animosity (108–10):

How to reduce animosity

- If someone is overly aggressive or keeps wandering off track, try to politely acknowledge valid reasons for such behavior: "I understand your concern about this, and it's probably something we should look at more closely." If you think the point has value, suggest a later meeting: "Why don't we take some time to think about this and schedule another meeting to discuss it?"
- Never attack or point the finger by using "aggressive 'you' talk": "You should," "You haven't," or "You need to realize." See page 221 for ways to avoid a blaming tone.

Ultimately, collaboration requires compromise and consensus: Each person must give a little. Before your meeting, review the persuasion guidelines on page 65; also, try really *listening* to what other people have to say.

Overcoming Differences by Active Listening

Listening is key to getting along, building relationships, and learning. Information expert Keith Devlin points out that "managers get around two-thirds of their knowledge from face-to-face meetings or telephone conversations and only one-third from documents and computers" (163). In one manager survey, the ability to listen was ranked second (after the ability to follow instructions) among thirteen communication skills sought in entry-level graduates (cited in Goby and Lewis 42).

Nearly half our time communicating at work is spent listening (Pearce, Johnson, and Barker 28). But poor listening behaviors cause us to retain only a fraction of what we hear. How effective are your listening behaviors? Assess them by using the questions below.

- Do I remember people's names after being introduced?
- Do I pay close attention to what is being said, or am I easily distracted?
- Do I make eye contact with the speaker, or stare off elsewhere?
- Do I actually appear interested and responsive, or bored and passive?
- Do I allow the speaker to finish, or do I interrupt?
- Do I tend to get the message straight, or misunderstand it?
- Do I remember important details from previous discussions, or do I forget who said what?
- Do I ask people to clarify complex ideas, or just stop listening?
- Do I know when to keep quiet, or do I insist on being heard?

Many of us seem more inclined to speak, to say what's on our minds, than to listen. We often hope someone else will do the listening. Effective listening requires *active* involvement—instead of merely passive reception, as explained in the following guidelines.

Guidelines for Active Listening

- **Don't dictate.** If you are the group moderator, don't express your view until everyone else has had a chance.
- **Be receptive.** Instead of resisting different views, develop a "learner's" mindset: take it all in first, and evaluate it later.
- **Keep an open mind.** Judgment stops thought (Hayakawa 42). Reserve judgment until everyone has had their say.
- **Be courteous.** Don't smirk, roll your eyes, whisper, fidget, or wisecrack.
- **Show genuine interest.** Eye contact is vital, and so is body language (nodding, smiling, leaning toward the speaker). Make it a point to remember everyone's name.
- **Hear the speaker out.** Instead of "tuning out" a message you find disagreeable, allow the speaker to continue without interruption (except to ask for clarification). Delay your own questions, comments, and rebuttals until the speaker has finished. Instead of blurting out a question or comment, raise your hand and wait to be recognized.
- **Focus on the message.** Instead of thinking about what you want to say next, try to get a clear understanding of the speaker's position.
- **Be agreeable.** Don't turn the conversation into a contest, and don't insist on having the last word.

(continues)

Guidelines (continued)

- **Ask for clarification.** If anything is unclear, say so: "Can you run that by me again?" To ensure accuracy, paraphrase the message: "So what you're saying is. . . . Is that right?" Whenever you respond, try repeating a word or phrase that the other person has just used.

- **Observe the 90/10 rule.** You rarely go wrong spending 90 percent of your time listening, and 10 percent speaking. President Calvin Coolidge claimed that "Nobody ever listened himself out of a job." Some historians would argue that "Silent Cal" listened himself right into the White House.

Source: Adapted from Armstrong 24+; Bashein and Markus 37; Cooper 78–84; Dumont and Lannon 648–51; Pearce, Johnson, and Barker 28–32; Sittenfeld 88; Smith 29.

Thinking Creatively

Today's rapidly changing workplace demands new and better ways of doing things:

Creativity is a vital asset

> More than one-fourth of U.S. companies employing more than 100 people offer some kind of creativity training to employees. (Kiely 33)

Creative thinking is especially productive in group settings, using one or more of the following techniques.

Brainstorming

Multiple ideas are better than one

When we begin working with a problem, we search for useful material: insights, facts, statistics, opinions, images—anything that sharpens our view of the problem and potential solutions ("How can we increase market share for Zappo software?"). *Brainstorming* is a technique for coming up with useful material. Its aim is to produce as many ideas as possible (on paper, screen, whiteboard, or the like).

A procedure for brainstorming

1. **Choose a quiet setting and agree on a time limit.**
2. **Decide on a clear and specific goal for the session.** For instance, "We need at least five good ideas about why we are losing top employees to other companies."
3. **Focus on the issue or problem.**
4. **As ideas begin to flow, record every one.** Don't stop to judge relevance or worth and don't worry about spelling or grammar.
5. **If ideas are still flowing at session's end, keep going.**
6. **Take a break.**
7. **Now confront your list.** Strike out what is useless and sort the remainder into categories. Include any new ideas that crop up.

 **Writing processes**

Although brainstorming can be done individually, it is especially effective in a group setting. Brainstorming online, using email or asynchronous "chat" software, can relieve social pressure on participants.

Brainwriting

An alternative to brainstorming, *brainwriting*, enables group members to record their ideas—anonymously—on slips of paper or on a networked computer file. Ideas are then exchanged or posted on a large screen for group comment (Kiely 35).

Mind-Mapping

A more structured version of brainstorming, *mind-mapping* (Figure 6.3A) helps visualize relationships. Group members begin by drawing a circle around the main issue or concept, centered on the paper or whiteboard. Related ideas are then added, each in its own box, connected to the circle by a ruled line (or "branch"). Other branches are then added, as lines to some other distinct geometric shape containing supporting ideas. Unlike a traditional outline, a mind-map does not require sequential thinking: as each idea pops up, it is connected to related ideas by its own branch. Mind-mapping software such as *Mindjet* automates this process of visual thinking.

A simplified form of mind-mapping is the *tree diagram* (Figure 6.3B), in which major topic, minor topics, and subtopics are connected by branches that indicate their relationships. Page 116 shows a sample tree diagram for a research project.

Storyboarding

A technique for visualizing the shape of an entire process (or a document) is *storyboarding* (Figure 6.3C). Group members write each idea and sketch each visual on a large index card. Cards are then displayed on a wall or bulletin board so that others can comment or add, delete, refine, or reshuffle ideas, topics, and visuals (Kiely 35–36). Page 203 shows a final storyboard for a long report.

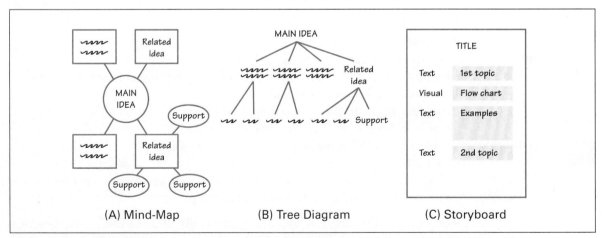

(A) Mind-Map   (B) Tree Diagram   (C) Storyboard

FIGURE 6.3 Visual Techniques for Thinking Creatively Each of these techniques produces a concrete mental image of an otherwise abstract process (i.e., the thinking process).

Reviewing and Editing Others' Work

Documents produced collaboratively are reviewed and edited extensively. *Reviewing* means evaluating how well a document connects with its audience and meets its purpose. Reviewers typically examine a document to make sure it includes these features:

What reviewers look for

- accurate, appropriate, useful, and legal content
- material organized for the reader's understanding
- clear, easy to read, and engaging style
- effective visuals and page design

In reviewing, you explain to the writer how you respond as a reader; you point out what works or doesn't work. This commentary helps a writer think about ways of revising. Criteria for reviewing various documents appear in checklists throughout this book.

Editing means actually "fixing" the piece by making it more precise and readable. Editors typically suggest improvements like these:

Ways in which editors "fix" writing

- rephrasing or reorganizing sentences
- clarifying a topic sentence
- choosing a better word or phrase
- correcting spelling, usage, or punctuation, and so on

(Criteria for editing appear in Chapter 13 and on pages 670–97)

NOTE   *Your job as a reviewer or editor is to help clarify and enhance a document—but without altering its original meaning.*

Guidelines for Peer Reviewing and Editing

- **Read the entire piece at least twice before you comment.** Develop a clear sense of the document's purpose and audience. Try to visualize the document as a whole before you evaluate specific parts.

- **Remember that mere mechanical correctness does not guarantee effectiveness.** Poor usage, punctuation, or mechanics do distract readers and harm the writer's credibility. However, a "correct" piece of writing might still contain faulty rhetorical elements (inferior content, confusing organization, or unsuitable style).

- **Understand the acceptable limits of editing.** In the workplace, editing can range from fine-tuning to an in-depth rewrite (in which case editors are cited prominently as consulting editors or coauthors). In school, however, rewriting a piece to the extent that it ceases to belong to its author may constitute plagiarism. (See pages 87, 636, 638.)

(continues)

Guidelines (continued)

- **Be honest but diplomatic.** Begin with something positive before moving to suggested improvements. Be supportive instead of judgmental.

- **Focus first on the big picture.** Begin with the content and the shape of the document. Is the document appropriate for its audience and purpose? Is the supporting material relevant and convincing? Is the discussion easy to follow? Does each paragraph do its job? Then discuss specifics of style and correctness (tone, word choice, sentence structure, and so on).

- **Always explain why something doesn't work.** Instead of "this paragraph is confusing," say "because this paragraph lacks a clear topic sentence, I had trouble discovering the main idea." (See page 43 for sample criteria.) Help the writer identify the cause of the problem.

- **Make specific recommendations for improvements.** Write out suggestions in enough detail for the writer to know what to do. Provide brief reasons for your suggestions.

- **Be aware that not all feedback has equal value.** Even professional editors can disagree. If different readers offer conflicting opinions of your own work, seek your instructor's advice.

 Effective electronic collaboration

Face-to-Face Versus Electronically Mediated Collaboration

For personal contact, face-to-face meetings are essential. But virtual meetings may allow some people to feel more secure about saying what they really think, by eliminating equality issues that crop up in face-to-face meetings. Also, "status cues" such as age, gender, appearance, or ethnicity are invisible online (Wojahn 747–48).

A number of technologies enable distributed teams to work together:

Tools for electronic collaboration

- **Email.** The most popular tool, email is great for keeping track of discussions.
- **Project management software.** Most large organizations use dedicated software, such as Microsoft Project, to manage complex team projects.
- **Instant messaging.** IM is a fast and easy way to get an answer to a quick question.
- **Groupware.** This special software is used for group authoring and editing.
- **Digital whiteboard.** A large screen allows participants to write, sketch, and erase in real time, from their own computers.
- **Web conferencing.** A password-protected site or company intranet (page 127) provides the medium.
- **Blogs.** Web logs allow users to post material in reverse chronological order and are increasingly used by teams to share and refine ideas.
- **Teleconferencing and videoconferencing.** In these live meetings, participants converse in real time.

Many cultures value the social (or relationship) function of communication as much as its informative function (Archee 41). Therefore, a recipient might prefer certain media, say, a phone conversation to text messaging or email.

Ethical Abuses in Workplace Collaboration

Teamwork versus survival of the fittest

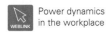
Power dynamics in the workplace

Our "lean" and "downsized" corporate world sends coworkers a conflicting message, encouraging teamwork while "rewarding individual stars, so that nobody has any real incentive to share the glory" (Fisher, "My Team Leader" 291). The resulting mistrust promotes unethical behavior such as the following.

Intimidating One's Peers

A dominant personality may intimidate peers into silence or agreement (Matson, "The Seven Sins" 30). Intimidated employees resort to "mimicking"—merely repeating what the boss says (Haskin, "Meetings without Walls" 55).

Claiming Credit for Others' Work

Workplace plagiarism occurs when the team or project leader claims all the credit. Even with good intentions, "the person who speaks for a team often gets the credit, not the people who had the ideas or did the work" (Nakache, 287–88). Team expert James Stern describes one strategy for avoiding plagiarism among coworkers:

How to ensure that the deserving get the credit

> Some companies list "core" and "contributing" team members, to distinguish those who did most of the heavy lifting from those who were less involved. (qtd. In fisher, "My Team Leader" 291)

Stern advises groups to decide beforehand who will get what credit.

Hoarding Information

Surveys reveal that the biggest obstacle to workplace collaboration is people's "tendency to hoard their own know-how" (Cole-Gomolski 6) when confronted with questions like these:

Information people need to do their jobs

- Whom do we contact for what?
- Where do we get the best price, the quickest repair, the best service?
- What's the best way to do X?

People hoard information when they think it gives them power or self-importance, or when having exclusive knowledge might provide job security (Devlin 179). In a worse case, they withhold information when they want to sabotage peers.

ON THE JOB... Collaborative Writing

■ *"Most of our writing happens in teams. Typically, our project teams (or sometimes just the Project Director) develop a detailed outline for a written product. The team then goes over it together and writing assignments are made (intentional use of the passive voice there). The assignments usually match the content areas for which team members have been responsible. The Project Director (generally me) is responsible for the introduction that describes the purpose or importance of the work and the conclusions/implications. The middle part is "technical" and I usually review those sections without getting into the details. We have a writing style that is consistent across most of our products. It takes about six months for team members to learn to write in that style. One of the biggest team writing challenges we have is the tendency for recent graduates to overwrite. They have learned in their academic programs to write very formally, with ponderous vocabulary and lots of passive voice. Our stuff has to get to the point in a hurry."*

—Paul Harder, President,
mid-sized consulting company

■ *"Unfortunately in my experience, whenever I've had to create documents with a team it's been a small agony. I am good at this process, but it only takes one clueless person on the team to grind the process to a halt. Usually these documentations or reports are created IN ADDITION TO your normal workload, so everyone involved is under pressure because every minute they're collaborating they're not doing the backlog of their normal workload. Then you get the weirdo or two who has a job of no timely responsibility and they find the meetings to be the high point of their careers to date, and they want to shine out and prolong the talking as much as possible, and then nothing gets done. I would much rather create these types of documents alone or with one or two sensible colleagues, and then put the shaped-up document out for review."*

—Terry Vilante, Chief Financial
Officer, small public relations company

■ *"My work in preparing user manuals is almost entirely collaborative. The actual process of writing takes maybe 30 percent of my time. I spend more time consulting with my information sources such as the software designers and field support people. I then meet with the publication and graphics departments to plan the manual's structure and format. As I prepare various drafts, I have to keep track of which reviewer has which draft. Because I rely on others' feedback, I circulate materials often. And so I write email memos on a regular basis. One major challenge is getting everyone involved to agree on a specific plan of action and then to stay on schedule so we can meet our publication deadline."*

—Pam Herbert,
Technical Writer, software firm

Exercises

 Exercises

1. Describe the role of collaboration in a company, organization, or campus group where you have worked or volunteered. Among the questions: What types of projects require collaboration? How are teams organized? Who manages the projects? How are meetings conducted? Who runs the meetings? How is conflict managed? Summarize your findings in a one- or two-page memo.

   Hint: If you have no direct experience, interview a group representative, say a school administrator or faculty member or editor of the campus newspaper. (See page 138 for interview guidelines.)

2. On the Web, examine the role of global collaboration in building the International Space Station. Summarize your findings in a memo to be shared with the class.

   Hint: You might begin by searching this site: <www.nasa .gov>.

Collaborative Projects

1. *Gender Differences:* Divide into small groups of mixed genders. Review page 102. Then test the hypothesis that women and men communicate differently in the workplace.

   Each group member prepares the following brief messages—without consulting with other members:

   - A thank-you note to a coworker who has done you a favor.
   - A note asking a coworker for help with a problem or project.
   - A note asking a collaborative peer to be more cooperative or to stop interrupting or complaining.
   - A note expressing impatience, frustration, confusion, or disapproval to members of your group.

   - A recommendation for a friend who is applying for a position with your company.
   - A note offering support to a coworker who is having a health problem.
   - A note to a new colleague, welcoming this person to the company.
   - A request for a raise, based on your hard work.
   - The meeting is out of hand, so you decide to take control. Write what you would say.
   - Some members of your group are dragging their feet on a project. Write what you would say.

   As a group, compare messages, draw conclusions about the original hypothesis, and appoint one member to present findings to the class.

2. *Listening Competence:* Use the questions on page 104 to:
   a. assess the listening behaviors of one member in your group during collaborative work,
   b. have some other member assess your behaviors, and
   c. do a self-assessment.

   Record the findings and compare each self-assessment with the corresponding outside assessment. Discuss findings with the class.

3. Use your email or instant messaging network to confer electronically on all phases of a collaborative project, including peer review (page 107).

   When your project is complete, write an explanation telling how electronic conferencing eased or hampered the group's efforts and how it improved or detracted from the overall quality of your document.

Service-Learning Project

Plan a group visit to one of the agencies or organizations your class is working with. Include in your planning document instructions detailing who will be in charge of taking notes, leading interviews or conversations, doing background research, and photographing the site. Review and edit the planning document until all of your team members feel comfortable and knowledgeable about their role in the agency visit.

The Research Process

CHAPTER 7
Thinking Critically about the Research Process   114

CHAPTER 8
Exploring Electronic and Hard Copy Sources   122

CHAPTER 9
Exploring Primary Sources   137

CHAPTER 10
Evaluating and Interpreting Information   149

CHAPTER 11
Summarizing and Abstracting Information   173

Thinking Critically about the Research Process

Asking the Right Questions

Exploring a Balance of Views

Achieving Adequate Depth in Your Search

Evaluating Your Findings

Interpreting Your Findings

Consider This Expert Opinion Is Not Always Reliable

Guidelines for Evaluating Expert Opinion

Major decisions in the workplace are based on careful research, with the findings recorded in a written report. Parts of the research process follow a recognizable sequence (Figure 7.1A). But research is not merely a numbered set of procedures. The procedural stages depend on the many decisions that accompany any legitimate inquiry (Figure 7.1B).[1]

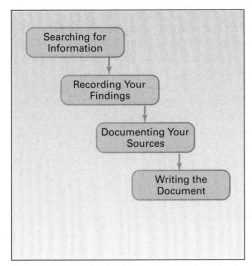

FIGURE 7.1A The Procedural Stages of the Research Process

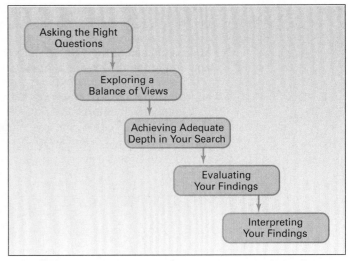

FIGURE 7.1B The Inquiry Stages of the Research Process

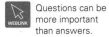
Questions can be more important than answers.

Asking the Right Questions

The answers you uncover will only be as good as the questions you ask. Suppose, for instance, you face the following scenario:

CASE: Defining and Refining a Research Question

You are the public health manager for a small, New England town in which high-tension power lines run within one hundred feet of the elementary school. Parents are concerned about danger from electromagnetic radiation (EMR) emitted by these power lines in energy waves known as electromagnetic fields (EMFs). Town officials ask you to research the issue and prepare a report to be distributed at the next town meeting in six weeks.

First, you need to identify your exact question or questions. Initially, the major question might be: *Do the power lines pose any real danger to our children?* After phone calls around town and discussions at the coffee shop, you discover that townspeople actually have three main questions about electromagnetic

---

[1] My thanks to University of Massachusetts Dartmouth librarian Shaleen Barnes for inspiring this chapter.

fields: *What are they? Do they endanger our children? If so, then what can be done?*

To answer these questions, you need to consider a range of subordinate questions, like those in the Figure 7.2 tree chart. Any *one* of those questions could serve as subject of a worthwhile research report on such a complex topic. As research progresses, this chart will grow. For instance, after some preliminary reading, you learn that electromagnetic fields radiate not only from power lines but from *all* electrical equipment, and even from the Earth itself. So you face this additional question: *Do power lines present the greatest hazard as a source of EMFs?*

You now wonder whether the greater hazard comes from power lines or from other sources of EMF exposure. Critical thinking, in short, has helped you to define and refine the essential questions.

Let's say you've chosen this question: Do electromagnetic fields from various sources endanger our children? Now you can consider sources to consult (journals, interviews, reports, Internet sites, database searches, and so on). Figure 7.3 illustrates likely sources for information on the EMF topic.

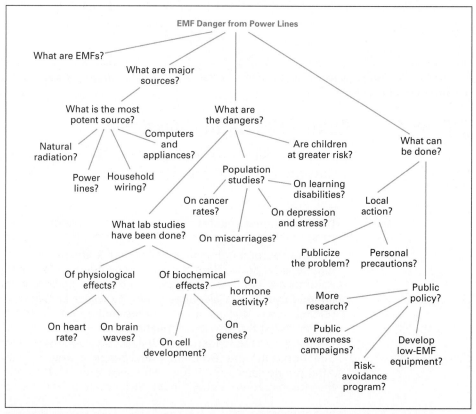

FIGURE 7.2 How the Right Questions Help Define a Research Problem You cannot begin to solve a problem until you have defined it clearly.

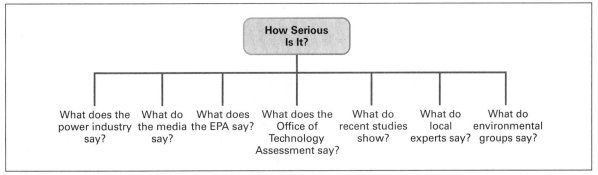

FIGURE 7.3 A Range of Essential Viewpoints No single source is likely to offer "the final word." Ethical researchers rely on evidence that represents a fair balance of views.

Exploring a Balance of Views

Instead of settling for the most comforting or convenient answer, pursue the *best* answer. Even "expert" testimony may not be enough, because experts can disagree or be mistaken. To answer fairly and accurately, consider a balance of perspectives from up-to-date and reputable sources:

Try to consider
all the angles.

- What do informed sources have to say about this topic?
- On which points do sources agree?
- On which points do sources disagree?

NOTE   *Recognize the difference between "balance" (sampling a full range of opinions) and "accuracy" (getting at the facts). Government or power industry spokespersons, for example, might present a more positive view (or "spin") of the EMF issue than the facts warrant. Not every source is equal, nor should we report points of view as though they were equal (Trafford 137).*

Achieving Adequate Depth in Your Search[2]

Balanced research examines a broad *range* of evidence; thorough research, however, examines that evidence in sufficient *depth*. Different sources of information about any topic occupy different levels of detail and dependability (Figure 7.4).

The depth of a
source often
determines its
quality

1. The surface level offers items from the popular media (newspapers, radio, TV, magazines, certain Internet discussion groups, blogs, and certain Web sites). Designed for general consumption, this layer of information often merely skims the surface of an issue.

---

[2] My thanks to University of Massachusetts Dartmouth librarian Ross LaBaugh for inspiring this section.

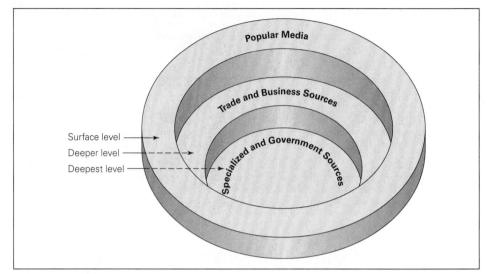

When to skim and when to drill down

FIGURE 7.4 Effective Research Achieves Adequate Depth

2. At the next level are trade, business, and technical publications or Web sites (*Frozen Food World*, *Publisher's Weekly*, Internet listservs, and so on). Designed for users who range from moderately informed to highly specialized, this layer of information focuses more on practice than on theory, on issues affecting the field, and on public relations. While the information is usually accurate, viewpoints tend to reflect a field's particular biases.

3. At a deeper level is the specialized literature (journals from professional associations—academic, medical, legal, engineering). Designed for practicing professionals, this layer of information focuses on theory as well as on practice, on descriptions of the latest studies (written by the researchers themselves and scrutinized by peers for accuracy and objectivity), on debates among scholars and researchers, and on reviews, critiques, and refutations of prior studies and publications.

Also at this deepest level are government sources and corporate documents available through the Freedom of Information Act (page 131). Designed for anyone willing to investigate its complex resources, this information layer offers hard facts and detailed discussion, and (in many instances) *relatively* impartial views.

NOTE   *Web pages, of course, offer links to increasingly specific levels of detail. But the actual "depth" and quality of a Web site's information depend on the sponsorship and reliability of that site (see page 153).*

How deep is deep enough? That depends on your purpose, your audience, and your topic. But the real story most likely resides at deeper levels. Research on the EMF issue, for example, would need to look beneath media headlines and biased special interests (say, electrical industry or environmental groups), focusing instead on studies by a wide range of experts.

Evaluating Your Findings

Not all findings have equal value. Some information might be distorted, incomplete, or misleading. Information might be tainted by *source bias*, in which a source understates or overstates certain facts, depending on whose interests that source represents (say, power company, government agency, parent group, or a reporter seeking headlines). To evaluate a particular finding, ask these questions:

Questions for evaluating a particular finding

- Is this information accurate, reliable, and relatively unbiased?
- Do the facts verify the claim?
- How much of the information is useful?
- Is this the whole or the real story?
- Do I need more information?

Instead of merely emphasizing findings that support their own biases or assumptions, ethical researchers seek out and report the most *accurate* answer.

Interpreting Your Findings

Once you have decided which of your findings seem legitimate, you need to decide what they all mean by asking these questions:

Questions for interpreting your findings

- What are my conclusions and do they address my original research question?
- Do any findings conflict?
- Are other interpretations possible?
- Should I reconsider the evidence?
- What, if anything, should be done?

For more advice on evaluating and interpreting data, see Chapter 10.

Consider This Expert Opinion Is Not Always Reliable

An expert is someone capable of doing the right thing at the right time. (Holyoak, qtd. in Woodhouse and Nieusma 23).

What We Expect from Experts

We consult experts to help us make informed decisions about complex issues:

- *What should we do about global warming?*
- *Where and how should we store nuclear waste?*
- *What is causing the massive die-off of frogs worldwide?*

How We Confer Expert Status

Researchers point out that "expert status is . . . in the eye of the beholder"—not necessarily based on a person's knowledge or *analytical skills,* but instead on that person's *linguistic skills*: use of technical language and persuasion strategies (Rifkin and Martin 31–36).

The Limits of Expert Opinion

Although experts like to proclaim their neutrality, in controversial issues outside influences often intervene (Rifkin and Martin 31–33):

(continues)

Consider This (continued)

- The expert might have a financial stake in the issue—say an environmental researcher funded by nuclear power companies.
- The expert might have a point of view that differs radically from mainstream, accepted, scientific opinion—for example, about risks or benefits of human cloning experiments.
- The expert might be venturing into areas beyond his expertise—for example, a real estate lawyer dabbling in copyright law.
- The expert can be mistaken—say, a meteorologist predicting a hurricane's path.

A Typical Case of Dueling Experts

For years, scientists and engineers have debated whether Yucca Mountain, Nevada, is appropriate for burying high-level nuclear waste. Some $3 billion worth of technical studies have assessed risks and benefits (Gross 134+).

Supporting Arguments

- *Storing nuclear waste in one secure facility is safer and cheaper than storing it at the various power plants.*
- *Many power plants are running out of storage space.*
- *The Yucca Mountain site is remote, has a dry climate and stable geology, and abuts a desert already contaminated by nuclear-weapons testing over 40 years ago.*

Opposing Arguments

- *Earthquake possibilities may have been greatly underestimated, given that tremors occur periodically in this area.*
- *Leaking waste could contaminate ground water.*
- *Some of this material will remain deadly for at least 10,000 years—a period longer than any written language (for warning) or "human-made edifice" has lasted.*

 Languages and cultures of expertise

Guidelines for Evaluating Expert Opinion

- **Look for common ground.** When opinions conflict, consult as many experts as possible and try to identify those areas in which they agree (Detjen 175).
- **Consider all reasonable opinions.** Science writer Richard Harris notes that "Often [extreme views] are either ignored entirely or given equal weight in a story. Neither solution is satisfying. . . . Putting [the opinions] in balance means . . . telling . . . where an expert lies on the spectrum of opinion. . . . The minority opinion isn't necessarily wrong—just ask Galileo" (170).
- **Be sure the expert's knowledge is relevant in this context.** Don't seek advice about a brain tumor from a podiatrist.
- **Don't expect certainty.** In complex issues, experts cannot *eliminate* uncertainty; they can only help us cope with it.
- **Expect special interest groups to produce their own experts to support their position.**
- **Learn all you can about the issue before accepting anyone's final judgment.**

NOTE *Never force a simplistic conclusion on a complex issue. Sometimes the best you can offer is an indefinite conclusion: "Although controversy continues over the extent of EMF hazards, we all can take simple precautions to reduce our exposure." A wrong conclusion is far worse than no definite conclusion at all.*

 ## Exercise

 More exercises

Begin researching for the analytical report (Chapter 24) due at semester's end.

Phase One: Preliminary Steps

a. Choose a topic that affects you, your workplace, or your community directly.
b. Develop a tree chart (page 116) to help you ask the right questions.
c. Complete an audience and use profile (page 35).
d. Narrow your topic, checking with your instructor for approval and advice.
e. Make a working bibliography to ensure sufficient primary and secondary sources.
f. List the information you already have about your topic.
g. Write a clear statement of purpose (page 47) and submit it in a research proposal (page 530) to your instructor.
h. Make a working outline.

Phase Two: Collecting, Evaluating, and Interpreting Data (Read Chapters 8–10 in preparation for this phase.)

a. In your research, begin with general works for an overview, and then consult more specific sources.
b. Skim the sources, looking for high points.
c. Take notes selectively (page 635). Use notecards or electronic file software.

d. Plan and administer questionnaires, interviews, and inquiries.
e. Whenever possible, conclude your research with direct observation.
f. Evaluate each finding for accuracy, reliability, fairness, and completeness.
g. Decide what your findings mean.
h. Use the checklist on page 170 to reassess your methods, interpretation, and reasoning.

Phase Three: Organizing Your Data and Writing the Report

a. Revise your working outline as needed.
b. Fully document all sources of information (page 634).
c. Write your final draft according to the checklist on page 170.
d. Proofread carefully. Add front and end matter (Chapter 25).

Due Dates: To Be Assigned by Your Instructor

List of possible topics due:
Final topic due:
Proposal memo due:
Working bibliography and working outline due:
Notecards (or note files) due:
Copies of questionnaires, interview questions, and inquiry letters due:
Revised outline due:
First draft of report due:
Final draft with supplements and documentation due:

CHAPTER 8

Exploring Electronic and Hard Copy Sources

Internet Sources

Intranets and Extranets

Guidelines for Researching on the Internet

Other Electronic Sources

Hard Copy Sources

Consider This Frequently Asked Questions about Copyright of Hard Copy Information

Consider This Information in Electronic Form Is Copyright Protected

On the Job . . . The Role of Research

Disciplinary research domains online

Although electronic searches for information are becoming the norm, a thorough search often requires careful examination of hard copy sources as well. Advantages and drawbacks of each search medium (Table 8.1) often provide good reason for exploring both.

	Benefits	Drawbacks
Hard Copy Sources	• organized and searched by librarians • often screened by experts for accuracy • easier to preserve and keep secure	• time-consuming and inefficient to search • offer only text and images • hard to update
Electronic Sources	• more current, efficient, and accessible • searches can be narrowed or broadened • can offer material that has no hard copy equivalent	• access to recent material only • not always reliable • user might get lost

TABLE 8.1 **Hard Copy versus Electronic Sources: Benefits and Drawbacks**

 NOTE

With many automated searches, a manual search of hard copy is usually needed as well. Even an electronic search by a trained librarian can miss improperly indexed material (Lang and Secic 174–75). In contrast, a manual search provides the whole "database" (the bound index or abstracts). As you browse, you often randomly discover something useful.

Database networks on the Web

Internet Sources

Information in virtually any format—journals, newspapers, and magazines; government documents and research reports; corporate Web sites; library databases—can be accessed on the Internet. "Googling" a research topic (using the *Google* search engine) is fast becoming the method of choice for almost all forms of research.

The Internet can provide sources ranging from electronic medical journals and national newspapers to adolescents who have their own blogs. You need to be sure that your information source is reliable. The following are the principal categories of information sources on the Internet.

Online News and Magazines

Most major news organizations offer online versions of their broadcast and print publications. Examples include online newspapers <www.nytimes.com>, the Web site for CNN <www.cnn.com>, and National Public Radio <www.npr.org>.

Major magazines also offer Web versions. Some news is available only electronically, as in the online magazines slate.com and About.com.

NOTE   *Make sure you understand how the publication obtains and reviews information. Is it a major news site, such as CNN, or is it a smaller site run by a special interest group? Each can be useful, but you must evaluate the source.*

Government Sites

Government organizations (local, state, federal) typically have a Web site and on-line access to research and reports. Examples include the Food and Drug Administration's electronic bulletin board at <www.fda.gov> on experimental drugs to fight AIDS, drug recalls, and countless related items; <www.fbi.gov> offers information about crime on college campuses. State and local sites provide information on auto licenses, state tax laws, and local property and land issues. From some of these sites you can link to specific government-sponsored research projects.

NOTE   *Check the date on the report or data; for instance, if you are using FBI information on college crime, make sure the data range fits with the research question you are trying to answer. Also, find out how often the site is updated.*

Community Discussion Groups and Bulletin Boards

For almost any topic there is a discussion group or bulletin board on the Web. Although such sites provide abundant information, you must determine how to evaluate it. For example, if you were studying a health-related issue such as stress among college students, you might want to visit a Yahoo group or other discussion site to learn how students develop strategies for coping with stress. The material you find may be insightful, but it may not represent an adequate range of responses from students in general.

NOTE   *Visit as many relevant sites as possible in order to get a broad perspective on the discussion.*

Blogs and Wikis

The *blog* (Web log) is a Web site where users post ideas and discussions, all displayed in reverse chronological order. Blogs can be used to connect to other similar discussions and to offer comment and give feedback. As with discussion groups (above), you will find more blogs than you can use, so you need to evaluate the information carefully. Blogs are great for real-time information from custom feeds and e-newsletters on preselected topics from sources, say, in health, science, technology, or business. One of them, Newsisfree.com, searches and updates the news from over 20,000 sources every 15 minutes. "Knowledge Centers" in various blogs offer the latest research reports on almost any topic imaginable. In the workplace, corporate blogs (page 352) are becoming a staple.

Colleges and universities host blogs as a way to support classroom teaching, provide space for student discussion, allow faculty to collaborate on research projects, and more. One excellent example is the University of Minnesota's UThink Project at <http://blog.lib.umn.edu/>.

A *wiki* (short for wikipedia) is a community encyclopedia where anyone can add to or edit the content of a listing. A popular wiki is <http://en.wikipedia.org/wiki/Main_Page>. The theory of a wiki is that if the information is wrong, someone will correct it. As with many Internet sites, wikis have no editor or gatekeeper to check the accuracy of the information,

NOTE *Use blogs and wikis with caution. Always check their information against several other peer-reviewed or traditional sources. Never lose sight of the fact that most of what is posted on a blog has not been evaluated objectively.*

Email Lists

Many topics can be researched by subscribing to an email list devoted to that content area. For instance, if you are studying food additives, you can probably find numerous email lists for this topic. Unlike the full Internet, email lists usually focus on the topic at hand, and subscribers are usually experts in the area.

NOTE *Email lists can be moderated or unmoderated. In a moderated list, each submission must be evaluated and approved by a reviewer before posting. An unmoderated list is generally less reliable.*

Library Chatrooms

Major libraries increasingly offer the research expertise of reference librarians via live chat. In response to a researcher query, the librarian locates the answer or guides the researcher to the appropriate sources. See, for example, the Santa Monica Public Library site at <www.smpl.org>.

Library Databases Searchable via the Internet

Almost all libraries have a Web site where you can search for books and articles, reserve material, and even pay overdue fines. Research libraries, such as those in colleges and universities, also have Web sites that let the user search not only the library itself but also the large databases (such as MEDLINE™) and CD-ROMs (such as *ProQuest*™) subscribed to by the library. (For more on these sources, see page 127.)

NOTE *Before initiating a database search, try to meet with your local reference librarian for a "tour" of the various databases and instructions for searching them effectively. Then you can use the Internet search engine from school or home.*

Other Types of Web Sites

Many other kinds of Web sites could be useful for research, including information feeds (see page 353), corporate information sites, advertising and marketing sites, and sites promoting specific points of view (lobbying and special interest groups). Remember that you must evaluate each Web site carefully. (See the Guidelines for Evaluating Sources on the Web, page 153.)

Guidelines for Researching on the Internet

- **Select keywords or search phrases that are varied and technical.** Some search terms generate more useful hits than others. In addition to "electromagnetic radiation," for example, try "electromagnetic fields," "power lines and health," or "electrical fields." Specialized terms (say, "vertigo" versus "dizziness") offer the best access to reliable sites.

- **Look for Web sites that are discipline-specific.** Specialized newsletters and trade publications offer good site listings. Compile a hotlist of the most relevant sites.

- **Expect limited results from any one search engine.** No single search engine can index more than a fraction of ever-increasing Web content.

- **Save or print what you need before it changes or disappears.** Always record the URL and your access date.

- **Download only what you need.** Unless they are crucial to your research, omit graphics, sound, and video files.

- **Before downloading *anything* from the Internet, consider the legal and ethical implications.** Ask yourself: "Am I violating someone's privacy (as in forwarding an email or a blog entry)?" or "Am I decreasing, in any way, the value of this material for its owner in any way?" For any type of commercial use, obtain written permission and credit the source exactly as directed by its owner. For information on copyright, see page 134.

- **Consider using information retrieval services such as *Inquisit* or *Dialog*.** For a monthly or per-page fee, users can download full texts of articles. Schools and companies often subscribe to these Internet-accessible databases. Check with your library.

- **Credit all sources.** For advice on citing Internet sources, see pages 648, 661.

Source: Adapted from Baker 57+; Branscum 78; Busiel and Maeglin 39–40, 76; Fugate, "Mastering" 40–41; Kawasaki, "Get Your Facts" 156; Matson, "(Search) Engines" 249–52.

Intranets and Extranets

An *intranet* is an in-house network that uses Internet technology to place a company's knowledge and expertise at any authorized user's fingertips. A customized intranet provides access to a company's library, price lists, progress reports, and the like. Organizations often have "yellow pages," listing the specialized knowledge possessed by each employee.

An *extranet* integrates a company's intranet with the global Internet. External users (customers, subcontractors, vendors) can browse nonrestricted areas of a company's site and download what they need. Extranet *firewall* software keeps out hackers and other uninvited users and limits outsider access, largely via password and encryption (coding) of sensitive information.

Other Electronic Sources

In addition to the Internet, other electronic technologies are used for storing and retrieving information. These technologies are accessible at libraries and, increasingly, via the Web.

Compact Discs

A single CD-ROM can store the equivalent of an entire encyclopedia and serves as a portable database, usually searchable via keyword. One useful CD-ROM for business information is *ProQuest™*: its *ABI/INFORM* database indexes countless journals; its *UMI* database indexes major U.S. newspapers. A useful CD-ROM for information about psychology, nursing, education, and social policy is *SilverPlatter™*.

NOTE   *In many cases, CD-ROM access via the Internet is restricted to users who have passwords for entering a particular library or information system.*

Online Retrieval Services

Libraries and corporations subscribe to three types of mainframe database services that are highly specialized and current, and often updated daily (Lavin 14).

Types of online databases

- *Bibliographic databases* list publications in a particular field and sometimes include abstracts for each entry.
- *Full-text databases* display the entire article or document (usually excluding graphics), and will print the article on command.
- *Factual databases* provide up-to-the-minute stock quotations, weather data, and credit ratings of major companies—among facts of all kinds.

Database networks such as *Dialog* are accessible via the Internet, for a fee. Specialized databases such as MEDLINE or ENVIROLINE offer free bibliographies and abstracts, and for a fee, copies of the full text. Ask your librarian for help searching online databases.

NOTE   *Never assume that computers yield the best material. Database specialist Charles McNeil points out that "the material in the computer is what is cheapest to put there." Reference librarian Ross LaBaugh warns of a built-in bias: "The company that assembles the database often includes a disproportionate number of its own publications." Like any collection of information, a database can reflect the biases of its assemblers.*

Hard Copy Sources

Traditional printed research tools are still of great value. Unlike much of what you may find on the Web (especially if you aren't careful about checking the source), most print research tools are carefully reviewed and edited before they are published. True, it may take more time to go to the library and look through a printed book, but it's often a better way to get solid information. Also, many of these printed sources are now available on the Web.

Where you begin your search depends on whether you are looking for background and basic facts or for the latest information.

NOTE   *Librarian Ross LaBaugh suggests beginning with the popular, general literature, then working toward journals and other specialized sources: "The more accessible the source, the less valuable it is likely to be."*

Reference Works

Reference sources provide basic facts

Reference works provide background that can lead to more specific information. Make sure the work is current by checking the most recent copyright date.

Bibliographies.   These comprehensive lists of publications on a given subject are generally issued yearly, or even more frequently. However, some quickly become dated. To locate bibliographies in your field, begin with the *Bibliographic Index,* a list (by subject) of major bibliographies. For everything published by the government in science and technology, consult *A Guide to U.S. Government Scientific and Technical Resources*. You can also find bibliographies on highly focused topics, such as *Health Hazards of Video Display Terminals: An Annotated Bibliography*.

Encyclopedias.   Encyclopedias provide basic information (which might be outdated). Examples include the *Encyclopedia of Building and Construction Terms* and the *Encyclopedia of Food Technology*.

Dictionaries.   Dictionaries can focus on specific disciplines or give biographical information. Examples include the *Dictionary of Engineering and Technology* and the *Dictionary of Scientific Biography*.

Handbooks.   These research aids offer condensed facts (formulas, tables, advice, examples) about a field. Examples include the *Civil Engineering Handbook* and *The McGraw-Hill Computer Handbook*.

Almanacs.   Almanacs contain factual and statistical data. Examples include the *World Almanac and Book of Facts* and the *Almanac for Computers*.

Directories.   Directories provide updated information about organizations, companies, people, products, services, or careers, often listing addresses and phone numbers. Examples include *The Career Guide: Dun's Employment Opportunities Directory,* and the *Directory of American Firms Operating in Foreign Countries*. For electronic versions, ask your librarian about *Hoover's Company Capsules* (for basic information on more than 13,000 companies) and *Hoover's Company Profiles* (for detailed information on roughly 3,400 companies).

NOTE   *Many of the reference works listed above are accessible free via the Internet. Go to the Internet Public Library at <www.ipl.org>.*

Card Catalog

Most library card catalogs aren't made up of cards anymore—rather, they are electronic and can be accessed through the Internet or at terminals in the library. You can search a library's holdings by subject, author, or title in that library's catalog system. Visit the library's Web site, or ask a librarian for help.

To search catalogs from libraries worldwide, go to the *Library of Congress Gateway* at <www.loc.gov> or *LibrarySpot* at <www.libraryspot.com>.

Guides to Literature

If you simply don't know which books, journals, indexes, and reference works are available for your topic, consult a guide to literature. For a general list of books in various disciplines, see Walford's *Guide to Reference Material* or Sheehy's *Guide to Reference Books*. For scientific and technical literature, see Malinowsky and Richardson's *Science and Engineering Literature: A Guide to Reference Sources*. Ask a librarian about guides for your discipline.

Indexes

Indexes list current works

Indexes are lists of books, newspaper articles, journal articles, or other works on a particular subject. Most are now searchable by computer.

Book Indexes.   Sample indexes include *Scientific and Technical Books and Serials in Print* (an annual listing) and *New Technical Books: A Selective List with Descriptive Annotations* (issued ten times yearly).

NOTE   *No book is likely to offer the very latest information, because of the time required to publish a book manuscript (from months to over one year).*

Newspaper Indexes.   Sample titles include the *New York Times Index* and the *Wall Street Journal Index*. Most newspapers and news magazines are searchable via their Web sites, and usually charge a fee for searches of past issues.

Periodical Indexes.   A periodical index lists articles from magazines and journals. For general information, consult the *Magazine Index* (an index on microfilm) and the *Reader's Guide to Periodical Literature* (updated every few weeks).

For specialized information, consult indexes that list articles by discipline, such as the *General Science Index* or *Business Periodicals Index*. Specific disciplines have their own indexes such as the *Index to Legal Periodicals* and the *International Nursing Index*. Ask a librarian.

Citation Indexes.   Citation indexes help answer this question: *Who else has said what about this published idea?* Using a citation index, you can track down the publications in which the original material has been cited, quoted, critiqued, verified, or otherwise amplified (Garfield 200). Examples include the *Social Science Citation Index* and *Web of Science (Science Citation Index Expanded)*, which cross-references articles on science and technology worldwide.

Technical Report Indexes.   Government and private-sector reports prepared worldwide offer specialized and current information. Examples include *Scientific and Technical Aerospace Reports* and the *Government Reports Announcements and Index*. Proprietary or security restrictions limit public access to certain corporate or government documents.

Patent Indexes.   Patents are issued to protect rights to new inventions, products, or processes. Information experts Schenk and Webster point out that patents are often overlooked as sources of current information: "Since . . . complete descriptions of the invention [must be] included in patent applications, one can assume that almost everything that is new and original in technology can be found in patents" (121). Sample indexes include the *Index of Patents Issued from the United States Patent and Trademark Office* and the *World Patents Index*. Patents in various technologies are searchable through databases such as *Hi Tech Patents, Data Communication,* and *World Patents Index*.

What happens when you are locked out of a source?

Indexes to Conference Proceedings.   Many of the papers presented at professional conferences are collected and then indexed in listings such as the *Index to Scientific and Technical Proceedings* and *Engineering Meetings*. The latest ideas or advances in a field often are unveiled at conferences, before appearing as journal publications.

Abstracts

By indexing and summarizing each article, abstracts can save you from having to track down a journal before deciding whether to read or skip the article. Abstracts usually are titled by discipline: *Biological Abstracts, Computer Abstracts,* and so on. For some current research, you might consult abstracts of doctoral dissertations in *Dissertation Abstracts International.* Most abstracts are searchable by computer.

Access Tools for U.S. Government Publications

The federal government publishes maps, periodicals, books, pamphlets, manuals, research reports, and other information, often searchable by computer. Examples include *Electromagnetic Fields in Your Environment, Major Oil and Gas Fields of the Free World,* and the *Journal of Research of the National Bureau of Standards.* Your best bet for tapping this complex resource is to request assistance from a librarian.

The basic access tools are the following:

- *The Monthly Catalog of the United States Government,* the major pathway to government publications and reports.
- *Government Reports Announcements and Index,* a listing (with summaries) of more than one million federally sponsored research reports published and patents issued since 1964.
- *The Statistical Abstract of the United States,* updated yearly, offers statistics on population, health, employment, and the like. It can be accessed via the Web. CD-ROM versions are now available.

Many unpublished documents are available under the Freedom of Information Act. The FOIA grants public access to all federal agency records except for classified documents, trade secrets, certain law enforcement files, records protected by personal privacy law, and the like. Contact the agency that would hold the records you seek: say, for workplace accident reports, the Department of Labor; for industrial pollution records, the Environmental Protection Agency; and so on.

Much government information is posted to the Web. For example, the Food and Drug Administration maintains a bulletin board at <www.fda.gov>

on experimental AIDS drugs, on drug recalls, and related items; the Department of Energy at <www.doe.gov> offers information on human radiation experiments. One gateway to government sites: the Library of Congress page at <www.loc.gov>.

Microforms

Microform technology allows vast quantities of printed information to be stored in rolls of microfilm or packets of microfiche. (This material is read on machines that magnify the reduced image.) Ask your librarian for assistance.

Consider This Frequently Asked Questions about Copyright of Hard Copy Information

Copyright laws ultimately have an ethical purpose: to balance the reward for intellectual labors with the public's right to use information freely.

1. *What is a copyright?*

   A copyright is the exclusive legal right to reproduce, publish, and sell a literary, dramatic, musical, or artistic work. Written permission must be obtained to use all copyrighted material.

2. *What are the limits of copyright protection?*

   Copyright protection covers the exact wording of the original, but not the ideas or information it conveys. For example, Einstein's theory of relativity has no protection but his exact wording does (Abelman 33; Elias 3). Also, paraphrasing Einstein's ideas but failing to cite him as the source would constitute plagiarism.

3. *How long does copyright protection last?*

   Works published before January 1, 1978 are protected for 95 years. Works published on or after January 1, 1978 are copyrighted for the author's life plus 70 years.

4. *Must a copyright be officially registered in order to protect a work?*

No. Protection begins as soon as a work is created.

5. *Must a work be published in order to receive copyright protection?*

   No.

6. *What is "fair use"?*

   "Fair use" is the legal and limited use of copyrighted material without permission. The source should, of course, be acknowledged. Fair use does not ordinarily apply to case studies, charts and graphs, author's notes, or private letters ("Copyright Protection" 30).

7. *How is fair use determined?*

   In determining fair use, the courts ask these questions:

   • *Is the material being used for commercial or for nonprofit purposes?* For example, nonprofit educational use is viewed more favorably than for-profit use.

   • *Is the copyrighted work published or unpublished?* Use of published work is viewed more favorably than use of unpublished essays, correspondence, and so on.

   • *How much, and which part, of the original work is being used?* The smaller the part, the more favorably its use will be viewed. Never considered fair, however, is the use of a part that "forms the core, distinguishable, creative effort of the work being cited" (*Author's Guide* 30).

• *How will the economic value of the original work be affected?* Any use that reduces the potential market value of the original will be viewed unfavorably.

8. *What is the exact difference between copyright infringement and fair use?*

Although using ideas from an original work is considered fair, a paraphrase that incorporates too much of the original expression can be infringement—even when the source is cited (Abelman 41). Reproduction of a government document that includes material previously protected by copyright (graphs, images, company logos, slogans) is considered infringement. The United States Copyright Office offers this caution:

There is no specific number of words, lines, or notes that may safely be taken without permission.

Acknowledging the source of the copyrighted material does not substitute for obtaining permission. ("Fair Use" 1–2)

When in doubt, obtain written permission.

 More on fair use.

9. *What is material in the "public domain"?*

"Public domain" refers to material not protected by copyright or material on which copyright has expired. Works published in the United States 95 years before the current year are in the public domain. Most government publications and commonplace information, such as height and weight charts or a metric conversion table are in the public domain. These works might contain copyrighted material (used with permission and properly acknowledged). If you are not sure whether an item is in the public domain, request permission. ("Copyright Protection" 31)

10. *What about international copyright protection?*

Copyright protection varies among individual countries, and some countries offer little or no protection for foreign works:

There is no such thing as an "international copyright" that will automatically protect an author's writings throughout the world. ("International Copyright" 1–2)

In the United States all foreign works that meet certain requirements are protected by copyright (Abelman 36).

 International copyright issues

11. *Who owns the copyright to a work prepared as part of one's employment?*

A work prepared in the service of one's employer or under written contract for a client is a "work made for hire." The employer or client is legally considered the author and therefore holds the copyright (Abelman 33–34). For example, a manual researched, designed, and written as part of one's employment would be a work made for hire.

For latest developments, visit the United States Copyright Office at: <www .loc.gov/ copyright>.

 Intellectual property issues

Consider This Information in Electronic Form Is Copyright Protected

Unanswered Questions

Copyright and fair use law is quite specific for printed works or works in other tangible form (paintings, photographs, music). But how do we define "fair use" (page 132) of intellectual property in electronic form? How does copyright protection apply? How do fair use restrictions apply to material used in multimedia presentations or to text or images that have been altered or reshaped to suit the user's specific needs?

Information obtained via email or discussion groups presents additional problems: Sources often do not wish to be quoted or named or to have early drafts made public. How do we protect source confidentiality? How do we avoid infringing on works in progress that have not yet been published? How do we quote and cite this material without violating ownership and privacy rights (Howard 40–41)?

Present Status of Electronic Copyright Law

Subscribers to commercial online services such as *Dialog* pay fees, and copyholders in turn receive royalties. But few specific legal protections exist for noncommercial types of electronic information. Since April 1989, however, most works are considered copyrighted as soon as they are produced in *any* tangible form—even if they carry no copyright notice. Fair use of electronic information generally is limited to brief excerpts that serve as a basis for response—for example, in a discussion group. Except for certain government documents, no Internet posting is in the "public domain" (page 133) unless it is expressly designated as such by its author (Templeton).

Until specific laws are enacted, the following uses of copyrighted material in electronic form can be considered copyright violations (Communication Concepts, Inc. 13; Elias 85, 86; Templeton):

• Downloading a work from the Internet and forwarding copies to other readers.
• Editing, altering, or incorporating an original work as part of your own document or multimedia presentation.
• Placing someone else's printed work online without the author's written permission.
• Reproducing and distributing original software or material from a privately owned database.
• Copying and forwarding an email message without the sender's authorization. The exact *wording* of an email message is copyrighted, but its *content* legally may be revealed—except for "proprietary information" (page 80).

Some copyright violations (say, reproducing and distributing trade secrets) may exceed the boundaries of civil law and be prosecuted as felonies (Templeton).

When in doubt, assume the work is copyrighted, and obtain written permission from the owner.

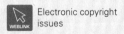 Electronic copyright issues

For more on electronic copyright issues, visit *The Copyright Website* at <http://www.benedict.com> and the University of Texas legal site at <http://www.utsystem.edu/OGC>.

ON THE *JOB...*   The Role of Research

■ *"If I have to research I look everywhere—books, on-line, databases, newsgroups, library, periodicals, etc. And I have to say—if you ever get stuck for information, do check out a newsgroup or mailing list about the sub-ject. Everyone interested in the subject will be there and someone will be able to get you started."*

—Lorraine Patsco,
Director of prepress
and multimedia production

■ *"Our writing is all about research. We hardly ever use the library. Mostly, the writing is about our own re-search. If other information is used, research assistants will find it on the Web. The Internet has changed my professional life dramatically for the better."*

—Paul Harder, President,
mid-sized consulting company

■ *"Our clients make investment decisions based on fea-sibility and strategy for marketing new products. Our job is to research consumer interest in these potential products (say, a new brand of low-calorie chocolate). In designing surveys, I have to translate the client's infor-mation needs into precise questions. I have to be certain that the respondents are answering* exactly *the question I had in mind, and not inventing their own version of the question. Then I have to take these data and trans-late them into accurate interpretations and recommen-dations for our clients."*

—James North, Senior Project Manager,
market research firm

■ *"As a freelance researcher, I search online databases and Web sites for any type of specialized information needed by my clients. For example, yesterday I did a search for a corporate attorney who needed the latest in-formation on some specific product-liability issues, plus any laws or court decisions involving specific products. For the legal research I accessed LEXIS, the legal database that offers full-text copies of articles and cases. For the liability issue I began with Dow-Jones News/Retrieval and then doubled-checked by going into the Dialog database."*

—Martha Casamonte,
Freelance Researcher

■ *"When researching a topic for a manual, I focus on usability, by trying to anticipate my audience's needs and asking the technical source person (usually a pro-grammer or a systems analyst) specific questions keyed to my audience's needs: Who performs the task? What materials are required? What does the task accomplish? What can go wrong? Otherwise, I would waste time soaking up like a sponge any and all information the source person feels like rattling off, whether it's impor-tant or not."*

—Pam Herbert, Technical Writer,
software firm

Exercise

   Exercises

Students in your major want a listing of at least *one* of each of the following discipline-specific sources: a major reference book, index, periodical, government publication, database, online newsgroup and discussion group. Prepare the list (in memo form) and include a brief paragraph describing each source.

Collaborative Projects

1. Divide into groups and prepare a comparative evaluation of literature search media. Each group member will select *one* of the resources listed below and create an individual bibliography (listing at least twelve recent and relevant works on a topic of interest selected by the group):

   - conventional print media
   - electronic catalogs
   - CD-ROM services
   - a commercial database service such as Dialog
   - the Internet and World Wide Web
   - an electronic consortium of local libraries, if applicable

   After recording the findings and keeping track of the time spent in each search, compare the ease of searching and quality of results obtained from each type of search on your group's selected topic. Which medium yielded the most current sources (page 150)? Which provided abstracts and full texts as well as bibliographic data? Which consumed the most time? Which provided the most dependable sources (page 151)? The most diverse or varied sources (page 117)? Which cost the most to use? Finally, which yielded the greatest *depth* of resources (page 117)?

   Prepare a report and present your findings to the class. (In conjunction with this project, your instructor may assign Chapter 24.)

2. Group yourselves according to major. Assume that several employers in your field are holding a job fair on campus next month and will be interviewing entry-level candidates. Each member of your group is assigned to develop a profile of *one* of these companies or organizations by researching its history, record of mergers and stock value, management style, financial condition, price/earnings ratio of its stock, growth prospects, products and services, multinational affiliations, ethical record, environmental record, employee relations, pension plan, employee stock options or profit-sharing plans, commitment to affirmative action, number of women in upper management, or any other features important to a prospective employee. The entire group will then edit each profile and assemble them in one single document to be used as a reference for students in your major.

Service-Learning Project

Two sites that provide information specific to service-learning and grant writing are the *Foundation Center* at <www.fdncenter.org> and *Donor's Forum* at <www.donorsforum.org>. Go to the *Foundation Center* site and click on "finding funders." Enter a search term that describes an issue your agency addresses (for example, "addiction" or "affordable housing"). Develop a list of ten foundations that look like primary sources of support for your agency. Detail these ten foundations in a one-page summary memo to the agency staff. (For more on grants and grant writing, see Chapter 23.)

CHAPTER 9

Exploring Primary Sources

Informative Interviews

Guidelines for Informative Interviews

Surveys and Questionnaires

Guidelines for Developing a Questionnaire

A Sample Questionnaire

Inquiry Letters, Phone Calls, and Email Inquiries

Public Records and Organizational Publications

Personal Observation and Experiments

Informative interviews, surveys and questionnaires, inquiry letters, official records, and personal observation are considered *primary sources* because they afford an original, firsthand study of a topic.

Informative Interviews

An excellent primary source for information unavailable in any publication is the interview, conducted in person, by telephone, or by email. Much of what an expert knows may never be published. Also, a respondent might refer you to other experts or sources of information.

Guidelines for Informative Interviews

Planning the Interview

- **Know exactly what you're looking for.** Write out your purpose.

  Purpose statement
  > I will interview Anne Hector, Chief Engineer at Northport Electric, to ask about the company's approaches to EMF risk avoidance—in the company as well as in the community.

- **Do your homework.** Learn all you can. Be sure the information this person might provide is unavailable in print.

- **Make arrangements by phone, letter, or email.** (See Karen Granger's letter on page 376.) Ask whether this person objects to being quoted or taped. If possible, submit your questions beforehand.

Preparing the Questions

 Resources on interviewing techniques

- **Make each question clear and specific.** Avoid questions that can be answered "yes" or "no":

  An unproductive question
  > In your opinion, can technology find ways to decrease EMF hazards?

  Instead, phrase your question to elicit a detailed response:

  A clear and specific question
  > Of the various technological solutions being proposed or considered, which do you consider most promising?

- **Avoid loaded questions.** A loaded question invites or promotes a particular bias:

  A loaded question
  > Wouldn't you agree that EMF hazards have been overstated?

  Ask an impartial question instead:

  An impartial question
  > In your opinion, have EMF hazards been accurately stated, overstated, or understated?

- **Save the most difficult, complex, or sensitive questions for last.**

- **Write out each question on a separate notecard.** Use the notecard to summarize the responses during the interview.

Conducting the Interview

- **Make a courteous start.** Express your gratitude; explain why you believe the respondent can be helpful; explain exactly how you will use the information.

- **Respect cultural differences.** Consider the level of formality, politeness, directness, and other behaviors appropriate in the given culture. (See pages 63–65.)

- **Let the respondent do most of the talking.**

- **Be a good listener.** For listening advice, see pages 103–05.

- **Stick to your interview plan.** If the conversation wanders, politely nudge it back on track (unless the peripheral information is useful).

- **Ask for clarification if needed.** Keep asking until you understand.

Clarifying questions

> —Could you go over that again?
> —What did you mean by [*word*]?

- **Repeat major points in your own words and ask if your interpretation is correct.** But do not put words into the respondent's mouth.

- **Be ready with follow-up questions.**

Follow-up questions

> —Why is it like that?
> —Could you say something more about that?
> —What more needs to be done?

- **Keep note taking to a minimum.** Record statistics, dates, names, and other precise data, but don't record every word. Jot key terms or phrases that can refresh your memory later.

Concluding the Interview

- **Ask for closing comments.** Perhaps these can point to additional information.

Concluding questions

> —Would you care to add anything?
> —Is there anyone else I should talk to?
> —Can you suggest other sources that might help me better understand this issue?

- **Request permission to contact your respondent again, if new questions arise.**

- **Invite the respondent to review your version for accuracy.** If the interview is to be published, ask for his/her approval of your final draft. Offer to provide copies of any document in which this information appears.

- **Say your thank-yous and leave promptly.**

- **As soon as possible, write a complete summary (or record one verbally).**

Source: Several guidelines are adapted from Blum 88; Dowd 13–14; Hopkins-Tanne 23, 26; Kotulak 147; Lambe 32; McDonald, "Covering Physics" 190; Rensberger 15; Young 114–16.

Figure 9.1 shows the partial text of an interview on persuasive challenges in the workplace. Notice how the interviewer probes, seeks clarification, and follows up on responses from XYZ's Director of Corporate Relations.

Surveys and Questionnaires

Surveys help you form impressions of the concerns, preferences, attitudes, beliefs, needs, or perceptions of a large, identifiable group (a *target population*) by studying representatives of that group (a *sample*).

Surveys help us make assessments like these

—Do consumers prefer brand A or brand B?

—What percentage of students feel safe on our campus?

—Are people able to use this product safely and efficiently?

NOTE   *A "census" is a survey of an entire target population.*

The tool for conducting surveys is the questionnaire. Whereas interviews allow for greater clarity and depth, questionnaires offer an inexpensive way to survey a large group. Respondents can answer privately and anonymously—and often more candidly than in an interview.

Defining the Survey's Purpose and Target Population

Why is this survey being done? What, exactly, is it measuring? How much background research do you need? How will survey findings be used? Who is the exact population being studied (the chronically unemployed, part-time students)?

Identifying the Sample Group

How will intended respondents be selected? How many respondents will there be? (Generally, the larger the sample surveyed, the more dependable the results, assuming a well-chosen and representative sample). Will the sample be randomly chosen? (In a random sample, each member of the target population stands an equal chance of being in the sample group.)

Qualitative and quantitative survey techniques

Defining the Survey Method

What type of data (opinions, ideas, facts, figures) will be collected? How will the survey be administered: in person, by mail, by phone? How will the data be collected, recorded, analyzed, and reported (Lavin 277)? Phone and in-person surveys yield fast results and high response rates, but respondents consider phone surveys annoying and, without anonymity, people are less candid. Electronic surveys, via a Web form or email, are least expensive, but here you cannot control how many times the same person might respond.

Probing and
following up

Q. *Would you please summarize your communication responsibilities?*

A. The corporate relations office oversees three departments: customer service (which handles claims, adjustments, and queries), public relations, and employee relations. My job is to supervise the production of all documents generated by this office.

Q. *Isn't that a lot of responsibility?*

A. It is, considering we're trying to keep some people happy, getting others to cooperate, and trying to get everyone to change their thinking and see things in a positive light. Just about every document we write has to be persuasive.

Seeking
clarification

Q. *What exactly do you mean by "persuasive"?*

A. The best way to explain is through examples of what we do. The customer service department responds to problems like these: Some users are unhappy with our software because it won't work for a particular application, or they find a glitch in one of our programs, or they're confused by the documentation, or someone wants the software modified to meet a specific need. For each of these complaints or requests, we have to persuade our audience that we've resolved the problem or that we're making a genuine effort to resolve it quickly.

The public relations department works to keep up our reputation through links outside the company. For instance, we keep in touch with this community, with consumers, the general public, government and educational agencies.

Seeking
clarification

Q. *Can you be more specific? "Keeping in touch" doesn't sound much like persuasion.*

A. Okay, right now we're developing programs with colleges and universities, in which we offer heavily discounted software, backed up by an extensive support network (regional consultants, an 800 phone hotline, and workshops). We're hoping to persuade them that our software is superior to our well-entrenched competitor's. And locally we're offering the same kind of service and support to business clients.

Following up

Q. *What about employee relations?*

A. Day to day we face the usual kinds of problems: trying to get 100 percent employee contributions to the United Way, or persuading employees to help out in the community, or getting them to abide by new company regulations restricting smoking or to limit personal phone calls. Right now, we're facing a real persuasive challenge. Because of market saturation, software sales have flattened across the board. This means temporary layoffs for roughly 28 percent of our employees. Our only alternative is to persuade *all* employees to accept a 10-percent salary and benefit cut until the market improves.

Probing

Q. *How, exactly, do you persuade employees to accept a cut in pay and benefits?*

A. Basically, we have to make them see that by taking the cut, they're really investing in the company's future—and, of course, in their own.

[The interview continues.]

FIGURE 9.1 Partial Text of an Informative Interview

Guidelines for Developing a Questionnaire

- **Decide on the types of questions.** Questions can take two forms: *open-ended* or *closed-ended*. Open-ended questions allow respondents to answer in any way they choose. Measuring the data gathered from such questions is more time-consuming, but they do provide a rich source of information. An open-ended question would be worded like this:

Open-ended question

| How much do you know about the level of electromagnetic radiation at our school?

   Closed-ended questions give people a limited number of choices, and the data gathered are easier to measure. Here are some types of closed-ended questions:

Are you interested in joining a group of concerned parents?
        YES _____   NO _____

Closed-ended questions

Rate your degree of concern about EMFs at our school.
        HIGH_____   MODERATE_____   LOW_____   NO CONCERN _____

Circle the number that indicates your view about the town's proposal to spend $20,000 to hire its own EMF consultant.
        1....2....3....4....5....6....7
Strongly   No   Strongly
Disapprove   Opinion   Approve

How often do you ...?
ALWAYS_____ OFTEN _____ SOMETIMES _____ RARELY _____ NEVER_____

To measure exactly where people stand on an issue, choose closed-ended questions.

- **Develop an engaging introduction and provide appropriate information.** Persuade respondents that the questionnaire relates to their concerns, that their answers matter, and that their anonymity is ensured:

A survey introduction

| Your answers will help our school board to speak accurately for your views at our next town meeting. All answers will be kept confidential. Thank you.

Researchers often include a cover letter with the questionnaire.
   Begin with the easiest questions, usually the closed-ended ones. Respondents who commit to these are likely to answer later, more difficult questions.

- **Make each question unambiguous.** All respondents should be able to interpret identical questions identically. An ambiguous question allows for misinterpretation:

An ambiguous question

| Do you favor weapons for campus police? YES_____ NO_____

"Weapons" might mean tear gas, clubs, handguns, tasers, or some combination of these. The limited "yes/no" format reduces an array of possible opinions to an either/or choice. Here is an unambiguous version:

A clear and
incisive question

_____ **Do you favor** (check all that apply):

_____ Having campus police carry mace and a club?

_____ Having campus police carry nonlethal "stun guns"?

_____ Having campus police store handguns in their cruisers?

_____ Having campus police carry small-caliber handguns?

_____ Having campus police carry large-caliber handguns?

_____ Having campus police carry no weapons?

_____ Don't know

To account for all possible responses, include options such as "Other," "Don't know," or an "Additional Comments" section.

- **Avoid biased questions:**

Should our campus tolerate the needless endangerment of innocent students by lethal weapons? YES_____ NO_____

A loaded
question

Emotionally loaded and judgmental words ("endangerment," "innocent," "tolerate," "needless,") are unethical in a survey because they manipulate people's responses (Hayakawa 40).

- **Make it brief, simple, and inviting.** Long questionnaires usually get few replies. And people who do reply tend to give less thought to their answers. Limit the number and types of questions. Include a stamped, return-addressed envelope, and stipulate a return date.

- **Have an expert review your questionnaire before use, whenever possible.**

A Sample Questionnaire

The student-written cover letter and questionnaire in Figures 9.2 and 9.3, sent to local company presidents, is designed to elicit responses that can be tabulated easily.

Written reports of survey findings often include an appendix (page 605) that contains a copy of the questionnaire as well as the tabulated responses.

Inquiry Letters, Phone Calls, and Email Inquiries

Letters, phone calls, or email inquiries to experts listed in Web pages can yield useful information from various agencies, legislators, companies, and other institutions.

NOTE   _Keep in mind that unsolicited inquiries, especially by phone or email, can be intrusive and offensive._

April 5, 20xx

House 10
University of Massachusetts, Dartmouth
North Dartmouth, MA 02747

Name, Title
Company Name
Address

Dear _____:

I am exploring ways to enhance relationships between UMD's Professional
Communication Program and the local business community.

Specific areas of inquiry:
1. the communication needs of local companies and industries
2. the feasibility of on-campus and in-house seminars for
   employees
3. the feasibility of expanding communication course offerings
   at UMD

Please take a few minutes to complete the attached survey. Your response
will provide an important contribution to my study.

All respondents will receive a copy of my report, scheduled to appear in
the fall issue of *The Business and Industry Newsletter*. Thank you.

Sincerely,

L.S. Taylor
Technical Communication Student

FIGURE 9.2 A Questionnaire Cover Letter

Communication Questionnaire

1. Describe your type of company (e.g., manufacturing, high tech)

   _____

2. Number of employees (Please check one.)

   _____ 0–4   _____ 25–50   _____ 100–150   _____ 300–450
   _____ 5–25   _____ 50–100   _____ 150–300   _____ 450+

3. What types of written communication occur in your company? (Label by frequency: daily, weekly, monthly, never.)

   _____ memos   _____ letters   _____ advertising
   _____ manuals   _____ reports   _____ newsletters
   _____ procedures   _____ proposals   _____ other (Specify.)
   _____ email   _____ catalogs   _____

4. Who does most of the writing? (Pls. give titles.) _____

5. Please characterize your employees' writing effectiveness.

   _____ good   _____ fair   _____ poor

6. Does your company have formal guidelines for writing?

   _____ no   _____ yes (Pls. describe briefly.) _____

7. Do you offer in-house communication training?

   _____ no   _____ yes (Pls. describe briefly.) _____

8. Please rank the usefulness of the following areas in communication training (from 1–10, 1 being
   most important).

   _____ organizing information   _____ audience awareness
   _____ summarizing information   _____ persuasive writing
   _____ editing for style   _____ grammar
   _____ document design   _____ researching
   _____ email etiquette   _____ Web page design
   _____ other (Pls. specify.) _____

9. Please rank these skills in order of importance (from 1–6, 1 being most important).

   _____ reading   _____ listening   _____ speaking to groups
   _____ writing   _____ collaborating   _____ speaking face-to-face

10. Do you provide tuition reimbursement for employees?

    _____ no   _____ yes

11. Would you consider having UMD communication interns work for you part-time?

    _____ no   _____ yes

12. Should UMD offer Saturday seminars in communication?

    _____ no   _____ yes

    Additional comments/suggestions: _____

    _____

FIGURE 9.3 A Questionnaire

Public Records and Organizational Publications

The Freedom of Information Act and state public-record laws grant public access to an array of government, corporate, and organizational documents. Obtaining these documents (from state or federal agencies) takes time—although more and more are available on the Web—but in them you can find answers to questions like these (Blum 90–92):

Public records may
hold answers to
tough questions

- Which universities are being investigated by the Department of Agriculture for mistreating laboratory animals?
- Are auditors for the Internal Revenue Service required to meet quotas?
- How often has a particular nuclear power plant been cited for safety violations?

Organization records (reports, memos, Web pages, and so on) are also good primary sources. Most organizations publish pamphlets, brochures, annual reports, or prospectuses for consumers, employees, investors, or voters.

NOTE   *Be alert for bias in company literature. If you were evaluating the safety measures at a local nuclear power plant, you would want the complete picture. Along with the company's literature, you would want to consult studies and reports from government agencies and publications from health and environmental groups.*

Techniques for
ethnographic
observations of
workplace
cultures

Personal Observation and Experiments

Observation should be your final step in primary research because you now know what to look for. Have a plan. Know how, where, and when to look, and jot down observations immediately. You might even take photos or draw sketches.

NOTE   *Even direct observation is not foolproof: you might be biased about what you see (focusing on wrong events or ignoring something important); or, people conscious of being observed might alter their normal behavior (Adams and Schvaneveldt 244).*

Unlike general observations, experiments are controlled forms of observation designed to verify an assumption (e.g., the role of fish oil in preventing heart disease) or to test something untried (the relationship between background music and productivity). Each field has its own guidelines for experimental design, including the requirement that all human medical trials be reviewed to ensure protection of the patients involved.

Finally, workplace research can involve the analysis of samples, such as water, soil, or air for contamination and pollution; foods for nutritional value; or plants for medicinal value. Investigators analyze material samples to find the cause of airline accidents; engineers analyze samples of steel, concrete, or other building materials to test for tensile strength or load-bearing capacity; medical specialists analyze tissue samples for disease. As a researcher, you may be able to access this information through interviews or published reports.

Exercises

 Exercises
WEBLINK

1. Revise these questions to make them appropriate for inclusion in a questionnaire:
   a. Would a female president do the job as well as a male?
   b. Don't you think that euthanasia is a crime?
   c. Do you oppose increased government spending?
   d. Do you think welfare recipients are too lazy to support themselves?
   e. Are teachers responsible for the decline in literacy among students?
   f. Aren't humanities studies a waste of time?
   g. Do you prefer Rocket Cola to other leading brands?
   h. In meetings, do you think men are more interruptive than women?
2. Identify and illustrate at least six features that enhance the effectiveness of the questionnaire in Figure 9.3. (Review pages 142–43 for criteria.)
3. Arrange an interview with someone in your field. Decide on areas for questioning: job opportunities, chances for promotion, working conditions, job satisfaction, and so on. Compose questions and conduct the interview. Summarize your findings in a memo to your instructor.

Collaborative Project

Divide into small groups and decide on a survey of views, attitudes, preferences, or concerns about some issue affecting your campus or the community. Expand on this short list of possible survey topics:

- campus alcohol policy
- campus safety
- facilities for disabled students
- campus racial or gender issues
- access to computers

Once you have identified your survey's exact purpose and your target population, follow these steps:

   a. Decide on the size and makeup of a randomly selected sample group.
   b. Develop a questionnaire. Design questions that are engaging, unambiguous, unbiased, and easy to answer and tabulate.
   c. Administer the survey to a representative sample group.
   d. Tabulate, analyze, and interpret the responses.
   e. Prepare a report summarizing your survey purpose, process, findings, and conclusions. Include a copy of the questionnaire as well as the tabulated responses.
   f. Appoint one group member to present your findings to the class.

In addition to reviewing pages 140–43, look over Chapter 10, especially the section on validity and reliability (page 166).

Service-Learning Project

Plan and conduct an on-site interview at the agency you are working with. In a memo to your instructor, summarize your findings.

CHAPTER 10

Evaluating and Interpreting Information

Evaluate the Sources

Guidelines for Evaluating Sources on the Web

Evaluate the Evidence

Guidelines for Evaluating Evidence

Interpret Your Findings

Consider This Standards of Proof Vary for Different
Audiences and Cultural Settings

Avoid Errors in Reasoning

Acknowledge the Limits of Research

Guidelines for Evaluating and Interpreting Information

Checklist: The Research Process

Not all information is equal. Not all interpretations are equal. For instance, if you really want to know how well the latest innovation in robotic surgery works, you need to check with other sources besides, say, its designer (from whom you could expect an overly optimistic or insufficiently critical assessment).

Whether you work with your own findings or the findings of other researchers, you need to decide if the information is valid and reliable. Then you need to decide what your information means. Figure 10.1 outlines your challenges, and the potential for error at any stage along the way.

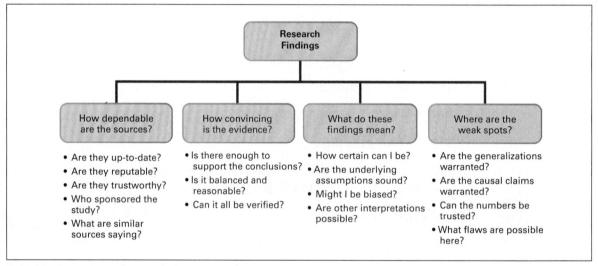

FIGURE 10.1 Decisions in Evaluating and Interpreting Information Collecting information is often the easiest part of the research process. Your larger challenge is in getting the exact information you need, making sure it's accurate, and figuring out what it means. Throughout this process, there is much room for the types of errors covered in this chapter.

Evaluate the Sources

Not all sources are equally dependable. A source might offer information that is out of date, inaccurate, incomplete, mistaken, or biased.

"Is the source up-to-date?"

- **Determine the currency of the source.** Certain types of information become outdated more quickly than others. For topics that focus on *technology* (Internet censorship, alternative cancer treatments), information more than a few months old may be outdated. But for topics that focus on *people* (student motivation, gender equality), historical perspective often helps.

  Even newly published books contain information that can be more than a year old, and journal articles typically undergo a lengthy process of peer review.

NOTE   *The most recent information is not always the most reliable—especially in scientific re-search, a process of ongoing inquiry in which what seems true today may be proven false tomorrow. Consider, for example, the recent discoveries of fatal side effects from some of the latest "miracle" drugs.*

"Is the printed source dependable?"

- **Assess the reputation of a printed source.** Assess a publication's reputation by checking its copyright page. Is the work published by a university, professional society, museum, or respected news organization? Do members of the editor-ial board have distinguished titles and degrees? Is the publication *refereed* (all submissions reviewed by experts before acceptance)? Does the bibliography or list of references indicate how thoroughly the author has researched the issue (Barnes)? You can also check citation indexes (page 130) to see what other ex-perts have said about this particular source. Many periodicals also provide brief biographies or descriptions of authors' earlier publications and achieve-ments.

"Is the electronic source trustworthy?"

- **Assess the dependability of an Internet or database source.** The Internet offers information that may never appear elsewhere; for example, from discussion lists and blogs. But much of this material may reflect the bias of the special-in-terest groups that provide it. Moreover, anyone can publish almost anything on the Internet—including misinformation—without having it verified, edited, or reviewed for accuracy. Don't expect to find everything you need on the Inter-net. (Pages 153–54 offer suggestions for evaluating sources on the Web.)

  Even in a commercial database such as *Dialog*, decisions about what to in-clude and what to leave out depend on the biases, priorities, or interests of those who assemble that database.

NOTE   *Because it advocates a particular point of view, a special-interest Web site (as in Figure 10.2) can provide useful clues about the ideas and opinions of its sponsors; however, don't rely on special-interest sites for factual information—unless the facts can be verified elsewhere ("Evaluating Internet-Based Information").*

"Who sponsored the study, and why?"

- **Consider the sponsorship and the motives for the study.** Much of today's re-search is paid for by private companies or special-interest groups that have their own agendas (Crossen 14, 19). Medical research may be sponsored by drug or tobacco companies; nutritional research, by food manufacturers; envi-ronmental research, by oil or chemical companies. Instead of a neutral and balanced inquiry, this kind of "strategic research" is designed to support one special interest or another (132–34). Research sponsored by opposing groups can produce opposing results.

  Also, those who pay for strategic research are not likely to publicize findings that contradict their original claims or opinions (for example: profits lower than expected, losses or risks greater than expected). Try to determine exactly what the sponsors of a particular study stand to gain or lose from the results (234).

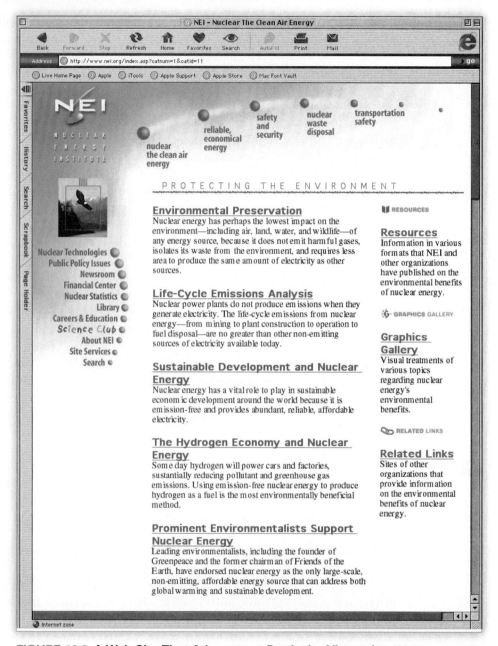

FIGURE 10.2 A Web Site That Advocates a Particular Viewpoint What concerns or issues are reflected in the content of this page? What public attitudes does this agency appear to be advocating?

Source: Home page from Nuclear Energy Institute, <www.nei.org>. Used courtesy of Nuclear Energy Institute.

Keep in mind that any research ultimately stands on its own merits. Thus, funding by a special interest should not automatically discredit an otherwise valid and reliable study.

Also, financing from a private company often sets the stage for beneficial research that might otherwise be unaffordable, as when research funded by Quaker Oats led to other studies proving that oats can lower cholesterol (Raloff, "Chocolate Hearts" 189).

"What are similar sources saying?"

• **Cross-check the source against other, similar sources.** Most studies have some type of flaw or limitation (page 166). Therefore, instead of relying on a single source or study, you should seek a consensus among various respected sources.

Guidelines for Evaluating Sources on the Web

• **Consider the site's domain type and sponsor.** The *domain* signifies where the site originates. Standard domain types in the United States:

.com = business/commercial organization
.edu = educational institution
.gov = government organization
.mil = military organization
.net = anyone with simple software and Internet access
.org = nonprofit organization

The domain type might signal a bias or hidden agenda. For example, a .com site might provide accurate information but also some type of sales pitch. An .org site might reflect a political or ideological bias. A tilde (~) in the address usually signifies a personal home page. Knowing a site's sponsor can help you evaluate its postings.

• **Identify the purpose of the site.** Is the intent merely to relay information, to sell something, or to promote an ideology or agenda?

• **Look beyond the style of a site.** Sometimes the most reliable material resides in the less attractive, text-only sites.

• **Assess the site's/material's currency.** When was the material created, posted, and updated?

• **Assess the author's credentials.** Check the author's reputation, expertise on the topic, and institutional affiliation (a university, major company, environmental group). Link to other sites that mention the author, by using search engines such as *Google,* or consult a citation index (page 130).

NOTE *Don't confuse an author (the person who wrote the material) with a Webmaster (the person who created and maintains the Web site).*

• **Decide whether the assertions/claims make sense.** Where, on the spectrum of expert opinion and accepted theory, does this author reside? Is each assertion supported by convincing evidence? Verify any extreme claim through other

(continues)

Guidelines (continued)

sources, such as a professor or an expert in the field. Also, consider whether your own biases might predispose you to accept certain ideas.

- **Compare the site with other sources.** Comparing similar sites helps you create a *benchmark* (a standard for evaluating any site based on the criteria in these guidelines). Ask a librarian for help.

- **Look for other indicators of quality.**

  —*Worthwhile content:* The material is technically accurate. All sources of data presented as "factual" are fully documented. (See page 151.)

  —*Sensible organization:* Organized for the user's understanding, the material reflects a clear line of reasoning.

  —*Readable style:* The writing is clear, concise, easy to understand and free of mechanical errors.

  —*Relatively objective coverage:* Opposing views are portrayed fairly and accurately. The tone is reasonable, with no name-calling ("radicals," "extremists," or the like).

  —*Expertise:* The author refers to related theory and other work in the field and uses specialized terminology accurately.

  —*Peer review:* The material has been evaluated and verified by experts.

  —*Up-to-date links to reputable sites.*

  —*Follow-up option:* The material includes a signature block or a link for contacting the author or organization.

Source: Adapted from Barnes; Busiel and Maeglin 39; Elliot; Fackelmann 397; Grassian; Hall 60–61; Hammett; Harris, Robert; Kapoun 4; Stemmer.

 Evaluating Web-based sources

Evaluate the Evidence

Evidence is any finding used to support or refute a particular claim. Although evidence can serve the truth, it can also distort, misinform, and deceive. For example:

Questions that invite distorted evidence

> How much money, material, or energy does recycling really save?
> How well are public schools educating children?
> Which investments or automobiles are safest?
> How safe and effective are herbal medications?

Competing answers to such questions often rest on evidence that has been chosen to support a particular view or agenda.

"Is there enough evidence?"

- **Determine the sufficiency of the evidence**. Evidence is sufficient when nothing more is needed to reach an accurate judgment or conclusion. Say you are researching the stress-reducing benefits of low-impact aerobics among employees at a fireworks factory. You would need to interview or survey a broad sample: people who have practiced aerobics for a long time; people of both genders, different ages, different occupations, different lifestyles before they began aerobics; and so on. But responses even from hundreds of practitioners might be insufficient unless those responses were supported by laboratory measurements of metabolic and heart rates, blood pressure, and so on.

NOTE   *Although anecdotal evidence ("This worked great for me!") might offer a good starting point for investigation, your personal experience rarely provides enough evidence from which to generalize. No matter how long you might have practiced aerobics, for instance, you need to determine whether your experience is representative.*

"Can the evidence be verified?"

"Is this claim too good to be true?"

"Is there a downside?"

Is the glass "half full" or "half empty"?

- **Differentiate hard from soft evidence**. "Hard evidence" consists of factual statements, expert opinion, or statistics that can be verified. "Soft evidence" consists of uninformed opinion or speculation, data that were obtained or analyzed unscientifically, and findings that have not been replicated or reviewed by experts.
- **Decide whether the presentation of evidence is balanced and reasonable.** Evidence may be overstated, say, when overzealous researchers exaggerate their achievements, without revealing the limitations of their study. Or vital facts may be omitted, as when acetaminophen pain relievers are promoted as "safe," even though acetaminophen is the leading cause of U.S. drug fatalities (Easton and Herrara 42–44). For more on information abuse, see pages 79–82.
- **Consider how the facts are being framed.** A *frame of reference* is a set of ideas, beliefs, or views that influences our interpretation or acceptance of other ideas. In medical terms, for example, is a "90-percent survival rate" more acceptable than a "10-percent mortality rate"? Framing sways our perception (Lang and Secic 239–40). For instance, what we now call a "financial recession" used to be a "financial depression"—a term which was coined as a euphemism for "financial panic" (P. Bernstein 183). For more on euphemisms, see page 235.

   Whether the language is provocative ("rape of the environment," "soft on terrorism"), euphemistic ("teachable moment" versus "mistake"), or demeaning to opponents ("bureaucrats," "tree huggers"), deceptive framing—all too common in political "spin" strategies—obscures the real issues.

Interpret Your Findings

Interpreting means trying to reach the truth of the matter: an overall judgment about what the findings mean and what conclusion or action they suggest.

   Unfortunately, research does not always yield answers that are clear or conclusive. Instead of settling for the most *convenient* answer, we pursue the most *reasonable* answer by critically examining a full range of possible meanings.

Identify Your Level of Certainty

Research can yield three distinct and very different levels of certainty:

1. The ultimate truth—the *conclusive answer:*

A practical
definition
of "truth"

What is truth?
Can there be
more than one
truth?

> Truth is *what is so* about something, as distinguished from what people wish, believe, or assert to be so. In the words of Harvard philosopher Israel Scheffler, truth is the view "which is fated to be ultimately agreed to by all who investigate."[1] The word *ultimately* is important. Investigation may produce a wrong answer for years, even for centuries. For example, in the second century A.D., Ptolemy's view of the universe placed the earth at its center—and though untrue, this judgment was based on the best information available at that time. And Ptolemy's view survived for 13 centuries, even after new information had discredited this belief. When Galileo proposed a more truthful view in the fifteenth century, he was labeled a heretic.
>
> One way to spare yourself further confusion about truth is to reserve the word *truth* for the final answer to an issue. Get in the habit of using the words *belief, theory,* and *present understanding* more often. (Ruggiero, 3rd ed. 21–22)

Conclusive answers are the research outcome we seek, but often we have to settle for answers that are less than certain.

2. The *probable answer:* the answer that stands the best chance of being true or accurate, given the most we can know at this particular time. Probable answers are subject to revision in light of new information. This is especially the case with *emergent science,* such as gene therapy or food irradiation.
3. The *inconclusive answer:* the realization that the truth of the matter is more elusive, ambiguous, or complex than we expected.

"Exactly how
certain are we?"

We need to decide what level of certainty our findings warrant. For example, we are *highly certain* about the perils of smoking and sunburn, *reasonably certain* about the health benefits of fruits and vegetables, but *less certain* about the perils of coffee drinking or the benefits of vitamin supplements.

Can you think of additional examples of information about which we are *highly, reasonably,* or *less* certain?

Examine the Underlying Assumptions

Assumptions are notions we take for granted, things we often accept without proof. The research process rests on assumptions like these: that a sample group accurately represents a larger target group, that survey respondents remember certain facts accurately, that mice and humans share enough biological similarities for

---

[1] From *Reason and Teaching.* New York: Bobbs-Merrill, 1973.

meaningful research. For a particular study to be valid, the underlying assumptions have to be accurate.

How underlying assumptions affect research validity

Consider this example: You are an education consultant evaluating the accuracy of IQ testing as a predictor of academic performance. Reviewing the evidence, you perceive an association between low IQ scores and low achievers. You then verify your statistics by examining a cross-section of reliable sources. Should you feel justified in concluding that IQ tests do predict performance accurately? This conclusion might be invalid unless you could verify the following assumptions:

1. That neither parents nor teachers nor children had seen individual test scores, which could produce biased expectations.
2. That, regardless of score, each child had completed an identical curriculum, instead of being "tracked" on the basis of his or her score.

NOTE *Assumptions are often easier to identify in someone else's thinking and writing than in our own. During collaborative discussions, ask group members to help you identify your own assumptions (Maeglin).*

Be Alert for Personal Bias

Personal bias is a fact of life

To support a particular version of the truth, our own bias might cause us to overestimate (or deny) the certainty of our findings.

> Unless you are perfectly neutral about the issue, an unlikely circumstance, at the very outset . . . you will believe one side of the issue to be right, and that belief will incline you to . . . present more and better arguments for the side of the issue you prefer. (Ruggiero 134)

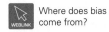 *Where does bias come from?*

Because personal bias is hard to transcend, *rationalizing* often becomes a substitute for *reasoning*:

Reasoning versus rationalizing

> You are reasoning if your belief follows the evidence—that is, if you examine the evidence first and then make up your mind. You are rationalizing if the evidence follows your belief—if you first decide what you'll believe and then select and interpret evidence to justify it. (Ruggiero 44)

Personal bias is often unconscious until we examine our own value systems, attitudes long held but never analyzed, assumptions we've inherited from our backgrounds, and so on. Recognizing our own biases is the crucial first step in managing them.

Consider Other Possible Interpretations

"What else could this mean?"

Perhaps other researchers would disagree about the meaning of certain findings. Settling on a final meaning can be difficult—and sometimes impossible. For example, issues such as the need for defense spending or the causes of inflation are always controversial and will never be resolved. Although we can get verifiable data and can reason persuasively on many subjects, no close reasoning by any expert and no supporting statistical analysis will "prove" anything about a controversial subject. Some problems are simply more resistant to solution than others, no matter how dependable the sources.

NOTE   *Not all interpretations are equally valid. Never assume that any interpretation that is possible is also allowable—especially in terms of its ethical consequences.*

Consider This Standards of Proof Vary for Different Audiences and Cultural Settings

How much evidence is enough to "prove" a particular claim? This often depends on whether the inquiry occurs in the science lab, the courtroom, or the boardroom, as well as on the cultural setting:

- **The scientist** demands evidence that indicates at least 95 percent certainty. A scientific finding must be evaluated and replicated by other experts. Good science looks at the entire picture. Findings are reviewed before they are reported. Even then, answers in science are never "final," but open-ended and ongoing.
- **The juror** demands evidence that indicates only 51 percent certainty (a "preponderance of the evidence"). Jurors are not scientists. Instead of the entire picture, jurors get only the information revealed by lawyers and witnesses. A jury bases its opinion on evidence that exceeds "reasonable doubt" (Monastersky, "Courting" 249;

Powell 32+). Based on such evidence, courts have to make decisions that are final.
- **The corporate executive** demands immediate (even if insufficient) evidence. In a global business climate of overnight developments (in world markets, political strife, natural disasters), business decisions are often made on the spur of the moment. On the basis of incomplete or unverified information—or even hunches—executives must react to crises and try to capitalize on opportunities (Seglin 54).
- **Specific cultures** have their own standards for credible evidence. "For example, African cultures rely on storytelling for authenticity. Arabic persuasion is dependent on universally accepted truths. And Chinese value ancient authorities over recent empiricism" (Byrd and Reid 109).

Avoid Errors in Reasoning

Finding the truth, especially in a complex issue or problem, often is a process of elimination, of ruling out or avoiding errors in reasoning. As we interpret, we make *inferences:* We derive conclusions about what we don't know by reasoning from what we do know (Hayakawa 37). For example, we might infer that a drug that boosts immunity in laboratory mice will boost immunity in humans, or that a rise in campus crime statistics is caused by the fact that young people have become more violent. Whether a particular inference is on target or dead wrong depends largely on our answers to one or more of these questions:

Questions for testing inferences

- To what extent can these findings be generalized?
- Is *Y* really caused by *X*?
- To what extent can the numbers be trusted, and what do they mean?

Three major reasoning errors that can distort our interpretations are faulty generalization, faulty causal reasoning, and faulty statistical reasoning.

Faulty Generalization

We engage in faulty generalization when we jump from a limited observation to a sweeping conclusion. Even "proven" facts can invite mistaken conclusions, as in the following examples:

Factual observations

1. "Some studies have shown that gingko [an herb] improves mental functioning in people with dementia [mental deterioration caused by maladies such as Alzheimer's Disease]" (Stix 30).
2. "For the period 1992–2005, two thirds of the fastest-growing occupations [called] for no more than a high-school degree" (Harrison 62).
3. "Adult female brains are significantly smaller than male brains—about 8% smaller, on average" (Seligman 74).

Invalid conclusions

1. Gingko is food for the brain!
2. Higher education . . . Who needs it?!
3. Women are the less intelligent gender.

"How much can we generalize from these findings?"

When we accept findings uncritically and jump to conclusions about their meaning (as in points 1 and 2, above) we commit the error of *hasty generalization*. When we overestimate the extent to which the findings reveal some larger truth (as in point 3, above) we commit the error of *overstated generalization*.

NOTE

We often need to generalize, and we should. For example, countless studies support the generalization that fruits and vegetables help lower cancer risk. But we ordinarily limit general claims by inserting qualifiers such as "usually," "often," "sometimes," "probably," "possibly," or "some."

 Some consequences of relativism

Faulty Causal Reasoning

Causal reasoning tries to explain why something happened or what will happen, often in very complex situations. Sometimes a *definite cause is apparent*

("The engine's overheating is caused by a faulty radiator cap"). We reason about definite causes when we explain why the combustion in a car engine causes the wheels to move, or why the moon's orbit makes the tides rise and fall. However, causal reasoning often explores *causes that are not so obvious, but only possible or probable.* In these cases, much analysis is needed to isolate a specific cause.

Suppose you want to answer this question: "Why does our college campus have no children's daycare facilities?" Brainstorming yields these possible causes:

"Did *X* possibly, probably, or definitely cause *Y?*"

- lack of need among students
- lack of interest among students, faculty, and staff
- high cost of liability insurance
- lack of space and facilities on campus
- lack of trained personnel
- prohibition by state law
- lack of government funding for such a project

Say you proceed with interviews, questionnaires, and research into state laws, insurance rates, and availability of personnel. You begin to rule out some items, and others appear as probable causes. Specifically, you find a need among students, high campus interest, an abundance of qualified people for staffing, and no state laws prohibiting such a project. Three probable causes remain: lack of funding, high insurance rates, and lack of space. Further inquiry shows that lack of funding and high insurance rates *are* issues. These obstacles, however, could be eliminated through new sources of revenue such as charging a modest fee per child, soliciting donations, and diverting funds from other campus organizations. Finally, after examining available campus space and speaking with school officials, you conclude that one definite cause is lack of space and facilities.

When you report on your research, be sure readers can draw conclusions identical to your own on the basis of the reasoning you present. Your reporting process might be diagrammed like this:

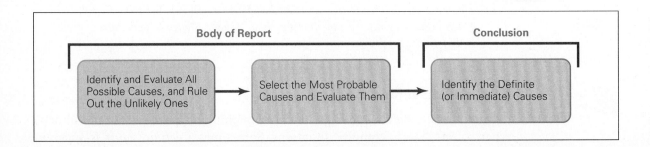

The persuasiveness of your causal argument will depend on the quality of evidence you bring to bear, as well as on how clearly you explain the links in the chain. Also, you must convince your audience you haven't overlooked important alternative causes.

NOTE *Anything but the simplest effect is likely to have more than one cause. You have to make the case that the cause you have isolated is the right one. In the daycare scenario, for example, you might argue that lack of space and facilities somehow is related to funding. And the college's inability to find funds or space might be related to student need or interest, which is not high enough to exert real pressure. Lack of space and facilities, however, appears to be the "immediate" cause.*

Here are common errors that distort or oversimplify cause-effect relationships:

Ignoring other causes | Investment builds wealth. [Ignores the roles of knowledge, wisdom, timing, and luck in successful investing.]

Ignoring other effects | Running improves health. [Ignores the fact that many runners get injured, and that some even drop dead while running.]

Inventing a causal sequence | Right after buying a rabbit's foot, Felix won the state lottery. [Posits an unwarranted causal relationship merely because one event follows another.]

Confusing correlation with causation | Women in Scandinavian countries drink a lot of milk. Women in Scandinavian countries have a high incidence of breast cancer. Therefore, milk must be a cause of breast cancer. [The association between these two variables might be mere coincidence and might obscure other possible causes, such as environment, fish diet, and genetic predisposition (Lemonick 85).]

Rationalizing | My grades were poor because my exams were unfair. [Denies the real causes of one's failures.]

Media Researcher Robert Griffin identifies three criteria for demonstrating a causal relationship:

Along with showing correlation [say, an association between smoking and cancer], evidence of causality requires that the alleged causal agent occurs prior to the condition it causes (e.g., that smoking precedes the development of cancers) and—the most difficult task—that other explanations are discounted or accounted for (240).

For example, epidemiological studies found this correlation: People who eat lots of broccoli, cauliflower, and other "cruciferous" vegetables have lower rates of some cancers. But other explanations (say, that big veggie eaters might have many other healthful habits as well) could not be ruled out until lab studies showed how a special protein in these vegetables actually protects human cells (Wang 182).

Faulty Statistical Reasoning

How numbers
can mislead

The purpose of statistical analysis is to determine the meaning of a collected set of numbers. In primary research, our surveys and questionnaires often lead to some kind of numerical interpretation ("What percentage of respondents prefer X?" "How often does Y happen?"). In secondary research, we rely on numbers collected by survey researchers.

Numbers seem more precise, more objective, more scientific, and less ambiguous than words. They are easier to summarize, measure, compare, and analyze. But numbers can be totally misleading. For example, radio or television phone-in surveys often produce distorted data: Although "90 percent of callers" might express support for a particular viewpoint, people who bother to respond tend to have the greatest anger or extreme feelings—representing only a fraction of overall attitudes (Fineman 24). Mail-in or Internet surveys can produce similar distortion. Before relying on any set of numbers, we need to know exactly where they come from, how they were collected, and how they were analyzed.

Common statistical
fallacies

Faulty statistical reasoning produces conclusions that are unwarranted, inaccurate, or deceptive. Following are typical fallacies.

"Exactly how well
are we doing?"

The Sanitized Statistic.   Numbers are manipulated (or "cleaned up") to obscure the facts. For instance, the College Board's 1996 "recentering" of SAT scores has raised the "average" math score from 478 to 500 and the average verbal score from 424 to 500 (boosts of almost 5 and 18 percent, respectively), although actual student performance remains unchanged (Samuelson 44).

"How many rats
was that?"

The Meaningless Statistic.   Exact numbers can be used to quantify something so inexact or vaguely defined that it should only be approximated (Huff 247; Lavin 278): "Boston has 3,247,561 rats." "Zappo detergent makes laundry 10 percent brighter." An exact number looks impressive, but it can hide the fact that certain subjects (child abuse, cheating in college, drug and alcohol abuse, eating habits) cannot be quantified exactly because respondents don't always tell the truth (because of denial or embarrassment or guessing). Or they respond in ways they think the researcher expects.

"Why is everbody
griping?"

Three ways of
reporting an
"average"

The Undefined Average.   The mean, median, and mode are confused in determining an average (Huff 244; Lavin 279). (1) The *mean* is the result of adding up the value of each item in a set of numbers, and then dividing by the number of items. (2) The *median* is the result of ranking all the values from high to low, then identifying the middle value (or the 50th percentile, as in calculating SAT scores). (3) The *mode* is the value that occurs most often in a set of numbers.

Each of these three measurements represents some kind of average. But unless we know which "average" (mean, median, or mode) is being presented, we cannot possibly interpret the figures accurately.

Assume, for instance, that we want to determine the average salary among female managers at XYZ Corporation (ranked from high to low):

Manager	Salary
"A"	$90,000
"B"	$90,000
"C"	$80,000
"D"	$65,000
"E"	$60,000
"F"	$55,000
"G"	$50,000

In the above example, the *mean* salary (total salaries divided by number of salaries) is $70,000; the *median* salary (middle value) is $65,000; the *mode* (most frequent value) is $90,000. Each is, legitimately, an "average," and each could be used to support or refute a particular assertion (for example, "Women managers are paid too little" or "Women managers are paid too much").

Research expert Michael R. Lavin sums up the potential for bias in the reporting of averages:

> Depending on the circumstances, any one of these measurements may describe a group of numbers better than the other two. . . . [But] people typically choose the value which best presents their case, whether or not it is the most appropriate to use. (279)

Although the mean is the most commonly computed average, this measurement is misleading when one or more values on either end of the scale (*outliers*) are extremely high or low. Suppose, for instance, that manager "A" (above) was paid a $200,000 salary. Because this figure deviates so far from the normal range of salary figures for "B" through "G," it distorts the average for the whole group, increasing the mean salary by more than 20 percent (Plumb and Spyridakis 636).

"Is 51 percent really a majority?"

The Distorted Percentage Figure.   Percentages are often reported without explanation of the original numbers used in the calculation (Adams and Schvaneveldt 359; Lavin 280): "Seventy-five percent of respondents prefer our brand over the competing brand"—without mention that only four people were surveyed.

NOTE   *In small samples, percentages can mislead because the percentage size can dwarf the number it represents: "In this experiment, 33% of the rats lived, 33% died, and the third rat got away." (Lang and Secic 41.) When your sample is small, report the actual numbers: "Five out of ten respondents agreed . . . ."*

Another fallacy in reporting percentages occurs when the *margin of error* is ignored. This is the margin within which the true figure lies, based on estimated sampling errors in a survey. For example, a claim that "most people surveyed prefer Brand X" might be based on the fact that 51 percent of respondents expressed this preference; but if the survey carried a 2 percent margin of error, the real figure could be as low as 49 percent or as high as 53 percent. In a survey with a high margin of error, the true figure may be so uncertain that no definite conclusion can be drawn.

"Which car should we buy?"

The Bogus Ranking.   This distortion occurs when items are compared on the basis of ill-defined criteria (Adams and Schvaneveldt 212; Lavin 284): "Last year, the Batmobile was the number-one selling car in America"—without mention that some competing car makers actually sold *more* cars to private individuals, and that the Batmobile figures were inflated by hefty sales—at huge discounts—to rental-car companies and corporate fleets. Unless we know how the ranked items were chosen and how they were compared (the *criteria*), a ranking can produce a seemingly scientific number based on a completely unscientific method.

"Does *X* actually cause *Y*?"

Confusion of Correlation with Causation.   *Correlation* is a numerical measure of the strength of the relationship between two variables (say smoking and increased lung cancer risk, or education and income). *Causation* is the demonstrable production of a specific effect (smoking causes lung cancer). Correlations between smoking and lung cancer or between education and income signal a causal relationship that has been demonstrated by many studies. But not every correlation implies causation. For instance, a recently discovered correlation between moderate alcohol consumption and decreased heart disease risk offers no sufficient proof that moderate drinking *causes* less heart disease.

In any type of causal analysis, be on the lookout for *confounding factors*, which are other possible reasons or explanations for a particular outcome. For instance, studies indicating that regular exercise improves health might be overlooking this confounding factor: healthy people tend to exercise more than those who are unhealthy ("Walking" 3–4).

Many highly publicized correlations are the product of *data mining:* In this process, computers randomly compare one set of variables (say, eating habits) with another set (say, range of diseases). From these countless comparisons, certain relationships or associations, are revealed (say, between coffee drinking and pancreatic cancer risk). As dramatic as such isolated correlations may be, they constitute no proof of causation and often lead to hasty conclusions (Ross, "Lies" 135).

NOTE   *Despite its limitations, data mining is invaluable for "uncovering correlations that require computers to perceive but that thinking humans can evaluate and research further" (Maeglin).*

Potential errors
in meta-analysis

The Biased Meta-Analysis. In a meta-analysis, researchers examine a whole range of studies that have been done on one topic (say, high-fat diets and cancer risk). The purpose of this "study of studies" is to decide the overall meaning of the collected findings. Because results ultimately depend on which studies have been included and which omitted, a meta-analysis can reflect the biases of the researchers who select the material. Also, because small studies have less chance of being published than large ones, they may get overlooked (Lang and Secic 174–76).

"How have
assumptions
influenced this
computer model?"

The Fallible Computer Model. Computer models process complex *assumptions* (see page 156) to predict or estimate costs, benefits, risks, and probable outcomes. But answers produced by any computer model depend on the assumptions (and data) programmed in. Assumptions might be influenced by researcher bias or the sponsors' agenda. For example, a prediction of human fatalities from a nuclear reactor meltdown might rest on assumptions about the availability of safe shelter, evacuation routes, time of day, season, wind direction, and the structural integrity of the containment unit. But these assumptions could be manipulated to overstate or understate the risk (Barbour 228). For computer-modeled estimates of accident risk (oil spill, plane crash) or of the costs and benefits of a proposed project or policy (International Space Station, welfare reform), consumers rarely know the assumptions behind the numbers.

"Do we all agree
on what these
terms mean?"

Misleading Terminology. The terms used to interpret statistics sometimes hide their real meaning. For instance, the widely publicized figure that people treated for cancer have a "50 percent survival rate" is misleading in two ways; (1) *Survival* to laypersons means "staying alive," but to medical experts, staying alive for only five years after diagnosis qualifies as survival; (2) the "50 percent" survival figure covers *all* cancers, including certain skin or thyroid cancers that have extremely high *cure rates,* as well as other cancers (such as lung or ovarian) that are rarely curable and have extremely low *survival rates* ("Are We" 6).

"Is this news
good, bad, or
insignificant?"

Even the most valid and reliable statistics require that we interpret the reality behind the numbers. For instance, the overall cancer rate today is "higher" than it was in 1910. What this may mean is that people are living longer and thus are more likely to die of cancer and that cancer today rarely is misdiagnosed—or mislabeled because of stigma ("Are We" 4). The finding that rates for certain cancers "double" after prolonged exposure to electromagnetic waves may really mean that cancer risk actually increases from 1 in 10,000 to 2 in 10,000.

The previous numbers may be "technically accurate" and may seem highly persuasive in the interpretations they suggest. But the actual "truth" behind these numbers is far more elusive. Any interpretation of statistical data carries the possibility that other, more accurate interpretations have been overlooked or deliberately excluded (Barnett 45).

Acknowledge the Limits of Research

Legitimate researchers live with uncertainty. They expect to be wrong far more often than right. Experimentation and exploration often produce confusion, mistakes, and dead ends. Following is a brief list of things that go wrong with research and interpretation.

Obstacles to Validity and Reliability

What makes a
survey valid

Validity and *reliability* determine the dependability of any research (Adams and Schvaneveldt 79–97; Burghardt 174–75; Crossen 22–24; Lang and Secic 154–55; Velotta 391). *Valid research* produces correct findings. A survey, for example, is valid when (1) it measures what you want it to measure, (2) it measures accurately and precisely, and (3) its findings can be generalized to the target population. Valid survey questions enable each respondent to interpret each question exactly as the researcher intended; valid questions also ask for information respondents are qualified to provide.

Why survey
responses can't
always be trusted

Survey validity depends largely on trustworthy responses. Even clear, precise, and neutral questions can produce mistaken, inaccurate, or dishonest answers. People often see themselves as more informed, responsible, or competent than they really are. Respondents are likely to suppress information that reflects poorly on their behavior, attitudes, or will power when answering such questions as "How often do you take needless sick days?" "Would you lie to get ahead?" "How much TV do you watch?" They might exaggerate or invent facts or opinions that reveal a more admirable picture when answering the following types of questions: "How much do you give to charity?" "How many books do you read?" "How often do you hug your children?" Even when respondents don't know, don't remember, or have no opinion, they often tend to guess in ways designed to win the researcher's approval.

What makes a
survey reliable

Reliable research produces findings that can be replicated. A survey is reliable when its results are consistent; for instance, when a respondent gives identical answers to the same survey given twice or to different versions of the same questions. Reliable survey questions can be interpreted identically by all respondents.

Much of your communication will be based on the findings of other researchers, so you will need to assess the validity and reliability of their research as well as your own.

Flaws in Research Studies

While some types of studies are more reliable than others, each type has limitations (Cohn 106; Harris, Richard 170–72; Lang and Secic 8–9; Murphy 143):

Common flaws
in epidemiologic
studies

- **Epidemiological studies.** Epidemiologists study various populations (human, animal, or plant) to find correlations (say, between computer use and cataracts). Conducted via observations, interviews, surveys, or records review, these studies are subject to faulty sampling techniques (page 140) and observer bias (seeing what one wants to see). Even with a correlation that is 99 percent certain, an epidemiological study alone doesn't "prove" anything. (The larger the study, however, the more credible.)

Common flaws in
laboratory studies

- **Laboratory studies.** Although a laboratory offers controlled conditions, these studies also carry limitations. For example, the reactions of experimental mice to a specific treatment or drug often are not generalizable to humans. Also, the reaction of an isolated group of cells does not always predict the reaction of the entire organism.

Common flaws
in clinical trials

- **Human exposure studies** *(clinical trials).* These studies compare one group of people receiving medication or treatment with an untreated group, the *control group*. Limitations include the possibility that the study group may be non-representative or too different from the general population in overall health, age, or ethnic background. (For example, the fact that gingko might slow memory loss in sick people doesn't mean it will boost the memory of healthy people.) Also, anecdotal reports are unreliable. Respondents often invent answers to questions such as "How often do you eat ice cream?" or "Do you sometimes forget to take your medication?"

Measurement Errors

How scientific
measurement
can go wrong

Regardless of the type of study, all measurements (of length, time, temperature, weight, population characteristics) are prone to error (Taylor 3–4). For example, technique can vary from measure to measure: in running a stopwatch or reading an instrument (say, a thermometer). Also, each observation differs with different observers or with the same observer in repeated observations. In some cases, the measuring device itself may be faulty: say, a watch that runs slow or an improperly calibrated instrument.

Deceptive Reporting

"Has bad or
embarrassing
news been
suppressed?"

One problem in reviewing scientific findings is "getting the story straight." Intentionally or not, the public often is given a distorted picture. For instance, although twice as many people in the United States are killed by medications as by auto accidents—and countless others harmed—doctors rarely report adverse drug reactions. For example, one Rhode Island study identified roughly 26,000 adverse reactions noted in doctors' files, of which only 11 had been reported to the Food and Drug Administration. (Freundlich 14).

"Is the topic 'too weird' for researchers?"

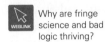 Why are fringe science and bad logic thriving?

Even bad science makes good news

Some promising but unconventional topics, such as herbal remedies, are rarely the topics of intensive research "partly because few 'respectable' scientists are willing to risk their reputations to do the testing required, and partly because few firms would be willing to pay for it if they were." Drug companies have little interest because "herbal medicines, not being new inventions, cannot be patented" ("Any Alternative?" 83).

Spectacular claims that are even remotely possible are more appealing than spectacular claims that have been disproven. Examples include "Giant Comet Headed for Earth!" and "Insects may carry the AIDS virus!

NOTE   *Does all this potential for error mean we shouldn't believe anything? Of course not. But we need to be discerning about what we do choose to believe. Critical thinking is essential.*

Guidelines for Evaluating and Interpreting Information

Evaluate the Sources

- **Check the posting or publication date.** The latest information is not always the best, but keeping up with recent developments is vital.

- **Assess the reputation of each printed source.** Check the copyright page for background on the publisher, the bibliography for the quality of research, and (if available) the author's brief biography.

- **Assess the quality of each electronic source.** See page 153.

- **Identify the study's sponsor.** If a study proclaiming the crashworthiness of the Batmobile has been sponsored by the Batmobile Auto Company, be skeptical.

- **Look for corroborating sources.** A single study rarely produces definitive findings. Learn what other sources say, why they agree or disagree, and where most experts stand.

Evaluate the Evidence

- **Decide whether the evidence is sufficient.** Evidence should surpass personal experience, anecdote, or media reports. Reasonable and informed observers should be able to agree on its credibility.

- **Look for a fair and balanced presentation.** Suspect any claims about "breakthroughs" or "miracle cures" or the like.

- **Try to verify the evidence.** Examine the facts that support the claims. Look for replication of findings.

Interpret Your Findings

- **Don't expect "certainty."** Complex questions are mostly open-ended, and a mere accumulation of facts doesn't "prove" anything. Even so, the weight of evidence usually suggests some reasonable conclusion.

- **Examine the underlying assumptions.** As opinions taken for granted, assumptions are easily mistaken for facts.

- **Identify your personal biases.** Examine your own assumptions. Don't ignore evidence simply because it contradicts your original assumptions.

- **Consider alternate interpretations.** What else might this evidence mean?

Check for Weak Spots

- **Scrutinize all generalizations.** Decide whether the evidence supports the generalization. Suspect any general claim not limited by a qualifier such as "often," "sometimes," or "rarely."

- **Treat causal claims skeptically.** Differentiate correlation from causation, as well as possible from probable or definite causes. Consider confounding factors (other explanations for the reported outcome).

- **Look for statistical fallacies.** Determine where the numbers come from, and how they were collected and analyzed—information that legitimate researchers routinely provide. Note the margin of error.

- **Consider the limits of computer analysis.** Data mining often produces intriguing but random correlations; a meta-analysis might be biased; a computer model is only as accurate as the assumptions and data programmed in.

- **Look for misleading terminology.** Examine terms that beg for precise definition in their specific context: "survival rate," "success rate," "customer satisfaction," "risk factor," and so on.

- **Interpret the reality behind the numbers.** Consider the possibility of alternative, more accurate, interpretations of the data.

- **Consider the study's possible limitations.** Small, brief studies are less reliable than large, extended ones; epidemiological studies are less reliable than laboratory studies (which have their own flaws); animal exposure studies are often not generalizable to human populations; and measurements are prone to error.

- **Look for the whole story.** Consider whether bad news may be underreported; good news, exaggerated; bad science, camouflaged and sensationalized; or research on promising but unconventional topics (say, alternative energy sources), ignored.

☑ **Checklist:** The Research Process

(Numbers in parentheses refer to the first page of discussion.)

Methods

☐ Did I ask the right questions? (115)

☐ Are the sources appropriately up-to-date? (150)

☐ Is each source reputable, trustworthy, relatively unbiased, and borne out by other, similar sources? (151)

☐ Does the evidence clearly support all of the conclusions? (154)

☐ Is a fair balance of viewpoints represented? (117)

☐ Can all of the evidence be verified? (155)

☐ Has the research achieved adequate depth? (117)

☐ Has the entire research process been valid and reliable? (166)

Reasoning

☐ Am I reasonably certain about the meaning of these findings? (156)

☐ Can I discern assumption from fact? (156)

☐ Am I reasoning instead of rationalizing? (157)

☐ Can I discern correlation from causation? (164)

☐ Is this the most reasonable conclusion (or merely the most convenient)? (155)

☐ Can I rule out other possible interpretations or conclusions? (157)

☐ Have I accounted for all sources of bias, including my own? (157)

☐ Are my generalizations warranted by the evidence? (159)

☐ Am I confident that my causal reasoning is accurate? (159)

☐ Can I rule out confounding factors? (164)

☐ Can all of the numbers, statistics, and interpretations be trusted? (162).

☐ Have I resolved (or at least acknowledged) any conflicts among my findings? (119)

☐ Can I rule out any possible error or distortion? (167)

☐ Am I getting the whole story, and getting it straight? (167)

☐ Should the evidence be reconsidered? (165)

Documentation

☐ Is the documentation consistent, complete, and correct? (634)

☐ Is all quoted material clearly marked throughout the text? (636)

☐ Are direct quotations used sparingly and appropriately? (636)

☐ Are all quotations accurate and integrated grammatically? (637)

☐ Are all paraphrases accurate and clear? (638)

☐ Have I documented all sources not considered common knowledge? (639)

Exercises

 Exercises

1. From print or broadcast media, personal experience, or the Internet, identify an example of each of the following sources of distortion or of interpretive error:

   - a study with questionable sponsorship or motives
   - reliance on insufficient evidence
   - unbalanced presentation
   - deceptive framing of facts
   - overestimating the level of certainty
   - biased interpretation
   - rationalizing
   - unexamined assumptions
   - faulty causal reasoning
   - hasty generalization
   - overstated generalization
   - sanitized statistic
   - meaningless statistic
   - undefined average
   - distorted percentage figure
   - bogus ranking
   - fallible computer model
   - misinterpreted statistic
   - deceptive reporting

   Hint: For examples of faulty (as well as correct) statistical reasoning in the news, check out Dartmouth College's *Chance Project* at <www. dartmouth.edu/~chance>.

   Submit your examples to your instructor along with a memo explaining each error, and be prepared to discuss your material in class.

2. Referring to the list in Exercise 1, identify the specific distortion or interpretive error in these examples:

   a. *The federal government excludes from unemployment figures an estimated 5 million people who remain unemployed after one year* (Morgenson 54).

   b. *Only 38.268 percent of college graduates end up working in their specialty.*

   c. *Sixty-six percent of employees we hired this year are women and minorities, compared to the national average of 40 percent.* No mention is made of the fact that only three people have been hired this year, by a company that employs 300 (mostly white males).

   d. *Are you pro-life (or pro-choice)?*

3. Identify confounding factors (page 164) that might have been overlooked in the following interpretations and conclusions:

   a. *One out of every five patients admitted to Central Hospital dies* (Sowell 120). Does this mean that the hospital is bad?

   b. *In a recent survey, rates of emotional depression differed widely among different countries—far lower in Asian than in Western countries* (Horgan 24+). Are these differences due to culturally specific genetic factors, as many scientists might conclude? Or is this conclusion *confounded* by other variables?

   c. *"Among 20-year-olds in 1979, those who said that they smoked marijuana 11 to 50 times in the past year had an average IQ 15 percentile points higher than those who said they'd only smoked once"* (Sklaroff and Ash 85). Does this indicate that pot increases brain power or could it mean something else?

   d. *Teachers are mostly to blame for low test scores and poor discipline in public schools.* How is our assessment of this claim affected by the following information? *From age 2 to 17, children in the U.S. average 12,000 hours in school, and 15,000 to 18,000 hours watching TV* ("Wellness Facts" 1).

4. Uninformed opinions are usually based on assumptions we've never really examined. Examples of popular assumptions that are largely unexamined:

   - "Bottled water is safer and better for us than tap water."
   - "Forest fires should always be prevented or suppressed immediately."
   - "The fewer germs in their environment, the healthier the children."
   - "The more soy we eat, the better."

Identify and examine one popular assumption for accuracy. For example, you might tackle the bottled water assumption by visiting the FDA Web site <www.fda.gov> and the Sierra Club site <www.sierra.org>, for starters. (Unless you get stuck, work with an assumption not listed above.) Trace the sites and links you followed to get your information, and write up your findings in a memo to be shared with the class.

Collaborative Projects

Exercises from the previous section may be done as collaborative projects.

Service-Learning Project

Divide into groups and identify a controversial environmental or technology issue (for example, the need to drill for oil and natural gas in the Alaskan Wildlife Refuge or the feasibility of the National Missile Defense System). Assume that your public-interest group publishes a monthly newsletter designed to give readers an accurate assessment of opposing claims about such issues. Using this chapter as a guide, review and evaluate the main arguments and counterarguments about the issue you've chosen. Prepare the text for a 1,500-word article that will appear in the newsletter, pointing out specific examples of questionable sources, interpretive error, or distorted reasoning.

CHAPTER 11

Summarizing and Abstracting Information

Purpose of Summaries

What Users Expect from a Summary

   Guidelines for Summarizing Information

A Situation Requiring a Summary

Forms of Summarized Information

Ethical Considerations in Summarizing Information

   Checklist: Usability of Summaries

On the Job . . . The Importance of Summaries

A *summary* is a short version of a longer document. Summaries are vital to people who have no time to read in detail everything that crosses their desks. Many busy readers are interested only in the big picture, and so most long reports are preceded by some type of summary.

 Summaries and hierarchies of power

Purpose of Summaries

On the job, you have to write concisely about your work. You might report on meetings or conferences, describe your progress on a project, or propose a money-saving idea. A routine assignment for many new employees is to provide superiors (decision makers) with summaries of the latest developments.

Researchers and people who must act on information need to identify quickly what is most important in a long document. A summary does three things: (1) shows what the document is all about; (2) helps users decide whether to read all of it, parts of it, or none of it; and (3) provides a framework for understanding the details of the longer document that follows.

An effective summary communicates the *essential message* accurately and in the fewest possible words. Consider, for example, this next passage and the summary that follows it:

The original passage

> Scientists know with virtual certainty that human activities are changing the composition of Earth's atmosphere. Increasing levels of greenhouse gases like carbon dioxide (CO_2) since pre-industrial times are well-documented and understood. The atmospheric buildup of CO_2 and other greenhouse gases is largely the result of human activities such as the burning of fossil fuels. Increasing greenhouse gas concentrations tend to warm the planet. A warming trend of about 0.7 to 1.5°F occurred during the 20th century in both the Northern and Southern Hemispheres and over the oceans. The major greenhouse gases remain in the atmosphere for periods ranging from decades to centuries. It is therefore virtually certain that atmospheric concentrations of greenhouse gases will continue to rise over the next few decades.
>
> *Source:* Adapted from *State of Knowledge*, U.S. Environmental Protection Agency <http://epa.gov/climatechange/science/stateofknowledge.html>.

In the previous passage, three ideas make up the essential message: (1) scientists are virtually certain that greenhouse gases largely produced by human activities are warming the planet; (2) rising temperatures worldwide during the 20th century have been demonstrated; and (3) this warming trend almost certainly will continue. A summary of the above passage might read like this:

A summarized version

> Scientists are virtually certain that greenhouse gases largely produced by human activities are warming the planet. Temperatures have risen worldwide during the 20th century and undoubtedly will continue.

NOTE *For letters, memos, or other short documents that can be read quickly, the only summary needed is usually an opening thesis or topic sentence that previews the contents.*

What Users Expect from a Summary

Whether you summarize your own documents (like the sample on page 548) or someone else's, users will have these expectations:

Elements of a usable summary

- **Accuracy:** Users expect a precise sketch of the content, emphasis, and line of reasoning from the original.
- **Completeness:** Users expect to consult the original document only for more detail—but not to make sense of the main ideas and their relationships.
- **Readability:** Users expect a summary to be clear and straightforward—easy to follow and understand.
- **Conciseness:** Users expect a summary to be informative yet brief, and they may stipulate a word limit (say, two hundred words).
- **Nontechnical style:** Unless they are all experts, users expect plain English.

Although the summary is written last, it is what readers of a long document turn to first. Take the time to do a good job.

Guidelines for Summarizing Information

- **Read the entire original.** When summarizing someone else's work, get a complete picture before writing a word.
- **Reread the original, underlining essential material.** Focus on the essential message: thesis and topic sentences, findings, conclusions, and recommendations.
- **Edit the underlined information.** Omit technical details, examples, explanations, or anything readers won't need for grasping the basics.
- **Rewrite in your own words.** Even if this first draft is too long, include everything essential for it to stand alone; you can trim later. In summarizing another's work, avoid direct quotations; if you must quote a crucial word or phrase, use quotation marks around the author's own words. Add no personal comments, except for brief definitions, if needed.
- **Edit your own version.** When you have everything readers need, edit for conciseness (See page 223).
  a. Cross out needless words—but keep sentences clear and grammatical:

Needless words omitted

| ~~As far as~~ artificial intelligence ~~is concerned, the~~ technology is ~~only~~ in its infancy.

(continues)

Guidelines (continued)

Needless prefaces
to be omitted

b. Cross out needless prefaces such as

> The writer argues . . . .
>
> Also discussed is. . . .

c. Use numerals for numbers, except to begin a sentence.
d. Combine related ideas in order to emphasize relationships. (See page 229.)

- **Check your version against the original.** Verify that you have preserved the essential message and added no comments—unless you are preparing an executive abstract (as on page 185).

- **Rewrite your edited version.** Add transitional expressions (page 693) to emphasize the connections. Respect any stipulated word limit.

- **Document your source.** Cite the full source below any summary not accompanied by its original. (See pages 640–69 for documentation formats.)

A Situation Requiring a Summary

The following case illustrates how the Guidelines for summarizing information can be applied.

CASE: Creating a Summary

Assume that you work in the information office of your state's Department of Environmental Management (DEM). In the coming election, citizens will vote on a referendum proposal for constructing the state's first nuclear power plant. Supporters argue that nuclear power would help solve the growing problem of acid rain and global warming from burning fossil fuels. Opponents argue that nuclear power is expensive and unsafe.

To clarify the issues, the DEM will mail a newsletter to each registered voter. You have been assigned to research the recent data and summarize it. One of the articles appears in Figure 11.1. You have underlined key phrases and noted your critical thinking responses in the margins.

Assume that in two early drafts of your summary, you rewrote and edited; for coherence and emphasis, you inserted transitions and combined related ideas. Figure 11.2 shows your final draft.

The version in Figure 11.2 is trimmed, tightened, and edited: word count is reduced to roughly 20 percent of original length. A summary this long serves well in many situations, but other audiences might want a briefer and more compressed summary—say, roughly 15 percent of the original—like the one in Figure 11.3.

Notice that the essential message remains intact; related ideas are again combined and fewer supporting details are included. Clearly, length is adjustable according to your audience and purpose.

1

U.S. Nuclear Power Industry: Background and Current Status

Combine as orienting statement (controlling idea)

Omit background details

Include causes of problem

The U.S. nuclear power industry, while currently generating more than 20 percent of the Nation's electricity, faces an uncertain future. No nuclear power plants have been ordered since 1978, and more than 100 reactors have been cancelled, including all ordered after 1973. No units are currently under active construction; the Tennessee Valley Authority's Watts Bar I reactor, ordered in 1970 and licensed to operate in 1996, was the last U.S. nuclear unit to be completed. The nuclear power industry's troubles include a slowdown in the rate of growth of electricity demand, high nuclear power plant construction costs, public concern about nuclear safety and waste disposal, and a changing regulatory environment.

Obstacles to Expansion

Include major cause

Omit nonvital details

Include key comparison

High construction costs are perhaps the most serious obstacle to nuclear power expansion. Construction costs for reactors completed within the last decade have ranged from $2 billion to $6 billion, averaging about $3,000 per kilowatt of electric generating capacity (in 1995 dollars). The nuclear industry predicts that new plant designs could be built for about half that amount, but construction costs would still substantially exceed the projected costs of coal- and gas-fired plants.

Omit speculation

Include key facts

Of more immediate concern to the nuclear power industry is the outlook for existing nuclear reactors in a deregulated electricity market. Electric utility restructuring, which is currently under way in several States, could increase the competition faced by existing nuclear plants. High operating costs and the need for costly improvements and equipment replacements have resulted in the permanent shutdown during the past decade of 10 U.S. commercial reactors before completion of their 40-year licensed operating periods. Several more reactors are currently being considered for early shutdown.

Include key facts and comparisons

Nevertheless, all is not bleak for the U.S. nuclear power industry, which currently comprises 109 licensed reactors at 68 plant sites in 38 states. Electricity production from U.S. nuclear power plants is greater than that from oil, natural gas, and hydropower, and behind only coal, which accounts for approximately 55 percent of U.S. electricity generation. Nuclear plants generate more than half the electricity in six states.

Include key fact

Omit nonvital details

Average operating costs of U.S. nuclear plants have dropped during the 1990s, and costly downtime has been steadily reduced. Licensed commercial

FIGURE 11.1 Article to Be Summarized

Source: Adapted from *Congressional Digest* Jan. 1998: 7+.

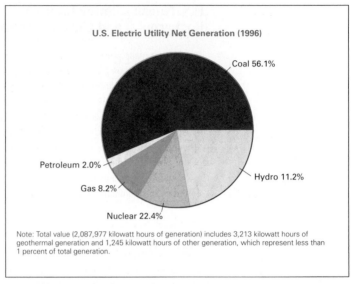

Source: U.S. Department of Energy, Energy Information Administration

reactors generated electricity at an average of 75 percent of their total capacity in 1996, slightly below the previous year's record.

Include key claim

    Global warming that may be caused by fossil fuels—the "greenhouse effect"—is cited by nuclear power supporters as an important reason to develop a new generation of reactors. But the large obstacles noted above must still be overcome before electric utilities will order new nuclear units.

Omit explanation

Include key fact

    Reactor manufacturers are working on designs for safer, less expensive nuclear plants, and the Nuclear Regulatory Commission (NRC) has approved new regulations to speed up the nuclear licensing process, consistent with the Energy Policy Act of 1992. Even so, the Energy Information Administration forecasts that no new U.S. reactors will become operational for a decade or more, if any are ordered at all.

Omit nonvital fact

Include key fact

Safety Concerns

Include key facts

Controversy over safety has dogged nuclear power throughout its development, particularly following the Three Mile Island accident in Pennsylvania and the April 1986 Chernobyl disaster in the former Soviet Union. In the United States, safety-related shortcomings have been identified in the construction quality of some plants, plant operation and maintenance,

Omit examples

FIGURE 11.1 *(Continued)*

equipment reliability, emergency planning, and other areas. In addition, mishaps have occurred in which key safety systems have been disabled. NRC's oversight of the nuclear industry is an ongoing issue: nuclear utilities often complain that they are subject to overly rigorous and inflexible regulation, but nuclear critics charge that NRC frequently relaxes safety standards when compliance may prove difficult or costly to the industry.

In terms of public health consequences, the safety record of the U.S. nuclear power industry has been excellent. In more than 2,000 reactor-years of operation in the United States, the only incident at a commercial power plant that might lead to any deaths or injuries to the public has been the Three Mile Island accident, in which more than half the core melted. Public exposure to radioactive materials released during that accident is expected to cause fewer than five deaths (and perhaps none) from cancer over the following 30 years.

An independent study released in September 1990 found no "convincing evidence" that the Three Mile Island accident had affected cancer rates in the area around the plant. However, a study released in February 1997 concluded that much higher levels of radiation may have been released during the accident than was previously believed.

The relatively small amounts of radioactivity released by nuclear plants during normal operation are not generally believed to pose significant hazards. Documented public exposure to radioactivity from nuclear power plant waste has also been minimal, although the potential long-term hazard of waste disposal remains controversial. There is substantial scientific uncertainty about the level of risk posed by low levels of radiation exposure; as with many carcinogens and other hazardous substances, health effects can be clearly measured only at relatively high exposure levels. In the case of radiation, the assumed risk of low-level exposure has been extrapolated mostly from health effects documented among persons exposed to high levels of radiation, particularly Japanese survivors of nuclear bombing.

The consensus among most safety experts is that a severe nuclear power plant accident in the United States is likely to occur less frequently than one every 10,000 reactor-years of operation. These experts believe that most severe accidents would have small public health impacts and that accidents causing as many as 100 deaths would be much rarer than once every 10,000 reactor-years. On the other hand, some experts challenge the complex calculations that go into predicting such accident frequencies, contending that accidents with serious public health consequences may be more frequent.

Include key claims

Include key fact

Include striking exception

Omit long explanation

Omit speculation

Include key issue

Omit explanation

Include key claim

Omit nonvital details

Include key claim

FIGURE 11.1 *(Continued)*

*Include key
claims*

Regulation

A fundamental concern in the nuclear regulatory debate is the performance of NRC in issuing and enforcing nuclear safety regulations. The nuclear industry and its supporters have regularly complained that unnecessarily stringent and inflexibly enforced nuclear safety regulations have burdened nuclear utilities and their customers with excessive costs. But many environmentalists, nuclear opponents, and other groups charge NRC with being too close to the nuclear industry, a situation that they say has resulted in lax oversight of nuclear power plants and routine exemptions from safety requirements.

Omit explanation

Primary responsibility for nuclear safety compliance lies with nuclear utilities, which are required to find any problems with their plants and report them to NRC. Compliance is monitored directly by NRC, which maintains at least two resident inspectors at each nuclear power plant. The resident inspectors routinely examine plant systems, observe the performance of reactor personnel, and prepare regular inspection reports. For serious safety violations, NRC often dispatches special inspection teams to plant sites.

Decommissioning and Life Extension

Include key fact

When nuclear power plants end their useful lives, they must be safely removed from service, a process called decommissioning. NRC requires nuclear utilities to make regular contributions to special trust funds to ensure that money is available to remove all radioactive material from reactors after they close. Because no full-sized U.S. commercial reactor has yet been completely decommissioned, which can take several decades, the cost of the process can only be estimated. Decommissioning cost estimates cited by a 1996 Department of Energy report, for one full-sized commercial reactor, ranged from about $150 million to $600 million in 1995 dollars.

Omit nonvital details

Include key fact

*Include striking
cost figure*

Omit speculation

It is assumed that U.S. commercial reactors could be decommissioned at the end of their 40-year operating licenses, although several plants have been retired before their licenses expired and others could seek license renewals to operate longer. NRC rules allow plants to apply for a 20-year license extension, for a total operating time of 60 years. Assuming a 40-year lifespan, more than half of today's 109 licensed reactors could be decommissioned by 2016.

FIGURE 11.1 *(Continued)*

U.S. Nuclear Power Industry: Background and Current Status

Although nuclear power generates more than 20 percent of U.S. electricity, no plants have been ordered since 1978, orders dating to 1973 are cancelled, and no units are now being built. Cost, safety, and regulatory concerns have led to zero growth in the industry.

Nuclear plant construction costs far exceed those for coal- and gas-fired plants. Also, high operating and equipment costs have forced permanent, early shutdown of 10 reactors, and the anticipated shutdown of several more.

On the positive side, the 109 licensed reactors in 38 states produce roughly 22 percent of the nation's electricity—more than oil, natural gas, and hydropower combined, and second only to coal, which produces roughly 55 percent. Also, nuclear power is cleaner than fossil fuels. Yet, despite declining costs and safer, less expensive designs, no new reactors could come online for at least a decade—even if any had been ordered.

Safety concerns persist about plant construction, operation, and maintenance, as well as equipment reliability, emergency planning, and NRC's (Nuclear Regulatory Commission) oversight of the industry. Scientists disagree over the extent of long-term hazards from low-level emissions during plant operation and from waste disposal.

Except for the 1979 partial meltdown at Three Mile Island, however, the U.S. nuclear power industry has an excellent safety record for more than 2,000 reactor-years of operation. Most experts estimate that a severe nuclear accident in the United States will occur less than once every 10,000 reactor-years, but other experts are less optimistic.

Central to the nuclear power controversy is the NRC's role in policing the industry and enforcing safety regulations. Industry supporters claim that overregulation has created excessive costs. But opponents charge the NRC with lax oversight and enforcement.

One final unknown involves "decommissioning": safely closing down an aging power plant at the end of its 40-year operating life, a lengthy process expected to cost $150 million to $600 million per reactor.

Source: Adapted from *Congressional Digest* Jan. 1988: 7+.

FIGURE 11.2 **A Summary of Figure 11.1** Word count in this version has been reduced to roughly 20 percent of the original.

U.S. Nuclear Power Industry: Background and Current Status

Although nuclear power generates more than 20 percent of U.S. electricity, cost, safety, and regulatory concerns have led to zero growth in the industry. Moreover, operating and equipment costs are forcing many permanent, early shutdowns.

On the positive side, nuclear reactors generate more of the nation's electricity than all other fossil fuels except coal—and with far less pollution. Yet, despite declining operating costs and safer, less expensive designs, no new reactors could come online for at least a decade—even if any had been ordered.

Safety concerns persist about plant construction, operation, and maintenance as well as equipment reliability, emergency planning, and NRC (Nuclear Regulatory Commission) oversight. Scientists disagree over the probability of a severe accident and the long-term hazards from normal, low-level emissions or from waste disposal. Except for the 1979 partial meltdown at Three Mile Island, however, the U.S. industry's safety record remains excellent.

Also controversial is the NRC's role in policing and enforcement. Industry supporters claim that excessive regulation has created excessive costs. But opponents charge the NRC with lax oversight and enforcement.

Finally, "decommissioning," safely closing down an aging power plant at the end of its operating life, is a lengthy and expensive process.

Source: Adapted from *Congressional Digest* Jan. 1988: 7+.

FIGURE 11.3 A More Compressed Summary of Figure 11.1 Word count is roughly 15 percent of the original.

Summaries in online documentation

Forms of Summarized Information

In preparing a report, proposal, or other document, you might summarize works of others as part of your presentation. But you will often summarize your own material as well. For instance, depending on its length, purpose, and audience, your document might include different forms of summarized information, in different locations, with different levels of detail: *closing summary*, *informative abstract*, *descriptive abstract*, or *executive abstract** (Figure 11.4).

---

*Adapted from David Vaughan. Although I take liberties with his classification, Vaughan helped clarify my thinking about the overlapping terminology that blurs these distinctions.

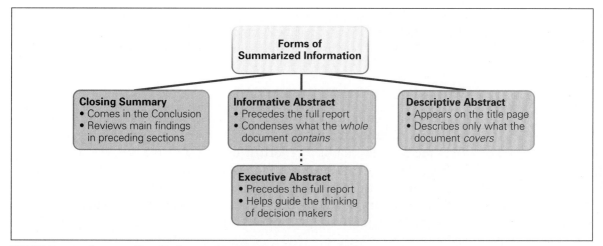

FIGURE 11.4 Summarized Information Assumes Various Forms

Closing Summary

A *closing summary* appears at the beginning of a long report's conclusion section. It helps readers review and remember the preceding major findings. This look back at "the big picture" also helps readers appreciate the conclusions and recommendations that typically follow the closing summary. (See pages 581 and 592 for examples.)

Informative Abstract ("Summary")

Readers often appreciate condensed versions of reports. Some of these readers like to see a capsule version before reading the complete document; others simply want to know basically what a report says without having to read the whole thing.

To meet reader needs, the *informative abstract* appears just after the title page. This summary tells essentially what the full version says: It identifies the need or issue that prompted the report; it describes the research methods used; it reviews the main facts and findings; and it condenses the conclusions and recommendations. (See page 604 for an example.)

NOTE   *Actually, the title "Informative Abstract" is not used much these days. You are more likely to encounter the title "Summary."*

The heading "Executive Summary" (or "Executive Abstract") is used for material summarized for managers who may not understand all the technical jargon a report might contain. (See page 184.) By contrast, a "Technical Summary" (or "Technical Abstract") is aimed at readers at the same technical level as the report's author. In short, you may need two or three levels of summary for report readers who have different levels of technical expertise.

(See Chapter 25 for more on the Summary section in a report.)

Descriptive Abstract ("Abstract")

Another, more compressed form of summarized information can precede the full report (usually one to three sentences on its title page): a *descriptive abstract* merely talks about a report; it doesn't give the report's main points. Such an abstract helps people decide whether to read the report. Thus a descriptive abstract conveys only the nature and extent of a document. It presents the broadest view and offers no major facts from the original. Compare, for example, the abstract that follows with the article summaries in Figures 11.2 and 11.3.

> The track record of the U.S. nuclear power industry is examined and reasons for its lack of growth are identified and assessed.

Because they tend to focus on methodology rather than results, descriptive abstracts are used most often in the sciences and social sciences.[*]

On the job, you might prepare informative abstracts for a boss who needs the information but who has no time to read the original. Or you might write descriptive abstracts to accompany a bibliography of works you are recommending to colleagues or clients (an annotated bibliography).

Executive Abstract

A special type of informative abstract, the *executive abstract* (or "executive summary") essentially "replaces" the entire report. Aimed at decision makers rather than technical audiences, an executive abstract generally has more of a persuasive emphasis: to convince readers to act on the information. Executive abstracts are crucial in cases when readers have no time to read the entire original document and when they expect the writer to help guide their thinking. ("Tell me how to think about this," instead of, "Help me understand this.") Unless the user stipulates a specific format, organize your executive abstract to answer these questions:

Users of an executive abstract have these questions

- What did you find?
- What does it mean?
- What should be done?

The executive abstract in Figure 11.5 addresses the problem of falling sales for a leading company in the breakfast cereal industry (Grant 223+).

---

[*]My thanks to Daryl Davis for this clarifying distinction.

"What did you find?"

"What does it mean?"

Status Report: Market Share for Goldilocks Breakfast Cereals (GBC)

In response to a request from GBC's Board of Directors, the accounting division analyzed recent trends in the company's sales volume and profitability.

Findings

- Even though GBC is the cereal industry leader, its sales for the past four years increased at a mere average of 2.5 percent annually, to $5.2 billion, and net income decreased 12 percent overall, to $459 million.

- This weak sales growth apparently results from consumer resistance to retail price increases for cereal, totaling 91 percent in slightly more than a decade, the highest increase of any processed-food product.

- GBC traditionally offers discount coupons to offset price increases, but consumers seem to prefer a lower everyday price.

- GBC introduces an average of two new cereal products annually (most recently, "Coconut Whammos" and "Spinach Crunchies"), but such innovations do little to increase consumer interest.

- A growing array of generic cereal brands have been underselling GBC's products by more than $1 per box, especially in giant retail outlets.

- This past June, GBC dropped its cereal prices by roughly 20 percent, but by this time the brand had lost substantial market share to generic cereal brands.

Conclusions

- Slow but progressive loss of market share threatens GBC's dominance as industry leader.

- GBC must regain consumer loyalty to reinvigorate its market base.

- Not only have discount coupon promotions proven ineffective, but the manufacturer's cost for such promotions can total as much as 20 percent of sales revenue.

- Our new cereal products have done more to erode than to enhance GBC's brand image.

FIGURE 11.5 An Executive Abstract This document might be the only section of the complete, 40 page report that will be read by many in its intended audience.

*"What should
be done?"*

> **Recommendations**
>
> To regain lost market share and ensure continued dominance, GBC should implement the following recommendations:
>
> 1. Eliminate coupon promotions immediately.
>
> 2. Curtail development of new cereal products, and invest in improving the taste and nutritional value of GBC's traditional products.
>
> 3. Capitalize on GBC's brand recognition with an advertising campaign to promote GBC's "best-sellers" as an "all-day" food (say, as a healthful snack or lunch or an inexpensive alternative to microwave dinners).
>
> 4. Examine the possibility of high-volume sales at discounted prices through giant retail chains.

FIGURE 11.5 *(Continued)*

Ethical Considerations in Summarizing Information

Information in a summary format is increasingly attractive to today's readers, who often feel bombarded by more information than they can handle. Consider, for example, the popularity of the *USA Today* newspaper, with its countless news items offered in brief snippets for overtaxed readers. In contrast, the *New York Times* offers lengthy text that is information rich but more time-consuming to digest.

 The ethics of summaries

A summary format is especially adaptable to the hypertext-linked design of Web-based documents. Instead of long blocks of text, Web users expect pages with concise modules, or "chunks," of information that stand alone, are easy to scan, and require little or no scrolling. (See Chapter 19 for more on Web page design.) Moreover, magazine Web sites such as *Forbes* or *The Economist* offer email summaries of their hard copy editions. And while capsules or "digests" of information are an efficient way to stay abreast of new developments, the abbreviated presentation carries potential pitfalls, as media critic Ilan Greenberg points out (650):

Ways in which summarized information can be unethical

- A condensed version of a complicated issue or event may provide a useful overview, but this superficial treatment can rarely communicate the issue's full complexity—that is, the complete story.
- Whoever summarizes a lengthy piece makes decisions about what to leave out and what to leave in, what to emphasize, and what to ignore. During the selection process, the original message could very well be distorted.

• In a summary of someone else's writing, the tone or "voice" of the original author disappears—along with that writer's way of seeing. In some cases, this can be a form of plagiarism.

A summary that fails to capture the real story

A summary's tip-of-the-iceberg view can alter any reader's accurate interpretation of the issue or event, as in the following headline that summarizes the story but distorts the facts: "Study: Cannabis Makes Drivers More Cautious." This headline from the August 21, 2000 *Ottawa Citizen* is accompanied by the following summary on page A1: "Driving while high is less dangerous than while fatigued or drunk." Unless they turn to page A2, readers never encounter the essential fact that "Experts agree that driving while high is not as safe as driving while sober."

Informed decisions about science and technological controversies (human cloning, bioengineered foods, global warming, estrogen therapy) require an informed public. And while summaries do have their place in our busy world, scanning headlines or abstracts is no substitute for detailed reading and careful weighing of the facts. The more complex the topic, the more readers need the whole story.

NOTE   *For more advice about quotations, paraphrases, and summaries (including examples), go to <www.wisc.edu/writing/Handbook/QuotingSources.html>.*

☑ Checklist: Usability of Summaries

Use this checklist to refine your summaries. (Page numbers in parentheses refer to first page of discussion.)

Content
☐ Does the summary contain only the essential message? (174)
☐ Does the summary make sense as an independent piece? (175)
☐ Is the summary accurate when checked against the original? (175)
☐ Is the summary free of any additions to the original? (176)
☐ Is the summary free of needless details? (175)
☐ Is the summary economical yet clear and comprehensive? (175)
☐ Is the source documented? (176)
☐ Does the descriptive abstract tell what the original is about? (184)

Organization
☐ Is the summary coherent? (206)
☐ Are there enough transitions to reveal the line of thought? (693)

Style
☐ Is the summary's level of technicality appropriate for its audience? (175)
☐ Is the summary free of needless words? (175)
☐ Are all sentences clear, concise, and fluent? (216)
☐ Is the summary written grammatically? (670)

ON THE JOB...   The Importance of Summaries

■ *"Every time I run a training session in corporate communication, participants tell horror stories about working weeks or months on a report, only to have it disappear somewhere up the management chain. We use copies of those 'invisible' reports as case studies, and invariably, the summary turns out to have been poorly written, providing readers few or no clues as to the report's significance. I'll bet companies lose millions because new ideas and recommendations get relegated to that stockpile of reports unread yearly in corporate America."*

—Frank Sousa,
Communications consultant

■ *"Distilling large amounts of information down to the essentials is a crucial part of my job. For example, I've just drafted an email inquiry to a Korean colleague I've never met, to ask about her new technique for increasing the durability and elasticity of rubberized road surfaces. This busy professional has little time to read my life story but she will need some background about my related work. Therefore, I'm including a one-page summary."*

—Jane R. Caswell, Civil Engineer

■ *"Virtually every branch of the legal profession relies on summarized information. For example, in preparation for courtroom litigation, law clerks research legal precedents, or prior rulings on the given type of case; then they prepare memoranda that summarize the judicial reasoning justifying each ruling. On the basis of these memoranda, the trial attorneys draft a legal brief, to be read by the presiding judge before the trial. This brief is essentially a summary of all the facts and points of law pertinent to the case that will be argued during the court proceedings. Done correctly, summaries are precision tools".*

—Scott Marvin, Attorney

■ *"In a large corporation, poorly written summaries can be very costly. For example, our top-level people often make decisions based on executive summaries of detailed staff reports. If the summary is unclear or incomplete, readers have to hunt through the full report of find what they need. Multiply this wasted time by the number of readers, and then consider the salaries these people earn!"*

—Margarite Samonas, Vice President,
Game software producer

Exercises

 Exercises

1. Find an article about your major field or area of interest and write both an informative abstract and a descriptive abstract of the article.
2. Select a long paper you have written for one of your courses; write an informative abstract and a descriptive abstract of the paper.
3. After reading the article in Figure 11.6 prepare a descriptive abstract and an informative abstract, using the guidelines on page 175. Identify a specific audience and use for your material.

A possible scenario: You are assistant communications manager for a leading software development company. Part of your job involves publishing a monthly newsletter for employees. Each issue includes a segment titled Good Health. After coming across this article, you decide to summarize it for the upcoming issue. You have 250–275 words of newsletter space to fill. Consider carefully what this audience does and doesn't need. In this situation, what information is most important?

Bring your abstracts to class and exchange them with a classmate for editing according to the checklist (page 187). Revise your edited copies before submitting them to your instructor.

Collaborative Project

Organize into small groups and choose a topic for discussion: an employment problem, a campus problem, plans for an event, suggestions for energy conservation, or the like. (A possible topic: Should employers have the right to require lie detector tests, drug tests, or AIDS tests for their employees?)

Discuss the topic for one class period, taking notes on significant points and conclusions. Afterward, organize and edit your notes in line with the directions for writing summaries. Next, write a summary of the group discussion in no more than 200 words. Finally, as a group, compare your individual summaries for accuracy, emphasis, conciseness, and clarity.

Service-Learning Project

Obtain a copy of the Annual Report or other public document describing the activities and mission of the agency for which you are working. Write an informative abstract of the report for a general, public audience.

Revealing *Trans* Fats

Scientific evidence shows that consumption of saturated fat, *trans* fat, and dietary cholesterol raises low-density lipoprotein (LDL), or "bad" cholesterol levels, which increases the risk of coronary heart disease (CHD). According to the National Heart, Lung, and Blood Institute of the National Institutes of Health, more than 12.5 million Americans have CHD, and more than 500,000 die each year. That makes CHD one of the leading causes of death in the United States.

The Food and Drug Administration has required that saturated fat and dietary cholesterol be listed on food labels since 1993. With *trans* fat added to the Nutrition Facts panel, you will know for the first time how much of all three—saturated fat, *trans* fat, and cholesterol—are in the foods you choose. Identifying saturated fat, *trans* fat, and cholesterol on the food label gives you information you need to make food choices that help reduce the risk of CHD. This revised label will be of particular interest to people concerned about high blood cholesterol and heart disease.

However, everyone should be aware of the risk posed by consuming too much saturated fat, *trans* fat, and cholesterol. But what is *trans* fat, and how can you limit the amount of this fat in your diet?

What is *Trans* Fat?

Basically, *trans* fat is made when manufacturers add hydrogen to vegetable oil—a process called hydrogenation. Hydrogenation increases the shelf life and flavor stability of foods containing these fats.

Trans fat can be found in vegetable shortenings, some margarines, crackers, cookies, snack foods, and other foods made with or fried in partially hydrogenated oils. Unlike other fats, the majority of *trans* fat is formed when food manufacturers turn liquid oils into solid fats like shortening and hard margarine. A small amount of *trans* fat is found naturally, primarily in dairy products, some meat, and other animal-based foods.

Trans fat, like saturated fat and dietary cholesterol, raises the LDL cholesterol that increases your risk for CHD. Americans consume on average 4 to 5 times as much saturated fat as *trans* fat in their diets.

Although saturated fat is the main dietary culprit that raises LDL, *trans* fat and dietary cholesterol also contribute significantly.

Are All Fats the Same?

Simply put: No. Fat is a major source of energy for the body and aids in the absorption of vitamins A, D, E, and K, and carotenoids. Both animal- and plant-derived food products contain fat, and when eaten in moderation, fat is important for proper growth, development, and maintenance of good health. As a food ingredient, fat provides taste, consistency, and stability and helps you feel full. In addition, parents should be aware that fats are an especially important source of calories and nutrients for infants and toddlers (up to 2 years of age), who have the highest energy needs per unit of body weight of any age group.

While unsaturated fats (monounsaturated and polyunsaturated) are beneficial when consumed in moderation, saturated and *trans* fats are not. Saturated fat and *trans* fat raise LDL cholesterol levels in the blood. Dietary cholesterol also raises

FIGURE 11.6 An Article to Be Summarized

Source: Excerpt from *FDA Consumer*, Sept.–Oct. 2003: 12–18.

LDL cholesterol and may contribute to heart disease even without raising LDL. Therefore, it is advisable to choose foods low in saturated fat, *trans* fat, and cholesterol as part of a healthful diet.

What Can You Do About Saturated Fat, *Trans* Fat, and Cholesterol?

When comparing foods, look at the Nutrition Facts panel, and choose the food with the lower amounts of saturated fat, *trans* fat, and cholesterol. Health experts recommend that you keep your intake of saturated fat, *trans* fat, and cholesterol as low as possible while consuming a nutritionally adequate diet. However, these experts recognize that eliminating these three components entirely from your diet is not practical because they are unavoidable in ordinary diets.

Where Can You Find *Trans* Fat on the Food Label?

You will find *trans* fat listed on the Nutrition Facts panel directly under the line for saturated fat.

How Do Your Choices Stack Up?

With the addition of *trans* fat to the Nutrition Facts panel, you can review your food choices and see how they stack up. (See the table illustrating total fat, saturated fat, *trans* fat, and cholesterol content per serving for selected food products.)

Don't assume similar products are the same. Be sure to check the Nutrition Facts panel because even similar foods can vary in calories, ingredients, nutrients, and the size and number of servings in a package.

How Can You Use the Label to Make Heart-Healthy Food Choices?

The Nutrition Facts panel can help you choose foods lower in saturated fat, *trans* fat, and cholesterol. Compare similar foods and choose the food with the lower combined saturated and trans fats and the lower amount of cholesterol.

Although the updated Nutrition Facts panel will list the amount of *trans* fat in a product, it will not show a Percent Daily Value (%DV). While scientific reports have confirmed the relationship between *trans* fat and an increased risk of CHD, none has provided a reference value for *trans* fat or any other information that the FDA believes is sufficient to establish a Daily Reference Value or a %DV.

There is, however, a %DV shown for saturated fat and cholesterol. To choose foods low in saturated fat and cholesterol, use the general rule of thumb that 5 percent of the Daily Value or less is low and 20 percent or more is high.

You can also use the %DV to make dietary trade-offs with other foods throughout the day. You don't have to give up a favorite food to eat a healthy diet. When a food you like is high in saturated fat or cholesterol, balance it with foods that are low in saturated fat and cholesterol at other times of the day.

FIGURE 11.6 *(Continued)*

PART THREE

Structure, Style, Graphics, and Page Design

CHAPTER 12
Organizing for Users 194

CHAPTER 13
Editing for Readable Style 215

CHAPTER 14
Designing Visual Information 252

CHAPTER 15
Designing Pages and Documents 297

Organizing for Users

Partitioning and Classifying

Outlining

Storyboarding

Paragraphing

Sequencing

Chunking

Creating an Overview

In order to follow your thinking, readers need a message organized in a way that makes sense to *them*. But data rarely materializes or thinking rarely occurs in neat, predictable sequences. Instead of forcing users to make sense of unstructured information, we shape this material for their understanding. As we organize, we face questions such as these:

Questions in organizing for users

- What relationships do the collected data suggest?
- What should I emphasize?
- In which sequence will users approach this material?
- What belongs where?
- What do I say first? Why?
- What comes next?
- How do I end?

To answer these questions, we rely on the organizing strategies discussed below.

Partitioning and Classifying

Partition and classification are each strategies for sorting things out. *Partition* deals with *one thing only*. It separates that thing into parts, chunks, sections, or categories for closer examination (say, a report partitioned into introduction, body, and conclusion).

Partition answers these user questions

- What are its parts?
- What is it made of?

Classification deals with *an assortment of things* that share certain similarities. It groups these things systematically (for example, grouping electronic documents into categories—reports, memos, Web pages).

Classification answers these user questions

- What relates to what?
- What belongs where?

Whether you choose to apply partition or classification depends on your purpose. For example, to describe a personal computer system to a novice, you might partition the system into *CPU, keyboard, printer, power cord,* and so on; for a seasoned user who wants to install an expansion card, you might partition the system into *processor-direct slot, video-in slot, communication slot,* and so on. On the other hand, if you have twenty-five software programs to arrange so you can easily locate the one you want, you will need to group them into smaller categories. You might want to classify programs according to function (*word processing, graphics, database management*) or according to expected frequency of use or relative ease of use—or some other basis.

In organizing a document, writers use partition and classification routinely, in a process we know as *outlining*.

Outlining

When written material is left in its original, unstructured form, people have to waste time in trying to understand it. However, when you prepare an outline, you move from a random list of items as they occurred to you to a deliberate map that will guide readers from point to point.

A Document's Basic Shape

Organize to make the document logical from the user's point of view. Begin with the basics: Useful writing of any length—a book, chapter, news article, letter, or memo—typically follows the *introduction, body, conclusion* pattern explained in Figure 12.1.

NOTE   *All readers expect a definite beginning, middle, and ending that provide orientation, discussion, and review. But specific people want these sections tailored to their expectations. Identify your readers' expectations by (a) anticipating their probable questions (pages 28–51), and (b) visualizing the sequence in which users would want these questions answered.*

Most word-processing programs enable you to work on your document and your outline simultaneously. An "outline view" of the document helps you to see relationships among ideas at various levels, to create new headings, to add text beneath headings, and to move headings and their subtext. You also can *collapse* the outline view to display the headings only. As a visual alternative to traditional outlining, many graphics programs allow you to display prose outlines as tree charts (page 271).

The Formal Outline

A simple list usually suffices for organizing a short document or starting a long one. In planning a long document, an author or team rarely begins with a formal outline. But eventually in the writing process, a long or complex document calls for much more than a simple list. Figure 12.2 shows a formal outline for the report examining the health effects of electromagnetic fields, on pages 572–82.

NOTE   *Long reports often begin directly with a statement of purpose. For the intended audience (i.e., generalists) of this report, however, the technical topic must first be defined so that users understand the context. Also, each level of division yields at least two items. If you cannot divide a major item into at least two subordinate items, retain only your major heading.*

A formal outline easily converts to a table of contents for the finished report, as shown in Chapter 25.

NOTE   *Because they serve mainly to guide the writer, minor outline headings (such as items [a] and [b] under II.A.1 in Figure 12.2) may be omitted from the table of contents or the report itself. Excessive headings make a document seem fragmented.*

INTRODUCTION

The introduction attracts attention, announces the viewpoint, and previews what will follow. A good introduction provides orientation to the text in any of these ways: explaining the background and the document's purpose; briefly identifying the intended audience and the writer's information sources; defining specialized terms or general terms that have special meaning in the document; accounting for limitations such as incomplete data; and previewing major topics in the body section. Some introductions are necessarily long and involved; others, short and to the point. If you don't know users well enough to know exactly what they need, use subheadings so they can read only what they want. All good introductions invite readers in.

BODY

The body explains and supports the viewpoint, achieving *unity* by remaining focused on the viewpoint and *coherence* by carrying a line of thought from sentence to sentence in logical order. The body delivers on the promise implied in your introduction ("show me!"). Here you present your data, discuss your evidence, lay out your case, or tell users what to do and how to do it. Body sections come in all different sizes, depending on how much users need and expect.

Body sections are titled to reflect their exact purpose: "Description and Function of Parts" for a mechanism description; "Required Steps" for a set of instructions; "Collected Data" for a feasibilty analysis, and so on.

CONCLUSION

The conclusion has various purposes: It might evaluate the significance of the report, reemphasize key points, take a position, predict an outcome, offer a solution, or suggest further study. If the issue is straightforward, the conclusion might be brief and definite; if the issue is complex or controversial, the conclusion might be lengthy and open-ended. Good conclusions give readers a clear perspective on what they have just read.

FIGURE 12.1 **The Typical Shape of a Workplace Document**

Children Exposed to EMFs: A Risk Assessment

I. INTRODUCTION
    A. Definition of electromagnetic fields
    B. Background on the health issues
    C. Description of the local power line configuration
    D. Purpose of this report
    E. Brief description of data sources
    F. Scope of this inquiry

II. DATA SECTION [Body]
    A. Sources of EMF exposure
        1. power lines
        2. home and office
            a. kitchen
            b. workshop [and so on]
        3. natural radiation
        4. risk factors
            a. current intensity
            b. source proximity
            c. duration of exposure
    B. Studies of health effects
        1. population surveys
        2. laboratory measurements
        3. workplace links
    C. Conflicting views of studies
        1. criticism of methodology in population studies
        2. criticism of overgeneralized lab findings
    D. Power industry views
        1. uncertainty about risk
        2. confusion about risk avoidance

FIGURE 12.2 A Formal Outline Using Alphanumeric Notation In an outline, *alphanumeric notation* refers to the use of letters and numbers.

E. Risk-avoidance measures

    1. nationally

    2. locally

III. CONCLUSION

    A. Summary and overall interpretation of findings

    B. Recommendations

FIGURE 12.2 *(Continued)*

In technical documents, alphanumeric notation often is replaced by decimal notation. Compare the following with the DATA SECTION from Figure 12.2.

Decimal notation
in a technical
document

2.0 DATA SECTION
    2.1 Sources of EMF Exposure
       2.1.1 home and office
          2.1.1.1 kitchen
          2.1.1.2 workshop [and so on]
       2.1.2 power lines
       2.1.3 natural radiation
       2.1.4 risk factors
          2.1.4.1 current intensity
          2.1.4.2 source proximity [and so on]

The decimal outline makes it easier to refer users to specifically numbered sections ("See section 2.1.2"). Decimal notation is usually preferred in the workplace.

You may wish to expand your *topic outline* into a *sentence outline,* in which each sentence serves as a topic sentence for a paragraph in the document:

A sentence
outline

2.0 DATA SECTION
    2.1 Although the 2 million miles of power lines crisscrossing the United States have been the focus of the EMF controversy, potentially harmful waves also are emitted by household wiring, appliances, electric blankets, and computer terminals.

Sentence outlines are used mainly in collaborative projects in which various team members prepare different sections of a long document.

NOTE   *The neat and ordered outlines in this book show the final **products** of writing and organizing, not the **process,** which is often initially messy and chaotic. Many writers don't start out with an outline at all! Instead, they scratch and scribble with pencil and paper or click away at the keyboard, making lots of false starts as they hammer out some kind of acceptable draft; only then do they outline to get their thinking straight.*

Not until the final draft of a long document do you compose the finished outline, which serves as a model for your table of contents, as a check on your reasoning, and as a way of revealing to readers a clear line of thinking.

NOTE

No single form of outline should be followed slavishly. The organization of any document ultimately is determined by the user's needs and expectations. In many cases, specific requirements about a document's organization and style are spelled out in a company's style guide (see page 301).

Organizing for Cross-Cultural Audiences

Cross-cultural awareness

Different cultures have different expectations as to how information should be organized. For instance, a paragraph in English typically begins with a topic sentence, followed by related supporting sentences; any digression from this main idea is considered harmful to the paragraph's *unity*. But some cultures consider digression a sign of intelligence or politeness. To native readers of English, the long introductions and digressions in certain Spanish or Russian documents might seem tedious and confusing, but a Spanish or Russian reader might view the more direct organization of English as abrupt and simplistic (Leki 151).

Expectations differ even among same-language cultures. British correspondence, for instance, typically expresses the bad news directly up front, instead of taking the indirect approach preferred in the United States. A bad news letter or memo appropriate for a U.S. audience could be considered evasive by British readers (Scott and Green 19).

The Report Design Worksheet

As an alternative to the audience and use profile sheet (page 35), the worksheet in Figure 12.3 can supplement your outline and help you focus on your audience and purpose.

Storyboarding

As you prepare a long document, one useful organizing tool is the *storyboard,* a sketch of the finished document. Much more specific and visual than an outline, a storyboard maps out each section (or module) of your outline, topic by topic, to help you see the shape and appearance of the entire document in its final form. Working from a storyboard, you can rearrange, delete, and insert material as needed—without having to wrestle with a draft of the entire document.

Storyboarding is especially helpful when people collaborate to prepare various parts of a document and then get together to edit and assemble their material. In such cases, storyboard modules may be displayed on whiteboards, posterboards, or flip charts. Figure 12.4 displays one storyboard module based on Section II.A of the outline on page 198.

NOTE

Try creating a storyboard after writing a full draft, for a bird's-eye view of the document's organization.

Report Design Worksheet

Preliminary Information

What is to be done? *A report on the health effects of electromagnetic radiation*

Whom is it to be presented to, and when? *Town Meeting, April 1*

Audience Analysis	Primary Audience	Secondary Audience
Position and title:	*town manager*	*selectpersons, various town officials, school board, parents, colleagues, friends*
Relationship to author or organization:	*employer*	
Technical expertise:	*nontechnical (for this topic)*	*nontechnical*
Personal characteristics:	*highly efficient; expects results*	*have strong views on the issue*
Attitude toward author or organization:	*is preparing my annual performance review*	*friendly and respectful; selectboard will vote on my contract renewal and pay raise*
Attitude toward subject:	*extremely concerned*	*same*
Effect of report on audience or organization:	*will be read closely and acted upon*	*will be discussed at town meeting*

User's Purpose

Why has audience requested it?	*wants to address any potential hazards without delay*	
What does audience plan to do with it?	*use the data to make an informed decision about action*	*confer with the town manager about the decision*
What should audience know beforehand to understand it as written?	*nothing special; history of the issue is reviewed in report*	*same*
What does audience already know?	*has read and heard very general information about the issue*	*same*
What amount and kinds of detail will audience find significant?	*clear description of the issue and careful review of the evidence*	*same*
What should audience know and/or be able to do after reading it?	*make a decision based on the best evidence available*	*advise the town manager about her decision*

FIGURE 12.3 **Report Design Worksheet**
Source: Based on a worksheet developed by Professor John S. Harris of Brigham Young University.

Writer's Purpose

Why am I writing?   *to communicate my research findings*

What effect(s) do I wish to achieve?   *to have my audience conclude that, while we await further research, we should take immediate and inexpensive steps toward risk avoidance and continue to assess EMF hazards throughout the school*

Design Specifications

Sources of data: *recently published research, including online and Internet sources; interviews with local authorities*

Tone: *semiformal*

Point of view: *mostly third person (except for recommendations)*

Needed visuals and supplements: *title page, letter of transmittal, table of contents, informative abstract, charts, graphs, and tables*

Appropriate format (letter, memo, etc.):   *formal report format with full heading system*

Basic organization (problem-causes-solution, etc.):   *causes-possible effects-conclusions and recommendations*

Main items in introduction: *Definition of electromagnetic fields*
Background on the health issue
Description of the local power line configuration
Purpose of report, and intended audience
Data sources
Scope of this inquiry

Main items in body: *Sources of EMF exposure*
Risk factors
Studies of health effects
Conflicting views of studies
Local power company views
Risk-avoidance measures

Main items in conclusion: *Summary of findings*
Overall interpretation of findings
Recommendations

Other Considerations: *no frills or complex technical data; this audience is interested in the "bottom line" as far as what action they should take*

FIGURE 12.3 *(Continued)*

section title	***Sources of EMF Exposure***
text	Discuss milligauss measurements as indicators of cancer risk
text	Brief lead-in to power line emissions
visual	EPS table comparing power line emissions at various distances
text	Discuss EMF sources in home and office
visual	Table comparing EMF emissions from common sources
text	Discuss major risk factors: Voltage versus current; proximity versus duration of exposure; sporadic, high-level exposure versus constant, low-level exposure
visual	Line graph showing strength of exposure in relation to distance from electrical appliances
text	Focus on the key role of proximity to the EMF source in risk assessment

Special considerations:

- *Define all specialized terms (current, voltage, milligauss, and so on) for a general audience.*
- *Emphasize that no "safe" level of EMF exposure has been established.*
- *Emphasize that even the earth's magnetic field emits significant electromagnetic radiation.*

FIGURE 12.4 One Module from a Storyboard Notice how the module begins with the section title, describes each text block and each visual, and includes suggestions about special considerations. (To see this section of the document in its final form, go to page 573)

Paragraphing

Readers look for orientation, for shapes they can recognize. But a document's larger design (introduction, body, conclusion) depends on the smaller design of each paragraph.

Although paragraphs have various shapes and purposes (paragraphs of introduction, conclusion, or transition), our focus here is on standard *support paragraphs*. Although it is part of the document's larger design, each support paragraph can usually stand alone in meaning.

The Support Paragraph

All the sentences in a standard support paragraph relate to the main point, which is expressed as the *topic sentence:*

Topic sentences

> As sea levels rise, New York City faces increasing risk of hurricane storm surge.
>
> A video display terminal can endanger the operator's health.
>
> Chemical pesticides and herbicides are both ineffective and hazardous.

Each topic sentence introduces an idea, judgment, or opinion. But in order to grasp the writer's exact meaning, people need explanation. Consider the third statement:

> Chemical pesticides and herbicides are both ineffective and hazardous.

Imagine that you are a researcher for the Epson Electric Light Company, assigned this question: Should the company (1) begin spraying pesticides and herbicides under its power lines, or (2) continue with its manual (and nonpolluting) ways of minimizing foliage and insect damage to lines and poles? If you simply responded with the preceding assertion, your employer would have further questions:

- Why, exactly, are these methods ineffective and hazardous?
- What are the problems? Can you explain?

To answer these questions and to support your assertion, you need a fully developed paragraph:

Introduction
(1-topic sentence)
Body (2–6)

> [1]**Chemical pesticides and herbicides are both ineffective and hazardous.** [2]Because none of these chemicals has permanent effects, pest populations invariably recover and need to be resprayed. [3]Repeated applications cause pests to develop immunity to the chemicals. [4]Furthermore, most of these products attack species other than the intended pest, killing off its natural predators, thus actually increasing the pest population. [5]Above all, chemical residues survive in the environment (and living tissue) for years, often carried hundreds of miles by wind and water. [6]This toxic legacy includes such biological effects as birth deformities, reproductive failures, brain damage, and cancer. [7]Although intended to control pest populations, these chemicals ironically threaten to make the human population their ultimate victims. [8]I therefore recommend continuing our manual control methods.

Conclusion (7–8)

Most standard support paragraphs in technical writing have an introduction-body-conclusion structure. They begin with a clear topic (or orienting) sentence stating a generalization. Details in the body support the generalization.

The Topic Sentence

ts

Users look to a paragraph's opening sentences for a framework. The topic sentence should appear *first* (or early) in the paragraph, unless you have good reason to place it elsewhere. Think of your topic sentence as "the one sentence you would keep if you could keep only one" (U.S. Air Force Academy 11). In some instances, a paragraph's main idea may require a "topic statement" consisting of two or more sentences, as in this example:

A topic statement can have two or more sentences

> The most common strip-mining methods are open-pit mining, contour mining, and auger mining. The specific method employed will depend on the type of terrain that covers the coal.

The topic sentence or topic statement should focus and forecast. Don't write *Some pesticides are less hazardous and often more effective than others* when you mean *Organic pesticides are less hazardous and often more effective than their chemical counterparts.* The first version is vague; the second helps us focus, tells us what to expect from the paragraph.

Paragraph Unity

¶un

A paragraph is unified when all its material belongs there—when every word, phrase, and sentence directly supports the topic sentence.

A unified paragraph

> **Solar power offers an efficient, economical, and safe solution to the Northeast's energy problems.** To begin with, solar power is highly efficient. Solar collectors installed on fewer than 30 percent of roofs in the Northeast would provide more than 70 percent of the area's heating and air-conditioning needs. Moreover, solar heat collectors are economical, operating for up to twenty years with little or no maintenance. These savings recoup the initial cost of installation within only ten years. Most important, solar power is safe. It can be transformed into electricity through photovoltaic cells (a type of storage battery) in a noiseless process that produces no air pollution—unlike coal, oil, and wood combustion. In contrast to its nuclear counterpart, solar power produces no toxic waste and poses no catastrophic danger of meltdown. Thus, massive conversion to solar power would ensure abundant energy and a safe, clean environment for future generations.

One way to damage unity in the paragraph above would be to veer from the focus on *efficient*, *economical*, and *safe* to material about the differences between active and passive solar heating or the advantages of solar power over wind power.

Every topic sentence has a key word or phrase that carries the meaning. In the pesticide-herbicide paragraph (page 204), the key words are *ineffective* and *hazardous*. Anything that fails to advance their meaning throws the paragraph—and the readers—off track.

Paragraph Coherence

In a coherent paragraph, everything not only belongs, but also sticks together: Topic sentence and support form a *connected line of thought*, like links in a chain.

Paragraph coherence can be damaged by (1) short, choppy sentences; (2) sentences in the wrong order; (3) insufficient transitions and connectors for linking related ideas; or (4) an inaccessible line of reasoning. Here is how the solar energy paragraph might become incoherent:

An incoherent paragraph

> Solar power offers an efficient, economical, and safe solution to the Northeast's energy problems. Unlike nuclear power, solar power produces no toxic waste and poses no danger of meltdown. Solar power is efficient. Solar collectors could be installed on fewer than 30 percent of roofs in the Northeast. These collectors would provide more than 70 percent of the area's heating and air-conditioning needs. Solar power is safe. It can be transformed into electricity. This transformation is made possible by photovoltaic cells (a type of storage battery). Solar heat collectors are economical. The photovoltaic process produces no air pollution.

In the above paragraph, the second sentence, about safety, belongs near the end. Also, because of short, choppy sentences and insufficient links between ideas, the paragraph reads more like a list than like a flowing discussion. Finally, a concluding sentence is needed to complete the chain of reasoning and to give readers a clear perspective on what they've just read.

Here, in contrast, is the original, coherent paragraph with sentences numbered for later discussion and with transitions and connectors shown in boldface. Notice how this version reveals a clear line of thought:

A coherent paragraph

> [1]Solar power offers an efficient, economical, and safe solution to the Northeast's energy problems. [2]**To begin with**, solar power is highly efficient. [3]Solar collectors installed on fewer than 30 percent of roofs in the Northeast would provide more than 70 percent of the area's heating and air-conditioning needs. [4]**Moreover**, solar heat collectors are economical, operating for up to twenty years with little or no maintenance. [5]**These savings** recoup the initial cost of installation within only ten years. [6]**Most important**, solar power is safe. [7]**It** can be transformed into electricity through photovoltaic cells (a type of storage battery) in a noiseless process that produces no air pollution—unlike coal, oil, and wood combustion. [8]**In contrast** to its nuclear counterpart, solar power produces no toxic waste and poses no danger of catastrophic meltdown. [9]**Thus**, massive conversion to solar power would ensure abundant energy and a safe, clean environment for future generations.

We can easily trace the sequence of thoughts in the previous paragraph:

1. The topic sentence establishes a clear direction.
2–3. The first reason is given and then explained.
4–5. The second reason is given and explained.

6–8.   The third and major reason is given and explained.

9.   The conclusion reemphasizes the main point.

To reinforce the logical sequence, related ideas are combined in individual sentences, and transitions and connectors signal clear relationships. The whole paragraph sticks together. For more on transitions and other connectors, see pages 693–94.

Paragraph Length

Paragraph length depends on the writer's purpose and the reader's capacity for understanding. Writing that contains highly technical information or complex instructions may use short paragraphs or perhaps a list. In writing that explains concepts, attitudes, or viewpoints, support paragraphs generally run from 100 to 300 words. But word count really means very little. What matters is *how thoroughly the paragraph makes your point.*

Try to avoid too much of anything. A clump of short paragraphs can make some writing seem choppy and poorly organized, but a stretch of long ones is tiring. A well-placed short paragraph—sometimes just one sentence—can highlight an important idea.

In writing displayed on computer screens, short paragraphs and lists are especially useful because they allow for easy scanning and navigation.

Associational or nonlinear structures

Sequencing

A logical sequence reveals a particular relationship: cause-and-effect, comparison-contrast, and so on. For instance, a progress report usually follows a *chronological* sequence (events in order of occurrence). An argument for a companywide exercise program would likely follow an *emphatic* sequence (benefits in order of importance—least to most, or vice versa).

A single paragraph usually follows one particular sequence. A longer document may use one sequence or a combination. Below are some common sequences.

Spatial Sequence

A spatial sequence begins at one location and ends at another. It is most useful in describing a physical item or a mechanism. You might describe the parts in the same sequence that readers would follow if they were actually looking at the item. Or you might follow the sequence in which each part functions: (left to right, inside to outside, top to bottom). The following description of a hypodermic needle proceeds from the needle's base (hub) to its point:

"What does it look like?"

> A hypodermic needle is a slender, hollow steel instrument used to introduce medication into the body (usually through a vein or muscle). It is a single piece composed of three parts, all considered sterile: the hub, the cannula, and the point. The hub is the lower, larger part of the needle that attaches to the necklike opening on the syringe barrel. Next is the cannula (stem), the smooth and slender central portion. Last is the point, which consists of a beveled (slanted) opening, ending in a sharp tip. The diameter of a needle's cannula is indicated by a gauge number; commonly, a 24–25 gauge needle is used for subcutaneous injections. Needle lengths are varied to suit individual needs. Common lengths used for subcutaneous injections are 3/8, 1/2, 5/8, and 3/4 inch. Regardless of length and diameter, all needles have the same functional design.

Product and mechanism descriptions (Chapter 21) almost always have some type of visual to amplify the verbal description.

Chronological Sequence

A chronological sequence follows the actual sequence of events. Explanations of how to do something or how something happened generally follow a strict time sequence: first step, second step, and so on.

"How is it done?"

> Instead of breaking into a jog too quickly and risking injury, take a relaxed and deliberate approach. Before taking a step, spend at least ten minutes stretching and warming up, using any exercises you find comfortable. (After your first week, consult a jogging book for specialized exercises.) When you've completed your warmup, set a brisk pace walking. Exaggerate the distance between steps, taking long strides and swinging your arms briskly and loosely. After roughly one hundred yards at this brisk pace, you should feel ready to jog. Immediately break into a very slow trot: lean your torso forward and let one foot fall in front of the other (one foot barely leaving the ground while the other is on the pavement). Maintain the slowest pace possible, just above a walk. *Do not bolt out like a sprinter!* The biggest mistake is to start fast and injure yourself. While jogging, relax your body. Keep your shoulders straight and your head up, and enjoy the scenery—after all, it is one of the joys of jogging. Keep your arms low and slightly bent at your sides. Move your legs freely from the hips in an action that is easy, not forced. Make your feet perform a heel-to-toe action: land on the heel; rock forward; take off from the toe.

Effect-to-Cause Sequence

Problem-solving analyses typically use a sequence that first identifies a problem and then traces its causes.

"How did this happen?"

> Modern whaling techniques nearly brought the whale population to the threshold of extinction. In the nineteenth century, invention of the steamboat increased hunters' speed and mobility. Shortly afterward, the grenade harpoon was invented so that whales could be killed quickly and easily from the ship's deck. In 1904, a whaling station

opened on Georgia Island in South America. This station became the gateway to Antarctic whaling for world nations. In 1924, factory ships were designed that enabled round-the-clock whale tracking and processing. These ships could reduce a ninety-foot whale to its by-products in roughly thirty minutes. After World War II, more powerful boats with remote sensing devices gave a final boost to the whaling industry. Numbers of kills had now increased far beyond the whales' capacity to reproduce.

Cause-to-Effect Sequence

A cause-to-effect sequence follows an action to its results. Below, the topic sentence identifies the causes, and the remainder of the paragraph discusses its effects.

"What will happen if I do this?"

Some of the most serious accidents involving gas water heaters occur when a flammable liquid is used in the vicinity. The heavier-than-air vapors of a flammable liquid such as gasoline can flow along the floor—even the length of a basement—and be explosively ignited by the flame of the water heater's pilot light or burner. Because the victim's clothing frequently ignites, the resulting burn injuries are commonly serious and extremely painful. They may require long hospitalization, and can result in disfigurement or death. *Never, under any circumstances, use a flammable liquid near a gas heater or any other open flame.* (Consumer Product Safety Commission)

Emphatic Sequence

Emphasis makes important things stand out. Reasons offered in support of a specific viewpoint or recommendation often appear in workplace writing, as in the pesticide-herbicide paragraph on page 204 or the solar energy paragraph on page 205. For emphasis, the reasons or examples are usually arranged in order of decreasing or increasing importance. In this paragraph, the most dramatic example appears last, for greatest emphasis.

"What should I remember about this?"

Although strip mining is safer and cheaper than conventional mining, it is highly damaging to the surrounding landscape. Among its effects are scarred mountains, ruined land, and polluted waterways. Strip operations are altering our country's land at the rate of 5,000 acres per week. An estimated 10,500 miles of streams have been poisoned by silt drainage in Appalachia alone. If strip mining continues at its present rate, 16,000 square miles of U.S. land will eventually be stripped barren.

Problem-Causes-Solution Sequence

The problem-solving sequence proceeds from description of the problem, through diagnosis, to solution. After outlining the cause of the problem, this next paragraph explains how the problem has been solved:

"How was the problem solved?"

On all waterfront buildings, the unpainted wood exteriors had been severely damaged by the high winds and sandstorms of the previous winter. After repairing the damage, we took protective steps against further storms. First, all joints, edges, and sashes were treated with water-repellent preservative to protect against water damage. Next, three coats of nonporous primer were applied to all exterior surfaces to prevent paint from blistering and peeling. Finally, two coats of wood-quality latex paint were applied over the nonporous primer. To keep coats of paint from future separation, the first coat was applied within two weeks of the priming coats, and the second within two weeks of the first. Two weeks after completion, no blistering, peeling, or separation has occurred.

Comparison-Contrast Sequence

Workplace writing often requires evaluation of two or more items on the basis of their similarities or differences.

"How do these items compare?"

The ski industry's quest for a binding that ensures good performance as well as safety has led to development of two basic types. Although both bindings improve performance and increase the safety margin, they have different release and retention mechanisms. The first type consists of two units (one at the toe, another at the heel) that are spring-loaded. These units apply their retention forces directly to the boot sole. Thus the friction of boot against ski allows for the kind of ankle movement needed at high speeds over rough terrain, without causing the boot to release. In contrast, the second type has one spring-loaded unit at either the toe or the heel. From this unit a boot plate travels the length of the boot to a fixed receptacle on its opposite end. With this plate binding, the boot has no part in release or retention. Instead, retention force is applied directly to the boot plate, providing more stability for the recreational skier, but allowing for less ankle and boot movement before releasing. Overall, the double-unit binding performs better in racing, but the plate binding is safer.

For comparing and contrasting more specific data on these bindings, two lists would be most effective.

The Salomon 555 offers the following features:

1. upward release at the heel and lateral release at the toe (thus eliminating 80 percent of leg injuries)
2. lateral antishock capacity of 15 millimeters, with the highest available return-to-center force
3. two methods of reentry to the binding: for hard and deep-powder conditions
4. five adjustments
5. (and so on)

The Americana offers these features:

1. upward release at the toe as well as upward and lateral release at the heel
2. lateral antishock capacity of 30 millimeters, with moderate return-to-center force
3. two methods of reentry to the binding

> 4. two adjustments, one for boot length and another for comprehensive adjustment for all angles of release and elasticity
>
> 5. (and so on)

Instead of this block structure (in which one binding is discussed and then the other), the writer might have chosen a point-by-point structure (in which points common to both items, such as "Reentry Methods" are listed together). The point-by-point comparison works best in feasibility and recommendation reports because it offers readers a meaningful comparison between common points.

Chunking

"Chunking" in electronic media

Each organizing technique discussed in this chapter is a way of *chunking* information: breaking it down into discrete, digestible units, based on the users' needs and the document's purpose. Well-chunked material generally is easier to follow and more visually appealing.

Chunking enables us to show which pieces of information belong together and how the various pieces are connected (Horn 187). For instance, the opening page of Chapter 7 divides the research process into two chunks:

A major topic chunked into subtopics

> • Procedural Stages
> • Inquiry Stages

Each of these units then divides into smaller chunks:

Subtopics chunked into smaller topics

> • Procedural Stages
>   Searching for Information
>   Recording Your Findings
>   Documenting Your Sources
>   Writing the Report
>
> • Inquiry Stages
>   Asking the Right Questions
>   Exploring a Balance of Views
>   Achieving Adequate Depth in Your Search
>   Evaluating Your Findings
>   Interpreting Your Findings

Any of these segments that become too long might be subdivided again.

NOTE *Chunking requires careful decisions about exactly how much is enough and what constitutes sensible proportions among the parts. Don't overdo it by creating such tiny segments that your document ends up looking fragmented and disconnected.*

Using visuals for chunking

In addition to chunking information verbally we can chunk it visually. Notice how the visual display on page 212 makes relationships immediately apparent. (For more on visual design, see Chapter 14.)

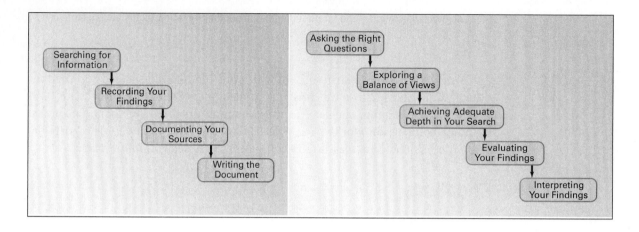

Finally, we can chunk information by using white space, shading, or other forms of page design. A well-designed page provides immediate cues about where to look and how to proceed. (For more on page design, see Chapter 15.)

Using page design
for chunking

Chunking is particularly useful in designing Web pages (Chapter 19).

Creating an Overview

Once you've settled on a final organization for your document, give readers an immediate preview of its contents by answering their intial questions:

What readers
want to know
immediately

- What is the purpose of this document?
- Why should I read it?
- What information can I expect to find here?

Readers will have additional, more specific questions as well (see page 28), but first they want to know what the document is all about and how it relates to them.

Overviews come in various shapes. The overview for this book, for example, appears on page xvii, under the heading "How This Book is Organized." An informative abstract of a long document also provides an overview, as on page 604. An overview for an oral presentation appears on page 614 as an introduction to that presentation. Whatever its shape, a good overview gives readers the "big picture" to help them navigate the document or presentation and understand its details.

Exercises

 Exercises

1. Locate, copy, and bring to class a paragraph that has the following features:
   - an orienting topic sentence
   - adequate development
   - unity
   - coherence
   - a recognizable sequence
   - appropriate length for its purpose and audience

   Be prepared to identify and explain each of these features in a class discussion.

2. For each of the following documents, indicate the most logical sequence. (For example, a description of a proposed computer lab would follow a spatial sequence.)
   - a set of instructions for operating a power tool
   - a campaign report describing your progress in political fund-raising
   - a report analyzing the weakest parts in a piece of industrial machinery
   - a report analyzing the desirability of a proposed oil refinery in your area
   - a detailed breakdown of your monthly budget to trim excess spending
   - a report investigating the reasons for student apathy on your campus
   - a report evaluating the effects of the ban on DDT in insect control
   - a report on any highly technical subject, written for a general audience
   - a report investigating the success of a no grade policy at other colleges
   - a proposal for a no-grade policy at your college

 ## Collaborative Project

1. Assume your group is preparing a report titled "The Negative Effects of Strip Mining on the Cumberland Plateau Region of Kentucky." After brainstorming and researching your subject, you all settle on these four major topics:
   - economic and social effects of strip mining
   - description of the strip-mining process
   - environmental effects of strip mining
   - description of the Cumberland Plateau

   Arrange these topics in the most sensible sequence.

   When your topics are arranged, assume that subsequent research and further brainstorming produce this list of subtopics:
   - method of strip mining used in the Cumberland Plateau region
   - location of the region
   - permanent land damage
   - water pollution

- lack of educational progress
- geological formation of the region
- open-pit mining
- unemployment
- increased erosion
- auger mining
- natural resources of the region
- types of strip mining
- increased flood hazards
- depopulation
- contour mining

Arrange these subtopics (and perhaps some sub-subtopics) under appropriate topic headings. Use decimal notation to create the body of a formal outline. Appoint one group member to present the outline in class.

Hint: Assume that your thesis is: "Decades of strip mining (without reclamation) in the Cumberland Plateau have devastated this region's environment, economy, and social structure."

2. Organize into small groups. Choose *one* of these topics, or one your group settles on, and then brainstorm to develop a formal outline for the body of a report. One representative from your group can present the final draft for class revision.

- job opportunities in your career field
- a physical description of the ideal classroom
- how to organize an effective job search
- how the quality of your higher educational experience can be improved
- arguments for and against a formal grading system
- an argument for an improvement you think this college needs most

CHAPTER 13

Editing for Readable Style

Editing for Clarity

Editing for Conciseness

Editing for Fluency

Finding the Exact Words

Adjusting Your Tone

Guidelines for Deciding about Tone

Guidelines for Nonsexist Usage

Guidelines for Inoffensive Usage

Considering the Cultural Context

Legal and Ethical Implications of Word Choice

Using Automated Editing Tools Effectively

Checklist: Style

On the Job . . . Revising a Document

No matter how technically appropriate your document, audience needs are not served unless your style is *readable:* sentences easy to understand and words precisely chosen.

A definition of style

Every bit as important as *what* you have to say is *how* you decide to say it. Your particular writing style is a blend of these elements:

What determines your style

- the way in which you construct each sentence
- the length of your sentences
- the way in which you connect sentences
- the words and phrases you choose
- the tone you convey

Readable style, of course, requires correct grammar, punctuation, and spelling. But correctness alone is no guarantee of readability. For example, this response to a job application is mechanically correct but hard to read:

Inefficient style

> We are in receipt of your recent correspondence indicating your interest in securing the advertised position. Your correspondence has been duly forwarded for consideration by the personnel office, which has employment candidate selection responsibility. You may expect to hear from us relative to your application as the selection process progresses. Your interest in the position is appreciated.

Notice how hard you have worked to extract information that could be expressed this simply:

Readable style

> Your application for the advertised position has been forwarded to our personnel office. As the selection process moves forward, we will be in touch. Thank you for your interest.

Inefficient style makes readers work harder than they should.

Style can be inefficient for many reasons, but it is especially inept when it does the following:

Ways in which style goes wrong

- makes the writing impossible to interpret
- takes too long to make the point
- reads like a Dick-and-Jane story from primary school
- uses imprecise or needlessly big words
- sounds stuffy and impersonal

Regardless of the cause, inefficient style results in writing that is less informative, less persuasive. Also, inefficient style can be unethical—by confusing or misleading the audience.

To help your audience spend less time reading, you must spend more time revising for a style that is *clear, concise, fluent, exact,* and *likable.*

Editing for Clarity

A clear sentence requires no more than a single reading. The following suggestions will help you edit for clarity.

| ref |

Avoid Ambiguous Pronoun References

Pronouns (*he, she, it, their,* and so on) must clearly refer to the noun they replace.

> AMBIGUOUS
> REFERENT
>
> Our patients enjoy the warm days while **they** last.
> *(Are the patients or the warm days on the way out?)*

Depending on whether the referent (or antecedent) for *they* is *patients* or *warm days,* the sentence can be clarified.

> CLEAR REFERENT
>
> While these warm days last, our patients enjoy them.
>
> *or*
>
> Our terminal patients enjoy the warm days.

> AMBIGUOUS
> REFERENT
>
> Jack resents his assistant because **he** is competitive.
> *(Who's the competitive one—Jack or his assistant?)*

> CLEAR REFERENT
>
> Because his assistant is competitive, Jack resents him.
>
> *or*
>
> Because Jack is competitive, he resents his assistant.

(See page 675 for more on pronoun references, and page 243 for avoiding sexist bias in pronoun use.)

| mod |

Avoid Ambiguous Modifiers

A modifier is a word (usually an adjective or adverb) or a group of words (usually a phrase or a clause) that provides information about other words or groups of words. If a modifier is too far from the words it modifies, the message can be ambiguous. Position modifiers to reflect your meaning.

> MISPLACED
> MODIFIER
>
> **Only** press the red button in an emergency. *(Does **only** modify **press** or **emergency**?)*

> REVISED
>
> Press **only** the red button in an emergency.
>
> *or*
>
> Press the red button in an emergency **only.**

Another problem with ambiguity occurs when a modifying phrase has no word to modify, as in the next example.

DANGLING MODIFIER	**Being so well known in the computer industry,** I would appreciate your advice.

The writer meant to say that the *reader* is well known, but with no word to connect to, the modifying phrase dangles. Eliminate the confusion by adding a subject:

REVISED	Because **you** are so well known in the computer industry, I would appreciate your advice.

(See page 678 for more on modifiers.)

EXERCISE 1

Edit each sentence below to eliminate ambiguities in pronoun reference or to clarify ambiguous modifiers.

    a.   Janice dislikes working with Claire because she's impatient.
    b.   Bill told Fred that he was mistaken.
    c.   Only use this phone in a red alert.
    d.   After offending our best client, I am deeply annoyed with the new manager.

---

st mod

Unstack Modifying Nouns

Too many nouns in a row can create confusion and reading difficulty. One noun can modify another (as in "software development"). But when two or more nouns modify a noun, the string of words becomes hard to read and ambiguous.

AMBIGUOUS	Be sure to leave enough time for a **training session participant** evaluation. *(Evaluation of the session or of the participants?)*

With no articles, prepositions, or verbs, readers cannot sort out the relationships among the nouns.

REVISED	Be sure to leave enough time **for** participants **to evaluate** the training session.

or

Be sure to leave enough time **to evaluate** participants in **the** training session.

wo

Arrange Word Order for Coherence and Emphasis

In coherent writing, everything sticks together; each sentence builds on the preceding sentence and looks ahead to the one that follows. In similar fashion, sentences generally work best when the beginning looks back at familiar information and the end provides the new (or unfamiliar) information:

Familiar		Unfamiliar
My dog	has	fleas.
Our boss	just won	the lottery.
This company	is planning	a merger.

The above pattern also emphasizes the new information. Every sentence has a key word or phrase that sums up the new information and that usually is emphasized best at the end of the sentence.

FAULTY EMPHASIS	We expect a **refund** because of your error in our shipment.
CORRECT	Because of your error in our shipment, we expect a **refund.**
FAULTY EMPHASIS	In a business relationship, **trust** is a vital element.
CORRECT	A business relationship depends on **trust.**

One exception to placing key words last occurs with an imperative statement (a command, an order, an instruction), with the subject [*you*] understood. For instance, each step in a list of instructions should begin with an action verb (*insert, open, close, turn, remove, press*).

CORRECT	**Insert** the diskette before activating the system.
	Remove the protective seal.

With the opening key word, users know immediately what action to take.

EXERCISE 2

Edit each sentence below to unstack modifying nouns or to rearrange word order for clarity and emphasis.

a. Develop online editing system documentation.
b. I recommend these management performance improvement incentives.
c. Our profits have doubled since we automated our assembly line.
d. Education enables us to recognize excellence and to achieve it.
e. In all writing, revision is required.
f. Sarah's job involves fault analysis systems troubleshooting handbook preparation.

---

av Use Active Voice Whenever Possible

In general, readers learn more quickly when communications are written in the active voice ("I did it") rather than the passive voice ("It was done by me"). In active voice sentences, a clear agent performs a clear action on a recipient:

The ethics of active and passive voice

	Agent	**Action**	**Recipient**
ACTIVE VOICE	Joe	lost	your report.
	Subject	**Verb**	**Object**

Passive voice, in contrast, reverses this pattern, placing the recipient of the action in the subject slot.

	Recipient	**Action**	**Agent**
PASSIVE VOICE	Your report	was lost	by Joe.
	Subject	**Verb**	**Prepositional phrase**

Sometimes the passive eliminates the agent altogether:

PASSIVE VOICE   Your report was lost. *(Who lost it?)*

Passive voice is unethical if it obscures the person or other agent when that responsible person or agent should be identified.

Some writers mistakenly rely on the passive voice because they think it sounds more objective and important—whereas it often makes writing wordy and evasive.

CONCISE AND DIRECT (ACTIVE)	**I underestimated** labor costs for this project. *(7 words)*
WORDY AND INDIRECT (PASSIVE)	Labor costs for this project **were underestimated by me.** *(9 words)*
EVASIVE (PASSIVE)	Labor costs for this project were underestimated.
	A **mistake was made** in your shipment. *(By whom?)*

In reporting errors or bad news, use the active voice, for clarity and sincerity.

The passive voice creates a weak and impersonal tone.

WEAK AND IMPERSONAL	An offer **will be made** by us next week.
STRONG AND PERSONAL	**We will make** an offer next week.

Use the active voice when you want action. Otherwise, your statement will have no power.

WEAK PASSIVE	If my claim is not settled by May 15, the Better Business Bureau **will be contacted,** and their advice on legal action **will be taken.**
STRONG ACTIVE	If you do not settle my claim by May 15, **I will contact** the Better Business Bureau for advice on legal action.

Notice how this active version emphasizes the new and significant information by placing it at the end.

Ordinarily, use the active voice for giving instructions.

| PASSIVE | The bid **should be sealed.**
Care **should be taken** with the dynamite. |
| ACTIVE | **Seal** the bid.
Be careful with the dynamite. |

Avoid shifts from active to passive voice in the same sentence.

| FAULTY SHIFT | During the meeting, project members **spoke** and **presentations were given.** |
| CORRECT | During the meeting, project members **spoke** and **gave** presentations. |

EXERCISE 3

Convert these passive voice sentences to concise, forceful, and direct expressions in the active voice.

    a. The evaluation was performed by us.
    b. Unless you pay me within three days, my lawyer will be contacted.
    c. Hard hats should be worn at all times.
    d. It was decided to reject your offer.
    e. Our test results will be sent to you as soon as verification is completed.

---

pv   Use Passive Voice Selectively

Use the passive voice when your audience has no need to know the agent.

| CORRECT PASSIVE | Mr. Jones **was brought** to the emergency room.
The bank failure **was publicized** statewide. |

Use the passive voice when the agent is not known or when the object is more important than the subject.

| CORRECT PASSIVE | Fred's article **was published** last week.
All policy claims **are kept** confidential. |

Prefer the passive when you want to be indirect or inoffensive (as in requesting the customer's payment or the employee's cooperation, or to avoid blaming someone—such as your supervisor) (Ornatowski 94).

| ACTIVE BUT
OFFENSIVE | **You have not paid** your bill.
You need to overhaul our filing system. |

| INOFFENSIVE | This bill **has not been paid.** |
| PASSIVE | Our filing system **needs to be overhauled.** |

Use the passive voice if the person behind the action needs to be protected.

| CORRECT PASSIVE | The criminal **was identified.** |
| | The embezzlement scheme **was exposed.** |

EXERCISE 4

The sentences below lack proper emphasis because of improper use of the active voice. Convert each to passive voice.

a. Joe's company fired him.
b. A power surge destroyed more than two thousand lines of our new applications program.
c. You are paying inadequate attention to worker safety.
d. You are checking temperatures too infrequently.
e. You did a poor job editing this report.

OS — Avoid Overstuffed Sentences

Give no more information in one sentence than readers can retain and process.

| OVERSTUFFED | Publicizing the records of a private meeting that took place three weeks ago to reveal the identity of a manager who criticized our company's promotion policy would be unethical. |

Clear things up by sorting out the relationships.

| REVISED | In a private meeting three weeks ago, a manager criticized our company's policy on promotion. It would be unethical to reveal the manager's identity by publicizing the records of that meeting. *(Other versions are possible, depending on the intended meaning.)* |

Even short sentences can be hard to interpret if they have too many details.

| OVERSTUFFED | Send three copies of Form 17-e to all six departments, unless Departments A or B or both request Form 16-w instead. |

EXERCISE 5

Unscramble this overstuffed sentence by making shorter, clearer sentences.

A smoke-filled room causes not only teary eyes and runny noses but also can alter people's hearing and vision, as well as creating dangerous levels of carbon monoxide, especially for people with heart and lung ailments, whose health is particularly threatened by secondhand smoke.

Editing for Conciseness

Concise writing conveys the most information in the fewest words. But it does not omit those details necessary for clarity. Use fewer words whenever fewer will do. But remember the difference between *clear writing* and *compressed writing* that is impossible to decipher.

COMPRESSED	Send new vehicle air conditioner compression cut-off system specifications to engineering manager advising immediate action.
CLEAR	The cut-off system for the air conditioner compressor on our new vehicles is faulty. Send the system specifications to our engineering manager so they can be modified.

First drafts rarely are concise. Trim the fat.

w   Avoid Wordy Phrases

Revising wordy phrases

Each phrase below can be reduced to one word.

due to the fact that	=	because
the majority of	=	most
readily apparent	=	obvious
a large number	=	many
aware of the fact that	=	know

red   Eliminate Redundancy

Spotting redundant phrases

A redundant expression says the same thing twice, in different words, as in *fellow colleagues*.

completely eliminate	**end** result
enter **into**	consensus **of opinion**
mental awareness	**utter** devastation
mutual cooperation	**the month of** August

rep   Avoid Needless Repetition

Unnecessary repetition clutters writing and dilutes meaning.

REPETITIOUS	In trauma victims, breathing is restored by **artificial respiration.** Techniques of **artificial respiration** include mouth-to-mouth **respiration** and mouth-to-nose **respiration.**

Repetition in the above passage disappears when sentences are combined.

CONCISE	In trauma victims, breathing is restored by artificial respiration, either mouth-to-mouth or mouth-to-nose.

NOTE   *Don't hesitate to repeat, or at least rephrase, material (even whole paragraphs in a longer document) if you feel that users need reminders. Effective repetition helps avoid cross-references like these: "See page 23" or "Review page 10."*

EXERCISE 6

Make these sentences more concise by eliminating wordy phrases, redundancy, and needless repetition.

a. I have admiration for Professor Jones.
b. Due to the fact that we made the lowest bid, we won the contract.
c. On previous occasions we have worked together.
d. We have completely eliminated the bugs from this program.
e. This report is the most informative report on the project.
f. This offer is the most attractive offer I've received.

---

th Avoid *There* Sentence Openers

Many *There is* or *There are* sentence openers can be eliminated.

WEAK   **There is** a danger of explosion in Number 2 mineshaft.

REVISED   Number 2 mineshaft is in danger of exploding.

Dropping such openers places the key words at the end of the sentence, where they are best emphasized.

NOTE   *Of course, in some contexts, proper emphasis would call for a* There *opener.*

CORRECT   People have often wondered about the rationale behind Boris's sudden decision. There were several good reasons for his dropping out of the program.

It Avoid Some *It* Sentence Openers

Avoid beginning a sentence with *It*—unless the *It* clearly points to a specific referent in the preceding sentence: "This document is excellent. It deserves special recognition."

WEAK   **It** is necessary to complete both sides of the form.

REVISED   Please complete both sides of the form.

pref Delete Needless Prefaces

Instead of delaying the new information in your sentence, get right to the point.

WORDY   **I am writing this letter because** I wish to apply for the position of copy editor.

CONCISE	Please consider me for the position of copy editor.
WORDY	**As far as artificial intelligence is concerned,** the technology is only in its infancy.
CONCISE	Artificial intelligence technology is only in its infancy.

EXERCISE 7

Make these sentences more concise by eliminating *There* and *It* openers and needless prefaces.

   a.   There was severe fire damage to the reactor.
   b.   There are several reasons why Jane left the company.
   c.   It is essential that we act immediately.
   d.   It has been reported by Bill that several safety violations have occurred.
   e.   This letter is to inform you that I am pleased to accept your job offer.
   f.   The purpose of this report is to update our research findings.

WV Avoid Weak Verbs

Prefer verbs that express a definite action: *open, close, move, continue, begin.* Avoid weak verbs that express no specific action: *is, was, are, has, give, make, come, take.*

NOTE

In some cases, such verbs are essential to your meaning: "Dr. Phillips is operating at 7 a.m." "Take me to the laboratory."

All forms of *to be* (*am, are, is, was, were, will, have been, might have been*) are weak. Substitute a strong verb for conciseness:

WEAK	My recommendation **is** for a larger budget.
STRONG	I **recommend** a larger budget.

Don't disappear behind weak verbs and their baggage of needless nouns and prepositions.

WEAK AND WORDY	Please **take into consideration** my offer.
CONCISE	Please **consider** my offer.

Strong verbs, or action verbs, suggest an assertive, positive, and confident writer. Here are examples of weak verbs converted to strong verbs:

has the ability to	=	can
give a summary of	=	summarize
make an assumption	=	assume
come to the conclusion	=	conclude
make a decision	=	decide

EXERCISE 8

Edit each of these wordy and vague sentences to eliminate weak verbs.

a. Our disposal procedure is in conformity with federal standards.
b. Please make a decision today.
c. We need to have a discussion about the problem.
d. I have just come to the realization that I was mistaken.
e. Your conclusion is in agreement with mine.

---

prep Avoid Excessive Prepositions

WORDY	The recommendation first appeared **in** the report written **by** the supervisor in January **about** that month's productivity.
CONCISE	The recommendation first appeared in the supervisor's productivity report for January.

Each prepositional phrase here can be reduced.

with the exception of	=	except for
in the near future	=	soon
at the present time	=	now
in the course of	=	during
in the process of	=	during (*or* in)

nom Fight Noun Addiction

Nouns manufactured from verbs (nominalizations) are harder to understand than the verbs themselves.

WEAK AND WORDY	We ask for the **cooperation** of all employees.
STRONG AND CONCISE	We ask that all employees **cooperate**.
WEAK AND WORDY	Give **consideration** to the possibility of a career change.
STRONG AND CONCISE	**Consider** a career change.

Besides causing wordiness, nominalizations can be vague—by hiding the agent of an action. Verbs are generally easier to read because they signal action.

WORDY AND VAGUE	A **valid requirement** for immediate action exists. *(Who should take the action? We can't tell.)*
PRECISE	We **must act** immediately.

Here are nominalizations restored to their action verb forms:

Trading nouns
for verbs

conduct an investigation of	=	investigate
provide a description of	=	describe
conduct a test of	=	test

Nominalizations drain the life from your style. In cheering for your favorite team, you wouldn't say "Blocking of that kick is a necessity!" instead of "Block that kick!"

NOTE   *Avoid excessive economy. For example, "Employees must cooperate" would not be an acceptable alternative to the first example in this section. But, for the final example, "Block that kick" would be.*

EXERCISE 9

Make these sentences more concise by eliminating needless prepositions, *to be* constructions, and nominalizations.

a. In the event of system failure, your sounding of the alarm is essential.
b. These are the recommendations of the chairperson of the committee.
c. Our acceptance of the offer is a necessity.
d. Please perform an analysis and make an evaluation of our new system.
e. A need for your caution exists.
f. Power surges are associated, in a causative way, with malfunctions of computers.

neg   ## Make Negatives Positive

A positive expression is easier to understand than a negative one.

INDIRECT AND WORDY
Please do not be late in submitting your report.

DIRECT AND CONCISE
Please submit your report on time.

Sentences with multiple negative expressions are even harder to translate:

CONFUSING AND WORDY
Do **not** distribute this memo to employees who have **not** received a security clearance.

CLEAR AND CONCISE
Distribute this memo only to employees who have received a security clearance.

Besides directly negative words (*no, not, never*), some indirectly negative words (*except, forget, mistake, lose, uncooperative*) also force readers to translate.

CONFUSING AND WORDY
Do not neglect to activate the alarm system.
My diagnosis was **not inaccurate**.

CLEAR AND   **Be sure** to activate the alarm system.
CONCISE   My diagnosis was **accurate.**

Some negative expressions, of course, are perfectly correct, as in expressing disagreement.

CORRECT NEGATIVES   This is **not** the best plan.
                      Your offer is **unacceptable.**

Prefer positives to negatives, though, whenever your meaning allows:

Trading negatives
for positives

did not succeed = failed
does not have   = lacks
did not prevent = allowed
not unless   = only if

cl   Clean Out Clutter Words

Clutter words stretch a message without adding meaning. Here are some of the most common: *very, definitely, quite, extremely, rather, somewhat, really, actually, currently, situation, aspect, factor.*

CLUTTERED   **Actually**, one **aspect** of a business **situation** that could **definitely** make me **quite** happy would be to have a **somewhat** adventurous partner who **really** shared my **extreme** attraction to risks.

CONCISE   I seek an adventurous business partner who enjoys risks.

qual   Delete Needless Qualifiers

Qualifiers such as *I feel, it seems, I believe, in my opinion,* and *I think* express uncertainty or soften the tone and force of a statement.

APPROPRIATE   Despite Frank's poor grades last year he will, **I think,** do well
QUALIFIER   in college.
                Your product **seems** to meet our needs.

But when you are certain, eliminate the qualifier so as not to seem tentative or evasive.

NEEDLESS   **It seems that** I've made an error.
QUALIFIERS   We **appear to** have exceeded our budget.

NOTE

In communicating across cultures, keep in mind that a direct, forceful style might be considered offensive (page 245).

EXERCISE 10

Make these sentences more concise by changing negatives to positives and by clearing out clutter words and needless qualifiers.

    a. Our design must avoid nonconformity with building codes.

    b. Never fail to wear protective clothing.

    c. We are currently in the situation of completing our investigation of all aspects of the accident.

    d. I appear to have misplaced the contract.

    e. Do not accept bids that are not signed.

    f. It seems as if I have just wrecked a company car.

Editing for Fluency

Fluent sentences are easy to read because they provide clear connections, variety, and emphasis. Their varied length and word order eliminate choppiness and monotony. Fluent sentences enhance *clarity,* emphasizing the most important ideas. Fluent sentences enhance *conciseness,* often replacing several short, repetitious sentences with one longer, more economical sentence. To write fluently, use the following strategies.

Combine Related Ideas

A series of short, disconnected sentences is not only choppy and wordy, but also unclear.

DISCONNECTED	Jogging can be healthful. You need the right equipment. Most necessary are well-fitting shoes. Without this equipment you take the chance of injuring your legs. Your knees are especially prone to injury. *(5 sentences)*
CLEAR, CONCISE, AND FLUENT	Jogging can be healthful if you have the right equipment. Shoes that fit well are most necessary because they prevent injury to your legs, especially your knees. *(2 sentences)*

Most sets of information can be combined to form different relationships, depending on what you want to emphasize. Imagine that this set of facts describes an applicant for a junior management position with your company.

- Roy James graduated from an excellent management school.
- He has no experience.
- He is highly recommended.

Assume that you are a personnel director, conveying your impression of this candidate to upper management. To convey a negative impression, you might combine the information in this way:

STRONGLY NEGATIVE EMPHASIS	Although Roy James graduated from an excellent management school and is highly recommended, **he has no experience.**

The *independent clause* (in boldface) receives the emphasis. (See also page 676, on subordination.) But if you are undecided yet leaning in a negative direction, you might write:

SLIGHTLY NEGATIVE EMPHASIS	Roy James graduated from an excellent management school and is highly recommended, **but** he has no experience.

In this sentence, the information both before and after *but* appears in independent clauses. Joining them with the coordinating word *but* suggests that both sides of the issue are equally important (or "coordinate"). Placing the negative idea last, however, gives it a slight emphasis. (See also page 675, on coordination.)

Finally, to emphasize strong support for the candidate, you could say this:

> Although Roy James has no experience, **he graduated from an excellent management school and is highly recommended.**

In the preceding example, the initial information is subordinated by *although*, giving the final information the weight of an independent clause.

NOTE   *Combine sentences only to simplify the reader's task. Overstuffed sentences with too much information and too many connections can be hard for readers to sort out. (See page 222.)*

EXERCISE 11

Combine each set of sentences below into one fluent sentence that provides the requested emphasis.

Examples:

SENTENCE SET	John is a loyal employee.
	John is a motivated employee.
	John is short-tempered with his colleagues.
COMBINED FOR POSITIVE EMPHASIS	Even though John is short-tempered with his colleagues, he is a loyal and motivated employee.
SENTENCE SET	This word processor has many features.
	It includes a spelling checker.
	It includes a thesaurus.
	It includes a grammar checker.
COMBINED TO EMPHASIZE THESAURUS	Among its many features, such as spelling and grammar checkers, this word processor includes a thesaurus.

a. The job offers an attractive salary.
    It demands long work hours.
    Promotions are rapid.
    (*Combine for negative emphasis.*)

b. The job offers an attractive salary.
   It demands long work hours.
   Promotions are rapid.
   (*Combine for positive emphasis.*)

c. Our office software is integrated.
   It has an excellent database management program.
   Most impressive is its word-processing capability.
   It has an excellent spreadsheet program.
   (*Combine to emphasize the word processor.*)

d. Company X gave us the lowest bid.
   Company Y has an excellent reputation.
   (*Combine to emphasize Company Y.*)

e. Superinsulated homes are energy efficient.
   Superinsulated homes create a danger of indoor air pollution.
   The toxic substances include radon gas and urea formaldehyde.
   (*Combine for a negative emphasis.*)

f. Computers cannot *think* for the writer.
   Computers eliminate many mechanical writing tasks.
   They speed the flow of information.
   (*Combine to emphasize the first assertion.*)

---

var Vary Sentence Construction and Length

Related ideas often need to be linked in one sentence, so that readers can grasp the connections:

DISCONNECTED	The nuclear core reached critical temperature. The loss-of-coolant alarm was triggered. The operator shut down the reactor.
CONNECTED	As the nuclear core reached critical temperature, triggering the loss-of-coolant alarm, the operator shut down the reactor.

But an idea that should stand alone for emphasis needs a whole sentence of its own:

CORRECT	Core meltdown seemed inevitable.

However, an unbroken string of long or short sentences can bore and confuse readers, as can a series with identical openings:

BORING AND REPETITIVE	There are some drawbacks about diesel engines. **They** are difficult to start in cold weather. **They** cause vibration. **They** also give off an unpleasant odor. **They** cause sulfur dioxide pollution.
VARIED	Diesel engines have some drawbacks. Most obvious are their noisiness, cold-weather starting difficulties, vibration, odor, and sulfur dioxide emission.

Similarly, when you write in the first person, overusing *I* makes you appear self-centered. (Some organizations require use of the third person, avoiding the first person completely, for all manuals, lab reports, specifications, product descriptions, and so on.)

Do not, however, avoid personal pronouns if they make the writing more readable (say, by eliminating passive constructions).

 ### Use Short Sentences for Special Emphasis

All this talk about combining ideas might suggest that short sentences have no place in good writing. Wrong. Short sentences (even one-word sentences) provide vivid emphasis. They stick in a reader's mind.

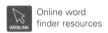 Online word finder resources

Finding the Exact Words

Too often, language can *camouflage* rather than communicate. People see many reasons to hide behind language, as when they do the following:

Situations in which people often hide behind language

- speak for their company but not for themselves
- fear the consequences of giving bad news
- are afraid to disagree with company policy
- make a recommendation some readers will resent
- worry about making a bad impression
- worry about being wrong
- pretend to know more than they do
- avoid admitting a mistake, or ignorance

Poor word choices produce inefficient and often unethical writing that resists interpretation and frustrates the audience. Use the following strategies to find words that are *convincing*, *precise*, and *informative*.

 ### Prefer Simple and Familiar Wording

Don't replace technically precise words with nontechnical words that are vague or imprecise. Don't write *a part that makes the computer run* when you mean *central processing unit*. Use the precise term, and then define it in a glossary for nontechnical readers:

GLOSSARY ENTRY   **Central processing unit:** the part of the computer that controls information transfer and carries out arithmetic and logical instructions.

In certain contexts, certain technical words are indispensable, but the nontechnical words usually can be simplified. For example, instead of *accoustically attenuating the food consumption area*, try *soundproofing the cafeteria*.

Besides being annoying, needlessly big or unfamiliar words can be ambiguous.

> AMBIGUOUS   Make an improvement in the clerical situation.

(Does this mean we should hire more clerical personnel or better personnel or train the personnel we have?)

Whenever possible, choose words you use and hear in everyday speaking:

Trading multiple syllables for fewer

demonstrate	=	show
endeavor	=	effort, try
frequently	=	often
subsequent to	=	after
utilize	=	use

Of course, now and then the complex or more elaborate word best expresses your meaning. For instance, we would not substitute *end* for *terminate* in referring to something with an established time limit.

> CORRECT   Our trade agreement **terminates** this month.

If a complex word can replace a handful of simpler words—and can sharpen your meaning—use it.

> WEAK   Six rectangular grooves **around the outside edge** of the steel plate **are needed for** the pressure clamps **to fit into.**
>
> INFORMATIVE AND PRECISE   Six rectangular grooves on the steel plate **perimeter accommodate** the pressure clamps.

EXERCISE 12

Edit these sentences for straightforward and familiar language.

  a. May you find luck and success in all endeavors.
  b. I suggest you reduce the number of cigarettes you consume.
  c. Within the copier, a magnetic reed switch is utilized as a mode of replacement for the conventional microswitches that were in use on previous models.
  d. A good writer is cognizant of how to utilize grammar in a correct fashion.
  e. I wish to upgrade my present employment situation.

---

jarg Avoid Useless Jargon

When jargon is appropriate

Every profession has its own shorthand and accepted phrases and terms. For example, *stat* (from the Latin "statim" or "immediately") is medical jargon for *Drop everything and deal with this emergency.* For computer buffs, a *glitch* is a momentary power surge that can erase the contents of internal memory; a *bug* is an error that causes a program to run incorrectly. Among specialists these terms are an economical way to communicate.

When jargon is inappropriate

But some jargon is useless in any context. In the world of useless jargon, people don't *cooperate* on a project; instead, they *interface* or *contiguously optimize their efforts*. Rather than *designing a model,* they *formulate a paradigm.*

A popular form of useless jargon is adding *-wise* to nouns, as shorthand for *in reference to* or *in terms of.*

> USELESS JARGON   **Expensewise** and **schedulewise,** this plan is unacceptable.
>
> REVISED   In terms of expense and scheduling, this plan is unacceptable.

Writers create another form of useless jargon when they invent verbs from nouns or from adjectives by adding an *-ize* ending: Don't invent *prioritize* from *priority;* instead use *to rank priorities.*

Useless jargon's worst fault is that it makes the person using it seem stuffy and pretentious or like someone with something to hide:

> PRETENTIOUS   Unless all parties interface synchronously within given parameters, the project will be rendered inoperative.
>
> POSSIBLE TRANSLATION   Unless we coordinate our efforts, the project will fail.

Before using any jargon, think about your specific audience and ask yourself: "Can I find an easier way to say exactly what I mean?" Only use jargon that improves your communication.

acr   ## Use Acronyms Selectively

Acronyms are words formed from the initial letter of each word in a phrase (as in *LOCA* from *l*oss *o*f *c*oolant *a*ccident) or from a combination of initial letters and parts of words (as in *bit* from *b*inary dig*it* or *pixel* from *pi*cture *ele*ment). Acronyms *can* communicate concisely—but only when the audience knows their meaning, and only when you use the term often in your document. Whenever you first use an acronym, spell out the words from which it is derived.

An acronym defined

> **Modem** ("modulator + demodulator"): a device that converts, or "modulates," computer data in electronic form into a sound signal that can be transmitted and then reconverted, or "demodulated," into electronic form for the receiving computer.

trite   ## Avoid Triteness

Worn-out phrases (clichés) make writers seem too lazy or too careless to find exact, unique ways of saying what they mean.

Worn out phrases

| make the grade | the chips are down |
| in the final analysis | not by a long shot |

close the deal	last but not least
hard as a rock	welcome aboard
water under the bridge	over the hill

EXERCISE 13

Edit these sentences to eliminate useless jargon and triteness.

a. To optimize your financial return, prioritize your investment goals.
b. The use of this product engenders a 50-percent repeat consumer encounter.
c. We'll have to swallow our pride and admit our mistake.
d. Managers who make the grade are those who can take daily pressures in stride.

euph

Avoid Misleading Euphemisms

A form of understatement, a euphemism is an expression aimed at politeness or at making unpleasant subjects seem less offensive. Thus, *we powder our noses* or *use the boys' room* instead of *using the bathroom; we pass away* or *meet our Maker* instead of *dying.*

When a euphemism is appropriate

When euphemisms avoid offending or embarrassing people, they are perfectly legitimate. Instead of telling a job applicant he or she is *unqualified,* we might say, *Your background doesn't meet our needs.* In addition, there are times when friendliness and interoffice harmony are more likely to be preserved with writing that is not too abrupt, bold, blunt, or emphatic (MacKenzie 2).

When a euphemism is deceptive

Euphemisms, however, are unethical if they understate the truth when only the truth will serve. In the sugarcoated world of misleading euphemisms, bad news disappears:

- Instead of being *laid off* or *fired,* workers are *surplused* or *deselected,* or the company is *downsized.*
- Instead of *lying* to the public, the government *engages in a policy of disinformation.*
- Instead of *wars* and *civilian casualties,* we have *conflicts* and *collateral damage.*

Plain talk is always better than deception. If someone offers you a job *with limited opportunity for promotion,* expect a *dead-end job.*

over

Avoid Overstatement

Exaggeration sounds phony. Be cautious when using superlatives such as *best, biggest, brightest, most,* and *worst.* Recognize the differences among *always, usually, often, sometimes,* and *rarely;* among *all, most, many, some,* and *few.*

OVERSTATED	You never listen to my ideas.
	This product will last forever.
MISLEADING	Assembly-line employees are doing shabby work.

Unless you mean *all employees,* qualify your generalization with *some,* or *most*—or even better, specify *20 percent.*

EXERCISE 14

Edit these sentences to eliminate euphemism, overstatement, or unsupported generalizations.

    a. I finally must admit that I am an abuser of intoxicating beverages.
    b. I was less than candid.
    c. This employee is poorly motivated.
    d. Most entry-level jobs are boring and dehumanizing.
    e. Clerical jobs offer no opportunity for advancement.
    f. Because of your absence of candor, we can no longer offer you employment.

---

ww   ## Avoid Imprecise Wording

Words listed as synonyms usually carry different shades of meaning. Do you mean to say *I'm slender, You're slim, She's lean,* or *He's scrawny?* The wrong choice could be disastrous.

    Imprecision can create ambiguity. For instance, is *send us more personal information* a request for more information that is personal or for information that is more personal? Does your client expect *fewer* or *less* technical details in your report? See Table 13.1 for words that are commonly confused.

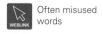

Often misused words

Similar Words	Used Correctly in a Sentence
Affect means "to have an influence on."	Meditation positively *affects* concentration.
Affect can also mean "to pretend."	Boris likes to *affect* a French accent.
Effect used as a noun means "a result."	Meditation has a positive *effect* on concentration.
Effect used as a verb means "to make happen" or "to bring about."	Meditation can *effect* an improvement in concentration.
Already means "before this time."	Our new laptops are *already* sold out.
All ready means "prepared."	We are *all ready* for the summer tourist season.
Among refers to three or more.	The prize was divided *among* the four winners.
Between refers to two.	The prize was divided *between* the two winners.
Continual means "repeated at intervals."	Our lower field floods *continually* during the rainy season.
Continuous means "without interruption."	His headache has been *continuous* for three days.

TABLE 13.1 Commonly Confused Words   *(continues)*

Similar Words	Used Correctly in a Sentence
Differ from refers to unlike things.	This plan *differs* greatly *from* our earlier one.
Differ with means "to disagree."	Mary *differs with* John about the feasibility of this project.
Disinterested means "unbiased" or "impartial."	Good science calls for *disinterested* analysis of research findings.
Uninterested means "not caring."	Junior high school students are often *uninterested* in science.
Eminent means "famous" or "distinguished."	Dr. Ostroff, the *eminent* physicist, is lecturing today.
Imminent means "about to happen."	A nuclear meltdown seemed *imminent*.
Farther refers to physical distance (a measurable quantity).	The station is 20 miles *farther*.
Further refers to extent (not measurable).	*Further* discussion of this issue is vital.
Fewer refers to things that can be counted.	*Fewer* than fifty students responded to our survey.
Less refers to things that can't be counted.	This survey had *less* of a response than our earlier one.
Imply means "to hint at" or "to insinuate."	This report *implies* that a crime occurred.
Infer means "to reason from evidence."	From this report, we can *infer* that a crime occurred.
It's stands for "it is."	*It's* a good time for a department meeting.
Its stands for "belonging to."	The cost of the project has exceeded *its* budget.
Lay means "to place or set something down." It always takes a direct object.	Please *lay* the blueprints on the desk.
Lie means "to recline." It takes no direct object.	This patient needs to *lie* on his right side all night.
(Note that the past tense of *lie* is *lay*.)	The patient *lay* on his right side all last night.
Precede means "to come before."	Audience analysis should *precede* a written report.
Proceed means "to go forward."	If you must wake the cobra, *proceed* carefully.
Principle is always a noun that means "basic rule or standard."	Ethical *principles* should govern all our communications.
Principal, used as a noun, means "the major person(s)."	All *principals* in this purchase must sign the contract.
Principal, used as an adjective, means "leading."	Martha was the *principal* negotiator for this contract.

TABLE 13.1 *(Continued)*

spec

Be Specific and Concrete

General words name broad classes of things, such as *job, computer,* or *person.* Such terms usually need to be clarified by more specific ones.

General terms traded for specific terms

job	=	senior accountant for Softbyte Press
person	=	Sarah Jones, production manager

The more specific your words, the more a reader can visualize your meaning.

Abstract words name qualities, concepts, or feelings (*beauty, luxury, depression*) whose exact meaning has to be nailed down by *concrete* words—words that name things we can visualize.

Abstract terms traded for concrete terms

a **beautiful** view	=	snowcapped mountains, a wilderness lake, pink ledge, ninety-foot birch trees
a **depressed** worker	=	suicidal urge, insomnia, feelings of worthlessness, no hope for improvement

Informative writing *tells* and *shows.*

GENERAL   One of our **workers** was **injured** by a **piece of equipment recently**.

SPECIFIC   **Alan Hill** suffered a **broken thumb** while working on a **lathe yesterday**.

Don't write *thing* when you mean *lever, switch, micrometer,* or *scalpel.*

NOTE   *In some instances, of course, you may wish to generalize for the sake of diplomacy. Instead of writing "Bill, Mary, and Sam have been tying up the office phones with personal calls," you might prefer to generalize: "Some employees. . . ."*

Most good writing offers both general and specific information. The most general material appears in the topic statement and sometimes in the conclusion because these parts, respectively, set the paragraph's direction and summarize its content.

EXERCISE 15

Edit these sentences to make them more precise and informative.

- a. Anaerobic fermentation is used in this report.
- b. Your crew damaged a piece of office equipment.
- c. His performance was admirable.
- d. This thing bothers me.

tone

Adjusting Your Tone

How tone is created

Your tone is your personal stamp—the personality that takes shape between the lines. The tone you create depends on (1) the distance you impose between yourself and the reader, and (2) the attitude you show toward the subject.

Assume, for example, that a friend is going to take over a job you've held. You're writing your friend instructions for parts of the job. Here is your first sentence:

Informal

> Now that you've arrived in the glamorous world of office work, put on your track shoes; this is no ordinary manager-trainee job.

That sentence imposes little distance between you and the reader (it uses the direct address, *you*, and the humorous suggestion to *put on your track shoes*). The ironic use of *glamorous* suggests just the opposite: that the job holds little glamor.

For a different reader (say, the recipient of a company training manual), you would choose some other opening:

Semiformal

> As a manager trainee at GlobalTech, you will work for many managers. In short, you will spend little of your day seated at your desk.

The tone now is serious, no longer intimate, and you express no distinct attitude toward the job. For yet another audience (clients or investors who will read an annual report), you might alter the tone again:

Formal

> Manager trainees at GlobalTech are responsible for duties that extend far beyond desk work.

Here the businesslike shift from second- to third-person address makes the tone too impersonal for any writing addressed to the trainees themselves.

We already know how tone works in speaking. When you meet someone new, for example, you respond in a tone that defines your relationship:

Tone announces interpersonal distance

> Honored to make your acquaintance. [*formal tone—greatest distance*]
> How do you do? [*formal*]
> Nice to meet you. [*semiformal—medium distance*]
> Hello. [*semiformal*]
> Hi. [*informal—least distance*]
> What's happening? [*informal—slang*]

Each of these greetings is appropriate in some situations, inappropriate in others.

Whichever tone you decide on, be consistent throughout your document.

INCONSISTENT TONE	My office isn't fit for a pig [*too informal*]: it is ungraciously unattractive [*too formal*].
REVISED	My office is so shabby that it's an awful place to work.

In general, lean toward an informal tone without using slang.

Besides setting the distance between writer and reader, your tone implies your *attitude* toward the subject *and* the reader.

Tone announces attitude

> We dine at seven.
> Dinner is at seven.

> Let's eat at seven.
> Let's chow down at seven.
> Let's strap on the feedbag at seven.
> Let's pig out at seven.

The words you choose tell readers a great deal about where you stand. For instance, in announcing a meeting to review your employee's job evaluation, would you invite this person to *discuss* the evaluation, *talk it over*, *have a chat*, or *chew the fat*? Decide how casual or serious your attitude should be.

Guidelines for Deciding about Tone

- **Use a formal or semiformal tone** in writing for superiors, professionals, or academics (depending on what you think the reader expects).
- **Use a semiformal or informal tone** in writing for colleagues and subordinates (depending on how close you feel to your reader).
- **Use an informal tone** when you want your writing to be conversational, or when you want it to sound like a person talking.
- **Avoid a negative tone** when conveying unpleasant information.
- **Above all, find out what tone your particular readers prefer.** When in doubt, do not be too casual!

Consider Using an Occasional Contraction

Unless you have reason to be formal, use (but *do not* overuse) contractions. Balance an *I am* with an *I'm*, a *you are* with a *you're*, and an *it is* with an *it's*. Keep in mind that contractions rarely are acceptable in formal business writing.

NOTE　　*The contracted version often sounds less emphatic than the two-word version—for example, "**Don't** handle this material without protective clothing" versus "**Do not** handle this material without protective clothing." If your message requires emphasis, do not use a contraction.*

Address Readers Directly

Use the personal pronouns *you* and *your* to connect with readers. Readers often relate better to something addressed to them directly.

IMPERSONAL TONE　　Students at this college will find the faculty always willing to help.

PERSONAL TONE　　As a student at this college, **you** will find the faculty always willing to help.

NOTE   *Use **you** and **your** only in letters, memos, instructions, and other documents intended to correspond directly with a reader. Using **you** and **your** in situations that call for first or third person, like description or narration, you might end up writing something awkward like this: "When you are in northern Ontario, you can see wilderness and lakes everywhere around you."*

EXERCISE 16

The sentences below suffer from pretentious language, unclear expression of attitude, missing contractions, or indirect address. Adjust the tone.

  a. Further interviews are a necessity to our ascertaining the most viable candidate.
  b. You are all invited to the company picnic!
  c. Employees must submit travel vouchers by May 1.
  d. Persons taking this test should use the HELP option whenever they need it.
  e. I am not unappreciative of your help.
  f. My disapproval is far more than negligible.

Use *I* and *We* When Appropriate

Instead of disappearing behind your writing, use *I* or *We* when referring to yourself or your organization.

Distant	The writer would like a refund.
Revised	**I** would like a refund.

A message becomes doubly impersonal when both writer and reader disappear.

Impersonal	The requested report will be sent next week.
Personal	**We** will send the report **you** requested next week.

Prefer the Active Voice

Because the active voice is more direct and economical than the passive voice, it generally creates a less formal tone. (Review pages 219–22 for use of active and passive voice.)

EXERCISE 17

These sentences have too few *I* or *We* constructions or too many passive constructions. Adjust the tone.

  a. Payment will be made as soon as an itemized bill is received.
  b. You will be notified.
  c. Your help is appreciated.
  d. Our reply to your bid will be sent next week.
  e. Your request will be given our consideration.
  f. This writer would like to be considered for your opening.

Emphasize the Positive

Whenever you offer advice, suggestions, or recommendations, try to emphasize benefits rather than flaws. (For more on delivering bad news, see page 372.)

CRITICAL TONE	Because of your division's lagging productivity, a management review may be needed.
ENCOURAGING TONE	A management review might help boost productivity in your division.

Avoid an Overly Informal Tone

How tone can be too informal

Achieving a conversational tone does not mean writing in the same way we would speak to friends at the local burger joint. *Substandard usage* ("He ain't got none," "I seen it today") is unacceptable in workplace writing; and so is *slang* ("hurling," "bogus," "bummed"). *Profanity* ("This idea sucks," "pissed off," "What the hell") not only conveys contempt for the audience but also triggers contempt for the person using it. *Colloquialisms* ("O.K.," "a lot," "snooze") tend to appear more in speaking than in writing.

How tone can offend

Tone is offensive when it violates the reader's expectations: when it seems disrespectful, tasteless, distant and aloof, too "chummy," casual, or otherwise inappropriate for the topic, the reader, and the situation.

When to use an academic tone

A formal or academic tone is appropriate in countless writing situations: a research paper, a job application, a report for the company president. In a history essay, for example, you would not refer to George Washington and Abraham Lincoln as "those dudes, George and Abe." Whenever you begin with rough drafting or brainstorming, your tone might be overly informal and is likely to require some adjustment during subsequent drafts.

bias   Avoid Personal Bias

If people expect an impartial report, try to keep your own biases out of it. Imagine that you have been assigned to investigate the causes of an employee-management confrontation at your company's Omaha branch. Your initial report, written for the New York central office, is intended simply to describe what happened. Here is how an unbiased description might begin:

A factual account

At 9:00 a.m. on Tuesday, January 21, eighty female employees set up picket lines around the executive offices of our Omaha branch, bringing business to a halt. The group issued a formal protest, claiming that their working conditions were repressive, their salary scale unfair, and their promotional opportunities limited.

Note the absence of implied judgments; the facts are presented objectively. A biased version of events, from a protestor's point of view, might begin this way:

A biased version

> Last Tuesday, sisters struck another blow against male supremacy when eighty women employees paralyzed the company's repressive and sexist administration for more than six hours. The timely and articulate protest was aimed against degrading working conditions, unfair salary scales, and lack of promotional opportunities for women.

Judgmental words (*male supremacy, repressive, degrading, paralyzed, articulate*) inject the writer's attitude about the event, even though it isn't called for. In contrast to this bias, the following version patronizingly defends the status quo:

A biased version

> Our Omaha branch was the scene of an amusing battle of the sexes last Tuesday, when a group of irate feminists, eighty strong, set up picket lines for six hours at the company's executive offices. The protest was lodged against alleged inequities in hiring, wages, working conditions, and promotion for women in our company.

(For more on how framing of the facts can influence reader opinions, see page 155.)

NOTE *Being unbiased doesn't mean remaining "neutral" about something you know to be wrong or dangerous (Kremers 59). If, for instance, you conclude that the Omaha protest was clearly justified, say so.*

 ## Avoid Sexist Usage

Language that makes unwarranted assumptions will offend readers. Women, for example, who receive a letter addressed to *Dear Sir* will probably throw the letter out before reading it. Avoid sexist usage such as referring to doctors, lawyers, and other professionals as *he* or *him*, while referring to nurses, secretaries, and homemakers as *she* or *her*. Words such as *foreman* or *fireman* automatically exclude women; terms such as *supervisor* or *firefighter* are far more inclusive.

> ## Guidelines for Nonsexist Usage
>
> - **Use neutral expressions** such as **chair** or **chairperson** rather than **chairman** and **postal worker** rather than **postman**.
> - **Rephrase to eliminate the pronoun,** but only if you can do so without altering your original meaning. For instance, change *A writer will succeed if **he** revises* to *A writer who revises succeeds.*
> - **Use plural forms** such as *Writers will succeed if **they** revise* (but *not A writer will succeed if **they** revise*). For pronoun-referent agreement, see page 675.
> - **Use occasional pairings** (*him or her, she or he, his or hers*): *A writer will succeed if **she or he** revises.*

(continues)

Guidelines (continued)

- **Drop condescending diminutive endings** such as *-ess* and *-ette* used to denote females (*poetess, drum majorette, actress*).

- **Use *Ms.* instead of *Mrs.* or *Miss,*** unless you know that person prefers a traditional title. Or omit titles: *Roger Smith and Jane Kelly; Smith and Kelly.*

- In quoting sources that ignore nonsexist standards, consider these options:
  a.   Insert [*sic*] ("thus" or "so") following the first instance of sexist usage;
  b.   use ellipses (see page 689) to omit sexist phrasing; or
  c.   paraphrase instead of quoting.

Avoid Offensive Usage of All Types

Usable communication should respect all people regardless of cultural, racial, ethnic, or national background; sexual and religious orientation; age or physical condition. References to individuals and groups should be as neutral as possible. Avoid any expression that is condescending or judgmental or that might violate a reader's sense of appropriateness.

EXERCISE 18

The sentences below suffer from negative emphasis, excessive informality, biased expressions, or offensive usage. Adjust the tone.

a.   If you want your workers to like you, show sensitivity to their needs.
b.   By not hesitating to act, you prevented my death.
c.   The union has won its struggle for a decent wage.
d.   The group's spokesman demanded salary increases.
e.   Each employee should submit his vacation preferences this week.
f.   While the girls played football, the men waved pom-poms.
g.   Aggressive management of this risky project will help you avoid failure.
h.   The explosion left me blind as a bat for nearly an hour.
i.   This dude would be an excellent employee if only he could learn to chill out.

Guidelines for Inoffensive Usage

- **Be as specific as possible,** when referring to a particular culture, about that culture's identity. Instead of *Latin American* or *Asian* or *Hispanic* prefer *Cuban American* or *Korean* or *Nicaraguan.* Use *United States* or *U.S.*, rather than *American.*

- **Avoid potentially judgmental expressions:** Instead of *third-world* or *undeveloped nations* or the *Far East*, prefer *developing* or *newly industrialized nations* or *East Asia.* Instead of *nonwhites,* refer to *people of color.*

- **Use person-first language** when referring to people with disabilities. Avoid terms that could be considered either pitying or overly euphemistic, such as *victim* or *differently abled*. Focus on the individual instead of the disability: *person who is blind* rather than *blind person*, or *person who has lost an arm* rather than *amputee*.
- **Avoid expressions that demean** those who have medical conditions: *retard, mental midget, insane idea, lame excuse, the blind leading the blind, able-bodied workers,* and so on.
- **Use age-appropriate designations** for both genders: *girl* or *boy* for people age fourteen or under; *young person, young adult, young man,* or *young woman* for those of high-school age; and *woman* or *man* for those of college age. (*Teenager* or *juvenile* carries certain negative connotations.) Instead of *the elderly*, prefer *older persons.*

Source: Adapted from the *Publication Manual of the American Psychological Association,* and Schwartz, Marilyn.

 Politically correct or necessary sensitivity?

EXERCISE 19

Find examples of overly euphemistic language (such as "chronologically challenged") or of insensitive language. Discuss examples in class.

 Cross-cultural and global communication

Considering the Cultural Context

The style guidelines in this chapter apply specifically to standard English in North America. But technical communication is a global process: Practices and preferences differ widely. For example, some cultures prefer long sentences and elaborate language, to convey an idea's full complexity. Others value expressions of respect, politeness, praise, and gratitude more than clarity or directness (Hein 125–26; Mackin 349–50).

Writing in non-English languages tends to be more formal than in English, and some languages rely heavily on passive voice (Weymouth 144). French readers, for example, may prefer an elaborate style that reflects sophisticated and complex modes of thinking. In contrast, our "plain English," conversational style might connote simplemindedness, disrespect, or incompetence (Thrush 277).

Documents to be translated into other languages pose special challenges: For example, in translation or in a different cultural context, some words have insulting or negative connotations, as when "male" and "female," in certain cultures, refer only to animals (Coe, "Writing for Other Cultures" 17). Notable translation disasters include the Chevrolet *Nova*—*no va* means "doesn't go" in Spanish—and the Finnish beer *Koff* for an English-speaking market (Gesteland 20; Victor 44). Many U.S. idioms (*breaking the bank, cutthroat competition, sticking your neck out*) and cultural references (*the crash of '29, Beantown*) make no sense outside of U.S. culture (Coe "Writing" 17–19). Slang (*bogus, fat city*) and colloquialisms (*You bet, Gotcha*) can seem too informal and crude.

In short, offensive writing (including inappropriate humor) can alienate audiences—with regard to you *and* your culture (Sturges 32).

Legal and Ethical Implications of Word Choice

 Ethics in technical communication

Chapter 5 (page 85) discusses how workplace writing is regulated by laws against libel, deceptive advertising, and defective information. One common denominator among these violations is poor word choice. We are each accountable for the words we use—intentionally or not—in framing the audience's perception and understanding. The following communication situations require particular care in word choice.

Situations in which word choice has ethical or legal consequences

- **Assessing risk.** Is the investment you are advocating "a sure thing" or merely "a good bet," or even "risky"? Are you announcing a "caution," a "warning," or a "danger"? Should methane levels in mineshaft #3 "be evaluated" or do "they pose a definite explosion risk"? Never downplay risks.
- **Offering a service or product.** Are you proposing to "study the problem," to "explore solutions to the problem," or to "eliminate the problem"? Do you "stand behind" your product or do you "guarantee" it? Never promise more than you can deliver.
- **Giving instructions.** Before inserting the widget between the grinder blades, should I "switch off the grinder" or "disconnect the grinder from its power source" or "trip the circuit breaker," or do all three? Always triple-check the clarity of your instructions.
- **Comparing your product with competing products.** Instead of referring to a competitor's product as "inferior," "second-rate," or "substandard," talk about your own "first-rate product" that "exceeds (or meets) standards." Never run down the competition.
- **Evaluating an employee** (T. Clark, "Teaching Students" 75–76). In a personnel evaluation, don't refer to the employee as a "troublemaker" or "unprofessional," or as "too abrasive," "too uncooperative," "incompetent," or "too old" for the job. Focus on the specific requirements of this job, and offer *factual* instances in which these requirements, or standards, have been violated: "Our monitoring software recorded five visits by this employee to X-rated Web sites during working hours." Or "This employee arrives late for work on average twice weekly, has failed to complete assigned projects on three occasions, and has difficulty working with others." Instead of expressing personal judgments,

offer the facts. Be sure everyone involved knows exactly what the standards are well beforehand. Otherwise, you risk violating federal laws against discrimination and libel (damaging someone's reputation) and facing lawsuits.

Using Automated Editing Tools Effectively

Many of the strategies in this chapter could be executed rapidly with word-processing software. By using the *global search and replace function,* you can command the computer to search for ambiguous pronoun references, overuse of passive voice, *to be* verbs, *There* and *It* sentence openers, negative constructions, clutter words, needless prefaces and qualifiers, overly technical language, jargon, sexist language, and so on. With an online dictionary or thesaurus, you can check definitions or see a list of synonyms for a word you have written. But these editing aids can be extremely imprecise.

Some people mistakenly assume that the computer can solve all grammar and spelling problems. This is simply not true. Both *its* and *it's* are spelled correctly, but only one of them means "it is". The same is true for *their* and *there* (*their* is a possessive pronoun, as in "their books," while *there* is an adverb, as in "There is my dog"). Spell checkers are great for finding words that are spelled incorrectly, but don't count on them to find words that are *used* incorrectly or for typos that create the wrong word but are correctly spelled words on their own, such as *howl* instead of *how.* Grammar checkers are also fine tools to help you locate possible problems, but do not rely on what the software tells you. For example, not every sentence that the grammar checker flags as "long" should be shortened. Use these tools wisely and with common sense. Also, ask someone to proofread your document. Some companies have full-time technical editors who are happy to look over your writing.

The limits of automation

NOTE   *None of the rules offered in this chapter applies universally. Ultimately, your own sensitivity to meaning, emphasis, and tone—the human contact—will determine the effectiveness of your writing style.*

☑ Checklist: Style

(Numbers in parentheses refer to the first page of the relevant section.)

Clarity

☐ Does each pronoun clearly refer to the noun it replaces? (217)

☐ Is each modifier close enough to the word(s) it explains? (217)

☐ Do most sentences begin with the familiar information and end with the new? (218)

☐ Are sentences in active rather than passive voice, unless the agent is immaterial? (219)

☐ Does each sentence provide only as much information as readers can easily process? (222)

Conciseness

☐ Is the piece free of wordiness, redundancy, or needless repetition? (223)

☐ Is it free of needless sentence openers and prefaces? (224)

☐ Have weak verbs been traded for verbs that express a definite action? (225)

☐ Have prepositions been trimmed and nominalizations restored to their verb forms? (226)

☐ Have negative constructions been converted to positive as needed? (227)

☐ Is the piece free of clutter words and needless qualifiers? (228)

Fluency

☐ Are related ideas subordinated or coordinated and combined appropriately? (229)

☐ Are sentences varied in construction and length? (231)

☐ Does an idea that should stand alone for emphasis get a sentence of its own? (231)

☐ Are short sentences used for special emphasis? (232)

Word Choice

☐ Is the wording simple, familiar, unambiguous, and free of useless jargon? (232)

☐ Is each acronym spelled out upon first use? (234)

☐ Is the piece free of triteness, misleading euphemisms, and overstatement? (234)

☐ Is the wording precise, with commonly confused words used correctly? (236)

☐ Are general or abstract terms clarified by more specific or concrete ones? (238)

Tone

☐ Is the tone appropriate and consistent for the situation and audience? (238)

☐ Is the level of formality what the intended audience would expect? (240)

☐ Is the piece free of implied bias or offensive language? (242)

☐ Does the piece display sensitivity to cultural differences? (245)?

☐ Is the word choice ethically and legally acceptable? (246)

ON THE JOB... Revising a Document

■ *"Deadlines affect how we approach the writing process. With plenty of time, we can afford the luxury of the whole process: careful decisions about audience, purpose, content, organization, and style—and plenty of revisions. At times, we have to take shortcuts."*

—Blair Cordasco,
Training Specialist
for an international bank

■ *"For short pieces, I outline in my head, draft, and revise. On my first draft of a short piece, I spend 40 to 50 percent of the time on the first one or two paragraphs and crank out the rest quickly. Then I revise two or three times, and tinker with the mechanics and format right up until printing. I usually don't bother to make a printout until I'm pretty close to a final product."*

—Bill Trippe,
Communications Specialist
for a military contract company

■ *"I usually have to just send it out there due to the fast pace of working in a crisis setting. I can't even use white out . . . have to cross things out so that they can be seen, because they are legal documents."*

—Emma Bryant,
Social Worker

■ *"The amount of time and energy I spend on revision depends on the type of document. Internal emails and memos get at least one careful review before being distributed. Needless to say, all letters and other documents to outside readers get detailed attention, to make sure that what is being said is actually what was intended. There's the issue of contractual obligations here—and also the issue of liability, if someone, say, were to misinterpret a set of instructions and were injured as a result. Also there's the issue of customer relations: Most people want to transact with businesses that display "likability" on the interpersonal front. They're fed up with talking only to machines and recordings, and with having only the machines and recordings talk back; so, getting the style just right is always a priority."*

—Andy Wallin, Communications Manager
for a maker of power tools

■ *"Working in a newsroom means that the story has to get out, and get out ASAP. However, we have to take the time to verify that the facts are accurate and to make the whole story fit the allotted space on the page. Much of our editing therefore involves careful checking for precision and lots of editing for conciseness.*

—Carole Cain, Copy Editor
for a large, daily newspaper

Exercises *(See also brief exercises throughout this chapter.)*

1. Go to the *University of Victoria's Hypertext Writer's Guide* <http://web.uvic.ca/wguide/>. Use the Table of Contents page to locate the section on *Audience and Tone*. Locate one item of information about audience and tone (or voice) not covered in this chapter. Take careful notes for a brief discussion of this information in class. Attach a copy of the relevant Web page(s) to your written notes.

2. Using the Checklist for Style (page 248), revise the following selections. (*Hint*: use the example on page 216 as a model for revision.)

   a. A Letter to a local newspaper.
   In the absence of definitive studies regarding the optimum length of the school day, I can only state my personal opinion based upon observations made by me and upon teacher observations that have been conveyed to me. Considering the length of the present school day, it is my opinion that the day is excessive length-wise for most elementary pupils, certainly for almost all of the primary children.

   To find the answer to the problem requires consideration of two ways in which the problem may be viewed. One way focuses upon the needs of the children, while the other focuses upon logistics, transportation, scheduling, and other limits imposed by the educational system. If it is necessary to prioritize these two ideas, it would seem most reasonable to give the first consideration to the primary reason for the very existence of the system, i.e., to meet the educational needs of the children the system is trying to serve.

   b. Various memos to employees.
   We are presently awaiting an on-site inspection of the designated professional library location by corporate representatives relative to electrical adaptations necessary for the computer installation. Meanwhile, all staff members are asked to respect the off-limits designation of the aforementioned location, as requested, due to the liability insurance provisions in regard to the computer.

   The new phone system has proven to be particularly interruptive to the administration office secretaries. It is highly imperative that you take particular note to ensure beyond the shadow of a doubt that all calls are of a business nature as far as possible. We are on a message unit cost system which is probationary at best, and the number of phones in our offices is considerably greater than any of our immediate office neighbors have. N.B.: The internal problem has been particularly vexing with phones not being properly replaced in cradles, constituting an additional dimension to an already perplexing internal telephone system dilemma of the greatest magnitude.

   Parents in general want their sons and daughters attending classes on a day-in day-out basis, not, as some may choose, on a staggered basis. It is your responsibility to bring pressure to bear on the students to attend your class and it is also your responsibility to be accountable for not bringing this pressure to bear, if such a situation in point of actual fact exists. In short, if a student can be excessively absent from your class without a reason justifiable to both you and the school administration in regard to this matter and this same student simply passes the course on the basis of having made up the work, then I submit that possibly, in such situations, it could be considered much wiser and of greater economy for the Town of Cobalt to offer a correspondence course in circumstances of this nature since the presence of the teacher and what he or she has to offer in the classroom evidently means little or nothing to both the student and/or the teacher involved.

Collaborative Project

Use a paper written for the course. In small groups, look for problems of clarity, conciseness, and fluency. Mark any grammatical errors. Then ask students with different word-processing programs to run the paper through the grammar and style check programs available to them. Compare the changes your group made with those suggested by the various programs. If the computer suggests changes that appear ungrammatical or incorrect, consult a good handbook for confirmation.

In your group, prepare a list of the advantages and disadvantages of the grammar and style checker programs. Note any topics covered in this chapter that your software programs miss. Are these programs always reliable? What conclusions can you draw from this exercise?

CHAPTER 14

Designing Visual Information

Why Visuals Matter

When to Use Visuals

Types of Visuals to Consider

How to Select Visuals

Tables

Graphs

   Guidelines for Displaying a Bar Graph

   Guidelines for Displaying a Line Graph

Charts

   Guidelines for Displaying a Pie Chart

Graphic Illustrations

Photographs

   Guidelines for Using Photographs

Software and Downloadable Images

Using Color

   Guidelines for Incorporating Color

Ethical Considerations

Cultural Considerations

   Guidelines for Fitting Visuals with Text

   Checklist: Usability of Visuals

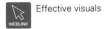 Effective visuals

In printed or online documents, in oral presentations or multimedia programs, visuals are a staple of communication today. Because they focus and organize information, visuals make the data easier to interpret and remember. Because they offer powerful new ways of looking at data, visuals reveal meanings that might otherwise remain buried in lists of facts and figures.

Why Visuals Matter

Our audiences
expect visuals

Readers want more than just raw information; they want the information processed for their understanding. People want to understand the message at a glance. Visuals help us answer many of the questions posed by readers as they process information:

Typical audience
questions in
processing
information

- Which information is most important?
- Where, exactly, should I focus?
- What do these numbers mean?
- What should I be thinking or doing?
- What should I remember about this?
- What does it look like?
- How is it organized?
- How is it done?
- How does it work?

When people look at a visual pattern, such as a graph, they see it as one large pattern—the Big Picture that conveys information quickly and efficiently. For instance, the line graph below has no verbal information. The axes are not labeled, nor is the topic identified. But one quick glance, without the help of any words or numbers, tells you that the trend, after a period of gradual rise, has risen sharply. The graph conveys information in a way plain text never could.

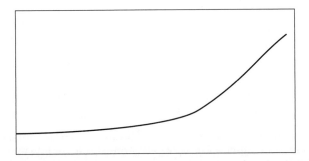

It certainly would be hard for audiences to visualize the trend depicted in the previous graph by just reading the long list of numbers in the following passage:

Technical data in prose form can be hard to interpret

> The time required for global population to grow from 5 to 6 billion was shorter than the interval between any of the previous billions. It took just 12 years for this to occur, just slightly less than the 13 years between the fourth and fifth billion, but much less time than the 118 years between the first and second billion. . . .

When we add all this information to the original graph, as in Figure 14.1, the numbers become much easier to comprehend and compare.

NOTE   *Visuals enhance—but they do not replace—essential discussion in your verbal text. In your discussion refer to the visual by number ("see Figure 1") and explain what to look for and what it means. For more on introducing and interpreting visuals in a document, see page 292.*

When to Use Visuals

Use visuals in situations like these

In general, you should use visuals whenever they make your point more clearly than text or when they enhance your text. Use visuals to clarify and enhance your discussion, not just to decorate your document. Use visuals to direct the audience's focus or help them remember something. There may be organizational reasons for using visuals; for example, some companies may always expect a chart or graph as part of their annual report. Certain industries, such as the financial sector, routinely use graphs and charts (such as the graph of the daily Dow Jones Industrial Average).

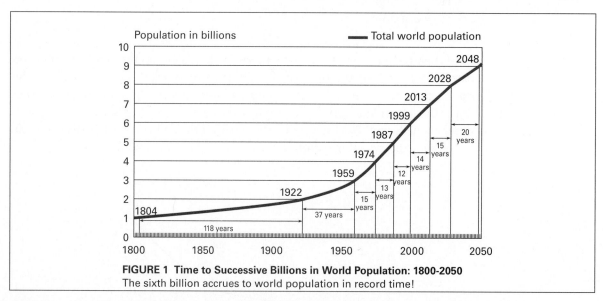

FIGURE 1 Time to Successive Billions in World Population: 1800-2050
The sixth billion accrues to world population in record time!

FIGURE 14.1 **A Graph that Conveys the Big Picture** This graph includes features essential to all types of visuals: (a) figure number for easy reference, (b) title that describes what readers are seeing, (c) caption that explains a key point, and (d) data source citation. More type-specific design elements are discussed later in this chapter.
Source: United Nations (1995b); U.S. Census Bureau, International Programs Center, International Database and Unpublished Tables.

Types of Visuals to Consider

The following overview sorts visual displays into four categories: tables, graphs, charts, and graphic illustrations. Common examples within each category are shown in the table below. Note how each type of visual offers a unique way of seeing, a different perspective for understanding and processing the information.

Types of Visuals and Their Uses

TABLES display organized data across columns and rows for easy comparison.

Numerical tables
Use to compare exact numerical values.

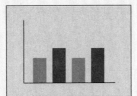

Prose tables
Use to organize verbal information.

GRAPHS translate numbers into shapes, shades, and patterns.

Bar graphs
Use to show comparisons.

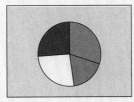

Line graphs
Use to show a trend over time, cost, or other variables.

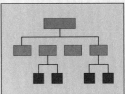

CHARTS depict relationships via geometric, arrows, lines, and other design elements.

Pie charts
Use to relate parts or percentages to the whole.

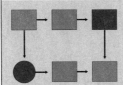

Organization charts
Use to show the hierarchy in a company.

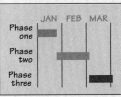

Flowcharts
Use to trace the steps (or decisions) in a procedure or process.

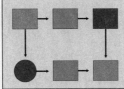

Gantt charts
Use to depict how the phases of a project relate.

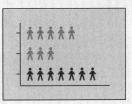

Tree charts
Use to show how the parts of an idea or concept relate.

Pictograms
Use icons or other graphic devices that represent the displayed items.

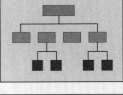

GRAPHIC ILLUSTRATIONS rely on pictures rather than on data or words.
Continued

Representational diagrams

Use to present a realistic but simplified view.

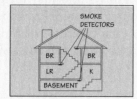

Cutaway diagrams

Use to show what is inside of a device or to help explain how a device works.

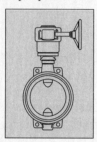

Maps

Use to help users visualize the position, location, and interrelationship of various data.

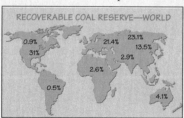

Exploded diagrams

Use to explain how an item is put together or how a user should assemble a product.

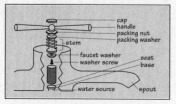

Symbols and icons

Use to make concepts understandable to broad audiences, including international audiences, children, and people who may have difficulty reading.

Schematic diagrams

Use to present the conceptual elements of a process or system—in depicting *function* instead of appearance.

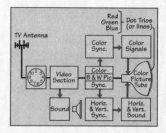

Photographs

Use to show exactly what something looks like.

Visualization

Use to create images out of highly abstract mathematical data.

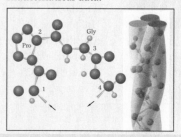

How to Select Visuals

To select the most effective display, answer these questions:

- **What is my purpose?**
  - To convey facts and figures alone, a table may be the best choice. But if I want my audience to draw conclusions from that data, I may want to use a graph or chart to show comparisons.
  - To show parts of a mechanism, I probably want to use an exploded or cutaway diagram, perhaps together with a labeled photograph.
  - To give directions, I may want to use a diagram.
  - To show relationships, my best choice may be a flow chart or graph.

- **Who is my audience?**
  - Expert audiences tend to prefer numerical tables, flowcharts, schematics, and complex graphs or diagrams that they can interpret for themselves.
  - General audiences tend to prefer basic tables, graphs, diagrams, and other visuals that direct their focus and interpret key points extracted from the data.
  - Cultural differences may come into play when selecting appropriate visuals.

- **What form of information will best achieve my purpose for this audience?**
  - Is my message best conveyed by numbers, shapes, words, pictures, symbols?
  - Will my audience most readily understand pictures or words? Line drawings or photographs? Symbols or numbers?

Although several alternatives might work, one particular type of visual (or a combination) usually is superior. The best option, however, may not be available. Your audience or organization may express its own preferences, or choices may be limited by lack of equipment (software, scanners, digitizers), insufficient personnel (graphic designers, technical illustrators), or budget. Regardless of the limitations, your basic task is to enable the audience to interpret the visual correctly.

    Although visual communication has global appeal, certain displays can be inappropriate in certain cultures. For more on cultural considerations in selecting visuals, see page 290.

Tables

A table is a powerful way to display dense textual information such as specifications or comparisons. Numerical tables such as Table 14.1 present *quantitative information* (data that can be measured). Prose tables present *qualitative information* (prose descriptions, explanations, or instructions). Table 14.2 combines numerical data, probability estimates, comparisons, and instructions.

Organizes data in columns and rows, for easy comparison

Death Rates for Heart Disease and Cancer 1970–2006				
	Number of Deaths (per 100,000)			
	Heart Disease		Cancer	
Year	Male	Female	Male	Female
1970	419	309	248	163
1980	369	305	272	167
1990	298	282	280	176
2000	256	260	257	206
2006	235	236	233	161
% change, 1970–2006	−43.9	−23.6	−6.0	−1.2

A caption explaining the numerical relationships

Both male and female death rates from heart disease decreased between 1970 to 2006, but males had nearly twice the rate of decrease. After increasing between 1970 and 1990, cancer death rates for both groups have decreased to slightly below their 1970 levels.

TABLE 14.1 Data Displayed in a Table Organizes data into columns and rows for easy comparison.

Source: Adapted from *Statistical Abstract of the United States: 2007 (126th ed.).* Washington: GPO. Tables 113, 115.

Displays numerical and verbal information

Radon Risk if You Smoke			
Radon level	If 1,000 people who smoked were exposed to this level over a lifetime . . .	The risk of cancer from radon exposure compares to . . .	WHAT TO DO: Stop smoking and . . .
20 pCi/L[a]	About 135 people could get lung cancer	←100 times the risk of drowning	Fix your home
10 pCi/L	About 71 people could get lung cancer	←100 times the risk of dying in a home fire	Fix your home
8 pCi/L	About 57 people could get lung cancer		Fix your home
4 pCi/L	About 29 people could get lung cancer	←100 times the risk of dying in an airplane crash	Fix your home
2 pCi/L	About 15 people could get lung cancer	←2 times the risk of dying in a car crash	Consider fixing between 2 and 4 pCi/L
1.3 pCi/L	About 9 people could get lung cancer	(Average indoor radon level)	(Reducing radon levels below 2 pCi/L is difficult)
0.4 pCi/L	About 3 people could get lung cancer	(Average outdoor radon level)	

Note: If you are a former smoker, your risk may be lower.
[a]picocuries per liter

TABLE 14.2 A Prose Table Displays numerical and verbal information.

Source: Home Buyer's and Seller's Guide to Radon. Washington: GPO, 1993.

NOTE   *Including a caption with your visual enables you to analyze or interpret the trends or key points you want readers to recognize (as in Table 14.1).*

Generating charts in Microsoft Excel

No table should be overly complex for its audience. Table 14.3 is hard for nonspecialists to interpret because it presents too much information at once. We can see how an unethical writer might use a complex table to bury numbers that are questionable or embarrassing (Williams 12). For laypersons, use fewer tables and keep them as simple as possible.

Can cause information overload for nontechnical audiences

Toxic Chemical Releases by Industry: 2003

[In millions of pounds (4,438.7 represents 4,438,700,000), except as indicated.]

Industry	1987 SIC[1] code	Total on- and off-site releases	On-site release			Off-site releases/ transfers to disposal
			Total[2]	Point source air emissions	Surface water discharges	
Total[3]	(X)	**4,438.7**	**3,920.7**	**1,381.3**	**222.6**	**518.0**
Metal mining	10	1,245.7	1,244.7	1.8	0.7	1.0
Coal mining	12	12.9	12.9	0.1	0.2	-
Food and kindred products	20	153.2	145.8	35.1	83.1	7.3
Tobacco products	21	3.2	2.8	2.4	0.1	0.4
Textile mill products	22	7.4	6.5	4.8	0.3	0.9
Apparel and other textile products	23	0.7	0.5	0.4	-	0.2
Lumber and wood products	24	33.0	31.0	27.0	0.1	2.0
Furniture and fixtures	25	6.2	6.1	5.4	0.0	0.1
Paper and allied products	26	215.0	209.6	146.2	18.7	5.3
Printing and publishing	27	15.0	14.7	7.4	-	0.3
Chemical and allied products	28	544.7	500.3	168.6	44.5	44.4
Petroleum and coal products	29	75.0	71.9	34.6	17.1	3.1
Rubber and misc. plastic products	30	75.3	65.8	51.3	0.1	9.5
Leather and leather products	31	2.1	1.0	0.7	0.0	1.1
Stone, clay, glass products	32	51.2	45.8	38.1	2.1	5.5
Primary metal industries	33	477.5	198.1	35.9	39.4	279.4
Fabricated metals products	34	58.6	38.8	23.7	2.3	19.8
Industrial machinery and equipment	35	14.3	10.7	4.1	0.2	3.6
Electronic, electric equipment	36	20.3	13.8	6.5	3.6	6.4
Transportation equipment	37	74.8	63.5	51.1	0.2	11.2
Instruments and related products	38	8.7	7.9	5.1	1.0	0.8
Miscellaneous	39	7.1	4.9	3.9	0.1	2.2

- Represents or rounds to zero. X Not applicable. [1]Standard Industrial Classification, see text, Section 12. Labor Force. [2]Includes on-site disposal to underground injection for Class I wells, Class II to V wells, other surface impoundments, land releases, and other releases, not shown separately. [3]Includes industries with no specific industry identified, not shown separately.

TABLE 14.3 A Complex Table

Source: Environmental Protection Agency, *Annual Toxics Release Inventory.*

Like all other parts of a document, visuals are designed with audience and purpose in mind (Journet 3). An accountant doing an audit might need a table listing exact amounts, whereas the average public stockholder reading an annual report would prefer the "big picture" in an easily grasped bar graph or pie chart (Van Pelt 1). Similarly, scientists might find the complexity of data shown in Table 14.3 perfectly appropriate, but a nonexpert audience (say, environmental groups) might prefer the clarity and simplicity of a chart.

Tables work well for displaying exact values, but often graphs or charts are easier to interpret. Geometric shapes (bars, curves, circles) are generally easier to remember than lists of numbers (Cochran et al. 25).

For specific information about creating tables, see How to Construct a Table on page 261.

NOTE   *Any visual other than a table is usually categorized as a figure, and so titled (Figure 1 Aerial View of the Panhandle Mine Site).*

Graphs

Graphs translate numbers into shapes, shades, and patterns. Graphs display, at a glance, the approximate values, the point being made about those values, and the relationship being emphasized. Graphs are especially useful for depicting comparisons, changes over time, patterns, or trends.

A graph's horizontal axis shows categories (the independent variables) to be compared, such as years within a period (1980, 1990, 2000). The vertical axis shows the range of values (the dependent variables) for comparing the categories, such as the number of deaths from heart failure in a given year. A dependent variable changes according to activity in the independent variable (say, a decrease in quantity over a set time, as in Figure 14.2).

Bar Graphs

Generally easy to understand, bar graphs show discrete comparisons, such as year-by-year or month-by-month. Each bar represents a specific quantity. You can use bar graphs to focus on one value or to compare values over time.

Simple Bar Graph.   A simple bar graph displays one trend or theme. The graph in Figure 14.2 shows one trend extracted from Table 14.1, male deaths from heart disease. If the audience needs exact numbers, you can record exact values above each bar.

Multiple-Bar Graph.   A bar graph can display two or three relationships simultaneously. Figure 14.3 contrasts two sets of data, to show comparative trends. Be sure to use a different pattern or color for each data set, and include a key (or *legend*) so that viewers will know which color or pattern corresponds with which data set.

HOW TO CONSTRUCT A TABLE

① **TABLE 14.4 ■ Federal Student Financial Assistance: 2002 – 2006**

STUB HEAD ② Number of Awards ③ (1000)[a]	COLUMN HEADS				
	2002	2003	2004	2005	2006[b]
Total	④ 55,525 ⑤	62,249	68,629	73,020	⑦ 76,604
⑥ Pell Grant	11,640	12,681	13,091	12,901	12,745
Opportunity Grant	1,033	1,064	975	985	⑧ (X)
Work-Study	1,097	1,106	1,194	1,184	1,172
Perkins Loan	1,460	1,638	1,263	1,137	1,135
Direct Student Loan	11,689	11,969	12,840	13,860	13,874
Family Educ. Loan	28,606	33,791	39,266	42,953	46,703

ROW HEADS

⑪

NOTE ⑨ [a]As of June 30. [b]Estimate. (X) Not available.

SRC ⑩ *Source:* U.S. Department of Education, Office of Postsecondary Education, unpublished data.
Statistical Abstract of the United States: 2007 (126th Edition). Washington: GPO. Table 279.

⑫

1. Number the table in its order of appearance and provide a title that describes exactly what is being measured.
2. Label stub, column, and row heads (*Number of Awards*; *2006*; *Pell Grant*) to orient readers.
3. Specify units of measurement or use familiar symbols and abbreviations ($, hr.). Define specialized symbols or abbreviations ($Å = angstrom$, $db = decibel$) in a footnote.
4. Compare data vertically (in columns) instead of horizontally (rows). Columns are easier to compare. Try to include row or column averages or totals, as reference points for comparing individual values.
5. Use horizontal rules to separate headings from data. In a complex table, use vertical rules to separate columns. In a simple table, use as few rules as clarity allows.
6. List items in a logical order (alphabetical, chronological, decreasing cost). Space listed items for easy comparison. Keep prose entries as brief as clarity allows.

7. Convert fractions to decimals. Align decimals and all numbers vertically. Keep decimal places for all numbers equal. Round insignificant decimals to whole numbers.
8. Use *x*, *NA*, or a dash to signify any omitted entry, and explain the omission in a footnote ("Not available," "Not applicable").
9. Use footnotes to explain entries, abbreviations, or omissions. Label footnotes with lowercase letters so readers do not confuse the notation with the numerical data.
10. Cite data sources beneath any footnotes. When adapting or reproducing a copyrighted table for a work to be published, obtain written permission.
11. If the table is too wide for the page, turn it 90 degrees with the left side facing page bottom. Or use two tables.
12. If the table exceeds one page, write "continues" at the bottom and begin the next page with the full title, "continued," and the original column headings.

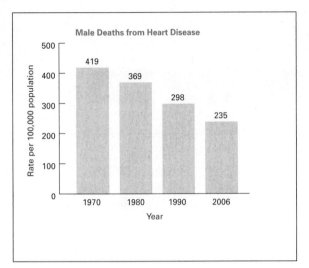

FIGURE 14.2 **A Simple Bar Graph** Shows a single relationship in the data

FIGURE 14.3 **A Multiple-Bar Graph** Shows two or more relationships

The more relationships you include, the more complex the graph becomes, so try to include no more than three on any one graph.

Horizontal-Bar Graph. Horizontal-bar graphs are good for displaying a large series of bars arranged in order of increasing or decreasing value, as in Figure 14.4. This format leaves room for labeling the categories horizontally (*Doctorate*, and so on).

Accommodates lengthy labels

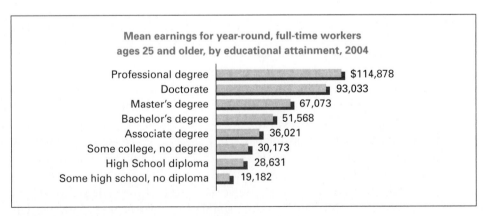

FIGURE 14.4 **A Horizontal-Bar Graph**
Source: Bureau of Labor Statistics.

Stacked-Bar Graph. Instead of displaying bars side-by-side, you can stack them. Stacked-bar graphs show how much each data set contributes to the whole.

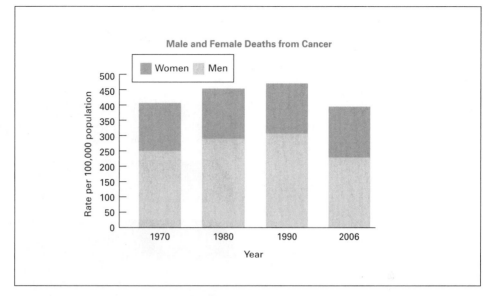

Compares the parts that make up each total

FIGURE 14.5 **A Stacked-Bar Graph**

Figure 14.5 displays other comparisons from Table 14.1. To avoid confusion, don't display more than four or five sets of data in a single bar.

100-Percent Bar Graph. A type of stacked-bar graph, the 100-percent bar graph shows the value of each part that makes up the 100-percent value, as in Figure 14.6. Like any bar graph, the 100-percent graph can have either horizontal or vertical bars.

Notice how bar graphs become harder to interpret as bars and patterns increase. For a general audience, the data from Figure 14.6 might be displayed in pie charts (page 269).

Deviation Bar Graph. Most graphs begin at a zero axis point, displaying only positive values. A deviation bar graph displays both positive and negative values, as in Figure 14.7. The vertical axis on the negative side of the zero baseline follows the same incremental division as the positive side.

3-D Bar Graph. Graphics software makes it easy to shade and rotate images for a three-dimensional view. The 3-D perspectives in Figure 14.8 engage our attention and visually emphasize the data.

NOTE   *Although 3-D graphs can enhance and dramatize a presentation, an overly complex graph can be misleading or hard to interpret. Use 3-D only when a two-dimensional version will not serve as well. Never sacrifice clarity and simplicity for the sake of visual effect.*

Compares
percentage values

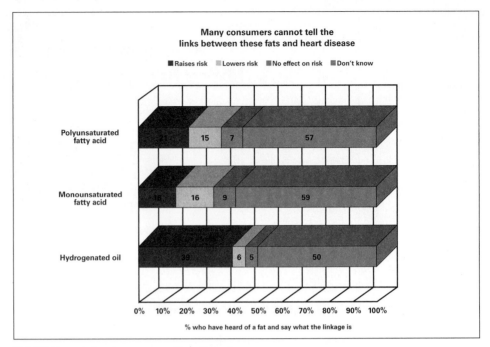

FIGURE 14.6 **A 100-percent Bar Graph**
Source: Center for Food Safety and Applied Nutrition, U.S. Food and Drug Administration.

Displays both
positive and
negative values

 Generating
charts in
Microsoft Excel

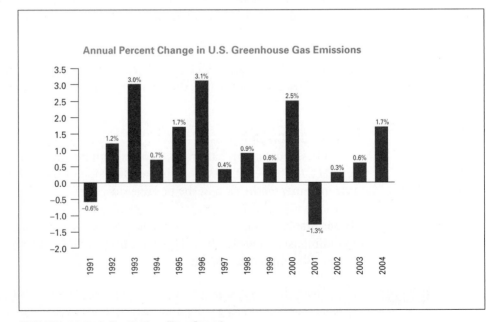

FIGURE 14.7 **A Deviation Bar Graph**
Source: U.S. Environmental Protection Agency.

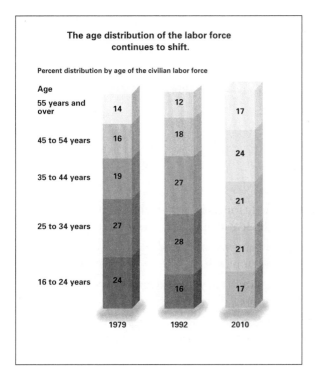

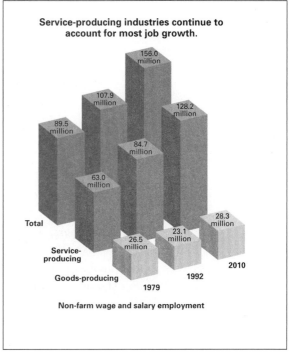

FIGURE 14.8 3-D Bar Graphs Adding a third axis creates the appearance of depth.
Source: Bureau of Labor Statistics.

Guidelines for Displaying a Bar Graph

- **Use a bar graph only to compare values that are noticeably different.** Small value differences will yield bars that look too similar to compare.

- **Keep the graph simple and easy to read.** Don't plot more than three types of bars in each cluster. Avoid needless visual details.

- **Number your scales in units familiar to the audience.** Units of 1 or multiples of 2, 5, or 10 are best (Lambert 45).

- **Label both scales** to show what is being measured or compared. If space allows, keep all labels horizontal for easier reading.

- **Label each bar or cluster of bars at its base.**

- **Use tick marks to show the points of division on your scale.** If the graph has many bars, extend the tick marks into *grid lines* to help readers relate bars to values. (Examples of tick marks and grid lines are shown on page 266.)

(continues)

Guidelines (continued)

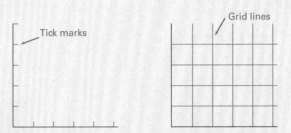

- **Make all bars the same width** (unless you are overlapping them).
- **Use a different pattern, color, or shade for each bar in a cluster in a multiple-bar graph.** Provide a key, or legend, identifying each pattern, color, or shade.
- **Use darker bars,** which are seen as larger, closer, and more important than lighter bars of the same size, to show emphasis *(Lambert 93).*
- **Refer to the graph by number ("Figure 1") in your text, and explain what the user should look for.** Or include a prose caption with the graph.
- **Cite data sources beneath the graph.** When adapting or reproducing a copyrighted graph for a work to be published, you must obtain written permission from the copyright holder.

Computer graphics programs, of course, automatically employ most of these design features. Anyone producing visuals, however, should know the conventions.

NOTE   *Failure to cite the creator of a visual or the information sources you used in making your own visual is plagiarism.*

Line Graphs

A line graph can accommodate many more data points than a bar graph (for example, a twelve-month trend, measured monthly). Line graphs help readers synthesize large bodies of information in which exact quantities don't need to be emphasized.

Simple Line Graph. A simple line graph, as in Figure 14.9, uses one line to plot time intervals (or categories) on the horizontal scale and values on the vertical scale.

Multiline Graph. A multiline graph displays several relationships simultaneously, as in Figure 14.10. Include a caption to explain the relationships readers are supposed to see and the interpretations they are supposed to make.

Displays one
relationship

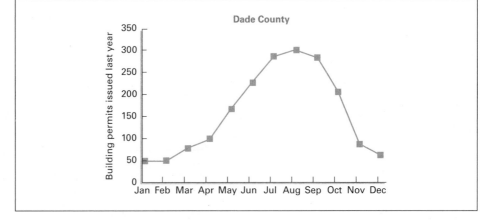

FIGURE 14.9 **A Simple Line Graph**

Displays multiple
relationships

A caption
explaining the
visual relationships

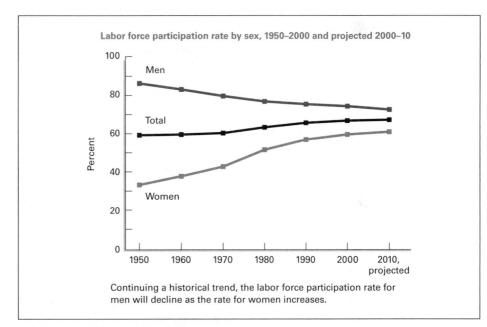

FIGURE 14.10 **A Multiline Graph**
Source: Bureau of Labor Statistics.

Deviation Line Graph.   Extend your vertical scale below the zero baseline to display positive and negative values in one graph, as in Figure 14.11. Mark values below the baseline in intervals parallel to those above it.

Band or Area Graph.   By shading in the area beneath the main plot lines, you can highlight specific information. Figure 14.12 is another version of the Figure 14.9 line graph.

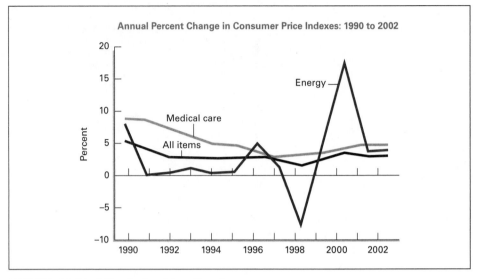

Displays both
negative and
positive values

FIGURE 14.11 **A Deviation Line Graph**

Source: Chart prepared by U.S. Bureau of the Census.

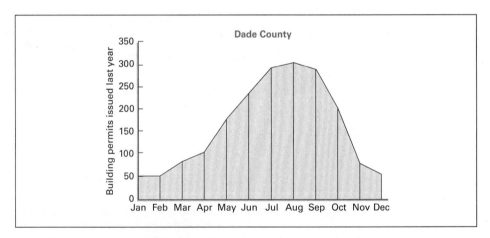

Shading adds
emphasis

FIGURE 14.12 **A Simple Band Graph**

Multiple Band Graph. The multiple bands in Figure 14.13 depict relationships among sums instead of the direct comparisons depicted in the Figure 14.10 multiline graph. Despite their visual appeal, multiple-band graphs are easy to misinterpret: In a multiline graph, each line depicts its own distance from the zero baseline. But in a multiple-*band* graph, the very top line depicts the *total* distance from the zero baseline, with each band below it being a part of that total. Always clarify these relationships for your audience.

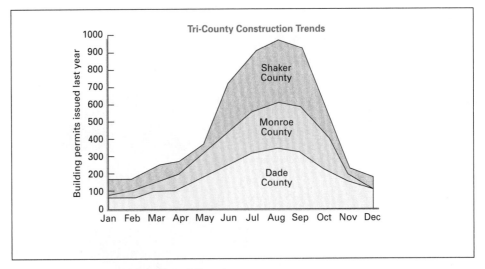

Each item is added to the one below it

FIGURE 14.13 A Multiple-Band Graph

Guidelines for Displaying a Line Graph

Follow the Guidelines for Displaying a Bar Graph (page 265), with these additions:

- **Display no more than three or four lines on one graph.**
- **Mark each individual data point used in plotting each line.**
- **Make each line visually distinct (using color, symbols, and so on).**
- **Label each line so users know what each one represents.**
- **Avoid grid lines that users could mistake for plotted lines.**

Charts

The terms *chart* and *graph* often are used interchangeably. Technically, a chart displays relationships (quantitative or cause-and-effect) that are not plotted on a coordinate system (x and y axes).

Pie Charts

Easy for almost anyone to understand, a pie chart displays the relationship of parts or percentages to the whole. Readers can compare the parts to each other as well as to the whole (to show how much was spent on what, how much income comes from which sources, and so on). Figure 14.14 shows a simple pie chart. Figure 14.15 is an exploded pie chart. Exploded pie charts help highlight various pieces of the pie.

Shows the relationships of parts or percentages to the whole

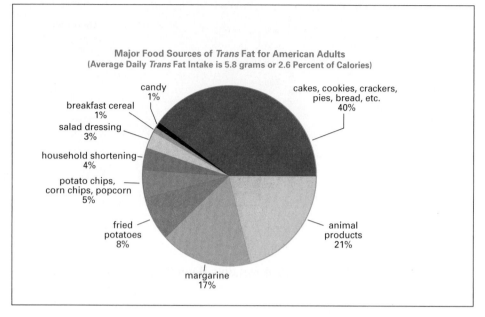

FIGURE 14.14 A Simple Pie Chart
Source: U.S. Food and Drug Administration.

Highlights various slices

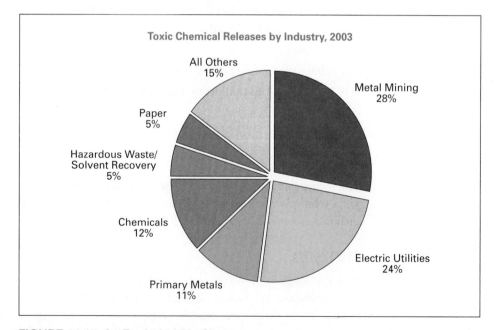

FIGURE 14.15 An Exploded Pie Chart
Source: U.S. Environmental Protection Agency. (See Table 14.3 for Data.)

- **Make sure the parts add up to 100 percent.**
- **Differentiate each slice clearly.** Use different colors or shades, or differentiate by "exploding" out various pie slices.
- **Include a key, or legend, to identify each slice.** Or you can label each slice directly.
- **Combine very small segments under the heading "Other."**
- **For easy reading, keep all labels horizontal.**

Organization Charts

An organization chart shows the hierarchy and relationships between different departments and other units in an organization, as in Figure 14.16.

Shows how different people or departments are ranked and related

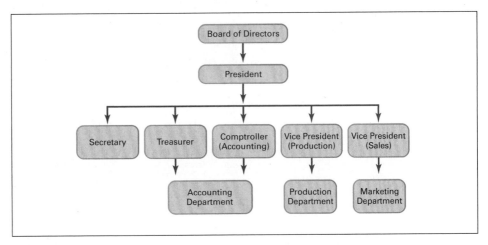

FIGURE 14.16 **An Organization Chart**

Flowcharts

A flowchart traces a procedure or process from beginning to end. Figure 14.17 traces the procedure for producing a textbook. (Another flowchart example appears on page 537.)

Tree Charts

Whereas flowcharts display the steps in a process, tree charts show how the parts of an idea or concept relate. Figure 14.18 displays part of an outline for this chapter so that users can better visualize relationships. The tree chart seems clearer and more interesting than the prose listing.

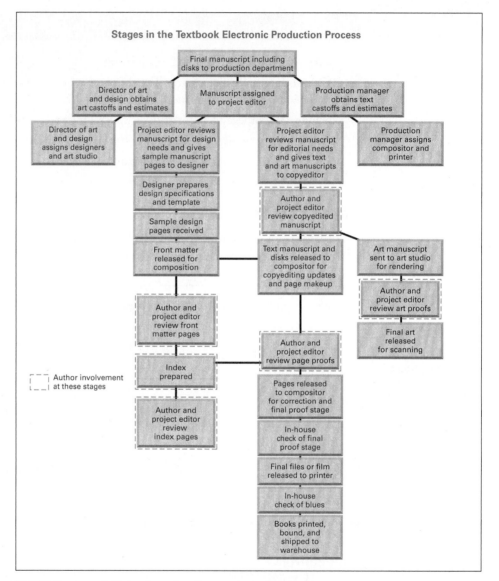

Depicts a sequence of events, activities, steps, or decisions

FIGURE 14.17 A Flowchart for Producing a Textbook
Source: Adapted from Harper & Row Author's Guide.

Gantt and PERT Charts

Named for engineer H. L. Gantt (1861–1919), a Gantt chart depicts how the parts of an idea or concept relate. A series of bars or lines (time lines) indicates start-up and completion dates for each phase or task in a project. Gantt charts are useful for planning a project (as in a proposal) and for tracking it (as in a progress report). The Gantt chart in Figure 14.19 illustrates the schedule for a manufacturing project.

Shows which items belong together and how they are connected

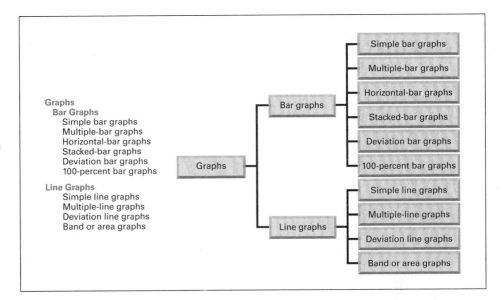

FIGURE 14.18 An Outline Converted to a Tree Chart

Depicts how the phases of a project relate to each other

 Project management

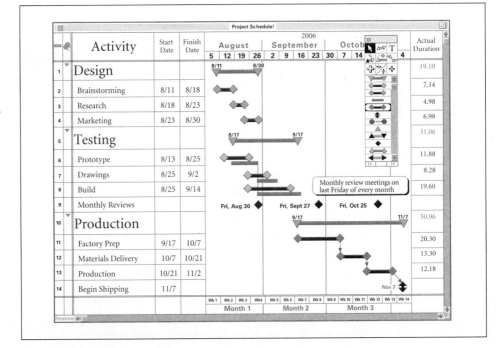

FIGURE 14.19 A Gantt Chart

Source: Chart created in *FastTrack Schedule*™. Reprinted by permission from AEC Software. Learn more about *FastTrack Schedule* at <www.aecsoftware.com>.

A PERT (Program Evaluation and Review Technique) chart uses geometric shapes and weighted arrows to outline a project's main activities and events (Figure 14.20). Both types of charts can be created with project management software such as *Microsoft Project*.

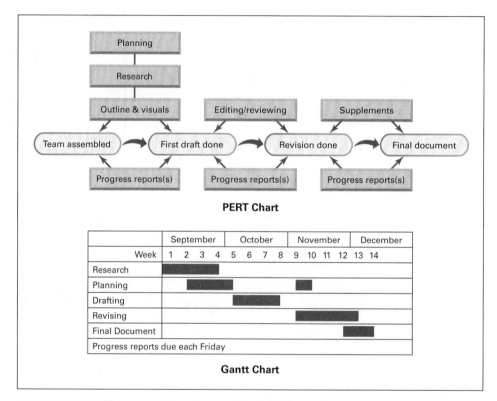

FIGURE 14.20 **Charts for Planning and Scheduling a Project** This PERT chart maps out the key activities (rectangles) and milestones (ovals) for a major technical report to be produced by a collaborative team. Heavy arrows indicate the *critical path* (straightest line) through the project. The Gantt chart specifies beginning and ending dates for each project phase and shows overlapping phases as well. Note that these are simplified versions; your own charts may need to include additional activities such as "updating," "usability testing," and "legal review."

Pictograms

Pictograms are something of a cross between a bar graph and a chart. Like line graphs, pictograms display numerical data, often by plotting it across x and y axes. But like a chart, pictograms use icons, symbols, or other graphic devices rather than simple lines or bars. In Figure 14.21 stick figures illustrate population changes during a given period. Pictograms are visually appealing and can be especially useful for nontechnical or multicultural audiences. Graphics software makes it easy to create pictograms.

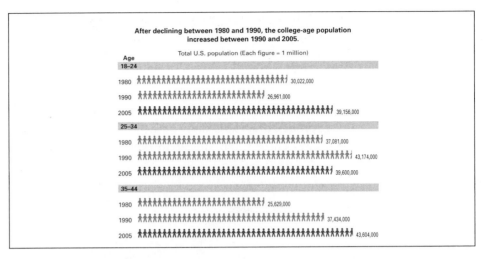

FIGURE 14.21 **A Pictogram**
Source: U.S. Bureau of the Census.

In place of lines and bars, icons and symbols lend appeal and clarity, especially for nontechnical or multicultural audiences

Graphic Illustrations

Illustrations can be diagrams, maps, drawings, icons, photographs, or any other visual that relies mainly on pictures rather than on data or words. For example, the diagram of a safety-belt locking mechanism in Figure 14.22 accomplishes what the verbal text alone cannot: it portrays the mechanism in operation.

Verbal text that requires a visual supplement

> The safety-belt apparatus includes a tiny pendulum attached to a lever, or locking mechanism. Upon sudden deceleration, the pendulum swings forward, activating the locking device to keep passengers from pitching into the dashboard.

Illustrations are invaluable when you need to convey spatial relationships or help your audience see what something actually looks like. Drawings can be more

Shows how the basic parts work together

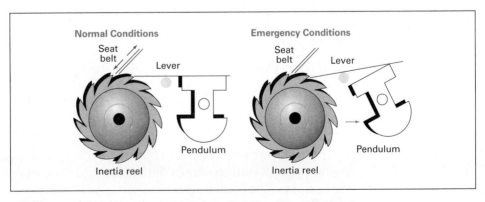

FIGURE 14.22 **A Diagram of a Safety-Belt Locking Mechanism**
Source: U.S. Department of Transportation.

effective than photographs because a drawing can simplify the view, omit unnecessary features, and focus on what is important.

Diagrams

Diagrams are especially effective for presenting views that could not be captured by photographing or observing the item.

Exploded diagrams show how the parts of an item are assembled, as in Figure 14.23. These often appear in repair or maintenance manuals. Notice how parts are numbered for the user's easy reference to the written instructions.

Shows how the parts are assembled

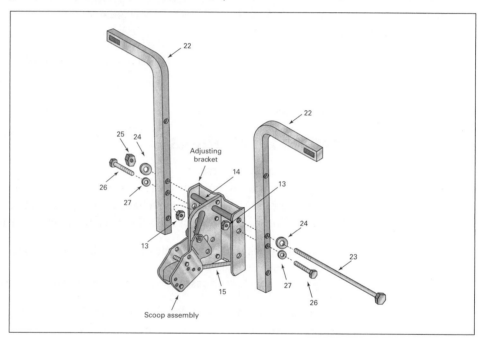

FIGURE 14.23 An Exploded Diagram of a Brace for an Adjustable Basketball Hoop
Source: Courtesy of Spalding.

Cutaway diagrams show the item with its exterior layers removed to reveal interior sections, as in Figure 14.24. Unless the specific viewing perspective is immediately recognizable (as in Figure 14.24), name the angle of vision: "top view," "side view," and so on.

Block diagrams are simplified sketches that represent the relationship between the parts of an item, principle, system, or process. Because block diagrams are designed to illustrate *concepts* (such as current flow in a circuit), the parts are represented as symbols or shapes. The block diagram in Figure 14.25 illustrates how any process can be controlled automatically through a feedback mechanism. Figure 14.26 shows the feedback concept applied as the cruise-control mechanism on a motor vehicle.

THE OPERATION

Incision

Transsphenoidal surgery is performed with the patient under general anesthesia and positioned on his back. The head is fixed in a special headrest, and the operation is monitored on a special x-ray machine (fluoroscope).

In the approach illustrated here (not used by all surgeons), a small incision is made in one side of the nasal septum **(Fig. 2)**. Part of the septum is then removed to provide access to the sphenoid sinus cavity **(Fig. 3)**.

Figure 2
Incision into nasal septum

PITUITARY GLAND (...) AND TUMOR

SPHENOID SINUS

NASAL SEPTUM

Figure 3
Removal of nasal septum to reach pituitary chamber

Shows what is inside

FIGURE 14.24 Cutaway Diagram of a Surgical Procedure

Source: Transsphenoidal Approach for Pituitary Tumor, © 1986 by The Ludann Co., Grand Rapids, MI.

Depicts a single concept

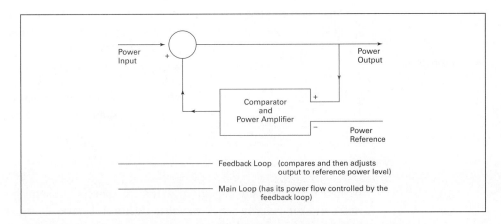

FIGURE 14.25 A Block Diagram Illustrating the Concept of Feedback

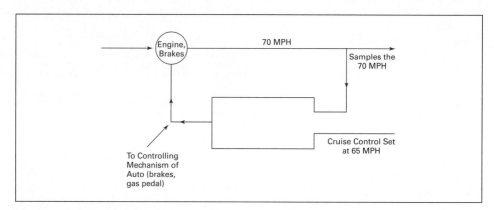

Depicts a specific application of the feedback concept

FIGURE 14.26 A Block Diagram Illustrating a Cruise-Control Mechanism

It is easy to create impressive-looking visuals by using electronic drawing programs, clip art, and image banks. However, specialized diagrams generally require the services of graphic artists or technical illustrators. The client requesting or commissioning the visual provides the art professional with an *art brief* (often prepared by writers and editors) that spells out the visual's purpose and specifications. The art brief is usually reinforced by a *thumbnail sketch*, a small, simple sketch of the visual being requested. (See Chapter 15 for thumbnail sketches also used in planning page layouts.) For example, part of the brief addressed to the medical illustrator for Figure 14.24 might read as follows:

An art brief for Figure 14.24

- **Purpose:** to illustrate transsphenoidal adenomectomy for laypersons
- **View:** full cutaway, sagittal
- **Range:** descending from cranial apex to a horizontal plane immediately below the upper jaw and second cervical vertebra
- **Depth:** medial cross-section
- **Structures omitted:** cranial nerves, vascular and lymphatic systems
- **Structures included:** gross anatomy of bone, cartilage, and soft tissue—delineated by color, shading, and texture

A thumbnail sketch of Figure 14.24

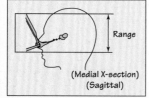

- **Structures highlighted:** nasal septum, sphenoid sinus, and sella turcica, showing the pituitary embedded in a 1.5 cm tumor invading the sphenoid sinus via an area of herniation at the base of the pituitary fossa

Maps

Besides being visually engaging, maps are especially useful for showing comparisons and for helping users *visualize* position, location, and relationships among various data. Figure 14.27 synthesizes statistical information in a format that is accessible and understandable. Color enhances the comparisons.

Shows the
geographic
distribution of data

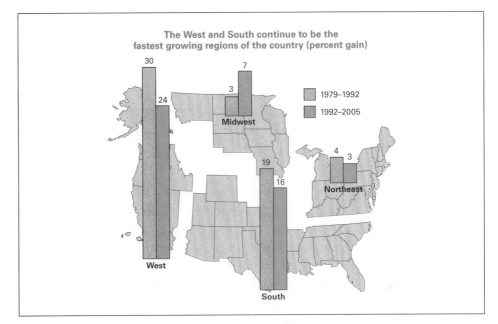

FIGURE 14.27 **A Map Rich in Statistical Significance**
Source: U.S. Bureau of the Census.

Photographs

Photographs are especially useful for showing exactly how something looks (Figure 14.28) or how something is done (Figure 14.29). Unlike a diagram, which highlights certain parts of an item, photographs show everything. So while a photograph

FIGURE 14.28 **Shows the Item's
Appearance** A Fixed-Platform Oil Rig.
Source: SuperStock.

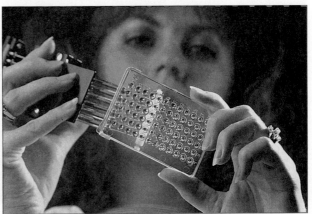

FIGURE 14.29 **Shows How Something Is Done**
Antibody Screening Procedure.
Source: SuperStock.

can be extremely useful, it also can provide too much detail or fail to emphasize the parts on which you want people to focus. For the most effective photographs, use a professional photographer who knows all about angles, lighting, lenses, and special film or digital editing options.

Guidelines for Using Photographs

- **Simulate the readers' angle of vision.** Consider how they would view the item or perform the procedure (Figure 14.30).

- **Label all the parts readers need to identify** (Figure 14.31).

- **Trim (crop) the photograph to eliminate needless detail** (Figures 14.32 and 14.33).

- **Supplement the photograph with diagrams.** This way, you can emphasize selected features. (Figures 14.34 and 14.35).

- **Provide a sense of scale for an object unfamiliar to readers.** Include a person, a ruler, or a familiar object (such as a hand) in the photo.

- **If your document will be published, attend to the legal aspects.** Obtain a signed release from any person in the photograph and written permission from the copyright holder. Cite the photographer and the copyright holder.

- **Explain what readers should look for in the photo.** Do this in your discussion or use a caption.

FIGURE 14.30 Shows a Realistic Angle of Vision
Titration in Measuring Electron-Spin Resonance.
Source: SuperStock.

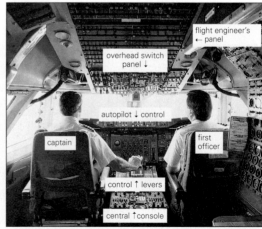

FIGURE 14.31 Shows Essential Features Labeled Standard Flight Deck for a Long-Range Jet.
Source: SuperStock.

FIGURE 14.33 **The Cropped Version of Figure 14.32**
Source: SuperStock.

FIGURE 14.32 **A Photograph That Needs to Be Cropped** Replacing the Microfilter Activation Unit.
Source: SuperStock.

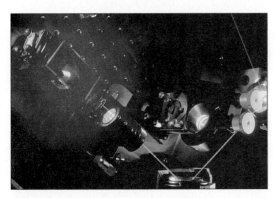

FIGURE 14.34 **Shows a Complex Mechanism** Sapphire Tunable Laser.
Source: SuperStock.

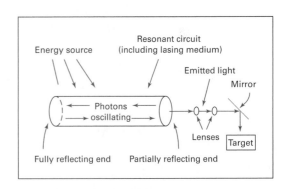

FIGURE 14.35 **A Simplified Diagram of Figure 14.34** Major Parts of the Laser.

 Basic photo editing techniques

Commercial vendors such as PhotoDisc, Inc. <www.photodisc.com> offer royalty-free stock photographs. (See page 283 for more Web sources.) For a fee, you can download photographs, edit and alter them as needed by using a program such as *Adobe Photoshop,* and then insert these images in your own documents.

NOTE   *Make sure you clearly understand what is legally and ethically permissible before including altered images.*

Software and Downloadable Images

Many of the tasks formerly done by graphic designers and technical illustrators now fall to people with little or no training. Whatever your career, you could be expected to produce high-quality graphics for conferences, presentations, and in-house publications. This text offers only a brief introduction to these matters. Your best bet is to take a graphic design class.

Using the Software

Knowing about the following categories of software definitely will enhance your abilities as a technical communicator.

A sampling of resources for electronic visual design

- **Graphics software,** such as *Adobe Illustrator* or *CorelDraw,* allows you to sketch, edit, and refine your diagrams and drawings.
- **Presentation software,** such as *Microsoft PowerPoint,* lets you create slides, computer presentations, and overhead transparency sheets. Using a program such as *Macromedia Director,* you can create multimedia presentations that include sound and video.
- **Spreadsheet software,** such as *Microsoft Excel,* makes it easy to create charts and graphs.
- **Word-processing programs,** such as *Corel WordPerfect* or *Microsoft Word,* include simple image editors ("draw" feature) and other tools for working with visuals. More sophisticated page layout programs, such as *Adobe InDesign,* also provide ways to work with visual design.

(For discussion of additional types of software, see pages 274 and 281.)

Using Symbols and Icons

Symbols and icons can convey information visually to a wide range of audiences. Because such visuals do not rely on text, they are often more easily understood by international audiences, children, or people who may have difficulty reading. Symbols and icons are used in airports and other public places as well as in documentation, manuals, or training material. Some of these images are developed and approved by the International Standards Organization (ISO). The ISO makes sure the images have universal appeal and conform to a single standard, whether used in a printed document or on an elevator wall.

How symbols and icons differ

The words *symbol* and *icon* are often used interchangeably. Technically, icons tend to resemble the thing they represent: an icon of a file folder on your computer, for example, looks like a real file folder. Symbols can be more abstract; symbols still get the meaning across but may not resemble, precisely, what they represent. Figure 14.36 shows some familiar icons and symbols.

FIGURE 14.36 Internationally Recognized Symbols
Source: Courtesy 4YEO.com, www.4yeo.com.

Limitations of clip art

Ready-to-use icons and symbols can be found in clip-art collections, from which you can import and customize images by using a drawing program. Because of its generally unpolished appearance, consider using clip art only for in-house documents or for situations in which schedule or budget preclude original artwork (Menz 5).

 NOTE

Be sure the image you choose is "intuitively recognizable" to multicultural users ("Using Icons" 3).

Using Web Sites for Graphics Support

Following is a sampling of useful Web sites and gateways for finding visuals.

- **Clip art:** <www.clipart.com>
- **Photographs:** <www.classicphotos.com> and <www.photolinks.net>
- **Art images:** <www.artresources.com>
- **Maps:** <http://plasma.nationalgeographic.com/mapmachine>
- **International symbols:** <www.iso.org>
- **Audio and video:** <www.streamingmediaworld.com>

NOTE

Be extremely cautious about downloading visuals (or any material, for that matter) from the Web and then using them. Review the copyright law (page 134). Originators of any work on the Web own the work and the copyright. Any photograph—including one offered as "free" clip art—is protected by copyright.

Using Color

Color often makes a presentation more interesting, focusing users' attention and helping them identify various elements. In Figure 14.19, for example, color helps users sort out the key schedule elements of a Gantt chart for a major project: activities, time lines, durations, and meetings.

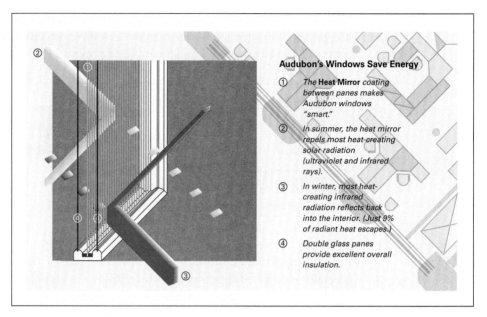

Audubon's Windows Save Energy

① The **Heat Mirror** coating between panes makes Audubon windows "smart."

② In summer, the heat mirror repels most heat-creating solar radiation (ultraviolet and infrared rays).

③ In winter, most heat-creating infrared radiation reflects back into the interior. (Just 9% of radiant heat escapes.)

④ Double glass panes provide excellent overall insulation.

FIGURE 14.37 Color Used as a Visualizing Tool
Source: Courtesy of National Audubon Society.

Color can help clarify a concept or dramatize how something works. In Figure 14.37 bright colors against a darker, duller background enable users to *visualize* the "heat mirror" concept.

Color can help clarify complex relationships. In Figure 14.38, a world map using distinctive colors allows users to make comparisons at a glance.

Color also can help guide users through the material. Used effectively on a printed page, color helps organize the user's understanding, provides orientation, and emphasizes important material.

On a Web page, color can mirror the site's main theme or "personality," orient the user, and provide cues for navigating the site. Figure 14.39 is a page from the National Oceanic and Atmospheric Administration. Sky-blue (or ocean-blue) as the dominant color (set against the blackness of outer space) reflects NOAA's mission in monitoring global climate. The striking image of the sun intersecting (or piercing) a depleted ozone shield helps underscore the urgency of ozone depletion as an environmental issue. In the masthead and elsewhere, subtle links in gray reversed type evoke the subtlety of the ozone depletion itself—a gradual, subtle process, but one with potentially grave consequences.

Following are just a few possible uses of color in page design (White, *Color* 39–44; Keyes 647–49). For more on designing pages, see Chapter 15.

Use Color to Organize.   Users look for ways of organizing their understanding of a document. Color can reveal structure and break material up into discrete blocks that are easier to locate, process, and digest.

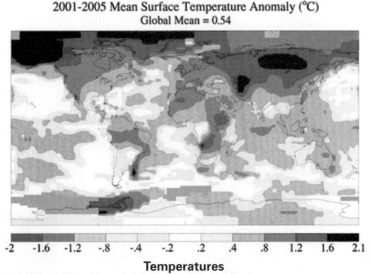

2001-2005 Mean Surface Temperature Anomaly (°C)
Global Mean = 0.54

-2   -1.6   -1.2   -.8   -.4   -.2   .2   .4   .8   1.2   1.6   2.1

Temperatures
Because of a rapid warming trend over the past 30 years, the Earth is now reaching and passing through the warmest levels seen in the last 12,000 years. This map shows temperatures from 2001–2005 compared to a base period of temperatures from 1951–1980. Dark red indicates the greatest warming and purple indicates the greatest cooling.

FIGURE 14.38 Colors Used to Show Relationships
Source: National Aeronautics and Space Administration (NASA)
<www.nasa.gov/images/content/158226main_mean_surface_temp_lg.jpg>.

How color reveals
organization

- A color background screen can set off like elements such as checklists, instructions, or examples.
- Horizontal colored rules can separate blocks of text, such as sections of a document or areas of a page.
- Vertical rules can set off examples, quotations, captions, and so on.

Color used
to organize

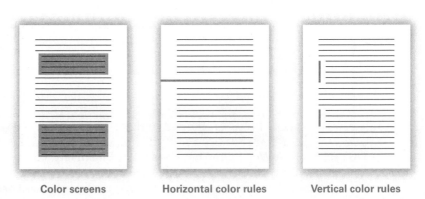

Color screens   Horizontal color rules   Vertical color rules

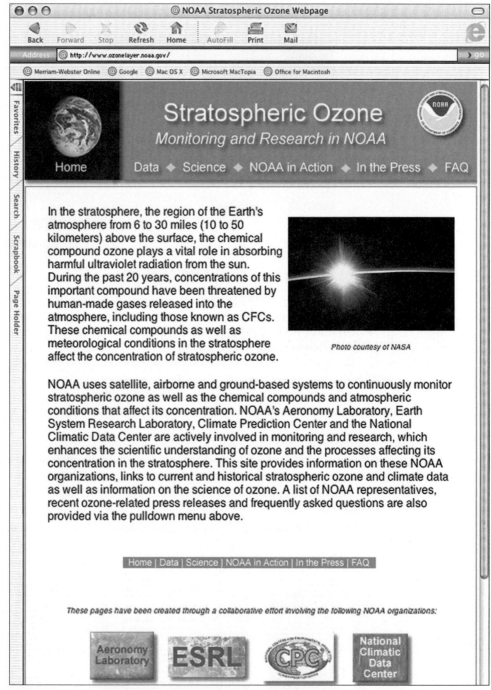

FIGURE 14.39 A Web Page That Uses Color Effectively For detailed explanation of how this design incorporates color effectively, refer to page 284.

Source: National Oceanic and Atmospheric Administration <www.ozonelayer.noaa.gov>.

Use Color to Orient.   Users look for signposts that help them find their place or locate what they need.

How color provides orientation

- Color can help headings stand out from the text and differentiate major from minor headings.
- Color tabs and boxes can serve as location markers.
- Color sidebars (for marginal comments), callouts (for labels), and leader lines (for connecting a label to its referent) can guide the eyes.

Color used to orient

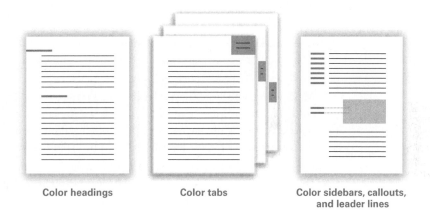

| Color headings | Color tabs | Color sidebars, callouts, and leader lines |

Use Color to Emphasize.   Users look for places to focus their attention in a document.

How color emphasizes

- Color type can highlight key words or ideas.
- Color can call attention to cross-references or to links on a Web page.
- A color, ruled box can frame a warning, caution, note, hint, or any other item that needs to stick in people's minds.

Color used to emphasize

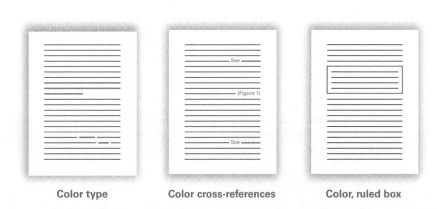

| Color type | Color cross-references | Color, ruled box |

Guidelines for Incorporating Color

- **Use color sparingly.** Color gains impact when used selectively. It loses impact when overused (*Aldus Guide* 39). Use no more than three or four distinct colors—including black and white (White, *Great Pages* 76).

- **Apply color consistently to like elements throughout your document** (Wickens 117).

- **Make color redundant.** Be sure all elements are first differentiated in black and white: by shape, location, texture, type style, or type size. Different readers perceive colors differently or, in some cases, not at all (White, *Great Pages* 76).

- **Use a darker color to make a stronger statement.** The darker the color the more important the material. Darker items can seem larger and closer than lighter objects of identical size.

- **Make color type larger or bolder than text type.** For text type, use a high-contrast color (dark against a light background). Color is less visible on the page than black ink on a white background. The smaller the image or the thinner the rule, the stronger or brighter the color should be (White, *Editing* 229, 237).

- **Create contrast.** For contrast in a color screen, use a very dark type against a very light background, say a 10- to 20-percent screen (Gribbons 70). The larger the screen area, the lighter the background color should be.

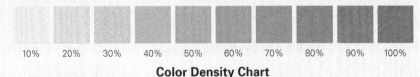

| 10% | 20% | 30% | 40% | 50% | 60% | 70% | 80% | 90% | 100% |

Color Density Chart

Ethical Considerations

Although you are perfectly justified in presenting data in its best light, you are ethically responsible for avoiding misrepresentation. Any one set of data can support contradictory conclusions. Even though your numbers may be accurate, your visual display could be misleading.

Present the Real Picture

Visual relationships in a graph should accurately portray the numerical relationships they represent. Begin the vertical scale at zero. Never compress the scales to reinforce your point.

Notice how visual relationships in Figure 14.40 become distorted when the value scale is compressed or fails to begin at zero. In version A, the bars accurately depict the numerical relationships measured from the value scale. In version B,

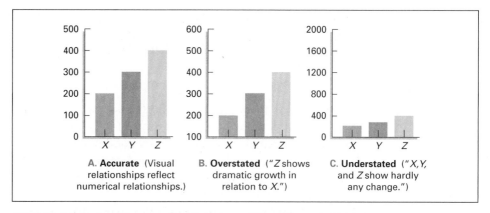

FIGURE 14.40 An Accurate Bar Graph and Two Distorted Versions Absence of a zero baseline in B shrinks the vertical axis and exaggerates differences among the data. In C, the excessive value range of the vertical axis dwarfs differences among the data.

item Z (400) is depicted as three times X (200). In version C, the scale is overly compressed, causing the shortened bars to understate the quantitative differences.

Deliberate distortions are unethical because they imply conclusions contradicted by the actual data.

Present the Complete Picture

Without getting bogged down in needless detail, an accurate visual includes all essential data. Figure 14.41 shows how distortion occurs when data that would provide

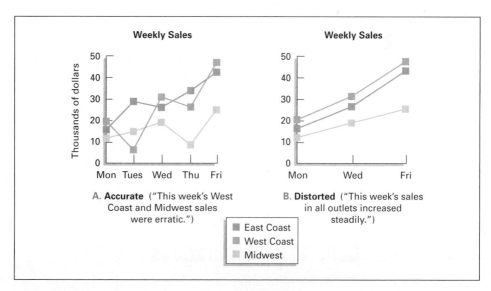

FIGURE 14.41 An Accurate Line Graph and a Distorted Version Selective omission of data points in B causes the lines to flatten, implying a steady increase rather than an erratic pattern of sales, as more accurately shown in A.

a complete picture are selectively omitted. Version A accurately depicts the numerical relationships measured from the value scale. In version B, too few points are plotted. Always decide carefully what to include and what to leave out.

Don't Mistake Distortion for Emphasis

When you want to emphasize a point (a sales increase, a safety record, etc.), be sure your data support the conclusion implied by your visual. For instance, don't use inordinately large visuals to emphasize good news or small ones to downplay bad news (Williams 11). When using clip art, pictograms, or drawn images to dramatize a comparison, be sure the relative size of the images or icons reflects the quantities being compared.

A visual accurately depicting a 100-percent increase in phone sales at your company might look like version A in Figure 14.42. Version B overstates the good news by depicting the larger image four times the size, instead of twice the size, of the smaller. Although the larger image is twice the height, it is also twice the *width*, so the total area conveys the visual impression that sales have *quadrupled*.

Visuals have their own rhetorical and persuasive force, which you can use to advantage—for positive or negative purposes, for the reader's benefit or detriment (Van Pelt 2). Avoiding visual distortion is ultimately a matter of ethics.

For additional guidance, use the planning sheet in Figure 14.43, and the checklist on page 293.

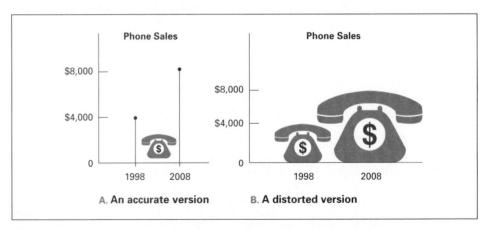

FIGURE 14.42 An Accurate Pictogram and a Distorted Version In B, the relative sizes of the images are not equivalent to the quantities they represent.

Cultural Considerations

Meaning is in the eye of the beholder

Visual communication can serve as a universal language—as long as the graphic or image is not misinterpreted. For example, not all cultures read left to right, so a chart designed to be read left to right that is read in the opposite direction could be

Focusing on Your Purpose

- What is this visual's purpose (to instruct, persuade, create interest)? _____

- What forms of information (numbers, shapes, words, pictures, symbols) will this visual depict? _____

- What kind of relationship(s) will the visual depict (comparison, cause-effect, connected parts, sequence of steps)? _____

- What judgment, conclusion, or interpretation is being emphasized (that profits have increased, that toxic levels are rising, that X is better than Y? _____ _____

- Is a visual needed at all? _____

Focusing on Your Audience

- Is this audience accustomed to interpreting visuals? _____

- Is the audience interested in specific numbers or an overall view? _____

- Should the audience focus on one exact value, compare two or more values, or synthesize a range of approximate values? _____

- Which type of visual will be most accurate, representative, accessible, and compatible with the type of judgment, action, or understanding expected from the audience? _____ _____

- In place of one complicated visual, would two or more straightforward ones be preferable? _____

- Are there any specific cultural considerations? _____

Focusing on Your Presentation

- What enhancements, if any, will increase audience interest (colors, patterns, legends, labels, varied typefaces, shadowing, enlargement or reduction of some features)? _____ _____

- Which medium—or combination of media—will be most effective for presenting this visual (slides, transparencies, handouts, large-screen monitor, flip chart, report text)? _____ _____

- For greatest utility and effect, where in the presentation does this visual belong? _____

FIGURE 14.43 A Planning Sheet for Preparing Visuals

misunderstood. Color is also a cultural consideration: For instance, U.S. audiences associate red with danger and green with safety. But in Ireland, green or orange carry strong political connotations. In Muslim cultures, green is a holy color (Cotton 169). Icons and symbols as well can have offensive connotations. Hand gestures are especially problematic: some Arab cultures consider the left hand unclean; a pointing index finger—on either hand—signifies rudeness in Venezuela or Sri Lanka (Bosley 5–6).

Guidelines for Fitting Visuals with Text

- **Place the visual where it will best serve your readers.** If it is central to your discussion, place the visual as close as possible to the material it clarifies. (Achieving proximity often requires that you ignore the traditional "top or bottom" design rule for placing visuals on a page.) If the visual is peripheral to your discussion or of interest to only a few readers, place it in an appendix. Tell readers when to consult the visual and where to find it.

- **Never refer to a visual that readers cannot easily locate.** In a long document, don't be afraid to repeat a visual if you discuss it a second time.

- **Never crowd a visual into a cramped space.** Frame the visual with plenty of white space, and position it on the page for balance. To achieve proportion with the surrounding text, consider the size of each visual and the amount of space it will occupy.

- **Number the visual and give it a clear title and labels.** Your title should tell readers what they are seeing. Label all the important material and cite the source of data or of graphics.

- **Match the visual to your audience.** Don't make it too elementary for specialists or too complex for nonspecialists.

- **Introduce and interpret the visual.** In your introduction, tell readers what to expect:

INFORMATIVE	As Table 2 shows, operating costs have increased 7 percent annually since 1990.
UNINFORMATIVE	See Table 2.

  Visuals alone make ambiguous statements (Girill, "Technical Communication and Art" 35); pictures need to be interpreted. Instead of leaving readers to struggle with a page of raw data, explain the relationships displayed. Follow the visual with a discussion of its important features:

INFORMATIVE	This cost increase means that . . . .

  Always tell readers what to look for and what it means.

- **Use prose captions to explain important points made by the visual.** Use a smaller type size so that captions don't compete with text type (*Aldus Guide* 35).

- **Eliminate "visual noise."** Excessive lines, bars, numbers, colors, or patterns will overwhelm readers. In place of one complicated visual, use two or more straightforward ones.
- **Be sure the visual can stand alone.** Even though it repeats or augments information already in the text, the visual should contain everything users will need to interpret it correctly.

☑ Checklist: Usability of Visuals

(Numbers in parentheses refer to the first page of discussion.)

Content

- [ ] Does the visual serve a valid purpose (clarification, not mere ornamentation)? (254)
- [ ] Is the level of complexity appropriate for the audience? (257)
- [ ] Is the visual titled and numbered? (261)
- [ ] Are all patterns identified by label or legend? (260)
- [ ] Are all values or units of measurement specified (grams per ounce, millions of dollars)? (261)
- [ ] Do the visual relationships represent the numeric relationships accurately? (288)
- [ ] Are captions and explanatory notes provided as needed? (259)
- [ ] Are all data sources cited? (261)
- [ ] Has written permission been obtained for reproducing or adapting a visual from a copyrighted source in any type of work to be published? (261)
- [ ] Is the visual introduced, discussed, interpreted, integrated with the text, and referred to by number? (292)
- [ ] Can the visual itself stand alone in terms of meaning? (293)

Style

- [ ] Is this the best type of visual for your purpose and audience? (257)
- [ ] Are all decimal points in each column of a table aligned vertically? (261)
- [ ] Is the visual uncrowded, uncluttered, and free of "visual noise"? (293)
- [ ] Is the visual engaging (patterns, colors, shapes), without being too busy? (293)
- [ ] Is color used tastefully and appropriately? (283)
- [ ] Is the visual ethically acceptable? (288)
- [ ] Does the visual respect users' cultural values? (290)

Placement

- [ ] Is the visual easy to locate? (292)
- [ ] Do all design elements (title, line thickness, legends, notes, borders, white space) achieve balance? (292)
- [ ] Is the visual positioned on the page to achieve balance? (292)
- [ ] Is the visual set off by adequate white space or borders? (292)
- [ ] Does the left side of a broadside table face page bottom? (261)
- [ ] Is the visual in the best location in the document? (292)

Exercises

  Exercises
WEBLINK

1. The following statistics are based on data from three colleges in a large western city. They compare the number of applicants to each college over six years.

   - In 2002, *X* college received 2,341 applications for admission, *Y* college received 3,116, and *Z* college 1,807.
   - In 2003, *X* college received 2,410 applications for admission, *Y* college received 3,224, and *Z* college 1,784.
   - In 2004, *X* college received 2,689 applications for admission, *Y* college received 2,976, and *Z* college 1,929.
   - In 2005, *X* college received 2,714 applications for admission, *Y* college received 2,840, and *Z* college 1,992.
   - In 2006, *X* college received 2,872 applications for admission, *Y* college received 2,615, and *Z* college 2,112.
   - In 2007, *X* college received 2,868 applications for admission, *Y* college received 2,421, and *Z* college 2,267.

   Display these data in a line graph, a bar graph, and a table. Which version seems most effective for someone who (a) wants exact figures, (b) wonders how overall enrollments are changing, or (c) wants to compare enrollments at each college in a certain year? Include a caption interpreting each version.

2. Devise a flowchart for a process in your field or area of interest. Include a title and a brief discussion.

3. Devise an organization chart showing the lines of responsibility and authority in an organization where you work.

4. Devise a pie chart to depict your yearly expenses. Title and discuss the chart.

5. Obtain enrollment figures at your college for the past five years by gender, age, race, or any other pertinent category. Construct a stacked-bar graph to illustrate one of these relationships over the five years.

6. In textbooks or professional journal articles, locate each of these visuals: a table, a multiple-bar graph, a multiple-line graph, a diagram, and a photograph. Evaluate each according to the revision checklist, and discuss the most effective visual in class.

7. Choose the most appropriate visual for illustrating each of these relationships.

   a. A comparison of three top brands of skis, according to cost, weight, durability, and edge control.
   b. A breakdown of your monthly budget.
   c. The changing cost of an average cup of coffee, as opposed to that of an average cup of tea, over the past three years.
   d. The percentage of college graduates finding desirable jobs within three months after graduation, over the last ten years.
   e. The percentage of college graduates finding desirable jobs within three months after graduation, over the last ten years—by gender.
   f. An illustration of automobile damage for an insurance claim.
   g. A breakdown of the process of corn-based ethanol production.
   h. A comparison of five cereals on the basis of cost and nutritive value.
   i. A comparison of the average age of students enrolled at your college in summer, day, and evening programs, over the last five years.
   j. Comparative sales figures for three items made by your company.

8. Display each of these sets of information in the visual format most appropriate for the stipulated audience. Complete the planning sheet in Figure 14.43 for each visual. Explain why you selected the type of visual as most effective for that audience. Include with each visual a caption that interprets and explains the data.

   a. (For general readers.) Assume that the Department of Energy breaks down energy consumption in the United States (by source) into these percentages: In 1970, coal, 18.5; natural gas, 32.8; hydro and geothermal, 3.1; nuclear, 1.2;

oil, 44.4. In 1980, coal, 20.3; natural gas, 26.9; hydro and geothermal, 3.8; nuclear, 4.0; oil, 45.0. In 1990, coal, 23.5; natural gas, 23.8; hydro and geothermal, 7.3; nuclear, 4.1; oil, 41.3. In 2000, coal, 20.3; natural gas, 25.2; hydro and geothermal, 9.6; nuclear, 6.3; oil, 38.6.

b. (For experienced investors in rental property.) As an aid in estimating annual heating and air-conditioning costs, here are annual maximum and minimum temperature averages from 1971 to 2007 for five Sunbelt cities (in Fahrenheit degrees): In Jacksonville, the average maximum was 78.4; the minimum was 57.6. In Miami, the maximum was 84.2; the minimum was 69.1. In Atlanta, the maximum was 72.0; the minimum was 52.3. In Dallas, the maximum was 75.8; the minimum was 55.1. In Houston, the maximum was 79.4; the minimum was 58.2. (From U.S. National Oceanic and Atmospheric Administration.)

c. (For the student senate.) Among the students who entered our school four years ago, here are the percentages of those who graduated, withdrew, or are still enrolled: In Nursing, 71 percent graduated; 27.9 percent withdrew; 1.1 percent are still enrolled. In Engineering, 62 percent graduated; 29.2 percent withdrew; 8.8 percent are still enrolled. In Business, 53.6 percent graduated; 43 percent withdrew; 3.4 percent are still enrolled. In Arts and Sciences, 27.5 percent graduated; 68 percent withdrew; 4.5 percent are still enrolled.

d. (For the student senate.) Here are the enrollment trends from 1995 to 2007 for two colleges in our university. In Engineering: 1995, 455 students enrolled; 1996, 610; 1997, 654; 1998, 758; 1999, 803; 2000, 827; 2001, 1046; 2002, 1200; 2003, 1115; 2004, 1075; 2005, 1116; 2006, 1145; 2007, 1177. In Business: 1995, 922; 1996, 1006; 1997, 1041; 1998, 1198; 1999, 1188; 2000, 1227; 2001, 1115; 2002, 1220; 2003, 1241; 2004, 1366; 2005, 1381; 2006, 1402; 2007, 1426.

9. Anywhere on campus or at work, locate a visual that needs revision for accuracy, clarity, appearance, or appropriateness. Look in computer manuals, lab manuals, newsletters, financial aid or admissions or placement brochures, student or faculty handbooks, newspapers, or textbooks. Using the planning sheet in Figure 14.43 and the checklist (page 293) as guides, revise the visual. Submit a copy of the original, along with a memo explaining your improvements. Be prepared to discuss your revision in class.

10. Locate a document (news, magazine, or journal article, brief instructions, or the like) that lacks adequate or appropriate visuals. Analyze the document and identify where visuals would be helpful. In a memo to the document's editor or author, provide an art brief and a thumbnail sketch (page 278) for each visual you recommend, specifying its exact placement in the document.

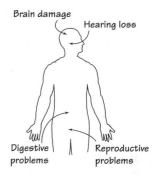

Source: U.S. Environmental Protection Agency. *Protect Your Family from Lead in Your Home,* 1995. 3.

Note: Be sure to provide enough detail for your audience to understand your suggestion clearly. For example, instead of merely recommending a "diagram of the toxic effects of lead on humans," stipulate a "diagram showing a frontal outline of the human body with the head turned sideways in profile view. Labels and arrows point to affected body areas to indicate brain damage, hearing problems, digestive problems, and reproductive problems."

11. Locate a Web page that uses color effectively to mirror the site's main theme or personality, to

orient the user, and to provide cues for easy navigation. Download the page and print it. Using the analysis of Figure 14.39 (page 284) as a model, prepare a brief memo justifying your choice.

Note: In a computer classroom, consider doing your presentation electronically.

 ## Collaborative Projects

1. Assume that your instructor is planning to purchase five copies of a graphics software package for students to use in designing their documents. The instructor has not yet decided which general-purpose package would be most useful. Your group's task is to test one package and to make a recommendation.

In small groups, visit your school's computer lab and ask for a listing of available graphics packages. Select one package and learn how to use it. Design at least four representative visuals. In a memo or presentation to your instructor and classmates, describe the package briefly and tell what it can do. Would you recommend purchasing this package for general-purpose use by writing students? Explain. Submit your report, along with the sample graphics you have composed.

2. Compile a list of six Web sites that offer graphics support by way of advice, image banks, design ideas, artwork catalogs, and the like. Provide the address for each site, along with a description of the resources offered and their approximate cost. Report your findings in the format stipulated by your instructor. See page 283 for URLs that will get you started.

CHAPTER 15

Designing Pages and Documents

Page Design in Workplace Documents

How Page Design Transforms a Document

Design Skills Needed in Today's Workplace

Creating a Usable Design
Guidelines for Highlighting for Emphasis
Guidelines for Using Headings

Audience Considerations in Page Design

Designing On-Screen Documents
Guidelines for Designing a Web Page
Checklist: Usability of Page Design

On the Job . . . Designing Documents

*P*age design, the layout of words and graphics, determines the look of a document. Well-designed pages invite users in, guide them through the material, and help them understand and remember the information.

In this electronic age the term "page" takes on broad meanings: On the computer screen, a page can scroll on endlessly. Also, *page* might mean a page of a report, but it can also mean one panel of a brochure or part of a reference card for installing printer software. The following discussion focuses mainly on traditional paper (printed) pages. See Designing On-Screen Documents later in this chapter for a discussion of pages in electronic documents.

How does page design affect workplace dynamics?

Page Design in Workplace Documents

Technical documents rarely get undivided attention

People read work-related documents only because they have to. If they have easier ways of getting the information, people will use them. In fact, busy users often only skim a document, or they refer to certain sections during a meeting or presentation. Amid frequent distractions, users want to be able to leave the document and then return and locate what they need easily.

NOTE

The so-called "paperless office" is largely a myth. In fact, information technology produces more paper than ever. Also, as computers generate more and more written messages, both electronic and hard copy, any document competes for audience attention. Overwhelmed by information overload, people resist any document that looks hard to get through.

Readers are attracted by documents that appear inviting and accessible

Before actually reading the document, people usually scan it for a sense of what it's about and how it's organized. An audience's first impression tends to involve a purely visual, esthetic judgment: "Does this look like something I want to read, or like too much work?" Instead of an unbroken sequence of paragraphs, users look for charts, diagrams, lists, various type sizes and fonts, different levels of headings, and other aids to navigation. Having decided at a glance whether your document is visually appealing, logically organized, and easy to navigate, users will draw conclusions about the value of your information, the quality of your work, and your overall credibility.

How Page Design Transforms a Document

To appreciate the impact of page design, consider Figures 15.1 and 15.2: Notice how the information in Figure 15.1 resists interpretation. Without design cues, we have no way of chunking that information into organized units of meaning. Figure 15.2 shows the same information after a design overhaul.

The Centers for Disease Control and Prevention (CDC) offer the following information on Chronic obstructive pulmonary disease, or COPD. COPD refers to a group of diseases that cause airflow blockage and breathing-related problems. It includes emphysema, chronic bronchitis, and in some cases asthma.

COPD is a leading cause of death, illness, and disability in the United States. In 2000, 11,900 deaths, 726,000 hospitalizations, and 1.5 million hospital emergency department visits were caused by COPD. An additional 8 million cases of hospital outpatient treatment or treatment by personal physicians were linked to COPD in 2000.

COPD has various causes. In the United States, tobacco use is a key factor in the development and progression of COPD, but asthma, exposure to air pollutants in the home and workplace, genetic factors, and respiratory infections also play a role. In the developing world, indoor air quality is thought to play a larger role in the development and progression of COPD than it does in the United States.

In the United States, an estimated 10 million adults had a diagnosis of COPD in 2000, but data from a national health survey suggest that as many as 24 million Americans are affected.

From 1980 to 2000, the COPD death rate for women grew much faster than the rate for men. For U.S. women, the rate rose from 20.1 deaths per 100,000 women to 56.7 deaths per 100,000 women over that 20-year span, while for men, the rate grew from 73.0 deaths per 100,000 men to 82.6 deaths per 100,000 men.

U.S. women also had more COPD hospitalizations (400,000) than men (322,000) and more emergency department visits (898,000) than men (551,000) in 2000. Additionally, 2000 marked the first year in which more women (59,936) than men (59,118) died from COPD.

However, the proportion of the U.S. population aged 25–54, both male and female, with mild or moderate COPD has declined over the past quarter century, suggesting that increases in hospitalizations and deaths might not continue.

The fact that women's COPD rates are rising so much faster than men's probably reflects the increase in smoking by women, relative to men, since the 1940s. In the United States, a history of currently or formerly smoking is the risk factor most often linked to COPD, and the increase in the number of women smoking in the past half-century is mirrored in the increase in COPD rates among women. The decreases in rates in both men and women aged 25–54 in the past quarter century reflect the decrease in overall smoking rates in the United States since the 1960s.

FIGURE 15.1 Ineffective Page Design This design provides no visual cues to indicate how the information is structured, what main ideas are being conveyed, or where readers should focus.

COPD

Facts About Chronic Obstructive Pulmonary Disease

What it is
Chronic obstructive pulmonary disease, or COPD, refers to a group of diseases that cause airflow blockage and breathing-related problems. It includes emphysema, chronic bronchitis, and in come cases asthma.

COPD is a leading cause of death, illness, and disability in the United States. In 2000, 119,000 deaths, 726,000 hospitalizations, and 1.5 million hospital emergency department visits were caused by COPD. An additional 8 million cases of hospital outpatient treatment or treatment by personal physicians were linked to COPD in 2000.

What causes it
In the United States, tobacco use is a key factor in the development and progression of COPD, but asthma, exposure to air pollutants in the home and workplace, genetic factors, and respiratory infections also play a role. In the developing world, indoor air quality is thought to play a larger role in the development and progression of COPD than it does in the United States.

Who has it
In the United States, an estimated 10 million adults had a diagnosis of COPD in 2000, but data from a national health survey suggest that as many as 24 million Americans are affected.

From 1980 to 2000, the COPD death rate for women grew much faster than the rate for men. For U.S. women, the rate rose from 20.1 deaths per 100,000 women to 56.7 deaths per 100,000 women over that 20-year span, while for men, the rate grew from 73.0 deaths per 100,000 men to 82.6 deaths per 100,000 men.

U.S. women also had more COPD hospitalizations (404,000) than men (322,000) and more emergency department visits (898,000) than men (551,000) in 2000. Additionally, 2000 marked the first year in which more women (59,936) than men (59,118) died from COPD.

However, the proportion of the U.S. population aged 25-54, both male and female, with mild or moderate COPD has declined over the past quarter century, suggesting that increases in hospitalizations and deaths might not continue.

Why women's COPD rates are rising so much faster than men's
These increases probably reflect the increase in smoking by women, relative to men, since the 1940s. In the United States, a history of currently or formerly smoking is the risk factor most often linked to COPD, and the increase in the number of women smoking over the past half-century is mirrored in the increase in COPD rates among women. The decreases in rates of mild and moderate COPD in both men and women aged 25-54 in the past quarter century reflect the decrease in overall smoking rates in the United States since the 1960s.

Page 1 of 2

DEPARTMENT OF HEALTH AND HUMAN SERVICES
CENTERS FOR DISEASE CONTROL AND PREVENTION
SAFER·HEALTHIER·PEOPLE™

FIGURE 15.2 Effective Page Design Notice how the masthead immediately identifies the subject (COPD) and the information source (CDC). The primary heading announces the type of information readers can expect. Subheadings indicate at a glance how this page is organized and how the ideas relate; color helps highlight these navigational cues and white space creates areas of emphasis.

Source: Centers for Disease Control and Prevention <www.cdc.gov/nceh/airpollution/copd/pdfs/copdfaq.pdf>.

Design Skills Needed in Today's Workplace

As more and more software is developed to help people with page layout and document design, you may be responsible for preparing actual publications as part of your job—often without the help of clerical staff, print shops, and graphic artists. In such cases, you will need to master a variety of technologies and to observe specific guidelines.

Desktop Publishing

Desktop publishing (DTP) systems such as *InDesign*, *Adobe Framemaker*, or *Quark* combine word processing, typesetting, and graphics. Using this software along with optical scanners, and laser printers, one person, or a group working collaboratively, controls the entire production cycle: designing, illustrating, laying out, and printing the final document (Cotton 36–47). Documents or parts of documents used repeatedly (*boilerplate*) can be retrieved when needed, or modified or inserted in some other document. With *groupware* (group authoring systems), writers from different locations can produce and distribute drafts online, incorporate reviewers' comments into their drafts, and publish documents collaboratively.

Electronic Publishing

Your work may involve electronic publishing (epublishing), in which you use programs such as *RoboHelp*, *Rainmaker*, or *Dreamweaver* to create documents in digital format for the Web, the company intranet, or as online help screens. You also might produce Portable Document Files, PDF versions of a document, using software such as *Buildfire*.

For projects that will be shared across different types of computer platforms, you might use markup languages. These languages use marks, or "tags," to indicate where the text should be bold, indented, italicized, and so on. Word-processing or page layout files from different programs or platforms are not always compatible, but with markup languages, once the tags are inserted, documents can be shared across many platforms.

Two examples of markup languages are standardized general markup language (SGML) and hypertext markup language (HTML). The first, SGML, is used for printed documents. The second, HTML, is used for hypertext pages—electronic documents such as online help screens or Web pages. For more on markup languages, see pages 426–27.

Using Style Sheets and Company Style Guides

Style sheets are specifications that ensure consistency across a single document or a set of documents. If you are working as part of a team, each writer needs to be using the same typefaces, fonts, headings, and other elements in identical fashion.

Possible style-sheet entries

- The first time you use or define a specialized term, highlight it with *italics* or **boldface**.
- In headings, capitalize prepositions of five or more letters ("Between," "Versus").

The more complex the document, the more specific the style sheet should be. All writers and editors should have a copy. Consider keeping the style sheet on a Web page for easy access and efficient updating.

In addition to style sheets for specific documents, some organizations produce style guides containing rules for proper use of trade names, appropriate punctuation, preferred formats for correspondence, and so on. Style guides help ensure a consistent look across a company's various documents and publications.

Creating a Usable Design

Approach your design decisions from the top down, as in Figure 15.3. First, consider the overall look of your pages; next, the shape of each paragraph; and finally, the size and style of individual words and letters (Kirsh 112).

NOTE   *All design considerations are influenced by the budget for a publication. For instance, adding a single color (say, to major heads) can double the printing cost.*

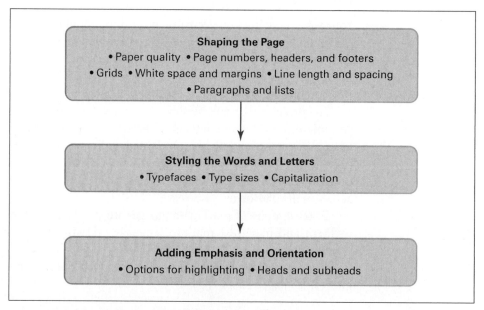

Shaping the Page
- Paper quality • Page numbers, headers, and footers
- Grids • White space and margins • Line length and spacing
- Paragraphs and lists

Styling the Words and Letters
- Typefaces • Type sizes • Capitalization

Adding Emphasis and Orientation
- Options for highlighting • Heads and subheads

FIGURE 15.3 A Flowchart for Decisions in Page Design A top-down design strategy moves from large elements to small.

If your organization prescribes no specific guidelines, the general design principles that follow should serve in most situations.

Shaping the Page

In shaping a page, consider its look, feel, and overall layout. The following suggestions will help you shape appealing and usable pages.

Use the Right Paper.   For routine documents (memos, letters, in-house reports) print in black, on low-gloss, white paper. Use rag-bond paper (20 pound or heavier) with a high fiber content (25 percent minimum).

For documents that will be published (manuals, marketing literature), consider the paper's grade and quality. Paper varies in weight, grain, and finish—from low-cost newsprint to specially coated paper with custom finishes. Choice of paper depends on the artwork to be included, the type of printing, and the intended esthetic effect: For example, you might choose specially coated, heavyweight, glossy paper for an elegant effect in an annual report (Cotton 73).

Use Consistent Page Numbers, Headers, and Footers.   For a long document, count your title page as page i, without numbering it, and number all front matter pages, including the table of contents and abstract, with lowercase roman numerals (ii, iii, iv). Number the first text page and subsequent pages with arabic numerals (1, 2, 3). Along with page numbers, *headers* or *footers* (or *running heads* and *feet*) appear in the top or bottom page margins, respectively. These provide chapter or article titles, authors' names, dates, or other publication information. (See page 315.)

Use a Grid.   Readers make sense of a page by looking for a consistent underlying structure, with the various elements located where they expect. With a view of a page's Big Picture, you can plan the size and placement of your visuals and calculate the number of lines available for written text. Most important, you can rearrange text and visuals repeatedly to achieve a balanced and consistent design (White, *Editing* 58). Figure 15.4 shows a sampling of grid patterns. A two-column grid is commonly used in manuals. (See the *Consider This* boxes in this text.) Brochures and newsletters typically employ a two- or three-column grid. Web pages (see page 430) often use a combined vertical/horizontal grid. Figure 15.2 uses a single-column grid, as do most memos, letters, and reports. (Grids are also used in storyboarding; see page 200.)

Figure 15.5 illustrates how a horizontal grid can transform the design of important medical information for consumers.

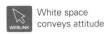 White space conveys attitude

Use White Space to Create Areas of Emphasis.   Sometimes, what makes a difference is what is *not* on the page. Areas of text surrounded by white space draw the reader's eye to those areas.

Well-designed white space imparts a shape to the whole document, a shape that orients readers and lends a distinctive visual form to the printed matter by keeping related elements together, by isolating and emphasizing important elements, and by providing breathing room between blocks of information.

Grids help readers make sense of material

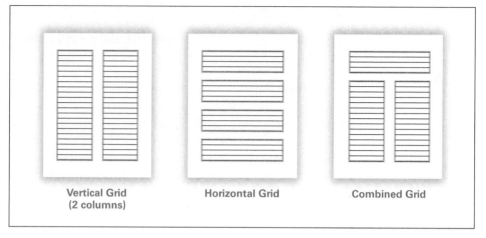

FIGURE 15.4 **Grid Patterns** By subdividing a page into modules, grids provide a blueprint for your page design as well as a coherent visual theme for the document's audience.

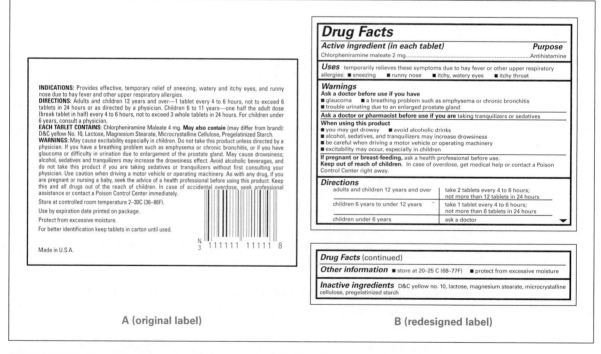

FIGURE 15.5 **Two Versions of a Consumer Label** The discrete horizontal modules in version B provide an underlying structure that is easy to navigate.

Source: Nordenberg, Tamar. "New Drug Label Spells It Out Simply." *FDA Consumer* (*Reprint*) *July 1999.*

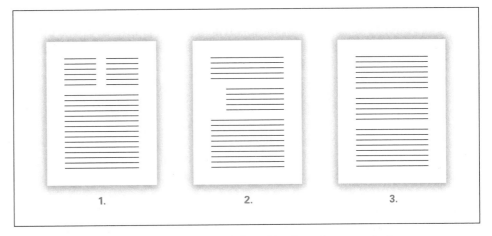

White space creates
areas of emphasis

1.   2.   3.

FIGURE 15.6 Use of White Space to Orient Readers In example 1, your eye
moves toward the "gutter" (the white space between the columns). In example 2,
the white space draws you to the middle paragraph. In example 3, white space falls
between each paragraph but is equally placed.

In the examples in Figure 15.6, notice how the white space pulls your eye toward the pages in different ways. Each example causes the reader to look at a different place on the page first. White space can keep a page from seeming too cluttered, and pages that look uncluttered, inviting, and easy to follow convey an immediate sense of user-friendliness.

Provide Ample Margins.   Small margins crowd the page and make the material look difficult. On your $8\frac{1}{2}$-by-11-inch page, leave margins of at least 1 or $1\frac{1}{2}$ inches. If the manuscript is to be bound in some kind of cover, widen the inside margin to two inches.

Headings, lines of text, or visuals that abut the right or left margin, without indentation, are designated as *flush right* or *flush left.*

Choose between *unjustified* text (uneven or "ragged" right margins) and *justified* text (even right margins). Each arrangement creates its own "feel."

Justified lines
are set flush
left and right

To make the right margin even in justified text, the spaces vary between words and letters on a line, sometimes creating channels or rivers of white space. The eyes are then forced to adjust continually to these space variations within a line or paragraph. Because each line ends at an identical vertical space, the eyes must work harder to differentiate one line from another (Felker 85). Moreover, to preserve the even margin, words at line's end are often hyphenated, and frequently hyphenated line endings can be distracting.

Unjustified lines
are set flush
left only

Unjustified text, on the other hand, uses equal spacing between letters and words on a line, and an uneven right margin (as traditionally produced by a typewriter). For some readers, a ragged right margin makes reading easier.

These differing line lengths can prompt the eye to move from one line to another (Pinelli 77). In contrast to justified text, an unjustified page looks less formal, less distant, and less official.

Justified text seems preferable for books, annual reports, and other formal materials. Unjustified text seems preferable for more personal forms of communication such as letters, memos, and in-house reports.

Keep Line Length Reasonable.   Long lines tire the eyes. The longer the line, the harder it is for the reader to return to the left margin and locate the beginning of the next line (White, *Visual Design* 25).

Notice how your eye labors to follow this apparently endless message that seems to stretch in lines that continue long after your eye was prepared to move down to the next line. After reading more than a few of these lines, you begin to feel tired and bored and annoyed, without hope of ever reaching the end.

Short lines force the eyes back and forth (Felker 79). "Too-short lines disrupt the normal horizontal rhythm of reading" (White, *Visual Design* 25).

Lines that are too
short cause your eye
to stumble from one
fragment to another
at a pace that too
soon becomes
annoying, if not
nauseating.

A reasonable line length is sixty to seventy characters (or nine to twelve words) per line for an $8\frac{1}{2}$-by-11-inch single-column page. The number of characters will depend on print size. Longer lines call for larger type and wider spacing between lines (White, *Great Pages* 70).

Line length, of course, is affected by the number of columns (vertical blocks of print) on your page. Two-column pages often appear in newsletters and brochures, but research indicates that single-column pages work best for complex, specialized information (Hartley 148).

Keep Line Spacing Consistent.   For any document likely to be read completely (letters, memos, instructions), single-space within paragraphs and double-space between. Instead of indenting the first line of single-spaced paragraphs, separate them with one line of space. For longer documents likely to be read selectively (proposals, formal reports), increase line spacing within paragraphs by one-half space. Indent these paragraphs or separate them with one extra line of space.

NOTE   *Although academic papers generally call for double spacing, most workplace documents do not.*

Tailor Each Paragraph to Its Purpose.   Users often skim a long document to find what they want. Most paragraphs, therefore, begin with a topic sentence forecasting the content. As you shape each paragraph, follow these suggestions:

Shape each
paragraph

- Use a long paragraph (no more than fifteen lines) for clustering material that is closely related (such as history and background, or any information best understood in one block).
- Use short paragraphs for making complex material more digestible, for giving step-by-step instructions, or for emphasizing vital information.
- Instead of indenting a series of short paragraphs, separate them by inserting an extra line of space.
- Avoid "orphans," leaving a paragraph's opening line at the bottom of a page, and "widows," leaving a paragraph's closing line at the top of the page.

Make Lists for Easy Reading.   Whenever you find yourself writing a series of related items within a paragraph, consider using a list instead, especially if you are describing a series of tasks or trying to make certain items easy to locate. Types of items you might list: advice or examples, conclusions and recommendations, criteria for evaluation, errors to avoid, materials and equipment for a procedure, parts of a mechanism, or steps or events in a sequence. Notice how the immediately preceding items, integrated into a sentence as an *embedded list*, become easier to grasp and remember when displayed below as a *vertical list.*

An embedded list is
part of the running
text

A vertical list
draws readers'
attention to the
content of the list

Types of items you might display in a vertical list:

- advice or examples
- conclusions and recommendations
- criteria for evaluation
- errors to avoid
- materials and equipment for a procedure
- parts of a mechanism
- steps or events in a sequence

A list of brief items usually needs no punctuation at the end of each line. A list of full sentences or questions requires appropriate punctuation after each item. For more on punctuating embedded and vertical lists, see page 691 or consult your organization's style guide.

Depending on the list's contents, set off each item with some kind of visual or verbal signal, as in Figure 15.7: If the items follow a strict sequence or chronology (say, parts of a mechanism or a set of steps), use arabic numbers (*1, 2, 3*) or the

Lists help readers
organize their
understanding

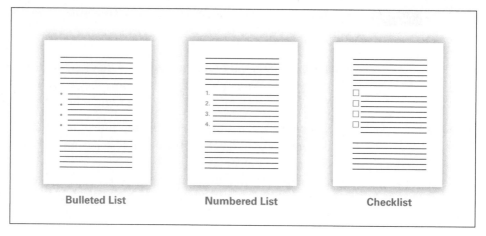

Bulleted List   **Numbered List**   **Checklist**

FIGURE 15.7 **Types of Vertical Lists** A bulleted list makes items easier to locate; a numbered list highlights the order of steps in a task; a checklist enumerates the conditions or requirements that need to be satisfied.

words *First, Second, Third.* If the items require no strict sequence (as in the sample list on page 307), use dashes, asterisks, or bullets. For a checklist, use open boxes.

Introduce your list with a forecasting phrase ("Topics to review for the exam:") or with a sentence ("To prepare for the exam, review the following topics:"). For more on introducing a list, see page 692.

Phrase all listed items in parallel grammatical form (page 679). When items suggest no strict sequence, try to impose some logical ranking (most to least important, alphabetical, or some such). Set off the list with extra white space above and below.

NOTE *A document with too many vertical lists appears busy, disconnected, and splintered (Felker 55). And long lists could be used by unethical writers to camouflage bad or embarrassing news (Williams 12).*

Using Typography Effectively

Typography, the art of type styling, consists of choices among various typefaces. *Typeface,* or *font,* refers to all the letters and characters in one particular family such as Times, Helvetica, or New York. Each typeface has its own *personality*: Some convey seriousness; others convey humor; still others convey a technical or businesslike quality. Choice of typeface can influence reading speed by as much as 30 percent (Chauncey 36).

All typefaces divide into two broad categories: *serif* and *sans serif* (Figure 15.8). Serifs are the fine lines that extend horizontally from the main strokes of a letter:

M serifs

Serif type makes printed body copy more readable because the horizontal lines "bind the individual letters" and thereby guide the reader's eyes from letter to letter. (White, *Visual Design* 14). Serif fonts look traditional, the sort you see in newspapers and formal reports.

Sans serif type is purely vertical . Clean looking and "businesslike," sans (French for "without") serif is ideal for technical material (numbers, equations, etc.), marginal comments, headings, examples, tables, and captions, and any other material set off from the body copy (White, *Visual Design* 16). Sans serif is also more readable in *projected* environments such as overhead transparencies and PowerPoint slides.

FIGURE 15.8 Serif Versus Sans Serif Typefaces Each version makes its own visual statement.

Font preferences are culturally determined

European readers generally prefer sans serif fonts, and other cultures have their own preferences as well. Learn all you can about the design conventions of the culture you are addressing.

Select an Appropriate Typeface. In selecting your typeface, consider the document's purpose. If the purpose is to help patients relax, choose a combination that conveys ease; fonts that imitate handwriting are often a good choice, but they can be hard to read if used in lengthy passages. If the purpose is to help engineers find technical data in a table or chart, use Helvetica or some other sans serif typeface—not only because numbers in sans serif type are easy to see but also because engineers will be more comfortable with fonts that look precise. Figure 15.9 offers a sampling of typeface choices.

For visual unity, use different sizes and versions (**bold,** *italic,* SMALL CAPS) of the same typeface throughout your document. For example, you might decide on Times for an audience of financial planners, investors, and others who expect a traditional font. In this case, use Times 14 point bold for the headings, 12 point regular (roman) for the body copy, and 12 point italic, sparingly, for emphasis.

If the document contains illustrations, charts, or numbers, use Helvetica 10 point for these; use a smaller size for captions (brief explanation of a visual) or sidebars (marginal comments). You can also use one typeface (say, Helvetica) for headings and another (say, Times) for body copy. In any case, use no more than two different typeface families in a single document—and use them consistently.

Times New Roman is a standard serif typeface.

Palatino is a slightly less formal serif alternative.

Helvetica is a standard sans serif typeface.

Arial seems a bit more readable than Helvetica.

Chicago makes a bold statement.

A font that imitates handwriting can be hard to read in long passages.

Ornate or whimsical fonts should generally be avoided.

FIGURE 15.9 **Sample Typefaces** Except for special emphasis, prefer conservative typefaces; the more ornate ones are harder to read and inappropriate for most workplace documents.

Use Type Sizes That Are Easy to Read. To map out a page, designers measure the size of type and other page elements (such as visuals and line length) in picas and points (Figure 15.10).

The height of a typeface, the distance from the top of the *ascender* to the base of the *descender*, is measured in points.

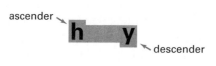

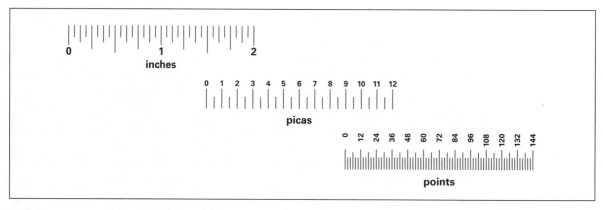

FIGURE 15.10 **Sizing the Page Elements** One pica equals roughly 1/6 of an inch and one point equals 1/12 of a pica (or 1/72 of an inch).

Select the
appropriate
point size

Standard type sizes for body copy run from 10 to 12 point, depending on the typeface. Use different sizes for other elements: headings, titles, captions, sidebars, or special emphasis. Whatever the element, use a consistent type size throughout your document. For overhead transparencies or computer projection in oral presentations, use 18 or 20 point type for body text and 20 or greater for headings. For Web pages and other electronic documents, see pages 318, 432.

Use Full Caps Sparingly. Long passages in full capitals (uppercase letters) are hard to recognize and remember because uppercase letters lack ascenders and descenders, and so all words in uppercase have the same visual outline (Felker 87). The longer the passage, the harder readers work to grasp your emphasis.

MY DOG HAS MANY FLEAS.

My dog has many fleas.

FULL CAPS are
good for
emphasis but they
make long
passages hard
to read

HARD	ACCORDING TO THE NATIONAL COUNCIL ON RADIATION PROTECTION, YOUR MAXIMUM ALLOWABLE DOSE OF LOW-LEVEL RADIATION IS 500 MILLIREMS PER YEAR.
EASIER	According to the National Council on Radiation Protection, your MAXIMUM allowable dose of low-level radiation is 500 millirems per year.

Use full caps as section headings (INTRODUCTION) or to highlight a word or phrase (WARNING: NEVER TEASE THE ALLIGATOR). As with other highlighting options discussed below, use them sparingly.

Purposes of
highlighting

Guidelines for Highlighting for Emphasis

To emphasize important elements such as headings, special terms, key points, or warnings, use white space, typography, color, and other graphic devices available on your word processor. Here are some basic options:

- You can indent (and use a smaller or a different type) to set off examples, explanations, or any material that should be differentiated from body copy.

- Using ruled horizontal lines, you can separate sections in a long document:

- Using ruled lines, broken lines, or ruled boxes, you can set off crucial information such as a warning or a caution. (See page 312 for an example.)

(continues)

Guidelines (continued)

Caution: Excessive highlights make a document look too busy.

(For more on background screens, ruled lines, and ruled boxes, see pages 284–87.)
    When using typographic devices for highlighting, keep in mind that some options are better than others:

Not all highlighting is equal

- **Boldface is good for emphasizing a single sentence or brief statement, and is seen by readers as "authoritative"** (*Aldus Guide* 42).

- *More subtle than boldface, italics can highlight words, phrases, book titles, or anything else one might otherwise underline. But long passages of italic type can be hard to read.*

- Small type sizes (usually sans serif) work well for captions and credit lines and as labels for visuals or to set off other material from the body copy.

- *Avoid large type sizes and dramatic typefaces—unless you really need to convey forcefulness.*

- Color is appropriate in some documents, but only when used sparingly. Pages 283–88 discuss how color can influence audience perception and interpretation of a message.

Whichever options you select, be consistent: Highlight all headings at one level identically; set off all warnings and cautions identically. And *never* mix too many highlights.

 Visual "chunking"

Using Headings for Access and Orientation

Readers of a long document often look back or jump ahead to sections that interest them most. Headings announce how a document is organized, point readers to what they need, and divide the document into accessible blocks or "chunks." An informative heading can help a person decide whether a section is worth reading. Besides cutting down on reading and retrieval time, headings help readers remember information.

Lay Out Headings by Level.   Like a good road map, your headings should clearly announce the large and small segments in your document. When you write your material, think of it in chunks and subchunks. In preparing any long document, you most likely have developed a formal outline (page 196). Use the logical divisions from your outline as a model for laying out the headings in your final draft.
    Figure 15.11 shows how headings vary in their position and highlighting, depending on their rank. However, because of space considerations, Figure 15.11 does not show that each higher-level heading yields at least two lower-level headings.

SECTION HEADING

In a formal report, center each section heading on the page. Use full caps and a type size roughly 4 points larger than body copy (say, 16 point section heads for 12 point body copy), in boldface. Avoid overly large heads, and use no other highlights, except possibly a second color.

Major Topic Heading

Place major topic headings at the left margin (flush left), and begin each important word with an uppercase letter. Use a type size roughly 2 points larger than body copy, in boldface. Start the copy immediately below the heading, or leave one space below the heading.

Minor Topic Heading

Set minor topic headings flush left. Use boldface, italics (optional), and a slightly larger type size than in the body copy. Begin each important word with an uppercase letter. Start the copy immediately below the heading, or leave one space below the heading.

Subtopic Heading. Incorporate subtopic headings into the body copy they head. Place them flush left and set them off with a period. Use boldface and roughly the same type size as in the body copy.

FIGURE 15.11 **One Recommended Format for Word-Processed Headings** Note that each head is set one extra line space below any preceding text. Also, different type sizes reflect different levels of heads.

Many variations of the heading format in Figure 15.11 are possible. For example, one such variation using decimal notation is shown in Figure 15.12. (For more on decimal notation, see page 199.)

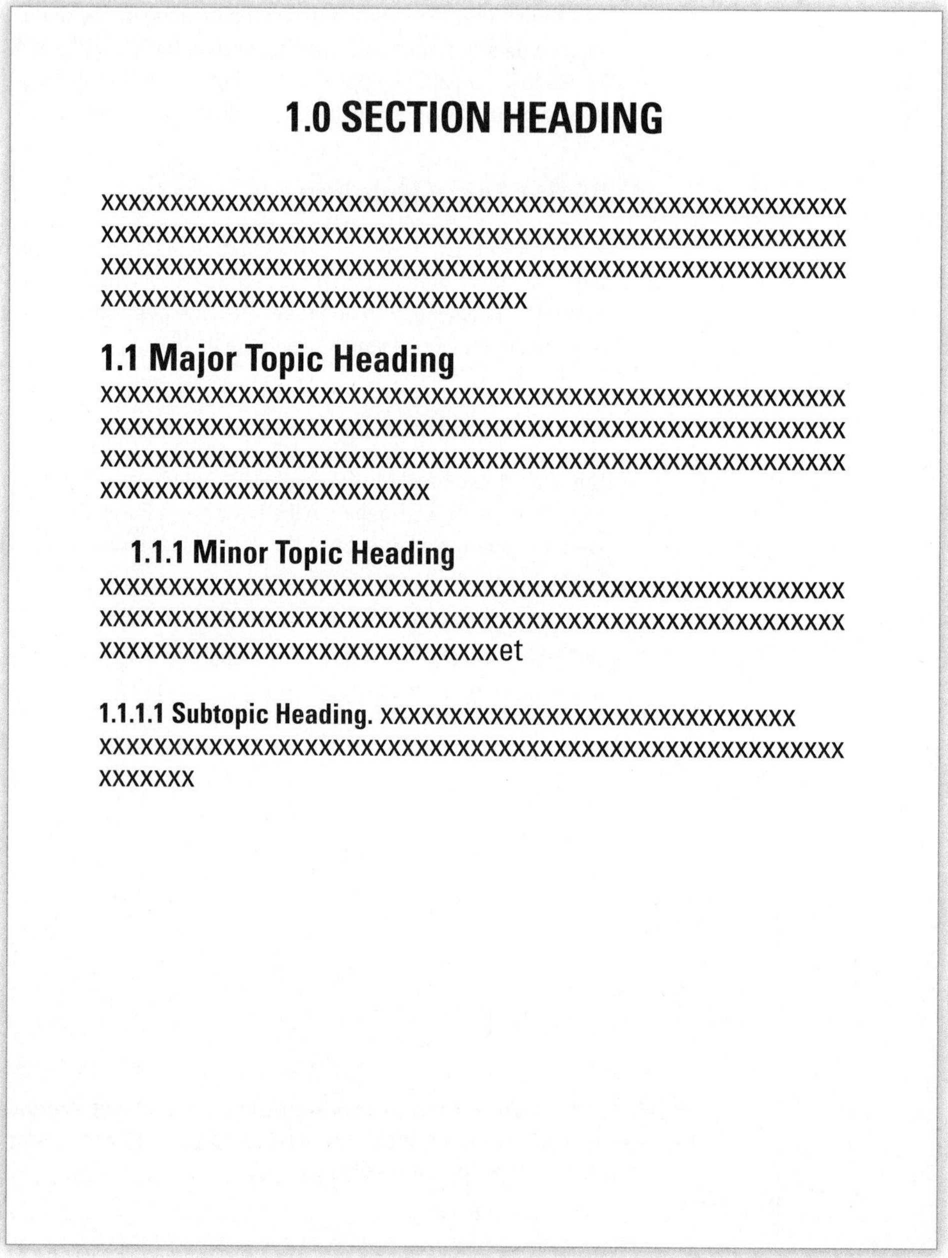

1.0 SECTION HEADING

xxxxxxxxxxxxxxxxxxxxxxxxxxxxxxxxxxxxxxxxxxxxxxxxxxxxxx
xxxxxxxxxxxxxxxxxxxxxxxxxxxxxxxxxxxxxxxxxxxxxxxxxxxxxx
xxxxxxxxxxxxxxxxxxxxxxxxxxxxxxxxxxxxxxxxxxxxxxxxxxxxxx
xxxxxxxxxxxxxxxxxxxxxxxxxxxxxxxxx

1.1 Major Topic Heading
xxxxxxxxxxxxxxxxxxxxxxxxxxxxxxxxxxxxxxxxxxxxxxxxxxxxxx
xxxxxxxxxxxxxxxxxxxxxxxxxxxxxxxxxxxxxxxxxxxxxxxxxxxxxx
xxxxxxxxxxxxxxxxxxxxxxxxxxxxxxxxxxxxxxxxxxxxxxxxxxxxxx
xxxxxxxxxxxxxxxxxxxxxxxxxx

1.1.1 Minor Topic Heading
xxxxxxxxxxxxxxxxxxxxxxxxxxxxxxxxxxxxxxxxxxxxxxxxxxxxxx
xxxxxxxxxxxxxxxxxxxxxxxxxxxxxxxxxxxxxxxxxxxxxxxxxxxxxx
xxxxxxxxxxxxxxxxxxxxxxxxxxxxxxxxxet

1.1.1.1 Subtopic Heading. xxxxxxxxxxxxxxxxxxxxxxxxxxxxxxxxxx
xxxxxxxxxxxxxxxxxxxxxxxxxxxxxxxxxxxxxxxxxxxxxxxxxxxxxx
xxxxxxx

FIGURE 15.12   **An Alternative Format for Headings**

Guidelines for Using Headings

- **Ordinarily, use no more than four levels of headings (section, major topic, minor topic, subtopic).** Excessive heads and subheads make a document seem cluttered or fragmented.

- **Divide logically.** Be sure that beneath each higher-level heading you have at least two headings at the next-lower level.

- **Insert one additional line of space above each heading.** For double-spaced text, triple-space before the heading and double-space after; for single-spaced text, double-space before the heading and single-space after.

- **Never begin the sentence right after the heading with "this," "it," or some other pronoun referring to the heading.** Make the sentence's meaning independent of the heading.

- **Never leave a heading floating as the final line of a page.** If at least two lines of text cannot fit below the heading, carry it over to the top of the next page.

- **Use running heads (headers) or feet (footers) in long documents.** Include a chapter or section heading across the top or bottom of each page (see Figure 15.13). In a document with single-sided pages, running heads or feet should always be placed consistently, typically flush right. In a document with double-sided pages, like a book, the running heads or feet should appear flush left on left-hand pages and flush right on right-hand pages.

Decide How to Phrase Your Headings.   Depending on your purpose, you can phrase your headings in various ways (*Writing User-Friendly Documents* 17):

Heading Type	Example	When to Use
Topic headings use a word or short phrase.	**Usable Page Design**	When you have lots of headings and want to keep them brief. Or to sound somewhat formal. Frequent drawback: too vague.
Statement headings use a sentence or explicit phrase.	**How to Create a Usable Page Design**	To assert something specific about the topic. Occasional drawback: wordy and cumbersome.
Question headings pose the questions in the same way readers are likely to ask them.	**How Do I Create a Usable Page Design?**	To invite readers in and to personalize the message, making people feel directly involved. Occasional drawbacks: too "chatty" for formal reports or proposals; overuse can be annoying.

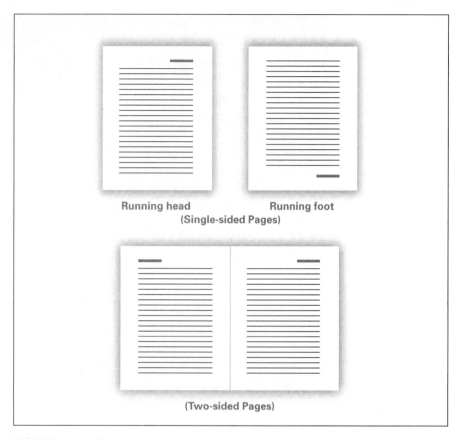

FIGURE 15.13 Running Heads and Feet For two-sided pages (say, in a book), running heads or feet on each left page would align toward the page's left side.

To avoid verbal clutter, brief *topic headings* can be useful in documents that have numerous subheads (as in a textbook or complex report)—as long as readers understand the context for each brief heading. *Statement headings* work well for explaining how something happens or operates (say, "How the Fulbright Scholarship Program Works"). *Question headings* are most useful for explaining how to do something because they address the actual questions users will have (say, "How Do I Apply for a Fulbright Scholarship?").

Phrase your headings to summarize the content as concisely as possible. But remember that a vague or overly general heading can be more misleading or confusing than no heading at all (Redish et al. 144). Compare, for example, a heading titled "Evaluation" versus "How the Fulbright Commission Evaluates a Scholarship Application"; the second version announces exactly what to expect.

Make Headings Visually Consistent and Grammatically Parallel. Feel free to vary the formats shown in Figures 15.11 and 15.12—as long as you are consistent.

When drafting your document, you can use the marks *h1*, *h2*, *h3*, and *h4* to indicate heading levels. All *h1* headings would then be set identically, as would each lower level of heading. For example, on a word-processed page, level one headings might use 14 point, bold upper case type, and be centered on the page; level two headings would then be 12 point, bold in upper and lower case and set flush left with the margin (or extended into the margin); level three headings would be 11 point bold, set flush left; level four would be 10 point bold, flush left, with the text run in (as in Figure 15.11).

Along with visual consistency, headings of the same level should also be grammatically parallel (see page 679). For example, if you phrase headings in the form of reader questions, make sure all are phrased in this way at that level. Or if you are providing instructions, begin each heading with the verb (shown in italics) that names the required action: "To avoid damaging your CDs: (1) *Clean* the CD drive heads. (2) *Store* CDs in appropriate containers. (3) *Keep* CDs away from magnets and heat."—and so on.

Audience Considerations in Page Design

In deciding on a format, work from a detailed audience and use profile (Wight 11). Know your audience and their intended use of your information. Create a design to meet their particular needs and expectations:

How users' needs determine page design

- If people will use your document for reference only (as in a repair manual), make sure you have plenty of headings.
- If users will follow a sequence of steps, show that sequence in a numbered list.
- If users will need to evaluate something, give them a checklist of criteria (as in this book, at the end of most chapters).
- If users need a warning, highlight the warning so that it cannot possibly be overlooked.
- If users have asked for a one-page report or résumé, save space by using a 10 point type size.
- If users will be facing complex information or difficult steps, widen the margins, increase all white space, and shorten the paragraphs.

Regardless of the audience, never make the document look "too intellectually intimidating" (White, *Visual Design* 4).

 Consider also your audience's cultural expectations. For instance, Arabic and Persian text is written from right to left instead of left to right (Leki 149). In other cultures, readers move up and down the page, instead of across. A particular culture might be offended by certain colors or by a typeface that seems too plain or too fancy (Weymouth 144). Ignoring a culture's design conventions can be interpreted as disrespect.

NOTE   *Even the most brilliant page design cannot redeem a document with worthless content, chaotic organization, or unreadable style. The value of any document ultimately depends on elements beneath the visual surface.*

Designing On-Screen Documents

Most of the techniques discussed so far in this chapter are appropriate for both paper and electronic documents. However, electronic documents (including Web pages, online help, PDF files, and CDs and other media) have some special design requirements.

Web Pages

Screen versus paper design

Each "page" of a Web document typically stands alone as a discrete "module," or unit of meaning. Instead of a traditional introduction-body-conclusion sequence of pages, material is displayed in screen-sized chunks, each linked as hypertext. Links essentially function as headings. Each link takes users to a deeper level (or a related level) of information. Also, to be read on a computer screen, pages must accommodate small screen size, reduced resolution, and reader resistance to scrolling—among other restrictions.

Guidelines for Designing a Web Page

- **Display the main point or topic close to the top of each page.**
- **Provide ample margins so that your text won't blur at the screen edges.**
- **Keep sentences and paragraphs shorter than for hard copy.**
- **Display links, hot buttons, and help options on each page.**
- **Provide a "Find" or "Search" option on each page.**
- **As with printed text headings, make your links consistent.** Use the same typeface and font for the same level heading. (Always test your links to be sure they actually work.)
- **Don't use underlining for emphasis.** Underlined text might be mistaken for a hyperlink.
- **Don't mix and match too many typefaces.**
- **Use sans serif type for body text.**
- **Don't use small type.** Anything under 12 point is hard to read on a screen.

These guidelines are embodied in Figure 15.14. For more on designing Web pages, see Chapter 19.

Special authoring software such as *Adobe FrameMaker* or *RoboHelp* automatically converts hard copy document format to various on-screen formats, chunked and linked for easy navigation. However, whenever possible, work with a professional Web designer to be sure your on-screen document looks and functions the way you want it to.

FIGURE 15.14 A User-Friendly Web Page A prominent heading announces the page's main topic. Then comes a graphic with links covering seasonal hazards. Topic heads throughout highlight links to key subtopics. Additional resources at page bottom include multilingual options and contact information. A quick scan of this page reveals the numerous resources available. Despite the many layers and types of information, the page is easy to navigate.

Source: Centers for Disease Control and Prevention <www.cdc.gov>.

NOTE

To learn about Web page design in full, you will need to take classes about this topic. Many organizations employ Webmasters or Web designers who can work with you in designing your pages.

Online Help

Like Web design, designing online help screens is a specialty. Many organizations, especially those that produce software, hire technical communicators who know how to produce online help screens. As with all page design, paper or electronic, producing online help screens requires consistency. For more on this topic see pages 510–12.

Adobe Acrobat™ and PDF Files

Unlike normal Web pages, which may display differently to different computers or browsers, PDF (Portable Document Format) documents retain their formatting and appear exactly as they were designed, both on the screen and when printed out. Also, unlike normal Web pages, PDF files cannot be altered or manipulated by other users, thus protecting the integrity of your document. Created with *Adobe Acrobat* software, PDF files can be placed on the Web. Users link to these just as they would to any Web site, using *Adobe Acrobat Reader* software, which usually can be downloaded free. PDF files also can be sent as email attachments (see page 349). PDF technology enables companies to make their user documentation and product manuals available to anyone with a Web connection without having to reproduce and distribute the actual manuals in hard-copy form. For more information about PDF, go to <www.adobe.com/products/acrobat>.

CDs and Other Media

You can't predict the types of media that will be used to deliver your documents. You may design an instruction manual or a customer information brochure with the intent of printing it, but the document may eventually be delivered and read on the Web, on a hand-held device (like an iPod, a Blackberry, or a Palm Pilot), or a CD. For a CD medium, you can use *Adobe Acrobat* and its PDF format to ensure that documents will look the same on the CD as they do in print. If designing for an iPod or Palm Pilot, you will need to work within the current specifications and software required for these devices. HTML is the standard language for creating Web pages (see page 426). In short, the best you can do is to identify as early as possible the media in which your document might be delivered, and work with your organization's design team to ensure that your intended audience will be able to access the information.

☑ Checklist: Usability of Page Design

(Numbers in parentheses refer to the first page of discussion.)

Shape of the Page

☐ Is the paper of the right quality? (303)

☐ Are page numbers, headers, and footers used consistently? (303)

☐ Does the grid structure provide a consistent visual theme? (303)

☐ Does the white space create areas of emphasis? (303)

☐ Are the margins ample? (305)

☐ Is line length reasonable? (306)

☐ Is the right margin unjustified? (305)

☐ Is line spacing appropriate and consistent? (306)

☐ Is each paragraph tailored to suit its purpose? (307)

☐ Are paragraphs free of "orphan" lines or "widows"? (307)

☐ Is a series of parallel items within a paragraph formatted as a list (numbered or bulleted, as appropriate)? (307)

Style of Words and Letters

☐ In general, are versions of a single typeface used throughout the document? (309)

☐ If different typefaces *are* used, are they used consistently? (309)

☐ Are typefaces and type sizes chosen for readability? (310)

☐ Do full caps highlight only single words or short phrases? (311)

Emphasis and Orientation

☐ Is the highlighting consistent and tasteful? (311)

☐ Do headings clearly announce the large and small segments in the document? (312)

☐ Are headings formatted to reflect their specific level in the document? (312)

☐ Is the phrasing of headings consistent with the document's purpose? (315)

☐ Are headings visually consistent and grammatically parallel? (316)

Audience Considerations

☐ Does this design meet the audience's needs and expectations? (317)

☐ Does this design respect the cultural conventions of the audience? (317)

ON THE JOB... Designing Documents

■ *"Sometimes I literally design documents (that is, textbooks or supplements) if a book I'm working on needs a light revision. I have a coworker who designs documents professionally though, so if I need something fancy, he designs it and I follow the specs. If an email is long and complex sometimes I try to impose some structure to it. If you are giving someone a written correspondence more than a page long, you probably should be worrying about the design of it. If you don't make things easy to follow, sometimes people panic and won't read what you've written."*

—Lorraine Patsco, Director of Prepress and Multimedia Production

■ *"As an editor of a journal and of two major publishing projects, I take a keen interest in design, or how information is displayed on the page. I tend to divide my essays into sections with headings in order to accentuate the main movements of my argument, and I often suggest to the other writers I edit that they do the same. If I am dealing with the study of a writer's revisions (which is a major part of my research), I develop graphics that allow readers to see the different revisions more clearly."*

—John Bryant, Professor of English

■ *"We are always thinking about design. I've just hired someone to help us come up with a new look to our stuff. Formatting, layout, font, graphics, artwork, color are* discussed every time we do a major piece. No one is really qualified to do this based on traditional academic training. So we have brought in a design person half-time to take on editorial and design responsibilities."

—Paul Harder, President, mid-sized consulting company

■ *"I help design everything from new company forms to letterheads and Web-based documents. But I spend much of my time designing our newsletters and writing some of the text. When I was hired, the company was mailing monthly fliers to its distributors. The fliers advertised new products, specials, and closeouts, and informed distributors of marketing or pricing changes. The problem was, all the distributors received the same fliers, regardless of whether they were a plumbing supply house, or sold electrical or construction supplies, or distributed only decorative hardware. Now we create newsletters targeted to specific distributors. We include interesting side bars, visuals, graphs on how a particular industry is doing, the history of a particular product and so on—whatever we hope will interest readers. They read those pieces and then look more closely at what we're selling."*

—Monique LeBleu, Marketing Specialist for a wholesaler of construction supplies

Exercises

 Exercises

1. Find an example of effective page design. Photocopy a selection (two or three pages), and attach a memo explaining to your instructor and classmates why this design is effective. Be specific in your evaluation. Now do the same for an example of ineffective page design, making specific suggestions for improvement. Bring your examples and explanations to class, and be prepared to discuss them.

   As an alternative assignment, imagine that you are a technical communication consultant, and address each memo to the manager of the organization that produced each document.

2. The following are headings from a set of instructions for listening. Rewrite the headings to make them parallel.

   - You Must Focus on the Message
   - Paying Attention to Nonverbal Communication
   - Your Biases Should Be Suppressed
   - Listen Critically
   - Listen for Main Ideas
   - Distractions Should Be Avoided
   - Provide Verbal and Nonverbal Feedback
   - Making Use of Silent Periods
   - Are You Allowing the Speaker Time to Make His or Her Point?
   - Keeping an Open Mind Is Important

3. Using the checklist on page design, redesign an earlier assignment or a document you've prepared on the job. Submit to your instructor the revision and the original, along with a memo explaining your improvements. Be prepared to discuss your design in class.

4. Anywhere on campus or at work, locate a document with a design that needs revision. Candidates include career counseling handbooks, financial aid handbooks, student or faculty handbooks, software or computer manuals, medical information, newsletters, or registration procedures. Redesign the document or a two- to five-page selection from it. Submit to your instructor a copy of the original, along with a memo explaining your improvements. Be prepared to discuss your revision in class.

5. Figure 15.15 shows two different designs for the same message. Which version is most effective, and why? List the specific elements in the improved version, and be prepared to discuss your list in class.

Collaborative Project

Working in small groups, redesign a document you select or your instructor provides. Prepare a detailed explanation of your group's revision. Appoint a group member to present your revision to the class.

§ 2653.31 Native group selections.

(a) Selections must not exceed the amount recommended by the regional corporation or 320 acres for each Native member of a group, or 7,680 acres for each Native group, whichever is less. Native groups must identify any acreage over that as alternate selections and rank their selections. Beyond the reservations in sections 2650.32 and 2650.46 of this Part, conveyances of lands in a National Wildlife Refuge are subject to the provisions of section 22(g) of ANCSA and section 2651.41 of this chapter as though they were conveyances to a village corporation.

(b) Selections must be contiguous and the total area selected must be compact except where separated by lands that are unavailable for selection. BLM will not consider the selection compact if it excludes lands available for selection within its exterior boundaries; or an isolated tract of public land of less than 640 acres remains after selection. The lands selected must be in quarter sections where they are available unless exhaustion of the group's entitlement does not allow the selection of a quarter section. The selection must include all available lands in less than quarter sections. Lands selected must conform as nearly as practicable to the United States lands survey system.

§ 2653.31 What are the selection criteria for Native group selections and what lands are available?

You may select only the amount recommended by the regional corporation or 320 acres for each Native member of a group, or 7,680 acres for each Native group, whichever is less. You must identify any acreage over 7,680 as alternate selections and rank their selection.

§ 2653.32 What are the restrictions in conveyances to Native groups?

Beyond the reservations described in this part conveyances of lands in a National Wildlife Refuge are subject to section 22(g) of ANCSA as though they were conveyances to a village.

§ 2653.33 Do Native group selections have to be contiguous?

Yes, selections must be contiguous. The total area you select must be compact except where separated by lands that are unavailable for selection. BLM will not consider your selection if:

(a) It excludes lands available for selection within its exterior boundaries; or

(b) An isolated tract of public land of less than 640 acres remains after selection.

§ 2653.34 How small a parcel can I select?

Select lands in quarter sections where they are available unless there is not enough left in your group's entitlement to allow this. Your selection must include all available lands in areas that are smaller than quarter sections. Conform your selections as much as possible to the United States land survey system.

FIGURE 15.15 **Two Different Designs for the Same Message**
Source: Writing User-Friendly Documents. Washington DC: U.S. Bureau of Land Management, 2001. 41.

PART FOUR

Specific Documents and Applications

CHAPTER **16**
Memo Reports and Electronic Correspondence 326

CHAPTER **17**
Workplace Letters 359

CHAPTER **18**
Employment Correspondence 388

CHAPTER **19**
Web Pages 425

CHAPTER **20**
Technical Definitions 439

CHAPTER **21**
Technical Descriptions and Specifications 462

CHAPTER **22**
Instructions and Procedures 490

CHAPTER **23**
Proposals 522

CHAPTER **24**
Formal Analytical Reports 560

CHAPTER **25**
Front Matter and End Matter in Long Documents 597

CHAPTER **26**
Oral Presentations 608

CHAPTER 16

Memo Reports and Electronic Correspondence

Documents in Hard-Copy Versus Digital Format

Informational Versus Analytical Reports

Formal Versus Informal Reports

Purpose of Memo Reports

Elements of a Usable Memo

Interpersonal Considerations in Writing a Memo

Direct Versus Indirect Organizing Patterns

Informational Reports in Memo Form

Analytical Reports in Memo Form

  Checklist: Usability of Memo Reports

Electronic Mail

  Guidelines for Using Electronic Mail

  Guidelines for Choosing Email Versus Paper,
    Telephone, or Fax

  Checklist: Email

Instant Messaging

Corporate Blogs and Wikis

For day-to-day operations in any sizable organization, memo reports and electronic correspondence are indispensable tools for communication.

Documents in Hard-Copy Versus Digital Format

Despite the proliferation of voice-mail systems, cell phones, personal digital assistants, iPods and Web sites, much of our electronic communication continues to be *written*. Though many of these documents are paperless, existing only in digital form, hard-copy text is unlikely to disappear anytime soon. In fact, documents prepared on paper are routinely transmitted electronically via fax or as an email attachment. Whether the message is cast as a brief memo or a long report, the paper document continues to serve as the standard for written communication in the workplace.

Informational Versus Analytical Reports

In the professional world, decision makers rely on two broad types of reports: Some reports focus primarily on *information* ("what we're doing now," "what we did last month," "what our customer survey found," "what went on at the department meeting"). Beyond merely providing information, many reports also include *analysis* ("what this information means for us," "what courses of action should be considered," "what we recommend, and why").

The role of analysis in a technical report

Analysis is the heart of technical communication: it involves evaluating your information, interpreting it accurately, drawing valid conclusions, and making persuasive recommendations. Although gathering and reporting information are essential workplace skills, *analysis* is ultimately what professionals largely do to earn their pay. And the results of any detailed analysis almost invariably get recorded in a written report. Chapter 24 covers formal analytical reports.

Formal Versus Informal Reports

For every long (formal) report, countless short (informal) reports lead to informed decisions on matters as diverse as the most comfortable office chairs to buy or the best recruit to hire for management training. Unlike long reports (Chapter 24), most short reports require no extended planning, are quickly prepared, contain little or no background information, and have no front or end matter (title page, table of contents, glossary, etc.). But despite their conciseness, short reports do provide the information and analysis that readers need.

Although various formats can be used, short reports most often take the form of a memorandum.

Purpose of Memo Reports

Memos have
many uses

Memos, the major form of communication in most organizations, leave a *paper trail* of directives, inquiries, instructions, requests, and recommendations, and daily reports for future reference.

Despite the explosive growth of email, paper memos continue to be used widely, especially when an email would be considered too informal or when the message is lengthy. (See page 350 for guidelines.) Different organizations have different preferences about paper memos versus email.

NOTE   *Email memos leave their own trail. Although generally less formal and more quickly written than paper documents, email messages are saved in both hard copy and online— and can inadvertently be forwarded to someone never intended to receive or read them.*

Memos have legal
and ethical
implications

Organizations rely on memos to trace decisions and responsibilities, track progress, and recheck data. Therefore, any memo you write can have far-reaching ethical and legal implications. Be sure your memo includes the date and your initials or signature. Also make sure that your information is specific, unambiguous, and accurate.

Elements of a Usable Memo

Because it often must compete for a busy recipient's attention, a memo needs to be easy to scan, file, and retrieve. A usable memo focuses on *one* main topic and is short and to the point. It provides all the information and analysis that the reader needs, but *no more* than the reader needs. And it is distributed to all the right people. The standard memo has heading guides that name the sender, recipient, date, and subject (often in caps or underlined for emphasis). Additional memo elements are shown in Figure 16.1.

Interpersonal Considerations in Writing a Memo

A form of "in-house" correspondence, memos circulate among colleagues, subordinates, and superiors to address questions like these:

What memo
recipients want
to know

- What are we doing right, and how can we do it better?
- What are we doing wrong, and how can we improve?
- Who's doing what, and when, and where?

Memo topics often involve evaluations or recommendations about policies, procedures, and, ultimately, the *people with whom we work*.

Because people are sensitive to criticism (even when it is merely implied) and often resistant to change, an ill-conceived or aggressive memo can spell disaster for

NAME OF ORGANIZATION

MEMORANDUM   Center this label on the page or set it flush left (as shown)

To: Name and title of recipient
From: Your name and title (and initials or signature), for verification
Date: (also serves as a chronological record for future reference)
Subject: ELEMENTS OF A USABLE MEMO (or, replace *SUBJECT* with *RE* for
               in reference to)

Subject Line
Be sure that the subject line clearly announces your purpose: (RECOMMENDATIONS FOR SOFTWARE
SECURITY UPGRADES) instead of (SOFTWARE SECURITY UPGRADES). Capitalize all major words or use
italics or boldface.

Memo Text
Unless you have reason for being indirect (see page 330), state your main point in the opening
paragraph. Provide a context the recipient can recognize. (*As you requested in our January
meeting, I am forwarding the results of our software security audit.*) For recipients unfamiliar
with the topic, begin with a brief background paragraph.

Headings
When the memo covers multiple subtopics, include headings (as shown here). Headings (see
page 312) help you organize and they help readers locate information quickly.

Graphic Highlights
To improve readability you might organize facts and figures in a table (see page 257) or in
bulleted or numbered lists (see page 307).

Paragraph and Line Spacing
Do not indent a paragraph's first line. Single-space within paragraphs and double-space between.

Subsequent Page Header
Be as brief as possible. If you must exceed one page, include a header on each subsequent
page, naming the recipient and date (*J. Baxter, 6/12/07, page 2*).

Copy, Distribution, and Enclosure Notations
These items are illustrated under "Letters" (see page 365), and used in the same way with
memos, as needed.

FIGURE 16.1   Elements of a Usable Memo Memo formats can differ across organizations and
professions, but most paper memos look like this. Because memos are often read rapidly by a busy
recipient, the various pieces of important information have to be in predictable locations.

its author. Consider, for instance, this evaluation of one company's training program for new employees:

A hostile
approach

> No one tells new employees what it's *really* like to work here—how to survive politically: for example, never tell anyone what you *really* think; never observe how few women are in management positions, or how disorganized things seem to be. New employees shouldn't have to learn these things the hard way. We need to demand clearer behavioral objectives.

Instead of emphasizing deficiencies, the following version focuses on the *benefits* of change:

A more
reasonable
approach

> New employees would benefit from a concrete guide to the personal and professional traits expected in our company. Training sessions could be based on the attitudes, manners, and behavior appropriate in business settings.

Here are some common interpersonal mistakes that can offend coworkers:

When memos
go wrong

- **Griping or complaining.** Everyone has problems of their own. Never complain without suggesting a solution.
- **Being too critical or judgmental.** Making someone look bad means making an enemy.
- **Sounding too formal or informal for the topic and audience.** A memo to the person in the next cubicle to ask for help on a project would be more personal and less formal than a memo to a company executive. (For more on tone, see pages 238–46).
- **Using the wrong medium.** Whether you deliver the memo via printed copy, email, or in person depends on your audience and situation. For example, an unsolicited recommendation for updating office software—or any topic that a recipient might perceive as a "delicate" or "sensitive" or as "out of the blue sky"—generally should be delivered in person, or at least prefaced by a phone call. (For more on choosing your medium, see page 350.)
- **Being too bossy.** The imperative mood is best reserved for instructions.
- **Neglecting to provide a copy to each appropriate person.** No one appreciates being left "out of the loop."

Before releasing any memo designed to influence people's thinking, review the Guidelines for Persuasion (Chapter 4) carefully.

NOTE   *Busy people are justifiably impatient with any memo that seems longer than it needs to be or that contains typos or grammar and spelling errors. Use your spelling and grammar checker, but also proofread carefully. (See page 21 for proofreading guidelines.)*

Direct Versus Indirect Organizing Patterns

In planning a memo, you can choose from two basic organizing patterns. First is the *direct* pattern, in which you begin with your main point (your request, recommendation, or position on the issue) and then present the details or analysis supporting your case. The second pattern is *indirect*, in which you lay out the details of your case before delivering the bottom line.

"Should the details or the bottom line come first?"

Readers generally prefer the direct approach, especially for analytical reports, because they can get right to your main point. For example, if the Payroll Division of a large company has to announce to employees that the delay in weekly paychecks was caused by a virus in the computer system, a direct approach would be appropriate. But when you need to convey bad news or make an unpopular request or recommendation (as in asking for a raise or announcing employee layoffs), you might consider an indirect approach so that you can present your case first. The danger of an indirect approach, however, is that readers could think you are being evasive. For more on direct versus indirect organizing patterns, see page 371.

Informational Reports in Memo Form

Among the informational reports that help keep organizations running from day to day are progress reports, periodic activity reports, and meeting minutes.

Progress Reports

Progress reports serve many purposes

Large organizations depend on progress reports (also called status reports) to monitor activities, problems, and progress on various projects. Some professions require regular progress reports (daily, weekly, monthly), while others only use such reports as needed for a specific project or task. Daily progress reports are vital in a business that assigns crews to many projects.

Managers use progress reports to evaluate a project and its supervisor, and to decide how to allocate funds. Managers also need to know about delays that could dramatically affect outcomes and project costs, and need information in order to coordinate the efforts of various groups working on a project.

When work is performed for an external client, the reports explain to the client how time and money are being spent and how difficulties have been overcome. The reports can therefore be used to assure the client that the project will be completed on schedule and on budget. Many contracts stipulate the dates and stages when progress will be reported. Failing to report on time may invoke contractual penalties.

Together, the project proposal (Chapter 23), progress reports (the number varies with the project's scope and length), and the final report (Chapter 24) provide a record and history of the project.

To inform managers and clients, progress reports should answer these questions:

What recipients of a progress report want to know

- How much has been accomplished since the last report?
- Is the project on schedule?
- If not, what went wrong? How was the problem corrected? How long will it take to get back on schedule?
- What else needs to be done? What is the next step?

- Have you encountered any unexpected developments?
- When do you anticipate completion? Or (on a long project) when do you anticipate completion of the next phase?

If the report is part of a series, you might also refer to prior problems or developments. Each report in a series should be organized identically.

Many organizations have forms for organizing progress reports. Otherwise, for clients or other outside recipients, a letter format (see page 365) is preferred. Reports for in-house recipients typically use a memo format, as in Figure 16.2.

BETA National

MEMORANDUM

To: P. J. Stone, Senior Vice President

From: B. Poret, Group Training Manager *B.P.*

Date: June 6, 20xx

Subject: *Progress Report: Training Equipment for New Operations Building*

Work Completed

Summarizes achievements to date

Our training group has met twice since our May 12 report to answer your questions in your May 16 memo. In our first meeting, we identified the types of training we anticipate.

Types of Training Anticipated

Details the achievements

- Divisional Surveys
- Divisional Systems Training
- Divisional Clerical Training (Continuing)
- Divisional Clerical Training (New Employees)
- Divisional Management Training (Seminars)
- Special/New Equipment Training

In our second meeting, we considered various areas for the training room.

Training Room

The frequency of training necessitates having a training room available daily. The large training room in the Corporate Education area (10th floor)

FIGURE 16.2 Progress Report (on the Job) Notice how lists increase readability by organizing the various sets of facts.

would be ideal. Please confirm that this room can be assigned to us on a full-time basis.

To support the training programs, we purchased this equipment:

- Audioviewer
- LCD monitor
- CD recorder and monitor
- CRT
- Software for computer-assisted instruction
- Slide projector
- Tape recorder

This equipment will facilitate training in varied modes, ranging from programmed and learner-controlled instruction to seminars and workshops.

Work Remaining

To support the training, we need to furnish the room appropriately. Because the types of training will vary, the furniture should provide a flexible environment. Outlined here are our anticipated furnishing needs.

- Tables and chairs that can be set up in many configurations. These would allow for individual or group training and large seminars.

- Portable room dividers. These would provide study space for training with programmed instruction, and allow for simultaneous training.

- Built-in storage space for audiovisual equipment as well as training supplies. This storage space should be multipurpose, providing work or display surfaces.

- A flexible lighting system, important for audiovisual presentations and individualized study.

- Independent temperature control, to ensure that the training room remains comfortable regardless of group size and equipment used.

The project is on schedule. As soon as we receive your approval of these specifications, we will proceed to the next step: sending out bids for room dividers and having plans drawn for the built-in storage space.

cc: R. S. Pike, SVP

Describes what remains to be done

Gives a rough timetable

FIGURE 16.2 *(Continued)*

As you work on a longer report or term project, your instructor might require a progress report. In Figure 16.3, Karen Granger documents the progress she has made on her term project: an evaluation of the Environmental Protection Agency's effectiveness in cleaning a heavily contaminated harbor at a major New England fishery. (For an additional example of this type of report as part of a course project in technical communication, see page 720.)

Progress Report

To: Dr. John Lannon

From: Karen P. Granger *KG*

Date: April 17, 20xx

Subject: Evaluation of the EPA's ***Remedial Action Master Plan***

Project Overview
As my term project, I have been evaluating the issues of politics, scheduling, and safety surrounding the EPA's published plan to remove Polychlorinated biphenyl (PCB) contaminants from New Bedford Harbor.

Work Completed

February 23:   Began general research on the PCB contamination of the New Bedford Harbor.

March 8:   Decided to analyze the *Remedial Action Master Plan* (*RAMP*) in order to determine whether residents are being studied to death " by the EPA.

March 9–19:   Drew a map of the harbor to show areas of contamination. Obtained the *RAMP* from Pat Shay of the EPA.

               Interviewed State Representative Grimes briefly by phone; Scheduled an in-depth interview with Grimes and environmental activist Sharon Dean on April 13. Interviewed Patricia Chase, President of the New England Sierra Club, briefly by phone.

March 24:   Obtained *Public Comments on the New Bedford RAMP,* a collection of reactions to the plan.

April 13:   Interviewed Grimes and Dean; searched Grimes's files for information. Also searched the files of Raymond Soares, New Bedford Coordinator, EPA.

Margin note: Summarizes achievements to date

FIGURE 16.3   **Progress Report on a Term Project**

J. Lannon, 4/17/xx, page 2

Work in Progress
Contacting by phone and email a cross section of respondents who have commented on the *RAMP*.

Work to Be Completed

Describes work
remaining, with
timetable

April 25:	Finish contacting commentators on the *RAMP*.
April 26:	Interview an EPA representative about the complaints that the commentators raised about the *RAMP*.
Date for Completion:	May 3, 20xx

Complications

Describes problems
encountered

The issue of PCB contamination is complicated and emotional. The more I uncovered, the more difficult I found it to remain impartial in my research and analysis. As a New Bedford resident, I expected to find that we are indeed being studied to death; because my research seems to support my initial impression, I am not sure I have remained impartial.

Lastly, the people I talk to do not always have the time to answer all my questions. Everyone, however, has been interested and encouraging, if not always informative.

FIGURE 16.3 *(Continued)*

Periodic Activity Reports

The periodic activity report resembles the progress report in that it summarizes activities over a specified time frame. But unlike progress reports, which summarize specific accomplishments on a given *project*, periodic reports summarize general activities during a given *period*. Manufacturers requiring periodic reports often have prepared forms, because most of their tasks are quantifiable (e.g., units produced). But most white-collar jobs do not lend themselves to prepared-form reports. You may have to develop your own format, as the next writer does.

Fran DeWitt's report (Figure 16.4) answers her boss's primary question: *What did you accomplish last month?* Her response has to be detailed and informative.

NOTE   *Both progress reports and periodic activity reports inform management and clients about what employees are doing and how well they are doing it. Therefore, accuracy, clarity, and appropriate detail are essential—as is the ethical dimension (Chapter 5). Make sure that recipients have all the vital facts—and that they understand these facts as clearly as you do.*

■ Mammon Trust

MEMORANDUM
Date: 6/18/xx
To: N. Morgan, Assistant Vice President
From: F. C. DeWitt *FCD*
Subject: **Recent Meetings for Computer-Assisted Instruction**

Gives overview of recent activities, and their purpose

For the past month, I've been working on a cooperative project with the Banking Administration Institute, Computron Corporation, and several banks. My purpose has been to develop training programs, specific to banking, appropriate for computer-assisted instruction (CAI).

We have focused on three major areas: Proof/Encoding Training for entry-level personnel, Productivity Skills for Management, and Banking Principles for Supervisors.

Gives details

I hosted two meetings for this task force. On June 6, we discussed Proof/Encoding Training, and on June 7, Productivity Training. The objective for the Proof/Encoding meeting was to compare ideas, information, and current training packages available on this topic. We are now designing a training course.

The objective of the meeting on Productivity was to discuss skills that increase productivity in banking (specifically Banking Operations). Discussion included instances in which computer-assisted instruction is appropriate for teaching productivity skills. Computron also discussed computer applications used to teach productivity. Other banks outlined their experiences with similar applications.

On June 10, I attended a meeting in Washington, D.C., to design a course in basic banking principles for high-level clerical/supervisory-level employees. We also discussed the feasibility of adapting this course to CAI. This type of training, not currently available through Corporate Education, would meet a definite supervisor/management need in the division.

Explains the benefits of these activities

My involvement in these meetings has two benefits. First, structured discussions with trainers in the banking industry provide an exchange of ideas, methods, and experiences. This involvement expedites development of our training programs because it saves me time on research. Second, automation will continue to affect future training practices. With a working knowledge of these systems and their applications, I now am able to assist my group in designing programs specific to our needs.

FIGURE 16.4   **Periodic Activity Report**

Meeting Minutes

Many team or project meetings require someone to record the proceedings. Minutes are the records of such meetings. Copies of minutes usually are distributed (often via email) to all members and interested parties, to track the proceedings and to remind members of their designated responsibilities. The appointed secretary records the minutes.

When you record minutes, answer these questions:

What recipients of minutes want to know

- What group held the meeting? When, where, and why?
- Who chaired the meeting? Who else was present?
- Were the minutes of the last meeting approved (or disapproved)?
- Who said what?
- Was anything resolved?
- Who made which motions and what was the vote? What discussion preceded the vote?
- Who was given responsibility for which tasks?

Minutes (Figure 16.5) are filed as part of an official record, and so must be precise, clear, highly informative, and free of the writer's personal commentary ("As usual,

Tells who attended

Summarizes discussion of each item

Minutes of Personnel Managers' Meeting
October 5, 20xx

Members Present
Harold Tweeksbury, Jeannine Boisvert, Sheila DaCruz, Ted Washington, Denise Walsh, Cora Parks, Cliff Walsh, Joyce Capizolo

Agenda

1. The meeting was called to order on Wednesday, October 5, at 10 A.M. by Cora Parks.

2. The minutes of the September meeting were approved unanimously.

3. The first order of new business was to approve the following policies for the Christmas season:

   a. Temporary employees should list their ID numbers in the upper-left corner of their receipt envelopes to help verification. Discount Clerical assistant managers will be responsible for seeing that this procedure is followed.

FIGURE 16.5 A Sample Set of Meeting Minutes Different organizations often have templates or special formats for recording minutes.

---

b. When temporary employees turn in their envelopes, personnel from Discount Clerical should spot-check them for completeness and legibility. Incomplete or illegible envelopes should be corrected, completed, or rewritten. *Envelopes should not be sealed.*

Tells who said what

Tells what was voted

4. Jeannine Boisvert moved that we also hold one-day training workshops for temporary employees in order to teach them our policies and procedures. The motion was seconded. Joyce Capizolo disagreed, saying that on-the-job training (OJT) was enough. The motion for the training session carried 6–3. The first workshop, which Jeannine agreed to arrange, will be held October 25.

5. Joyce Capizolo requested that temporary employees be sent a memo explaining the temporary employee discount procedure. The request was converted to a motion and seconded by Cliff Walsh. The motion passed by a 7–2 vote.

6. Cora Parks adjourned the meeting at 11:55 A.M.

FIGURE 16.5 *(Continued)*

Ms. Jones disagreed with the committee") or judgmental words ("good," "poor," "irrelevant").

Analytical Reports in Memo Form

The reports discussed so far in this chapter focus on factual information. Now the focus shifts to short analytical reports, all of which logically arrive at a conclusion derived from the information. Readers of analytical reports want more than the facts; they want to know what the facts mean and, often, what action the facts suggest. Common types of short (or informal) analytical reports include feasibility reports, recommendation reports, and justification reports.

Feasibility Reports

"Should we or shouldn't we?"

Feasibility reports are used when decision makers need to assess whether an idea or plan or course of action is realistic and practical: "How *doable* is this idea?" Although a particular course of action might be *possible*, it might not be *practical*—because such action might be too costly or hazardous or poorly timed, among other reasons. For example, a maker of precision tools might examine the feasibility of automating several key manufacturing processes. While automating these tasks would lower costs and increase productivity for the short term, the dampening effect of layoffs on company morale could lead, over the long term, to reduced productivity as well as quality control problems.

A feasibility analysis provides answers to questions like these:

What recipients of a feasibility report want to know

- Is this course of action likely to succeed?
- Why or why not?
- What are the assessment criteria (e.g., cost, safety, productivity)?
- Do the benefits outweigh the drawbacks or risks?
- What are the pros and cons?
- What alternatives do we have?
- Can we get the funding?
- Should we do anything at all? Should we wait?

Readers of a feasibility analysis look for answers at or near the beginning of the document, followed by the supporting evidence and reasoning.

NOTE   *An assessment of feasibility often requires two additional types of analysis: an examination of what caused a problem or situation and a comparison of two or more alternative solutions or courses of action. For detailed discussion of these three analytical approaches, see pages 562–64.*

In Figure 16.6, a securities analyst for a state pension fund reports to the fund's manager on the feasibility of investing in a rapidly growing computer maker. (Notice

State Pension Fund

MEMORANDUM

To: Mary K. White, Fund Manager

From: Martha Mooney *MM*

Date: April 1, 20xx

Subject: **The Feasibility of Investing in WBM Computers, Inc.**

Gives brief background

Our zero-coupon bonds, comprising 3.5 percent of State Pension Fund's investment portfolio, will mature on April 15. Current inflationary pressures are making fixed-income investments less attractive than equities. As you

FIGURE 16.6   A Feasibility Analysis

requested, I have researched and compared the feasibility of various investment alternatives based on these criteria: market share, earnings, and dividends.

Recommendation

Makes a direct recommendation

Given its established market share, solid earnings, and generous dividends, WBM Computers, Inc. is a sound and promising company. I recommend that we invest our maturing bond proceeds in WBM's Class A stock.

Market Share

Explains the criteria supporting the recommendation

Although only ten years old, WBM successfully competes with well established computer makers. WBM's market share has grown steadily for the past five years. For this past year, total services and sales ranked 367th in the industrial United States, with orders increasing from $750 million to $1.25 billion. Net income places WBM 237th in the country, and 13th on return to investors.

Earnings

WBM's margin for profit on sales is 9 percent, a roughly steady figure for the past three years. Whereas 1997 earnings were only $ .09 per share, this year's earnings are $1.36 per share. Included in these ten-year earnings is a two-for-one stock split issued on November 2, 2004. Barring a global downturn in computer sales, WBM's outlook for continued strong earnings is promising.

Dividends

Investors are offered two types of common stock, listed on the American Stock Exchange. The assigned par value of both classes is $.50 per share. Class A stock pays an additional $.25 per share dividend but restricts voting privileges to one vote for every ten shares held by the investor. Class B stock is not entitled to the extra dividend but carries full voting rights. The additional dividend from Class A shares would enhance income flow into our portfolio.

Encourages reader action

WBM shares now trade at 14 times earnings, with a current share price of $56.00, a relative bargain in my estimation. An immediate investment would add strength and diversity to our portfolio.

FIGURE 16.6 *(Continued)*

the technical language, appropriate for an audience familiar with the specialized terminology of finance.)

Feasibility analysis is an essential basis for any well-conceived recommendation. Notice how the following recommendation and justification reports include implicit considerations of feasibility. Before people will accept your recommendation, you have to persuade them that this is a good idea.

Recommendation Reports

Recommendation reports interpret data, draw conclusions, and recommend a convincing and realistic course of action, usually in response to a specific problem or need. The following recommendation report is addressed to the writer's supervisor. This is just one example of a short report used to examine a problem and recommend a solution.

Sample memos

CASE: A Problem-Solving Recommendation

Bruce Doakes is assistant manager of occupational health and safety for a major airline that employs over two hundred reservation and booking agents. Each agent spends eight hours daily seated at a workstation that has a computer, telephone, and other electronic equipment. Many agents have complained of chronic discomfort from their work: headache, eyestrain and irritation, blurred or double vision, backache, and stiff neck and joints.

Bruce's boss asked him to study the problem and recommend improvements in the work environment. Bruce surveyed employees and consulted ophthalmologists, chiropractors, orthopedic physicians, and the latest publications on ergonomics (tailoring work environments for employees' physical and psychological well-being). After completing his study, Bruce composed his reports (Figure 16.7), which had to be persuasive as well as informative.

For more examples and advice on formulating, evaluating, and refining your recommendations, see pages 567–71.

Justification Reports

Many recommendation reports respond to reader requests for a solution to a problem (as in Figure 16.7); others originate with the writer, who has recognized a problem and has come up with a solution. This latter type is often called a *justification report*; such reports justify the writer's position by answering this key question for recipients: *Why should we?*

Unless you except total resistance to your idea, get to the point quickly and make your case (as in Figure 16.8) by using some version of the direct organizational plan that is described on page 345.

• TRANS GLOBE AIRLINES •

MEMORANDUM

To: R. Ames, Vice President, Personnel

From: B. Doakes, Health and Safety *BD*

Date: August 15, 20xx

Subject: **Recommendations for Reducing Agents' Discomfort**

Provides immediate orientation by giving brief background and main point

In our July 20 staff meeting, we discussed physical discomfort among reservation and booking agents, who spend eight hours daily at automated workstations. Our agents complain of headaches, eyestrain and irritation, blurred or double vision, backaches, and stiff joints. This report outlines the apparent causes and recommends ways of reducing discomfort.

Causes of Agents' Discomfort

Interprets findings and draws conclusions

For the time being, I have ruled out the computer display screens as a cause of headaches and eye problems for the following reasons:

1. Our new display screens have excellent contrast and no flicker.

2. Research findings about the health effects of low-level radiation from computer screens are inconclusive.

The headaches and eye problems seem to be caused by the excessive glare on display screens from background lighting.

Other discomforts, such as backaches and stiffness, apparently result from the agents' sitting in one position for up to two hours between breaks.

Recommended Changes

Makes general recommendations

We can eliminate much discomfort by improving background lighting, workstation conditions, and work routines and habits.

Background Lighting. To reduce the glare on display screens, these are recommended changes in background lighting:

FIGURE 16.7   A Recommendation Memo Before making any recommendation, be sure you've gathered the right information. For this report, the writer did enough research to rule out one cause of the problem (computer display screens as the cause of employee headaches) before settling on the actual cause (excessive glare on display screens from background lighting).

R. Ames, 8/15/xx, page 2

Expands on each
recommendation

1. Decrease all overhead lighting by installing lower-wattage bulbs.

2. Keep all curtains and adjustable blinds on the south and west windows at least half-drawn, to block direct sunlight.

3. Install shades to direct the overhead light straight downward, so that it is not reflected by the screens.

Workstation Conditions.   These are recommended changes in the workstations:

1. Reposition all screens so light sources are neither at front nor back.

2. Wash the surface of each screen weekly.

3. Adjust each screen so the top is slightly below the operator's eye level.

4. Adjust all keyboards so they are 27 inches from the floor.

5. Replace all fixed chairs with pneumatic, multi-task chairs.

Work Routines and Habits.   These are recommended changes in agents' work routines and habits:

1. Allow frequent rest periods (10 minutes each hour instead of 30 minutes twice daily).

2. Provide yearly eye exams for all terminal operators, as part of our routine healthcare program.

3. Train employees to adjust screen contrast and brightness whenever the background lighting changes.

4. Offer workshops on improving posture.

Discusses benefits
of following the
recommendations

These changes will give us time to consider more complex options such as installing hoods and antiglare filters on terminal screens, replacing fluorescent lighting with incandescent, covering surfaces with nonglare paint, or other disruptive procedures.

cc: J. Bush, Medical Director
    M. White, Manager of Physical Plant

FIGURE 16.7 *(Continued)*

MEMORANDUM

To: D. Spring, President

            Greentree Bionomics, Inc. (GBI)

From: M. Noll, Chief, Biology Division *MN*

Date: April 18, 20xx

Subject: **The Need to Hire Additional Personnel**

Introduction and Recommendation

Opens with the problem

With 56 active employees, GBI has been unable to keep up with scheduled contracts. As a result, we have a contract backlog of roughly $700,000. This backlog is caused by understaffing in the biology and chemistry divisions.

Recommends a solution

To increase production and ease the workload, I recommend that we hire three general laboratory assistants.

Expands on the recommendation

The lab assistants would be responsible for cleaning glassware and general equipment; feeding and monitoring fish stocks; preparing yeast, algae, and shrimp cultures; preparing stock solutions; and assisting scientists in various tests and procedures.

Benefits and Costs

Three full-time lab assistants would have a positive effect on overall productivity:

Shows how benefits would offset costs

- Dirty glassware would no longer pile up, and the fish holding tanks could be cleaned daily (as they should be) instead of weekly.

- Because other employees would no longer need to work more than forty hours weekly, morale would improve.

- Research scientists would be freed from general maintenance work (cleaning glassware, feeding and monitoring the fish stock, etc.) Given more time to perform and report on client tests, the researchers could eliminate their chronic backlog.

- With our backlog eliminated, clients would no longer have cause to be impatient.

FIGURE 16.8   A Justification Report   The tone here is confident yet diplomatic—appropriate for an unsolicited recommendation to an executive. For more on connecting with a reluctant audience, see Chapter 4.

> D. Spring, 4/18/xx, page 2
>
> Costs: Initial yearly salaries (at $12.00/hour) for three lab assistants would
> come to $74,880; medical insurance would add roughly $30,000. Francine
> Flynn, in Billing and Accounting, assures me that this expenditure would be
> more than offset by anticipated growth in revenue.
>
> **Conclusion**
> Increased productivity at GBI is essential to maintaining good client
> relations. These additional personnel would allow us to continue a
> reputation of prompt and efficient service, thus ensuring our steady growth
> and development.
>
> Could we meet sometime next week to discuss this in detail? I will contact
> you on Monday.

Encourages
acceptance of the
recommendation

FIGURE 16.8 *(Continued)*

How to organize
a justification
report

1. State the problem and your recommendations for solving it.
2. Highlight the benefits of your plan before you present the *costs;* the "bottom
   line" is often a deterrent.
3. If needed, explain how your plan can be implemented.
4. Conclude by encouraging the reader to act.

NOTE   *Unsolicited recommendations present a complex persuasive challenge and they **always** carry the possibility of inviting a hostile or defensive response from a surprised or offended recipient. ("Who asked for your two cents worth?") Never come across as presumptuous! Give readers notice beforehand; feel them out on the issue.*

☑ Checklist: Usability of Memo Reports

(Numbers in parentheses refer to the first page of discussion.)

Ethical, Legal, and Interpersonal Considerations
☐ Is the information specific, accurate, and unambiguous? (328)
☐ Does the medium (paper, fax, email, phone, in person) fit the situation? (330)
☐ Is the message inoffensive to all parties? (328)
☐ Are all appropriate parties receiving a copy? (330)

(continues)

Checklist (continued)

Organization

☐ Is the important information in an area of emphasis? (329)

☐ Is the direct or indirect pattern used appropriately to present the report's bottom line? (330)

☐ Is the material "chunked" into easily digestible parts? (211)

Format

☐ Does the memo have a complete heading? (328)

☐ Does the subject line announce the memo's content and purpose? (329)

☐ Are paragraphs single spaced within and double spaced between? (329)

☐ Do headings announce subtopics, as needed? (329)

☐ If more than one reader is receiving a copy, does the memo include a distribution notation (cc:) to identify other recipients? (329)

☐ Does the document's appearance create a favorable impression? (329)

Content

☐ Is the information based on careful research? (342)

☐ Is the message brief and to the point? (327)

☐ Are tables, charts, and other graphics used as needed? (329)

☐ Are recipients given enough information to make an *informed* decision? (38)

☐ Are the conclusions and recommendations clear? (567)

Style

☐ Is the writing clear, concise, fluent, exact, and likable? (215)

☐ Is the tone appropriate? (330)

☐ Has the memo been carefully proofread? (21)

 Email in the workplace

The changing face of email

Electronic Mail

The standard email format (Figure 16.9) resembles that of a paper memo, with "To," "From," Date," and "Subject" fields. But email tends to be more informal and conversational, and, until recently, has been largely used for relatively simple messages. Even writers who are extremely careful with traditional paper correspondence sometimes ignore spelling and grammar as they dash off various emails. However, as audiences and uses for email broaden and as the software evolves, email messages, especially in the workplace, are starting to look more polished; writers are paying greater attention to style and correctness. Also, provisions for attaching more complex documents mean that fully formatted documents can be sent by email.

Current Folder: **INBOX**	**Sign Out**

Compose   Addresses   Folders   Options   Search   Help   Calendar

Message List | Delete   Previous | Next   **Forward | Forward as Attachment | Reply | Reply All**

Subject:	Elements of a Typical Email Message
From:	ergo@comcast.net
Date:	Sat, February 24, 2007 2:25 pm
To:	ergo@valinet.com
Cc:	rdumas@comcast.net
Priority:	Normal
Options:	**View Full Header	View Printable Version	Download this as a file	Add to Addressbook**

```
HEADER INFORMATION
Besides the standard fields from a memo (To, From, Date, Subject), the email
header includes a list of recipients who were sent a courtesy copy (CC) and
the exact time the message was sent. Depending on the program, additional
information (host server, priority status, etc.) may be included.

MESSAGE BODY
To avoid scrolling, try to limit the message to one page. For readability,
keep the paragraphs short.

GRAPHIC HIGHLIGHTING
Use headings, bullets, and numbered lists to break up a long message.

ATTACHMENTS
Send formatted documents, software, photographs, scanned images, and other
files as attachments to your message.

SIGNATURE BLOCK
Your name, title, company, and contact information can be added automatically
to each email message. For example:

Harvey C. Keck
Manager, Customer Relations
Apex, Inc.
Tel. 641-555-9871; Fax: 641-555-8791
```

FIGURE 16.9   Elements of a Typical Email Message

Email Benefits

Compared to phone, fax, or conventional mail (or even face-to-face conversation, in some cases), email can offer real advantages:

Email advantages in the workplace

- **Lack of real-time constraints.** Email allows people to communicate at any time.
- **Efficient filing, retrieval, and forwarding.** Email messages can be filed for future reference, cut and pasted into other documents, and forwarded.

- **Attachments.** Documents or files can be attached and downloaded, usually with original formatting intact.
- **Democratic communication.** Email allows anyone in an organization to contact anyone else. The filing clerk could conceivably email the company president directly, whereas a conventional memo or phone call would be routed through management or screened by assistants (D. Goodman 33–35).
- **Creative thinking.** When brainstorming via email, users communicate spontaneously—usually without worrying about page design, paragraph structure, or perfect phrasing. This rapid and relatively free exchange of views can lead to new insights or ideas (Bruhn 43).
- **Collaboration and research.** Teams can keep in touch, and researchers can contact people for answers they need.

Email Copyright Issues

Any email message you receive is copyrighted by the person who wrote it. Under current law, forwarding this message to anyone for any purpose is a violation of the owner's copyright. The same is true for reproducing an email message as part of any type of publication—unless your use of this material falls within the boundaries of "fair use." (See pages 132, 134.)

Email Privacy Issues

Gossip, personal messages, risqué jokes, or complaints about the boss or a colleague—all might reach unintended recipients. While phone companies and other private carriers are governed by laws protecting privacy, no such legal protection yet exists for Internet communication (Peyser and Rhodes 82). The Electronic Privacy Act of 1986 offers limited protection against unauthorized reading of another person's email, but employers are exempt (Extejt 63).

Employers are legally entitled to monitor employee email

> In some instances it may be proper for an employer to monitor E-mail, if it has evidence of safety violations, illegal activity, racial discrimination, or sexual improprieties, for instance. Companies may also need access to business information, whether it is kept in an employee's drawer, file cabinet, or computer E-mail. (Bjerklie 15)

Email privacy can be compromised in other ways as well:

Email offers no privacy

- Everyone on a group mailing list—intended recipient or not—automatically receives a copy.
- Even when "deleted" from the system, messages can live on, saved in a backup file.
- Forwarding email without the author's consent violates that person's privacy.

- Anyone with access to your network and password can read your document, alter it, use parts of it out of context, pretend to be its author, forward it, plagiarize your ideas, or even author a document or conduct illegal activity in your name. (One partial safeguard is encryption software, which scrambles the message, and only people who possess the code can unscramble it. Another strategy is to circulate any sensitive document as an attachment in Adobe *Portable Document File* format. PDF format prevents the document from being altered.)

Guidelines for Using Electronic Mail*

Observe the Rules of "Netiquette"

- **Check and answer your email daily.** If you're really busy, at least acknowledge receipt and respond later.
- **Check your distribution list before each mailing.** Deliver your message to all intended recipients—but no unintended ones.
- **Spell each recipient's name correctly.**

Consider the Ethical, Legal, and Interpersonal Implications

- **Assume that your email is permanent and readable by anyone any time.** "Forensic software" can find and revive deleted files.
- **Avoid wisecracks and rude remarks (flaming).** Any email judged harassing or discriminatory can have dire legal consequences.
- **Don't use email to send confidential information.** Avoid complaining, evaluating, or criticizing, and handle anything that should be kept private (say, an employee reprimand) in some other way.
- **Don't use your employer's email network for anything not work related.**
- **Before you forward a message, obtain permission from the sender.**

Make the Message Readable

- **Use an explicit subject line.** Instead of "Test Data" or "Data Request," announce your purpose clearly: "Request for Beta Test Data for Project 16."
- **Refer clearly to the message to which you are responding:** "Here are the Project #16 Beta test data you requested on Oct. 10."
- **Keep sentences and paragraphs short.**
- **Don't indent paragraphs.** Double space between them.

*Adapted from Bruhn 43; D. Goodman 33–35, 167; "Email Etiquette" 3; Gurak and Lannon, 3rd ed. 186; Kawasaki, "The Rules" 286; D. Munger; Nantz and Drexel 45–51; Peyser and Rhodes 82.

(continues)

Guidelines (continued)

- **Don't write in FULL CAPS—unless you want to SCREAM.**
- **Use graphic highlighting.** Headings, bullets and lists, boldface, and italics improve readability.
- **For someone you don't know or someone in authority, use a formal salutation and closing.** See pages 362–63.
- **Use emoticons and abbreviations sparingly.** Use smiley faces [:-)] and other emoticons strictly in informal messages to people you know well. The same goes for common email abbreviations such as BTW or HAND—("by the way," "have a nice day").
- **Close with a signature section.** Include your contact information and, if you have the technology, your electronic signature.
- **Don't send huge or specially formatted attachments without checking with the recipient** which file types (*simple text, PDF, Rich Text Format*) the recipient's browser can handle.
- **Proofread before hitting the SEND button.** Every message reflects your image.

Guidelines for Choosing Email Versus Paper, Telephone, or Fax

Email is excellent for reaching a lot of people quickly with a relatively brief, informal message. And it is preferable to fax transmission when you wish to preserve the professional look of any well-formatted attachments. But there are often good reasons to transmit your message in traditional fashion, on paper—or to speak with the recipient directly.

- **Don't use email when a more personal medium is preferable.** Sometimes an issue is best resolved by a phone call, or even voice mail
- **Don't use email for a complex message.** In contrast to a rapid-fire email message, preparing a paper document is more deliberate, giving you a chance to choose words carefully, and to revise. Also, a well-crafted letter or memo is likely to be read more attentively. For in-house recipients, attach your paper document to an introductory email.
- **Don't use email for most formal correspondence.** Don't use email to apply for or to resign from a job, request a raise, or respond to a formal letter unless recipients specifically request this method. Don't use it to send a thank-you or a follow-up after a job interview. (See Chapters 17 and 18 for formal letters and for job hunting.)

☑ Checklist: Email

(These criteria are discussed on pages 349–50.)

Netiquette
☐ Do you check and answer your email daily?

☐ Have you reviewed your distribution list before mailing?

☐ Is each recipient's name spelled correctly?

☐ Have you chosen an alternative medium for any formal correspondence?

Ethical, Legal, and Interpersonal Considerations
☐ Have you avoided writing anything incriminating?

☐ Have wisecracks and flaming been avoided?

☐ Have you avoided sending confidential information?

☐ Are you keeping personal correspondence out of the workplace network?

☐ Before forwarding a message, have you obtained the sender's permission?

☐ Is email the most appropriate medium in this situation?

Readability
☐ Is there an explicit subject line?

☐ Do you refer clearly to the message to which you are responding?

☐ Are sentences and paragraphs short?

☐ Do you avoid paragraph indentations and FULL CAPS?

☐ Are graphic highlights used as needed to improve readability?

☐ Are formal salutations and closings used, when appropriate?

☐ Are smiley faces and abbreviations used sparingly?

☐ Before sending a long attachment, have you checked with the recipient?

☐ Have you included a signature block?

☐ Have you proofread carefully?

Instant Messaging

A faster medium than email, instant messaging (IM) allows for text-based conversation in real time: The user types a message in a pop-up box and the recipient can respond instantly. IM groupware enables multiple users to converse and collaborate from various locations. According to *Fortune* magazine, "instant messaging is rising fast in corporate America," rapidly displacing email for routine communication (Varchaver 102). Although it is useful for brief, rapid exchanges, IM is not a good medium for the kind of written communication that requires careful planning, composing, and editing.

The limitations of instant messaging

While instant messaging has been popular among teens and college students, its more recent advent as a business tool means that few rules govern its use. Also, most current IM software does not automatically save these messages electronically. But as IM becomes more pervasive in the workplace, companies will likely monitor its use by employees and then save all messages as a permanent record.

Corporate Blogs and Wikis

Blogs are no longer only for casual chats or for sounding off

Interactive online forums, or *blogs* (short for "Web logs"; see also page 124) began as social networking sites, and recently have played key roles in the national political debate and in "citizen journalism." At their worst, blogs are opinion-based chat rooms for raving about the issues; at their best, they are knowledge-based resources for acquiring useful information, for completing meaningful tasks, and for enhancing customer relations. As part of a company's *intranet* and *extranet* (see page 127), corporate blogs play an increasing role in mainstream workplace communication. Major companies including Intel, Boeing, Xerox, and Texas Instruments have their own blogs. Increasing numbers of corporate blogs are tracked on the Fortune 500 Business Blogging Wiki <http://www.socialtext.net/bizblogs/index.cgi>.

Internal Blogs

How a blog can enhance a company's internal conversation

Internal corporate blogs enhance both workflow and morale. In large organizations, blogs can provide an alternative to email for routine in-house communication. Anyone in the network can either post a message or comment on other messages. In the (virtual) blogging environment, meetings can be conducted, employee training can be delivered, and updates about company developments can be circulated. Blogs are especially useful for rapid sharing of knowledge: say someone in the company's shipping department has an idea for using biodegradable packaging materials for its laptop computers, or someone in personnel asks for ideas about yoga and other relaxation workshops for stressed-out employees. In short, blogs can enhance company morale and team spirit via ongoing conversation.

How wikis differ from standard blogs

A *wiki* is a type of blog in which users not only can comment on earlier postings, but also can edit them as well. Despite the potential for abuse created by such alterations, a well managed wiki network can be a valuable tool for collaboration among trustworthy users. To ensure that serial edits do not end up distorting the original posting, copies of the original along with each subsequent edit can be filed for later reference.

External Blogs

How a blog can enhance a company's public conversation

In the public context, *external* blogs can facilitate customer feedback, enhance marketing and public relations, and basically help personalize a large corporation in the eyes of customers and consumers. Blogs give big business a chance to show an intimate, informal side; to respond amiably and quickly to customer concerns; and to contribute to public dialogue on issues of the day. Ultimately, blogs help put a human face on the corporation; in fact, CEO blogs often display an actual photo of the blog's creator. *Tone,* of course, is critical in a corporate blog; it needs to sound friendly, welcoming, and sincere.

RSS Feeds

How RSS technology works

Up-to-date information depends on a continual information stream. Corporate bloggers can follow the latest postings from preselected web sites by subscribing to RSS (Rich Site Summary, see Figure 16.10) feeds. An RSS feed is a retrieval program that monitors selected sites, identifies the information most relevant to the individual subscriber, and delivers, usually via email, a list of pertinent links. RSS technology is based on XML, a programming code that enables the delivery of information in a standardized format readable by any computer. The feed in XML format is then decoded by an RSS reader or *aggregator,* one of many easily downloadable programs such as *NewsFire, Aggregato,* or *Google Reader.* Once the aggregator is downloaded, the user can specify the sites from which to receive automatic newsfeeds.

Ethical, Legal, and Privacy Issues

It is no secret that the blogosphere's freewheeling ambience creates potential for information abuses. One such example is "stealth marketing," in which bloggers who publish supposedly objective product reviews fail to disclose the free merchandise or cash payments received for their flattering portrayals.

People need to be able to trust the information they receive. Furthermore, in workplace settings, people need to be able to trust the discretion of coworkers and colleagues. As with email, any employee who discusses proprietary matters (see page 80) or who posts defamatory comments can face serious legal consequences—not to mention being fired. Also like email, blogging carries the potential for violations of copyright or privacy (see page 348). To avoid such problems, corporate blogs often have a moderator who screens any comment before it is posted. (For more on unethical communication, see Chapter 5.)

To reinforce ethical, legal, and privacy standards, companies such as IBM have established explicit policies that govern corporate blogging. See, for example, "Guidelines for IBM Bloggers" at <www.snellspace.com/IBM_Blogging_Policy_and_Guidelines.pdf>.

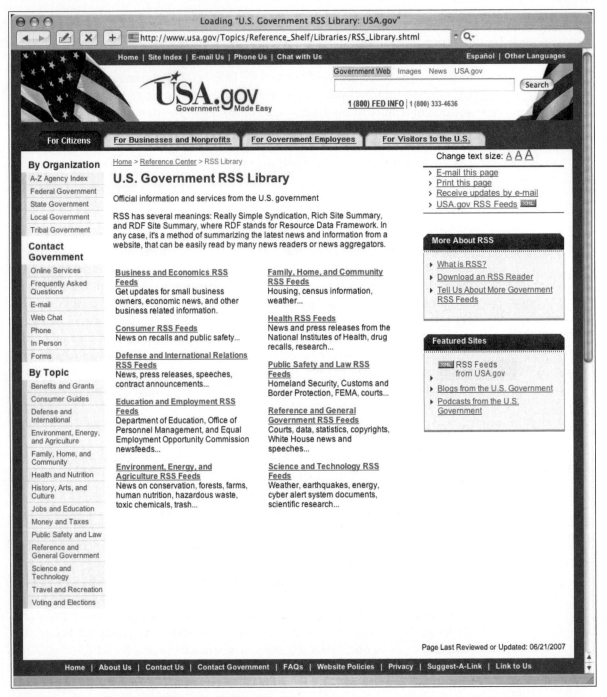

FIGURE 16.10 An Access Page for RSS Feeds This gateway to government sources leads to countless Web sites in each major category, organized by topic.

Source: U.S.A. gov <www.usa.gov/Topics/Reference_Shelf/Libraries/RSS_Library.shtml>.

Exercises

1. We would all like to see changes in our schools' policies or procedures, whether they are changes in our majors, school regulations, social activities, grading policies, or registration procedures. Find some area of your school that needs obvious changes, and write a justification report to the person who might initiate that change. Explain why the change is necessary and describe the benefits. Follow the format on pages 344–45.

2. Think of an idea you would like to see implemented in your job (e.g., a way to increase productivity, improve service, increase business, or improve working conditions). Write a justification memo, persuading your audience that your idea is worthwhile.

3. Write a memo to your employer, justifying reimbursement for this course. *Note:* You might have written another version of this assignment for Exercise 2 in Chapter 1. If so, compare early and recent versions for content, organization, style, and format.

4. Identify a dangerous or inconvenient area or situation on campus or in your community (endless cafeteria lines, a poorly lit intersection, slippery stairs, a poorly adjusted traffic light). Observe the problem for several hours during a peak use period. Write a justification report to a *specifically identified* decision maker, describing the problem, listing your observations, making recommendations, and encouraging reader support or action.

5. In a memo to your instructor, outline your progress on your term project.

6. Keep accurate minutes for one class session (preferably one with debate or discussion). Submit the minutes in memo form to your instructor.

7. Recommendation report (choose one)

   a. You are a consulting engineer to an island community of two hundred families suffering a severe shortage of fresh water. Some islanders have raised the possibility of producing drinking water from salt water (desalination). Write a report for the town council, summarizing the process and describing instances in which desalination has been used successfully or unsuccessfully. Would desalination be economically feasible for a community this size? Recommend a course of action.

   b. You are an investment broker for a major firm. A longtime client calls to ask your opinion. She is thinking of investing in a company that is fast becoming a leader in nanotechnology. "Should I invest in this technology?" your client wants to know. Find out, and give her your recommendations in a short report.

   c. The buildings in the condominium complex you manage have been invaded by carpenter ants. Can the ants be eliminated by any insecticide *proven* nontoxic to humans or pets? (Many dwellers have small children and pets.) Find out, and write a report making recommendations to the maintenance supervisor.

   d. Dream up a scenario of your own in which information and recommendations would make a real difference. (Perhaps the question could be one you've always wanted answered.)

8. Individually or in small groups, decide whether each of the following documents would be appropriate for transmission via a company email network. Be prepared to explain your decisions.

   Sarah Burnes's memo about benzene levels (page 17)
   The "Rational Connection" memo (page 54)
   The "better" memo to the maintenance director (page 57)
   Tom Ewing's letter to a potential customer (page 68)
   The medical report written for expert readers (page 29)
   A memo reporting illegal or unethical activity in your company

A personal note to a colleague

A request for a raise or promotion

Minutes of a meeting

Announcement of a no-smoking policy

An evaluation or performance review of an employee

A reprimand to an employee

A notice of a meeting

Criticism of an employee or employer

A request for volunteers

A suggestion for change or improvement in company policy or practice

A gripe

A note of praise or thanks

A message you have received and have decided to forward to other recipients

9. Locate one or more blogs related to technical communication. You might begin with the following sites (but find others on your own):

<http://blogs.adobe.com/techcomm/>

<http://wordpress.com/tag/
technical-writing/>

Write a brief analysis of a chosen blog, its content areas, and its value to technical communicators.

10. Do some online research to find out how corporations are using blogs for workplace communication and what functions they are serving. Write a persuasive memo to argue that your company or organization should launch a blog, what it should include, who its audiences should be, and what role it would serve in internal and/or external communication. You might begin with the following site:

<http://www.successful-blog.com/1/
blogs-the-new-black-in-corporate-
communication/>

 ## Collaborative Projects

1. Organize into groups of four or five and choose a topic for which group members can agree on a position. Here are some possibilities:

- Should your college abolish core requirements?
- Should every student in your school pass a writing proficiency exam before graduating?
- Should campus police carry guns?
- Should school security be improved?
- Should students with meal tickets be charged according to the type and amount of food they eat, instead of paying a flat fee?

As a group, decide your position on the issue, and brainstorm collectively to justify your recommendation to a stipulated primary audience in addition to your classmates and instructor. Complete an audience and use profile (page 35), and compose a justification report. Appoint one member to present the report in class.

2. Divide into groups and respond to the following scenario:

As a legal safeguard against discriminatory, harassing, or otherwise inappropriate email messages, a legal consultant to your company or college has proposed a plan for electronic monitoring of email use at your organization. Your employer or college dean has asked your team to study the issue and to answer this question: "Should we support this plan?" Among the many subordinate questions to consider:

- What are the rights of the people who would be monitored?
- What are the rights of the organization?
- Is the plan ethical?
- Could the plan backfire? Why?
- How would the plan affect people's perception of the organization?
- Should monitoring be done selectively or routinely?
- Should the entire organization be given a voice in the decision?
- Are there acceptable alternatives to monitoring?

Begin by reviewing Chapters 5 and 6 and consulting Figure 24.3. Then do the research and prepare a memo that makes a persuasive case for your team's recommendation.

Web sites that address privacy issues:

- *Electronic Privacy Information Center,* a public interest research center at <http://www.epic.org>.

- *Privacy International,* a human rights group at <http://www.privacyinternational.org>.
- *Computer Professionals for Social Responsibility,* a public interest group at <http://www.cpsr.org>.

CHAPTER 17

Workplace Letters

Elements of Usable Letters

Interpersonal Considerations in Workplace Letters

Conveying Bad or Unwelcome News

Guidelines for Conveying Bad News

Inquiry Letters

Guidelines for Writing an Inquiry

Claim Letters

Guidelines for Routine Claim Letters

Guidelines for Arguable Claim Letters

Adjustment Letters

Guidelines for Granting Adjustments

Guidelines for Refusing Adjustments

Checklist: Usability of Letters

We often have good reason to correspond in a more formal and personal medium than a memo or email message. A well-crafted letter is appropriate in situations like these:

When to send a
letter instead of a
memo or email

- To personalize your correspondence, conveying the sense that this message is prepared exclusively for your recipient
- To convey a dignified, professional impression
- To act as a representative of your company or organization
- To present a reasoned, carefully constructed case
- To respond to clients, customers, or anyone outside your organization
- To provide an official notice or record (as in a letter announcing legal action or confirming a verbal agreement)

Because a letter often has a *persuasive* purpose (see Chapter 4), proper tone is essential for connecting with the recipient. Because your signature certifies your approval—and your responsibility—for the message (which may serve as a legal document, as in Figure 17.1), precision is crucial.

This chapter covers three common letter types: inquiry letters, claim letters, and adjustment letters. (Job application letters and letters of transmittal are discussed in Chapters 18 and 25, respectively.)

Elements of Usable Letters

Most workplace letters have the same basic components. This conventional and predictable arrangement enables recipients to locate what they need immediately, as in Figure 17.1.

Standard Parts of Letters

Many organizations have their own formats for letters; so, depending on where you work, some of these parts may appear at different locations on the page. But in general a letter contains the elements listed here.

Heading and Date.   If your stationery has a company letterhead, simply include the date a few lines below the letterhead, flush against the right or left margin. On blank stationery, include your return address and the date (but not your name):

Street address
City, state, zip
Month, day, year

154 Sea Lane
Harwich, MA 02163
July 15, 20xx

Use the Postal Service's two-letter state abbreviations (MA for Massachusetts, WY for Wyoming, etc.) in your heading, in the inside address, and on the envelope.

Heading	LEVERETT LAND & TIMBER COMPANY, INC. creative land use
	18 River Rock Road quality building materials
	Leverett, MA 01054 architectural construction

Date

January 17, 20xx

Inside address

Mr. Thomas E. Muffin
Clearwater Drive
Amherst, MA 01022

Salutation

Dear Mr. Muffin:

Body text

I have examined the damage to your home caused by the ruptured water pipe and consider the following repairs to be necessary and of immediate concern:

> Exterior:
> Remove plywood soffit panels beneath overhangs
> Replace damaged insulation and plumbing
> Remove all built-up ice within floor framing
> Replace plywood panels and finish as required

> Northeast Bedroom—Lower Level:
> Remove and replace all sheetrock, including closet
> Remove and replace all door casings and baseboards
> Remove and repair windowsill extensions and moldings
> Remove and reinstall electric heaters
> Respray ceilings and repaint all surfaces

This appraisal of damage repair does not include repairs and/or replacements of carpets, tile work, or vinyl flooring. Also, this appraisal assumes that the plywood subflooring on the main level has not been severely damaged.

Leverett Land & Timber Company, Inc. proposes to furnish the necessary materials and labor to perform the described damage repairs for the amount of six thousand one hundred and eighty dollars ($6,180).

Complimentary
closing

Sincerely,

Signature

P.A. Jackson

Gerald A. Jackson, President

Typist's initials

GAJ/ob

Enclosure notation

Encl. Itemized estimate

Phone: 410-555-9879   Fax: 410-555-6874   Email: llt@yonet.com

FIGURE 17.1 A Standard Design for a Workplace Letter This writer is careful to stipulate not only the exact repairs and costs, but also those items excluded from his estimate. In the event of legal proceedings, a formal letter signifies a contractual obligation on the sender's part.

Inside Address.   Two to six line spaces below the heading, flush against the left margin, is the inside address (the address to which you are sending the letter).

Name/position
Organization
Street address
City, state, zip

| Dr. Ann Mello, Dean of Students
| Western University
| 30 Mogul Hill Road
| Stowe, VT 51350

Whenever possible, address a specifically named recipient, and include the person's title. Using "Mr." or "Ms." before the name is optional. (See page 243 for avoiding sexist usage in titles and salutations.)

NOTE   *Depending on the letter's length, adjust the vertical placement of your return address and inside address to achieve a balanced page.*

Salutation.   The salutation, two line spaces below the inside address, begins with *Dear* and ends with a colon (*Dear Ms. Smith:*). If you don't know the recipient's name, use the position title (*Dear Manager*) or, preferably, an attention line (page 364). Only address the recipient by first name if that is the way you would address that individual in person.

Typical
salutations

| Dear Ms. Smith:
| Dear Managing Editor:
| Dear Professor Trudeau:

No satisfactory guidelines exist for addressing several people within an organization. *Gentlemen* or *Dear Sirs* implies bias. *Ladies and Gentlemen* sounds too much like the beginning of a speech. *Dear Sir or Madam* is old-fashioned. *To Whom It May Concern* is vague and impersonal. Your best bet is to eliminate the salutation by using an attention line.

 NOTE   *For international audiences, an inappropriate salutation is highly offensive. In France or England, for example, a person's title should be used in the greeting, as in "Monsieur le Professeur Larrouse" (Sabath 164); in England, "Dear Madam" and "Dear Sir" continue to be acceptable for people not known well by the writer (Scott 55). Whenever possible, learn about your recipient's culture and preferences beforehand.*

The shape of
workplace letters

Body Text.   Begin the text of your letter two line spaces below the salutation or subject line. Workplace letters typically include (1) a brief introductory paragraph (five or fewer lines) that identifies your purpose and connects with the recipient's interest, (2) one or more discussion paragraphs that present details of your message, and (3) a concluding paragraph that sums up and encourages action.

Keep the paragraphs short, usually fewer than eight lines. If a paragraph goes beyond eight lines, or if the paragraph contains detailed supporting facts or examples, as in Figure 17.1, consider using a vertical list.

Complimentary Closing.   The closing, two line spaces (returns) below the last line of text, should parallel the level of formality used in the salutation and should reflect your relationship to the recipient (polite but not overly intimate). *Yours truly* and *Sincerely* are the most common. Others, in order of decreasing formality, include:

Complimentary
closings

> Respectfully,
>
> Cordially,
>
> Best wishes,
>
> Warmest regards,
>
> Regards,
>
> Best,

Align the closing with the letter's heading.

Signature.   Type your full name and title on the fourth and fifth lines below and aligned with the closing. Sign in the triple space between the closing and your typed name.

The signature block

> Sincerely yours,
>
> *Martha S. Jones*
>
> Martha S. Jones
> Personnel Manager

If you are representing your company or a group that bears legal responsibility for the correspondence, type the company's name in full caps two line spaces below your complimentary closing; place your typed name and title four line spaces below the company name and sign in the triple space between.

Signature block
representing the
company

> Yours truly,
> HASBROUCK LABORATORIES
>
> *Lester Fong*
>
> L. H. Fong
> Research Associate

Specialized Parts of Letters

Some letters have one or more of the following specialized parts. (Examples appear in the sample letters in this chapter.)

Attention Line.   Use an attention line when you write to an organization and do not know your recipient's name, but are directing the letter to a specific department or position.

Glaxol Industries, Inc.
232 Rogaline Circle
Missoula, MT 61347

ATTENTION: <u>Director of Research and Development</u>

An attention line can replace your salutation

Drop two line spaces below the inside address and place the attention line either flush with the left margin or centered on the page.

Subject Line.   Typically, subject lines are used with memos, but if the recipient is not expecting your letter, a subject line is a good way of catching a busy reader's attention.

A subject line can attract attention

SUBJECT: <u>Placement of the Subject Line</u>

Place the subject line below the inside address or attention line with one line space before and after it. You can underline or highlight the subject to make it more prominent.

Typist's Initials.   If someone else types your letter for you (common in the days of typewriters but rare today), your initials (in CAPS) and your typist's initials (in lower case) appear below the typed signature, flush with the left margin.

Typist's initials

JJ/pl

Enclosure Notation.   If you enclose other documents with your letter, indicate this one line space below the initials (or writer's name and position), flush against the left margin. State the number of enclosures.

Enclosure noted

Enclosure
Enclosures 2
Encl. 3

If the enclosures are important documents such as legal certificates, checks, or specifications, name them in the notation.

Enclosure named

Enclosures: 2 certified checks, 1 set of KBX plans

Distribution Notation.   If you distribute copies of your letter to other recipients, indicate this by inserting the notation "Copy" or "cc" one line below the previous line (such as an enclosure line). The "cc" notation once stood for "carbon copy," but no one uses carbon paper any more, so now it is said to stand for "courtesy copy."

> cc: office file
>   Melvin Blount
>
> c: S. Furlow
>   B. Smith

Most copies are distributed on an *FYI* (*For Your Information*) basis, but writers sometimes use the distribution notation to maintain a paper trail or to signal the primary recipient that this information is being shared with others (e.g., superiors, legal authorities).

Postscript.   A postscript (typed or handwritten) draws attention to a point you wish to emphasize or adds a personal note. Do not use a postscript if you forget to mention a point in the body of the letter. Rewrite the body section instead.

A postscript

> P. S. Because of its terminal position in your letter, a postscript can draw attention to
>   a point that needs reemphasizing.

Place the postscript two line spaces below any other notation, and flush against the left margin. Because readers often regard postscripts as sales gimmicks, use them sparingly in professional correspondence.

Design Features

The following design features help make workplace letters look inviting, accessible, and professional.

Letter Format.   Although several formats are acceptable, and your company may have its own, the two most popular formats for workplace letters are *modified block* (Figure 17.2) and *block* (Figure 17.3). One additional format, the simplified format (Figure 17.7), replaces the salutation with a subject line, eliminates the complimentary closing, and retains the writer's signature and typed name.

Word-Processing Templates.   Most word-processing software allows you to select from templates, or predesigned letter formats, as in Figure 17.4. These templates provide fields for you to insert your name, your company name, and your message. Some templates provide background artwork or other decorative features. As

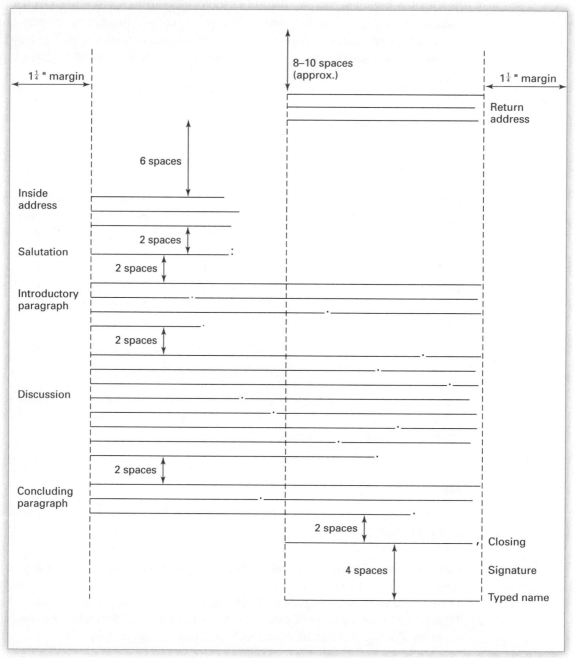

FIGURE 17.2 Modified Block Format In this traditional format, the first line of a paragraph is not indented. Single-spaced paragraphs are separated by one line space. The return address, complimentary closing, and signature align at page center.

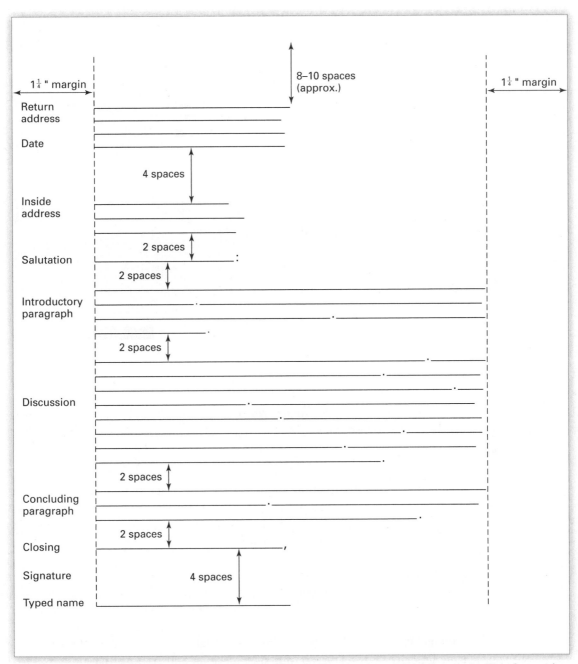

FIGURE 17.3 **Block Format** In the block format, every line begins at the left margin. This format is popular because it looks businesslike and saves keying time because it eliminates the need to tab and center.

 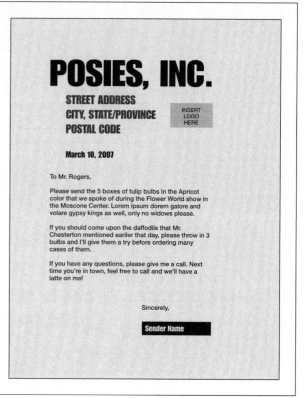

FIGURE 17.4 Sample of Letter Templates in Microsoft Word Customize a template to suit your needs.
Source: Reprinted with permission from Microsoft Corp.

tempting as it may be to simply choose a template, make sure the one you use is appropriate for your audience and purpose. Unless the situation specifically calls for a decorative format, strive for a tasteful, conservative look. When in doubt, ignore the templates and work from a blank document.

Quality Stationery. Use high-quality, 20-pound bond, $8\frac{1}{2}'' \times 11''$ white stationery with a minimum fiber content of 25 percent. Even though countless varieties of colored, specially textured paper are available, your safest bet is white stationery.

Uniform Margins and Spacing. When using stationery without a letterhead, frame your letter with $1\frac{1}{2}$-inch top and side margins and bottom margins of 1 to $1\frac{1}{2}$ inches. Use single spacing within paragraphs and double spacing between. Vary these guidelines based on the amount of space required by the letter's text, but strive for a balanced look.

Headers for Subsequent Pages.   Head each additional page with a notation identifying the recipient, date, and page number.

Subsequent-page
header

| Adrianna Fonseca, June 25, 20xx, p. 2

Align your header with the right-hand margin. See page 69 for an example.

NOTE   *Never use an additional page solely for the closing section. Instead, reformat the letter so that the closing appears on the first page, or so that at least two lines of text appear above the closing on the subsequent page.*

The Envelope.   Your envelope (usually a #10 envelope) should be of the same quality as your stationery. Place the recipient's name and address at a fairly central point on the envelope. Place your own name and address in the upper-left corner. Single space these elements. Your word processor likely has an envelope printing function that will automatically place these elements. (See your printer's operating manual for instructions.)

Interpersonal Considerations in Workplace Letters

In addition to presenting an accessible and inviting design, an effective letter enhances the relationship between sender and recipient. Interpersonal elements forge a *human* connection.

Focus on Your Recipient's Interests: The "You" Perspective

In speaking face-to-face, you unconsciously modify your statements and expression as you read the listener's signals: a smile, a frown, a raised eyebrow, a nod. In a phone conversation, the voice can signal approval, dismay, anger, or confusion. In writing a letter, however, you can easily forget that a flesh-and-blood person will be reacting to what you are saying—or seem to be saying.

A letter displaying a "you" perspective subordinates the writer's interests and concerns to those of the reader. In addition to focusing on the information that is important to the reader, the "you" perspective conveys respect for that person's feelings and attitudes.

To achieve a "you" perspective, put yourself in the place of the person who will read your correspondence; ask yourself how this recipient will react to what you have written. Even a single word, carelessly chosen, can offend. In trying to correct a billing error, for example, you might feel tempted to write this:

A needlessly
offensive tone

| Our record keeping is very efficient, so this is obviously your error.

Such an accusatory tone might be appropriate after numerous failed attempts to achieve satisfaction on your part, but in your initial correspondence it would be offensive. Here is a more considerate version:

A tone that conveys the "you" perspective

> If my paperwork is wrong, please let me know and I will send you a corrected version immediately.

Instead of indicting the reader, this second version conveys respect for the reader's viewpoint.

Use Plain English

Avoid *letterese,* the stuffy, puffed-up phrases some writers think they need to make their communications sound important.

Letterese

> Humbly thanking you in anticipation of your kind assistance, I remain
>
> Faithfully yours,

Instead you might simply write this.

Clear phrasing

> I will appreciate your help.

Here are a few of the old standards with some clearer, more direct translations.

Plain-English translations

Letterese	Plain-English
As per your request	As you requested
Contingent upon receipt of	As soon as we receive
Please be advised that I	I
In accordance with your request	As you requested
Due to the fact that	Because

Be natural. Write as you would speak in a classroom or office.

NOTE   *Comunications expert Laura Gurak notes that "in the legal profession (and others), certain phrases such as these are known as 'terms of art' and connote a specific meaning. In these cases, you may not be able to avoid such [elaborate] phrases." (Gurak and Lannon, 3rd ed. 202)*

Focus on the Human Connection

As you plan, write, and revise, answer these questions:

Questions for connecting with the recipient

- What do I want this person to do, think, or feel? Offer a job, give advice or information, follow instructions, grant a favor, accept bad news?

- Exactly what information does this person expect? Do I need to give measurements, dates, costs, model numbers, enclosures, other details?
- To whom am I writing? When possible, write to a person, not a title.
- What is my relationship to this person? Is this a potential employer, an employee, a person doing a favor, a person whose products are disappointing, an acquaintance, an associate, a stranger?

Anticipate the Recipient's Reaction

After you have written a draft, answer the following three questions, which pertain to the *effect* of your letter. Will the recipient feel inclined to respond favorably?

Questions for anticipating the recipient's reaction

- How will this person react? With anger, hostility, pleasure, confusion, fear, guilt, resistance, satisfaction?
- What impression of me does this letter convey? Do I seem intelligent, courteous, friendly, articulate, pretentious, illiterate, confident?
- Am I ready to sign my letter with confidence? Think about it.

Decide on a Direct or Indirect Organizing Pattern

The reaction you anticipate should determine the organizational plan of your letter: either *direct* or *indirect*.

Questions for organizing your message

- Will the recipient feel pleased, angry, or neutral?
- Will the message cause resistance, resentment, or disappointment?

When to be direct

The direct pattern puts the main point in the first paragraph, followed by the explanation. Be direct when you expect the recipient to react with approval or when you want to convey immediately the point of your letter (e.g., in good news, inquiry, or application letters—or other routine correspondence).

When to be indirect

If you expect the reader to resist or to need persuading, or if this person is from a different culture, consider an indirect plan. Give the explanation *before* the main point (as in requesting a pay raise or refusing a request).

Research indicates that "readers will always look for the bottom line" (*Writing User-Friendly Documents* 14). Therefore, a direct pattern, even for certain types of bad news, may be preferable—as in complaining about a faulty product. For more on conveying bad news, see the next section in this chapter.

NOTE   *Whenever you consider using an indirect pattern, think carefully about its ethical implications. Never try to deceive the recipient—and never create an impression that you have something to hide.*

For more on direct versus indirect organizing patterns, see page 330.

Conveying Bad or Unwelcome News

During your career you will have to say no to customers, employees, and job applicants. You will have to make difficult requests, such as asking employees to accept higher medical insurance premiums or seeking an interview with a beleaguered official. You may have to notify consumers or shareholders about accidents or product recalls; you may need to apologize for errors; the list of possibilities goes on. In conveying bad news, you face a *persuasive* challenge (see Chapter 4): You must convince people to accept your message. As the bearer of unwelcome news and requests, you will need to offer reasonable explanations, incentives, or justifications—and you will need to be diplomatic.

In each instance, you will have to decide whether to build your case first or get right to the main point. This will depend on the situation: If you are requesting a refund for a faulty printer, for example, you will probably want a direct approach, because the customer service person, who could easily receive hundreds of letters each day, will get to your point quickly. But if you are announcing a 15-percent increase in your client service fees, you might want readers to process your justification first.

The following general guidelines apply to many situations you will face; they also complement the guidelines for each specific type of letter covered in this chapter.

Guidelines for Conveying Bad News*

- **Don't procrastinate.** As much as people may dislike the news, they will feel doubly offended after being kept in the dark.

- **Never just blurt it out.** Set a considerate tone by prefacing your bad news with considerate terms such as *I regret*, *We're sorry*, or *Unfortunately*. Instead of flatly proclaiming *Your application has been denied*, give recipients information they can use: *Unfortunately, we are unable to offer you admission to this year's Program. This letter will explain why we made this decision and how you can reapply.* Provide a context that leads into your explanation.

- **Give a clear and honest explanation.** Don't make things worse by fogging or dodging the issue. (See the Guidelines for Persuasion, page 65).

- **When you need to apologize, do so immediately.** Place your apology right up front. Don't say *An error was made in calculating your construction bill*. Do say *We are sorry we made a mistake in calculating your construction bill*. Don't try to camouflage the error. Don't offer excuses or try to shift the blame.

- **Use the passive voice to avoid accusations but not to dodge responsibility.** Instead of *You used the wrong bolts*, say *The wrong bolts were used*.

- **Do not use "you" to blame the reader.** Instead of *You did not send a deposit*, say *We have not received your deposit*.

*Guidelines adapted from Dumont and Lannon 206–21; U.S. Bureau of Land Management; Timmerman and Harrison 382–87.

- **Keep it personal.** Avoid patronizing or impersonal jargon such as *company policy* or *circumstances beyond our control*.

- **Consider the format.** Take plenty of time to write and revise the letter, even by hand, if a personal note is warranted. For exceedingly bad news—say, denial of a promotion—consider sending the letter and following up with a meeting. Never use form letters for important matters, and don't use a formal letter for a relatively minor issue; for example, to notify employees that a company softball game has been cancelled, an email would be sufficient.

- **Consider the medium.** Don't be like one major electronics retailer who used an email list to notify hundreds of workers that they were laid off, effective immediately.

Inquiry Letters

Model letters

Inquiry letters may be *solicited* or *unsolicited*. You might write the first type as a consumer, to request information about an advertised product or service. Such letters are welcomed because the recipient stands to benefit from your interest. In such cases, you can afford to be brief and direct: *Please send me your brochure on . . .* or the like.

Other inquiries will be unsolicited; that is, not in response to an ad, but to request some type of information that you need in your work. This type of letter imposes on the recipient, asking this busy person to spend the time to read your letter, consider your request, collect the information, and write a response. You therefore should apologize for any imposition, express appreciation, and state a reasonable request clearly and concisely—long, involved inquiries are unlikely to be answered.

Guidelines for Writing an Inquiry

- **Don't wait until the last minute.** Give the recipient reasonable time to respond.

- **Whenever possible, write to a specific, named person.** If you must, phone the organization beforehand, asking to whom you should address your inquiry.

- **Do your homework beforehand, so you can ask the right questions.** A vague request such as *Please send me all your data on . . .* is likely to be ignored. Don't ask questions whose answers are readily available elsewhere.

- **Keep the introduction short and to the point.** Follow the direct approach and state clearly at the outset who you are, what you are requesting, and why. Maintain the "you" perspective.

- **In the body (or discussion) section, write specific questions that are easy to understand and answer.** If you have multiple questions, put them in a numbered list, to help readers organize their answers and to increase your chances

(continues)

Guidelines (continued)

of getting all the information you want. Consider leaving space for responses below each question. (For more than five questions, consider using an attached questionnaire.) Provide multiple ways for the recipient to reach you: email, fax, phone, surface mail.

• **Conclude by explaining briefly how you plan to use the information, and, if possible, how your respondent might benefit.** Specify a date by which you need a response. Offer to provide a copy of the finished document. Close by expressing your appreciation.

• **Don't forget the stamped, return-addressed envelope.**

CASE: Requesting Information

Technical writing student Al Greene is preparing a report on the feasibility of harnessing solar energy for home heating in northern climates. After learning that a nonprofit research group has been experimenting with solar applications, Al decides to write for details (Figure 17.5). Notice the features throughout that are designed to make the respondent's task as easy as possible.

234 Western Road
Fargo, ND 27116
March 10, 20xx

Rachel Cowans
Director of Energy Systems
The Earth Research Institute
Persham, ME 04619

Dear Ms. Cowans:

States the
purpose

As a student at Evergreen College, I am preparing a report (April 15 deadline) on the feasibility of solar energy for home heating in northern climates.

Makes a
reasonable
request

While gathering data on home solar heating, I encountered references (in *Scientific American* and elsewhere) to your groups pioneerin g work in solar energy systems. Would you please allow me to benefit from your experience? I hate to impose on your valuable time, but your answers to the following questions would be a great help.

FIGURE 17.5 An Unsolicited Inquiry

Presents a list of specific questions

Leaves space for response to each question

1. At this stage of development, do you consider active or passive heating more practical? (Please explain briefly.)

2. Do you expect to surpass the 60 percent limit of heating needs supplied by the active system? If so, at what level of efficiency and how soon?

3. What is the cost of materials for building your active system, per cubic foot of living space?

4. What metal do you use in collectors, to obtain the highest thermal conductivity at the lowest maintenance costs?

Provides complete contact information

Please record your answers in the spaces provided and drop the return envelope in the mail. If an alternative way to respond is more convenient, here is my contact information: phone—555-986-6578 (collect); fax—555-986-5432; email—agreene245@hotmail.com.

Tells how the material will be used, and offers to share findings

Your answers, along with any recent findings you can share, will enrich a learning experience I hope to apply after graduation by building my own solar-heated home. I would be glad to send you a copy of my report, along with the house plans I have designed. Thank you.

Sincerely,

Alan Greene

Alan Greene

FIGURE 17.5 *(Continued)*

If your questions are too numerous or complex to be answered in print, you might request an interview (assuming the respondent is nearby), as our next writer decides to do.

CASE: Requesting an Interview

In preparing her report, student Karen Granger seeks a state representative's "opinions on the EPA's progress" in cleaning up local contamination. Anticipating a complex answer, she asks for an interview (Figure 17.6). By presenting an overview of the many questions surrounding this complicated issue, Karen implicitly justifies her interview request.

82 Mountain Street
New Bedford, MA 02720
March 8, 20xx

The Honorable Roger R. Grimes
Massachusetts House of Representatives
Boston, MA 02202

Dear Representative Grimes:

As a University of Massachusetts technical writing student, I am preparing a report evaluating the EPA's progress in cleaning up PCB contamination in New Bedford Harbor.

In my research, I encounter your name repeatedly. Your dedicated work has had a definite influence on this situation, and I am hoping to benefit from your knowledge.

I was surprised to learn that, although this contamination is considered the most extensive anywhere, the EPA has not moved beyond conducting studies. My own study questions the need for such extensive data gathering. Your opinion, as I can ascertain from the news media, is that the EPA is definitely moving too slowly.

The EPA refutes that argument by asserting they simply do not yet have the information necessary to begin a clean-up operation.

As a New Bedford resident, I am very interested in your opinions on the EPA's progress. Could you find time in your busy schedule to grant me an interview? With your permission, I will phone your office in a few days to ask about arranging an appointment.

I would deeply appreciate your assistance and will gladly send you a copy of my report.

Very truly yours,

Karen P. Granger

Karen P. Granger

FIGURE 17.6   Request for an Informative Interview

Choosing Your Medium

Selecting the appropriate medium for an unsolicited inquiry is crucial. Since you are asking for a favor—typically from someone who neither knows you personally nor expects your inquiry—the recipient's willingness to help becomes essential. Although our wired world offers alternatives to a hard-copy letter, consider carefully whether the recipient's impression to a particular medium is likely to be favorable or unfavorable.

Telephone and Email Inquiries

Why inquiries via regular mail may be preferable

Unsolicited inquiries via telephone, email, or fax can be efficient and productive but they also can be seen as unwelcome and intrusive. A traditional, carefully crafted letter implies greater respect for the recipient's privacy and provides a certain distance from which that person can contemplate a response—or even decide not to respond.

Etiquette for telephone or email inquiries

One alternative is to inquire by traditional letter and to invite a response by phone (collect), fax, or email, if your recipient prefers. Or, if you must inquire via telephone or email, consider this suggestion: Establish a brief initial contact in which you apologize for any intrusion and then ask if the respondent is willing to answer your questions at a convenient future time. In this or any communication, never sacrifice goodwill in the interest of efficiency.

Claim Letters

In the business and professional world, things do not always run smoothly. And when mistakes are made or promises are broken, the client or customer must often compose a formal letter to address the issue and to request a satisfactory resolution.

Claim (or complaint) letters request adjustments for defective goods or poor services, or they complain about unfair treatment or the like. Such letters fall into two groups: *routine claims* and *arguable claims*. The two types call for different approaches.

Routine claim letters follow a direct organizational plan because the customer's claim is not debatable. Arguable claims, on the other hand, present much more of a persuasive challenge because they convey unwelcome news and they are open to interpretation; an arguable claim, therefore, typically follows an indirect organizational plan. (For more on direct versus indirect organization, see pages 371, 372).

Routine Claims

Routine claims generally can be straightforward because the claim is backed by a contract, guarantee, or the company's reputation. Most companies will promptly grant any reasonable request.

Guidelines for Routine Claim Letters

- **Use a direct organization plan.** Describe the request or problem in your introductory paragraph; then explain the problem clearly in the body section. Close courteously, restating the action you request.

- **Make your tone polite and reasonable.** Your goal is not to sound off but to achieve results: a refund, a replacement, an apology. Press your claim objectively yet firmly by explaining it clearly and by stipulating the *reasonable* action that will satisfy you. Do not insult the reader or revile the firm.

- **Explain the problem in enough detail to clarify the basis for your claim.** Explain that your new alarm clock never rings instead of merely saying it's defective. Identify the faulty item clearly, giving serial and model numbers, and date and place of purchase. Then propose a fair adjustment.

- **Conclude by expressing goodwill and confidence in the company's integrity.** Do not threaten repercussions for inaction.

CASE: Making a Routine Claim

Jeffrey Ryder does not ask whether the firm will honor his claim (Figure 17.7); he assumes it will, and asks directly how to return his defective skis for repair. (Although 19 years separated the purchase from the claim on a lifetime guarantee, the company honored the claim without question, and Jeff had his skis relaminated.)

The attention line directs the claim to the appropriate department. The subject line, and its reemphasis in the first sentence, makes clear the nature of the claim.

Box 2641-A
Pocatello, Idaho 83201
April 13, 20xx

Hart Ski Manufacturing Company
P.O. Box 3049
St. Paul, MN 55165

Attention: Consumer Affairs Department

Subject: Delaminated Skis

FIGURE 17.7 Routine Claim Letter

States problem
and action desired

Provides details

Explains basis
for claim

Courteously states
desired action

This winter, my Tornado skis began to delaminate. I want to take advantage of your lifetime guarantee to have them relaminated.

I bought the skis from the Ski House in Erving, Massachusetts, in November 1989. Although I no longer have the sales slip, I did register them with you. The registration number is P9965.

I'm aware that you no longer make metal skis, but as I recall, your lifetime guarantee on the skis I bought was a major selling point. Only your company and one other were backing their skis so strongly.

Would you please let me know how to go about returning my delaminated skis for repair?

Yours truly,

Jeffery Ryder

Jeffery Ryder

FIGURE 17.7 *(Continued)*

Arguable Claims

When your request has been refused or ignored, or is in some way unusual or debatable, you must *persuade* the recipient to grant your claim. Say your parked car is wrecked by a drunk driver, and the insurance company appraises the car at $3,500. But two months earlier you had the engine rebuilt, a muffler system installed, and the front end repaired. By accepting the $3,500 you would lose roughly $1,000. You would need to write a claim letter requesting a fair adjustment.

Guidelines for Arguable Claim Letters

- **Use an indirect organizing pattern.** People are more likely to respond favorably *after* reading your explanation. Begin with a neutral statement both parties can agree to—but that also serves as the basis for your request: for example, *Customer goodwill is often an intangible quality, but a quality that brings tangible benefits.*
- **Once you've established agreement, explain and support your claim.** Include enough information for a fair evaluation: date and place of purchase, order or policy number, dates of previous letters or calls, and background.
- **Conclude by requesting a** *specific action* (**a credit to your account, a replacement, a rebate**). Ask politely but assertively.

CASE: Making an Arguable Claim

Sandra Alvarez uses a tactful and reasonable tone and an indirect pattern to present her argument (Figure 17.8). This writer is courteous but somewhat forceful, to reflect her insistence on an acceptable adjustment.

◆**Office Systems, Inc.**◆
657 High Street
Tulsa, OK 74120

Fax (302) 655-5551   Phone (302) 655-5550   Email osys@sys.com

January 23, 20xx

Consumer Affairs Department
Hightone Office Supplies
93 Cattle Drive
Houston, Texas 77028

ATTENTION: Ms. Dionne Dubree

Establishes early agreement

Your company has an established reputation as a reliable wholesaler of office supplies. For eight years we have counted on that reliability, but a recent episode has left us annoyed and disappointed.

On January 29, we ordered 5 cartons of 700 MB "hp" CDs (#A74–866) and 13 cartons of Epson MX 70/80 black cartridges (#A19–556).

Presents facts to support claim

On February 5, the order arrived. But instead of the 700 MB "hp" CDs ordered, we received 650 MB Everlast CDs. And the Epson ribbons were blue, not the black we had ordered. We returned the order the same day.

Offers more support

Also on the 5th, we called John Fitzsimmons at your company to explain our problem. He promised delivery of a corrected order by the 12th. Finally, on the 22nd, we did receive an order—the original incorrect one—with a note claiming that the packages had been water damaged while in our possession.

FIGURE 17.8 Arguable Claim Letter

Includes all relevant
information

Sticks to the facts—
accuses no one

Requests a specific
adjustment

Stipulates a
reasonable
response time

> Our warehouse manager insists the packages were in perfect condition when he released them to the shipper. Because we had the packages only five hours, and had no rain on the 5th, we are certain the damage did not occur here.
>
> Responsibility for damages therefore rests with either the shipper or your warehouse staff. What bothers us is our outstanding bill from Hightone ($2,049.50) for the faulty shipment. We insist that the bill be canceled and that we receive a corrected statement. Until this misunderstanding, our transactions with your company were excellent. We hope they can be again.
>
> We would appreciate having this matter resolved before the end of this month.
>
> Yours truly,
>
> *Sandra Alvarez*
>
> Sandra Alvarez
> Manager, Accounting

FIGURE 17.8 (*Continued*)

Adjustment Letters

Even though the vast majority of people never bother to make a formal complaint, companies generally will make a requested adjustment that seems reasonable. Rather than quibbling over questionable claims, companies usually honor the request. The resultant goodwill usually outweighs the cost of granting a few suspect claims. Of course, if the claim is unreasonable or unfounded, the adjustment should be refused (Figure 17.10).

Granting Adjustments

The goal of adjustment letters is to keep customers satisfied. In fact, reputable firms welcome claim letters, to help them assess their products and services. If a claim warrants an adjustment, be sure to grant it willingly and positively.

Guidelines for Granting Adjustments

- **Begin with the good news.** A sincere apology helps rebuild customers' confidence.
- **Explain what went wrong and how the problem will be corrected.** Without an honest explanation, you leave the impression that such problems are common or beyond your control.
- **Never blame employees as scapegoats.** To blame someone in the firm reflects poorly on the firm itself.
- **Do not promise that the problem never will recur.** Mishaps are inevitable.
- **End on a positive note.** Focus on the solution, not the problem.

CASE: Granting an Adjustment

Jane Duval apologizes graciously for a mistake (Figure 17.9). She omits an explanation because the error is obvious: Someone sent the wrong software. Once the reader has the information and the apology, Duval shifts attention to the gift certificate. Note the "you" perspective and the friendly tone.

Software Unlimited
421 Fairview Road
Tulsa, Oklahoma 74321

May 2, 20xx

Mr. James Morris
P.O. Box 176
543 So. Main Street
Little Rock AR 54701

Dear Mr. Morris:

Apologies immediately

Your software should arrive by May 15. Sorry for the mixup. We don't make a practice of sending Apple software to HP owners, but we do slip up once in awhile.

FIGURE 17.9 **Letter Granting an Adjustment**

**Offers
compensation**

To show our appreciation for your patience and understanding, I've enclosed a $50 gift certificate. You can give it to a friend or apply it toward your next order. If you order by phone, just give the operator the certificate number, and he will credit your account.

**Looks toward
the future**

Keep your certificate handy because you will be getting our new catalog soon. It features 15 new business and utility programs that you might find useful.

Sincerely,

Jane Duval

Jane Duval
Sales Manager

Enc. Gift Certificate

FIGURE 17.9 (*Continued*)

Refusing Adjustments

Favorable adjustments enhance a company's reputation. But when the customer has misused the product or is mistaken about company procedures or services, you must write a refusal.

Guidelines for Refusing Adjustments

- **Use an indirect organizational plan.** Explain diplomatically and clearly why you are refusing the request. Your goal is to convince the reader that your refusal results from a thorough analysis of the situation.
- **Be sure the refusal is unambiguous.** Don't create unrealistic expectations by beating around the bush.
- **Avoid a patronizing or accusing tone.** Use the passive voice so as not to accuse the claimant, but do not hide behind the passive voice (see page 221).
- **Close courteously and positively.** Offer an alternative or compromise, when it is feasible to do so.

CASE: Refusing an Adjustment

In refusing to grant a refund for a 10-speed bicycle, Anna Jenkins faces a delicate balance (Figure 17.10): on the one hand she must explain clearly why she cannot grant the adjustment; on the other, she must diplomatically point out that the customer is mistaken.

 **People Power, Inc.**

101 Salem Street, Springfield, Illinois 32456

March 8, 20xx

Mrs. Alma Gower
32 Wood Street
Lewiston, IL 32432

Dear Mrs. Gower:

When we advertise the Windspirit as the toughest, most durable ten-speed, we stress it's a racing or cruising bike built to withstand the long, grueling miles of intense competition. The bike is built of the strongest, yet lightest, alloys available, and each part is calibrated to within 1/1000 of an inch. That's why we guarantee the Windspirit against defects resulting from the strain of competitive racing.

The Windspirit, though, is not built to withstand the impact of ramp jumps such as those attempted by your son. The rims and front fork would have to be made from a much thicker gauge alloy, thereby increasing weight and decreasing speed. Since we build racing bikes, such a compromise is unacceptable

To ensure that buyers are familiar with the Windspirit's limits, in the owner's manual we stress that the bike should be carried over curbings and similar drops because even an eight-inch drop could damage the front rim. Damage from such drops is not considered normal wear and so is not covered by our guarantee.

Since your son appears to be more interested in a bike capable of withstanding the impact of high jumps, you could recoup a large part of the Windspirit's price by advertising it in your local newspaper. Many novice racers would welcome the chance to buy one at a reduced price. Or, if you prefer having it repaired, you could take it to Jamie's Bike Shop, the dealer closest to you.

Yours truly,

Anna Jenkins

Anna Jenkins
Manager, Customer Services

Margin annotations:
- Explanation
- Writer doesn't accuse; she explains in a friendly tone
- Refusal
- Helpful close

FIGURE 17.10 Letter Refusing an Adjustment Although Mrs. Gower may not be pleased by the explanation, it is thorough and reasonable.

☑ Checklist: Usability of Letters

(Numbers in parentheses refer to the first page of discussion.)

Content

☐ Does the situation call for a formal letter rather than a memo or email? (360)

☐ Is the letter addressed to the correct and specifically named person? (362)

☐ Have you determined the position or title of your recipient? (362)

☐ Does the letter contain all the standard parts? (360)

☐ Does the letter have all needed specialized parts? (364)

☐ Is the letter's main point clearly stated? (362)

☐ Is all the necessary information included? (38)

Arrangement

☐ Does the introduction engage the reader and preview the body section? (362)

☐ Is the direct or indirect pattern used appropriately? (371)

☐ Does the conclusion encourage the reader to act? (362)

☐ Is the format acceptable and correct? (365)

Style

☐ Does the letter reflect a "you" perspective throughout? (369)

☐ Is the letter in conversational language (free of letterese)? (370)

☐ Does the tone reflect your relationship with the recipient? (240)

☐ Is the letter designed for a tasteful, conservative look? (368)

☐ Is the style clear, concise, fluent, exact, and likable? (215)

☐ Have you proofread with extreme care? (21)

Exercises

1. Bring to class a copy of a business letter addressed to you or a friend. Compare letters. Choose the most and least effective.

2. Write and mail an unsolicited letter of inquiry about the topic you are investigating for an analytical report or research assignment. In your letter you might request brochures, pamphlets, or other informative literature, or you might ask specific questions. Submit a copy of your letter, and the response, to your instructor.

3. a. As a student in a state college, you learn that your governor and legislature have cut next year's operating budget for all state colleges by 20 percent. This cut will cause the firing of young and popular faculty members; drastically reduce admissions, financial aid, and new programs; and wreck college morale. Write a claim letter to your governor or representative, expressing your strong disapproval and justifying a major adjustment in the proposed budget.

   b. Write a claim letter to a politician about some issue affecting your school or community.

   c. Write a claim letter to an appropriate school official to recommend action on a campus problem.

4. Write a complaint letter about a problem you've had with goods or service. State your case clearly and objectively, and request a specific adjustment.

5. *For Class Discussion:* Under what circumstances might it be acceptable to contact a potential inquiry respondent by email? When should you just leave the person alone?

6. These sentences need to be overhauled before being included in a letter. Identify the weakness in each statement, and revise as needed. For example, you would revise the accusatory *You were not very clear* to *We did not understand your message.*

   a. I need all the information you have about methane-powered engines.

   b. You morons have sent me the wrong software!

   c. It is imperative that you let me know of your decision by January 15.

   d. I have become cognizant of your experiments and wish to ask your advice about the following procedure.

   e. You will find the following instructions easy enough for an ape to follow.

   f. As per your request I am sending the country map.

   g. I am in hopes that you will call soon.

   h. We beg to differ with your interpretation of this leasing clause.

Collaborative Project

Working in groups, respond to one of the following scenarios. Appoint one group member to present the letter in class.

   a. As director of Consumer Affairs, you've received an adjustment request from Brian Maxwell. Two years ago, he bought a pair of top-of-the-line Gannon speakers. Both speakers, he claims, are badly distorting bass sounds, and he states that his local dealer refuses to honor the three-year warranty. After checking, you find that the dealer refused because someone had obviously tampered with the speakers. Two lead wires had been respliced; one of the booster magnets was missing; and the top insulation also was missing from one of the speaker cabinets. Your warranty specifically states that if speakers are removed from the cabinet or subjected to tampering in any way, the warranty is void. You must refuse the adjustment; however, because Maxwell bought the speakers from a factory-authorized dealer, he is entitled to a 30 percent discount on repairs. Write the refusal, offering this alternative. His address: 691 Concord Street, Biloxi, MS 71690.

   b. Luke Harrington wants a $1200 refund for four Douglas Fir trees that have died since your workers planted them in his yard two years ago. Because you guarantee your transplants for three years, he wants his money returned. After checking Harrington's contract, you recall his problem: you wouldn't guarantee the five Douglas Firs he ordered because he wanted them planted in a wet, marshy area, and Douglas Firs need well-drained soil. A check of Harrington's lot confirms that four trees planted in the wet area have died of root rot. Write him, reminding him of the contract, and refusing the adjustment. As you did two years ago, suggest that he plant balsam firs in the wet area. Although balsam needles are slightly darker than the Douglas Firs', both trees have the shape he wants. The balsams would retain the symmetry of his tree line. Harrington's address: 921 Daisy Lane, Churchill, MO 61516.

   c. Kim Kurt has mailed back a red silk blouse she brought through your catalogue three months ago. Ms. Kurt claims that the blouse is defective, and she wants a $97.25 adjustment to her credit card. Your textile technologist has discovered that the blouse was washed at least twice with a harsh detergent, and that detergent residue remained in the fibers, causing further breakdown. The care label states the blouse must be washed by hand with a mild detergent. Refuse the adjustment, but don't accuse–explain. For resale, mention you're having a sale this week on blouses that have the look and feel of silk, cost only $\frac{1}{2}$ the price, and can be machine washed. Her address is 391 Beacon Street, Selma, AL 51321.

d. As superintendent of a large warehouse, you've just received a return on a six-month-old shipment of nuts, bolts, and other fasteners from a hardware retailer who wants a credit on the return. An inspection of the goods shows they've been water damaged, and many of the fasteners are rusted. Since you're not responsible for the damage, you can't give the dealer credit. The cartons in which the goods were shipped aren't water damaged, so the shipper doesn't appear responsible either. Write to Glen Harper, Harper Hardware, 100 East Elm Street, Trenton, NJ 31267. Explain the situation and suggest how he could sell the merchandise to recoup some of his money.

CHAPTER 18

Employment Correspondence

Employment Outlook in the Twenty-First Century

Prospecting for Jobs

Preparing Your Résumé

Guidelines for Résumés

Preparing Your Job Application Letter

Guidelines for Job Application Letters

Consider This: How Applicants Are Screened for Personal Qualities

Submitting Electronic Résumés

Guidelines for Preparing a Scannable Résumé

Support for the Application

Guidelines for Preparing a Portfolio

Employment Interviews

Guidelines for Surviving a Job Interview

Checklist: Résumés

Checklist: Job Application Letters

Whether you are applying for your first professional job or changing careers, you must market your skills effectively. Your résumé and letter of application must stand out among the competition.

Employment Outlook in the Twenty-First Century

In today's workplace, the name of the game is *change* (as page 10 shows in detail). The U.S. Labor Department estimates that "a typical 32-year-old has already held 9 jobs" (Conlin 170). What this means is that the typical "employee" is becoming someone who works for various employers just long enough to complete a particular project (Bolles 141). These "free agents" have been increasing from 26 percent of the U.S. workforce to an estimated 41 percent during this decade (Conlin 170).

In addition, more and more jobs (ranging from accounting to reading X-rays) are being "outsourced" to other countries that have far lower labor costs. Other type of jobs (such as programming or data processing) are being automated, in many cases.

A glimpse at your job future

Whatever your major, the message is clear: (1) expect multiple employers and careers, and (2) expect to rely on skills that involve working well with others, life-long learning, and adapting to rapid change. (For more on these "portable" skills, review page 10.)

NOTE

Although email and online job listings and résumé postings have provided new tools for job seekers, today's job searches require the same basic approach and communication skills that people have relied on for decades.

Prospecting for Jobs

Begin your employment search by studying the job market to identify careers and jobs for which you best qualify.

Assess Your Skills and Aptitudes

Beyond the portable skills mentioned above, what specific qualities can you bring to the job search?

Identify your assets

- Do you have skills in leadership or in group projects (as demonstrated in employment, social organizations, or extracurricular activities)?
- Do you speak a second language? Have musical or artistic talent?
- Do you communicate well? Are you a good listener?
- Can you perform under pressure?
- Have you done anything special or out of the ordinary?

Besides helping focus your search, answers to the previous questions will be handy when you write your résumé and prepare for interviews.

Research the Job Market

Launch your search early. Don't wait for the job to come to you. Begin by scanning the Help Wanted section in major Sunday newspapers for job descriptions, salaries, and qualifications. The Web provides an endless resource for job seekers. Check out, for example, the Bureau of Labor Statistics at <http://www.bls.gov>. (For more on Internet job sites, see pages 391, 392). Also, consult specific resources such as these, increasingly available in electronic versions:

Know what is available

- *Fortune, Business Week, Forbes,* the *Wall Street Journal,* or trade publications in your field—for latest developments and the big picture on business, economy, or technology. Specific topics and companies can be searched in the *Business Index.*
- *Occupational Outlook Handbook* and its quarterly update, *Occupational Outlook Quarterly,* published by the U.S. Department of Labor—for occupations, qualifications, employment prospects, and salaries.
- *Almanac of Jobs and Salaries, Dun's Employment Opportunities Directory*, or *Federal Career Opportunities*—for government and private-sector organizations that hire college graduates.
- *Moody's Industrial Index* or Standard and Poor's *Register of Corporations*—for company locations, major subsidiaries, products, executive officers, and assets.
- *Annual reports*—for a company's subsidiaries, financial health, innovations, performance, and prospects. (Many libraries collect annual reports.)

Ask a reference librarian to suggest additional resources in your field.

Launch your search well before your senior year to learn whether certain courses make you more marketable. If you are changing jobs or careers, employers will be interested in what you have accomplished *since* college. Be prepared to show how your experience is relevant to the new job.

You might also register with an employment agency. A fee is payable after you are hired, but employers often pay this fee. Ask about fee arrangements *before* you sign up. Consider investing in a *career coach,* an expert in grooming job seekers.

Search Online

Online career sites

The computer and the Web continue to improve the quality and speed of contact between jobseekers and employers. Beyond ease and efficiency, online job hunting offers some clear benefits:

Benefits of online job searches

- You can search for jobs worldwide.
- You can focus your search by region, industry, or job category.
- You can research companies comprehensively from many perspectives.

- You can create your own Web site, with hyperlinks to samples of your work, employment references, or other supporting material.
- You can search "passively" and discretely (say, while employed elsewhere) by specifying preferences for salary, region, types of industry, and then receive an email message when the service provider identifies an opening that matches your "profile" (Justin Martin, "Changing Jobs?" 206).
- Your search can be ongoing, in that your résumé remains part of an active computer file until you delete it.

NOTE   *Even the largest job-posting sites represent only a fraction of all jobs available; don't overlook traditional job-hunting sources listed on page 393 and in Figure 18.1.*

Most major companies recruit on sites such as these:

WEBLINK Electronic job hunting

A sampling of job sites on the Web

- *CareerBuilder* <http://www.careerbuilder.com> provides access to employer Web sites, posting of résumés, a career test, career advice, and domestic and international job listings.
- *CareerPath.com* <http://www.careerpath.com> posts job listings from major newspapers nationwide, and enables jobseekers to post résumés free.
- *College Grad Job Hunter* at <http://www.collegegrad.com> focuses on entry-level job hunting for students and recent graduates.

Most Commonly Used Job-Search Methods

Percent of Total Job-seekers Using the Method	Method	Effectiveness Rate*
66.0%	Applied directly to employer	47.7%
50.8	Asked friends about jobs where they work	22.1
41.8	Asked friends about jobs elsewhere	11.9
28.4	Asked relatives about jobs where they work	19.3
27.3	Asked relatives about jobs elsewhere	7.4
45.9	Answered local newspaper ads	23.9
21.0	Private employment agency	24.2
12.5	School placement office	21.4
15.3	Civil Service test	12.5
10.4	Asked teacher or professor	12.1
1.6	Placed ad in local newspaper	12.9
6.0	Union hiring hall	22.2

*A percentage obtained by dividing the number of jobseekers who actually found work using the method, by the total number of jobseekers who tried to use that method, whether successfully or not.

FIGURE 18.1   How People Usually Find Jobs

Source: Tips for Finding the Right Job. U.S. Department of Labor.

- Gateway sites for job hunters offer countless targeted resources that have been organized for easy navigation and evaluated for usefulness (Bolles 10–11). Two of the highly regarded gateway employment sites are *The Riley Guide* at <http://www.rileyguide.com> and *JobHunt: A Meta-list of Online Search Resources and Services* at <http://www.job-hunt.org>.

Online recruiting centers such as the Employment Guide site at <http://www.employment-guide.com> match applicants with employers in engineering, marketing, data processing, and technical fields worldwide. Countless specialized sites include *Boston Job Bank, College Grad Job Hunter, Euro-jobs On-line, HiTechCareers, Hospitality Industry Job Exchange, Jobs in Atomic and Plasma Physics,* and *Positions in Bioscience and Medicine.*

Major companies such as Johnson & Johnson, Boeing, John Deere, and IBM post openings on their own Web sites. You can visit a company's site, learn about its history, products, and priorities, search its job listings, email your résumé and application letter, and arrange an interview.

NOTE   *For a company's real story, look beyond its Web site (for which information has been selected to paint the rosiest possible picture). To see what industry analysts think about the company's prospects, consult an impartial research site such as* Hoover's Online *at* <http://www.hoovers.com>. *Here, in addition to relatively objective financial and management profiles, you can access recent articles about the company (Justin Martin, "Changing Jobs?" 208). For more on researching a company, see pages 390 and 417.*

Web sites maintained by professional organizations offer additional job listings, along with career advice and industry prospects. Some sites also allow for posting of interactive, hyperlinked résumés.

Professional organizations on the Web

- Society for Technical Communication <http://www.stc.org>
- International Television and Video Association <http://www.itva.org>
- Institute for Electrical and Electronic Engineers <http://www.ieee.org>

For internship postings and other related information, go to the *InternWeb.com* site at <http://www.internweb.com>, the *RisingStar Internships* site at <http://www.rsinternships.com>, and the *InternshipPrograms.com* site at <http://www.internships.wetfeet.com/home.asp>.

NOTE   *Record each date and site at which you post an online résumé (or fill out an onscreen application) so you can keep track of responses and edit or delete your material as needed (Curry 100).*

Learn to Network

Do all the *networking* you can. Former recruiter Brad Karsh offers recent graduates this advice: "Your best chance of getting a job is through someone who knows someone. Use your college alumni network. Find out who is working in the field you want to enter, and call them" (qtd. in Fisher, "I Didn't" 178). Karsh also advises that you consult family friends about whom they might know. (For more advice, visit Karsh's job-search Web site for recent grads at <http://www.jobbound.com>.)

Here are additional suggestions for networking:

How to make contacts

- Visit your college placement service. Openings and job fair notices are posted there; interviews are scheduled; and counselors provide job-hunting advice. Sign up for interviews with recruiters who visit the campus. Go to job fairs.
- Speak with people in your field to get an inside view and practical advice.
- Seek advice from faculty who do outside consulting or who have worked in business, industry, or government.
- Look for a summer job or internship in your field; this experience may count as much as your academic credentials.
- Do related volunteer work. (Visit <http://www.volunteermatch.org> for organizations that seek volunteers.)
- Register with agencies that provide temporary staffing. Even the most humble and temporary job offers the chance to make contacts and could be a way of getting your foot in the door.
- Join a professional organization in your field. Student memberships usually are available at reduced fees. Such affiliations can generate excellent contacts, and they look good on your résumé. Try to attend meetings of the local chapter.

Notice that several job-search methods in Figure 18.1 include talking with people and exploring useful contacts.

Once you have a clear picture of where you fit into the job market, you must answer the big question asked by all employers: *What do you have to offer?* Your answer must be a highly polished presentation of yourself, your education, work history, interests, and skills—in short, your résumé.

Preparing Your Résumé

What employers expect in a résumé

Employers initially spend only 15 to 45 seconds looking at a résumé; during this scan, they are looking for a persuasive answer to this question: *What can you do for us?* Employers are impressed by a résumé that looks good, reads easily, and provides information the employer needs to determine if the applicant should be interviewed. Résumés that are mechanically flawed, cluttered, sketchy, or hard to follow will simply get discarded. Make your résumé perfect!

Typical Components of a Résumé

A résumé has several basic components: contact information, objectives, education, work experience, personal data, personal interests, and references.

Contact Information.   Be sure to provide current information that lets prospective employers know where they can reach you; if you are between addresses, provide both and check each contact point regularly. Be sure that both your email address and phone number are accurate. If you use an answering machine or voice mail, record an outgoing message that sounds friendly and professional.

Job and Career Objectives.   Spell out the kind of job you want. Your objectives project an image to your potential employer of who you are. Avoid vague statements such as *A position in which I can apply my education and experience.* Instead, be specific: *Intensive-care nursing in a teaching hospital, with the eventual goal of supervising and instructing.* Prepare different statements to focus on the requirements of different jobs. State your immediate and long-range goals, including any plans to continue your education. If the company has branches, include *Willing to relocate.*

One hiring officer for a major computer firm offers this advice: "A statement should show that you know the type of work the company does and the type of position it needs to fill" (Beamon, qtd. in Crosby, *Résumés* 3).

NOTE   *Below career objectives, you might insert a summary of qualifications (Figure 18.5). This section is vital in a computer-scannable résumé (Figure 18.9), but even in a conventional résumé, a "Qualifications" section can highlight your strengths. Make the summary specific and concrete: replace "proven leadership" with "team and project management," "special-event planning," or "instructor-led training"; replace "persuasive communicator" with "fundraising," "publicity campaigns," "environmental/public-interest advocacy," and "door-to-door canvassing." In short, allow the reader to* **visualize** *your activities.*

Education.   If your education is more substantial than your work experience, place it first. Begin with your most recent school, and work backward. Include the name of the school, degree completed, year completed, and your major and minor if applicable. (Omit high school—unless the high school's prestige or your achievements warrant its inclusion). List any courses that have directly prepared you for the job you seek. If your class rank is in the upper 30 percent and your grade point average is 3.0 or above, list them. Include schools or specialized training during military service. If you finance part or all of your education by working, say so (here or in your cover letter), indicating the percentage of your contribution.

Work Experience.   If your experience relates to the job you seek, list it before your education. List your most recent job and then earlier ones. Include the dates you were employed, the employers' names, and their contact information. Indicate whether the job was full-time, part-time (include number of hours weekly), or seasonal. Describe your exact duties in each job, indicating promotions. If it is to your advantage, specifically state why you left each job. Include military experience and relevant volunteer work. If you have no paid experience, emphasize your education, including internships and special projects; convince prospective employers that you have potential.

Personal Data.   By law, you are not required to include a photograph or reveal your sex, religion, race, age, national origin, disability, or marital status. But if you believe that any of this information could advance your prospects, you should include it.

Personal Interests, Awards, and Skills.   List any hobbies and interests that are *relevant* to the position you are applying for, such as memberships in organizations. Note any special recognition you have received. List work-related skills, say, in foreign language, typing, first aid, or computers. Be selective: List only those items that reflect the qualities employers seek.

References.   List three to five people *who have agreed to provide* strong assessments of your qualifications and personal qualities. References may be asked to provide letters or email responses or to complete reference forms. Other requests will be made by telephone calls from employers doing reference checks. In any case, it's a good idea to keep your own file containing letters from each of your references.

How to choose references

Select references who can speak genuinely about your ability and character. Choose among former employers, professors, and community figures who know you well enough to speak concretely on your behalf. Do not choose family members or friends not in your field.

How to request a reference

A lukewarm reference is more damaging than no reference at all.   Don't merely ask, *Could you please be one of my references?* This is hard to refuse, but a person who doesn't know you well or who is unimpressed by your work might write a letter that does more harm than good. Instead, make an explicit request: *Do you know me and my work well enough to write a strong letter of reference? If so, would you be one of my references?* This second version provides the option of declining gracefully; otherwise, it elicits a firm commitment to a positive recommendation.

Letters of recommendation are time-consuming to write. Few people have time to write individual letters to every prospective employer. Ask for only one letter, with no salutation. Your reference keeps a copy, you keep the original for your personal dossier (to reproduce as necessary), and a copy goes to the placement office for your placement dossier. Because the law permits you to read all material in your dossier, this arrangement provides you with your own copy of your credentials. (The dossier is discussed later in this chapter.)

NOTE

Under some circumstances you may—if you wish to—waive the right to examine your references. Some applicants, especially those applying to professional schools, as in medicine and law, waive this right in concession to a general feeling that a letter writer who is assured of confidentiality is more likely to provide a balanced, objective, and reliable assessment of a candidate. Before you decide, seek the advice of your major adviser or a career counselor.

If the people you select as references live elsewhere, you might make your request by letter (or email), as shown in Figure 18.2.

[Heading/inside address]

Dear Mr. Knight:

From September 19xx to August 20xx, I worked at Teo's Restaurant as a waiter, cashier, and then assistant manager. Because I enjoyed my work, I decided to study for a career in the hospitality field.

In three months I will graduate from San Jose City College with an A.A. degree in Hotel and Restaurant Management. Next month I begin my job search. Do you remember me and my work enough to write a strong letter of recommendation? If so, would you kindly serve as one of my references?

Please address your salutation "To Whom It May Concern." If you could send me the original letter, I will forward a copy to my college placement office.

To update you on my recent activities, I've enclosed my résumé. If I can answer any questions, please contact me by phone (collect) at 214-316-2419 or by email at jpur@valnet.com.

Thank you for your help and support.

Sincerely,

James D. Purdy

James D. Purdy

FIGURE 18.2   Request for Employment Reference (To save space, the heading and inside address are omitted here.)

Opinion is divided about whether names and addresses of references should appear in a résumé. If saving space is important, simply state, *References available on request,* keeping your résumé only one page long, but if the résumé already takes up more than one page, you probably should include that information. (A prospective employer might recognize a name, and thus notice you among the crowd of applicants.) If you are changing careers, a full listing of references is vital.

If you don't list references on your résumé, prepare a separate reference sheet that you can provide on request. Beneath your personal contact information, repeated from the résumé, list each reference, including the person's title, company address, and contact information (Crosby, *Résumés* 6).

Portfolio.   To illustrate your skills, organize samples of your relevant work in a leather or leather-like notebook. Depending on your field, the portfolio might contain sample documents you've written or edited (such as reports, articles, or manuals) or other evidence of related skills (such as engineering drawings or software documentation). Portfolios are obviously more appropriate for jobs that generate actual writing or visual samples—say, for graphic artists or marketing specialists rather than for resort or hotel managers. If you do have a portfolio, indicate this on your résumé, followed by *Available on request.* (See the suggestions for preparing a portfolio on page 416.)

Résumés from a Template.   Programs such as *Microsoft Word* provide electronic templates that can be filled in with an individual's own personal data. Such programs organize the information keyed into the template, and the organization can be easily changed as needed.

Organizing Your Résumé

Emphasize your assets

Model résumés

Organize your résumé to convey the strongest impression of your qualifications, skills, and experience. Your experience will dictate the organization of your resume. To show a pattern of job experience, you should use *reverse chronological organization* (Figure 18.3), in which you list your most recent experience first and then move backward toward earlier experiences. If you have limited experience or gaps in your job record, you should use *functional organization* (Figure 18.4), which allows you to focus on skills, abilities, and activities instead of employment chronology. *Combined organization* (Figure 18.5), also called *modified functional,* is often used when résumés are to be electronically scanned; this method combines highlighting specific job skills with reverse chronological ordering.

Sample Résumés for Different Situations

Based on the situation and the writer' purpose, each of three résumés that follow illustrates one of the three different standard types of organization: reverse chronological, functional, and modified-functional.

CASE: Composing a Reverse Chronological Résumé

Daniel Lannon is about to graduate from law school and is seeking an entry-level position in environmental law. He designs his résumé to highlight his diverse achievements and to emphasize a steady pattern of relevant employment (Figure 18.3).

CASE: Composing a Functional Résumé

Carol Chasone will soon graduate from a regional university with a major in marketing and a minor in graphic design. She hopes to work in marketing/communications, but has limited work experience. She has spent two weeks compiling information for her résumé and obtaining commitments from four references. Figure 18.4 shows her final draft.

CASE: Composing a Modified Functional Résumé

Karen Granger seeks a summer internship with a software company, in which she can further her practical experience. To highlight her skills as well as her experience, Karen's résumé combines features of reverse chronological and functional resumes (Figure 18.5).

Guidelines for Résumés

- **Begin your résumé well before your job search**. Your final version can be printed for various similar targets—but each new type of job requires a new résumé tailored to fit the advertised demands of that job.

- **Try to limit your résumé to a single page, but keep it uncluttered and tasteful.** If you are changing jobs or careers, or if the résumé looks cramped, you might need a second page.

- **Use good white paper.**

- **Stick to material that shows what you can offer.** Don't merely list *everything*.

- **Never "invent" credentials.** Make yourself look as good as the facts allow. Distortions are unethical and counterproductive. Companies routinely investigate claims made in a résumé, and people who have lied are fired.

- **Do not raise the topic of salary**. Wait until your interview, or later.

- **Avoid complete sentences.** They take up too much room.

(continues on page 402)

DANIEL M. LANNON
3598 Seal Blvd.
Bloomington, Indiana 42167

(710) 555-5555   dlannon@indiana.edu

OBJECTIVE
  Entry-level position in environmental regulation and litigation.

EDUCATION
  University of Indiana School of Law, Bloomington, IN
  Expected Graduation: May, 2008
  GPA: 3.4/4.0, 2nd Year Class Rank: 78/173
  Co-Director of Street Law: Landlord-Tenant Pro-Bono Program
  Treasurer of Environmental Law Forum
  Member of Family Law in Practice

  Calvin College, New Haven, Connecticut
  B.A. in Anthropology, English minor, 2002
  GPA 3.3/4.0, Graduated with Honors in Major (GPA: 3.6); Dean's List every college semester.
  Served on Student Activities Committee and as House Council and Environmental Coordinator;
  co-chaired Campus Recycling Committee and managed $22,000 recycling budget.

  University College Cork, Cork, Ireland
  GPA 3.0/4.0, Fall 2000
  Took courses in European Archaeology and participated in home-stay program with local Irish family.

EXPERIENCE
  Advanced Educational Systems, Indianapolis, IN
  Law Clerk, August 2006–December 2007. In this major education/childcare corporation, my work
  included contract review, editing, and drafting; preparing a journal supplement; drafting
  cease–and–desist letters to parties who use AES trademarked materials illegally; legal research and
  drafting memoranda regarding employment, tax, real estate, marketing, intellectual property, and
  licensing.

  Leonard, Moran, Lang & Holmes, P.C., Indianapolis, IN
  Law Clerk, May 2006–August 2006. Responsibilities included extensive legal research, preparation for
  litigation, assistance with case preparation, and pro-bono assistance for clients in need.

  Leonard, Moran, Lang & Holmes, P.C., Indianapolis, IN
  Office Assistant, July 2003–July 2005. At family law firm, managed files and supplies, assisted with trial
  preparation by organizing and categorizing exhibits, preparing exhibit lists, and performing legal
  research and clerical duties. Also attended CLE attorney meetings.

  Catering Edge @ the Sports Stadium, Indianapolis, IN
  VIP courtside-seat server, October 2002–June 2003. Indiana Pacers home games.

  PIRG/Sierra Club, Amherst, MA & Burlington, VT
  Field Manager/Canvasser, June 1998–August 1999. Gained advocacy experience working for grassroots
  groups doing canvasser training, VIP communications, and legislative interaction.

HOBBIES & PERSONAL INTERESTS
  Basic fluency in French. Performed in improvisational comedy group in college. Hobbies include jazz/
  blues guitar, fishing, basketball, and following Indiana sports teams.

REFERENCES
  Available on request.

FIGURE 18.3 **A Reverse Chronological Résumé** Use this format to show a clear pattern of job
experience.

Carol R. Chasone
642 Eagle Lane
Eugene, OR 97405
(503-314-5555)
crchasone@eor.edu

OBJECTIVE	Position in marketing/communications with opportunity for advancement
SALES/ MARKETING SKILLS	• Wrote recruiting letter currently used by the Eugene Chamber of Commerce • Designed posters for promoting industrial development in Central Oregon • Assisted Chamber President in promoting the organization's activities • Recruited 7 speakers for Chamber meetings • Wrote 3 public-relations pieces about a local hospital, for area newspapers
COMMUNICATION AND DOCUMENT DESIGN SKILLS	• Conducted demographic study of small businesses in Southwestern OR • Presented study findings to Eugene Chamber of Commerce • Wrote 15-page report on results of demographic study • Designed and wrote two brochures to promote the Small Business Institute • Designed 5 issues of *Patient Care*, 16-page in-house hospital newsletter • Wrote 8 articles and conducted 3 interviews for the newsletter • Designed 6 posters for in-service hospital programs
ORGANIZATIONAL/ MANAGEMENT SKILLS	• Coordinated all weekly Chamber meetings for Feb., March, April, and May • Attended 2 seminars (Houston, Seattle) for hospital public relations • Trained and supervised 3 new interns at the Small Business Institute • Scheduled and chaired weekly intern meetings
EDUCATION	Eastern Oregon University, Eugene OR B.S. in Marketing; Graphic Design minor—May 2008 GPA: 3.3/4.0; Dean's List, 5 semesters Contract Learning: Eugene Chamber of Commerce, Fall 2007 Internships: EOU's Small Business Institute, Spring 2007; Mercy Hospital, Fall 2007
EMPLOYMENT	Personal trainer (part-time and summers 2005–2007)—Acme Gym, Eugene Caddy and Pro Shop salesperson—Eugene Golf Club, summers, 2002–2004
INTERESTS	Golf, fitness, modern dance, oil painting, photography
REFERENCES	Available on request

FIGURE 18.4 A Functional Résumé Use this format to focus on skills and potential instead of employment chronology. (Note that certain items in the above skills categories overlap.)

Karen P. Granger
82 Mountain Street
New Bedford, MA 02720
Telephone (617) 864-9318
Email: kgrang@swis.net

Objective   A summer internship documenting software.

Qualifications   Software and hardware documentation. Editing. Desktop publishing. Usability
                         testing. Computer science. Internet research. World Wide Web collaboration.
                         Networking technology. Instructor-led training. DEC 20 mainframe and VAX
                         11/780 systems. *InDesign*, Adobe *FrameMaker*, *RoboHelp*, Webworks *Publisher*,
                         PowerPoint, *Excel*, and *Lotus Notes* software. Logo, Pascal, HTML, and C++
                         program languages.

Education   Attending University of Massachusetts Dartmouth; B.A. expected January 2009.
                         Major: English/Communications. Minor: Computer Science. Dean's List,
                         all semesters. GPA: 3.54. Class rank 110 of 1,792.

Experience
Writing   **Writing/Reading Center, UMD.** Tutored writing and word processing for
Tutor   individuals and groups. Edited WRC student newsletter. Trained new tutors.
                         Cowrote and acted in a video about the WRC. Designed WRC home page for
                         World Wide Web. Fall 2005–present.

Intern   **Conway Communications, Inc.,** 39 Wall Street, Marlboro, MA 02864.
Technical Writer   Learned local area network (LAN) technology and Conway's product line.
                         Wrote, designed, and tested five hardware upgrade manuals. Produced a hardware
                         installation/maintenance manual from another writer's work. Specified and
                         approved all illustrations. Designed a fully linked home page and online help for
                         the company intranet. Summers 2006, 2007.

Managing   **The Torch,** UMD weekly newspaper. Organized staff meetings, generated story
Editor   ideas, wrote articles and editorials, edited articles, and supervised page layout and
                         paste-up. Fall 2006–present.

Achievements   Writing samples published in Dr. John M. Lannon's *Technical Communication,*
                         11th ed. (Longman, 2008); Massachusetts State Honors Scholarship, 2005–2008.

Activities   Student member, Society for Technical Communication and American Society for
                         Training and Development; student representative, College Curriculum
                         Committee; UMD Literary Society.

References   Available on request.
and Portfolio

FIGURE 18.5 A Résumé with Combined Organization Use this format to retain the reverse
chronological pattern employers prefer while also highlighting your skills and qualifications.
(Because this applicant is seeking a position in writing and editing, she indicates that her writing
portfolio is available.)

Guidelines (continued from page 398)

- **Use action verbs and key words.** Action verbs (*supervised, developed, built, taught, installed, managed, trained, solved, planned, directed*) stress your ability to produce results. If your résumé is likely to be scanned electronically, list key words as nouns (*leadership skills, software development, data processing, editing*) immediately below your contact information. (For more on preparing electronic résumés, see page 409.)
- **Use punctuation to clarify and emphasize, but not to be "artsy."** Abbreviate only when you have identified the referent beforehand.
- **Proofread, proofread, proofread.** By relying on your computer's spell checker, you might end up expressing pride in receiving a "plague" instead of a "plaque," in receiving a "bogus award" instead of a "bonus award" or in "ruining" your own business instead of "running" it.

Preparing Your Job Application Letter

Include a cover letter with each résumé you send. In the words of one employment expert, "Sending a résumé without a cover letter is like starting an interview without shaking hands" (Crosby, *Résumés* 12).

Although it elaborates on your résumé, your cover letter must emphasize personal qualities and qualifications in a convincing way. In the résumé you present raw facts; in the cover letter you relate these facts to the company to which you are applying. The tone and insight you bring to your discussion suggest a good deal about who you are.

A good cover letter complements your résumé by explaining how your credentials fit this particular job; it also conveys a sufficiently informed and professional—and likable—persona for the prospective employer to decide that you should be interviewed. Another purpose is to highlight specific qualifications or skills. For example, you may have "C++ programming" listed on your résumé under the category "Programming Languages." But for one particular job application, you may wish to call attention to this item in your cover letter.

> You will note on my résumé that I am experienced with C++ programming. In fact, I also tutor C++ programming students in our school's Learning Center.

Sometimes you will apply for positions advertised in print or by word of mouth (solicited applications). At other times you will write prospecting letters to organizations that have not advertised but might need someone like you (unsolicited applications). In either case, tailor your letter to the situation.

NOTE   *Most of your letters, whether solicited or unsolicited, can be based on one working model, or prototype, which you have diligently prepared in advance. For more on preparing the prototype letter, see page 408.*

The Solicited Application Letter

Although application letters have components common to all business letters (Chapter 17), shaping your message persuasively requires special consideration.

Introduction.   Create a confident tone by stating directly your reason for writing. Remember that you are talking *to* someone; use the pronoun "you" instead of awkward or impersonal constructions such as "one can see from the enclosed résumé...."

In five lines or fewer, do the following things: name the job you're applying for and where you have seen it advertised; in one sentence, identify yourself and your background; and, if possible, establish a connection by mentioning a mutual acquaintance who encouraged you to apply—but only if that person has given permission.

Body.   Spell out your case. Without merely repeating your résumé, relate your qualifications specifically to the job for which you are applying. Try not to come across as a jack-of-all-trades. Instead of referring to *much experience* or *increased sales*, stipulate *three years of experience* or *a 35 percent increase in sales between June and October 2008*. Support all claims with evidence. Instead of *I have leadership skills*, say *I was student senate president during my senior year and captain of the lacrosse team*. Credible claims always require concrete support. (For more on supporting your claims, see page 60.)

Conclusion.   Restate your interest in the position and emphasize your willingness to retrain or relocate (if necessary). If the job is nearby, request an interview; otherwise, request a phone call, stating times you can be reached. Your conclusion should leave the prospective employer with the distinct impression that you are someone who is worth knowing.

CASE: Composing a Solicited Application Letter

The sample letters in Figures 18.6 and 18.7 each respond to advertised openings. In the first example, Daniel Lannon, our law student, customizes his letter to highlight features on his résumé (Figure 18.6) that relate specifically to an advertised entry-level opening for an environmental attorney with a regional utility company. Using a direct approach. Lannon wisely emphasizes practical experience because his background is varied and substantial. An applicant with less work experience would emphasize skills and education instead, focusing on related courses and activities.

In the second example, Karen Granger expands upon her résumé (Figure 18.7) in her quest for an internship in software documentation.

Since the recipient in each of these situations is expecting solicited letters, each writer uses a direct approach, to get right to the point.

February 15, 2008

3598 Seal Blvd.
Bloomington IN 42167

Edward R. Elwood, Hiring Attorney
Booneville Power Administration
P.O. Box 3123
Indianapolis, IN 42159-3123

Dear Mr. Elwood:

Writer identifies self and purpose

Your advertisement for an entry-level environmental attorney, in the January issue of *Indiana Law*, immediately caught my attention because my background qualifies me for precisely such a position. Please consider my application. I am a third-year law student with experience in private practice as well as in-house counsel work for a large educational corporation.

Relates specific qualifications to the job opening

After my first year of law school I clerked for the family law firm of Leonard, Moran, Lang, and Holmes, P.C. The mid-size private practice setting helped me develop many basic legal skills, particularly in research and writing, discovery organization, and drafting of pleadings. Following this clerkship, I worked in-house for Advanced Educational Systems for three semesters and one summer. AES operates childcare facilities nationwide. The childcare industry, much like the utility industry, is highly regulated on both state and federal levels, and I think my experience with regulatory issues could serve the needs of Booneville Power Administration.

Expresses confidence and enthusiasm throughout

My work in grassroots environmental advocacy, described in the enclosed résumé, could be a further asset to BPA's public outreach efforts towards energy conservation programs, renewable-resource development, and fuel cell technology.

Follow-up

Thank you for considering my candidacy. I would welcome the opportunity to speak with you in person.

Sincerely,

Daniel M. Lannon

Daniel M. Lannon

Enclosure

FIGURE 18.6 A Solicited Job Application Letter

March 28, 2008

82 Mountain Street
New Bedford, MA 02720

Roger W. White, Personnel Manager
The Birchwood Group
16 Cape Cod Way
Hyannis, MA 04156

Dear Mr. White:

Begins by stating purpose

I read in *InternWeb.com* that your company offers a summer documentation internship. Because of my education and previous technical writing employment, I am very interested in such a position.

Identifies herself and college background

In January 2009, I will graduate from the University of Massachusetts with a B.A. in English/Writing. I have prepared specifically for a computer documentation career by taking computer science, math, and technical communication courses.

Expands on background

In one writing course, the Computer Documentation Seminar, I wrote three software manuals. One manual uses a tutorial to introduce beginners to the Macintosh and *Microsoft Word*. The other manuals describe two Windows applications that arrived at the university's computer center with no documentation.

Describes work experience

The enclosed résumé describes my work as the intern technical writer with Conway Communications, Inc. for two summers. I learned local area networking (LAN) by documenting Conway's LAN hardware and software. I was responsible for several projects simultaneously and spent much of my time talking with engineers and testing procedures. If you would like samples of my writing, please let me know.

Explains interest in this job

Although Conway has invited me to return next summer and to work full-time after graduation, I would like more varied experience before committing myself to permanent employment. I know I could make a positive contribution to Birchwood Group, Inc. May I phone you next week to arrange a meeting?

Sincerely,

Karen P. Granger

Karen P. Granger

FIGURE 18.7 A Solicited Internship Application Letter Since recipients expect solicited letters, use a direct approach. Get right to the point.

The Unsolicited Application Letter

Do not limit your search to advertised openings. (Fewer than 20 percent of all job openings are advertised.) Unsolicited letters are a good way to uncover possibilities beyond the Help Wanted section.

Drawbacks of unsolicited applications

Unsolicited applications do have drawbacks: (1) You can waste time writing to organizations that have no openings, and (2) you cannot tailor your letter to specific requirements. But there also are advantages: For advertised openings, you compete with legions of applicants, whereas your unsolicited letter might arrive just as an opening materializes. Even employers with no openings often welcome and file impressive applications or pass them to another employer who has an opening.

Advantages of unsolicited applications

Spark reader interest

Because an unsolicited letter arrives unexpectedly, you need to get the reader's immediate attention. Don't begin: "I am writing to inquire about the possibility of obtaining a position with your company." If you can't establish a connection through a mutual acquaintance, use a forceful opening:

Open forcefully

> Marketing Research, Marketing Management, Principles of Marketing, Business and Technical Communication, Visual Design, Photography, Typography: I believe such courses, along with two internships and relevant employment background, have given me the theoretical background and practical experience you seek.

Address your letter to the person most likely in charge of hiring. (Consult company Web sites or the business directories listed on page 390 for names of company officers.) Then call the company to verify the person's name and title.

CASE: Composing an Unsolicited Application Letter

Carol Chasone's unsolicited letter in Figure 18.8 demonstrates her initiative, expands on her résumé (Figure 18.4), and shows how she has applied her education. She addresses her letter to a specifically named person, the personnel director whom she has confirmed is in charge of hiring at this firm. She includes a Subject line (see page 364) to announce immediately the purpose of her letter.

Since her recipient will not expect this unsolicited letter, Chasone employs an indirect approach. She builds her case before asking for a job. But she does not beat around the bush because her reader would quickly lose interest.

NOTE   *Write to a specific person—not to a generic recipient such as "Director of Human Resources" or "Personnel Office." If you don't know who does the hiring, phone the company and ask for that person's name and title, and be sure you get the spelling right.*

March 1, 2008

642 Eagle Lane
Eugene, OR 97405

Martha LaFrance, Personnel Director
Zithro Marketing Associates
132 Main Street
Portland, OR 42290

Dear Ms. LaFrance:

RE: Inquiry about a Marketing/Communications Position with Your Firm

Highlights special skills

Marketing Research, Marketing Management, Principles of Marketing, Business and Technical Communication, Visual Design, Photography, Typography: I believe such courses, along with two internships and relevant employment, have given me the theoretical background and practical experience employers would seek.

Focuses on experience

My experience includes writing and analyzing surveys, researching market trends, speaking before groups, prospecting for potential sales, and creating promotional materials. Could your firm use the services of an entry-level employee with this type of experience?

Relates background to employer's needs

Through internships with Mercy Hospital and the Small Business Institute, I have done public relations work, assisted in publishing the newsletter, written ads and public relations stories for local newspapers, interviewed key personnel, prepared layout and copy, and edited text. While working for the Chamber of Commerce, I wrote promotional letters, designed brochures and posters, organized events, and collaborated in promoting the organization's goals. Jobs as personal trainer and as salesperson not only have covered 75 percent of my college expenses but also have taught me a great deal about motivating and getting along with people.

Focuses on relevant personal traits

My references will confirm that I am conscientious, disciplined, energetic, and reliable—someone willing to take on new projects and prepared to adapt quickly.

Encourages follow-up

If you have an opening and you feel that I could make worthwhile contributions to your firm, I would welcome an interview at your convenience.

Sincerely,

Carol R. Chasone

Carol R. Chasone
Enc: Résumé

FIGURE 18.8 An Unsolicited Application Letter

Guidelines for Job Application Letters

- **Develop an excellent prototype letter.** Presenting a clear and concise picture of who you are, what you have to offer, and what makes you special is arguably the hardest—but most essential—part of the application process. Revise this prototype, or model, until it represents you in the best possible light. (See also page 709 on personal statements.) Don't look for shortcuts.

- **Customize each letter for the specific job opening.** Although you can base letters to different employers on the same basic prototype—with appropriate changes—prepare each letter afresh.

- **Use great caution in adapting sample letters.** There are plenty of free, online versions of sample letters that give some ideas for approaching your own situation, but you should never borrow them wholesale. Many employers will spot a "canned" letter immediately.

- **Create a dynamic tone with active voice and action verbs.** Instead of *Management responsibilities were steadily given to me*, say *I steadily assumed management.* . . . Be confident without seeming arrogant.

- **Never be vague.** Help readers visualize: Instead of *I am familiar with the 1022 interactive database system and RUNOFF, the text processing system*, say *As a lab grader, I kept grading records on the 1022 database management system and composed lab procedures on the RUNOFF text-processing system.*

- **Never exaggerate.** Liars get busted.

- **Convey some enthusiasm.** An enthusiastic attitude can sometimes be as important as your background (as in Figure 18.8).

- **Avoid flattery.** Don't say *I am greatly impressed by your remarkable company.*

- **Write in plain English.** Avoid letterese (page 370).

- **Be Concise.** Review pages 223–28. Limit your letters to one page, whenever possible.

- ***Never* settle for a first draft—or a second or third!** This letter is your model for letters serving in various circumstances. Make it perfect and do not exceed one page—unless your discussion truly warrants the additional space.

- **Never send a photocopied letter.** Although you can base letters to similar employers on one model—with appropriate changes—each letter should be prepared anew.

- **Proofread, proofread, proofread.**

Consider This How Applicants Are Screened for Personal Qualities

As many as 25 percent of résumés contain falsified credentials, such as a nonexistent degree or a contrived affiliation with a prestigious school (Parrish 1+). A security director for one major employer estimates that 15 to 20 percent of job applicants have something personal to hide: a conviction for drunk driving or some other felony, trouble with the IRS, bad credit, or the like (Robinson 285).

With yearly costs of employee dishonesty or bad judgment amounting to billions of dollars, companies use preemployment screening for integrity, emotional stability, and a host of other personal qualities (Hollwitz and Pawlowski 203, 209).

Screening often begins with a background check of education, employment history, and references. One corporation checks up to ten references (from peers, superiors, and subordinates) per candidate (Justin Martin, "So" 78). In addition, roughly 95 percent of corporations check on the applicant's character, trustworthiness, and reputation: they may examine driving, credit, and criminal records, and interview neighbors and coworkers (Robinson 285).

The law affords some protection by requiring employers to notify the applicant before checking on character, reputation, and credit history and to provide a copy of any report that leads to a negative hiring decision (Robinson 285). Once an applicant is hired, however, the picture changes: more than 50 percent of companies provide personal information to credit agencies, banks, and landlords without informing employees, and 40 percent don't inform employees about what kinds of records are being kept on them (Karaim 72).

Beyond screening for background, employers use aptitude and personality tests to pinpoint desirable qualities. A sampling of test questions (Garner 86; Kane 56; Justin Martin, "So" 77, 78):

- *Ability to perform under pressure:* "Do you get nervous and confused at busy intersections?"
- *Emotional stability and even temper:* "Do you honk your horn often while driving?"
- *Sense of humor:* "Tell us a joke."
- *Ability to cope with people in stressful situations:* "Do you like to argue and debate?" "Are you good at taking control in a crisis?"
- *Persuasive skills:* "Write a brief memo to a client, explaining why X [stipulated on the test] can't be done on time."
- *Presentation skills:* "Prepare and give a five-minute speech on some aspect of the industry as it relates to this company."

These tests may be given online, before an applicant is considered for an interview.

Above all, most employers look for candidates who are *likable*. One employer checks with each person an applicant speaks with during the company visit—including the receptionist. Another employer has candidates join in a company softball game (Justin Martin, "So" 77).

Evolving conventions of electronic résumés

Submitting Electronic Résumés

An estimated 94 percent of leading U.S. corporations ask job applicants to submit their résumés online ("The Art of" 86), as do countless other large and midsize employers. Electronic storage of online or hard copy résumés is an efficient way to screen applicants, compile an applicant database (for possible later openings), and evaluate all applicants as fairly and objectively as possible.

How Scanning Works

An optical scanner feeds in the printed page, stores it as a file, and searches for keywords associated with the job opening (nouns instead of traditional "action verbs"). Those résumés containing the most relevant keywords ("hits") make the final cut.

Guidelines for Preparing a Scannable Résumé

- **Using nouns as keywords, list skills, qualifications, and job titles.** Help Wanted ads or postings by similar employers are good sources for keywords.

- **List specialized skills.** Use terms such as *C++ programming, database management, user documentation, graphic design, fluid mechanics, editing, surveying, soil testing.*

- **List general skills.** Use terms such as *teamwork coordination, conflict management, report and proposal writing, oral presentations, troubleshooting, bilingual in Spanish and English.*

- **List credentials and job titles.** Be specific: *board-certified in Medical Technology, B.S. Electrical Engineering, top 5 percent of class, manager, supervisor, intern, project leader, technician.*

- **List synonymous versions of key terms.** To increase your chances of a hit use terms such as these: *procurement and purchasing multimedia, and hypermedia, Web page design and XML, management and supervision.*

- **Keep the print simple.** Use standard typefaces such as Optima, Courier, Futura, Helvetica, or Times. Depending on the font, choose a type size ranging from 10 to 14 points. Avoid small print. For example, you might use 12-point Helvetica for headings and 12-point Times Roman for body text.

- **Avoid fancy highlighting.** Use **boldface** or FULL CAPS for emphasis. Avoid italics, underlines, bullets, slashes, dashes, parentheses, or ruled lines.

- **Avoid a two-column format.** Multiple columns can be jumbled by scanners that read across the page.

- **Do not fold or staple pages.**

- **Consider submitting two versions.** Submit a traditionally designed résumé and a scannable version—or include a keyword section. Or, submit a PDF version via email and bring hard copies to the interview. (Figure 18.9 shows a scannable version of Figure 18.5.)

NOTE   *Don't hesitate to make your scannable résumé longer than your hard copy version (but no more than three pages total). The longer the résumé being scanned, the more hits possible.*

Types of Electronic Résumés

Following are types of electronic résumés you might submit. (See also Table 18.1, on page 414.)

Email Résumés.   Submit your résumé directly as email text or attach a PDF version. Check with the recipient beforehand. Not all systems can receive or decode attached files—so when in doubt, paste your résumé directly into your email message (and reformat as needed).

Arrange lines that other systems can differentiate. To indent, use the space bar instead of tabs. Instead of allowing lines to "wrap around," end each line by hitting the Return key.

ASCII Résumés.   One way to ensure your résumé can be read by any computer is to create an ASCII version (or "text file"). Select "Save As Text Only" from your desktop menu, and reformat your ASCII page as needed (Robart 14). When you do send an ASCII version, career expert Martin Kimeldorf suggests you include at the end a sentence like this: "A fully formatted hard copy version of this document is available upon request" (qtd. in Bolles 60).

NOTE   *When submitting a résumé in electronic form, include a cover letter, either as an email document or an attractively formatted attachment. If you do send these documents as attachments, be sure they can be translated by the recipient's software. Indicate the software (and version) you have used, or ask the employer to specify the desired software (Robart 13). When in doubt, send your material as email text, or attach an ASCII version as well.*

Searchable Résumés.   Consider placing a hyperlinked résumé on your own Web site or that of your school or professional society. (This might include an online portfolio containing a personal statement (see page 709), and indicators of your talents.) Figure 18.10 shows a searchable version of Karen Granger's résumé (Figures 18.5 and 18.9). Include the Web address for the searchable résumé on your hard copy or scannable résumé. Some employers refuse to track down a résumé on a Web page, so be sure to provide other delivery options as well (Robart 13–14).

KAREN P. GRANGER
82 Mountain Street
New Bedford, MA 02720
Telephone (617) 864-9318
Email: kgrang@swis.net

OBJECTIVE
A summer internship in software documentation.

QUALIFICATIONS
Software and hardware documentation. Editing. Desktop publishing. Usability testing. Computer science. Internet research. World Wide Web collaboration. Networking technology. Instructor-led training. DEC 20 mainframe and VAX 11/780 systems. *InDesign*, Adobe *FrameMaker*, *RoboHelp*, Webworks *Publisher*, *PowerPoint*, *Excel*, and *Lotus Notes* software. Logo, Pascal, HTML, and C++ program languages.

EDUCATION
UNIVERSITY OF MASSACHUSETTS DARTMOUTH: B.A. expected Jan. 2009. English and Communications major. Computer Science minor. GPA: 3.54. Class rank: top 7 percent.

EXPERIENCE
WRITING AND READING CENTER, UMD: Tutor. Individual and group instruction in writing and word processing. Training new tutors. Newsletter editing. Scriptwriting and acting in a training video. Designing home page. Fall 2005–present.

CONWAY COMMUNICATIONS, INC., 39 Wall Street, Marlboro, MA 02864: Intern Technical Writer. LAN technology. Writing, designing, and testing hardware upgrade manuals. Designing and publishing of installation and maintenance manual. Specifying art and illustrations. Designing a fully linked home page and online help for the company intranet. Summers 2006 and 2007.

THE TORCH, UMD WEEKLY NEWSPAPER: Managing Editor. Responsible for conducting staff meetings, generating story ideas, writing editorials and articles, and for supervising page layout, paste-up, and copyediting. Fall 2006–present.

ACHIEVEMENTS AND AWARDS
Writing samples published in John M. Lannons TECHNICAL COMMUNICATION, 11th ed., Lon gman, 2008. Massachusetts State Honors Scholarship, 2005–2007. Dean's list, each semester.

ACTIVITIES
Student member: Society for Technical Communication, American Society for Training and Development. Student representative, College Curriculum Committee. UMD Literary Society.

REFERENCES AND WRITING PORTFOLIO
Available on request.

FIGURE 18.9   **A Computer-Scannable Résumé**   Notice the standard print and the absence of fancy highlighting.

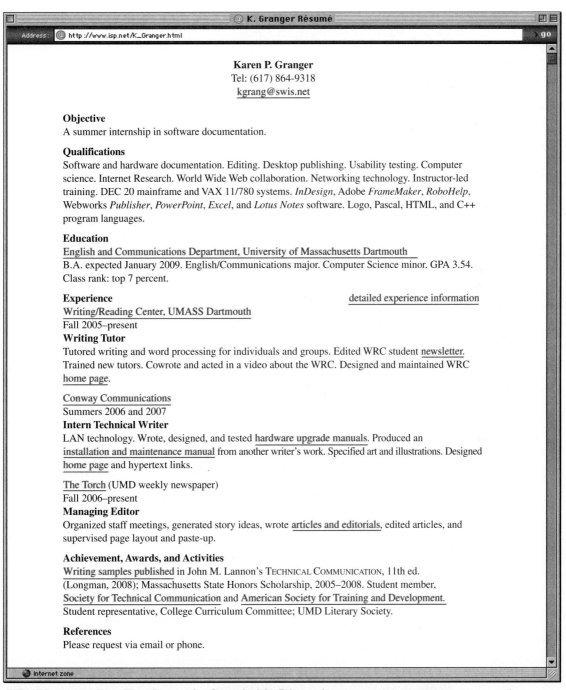

FIGURE 18.10   The First Page of a Searchable Résumé Links connect to various types of information, including several links to Karen's writing portfolio. For security reasons, personal contact information is limited to the applicant's phone number and email address.

NOTE   *Be sure your searchable résumé can download quickly. Complex graphics and multi-media download slowly. Also, verify that all links are functioning*

Purpose	Preferred Form
• For applying via traditional mail, fax, or email attachment; and for job interviews	• Attractively formatted and highlighted word-processed document, or scannable version, or both
• For translation by any computer	• ASCII (text only) file
• For use as a Web page or as an online posting on a Web site job board or database	• Hyperlinked document with links to materials supporting your application, or ASCII version, or both
• For applying via email	• Direct pasting into email, or word-processed/ PDF attachment, or ASCII version

TABLE 18.1 Preferred Forms of Résumés for Different Purposes

Protecting Privacy and Security When You Post a Résumé Online

Indiscriminate posting of résumés as Web pages or on job boards can be hazardous to your career or your welfare. If you already have a job, your present employer could discover that you're looking elsewhere. More important, placing certain information about yourself on the Internet can be dangerous.

Your safest bet is to limit the contact and personal information you list on your personal home page. Job expert Richard Bolles suggests including only your email address and phone number; home and work addresses and names of past employers and references can be supplied *after* a potential employer has contacted you by phone or email (60). In a hyperlinked résumé, withholding information about employers, schools, or training programs is often impossible. But personal contact information and names of references can still be protected, as shown in Figure 18.10.

Some résumé-posting sites are more private than others. On a site such as *E.SPAN* <http://www.espan.com>, for example, you can conceal your contact information and your name. Moreover, you must give permission (via email) before the résumé can be sent to an employer who requests it (Imperato 197). Other sites offer similar options for anonymity while some offer no privacy at all. Learn about a site's policy by checking the site's privacy statement.

Protecting Your Good Name Online

If you visit social networking sites such as *YouTube, Facebook,* or *MySpace,* or if you maintain your own blog, beware of inadvertently creating a shadow résumé that could haunt you for life. Whatever you post online—or whatever anyone else posts about you—is fair game for employers or anyone else seeking your personal information. All it takes is a few minutes and a simple *Google* search. Major companies also routinely use such resources as *Zoominfo.com,* a search engine that mines the Web to compile information on present or prospective employees.

To protect yourself, visit only sites that offer privacy options. Avoid inflammatory comments—and, or course, party stories. Try Googling your own name; if you already have an unflattering or incorrect online profile, do whatever you can to update the profile or delete it, if possible. Also, consider registering with *Zoominfo, Linkedin.com,* or *Ziigs.com* to create a profile that you can check, update, and correct at any time.

Support for the Application

An employer impressed by your résumé and cover letter will want answers to these three questions: How highly do other people think of you and your work? What evidence can you show as proof of your skills? Are you as likable in person as you seem on paper? These questions will be answered, respectively, by your dossier, portfolio, and job interview.

Your Dossier

Your dossier contains your credentials: college transcript, recommendation letters, and other items (such as a scholarship award or commendation letter) that document your achievements. Prospective employers who decide to follow up on your application will request your dossier. By collecting recommendations in one folder, you spare your references from writing the same letter repeatedly.

Your college placement office will keep your dossier (or placement folder) on file and send copies to employers. Always keep your own copy as well. Then, if an employer requests your dossier, you can photocopy and mail it, advising your recipient that the official placement copy is on the way.

NOTE   *This is not needless repetition! Most employers establish a specific timetable for (1) advertising an opening, (2) reading letters and résumés, (3) requesting and reviewing dossiers, (4) holding interviews, and (5) making an offer. Timing is crucial. Too often, dossier requests may sit on someone's desk and may even get lost in a busy placement office. Weeks can pass before your dossier is mailed. In these situations the only loser is you.*

Your Professional Portfolio

Examples of portfolio formatting

An organized, professional-looking portfolio shows you can apply your skills and makes you stand out as a job candidate. Also, the portfolio gives you concrete material to discuss during job interviews.

As you create your portfolio, seek advice and feedback from major professors and other people in the field. For online portfolio advice, go to <http://www.talentnet.com> and <http://www.prospring.net>.

<table>
<tr><td style="vertical-align:top">How to prepare a portfolio</td><td>

Guidelines for Preparing a Portfolio

- **Collect materials relevant to the job.** Gather documents or graphics you've prepared in school or on the job, presentations you've given, and projects or experiments you've worked on. Possible items: campus newspaper articles, reports on course projects, papers that earned an "A", examples of persuasive argument, documents from an internship, visuals you've designed for an oral presentation, and so on. Select samples that relate to the job you seek.

- **Sort your materials according to the major requirements of the job.** If requirements include desktop publishing, editing, and marketing, select two or three items for each category (a brochure you've designed, pages from a manual you've edited, slides from an oral presentation, and so on).

- **Assemble your portfolio.** Encase each page in its own clear plastic envelope in a portfolio-type notebook. Place your résumé first, followed by a table of contents giving the title of each item and one or two brief sentences about the item's purpose and audience. Use divider pages to group the items. Reassemble items for various job requirements.

- **Make copies as employers request.** When an employer requests the portfolio before the interview, send a photocopy. In case you need to leave a copy after your interview, bring one along with the original, bound portfolio.

- *Consider posting an electronic version.* If your portfolio materials can all be converted to a digital format, post the portfolio on your Web site. (Your career placement office may provide a portfolio template.)

</td></tr>
</table>

Employment Interviews

An employer impressed by your credentials will arrange an interview. The interview's purpose is to confirm the employer's impressions from your application letter, résumé, and references.

Interviews come in various shapes and sizes. They can be face-to-face or via telephone or video conference. You might meet with one interviewer, a hiring committee, or several committees in succession. You might be interviewed alone or as part of a group of candidates. Interviews can last one hour or less, a full day, or several days. The interview can range from a pleasant chat to a grueling interrogation. Some interviewers may antagonize you deliberately to observe your reaction. Unprepared interviewees make mistakes like the following (Dumont and Lannon 620):

How people fail job interviews

- know little about the company or what role they would play as an employee
- have inflated ideas about their own worth
- have little idea of how their education prepares them for work
- dress inappropriately
- exhibit no self-confidence
- have only vague ideas of how they could benefit the employer
- inquire only about salary and benefits
- speak negatively of former employers or coworkers

Careful preparation is the key to a productive interview.

How to research an organization

Prepare by learning about the company in trade journals, industrial indexes, and other resources listed on page 390. Request company literature, including its annual report. Speak with people who know about the company. Visit the company's Web site and, for a more objective view, do a keyword search (using the company's name) of various business magazine Web sites such as <http://money.cnn.com/magazines/fortune.com>, <http://www.forbes.com>, or <http://www.businessweek.com>; there you can find articles about a company's financial health, working conditions, environmental record, chance of merger (which often means big layoffs), or impending crises (an automaker's tire recall, for example), and the like. Once you've done all this, ask yourself, "Does this job seem like a good fit?"

NOTE *Taking the wrong job can be far worse than taking no job at all—especially for a recent graduate trying to build credentials.*

Once you've learned enough to decide that you actually want to work for this employer, prepare—and practice—specific answers to the obvious questions:

Questions to expect in a job interview

- Why does this job appeal to you?
- What do you know about our company?
- What do you know about our core values (say, informal management structure, commitment to diversity or the environment)?
- What do you know about the expectations and demands of this job?
- What are the major issues affecting this industry?
- How would you describe yourself?
- What do you see as your biggest weakness? Biggest strength?
- Can you describe an instance in which you came up with a new and better way of doing something?
- What are your short-term and long-term career goals?

Plan direct answers to questions about your background, training, experience, and salary requirements.

Prepare your own list of *well-researched* questions about the job and the organization; you will be invited to ask questions, and what you ask can be as revealing as any answers you give.

NOTE   *Being truthful during a job interview is not only ethical but also smart. Companies routinely verify an applicant's claims about education, prior employment, positions held, salary, and personal background. Say you have some past infraction such as a bad credit rating or a brush with the law, or some pressing personal commitment such as caring for an elderly parent or a disabled child. Experts suggest that it's better to air these issues right up front—before the employer finds out from other sources. The employer will appreciate your honesty and you will know exactly where you stand before accepting the job (Fisher, "Truth" 292). For more on how employers screen applicants for personal qualities, see page 409.*

Guidelines for Surviving a Job Interview

The Face-to-Face Interview

- **Get your timing right.** Confirm the interview's exact time and location. Give yourself ample time to get there. Arrive early but no more than 10 minutes or so.

  NOTE   *If you are offered a choice of interview times, choose mid-morning over late afternoon: According to an Accountemps survey of 1,400 managers, 69 percent prefer mid-morning for doing their hiring, whereas only 5 percent prefer late afternoon (Fisher, "My Company" 184).*

- **Don't show up empty-handed.** Have a briefcase, pen, and notepad. Have your own questions organized and written out. Bring extra copies of your résumé (unfolded) and a portfolio (if appropriate) with examples of your work.

- **Make a positive first impression:**

  - Come dressed as if you already work for the company.
  - Learn the name of your interviewer beforehand, so you can greet this person by name—but never by first name unless invited.
  - Extend a firm handshake, smile, and look the interviewer in the eye.
  - Wait to be asked to take a chair.
  - Relax but do not slouch.
  - Keep your hands in your lap.
  - Do not fiddle with your face, hair, or other body parts.
  - Maintain eye contact much of the time, but don't stare.

- **Don't worry about having all the answers.** When you don't know the answer to a question, say so, and relax. Interviewers typically do about 70 percent of the talking (Kane 56).

- **Avoid abrupt yes or no answers—-as well as life stories.** Keep answers short and to the point.

- **Don't answer questions by merely repeating the material on your résumé.** Instead, explain how specific skills and types of experience could be assets to this particular employer. For evidence, refer to your portfolio whenever possible.

- **Remember to smile often and to be friendly and attentive throughout.** In the end, people hire the candidate they **like** the best!

- **Never criticize a previous employer.** Above all, interviewers like people who have positive attitudes.

- **Prepare to ask intelligent questions.** When questions are invited, focus on the nature of the job: travel involved, specific responsibilities, typical job assignments, opportunities for further training, types of clients, and so on. Avoid questions that could easily have been answered by your own prior research.

- **Don't be afraid to allow silence.** An interviewer may simply stop talking, just to observe your reaction to silence. If you have nothing more to say or ask, don't feel compelled to speak. Let the interviewer make the next move.

- **Take a hint.** When your interviewer hints that the meeting is ending (perhaps by checking a watch), restate your interest, ask when a hiring decision is likely to be made, thank the interviewer, and leave.

- **Show some class.** If you are invited to lunch, don't order the most expensive dish on the menu; don't order an alcoholic beverage; don't smoke; don't salt your food before tasting it; don't eat too quickly; don't put your elbows on the table; don't speak with your mouth full; and don't order a huge dessert. And try to order last.

- **Follow up as soon as possible.** Send a thank-you note (page 420).

The Telephone Interview

Many employers interview candidates initially by phone. (They usually call beforehand to arrange a time.) A phone interview gives you the chance of making a good first impression by speaking from your home turf and having all your backup materials organized within easy reach. A few guidelines (Crosby, *Employment* 20–21; Ford, "Phone" 19):

- **If you have "call waiting," disable it temporarily, to avoid beeping and interruptions.** On most phones, press *70 as soon as the call connects.

(continues)

Guidelines (continued)

- **Arrange all your materials where you can reach them.** Have your list of questions, job description, talking points, résumé, pen, paper, and anything else you might need. Tape things on the walls, spread them on the floor, or use whatever arrangement works for you.
- **Sit in a straight-backed chair or remain standing.** These postures may help you speak more emphatically and confidently. They are also likely to keep you more attentive and businesslike than if you were lounging in a comfy armchair.
- **Identify the interviewer clearly.** Ask for the interviewer's name (spelled) and contact information, including email, and a mailing address (to which you can send a thank-you letter).
- **As the interview ends, encourage further contact.** Restate your interest in the position and your desire to visit the organization and meet people in person.
- **Send your thank-you letter as soon as possible.**

The Follow-Up Letter

Within a day or so after the interview, send a thank-you letter. Not only is this courteous, but it also reinforces a positive impression. Keep your letter brief, but try to personalize your connection with the reader (Crosby, *Employment* 20):

What to say in a follow-up letter

- Open by thanking the interviewer and reemphasizing your interest in the position.
- Refer to some details from the interview or some aspect of your visit that would help the interviewer reconnect in his/her mind with you specifically. (If you forgot to mention something important during the interview, include it here—briefly.)
- Close with genuine enthusiasm, and make it easy for the reader to respond.

Here is the text of one letter from James Purdy, an entry-level candidate in hotel-restaurant management, following up on his recent interview at a major resort:

Refresh the employer's memory

Thank you for your hospitality during my Tuesday visit to Greenwoods resort. I am very interested in the restaurant-management position, and was intrigued by our discussion about developing an eclectic regional cuisine.

Everything about my tour was enjoyable, but I was especially impressed by the friendliness and professionalism of the resort staff. People seem to love working here, and it's not hard to see why.

I'm convinced I would be a productive employee at Greenwood, and would welcome the chance to prove my abilities. If you need additional information, please call me at (214) 316-5555.

NOTE *Employment expert Olivia Crosby offers these suggestions: Instead of following up via email, send hard copy, either in a business-letter format or as a tasteful, handwritten note. Write to each person with whom you spoke or to the person in charge of the group interview. Be sure to spell each person's name correctly and to proofread repeatedly (Employment 20).*

Letters of Acceptance or Refusal

You may receive a job offer by phone or letter. If by phone, request a written offer, and respond with a formal letter of acceptance. This letter may serve as part of your contract; spell out the terms you are accepting. Here is Purdy's letter of acceptance:

Accept an offer with enthusiasm

> I am delighted to accept your offer of a position as assistant recreation supervisor at Liberty International's Lake Geneva Resort, with a starting salary of $44,500.
>
> As you requested, I will phone Bambi Druid in your personnel office for instructions on reporting date, physical exam, and employee orientation.
>
> I look forward to a long and satisfying career with Liberty International.

You may have to refuse offers. Even if you refuse by phone, write a prompt and cordial letter of refusal, explaining your reasons, and allowing for future possibilities. Purdy handled one refusal this way:

Decline an offer diplomatically

> Although I thoroughly enjoyed my visit to your company's headquarters, I have to decline your offer of a position as assistant desk manager of your London hotel.
>
> I've decided to accept a position with Liberty International because the company has offered me the chance to participate in its manager-trainee program. Also, Liberty will provide tuition for courses in completing my B.S. degree in hospitality management.
>
> If any future openings should materialize at your Aspen resort, however, I would appreciate your considering me again as a candidate.
>
> Thank you for your confidence in me.

 More job hunting resources

A courteous refusal and explanation can let the employer know why an applicant has choosen a competing employer. This is information that companies appreciate in order to remain competitive in the hiring market. Also, you may discover later that you dislike the job you accepted and may wish to explore old contacts. Your thoughtful refusal leaves the door open.

☑ Checklist: Résumés

(Numbers in parentheses refer to the first page of discussion.)

Content

☐ Is all your contact information accurate? (394)

☐ Does your statement of objective show a clear sense of purpose? (394)

☐ If you are willing to relocate, have you so indicated? (394)

☐ Do you include a summary of skills or qualifications, as needed? (394)

☐ Is your educational background clear and complete? (394)

☐ Do you accurately describe your previous jobs? (394)

☐ Are personal data and interests included, as appropriate? (395)

☐ Do you list references or offer to provide them? (395)

☐ Do you offer to provide a portfolio, as appropriate? (397)

☐ Are you being scrupulously honest? (398)

Arrangement

☐ Do you place your strongest qualifications in positions of emphasis? (397)

☐ Are education versus experience presented in the most appropriate sequence? (394)

☐ Does your résumé's organization (chronological, functional, or combined) put your best characteristics forward? (397)

☐ If you have a scannable résumé, does it use key words effectively? (410)

☐ If your résumé has hyperlinks, are they all functioning? (414)

Overall

☐ Do you limit the résumé to a single page, if possible? (398)

☐ Is the résumé uncluttered and tasteful? (398)

☐ Do you use quality paper? (398)

☐ Do you use phrases instead of complete sentences? (398)

☐ Do you use action verbs and descriptive words? (402)

☐ Do you punctuate effectively? (402)

☐ Have you proofread exhaustively? (21)

☑ Checklist: Job Application Letters

(Numbers in parentheses refer to the first page of discussion.)

Content

☐ Is your letter addressed to a specifically named person? (406)

☐ If your letter is solicited, do you indicate how you heard about the job? (403)

☐ If your letter is unsolicited, does it have a forceful opening? (406)

☐ Do you make your case without merely repeating your résumé? (402)

☐ Do you support all claims with evidence? (403)

☐ Do you avoid flattery? (408)

☐ Are you being scrupulously honest? (408)

Arrangement

☐ Does your introduction get directly to the point? (403)

☐ Does the body section expand on qualifications sketched in your résumé? (403)

☐ Does the conclusion restate your interest and request specific action? (403)

Overall

☐ Do you limit the letter to a single page, whenever possible? (408)

☐ Is your letter free of "canned" expressions? (408)

☐ Is your tone confident without being arrogant? (408)

☐ Do you convey enthusiasm? (408)

☐ Do you write in plain English? (370)

☐ Have you trimmed all the fat? (223)

☐ Have you prepared a fresh letter for each job? (408)

☐ Have you proofread exhaustively? (21)

Exercises

1. Write a five hundred to seven hundred word personal statement applying to a college for transfer or for graduate or professional school admission. Cover two areas: (1) what you can bring to this school by way of attitude, background, and talent; and (2) what you expect to gain in personal and professional growth. (See pages 709–16)

2. Write a letter applying for a part-time or summer job, in response to a specific ad. Choose an organization related to your career goal. Identify the exact hours and calendar period during which you are free to work.

3. Most of the following sentences need to be overhauled before being included in a letter. Identify the weakness in each statement, and revise as needed.

> Pursuant to your ad, I am writing to apply for the internship.
>
> It is imperative that you let me know of your decision by January 15.

You are bound to be impressed by my credentials.

I could do wonders for your company.

I humbly request your kind consideration of my application for the position of junior engineer.

If you are looking for a winner, your search is over!

I would love to work for your wonderful company.

I am in hopes that you will call soon.

I am impressed by the high salaries paid by your company.

 Collaborative Projects

1. Form groups according to college majors. Prepare a set of instructions for entry-level jobseekers in your major, telling them how to launch their search. Base at least part of your advice on your analysis of Figure 18.1. Limit your document to one double-sided page, using an inviting and accessible design and any visuals you consider appropriate. Appoint one group member to present your final document to the class.

2. Divide into groups and prepare a listing of five Web sites that jobseekers should visit for advice about cover letters and résumés, including on-line postings. Include a one-paragraph summary of the material to be found on each site. Compare the findings of your group with others in your class. In addition to sites mentioned in this chapter, here are other sources where you might begin:

Web Resources for Résumés and Cover Letters

<http://www.jobstar.org/tools/resume>
<http://www.eresumes.com>

Note: Expand your search beyond these sites.

3. Divide into groups and prepare a Web site guide for entry-level jobseekers in your field, based on answers to questions like these:

"Where can I find listings for job opportunities in our state or region?"

"Where can I find listings for internships in our field?"

"What Web site focuses on jobs in our field?" (such as hi-tech)

"Where can I find listings for temporary or contract work in our field?"

Once you've identified ten likely questions, list one site that could answer each question. For example:

<http://www.craigslist.com> for jobs in a particular region

<http://www.careerbuildercollege.com> for internship opportunities

<http://www.firsttuesday.com> for hi-tech jobs

<http://www.net-temps.com> for contract or temporary jobs

Note: Expand your search beyond these sites.

Report your findings in a memo to your instructor and classmates.

CHAPTER 19

Web Pages

HTML: Hypertext Markup Language

Elements of a Usable Web Site

Guidelines for Creating a Web Site

Privacy Issues in Online Communication

Checklist: Usability of Web Sites

Providing information online has become a critical communication strategy for several reasons.[1] Once text is printed it remains the same for as long as the paper or the disk it was printed on lasts. If the text needs to be updated, a new (and costly) print run has to be made. At the same time, printed copy takes up space and costs money to distribute. But information that is saved on a server and delivered fresh to each user upon request takes up negligible physical space, can be updated for only the cost of the labor, and can in fact be updated automatically, without direct human intervention. Moreover, one can be relatively confident that only the most current information is circulating.

Writing for the Web is a complex topic and one that ceaselessly changes as the technologies used to deliver it change. Writing online requires regular training and a wide range of skills including visual rhetoric, information design, and computer–human interaction, or usability. It is primarily a collaborative activity, often involving content providers, information architects, graphic designers, computer programmers, and marketers. Nevertheless, especially in small businesses and nonprofit organizations, online writing often becomes the responsibility of the communications person or staff. This chapter introduces the basics of writing for the Web.

HTML: Hypertext Markup Language

In a hypertext system, a topic can be explored from any angle, at any level of detail. The typical Web site contains chunks of related topics organized in a network (or web) of files linked electronically. The files themselves might be printed words, graphics, sound, video, or animation.

Any document, whether typeset, served over the Web, or even handwritten, has a structure that can be labeled. With a letter, for example, the markup would consist of Date, Addressee, Return Address, Salutation, Body, Closing, Signature. Information designed to be presented online is labeled in Hypertext Markup Language (HTML). HTML consists of a set of tags used to label the structure of a document and so make it theoretically possible for a document to be read in the same basic format on any computer regardless of operating system or browser.

This HTML code appears as inserted commands, or tags, which, when read by a Web browser (such as *Internet Explorer*), cause the specified formatting features to appear on the user's screen. For example, a line of text tagged as follows:

```
<b><c>Ethical Issues in Genomic Research</b></c>
```

would appear as bold (<b>) and centered (<c>) when viewed through a browser:

---

[1]My thanks to Professor George Pullman, Georgia State University, for many of the ideas in this chapter.

| Ethical Issues in Genomic Research

The slash tags at the end of the text (</b> and </c>) tell the browser to turn off the boldface and centering features until these codes are used again.

In the Web's early days, HTML coding was done by experts. Today, it is easy to write a Web page with little or no knowledge of HTML. You can use software such as *Dreamweaver*, or even most word-processing programs, to create a Web page, much as you would create a word-processing document. The software then translates your document into HTML code. For more on HTML, visit <http://www.w3schools.com>.

Even though Web sites are technically easy to produce, effective design is no simple matter. Many sites created by novices are poorly designed and hard to use. Web design is the subject of many books, classes, and workshops. Figure 19.1 shows a page from the Usability.gov Web site, which offers a wealth of information on this topic.

Following are some basic design considerations for creating a usable Web site.

Elements of a Usable Web Site

Although more diverse than typical users of paper documents, Web users share common expectations. Following are basic usability requirements.

- **Accessibility.** Users expect a site to be easy to enter, navigate, and exit. Instead of reading word for word, they tend to skim, looking for key material without having to scroll through pages of text. They look for chances to interact, and they want to download material at a reasonable speed.

- **Worthwhile Content.** Users expect the site to contain all the explanations they need. They want material that is accurate and up-to-date (say, product and price updates). They expect clear error messages that spell out appropriate corrective action. They look for links to other, high-quality sites as indicators of credibility. They look for an email address and other contact information to be prominently displayed.

- **Sensible Arrangement.** Users want to know where they are and where they are going. They expect a recognizable design and layout, with links easily navigated forward or backward, back links to the home page, and no dead ends. They look for navigation bars and hot buttons to be explicitly labeled ("Company Information," "Ordering," "Job Openings," and so on).

  Instead of a traditional introduction, discussion, and conclusion, users expect the main point right up front. Because they hate to scroll, users often read only what is on the first screen, "above the fold."

- **Good Writing and Page Design.** Users expect a writing style that is easy to read and error-free. They look for concise pages that are quick to scan, with short sentences and paragraphs, headings, and bulleted lists. Instead of having to wade through overstatement and exaggeration to "get at the facts," users expect restrained, impartial language (Nielsen, "Be Succinct" 2). Figure 19.2 illustrates the effect of good writing on usability.

- **Good Graphics and Special Effects.** Some users look for images or multimedia special effects—as long as they are neither excessive nor gratuitous. Other users disable their browser's visual capability (to save memory and downloading time); they look for a prose equivalent of each visual (*visual/prose redundancy*). Users expect to recognize each icon and screen element—hot buttons, links, help options, and the like. Figure 19.3 is an updated version of an award-winning Web page designed for usability. Figure 19.4 shows a highly simplified but usable design.

The guidelines on page 432 offer suggestions for incorporating these elements.

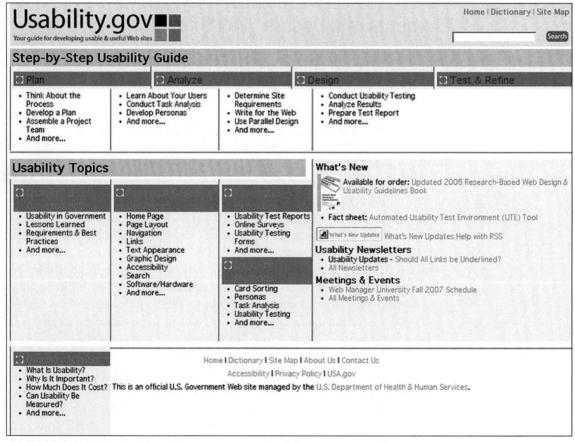

FIGURE 19.1 An Online Usability Resource This site offers up-to-date coverage of usability issues.
Source: From <http://usability.gov>.

Site Version	Sample Paragraph	Usability Improvement (relative to control condition)
Promotional writing (control condition) using the "marketese" found on many commercial Web sites	Nebraska is filled with internationally recognized attractions that draw large crowds of people every year, without fail. In 1996, some of the most popular places were Fort Robinson State Park (355,000 visitors), Scotts Bluff National Monument (132,166), Arbor Lodge State Historical Park & Museum (100,000), **Carhenge** (86,598), Stuhr Museum of the Prairie Pioneer (60,002), and Buffalo Bill Ranch State Historical Park (28,446).	0% (by definition)
Concise text with about half the word count as the control condition	In 1996, six of the best-attended attractions in Nebraska were Fort Robinson State Park, Scotts Bluff National Monument, Arbor Lodge State Historical Park & Museum, **Carhenge**, Stuhr Museum of the Prairie Pioneer, and Buffalo Bill Ranch State Historical Park.	58%
Scannable layout using the same text as the control condition	Nebraska is filled with internationally recognized attractions that draw large crowds of people every year, without fail. In 1996, some of the most popular places were • Fort Robinson State Park (355,000 visitors) • Scotts Bluff National Monument (132,166) • Arbor Lodge State Historical Park & Museum (100,000) • **Carhenge** (86,598) • Stuhr Museum of the Prairie Pioneer (60,002) • Buffalo Bill Ranch State Historical Park (28,446)	47%
Objective language using neutral rather than subjective, boastful, or exaggerated language (otherwise the same as the control condition)	Nebraska has several attractions. In 1996, some of the most visited places were Fort Robinson State Park (355,000 visitors), Scotts Bluff National Monument (132,166), Arbor Lodge State Historical Park & Museum (100,000), **Carhenge** (86,598), Stuhr Museum of the Prairie Pioneer (60,002), and Buffalo Bill Ranch State Historical Park (28,446).	27%
Combined version using all three improvements in writing style together: concise, scannable, and objective	In 1996, six of the most visited places in Nebraska were • Fort Robinson State Park • Scotts Bluff National Monument • Arbor Lodge State Historical Park & Museum • **Carhenge** • Stuhr Museum of the Prairie Pioneer • Buffalo Bill Ranch State Historical Park	124%

FIGURE 19.2 The Effect of Good Writing on Usability

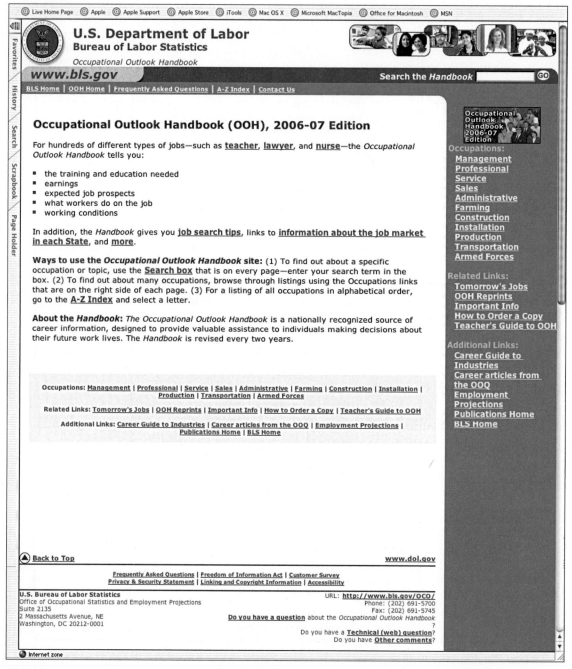

FIGURE 19.3 An Award-Winning Web Page A previous version of this home page received an Award of Excellence from the Society for Technical Communication. Notice the prominence of the search feature and the dominance of text over graphics.

Source: U.S. Bureau of Labor Statistics, <http://www.bls.gov/oco/>.

FIGURE 19.4 A Simplified Design Typical visitors to this site are seeking direct access to legal information, without design frills. All the links, therefore, are grouped under topic headings, as one would find in the index to a book.

Source: U.S. Equal Employment Opportunity Commission <http://www.eeoc.gov>.

Guidelines for Creating a Web Site

NOTE *Organizational Web sites are generally developed by a Web team: content developers, graphic designers, programmers, and managers. Whether or not you are an actual team member, expect a collaborative role in your organization's site development and maintenance.*

Planning Your Site

- **Identify the intended audience.** Are they potential customers seeking information, people buying a product or service, customers seeking product support? Will different audiences need different material?

- **Decide on the site's purpose.** Is it to publish information, sell a product, promote an idea, solicit customer feedback, advertise talents, create goodwill? Should the site convey a "cool," cutting-edge image, employing the latest Web technologies (animation, interaction, fancy design)?

- **Decide on what the site will contain.** Will it display only print or also graphics, audio, and video? Will links be provided and, if so, how many and to where? Will user feedback be solicited and, if so, in what form: surveys, email comments, or other?

- **Decide on the level of user interaction.** Will this be a document-only site, offering only downloading? Will it offer dynamic marketing (Dulude 69): online FAQs, technical support, downloadable software, online catalogs? Will an email button be included?

- **Visit other sites for design ideas.** When you find an attractive, navigable site (or the opposite), analyze what works or doesn't work in terms of typography, color, layout, graphics, highlighting, and overall design (Fugate, "Wowing" 33). For a look at award-winning Web sites, go to *Webby Awards* at <http://www.webbyawards.com> (Figure 19.5).

Laying Out Your Pages

- **Chunk your information.** Break long paragraphs into shorter passages that are easy to access and quick to read. Chunking is also used in paper documents (see Chapter 12), but it is especially important for Web documents.

- **Design your pages (Chapter 15) to guide the user.** Highlight important material with headings, lists, type styles, color, and white space. Prefer sans serif fonts (page 308). Use storyboards (page 200) to sketch each page. Limit page size to 30K, to speed downloading.

- **Use graphics that download quickly.** Avoid excessive complexity and color, especially in screen backgrounds. Keep maximum image size below 30K. Create an individual file for each graphic, and use thumbnail sketches on the home page, with links to each image (Fugate, "Wowing" 33).

- **Include text-only versions of all visual information.** Some users turn off the graphics function on their browsers.

- **Make the content broadly accessible.** Some people may want to choose how the content of your site appears on their screen: for example, people with limited vision or those using hand-held devices or older browsers. For options, consult the *World Wide Web Consortium's Content Accessibility Guidelines 1.0* at <www.w3.org/TR/WAI-WEBCONTENT>.

- **Organize so that users can follow the information flow.** Use a top-down approach, with the site's main purpose announced by the most prominent item. Structure each hypertext node as an "inverse pyramid," like a newspaper article, in which the major news/conclusion appears first (say, "The jury deliberated only two hours before returning a guilty verdict"), followed by the details (Nielsen, "Inverted Pyramids"). Also, think hard about what users need, and give them only that.

  To identify academic and research sites that offer excellent content, go to the *Internet Scout Project* at <http://scout.wisc.edu> (Figure 19.6).

- **Provide orientation.** Place the most important material up front and create links to detailed information. Date each page to announce the exact time of each update—or include a "What's New" head, so users can keep track of changes.

- **Provide navigational aids.** Always link back to the home page. Don't overwhelm the user with excessive choices. Label each link explicitly (say "Product Updates," instead of "Click here"). Use the color blue for denoting links not yet visited and red for links already visited by that user (Fugate, "Wowing" 34).

- **Sharpen the style.** Make your online text at least 50 percent shorter than its hard copy equivalent. Try to summarize (Chapter 11). Use short sentences and paragraphs.

- **Show cultural sensitivity.** A site that is truly "international," enables anyone anywhere to feel at home (Nielsen, "Global"). For example, avoid sarcasm or irreverence (offensive in many cultures) and topical references such as "bear markets," "the Wild West," and "Super Bowl."

- **Include an alternate, printer-based style sheet or a link to a printable version of the content.** Use a PDF file (page 320) for content that needs to appear exactly like the original paper document. Provide a link for downloading the free Adobe *Acrobat Reader*™ that enables users to view and print the document in its original format.

Checking, Testing, and Monitoring Your Site

- **Check your site.** Verify the accuracy of numbers, dates, and data; check for broken links and for spelling or grammar errors.

(continues)

Guidelines (continued)

- **Attend to legal considerations.** Have your legal department approve all material before you post it. Obtain written permission before linking to other Web pages or borrowing any graphic from a site. Display a privacy notice that explains how each transaction is being recorded, collected, and used. To protect your own intellectual property, display a copyright notice on every page (Evans, "Whose" 48, 50). For more on Internet copyright, fair use, privacy, and other legal issues, go to <http://www.publaw.com>.

- **Test your site for usability.** Test with unfamiliar users and record their problems and questions. What do users like and dislike? Can they navigate effectively to get to what they need? Are the icons recognizable? Is the site free of needless complexity or interactivity? For more on usability testing, see pages 42, 512.

- **Maintain your site.** Review and update the site often and redesign as needed. If the site accommodates email queries, respond within one business day.

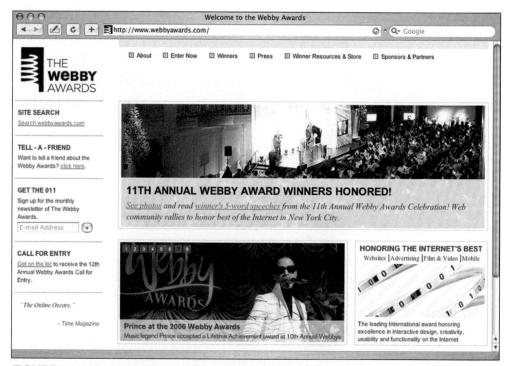

FIGURE 19.5 Listing of Award-Winning Sites The Webby Awards are the equivalent of the Oscars for Web sites. This site includes archives of previous winners, offering a revealing chronicle of the evolution of Web design.

Source: The Webby Awards <http://www.webbyawards.com/main>. Reprinted with permission.

FIGURE 19.6 A Listing of Sites That Offer High-Quality Content Based at the University of Wisconsin-Madison, the *Internet Scout Project* publishes its weekly *Scout Report*, providing reviews and links to top Web sites in Science and Engineering, Social Sciences and Humanities, and Business and Economics.
Source: Copyright 2007 *Internet Scout Project* <http://scout.wisc.edu>. Reprinted with permission.

NOTE *These guidelines scratch only the surface of Web design issues. For detailed advice, consult:* the Web Style Guide *at* <http://www.webstyleguide.com> *or* IBM's Web Design Guidelines *at* <http://www–03.ibm.com/easy/page1572/>.

Privacy Issues in Online Communication

Information sharing between computers makes the Internet and World Wide Web possible. For instance, when someone visits a site, the host computer needs to know what browser is being used. Also, for improved client service, a host site often tracks the links visitors follow, the files they open or download, and the pages they visit most often (Reichard 106). This user information is captured via "cookies" (files the Web site sends to any computer that has connected to the host site), which record that person's usage data. Too often, however, more information gets "shared" than the user intended (James-Catalano 32). Commercial U.S. sites routinely share customer information with other companies.

Servers and sites often display privacy notices explaining how usage patterns or transactions are being collected and used. But even the most stringent privacy policies offer limited protection. Any transaction is routed through various browsers and servers and can be intercepted along the way.

In the U.S., electronic monitoring of employees is becoming standard practice. Some types of workplace monitoring arguably have legitimate purposes; page 348, for example, lists arguments for monitoring of email. Employers also claim to have valid reasons for monitoring workplace Web sites:

Claims in support of monitoring workplace Web sites

- **Troubleshooting.** Monitoring software (*AlertPage, Net.Medic*) can scan a company site for broken links, and identify server glitches, software bugs, modem problems, or faulty hardware connections (Reichard 106).
- **Productivity.** Companies track intranet use for the number of queries per employee, types of questions, and the time required for people to find what they need. These data help Webmasters decide whether the search mechanism (user interface) can be improved or whether online documents can be written more clearly (Cronin, "Knowing" 103). Monitoring can also reveal software bugs or recurring errors by employees who might require further training.
- **Security.** Software can track employees' visits to other Web sites, as well as files opened for recreational or personal use, email sent and received, and can even provide snapshots of an employee's computer screen (Karaim 73). Such monitoring can be a justifiable precaution against employee theft, drug abuse, security violations (such as publishing trade secrets on the Internet)—or wasted time. After losing millions of worker hours yearly to computer game-playing, corporations increasingly are addressing the problem by investing in corporate training video games.

Privacy abuses in workplace monitoring

Beyond its legitimate uses, monitoring also carries potential for privacy abuses. Employers have more freedom to violate employee privacy than the police (Karaim 72). Andre Bacard, author of *The Computer Privacy Handbook,* notes that supervisors can "tap an employee's phones, monitor her e-mail, watch her on closed-circuit TV, and search her computer files, without giving her notice" (qtd. in Karaim 72).

✓ Checklist: Usability of Web Sites

(These criteria are discussed on pages 318–20 and on pages 432–34.)

Accessibility

☐ Is the site easy to enter, navigate, and exit?

☐ Is required scrolling kept to a minimum?

☐ Is the information chunked for easy access and quick reading?

☐ Is downloading speed reasonable?

☐ If interaction is offered, is it useful—not superfluous?

☐ Does the site avoid overwhelming the user with excessive choices?

Content

☐ Are all needed explanations, error messages, and help screens provided?

☐ Is the time of each update clearly indicated?

☐ Is everything accurate and up-to-date?

☐ Are links connected to high-quality sites?

☐ Does everything belong (nothing excessive or needlessly complex)?

☐ Is an email button or other contact method prominently displayed?

☐ Does the content accommodate international users?

Arrangement

☐ Is the document organized top-down?

☐ Are navigation bars, hot buttons, help options, and links to PDF files clearly displayed and labeled?

☐ Are links easily navigated—backward and forward—with links back to the home page?

Writing and Page Design

☐ Is the text easy to scan, with short sentences and paragraphs, and do headings, lists, typography, and color highlight important material?

☐ Is overall word count roughly one-half of the hard copy equivalent?

☐ Are all sentences short enough to facilitate reading and understanding?

☐ Are links structured according to a logical hierarchy of importance?

Graphics and Special Effects

☐ Is each graphic easy to download?

☐ Is each graphic backed up by a text-only version?

☐ Is each graphic or special effect necessary?

Legal and Technical Considerations

☐ Does the site display a privacy notice that explains how transactions are recorded, collected, and used?

☐ Does each page of the site display a copyright notice?

☐ Has written permission been obtained for each link to other sites and for each borrowed graphic element?

☐ Has all posted material received prior legal approval?

☐ Has the site been tested to ensure that it is functional and usable?

Individual or Collaborative Projects

1. Consult the previous checklist and evaluate a Web site for usability. Begin by deciding on specific information you seek (such as "internship opportunities," "special programs," "campus crime statistics," or "average SAT scores of admitted students") and use this as a basis for your assessment.

   Report any problems or suggest improvements in a memo to a designated decision maker. (Your instructor might ask different groups to evaluate the same site and to compare their findings in class.)

2. Download and print pages from a Web site. Edit these pages to improve their layout and writing style. Submit copies to your instructor.

3. Examine Web sites from three or four competing companies (say, computer makers IBM™, Apple™, Gateway™, Dell™, and Compaq™—or automakers, and so on). Which site seems most effective; least effective; why? Report your findings in a memo to your classmates.

4. Think of a specific procedure for which you might need help as you prepare a document (say, positioning text and graphics on a page or creating a table). Compare your word-processing software's online help information on this topic with the information in the paper manual. Which version is easier to use? In which can you find the help you need more quickly? Write a short report comparing the two media. Illustrate your comparison with hard copy examples and printouts of online examples.

5. Locate Web sites that originate from three different areas of the globe (say, Europe, East Asia, and the Middle East). In addition to different languages, what other differences seem to stand out in terms of a given site's content, arrangement, design, and special effects? Consider, for example, politeness of tone, ratio of text to visuals, use of colors and type styles, privacy policies, and relative ease of navigation.

   Summarize your main points, bookmark each site, and be prepared to discuss and illustrate your findings in class, preferably via interactive demonstration on the computer. If this is impossible, distribute printouts.

6. Return to Figure 19.3 and make a list of the specific features that make this an award-winning Web page. Discuss and illustrate your findings in class by using printouts or via interactive demonstration on the computer.

Service-Learning Project

Working in groups, offer to design or redesign a Web site for your school or for a community service organization.

CHAPTER 20

Technical Definitions

Purpose of Technical Definitions

Levels of Detail in a Definition

Expansion Methods

Situations Requiring Definitions

Placement of Definitions

    Guidelines for Defining Clearly and Precisely

    Checklist: Usability of Definitions

Definitions explain a term or concept that is specialized or unfamiliar to an audience. In many cases, a term may have more than one meaning, and a clearly written definition tells readers exactly how the term is being used. Unless you are sure your audience knows the exact meaning you intend, always define a term the first time you use it.

Purpose of Technical Definitions

What users of a technical definition want to know

Definitions answer the question What, exactly, are we talking about? by spelling out the precise meaning of a term that can be interpreted in different ways; for example, a person buying a new computer needs to understand exactly what "manufacturer's guarantee" or "expandable memory" means in the context of that purchase.

Definitions can also answer the question What, exactly, is it? by explaining what makes an item, concept, or process unique; for example, an engineering student needs to understand the distinction between "elasticity" and "ductility." Inside or outside any field, people have to grasp precisely what "makes a thing what it is and distinguishes that thing from all other things" (Corbett 38).

Definitions have legal implications

Contracts are detailed (and legally binding) definitions of the specific terms of an agreement. If you lease an apartment or a car, for example, the printed contract will define both the *lessee's* and *lessor's* specific responsibilities. An employment contract will spell out responsibilities for both employer and employee. Many other documents, such as employee handbooks, are considered implied contracts ("Handbooks" 5). In preparing an employee handbook for your company, you would need to define such terms as "acceptable job performance" on the basis of clear objectives that each employee can understand, such as "submitting weekly progress reports, arriving on time for meetings," and so on ("Performance Appraisal" 5–6). Because you are legally responsible for any document you prepare, clear and precise definitions are essential.

Definitions have ethical implications

Definitions have ethical requirements, too. For example, on January 28, 1986, the space shuttle *Challenger* exploded 73 seconds after launch, killing all seven crew members. (Two rubber O-ring seals in a booster rocket had failed, allowing hot exhaust gases to escape and igniting the adjacent fuel tank.) Hours earlier—despite vehement objections from the engineers—management had decided that going ahead with the launch was a risk worth taking. This definition of "acceptable risk" was based not on the engineering facts but rather on bureaucratic pressure to launch on schedule. Agreeing on meaning in such cases rarely is easy, but you are ethically bound to convey an accurate interpretation of the facts as you understand them.

Definitions have societal implications

Clear and accurate definitions help the general public understand and evaluate complex technical and social issues. For example, we hear and read plenty about the debates over genetic engineering. But as a first step in understanding this debate, we would need at least the following basic definition:

A general but
informative
definition

> Genetic engineering refers to [an experimental] technique through which genes can be isolated in a laboratory, manipulated, and then inserted stably into another organism. Gene insertion can be accomplished mechanically, chemically, or by using biological vectors such as viruses. (Office of Technology Assessment 20)

Of course, to follow the debate, we would need increasingly more detailed information (about specific procedures, risks, benefits, and so on). But the above definition gets us started, by enabling us to *visualize* the basic concept.

Levels of Detail in a Definition

How much detail will your audience need to grasp your exact meaning? Can you define the term by using a synonym or will you need a full sentence, an entire paragraph, or even several pages?

Parenthetical Definition

Often, you can clarify the meaning of a word by using a more familiar synonym or a clarifying phrase:

Parenthetical
definitions

> The *leaching field* (sievelike drainage area) requires crushed stone.
>
> The trees on the site are mostly *deciduous* (shedding foliage at season's end).

NOTE   *Your language in a definition needs to match the particular audience's level of experience. An audience of medical technicians, for example, will easily understand jargon (page 233) related to their field. But nonexperts will need language they find familiar. Therefore, for general readers do not write:*

> A tumor is a neoplasm.
>
> A solenoid is an inductance coil that serves as a tractive electromagnet.

NOTE   *Although the term* neoplasm *would make sense to most medical professionals, for audiences outside that field, you would need to use less technical language. Likewise, the solenoid definition would be appropriate for an engineering manual but too technical for general readers. Instead for general readers you might write:*

> A tumor is a growth of cells that occurs independently of surrounding tissue and serves no useful function.
>
> A solenoid is a coil that converts electrical energy to magnetic energy capable of performing mechanical functions.

On a Web page or online help system, these types of short definitions can be linked to the main word or phrase. A user who clicks on "leaching field," say, would be taken to a window containing the definition and other important information.

Sentence Definition

More complex terms may require a *sentence definition* (which may be stated in more than one sentence). These definitions follow a fixed pattern: (1) the name of the item to be defined, (2) the class to which the item belongs, and (3) the features that differentiate the item from all others in its class.

Elements of sentence definitions

ITEM	CLASS	DISTINGUISHING FEATURES
carburetor	a mixing device . . .	in gasoline engines that blends air and fuel into a vapor for combustion within the cylinders
diabetes	a metabolic disease . . .	caused by a disorder of the pituitary gland or pancreas and characterized by excessive urination, persistent thirst, and inability to metabolize sugar
stress	an applied force . . .	that strains or deforms a body
fiber optics	a technology . . .	that uses light energy to transmit voices, video images, and data via hair-thin glass fibers

These elements are combined into one or more complete sentences:

A complete sentence definition

Diabetes is a metabolic disease caused by a disorder of the pituitary gland or pancreas. This disease is characterized by excessive urination, persistent thirst, and inability to metabolize sugar.

Sentence definition is especially useful if you need to stipulate your precise working meaning of a term that has several possible meanings. State your working definitions at the beginning of your document:

A working definition

Throughout this report, the term "disadvantaged student" means . . .

Brief definitions are fine when the audience requires only a general understanding. For example, the sentence definition on page 441 about the leaching field might be adequate in a progress report to a client whose house you are building. But a document that requires more detail, such as a public health report on groundwater contamination from leaching fields, would call for an expanded definition.

Expanded Definition

The sentence definition of "solenoid" on page 441 is good for a layperson who simply needs to know what a solenoid is. An instruction manual for mechanics, however, would define solenoid in much greater detail (page 449); mechanics need to know how a solenoid works and how to use and repair it.

The problem with defining an abstract and general word, such as "condominium" or "loan," is different. "Condominium" is a vaguer term than leaching field (leaching field A is pretty much like leaching field B) because the former refers to many types of ownership agreements, and so requires expanded definition for almost any audience.

Depending on audience and purpose, an expanded definition may be a short paragraph or may extend to several pages. For example, Figure 20.1, aimed at a general audience, employs only two paragraphs (aided by visuals) to define the differences between two weapons of mass destruction. However, if a complex device, such as a digital dosimeter (used for measuring radiation exposure), is being introduced to an audience who needs to understand how this instrument works, your definition would require at least several paragraphs, if not pages.

DIRTY VERSUS NUCLEAR BOMBS

People sometimes confuse radiological with nuclear weapons.

A DIRTY BOMB is likely to be a primitive device in which TNT or fuel oil and fertilizer explosives are combined with highly radioactive materials. The detonated bomb vaporizes or aerosolizes the toxic isotopes, propelling them into the air.

High explosives

Radioactive materials

A FISSION BOMB is a more sophisticated mechanism that relies on creating a runaway nuclear chain reaction in uranium 235 or plutonium 239. One type features tall, inward-pointing pyramids of plutonium surrounded by a shell of high explosives. When the bomb goes off, the explosives produce an imploding shock wave that drives the plutonium pieces together into a sphere containing a pellet of beryllium/polonium at the center, creating a critical mass. The resulting fission reaction causes the bomb to explode with tremendous force, sending high-energy electromagnetic waves and fallout into the air.

High explosives

Beryllium/ polonium core

Plutonium pieces

Heavy casing

FIGURE 20.1 An Expanded Definition In this example, two items are defined, to clarify an important distinction for the general public.

Source: From "Weapons of Mass Disruption," text by Michael A. Levi and Henry C. Kelly, illustrations by Sara Chen. Published in *Scientific American*, November 2002. Illustrations copyright © 2002 by Sara Chen. Text copyright © 2002 by Scientific American, Inc. Reprinted with permission. All rights reserved.

Expansion Methods

How you expand a definition depends on the audience questions you can anticipate (Figure 20.2). Begin with a sentence definition, and then select from the following expansion strategies.

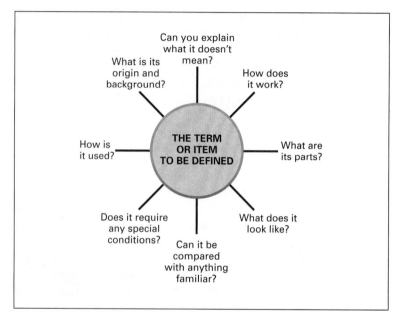

FIGURE 20.2 Directions in Which a Definition Can Be Expanded

Etymology

Sometimes, a word's origin (its development and changing meanings) can help users understand its meaning. "Biological control" of insects, for example, is derived from the Greek "bio," meaning "life" or "living organism" and the Latin "contra," meaning "against" or "opposite." Biological control, then, is the use of living organisms against insects. College dictionaries contain etymological information, but your best bets are *The Oxford English Dictionary* (or its Web site) and dictionaries of science, technology, and business.

Some terms are acronyms, derived from the first letters or parts of several words. *Laser* is an acronym for *light amplification by stimulated emission of radiation*.

Other terms developed as jargon. For instance, "bug" (jargon for "programming error") comes from an early computer malfunction at Harvard caused by a dead bug blocking the contacts of an electrical relay. Because programmers typically hated to admit mistakes, the term became a euphemism for "error." And "debugging," of course, means to eliminate errors in a program.

History and Background

The meaning of specialized terms such as "radar," "bacteriophage," "silicon chips," or "X-ray" can often be clarified through a background discussion: discovery or history of the concept, development, method of production, applications, and so on. Specialized encyclopedias are a good background source.

"Where did it come from?"

> The idea of lasers . . . dates back as far as 212 B.C., when Archimedes used a [magnifying] glass to set fire to Roman ships during the siege of Syracuse. (Gartaganis 22)

"How was it perfected?"

> The early researchers in fiber optic communications were hampered by two principal difficulties—the lack of a sufficiently intense source of light and the absence of a medium which could transmit this light free from interference and with a minimum signal loss. Lasers emit a narrow beam of intense light, so their invention in 1960 solved the first problem. The development of a means to convey this signal was longer in coming, but scientists succeeded in developing the first communications-grade optical fiber of almost pure silica glass in 1970. (Stanton 28)

For students and researchers who want in-depth information, history and background is appropriate. However, for users trying to perform a task, history and background can be cumbersome and unnecessary. If you wanted to install a new modem you might be interested in a quick sentence explaining that "modem" stands for "modulator-demodulator." But you would not really care about the history of how modems were developed.

Negation

Some definitions can be clarified by an explanation of what the term *does not* mean:

"What does this term not mean?"

> Raw data is not "information"; data only becomes information after it has been evaluated, interpreted, and applied.

Operating Principle

Anyone who wants to use a product correctly will need to know how it operates:

"How does it work?"

> A classic thermometer works on the principle of heat expansion: As the temperature of the bulb increases, the mercury inside expands, forcing a mercury thread up into the hollow stem.

> Basically, a laser [uses electrical energy to produce] coherent light, light in which all the waves are in phase with each other, making the light hotter and more intense. (Gartaganis 23)

Even abstract concepts or processes can be explained on the basis of their operating principle:

> Economic inflation is governed by the principle of supply and demand: If an item or service is in short supply, its price increases in proportion to its demand.

Analysis of Parts

When users need to understand a complex item or concept, be sure to explain each part or element:

"What are its
parts?"

> The standard frame of a pitched-roof wooden dwelling consists of floor joists, wall studs, roof rafters, and collar ties.
>
> Psychoanalysis is an analytic and therapeutic technique consisting of four parts: (1) free association, (2) dream interpretation, (3) analysis of repression and resistance, and (4) analysis of transference.

In discussing each part, of course, you would further define specialized terms such as "floor joists" and "repression."

Analysis of parts is especially useful for explaining a technical concept to laypersons. This next analysis helps explain the physics of lasing by dividing the process into three discrete parts:

1. [Lasers require] a source of energy, [such as] electric currents or even other lasers.
2. A resonant circuit . . . contains the lasing medium and has one fully reflecting end and one partially reflecting end. The medium—which can be a solid, liquid, or gas—absorbs the energy and releases it as a stream of photons [electromagnetic particles that emit light]. The photons . . . vibrate between the fully and partially reflecting ends of the resonant circuit, constantly accumulating energy—that is, they are amplified. After attaining a prescribed level of energy, the photons can pass through the partially reflecting surface as a beam of coherent light and encounter the optical elements.
3. Optical elements—lenses, prisms, and mirrors—modify size, shape, and other characteristics of the laser beam and direct it to its target. (Gartaganis 23)

Figure 1 shows the three parts of a laser.

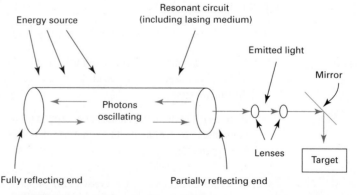

FIGURE 1 Description of a Simple Laser

Visuals

Well-labeled visuals (such as the previous laser drawing) help clarify definitions. Always introduce your visual and explain it. If your visual is borrowed, credit the source. Unless the visual takes up one whole page or more, do not place it on a separate page. Include the visual near its discussion.

Comparison and Contrast

By comparing or contrasting new information to information your audience already understands, you help create a link from their current knowledge to the new ideas. For example, for a group of nonexperts, you could explain how earthquakes start by using the following *analogy* (a type of comparison, discussed below). To help nonexperts visualize an optical cable, you could use the second analogy.

"Does it resemble anything familiar?"

> Imagine an enormous block of gelatin with a vertical knife slit through the middle of its lower half. Gigantic hands are slowly pushing the right side forward and pulling the left side back along the slit, creating a strain on the upper half of the block that eventually splits it. When the split reaches the upper surface, the two halves of the block spring apart and jiggle back and forth before settling into a new alignment. ("Earthquake Hazard Analysis" 8)

> The average diameter of an optical cable is around two-thousandths of an inch, making it about as fine as a hair on a baby's head (Stanton 29–30).

Whereas *analogy* shows some essential similarity between two things in different classes (say, computer memory and post-office boxes, or a dorm room and a junkyard), *comparison* shows similarities between two things in the same class (say, two teachers or two medications). This next example, for instance, compares optical fiber cable to conventional copper cable:

"How does it differ from comparable things?"

> Beams of laser light coursing through optical fibers of the purest glass can transmit many times more information than [conventional] communications systems. . . . A pair of optical fibers has the capacity to carry more than 10,000 times as many signals as conventional copper cable. A $\frac{1}{2}$-inch optical cable can carry as much information as a copper cable as thick as a person's arm. . . .
>   Not only does fiber optics produce a better signal, [but] the signal travels farther as well. All communications signals experience a loss of power, or attenuation, as they move along a cable. This power loss necessitates placement of repeaters at one- or two-mile intervals of copper cable in order to regenerate the signal. With fiber, repeaters are necessary about every thirty or forty miles, and this distance is increasing with every generation of fiber. (Stanton 27–28)

Here is a combined comparison and contrast:

"How is it both
similar and
different?"

> Fiber optics technology results from the superior capacity of light waves to carry a communications signal. Sound waves, radio waves, and light waves can all carry signals; their capacity increases with their frequency. Voice frequencies carried by telephone operate at 1000 cycles per second, or hertz. Television signals transmit at about 50 million hertz. Light waves, however, operate at frequencies in the hundreds of trillions of hertz. (Stanton 28)

Required Materials or Conditions

Some items or processes need special materials and handling, or they may have other requirements or restrictions. An expanded definition should include this important information.

"What is needed to
make it work (or
occur)?"

> Besides training in engineering, physics, or chemistry, careers in laser technology require a strong background in optics (study of the generation, transmission, and manipulation of light).

Abstract concepts might also be defined in terms of special conditions:

> To be held guilty of libel, a person must have defamed someone's character through written or pictorial statements.

Example

Familiar examples showing types or uses of an item can help clarify your definition. This example shows how laser light is used as a heat-generating device:

"How is it used
or applied?"

> Lasers are increasingly used to treat health problems. Thousands of eye operations involving cataracts and detached retinas are performed every year by ophthalmologists. . . . Dermatologists treat skin problems. . . . Gynecologists treat problems of the reproductive system, and neurosurgeons even perform brain surgery—all using lasers transmitted through optical fibers. (Gartaganis 24–25)

The next example shows how laser light is used to carry information:

> The use of lasers in the calculating and memory units of computers, for example, permits storage and rapid manipulation of large amounts of data. And audiodisc players use lasers to improve the quality of the sound they reproduce. The use of optical cable to transmit data also relies on lasers. (Gartaganis 25)

Examples are a powerful communication tool—as long as they are tailored to your audience's level of understanding.

Whichever expansion strategies you use, be sure to document your information sources, as shown in "A Quick Guide to Documentation" (page 633).

NOTE   *An increasingly familiar (and user-friendly) format for expanded definition, especially for Web users, is a listing of Frequently Asked Questions (FAQ), which organizes chunks of information as responses to questions users are likely to ask. This question-and-answer* *format creates a conversational style and conveys to users the sense that their particular concerns are being addressed. Consider using a FAQ list whenever you want to increase user interest and decrease resistance. For an example posted to a Web site, see Figure 20.4, page 452.*

Situations Requiring Definitions

The following definitions employ expansion strategies appropriate to their audiences' needs (and labeled in the margin). Each definition, like a good essay, is unified and coherent: Each paragraph is developed around one main idea and logically connected to other paragraphs. Visuals are incorporated. Transitions emphasize the connection between ideas. Each definition is at a level of technicality that connects with the intended audience. Each example is preceded by an audience and use profile based on the worksheet on page 35.

CASE: Preparing an Expanded Definition for Semitechnical Readers

---

Audience and Use Profile. The intended users of this material (Figure 20.3) are beginning student mechanics. Before they can repair a solenoid, they will need to know where the term *solenoid* comes from, what a solenoid looks like, how it works, how its parts operate, and how it is used. This definition is designed as an *introduction,* so it offers only a general (but comprehensive) view of the mechanism.

Because the users are not engineering students, they do *not* need details about electromagnetic or mechanical theory (e.g., equations or graphs illustrating voltage magnitudes, joules, lines of force).

SOLENOID

Formal sentence definition

Etymology

A solenoid is an electrically energized coil that forms an electromagnet capable of performing mechanical functions. The term "solenoid" is derived from the word "sole," which in reference to electrical equipment means "a part of," or "contained inside, or with, other electrical equipment." The Greek word *solenoides* means "channel," or "shaped like a pipe."

Description and analysis of parts

A simple plunger-type solenoid consists of a coil of wire attached to an electrical source and an iron rod, or plunger, that passes in and out of the coil along the axis of the spiral. A return

FIGURE 20.3 An Expanded Definition for Semitechnical Readers

spring holds the rod outside the coil when the current is deenergized, as shown in Figure 1.

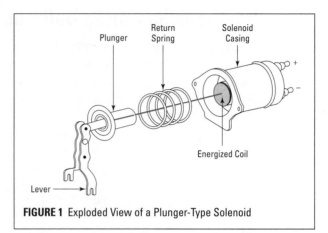

FIGURE 1 Exploded View of a Plunger-Type Solenoid

Special conditions
and operating
principle

When the coil receives electric current, it becomes a magnet and thus draws the iron rod inside, along the length of its cylindrical center. With a lever attached to its end, the rod can transform electrical energy into mechanical force. The amount of mechanical force produced is the product of the number of turns in the coil, the strength of the current, and the magnetic conductivity of the rod.

Example and
analysis of parts

The plunger-type solenoid in Figure 1 is commonly used in the starter-motor of an automobile engine. This type is 4.5 inches long and 2 inches in diameter, with a steel casing attached to the casing of the starter-motor. A linkage (pivoting lever) is attached at one end to the iron rod of the solenoid, and at the other end to the drive gear of the starter, as shown in Figure 2. When the ignition key is turned, current from the battery is supplied to the solenoid coil, and the iron rod is drawn inside the coil, thereby shifting the attached linkage. The linkage, in turn, engages the drive gear, activated by the starter-motor, with the flywheel (the main rotating gear of the engine).

Explanation of
visual

Comparison of
sizes and
applications

Because of the solenoid's many uses, its size varies according to the work it must do. A small solenoid will have a small wire coil, hence a weak magnetic field. The larger the coil, the stronger the

FIGURE 20.3 *(Continued)*

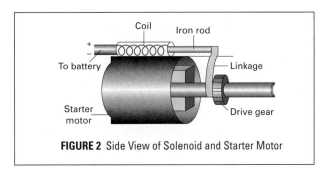

FIGURE 2 Side View of Solenoid and Starter Motor

magnetic field; in this case, the rod in the solenoid can do harder work. An electronic lock for a standard door would, for instance, require a much smaller solenoid than one for a bank vault.

FIGURE 20.3 *(Continued)*

The audience for the following definition is too diverse to identify precisely, so the writer wisely addresses the lowest level of technicality—to ensure that all readers will understand.

CASE: Preparing an Expanded Definition for Nontechnical Readers

Audience and Use Profile. The following definition (Figure 20.4) is written and posted online for hi-tech investors and other readers interested in new and promising technologies.

To understand *nanotechnology* and its implications, readers need an overview of what it is and how it developed, as well as its potential uses, present applications, health risks, and impact on the workforce. Question-type headings pose the questions in the same way readers are likely to ask them. Parenthethical definitions of *nanometer* and *micrometer* provide an essential sense of scale. This audience would have little interest in the physics or physical chemistry involved, such as *carbon nanotubes* (engineered nanoparticles), *nanolasers* (advanced applications) or *computational nanotechnology* (theoretical aspects). They simply need the broadest possible picture.

Sentence definition

Parenthetical
definitions

Comparison

NANOTECHNOLOGY

What Is Nanotechnology?

Nanotechnology refers to the understanding and control of matter at dimensions of roughly 1 to 100 nanometers to produce new structures, materials, and devices. (A nanometer, μm, equals one-billionth of a meter; a sheet of paper is about 100,000 nanometers thick.) For further perspective, the diameter of DNA, our genetic material, is in the 2.5 nanometer range, while red blood cells are roughly 2.5 micrometers (a micrometer, mm, equals one-millionth of a meter), as shown in Figure 1.

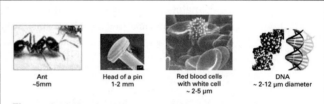

| Ant
~5mm | Head of a pin
1-2 mm | Red blood cells
with white cell
~ 2-5 μm | DNA
~ 2-12 μm diameter |

Figure 1 The Scale of Things—Nanometers and More
Source: Adapted from U.S. Dept. of Energy
<www.nano.gov/html/facts/the_scale-of-things.html>.

Contrast and
operating principle

History

At the nanoscale level, the physical, chemical, and biological properties of materials differ from the properties of individual atoms and molecules or bulk matter. Nanotechnology research is directed toward understanding and creating improved materials, devices, and systems that exploit these new properties.

How did it develop?

Nanoscale science was enabled by advances in microscopy, most notably the electron, scanning-tunnel, and atomic-force microscopes, among others.

Examples

How is it used?

The use of nanoparticles is being researched and applied in many areas of technology and medicine, such as the following:

FIGURE 20.4 An Expanded Definition for Nontechnical Readers

Source: Adapted from Documents at the National Nanotechnology Intitiative
<www.nano.gov>.

Examples

- Developing new optical and electronic devices
- Improving energy storage and efficiency
- Advancing new methods of medical imaging, treatment, and drug delivery

Scientists predict nanotechnology could revolutionize many industries. For example, nanotechnology is expected to enable the production of smaller, cheaper, and more accurate sensors. The sensors could detect environmental pollutants, indicate exposure to toxic substances in the workplace, check food safety, and assess structural damage in buildings.

Examples

What products available today have resulted from nanoscience?

While nanotechnology is in the "pre-competitive" stage (meaning its applied use is limited), nanoparticles are being used in a number of products. Today, most computer hard drives contain giant magnetoresistance (GMR) heads that, through nanothin layers of magnetic materials, allow for a tenfold increase in storage capacity. Other applications include sunscreens and cosmetics, water filters, and landmine detectors.

Comparison

Is there a risk in the workplace?

Nanomaterials may interact with the body in ways different than more conventional materials, because of their extremely small size. For example, studies have established that the comparatively large surface area of inhaled nanoparticles can increase their toxicity. Such small particles can penetrate deep into the lungs and may move to other parts of the body, including the brain.

Special conditions

Many knowledge gaps remain before we fully understand how to work safely with these materials. Until these and other research questions are answered, we should be extremely cautious when working with nanomaterials.

Special conditions

What are future workforce needs?

The National Science Foundation has estimated that 2 million workers will be needed to support nanotechnology industries worldwide within 15 years.

FIGURE 20.4 *(Continued)*

Placement of Definitions

Poorly placed definitions interrupt the information flow. Each time an audience encounters an unfamiliar term or concept, it should be defined in the same area on the page or screen. In a printed text, do this by placing a brief, parenthetical definition immediately after the term or in the outside margin. On a Web page, you would use a hypertext link.

More than three or four definitions on one page or screen will be disruptive. For a paper document, rewrite them as sentence definitions and place them in a "Definitions" section of your introduction or in a glossary. For a Web page, provide a link to a separate glossary page, as in Figure 20.5.

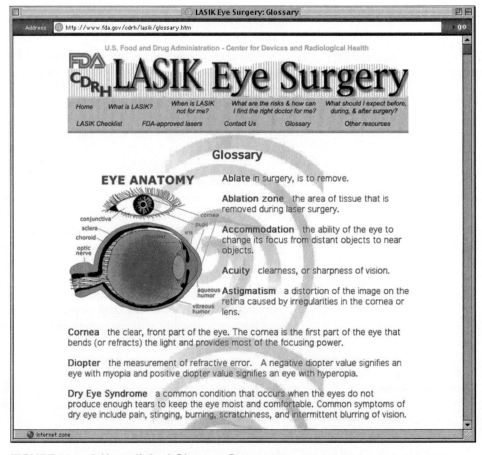

FIGURE 20.5 A Hyperlinked Glossary Page Links clearly displayed below the site's masthead on each page enable users to access the glossary and then return to any of the main pages in an instant.

Source: U.S. Food and Drug Administration <www.fda.gov/cdrh/lasik/glossary/htm>.

Depending on its role in the document, place an expanded definition in one of these locations:

- If the definition is essential to understanding the whole document, place it in the introduction as in Figure 1.1 (page 3).
- When the definition clarifies a major part of your discussion, place it in that section of your document but avoid doing this too often in a paper document. In a hyperlinked document, such as Figure 20.6, users can click on the item,

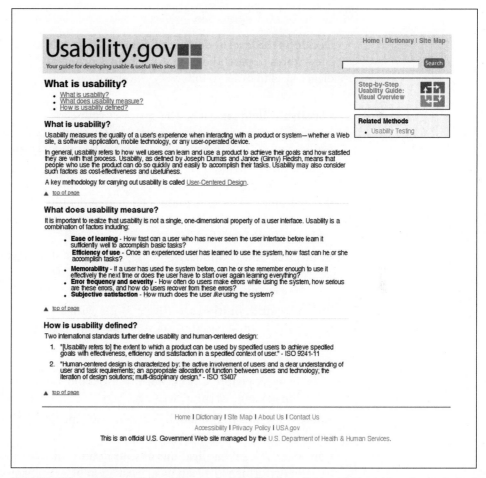

FIGURE 20.6 A Hyperlinked Expanded Definition Embedded within a hyperlinked network, this one-page definition provides forward links to deeper levels (such as *User-centered Design*) as well as backward links to main pages—all without disrupting the discussion of "Usability."
Source: From <http://Usability.gov>.

read about it (and possibly explore deeper links), and then return to their place on the original page.

- If the definition serves only as a reference, place it in an appendix.

In online documentation (page 510), one option for making definitions available when they are needed is the "pop-up note": The term to be defined is highlighted in the text, to indicate that its definition can be called up and displayed in a small window on the actual text screen (Horton, "Is Hypertext" 25).

Guidelines for Defining Clearly and Precisely

- **Decide on the level of detail.** Definitions vary greatly in length and detail, from a few words in parentheses to a multipage document. How much does this audience need in order to follow your explanation or grasp your point in this particular situation?

- **Classify the item precisely.** The narrower your class, the clearer your meaning. *Stress* is classified as an applied force; to say that stress "is what . . ." or "takes place when . . ." fails to denote a specific classification. Diabetes is precisely classified as a *metabolic disease*, not as a *medical term*.

- **Differentiate the item accurately.** If the distinguishing features are too broad, they will apply to more than this one item. A definition of *brief* as a "legal document used in court" fails to differentiate brief from all other legal documents (*wills*, *affidavits*, and the like).

- **Avoid circular definitions.** Do not repeat, as part of the distinguishing feature, the word you are defining. "Stress is an applied force that places stress on a body" is a circular definition.

- **Expand your definition selectively.** Begin with a sentence definition and select the best combination of development strategies for your audience and purpose.

- **Use visuals to clarify your meaning.** No matter how clearly you explain, as the saying goes, a picture can be worth a thousand words—even more so when used with readable, accurate writing.

- **Know "how much is enough."** Don't insult people's intelligence by giving needless details or spelling out the obvious.

- **Consider the legal implications of your definition.** What does an "unsatisfactory job performance" mean in an evaluation of a company employee: that the employee could be fired, required to attend a training program, or given one or more chances to improve ("Performance Appraisal 3–4")? Failure to spell out your meaning invites a lawsuit.

- **Consider the ethical implications of your definition.** Be sure your definition of a fuzzy or ambiguous term such as "safe levels of exposure" or "conservative investment" or "acceptable risk" is based on fair and accurate interpretation of the facts. Consider, for example, a recent U.S. cigarette company's claim that cigarette smoking in the Czech Republic promoted "fiscal benefits," defined, in this case, by the fact that smokers die young, thus eliminating pension and health care costs for the elderly!

- **Place your definition in an appropriate location.** Allow users to access the definition and then return to the main text with as little disruption as possible.

✓ Checklist: Usability of Definitions

(Numbers in parentheses refer to the first page of discussion.)

Content

☐ Is the type of definition (parenthetical, sentence, expanded) suited to its audience and purpose? (441)

☐ Does the definition adequately classify the item? (456)

☐ Will the level of technicality connect with the audience? (441)

☐ Have you avoided circular definitions? (456)

☐ Does the sentence definition describe features that distinguish the item from all other items in the same class? (442)

☐ Is the expanded definition developed adequately for its audience? (443)

☐ Is the expanded definition free of needless details for its audience? (449)

☐ Are visuals used adequately and appropriately? (447)

☐ Are all information sources properly documented? (634)

☐ Is the definition ethically and legally acceptable? (456)

Arrangement

☐ Is the expanded definition unified and coherent (like an essay)? (449)

☐ Are transitions between ideas adequate? (693)

☐ Is the definition placed at an appropriate location in the document? (454)

Style and Page Design

☐ Is the definition in plain English? (232)

☐ Are sentences clear, concise, and fluent? (216)

☐ Is word choice precise? (236)

☐ Is the definition grammatical? (670)

☐ Is the page design inviting and accessible? (297)

Exercises

1. Sentence definitions require precise classification and differentiation. Is each of these definitions adequate for a layperson? Rewrite those that seem inadequate. Consult print or online sources as needed, and cite your sources as shown in "A Quick Guide to Documentation" (page 634).

   a. Avian flu is a serious threat.
   b. A transistor is a device used in transistorized electronic equipment.
   c. Bubonic plague is caused by an organism known as *Pasteurella pestis*.
   d. Mace is a chemical aerosol spray used by the police.
   e. A Geiger counter measures radioactivity.
   f. A cactus is a succulent.
   g. In law, an indictment is a criminal charge against a defendant.
   h. Lunar power is a potential energy source.
   i. Friction is a force between two bodies.
   j. Luffing is what happens when one sails into the wind.
   k. A frame is an important part of a bicycle.
   l. To meditate is to exercise mental faculties in thought.

2. Using reference books as necessary, write sentence definitions for five of these terms or five from your field. Cite your sources, as shown in "A Quick Guide to Documentation" (page 634).

stem cell	angioplasty
biofuels	dark matter
bioinformatics	oil shale
genome	chemotherapy
hybrid electric vehicle	estuary
marsh	green buildings
artificial intelligence	neutrino
ricin	hypothermia
anorexia nervosa	heat sink
coal gasification	aquaculture
hemodialysis	nuclear fission

3. Select a term from the list in Exercise 2 or from an area of interest. Identify an audience and purpose. Complete an audience and use profile sheet (page 35). Begin with a sentence definition of the term. Then write an expanded definition for a first-year student in that field. Next, write a definition of the same term for a layperson (client, patient, or other interested party). Leave a margin at the left of your page to list expansion strategies. Use at least four expansion strategies in each version, including at least one visual or an *art brief* (page 278) and a rough diagram. In preparing each version, consult no fewer than four outside references. Cite and document each source as shown in "A Quick Guide to Documentation" (page 634). Submit, with your two versions, an explanation of your changes from the first version to the second.

4. Convert your expanded definition from Exercise 3 into a Web page. Include links to your information sources.

5. Why is the reliability of Wikipedia questioned? Discuss your findings in class.

6. Figure 20.7 shows a page from a brochure titled *Cogeneration*. The brochure provides an expanded definition for potential users of fuel conservation systems engineered and packaged by Ewing Power Systems. The intended users are plant engineers and other technical experts unfamiliar with cogeneration.

   Another page of the brochure is designed in a question-and-answer format (FAQ list) for laypersons. Figure 20.8 shows parts of that page.

   Identify each expansion strategy in Figures 20.7 and 20.8. Is each definition appropriate for its intended audience? Why, or why not? Discuss your evaluation in class.

TECHNICAL CONSIDERATIONS

Turbine generator sets make electricity by converting a steam pressure drop into mechanical power to spin the generator. Conceptually, steam turbines work much the same way as water turbines. Just as water turbines take the energy from water as it flows from a high elevation to a lower elevation, steam turbines take the energy from steam as it flows from high pressure to low pressure. The amount of energy that can be converted to electricity is determined by the difference between the inlet pressure and the exhaust pressure (pressure drop) and the volume of steam flowing through the turbine.

Steam turbines have been used in industry in a variety of applications for decades and are the most common way utilities generate electricity. Exactly how a steam turbine generator can be used in your plant depends upon your circumstances.

IF YOU USE WASTE AS A BOILER FUEL

If you use wood waste or incinerator waste as a boiler fuel you can afford to condense turbine exhaust steam in a condenser. This allows you to convert waste fuel into electricity.

The simplest form of a condensing turbine generator set is the Ewing Power Systems C Series. All surplus steam enters the turbine at high pressure and exhausts to a condenser at a very low pressure, usually a vacuum. Because of the very low exhaust pressure, the pressure drop through the turbine is greater and more energy is extracted from each pound of steam. This is the same basic design as utilities use to produce power. The condenser can be either air or water cooled. In water cooled systems the "cooling" water can be hot enough for use as process hot water or for space heat.

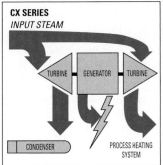

In situations where there is surplus fuel and also a need for low pressure process steam, the Ewing Power Systems CX Series is the system of choice. This arrangement includes a back pressure turbine and a condensing turbine connected to a common generator. Low pressure process or space heating loads are met with the back pressure turbine while surplus steam is directed to the condensing turbine to maximize power production.

IF YOU PURCHASE BOILER FUEL SUCH AS OIL OR GAS

If oil or gas is used as boiler fuel the best use of a turbine is as a replacement for a steam pressure reducing valve. Many plants produce steam at high pressure and then use some or all of the steam at low pressure after passing it through a pressure reducing valve. Other plants have high pressure boilers but run them at low pressure because they do not need high pressure steam for their process. In either case, a turbine generator can turn the pressure drop energy potential into electricity.

The Ewing Power Systems BP Series turbine generator sets are designed for pressure reducing (back pressure) applications. Very little energy is consumed by the turbine, so most of the inlet steam is available for process. The turbine generator uses about 3631 BTU's per hour for each kilowatt-hour produced. At 40 cents per gallon for No. 6 fuel oil and 85% boiler efficiency, it will cost about 1.1 cents per kilowatt-hour to generate your own power with a BP Series turbine. Generating costs for gas-fired boilers are similar.

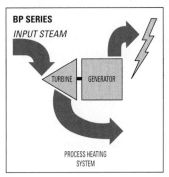

To generate power at this very low cost, all the exhaust steam must be used productively. Generator output is therefore completely governed by process steam demand. For example, if steam is used for space heating you will make more electricity on cold days than on warmer days because more steam will flow through the turbine.

ELECTRICAL CONSIDERATIONS

In most cases the generator will be connected to your plant electrical system and to your utility. This means that you will not give up the security of utility power. It also means that you do not have to generate *all* your own power; most cogeneration systems provide only part of the plant load. The more power the generator is making, the less you buy from the utility. If you make more power than you use, you will be able to sell the excess to the utility. If your generator is off-line for any reason, you will be able to buy power from the utility, just as you do now.

There are two primary generator designs: induction and synchronous. Induction generators are similar to induction motors and are much simpler than synchronous generators. Synchronous generators require more elaborate controls and are usually more expensive but offer the advantage of stand-alone capability. Whereas induction generators cannot operate unless they are connected to a utility grid, synchronous sets can be operated in isolation as emergency units or when it is economically advantageous to avoid interconnection with the utility.

All turbine generator sets from Ewing Power Systems include a complete electrical control panel. Our standard panels meet most utility interconnection requirements and we will customize the panel to meet unusual requirements. Synchronous panels can be built for full utility paralleling, stand-alone capability, or both.

FIGURE 20.7 Expanded Definition in a Technical Brochure

Source: Used with permission of Turbosteam Corporation, Turners Falls, MA.

Q. What is cogeneration?

A. It is the simultaneous production of electricity and useful thermal energy. This means that you can generate electricity with the same steam you are now using for heating or process. *You can use the same steam twice.* In modern usage cogeneration has also come to mean using waste fuel for in-plant electricity generation.

Q. How does it save money?

A. Cogeneration saves money by allowing you to produce your own electricity for a fraction of the cost of utility power. Cogenerated power is cheaper because cogeneration systems are much more efficient than central utility plants. By using the same steam twice, cogeneration systems can achieve efficiencies of up to 80%, whereas the best utilities can do is about 40%.

Q. Are there other benefits to cogeneration?

A. Yes. For companies using waste fuel, elimination of waste disposal can be a very important benefit. Depending upon design, a cogeneration system can provide emergency standby power and can smooth out boiler load swings.

Q. Is cogeneration new?

A. No. It's been done ever since the beginning of the electrification of industrial America. Originally, most electric power was cogenerated by individual manufacturers, not the utilities. In the 1920s and '30s, as cheaper utility electricity became available, cogeneration waned. With cheap oil available, power rates continued to decline through the 1950s and '60s. Then came the Arab Oil Embargos. Everything changed abruptly. Since then electricity prices have risen steadily. Further upward pressure was produced by some utilities' nuclear power plant building programs. Now many companies are getting back to their original source of power: cogeneration.

FIGURE 20.8 Expanded Definition in a FAQ List Format
Source: Used with permission of Turbosteam Corporation, Turners Falls, MA.

Collaborative Projects

1. Divide into small groups by majors or interests. Appoint one person as group manager. Decide on an item, concept, or process that would require an expanded definition for laypersons; some examples follow.

   From computer science: an algorithm, binary coding, or systems analysis

   From nursing: a pacemaker, coronary bypass surgery, or natural childbirth

   Complete an audience and use profile (page 451).

   Once your group has decided on the appropriate expansion strategies, the group manager will assign each member to work on one or two specific strategies as part of the definition. As a group, edit and incorporate the collected material into an expanded definition, revising as often as needed.

   Your instructor may stipulate a brochure format for your definition, as in Figure 20.9. (For more on this format, refer to "brochures" in this book's Index.)

   The group manager will assign one member to present the definition in class.

Service-Learning Project

Revise the flyer/fact sheet you prepared for Chapter 3 (page 47) to publicize your public service organization. Use all appropriate expansion strategies to show your readers "Who we are" and "What we do."

Hint: To decrease reader resistance and to help people identify with the issue, consider presenting your definition in the form of a FAQ list.

What is a generic drug?

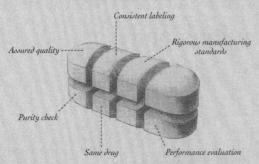

Consistent labeling

Assured quality

Rigorous manufacturing standards

Purity check

Same drug

Performance evaluation

When a brand-name drug's patent protection expires, generic versions of the drug can be approved for sale. The generic version works like the brand-name drug in dosage, strength, performance and use, and must meet the same quality and safety standards. All generic drugs must be reviewed and approved by FDA.

How does FDA ensure that my generic drug is as safe and effective as the brand-name drug?

All generic drugs are put through a rigorous, multi-step review process that includes a review of scientific data on the generic drug's ingredients and performance. FDA also conducts periodic inspections of the manufacturing plant, and monitors drug quality—even after the generic drug has been approved.

If generic drugs and brand-name drugs have the same active ingredients, why do they look different?

Generic drugs look different because certain inactive ingredients, such as colors and flavorings, may be different. These ingredients do not affect the performance, safety or effectiveness of the generic drug. They look different because trademark laws in the U.S. do not allow a generic drug to look exactly like other drugs already on the market.

Is my generic drug made by the same company that makes the brand-name drug?

It is possible. Brand-name firms are responsible for manufacturing approximately 50 percent of generic drugs.

Are generic drugs always made in the same kind of facilities as brand-name drugs?

Yes. All generic drug manufacturing facilities must meet FDA's standards of good manufacturing practices. FDA will not permit drugs to be made in substandard facilities. FDA conducts about 3,500 inspections a year to ensure standards are met.

FDA makes it tough to become a generic drug in America so you can feel confident about taking your generic drugs. If you still want to learn more, talk with your doctor, pharmacist or other health care professional. Or call **1-888-INFO-FDA** or visit **www.fda.gov/cder** today.

U.S. Food and Drug Administration

Generic Drugs: Safe. Effective. FDA Approved.

FIGURE 20.9 A Definition for Laypersons, Designed as a Two-Column Brochure
Source: U.S. Department of Health and Human Services. Food and Drug Administration.

CHAPTER 21

Technical Descriptions and Specifications

Purposes and Types of Technical Description

Objectivity in Technical Description

Elements of a Usable Description

An Outline and Model for Product Description

A Situation Requiring Product Description

An Outline for Process Description

A Situation Requiring Process Description

Specifications

Technical Marketing Literature

    Checklist: Usability of Technical Descriptions

Description (creating a picture with words and images) is part of all writing. But technical descriptions convey information about a product or mechanism to someone who will use it, operate it, assemble it, or manufacture it, or to someone who has to know more about it. Any item can be visualized from countless different perspectives. Therefore, how you describe something—your perspective—depends on your purpose and the user's needs.

Purposes and Types of Technical Description

What users of a technical description want to know

Description, like definition (Chapter 20), answers the question What is it? But to help users "visualize," description answers additional questions that include What does it do? What does it look like? What is it made of? How does it work? How does it happen? Definition and description depend on each other and provide the foundation for virtually any type of technical explanation.

Product versus process descriptions

Technical descriptions divide into two basic types: *product* descriptions and *process* descriptions. Anyone learning to use a particular device (say, a stethoscope) relies on product description. Anyone wanting to understand the steps or stages in a complex event (say, how lightning is produced) relies on process description.

The product description in Figure 21.1, part of an owner's manual, gives do-it-yourself homeowners a clear image of the overall device and its parts. The accompanying process description in Figure 21.2 shows the device in action.

Objectivity in Technical Description

A description can be mainly *subjective* or *objective*: based on feelings or fact. Subjective description aims at expressing feelings, attitudes, and moods. You create an *impression* of your subject: ("The weather was miserable"), more than communicating factual information about it ("All day, we had freezing rain and gale-force winds"). Objective description presents an impartial view, filtering out personal impressions and focusing on observable details.

Descriptions have ethical implications

Except for promotional writing, technical descriptions should be impartial, if they are to be ethical. Pure objectivity is, of course, humanly impossible. Each writer filters the facts and their meaning through his or her own perspective, and therefore chooses what to put in and what to leave out. Nonetheless, we are expected to communicate the facts as we know and understand them. Even positive claims made in promotional writing (for example, "reliable," "rugged," and so on in Figure 21.11, page 487) should be based on objective and verifiable evidence.

NOTE   *Being objective does not mean forsaking personal evaluation in cases in which a product may be unsafe or unsound. An ethical communicator "is obligated to express her or his opinions of products, as long as these opinions are based on objective and responsible research and observation" (MacKenzie 3).*

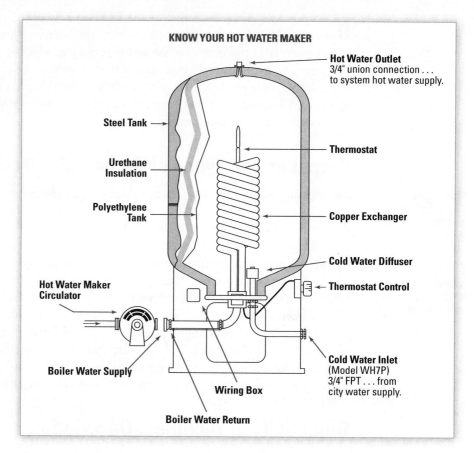

FIGURE 21.1 A Product Description This description allows users to visualize the basic parts of the hot water maker and their relationships.
Source: Courtesy of AMTROL Inc.

The following suggestions will help you remain as impartial as possible in preparing a technical description.

Record the Details That Enable Readers to Visualize the Item.   Ask these questions: What could any observer recognize? What would a camera record? Avoid details that provide no distinct visual image:

Subjective

| His office has an *awful* view, *terrible* furniture, and a *depressing* atmosphere.

This next version provides a clear and exact picture:

Objective

| His office has broken windows looking out on a brick wall, a rug with a six-inch hole in the center, missing floorboards, broken chairs, and a ceiling with chunks of plaster missing.

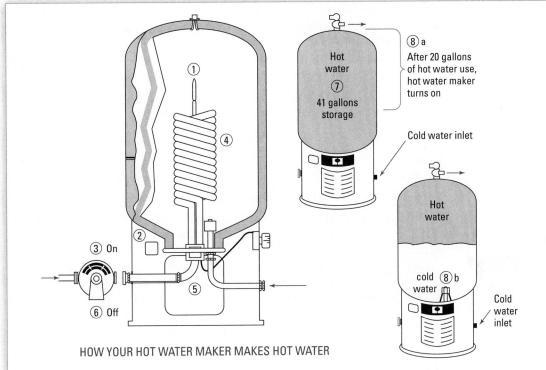

HOW YOUR HOT WATER MAKER MAKES HOT WATER

1. The thermostat calls for energy to make hot water in your Hot Water Maker.

2. The built-in relay signals your boiler/burner to generate energy by heating boiler water.

3. The Hot Water Maker circulator comes on and circulates hot boiler water through the inside of the Hot Water Maker heat exchanger.

4. Heat energy is transferred, or "exchanged" from the boiler water inside the exchanger to the water surrounding it in the Hot Water Maker.

5. The boiler water, after the maximum of heat energy is taken out of it, is returned to the boiler so it can be reheated.

6. When enough heat has been exchanged to raise the temperature in your Hot Water Maker to the desired temperature, the thermostat will de-energize the relay and turn off the Hot Water Maker circulator and your boiler/burner. This will take approximately 23 minutes—when you first start up the Hot Water Maker.

During use, reheating will be approximately 9–12 minutes.

7. You now have 41 gallons of hot water in storage . . . ready for use in washing machines, showers, sinks, etc. This 41 gallons of hot water will stay hot up to 10 hours, if you don't use it, without causing your boiler/burner to come on. (Unless, of course, you need it for heating your home in the winter.)

8. When you do use hot water, you will be able to use approximately 20 gallons, before the Hot Water Maker turns on. Then you will still have 21 gallons of hot water left for use, as your Hot Water Maker "recoups" 20 gallons of cold water. This means, during normal use (3 1/2 GPM Flow), you will never run out of hot water.

You can expect substantial energy savings with your Hot Water Maker, as its ability to store hot water and efficiently transfer energy to make more hot water will keep your boiler off for longer periods of time.

FIGURE 21.2 A Process Description This description allows users to visualize the sequence of events in producing the hot water.
Source: Courtesy of AMTROL Inc.

Use Precise and Informative Language.   Use high-information words that enable readers to *visualize*. Instead of "large," "long," and "near," give exact measurements, weights, dimensions, and ingredients. Specify location and spatial relationships: "above," "oblique," "behind," "tangential," "adjacent," "interlocking," "abutting," and "overlapping." Specify position: "horizontal," "vertical," "lateral," "longitudinal," "in cross-section," "parallel." Avoid judgmental words ("impressive," "poor"), unless your judgment is requested and can be supported by facts.

Indefinite	Precise
a late-model car	a 2008 Lexus ES 300
an inside view	a cross-sectional, cutaway, or exploded view
next to the foundation	adjacent to the right side
a small red thing	a red activator button with a 1-inch diameter and a concave surface

NOTE   *Never confuse precise language with overly complicated technical terms or needless jargon. Don't say "phlebotomy specimen" instead of "blood," "thermal attenuation" instead of "insulation," or "proactive neutralization" instead of "damage control." The clearest description uses precise but plain language. General readers prefer nontechnical language—as long as the simpler words do the job. Always think about your specific reader's needs.*

Elements of a Usable Description

Clear and Limiting Title

Give an immediate forecast

An effective title promises exactly what the document will deliver—no more and no less. For example, the title "A Description of a Velo Ten-Speed Racing Bicycle" promises a comprehensive description. If you intend to describe the braking mechanism only, be sure your title so indicates: "A Description of the Velo's Center-Pull Caliper Braking Mechanism."

Appropriate Level of Detail and Technicality

 How is technicality culturally situated?

Give users exactly and only what they need

Give enough detail to convey a clear picture, but do not burden readers needlessly. Identify your audience and its reasons for using your description. Focus carefully on your purpose.

The descriptions of the hot water maker in Figures 21.1 and 21.2 focus on *what this model looks like, what it's made of,* and *how it works.* Its intended audience of do-it-yourselfers will know already what a hot water maker is and what it does. That audience will need no background. (A description of *how this product was put together* appears with the installation and maintenance instructions later in the owner's manual.)

In contrast, *specifications* (page 479) for manufacturing the hot water maker would describe each part in exacting detail (e.g., the steel tank's required thickness and pressure rating as well as required percentages of iron, carbon, and other constituents in the steel alloy).

Visuals

Let the visual
repeat, restate, or
reinforce the prose

Use drawings, diagrams, or photographs generously—with captions and labels that help users interpret what they are seeing. Notice how the diagram in Figure 21.3 combines words and images to provide a simple but dynamic picture of a process in action.

NOTE *Economy in a visual often equals clarity. Avoid verbal and visual clutter. The experiment described in the caption to Figure 21.3, for example, demonstrates why it's important to "minimize distracting detail" (Rowan 214).*

Visuals generated by computers (for example, 3-D drawing or architectural drafting programs) are particularly appropriate for technical descriptions. Other sources for descriptive graphics include clip art, electronic scanning, and downloading from the Internet. (See page 283 for a sampling of useful Web sites and discussion of legal issues regarding the use of computer graphics.)

Clearest Descriptive Sequence

Organize for
the user's
understanding

Any item or process usually has its own logic of organization, based on (1) the way it appears as a static object, (2) the way its parts operate in order, or (3) the way its parts are assembled. We describe these relationships, respectively, in spatial, functional, or chronological sequence.

A spatial sequence
parallels the user's
angle of vision in
viewing the item

Spatial Sequence.   Part of all physical descriptions, a spatial sequence answers these questions: *What does it do? What does it look like? What parts and materials is it made of?* Use this sequence when you want users to visualize a static item or a mechanism at rest (an office interior, a document, the Statue of Liberty, a plot of land, a chainsaw, or a computer keyboard). Can readers best visualize this item from front to rear, left to right, top to bottom? (What logical path do the parts create?) A retractable pen would logically be viewed from outside to inside. The specifications in Figure 21.6 (page 480) proceed from the ground upward.

A functional
sequence parallels
the order in which
parts operate

Functional Sequence.   The functional sequence answers: *How does it work?* It is best used in describing a mechanism in action, such as a 35-millimeter camera, a nuclear warhead, a smoke detector, or a car's cruise-control system. The logic of the item is reflected by the order in which its parts function. Like the hot water

The Process of Lightning

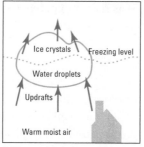

1. Warm moist air rises, water vapor condenses and forms cloud.

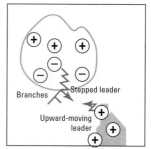

4. Two leaders meet; negatively charged particles rush from cloud to ground.

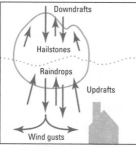

2. Raindrops and ice crystals drag air downward.

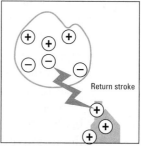

5. Positively charged particles from the ground rush upward along the same path.

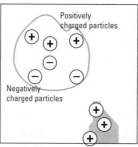

3. Negatively charged particles fall to bottom of cloud.

FIGURE 21.3 A Process Description That Minimizes Distracting Detail In an experiment, students who were given this visual alone were better able to understand the process of lightning than students who were given 550 words of text along with the visual.

Source: From *Journal of Educational Psychology*, 88, by Richard E. Mayer, et al. Copyright © 1996 by the American Psychological Association. Reprinted by permission of the American Psychological Association and Richard E. Mayer.

maker in Figure 21.2, a mechanism usually has only one functional sequence. The stethoscope description on page 470 follows the sequence of parts through which sound travels.

In describing a solar home-heating system, you would begin with the heat collectors on the roof, moving through the pipes, pumping system, and tanks for the heated water, to the heating vents in the floors and walls—from source to outlet. After this functional sequence of operating parts, you could describe each part in a spatial sequence.

A chronological sequence parallels the order in which parts are assembled or stages occur

Chronological Sequence. A chronological sequence answers: *How is it assembled? How does it work? How does it happen?* Use the chronological sequence for an item that is best visualized in terms of its order of assembly (such as a piece of furniture, an umbrella tent, or a prehung window or door unit). Architects might find a spatial sequence best for describing a proposed beach house to clients; however, they would use a chronological sequence (of blueprints) for specifying for the builder the prescribed dimensions, materials, and construction methods at each stage of the process.

NOTE

You can combine these sequences as needed. For example, in describing an automobile jack (for a car owner's manual) you would employ a spatial sequence to help users recognize this item, a functional sequence to show them how it works, and a chronological sequence to help them assemble and use it correctly.

An Outline and Model for Product Description

Description of a complex mechanism almost invariably calls for an outline. This model is adaptable to any description.

    I. **Introduction: General Description**[1]
       A. Definition, Function, and Background of the Item
       B. Purpose (and Audience—for classroom only)
       C. Overall Description (with general visuals, if applicable)
       D. Principle of Operation (if applicable)
       E. Preview of Major Parts

    II. **Description and Function of Parts**
       A. Part One in Your Descriptive Sequence
         1. Definition
         2. Shape, dimensions, material (with specific visuals)
         3. Subparts (if applicable)
         4. Function

---

[1]In most descriptions, the subdivisions in the introduction can be combined and need not appear as individual headings in the document.

5. Relation to adjoining parts
6. Mode of attachment (if applicable)
B. Part Two in Your Descriptive Sequence (and so on)

III. Conclusion and Operating Description
A. Summary (used only in a long, complex description)
B. Interrelation of Parts
C. One Complete Operating Cycle

You might modify, delete, or combine certain components of this outline to suit your subject, purpose, and audience.

Introduction: General Description

Give users only as much background as they need to get the picture.

A DESCRIPTION OF THE STANDARD STETHOSCOPE

Definition and function

History and background

Purpose and audience

Overall view and principle of operation

Preview of major parts

Visual reinforces the prose

The stethoscope is a listening device that amplifies and transmits body sounds to aid in detecting physical abnormalities.

This instrument has evolved from the original wooden, funnel-shaped instrument invented by a French physician, R. T. Laënnec, in 1819. Because of his female patients' modesty, he found it necessary to develop a device, other than his ear, for auscultation (listening to body sounds).

This description explains to the beginning paramedical or nursing student the structure, assembly, and operating principle of the stethoscope.

The standard stethoscope, roughly 24 inches long and weighing about 5 ounces, consists of a sensitive sound-detecting and amplifying device whose flat surface is pressed against a bodily area. This amplifying device is attached to rubber and metal tubing that transmits the body sound to a listening device inserted in the ear.

The stethoscope's Y-shaped structure contains seven interlocking pieces: (1) diaphragm contact piece, (2) lower tubing, (3) Y-shaped metal piece, (4) upper tubing, (5) U-shaped metal strip, (6) curved metal tubing, and (7) hollow ear plugs. These parts form a continuous unit (Figure 1).

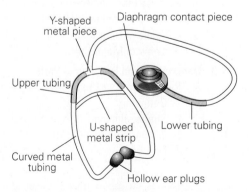

FIGURE 1 Stethoscope with Diaphragm Contact Piece (Front View)

Description and Function of Parts

The body of your text describes each major part. After arranging the parts in sequence, follow the logic of each part. Provide only as much detail as users need, as in the following description of one of the stethoscope's major parts.

Readers of this description will use a stethoscope daily, so they need to know how it works, how to take it apart for cleaning, and how to replace worn or broken parts. (Specifications for the manufacturer would require many more technical details—dimensions, alloys, curvatures, tolerances, and so on.)

Definition, size, shape, and material

Subparts

DIAPHRAGM CONTACT PIECE.   The diaphragm contact piece is a shallow metal bowl, about the size of a silver dollar (and twice its thickness). Various body sounds are captured in the bowl, causing the plastic diaphragm to vibrate.

Three separate parts make up the piece: hollow steel bowl, plastic diaphragm, and metal frame (Figure 2).

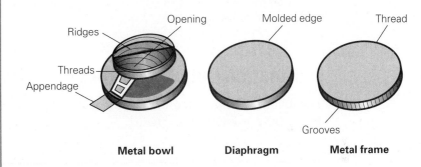

FIGURE 2 Exploded View of a Diaphragm Contact Piece

The stainless steel metal bowl has a concave inner surface, with concentric ridges that funnel sound toward an opening in the tapered base, then out through the hollow appendage. Lateral threads ring the outer circumference of the bowl to accommodate the interlocking metal frame. A fitted diaphragm covers the bowl's upper opening.

The diaphragm is a plastic disk, 2 millimeters thick, 4 inches in circumference, with a molded lip around the edge. It fits flush over the metal bowl and vibrates sound toward the ridges. A metal frame that screws onto the bowl holds the diaphragm in place.

Function and relation to adjoining parts

Mode of attachment

A stainless steel frame fits over the disk and metal bowl. A $\frac{1}{4}$-inch ridge between the inner and outer edge accommodates threads for screwing the frame to the bowl. The frame's outside circumference is notched with equally spaced, perpendicular grooves—like those on the edge of a dime—to provide a gripping surface.

> The diaphragm contact piece receives, amplifies, and transmits sound through the system of attached tubing. The piece attaches to the lower tubing by an appendage on its apex (narrow end), which fits inside the tubing.

Each part of the stethoscope, in turn, is described according to its own logic of organization.

Summary and Operating Description

Conclude by explaining how the parts work together to make the whole item function.

How parts
interrelate

One complete
operating cycle

> The seven major parts of the stethoscope provide support for the instrument, flexibility of movement for the operator, and ease in use.
>
> In an operating cycle, the diaphragm contact piece, placed against the skin, picks up sound impulses from the body's surface. These impulses cause the plastic diaphragm to vibrate. The amplified vibrations, in turn, are carried through a tube to a dividing point. From here, the amplified sound is carried through two separate but identical series of tubes to hollow ear plugs.

A Situation Requiring Product Description

The following description of a solar collector, aimed toward a general audience, adapts the previous outline model.

CASE: Composing a Mechanism Description for a Nontechnical Audience

---

The Situation.   Roxanne Payton is a mechanical engineer specializing in non-polluting energy technologies. Roxanne prepared this description (Figure 21.4) as part of an informational booklet on solar energy systems distributed by her company, Eco-Solutions.

Audience and Use Profile.   The audience here will be homeowners or potential homeowners interested in incorporating solar flat-plate collectors as a heating source. Although many of these people probably lack technical expertise, they presumably have some general knowledge about active solar heating systems and principles. Therefore, this description will focus on the collectors rather than on the entire system, while omitting specific technical data (say, the heat conducting and corrosive properties of copper versus aluminum in the absorber plates). The engineer who designed the collector would include such data in research-and-development reports for the manufacturer. Informed laypersons, however, need only the information that will help them visualize and understand how a basic collector operates.

Definition and
function

Background

Overall view and
operating principle

List of major parts
(spatial sequence)

First major part
(definition, shape,
and material)

DESCRIPTION OF A STANDARD FLAT-PLATE SOLAR COLLECTOR

Introduction—General Description

A flat-plate solar collector is an energy gathering device that absorbs sunlight
and converts it into heat. Depending on a site's geographical location, a
flat-plate collection system can provide between 30 and 80 percent of a
home's hot water and space heating.

The flat-plate collector has found the widest application in the solar energy
industry because it is inexpensive to fabricate, install, and maintain as
compared with higher-temperature heat collection plates. Flat-plate
collectors can easily be incorporated into traditional or modern building
design, provided that the tilt and orientation are properly calculated.
Collectors work best if they face the sun directly, a few degrees west of due
south, tilted up at an angle that equals the latitude of the site plus 10 degrees.
By using direct as well as diffuse solar radiation, flat-plate collectors can
attain 250 degrees Fahrenheit—well above the temperatures needed for
space heating and domestic hot water.

A standard collection unit is rectangular, nine feet long by four feet wide by
four inches high. The collector operates on a heat-transfer principle: the sun's
rays strike an absorber plate, which in turn transfers its heat to fluid
circulating through adjacent tubes.

Five main parts make up the flat-plate collector: enclosure, glazing (and
frame), absorber plate, flow tubes holding the transfer fluid, and insulation
(Figure 1).

Flat Plate Collector

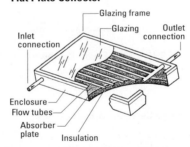

FIGURE 1   A Flat-Plate Collector (Cutaway View)

Source: Solar Water Heating. U.S. Department of Energy, March 1996.

Description of Parts and Their Function

ENCLOSURE.   The enclosure is a rectangular metal or plastic tray that serves as
a container for the remaining (four) main parts of the collector. It is mounted
on a home's roof at a precise angle for absorbing solar rays.

FIGURE 21.4 A Mechanism Description for a Nontechnical Audience
Readers are given only as much detail as they need to understand and
visualize the item. Diagrams are especially effective descriptive tools because
they simplify the view by removing unnecessary features; labels help readers
interpret what they are seeing.

Second major
part, etc.

Description of a Standard Flat-Plate Solar Collector   2

GLAZING (AND FRAME). The glazing consists of one or more layers of transparent plastic or glass that allow the sun's rays to shine on the absorber plate. This part also provides a cover for the enclosure and serves as insulation by trapping the heat that has been absorbed. An insulated frame secures the glazing sheet to the enclosure.

ABSORBER PLATE. The metallic absorber plate, coated in black for maximum efficiency, absorbs solar radiation and converts it into heat energy. This plate is the heat source for the transfer fluid in the adjacent tubing.

FLOW TUBES AND TRANSFER FLUID. The captured solar heat is removed from the absorber by means of a transfer medium; generally, treated water. The transfer medium is heated as it passes through flow tubes attached to the absorbing plate and then transported to points of use in the home or to storage, depending on energy demand.

INSULATION. Fiberglass insulation surrounds the bottom, edges, and sides of the collector, to retain absorbed energy and limit heat loss.

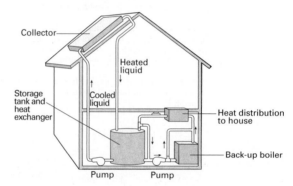

FIGURE 2 How Solar Energy Is Captured and Distributed Throughout a Home
Source: Adapted from *Converting a Home to Solar Heat*. U.S. Department of Energy, December 1995.

One complete
operating cycle
(functional
sequence)

Operating Description and Conclusion

In one operating cycle, solar rays penetrate the glazing to heat the absorber plate (Figure 2). Insulation helps retain the heat. The absorber plate, in turn, heats a liquid circulating through attached flow tubes, which is then pumped to a heat exchanger. The heat exchanger transfers the heat to the water in a storage tank, pumped to various uses in the home. The cooled liquid is then pumped back to the collector to be re-heated.

A conclusion
emphasizing the
collector's
efficiency

The solar energy annually striking the roof of a typical house is ten times greater its annual heat demand. Properly designed and installed, a flat-plate solar system can provide a large percentage of a house's space heating and domestic hot water.

FIGURE 21.4 *(Continued)*

More models of process description

An Outline for Process Description

A description of how things work or happen divides the process into its parts or principles. Colleagues and clients need to know how stock and bond prices are governed, how your bank reviews a mortgage application, how an optical fiber conducts an impulse, and so on. A process description must be detailed enough to allow users to follow the process step by step.

Much of your college writing explains how things happen. Your audience is the professor, who will evaluate what you have learned. Because this person knows *more* than you do about the subject, you often discuss only the main points, omitting details.

But your real challenge comes in describing a process for audiences who know *less* than you do, and who are neither willing nor able to fill in the blank spots; you then become the teacher, and the audience members become your students.

Introduce your description by telling what the process is, and why, when, and where it happens. In the body, tell how it happens, analyzing each stage in sequence. In the conclusion, summarize the stages, and describe one full cycle of the process.

Sections from the following general outline can be adapted to any process description:

I. **Introduction**
   A. Definition, Background, and Purpose of the Process
   B. Intended Audience (usually omitted for workplace audiences)
   C. Prior Knowledge Needed to Understand the Process
   D. Brief Description of the Process
   E. Principle of Operation
   F. Special Conditions Needed for the Process to Occur
   G. Definitions of Special Terms
   H. Preview of Stages

II. **Stages in the Process**
   A. First Major Stage
      1. Definition and purpose
      2. Special conditions needed for the specific stage
      3. Substages (if applicable)
         a.
         b.
   B. Second Stage (and so on)

III. **Conclusion**
   A. Summary of Major Stages
   B. One Complete Process Cycle

Adapt this outline to the process you are describing.

A Situation Requiring Process Description

The following document is patterned after the sample outline.

CASE: Composing a Process Description for a Nontechnical Audience

---

The Situation. Bill Kelly belongs to an environmental group studying the problem of acid rain in its Massachusetts community. (Massachusetts is among the states most affected by acid rain.) To gain community support, the environmentalists must educate citizens about the problem. Bill's group is publishing and mailing a series of brochures. The first brochure explains how acid rain is formed (Figure 21.5).

Audience and Use Profile. Some will already be interested in the problem; others will have no awareness (or interest). Therefore, explanation is given at the lowest level of technicality (no chemical formulas, equations). But the explanation needs to be vivid enough to appeal to less aware or less interested readers. Visuals create interest and illustrate simply. To give an explanation thorough enough for broad understanding, the process is divided into three chronological steps: how acid rain develops, spreads, and destroys.

<table>
<tr>
<td width="25%" valign="top">

Definition

Purpose

Brief description
of the process

Preview of stages

First stage

</td>
<td valign="top">

HOW ACID RAIN DEVELOPS, SPREADS, AND DESTROYS

Introduction
Acid rain is environmentally damaging rainfall that occurs after fossil fuels burn, releasing nitrogen and sulfur oxides into the atmosphere. Acid rain increases the acidity level of waterways because these nitrogen and sulfur oxides combine with the air's normal moisture. The resulting rainfall is far more acidic than normal rainfall. Acid rain is a silent threat because its effects, although slow, are cumulative.

Power plants burning oil or coal are primary causes of acid rain. The burnt fuel is not completely expended, and residue enters the atmosphere. Although this residue contains several potentially toxic elements, sulfur oxide and, to a lesser extent, nitrogen oxide are the major problems: These chemical culprits combine with moisture to form sulfur dioxide and nitric acid, which then rain down to earth.

The major steps explained here are (1) how acid rain develops, (2) how acid rain spreads, and (3) how acid rain destroys.

The Process
HOW ACID RAIN DEVELOPS.   Once fossil fuels have been burned, their usefulness ends. Unfortunately, it is here that the acid rain problem begins. (Figure 1 illustrates how acid rain develops.).

</td>
</tr>
</table>

FIGURE 21.5 A Process Description for a Nontechnical Audience Readers can follow the process as it unfolds.

How Acid Rain Develops, Spreads, and Destroys   2

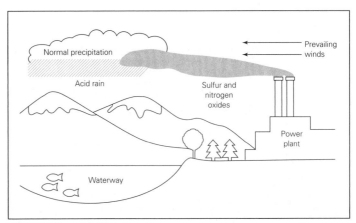

FIGURE 1 How Acid Rain Develops

Definition

Acid level is measured by pH readings. The pH scale runs from 0 through 14—a pH of 7 is neutral. (Distilled water has a pH of 7.) Numbers above 7 indicate increasing alkalinity. (Household ammonia has a pH of 11.) Numbers below 7 indicate increasing acidity. Movement in either direction on the scale means multiplying by 10. Lemon juice, with a pH value of 2, is 10 times more acidic than apples, with a pH of 3, and 1,000 times more acidic than carrots, with a pH of 5.

Because of carbon dioxide (an acid substance) normally present in air, unaffected rainfall has a pH of 5.6. At this time, the pH of precipitation in the northeastern United States and Canada is between 4.5 and 4. In Massachusetts, rain and snowfall have an average pH reading of 4.1. A pH reading below 5 is considered abnormally acidic, and therefore a threat to aquatic populations.

Second stage

How Acid Rain Spreads. Although we might expect areas containing power plants to be most severely affected, acid rain can in fact travel thousands of miles from its source. Stack gases escape and drift with the wind currents, traveling great distances before they return to earth as acid rain.

For an average of two to five days after emission, the gases follow the prevailing winds far from the point of origin. Estimates show that about 50 percent of the acid rain that affects Canada originates in the United States; conversely, 15 to 25 percent of U.S. acid rain originates in Canada.

The tendency of stack gases to drift makes acid rain a widespread menace. More than 200 lakes in the Adirondacks, hundreds of miles from any industrial center, cannot support life because their water has become so acidic.

Third stage

Substage

How Acid Rain Destroys. Acid rain causes damage wherever it falls. It erodes various types of building rock such as limestone, marble, and mortar. Damage to buildings, houses, monuments, statues, and cars is

FIGURE 21.5 *(Continued)*

Substage

widespread. Many priceless monuments have already been destroyed, and even trees of some varieties are dying in large numbers.

More important is acid rain damage to waterways. (Figure 2 illustrates how a typical waterway is infiltrated.) Acid rain gradually but dramatically lowers the pH in lakes and streams, eventually making a waterway so acidic that it dies. In areas with natural acid-buffering elements such as limestone, the dilute acid has less effect. The northeastern United States and Canada, however, lack this natural protection, and so are continually vulnerable.

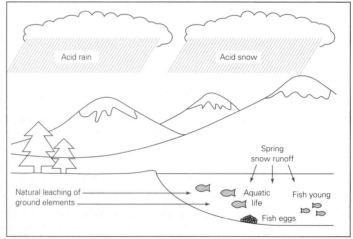

FIGURE 2 How Acid Rain Destroys

The pH level in an affected waterway drops so low that some species cease to reproduce. A pH of 5.1 to 5.4 means that entire fisheries are threatened: once a waterway reaches a pH of 4.5, fish reproduction ceases. Because each creature is part of the overall food chain, loss of one element in the chain disrupts the whole cycle.

In the northeastern United States and Canada, the acidity problem is compounded by the runoff from acid snow. During winter, acid snow sits with little melting, so that by spring thaw, the acid released is greatly concentrated. Aluminum and other heavy metals normally present in soil are also released by acid rain and runoff. These concentrated toxins leach into waterways, affecting fish in all stages of development.

Summary

Acid rain develops from nitrogen and sulfur oxides emitted by the burning of fossil fuels. In the atmosphere, these oxides combine with ozone and water to form precipitation with a low pH. This acid precipitation returns to earth miles from its source, damaging waterways that lack natural buffering agents. The northeastern United States and Canada are the most severely affected areas in North America.

One complete cycle

FIGURE 21.5 *(Continued)*

Model specifications

Specifications

Airplanes, bridges, smoke detectors, and countless other technologies are produced according to certain *specifications*. A particularly exacting type of description, specifications (or "specs") prescribe standards for performance, safety, and quality. For almost any product and process, specifications spell out the following:

Specifications describe products and processes

- methods for manufacturing, building, or installing a product
- materials and equipment to be used
- size, shape, and weight of the product
- specific testing, maintenance, and inspection procedures

Specifications are often used to ensure compliance with a particular safety code, engineering standard, or government or legal ruling.

Specifications have ethical and legal implications

Because specifications define an "acceptable" level of quality, any product "below specifications" may provide grounds for a lawsuit. When injury or death results (as in a bridge collapse or an airline accident), the contractor, subcontractor or supplier is criminally liable.

How specifications originate

Federal and state regulatory agencies routinely issue specifications to ensure safety. For example, the Consumer Product Safety Commission specifies that power lawn mowers be equipped with a "kill switch" on the handle, a blade guard to prevent foot injuries, and a grass thrower that aims downward to prevent eye and facial injury. This same agency issues specifications for baby products, as in governing the fire retardancy of pajama fabric. Passenger airline specifications for aisle width, seat belt configurations, and emergency equipment are issued by the Federal Aviation Administration. State and local agencies issue specifications in the form of building codes, fire codes, and other standards for safety and reliability.

Government departments (Defense, Interior, etc.) issue specifications for all types of military hardware and other equipment. A set of NASA specifications for spacecraft parts can be hundreds of pages long, prescribing the standards for even the smallest nuts and bolts, down to screw-thread depth and width in millimeters.

The private sector issues specifications for countless products or projects, to help ensure that customers get exactly what they want. Figure 21.6 shows partial specifications drawn up by an architect for a medical clinic building. This section of the specs covers only the structure's "shell." Other sections detail the requirements for plumbing, wiring, and interior finish work.

Specifications like those in Figure 21.6 must be clear enough for *identical* interpretation by a broad audience (Glidden 258–59).

Specifications address a diverse audience

- **The customer,** who has the big picture of what is needed and who wants the best product at the best price
- **The designer** (architect, engineer, computer scientist, etc.), who must translate the customer's wishes into the actual specification
- **The contractor or manufacturer,** who won the job by making the lowest bid, and so must preserve profit by doing only what is prescribed

**Ruger, Filstone, and Grant
Architects**

MATERIAL SPECIFICATIONS FOR THE POWNAL CLINIC BUILDING

Foundation
   footings: 8" x 16" concrete (load-bearing capacity: 3,000 lbs. per sq. in.)
   frost walls: 8" x 4' @ 3,000 psi
   slab: 4" @ 3,000 psi, reinforced with wire mesh over vapor barrier

Exterior Walls
   frame: eastern pine #2 timber frame with exterior partitions set inside posts
   exterior partitions: 2" x 4" kiln-dried spruce set at 16" on center
   sheathing: 1/4" exterior-grade plywood
   siding: #1 red cedar with a 1/2" x 6" bevel
   trim: finished pine boards ranging from 1" x 4" to 1" x 10"
   painting: 2 coats of Clear Wood Finish on siding; trim primed and finished with one
               coat of bone white, oil base paint

Roof System
   framing: 2" x 12" kiln-dried spruce set at 24" on center
   sheathing: 5/8" exterior-grade plywood
   finish: 240 Celotex 20-year fiberglass shingles over #15 impregnated felt roofing paper
   flashing: copper

Windows
   Anderson casement and fixed-over-awning models, with white exterior cladding,
   insulating glass and screens, and wood interior frames

Landscape
   driveway: gravel base, with 3" traprock surface
   walks: timber defined, with traprock surface
   cleared areas: to be rough graded and covered with wood chips
   plantings: 10 assorted lawn plants along the road side of the building

FIGURE 21.6 Specifications for a Building Project (Partial) These specifications ensure that all parties agree on the specific materials to be used.

- **The supplier,** who must provide the exact materials and equipment
- **The workforce,** who will do the actual assembly, construction, or installation (managers, supervisors, subcontractors, and workers—some working on only one part of the product, such as plumbing or electrical)
- **The inspectors** (such as building, plumbing, or electrical inspectors), who evaluate how well the product conforms to the specifications

Each of these parties needs to understand and agree on exactly *what* is to be done and *how* it is to be done. In the event of a lawsuit over failure to meet specifications, the readership broadens to include judges, lawyers, and jury. Figure 21.7 depicts how a set of clear specifications unifies all users (their various viewpoints, motives, and levels of expertise) in a shared understanding.

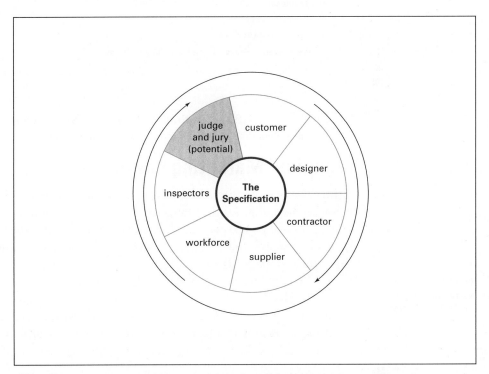

FIGURE 21.7 Users and Potential Users of Specifications

In addition to guiding a product's design and construction, specifications can facilitate the product's use and maintenance. For instance, specifications in a computer manual include the product's performance limits, or *ratings:* its power requirements; its processing and storage capacity; operating environment requirements; the makeup of key parts; and so on. Product support literature for appliances, power tools, and other items routinely contains ratings to help customers select a good operating environment or replace worn or defective parts (Riney 186). The ratings in Figure 21.8 are taken from the owner's manual for an ink jet printer.

General specifications

Marking engine

- Thermal ink jet engine

Resolution

- 360 dots per inch (dpi) for text and graphics (180 dpi for draft quality)

Engine speed

- Printing speed depends on the images printed and on the Macintosh computer used.

Connector cable

- Apple System/Peripheral-8 cable

Interface

- High-speed serial (RS-422)
- Optional LocalTalk

Paper feed in pounds (lb.) and grams/meter^2 (g/m^2)

- Sheet feeder holds up to 100 sheets of 20-lb. (75-g/m^2) paper or 15 envelopes.

FIGURE 21.8 Specifications for the Color StyleWriter™ 2400
Source: Reprinted by permission of Apple Computer, Inc.

Technical Marketing Literature

Technical marketing literature is designed to sell a technical or scientific product or service to audiences that range from novice to highly informed. Descriptions and specifications are essential marketing tools because they help potential customers to visualize the product or service and to recognize how its special features can fit their exact needs.

Even though technical marketing has persuasion as its main goal, readers dislike a "hard-sell approach." They expect upbeat promotional claims such as "durable finish" and "performance of a lifetime" to be backed up by solid evidence: for example, results of objective product testing, performance ratings, and data that indicate how the product meets or exceeds industry specifications.

> Technical marketing audiences expect a factual presentation

NOTE

Unlike proposals (Chapter 23), which are also used to sell a product or service, technical marketing materials tend to be less formal and more dynamic, colorful, and varied. A typical proposal is tailored to one client's needs and follows a fairly standard format; marketing literature, on the other hand, uses a wide variety of formats to present the product in its best light for a broad array of audiences and needs.

Marketing documents run the gamut from simple "fact sheets" to glossy booklets with colorful photographs and other visuals. Here are some common types of documents.

> Common formats for technical marketing documents

- **Brochures** are a popular marketing medium. The six-panel foldout brochure in Figure 21.9 is designed to promote a brand of windows and

Outside panels

Inside panels

FIGURE 21.9 A Technical Marketing Brochure First, the upbeat message and engaging photos in outside Panel A immediately place the product in an aesthetic light. Next, inside Panel A stresses product benefits (energy savings, beauty, and versatility) followed by an attractive photo. Next, inside Panel B—the brochure's center—focuses on technical features and options, with contact information prominently displayed. Following a graphic depicting insulating glass in action, inside Panel C describes the standards that Marvin products meet. Next, outside Panel C shows cross-sections of various insulating options. Finally, striking photos in outside Panel B echo the aesthetic focus of the opening panel.

Source: Used by permission of Marvin Windows and Doors.

doors by emphasizing their energy efficiency as well as their beauty; product appeal is enhanced by a visual background of striking product designs and various weather conditions and settings. Good brochures feature panels that provide a logical sequence, with each panel offering its own discrete "chunk" (page 211) of information about the product (Hilligoss 71). The balance of technical and aesthetic details creates a persuasive message something like this: "Marvin products not only look great but also work great."

- **Web pages** are especially effective for technical marketing. A visitor can explore the links of particular interest, read or download the material, and easily return to the site's home page. As a marketing tool, Web pages offer these advantages: product information can easily be updated; customers can interact to ask questions or place orders directly online; and through animation, the product can be shown in operation. Figure 21.10 shows a web-based description of one of the products ("Double Hung combinations") referenced in Figure 21.11.

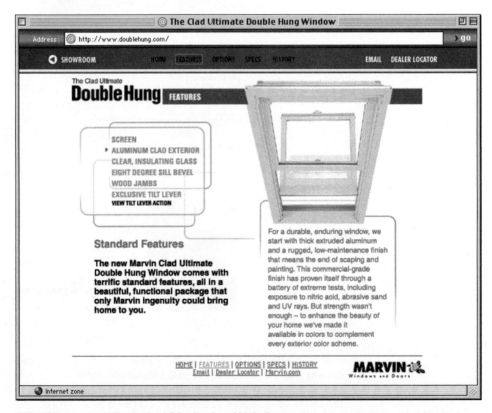

FIGURE 21.10 A Technical Marketing Web Page This description provides links to product details (such as "Specs"), background on the company, and contact and ordering information. Clicking on "View Tilt Lever Action" provides an animated view of this mechanism.

Source: Used by permission of Marvin Windows and Doors <www.marvin.com>.

- **Fact sheets** offer basic data about the product or service in a straightforward, un-adorned format, usually on a single $8\frac{1}{2} \times 11$-inch page, sometimes using both sides of the page. Figure 21.11 displays a double-sided fact sheet that accompanies the expanded definition in Figures 20.7 and 20.8 (pages 459, 460). Even though this sheet contains a great deal of technical information, it is designed to be inviting and navigable: visuals are engaging and easy to interpret; paragraphs are concise and readable; headings provide a clear forecast of each section; and the most complex data is chunked into clearly labeled lists (Hilligoss 63).
- **Business letters** are the most personal type of marketing document. See, for example, how Tom Ewing's letter on page 68 creates a human connection with a potential customer.

(For an intimate look at technical marketing as a career, see Richard Larkin's report in Chapter 24.)

☑ Checklist: Usability of Technical Descriptions

(Numbers in parentheses refer to first page of discussion.)

Content

☐ Does the title promise exactly what the description delivers? (466)

☐ Are the item's overall features described, as well as each part? (469)

☐ Is each part defined before it is discussed? (469)

☐ Is the function of each part explained? (469)

☐ Do visuals appear whenever they can provide clarification? (467)

☐ Will users be able to visualize the item? (463)

☐ Are any details missing, needless, or confusing for this audience? (466)

☐ Is the description ethically acceptable? (463)

Arrangement

☐ Does the description follow the clearest possible sequence? (467)

☐ Are relationships among the parts clearly explained? (470)

Style and Page Design

☐ Is the description sufficiently impartial? (463)

☐ Is the language informative and precise? (466)

☐ Is the level of technicality appropriate for the audience? (466)

☐ Is the description in plain English? (232)

☐ Is each sentence clear, concise, and fluent? (216)

☐ Is the description grammatical? (670)

☐ Is the page design inviting and accessible? (297)

Exercises

1. Select an item from the following list or a device used in your major field. Using the general outline (page 469) as a model, develop an objective description. Include (a) all necessary visuals, (b) an "art brief" (page 278) and a rough diagram for each visual, or (c) a "reference visual" (a copy of a visual published elsewhere) with instructions for adapting your visual from that one. (If you borrow visuals from other sources, provide full documentation.) Write for a specific use by a specified audience. Attach your written audience and use profile (based on the worksheet, page 35) to your document.

> PDA (personal digital assistant)
> soda-acid fire extinguisher
> breathalyzer
> sphygmomanometer
> transit
> Skinner box
> distilling apparatus
> specific brand of woodstove
> photovoltaic panel
> catalytic converter

Remember, you are simply describing the item, its parts, and its function: *do not* provide directions for its assembly or operation.

As an optional assignment, describe a place you know well. You are trying to convey a visual image, not a mood; therefore, your description should be impartial, discussing only observable details.

2. The flat-plate collector description in this chapter is aimed toward a general audience. Evaluate it using the usability checklist. In one or two paragraphs, discuss your evaluation, and suggest revisions.

3. Figure 21.11 is designed to promote as well as describe a technical product. Answer the following questions about the document:

    • When read in conjunction with Figures 20.7 and 20.8, is Figure 21.11 an effective introduction to this particular product for its intended audience of engineers and other technical experts? Why or why not?

    • Is the overall page design effective? Why or why not? Be specific. (See Chapter 15 and "Using Color," pages 283–88.)

    • Are the visuals adequate and appropriate? Why or why not? (See Chapter 14.) Why aren't the diagrams on the first page labeled more extensively?

    • Is this a sufficiently impartial description? Why or why not? Given its purpose as a marketing document, is the description ethically appropriate? (See Chapter 5.)

    Be prepared to discuss your analysis and evaluation in class.

4. Locate a description and specifications for a particular brand of automobile or some other consumer product. Evaluate this material for promotional and descriptive value and ethical appropriateness.

5. Select a specialized process that you understand well and that has several distinct steps. Using the process description on pages 476–78 as a model, explain this process to classmates who are unfamiliar with it. Begin by completing an audience and use profile (page 35). Possible topics: how the body metabolizes alcohol, how economic inflation occurs, how the federal deficit affects our future, how a lake or pond becomes a swamp, how a volcanic eruption occurs, how the greenhouse effect contributes to global warming.

Collaborative Projects

1. Divide into groups. Assume your group works in the product development division of a diversified manufacturing company.

    Your division has just thought of an idea for an inexpensive consumer item with a potentially vast market. (Choose one from below.)

> flashlight
> nail clippers

C Series System Description

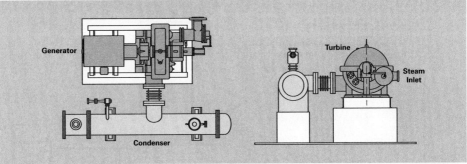

The Ewing Power Systems C Series is a complete single-stage condensing turbine generator package designed for use where maximum electricity production is desired and surplus steam is available. High-pressure steam passes through the turbine and exits at a vacuum pressure to a close-coupled condenser. The condenser may be either water cooled or air cooled. In water-cooled systems the cooling water can be used for heating or the heat can be dissipated in a cooling tower. This series is ideal for converting waste fuel into valuable electricity. It is generally not suited for applications where oil or gas is the primary boiler fuel unless the condenser cooling water will be used for heating.

Features and Specifications

Turbine Features
- Coppus RLHA turbine, fully proven in world-wide applications
- Integrated steam control system including all transmitters, actuators, and controllers
- Dual electronic and mechanical overspeed trip mechanisms
- Hand valves for maximum operating efficiency
- Very low maintenance
- Rugged, reliable design, 20 year minimum service life
- Meets all applicable NEMA and API specifications

Steam Specifications
- Recommended Inlet Pressure
  - Maximum: 700 psig
  - Minimum: 14 psig
- Recommended Exhaust Pressure
  - Maximum: 0 psig (14.7 psia)
  - Minimum: –10 psig (4.7 psia)
- Steam Flow
  2,500 pounds of steam per hour (75 boiler horsepower) or greater

Generator Features
- Louis Allis induction generator, renowned for high efficiency and dependability*
- Models from 55 kW to 800 kW continuous duty at 480 volts
- Models to 2,000 kW at higher voltages
- Extra high efficiency design is standard

*Synchronous generators also available

Standard Prewired Electrical Controls
- Shunt trip, 3-pole, motor-operated circuit breaker with stored energy trip mechanism
- Utility Grade Protective Relays
  - Over/under Voltage
  - Over/under Frequency
  - Ground overcurrent
- Stator thermostats
- Time delay relay to disconnect on motoring
- Pilot lights for operating and trip status
- Ammeter and voltmeter
- Digital tachometer
- Kilowatt meter
- Synchronous panels available

NOTE: *We will customize our control panels to meet the interconnection requirements of any utility.*

Condenser Features
- Air-cooled models
  - Specially designed to minimize power consumption
  - Freeze protection system
  - Standard design is for 97°F ambient, higher temperatures available
- Water-cooled models
  - Includes cooling tower
  - Steel shell and tubesheet and admiralty brass tubes
  - Integral hot-well
- Both models include:
  - Steam ejector to remove non-condensables
  - Condensate pump

(EWING POWER SYSTEMS)

FIGURE 21.11 A Technical Marketing Fact Sheet After a product diagram and a brief introduction to the C Series Cogeneration System, the description focuses on the product's major components and specifications.

Source: Used with permission of Turbosteam Corporation, Turners Falls, MA.

Typical System Schematic

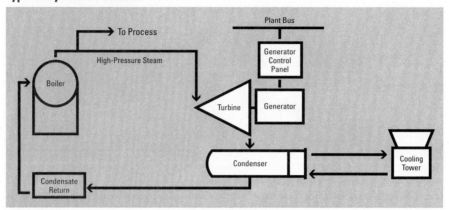

C Series with water-cooled condenser and cooling tower.

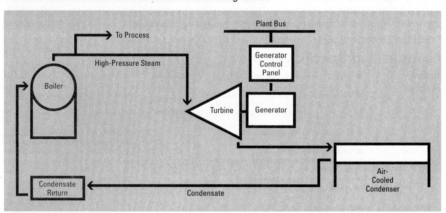

C Series with air-cooled condenser.

Services

In addition to supplying the finest available equipment, Ewing Power Systems also provides complete engineering services. We recognize that you may not be familiar with many of the engineering details of cogeneration so we go to extra lengths to assure our systems will meet your specific requirements for steam and electricity and will provide detailed prints and installation supervision. We will also work with your local utility to assure that your system is designed to take maximum advantage of their rate structure and will meet all their technical requirements. These engineering services, together with our complete economic analysis, assure that your cogeneration system will provide the shortest possible payback.

EWING POWER SYSTEMS

5 North Street • South Deerfield, MA 01373-0566

FIGURE 21.11 *(Continued)* Representational diagrams depict the sequence of events in the cogeneration process and a brief closing paragraph describes the support services offered by the vendor.

retractable ballpoint pen

scissors

stapler

any simple mechanism

Your group's assignment is to prepare three descriptions of this invention:

a. for company executives who will decide whether to produce and market the item

b. for the engineers, machinists, and so on who will design and manufacture the item

c. for the customers who might purchase and use the item

Before writing for each audience, complete audience and use profiles (page 35).

Appoint a group manager, who will assign tasks (visuals, typing, etc.) to members. When the descriptions are fully prepared, the group manager will appoint one member to present them and explain their differences in class.

2. Assume your group is an architectural firm designing buildings at your college. Develop a set of specifications for duplicating the interior of the classroom in which this course is held. Focus only on materials, dimensions, and equipment (whiteboard, desk, etc.) and use visuals as appropriate. Your audience includes the firm that will construct the classroom, teachers, and school administrators. Use the same format as in Figure 21.6, or design a better one. Appoint one member to present the completed specifications in class. Compare versions from each group for accuracy and clarity.

3. As a group, select a particular product (cell phone, sound system, laptop computer, video game) for which descriptions and specifications are available (in product manuals or brochures). Using Figure 21.11 as a model, design a marketing document that describes and promotes this product in a one-page, double-sided format. Include (a) all necessary visuals, (b) an "art brief" (page 278) and a rough diagram for each visual, or (c) a "reference visual" with instructions for adapting your visual from that one. (If you borrow visuals from other sources, provide full documentation.)

4. Select a specialized process you understand well (how gum disease develops, how an earthquake occurs, how steel is made, how a computer compiles and executes a program). Write a brief description of the process. Include visuals, as stipulated in Exercise 3 above. Exchange your description with a classmate in another major. Study your classmate's explanation for fifteen minutes and then write the same explanation in your own words, referring to your classmate's paper as needed. Now, evaluate your classmate's version of your original explanation for accuracy. Does it show that your explanation was understood? If not, why not? Discuss your conclusions in a memo to your instructor, submitted with all samples.

CHAPTER 22

Instructions and Procedures

Purpose of Instructional Documents

Formats for Instructional Documents

Faulty Instructions and Legal Liability

Elements of Usable Instructions

Guidelines for Providing Appropriate Detail

Guidelines for Designing Instructions

An Outline for Instructions

A Situation Requiring Instructions

Online Documentation

Testing the Usability of Your Document

Procedures

Checklist: Usability of Instructions

Instructions spell out the steps required for completing a task or series of tasks (say, installing printer software on your hard drive or operating an electron microscope). The audience for a set of instructions might be someone who doesn't know how to perform the task or someone who wants to perform it better. In either case, effective instructions enable users to get the job done safely and efficiently.

Procedures, a special type of instruction, serve as official guidelines for people who typically are already familiar with a given task (say, evacuating a high-rise building). Procedures ensure that all members of a group (say, employers or employees) coordinate their activities in performing the task.

Purpose of Instructional Documents

The role of instructions on the job

Almost anyone with a responsible job writes and reads instructions. For example, you might instruct a new employee in activating his or her voice mail system, or a customer in shipping radioactive waste. The employee going on vacation writes instructions for the person filling in. Computer users routinely consult hard copy or online manuals (or *documentation*) for all sorts of tasks. Whatever their task, users will have basic questions:

What users expect to learn from a set of instructions

- Why am I doing this?
- How do I do it?
- What materials and equipment will I need?
- Where do I begin?
- What do I do next?
- What could go wrong?

Because they focus squarely on the *user*—the person who will "read" and then "do"—instructions must meet the highest standards of excellence.

Formats for Instructional Documents

Instructional documents take various formats, in hard copy or electronic versions. Here are some of the most commonly used:

Common formats for instructional documents

- **Instructional brochures** (Figure 22.1) can be displayed, handed out, mailed, or otherwise distributed to a broad audience. They are especially useful for advocating procedures that increase health and safety.
- **Manuals** (Figure 22.2) contain instructions for all sorts of tasks. A manual also may contain descriptions and specifications for the product, warnings, maintenance and troubleshooting advice, and any other information the user is likely to need. For complex products (say, a word-processing program) or procedures (say, cleaning up a hazardous-waste site), the manual can be a sizable book. In a recent trend, briefer manuals contain the basic operating tips and the more lengthy information is provided as online documentation (page 492).

- **Brief reference cards** (Figure 22.3) typically fit on a single page or less. The instructions usually focus on the basic steps for users who want only enough information to start on a task and to keep moving through it.
- **Hyperlinked instructions** (Figure 22.4) enable users to explore various levels and layers of information and to choose the layer or layers that match their exact needs.
- **Online documentation** (Figure 22.9) provides the entire contents of a hard copy manual at the click of a key or mouse button. Whereas less experienced users tend to prefer paper documentation, online help is especially popular among more experienced users.

Regardless of its format, any set of instructions must meet the strict legal and usability requirements discussed on the following pages.

BAC (foodborne bacteria) could make you and those you care about sick. In fact, even though you can't see BAC—or smell him, or feel him—he and millions more like him may have already invaded the food you eat. But you have the power to *Fight BAC!*.

Foodborne illness can strike anyone. Some people are at a higher risk for developing foodborne illness, including pregnant women, young children, older adults and people with weakened immune systems. For these people the following four simple steps are critically important:

 CLEAN: *Wash hands and surfaces often*

Bacteria can be spread throughout the kitchen and get onto hands, cutting boards, utensils, counter tops and food. To *Fight BAC!*, always:

- Wash your hands with warm water and soap for at least 20 seconds before and after handling food and after using the bathroom, changing diapers and handling pets.
- Wash your cutting boards, dishes, utensils and counter tops with hot soapy water after preparing each food item and before you go on to the next food.
- Consider using paper towels to clean up kitchen surfaces. If you use cloth towels wash them often in the hot cycle of your washing machine.
- Rinse fresh fruits and vegetables under running tap water, including those with skins and rinds that are not eaten.
- Rub firm-skin fruits and vegetables under running tap water or scrub with a clean vegetable brush while rinsing with running tap water.

 SEPARATE: *Don't cross-contaminate*

Cross-contamination is how bacteria can be spread. When handling raw meat, poultry, seafood and eggs, keep these foods and their juices away from ready-to-eat foods. Always start with a clean scene— wash hands with warm water and soap. Wash cutting boards, dishes, countertops and utensils with hot soapy water.

- Separate raw meat, poultry, seafood and eggs from other foods in your grocery shopping cart, grocery bags and in your refrigerator.
- Use one cutting board for fresh produce and a separate one for raw meat, poultry and seafood.
- Never place cooked food on a plate that previously held raw meat, poultry, seafood or eggs.

 COOK: *Cook to proper temperatures*

Food is safely cooked when it reaches a high enough internal temperature to kill the harmful bacteria that cause illness. Refer to the chart on the back of this brochure for the proper internal temperatures.

- Use a food thermometer to measure the internal temperature of cooked foods. Make sure that meat, poultry, egg dishes, casseroles and other foods are cooked to the internal temperature shown in the chart on the back of this brochure.
- Cook ground meat or ground poultry until it reaches a safe internal temperature. Color is not a reliable indicator of doneness.
- Cook eggs until the yolk and white are firm. Only use recipes in which eggs are cooked or heated thoroughly.
- When cooking in a microwave oven, cover food, stir and rotate for even cooking. Food is done when it reaches

the internal temperature shown on the back of this brochure.

- Bring sauces, soups and gravy to a boil when reheating.

 CHILL: *Refrigerate promptly*

Refrigerate foods quickly because cold temperatures slow the growth of harmful bacteria. Do not over-stuff the refrigerator. Cold air must circulate to help keep food safe. Keeping a constant refrigerator temperature of 40°F or below is one of the most effective ways to reduce the risk of foodborne illness. Use an appliance thermometer to be sure the temperature is consistently 40°F or below. The freezer temperature should be 0°F or below.

- Refrigerate or freeze meat, poultry, eggs and other perishables as soon as you get them home from the store.
- Never let raw meat, poultry, eggs, cooked food or cut fresh fruits or vegetables sit at room temperature more than two hours before putting them in the refrigerator or freezer (one hour when the temperature is above 90°F).
- Never defrost food at room temperature. Food must be kept at a safe temperature during thawing. There are three safe ways to defrost food: in the refrigerator, in cold water, and in the microwave. Food thawed in cold water or in the microwave should be cooked immediately.
- Always marinate food in the refrigerator.
- Divide large amounts of leftovers into shallow containers for quicker cooling in the refrigerator.
- Use or discard refrigerated food on a regular basis. Check USDA cold storage information at **www.fightbac.org** for optimum storage times.

FIGURE 22.1   A Foldout Instructional Brochure The three inside panels of this *Fight BAC!* brochure offer "Four Simple Steps to Food Safety."

Source: Used by permission of Partnership for Food Safety Education <www.fightbac.org>.

FIGURE 22.2
Table of Contents from the *Sharp Compact Copier Operation Manual*

Source: Reproduced by permission of Sharp Electronics Corporation.

INTRODUCTION

Welcome to the world of compact copying on the Z-85II Copier. The Sharp Z-85II has been designed for greater copying versatility while occupying a minimum amount of space and featuring intuitive operating ease. Special features include:

- One enlargement and two reduction ratios
- Stationary Platen
- Auto start mode
- Two-way paper feed
- Automatic exposure control
- Color copying

To get full use of all Copier features, be sure to familiarize yourself with this Manual and the Copier. For quick reference during Copier use, keep the Manual in a handy location.

CONTENTS

Page
- UNPACKING 2
- A WORD ON COPIER INSTALLATION 3
- CAUTIONS 3
- SET-UP 4
- MAKING COPIES 6
- SPECIAL PAPERS (MANUAL BY-PASS FEED) 8
- TWO-SIDED COPYING 9
- COLOR COPYING 10
- ▣ LOADING COPY PAPER 11
- ⌁ MISFEED REMOVAL 12
- ⁂ TD CARTRIDGE REPLACEMENT 13
- ◐DRUM CARTRIDGE REPLACEMENT 14
- USER MAINTENANCE 15
- COPIER TROUBLE? 16
- MOVING INSTRUCTIONS 18
- SUPPLIES AND ACCESSORIES PART NUMBERS . . 18
- SPECIFICATIONS 19

1

FIGURE 22.3   A Brief Reference Card

Source: Adapted from United States Office of Government Ethics <www.usoge.gov>.

INSTRUCTOR TIP
Talking Too Fast

Instructors who constantly talk at a fast pace are likely to frustrate the participants. Also, participants tend to tune out if instructors make listening uncomfortable. It's your job to make it easy and comfortable for the participants to listen. The following strategies are suggested to help you slow down and deliver a very effective presentation:

- **Breathe.** Taking slow, deep breaths relaxes you. It helps you deal with that extra adrenaline inside of you. Breathing will help you slow down and also give you more energy for your voice. It's a fact that when adrenaline is flowing, your sense of time is distorted, and what seems natural to you may look like fast forward to your participants.

- **Pause to punctuate speech.** If you habitually talk fast, you need to pause to punctuate your speech. The most natural punctuation for speech is the pause you take when you reach for a breath. Speech, without pausing for punctuation is unclear and hard to listen to. Listeners are uncomfortable and are not allowed a chance to ponder and absorb the information.

- **Use props to help slow you down.** Use a flipchart or a PowerPoint slide to help you focus on main issues and to let you know when it is time to pause before going on to another topic.

Using these strategies enables you to hold the attention of your participants and deliver your points more powerfully and persuasively.

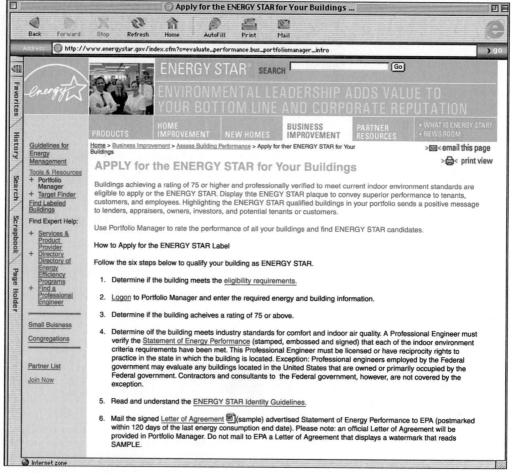

FIGURE 22.4   A Set of Web-Based (Hyperlinked) Instructions Note the links to specific steps.

Source: U.S. Environmental Protection Agency <http://www.energystar.gov>.

Liability and public relations

Faulty Instructions and Legal Liability

Instructional documents carry profound ethical and legal obligations on the part of those who prepare such documents. As many as 10 percent of workers are injured each year on the job (Clement 149). Certain medications produce depression that can lead to suicide (Caher 5). Countless injuries also result from misuse of consumer products such as power tools, car jacks, or household cleaners—types of misuse that are often caused by defective instructions.

Any person injured because of unclear, inaccurate, or incomplete instructions can sue the writer as well as the manufacturer. Courts have ruled that a writing defect in product support literature carries the same type of liability as a design or manufacturing defect in the product itself (Girill, "Technical Communication and Law" 37).

Those who prepare instructions are potentially liable for damage or injury resulting from information omissions such as the following (Caher 5–7; Manning 13; Nordenberg 7):

Examples of faulty instructions that create legal liability

- **Failure to instruct and caution users in the proper use of a product:** for example, a medication's proper dosage or possible interaction with other drugs or possible side effects.
- **Failure to warn against hazards from proper use of a product:** for example, the risk of repetitive stress injury resulting from extended use of a computer keyboard.
- **Failure to warn against the possible misuses of a product:** for example, the danger of child suffocation posed by plastic bags or the danger of toxic fumes from spray-on oven cleaners.
- **Failure to explain a product's benefits and risks in language that average consumers can understand.**
- **Failure to convey the extent of risk with forceful language.**
- **Failure to display warnings prominently.**

Some legal experts argue that defects in the instructions carry even greater liability than defects in the product because they are more easily demonstrated to a nontechnical jury (Bedford and Stearns 128).

NOTE

Among all technical documents, instructions have the strictest requirements for giving users precisely what they need precisely when they need it. To design usable instructions, you must have a clear sense of (a) the specific tasks you want users to accomplish, (b) the users' abilities and limitations, and (c) the setting/circumstances in which users will be referring to this document. For advice on analyzing the tasks, users, and setting, see pages 36–41.

Elements of Usable Instructions

Clear and Limiting Title

Give an immediate forecast

Be sure your title provides a clear and exact preview of the required task. For example, the title "Instructions for Cleaning the Drive Head of a Laptop Computer" tells people what to expect: instructions for a specific procedure involving one selected part. But the title "The Laptop Computer" gives no such forecast; a document so titled might contain a history of the laptop, a description of each part, or a wide range of related information.

Informed Content

Know the procedure

Make sure that you know exactly what you are talking about. Ignorance, inexperience, or misinformation on your part makes you no less liable for faulty or inaccurate instructions:

Ignorance
provides no
legal excuse

> If the author of [a car repair] manual had no experience with cars, yet provided faulty instructions on the repair of the car's brakes, the home mechanic who was injured when the brakes failed may recover [damages] from the author. (Walter and Marsteller 165)

Unless you have performed the task often, do not try to write instructions for it.

Visuals

Instructions often include a persuasive dimension: to promote interest, commitment, or action. In addition to showing what to do, visuals attract the user's attention and help keep words to a minimum.

Types of visuals especially suited to instructions include icons, representational and schematic diagrams, flowcharts, photographs, and prose tables.

Visuals generated by computers are especially useful for instructions. Other sources for instructional graphics include clip art, electronic scanning, and downloading from the Internet. (Page 283 describes useful Web sites and discusses legal issues in the use of computer graphics.)

To use visuals effectively, consider these suggestions:

How to use
instructional
visuals

- Illustrate any step that might be hard for users to visualize. The less specialized your users, the more visuals they are likely to need.
- Parallel the user's angle of vision in performing the activity or operating the equipment. Name the angle (side view, top view) if you think people will have trouble figuring it out for themselves.
- Avoid illustrating any action simple enough for users to visualize on their own, such as "PRESS RETURN" for anyone familiar with a keyboard.

Figure 22.5 presents an array of visuals and their specific instructional functions. Each of these visuals is easily constructed and some could be further enhanced, depending on your production budget and graphics capability. Writers and editors often provide the graphic designer or art department with an *art brief* (page 278) and a rough sketch describing the visual and its purpose.

 What level of
technicality is
culturally
appropriate?

Appropriate Level of Detail and Technicality

Unless you know your users have the relevant background and skills, write for general readers, and do three things:

Provide exactly and
only what users
need

1. Give them enough background to understand why they need your instructions.
2. Give them enough detail to understand *what* to do.
3. Give them enough examples to visualize each step clearly.

These three procedures are explained and illustrated on pages 499–502.

HOW TO LOCATE SOMETHING

Installing a communication card

1 If your communication card has ports for connecting equipment, remove the plastic access cover from the vertical plate.

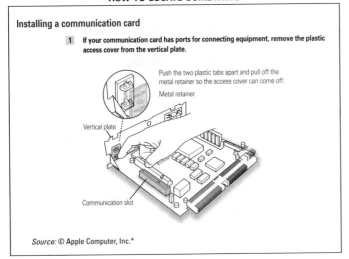

Push the two plastic tabs apart and pull off the metal retainer so the access cover can come off.

Metal retainer

Vertical plate

Communication slot

Source: © Apple Computer, Inc.*

HOW TO OPERATE SOMETHING

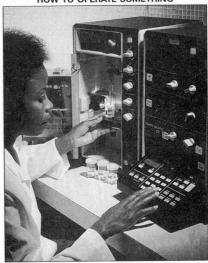

Source: Superstock

HOW TO REPAIR SOMETHING

This   Or this   Not this

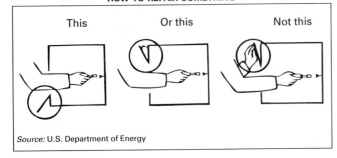

Source: U.S. Department of Energy

HOW TO ASSEMBLE SOMETHING

Extension Cord Retainer

1. Look into the end of the Switch Handle and you will see 2 slots. The WIDER end of the Retainer goes into the TOP slot (Figure 8).
2. Plug extension cord into Switch Handle and weave cord into Retainer, leaving a little slack (Figure 9).

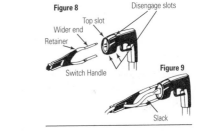

Figure 8

Disengage slots

Wider end

Top slot

Retainer

Switch Handle

Figure 9

Slack

Source: Courtesy of Black & Decker® (U.S.), Inc.

HOW TO POSITION SOMETHING

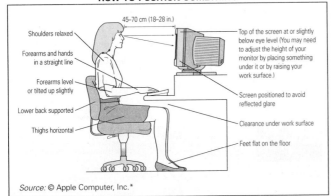

45–70 cm (18–28 in.)

Shoulders relaxed

Forearms and hands in a straight line

Forearms level or tilted up slightly

Lower back supported

Thighs horizontal

Top of the screen at or slightly below eye level (You may need to adjust the height of your monitor by placing something under it or by raising your work surface.)

Screen positioned to avoid reflected glare

Clearance under work surface

Feet flat on the floor

Source: © Apple Computer, Inc.*

HOW TO AVOID DAMAGE OR INJURY

△ **Important:** The fixing assembly in the printer operates at very high temperatures. When you need to open the printer, be careful not to touch the fixing assembly.△

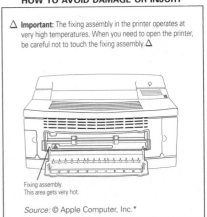

Fixing assembly. This area gets very hot.

Source: © Apple Computer, Inc.*

FIGURE 22.5 **Common Types of Instructional Visuals and Their Functions**

HOW TO DIAGNOSE AND SOLVE PROBLEMS

GENERAL TROUBLESHOOTING CHART

If the amplifier is otherwise operating satisfactorily the more common causes of trouble may generally be attributed to the following:

1. Incorrect connections or loose terminal contacts. Check the speakers, record player, tape deck, antenna and line cord.
2. Improper operation. Before operating any audio component, be sure to read the instructions.

3. Improper location of audio components. The proper positioning of components, such as speakers and turntable, is vital to stereo.
4. Defective audio components.

Following are some other common causes of malfunction and what to do about them. If the amplifier is otherwise operating satisfactorily the more common

PROGRAM	SYMPTOM	PROBABLE CAUSE	WHAT TO DO
AM, FM or MPX reception	a. Constant or intermit-tent noise heard at certain times or in a certain area	* Discharge or oscillation caused by electrical appli-ances, such as fluorescent lamps, TV sets, D.C. mo-tors, rectifier and oscillator * Natural phenomena, such as atmospherics, static, and thunderbolt * Insufficient antenna input due to reinforced concrete walls or long distance from the station * Wave interference from	* Attach a noise limiter to the elec-trical appliance that causes the noise, or attach it to the power source of the amplifier. * Install an outdoor antenna and ground the amplifier to raise the signal-to-noise ratio. * Reverse the power cord plug-receptacle connections. * If the noise occurs at a certain frequency, attach a wave trap to the ANT. input. * Place the set away from other electrical appliances.

Source: Courtesy of Sansui Electronic Co. Ltd.

HOW TO PROCEED SYSTEMATICALLY

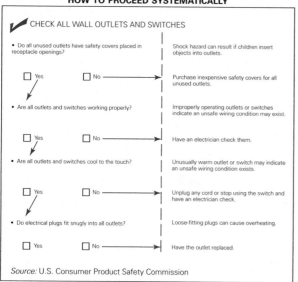

✓ CHECK ALL WALL OUTLETS AND SWITCHES

- Do all unused outlets have safety covers placed in receptacle openings? — Shock hazard can result if children insert objects into outlets.

☐ Yes   ☐ No → Purchase inexpensive safety covers for all unused outlets.

- Are all outlets and switches working properly? — Improperly operating outlets or switches indicate an unsafe wiring condition may exist.

☐ Yes   ☐ No → Have an electrician check them.

- Are all outlets and switches cool to the touch? — Unusually warm outlet or switch may indicate an unsafe wiring condition exists.

☐ Yes   ☐ No → Unplug any cord or stop using the switch and have an electrician check.

- Do electrical plugs fit snugly into all outlets? — Loose-fitting plugs can cause overheating.

☐ Yes   ☐ No → Have the outlet replaced.

Source: U.S. Consumer Product Safety Commission

HOW TO MAKE THE RIGHT DECISIONS

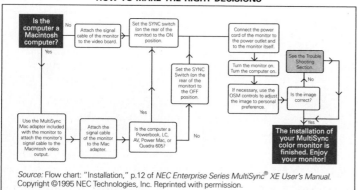

Source: Flow chart: "Installation," p.12 of *NEC Enterprise Series MultiSync® XE User's Manual.* Copyright ©1995 NEC Technologies, Inc. Reprinted with permission.

FIGURE 22.5 *(Continued)*

HOW TO IDENTIFY SAFE OR ACCEPTABLE LIMITS

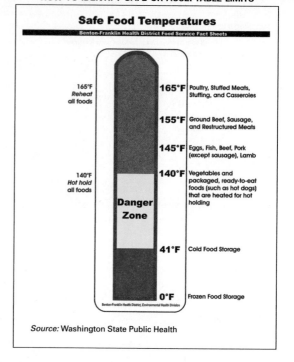

Source: Washington State Public Health

WHY ACTION IS IMPORTANT

 Hidden air leaks can account for up to 50 percent of a typical home's heat loss.

 Total area of all air leaks can add up to 10 to 20 square feet; that's like leaving a door open all winter.

 Insulation alone does not seal air leaks.

 Sealing air leaks helps insulation do its job.

 Insulation not only keeps heat inside the house in winter but also keeps heat out in the summer.

 The greatest heat loss or gain occurs through the attic. Sealing attic air leaks and installing attic insulation reduces energy costs and increases comfort.

 Insufficient attic ventilation can cause moisture buildup that ruins attic insulation and rots wood.

Source: Courtesy of Mass-Save-www.masssave.com. Copyright © 1993, 2005. Reprinted with permission of MassSAVE.

Provide Background. Begin by explaining the purpose of the task.

Tell users why they are doing this

> You might easily lose information stored on a hard disk if:
>
> • the disk is damaged by repeated use, jarring, moisture, or extreme temperature;
> • the disk is erased by a power surge, a computer malfunction, or a user error; or
> • the stored information is scrambled by a nearby magnet (telephone, computer terminal, or the like).
>
> Always make a backup copy of any disk that contains important material.

Also, state your assumptions about the user's level of technical understanding.

Spell out what users should already know

> To follow these instructions, you should be able to identify these parts of a Macintosh system: computer, monitor, keyboard, mouse, compact disk (CD) drive, and recordable compact disk.

Define any specialized terms that appear in your instructions.

Tell users what each key term means

> *Initialize:* Before you can store or retrieve information on a new disk, you must initialize the blank disk. Initializing creates a format the computer can understand—a directory of specific memory spaces (like post office boxes) on the disk where you can store information and retrieve it as needed.

When the user understands *what* and *why,* you are ready to explain *how* the user can complete the task.

Provide Adequate Detail. Include enough detail for users to understand and perform the task successfully, but omit general information that users probably know.

Make instructions complete but not excessive

> **FIRST AID FOR ELECTRICAL SHOCK**
>
> 1. Check vital signs.
> 2. Establish an airway.
> 3. Administer CPR as needed.
> 4. Treat for shock.

Inadequate detail for laypersons

Not only are the above details inadequate, but terms such as "vital signs" and "CPR" are too technical for laypersons. Such instructions posted for workers in a high-voltage area would be useless. Illustrations and explanations are needed, as in the partial instructions in Figure 22.6 for item 3 above, administering CPR.

Don't assume that people know more than they really do, especially when you can perform the task almost automatically. (Think about when a relative or friend taught you to drive a car—or perhaps you tried to teach someone else.) Always assume that the user knows less than you. A colleague will know at least a little less; a layperson will know a good deal less—maybe nothing—about this procedure.

Adequate detail for
laypersons

Methods of Cardiopulmonary Resuscitation (CPR)

Mouth-to-Mouth Breathing

Step 1: If there are no signs of breathing or there is no significant pulse, place one hand under the victim's neck and gently lift. At the same time, push with the other hand on the victim's forehead. This will move the tongue away from the back of the throat to open the airway. If available, a plastic "stoma," or oropharyngeal airway device, should be inserted now.

Step 2: While maintaining the backward head tilt position, place your cheek and ear close to the victim's mouth and nose. Look for the chest to rise and fall while you listen and feel for breathing. Check for about 5 seconds.

Step 3: Next, while maintaining the backward head tilt, pinch the victim's nose with the hand that is on the victim's forehead to prevent leakage of air, open your mouth wide, take a deep breath, seal your mouth around the victim's mouth, and blow into the victim's mouth with four quick but full breaths. For an infant, give gentle puffs and blow through the mouth and nose *and* do not tilt the head back as far as for an adult.

If you do not get an air exchange when you blow, it may help to reposition the head and try again.

If there is still no breathing, give one breath every 5 seconds for an adult and one gentle puff every 3 seconds for an infant until breathing resumes.

If the victim's chest fails to expand, the problem may be an airway obstruction. Mouth-to-mouth respiration should be interrupted briefly to apply first aid for choking.

Step 1   Step 2   Step 3

FIGURE 22.6   Adequate Detail for Laypersons

Source: Reprinted with permission from *New York Public Library Desk Reference, 3rd ed.,* copyright © 1998, 1993, 1989 by The New York Public Library and the Stonesong Press, Inc.

Exactly how much information is enough? The following suggestions can help you find an answer:

Guidelines for Providing Appropriate Detail

- **Give everything users need.** The instructions must be able to stand alone.
- **Give only what users need.** Don't tell them how to build a computer when they only need to know how to copy a disk.
- **Instead of focusing on the *product,* focus on the *task.*** "How does it work?" "How do I use it?" or "How do I do it?" (Grice, "Focus" 132).
- **Omit steps that are obvious to users.** Seat yourself at the computer.
- **Divide the task into simple steps and substeps.** Allow users to focus on one step at a time.
- **Adjust the *information rate.*** This is "the amount of information presented in a given page." (Meyer 17) adjusted to the user's background and the difficulty of the task. For complex or sensitive steps, slow the information rate. Don't make users do too much too fast.
- **Reinforce the prose with visuals.** Don't be afraid to repeat information if it saves users from flipping pages.
- **Keep it simple.** When writing instructions for consumer products, assume "a barely literate reader" (Clement 151).
- **Recognize the persuasive dimension of the instructions.** Users may need persuading that this procedure is necessary or beneficial, or that they can complete this procedure with relative ease and competence.

Give plenty
of examples

Offer Examples. Instructions require specific examples (how to load a program, how to order a part) to help users follow the steps correctly:

> To load your program, type this command:
>
> Load "Style Editor"
>
> Then press RETURN.

Like visuals, examples *show* users what to do. Examples, in fact, often appear as visuals.

Include Troubleshooting Advice. Anticipate things that commonly go wrong when this task is performed—the paper jams in the printer, the tray of the CD-ROM drive won't open, or some other malfunction. Explain the probable cause(s) and offer solutions.

Explain what to do when things go wrong

| *Note:* IF *X* doesn't work, first check *Y* and then do *Z.*

Logically Ordered Steps

Organize for the user's understanding

Instructions are almost always arranged in chronological order, with warnings and precautions inserted for specific steps.

Show how the steps are connected

| You can't splice two wires to make an electrical connection until you have removed the insulation. To remove the insulation, you will need. . . .

Notes and Hazard Notices

Alert users to special considerations and hazards

Following are the only items that normally should interrupt the steps in a set of instructions (Van Pelt 3):

- A *note* clarifies a point, emphasizes vital information, or describes options or alternatives.

| NOTE: If you don't name a newly initialized disk, the computer automatically names it "Untitled."

While a note is designed to enhance performance and prevent error, the following hazard notices—ranked in order of severity—are designed to prevent damage, injury, or death.

- A *caution* prevents possible mistakes that could result in injury or equipment damage:

The least forceful notice

| CAUTION: A momentary electrical surge or power failure will erase the contents of internal memory. To avoid losing your work, every few minutes save on a backup disk what you have just typed into the computer.

- A *warning* alerts users to potential hazards to life or limb:

A moderately forceful notice

| WARNING: To prevent electrical shock, always disconnect your printer from its power source before cleaning internal parts.

- A *danger* notice identifies an immediate hazard to life or limb:

The most forceful notice

| DANGER: The red canister contains DEADLY radioactive material. **Do not break the safety seal** under any circumstances.

Content requirements for hazard notices

Inadequate notices of warning, caution, or danger are a common cause of lawsuits (page 494). Each hazard notice is legally required to (1) describe the specific hazard, (2) spell out the consequences of ignoring the hazard, and (3) offer instruction for avoiding the hazard (Manning 15).

Visual requirements for hazard notices

Even the most emphatic verbal notice might be overlooked by an impatient or inattentive user. Direct the user's attention with symbols, or icons, as a visual signal (Bedford and Stearns 128):

Use hazard symbols

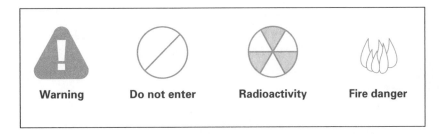

| Warning | Do not enter | Radioactivity | Fire danger |

Visibility requirements for hazard notices

Keep the hazards prominent in the user's awareness: Preview the hazards in your introduction and place each notice, *clearly highlighted* (by a ruled box, a distinct typeface, larger typesize, or color), immediately before the respective step.

NOTE   *Use hazard notices only when needed; overuse will dull their effect, and readers may overlook their importance.*

Readability

Make instructions immediately readable

Instructions must be understood on the first reading because users usually take *immediate* action.

Like descriptions (page 466), instructions name parts, use location and position words, and state exact measurements, weights, and dimensions. Instructions additionally require your strict attention to phrasing, sentence structure, and paragraph structure.

Use Direct Address, Active Voice, and Imperative Mood. To emphasize the user's role, write instructions in the second person, as direct address.

In general, begin all steps and substeps with action verbs, using the *active voice* and *imperative mood* ("Insert the disk" instead of "The disk should be inserted" or "You should insert the disk").

Indirect or confusing

- The user keys in his or her access code.
- You should key in your access code.
- It is important to key in the access code.
- The access code is keyed in.

In this next version, the opening verb announces the specific action required.

Clear and direct

Key in your access code.

In certain cases, you may want to provide a clarifying word or phrase that precedes the verb (*Read Me* 130):

Information that might precede the verb

- [To log on,] **key in** your access code.
- [If your screen displays an error message,] **restart** the computer.
- [Slowly] **scan** the seal for gamma ray leakage.
- [In the Edit menu,] **click** on Paste.

 NOTE   *Certain cultures consider the direct imperative bossy and offensive. For cross-cultural audiences, you might rephrase an instruction as a declarative statement: from "Key in your access code" to "The access code should be keyed in." Or you might use an indirect imperative such as "Be sure to key in your access code" (Coe, "Writing" 18).*

Use Short and Logically Shaped Sentences.   Use shorter sentences than usual, but never "telegraph" your message by omitting articles (*a, an, the*). Use one sentence for each step, so that users can perform one step at a time.

If a single step covers two related actions, describe these actions in their required sequence:

Confusing | Before switching on the computer, insert the CD in the drive.

Logical | Insert the CD in the drive; then switch on the computer.

Simplify explanations by using a familiar-to-unfamiliar sequence:

Hard | You must initialize a blank CD before you can store information on it.

Easier | Before you can store information on a blank CD, you must initialize the CD.

Use Parallel Phrasing.   Parallelism is important in all writing, but especially so in instructions, because repeating grammatical forms emphasizes the step-by-step organization. Parallelism also increases readability and lends continuity to the instructions.

Not parallel | To log on to the VAX 380, follow these steps:

1. Switch the terminal to "on."
2. The CONTROL key and C key are pressed simultaneously.
3. Typing LOGON, and pressing the ESCAPE key.
4. Type your user number, and then press the ESCAPE key.

All steps should be in identical grammatical form:

Parallel

> To log on to the VAX 380, follow these steps:
>
> 1. Switch the terminal to "on."
> 2. Press the CONTROL key and C key simultaneously.
> 3. Type LOGON, and then press the ESCAPE key.
> 4. Type your user number, and then press the ESCAPE key.

Phrase Instructions Affirmatively. Research shows that users respond more quickly and efficiently to instructions phrased affirmatively rather than negatively (Spyridakis and Wenger 205).

Negative

> Verify that your disk is not contaminated with dust.

Affirmative

> Examine your disk for dust contamination.

Use Transitions to Mark Time and Sequence. Transitional expressions (see page 693) provide a bridge between related ideas. Some transitions ("first," "next," "meanwhile," "finally," "ten minutes later," "the next day," "immediately afterward") mark time and sequence. They help users understand the step-by-step process, as in the next example.

> **PREPARING THE GROUND FOR A Tent**
>
> Begin by clearing and smoothing the area that will be under the tent. This step will prevent damage to the tent floor and eliminate the discomfort of sleeping on uneven ground. **First,** remove all large stones, branches, or other debris within a level area roughly 10 × 10 feet. Use your camping shovel to remove half-buried rocks that cannot easily be moved by hand. **Next,** fill in any large holes with soil or leaves. **Finally,** make several light surface passes with the shovel or a large, leafy branch to smooth the area.

Transitions enhance continuity

Effective Design

Instructions rarely get undivided attention. The reader, in fact, is doing two things more or less at once: interpreting the instructions and performing the task. An effective instructional design conveys the sense that the task is within a qualified user's range of abilities.

Guidelines for Designing Instructions

- **Use informative headings.** Tell readers what to expect; emphasize what is most important; provide cues for navigation. A heading such as "How to Initialize Your Compact Disk" is more informative than "Compact Disk Initializing."
- **Arrange all steps in a numbered list.** Unless the procedure consists of simple steps (as in "Preparing the Ground for a Tent," above), list and number each step. Numbered steps not only announce the sequence of steps, but also help users remember where they left off. (For more on using lists, see page 307.)
- **Separate each step visually.** Single-space within steps and double-space between.

(continues)

Guidelines (continued)

- **Make warning, caution, and danger notices highly visible.** Use ruled boxes or highlighting, and plenty of white space.

- **Make visual and verbal information redundant.** Let the visual repeat, restate, or reinforce the prose.

- **Keep the visual and the step close together.** If room allows, place the visual right beside the step; if not, right after the step. Set off the visual with plenty of white space.

- *Consider a multicolumn design.* If steps are brief and straightforward and require back-and-forth reference from prose to visuals, consider multiple columns (Figure 22.7).

- **Keep it simple.** Users can be overwhelmed by a page with excessive or inconsistent designs.

- **For lengthy instructions, consider a layered approach.** In a complex manual, for instance, you might add a "Quick-Use Guide" for getting started, with cross-references to pages containing more detailed and technical information.

For additional design considerations, see Chapter 15.

Connecting cables

▲ **Warning:** When making SCSI connections, always turn off power to all devices in the chain. Failure to do so can cause the loss of information and damage to your equipment.▲

1. **Shut down your PowerBook and all SCSI devices in the chain.**

2. **To connect the first device, use an Apple HDI-30 SCSI System Cable.**

   Attach the smaller end of the cable to your computer's SCSI port (marked with the icon◈) and the larger end of the cable to either SCSI port on the device.

3. **To connect the next device, use a SCSI peripheral interface cable.**

   Both cable connectors are the same. Attach one connector to the available SCSI port on the first device, and the other connector to either SCSI port on the next device.

4. **Repeat step 3 for each additional device you want to connect.**

The illustration shows where to add cable terminators.

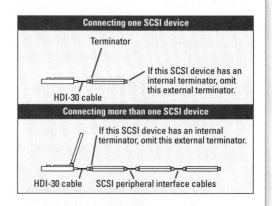

△ **Important:** The total length of an SCSI chain should not exceed 20 feet (6 meters). Apple SCSI cables are designed to meet this restriction. If you are using SCSI cables from another vendor, check the length of the chain.△

Once your SCSI devices are connected, always turn them on before turning on your PowerBook. If you turn the computer on first, it may not be able to start up, or it may not recognize the SCSI devices.

FIGURE 22.7 A Multicolumn Design

Source: Reprinted by permission of Apple Computer, Inc.

NOTE   *Online instructions have their own design requirements, discussed on page 510. Also, despite the increasing popularity of online documentation, many users continue to find printed manuals more convenient and easier to navigate (Foster 10).*

Sample instructions

An Outline for Instructions

You can adapt the following outline to any instructions. Here are the possible components to include:

I. Introduction
   A. Definition, Benefits, and Purpose of the Procedure
   B. Intended Audience (often omitted for workplace audiences)
   C. Prior Knowledge and Skills Needed by the Audience
   D. Brief Overall Description of the Procedure
   E. Principle of Operation
   F. Materials, Equipment (in order of use), and Special Conditions
   G. Working Definitions (always in the introduction)
   H. Warnings, Cautions, Dangers (previewed here and spelled out at steps)
   I. List of Major Steps

II. Required Steps
   A. First Major Step
      1. Definition and purpose
      2. Materials, equipment, and special conditions for this step
      3. Substeps (if applicable)
         a.
         b.
   B. Second Major Step (and so on)

III. Conclusion
   A. Review of Major Steps (for a complex procedure only)
   B. Interrelation of Steps
   C. Troubleshooting or Follow-up Advice (as needed)

This outline is only tentative; you might modify, delete, or combine some components, depending on your subject, purpose, and audience.

Introduction

The introduction should help users to begin "doing" as soon as they are able to proceed safely, effectively, and confidently (van der Meij and Carroll 245–46). Most users are interested primarily in "how to use it or fix it," and will require only a general understanding of "how it works." You don't want to bury users in a long introduction, nor do you want to set them loose on the procedure without adequate preparation. Know your audience—what they need and don't need.

Body: Required Steps

In the body section (labeled Required Steps), give each step and substep in order. Insert warnings, cautions, and notes as needed. Begin each step with its definition or purpose or both. Users who understand the reasons for a step will do a better job. A numbered list is an excellent way to segment the steps. Or, begin each sentence in a complex stage on a new line.

Conclusion

The conclusion of a set of instructions has several possible functions:

- You might summarize the major steps in a long and complex procedure, to help users review their performance.
- You might describe the results of the procedure.
- You might offer follow-up advice about what could be done next or refer the user to further sources of documentation.
- You might give troubleshooting advice about what to do if anything goes wrong.

You might do all these things—or none of them. If your procedural section has given users all they need, omit the conclusion altogether.

A Situation Requiring Instructions

Kerry Wright created instructions for operating a fire extinguisher (Figure 22.8) patterned after the general outline shown earlier.

CASE: Preparing Instructions for a Nontechnical Audience

The Situation. These instructions will appear as part of a packet of brochures given to new employees at Global BioMedical, Inc., maker of medical laboratory instrumentation.

Audience and Use Profile. This document is aimed at users who have varying measures of expertise in their own specialties (biomedical engineering, clinical chemistry, electronics), but who likely have given little thought to operating a fire extinguisher when mere seconds can make the difference between a small, easily contained fire and an inferno. Basic information here will be essential: how the device works in general, how a "multipurpose extinguisher" works specifically, and how to use it.

Visuals illustrate each step that might be hard for users to picture, and they parallel the user's angle of vision in performing the activity. The conclusion, for these users, will be brief and to the point—a simple emphasis on troubleshooting and safety.

1

How to Operate a Multipurpose Dry-Chemical Fire Extinguisher

Introduction

The Occupational Safety and Health Administration (OSHA) requires that all employees know how to operate a fire extinguisher and how to recognize the hazards associated with small or developing fires.

Portable fire extinguishers in our buildings are easily found in various areas: public hallways, laboratories, mechanical rooms, break rooms, chemical storage areas, company vehicles, and other areas that contain flammable liquids. Please note the specific location of extinguishers in each of these areas.

Portable fire extinguishers apply an extinguishing agent that will either cool burning fuel, displace or remove oxygen, or stop the chemical reaction so a fire cannot continue to burn. When the extinguisher handle is compressed, it opens an inner canister of high-pressure gas that forces the extinguishing agent from the main cylinder through a siphon tube and out the nozzle (Figure 1). A fire extinguisher works much like a can of hair spray.

FIGURE 1 How a fire extinguisher works

All of our fire extinguishers are *multipurpose dry-chemical extinguishers*. This type of extinguisher puts out fires by coating the fuel with a thin layer of fire-retardant powder, separating the fuel from the oxygen. The powder also works to interrupt the chemical reaction, making these extinguishers extremely effective for ordinary combustibles (such as wood or paper), flammable liquids, and electrical equipment.

These instructions cover four simple steps in operating the extinguisher safely and effectively: Pull, Aim, Squeeze, and Sweep.

Margin annotations:

Title announces document's purpose

Intended audience

Equipment locations

General operating description

Visual reinforces the prose

Specific operating description

Preview of major steps

FIGURE 22.8 A Set of Instructions for a Nontechnical Audience

Source: Text and figures adapted from the Occupational Safety and Health Administration <www.osha.gov>.

Prominent warning
alerts users **before**
they take action

> **WARNING:** At the first sign of fire, sound the alarm and call the fire department. Before approaching the fire, identify a safe evacuation path. **Never** allow the fire, heat, or smoke to come between you and your evacuation path. **If you have the slightest doubt about your ability to fight a fire. . .** EVACUATE **IMMEDIATELY!**

Repeat preview of
major steps

Using the Fire Extinguisher

Even though extinguishers come in a number of shapes and sizes, they all operate in a similar manner. Here is an easy acronym to remember for rapid and safe fire extinguisher use: PASS—Pull, Aim, Squeeze, and Sweep (Figure 2).

Boldface headings
provide a rapid
overview

1. **PULL** . . . Pull the pin. This will also break the tamper seal.

2. **AIM** . . . Aim low, pointing the extinguisher nozzle (or its horn or hose) at the base of the fire.

3. **SQUEEZE**... Squeeze the handle to release the extinguishing agent.

Numbered steps
guide users

Examples **show**
what to do

Visuals and steps
are together

4. **SWEEP**... Sweep from side to side at the base of the fire until it appears to be out. Watch the area. If the fire reignites, repeat steps 2–4.

Conclusion

Your first concern is **safety:** Always back away from an extinguished fire in case it flames up again. Evacuate immediately if the extinguisher is empty and the fire is not out. Evacuate immediately if the fire worsens.

Troubleshooting
and safety
advice

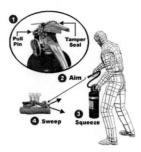

FIGURE 2 The PASS Technique

FIGURE 22.8 *(Continued)*

Online Documentation

Instead of computers and software coming with bulky printed manuals, the computer itself is increasingly the preferred instructional medium. Online documentation (Figure 22.9) explains how a particular system works and how to use it. Online help is designed to support specific tasks and to answer specific questions, as in the examples that follow.

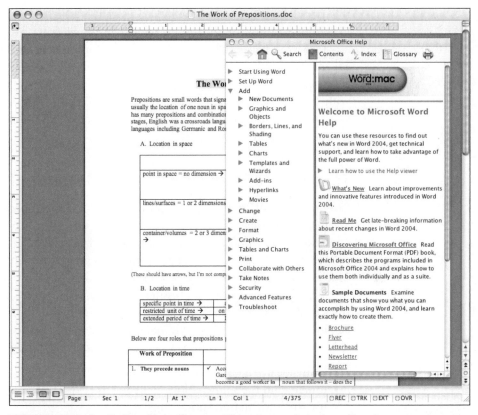

FIGURE 22.9 An Online Help Screen This electronic index offers instant access to any of the topics in the entire online manual.

Source: Microsoft product screen shot reprinted with permission from Microsoft Corporation.

Examples of online documentation

- error messages and troubleshooting advice
- reference guides to additional information or instructions
- tutorial lessons that include interactive exercises with immediate feedback
- help and review options to accommodate different learning styles
- link to software manufacturer's Web site

Instead of leafing through a printed manual, users find what they need by typing a simple command, clicking a mouse button, using a help menu, or following an electronic prompt.

The cost of producing and distributing printed materials makes online documentation attractive to software producers. Also, because most business software is sold on a subscription basis, with a new version coming out every sixteen months or so, providing paper documentation becomes increasingly cost prohibitive.

Special software such as *RoboHelp* or *Doc-to-Help* can convert print material into online help files that appear (a) as dialog boxes that ask the user to input a response or click on an option, or (b) as pop-up or balloon help that appears when the user clicks on an icon or points to an item on the screen for more information. (Explore, for example, the online help resources on your own computer.)

Like Web pages (Chapter 19), online information should be written in well-organized chunks (page 211). It should never be paper documentation merely converted into an electronic file, for this reason: some tasks that users perform with the paper document may not be possible with the online version without substantial modifications. In short, creating effective online documentation requires much training and practice.

Testing the Usability of Your Document

Companies routinely measure the usability of their products, including the *documentation* that accompanies the product (warnings, explanations, assembly or operating instructions, and other elements of a product manual). To keep their customers—and to avoid lawsuits—companies go to great lengths to eliminate flaws or to anticipate all the ways a product might fail or be misused. (Refer also to page 42.)

The purpose of usability testing is to keep what works in a product or document and to fix what doesn't. For a document (whether in hard copy or online) to achieve its objectives—as previewed on page 26 and restated here—users must be able to do at least three things (Coe, *Human Factors* 193; Spencer 74):

What a usable document enables readers to do

- easily locate the information they need
- understand the information immediately
- use the information successfully

To measure usability in a set of instructions, for instance, we ask this question: Do these instructions enable users to carry out the task safely, efficiently, and accurately?

How Usability Testing Is Done

Usability testing usually occurs at two levels (Petroski 90): (1) *alpha testing*, by the product's designers or the document's authors, and (2) *beta testing*, by the actual users of the product or document. At the beta level, two types of testing can be done: *qualitative* and *quantitative*.

Qualitative testing shows what works and what doesn't

Qualitative Testing. To identify which parts of the document work or don't work, observe how users react to the document or what they say or do. ("Testing Your Documents" 1–2):

Two types of qualitative testing

- **Use focus groups.** Based on a list of targeted questions about the document's content, organization, style, and design (Figure 22.10), users discuss what information they think is missing or excessive, what they like or dislike, and what they find easy or hard to understand. They might also suggest revisions for graphics, format, or level of technicality.

Basic Usability Survey

1. Briefly describe why this document is used. _____
_____

2. Evaluate the *content:*
   - Identify any irrelevant information. _____
   _____

   - Indicate any gaps in the information. _____
   _____

   - Identify any information that seems inaccurate. _____
   _____

   - List other problems with the content. _____
   _____

3. Evaluate the *organization:*
   - Identify anything that is out of order or hard to locate or follow. _____
   _____

   - List other problems with the organization. _____
   _____

4. Evaluate the *style:*
   - Identify anything you misunderstood on first reading. _____
   _____

   - Identify anything you couldn't understand at all. _____
   _____

   - Identify expressions that seem wordy, inexact, or too complex. _____
   _____

   - List other problems with the style. _____
   _____

5. Evaluate the *design:*
   - Indicate any headings that are missing, confusing, or excessive. _____
   _____

   - Indicate any material that should be designed as a list. _____
   _____

   - Give examples of material that might be clarified by a visual. _____
   _____

   - Give examples of misleading or overly complex visuals. _____
   _____

   - List other problems with design. _____
   _____

6. Identify anything that seems misleading or that could create legal problems or
   cross-cultural misunderstanding. _____

7. Please suggest other ways of making this document easier to use. _____

FIGURE 22.10 A Basic Usability Survey Versions of these questions can serve as a basis for beta testing (by the document's users). Notice how the phrasing encourages responses containing examples, instead of merely "yes" or "no."

Source: Adapted from Carliner, "Demonstrating Effectiveness" 258; Daugherty 17–18; Hart 53–57.

Methods of qualitative testing

- **Use protocol analysis.** In a one-on-one interview, a user reads a section of a document and then explains what that section means or what seems useful or confusing. Or, the interviewer observes how the person actually reads the document, for example, how often she/he flips pages or refers to the index or table of contents (Ostrander 20).

Quantitative testing shows whether the document succeeds as a whole

Methods of quantitative testing

Quantitative Testing.   Assess a document's overall effectiveness by using a *control group:* Compare success rates among people using different versions of your document, or count the number of people who performed the task accurately ("Testing Your Documents" 2–4). Or measure the time required to complete a task and the types and frequency of user errors (Hughes 489). Quantitative testing yields numerical data, but is more complicated and time-consuming than qualitative testing.

Usability Testing in the Classroom

Ideally, usability tests occur in a setting that simulates the actual situation, with people who will actually use the document (Redish and Schell 67; Ruhs 8). But even in a classroom setting you can assess a document's effectiveness: For alpha testing, use the Checklist for Usability of Instructions (page 517); for beta testing, use a version of Figure 22.10;

NOTE   *See also the generic Checklist for Usability (page 43) for criteria shared by many technical documents. In addition, specific elements (visuals, page design) and document types (proposals, memos, instructions) have their own usability criteria. These are detailed in the individual checklists for usability throughout this book (for example, pages 293, 555, 594).*

Procedures

The difference between instructions and procedures

Instructions show an uninitiated user how to perform a task. *Procedures,* on the other hand, provide rules and guidance for people who usually know how to perform the task but who are required to follow accepted practice. To ensure that everyone does something in exactly the same way, procedures typically are aimed at groups of people who need to coordinate their activities so that everyone's performance meets a certain standard. Consider, for example, police procedures for properly gathering evidence from a crime scene: strict rules stipulate how evidence should be collected and labeled and how it should be preserved, transported, and stored. Evidence shown to have been improperly handled is routinely discredited in a courtroom.

Procedures help ensure safety

Procedures are useful in situations in which certain tasks need to be standardized. For example, if different people in your organization perform the same task at different times (say, monitoring groundwater pollution) with different equipment, or under different circumstances, this procedure may need to be standardized to ensure that all work is done with the same accuracy and precision. A document known as a *Standard Operating Procedure (SOP)* becomes the official guideline for that task (Gurak and Lannon, 3rd ed. 237), as shown in Figure 22.11.

Procedures help keep everyone "on the same page"

Organizations also need to follow strict safety procedures, say, as defined by the U.S. Occupational Safety and Health Administration (OSHA). As laws and policies change, such procedures are often updated. The written procedures must be posted for employees to read. Figure 22.12 shows one page outlining OSHA regulations for evacuating high-rise buildings.

The steps in a procedure may or may not need to be numbered. This will depend on whether steps must be performed in strict sequence, as in Figure 22.11 versus Figure 22.12.

V. SOIL AND GROUNDWATER ASSESSMENT

H. DECONTAMINATION PROCEDURES

The equipment decontamination procedures used during the fieldwork must be described in the site assessment report. The following procedures, at a minimum, must be used for both soil and groundwater sampling equipment:

1. **Drilling or Other Equipment**
   The drilling bits and augers must be steam cleaned between each boring and after each use.
2. **Sampling Equipment**
   a. Reusable bailers must be steam cleaned or one-time-use disposable bailers must be used.
   b. The cord used with the bailers must be discarded after each use.
   c. Sampling equipment that is not steam cleaned must be initially washed with a non-phosphate detergent, rinsed twice with tap water, and final rinsed with deionized or distilled water.
3. **Rinseate**
   The soil and water from washing, rinsing, and steam cleaning must be properly containerized and labeled for disposal.

FIGURE 22.11 A Standard Operating Procedure Part of a manual for dealing with leaking underground fuel tanks, this SOP is aimed at technicians already familiar with techniques such as "steam cleaning" and "containerizing." However, to prevent contamination of testing equipment, each technician needs to follow that strict sequence of steps.

Source: Ventura County LUFT Guidance Manual. Ventura, CA. April 2001.

Evacuating High-Rise Buildings

The National Fire Protection Association defines "high-rise building" as a building greater than 75 feet (25 m) in height where the building height is measured from the lowest level of fire department vehicle access to the floor of the highest occupiable story. Appropriate exits, alarms, emergency lighting, communication systems, and sprinkler systems are critical for employee safety. When designing and maintaining exits, it is essential to ensure that routes leading to the exits, as well as the areas beyond the exits, are accessible and free from materials or items that would impede individuals from easily and effectively evacuating. State and local building code officials can help employers ensure that the design and safety systems are adequate.

When there is an emergency, getting workers out of high-rise buildings poses special challenges. Preparing in advance to safely evacuate the building is critical to the safety of employees who work there.

What actions should employers take to help ensure safe evacuations of high-rise buildings?

- Don't lock fire exits or block doorways, halls, or stairways.
- Test regularly all back-up systems and safety systems, such as emergency lighting and communication systems, and repair them as needed.
- Develop a workplace evacuation plan, post it prominently on each floor, and review it periodically to ensure its effectiveness.
- Identify and train floor wardens, including back-up personnel, who will be responsible for sounding alarms and helping to evacuate employees.
- Conduct emergency evacuation drills periodically.
- Establish designated meeting locations outside the building for workers to gather following an evacuation. The locations should be a safe distance from the building and in an area where people can assemble safely without interfering with emergency response teams.
- Identify personnel with special needs or disabilities who may need help evacuating and assign one or more people, including back-up personnel, to help them.
- Ensure that during off-hour periods, systems are in place to notify, evacuate, and account for off-hour building occupants.
- Post emergency numbers near telephones.

What should workers know before an emergency occurs?

- Be familiar with the worksite's emergency evacuation plan;
- Know the pathway to at least two alternative exits from every room/area at the workplace;
- Recognize the sound/signaling method of the fire/evacuation alarms;
- Know who to contact in an emergency and how to contact them;
- Know how many desks or cubicles are between your workstation and two of the nearest exits so you can escape in the dark if necessary;
- Know where the fire/evacuation alarms are located and how to use them; and
- Report damaged or malfunctioning safety systems and back-up systems

What should employers do when an emergency occurs?

- Sound appropriate alarms and instruct employees to leave building.
- Notify police, firefighters, or other appropriate emergency personnel.
- Take a head count of employees at designated meeting locations, and notify emergency personnel of any missing workers.

What should employees do when an emergency occurs?

- Leave the area quickly but in an orderly manner, following the worksite's emergency evacuation plan. Go directly to the nearest fire-free and smoke-free stairwell recognizing that in some circumstances the only available exit route may contain limited amounts of smoke or fire.

FIGURE 22.12 Safety Procedures This page defines general safety and evacuation procedures to be followed by employers and employees. Each building in turn is required to have its own specific procedures, based on such variables as location, design, and state law.

Source: U.S. Occupational Safety and Health Administration, 2007 <www.osha.gov>.

☑ Checklist: Usability of Instructions

Use this checklist to evaluate the usability of instructions. (Numbers in parentheses refer to the first page of discussion.)

Content

☐ Does the title promise exactly what the instructions deliver? (495)

☐ Is the background adequate for the intended audience? (496)

☐ Do explanations enable users to understand what to do? (496)

☐ Do examples enable users to see how to do it correctly? (496)

☐ Are the definition and purpose of each step given as needed? (508)

☐ Is all needless information omitted? (501)

☐ Are all obvious steps omitted? (501)

☐ Do notes, cautions, or warnings appear whenever needed, before or with the step? (502)

☐ Is the information rate appropriate for the user's abilities and the difficulty of this procedure? (501)

☐ Are visuals adequate for clarifying the steps? (496)

☐ Do visuals repeat prose information whenever necessary? (506)

☐ Is everything accurate? (495)

Organization

☐ Is the introduction adequate without being excessive? (507)

☐ Do the instructions follow the exact sequence of steps? (502)

☐ Is each step numbered, if appropriate? (505)

☐ Is all the information for a particular step close together? (506)

☐ For a complex step, does each sentence begin on a new line? (508)

☐ For lengthy instructions, is a layered approach, with a brief reference card, more appropriate? (506)

☐ Is the conclusion necessary and, if necessary, adequate? (508)

Style

☐ Does the familiar material appear *first* in each sentence? (504)

☐ Do steps generally have short sentences? (504)

☐ Does each step begin with an action verb? (503)

☐ Are all steps in the active voice and imperative mood? (503)

☐ Do all steps have parallel phrasing? (504)

☐ Are transitions adequate for marking time and sequence? (505)

Page Design

☐ Does each heading clearly tell users what to expect? (505)

☐ On a typed page, are steps single-spaced within, and double-spaced between? (505)

☐ Is the overall design simple and accessible? (506)

☐ Are notes, cautions, or warnings set off or highlighted? (506)

☐ Are visuals beside or near the step, and set off by white space? (506)

Exercises

1. Improve readability by revising the diction, voice, and design of these instructions.

   What to Do Before Jacking Up Your Car
   Whenever the misfortune of a flat tire occurs, some basic procedures should be followed before the car is jacked up. If possible, your car should be positioned on as firm and level a surface as is available. The engine has to be turned off; the parking brake should be set; and the automatic transmission shift lever must be placed in "park" or the manual transmission lever in "reverse." The wheel diagonally opposite the one to be removed should have a piece of wood placed beneath it to prevent the wheel from rolling. The spare wheel, jack, and lug wrench should be removed from the luggage compartment.

2. Select part of a technical manual in your field or instructions for a general audience and make a copy of the material. Using the checklist on page 517, evaluate the sample's usability. In a memo to your instructor, discuss the strong and weak points of the instructions. Or be prepared to explain in class why the sample is effective or ineffective.

3. Assume that colleagues or classmates will be serving six months as volunteers in agriculture, education, or a similar capacity in a developing country. Do the research and create a set of procedures that will prepare users for avoiding diseases and dealing with medical issues in that specific country. Topics might include safe food and water, insect protection, vaccinations, medical emergencies, and the like. Be sure to provide background on the specific health risks travelers will face. Design your instructions as a two-sided brief reference card, as a chapter to be included in a longer manual, or in some other format suggested by your instructor.

   Hint: Begin your research for this project by checking out the National Center for Disease Control's Web site at <www.cdc.gov/travel/>.

4. Choose a topic from the following list, your major, or an area of interest. Using the general outline in this chapter as a model, outline instructions for a task that requires at least three major steps. Address a general audience, and begin by completing an audience and use profile. Include (a) all necessary visuals, (b) an "art brief" (page 278) and a rough diagram for each visual, or (c) a "reference visual" (a copy of a visual published elsewhere) with instructions for adapting your visual from that one. (If you borrow visuals from other sources, provide full documentation.)

planting a tree	hitting a golf ball
hot-waxing skis	removing the rear
hanging wallpaper	wheel of a bicycle
filleting a fish	avoiding hypothermia

5. Assume that you are assistant to the communications manager for a manufacturer of outdoor products. Among the company's best-selling items are its various models of gas grills. Because of fire and explosion hazards, all grills must be accompanied by detailed instructions for safe assembly, use, and maintenance.

   One of the first procedures in the manual is the "leak test," to ensure that the gas supply-and-transport apparatus is leak free. One of the engineers has prepared the instructions in Figure 22.13. Before being published in the manual, they must be approved by communications management. Your boss directs you to evaluate the instructions for accuracy, completeness, clarity, and appropriateness, and to report your findings in a memo. Because of the legal implications, your evaluation must spell out all positive and negative details of content, organization, style, and design. (Use the checklist on page 517 as a guide.) The boss is busy and impatient, and expects your report to be no longer than two pages. Do the evaluation and write the memo.

6. Select any one of the instructional visuals in Figure 22.5 and write a prose version of those instructions—without using visual illustrations or special page design. Bring your version to class and be prepared to discuss the conclusions you've derived from this exercise.

Tank must be filled prior to this step (See "Propane Tank" section for details about filling this tank)

Leak Test Check List

- Tank valve (all over) including area that screws into the tank
- Regulator fitting
- Hose connections (3 places)
- Valves (4 places)

SAFETY!

All models must be Leak Tested! Take the hose, valve, and regulator assembly outdoors in a well ventilated area. Keep away from open flames or sparks. Do Not smoke during this test. Use only a soap and water solution to test for leaks.

1. Have propane tank filled with propane gas only by a reputable propane gas dealer.
2. Attach regulator fitting to tank valve.
   - Regulator fitting has left-hand threads. Turn counterclockwise to attach.
3. Tighten regulator fitting securely with wrench.
4. Place the two matching control knobs onto the valve stems.
5. Turn the control knobs to the right, clockwise. This is the **"Off"** position.
6. Make a solution of half liquid detergent and half water.
7. Turn gas supply "ON" at the tank valve (counterclockwise).
8. Brush soapy mixture on all connections listed in the **Leak Test Check List**.
9. Observe each place for bubbles caused by leaks.
10. Tighten any leaking connections, if possible.
    - If leak cannot be stopped. **Do Not Use Those Parts!** Order new parts.
11. Turn gas supply **"Off"** at the tank valve.
12. Push in and turn control knobs to the left ("HI" position) to release pressure in hose.
13. Disconnect the regulator fitting from the tank valve.
    - Regulator fitting has left-hand threads. Turn fitting clockwise to disconnect.
14. Leave tank outdoors and return to the grill assembly with valve, hose, and regulator.

FIGURE 22.13 Instructions for Leak Testing a Grill

Source: Instructions reprinted by permission of Thermos® Division.

7. Find a set of instructions or some other technical document that is easy to use. Assume that you are Associate Director of Communications for the company that produced this document and you are doing a final review before the document is released. With the checklist for usability as a guide, identify those features that make the document usable and prepare a memo to your boss that justifies your decision to release the document.

   Following the identical scenario, find a document that is hard to use, and identify the features that need improving. Prepare a memo to your boss that spells out the needed improvements. Submit both memos and the examples to your instructor.

Collaborative Projects

1. Draw a map of the route from your classroom to your dorm, apartment, or home—whichever is closest. Be sure to include identifying landmarks. When your map is completed, write instructions for a classmate who will try to duplicate your map from the information given in your written instructions. Be sure your classmate does not see your map! Exchange your instructions and try to duplicate your classmate's map. Compare your results with the original map. Discuss your conclusions about the usability of these instructions.

2. Divide into small groups and visit your computer center, library, or any place on campus or at work where you can find operating manuals for computers, lab or office equipment, or the like. (Or look through the documentation for your own computer hardware or software.) Locate fairly brief instructions that could use revision for improved content, organization, style, or format. Choose instructions for a procedure you are able to carry out. Make a copy of the instructions, test them for usability, and revise as needed. Submit all materials to your instructor, along with a memo explaining the improvements. Or be prepared to discuss your revision in class.

3. Test the usability of a document prepared for this course.

   a. As a basis for your *alpha test*, adapt the Audience and Use Profile Sheet on page 35, the general checklist for usability (43), and whichever specific checklist applies to this particular document (as on page 517, for example).

   b. As a basis for your *beta test*, adapt the Usability Survey on page 513.

   c. Revise the document based on your findings. Obtain your data qualitatively, through focus group discussions and/or protocol analysis.

   Appoint a group member to explain the usability testing procedure and the results to the class.

4. Working in small groups, revise Figure 22.14 for improved usability. Appoint one member to present your group's version to the class, explaining the specific criteria used for revision.

Service-Learning Project

Do the research and prepare a set of instructions that will show general readers how to become more environmentally informed consumers and how to find, identify, evaluate, and compare environmentally friendly consumer goods such as appliances, building materials, and household products. Design your instructions as a foldout brochure (page 492) or a one-page (double-sided) handout, or in a format requested by your instructor. *Hint:* Begin your research by checking out the following Web sites:

- *The Environment at MIT Goods* at <http://tbe.mit.edu/environment/reduce/env_living.html/>
- The U.S. Environmental Protection Agency's *Energy Star* site at <http://www.energystar.gov>
- *Shopping tips for the Ethical consumer* site at <www.ethicalconsumer.org/aboutec/tentips.html>
- *Green Marketplace* at <www.greenmarketplace.com>

Proper Care Gives Safer Wear

- Follow, and save, the directions that come with your lenses. If you didn't get a patient information booklet about your lenses, request it from your eye-care practitioner.

- Use only the types of lens-care enzyme cleaners and saline solutions your practitioner okays.

- Be exact in following the directions that come with each lens-care product. If you have questions, ask your practitioner or pharmacist.

- Wash and rinse your hands before handling lenses. Fragrance-free soap is best.

- Clean, rinse, and disinfect reusable lenses each time they're removed, even if this is several times a day.

- Clean, rinse, and disinfect again if storage lasts longer than allowed by your disinfecting solution.

- Clean, rinse, and air-dry the lens case each time you remove the lenses. Then put in fresh solution. Replace the case every six months.

- Get your practitioner's okay before taking medicines or using topical eye products, even those you buy without a prescription.

- Remove your lenses and call your practitioner right away if you have vision changes, redness of the eye, eye discomfort or pain, or excessive tearing.

- Visit your practitioner every six months (more often if needed) to catch possible problems early.

Caring for Contact Lenses

Clean — Remove surface dirt

Rinse — Rinse away dirt

Enzyme — Remove deep deposits

Disinfect/Store — Eliminate bacteria

Rinse — Rinse dirt away

Wet — Prepare lens surface

Insert

Lubricate/Rewet

Clean Lens Case

Watch Out:

- Never use saliva to wet your lenses.

- Never use tap water, distilled water, or saline solution made at home with salt tablets for any part of your lens care. Use only commercial sterile saline solution.

- Never mix different brands of cleaner or solution.

- Never change your lens-care regimen or products without your practitioner's okay.

- Never let cosmetic lotions, creams, or sprays touch your lenses.

- Never wear lenses when swimming or in a hot tub.

- Never wear daily-wear lenses during sleep, not even a nap.

- Never wear your lenses longer than prescribed by your eye-care practitioner. ■

FIGURE 22.14 Procedure for Caring for Contact Lenses

Source: Farley, Dixie. "Keeping an Eye on Contact Lenses." *FDA Consumer* Mar.–Apr. 1998: 17–21.

CHAPTER 23

Proposals

How Proposals and Reports Differ in Purpose

The Proposal Audience

The Proposal Process

Proposal Types

Elements of a Persuasive Proposal

An Outline and Model for Proposals

A Situation Requiring a Proposal

   Checklist: Usability of Proposals

Proposals attempt to *persuade* an audience to take some form of action: to authorize a project, accept a service or product, or otherwise support a specific plan for solving a problem or improving a situation.

Your own proposal might consist of a letter to your school board to suggest changes in the English curriculum; it may be a memo to your firm's vice president to request funding for a training program for new employees; or it may be an extensive document to the Defense Department to bid on a guided-missile contract (competing with proposals from other firms). As a student or as an intern at a nonprofit agency, you might submit a *grant proposal*, requesting financial support for a research or community project.

You might work alone or collaboratively, as part of a team. Developing and writing the proposal might take hours or months. If your job depends on funding from outside sources, proposals might be the most important documents you produce.

How Proposals and Reports Differ in Purpose

While they may contain many of the same basic elements as a report, proposals have a primarily *persuasive* purpose: to move people to say "Yes. Let's move ahead on this." Of course, reports can also contain persuasive elements, as in recommending a specific course of action or justifying an equipment purchase. But reports typically serve a variety of *informative* purposes as well—such as keeping track of progress, explaining why something happened, or predicting an outcome.

Proposals rely on persuasion

A report often precedes a proposal: for example, a report on high levels of chemical pollution in a major waterway typically leads to various proposals for cleaning up that waterway. In short, once the report has *explored* a particular need, a proposal will be developed to *sell* the idea for meeting that need.

The Proposal Audience

In science, business, government, or education, proposals are written for decision makers: managers, executives, directors, clients, board members, or community leaders. Inside or outside your organization, these people review various proposals and then decide whether a specific plan is worthwhile, whether the project will materialize, or whether the service or product is useful.

Before accepting a particular proposal, reviewers look for persuasive answers to these basic questions:

What proposal reviewers want to know

- What exactly is the problem or need, and why is this such a big deal?
- Why should we spend time, money, and effort on this?
- What exactly is your plan, and how do we know it is feasible?

> • Why should we accept the items that seem wrong or costly about your plan?
>
> • What action are we supposed to take?

Connect with your audience by addressing the previous questions early and systematically. Here are the tasks involved:

A proposal
involves
these basic
persuasive tasks

1. **Spell out the problem (and its causes) clearly and convincingly.** Supply enough detail for your audience to appreciate the problem's importance.
2. **Point out the benefits of solving the problem.** Explain specifically to your readers what they stand to gain.
3. **Offer a realistic, cost-effective solution.** Stick to claims or assertions you can support. (For more on feasibility, see pages 338 and 563.)
4. **Address anticipated objections to your solution.** Consider carefully your audience's level of skepticism about this issue.
5. **Induce your audience to act.** Decide exactly what you want your readers to do and give reasons why they should be the ones to take action.

Pages 534–39 offer examples and strategies for completing each of these tasks.

The Proposal Process

Proposals in
the commercial
sector

Stages in the
proposal process

The basic proposal process can be summarized like this: someone offers a plan for something that needs to be done. This process has three stages:

1. Client X needs a service or product.
2. Firms A, B, and C propose a plan for meeting the need.
3. Client X awards the job to the firm offering the best proposal.

Following is a typical scenario.

CASE: Submitting a Competitive Proposal

You manage a mining engineering firm in Tulsa, Oklahoma. You regularly read the *Commerce Business Daily*, an essential online reference tool for anyone whose firm seeks government contracts. This publication lists the government's latest needs for services (salvage, engineering, maintenance) and for *supplies*, *equipment,* and *materials* (guided missiles, engine parts, and so on). On Wednesday, February 19, you spot this announcement:

> **Development of Alternative Solutions to Acid Mine Water Contamination from Abandoned Lead and Zinc Mines** near Tar Creek, Neosho River, Ground Lake, and the Boone and Roubidoux aquifers in northeastern Oklahoma. This will include assessment of environmental effects of mine drainage followed by development and evaluation of alternate solutions to alleviate acid mine drainage in receiving streams. An optional portion of the contract to be bid on as an add-on and awarded at the discretion of the OWRB will be to prepare an Environmental Impact Assessment for each of three

alternative solutions as selected by the OWRB. The project is expected to take six months to accomplish, with an anticipated completion date of September 30, 20XX. The projected effort for the required task is thirty person-months. The request for proposal is available at www.owrb.gov. Proposals are due March 1.

Oklahoma Water Resources Board
P.O. Box 53585
1000 Northeast 10th Street
Oklahoma City, OK 73151
(405) 555–2541

 RFPs and how to respond

Your firm has the personnel, experience, and time to do the job, so you decide to compete for the contract. Because the March 1 deadline is fast approaching, you immediately download the request for proposal (RFP). The RFP will give you the guidelines for developing and submitting the proposal—guidelines for spelling out your plan to solve the problem (methods, timetables, costs).

You then get right to work with the two staff engineers you have appointed to your proposal team. Because the credentials of your staff could affect the client's acceptance of the proposal, you ask team members to update their résumés for inclusion in an appendix to the proposal.

In situations like the one above, the client will award the contract to the firm submitting the best proposal, based on the following criteria (and perhaps others):

Criteria by which reviewers evaluate proposals

- understanding of the client's needs, as described in the RFP
- clarity and feasibility of the plan being offered
- quality of the project's organization and management
- ability to complete the job by deadline
- ability to control costs
- firm's experience on similar projects
- qualifications of staff to be assigned to the project
- firm's record for similar projects

A client's specific evaluation criteria are often listed (in order of importance or on a point scale) in the RFP. Although these criteria may vary, every client expects a proposal that is *clear*, *informative*, and *realistic*.

Proposals in the nonprofit sector

In contrast to proposals prepared for commercial purposes, museums, community service groups, and other nonprofit organizations prepare *grant proposals* that request financial support for worthwhile causes. Government and charitable granting agencies such as the Department of Health and Human Services, the Department of Agriculture, or the Pugh Charitable Trust solicit proposals for funding in areas such as medical research, educational TV programming, and rural development. Submission and review of grant proposals follow the same basic process used for commercial proposals. Figure 23.1 shows part of a request for funding proposals. This RFP was issued by a U.S. government health organization.

Submitting paperless proposals

In both the commercial and nonprofit sectors, the proposal process increasingly occurs online. The National Science Foundation's *Fastlane* Web site

Examples of electronic proposals

<www.fastlane.nsf.gov>, for example, allows grant applicants to submit proposals in electronic format. This enables applicants to include sophisticated graphics, to revise budget estimates, to update other aspects of the plan as needed, and to maintain real-time contact with the granting agency while the proposal is being reviewed.

Proposal Types

Proposal types classified by origin

Proposals are classified according to *origin*, *audience*, and *purpose*. Based on its origin, a proposal is either *solicited* or *unsolicited*. Solicited proposals are those requested by a potential client or your employer, as in the engineering firm example on page 524. Unsolicited proposals are not specifically requested. For example, if you are creating a new Web site development service in your town, you might send out short proposals to area businesses, to suggest methods for online advertising and sales.

RFP No. NIH-NHLBI-HR-01-01

"Clinical Centers for the Clinical Network for the Treatment of the Adult Respiratory Distress Syndrome (ARDS)"

The National Heart, Lung, and Blood Institute (NHLBI) is soliciting proposals for clinical centers to participate in the "Clinical Centers for the Clinical Network for the Treatment of the Adult Respiratory Distress Syndrome (ARDS)." The objective of ARDSnet is to test novel therapies for the prevention and treatment of adult respiratory distress syndrome and acute lung injury (ARDS/ALI). The ARDSnet has developed a protocol to test the role of the pulmonary artery catheter (PAC) in the clinical management of ARDS/ALI. The ARDSnet investigators and NHLBI staff have determined that enrollment in the protocol will be challenging and that additional sites are required to complete this protocol in a reasonable time frame. It is anticipated that this solicitation will award up to ten (10) additional Critical Care Treatment Groups (CCTG) to participate in the *PAC protocol*. Each new CCTG will enroll approximately 30 patients/year during Phase II (24 months).

FIGURE 23.1 Request for Proposal The complete, 44-page RFP includes a project history and background. It also stipulates the types, frequency, and format of reports required, completion dates for various phases of the project, guidelines for submitting the proposal, and additional evaluation factors (such as the diversity of people in the study population and the proposal offeror's record of performance on past projects).

Source: Adapted from the National Institutes of Health Archive <www.nhlbi.nih.gov/funding/inits.archive>.

STATEMENT OF WORK

Independently, and not as an agent of the Government, the contractor shall furnish all the necessary services, qualified personnel, material, equipment, and facilities, not otherwise provided by the Government as needed to perform the statement of work below. Specifically, the contractor shall:

Train a staff to conduct the Pulmonary Artery Catheter (PAC) study as outlined in the protocol and manual of operations.

Participate with other study investigators in a clinical study of the PAC in the treatment of Acute Respiratory Distress Syndrome (ARDS) and Acute Lung Injury (ALI) according to the protocol and manual of operations. The protocol, manual of operations and any amendments thereto are incorporated herein, by reference, as part of the contract.

Enroll and treat a minimum of 30 patients, 13 years of age or older, with ARDS or ALI according to the PAC protocol. The patients will have a gender and racial composition similar to the population of patients that are available for study.

Perform follow-up assessment on the subjects in the manner specified in the manual of operations.

Collect the subject data as specified by the protocol and forward the data to the Clinical Coordinating Center (CCC) in accordance with procedures in the manual of operations.

Participate in the Steering Committee to monitor progress on the study.

Interact with the CCC to provide data and information necessary for data analysis work with other study investigators in the preparation and writing of reports and manuscripts for publication.

Work with other study investigators in the preparation and writing of reports and manuscripts for publication.

FIGURE 23.1 (*Continued*)

Proposal types classified by audience

Proposal types classified by purpose

Based on its audience, a proposal may be *internal* or *external*—written for members of your organization or for clients and funding agencies. (The situation in the case on page 524 calls for an external proposal.)

Based on its purpose, a proposal may be a *planning*, *research*, or *sales* proposal. This last classification by no means accounts for all variations among proposals, but these purposes are most common. Some proposals may in fact fall within all three of these categories. A discussion of each type begins on page 528.

TECHNICAL EVALUATION CRITERIA

Proposals submitted in response to this solicitation will be reviewed by a peer group of scientists under the auspices of the Review Branch, Division of Extramural Affairs, NHLBI, and subsequently by a review group within NHLBI. The evaluation criteria are used by the Technical Evaluation Committee when reviewing the technical proposals. The criteria below are listed in the order of relative importance with weights assigned for evaluation purposes.

Weight	Criterion
40%	Ability to enroll 30 patients with ARDS/ALI per year. Offerors shall describe their previous experience enrolling patients with ARDS or patients at risk of developing ARDS into multi-center treatment trials. If previous enrollment has been less than 30 patients a year, practical procedures must be proposed to identify and screen adequate numbers of prospective subjects.
30%	Adequacy of experience and competence of the professional and technical staff pertinent to the study, including experience in clinical studies of ARDS. In particular, the PI is expected to be expert in the treatment of critically ill patients with ARDS and also to have previously participated in multi-center treatment trials.
30%	Adequacy of laboratory/clinical facilities available, including all participating institutions. Description of the facilities and means of assuring quality control of patient care. Adequacy of plans for study coordination, including quality control of data entry.

FIGURE 23.1 (*Continued*)

Planning Proposal

The purpose of a planning proposal is to provide solutions to a problem or suggestions for improvement. Typical subjects of a planning proposal might take the form of a request for funding to expand the campus newspaper, an architectural plan for new facilities at a ski area, or a plan to develop energy alternatives to fossil fuels.

CASE: Developing a Planning Proposal

The XYZ Corporation has contracted a team of communication consultants to design in-house writing workshops, and the consultants must persuade the client (the company's education officer) that their methods will succeed. After briefly introducing the problem, the authors develop their proposal under two headings and several subheadings, making the document easy to read and to the point. Because this proposal is external, it takes the form of a letter (Figure 23.2).

States purpose

Identifies problem

Proposes solution

Details what
will be done

Details how it will
be done

Dear Mary:

Thanks for sending the writing samples from your technical support staff. Here is what we're doing to design a targeted approach.

Needs Assessment

After conferring with technicians in both Jack's and Terry's groups and analyzing their writing samples, we identified this hierarchy of needs:

- improving readability
- achieving precise diction
- summarizing information
- organizing a set of procedures
- formulating various memo reports
- analyzing audiences for upward communication
- writing persuasive bids for transfer or promotion
- writing persuasive suggestions

Proposed Plan

Based on the needs listed above, we have limited our instruction package to seven carefully selected and readily achievable goals.

Course Outline.   Each three-hour session is structured as follows:

1. achieving sentence clarity and conciseness
2. achieving fluency and precise diction
3. writing summaries and abstracts
4. outlining manuals and procedures
5. editing manuals and procedures
6. designing various reports for various purposes
7. analyzing the audience and writing persuasively

Classroom Format.   The first three meetings will be lecture-intensive with weekly exercises to be done at home and edited in class. The remaining four weeks will combine lectures and exercises with group

FIGURE 23.2 A Planning Proposal

Sets realistic expectations **Encourages reader response**	editing of work-related documents. We also plan to remain flexible so we can respond to needs that arise. **Limitations** Given our limited contact time, we cannot realistically expect to turn out a batch of polished communicators. By the end of the course, however, our students will have begun to appreciate writing as a deliberate process. If you have any suggestions for refining this plan, please let us know.

FIGURE 23.2 (*Continued*)

Notice that the word choice ("thanks," "what we're doing," "Jack and Terry") creates an informal, familiar tone—appropriate in this external document only because the consultants and client have spent many hours in conferences, luncheons, and phone conversations. Notice also that the "Limitations" section indicates that these authors are careful to promise no more than they can deliver.

Research Proposal

Research (or grant) proposals request approval (and often funding) for some type of study. A university chemist might address a research proposal to the Environmental Protection Agency for funds to identify toxic contaminants in local groundwater. Research proposals are solicited by many government and private agencies: National Science Foundation, National Institutes of Health, and others. Each granting agency has its own requirements and guidelines for proposal format and content. Successful research proposals follow those guidelines and carefully articulate the goals of the project.

Other research proposals might be submitted by students requesting funds or approval for independent study, field study, or a thesis project. A technical communication student usually submits a relatively brief research proposal that will lead to the term project (See, for example, the formal funding (or grant) proposal that begins on page 546 or the analytical report that begins on page 585).

CASE: Developing a Research Proposal

Tom Dewoody requests his instructor's authorization to do a feasibility study (Chapter 24) that will produce an analytical report for potential investors. Dewoody's proposal clearly answers the questions about *what, why, how, when,* and *where.* Because this proposal is internal, it is cast informally as a memo (Figure 23.3).

To: Dr. John Lannon
From: T. Sorrells Dewoody
Date: March 16, 20XX
Subject: *Proposal for Determining the Feasibility of Marketing Dead Western White Pine*

Introduction

Over the past four decades, huge losses of western white pine have occurred in the northern Rockies, primarily attributable to white pine blister rust and the attack of the mountain pine beetle. Estimated annual mortality is 318 million board feet. Because of the low natural resistance of white pine to blister rust, this high mortality rate is expected to continue indefinitely.

If white pine is not harvested while the tree is dying or soon after death, the wood begins to dry and check (warp and crack). The sapwood is discolored by blue stain, a fungus carried by the mountain pine beetle. If the white pine continues to stand after death, heart cracks develop. These factors work together to cause degradation of the lumber and consequent loss in value.

Statement of Problem

White pine mortality reduces the value of white pine stumpage because the commercial lumber market will not accept dead wood. The major implications of this problem are two: first, in the face of rising demand for wood, vast amounts of timber lie unused; second, dead trees are left to accumulate in the woods, where they are rapidly becoming a major fire hazard here in northern Idaho and elsewhere.

Proposed Solution

One possible solution to the problem of white pine mortality and waste is to search for markets other than the conventional lumber market. The last few years have seen a burst of popularity and growing demand for weathered barn boards and wormy pine for interior paneling. Some firms around the country are marketing defective wood as specialty products. (These firms call the wood from which their products come "distressed," a term I will use hereafter to refer to dead and defective white pine.) Distressed white pine quite possibly will find a place in such a market.

Scope

To assess the feasibility of developing a market for distressed white pine, I plan to pursue six areas of inquiry:

Opens with background and causes of the problem

Describes problem

Describes one possible solution

Defines scope of the proposed study

FIGURE 23.3 A Research Proposal

1. What products presently are being produced from dead wood, and what are the approximate costs of production?
2. How large is the demand for distressed-wood products?
3. Can distressed white pine meet this demand as well as other species meet it?
4. Does the market contain room for distressed white pine?
5. What are the costs of retrieving and milling distressed white pine?
6. What prices for the products can the market bear?

Methods

My primary data sources will include consultations with Dr. James Hill, Professor of Wood Utilization, and Dr. Sven Bergman, Forest Economist—both members of the College of Forestry, Wildlife, and Range. I will also inspect decks of dead white pine at several locations and visit a processing mill to evaluate it as a possible base of operations. I will round out my primary research with a letter and telephone survey of processors and wholesalers of distressed material.

Secondary sources will include publications on the uses of dead timber, and a review of a study by Dr. Hill on the uses of dead white pine.

My Qualifications

I have been following Dr. Hill's study on dead white pine for two years. In June of this year I will receive my B.S. in forest management. I am familiar with wood milling processes and have firsthand experience at logging. My association with Drs. Hill and Bergman gives me the opportunity for an in-depth feasibility study.

Conclusion

Clearly, action is needed to reduce the vast accumulations of dead white pine in our forests—among the most productive forests in northern Idaho. By addressing the six areas of inquiry mentioned earlier, I can determine the feasibility of directing capital and labor to the production of distressed white pine products. With your approval I will begin research at once.

Describes how study will be done

Mentions literature review

Cites a major reference and gives the writer's qualifications for this project

Encourages reader acceptance

FIGURE 23.3 *(Continued)*

Sales Proposal

The sales proposal is a marketing tool that offers a service or product. The offer may be solicited or unsolicited. If the proposal is solicited, several firms may be competing for the contract, so your proposal may be ranked against others by a committee. Because sales proposals are addressed to readers outside your organization, they are cast as letters if they are brief (as on page 533). Long sales proposals, like long reports, are formal documents with supplements (cover letter, title page, table of contents). A successful sales proposal persuades customers that your product or service surpasses those offered by competitors.

CASE: Developing a Sales Proposal

Frank Castellano uses this proposal letter (Figure 23.4) to explain why his machinery is best for the job, how the job can be done efficiently, what qualifications his company can offer, and what costs are involved. To protect himself from shouldering unexpected expenses, he points out one variable (subsurface ledge) that might increase costs.

Describes the subject and purpose

Gives the writer's qualifications

Explains how the job will be done

Maintains a confident tone throughout

Gives a qualified cost estimate

Encourages reader acceptance by emphasizing economy and efficiency

Subject: *Proposal to Dig a Trench and Move Boulders at Bliss Site*

Dear Mr. Haver:

I've inspected your property and would be happy to undertake the landscaping project necessary for the development of your farm.

The backhoe I use cuts a span 3 feet wide and can dig as deep as 18 feet—more than an adequate depth for the mainline pipe you wish to lay. Because this backhoe is on tracks rather than tires, and is hydraulically operated, it is particularly efficient in moving rocks. I have more than twelve years of experience with backhoe work and have completed many jobs similar to this one.

After examining the huge boulders that block access to your property, I am convinced they can be moved only if I dig out underneath and exert upward pressure with the hydraulic ram while you push forward on the boulders with your D-9 Caterpillar. With this method, we can move enough rock to enable you to farm that now inaccessible tract. Because of its power, my larger backhoe will save you both time and money in the long run.

This job should take 12 to 15 hours, unless we encounter subsurface ledge formations. My fee is $200 per hour. The fact that I provide my own dynamiting crew at no extra charge should be an advantage to you because you have so much rock to be moved.

Please phone me anytime for more information. I'm sure we can do the job economically and efficiently.

FIGURE 23.4 A Sales Proposal

NOTE   *Never underestimate costs by failing to account for, and acknowledge all, variables—a sure way to lose money or clients.*

The proposal categories (planning, research, and sales) discussed in this section are neither exhaustive nor mutually exclusive. A research proposal, for example, may request funds for a study that will lead to a planning proposal. The Vista proposal partially shown below combines planning and sales features; if clients accept the preliminary plan, they will hire the firm to install the automated system.

Elements of a Persuasive Proposal

Proposal reviewers expect a clear, informative, and realistic presentation. They will evaluate your proposal on the basis of the following quality indicators. (See also the criteria listed on page 525.)

A Forecasting Title

Overworked reviewers facing a stack of proposals might very well decide to focus on those "with the most intriguing titles" (Friedland and Folt 53). In any case, your title should clearly announce the proposal's purpose and content. Don't be vague.

Unclear

> Proposed Office Procedures for Vista Freight, Inc.

Revised

> A Proposal for Automating Vista's Freight Billing System

Don't write "Recommended Improvements" when you mean "Recommended Wastewater Treatment."

Clear Understanding of the Audience's Needs

Focus on the problem and the objective

The proposal audience wants specific suggestions for meeting their specific needs. Their biggest question is "What will this plan do for me?" Show that you clearly understand your clients' problems and their expectations, and then offer an appropriate solution.

In the following proposal for automating office procedures at Vista, Inc., Gerald Beaulieu begins with a clear assessment of needs and then moves quickly into a proposed plan of action.

Gives background

> **Statement of the Problem**
> Vista provides two services. (1) It locates freight carriers for its clients. The carriers, in turn, pay Vista a 6 percent commission for each referral. (2) Vista handles all shipping paperwork for its clients. For this auditing service, clients pay Vista a monthly retainer.

Describes problem
and its effects

Although Vista's business has increased steadily for the past three years, record keeping, accounting, and other paperwork are still done manually. These inefficient procedures have caused a number of problems, including late billings, lost commissions, and poor account maintenance. Updated office procedures seem crucial to competitiveness and continued growth.

A clear statement of
what is being
proposed enables
readers to visualize
the results

Objective
This proposal offers a realistic and effective plan for streamlining Vista's office procedures. We first identify the burden imposed on your staff by the current system, and then we show how to reduce inefficiency, eliminate client complaints, and improve your cash flow by automating most office procedures.

A Clear Focus on Benefits

Spell out
the benefits

Do a detailed audience analysis to identify readers' major concerns and to anticipate likely questions and objections. Show your audience that you understand what they (or their organization) will gain by adopting your plan. The following bulleted list spells out exactly what tasks Vista employees will be able to accomplish once the proposed plan is implemented.

Relates benefits
directly to client's
needs

Once your automated system is operational, you will be able to

- identify cost-effective carriers
- coordinate shipments (which will ensure substantial client discounts)
- print commission bills
- track shipments by weight, miles, fuel costs, and destination
- send clients weekly audit reports on their shipments
- bill clients on a 25-day cycle
- produce weekly or monthly reports

Additional benefits include eliminating repetitive tasks, improving cash flow, and increasing productivity.

(Each of these benefits will be described at length later in the "Plan" section.)

Honest and Supportable Claims

Promise only
what you can
deliver

Because they typically involve large sums of money as well as contractual obligations, proposals require a solid ethical and legal foundation. Clients in these situations often have doubts or objections about time and financial costs and a host of other risks involved whenever any important project is undertaken. Your proposal needs to address these issues openly and honestly. For example, if you are proposing to install customized virus-protection software, be clear about what this software cannot accomplish under certain circumstances. False or exaggerated promises not only damage a writer's or a company's reputation, but also invite lawsuits. (For more on supporting your claims, see page 60.)

WEBLINK Ethics in
proposals

Here is how the Vista proposal qualifies its promises:

Anticipates a major objection and offers a realistic approach

> As countless firms have learned, imposing automated procedures on employees can create severe morale problems—particularly among senior staff who feel coerced and often marginalized. To diminish employee resistance, we suggest that your entire staff be invited to comment on this proposal. To help avoid hardware and software problems once the system is operational, we have included recommendations and a budget for staff training. (Adequate training is essential to the automation process.)

If the best available solutions have limitations, say so. Notice how the above solutions are qualified ("diminish" and "help avoid" instead of "eliminate") so as not to promise more than the plan can achieve.

A proposal can be judged fraudulent if it misleads potential clients by

Major ethical and legal violations in a proposal

- making unsupported claims,
- ignoring anticipated technical problems, or
- knowingly underestimating costs or time requirements.

For a project involving complex tasks or phases, provide a realistic timetable (perhaps using a Gantt chart, page 272) to show when each major phase will begin and end. Also provide a realistic, accurate budget, with a detailed cost breakdown (for supplies and equipment, travel, research costs, outside contractors, or the like) to show clients exactly how the money is being spent. For a sample breakdown of costs, see the construction repair proposal (Figure 18.1).

NOTE *Be absolutely certain that you spend every dollar according to the allocations that have been stipulated. For example, if a grant award allocates a certain amount for "a research assistant," be sure to spend that exact amount for that exact purpose—unless you receive written permission from the granting agency to shift funds for other purposes. Keep strict accounting of all the money you spend. Proposal experts Friedland and Folt remind us that "Financial misconduct is never tolerated, regardless of intent" (161). Even an innocent mistake or accounting lapse on your part can lead to charges of fraud.*

Appropriate Detail

Provide adequate but not excessive detail

Vagueness in a proposal is fatal. Spell everything out. Instead of writing, "We will install state-of-the-art equipment," enumerate the products or services to be provided.

Spells out what will be provided

> To meet your automation requirements, we will install twelve Power Macintosh G4 computers with 60-Gigabyte hard drives. The system will be networked for rapid file transfer between offices. The plan also includes interconnection with four Hewlett-Packard 5 MP printers, and one HP Desk Jet 1600 CM color printer.

To avoid misunderstandings that could produce legal complications, a proposal must elicit *one* interpretation only.

Place support material (maps, blueprints, specifications, calculations) in an appendix so as not to interrupt the discussion.

NOTE *While concrete and specific detail is vital, never overburden reviewers with needless material. A precise audience analysis (Chapter 3) can pinpoint specific information needs.*

Readability

Make the proposal inviting and easy to understand

A readable proposal is straightforward, easy to follow, and understandable. Avoid language that is overblown or too technical for your audience. Review Chapter 13 for style strategies.

Convincing Language

Sell your ideas

Your proposal should move people to action. Review Chapter 4 for persuasion guidelines. Keep your tone confident and encouraging, not bossy and critical. For more on tone, see pages 238–46.

Visuals

Emphasize key points in your proposal with relevant tables, flowcharts, and other visuals (Chapter 14), properly introduced and discussed.

Gives a framework for interpreting the visual

As the flowchart (Figure 1) illustrates, Vista's routing and billing system creates redundant work for your staff. The routing sheet alone is handled at least six times. Such extensive handling leads to errors, misplaced paperwork, and late billing.

Visual repeats, restates, or reinforces the prose

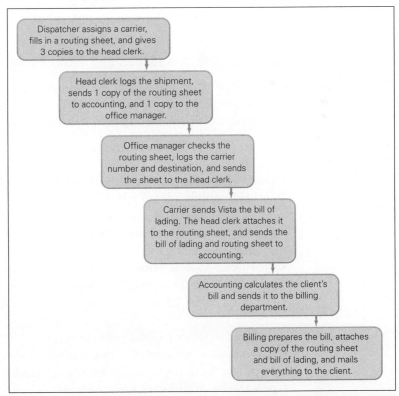

FIGURE 1 Flowchart of Vista's Manual Routing and Billing System

Accessible Page Design

Make the
audience's job
easy

Yours might be one of several proposals being reviewed. Help the audience to get in quickly, find what they need, and get out. Review Chapter 15 for design strategies.

Supplements Tailored for a Diverse Audience

Analyze the
specific needs
and interests of
each major
reviewer

A single proposal often addresses a diverse audience: executives, managers, technical experts, attorneys, politicians, and so on. Various reviewers are interested in various parts of your proposal. Experts look for the technical details. Others might be interested in the recommendations, costs, timetable, or expected results, but they will need an explanation of technical details as well.

How to give each
major reviewer
what he or she
expects

If the primary audience is expert or informed, keep the proposal text itself technical. For uninformed secondary reviewers (if any), provide an informative abstract, a glossary, and appendixes explaining specialized information. If the primary audience has no expertise and the secondary audience does, write the proposal itself for laypersons, and provide appendixes with the technical details (formulas, specifications, calculations) that experts will use to evaluate your plan. See Chapter 25 for specific supplements.

If you are unsure about which supplements to include in an internal proposal, ask the intended audience or study other proposals. For a solicited proposal (to an outside agency), follow the agency's instructions exactly.

Proper Citation of Sources and Contributors

Proposals rarely emerge from thin air. Whenever appropriate, especially for topics that involve ongoing research, you need to credit key information sources and contributors. Proposal experts Friedland and Folt offer these suggestions (22, 134–36):

How to cite
sources and
contributors

- **Review the literature on this topic.** Limit your focus to the major background studies.
- **Don't cite sources of "common knowledge" about this topic.** Information available in multiple sources or readily known in your discipline usually qualifies as common knowledge. (For more, see page 639).
- **Provide adequate support for your plan.** Cite all key sources that serve to confirm your plan's feasibility.
- **Provide up-to-date principal references.** Although references to earlier, groundbreaking studies are important, recent studies can be most essential.
- **Present a balanced, unbiased view.** Acknowledge sources that differ from or oppose your point of view; explain the key differences among the various viewpoints before making your case.
- **Give credit to all contributors.** Recognize everyone who has worked on or helped with this proposal: for example, coauthors, editors, data gatherers, and people who contributed various ideas.

Proper citation is not only an ethical requirement, but also an indicator of your proposal's feasibility. See "A Quick Guide to Documentation" (page 634) for more on citation techniques.

 Oral proposals in *PowerPoint*

An Outline and Model for Proposals

Depending on a proposal's complexity, each section contains some or all of the components listed in the following general outline:

  I. Introduction
    A. Statement of Problem and Objective/Project Overview
    B. Background and Review of the Literature (as needed)
    C. Need
    D. Benefits
    E. Qualifications of Personnel
    F. Data Sources
    G. Limitations and Contingencies
    H. Scope

 II. Plan
    A. Objectives and Methods
    B. Timetable
    C. Materials and Equipment
    D. Personnel
    E. Available Facilities
    F. Needed Facilities
    G. Cost and Budget
    H. Expected Results
    I. Feasibility

III. Conclusion
    A. Summary of Key Points
    B. Request for Action

IV. Works Cited

These components can be rearranged, combined, divided, or deleted as needed. Not every proposal will contain all components; however, each major section must persuasively address specific information needs as illustrated in the sample proposal that begins on page 540.

Introduction

From the beginning, your goal is *to sell your idea*—to demonstrate the need for the project, your qualifications for tackling the project, and your clear understanding of what needs to be done and how to proceed. Readers quickly lose interest in a wordy, evasive, or vague introduction.

Following is the introduction for a planning proposal titled "Proposal for Solving the Noise Problem in the University Library." Jill Sanders, a library work-study student, addresses her proposal to the chief librarian and the administrative staff. Because this proposal is unsolicited, it must first make the problem vivid through details that arouse concern and interest. This introduction is longer than it would be in a solicited proposal, whose audience would already agree on the severity of the problem.

NOTE   *Title page, informative abstract, table of contents, and other supplements that ordinarily accompany long proposals of this type are omitted here to save space. See Chapter 25 for discussion and examples of each type of document supplement.*

INTRODUCTION

Statement of Problem

Concise descriptions of problem and objective immediately alert the readers

During the October 20XX Convocation at Margate University, students and faculty members complained about noise in the library. Soon afterward, areas were designated for "quiet study," but complaints about noise continue. To create a scholarly atmosphere, the library should take immediate action to decrease noise.

Objective

This proposal examines the noise problem from the viewpoint of students, faculty, and library staff. It then offers a plan to make areas of the library quiet enough for serious study and research.

Sources

This section comes early because it is referred to in the next section

My data come from a university-wide questionnaire; interviews with students, faculty, and library staff; inquiry letters to other college libraries; and my own observations for three years on the library staff.

Details of the Problem

Details help readers to understand the problem

This subsection examines the severity and causes of the noise.

Severity. Since the 20XX Convocation, the library's fourth and fifth floors have been reserved for quiet study, but students hold group study sessions at the large tables and disturb others working alone. The constant use of computer terminals on both floors adds to the noise, especially when students converse. Moreover, people often chat as they enter or leave study areas.

On the second and third floors, designed for reference, staff help patrons locate materials, causing constant shuffling of people and books, as well as loud conversation. At the computer service desk on the third floor, conferences between students and instructors create more noise.

Shows how campus feels about problem

The most frequently voiced complaint from the faculty members interviewed was about the second floor, where people using the Reference and Government Documents services converse loudly. Students complain about the lack of a quiet spot to study, especially in the evening, when even the "quiet" floors are as noisy as the dorms.

Shows concern is widespread and pervasive	More than 80 percent of respondents (530 undergraduates, 30 faculty, 22 graduate students) to a university-wide questionnaire (Appendix A) insisted that excessive noise discourages them from using the library as often as they would prefer. Of the student respondents, 430 cited quiet study as their primary reason for wishing to use the library.

The library staff recognizes the problem but has insufficient personnel. Because all staff members have assigned tasks, they have no time to monitor noise in their sections. |

Causes.   Respondents complained specifically about these causes of noise (in descending order of frequency):

Identifies specific causes	1. Loud study groups that often lapse into social discussions.
2.   General disrespect for the library, with some students' attitudes characterized as "rude," "inconsiderate," or "immature."
3.   The constant clicking of computer terminals on all five floors, and of laptops on the first three.
4.   Vacuuming by the evening custodians.

All complaints converged on lack of enforcement by library staff. Because the day staff works on the first three floors, quiet-study rules are not enforced on the fourth and fifth floors. Work-study students on these floors have no authority to enforce rules not enforced by the regular staff. Small, black-and-white "Quiet Please" signs posted on all floors go unnoticed, and the evening security guard provides no deterrent.

Needs

This statement of need evolves logically and persuasively from earlier evidence	Excessive noise in the library is keeping patrons away. By addressing this problem immediately, we can help restore the library's credibility and utility as a campus resource. We must reduce noise on the lower floors and eliminate it from the quiet-study floors.

Scope

Previews the plan	The proposed plan includes a detailed assessment of methods, costs and materials, personnel requirements, feasibility, and expected results.

Body

The body (or plan section) of your proposal will receive the most audience attention. The main goal of this section is to prove your plan will work. Here you spell out your plan in enough detail for the audience to evaluate its soundness. If this section is vague, your proposal stands no chance of being accepted. Be sure your plan is realistic and that it promises no more than you can deliver.

PROPOSED PLAN

This plan takes into account the needs and wishes of our campus community, as well as the available facilities in our library.

Phases of the Plan

Noise in the library can be reduced in three complementary phases: (1) improving publicity, (2) shutting down and modifying our facilities, and (3) enforcing the quiet rules.

Improving Publicity.   First, the library must publicize the noise problem. This assertive move will demonstrate the staff's interest. Publicity could include articles by staff members in the campus newspaper, leaflets distributed on campus, and a freshman library orientation acknowledging the noise problem and asking cooperation from new students. All forms of publicity should detail the steps being taken by the library to solve the problem.

Shutting Down and Modifying Facilities.   After notifying campus and local newspapers, you should close the library for one week. To minimize disruption, the shutdown should occur between the end of summer school and the beginning of the fall term.

During this period, you can convert the fixed tables on the fourth and fifth floors to cubicles with temporary partitions (six cubicles per table). You could later convert the cubicles to shelves as the need increases.

Then you can take all unfixed tables from the upper floors to the first floor, and set up a space for group study. Plans are already under way for removing the computer terminals from the fourth and fifth floors.

Enforcing the Quiet Rules.   Enforcement is the essential long-term element in this plan. No one of any age is likely to follow all the rules all the time—unless the rules are enforced.

First, you can make new "Quiet" posters to replace the present, innocuous notices. A visual-design student can be hired to draw up large, colorful posters that attract attention. Either the design student or the university print shop can take charge of poster production.

Next, through publicity, library patrons can be encouraged to demand quiet from noisy people. To support such patron demands, the library staff can begin monitoring the fourth and fifth floors, asking study groups to move to the first floor, and revoking library privileges of those who refuse. Patrons on the second and third floors can be asked to speak in whispers. Staff members should set an example by regulating their own voices.

Costs and Materials

- The major cost would be for salaries of new staff members who would help monitor. Next year's library budget, however, will include an allocation for four new staff members.

- A design student has offered to make up four different posters for $200. The university printing office can reproduce as many posters as needed at no additional cost.

Margin notes:

Tells how plan will be implemented

Describes first phase

Describes second phase

Describes third phase

Estimates costs and materials needed

- Prefabricated cubicles for 26 tables sell for $150 apiece, for a total cost of $3,900.
- Rearrangement on various floors can be handled by the library's custodians.

The Student Fee Allocations Committee and the Student Senate routinely reserve funds for improving student facilities. A request to these organizations would presumably yield at least partial funding for the plan.

Personnel

The success of this plan ultimately depends on the willingness of the library administration to implement it. You can run the program itself by committees made up of students, staff, and faculty. This is yet another area where publicity is essential to persuade people that the problem is severe and that you need their help. To recruit committee members from among students, you can offer Contract Learning credits.

The proposed committees include an Antinoise Committee overseeing the program, a Public Relations Committee, a Poster Committee, and an Enforcement Committee.

Feasibility

On March 15, 20XX, I mailed survey letters to twenty-five New England colleges, inquiring about their methods for coping with noise in the library. Among the respondents, sixteen stated that publicity and the administration's attitude toward enforcement were main elements in their success.

Improved publicity and enforcement could work for us as well. And slight modifications in our facilities, to concentrate group study on the busiest floors, would automatically lighten the burden of enforcement.

Benefits

Publicity will improve communication between the library and the campus. An assertive approach will show that the library is aware of its patrons' needs and is willing to meet those needs. Offering the program for public inspection will draw the entire community into improvement efforts. Publicity, begun now, will pave the way for the formation of committees.

The library shutdown will have a dual effect: it will dramatize the problem to the community, and it will provide time for the physical changes. (An antinoise program begun with carpentry noise in the quiet areas would hardly be effective.) The shutdown will be both a symbolic and a concrete measure, leading to reopening of the library with a new philosophy and a new image.

Continued strict enforcement will be the backbone of the program. It will prove that staff members care enough about the atmosphere to jeopardize their friendly image in the eyes of some users, and that the library is not afraid to enforce its rules.

Conclusion

The conclusion reaffirms the need for the project and induces the audience to act. End on a strong note, with a conclusion that is assertive, confident, and encouraging—and keep it short.

Margin notes:

Describes personnel needed

Assesses probability of success

Offers a realistic and persuasive forecast of benefits

CONCLUSION AND RECOMMENDATION

Reemphasizes
need and
feasibility and
encourages
action

> The noise in Margate University Library has become embarrassing and annoying to the whole campus. Forceful steps are needed to restore the academic atmosphere.
>
> Aside from the intangible question of image, close inspection of the proposed plan will show that it will work if the recommended steps are taken and—most important—if daily enforcement of quiet rules becomes a part of the library's services.

In long, formal proposals, especially those beginning with a comprehensive abstract, the conclusion can be omitted.

A Situation Requiring a Proposal

The proposal that follows (page 546) can be considered a form of grant proposal, since it requests funding for a nonprofit enterprise. As in any funding proposal, a precise, realistic plan and an itemized budget provide the essential justification for the requested financial support.

CASE: Preparing a Formal Proposal

The Situation. Southeastern Massachusetts University's newspaper, the SMU *Torch*, is struggling to meet rising costs. The paper's yearly budget is funded by the Student Fee Allocation Committee which disburses money to various campus organizations. Drastic budget cuts have resulted in reduced funding for all state schools. As a result, the newspaper has received no funding increase for the last three years. Meanwhile, production costs keep rising.

Bill Trippe is the *Torch's* business manager. His task is to justify a requested increase of 20.6 percent for the coming year's budget. Before drafting his proposal (Figure 23.5), Bill constructs a detailed profile of his audience (based on the worksheet, page 35).

Audience Identity and Needs. My primary audience includes all members of the Student Fee Allocation Committee. My secondary audience is the newspaper staff, who will implement the proposed plan—if it is approved by the allocations committee.

The primary audience will use my document as perhaps the sole basis for deciding whether to grant the additional funds. Most of these readers have overseen the newspaper budget for years, and so they already know quite a bit about our overall operation. But they still need an item-by-item explanation of the conditions created by our problems with funding and ever-increasing costs. Probable questions I can anticipate:

• *Why should the paper receive priority over other campus organizations?*
• *Just how crucial is the problem?*

• *Are present funds being used efficiently?*
• *Can any expenses be reduced?*
• *How would additional funds be spent?*
• *How much will this increase cost?*
• *Will the benefits justify the cost?*

Attitude and Personality.   My primary audience often has expressed interest in this topic. But they are likely to object to any request for more money by arguing that everyone has to economize in these difficult times. I guess I could characterize their attitude as both receptive and hesitant. (Almost every campus organization is trying to make a case for additional funds.)

I do know most committee members pretty well, and they seem to respect my management skills. But I still need to spell out the problem and propose a realistic plan, showing that the newspaper staff is sincere in its intention to eliminate nonessential operating costs. At a time when everyone is expected to make do with less, I need to make an especially strong case for salary increases (to attract talented personnel).

Expectations about the Document.   My audience has requested (solicited) this proposal, and so I know it will be carefully read—but also scrutinized and evaluated for its soundness! Especially in a budget request, my audience expects no shortcuts; I'll have to itemize every expense. The Costs section then could be the longest part of the proposal.

And to further justify the requested budget, I can demonstrate just how well the newspaper manages its present funds. In the Feasibility section, I'll give a detailed comparison of funding, expenditures, and the size of the *Torch* in relation to the newspapers of the four other local colleges. This section should be the "clincher" because these facts are most likely to persuade the committee that my plan is cost-effective. To avoid clutter, I'll add an appendix with a table of figures for the comparison above.

To organize my document, I will (1) identify the problem, (2) establish need, (3) propose a solution, (4) show that the plan is cost-effective, and (5) conclude with a request for action. My audience here expects a confident and businesslike—but not stuffy—tone. I want to be sure that everything in this proposal encourages readers to support our budget request.

**A Funding Proposal
for
The SMU *Torch***
(20XX–XX)

Prepared for
The Student Fee Allocation Committee
Southeastern Massachusetts University
North Dartmouth, Massachusetts

by
William Trippe
Torch Business Manager

May 1, 20XX

FIGURE 23.5 A Funding Proposal

The SMU *Torch*

Old Westport Road
North Dartmouth, Massachusetts 02747

May 1, 20XX

Charles Marcus, Chair
Student Fee Allocation Committee
Southeastern Massachusetts University
North Dartmouth, MA 02747

Dear Dean Marcus:

No one needs to be reminded about the effects of increased costs on our campus community. We are all faced with having to make do with less.

Accordingly, we at the *Torch* have spent long hours devising a plan to cope with increased production costs—without compromising the newspaper's tradition of quality service. I think you and your colleagues will agree that our plan is realistic and feasible. Even the "bare-bones" operation that will result from our proposed spending cuts, however, will call for a $7,710.27 increase in next year's budget.

We have received no funding increase in three years. Our present need is absolute. Without additional funds, the *Torch* simply cannot continue to function as a professional newspaper. I therefore submit the following budget proposal for your consideration.

Respectfully,

William Trippe

William Trippe
Business Manager, SMU *Torch*

FIGURE 23.5 *(Continued)*

TABLE OF CONTENTS

PAGE

LETTER OF TRANSMITTAL ii

INFORMATIVE ABSTRACT iv

INTRODUCTION 1
      Overview 1
      Background 1
      Statement of Problem 1
      Need 2
      Scope 2

PROPOSED PLAN 2
      Methods 2
      Costs 3
      Feasibility 5
      Personnel 5

CONCLUSION 5

APPENDIX (Comparative Performance) 6

FIGURE 23.5 *(Continued)*

INFORMATIVE ABSTRACT

The SMU *Torch*, the student newspaper at Southeastern Massachusetts University, is crippled by inadequate funding, having received no budget increase in three years. Increased costs and inadequate funding are the major problems facing the *Torch*. Increases in costs of technology upgrades and in printing have called for cutbacks in production. Moreover, our low staff salaries are inadequate to attract and retain qualified personnel. A nominal pay increase would make salaries more competitive.

Our staff plans to cut costs by reducing page count and by hiring a new press for the *Torch*'s printing work. The only proposed cost increase (for staff salaries) is essential.

A detailed breakdown of projected costs establishes the need for a $7,710.27 budget increase to keep the paper a weekly publication with adequate page count to serve our campus.

Compared with similar newspapers at other colleges, the *Torch* makes much better use of its money. The comparison figures in the Appendix illustrate the cost-effectiveness of our proposal.

FIGURE 23.5 *(Continued)*

INTRODUCTION

Overview

Our campus newspaper faces the contradictory challenge of surviving ever-growing production costs while maintaining its reputation for quality. The following proposal addresses that crisis. This plan's ultimate success, however, depends on the Allocation Committee's willingness to approve a long-overdue increase in the *Torch's* upcoming yearly budget.

Background

In ten years, the *Torch* has grown in size, scope, and quality. Roughly 6,000 copies (24 pages/issue) are printed weekly for each fourteen-week semester. Each week, the *Torch* prints national and local press releases, features, editorials, sports articles, announcements, notices, classified ads, a calendar column, and letters to the editor. A vital part of university life, our newspaper provides a forum for information, ideas, and opinions—all with the highest professionalism. This year we published a Web-based version as well.

Statement of Problem

With much of its staff about to graduate, the *Torch* faces next year with rising costs in every phase of production, and the need to replace outdated and worn equipment.

Our newspaper also suffers from a lack of student involvement: Despite gaining valuable experience and potential career credentials, few students can be expected to work without some kind of remuneration. Most staff members do receive minimal weekly salaries: from $20 for the distributor to $90 for the Editor-in-Chief. But salaries averaging barely $3 per hour cannot possibly compete with the minimum wage. Since more and more SMU students must work part-time, the *Torch* will have to make its salaries more competitive.

The newspaper's operating expenses can be divided into four categories: hardware and software upgrades, salaries, printing costs, and miscellaneous (office supplies, mail, and so on). The first three categories account for nearly 90 percent of the budget. Over the past year, costs in all categories have increased: from as little as 2 percent for miscellaneous expenses to as much as 19 percent for technology upgrades. Printing costs (roughly one-third of our total budget) rose 9 percent in the past year, and another price hike of 10 percent has just been announced.

FIGURE 23.5 *(Continued)*

Need

Despite growing production costs, the *Torch* has received no increase in its yearly budget allocation ($37,400) in three years. Inadequate funding is virtually crippling our newspaper.

Scope

The following plan includes

1. Methods for reducing production costs while maintaining the quality of our staff
2. Projected costs for technology upgrades, salaries, and services during the upcoming year
3. A demonstration of feasibility, showing our cost-effectiveness
4. A summary of attitudes shared by our personnel

PROPOSED PLAN

The following plan is designed to trim operating costs without compromising quality.

Methods

We can overcome our budget and staffing crisis by taking these steps:

Reducing Page Count. By condensing free notices for campus organizations, abolishing "personal" notices, and limiting press releases to one page, we can reduce page count per issue from 24 to 20, saving nearly 17 percent in production costs. (Items deleted from hard copy could be linked as add-ons in the *Torch*'s Web-based version.)

Reducing Hard-Copy Circulation. Reducing circulation from 6,000 to 5,000 copies barely will cover the number of full-time SMU students, but will save nearly 17 percent in printing costs. The steadily increasing hits on our Web site suggests that more and more readers are using the electronic medium. (We are designing a fall survey that will help determine how many readers rely on the Web-based version.)

Hiring a New Press. We can save money by hiring Arrow Press for printing. Other presses (including our present printer) bid at least 25 percent higher than Arrow. With its state-of-the art production equipment, Arrow will import our "camera-ready" digital files to produce the hard-copy version. Moreover, no other company offers the rapid turnover time (from submission to finished product) that Arrow promises.

FIGURE 23.5 *(Continued)*

Upgrading Our Desktop Publishing Technology. To meet Arrow's specifications for submitting digital files, we must upgrade our equipment. Upgrade costs will be largely offset the first year by reduced printing costs. Also, this technology will increase efficiency and reduce labor costs, resulting in substantial payback on investment.

Increasing Staff Salaries. Although we seek talented students who expect little money and much experience, salaries for all positions must increase by an average of 25 percent. Otherwise, any of our staff could earn as much money elsewhere by working only a little more than half the time. In fact, many students could exceed the minimum wage by working for local newspapers. To illustrate: The *Standard Beacon* pays $60 to $90 per news article and $30 per photo; the *Torch* pays nothing for articles and $6 per photo.

A striking example of low salaries is the $4.75 per hour we pay our desktop publishing staff. Our present desktop publishing cost of $3,038 could be as much as $7,000 or even higher if we had this service done by an outside firm, as many colleges do. Without this nominal salary increase, we cannot possibly attract qualified personnel.

Costs

Our proposed budget is itemized in Table 1, but the main point is clear: If the *Torch* is to remain viable, increased funding is essential for meeting projected costs.

Table 1   Projected Costs and Requested Funding for Next Year's *Torch* Budget

PROJECTED COSTS

Hardware/Software Upgrades	
Macintosh G5 (1.8 GHz) Processor	$2,494.98
23-inch Apple™ HD Display (w/rebates)	1,499.98
LaCie™ 160 GB 7200 RPM USB Hard Drive	219.99
Olympus™ Stylus 410 4MP Digital Camera	349.99
Mikrotek™ ScanMaker 6100 Pro	299.99
Extensis™ Photo Imaging Suite	499.98
Microsoft™ Office 2007 Professional-Upgrade	289.97
QuarkEXPress™ 6 software (discounted)	729.97
Adobe™ Photoshop™ CS-Upgrade	169.97
Adobe™ Illustrator™ CS-Upgrade	169.99
Macromedia™ Dreamweaver™ MX2004-Upgrade	199.98
Subtotal	**$6,924.79**

FIGURE 23.5 *(Continued)*

Funding Proposal   4

Wages and Salaries

Desktop-publishing staff (35 hr/wk at $6.00/hr x 28 wk)	$5,880.00
Editor-in-Chief	3,150.00
News Editor	1,890.00
Features Editor	1,890.00
Advertising Manager	2,350.00
Advertising Designer	1,575.00
Webmaster	2,520.00
Layout Editor	1,890.00
Art Director	1,260.00
Photo Editor	1,890.00
Business Manager	1,890.00
Distributor	560.00
Subtotal	**$26,745.00**

Miscellaneous Costs

Graphics by SMU art students (3/wk @ $10 each)	$ 840.00
Mailing	1,100.00
Telephone	1,000.00
Campus print shop services	400.00
Copier fees	100.00
Subtotal	**$3,440.00**

Fixed Printing Costs (5,000 copies/wk x 28/wk)	**$24,799.60**

TOTAL YEARLY COSTS	**$61,909.39**
Expected Advertising Revenue ($600/wk x 28 wks)	**($16,800.00)**
Total Costs Minus Advertising Revenue	**$45,109.39**

TOTAL FUNDING REQUEST	**$45,109.39**

FIGURE 23.5 *(Continued)*

Feasibility

Beyond exhibiting our need, we feel that the feasibility of this proposal can be measured through an objective evaluation of our cost-effectiveness: Compared with newspapers at similar schools, how well does the *Torch* use its funding?

In a survey of the four area college newspapers, we found that the *Torch*—by a sometimes huge margin—makes the best use of its money per page. Table 1A in the Appendix shows, that of the five newspapers, the *Torch* costs students the least, runs the most pages weekly, and spends the least money per page, *despite a circulation two to three times the size of the other papers.*

The *Torch* has the lowest yearly cost of all five newspapers, despite having the largest circulation. With the requested budget increase, the cost would rise by only $0.88, for a yearly cost of $9.00 to each student. Although Alden College's newspaper costs each student $8.58, it is published only every third week, averages 12 pages per issue, and costs more than $71.00 yearly per page to print—in contrast to our yearly printing cost of $55.65 per page. As the figures in the Appendix demonstrate, our cost management is responsible and effective.

Personnel

The *Torch* staff is determined to maintain the highest professionalism. Many are planning careers in journalism, writing, editing, advertising, photography, Web design, or public relations. In any *Torch* issue, the balanced, enlightened coverage is evidence of our judicious selection and treatment of articles and our shared concern for quality.

CONCLUSION

As a broad forum for ideas and opinions, the *Torch* continues to reflect a seriousness of purpose and a commitment to free and responsible expression. Its role in the campus community is more vital than ever during these troubled times.

Every year, allocations to student organizations increase or decrease based on need. Last year, for example, eight allocations increased by an average of $4,332. The *Torch* has received no increase in three years.

FIGURE 23.5 *(Continued)*

Presumably, increases are prompted by special circumstances. For the *Torch*, these circumstances derive from increasing production costs and from the need to update vital equipment. We respectfully urge the Committee to respond to the *Torch*'s legitimate and proven needs by increasing next year's allocation to $45,109.39.

APPENDIX (Comparative Performance)

Table 1A Allocations and Performance of Five Massachusetts College Newspapers

	Stonehorse College	Alden College	Simms University	Fallow State	SMU
Enrollment	1,600	1,400	3,000	3,000	5,000
Fee paid (per year)	$65.00	$85.00	$35.00	$50.00	$65.00
Total fee budget	$104,000	$119,000	$105,000	$150,000	$325,000
Newspaper budget	$18,300	$8,580	$36,179	$52,910	$37,392
					$45,109[a]
Yearly cost per student	$12.50	$8.58	$16.86	$24.66	$8.12
					$9.00[a]
Publication rate	Weekly	Every third week	Weekly	Weekly	Weekly
Average no. of pages	8	12	18	12	24
Average total pages	224	120	504	336	672
					560[a]
Yearly cost per page	$81.60	$71.50	$71.78	$157.47	$55.65
					$67.12[a]

[a]These figures are next year's costs for the SMU *Torch*.

Source: Figures were quoted by newspaper business managers in April 20XX.

FIGURE 23.5 *(Continued)*

☑ Checklist: Usability of Proposals

(Numbers in parentheses refer to the first page of discussion.)

Content

☐ Are all required proposal components included? (539)

☐ Does the title forecast the proposal's subject and purpose? (534)

☐ Is the background section appropriate for this audience's needs? (534)

☐ Is the problem clearly identified? (535)

☐ Is the objective clearly identified? (535)

☐ Does the proposal demonstrate a clear understanding of the client's problems and expectations? (534)

☐ Is the proposed plan, service, or product stated clearly? (535)

☐ Are the claims honest and supportable? (535)

☐ Does the proposal maintain a clear focus on benefits? (535)

☐ Does it address anticipated objections? (536)

☐ Are the proposed solutions feasible and realistic? (524)

☐ Are all foreseeable limitations and contingencies identified? (536)

☐ Is every *relevant* detail spelled out? (536)

☐ Is the cost and budget section accurate and easy to understand? (536)

☐ Are visuals used effectively? (537)

☐ Is each source and contribution properly cited? (538)

☐ Is the proposal ethically acceptable? (535)

Arrangement

☐ Does the introduction offer clear orientation to the problem and the plan? (539)

☐ Does the body section explain *how*, *where*, *when*, and *how much*? (541)

☐ Does the conclusion encourage acceptance of the proposal? (543)

☐ Are there clear transitions between related ideas? (693)

☐ Does the long proposal have adequate supplements to serve the needs of different readers? (538)

Style and Page Design

☐ Is the level of technicality appropriate for primary readers? (537)

☐ Does the tone encourage acceptance of the proposal? (537)

☐ Is the writing clear, concise, and fluent? (216)

☐ Is the language precise? (236)

☐ Is the proposal grammatical? (670)

☐ Is the page design inviting and accessible? (538)

Exercises

1. Assume that the head of your high school English department has asked you, as a recent graduate, for suggestions about revising the English curriculum to prepare students for writing. Write a proposal, based on your experience since high school. (Primary audience: the English department head and faculty; secondary audience: the school committee.) Review the outline on page 539 before selecting specific proposal components.

2. After identifying your primary and secondary audience, compose a short planning proposal for improving an unsatisfactory situation in the classroom, on the job, or in your dorm or apartment (e.g., poor lighting, drab atmosphere, health hazards, poor seating arrangements). Choose a problem or situation whose resolution is more a matter of common sense and lucid observation than of intensive research. Be sure to (a) identify the problem clearly, give a brief background, and stimulate interest; (b) clearly state the methods proposed to solve the problem; and (c) conclude with a statement designed to gain audience support for your proposal.

3. Write a research proposal to your instructor (or an interested third party) requesting approval for the final term project (an analytical report or formal proposal). Verify that adequate primary and secondary sources are available. Convince your audience of the soundness and usefulness of the project.

4. As an alternate term project to the formal analytical report (Chapter 24), develop a long proposal for solving a problem, improving a situation, or satisfying a need in your school, community, or job. Choose a subject sufficiently complex to justify a formal proposal, a topic requiring research (mostly primary). Identify an audience (other than your instructor) who will use your proposal for a specific purpose. Compose an audience and use profile, using the sample on page 544 as a model. Here are possible subjects for your proposal:

   - improving living conditions in your dorm or fraternity/sorority
   - creating a student-oriented advertising agency on campus
   - creating a daycare center on campus
   - creating a new business or expanding a business
   - saving labor, materials, or money on the job
   - improving working conditions
   - improving campus facilities for the disabled
   - supplying a product or service to clients or customers
   - increasing tourism in your town
   - eliminating traffic hazards in your neighborhood or on campus
   - reducing energy expenditures on the job
   - improving security in dorms or in the college library
   - improving in-house training or job orientation programs
   - creating a one-credit course in job hunting or stress management for students
   - improving tutoring in the learning center
   - making the course content in your major more relevant to student needs
   - creating a new student government organization
   - finding ways for an organization to raise money
   - improving faculty advising for students
   - purchasing new equipment
   - improving food service on campus
   - easing first-year students through the transition to college
   - changing the grading system at your school
   - establishing more equitable computer terminal use
   - designing a Web site for your employer or an organization to which you belong

Service-Learning Project[1]

In your nonprofit organization or your school, identify a particular need or project that requires outside funding. Search the Web to locate an appropriate

---

[1]This exercise was inspired by Roger H. Munger's article listed in Works Cited.

funding program. Start by using words such as *proposal*, *grant*, or *funding* along with keywords that describe your project, such as *remedial programs*, *adolescent drug treatment*, and so on.

For a general listing of foundations that provide grants, go to the *Foundation Center* at <www.fdncenter.org>. For sources of education funding, go to <www.ed.gov/fund/grant/find/edlite-forecast.html>. For sources of science funding, go to the *National Science Foundation* at <www.nsf.gov>. For grant sources for nonprofit or public service organizations, go to

"*The Grant Getting Page*" <http://tigger.uic.edu/depts/ovcr/research/proposals> shown in Figure 23.6.

Prepare a short report for your agency that describes the types of projects funded by your chosen source, the average amount of a grant, the number of proposals submitted in a given year, the number of grants awarded, and the specific criteria this funding program uses in evaluating different proposals. Persuade your fellow members that your organization could qualify for a grant from this source. Attach copies of relevant Web pages to your document.

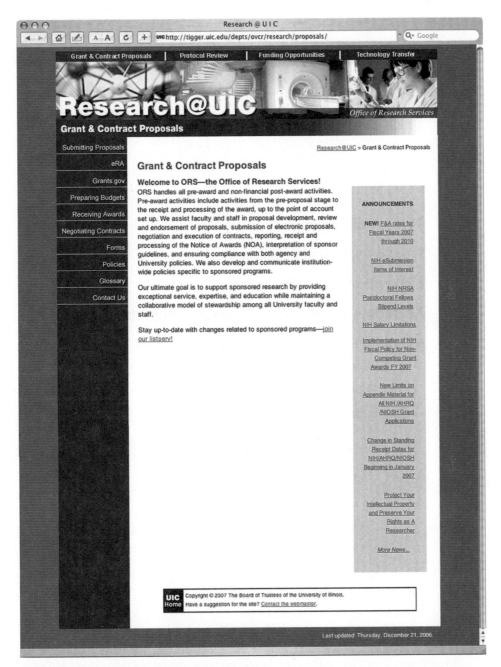

FIGURE 23.6 "The Grant Getting Page" This Web site offers a good starting point for applicants seeking funding from federal and nonprofit granting agencies. *Source:* Used by permission of The University of Illinois at Chicago.

CHAPTER 24

Formal Analytical Reports

Purpose of Analysis

Typical Analytical Problems

Elements of a Usable Analysis

An Outline and Model for Analytical Reports

A Situation Requiring an Analytical Report

Guidelines for Reasoning through an Analytical Problem

Checklist: Usability of Analytical Reports

The formal analytical report, like the shorter versions discussed in Chapter 16, usually leads to recommendations. The formal report replaces the memo when the topic requires lengthy discussion. Formal reports generally include a title page, table of contents, a system of headings, a list of references or works cited, and other front-matter and end-matter supplements discussed in Chapter 25.

An essential component of workplace problem solving, analytical reports are designed to answer these questions:

What readers of an analytical report want to know

- Based on the information gathered about this issue, what do we know?
- What conclusions can we draw?
- What should we do or not do?

Assume, for example, that you receive this assignment from your supervisor:

A typical analytical problem

> Recommend the best method for removing the heavy-metal contamination from our company dump site.

First, you will have to learn everything you can about the nature and extent of the problem. Then you will compare the advantages and disadvantages of various options based on the criteria you are using to assess feasibility: say, cost-effectiveness, time required versus time available for completion, potential risk to the public and the environment. For example, the cheapest option might also pose the greatest environmental risk and could result in heavy fines or criminal charges. But the safest option might simply be too expensive for this struggling company to afford. Or perhaps the Environmental Protection Agency has imposed a legal deadline for the cleanup. In making your recommendation, you will need to weigh all the criteria (cost, safety, time) very carefully, or you could land in jail.

Recommendations have legal and ethical implications

The above situation calls for critical thinking (Chapter 2) and research (Chapters 7–10). Besides interviewing legal and environmental experts, you might search the literature and the Web. From these sources you can discover whether anyone has been able to solve a problem like yours, or learn about the newest technologies for toxic waste cleanup. Then you will have to decide how much, if any, of what others have done applies to your situation. (For more on analytical reasoning, see pages 562, 567.)

Purpose of Analysis

Using analysis on the job

You may be assigned to evaluate a new assembly technique on the production line, or to locate and purchase the best equipment at the best price. You might have to identify the cause behind a monthly drop in sales, the reasons for low employee morale, the causes of an accident, or the reasons for equipment failure. You might need to assess the feasibility of a proposal for a company's expansion or merger or investment.

The list is endless, but the procedure is always the same: (1) asking the right questions, (2) searching the best sources, (3) evaluating and interpreting your findings, and (4) drawing conclusions and making recommendations.

Typical Analytical Problems

Far more than an encyclopedia presentation of information, the analytical report traces your inquiry, your evidence, and your reasoning to show exactly how you arrived at your conclusions and recommendations.

Workplace problem solving calls for skills in three broad categories: *causal analysis, comparative analysis,* and *feasibility analysis.* Each approach relies on its own type of reasoning.

Causal Analysis: "Why Does *X* Happen?"

Designed to attack a problem at its source, the causal analysis answers questions like this: *Why do so many apparently healthy people have sudden heart attacks?*

CASE: The Reasoning Process in Causal Analysis

Identify the
problem

Medical researchers at the world-renowned Hanford Health Institute recently found that 20 to 30 percent of deaths from sudden heart attacks occur in people who have none of the established risk factors (weight gain, smoking, diabetes, lack of exercise, high blood pressure, or family history).

Examine possible
causes

To better identify people at risk, researchers are now tracking down new and powerful risk factors such as bacteria, viruses, genes, stress, anger, and depression.

Recommend
solutions

Once researchers identify these factors and their mechanisms, they can recommend preventive steps such as careful monitoring, lifestyle and diet changes, drug treatment, or psychotherapy (H. Lewis 39–43).

A different version of causal analysis employs reasoning from effect to cause, to answer questions like this: What are the health effects of exposure to electromagnetic radiation? For more on causal reasoning, see pages 159–61 and 593.

NOTE   *Keep in mind that faulty causal reasoning is extremely common, especially when we ignore other possible causes or we confuse correlation with causation (page 164).*

Comparative Analysis: "Is *X* or *Y* Better for Our Purpose?"

Designed to rate competing items on the basis of specific criteria, the comparative analysis answers questions like this: *Which type of security (firewall/encryption) program should we install on our company's computer system?*

Identify the
criteria

Rank the
criteria

Compare items
according to the
criteria, and
recommend the
best one

 Model
feasibility
studies

Consider the
strength of
supporting
reasons

Consider the
strength of
opposing reasons

CASE: The Reasoning Process in Comparative Analysis

XYZ Corporation needs to identify exactly what information (personnel files, financial records) or functions (in-house communication, file transfer) it wants to protect from whom. Does it need both virus and tamper protection? Does it wish to restrict network access or encrypt (scramble) email and computer files so they become unreadable to unauthorized persons? Does it wish to restrict access to or from the Web? In addition to the level of protection, how important are ease of maintenance and user-friendliness?

After identifying their specific criteria, XYZ decision makers need to rank them in order of importance (for example, 1. tamper protection, 2. user-friendliness, 3. secure financial records, and so on).

On the basis of these ranked criteria, XYZ will assess relative strengths and weaknesses of competing security programs and recommend the best one (Schafer 93–94).

For more on comparative analysis, see page 593.

Feasibility Analysis: "Is This a Good Idea?"

Designed to assess the practicality of an idea or a plan, the feasibility analysis answers questions such as this: *Should healthy, young adults be encouraged to receive genetic testing to measure their susceptibility to various diseases?*

CASE: The Reasoning Process in Feasibility Analysis

As a step toward "[translating] genetic research into health care," a National Institutes of Health (NIH) study is investigating the feasibility of offering genetic testing to healthy, young adults at little or no cost. The testing focuses on diseases such as melanoma, diabetes, heart disease, and lung cancer. This study will measure not only the target audience's interest but also how those people tested "will interpret and use the results in making their own health care decisions in the future."

Arguments in favor of testing include the following:

- Young people with a higher risk for a particular disorder might consider preventive treatments.
- Early diagnosis and treatment could be "personalized," tailored to an individual's genetic profile.
- Low-risk test results might "inspire healthy people to stay healthy" by taking precautions such as limiting sun exposure, or changing their dietary, exercise, and smoking habits.

Arguments against testing include the following:

- The benefits of early diagnosis and treatment for a small population might not justify the expense of testing the population at large.
- False positive results are always traumatic, and false negative results could be disastrous.

- Any positive result could subject a currently healthy, young person to biased treatment from employers or disqualification for health and life insurance (National Institutes of Health; Notkins 74, 79).

Weigh the pros and cons and recommend a course of action

After assessing the benefits and drawbacks of testing in this situation, NIH decision makers can make the appropriate recommendations.

For more on feasibility analysis, see pages 338–41 and 594.

Combining Types of Analysis

Analytical categories overlap considerably. Any one study may in fact require answers to two or more of the previous questions. The sample report on pages 585–92 is both a feasibility analysis and a comparative analysis. It is designed to answer these questions: *Is technical marketing the right career for me? If so, which is my best option for entering the field?*

Elements of a Usable Analysis

The formal analytical report incorporates many elements from documents in earlier chapters, along with the suggestions that follow.

Clearly Identified Problem or Goal

Define your goal

To solve any problem or achieve any goal, you must first identify it precisely. Always begin by defining the main questions and thinking through any subordinate questions they may imply. Only then can you determine what to look for, where to look, and how much information you will need.

Your employer, for example, might pose this question: Will a low-impact aerobics program significantly reduce stress among my employees? The aerobics question obviously requires answers to three other questions: What are the therapeutic claims for aerobics? Are they valid? Will aerobics work in this situation? With the main questions identified, you can formulate a goal (or purpose) statement:

Goal statement

> My goal is to examine and evaluate claims about the therapeutic benefits of low-impact aerobic exercise.

Words such as *examine* and *evaluate* (or *compare, identify, determine, measure, describe,* and so on) help readers understand the specific analytical activity that forms the subject of the report. (For more on asking the right questions, see pages 115–16.)

Adequate but Not Excessive Data

Decide how much is enough

A superficial analysis is basically worthless. Worthwhile analysis, in contrast, examines an issue in depth (as discussed on pages 117–18). In reporting on your analysis, however, you filter that material for the audience's understanding, deciding what to include and what to leave out. "Do decision makers in this situation need a closer look or am I presenting excessive detail when only general information is needed?" Is it possible to have too much information? In some cases, yes—as behavioral expert Dietrich Dorner explains:

Excessive
information
hampers decision
making

> The more we know, the more clearly we realize what we don't know. This probably explains why . . . organizations tend to [separate] their information-gathering and decision-making branches. A business executive has an office manager; presidents have . . . advisers; military commanders have chiefs of staff. The point of this separation may well be to provide decision makers with only the bare outlines of all the available information so they will not be hobbled by excessive detail when they are obliged to render decisions. Anyone who is fully informed will see much more than the bare outlines and will therefore find it extremely difficult to reach a clear decision. (99)

Confusing the issue with excessive information is no better than recommending hasty action on the basis of inadequate information (Dorner 104).

When you might
consult an abstract
or summary instead
of the complete
work

As you research the issue you may want to filter material for your own understanding as well. Whether to rely on the abstract or summary or to read the complete text of a specialized article or report depends on the question you're trying to answer and the level of technical detail your readers expect. If you are expert in the field, writing for other experts, you probably want to read the entire document in order to assess the methods and reasoning behind a given study. But if you are less than expert, a summary or abstract of this study's findings might suffice. The fact sheet in Figure 24.1, for example, summarizes a detailed feasibility study for a general reading audience. Readers seeking more details, including nonclassified elements of the complete report, could visit the Transportation Security Administration's Web site at <www.tsa.gov>.

NOTE   *If you have relied merely on the abstract or summary instead of the full article, be sure to indicate this ("Abstract," "Press Release" or the like) when you cite the source in your report (as shown on pages 645, 653).*

Accurate and Balanced Data

Give readers all
they need to make
an informed
judgment

Avoid stacking the evidence to support a preconceived point of view. Assume, for example, that you are asked to recommend the best chainsaw brand for a logging company. Reviewing test reports, you come across this information:

> Of all six brands tested, the Bomarc chainsaw proved easiest to operate. However, this brand also offers the fewest safety features.

In citing these equivocal findings, you need to present both of them accurately, and not simply the first—even though the Bomarc brand may be your favorite. Then argue for the feature (ease of use or safety) you think should receive priority. (Refer to pages 117 and 155 for exploring and presenting balanced and reasonable evidence.)

FACT SHEET: Train and Rail Inspection Pilot, Phase I

U.S. DEPARTMENT OF HOMELAND SECURITY
Transportation Security Administration
FOR IMMEDIATE RELEASE – June 7, 2004
TSA Press Office: (571) 227-2829

Objective:
Implement a pilot program to determine the feasibility of screening passengers, luggage and carry-on bags for explosives in the rail environment.

TRIP I Background:
- Secretary Ridge announced TRIP on March 22, 2004, to test new technologies and screening concepts.
- The program is conducted in partnership with the Department of Transportation, Amtrak, Maryland Rail Commuter and Washington D.C.'s Metro.
- The New Carrollton, Md. station was selected because it serves multiple types of rail operations and is located close to Washington, D.C.

TRIP I Facts:
- Screening for Phase I of TRIP began on May 4 and was completed on May 26, 2004.
- A total of 8,835 passengers and 9,875 pieces of baggage were screened during the test.
- The average time to wait in line and move through the screening process was less than 2 minutes.
- Customer Feedback cards reflect a 93 percent satisfaction rate with both the screening process and the professional demeanor of TSA personnel.

Lessons Learned:
- Results indicate efficient checkpoints throughout with minimal customer inconvenience.
- Passengers were overwhelmingly receptive to the screening process.
- Providing a customer service representative on-site during all screening operations helped Amtrak ensure passengers received outstanding customer service.
- Skilled TSA screeners from the agency's National Screening Force were able to quickly transition to screening in the rail environment.
- Most importantly, Phase I showed that currently available technology could be utilized to screen for explosives in the rail environment.

FIGURE 24.1   A Summary Description of a Feasibility Study Notice that the criteria for assessing feasibility include passenger wait times, passenger receptiveness to screening, and—most important—effectiveness of screening equipment in this environment.
Source: Transportation Security Administration. Press Release.

Fully Interpreted Data

Explain the significance of your data

Interpretation shows the audience "what is important and what unimportant, what belongs together and what does not" (Dorner 44). For example, you might interpret the chainsaw data from page 565 in this way:

Explain the meaning of your evidence

> Our logging crews often work suspended by harness, high above the ground. Also, much work is in remote areas. Safety features therefore should be our first requirement in a chainsaw. Despite its ease of operation, the Bomarc saw does not meet our safety needs.

By saying "therefore" you engage in analysis—not just information sharing. Don't merely list your findings, explain what they mean. (Refer to pages 155–58.)

Subordination of Personal Bias

To arrive at the *truth* of the matter (page 156), you need to see clearly. Don't let your biases fog up the real picture. Each stage of analysis requires decisions about what to record, what to exclude, and where to go next. You must evaluate your data (Is this reliable and important?), interpret your evidence (What does it mean?), and make recommendations (What action is needed?). An ethically sound analysis presents a balanced and reasonable assessment of the evidence. Do not force viewpoints that are not supported by dependable evidence. (Refer to page 119.)

Evaluate and interpret evidence impartially

Appropriate Visuals

Use visuals generously

Graphs are especially useful in an analysis of trends (rising or falling sales, radiation levels). Tables, charts, photographs, and diagrams work well in comparative analyses. Be sure to accompany each visual with a fully interpreted "story."

NOTE   *As the simplicity of Figure 24.2 and its brief caption illustrate, a powerful visual does not need to be complex and fancy, nor its accompanying story long and involved. Sometimes, less can be more.*

Valid Conclusions and Recommendations

Be clear about what the audience should think and do

Along with the informative abstract (page 603), conclusions and recommendations are the sections of a long report that receive the most audience attention. The goal of analysis is to reach a valid conclusion—an overall judgment about what all the material means (that X is better than Y, that B failed because of C, that A is a good plan of action). On the bottom of the next page is the conclusion of a report on the feasibility of installing an active solar heating system in a large building.

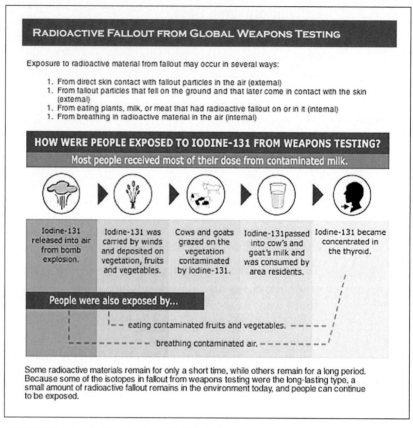

FIGURE 24.2   A Simple but Richly Informative Visual

Source: Adapted from *Radiation Studies*, Centers for Disease Control (CDC)
<www.cdc.gov/nceh/radiation/fallout/RF-GWT_exposure.htm>.

Offer a final
judgment

1. Active solar space heating for our new research building is technically feasible because the site orientation will allow for a sloping roof facing due south, with plenty of unshaded space.

2. It is legally feasible because we are able to obtain an access easement on the adjoining property, to ensure that no buildings or trees will be permitted to shade the solar collectors once they are installed.

3. It is economically feasible because our sunny, cold climate means high fuel savings and faster payback (fifteen years maximum) with solar heating. The long-term fuel savings justify our short-term installation costs (already minimal because the solar system can be incorporated during the building's construction—without renovations).

Conclusions are valid when they are logically derived from accurate interpretations.

Having explained *what it all means*, you then recommend *what should be done.* Taking all possible alternatives into account, your recommendations urge the most feasible option (to invest in *A* instead of *B*, to replace *C* immediately, to follow plan *A*, or the like). Here are the recommendations based on the previous interpretations:

Tell what should be done

1. I recommend that we install an active solar heating system in our new research building.
2. We should arrange an immediate meeting with our architect, building contractor, and solar heating contractor. In this way, we can make all necessary design changes before construction begins in two weeks.
3. We should instruct our legal department to obtain the appropriate permits and easements immediately.

Recommendations are valid when they propose an appropriate response to the problem or question.

Because they culminate your research and analysis, recommendations challenge your imagination, your creativity, and—above all—your critical thinking skills. What strikes one person as a brilliant suggestion might be seen by others as irresponsible, offensive, or dangerous. (Figure 24.3 depicts the kinds of decisions writers encounter in formulating, evaluating, and refining their recommendations.)

NOTE   *Keep in mind that solving one problem might create new and worse problems—or unintended consequences. For example, to prevent crop damage by rodents, an agriculture specialist might recommend trapping and poisoning. While rodent eradication may increase crop yield temporarily, it also increases the insects these rodents feed on—leading eventually to even greater crop damage. In short, before settling on any recommendation, try to anticipate its "side effects and long-term repercussions" (Dorner 15).*

When you do achieve definite conclusions and recommendations, express them with assurance and authority. Unless you have reason to be unsure, avoid noncommittal statements ("It would seem that" or "It looks as if"). Be direct and assertive ("The earthquake danger at the reactor site is acute," or "I recommend an immediate investment"). Announce where you stand.

If, however, your analysis yields nothing definite, do not force a simplistic conclusion on your material (pages 119–21). Instead, explain the limitations ("The contradictory responses to our consumer survey prevent me from reaching a definite conclusion. Before we make any decision about this product, I recommend a full-scale market analysis"). The wrong recommendation is far worse than no recommendation at all. (Refer to Chapter 10, pages 168–69 for helpful guidelines.)

Self-Assessment

Assess your analysis continuously

The more we are involved in a project, the larger our stake in its outcome—making self-criticism less likely just when it is needed most! For example, it is

Consider All the Details

- What exactly should be done—if anything at all?
- How exactly should it be done?
- When should it begin and be completed?
- Who will do it, and how willing are they?
- What equipment, material, or resources are needed?
- Are any special conditions required?
- What will this cost, and where will the money come from?
- What consequences are possible?
- Whom do I have to persuade?
- How should I order my list (priority, urgency, etc.)?

Locate the Weak Spots

- Is anything unclear or hard to follow?
- Is this course of action unrealistic?
- Is it risky or dangerous?
- Is it too complicated or confusing?
- Is anything about it illegal or unethical?
- Will it cost too much?
- Will it take too long?
- Could anything go wrong?
- Who might object or be offended?
- What objections might be raised?

Make Improvements

- Can I rephrase anything?
- Can I change anything?
- Should I consider alternatives?
- Should I reorder my list?
- Can I overcome objections?
- Should I get advice or feedback before I submit this?

FIGURE 24.3   How to Think Critically About Your Recommendations

Source: Adapted from *The Art of Thinking*, 8th ed. by Vincent R. Ruggiero, copyright © 2006. Reprinted by permission of Pearson Education, Inc.

hard to admit that we might need to backtrack, or even start over, in instances like these (Dorner 46):

Things that might go wrong with your analysis

- During research you find that your goal isn't clear enough to indicate exactly what information you need.
- As you review your findings, you discover that the information you have is not the information you need.

It is even harder to test our recommendations and admit they are not working:

- After making a recommendation, you discover that what seemed like the right course of action turns out to be the wrong one.

If you meet such obstacles, acknowledge them immediately, and revise your approach as needed.

 Model reports

An Outline and Model for Analytical Reports

Whether you outline earlier or later, the finished report depends on a good outline. This model outline can be adapted to most analytical reports.

I. **Introduction**
  A. Definition, Description, and Background
  B. Purpose of the Report, and Intended Audience
  C. Method of Inquiry
  D. Limitations of the Study
  E. Working Definitions (here or in a glossary)
  F. Scope of the Inquiry (topics listed in logical order)
  G. Conclusion(s) of the Inquiry (briefly stated)

II. **Collected Data**
  A. First Topic for Investigation
    1. Definition
    2. Findings
    3. Interpretation of findings
  B. Second Topic for Investigation
    1. First subtopic
      a. Definition
      b. Findings
      c. Interpretation of findings
    2. Second subtopic (and so on)

III. **Conclusion**
  A. Summary of Findings
  B. Overall Interpretation of Findings (as needed)
  C. Recommendations (as needed and feasible)

(This outline is only tentative. Modify the components as necessary.)

Two sample reports in this chapter follow the model outline. The first one, "Children Exposed to Electromagnetic Radiation: A Risk Assessment" (minus the document supplements that ordinarily accompany a long report), begins on this page. The second report, "The Feasibility of a Career in Technical Marketing," appears in Figure 24.4. Supplements (front and end matter) for this report appear in Chapter 25 and on page 665.

Each report responds to slightly different questions. The first tackles these questions: *What are the effects of* X *and what should we do about them?* The second tackles two questions: *Is* X *feasible, and which version of* X *is better for my purposes?* At least one of these reports should serve as a model for your own analysis.

Introduction

The introduction engages and orients the audience and provides background as briefly as possible for the situation. Often, writers are tempted to write long introductions because they have a lot of background knowledge about the issue. But readers generally don't need long history lessons on the subject.

Identify your topic's origin and significance, define or describe the problem or issue, and explain the report's purpose. (Generally, stipulate your audience only in the version your instructor will read and only if you don't attach an audience and use profile.) Briefly identify your research methods (interviews, literature searches, and so on) and explain any limitations or omissions (person unavailable for interview, research still in progress, and so on). List working definitions, but if you have more than two or three, use a glossary. List the topics you have researched. Finally, briefly preview your conclusion; don't make readers wade through the entire report to find out what you recommend or advise.

NOTE   *Not all reports require every component. Give readers only what they need and expect.*

As you read the following introduction, think about the elements designed to engage and orient the audience (i.e., local citizens), and evaluate their effectiveness. (Review pages 115–16 for the situation that gave rise to this report.)

CHILDREN EXPOSED TO ELECTROMAGNETIC RADIATION: A RISK ASSESSMENT

LAURIE A. SIMONEAU

Introduction

Definition and background of the problem

Wherever electricity flows—through the largest transmission line or the smallest appliance—it emits varying intensities of charged waves: an *electromagnetic field* (EMF). Some medical studies have linked human exposure to EMFs with definite physiologic changes and possible illness including cancer, miscarriage, and depression.

Description
of the problem

Experts disagree over the health risk, if any, from EMFs. Some question whether EMF risk is greater from high-voltage transmission lines, the smaller distribution lines strung on utility poles, or household appliances. Conclusive research may take years; meanwhile, concerned citizens worry about avoiding potential risks.

In Bocaville, four sets of transmission lines—two at 115 Kilovolts (kV) and two at 500 kV—cross residential neighborhoods and public property. The Adams elementary school is less than 100 feet from this power line corridor. EMF risks—whatever they may be—are thought to increase with proximity.

Purpose and
methods of
this inquiry

Based on examination of recent research and interviews with local authorities, this report assesses whether potential health risks from EMFs seem significant enough for Bocaville to (a) increase public awareness, (b) divert the transmission lines that run adjacent to the elementary school, and (c) implement widespread precautions in the transmission and distribution of electrical power throughout Bocaville.

Scope of
this inquiry

This report covers five major topics: what we know about various EMF sources, what research indicates about physiologic and health effects, how experts differ in evaluating the research, what the power industry and the public have to say, and what actions are being taken locally and nationwide to avoid risk.

Conclusions
of the inquiry
(briefly stated)

The report concludes by acknowledging the ongoing conflict among EMF research findings and by recommending immediate and inexpensive precautionary steps for our community.

Body

The body section describes and explains your findings. Present a clear and detailed picture of the evidence, interpretations, and reasoning on which you will base your conclusion. Divide topics into subtopics, and use informative headings as aids to navigation.

NOTE

Remember your ethical responsibility for presenting a fair *and* balanced *treatment of the material, instead of "loading" the report with only those findings that support your viewpoint. Also, keep in mind the body section can have many variations, depending on the audience, topic, purpose, and situation.*

As you read the following section, evaluate how effectively it informs readers, keeps them on track, reveals a clear line of reasoning, and presents an impartial analysis.

Data Section

First topic

Definition

Sources of EMF Exposure
Electromagnetic intensity is measured in *milligauss* (mG), a unit of electrical measurement. The higher the mG reading, the stronger the field. Studies suggest that consistent exposure above 1–2 mG may increase cancer risk significantly, but no scientific evidence concludes that exposure even below 2.5 mG is safe.

Findings

Table 1 gives the EMF intensities from electric power lines at varying distances during average and peak usage.

Table 1　EMF Emissions from Power Lines (in milligauss)

Types of Transmission Lines	Maximum on Right-of-Way	Distance from lines			
		50'	100'	200'	300'
115 Kilovolts (kV)					
Average usage	30	7	2	0.4	0.2
Peak usage	63	14	4	0.9	0.4
230 Kilovolts (kV)					
Average usage	58	20	7	1.8	0.8
Peak usage	118	40	15	3.6	1.6
500 Kilovolts (kV)					
Average usage	87	29	13	3.2	1.4
Peak usage	183	62	27	6.7	3.0

Source: United States Environmental Protection Agency. *EMF in Your Environment.* Washington: GPO, 1992. Data from Bonneville Power Administration.

Interpretation

　　As Table 1 indicates, EMF intensity drops substantially as distance from the power lines increases.

　　Although the EMF controversy has focused on 2 million miles of power lines criss-crossing the country, potentially harmful waves are also emitted by household wiring, appliances, computer terminals—and even from the earth's natural magnetic field. The background magnetic field (at a safe distance from any electrical appliance) in the average American home varies from 0.5 to 4.0 mG (United States Environmental 10). Table 2 compares intensities of various sources.

Interpretation

　　EMF intensity from certain appliances tends to be higher than from transmission lines because of the amount of current involved.

Table 2　EMF Emissions from Selected Sources (in milligauss)

Source	*Range*[a,b]
Earth's magnetic field	0.1–2.5
Blowdryer	60–1400
Four in. from TV screen	40–100
Four ft from TV screen	0.7–9
Fluorescent lights	10–12
Electric razor	1200–1600
Electric blanket	2–25
Computer terminal (12 inches away)	3–15
Toaster	10–60

[a]Data from Brodeur, Paul. "Annals of Radiation: The Cancer at Slater School." *The New Yorker* 7 Dec. 1992: 88; Miltane, John. Interview 5 Apr. 2007; National Institute of Environmental Health. *Questions and Answers about EMF.* Washington: GPO, 1995:3.

[b]Readings are made with a gaussmeter, and vary with technique, proximity of gaussmeter to source, its direction of aim, and other random factors.

Definitions

Finding

Voltage measures the speed and pressure of electricity in wires, but *current* measures the volume of electricity passing through wires. Current (measured in *amperage*) is what produces electromagnetic fields. The current flowing through a transmission line typically ranges from 200 to 400 amps. Most homes have a 200-amp service. This means that if every electrical item in the house were turned on at the same time, the house could run about 200 amps—almost as high as the transmission line. Consumers then have the ability to put 200 amps of current-flow into their homes, while transmission lines carrying 200 to 400 amps are at least 50 feet away (Miltane).

Proximity and duration of exposure, however, are other risk factors. People are exposed to EMFs from home appliances at close proximity, but appliances run only periodically: exposure is therefore sporadic, and intensity diminishes sharply within a few feet (Figure 1).

As Figure 1 indicates, EMF intensity drops dramatically over very short distances from the typical appliance.

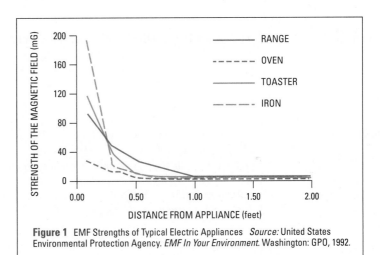

Figure 1 EMF Strengths of Typical Electric Appliances *Source:* United States Environmental Protection Agency. *EMF In Your Environment.* Washington: GPO, 1992.

Finding

Power line exposure, on the other hand, is at a greater distance (usually 50 feet or more), but it is constant. Moreover, its intensity can remain strong well beyond 100 feet (Miltane).

Interpretation

Research has yet to determine which type of exposure might be more harmful: briefly, to higher intensities or constantly, to lower intensities. In any case, proximity seems most significant because EMF intensity drops rapidly with distance.

Second topic

Physiologic Effects and Health Risks from EMF Exposure
Research on EMF exposure falls into two categories: epidemiologic studies and laboratory studies. The findings are sometimes controversial and inconclusive, but also disturbing.

First subtopic

Definition

General findings

Epidemiologic Studies.   Epidemiologic studies look for statistical correlations between EMF exposure and human illness or disorders. Of 77 such studies in recent decades, over 70 percent suggest that EMF exposure increases the incidence of the following conditions (Pinsky 155–215):

- cancer, especially leukemia and brain tumors
- miscarriage
- stress and depression
- learning disabilities
- heart attacks

For example, a 38-year study of nearly 140,000 electrical employees in the United States indicates that those who routinely worked in high-EMF environments were about three times more likely to die from heart attacks than coworkers in low-EMF environments (Raloff, "Electromagnetic . . . Hearts" 70).

    Following are summaries of four noted epidemiologic studies implicating EMFs in cancer.

Detailed findings

A Landmark Study of the EMF/Cancer Connection.   A 1979 Denver study by Wertheimer and Leeper was the first to implicate EMFs as a cause of cancer. Researchers compared hundreds of homes in which children had developed cancer with similar homes in which children were cancer free. Victims were two to three times as likely to live in "high-current homes" (within 130 feet of a transmission line or 50 feet of a distribution line).

Critique of findings

    This study has been criticized because (1) it was not "blind" (researchers knew which homes cancer victims were living in), and (2) researchers never took gaussmeter readings to verify their designation of "high-current" homes (Pinsky 160–62; Taubes 96).

Detailed findings

Follow-up Studies.   Several major studies of the EMF/cancer connection have confirmed Wertheimer's findings:

- In 1988, Savitz studied hundreds of Denver houses and found that children with cancer were 1.7 times as likely to live in high-current homes. Unlike his predecessors, Savitz did not know whether a cancer victim lived in the home being measured, and he took gaussmeter readings to verify that houses could be designated "high-current" (Pinsky 162–63).
- In 1990, London and Peters found that Los Angeles children had 2.5 times more risk of leukemia if they lived near power lines (Brodeur 115).
- In 1992, a massive Swedish study found that children in houses with average intensities greater than 1 mG had twice the normal leukemia risk; at greater than 2 mG, the risk nearly tripled; at greater than 3 mG, it nearly quadrupled (Brodeur 115).
- Most recently, in 2002, British researchers evaluated findings from 34 studies of power line EMF effects (a *meta-analysis*). This study found "a degree of consistency in the evidence suggesting adverse health effects of living near high voltage powerlines" (Henshaw et al. 1).

Detailed findings

Workplace Studies. More than 80 percent of 51 studies from 1981 to 1994—most notably a 1992 Swedish study—concluded that electricians, electrical engineers, and power line workers constantly exposed to an average of 1.5 to 4.0 mG had a significantly elevated cancer risk (Brodeur 115; Pinsky 177–209).

Notable Recent Studies. Three recent workplace studies seem to support or even amplify the above findings.

- A 1994 University of Southern California study indicates that high workplace exposure to EMFs triples the risk of Alzheimer's disease (Des Marteau 38).
- A 1995 University of North Carolina study of 138,905 electric utility workers concluded that occupational EMF exposure roughly doubles brain cancer risk. This study, however, found no increased leukemia risk (Cavanaugh 8; Moore 16).
- A Canadian study of electrical-power employees published in 2000 indicates that those who had worked in strong electric fields for more than 20 years had "an eight- to tenfold increase in the risk of leukemia," along with a significantly elevated risk of lymphoma ("Strong Electric Fields" 1–2).

Interpretation

Although none of the above studies can be said to "prove" a direct cause-effect relationship, their strikingly similar results suggest a conceivable link between prolonged EMF exposure and illness.

Second subtopic

Laboratory Studies. Laboratory studies assess cellular, metabolic, and behavioral effects of EMFs on humans and animals. EMFs directly cause the following physiologic changes (Brodeur 88; Pinsky 24–29; Raloff, "EMFs'" 30):

General findings

- reduced heart rate
- altered brain waves
- impaired immune system
- interference with the synthesis of genetic material
- disrupted regulation of cell growth
- interaction with the biochemistry of cancer cells
- altered hormonal activity
- disrupted sleep patterns

These changes are documented in the following summaries of several significant laboratory studies.

EMF Effects on Cell Chemistry. Recent studies have demonstrated previously unrecognized effects on cell growth and division.

Detailed findings

- A 1995 University of Wisconsin study showed that cell metabolism is influenced by electromagnetic fields—the extent of effect depending on a cell's age and health. While this type of cellular stress does not appear to initiate cancer, it might help promote growth of an existing tumor (Goodman, Greenebaum, and Marron 279–338).

• A 2000 study by Michigan State University found that EMFs equal to the intensity that occurs "within a few feet" of outdoor power lines caused cells with cancer-related genetic mutations to multiply rapidly (Sivitz 196).

EMF Effects on Hormones.   Several studies have found that EMF exposure (say, from an electric blanket) inhibits production of melatonin, a hormone that fights cancer and depression, stimulates the immune system, and regulates bodily rhythms.

Detailed findings

• A 1997 study at the Lawrence National Laboratory found that EMF exposure can suppress both melatonin and the hormonelike, anticancer drug Tamoxifen (Raloff, "EMFs'" 30). A 2004 British study of Oxford University, however, found no association between decreased melatonin levels and breast cancer (Travis).

• In 1996, physiologist Charles Graham found that EMFs elevate female estrogen levels and depress male testosterone levels—hormone alterations associated respectively, with risk of breast or testicular cancer (Raloff, "EMFs'" 30).

Detailed findings

EMF Effects on Life Expectancy.   A 1994 South African study at the University of the Orange Free State measured the life span of mice exposed to EMFs. Both first and second generations of exposed mice showed significantly shortened life expectancy (de Jager and de Bruyn 221–24).

Detailed findings

EMF Effects on Behavior.   Recent studies indicate that people who live adjacent to power lines have roughly twice the normal rate of depression (Pinsky 31–32). Also, rats exposed to EMFs exhibit slower rates of learning (Beardsley 20).

Interpretation

Although laboratory studies seem more conclusive than the epidemiologic studies, what these findings *mean* is debatable.

Third topic

Debate over Quality, Cost, and Status of EMF Research
Experts differ over the meaning of EMF research findings largely because of the following limitations attributed to various studies.

First subtopic

Limitations of Various EMF Studies.   Epidemiologic studies are criticized for overstating evidence. For example, some critics claim that so-called EMF-cancer

Critiques of population studies

links are produced by "data dredging" (making countless comparisons between cancers and EMF sources until random correlations appear) (Taubes 99). Other critics argue that news media distort the issue by publicizing positive findings while often ignoring negative or ambiguous findings (N. Goodman). Some studies are also accused of mistaking *coincidence* for *correlation,* without exploring "confounding factors" (e.g., exposure to toxins or to other adverse conditions—including the earth's natural magnetic field) (Moore 16).

Response to critiques

Supporters of EMF research respond that the sheer volume of epidemiologic evidence seems overwhelming (Kirkpatrick 81, 83). Moreover, the Swedish studies cited earlier seem to invalidate the above criticisms (Brodeur 115).

Critiques of lab studies

Laboratory studies are criticized—even by scientists who conduct them—because effects on an isolated culture of cells or on experimental animals do not always equal effects on the total human organism (Jauchem 190–94).

Response to
critiques

> Until recently critics argued that no scientist had offered a reasonable hypothesis to explain the possible health effects (Palfreman 26). However, a 2004 University of Washington study showed that a weak electromagnetic field can break DNA strands and lead to brain cell death in rats, presumably because of cell-damaging agents known as free radicals (Lai and Singh).

Second subtopic
Cost objections

> **Costs of EMF Research.**   Critics claim that research and publicity about EMFs are becoming a profit venture, spawning "a new growth industry among researchers, as well as marketers of EMF monitors" ("Electrophobia" I). Environmental expert Keith Florig identifies adverse economic effects of the EMF debate that include decreased property values, frivolous lawsuits, expensive but needless "low field" consumer appliances, and costly modifications to schools and public buildings (Monmonier 190).

Third subtopic

Conflicting
scientific opinions

> **Present Status of EMF Research.**   In July 1998, an editor at the *New England Journal of Medicine* called for ending EMF/cancer research. He cited studies from the National Cancer Institute and other respected sources that showed "little evidence" of any causal connection. In a parallel development, federal and industry funding for EMF research has been reduced drastically (Stix 33). But, in August 1998, experts from the Energy Department and the National Institute of Environmental Health Sciences (NIEHS) announced that EMFs should be officially designated a "possible human carcinogen" (Gross 30).
>
> However, one year later, in a report based on its seven-year review of EMF research, NIEHS concluded that "the scientific evidence suggesting that . . . EMF exposures pose any health risk is weak." But the report also conceded that such exposure "cannot be recognized at this time as entirely safe" (1–2). In 2005, the National Cancer Institute fueled the controversy, concluding that the EMF-cancer connection is supported by only "limited evidence" and "inconsistent associations" (1).
>
> Most recently, noted epidemiologist Daniel Wartenberg has testified in support of the "Precautionary Principle," arguing that policy decisions should be based on "the possibility of risk." Specifically, Wartenberg advocates "prudently lowering exposures of greatest concern [i.e., of children] in case the possible risk is shown eventually to be true" (6).

Interpretation

> In short, after more than twenty-five years of study, the EMF/illness debate continues, even among respected experts. While most scientists agree that EMFs exert measurable effects on the human body, they disagree about whether a real hazard exists. Given the drastic cuts in research funding, definite answers are unlikely to appear anytime soon.

Fourth topic

> **Views from the Power Industry and the Public**
> While the experts continue their debate, other viewpoints are worth considering as well.

Findings

> **The Power Industry's Views.**   The Electrical Power Research Institute (EPRI), the research arm of the nation's electric utilities, claims that recent EMF studies have provided valuable but inconclusive data that warrant further study (Moore 17).

What does our local power company think about the alleged EMF risk? Marianne Halloran-Barney, Energy Service Advisor for County Electric, expressed this view in an email correspondence:

Findings

> There are definitely some links, but we don't know, really, what the effects are or what to do about them. . . . There are so many variables in EMF research that it's a question of whether the studies were even done correctly. . . . Maybe in a few years there will be really definite answers.

Echoing Halloran-Barney's views, John Miltane, Chief Engineer for County Electric, added this political insight:

> The public needs and demands electricity, but in regard to the negative effects of generation and transmission, the pervasive attitude seems to be "not in my back yard!" Utilities in general are scared to death of the EMF issue, but at County Electric we're trying to do the best job we can while providing reliable electricity to 24,000 customers.

Interpretation

Public Perception.   Industry views seem to parallel the national perspective among the broader population: Informed people are genuinely concerned, but remain unsure about what level of anxiety is warranted or what exactly should be done.

Finding

A 1998 survey by the Edison Electric Institute did reveal that EMFs are considered a serious health threat by 33 percent of the American public (Stix 33).

Fifth topic

Risk-Avoidance Measures Being Taken
Although conclusive answers may require decades of research, concerned citizens are already taking action against potential EMF hazards.

First subtopic

Risk Avoidance Nationwide.   Here are steps taken by various communities to protect schoolchildren from EMF exposure:

Findings

- Hundreds of individuals and community groups have taken legal action to block proposed construction of new power lines. A single Washington law firm has defended roughly 140 utilities in cases related to EMFs (Dana and Turner 32).

- Houston schools "forced a utility company to remove a transmission line that ran within 300 feet of three schools. Cost: $8 million" (Kirkpatrick 85).

- California parents and teachers are pressuring reluctant school and public health officials to investigate cancer rates in the roughly 1,000 schools located within 300 feet of transmission lines, and to close at least one school (within 100 feet) in which cancer rates far exceed normal (Brodeur 118).

Although critics argue that the questionable risks fail to justify the costs of such measures, widespread concern about EMF exposure continues to grow.

Second subtopic
Findings

Risk Avoidance Locally.   Local awareness of the EMF issue seems low. The main public concern seems to be with property values. According to Halloran-Barney, County Electric receives one or two calls monthly from concerned customers, including people buying homes near power lines. The lack of public awareness adds another dimension to the EMF problem: People can't avoid a health threat that they don't know exists.

John Miltane stresses that County Electric takes the EMF issue very seriously: Whenever possible, new distribution lines are run underground and configured to diminish EMF intensity:

> Although EMFs are impossible to eliminate altogether, we design anything we build to emit minimal intensities. . . . Also, we are considering underground cable (at $1,200 per ft.) to replace 8,000 feet of transmission lines, but the bill would ring up to nearly $10 million, for the cable alone, without labor: You don't get environmental stuff for free, which is one of the problems.

Interpretation

Before risk avoidance can be considered on a broader community level, the public must first be informed about EMFs and the associated risks of exposure.

Conclusion

The conclusion is likely to interest readers most because it answers the questions that originally sparked the analysis.

NOTE   *Many workplace reports are submitted with the conclusion preceding the introduction and body sections.*

In the conclusion, you summarize, interpret, and recommend. Although you have interpreted evidence at each stage of your analysis, your conclusion presents a broad interpretation and suggests a course of action, where appropriate. The summary and interpretations should lead logically to your recommendations.

Elements of a logical conclusion

- The summary accurately reflects the body of the report.
- The overall interpretation is consistent with the findings in the summary.
- The recommendations are consistent with the purpose of the report, the evidence presented, and the interpretations given.

NOTE   *Don't introduce any new facts, ideas, or statistics in the conclusion.*

As you read the following conclusion, evaluate how effectively it provides a clear and consistent perspective on the whole document.

Conclusion

Summary and Overall Interpretation of Findings

Review of major findings

Electromagnetic fields exist wherever electricity flows; the stronger the current, the higher the EMF intensity. While no "safe" EMF level has been identified, long-term exposure to intensities greater than 2.5 milligauss is considered dangerous. Although home appliances can generate high EMFs during use, power lines can generate constant EMFs, typically at 2 to 3 milligauss in buildings within 150 feet. Our elementary school is less than 100 feet from a high-voltage power line corridor.

An overall
judgment about
what the findings
mean

Notable epidemiologic studies implicate EMFs in increased rates of medical disorders such as cancer, miscarriage, stress, depression, and learning disabilities—all directly related to intensity and duration of exposure. Laboratory studies show that EMFs cause the kinds of cellular, metabolic, and behavioral changes that could produce these disorders.

Though still controversial and inconclusive, most of the various findings are strikingly similar and they underscore the need for more research and for risk avoidance, especially as far as children are concerned. Especially striking are the 1997 and 2004 discoveries of a direct biological link between EMF exposure and DNA damage.

Concerned citizens nationwide are beginning to prevail over resistant school and health officials and utility companies in reducing EMF risk to schoolchildren. And even though our local power company is taking reasonable risk-avoidance steps, our community can do more to learn about the issues and diminish potential risk.

Recommendations

The National Institute of Environmental Health Sciences cautions that the health evidence against EMF exposure "is insufficient to warrant aggressive regulatory concern" (NIEHS 2). In light of this "official" position, any type of government regulation anytime soon seems highly unlikely. Also, considering the limitations of what we know, drastic and enormously expensive actions (such as burying all the town's power lines or increasing the height of utility towers) seem inadvisable. In fact, these might turn out to be the wrong actions.

Despite this climate of uncertainty, however, our community still can take some immediate and inexpensive steps to address possible EMF risk:

A feasible and
realistic course of
action

- The school playground should be relocated to the side of the school most distant from the power lines.
- Children should be discouraged from playing near any power lines.
- A version of this report should be distributed to all Bocaville residents.
- Our school board should hire a qualified contractor to take milligauss readings throughout the elementary school, to determine the extent of the problem, and to suggest reasonable corrective measures.
- Our Town Council should meet with County Electric Company representatives to explore options and costs for rerouting or burying the segment of the power lines near the school.
- A town meeting should then be held to answer citizens' questions and to solicit opinions.
- A committee (consisting of at least one physician, one engineer, and other experts) should be appointed to review emerging research as it relates to our school and town.

A closing call
to action

As we await conclusive answers, we need to learn all we can about the EMF issue, and to do all we can to diminish this potentially significant health issue.

NOTE   *The Works Cited section for the preceding report appears on pages 653–54. This author uses MLA documentation style.*

Supplements

Submit your completed report with these supporting components, in this order:

Front matter precedes the report

- title page
- letter of transmittal
- table of contents
- list of tables and figures
- abstract
- report text (introduction, body, conclusion)
- glossary (as needed)

End matter follows the report

- appendices (as needed)
- Works Cited page (or alphabetical or numbered list of references)

For discussion and examples of the above items, see Chapter 25.

A Situation Requiring an Analytical Report

The formal report that follows, patterned after the model outline, combines a feasibility analysis with a comparative analysis.

CASE: Preparing a Formal Report

The Situation. Richard Larkin, author of the following report, has a work-study job fifteen hours weekly in his school's placement office. His boss, John Fitton (placement director), likes to keep up with trends in various fields. Larkin, an engineering major, has developed an interest in technical marketing and sales. Needing a report topic for his writing course, Larkin offers to analyze the feasibility of a technical marketing and sales career, both for his own decision making and for technical and science graduates in general. Fitton accepts Larkin's offer, looking forward to having the final report in his reference file for use by students choosing careers. Larkin wants his report to be useful in three ways: (1) to satisfy a course requirement, (2) to help him in choosing his own career, and (3) to help other students with their career choices.

With his topic approved, Larkin begins gathering his primary data, using interviews, letters of inquiry, telephone inquiries, and lecture notes. He supplements these primary sources with articles in recent publications. He will document his findings in APA (author-date) style.

As a guide for designing his final report (Figure 24.4), Larkin completes the following audience and use profile (based on the worksheet on page 35).

Audience Identity and Needs. My primary audience consists of John Fitton, Placement Director, and the students who will refer to my report. The secondary audience is my writing instructor.

Because he is familiar with the marketing field, Fitton will need very little background to understand my report. Many student readers, however, will have questions like these:

- What, exactly, is technical marketing and sales?
- What are the requirements for this career?
- What are the pros and cons of this career?
- Could this be the right career for me?
- How do I enter the field?

Attitude and Personality.   Readers likely to be affected by this document are students making career choices. I expect readers' attitudes will vary:

- Some readers should have a good deal of interest, especially those seeking a people-oriented career.
- Others might be only casually interested as they investigate a range of possible careers.
- Some readers might be skeptical about something written by a fellow student instead of by some expert. To connect with all these people, I need to persuade them that my conclusions are based on reliable information and careful reasoning.

Expectations about the Document.   All readers expect me to spell things out, but to be concise. Visuals will help compress and emphasize material throughout.

Essential information will include an expanded definition of technical marketing and sales, the skills and attitudes needed for success, the career's advantages and drawbacks, and a description of various paths for entering the career.

This report combines feasibility and comparative analysis, so I'll want to structure the report to reveal a clear line of reasoning: in the feasibility section, reasons for and reasons against; in the comparison section, a block structure and a table that compares the four entry paths point by point. The report will close with recommendations based solidly on my conclusions.

For various readers who might not wish to read the entire report, I will include an informative abstract.

NOTE   *This report's front matter (title page, informative abstract, and so on) and end matter are shown and discussed in Chapter 25 and on pages 665, 666.*

Feasibility Analysis of a Career in Technical Marketing

INTRODUCTION

In today's global business climate, graduates in science and engineering face narrowing career opportunities because of "offshoring" of hi-tech jobs to low-wage countries. Government research indicates that more than two-thirds of the 40 occupations "most prone to offshoring" are in science and engineering (Bureau of Labor Statistics [BLS], 2006a, p. 14). Experts Hira and Hira suggest that the offshoring situation threatens the livelihood of some of the best-paid workers in America (2005, p. 12). University career counselor Troy Behrens offers these disturbing numbers: "The U.S. will graduate 30,000 engineers this year. India and China will graduate 3 million" (cited in Jacobs, 2007). One research firm, Gartner, predicts that spending on outsourced engineering will multiply tenfold within 3 years (Dolan, 2007, p. 74).

Given such bleak prospects, graduates might consider alternative careers. Technical marketing is one field that combines science and engineering expertise with "people skills"— those least likely to be offshored (BLS, 2006a, p. 12). Engineers, for example, might seek jobs as *sales engineers*, specially trained professionals who market and sell highly technical products and services (BLS, 2006b).

What specific type of work do technical marketers perform? *The Occupational Outlook Handbook* offers this job description:

> They usually sell products whose installation and optimal use requires a great deal of technical expertise and support. . . . Additionally, they provide information on their firm's products, help prospective and current buyers with technical problems, recommend improved materials and machinery . . . , design plans of proposed machinery layouts, estimate cost savings, and suggest training schedules for employees (BLS, 2006b).

(For a more detailed job description, refer to "The Technical Marketing Process," on page 2.)

Undergraduates interested in technical marketing need answers to basic questions:

- *Is this the right career for me?*
- *If so, how do I enter the field?*

To help answer these questions, this report analyzes information from professionals and from the literature. After defining *technical marketing,* the analysis examines employment outlook, required skills and personal qualities, career benefits and drawbacks, and entry options.

FIGURE 24.4 An Analytical Report

COLLECTED DATA

Key Factors in a Technical Marketing Career

Anyone considering technical marketing needs to assess whether this career fits his or her interests, abilities, and aspirations.

THE TECHNICAL MARKETING PROCESS. Technical marketing involves far more than sales work. According to a classic definition, the process itself (identifying, reaching, and selling to customers) entails six key activities (Cornelius & Lewis, 1983, p. 44):

1. *Market research:* assessing size and character of the product's target market.
2. *Product development and management:* producing the goods to fill a market need.
3. *Cost determination and pricing:* measuring every expense in the production, distribution, advertising, and sales of the product, to determine its price.
4. *Advertising and promotion:* developing all strategies for reaching customers.
5. *Product distribution:* coordinating all elements of a technical product or service, from its conception through its final delivery to the customer.
6. *Sales and technical support:* creating and maintaining customer accounts, and servicing and upgrading products.

Fully engaged in all these activities, the technical marketing professional gains a detailed understanding of the industry, the product, and the customer's needs (Figure 1).

Figure 1 The Technical Marketing Process

Source: Selected information from "Services for Clients." Technology Marketing Group, Inc. (1998). <www.technology-marketing.com>

FIGURE 24.4 *(Continued)*

Feasibility Analysis   **3**

EMPLOYMENT OUTLOOK. For graduates with the right combination of technical and personal qualifications, the employment outlook for technical marketing appears excellent. While engineering jobs will increase at less than the average growth rate for jobs requiring a Bachelor's degree, marketing jobs will exceed the average rate (Figure 2).

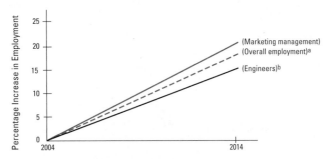

Figure 2 The Employment Outlook for Technical Marketing

[a]Jobs requiring a Bachelor's degree.

[b]Excluding outlying rates for specialties at the positive end of the spectrum (environmental engineers: +30%; software engineers: +10%).

Source: Data from U.S. Department of Labor. Bureau of Labor Statistics. Retrieved April 25, 2007, from http://www.bls.gov/EMP/optd/optd001.pdf

Although highly competitive, these marketing positions call for the very kinds of technical, analytical, and problem-solving skills that engineers can offer—especially in an automated environment.

TECHNICAL SKILLS REQUIRED. Computer networks, interactive media, and multimedia will increasingly influence the way products are advertised and sold. Also, marketing representatives increasingly work from a "virtual" office. Using laptop computers, fax networks, personal digital assistants, and other devices, representatives in the field have real-time access to electronic catalogs of product lines, multimedia presentations, pricing for customized products, inventory data, product distribution channels, and customized sales contacts (Tolland, 2007).

With their rich background in computer, technical, and problem-solving skills, engineering graduates are ideally suited for (a) working in automated environments, and (b) implementing and troubleshooting these complex and often sensitive electronic systems.

FIGURE 24.4 *(Continued)*

Feasibility Analysis   **4**

OTHER SKILLS AND QUALITIES REQUIRED. *BusinessWeek's* Peter Coy offers this distinction between routine versus non routine work:

> The jobs that will pay well in the future will be ones that are hard to reduce to a recipe. These attractive jobs—from factory floor management to sales to teaching to the professions—require flexibility, creativity, and lifelong learning. They generally also require subtle and frequent interactions with other people, often face to face. (2004, p. 50)

Technical marketing is just such a job: it involves few "cookbook-type" tasks and it requires a firm grasp of "people skills." Besides a strong technical background, success in this field calls for a generous blend of those traits summarized in Figure 3.

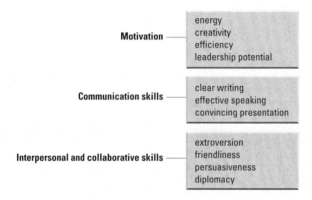

Figure 3 Requirements for a Technical Marketing Career

Motivation is essential for marketing work. Professionals must be energetic and able to function with minimal supervision. Career counselor Phil Hawkins describes the ideal candidates as people who can plan and program their own tasks, who can manage their time, and who have no fear of hard work (personal interview, February 11, 2007). Leadership potential, as demonstrated by extracurricular activities, is an asset.

Motivation alone provides no guarantee of success. Marketing professionals are paid to communicate the value of their products and services, both orally and in writing. They routinely prepare documents ranging from sales proposals to product descriptions to user manuals. Successful job candidates typically have taken courses in advertising, public speaking, technical writing, and –increasingly– foreign language (BLS, 2006c).

FIGURE 24.4 *(Continued)*

Skilled oral presentation is vital to any sales effort, as Phil Hawkins points out. Technical marketing professionals need to speak confidently and persuasively—to represent their products and services in the best light (personal interview, February 11, 2007). Sales presentations often involve public speaking at conventions, trade shows, and similar forums.

The ultimate requirement for success in marketing is interpersonal and collaborative skills: "tact, good judgement, and exceptional ability to establish and maintain effective personal relationships with supervisory and professional staff members and client firms" (BLS, 2006c).

ADVANTAGES OF THE CAREER. As shown in Figure 1, technical marketing offers diverse experience in every phase of a company's operation, from a product's design to its sales and service. Such broad exposure provides excellent preparation for countless upper-management positions. In fact, sales engineers with solid experience often open their own businesses as freelance "manufacturers' agents" representing a variety of companies who have no marketing staff of their own. In effect their own bosses, manufacturers' agents are free to choose, from among many offers, the products they wish to represent (Tolland, 2007).

Another career benefit is the attractive salary. In addition to typically receiving a base pay plus commissions, marketing professionals are reimbursed for business expenses. Other employee benefits often include health insurance, a pension plan, and a company car. In 2004, the median annual earnings for sales engineers ranged from $53,270 for professional and commercial equipment sales to $86,980 for computer systems design services. The highest 10 percent earned more than $117,260 annually (BLS, 2006b).

The interpersonal and communication skills that marketing professionals develop are highly portable. This is vital in our rapidly shifting economy, in which job security is disappearing in the face of more and more temporary positions (Tolland, 2007).

DRAWBACKS OF THE CAREER. Technical marketing is by no means a career for every engineer. Sales engineer Roger Cayer cautions that personnel might spend most of their time traveling to meet potential customers. Success requires hard work over long hours, evenings, and occasional weekends. Above all, the job is stressful because of constant pressure to meet sales quotas (phone interview, February 8, 2007). Anyone considering this career should be able to work and thrive in a highly competitive environment. The Bureau of Labor Statistics (2006c) adds that the expanding global economy means that "international travel, to secure contracts with foreign customers, is becoming more important"—typically placing more pressure on an already hectic schedule.

FIGURE 24.4 *(Continued)*

A Comparison of Entry Options

Engineers and other technical graduates enter technical marketing through one of four options. Some join small companies and learn their trade directly on the job. Others join companies that offer formal training programs. Some begin by getting experience in their technical specialty. Others earn a graduate degree beforehand. These options are compared below.

OPTION 1: ENTRY-LEVEL MARKETING WITH ON-THE-JOB TRAINING. Smaller manufacturers offer marketing positions in which people learn on the job. Elaine Carto, president of ABCO Electronics, believes small companies offer a unique opportunity; entry-level salespersons learn about all facets of an organization, and have a good possibility for rapid advancement (personal interview, February 10, 2007). Career counselor Phil Hawkins says, "It's all a matter of whether you prefer to be a big fish in a small pond or a small fish in a big pond" (personal interview, February 11, 2007).

Entry-level marketing offers immediate income and a chance for early promotion. But one disadvantage might be the loss of any technical edge one might have acquired in college.

OPTION 2: A MARKETING AND SALES TRAINING PROGRAM. Formal training programs offer the most popular entry into sales and marketing. Large to mid-size companies typically offer two formats: (a) a product-specific program, focused on a particular product or product line, or (b) a rotational program, in which trainees learn about an array of products and work in the various positions outlined in Figure 1. Programs last from weeks to months. Intel Corporation, for example, offers 30-month training programs titled "Sales and Marketing Rotation," to prepare new graduates for positions as technical sales engineer, marketing technical engineer, and technical applications engineer.

Like direct entry, this option offers the advantage of immediate income and early promotion. With no chance to practice in their technical specialty, however, trainees might eventually find their technical expertise compromised.

OPTION 3: PRIOR EXPERIENCE IN ONE'S TECHNICAL SPECIALTY. Instead of directly entering marketing, some candidates first gain experience in their specialty. This option combines direct exposure to the workplace with the chance to sharpen technical skills in practical applications. In addition, some companies, such as Roger Cayer's, will offer marketing and sales positions to outstanding staff engineers, as a step toward upper management (phone interview, February 8, 2007).

FIGURE 24.4 *(Continued)*

Feasibility Analysis   **7**

Although the prior-experience option delays a candidate's entry into technical marketing, industry experts consider direct workplace and technical experience key assets for career growth in any field. Also, work experience becomes an asset for applicants to top MBA programs (Shelley, 1997, pp. 30–31).

OPTION 4: GRADUATE PROGRAM. Instead of direct entry, some people choose to pursue an MS degree in their specialty or an MBA. According to engineering professor Mary McClane, MS degrees are usually unnecessary for technical marketing unless the particular products are highly complex (personal interview, April 2, 2007).

In general, jobseekers with an MBA have a distinct competitive advantage. More significantly, new MBAs with a technical bachelor's degree and one to two years of experience command salaries from 10 to 30 percent higher than MBAs who lack work experience and a technical bachelor's degree. In fact, no more than 3 percent of job candidates offer a "techno-MBA" specialty, making this unique group highly desirable to employers (Shelley, 1997, p. 30). A motivated student might combine graduate degrees. Dora Anson, president of Susimo Cosmic Systems, sees the MS/MBA combination as ideal preparation for technical marketing (2007).

One disadvantage of a full-time graduate program is lost salary, compounded by school expenses. These costs must be weighed against the prospect of promotion and monetary rewards later in one's career.

AN OVERALL COMPARISON BY RELATIVE ADVANTAGE. Table 1 compares the four entry options on the basis of three criteria: immediate income, rate of advancement, and long-term potential.

Table 1 Relative Advantages Among Four Technical-Marketing Entry Options

	Relative Advantages		
Option	Early, immediate income	Greatest advancement in marketing	Long-term potential
Entry level, no experience	yes	yes	no
Training program	yes	yes	no
Practical experience	yes	no	yes
Graduate program	no	no	yes

FIGURE 24.4 *(Continued)*

CONCLUSION

Summary of Findings

Technical marketing and sales requires solid technical background, motivation, communication skills, and interpersonal skills. This career offers job diversity and excellent income potential, balanced against hard work and relentless pressure to perform.

College graduates interested in this field confront four entry options: (1) direct entry with on-the-job training, (2) a formal training program, (3) prior experience in a technical specialty, and (4) graduate programs. Each option has benefits and drawbacks based on immediacy of income, rate of advancement, and long-term potential.

Interpretation of Findings

For graduates with a strong technical background and the right skills and motivation, technical marketing offers attractive career prospects. Anyone contemplating this field, however, needs to enjoy customer contact and thrive in a competitive environment.

Those who decide that technical marketing is for them can choose various entry options:

- For hands-on experience, direct entry is the logical option.
- For sophisticated sales training, a formal program with a large company is best.
- For sharpening technical skills, prior work in one's specialty is invaluable.
- If immediate income is not vital, graduate school is an attractive option.

Recommendations

If your interests and abilities match the requirements, consider these suggestions:

1. For a firsthand view, seek the advice and opinions of people in the field. You might begin by contacting professional organizations such as the Manufacturers' Agents National Association at www.manaonline.org.
2. Before settling on an entry option, consider all its advantages and disadvantages and decide whether this option best coincides with your career goals. (Of course, you can always combine options during your professional life.)
3. When making any career decision, consider career counselor Phil Hawkins' advice: "Listen to your brain and your heart" (personal interview, February 11, 2007). Choose options that offer not only professional advancement but also personal satisfaction.

REFERENCES

[The complete list of references is shown and discussed on pages 665, 666.]

FIGURE 24.4 *(Continued)*

Guidelines for Reasoning through an Analytical Problem

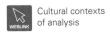 Cultural contexts of analysis

Audiences approach an analytical report with this basic question:

| *Is this analysis based on sound reasoning?*

Whether your report documents a causal, comparative, or feasibility analysis (or some combination) you need to trace your line of reasoning so that readers can follow it clearly.

As you prepare your report, refer to the usability checklist on page 594 and observe the following guidelines:

For Causal Analysis

1. **Be sure the cause fits the effect.** Keep in mind that faulty causal reasoning is extremely common, especially when we ignore other possible causes or we confuse mere coincidence with causation. For more on this topic, see pages 159–61.

2. **Make the links between effect and cause clear.** Identify the immediate cause (the one most closely related to the effect) as well as the distant cause(s) (the ones that precede the immediate cause). For example, the immediate cause of a particular airplane crash might be a fuel-tank explosion, caused by a short circuit in frayed wiring, caused by faulty design or poor quality control by the manufacturer. Discussing only the immediate cause often just scratches the surface of the problem.

3. **Clearly distinguish between possible, probable, and definite causes.** Unless the cause is obvious, limit your assertions by using *perhaps, probably, maybe, most likely, could, seems to, appears to,* or similar qualifiers that prevent you from making an insupportable claim.

For Comparative Analysis

1. **Rest the comparison on clear and definite criteria: costs, uses, benefits/ drawbacks, appearance, results.** In evaluating the merits of competing items, identify your specific criteria (cost, ease of use, durability, and so on) and rank these criteria in order of importance.

2. **Give each item balanced treatment.** Discuss points of comparison for each item in identical order.

3. **Support and clarify the comparison or contrast through credible examples.** Use research, if necessary, for examples that readers can visualize.

4. **Follow either a block pattern or a point-by-point pattern.** In the block pattern, first one item is discussed fully, then the next. Choose a block pattern when the overall picture is more important than the individual points.

   In the point-by-point pattern, one point about both items is discussed, then the next point, and so on. Choose a point-by-point pattern when specific points might be hard to remember unless placed side by side.

(continues)

Guidelines (continued)

Block pattern	**Point-by-point pattern**
Item A	first point of A/first point of B, etc.
first point	
second point, etc.	
Item B	second point of A/second point of B, etc.
first point	
second point, etc.	

For illustration of each of these patterns in an actual document, see pages 210–11.

5. **Order your points for greatest emphasis.** Try ordering your points from least to most important or dramatic or useful or reasonable. Placing the most striking point last emphasizes it best.

6. **In an evaluative comparison ("X is better than Y"),** offer your final judgment. Base your judgment squarely on the criteria presented.

For Feasibility Analysis

1. **Consider the strength of supporting reasons.** Choose the best reasons for supporting the action or decision being considered—based on your collected evidence.

2. **Consider the strength of opposing reasons.** Remember that people—including ourselves—usually see only what they want to see. Avoid the temptation to overlook or downplay opposing reasons, especially for an action or decision that you have been promoting. Consider alternate points of view; examine and evaluate all the evidence.

3. **Recommend a realistic course of action.** After weighing all the pros and cons, make your recommendation—but be prepared to reconsider if you discover that what seemed like the right course of action turns out to be the wrong one.

 Usability testing

✔ Checklist: Usability of Analytical Reports

For evaluating your research methods and reasoning, refer also to the checklist on page 170. (Numbers in parentheses refer to the first page of discussion.)

Content

☐ Does the report address a clearly identified problem or goal? (564)

☐ Is the report's length and detail appropriate for the subject? (564)

☐ Is there enough information for readers to make an informed decision? (565)

☐ Are all limitations of the analysis clearly acknowledged? (569)

☐ Is the information accurate, unbiased, and complete? (565)

☐ Are visuals used whenever possible to aid communication? (568)

☐ Are all necessary report components included? (571)

☐ Are all data fully interpreted? (567)

☐ Are the conclusions logically derived from accurate interpretation? (568)

☐ Do the recommendations constitute an appropriate and reasonable response to the question or problem? (569)

☐ Is each source and contribution properly cited? (634)

☐ Is all needed front and end matter included? (598)

Arrangement

☐ Is there a distinct introduction, body, and conclusion? (571)

☐ Does the introduction provide sufficient orientation to the issue or problem? (572)

☐ Does the body section present a clear picture of the evidence and reasoning? (573)

☐ Does the conclusion answer the question that originally sparked the analysis? (581)

☐ Are there clear transitions between related ideas? (693)

Style and Page Design

☐ Is the level of technicality appropriate for the primary audience? (28)

☐ Are headings informative and adequate? (312)

☐ Is the writing clear, concise, and fluent? (216)

☐ Is the language convincing, precise, and informative? (232)

☐ Is the report grammatical? (670)

☐ Is the page design inviting and accessible? (298)

 Exercise

Prepare an analytical report, using these guidelines:

a. Choose a subject for analysis from the list of questions at the end of this exercise, from your major, or from a subject of interest.

b. Identify the problem or question so that you will know exactly what you are seeking.

c. Restate the main question as a declarative sentence in your statement of purpose.

d. Identify an audience—other than your instructor—who will use your information for a specific purpose.

e. Hold a private brainstorming session to generate major topics and subtopics.

f. Use the topics to make an outline based on the model outline in this chapter. Divide as far as necessary to identify all points of discussion.

g. Make a tentative list of all sources (primary and secondary) that you will investigate. Verify that adequate sources are available.

h. In a proposal memo to your instructor, describe the problem or question and your plan for analysis. Attach a tentative bibliography.

i. Use your working outline as a guide to research and observation. Evaluate sources and evidence, and interpret all evidence fully. Modify your outline as needed.

j. Submit a progress report to your instructor describing work completed, problems encountered, and work remaining.

k. Compose an audience and use profile. (Use the sample on page 583 as a model, along with the profile worksheet on page 35.)

l. Write the report for your stated audience. Work from a clear statement of purpose, and be sure that your reasoning is shown clearly. Verify that your evidence, conclusions, and recommendations are consistent. Be especially careful that your recommendations observe the critical-thinking guidelines in Figure 24.3.

m. After writing your first draft, make any needed changes in the outline and revise your report according to the revision checklist. Include all necessary supplements.

n. Exchange reports with a classmate for further suggestions for revision.

o. Prepare an oral report of your findings for the class as a whole.

Base your analysis on a question similar to these:

- What has and hasn't been done to protect a nearby port, nuclear plant, or chemical plant from sabotage or attack?
- How adequate is your area's evacuation plan?
- How can local hospitals reduce medical errors?
- Who are the biggest polluters in your area, and what can be done?
- How should your state deal with discarded computers and other "ewaste"?
- What can local schools do to stem the obesity epidemic?
- Is mass smallpox vaccination a good idea?
- How safe is our food supply, and what can be done to protect it?
- How should we deal with the Mad-Cow threat?
- Which gender is the more competitive, and what could this difference mean in the workplace?
- How will digital convergence change our work and our world?

- Which diets should be avoided, and why?
- How can future skyscrapers be made safer?
- Can wind power be profitable?
- Are efforts to deflect incoming asteroids worth the cost?
- Stem cell research: What progress has been made so far? Prospects?
- Can nuclear power plants be dismantled safely?
- What are the unintended consequences of banning DDT, or some other major policy decision?
- What are pros and cons of distance learning?
- Are treatments such as homeopathy or acupuncture feasible alternatives to traditional medicine?
- Are irradiated or genetically modified foods safe?
- What are the pros and cons of legalizing gambling in your state?
- Which should you buy: a condominium or a house?
- Should you move to a different part of the country or the world?
- How have budget cuts affected your public schools?
- Is police protection adequate in your area?
- How should people prepare for long-term job prospects in your field?
- In which fields are women paid less than men? Why?
- What are pros and cons of home birth (vs. hospital delivery).
- How can tourism be promoted in your area?
- Should you work before graduate school?

 Collaborative Projects

1. Divide into small groups. Choose a topic for group analysis—preferably, a campus issue—and brainstorm. Draw up a working outline that could be used as an analytical report on this subject.

2. Prepare a questionnaire based on your work above, and administer it to members of your campus community. Report the findings of your questionnaire and your conclusions and recommendations. (Review pages 140–45, on questionnaires and surveys.)

CHAPTER 25

Front Matter and End Matter in Long Documents

Cover

Title Page

Letter of Transmittal

Table of Contents

List of Tables and Figures

Abstract or Executive Summary

Glossary

Appendices

Documentation

A long document must be easily accessible and must accommodate users with different interests. Preceding the report is *front matter:* The cover, title page, letter of transmittal, table of contents, and abstract give summary information about the content of the document. Following the report (as needed) is *end matter:* The glossary, appendices, and list of works cited can either provide supporting data or help users understand technical sections. Users can refer to any of these supplements or skip them altogether, according to their needs.

Cover

Use a sturdy, plain cover with page fasteners. With the cover on, the open pages should lie flat. Use covers only for long documents.

Center the report title and your name four to five inches below the top of your page. (Many workplace reports include the company name and logo instead of the report author's name).

> THE FEASIBILITY OF A TECHNICAL MARKETING CAREER:
> AN ANALYSIS
> by
> Richard B. Larkin, Jr.

Title Page

The title page lists the report title, author's name, name of person(s) or organization to whom the report is addressed, and date of submission.

The title announces the report's purpose and subject by using descriptive words such as "analysis," "instructions," "proposal," "feasibility," "description," "progress." Do not number your title page but count it as page i of the front matter. Center the title and all other lines (Figure 25.1).

Letter of Transmittal

Include a letter of transmittal with any formal report or proposal addressed to a specific reader. As a gesture of courtesy, your letter might

What to include in a letter of transmittal

- acknowledge those who helped with the report
- thank the recipient for any special assistance
- refer to sections of special interest
- discuss the limitations of your study, or any problems gathering data
- discuss possible follow-up investigations
- offer personal (or off-the-record) observations
- suggest some special uses for the information
- urge the recipient to immediate action

The transmittal letter is tailored to a particular audience, as is Richard Larkin's in Figure 25.2. If a report is being sent to a number of people who are variously

Feasibility Analysis
of a Career
in Technical Marketing

for

Professor J. M. Lannon
Technical Writing Instructor
University of Massachusetts
North Dartmouth, Massachusetts

by

Richard B. Larkin, Jr.
English 266 Student

May 1, 20XX

FIGURE 25.1 **Title Page for a Formal Report**

165 Hammond Way
Hyannis, MA 02457
April 29, 20XX

John Fitton
Placement Director
University of Massachusetts
North Dartmouth, MA 02747

Dear Mr. Fitton:

Here is my report, Feasibility Analysis of a Career in Technical Marketing. In preparing this report, I've learned a great deal about the requirements and modes of access to this career, and I believe my information will help other students as well. Thank you for your guidance and encouragement throughout this process.

Although committed to their specialties, some technical and science graduates seem interested in careers in which they can apply their technical knowledge to customer and business problems. Technical marketing may be an attractive choice of career for those who know their field, who can relate to different personalities, and who communicate well.

Technical marketing is competitive and demanding, but highly rewarding. In fact, it is an excellent route to upper-management and executive positions. Specifically, marketing work enables one to develop a sound technical knowledge of a company's products, to understand how these products fit into the marketplace, and to perfect sales techniques and interpersonal skills. This is precisely the kind of background that paves the way to top-level jobs.

I've enjoyed my work on this project, and would be happy to answer any questions. Please phone me at 690-555-1122 anytime.

Sincerely,

Richard B. Larkin

Richard B. Larkin, Jr.

FIGURE 25.2 Letter of Transmittal for a Formal Report

qualified and bear various relationships to the writer, individual letters of transmittal may vary.

How to prepare
the transmittal
letter

Begin your letter by referring to the user's original request, and introduce your report by name. Briefly review the reasons for your report or include a short abstract. Maintain a confident and positive tone. Indicate pride and satisfaction in your work. Avoid implied apologies, such as "I hope this report meets your expectations."

In the body section, include items from the above-mentioned list of possibilities (acknowledgments, special problems). Although your abstract or executive summary will summarize major findings, conclusions, and recommendations, your letter gives a brief and personal overview of the *entire project*.

End on a positive theme: "I believe that the data in this report are accurate, that they have been analyzed rigorously and impartially, and that the recommendations are sound." Express your willingness to answer questions or discuss findings. Show how the reader can get in touch quickly with the writer.

NOTE   *For college reports, the letter of transmittal usually follows the title page and is bound as part of the report. For workplace reports, the letter usually is not bound in the report but is presented separately.*

Table of Contents

Help readers find the information they're looking for by providing a table of contents. In designing your table of contents, follow these guidelines:

How to prepare a
table of contents

- List front matter (transmittal letter, abstract), numbering the pages with lowercase roman numerals. (The title page, though not listed, is counted page i.) Number glossary, appendix, and endnote pages with arabic numerals, continuing the page sequence of your report proper, in which page 1 is the first page of the report text.
- Include no headings in the table of contents not listed as headings or subheadings in the report; the report may, however, contain subheadings not listed in the table of contents.
- Phrase headings in the table of contents exactly as in the report.
- List headings at various levels in varying type styles and indention.
- Use *leader lines* (. . . . .) to connect headings to page numbers. Align rows of leader lines vertically, each above the other.

Figure 25.3 shows the table of contents for Richard Larkin's feasibility analysis.

With some word-processing programs you can generate a table of contents automatically provided that you have assigned styles or codes to all of the headings in your report. If your word-processing program does not have this feature, compose the table of contents by assigning page numbers to headings from your iii

CONTENTS

LETTER OF TRANSMITTAL ii

FIGURES AND TABLES iv

ABSTRACT v

INTRODUCTION 1

COLLECTED DATA 2

    Key Factors in a Technical Marketing Career 2

        The Technical Marketing Process 2

        Employment Outlook 3

        Technical Skills Required 3

        Other Skills and Qualities Required 4

        Advantages of the Career 5

        Drawbacks of the Career 5

    A Comparison of Entry Options 6

        Option 1:   Entry-Level Marketing with On-the-Job Training 6

        Option 2:   A Marketing and Sales Training Program 6

        Option 3:   Prior Experience in One's Technical Specialty 6

        Option 4:   Graduate Program 7

        An Overall Comparison by Relative Advantage 7

CONCLUSION 8

    Summary of Findings 8

    Interpretation of Findings 8

    Recommendations 8

REFERENCES 8

FIGURE 25.3 **Table of Contents for a Formal Report**

outline. Keep in mind, however, that not all levels of outline headings should appear in your table of contents or your report. Excessive headings can fragment the discussion.

List of Tables and Figures

Following the table of contents is a list of tables and figures, if needed. When a report has four or more visuals, place this list on a separate page. List the figures first, then the tables. Figure 25.4 shows the list of tables and figures in Larkin's report.

TABLES AND FIGURES

Figure 1   The Technical Marketing Process 2

Figure 2   The Employment Outlook for Technical Marketing 3

Figure 3   Requirements for a Technical Marketing Career 4

Table 1   Relative Advantages among Four Technical-Marketing
           Entry Options 7

FIGURE 25.4 **A List of Tables and Figures for a Formal Report**

Abstract or Executive Summary

Reports are often read by many people: researchers, managers, executives, customers. For readers who are interested only in the big picture, the entire report may not be relevant. Many readers who don't have the time or willingness to read your entire report will consider the informative abstract the most useful part of the material you present. In addition to the Chapter 11 guidelines for summarizing information, follow these suggestions for preparing your abstract[1]:

How to prepare an informative abstract

- Make sure your abstract stands alone in terms of meaning.
- Write for a general audience. Readers of the abstract are likely to vary in expertise, perhaps more than those who read the report itself; therefore, adjust the vocabulary to suit the intended reader. When you send report copies to readers with varying levels of expertise, write a different summary for each type of reader.

---

[1] My thanks to Professor Edith K. Weinstein for these suggestions.

- Add no new information. Simply present the report's highlights.
- Present your information in the following sequence:
  a. Identify the issue or need that led to the report.
  b. Offer key facts, statistics, and findings—material your reader *must* know.
  c. Include a condensed conclusion and recommendations, if any.

The informative abstract in Figure 25.5 accompanies Richard Larkin's report.

NOTE   *This item can be called many different names including summary, abstract, informative abstract, executive summary, executive abstract, or report synopsis.*

ABSTRACT

The feasibility of technical marketing as a career is based on a college graduate's interests, abilities, and expectations, as well as on possible entry options.

Technical marketing is a feasible career for anyone who is motivated, who can communicate well, and who knows how to get along. Although this career offers job diversity and potential for excellent income, it entails almost constant travel, competition, and stress.

College graduates enter technical marketing through one of four options: entry-level positions that offer hands-on experience, formal training programs in large companies, prior experience in one's specialty, or graduate programs. The relative advantages and disadvantages of each option can be measured in resulting immediacy of income, rapidity of advancement, and long-term potential.

Anyone considering a technical marketing career should follow these recommendations:

- Speak with people who work in the field.
- Weigh the implications of each entry option carefully.
- Consider combining two or more options.
- Choose options for personal as well as professional benefits.

FIGURE 25.5 Informative Abstract

Glossary

A glossary alphabetically lists specialized terms and their definitions. A glossary makes key definitions available to laypersons without interrupting technical readers. Use a glossary if your report contains more than five or six technical terms that may not be understood by all audience members. If fewer than five terms need defining, place them in the report introduction as working definitions, or use footnote definitions. If you use a separate glossary, announce its location: "(See the glossary at the end of this report)."

Follow these suggestions for preparing a glossary:

How to prepare a glossary

- Define all terms unfamiliar to an intelligent layperson. When in doubt, overdefining is safer than underdefining.
- Define all terms that have a special meaning in your report ("In this report, a small business is defined as . . .").
- Define all terms by giving their class and distinguishing features (page 442), unless some terms need expanded definitions.
- List all terms in alphabetical order. Highlight each term and use a colon to separate it from its definition.
- On first use, place an asterisk in the text by each item defined in the glossary.
- List your glossary and its first page number in the table of contents.

Figure 25.6 shows part of a glossary for a comparative analysis of two natural childbirth techniques, written by a nurse practitioner for expectant mothers and student nurses. (For a hyperlinked glossary, see page 454.)

GLOSSARY

Analgesic: a medication given to relieve pain during the first stage of labor.

Cervix: the neck-shaped anatomical structure that forms the mouth of the uterus.

Dilation: cervical expansion occurring during the first stage of labor.

Episiotomy: an incision of the outer vaginal tissue, made by the obstetrician just before the delivery, to enlarge the vaginal opening.

First stage of labor: the stage in which the cervix dilates and the baby remains in the uterus.

Induction: the stimulating of labor by puncturing the membranes around the baby or by giving an oxytoxic drug (uterine contractant), or by doing both.

FIGURE 25.6 A Partial Glossary

Appendices

Add one or more appendices to your report if you have large blocks of material or other documents that are relevant but will bog readers down if placed in the middle of the report itself. (Page 555 shows an appendix to a funding proposal.) Items that belong in an appendix might include the following:

What an
appendix might
include

- complex formulas
- details of an experiment
- interview questions and responses
- long quotations (one or more pages)
- maps
- material more essential to secondary readers than to primary readers
- photographs
- related correspondence (letters of inquiry, and so on)
- sample questionnaires and tabulated responses
- sample tests and tabulated results
- some visuals occupying more than one full page
- statistical or other measurements
- texts of laws and regulations

Do not stuff appendices with needless information or use them unethically for burying bad or embarrassing news that belongs in the report proper. In preparing your appendices, follow these suggestions:

How to prepare
an appendix

- Include only relevant material.
- Use a separate appendix for each major item.
- Title each appendix clearly: "Appendix A: Projected Costs."
- Use appendices sparingly. Four or five appendices in a ten-page report indicates a poorly organized document.
- Limit an appendix to a few pages, unless more length is essential.
- Mention the appendix early in the introduction, and refer to it at appropriate points in the report: "(see Appendix A)."

Users should be able to understand your report without having to turn to the appendix. Distill essential facts from your appendix and place them in your report text.

IMPROPER **REFERENCE**	The whale population declined drastically between 1996 and 2007 (see Appendix B for details).
PROPER **REFERENCE**	The whale population declined by 16 percent from 1996 to 2007 (see Appendix B for statistical breakdown).

Documentation

In the endnotes or works cited pages, list each of your outside references in alphabetical order or in the same numerical order as they are cited in the report proper. See "A Quick Guide to Documentation" (page 634) for discussion.

Exercises

1. These titles are intended for investigative, research, or analytical reports. Revise each inadequate title to make it clear and accurate.
   a. The Effectiveness of the Prison Furlough Program in Our State
   b. Drug Testing on the Job
   c. The Effects of Nuclear Power Plants
   d. Woodburning Stoves
   e. Interviewing
   f. An Analysis of Vegetables (for a report assessing the physiological effects of a vegetarian diet)
   g. Wood as a Fuel Source
   h. Oral Contraceptives
   i. Lie Detectors and Employees

2. Prepare a title page, letter of transmittal (for a specific reader who can use your information in a definite way), table of contents, and informative abstract for a report you have written earlier.

3. Find a short but effective appendix in one of your textbooks, in a journal article in your field, or in a report from your workplace. In a memo to your instructor and classmates, explain how the appendix is used, how it relates to the main text, and why it is effective. Attach a copy of the appendix to your memo. Be prepared to discuss your evaluation in class.

CHAPTER 26

Oral Presentations

Advantages and Drawbacks of Oral Reports

Avoiding Presentation Pitfalls

Planning Your Presentation

Preparing Your Presentation

Guidelines for Readable Visuals

Guidelines for Understandable Visuals

Guidelines for Using Presentation Software

Delivering Your Presentation

Guidelines for Presenting Visuals

Guidelines for Managing Listener Questions

Consider This Cross-Cultural Audiences May Have Specific Expectations

Checklist: Oral Presentations

We all need to present our ideas effectively in person. Oral presentations vary in style, range, complexity, and formality. They may include convention speeches, reports at national meetings, reports via teleconferencing networks, technical briefings for colleagues, and speeches to community groups. These talks may be designed to inform (say, to describe new government safety requirements), to persuade (say, to induce company officers to vote a pay raise), or to do both. The higher your status, on the job or in the community, the more you can expect to give oral presentations.

Advantages and Drawbacks of Oral Reports

Advantages

Unlike written documents, oral presentations are truly interactive. In face-to-face communication, you can rely on body language, vocal tone, eye contact, and other elements of human chemistry—a likable personality can have a powerful effect on audience receptiveness. Also, oral presentations provide for give-and-take, which does not happen with traditional written documents. As you see how your audience reacts, you can adjust your presentation accordingly and answer questions immediately.

Drawbacks

In a written report you generally have plenty of time to think about what you're saying and how you're saying it, and to revise until the message is just right. For an oral report, one attempt is basically all you get, and all this pressure makes it easier to stumble. (People consistently rank fear of public speaking higher than fear of dying!) Also, an oral report is limited in the amount and complexity of information it can present. Readers of a written report can follow their own pace and direction, going back and forth, perhaps skimming some sections and studying others. In an oral presentation, you establish the pace and the information flow, thereby creating the risk of "losing" or boring the listeners.

Avoiding Presentation Pitfalls

An oral presentation is only the tip of a pyramid built from many earlier labors. But such presentations often serve as the concrete measure of your overall job performance. In short, your audience's only basis for judgment may be the brief moments during which you stand before them.

The podium or lectern can be a lonely and intimidating place. In the words of two experts, "most persons in most presentational settings do not perform well" (Goodall and Waagen 14–15). Despite the fact that they can help make or break a person's career, oral presentations often turn out to be boring, confusing, unconvincing, or too long. Many are delivered ineptly, with the presenter losing her or his place, fumbling through notes, apologizing for forgetting something, or generally seeming disorganized and unprofessional. Table 26.1 lists some of the things that go wrong.

Speaker • • •	Visuals * * *	Setting ■ ■ ■
• makes no eye contact	* are nonexistent	■ is too noisy
• seems like a robot	* are hard to see	■ is too hot or cold
• hides behind the lectern	* are hard to interpret	■ is too large or small
• speaks too softly/loudly	* are out of sequence	■ is too bright for visuals
• sways, fidgets, paces	* are shown too rapidly	■ is too dark for notes
• rambles or loses her/his place	* are shown too slowly	■ has equipment missing
• never gets to the point	* have typos/errors	■ has broken equipment
• fumbles with notes or visuals	* are word-filled	
• has too much material		

TABLE 26.1 Common Pitfalls in Oral Presentations

Avoid difficulties through careful analysis, planning, and preparation.

Planning Your Presentation

Forge a relationship with the listeners; establish rapport; and persuade listeners their time has been well spent.

Analyze Your Listeners

Assess your listeners' needs, knowledge, concerns, level of involvement, and possible objections (Goodall and Waagen 16). Many audiences include people with varied technical backgrounds. Unless you have a good idea of each person's background, speak to a general, heterogeneous audience, as in a classroom of mixed majors.

Work from an Explicit Purpose Statement

Formulate, on paper, a statement of purpose in two or three sentences. Why, exactly, are you speaking on this subject? Who are your listeners? What do you want the listeners to think, know, or do? (A solid purpose statement can also serve as the introduction to your presentation.)

Assume, for example, that you represent an environmental engineering firm that has completed a study of groundwater quality in your area. The organization that sponsored your study has asked you to give an oral version of your written report, titled "Pollution Threats to Local Groundwater," at a town meeting.

After careful thought, you settle on this purpose statement:

Purpose
statement

> *PURPOSE:* By informing Cape Cod residents about the dangers to the Cape's freshwater supply posed by rapid population growth, this report is intended to increase local interest in the problem.

Now you are prepared to focus on the listeners and the speaking situation by asking these questions:

Questions for analyzing your listeners and purpose

- Who are my listeners (strangers, peers, superiors, clients)?
- What is their attitude toward me or the topic (hostile, indifferent, needy, friendly)?
- Why are they here (they want to be here, they are forced to be here, they are curious)?
- What kind of presentation do they expect (brief, informal; long, detailed; lecture)?
- What do these listeners already know (nothing, a little, a lot)?
- What do they need or want to know (overview, bottom line, nitty gritty)?
- How large is their stake in this topic (about layoffs, new policies, pay raises)?
- Do I want to motivate, mollify, inform, instruct, or warn my listeners?
- What are their biggest concerns or objections about this topic?
- What do I want them to think, know, or do?

Analyze Your Speaking Situation

The more you can discover about the circumstances, the setting, and the constraints for your presentation, the more deliberately you will be able to prepare.

Ask yourself these questions:

Questions for analyzing your speaking situation

- How much time will I have to speak?
- Will other people be speaking before or after me?
- How formal or informal is the setting?
- How large is the audience?
- How large is the room?
- How bright and adjustable is the lighting?
- What equipment is available?
- How much time do I have to prepare?

Later parts of this chapter explain how to incorporate your answers to the questions in your preparation.

Select a Delivery Method

Your presentation's effectiveness will depend largely on *how* it connects with listeners. Different types of delivery create different connections.

The Memorized Delivery.   This type of delivery takes a long time to prepare, offers no chance for revision during the presentation, and spells disaster if you lose your place. Avoid a memorized delivery in most workplace settings.

The Impromptu Delivery.   An impromptu (off-the-cuff) delivery can be a natural way of connecting with listeners—but only when you really know your material, feel comfortable with your audience, and are in an informal speaking situation (group brainstorming, or a response to a question: "Tell us about your team's progress on the automation project"). Avoid impromptu deliveries for complex information—no matter how well you know the material. If you have little warning beforehand, at least jot a few notes about what you want to say.

The Scripted Delivery.   For a complex technical presentation, a conference paper, or a formal speech, you may want to read your material verbatim from a prepared script. Scripted presentations work well if you have many details to present, are talkative, or have a strict time limit (e.g., at a conference), or if this audience makes you nervous. Consider a scripted delivery when you want the content, organization, and style of your presentation to be as near perfect as possible.

Although a scripted delivery helps you control your material, it offers little chance for audience interaction and it can be boring.

If you *do* plan to read aloud, allow ample preparation time. Leave plenty of white space between lines and paragraphs. Rehearse until you are able to glance up from the script periodically without losing your place. Plan on roughly two minutes per double-spaced page.

Role of Microsoft *PowerPoint* in presentations

The Extemporaneous Delivery.   An extemporaneous delivery is carefully planned, practiced, and based on notes that keep you on track. In this natural way of addressing an audience, you glance at your material and speak in a conversational style. Extemporaneous delivery is based on key ideas in sentence or topic outline form, often projected as overhead transparencies or as slides generated from presentation software such as Microsoft *PowerPoint*™.

The dangers in extemporaneous delivery are that you might lose track of your material, forget something important, say something unclearly, or exceed your time limit. Careful preparation is the key.

Table 26.2 summarizes the various uses and drawbacks of the most common types of delivery. In many instances, some combination of methods can be effective. For example, in an orientation for new employees, you might prefer the flexibility of an extemporaneous format but also read a brief passage aloud from time to time (e.g., excerpts from the company's formal code of ethics).

Preparing Your Presentation

To stay in control and build confidence, plan the presentation systematically. We will assume here that your presentation is extemporaneous.

Research Your Topic

Be prepared to support each assertion, opinion, conclusion, and recommendation with evidence and reason. Check your facts for accuracy. Begin gathering material

Delivery Method	* Main Uses*	• Main Drawbacks •
IMPROMPTU (inventing as you speak)	* in-house meetings * small, intimate groups * simple topics	• offers no chance to prepare • speaker might ramble • speaker might lose track
SCRIPTED (reading verbatim from a written work)	* formal speeches * large, unfamiliar groups * strict time limit * cross-cultural audiences * highly nervous speaker	• takes a long time to prepare • speaker can't move around • limits human contact • can appear stiff and unnatural • might bore listeners • makes working with visuals difficult
EXTEMPORANEOUS (speaking from an outline of key points)	* face-to-face presentations * medium-sized, familiar groups * moderately complex topics * somewhat flexible time limit * visually based presentations	• speaker might lose track • speaker might leave something out • speaker might get tongue-tied • speaker might exceed time limit • speaker might fumble with notes, visuals, or equipment

TABLE 26.2 A Comparison of Oral Presentation Methods

well ahead of time. Use summarizing techniques from Chapter 11. If your presentation is merely a spoken version of a written report, you can simply expand your outline for the written report into a sentence outline.

Aim for Simplicity and Conciseness

Boil the material down to a few main points. Listeners' normal attention span is about twenty minutes. Time yourself in practice sessions and trim as needed. (If the situation requires a lengthy presentation, plan a short break, with refreshments if possible, about halfway.)

Anticipate Audience Questions

Consider those parts of your presentation that listeners might question or challenge. You might need to clarify or justify information that is new, controversial, disappointing, or surprising.

 Alternative forms of outlining by storyboard in *PowerPoint*

Outline Your Presentation

Review Chapter 12 for organizing and outlining strategies. Each sentence in the following presentation outline is a topic sentence for a paragraph that a well-prepared speaker can develop in detail.

Pollution Threats to Local Groundwater

ARNOLD BORTHWICK

I. Introduction to the Problem
    A. Do you know what you are drinking when you turn on the tap and fill a glass?
    B. The quality of our water is good, but not guaranteed to last forever.
    C. Cape Cod's rapid population growth poses a serious threat to our freshwater supply. (Visual #1)
    D. Measurable pollution in some town water supplies has already occurred. (Visual #2)
    E. What are the major causes and consequences of this problem and what can we do about it? (Visual #3)

II. Description of the Aquifer
    A. The groundwater is collected and held in an aquifer.
        1. This porous rock formation creates a broad, continuous arch beneath the entire Cape. (Visual #4)
        2. The lighter freshwater flows on top of the heavier saltwater.
    B. This type of natural storage facility, combined with rapid population growth, creates potential for disaster.

III. Hazards from Sewage and Landfills
    A. With increasing population, sewage and solid waste from landfill dumps increasingly invade the aquifer.
    B. The Cape's sandy soil promotes rapid seepage of wastes into the groundwater.
    C. As wastes flow naturally toward the sea, they can invade the drawing radii of town wells. (Visual #5)

IV. Hazards from Saltwater Intrusion
    A. Increased population also causes overdraw on some town wells, resulting in saltwater intrusion. (Visual #6)
    B. Salt and calcium used in snow removal add to the problem by seeping into the aquifer from surface runoff.

V. Long-Term Environmental and Economic Consequences
    A. The environmental effects of continuing pollution of our water table will be far-reaching. (Visual #7)
        1. Drinking water will have to be piped in more than 100 miles from Quabbin Reservoir.
        2. The Cape's beautiful freshwater ponds will be unfit for swimming.
        3. Aquatic and aviary marsh life will be threatened.
        4. The Cape's sensitive ecology might well be damaged beyond repair.
    B. Such environmental damage would, in turn, spell economic disaster for Cape Cod's major industry—tourism.

VI. Conclusion and Recommendations
   A. This problem is becoming more real than theoretical.
   B. The conclusion is obvious: If the Cape is to survive ecologically and financially, we must take immediate action to preserve our *only* water supply.
   C. These recommendations offer a starting point for action. (Visual #8)
      1. Restrict population density in all Cape towns by creating larger building lot requirements.
      2. Keep strict watch on proposed high-density apartment and condominium projects.
      3. Create a committee in each town to educate residents about water conservation.
      4. Prohibit salt, calcium, and other additives in sand spread on snow-covered roads.
      5. Explore alternatives to landfills for solid waste disposal.
   D. Given its potential effects on our quality of life, such a crucial issue deserves the active involvement of every Cape resident.

If you are not using *PowerPoint* or another program that creates notes for you, transfer your presentation outline to notecards (one side only, each card numbered and perhaps color-coded), which you can hold in one hand and shuffle as needed. Or insert the outline pages in a looseleaf binder for easy flipping. Type or print clearly, leaving enough white space to locate material at a glance.

Plan Your Visuals

Visuals increase listeners' interest, focus, understanding, and memory. Select visuals that will clarify and enhance your talk—without making you fade into the background. Make the following decisions.

Decide Where Visuals Will Work Best. Use visuals to emphasize a point and whenever *showing* would be more effective than just *telling*.

Decide Which Visuals Will Work Best. Will you need numerical or prose tables, graphs, charts, graphic illustrations, computer graphics? How complex should these visuals be? Should they impress or simply inform? Use the visual planning sheet in Chapter 14 (page 291) to guide your decisions.

Decide How Many Visuals Are Appropriate. Prefer an array of lean and simple visuals that present material in digestible amounts instead of one or two overstuffed visuals that people end up staring at endlessly.

Create a Storyboard. A presentation storyboard is a double-column format in which your discussion is outlined in the left column, aligned with the specific supporting visuals in the right column (Figure 26.1).

Pollution Threats to Local Groundwater

1.0 Introduce the Problem

    1.1   Do you know what you are drinking when you turn on the tap and fill the glass?

    1.2   The quality of our water is good, but not guaranteed to last forever.

    1.3   Cape Cod's rapid population growth poses a serious threat to our freshwater supply.   (slide: *a line graph showing twenty-year population growth*)

    1.4   Measurable pollution in some town water supplies has already occurred.   (slide: *two side-by-side tables showing twenty-year increases in nitrate and chloride concentrations in three town wells*)

    1.5   What are the major causes and consequences of this problem and what can we do about it?   (poster: *a multicolored list that previews my five subtopics*)

2.0 Describe the Aquifer

    2.1   The groundwater is collected and held in an aquifer.

        2.1.1.   This porous rock formation creates a broad, continuous arch beneath the entire Cape.   (slide: *a cutaway view of the aquifer's geology*)

FIGURE 26.1   **A Partial Storyboard**

Decide Which Visuals Can Realistically Be Created.   Fit each visual to the situation. The visuals you select will depend on the room, the equipment, and the production resources available.

Fit each visual to the situation

How large is the room and how is it arranged? Some visuals work well in small rooms, but not large ones, and vice versa. How well can the room be darkened? Which lights can be left on? Can the lighting be adjusted selectively? What size should visuals be, to be seen clearly by the whole room? (A smaller, intimate room is usually better than a room that is too big.)

What hardware is available (opaque projector, overhead projector, film projector, videotape player, terminal with large-screen monitor)? What graphics programs are available? Which program is best for your purpose and listeners? How far in advance does this equipment have to be requested?

What resources are available for producing the visuals? Can drawings, charts, graphs, or maps be created as needed? Can transparencies (for overhead projection) be made or slides produced? Can handouts be typed and reproduced? Can multimedia displays be created?

Select Your Media. Fit the medium to the situation. Which medium or combination is best for the topic, setting, and listeners? How fancy do listeners expect the presentation to be? Which media are appropriate for this occasion?

Fit the medium
to the situation

- For a weekly meeting with colleagues in your department, scribbling on a blank transparency, chalkboard, or dry-erase markerboard might suffice.
- For interacting with listeners, you might use a chalkboard to record audience responses to your questions.
- For immediate orientation, you might begin with a poster listing key visuals/ideas/themes to which you will refer repeatedly.
- For helping listeners take notes, absorb technical data, or remember complex material, you might distribute a presentation outline as a preview or provide handouts.
- For displaying and discussing written samples listeners bring in, you might use an opaque projector.
- For a presentation to investors, clients, or upper management, you might require polished and professionally prepared visuals, including computer graphics, such as an electronic slide presentation using *PowerPoint* software.

Figure 26.2 presents the various common media in approximate order of availability and ease of preparation.

NOTE *Keep in mind that the more technology you use in your presentation, the more prepared you must be.*

Prepare Your Visuals

As you prepare visuals, focus on economy, clarity, and simplicity.

Be Selective. Use a visual only when it truly serves a purpose. Use restraint in choosing what to highlight with visuals. Try not to begin or end the presentation with a visual. At those times, listeners' attention should be focused on the presenter instead of the visual.

Make Visuals Easy to Read and Understand. Think of each visual as an image that flashes before your listeners. They will not have the luxury of studying the visual at leisure. Listeners need to know at a glance what they are looking at and what it means. In addition to being able to *read* the visual, listeners need to *understand* it. See the guidelines on page 620.

When your material is extremely detailed or complex, prepare and handouts to each listener so that people can jot notes as you discuss specific material. For more on using and managing handouts effectively, refer to page 626.

Whiteboard/Chalkboard

Uses
- simple, on-the-spot visuals
- recording audience responses
- informal settings
- small, well-lighted rooms

Tips
- copy long material in advance
- make it legible and visible to all
- use washable markers on markerboard
- speak to the listeners—not to the board

Handouts

Uses
- present complex material
- help listeners follow along
- help listeners take notes
- help listeners remember

Tips
- staple or bind the packet
- number the pages
- try saving for the end
- if you must distribute up front, ask audience to await instructions before reading the material

Poster

Uses
- overviews, previews, emphasis
- recurring themes
- formal or informal settings
- small, well-lighted rooms

Tips
- use 20" x 30" posterboard (or larger)
- use intense, washable colors
- keep each poster simple and uncrowded
- arrange/display posters in advance
- make each visible to the whole room
- point to what you are discussing

Opaque Projection

Uses
- direct display of paper documents
- samples listeners bring in
- pages from books, reports
- informal settings
- very small and dark rooms
- when spontaneity is more important than image quality

Tips
- allow projector to warm up
- don't shut off projector until you're done
- never stare at a bright bulb
- use a light source for viewing your notes
- use a laser or telescoping pointer
- place audience close enough to see clearly

Flip Chart

Uses
- a sequence of visuals
- back-and-forth movement
- formal or informal settings
- small, well-lighted rooms

Tips
- use an easel pad and easel
- use intense, washable colors
- work from a storyboard
- check your sequence beforehand
- point to what you are discussing

FIGURE 26.2   **Selecting Media for Visual Presentations**

Film and Video

Uses
- necessary display of moving images
- coordinated sound and visual images aid understanding and help persuade

Tips
- carefully introduce segment to be shown; tell viewers what to see or expect
- show only those segments needed to make your points
- if the segment is complex, or happens very quickly, play it more than once
- where appropriate, use video slow-motion replay
- always practice with the segment beforehand

Overhead Projection

Uses
- on-the-spot or prepared visuals
- overlaid visuals[1]
- formal or informal settings
- small- or medium-sized rooms
- rooms needing to remain lighted

Tips
- use cardboard mounting frames for your acetate transparencies
- write discussion notes on each frame
- check your sequence beforehand
- turn projector off when not using it
- face the audience—not the screen
- point directly on the transparency
- use erasable color markers to highlight items as you discuss them

Slide Projection

Uses
- professional-quality visuals
- formal setting
- small or large dark rooms

Tips
- work from a storyboard
- check the slide sequence beforehand
- use a light source for viewing your notes
- use a laser or telescoping pointer

Computer Projection

Uses
- sophisticated charts, graphs, maps
- multimedia presentations
- formal settings
- small, dark rooms

Tips
- take lots of time to prepare/practice
- work from a storyboard
- check the whole system beforehand
- have a default plan in case something goes wrong

1. The overlay technique begins with one transparency showing a basic image, over which additional transparencies (with coordinated images, colors, labels, and so on) are added to produce an increasingly complex image.

FIGURE 26.2 *(Continued)*

Guidelines for Readable Visuals

- Make visuals large enough to be read anywhere in the room.
- Don't cram too many words, ideas, designs, or type styles into one visual.
- Distill the message into the fewest words and simplest images possible.
- Chunk material into small sections.
- Summarize with key words, phrases, or short sentences.
- Use 18–24 point type size and sans serif typeface.

Guidelines for Understandable Visuals

- Display only one point per visual—unless previewing or reviewing.
- Give each visual a title that announces the topic.
- Use color, sparingly, to highlight key words, facts, or the bottom line.
- Use the brightest color for what is most important.
- Label each part of a diagram or illustration.
- Proofread each visual carefully.

Look for Alternatives to Word-Filled Visuals.   Instead of just presenting overhead versions of printed pages, explore the full *visual* possibilities of your media. For example, anyone who tries to write a verbal equivalent of the visual message in Figure 26.3 will soon appreciate the power of images in relation to words alone. For more on visual representation, see Chapter 14.

Consider the Available Technology

Using digital and video cameras, Web sites, and presentation software, you can create dynamic presentations that appeal to multiple senses. Using remote-controlled transparency feeder and laser pointer, you can deliver a smooth and elegant presentation. Despite the possibilities inherent in the technology, you are still responsible for a presentation that is well researched and professionally delivered.

Use *PowerPoint* or Other Software Wisely

Using presentation software such as Microsoft *PowerPoint*, you can produce professional-quality slides and then show them electronically.

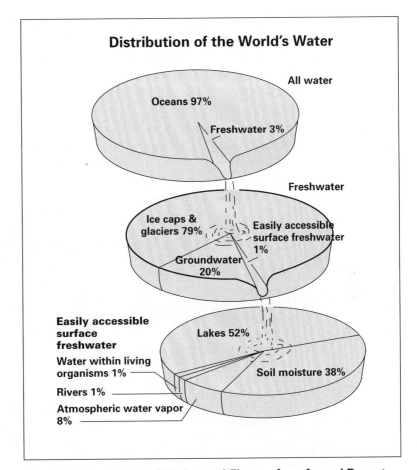

Distribution of the World's Water

All water

Oceans 97%

Freshwater 3%

Freshwater

Ice caps & glaciers 79%

Easily accessible surface freshwater 1%

Groundwater 20%

Easily accessible surface freshwater

Water within living organisms 1%

Rivers 1%

Atmospheric water vapor 8%

Lakes 52%

Soil moisture 38%

FIGURE 26.3   A List of Tables and Figures for a formal Report

Source: "Distribution of the World's Water," as appeared in *WWF Atlas of the Environment* by Geoffrey Lean and Don Hinrichsen. Copyright © 1994 Banson Marketing Ltd.

Images can be more powerful than words

A sampling of *PowerPoint's* design and display features

 Models of *PowerPoint* presentations

- Create slide designs in various colors, shading, and textures.
- Create drawings or graphs and import clip art, photographs, or other images.
- Create animated text and images: say, bullets that flash one-at-a-time on the screen or bars and lines on a graph that are highlighted individually, to emphasize specific characteristics of the data.
- Create dynamic transitions between each slide, such as having one slide dissolve toward the right side of the screen as the following slide uncovers from the left.
- Amplify each slide with speaker notes that are invisible to the audience.
- Sort your slides into various sequences.
- Precisely time your entire presentation.
- Show your presentation directly on the computer screen or large-screen projector, online via the Web, as overhead transparencies, or as printed handouts. (Figure 26.2 shows printed versions of *PowerPoint* slides.)

Because of its many features, *PowerPoint* (Figure 26.4) has become the most widely used presentation software. The latest versions accommodate hyperlinked and embedded media, including prerecorded sections. In a world in which images are everywhere, and electronic communication is the mode, *PowerPoint* is often regarded—rightly or wrongly—as "an indispensable corporate survival tool" (Nunberg 330).

The *PowerPoint* debate

PowerPoint advocates argue that bullet-style points help structure the story or the argument and help the presenter organize and stay on course. Critics argue that the mere content outline provided by the slides can oversimplify complex issues and that an endless list of bullets or animations, colors, and sounds can distract the audience from the deeper message.

CASE: *PowerPoint* and the Space Shuttle *Columbia* Disaster

On February 1, 2003, the space shuttle *Columbia* burned up upon reentering the Earth's atmosphere. The *Columbia* had suffered damage during launch when a piece of insulating foam had broken off the shuttle and damaged the wing.

While *Columbia* was in orbit, NASA personnel tried to assess the damage and to recommend a course of action. It was decided that the damage did not seem serious enough to pose a significant threat, and reentry proceeded on schedule. (Lower-level suggestions that the shuttle fly close to a satellite that could have photographed the damage, for a clearer assessment, were overlooked and ultimately ignored by the decision makers.)

The *Columbia* Accident Investigation Board concluded that a *PowerPoint* presentation to NASA officials had played a role in the disaster: Engineers presented their findings in a series of confusing and misleading slides that obscured errors in their own engineering analysis. Design expert Edward Tufte points out that one especially crucial slide was so crammed with data and bullet points and so lacking in analysis that it was impossible to decipher accurately (8–9).

The Board's findings:

As information gets passed up an organization's hierarchy, from people who do analysis to mid-level managers to high-level leadership, key explanations and supporting information are filtered out. In this context, it is easy to understand how a senior manager might read this *PowerPoint* slide and not realize that it addresses a life-threatening situation.

At many points during its investigation, the Board was surprised to receive similar presentation slides from NASA officials in place of technical reports. The Board views the endemic use of *PowerPoint* briefing slides instead of technical papers as an illustration of the problematic methods of technical communication at NASA. (Columbia Accident, *Report* 191)

In the end, technological tools are merely a *supplement* to your presentation; they are no *substitute* for the facts, ideas, examples, numbers, and interpretations that make up the clear and complete message audiences expect.

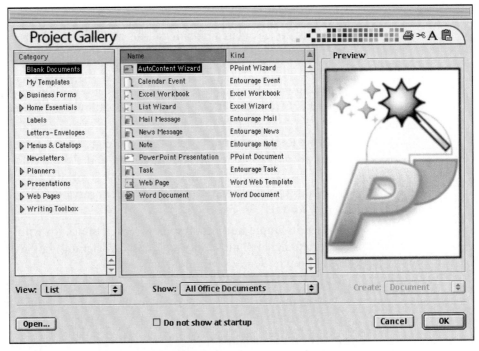

FIGURE 26.4 *PowerPoint* **Software's Opening Screen** From this gateway screen, even inexperienced users can explore topic categories (say, "Presenting a Technical Report," "Reporting Progress," or "Communicating Bad News"). Users can also find ideas for slide content and schemes for organizing their presentation. *Source:* Microsoft product screen shots reprinted by permission from Microsoft Corporation.

Check the Room and Setting Beforehand

Make sure you have enough space, electrical outlets, and tables for your equipment. If you will be addressing a large audience by microphone and plan to point to features on your visuals, be sure the microphone is movable. Pay careful attention to lighting, especially for chalkboards, flip charts, and posters. Don't forget a pointer if you need one.

Guidelines for Using Presentation Software

- **Have a backup plan in case the technology fails.** Be prepared to give the presentation without the software.
- **Prepare a handout.** In case of system failure, you can distribute a handout of your slides so listeners can follow along. In any event, by not having to summarize

(continues)

Guidelines (continued)

each slide as you are presenting it, the audience can devote its attention to your commentary. If you save the handout for the end, tell your audience up-front.

- **Avoid slide overload (too many slides for the time allotted, too many words per slide).** Aim for no more than one content slide per minute, 7 lines per slide, 7 words per line. Use phrases instead of complete sentences. Keep bulleted lists grammatically parallel.

- **Don't let the medium obscure the message.** The audience should be focused on what you have to say, and not on the slide. Avoid colors and backgrounds that distract from the content. Avoid the whooshing and whiz-bang and other sounds unless absolutely necessary. Be conservative with any design and display feature.

- **Keep it simple but not simplistic.** Spice things up with a light dose of imported digital photos, charts, graphs, or diagrams, but avoid images that look so complex that they require detailed study.

- **Keep viewers oriented.** Open with a slide that previews the main topics in your presentation. Use divider slides as transitions from one topic to the next. Close with a "Conclusion" or "Questions?" slide.

- **Set a comfortable pace.** Present one idea per slide, bringing bullets on one at a time. Give viewers time to digest the data.

- **Avoid merely reciting the slides.** Instead, discuss each slide, with specific examples and details that round out the idea—but try not to digress or ramble.

NOTE   *See also the general guidelines for preparing and presenting visuals (pages 620 and 627.)*

Rehearse Your Delivery

Hold ample practice sessions to learn the geography of your report. Try to rehearse at least once in front of friends, or use a full-length mirror and a tape recorder. Assess your delivery from listeners' comments or from your taped voice (which will sound high to you). Use the evaluation sheet on page 631 as a guide.

If at all possible, rehearse using the actual equipment (overhead projector and so on) in the actual setting, to ensure that you have all you need and that everything works. Rehearsing a computer-projected presentation is essential.

Delivering your Presentation

You have planned and prepared carefully. Now consider the following simple steps to make your actual presentation enjoyable instead of terrifying.

Cultivate the Human Landscape

A successful presentation involves relationship building with the audience.

Get to Know your Audience.   Try to meet some audience members before your presentation. We all feel more comfortable with people we know. Don't be afraid to smile.

Display Enthusiasm and Confidence.   Nobody likes a speaker who seems half dead. Clean up verbal tics ("er," "ah," "uuh"). Overcome your shyness; research indicates that shy people are seen as less credible, trustworthy, likable, attractive, and knowledgeable.

Be Reasonable.   Don't make your point at someone else's expense. If your topic is controversial (layoffs, policy changes, downsizing), decide how to speak candidly and persuasively with the least chance of offending anyone. For example, in your presentation about groundwater pollution (page 614), you don't want to attack the developers, since the building trade is a major producer of jobs, second only to tourism, on Cape Cod. Avoid personal attacks.

Don't Preach.   Speak like a person talking—not someone giving a sermon or the Gettysburg Address. Use *we, you, your, our,* to establish commonality with the audience. Avoid jokes or wisecracks.

Keep Your Listeners Oriented

Help your listeners to focus their attention and organize their understanding. Give them a map, some guidance, and highlights.

Open with a Clear and Engaging Introduction.   The introduction to a presentation is your chance to set the stage. For most presentations, you have three main tasks:

1. Show the listeners how your presentation has meaning for them. Show how your topic affects listeners personally by telling a quick story, asking a question, or referring to a current event or something else the audience cares about.
2. Establish your credibility by stating your credentials or explaining where you obtained your information.
3. Preview your presentation by listing the main points and the overall conclusion.

An introduction following this format might sound something like this:

An appeal to listeners' concerns

A presentation preview

> Do you know what you are drinking when you turn on the tap and fill a glass? The quality of Cape Cod's drinking water is seriously threatened by rapid population growth. My name is Arnold Borthwick, and I've been researching this topic for a term project. Today, I'd like to share my findings with you by discussing three main points: specific causes of the problem, the foreseeable consequences, and what we can do to avoid disaster.

Outline your main points by using an opening visual such as a poster, transparency, slide, or handout.

Give Concrete Examples.   Good examples are informative and persuasive.

A concrete
example

> Overdraw from town wells in Maloket and Tanford (two of our most rapidly growing towns) has resulted in measurable salt infusion at a yearly rate of 0.1 mg per liter.

Use examples that focus on listener concerns.

Provide Explicit Transitions.   Alert listeners whenever you are switching gears:

Explicit
transitions

> For my next point. . . .
>
> Turning now to my second point. . . .
>
> The third point I want to emphasize. . . .

Repeat key points or terms to keep them fresh in listeners' minds.

Review and Interpret.   Last things are best remembered. Help listeners remember the main points:

A review of
main points

> To summarize the dangers to our groundwater, . . .

Also, be clear about what this material means. Be emphatic about what listeners should be doing, thinking, or feeling:

An emphatic
conclusion

> The conclusion is obvious: If the Cape is to survive, we must. . . .

Try to conclude with a forceful answer to this implied question from each listener: "What does this all mean to me personally?"

Manage Your Visuals

Presenting visuals effectively is a matter of good timing and careful management.

Prepare Everything Beforehand.   If you plan to draw on a chalkboard or poster, do the drawings beforehand (in multicolors). Otherwise, listeners will be sitting idly while you draw away.

Prepare handouts if you want listeners to remember or study certain material. Distribute these *after* your talk. (You want the audience to be looking at and listening to you, instead of reading the handout.) Distribute handouts before or during the talk only if you want listeners to take notes—or if your equipment breaks down. When you do distribute handouts beforehand, ask listeners to await your instructions before they turn to a particular page.

Use transparency mounting frames for easy handling (the white cardboard frames allow you to number the transparencies and prepare notes for yourself on the frame).

Increasingly available are automatic transparency feeders with a remote control, making your transparency presentation work like a slide show. This device attaches easily to your overhead projector and allows you to reveal each point, line by line.

Arrange Everything Beforehand.   Make sure you organize your media materials and the physical layout beforehand, to avoid fumbling during the presentation. Check your visual sequence against your storyboard.

Follow a Few Simple Guidelines.   Make your visuals part of a seamless presentation. Avoid listener distraction, confusion, and frustration by observing the following suggestions.

Guidelines for Presenting Visuals

- Try not to begin with a visual.
- Try not to display a visual until you are ready to discuss it.
- Tell viewers what they should be looking for in the visual.
- Point to what is important.
- Stand aside when discussing a visual, so everyone can see it.
- Don't turn your back on the audience.
- After discussing the visual, remove it promptly.
- Switch off equipment that is not in use.
- Try not to end with a visual.

Manage Your Presentation Style

Think about how you are moving, how you are speaking, and where you are looking. These are all elements of your personal style.

Use Natural Movements and Reasonable Postures.   Move and gesture as you normally would in conversation, and maintain reasonable postures. Avoid foot shuffling, pencil tapping, swaying, slumping, or fidgeting.

Adjust Volume, Pronunciation, and Rate.   With a microphone, don't speak too loudly. Without one, don't speak too softly. Be sure you can be heard clearly without shattering eardrums. Ask your audience about the sound and speed of your delivery after a few sentences.

Nervousness causes speakers to gallop along and mispronounce words. Slow down and pronounce clearly. Usually, a rate that seems a bit slow to you will be just right for listeners.

Maintain Eye Contact.   Look directly into listeners' eyes. With a small audience, eye contact is one of your best connectors. As you speak, establish eye contact with as many listeners as possible. With a large group, maintain eye contact with those in the first rows. Establish eye contact immediately—before you even begin to speak—by looking around.

Manage Your Speaking Situation

Do everything you can to keep things running smoothly.

Be Responsive to Listener Feedback.   Assess listener feedback continually and make adjustments as needed. If you are laboring through a long list of facts or figures and people begin to doze or fidget, you might summarize. Likewise, if frowns, raised eyebrows, or questioning looks indicate confusion, skepticism, or indignation, you can backtrack with a specific example or explanation. By tuning in to your audience's reactions, you can keep listeners on your side.

Stick to Your Plan.   Say what you came to say, then summarize and close—politely and on time. Don't punctuate your speech with digressions that pop into your head. Unless a specific anecdote was part of your original plan to clarify a point or increase interest, avoid excursions. We often tend to be more interested in what we have to say than our listeners are! Don't exceed your time limit.

Leave Listeners with Something to Remember.   Before ending, take a moment to summarize the major points and reemphasize anything of special importance. Are listeners supposed to remember something, have a different attitude, take a specific action? Let them know! As you conclude, thank your listeners.

 Global communication

Allow Time for Questions and Answers.   At the very beginning, tell your listeners that a question-and-answer period will follow. Use the following suggestions for managing listener questions diplomatically and efficiently.

Guidelines for Managing Listener Questions

- Announce a specific time limit for the question period.
- Listen carefully to each question.
- If you can't understand a question, ask that it be rephrased.

- **Repeat every question, to ensure that everyone hears it.**
- **Be brief in your answers.**
- **If you need extra time for an answer, arrange for it after the presentation.**
- **If anyone attempts lengthy debate, offer to continue after the presentation.**
- **If you can't answer a question, say so and move on.**
- **End the session with a clear signal. Say something such as, "We have time for one more question."**

Consider This: Cross-Cultural Audiences May Have Specific Expectations

 Imagine that you've been assigned to represent your company at an international conference or before international clients (e.g., of passenger aircraft or mainframe computers). As you plan and prepare your presentation, remain sensitive to various cultural expectations.

For example, some cultures might be offended by a presentation that gets right to the point without first observing formalities of politeness, well wishes, and the like.

Certain communication styles are welcomed in some cultures, but considered offensive in others. In southern Europe and the Middle East, people expect direct and prolonged eye contact as a way of showing honesty and respect. In Southeast Asia, this may be taken as a sign of aggression or disrespect (Gesteland 24). A sampling of the questions to consider:

- *Should I smile a lot or look serious? (Hulbert, "Overcoming" 42)*
- *Should I rely on expressive gestures and facial expressions?*

- *How loudly or softly, rapidly or slowly should I speak?*
- *Should I come out from behind the podium and approach the audience or keep my distance?*
- *Should I get right to the point or take plenty of time to lead into and discuss the matter thoroughly?*
- *Should I focus only on the key facts or on all the details and various interpretations?*
- *Should I be assertive in offering interpretations and conclusions, or should I allow listeners to reach their own conclusions?*
- *Which types of visuals and which media might or might not work?*
- *Should I invite questions from this audience, or would this be offensive?*

To account for language differences, prepare a handout of your entire script for distribution after the presentation, along with a copy of your visuals. This way, your audience will be able to study your material at their leisure.

Exercises

1. In a memo to your instructor, identify and discuss the kinds of oral reporting duties you expect to encounter in your career.

2. Prepare an oral presentation for your class, based on your written long report. Develop a sentence outline and a storyboard that includes at least three visuals. If your instructor requests, create one or more of your presentation visuals using *PowerPoint* software. (For a step-by-step guide to getting started on *PowerPoint,* select "AutoContent Wizard" from the opening screen. See Figure 26.4.)

Practice your presentation with a tape recorder, video camera, or a friend. Use the checklist on page 631 to assess and refine your delivery.

3. Observe a lecture or speech, and evaluate it according to the Checklist (page 631). Write a memo to your instructor (without naming the speaker), identifying strong and weak areas and suggesting improvements.

4. In an oral presentation to the class, present your findings, conclusions, and recommendations from the analytical report assignment in Chapter 24.

Checklist for Oral Presentations

Presentation Evaluation for (name/topic) _____

Comments

Content
- ☐ Stated a clear purpose. _____
- ☐ Created interest in the topic. _____
- ☐ Showed command of the material. _____
- ☐ Supported assertions with evidence. _____
- ☐ Used adequate and appropriate visuals. _____
- ☐ Used material suited to this audience's _____
  needs, knowledge, concerns, and interests. _____
- ☐ Acknowledged opposing views. _____
- ☐ Gave the right amount of information. _____

Organization
- ☐ Began with a clear overview. _____
- ☐ Presented a clear line of reasoning. _____
- ☐ Moved from point to point effectively. _____
- ☐ Stayed on course. _____
- ☐ Used transitions effectively. _____
- ☐ Avoided needless digressions. _____
- ☐ Summarized before concluding. _____
- ☐ Was clear about what the listeners _____
  should think or do.

Style
- ☐ Dressed appropriately. _____
- ☐ Seemed confident, relaxed, and likable. _____
- ☐ Seemed in control of the speaking situation. _____
- ☐ Showed appropriate enthusiasm. _____
- ☐ Pronounced, enunciated, and spoke well. _____
- ☐ Used no slang whatsoever. _____
- ☐ Used appropriate gestures, tone, _____
  volume, and delivery rate.
- ☐ Had good posture and eye contact. _____
- ☐ Interacted with the audience. _____
- ☐ Kept the audience actively involved. _____
- ☐ Answered questions concisely and convincingly. _____

Overall professionalism: Superior _____ **Acceptable** _____ **Needs work** _____

Evaluator's signature: _____

FIGURE 26.5   An Evaluation Checklist for Oral Presentations

PART FIVE

Resources for Writers

A Quick Guide to Documention   634

A Quick Guide to Grammar, Usage, and Mechanics   670

A Casebook: The Writing Process Illustrated   698

Is It Plagiarism?
Test Yourself on In-text (Parenthetical) References   735

A Quick Guide to Documentation

Taking Notes

Guidelines for Recording Research Findings

Quoting the Work of Others

Guidelines for Quoting the Work of Others

Paraphrasing the Work of Others

Guidelines for Paraphrasing

What You Should Document

How You Should Document

MLA Documentation Style

APA Documentation Style

CSE and Other Numbered Documentation Styles

Taking Notes

Researchers increasingly take notes on a laptop, using file programs or database management software that allows notes to be filed, shuffled, and retrieved by author, title, topic, date, or key words. You can also take notes in a single word-processing file, then use the "find" command to locate notes quickly. Whether you use a computer or notecards, your notes should be easy to organize and reorganize.

Guidelines for Recording Research Findings

- **Make a separate bibliography listing for each work you consult.** Record that work's complete entry, (Figure QG.1), using the citation format that will appear in your document. (See pages 642–69 for sample entries.) Record the information accurately so that you won't have to relocate a source at the last minute.

Record each bibliographic citation exactly as it will appear in your final report

> Pinsky, Mark A. The EMF Book: What You Should Know about Electromagnetic Fields, Electromagnetic Radiation, and Your Health. New York: Warner, 1995.

FIGURE QG.1 **Recording a Bibliographic Citation**

When searching online, you can often print out a work's full bibliographic record or save it to disk, to ensure an accurate citation.

- **Skim the entire work to locate relevant material.** Look over the table of contents and the index. Check the introduction for an overview or thesis. Look for informative headings.
- **Go back and decide what to record.** Use a separate entry for each item.
- **Be selective.** Don't copy or paraphrase every word. (See the Guidelines for Summarizing, page 175.)
- **Record the item as a quotation or paraphrase.** When quoting others directly, be sure to record words and punctuation accurately. When restating material in your own words, preserve the original meaning and emphasis.

Quoting the Work of Others

You must place quotation marks around all exact wording you borrow, whether the words were written, spoken (as in an interview or presentation), or appeared in electronic form. Even a single borrowed sentence or phrase, or a single word used in a special way, needs quotation marks, with the exact source properly cited. These sources include people with whom you collaborate.

Plagiarism is often unintentional

    If your notes don't identify quoted material accurately, you might forget to credit the source. Even when this omission is unintentional, you face the charge of *plagiarism* (misrepresenting as your own the words or ideas of someone else). Possible consequences of plagiarism include expulsion from school, loss of a job, and a lawsuit.

The perils of buying plagiarized work online

    It's no secret that any cheater can purchase reports, term papers, and other documents on the Web. But antiplagiarism Web sites, such as <plagiarism.org> now enable professors to cross-reference a suspicious paper against previously published material, flagging and identifying each plagiarized source.

Guidelines for Quoting the Work of Others

Expressions that warrant direct quotation

- **Use a direct quotation only when absolutely necessary.** Sometimes a direct quotation is the only way to do justice to the author's own words:

  > "Writing is a way to end up thinking something you couldn't have started out thinking" (Elbow 15).

  > Think of the topic sentence as "the one sentence you would keep if you could keep only one" (USAF Academy 11).

  Consider quoting directly for these purposes:

Reasons for quoting directly

  —to preserve special phrasing or emphasis
  —to preserve precise meaning
  —to preserve the original line of reasoning
  —to preserve an especially striking or colorful example
  —to convey the authority and complexity of expert opinion
  —to convey the original's voice, sincerity, or emotional intensity

- **Ensure accuracy.** Copy the selection word for word; record the exact page numbers; and double-check that you haven't altered the original expression in any way (Figure QG.2).

- **Keep the quotation as brief as possible.** For conciseness and emphasis, use *ellipses:* Use three spaced periods (. . .) to indicate each omission within a single sentence. Add a fourth period to indicate each omission that includes the end of a sentence or multi-sentence sections of text.

Ellipsis within and between sentences

  > Use three . . . periods to indicate each omission within a single sentence. Add a fourth period to indicate . . . the end of a sentence. . . .

Pinsky, Mark A. pp. 29–30.

"Neither electromagnetic fields nor electromagnetic radiation cause cancer per se, most researchers agree. What they may do is promote cancer. Cancer is a multistage process that requires an 'initiator' that makes a cell or group of cells abnormal. Everyone has cancerous cells in his or her body. Cancer— the disease as we think of it—occurs when these cancerous cells grow uncontrollably."

FIGURE QG.2 **Recording a Quotation**

The elliptical passage must be grammatical and must not distort the original meaning. (For additional guidelines, see page 689.)

- **Use square brackets to insert your own clarifying comments or transitions.**

> "Job stress [in aircraft ground control] can lead to disaster."

- **Embed quoted material in your sentences clearly and grammatically.** Introduce integrated quotations with phrases such as "Jones argues that," or "Gomez concludes that." More importantly, use a transitional phrase to show the relationship between the quoted idea and the sentence that precedes it:

> One investigation of age discrimination at select Fortune 500 companies found that "middle managers over age 45 are an endangered species" (Jablonski 69).

Your integrated sentence should be grammatical:

> "The present farming crisis," Marx argues, "is a direct result of rampant land speculation" (41).

(For additional guidelines, see page 688.)

- **Quote passages four lines or longer in block form.** Avoid relying on long quotations except in these instances:

—to provide an extended example, definition, or analogy (see page 9)
—to analyze or discuss an idea or concept (see page 555)

Double-space a block quotation and indent the entire block ten spaces. Do not indent the first line of the passage, but do indent first lines of subsequent paragraphs three spaces. Do not use quotation marks.

- **Introduce the quotation and discuss its significance.**

> Here is a corporate executive's description of some audiences you can expect to address:

- **Cite the source of each quoted passage.**

Sidebar annotations:

Place quotation marks around all directly quoted material

Brackets setting off the added words within a quotation

An introduction that unifies a quotation with the discussion

Quoted material integrated grammatically with the writer's words

Reasons for quoting a long passage

An introduction to quoted material

Research writing is a process of independent thinking in which you work with the ideas of others in order to reach your own conclusions; unless the author's exact wording is essential, try to paraphrase, instead of quoting, borrowed material.

Paraphrasing the Work of Others

Paraphrasing means more than changing or shuffling a few words; it means restating the original idea in your own words—sometimes in a clearer, more direct, and emphatic way—and giving full credit to the source.

Faulty paraphrasing is a form of plagiarism

To borrow or adapt someone else's ideas or reasoning without properly documenting the source is plagiarism. To offer as a paraphrase an original passage that is only slightly altered—even when you document the source—also is plagiarism. Equally unethical is offering a paraphrase, although documented, that distorts the original meaning.

Guidelines for Paraphrasing

- **Refer to the author early in the paraphrase,** to indicate the beginning of the borrowed passage.
- **Retain key words from the original,** to preserve its meaning.
- **Restructure and combine original sentences** for emphasis and fluency.
- **Delete needless words from the original,** for conciseness.
- **Use your own words and phrases** to clarify the author's ideas.
- **Cite (in parentheses) the exact source,** to mark the end of the borrowed passage and to give full credit.
- **Be sure to preserve the author's original intent** (Weinstein 3).

Figure QG.3 shows an entry paraphrased from Figure QG.2. Paraphrased material is not enclosed within quotation marks, but it is documented to acknowledge your debt to the source. The paraphrase in the figure is adapted from the quote on p. 637.

What You Should Document

Document any insight, assertion, fact, finding, interpretation, judgment, or other "appropriated material that readers might otherwise mistake for your own" (Gibaldi and Achtert 155)—whether the material appears in published form or not. Specifically, you must document these sources:

Pinsky, Mark A.

Pinsky explains that electromagnetic waves probably do not directly cause cancer. However, they might contribute to the uncontrollable growth of those cancer cells normally present—but controlled—in the human body (29–30).

Signal the beginning of the paraphrase by citing the author, and the end by citing the source.

FIGURE QG.3 **Recording a Paraphrase**

Sources that require documentation

- any source from which you use exact wording
- any source from which you adapt material in your own words
- any visual illustration: charts, graphs, drawings, or the like (see Chapter 14 for documenting visuals)

How to document a confidential source

In some instances, you might have reason to preserve the anonymity of unpublished sources: for example, to allow people to respond candidly without fear of reprisal (as with employee criticism of the company), or to protect their privacy (as with certain material from email inquiries or electronic discussion groups). You must still document the fact that you are not the originator of this material. Do this by providing a general acknowledgment in the text such as "A number of employees expressed frustration with . . ." along with a general citation in your list of references or works cited such as "Interviews with Polex employees, May 2007."

Common knowledge need not be documented

You don't need to document anything considered *common knowledge:* material that appears repeatedly in general sources. In medicine, for instance, it has become common knowledge that foods containing animal fat contribute to higher blood cholesterol levels. So in a report on fatty diets and heart disease, you probably would not need to document that well-known fact. But you would document information about how the fat/cholesterol connection was discovered, what subsequent studies have found (say, the role of saturated versus unsaturated fats), and any information for which some other person could claim specific credit. If the borrowed material can be found in only one specific source, not in multiple sources, document it. When in doubt, document the source.

How You Should Document

Cite borrowed material twice: at the exact place you use that material, and at the end of your document. Documentation practices vary widely, but all systems work almost identically: a brief reference in the text names the source and refers readers to the complete citation, which allows readers to retrieve the source.

Style guides from various disciplines

Many disciplines, institutions, and organizations publish their own style guides or documentation manuals. This chapter illustrates citations and entries for three styles widely used for documenting sources in their respective disciplines:

- Modern Language Association (MLA) style, for the humanities
- American Psychological Association (APA) style, for the social sciences
- Council of Science Editors (CSE) style, for the natural and applied sciences

Unless your audience has its own preference, any of these three styles can be adapted to most research writing. Use one style consistently throughout the document.

MLA Documentation Style

Traditional MLA documentation of sources used superscript numbers (like this:[1]) in the text, followed by full references at the bottom of the page (footnotes) or at the end of the document (endnotes) and, finally, by a bibliography. But a more current form of documentation appears in the *MLA Handbook for Writers of Research Papers, 6th ed.,* New York: Modern Language Association, 2003. Footnotes or endnotes are now used only to comment on material in the text or on sources, or to suggest additional sources.

Use this alternative to footnotes and bibliographies

In MLA style, in-text parenthetical references briefly identify each source. Full documentation then appears in a Works Cited section at the end of the document. The parenthetical reference usually includes the author's surname and the exact page number where the borrowed material can be found:

Cite a source briefly in text and fully at the end

Parenthetical reference in the text

> One notable study indicates an elevated risk of leukemia for children exposed to certain types of electromagnetic fields (Bowman et al. 59).

Readers seeking the complete citation for Bowman can refer easily to the Works Cited section, listed alphabetically by author:

Full citation at document's end

> Bowman, J. D., et al. "Hypothesis: The Risk of Childhood Leukemia Is Related to Combinations of Power-Frequency and Static Magnetic Fields." Bioelectromagnetics 16.1 (1995): 48-59.

This complete citation includes page numbers for the entire article.

MLA Parenthetical References

For clear and informative parenthetical references, observe these rules:

How to cite briefly in text

- If your discussion names the author, do not repeat the name in your parenthetical reference; simply give the page number(s):

Citing page
numbers only

> Bowman et al. explain how their study indicates an elevated risk of leukemia for children exposed to certain types of electromagnetic fields (59).

- If you cite two or more works in a single parenthetical reference, separate the citations with semicolons:

Three works in a
single reference

> (Jones 32; Leduc 41; Gomez 293-94)

- If you cite two or more authors with the same surnames, include the first initial in your parenthetical reference to each author:

Two authors with
identical surnames

> (R. Jones 32)
>
> (S. Jones 14–15)

- If you cite two or more works by the same author, include the first significant word from each work's title, or a shortened version:

Two works by
one author

> (Lamont, <u>Biophysics</u> 100–01)
>
> (Lamont, <u>Diagnostic Tests</u> 81)

- If the work is by an institutional or corporate author or if it is unsigned (that is, the author is unknown), use only the first few words of the institutional name or the work's title in your parenthetical reference:

Institutional,
corporate, or
anonymous
author

> (American Medical Assn. 2)
>
> ("Distribution Systems" 18)

To avoid distracting the reader, keep each parenthetical reference brief. (The easiest way to keep parenthetical references brief is to name the source in your discussion and to place only the page number(s) in parentheses.)

Where to place a
parenthetical
reference

For a paraphrase, place the parenthetical reference *before* the closing punctuation mark. For a quotation that runs into the text, place the reference *between* the final quotation mark and the closing punctuation mark. For a quotation set off (indented) from the text, place the reference two spaces *after* the closing punctuation mark.

MLA Works Cited Entries

How to space and
indent entries

The Works Cited list includes each source that you have paraphrased or quoted. In preparing the list, type the first line of each entry flush with the left margin. Indent the second and subsequent lines five spaces. Use one character space after any period, comma, or colon. Double-space within and between each entry.

How to cite fully
at the end

Following are examples of complete citations as they would appear in the Works Cited section of your document. Shown below each citation is its corresponding parenthetical reference as it would appear in the text.

INDEX TO SAMPLE MLA WORKS CITED ENTRIES

Books

1. Book, single author
2. Book, two or three authors
3. Book, four or more authors
4. Book, anonymous author
5. Multiple books, same author
6. Book, one or more editors
7. Book, indirect source
8. Anthology selection or book chapter

Periodicals

9. Article, magazine
10. Article, journal with new pagination each issue
11. Article, journal with continuous pagination
12. Article, newspaper

Other Sources

13. Encyclopedia, dictionary, other alphabetical reference
14. Report
15. Conference presentation
16. Interview, personally conducted
17. Interview, published

18. Letter or memo, unpublished
19. Questionnaire
20. Brochure or pamphlet
21. Lecture, speech, address, or reading
22. Government document
23. Document with corporate or foundation authorship
24. Map or other visual
25. Unpublished dissertation, report, or miscellaneous items

Electronic Sources

26. Reference database
27. Computer software
28. CD-ROM
29. Email discussion group
30. Newsgroup
31. Personal email
32. Web site
33. Print article posted online
34. Real-time communication
35. Online abstract
36. General reference to a site

What to include in
an MLA citation for
a book

MLA Works Cited Entries for Books.   Any citation for a book should contain the following information: author, title, editor or translator, edition, volume number, and facts about publication (city, publisher, date).

1. Book, Single Author—MLA

> Kerzin-Fontana, Jane B. Technology Management: A Handbook. 3rd ed.
>
> Delmar, NY: American Management Assn., 2007.

Parenthetical reference: (Kerzin-Fontana 3-4)

Identify the state of publication by U.S. Postal Service abbreviations. For well-known U.S. cities, omit the state. If several cities are listed on the title page, give only the first. For unfamiliar cities in Canada, include the two-letter abbreviation for the province. For unfamiliar cities in other countries, include an abbreviation of the country name.

2. Book, Two or Three Authors—MLA

> Aronson, Linda, Roger Katz, and Candide Moustafa. Toxic Waste Disposal
> Methods. New Haven: Yale UP, 2007.

Parenthetical reference: (Aronson, Katz, and Moustafa 121-23)

Shorten publisher's names, as in "Simon" for Simon & Schuster, "GPO" for Government Printing Office, or "Yale UP" for Yale University Press. For page numbers with more than two digits, give only the final two digits for the second number when the preceding digits are identical.

3. Book, Four or More Authors—MLA

> Santos, Ruth J., et al. Environmental Crises in Developing Countries.
> New York: Harper, 2006.

Parenthetical reference: (Santos et al. 9)

"Et al." is the abbreviated form of the Latin "et alia," meaning "and others."

4. Book, Anonymous Author—MLA

> Structured Programming. Boston: Meredith, 2007.

Parenthetical reference: (Structured 67)

5. Multiple Books, Same Author—MLA

> Chang, John W. Biophysics. Boston: Little, 2005.
>
> ---. Diagnostic Techniques. New York: Radon, 1997.

Parenthetical references: (Chang, Biophysics 123-26), (Chang, Diagnostic 87)

When citing more than one work by the same author, do not repeat the author's name; simply type three hyphens followed by a period. List the works alphabetically by title.

6. Book, One or More Editors—MLA

> Morris, A. J., and Louise B. Pardin-Walker, eds. Handbook of New
> Information Technology. New York: Harper, 2007.

Parenthetical reference: (Morris and Pardin-Walker 34)

For more than three editors, name only the first, followed by "et al."

7. Book, Indirect Source—MLA

```
Kline, Thomas. Automated Systems. Boston: Rhodes, 2002.

Stubbs, John. White-Collar Productivity. Miami: Harris, 2007.
```

Parenthetical reference: (qtd. in Stubbs 116)

When your source (as in Stubbs, above) has quoted or cited another source, list each source in its appropriate place on your Works Cited page. Use the name of the original source (here, Kline) in your text and precede your parenthetical reference with "qtd. in," or "cited in" for a paraphrase.

8. Anthology Selection or Book Chapter—MLA

```
Bowman, Joel P. "Electronic Conferencing." Communication and
     Technology: Today and Tomorrow. Ed. Al Williams. Denton, TX:
     Assn. for Business Communication, 1994, 123-42.
```

Parenthetical reference: (Bowman 129)

The page numbers in the complete citation are for the selection cited from the anthology.

MLA Works Cited Entries for Periodicals.   Give all available information in this order: author, article title, periodical title, volume or number (or both), date (day, month, year), and page numbers for the entire article—not just pages cited.

What to include in an MLA citation for a periodical

9. Article, Magazine—MLA

```
DesMarteau, Kathleen. "Study Links Sewing Machine Use to Alzheimer's
     Disease." Bobbin Oct. 1994: 36-38.
```

Parenthetical reference: (DesMarteau 36)

No punctuation separates the magazine title and date. Nor is the abbreviation "p." or "pp." used to designate page numbers.

If no author is given, list all other information:

```
"Distribution Systems for the New Decade." Power Technology Magazine
     18 Oct. 2007: 18+.
```

Parenthetical reference: ("Distribution Systems" 18)

This article begins on page 18 and continues on page 21. When an article does not appear on consecutive pages, give only the number of the first page, followed immediately by a plus sign. Use a three-letter abbreviation for any month spelled with five or more letters.

10. Article, Journal with New Pagination Each Issue—MLA

```
Thackman-White, Joan R. "Computer-Assisted Research." American
     Librarian 51.1 (2006): 3-9.
```

Parenthetical reference: (Thackman-White 4-5)

Because each issue for a given year will have page numbers beginning with "1," readers need the number of this issue. The "51" denotes the volume number; "1" denotes the issue number. Omit "The," "A," or "An" if it is the first word in a journal or magazine title.

11. Article, Journal with Continuous Pagination—MLA

```
Barnstead, Marion H. "The Writing Crisis." Journal of Writing Theory 12
     (2007): 415-33.
```

Parenthetical reference: (Barnstead 415-16)

When page numbers continue from one issue to the next for the full year, readers won't need the issue number, because no other issue in that year repeats these same page numbers. (Include the issue number, however, if you think it will help readers retrieve the article more easily.) The "12" denotes the volume number.

How to cite an abstract

If, instead of the complete work, you are citing merely an abstract found in a bound collection of abstracts, and not the full article, include the information on the abstracting service right after the information on the original article.

```
Barnstead, Marion H. "The Writing Crisis." Journal of Writing Theory
     12 (2007): 415-33. Rhetoric Abstracts 67 (2005): item 1354.
```

If you are citing an abstract that appears before the printed article, add "Abstract," followed by a period, immediately after the original work's page number(s).

12. Article, Newspaper—MLA

```
Baranski, Vida H. "Errors in Technology Assessment." Boston Times
     15 Jan. 2006, evening ed., sec. 2: 3.
```

Parenthetical reference: (Baranski 3)

When a daily newspaper has more than one edition, cite the edition after the date. Omit any introductory article in the newspaper's name (not *The Boston Times*). If no author is given, list all other information. If the newspaper's name does not include the city of publication, insert it, using brackets: *Sippican Sentinel* [Marion, MA].

What to include in MLA citations for a miscellaneous source

MLA Works Cited Entries for Other Kinds of Materials. Miscellaneous sources range from unsigned encyclopedia entries to conference presentations to government publications. A full citation should give this information (as available): author, title, city, publisher, date, and page numbers.

13. Encyclopedia, Dictionary, Other Alphabetical Reference—MLA

"Communication." The Business Reference Book 2007.

Parenthetical reference: ("Communication")

Begin a signed entry with the author's name. For any work arranged alphabetically, omit page numbers in the citation and the parenthetical reference. For a well-known reference book, include only an edition (if stated) and a date. For other reference books, give the full publication information.

14. Report—MLA

Electrical Power Research Institute (EPRI). Epidemiologic Studies of
         Electric Utility Employees. (Report No. RP2964.5). Palo Alto, CA:
         EPRI, Nov. 1994.

Parenthetical reference: (Electrical Power Research Institute [EPRI] 27)

If no author is given, begin with the organization that sponsored the report.

For any report or other document with group authorship, as above, include the group's abbreviated name in your first parenthetical reference, and then use only that abbreviation in any subsequent reference.

15. Conference Presentation—MLA

Smith, Abelard A. "Radon Concentrations in Molded Concrete." First
         British Symposium in Environmental Engineering. London, 11-13
         Oct. 2006. Ed. Anne Hodkins. London: Harrison, 2007. 106-21.

Parenthetical reference: (Smith 109)

This citation is for a presentation that has been included in the published proceedings of a conference. For an unpublished presentation, include the presenter's name, the title of the presentation, and the conference title, location, and date, but do not underline or italicize the conference information.

16. Interview, Personally Conducted—MLA

Nasser, Gamel. Chief Engineer for Northern Electric. Personal
         interview. Rangeley, ME. 2 Apr., 2007.

Parenthetical reference: (Nasser)

17. Interview, Published—MLA

Lescault, James. "The Future of Graphics." Executive Views of
         Automation. Ed. Karen Prell. Miami: Haber, 2007. 216-31.

Parenthetical reference: (Lescault 218)

The interviewee's name is placed in the entry's author slot.

18. Letter or Memo, Unpublished—MLA

Rogers, Leonard. Letter to the author. 15 May 2007.

Parenthetical reference: (Rogers)

19. Questionnaire—MLA

Taylor, Lynne. Questionnaire sent to 612 Massachusetts business
executives. 14 Feb. 2007.

Parenthetical reference: (Taylor)

20. Brochure or Pamphlet—MLA

Investment Strategies for the 21st Century. San Francisco: Blount
Economics Assn., 2004.

Parenthetical reference: (Investment)

If the work is signed, begin with its author.

21. Lecture, Speech, Address, or Reading—MLA

Dumont, R. A. "Managing Natural Gas." Lecture. University of
Massachusetts at Dartmouth, 15 Jan. 2006.

Parenthetical reference: (Dumont)

If the lecture title is not known, write Address, Lecture, or Reading—without quotation marks. Include the sponsor and the location if available. For citing the transcript of testimony (say, before a committee), see page 654.

22. Government Document—MLA

Virginia. Highway Dept. Standards for Bridge Maintenance. Richmond:
Virginia Highway Dept., 2007.

Parenthetical reference: (Virginia Highway Dept. 49)

If the author is unknown (as here), list the information in this order: name of the government, name of the issuing agency, document title, place, publisher, and date.

For any congressional document, identify the house of Congress (Senate or House of Representatives) before the title, and the number and session of Congress after the title:

> United States Cong. House, Armed Services Committee. <u>Funding for the</u>
> <u>Military Academies</u>. 108th Congress, 2nd sess. Washington: GPO, 2006.

Parenthetical reference: (U.S. Cong. 41)

GPO is the abbreviation for the U.S. Government Printing Office.

For an entry from the *Congressional Record,* give only date and pages:

> <u>Cong. Rec.</u> 10 Mar. 2004: 2178-92.

Parenthetical reference: (<u>Cong. Rec.</u> 2184)

23. Document with Corporate or Foundation Authorship—MLA

> Hermitage Foundation. <u>Global Warming Scenarios for the Year 2030</u>.
> Washington: Natl. Res. Council, 2005.

Parenthetical reference: (Hermitage Foun. 123)

24. Map or Other Visual—MLA

> "Deaths Caused by Breast Cancer, by County." Map. <u>Scientific American</u>
> Oct. 1995: 32D.

Parenthetical reference: ("Deaths Caused")

If the creator of the visual is listed, give that name first. Identify the type of visual (Map, Graph, Table, Diagram) immediately following its title.

25. Unpublished Dissertation, Report, or Miscellaneous Items—MLA

> Author (if known). "Title." Sponsoring organization or publisher, date.

For any work that has group authorship (corporation, committee, task force), cite the name of the group or agency in place of the author's name.

MLA Works Cited Entries for Electronic Sources.   Electronic sources include Internet sites, reference databases, CD-ROMs, computer software, and email. Any citation for an electronic source should allow readers to identify the original source (printed or electronic) and trace a clear path for retrieving the material. Provide all available information in the following order:

What to include in an MLA citation for an electronic source

1. Name of author, editor, or creator of the electronic work or site.
2. Title of the document. For online postings, such as email discussion lists or newsgroups, give the title of the posting followed by the words "Online posting." For CD-ROM or software, give the title of the document or software followed by "CD-ROM" or "Diskette."

3. Publication information of the original printed version (as in the previous entries), if such a version exists.
4. Information about the electronic publication, including the title of the site or database (as in "MEDLINE") and the date of the posting or the last update of the site. Name the sponsoring organization or provider of the CD-ROM (as in "ProQuest") or reference database service (as in "Dialog").
5. The date you accessed the source.
6. The full and accurate electronic address. For Internet sources, provide the complete URL (Uniform Resource Locator), enclosed in angle brackets (< >). Include page numbers only if the electronic document shows page numbers from the original print version. Include paragraph numbers only if they appear in the original Internet document.

NOTE   *When a URL continues from one line to the next, break it only after a slash. Do not insert a hyphen.*

26. Reference Database—MLA

> Sahl, J. D. "Power Lines, Viruses, and Childhood Leukemia." Cancer Causes
>> Control 6.1 (Jan. 1995): 83. MEDLINE. Online. Dialog. 7 Nov. 2007.

Parenthetical reference: (Sahl 83)

For entries with a printed equivalent, begin with publication information, then the database title (underlined or italicized), the "Online" designation to indicate the medium, and the service provider (or URL or email address) and the date of access. The access date is important because frequent updatings of databases can produce different versions of the material.

For entries with no printed equivalent, give the title and date of the work in quotation marks, followed by the electronic source information:

> Argent, Roger R. "An Analysis of International Exchange Rates for
>> 2005." Accu-Data. Online. Dow Jones News Retrieval. 10 Jan. 2006.

Parenthetical reference: (Argent)

If the author is not known, begin with the work's title.

27. Computer Software—MLA

> Virtual Collaboration. Diskette. New York: Pearson, 2007.

Parenthetical reference: (Virtual)

Begin with the author's name, if known.

28. CD-ROM—MLA

> Canalte, Henry A. "Violent-Crime Statistics: Good News and Bad News."
>
>   Law Enforcement Feb. 1995: 8. ABI/INFORM. CD-ROM. ProQuest.
>
>   Sept. 2007.

Parenthetical reference: (Canalte 8)

If the material is also available in print, begin with the information about the printed source, followed by the electronic source information: name of the database (underlined), CD-ROM designation, vendor name, and electronic publication date. If the material has no printed equivalent, list its author (if known) and title (in quotation marks), followed by the electronic source information.

For CD-ROM reference works and other material not routinely updated, give the title of the work, followed by the CD-ROM designation, place, electronic publisher, and date:

> Time Almanac. CD-ROM. Washington: Compact, 2004.

Parenthetical reference: (Time Almanac 74)

Begin with the author's name, if known.

29. Email Discussion Group—MLA

> Korsten, A. "Major Update of the WWWVL Migration and Ethnic Relations."
>
>   7 Apr. 1998. Online posting. ERCOMER News. 8 Apr. 2003.
>
>   <www.ercomer.org/archive/ercomer-news/0002.html>.

Parenthetical reference: (Korsten)

Begin with the author's name (if known), followed by the title of the work (in quotation marks), publication date, the Online posting designation, title of discussion group (underlined), date of access, and the URL. The parenthetical reference includes no page number because none is given in an online posting.

30. Newsgroup—MLA

> Dorsey, Michael. "Environmentalism or Racism." 25 Mar. 1998. Online
>
>   posting. 1 Apr. 2002 <news:alt.org.sierra-club>.

Parenthetical reference: (Dorsey)

31. Personal Email—MLA

> Wallin, John Luther. "Frog Reveries." Email to the author. 12 Oct. 2007.

Parenthetical reference: (Wallin)

Cite personal email as you would printed correspondence. If the document has a subject line or title, enclose it in quotation marks. For publicly posted email (say, a newsgroup or discussion list) include the address and date of access.

32. Web Site—MLA

> Dumont, R. A. "An Online Course in Technical Writing." Course Home
>> Page. Fall 2006. Dept. of English, UMASS Dartmouth. 6 Jan. 2007.
>> <www.umassd.edu/englishdepartment.html.>.

Parenthetical reference: (Dumont)

Begin with the author's name (if known), followed by title of the work, posting date, name of Web site, date of access, and Web address (in angle brackets).

33. Print Article Posted Online—MLA

> Jeffers, Anna D. "NAFTA's Effects on the U.S. Trade Deficit." <u>Sultana</u>
>> <u>Business Quarterly</u> 3.4 (2006): 65-74. April 2007.
>> <www.sol.org/sbc/2004vol3/jeffers2.html>.

Parenthetical reference: (Jeffers 66)

34. Real-Time Communication—MLA

Synchronous communication occurs in "real-time" forums and MUDs (multi-user dungeons), MOOs (MUD object-oriented software), FTP (file transfer protocols), chatrooms, and instant messaging.

> "Online Debate on Global Warming." 3 Apr. 2004. Frank Findle at
>> EarthWatchMOO. 10 May 2004. <www.ab.liu/orb/globalwarm_3_4-04.htm>.

Parenthetical reference: ("Online Debate")

35. Online Abstract—MLA

> Lane, Amanda D., et al. "The Promise of Microcircuits." <u>Journal of</u>
>> <u>Nanotechnology</u> 12.2 (2004). Abstract. 11 May 2004.
>> <http://www.jnt.org/abt/0105ab.htm>.

Parenthetical reference: (Lane et al.)

36. General Reference to a Site—MLA

When you are referring to a site in general instead of a specific document, include the address in your discussion and *not* in the list of Works Cited.

> For the latest information about worldwide research in electromagnetic radiation, go to Microwave News at <www.microwavenews.com>.

MLA Sample Works Cited Pages

On a separate page at the document's end arrange entries alphabetically by author's surname. When the author is unknown, list the title alphabetically according to its first word (excluding introductory articles). For a title that begins with a digit ("5," "6," etc.), alphabetize the entry as if the digit were spelled out.

The list of works cited in Figure QG.4 accompanies the report on electromagnetic fields, pages 572–82. In the left margin, colored numbers refer to the elements discussed below. Bracketed labels identify different types of sources cited.

Discussion of Figure QG.4

1. Center Works Cited title at the page top. Double-space entries. Number Works Cited pages consecutively with text pages.
2. Indent five spaces for the second and subsequent lines of an entry.
3. Place quotation marks around article titles. Underline or italicize periodical or book titles. Capitalize the first letter of key words in all titles (also—but only when the first or last word in a title—articles, prepositions, and conjunctions). When an article skips pages in a publication, give only the first page number followed by a plus sign.
4. Do not cite a magazine's volume number, even if it is given.
5. For a CD-ROM database that is updated often (such as *ProQuest*), conclude your citation with the date of electronic publication.
6. For additional perspective beyond "establishment" viewpoints, examine "alternative" publications (such as the *Amicus Journal* and *In These Times*).
7. In citing an online database, include the date you accessed the source.
8. Use a period and one space to separate a citation's three major items (author, title, publication data). Skip one space after a comma or colon. Use no punctuation to separate magazine title and date.
9. Alphabetize hyphenated surnames according to the name that appears first.
10. Use the first author's name and "et al." for works with four or more authors or editors. When citing an abstract instead of the complete article, indicate this by inserting "Abstract" after the page numbers of the original.
11. For a journal with new pagination in each issue include the issue number after the volume number and separated by a period. For example, 26.4 would signify volume 26, issue 4. For page numbers of more than two digits, give only the final differing digits in the second number (but never less than two digits).
12. Use three-letter abbreviations for months with five or more letters.
13. For government reports, name the sponsoring agency and include all available information for retrieving the document.
14. When the privacy of the electronic source is not an issue (e.g., a library versus an email correspondent), include the electronic address in your entry.

Works Cited

Beardsley, Tim. "Say That Again?" Scientific American Dec. 1997: 20.   *[magazine article]*

Brodeur, Paul. "Annals of Radiation: The Cancer at Slater School." New Yorker 7 Dec. 1992: 86+.

Cavanaugh, Herbert A. "EMF Study: Good News and Bad News." Electrical World Feb. 1995: 8.
        ABI/INFORM. CD-ROM. ProQuest. Sept. 2004.   *[trade magazine article from database]*

Dana, Amy, and Tom Turner. "Currents of Controversy." Amicus Journal Summer 1993: 29–32.

de Jager, L., and L. de Bruyn. "Long-Term Effects of a 50 HZ Electric Field on the Life
        Expectancy of Mice." Review of Environmental Health 10.3 (1994): 221–24. MEDLINE.
        DIALOG. 8 May 2007 <www.dialog.com>.   *[database article]*

DesMarteau, Kathleen. "Study Links Sewing Machine Use to Alzheimer's Disease." Bobbin
        Oct. 1994: 36–38. ABI/INFORM. CD-ROM. ProQuest. Aug. 2004.

"Electrophobia: Overcoming Fears of EMFs." University of California Wellness Letter Nov. 1994:1.
                                                              [newsletter]

Goodman, E. M., B. Greenebaum, and M. T. Marron. "Effects of Electromagnetic Fields on Molecules
        and Cells." International Review of Cytology 158 (1995): 279–338. MEDLINE. DIALOG. 8 Mar.
        2007 <www.dialog.com>.

Goodman, Neville W. "The Media and The Power Line Scare." 23 Jan. 2004. 12 Mar. 2007
        <www.healthwatch-uk.org/nlett21.html#power>.   *[Web page]*

Gross, Liza. "Current Risks." Sierra May-June 1999: 30+.

Halloran-Barney, Marianne B. Energy Service Advisor for County Electric. Email to the author.
        3 Apr. 2007.   *[personal email inquiry]*

Henshaw, D. L., et.al. "Does Our Electricity Distribution System Pose a Serious Risk to Public
        Health?" Medical Hypotheses 59.1 (2002): 39–51. Abstract. 22 April 2007
        <www.electric-fields.bris.ac.uk/MedHypoth.htm>.   *[online abstract]*

Jauchem, J. "Alleged Health Effects of Electromagnetic Fields: Misconceptions in the Scientific
        Literature." Journal of Microwave Power and Electromagnetic Energy 26.4 (1991): 189–95.

Kirkpatrick, David. "Can Power Lines Give You Cancer?" Fortune 31 Dec. 1990: 80-85.

Lai, Henry, and Narendra D. Singh. "Magnetic-Field-Induced DNA Strand Breaks in Brain Cells
        of the Rat." Environmental Health Perspectives 112.6 (2004): 687–94. Abstract. 22 Apr. 2007
        <www.ehp.niehs.nih.gov/docs/2004/6355/abstract.html>.   *[Web page]*

FIGURE QG.4 A List of Works Cited (MLA Style)

Miltane, John. Chief Engineer for County Electric. Personal interview. 5 Apr. 2007.

Monmonier, Mark. Cartographies of Danger: Mapping Hazards in America. Chicago: U of Chicago P,

   1997: 190.   *[book–one author]*

Moore, Taylor. "EMF Health Risks: The Story in Brief." EPRI Journal Mar./Apr. 1995: 7–17.

National Cancer Institute. Magnetic Field Exposure and Cancer (Fact Sheet No. 346).

   21 April 2005. 12 April 2007 <www.cancer.gov/cancer topics/factsheet/Risk/magnetic-fields>.

NIEHS EMF-RAPID Program Staff. Health Effects from Exposure to Power Line Frequency Electric

   and Magnetic Fields (NIH Publication No. 99-4493). Research Triangle Park, NC: National

   Institute of Environmental Health Sciences. 4 May 1999. 11 Mar. 2007

   <www.niehs.nih.gov/emfrapid>.   *[govt. report posted online]*

Palfreman, John. "Apocalypse Not." Technology Review 24 April 1996: 24–33.

Pinsky, Mark A. The EMF Book: What You Should Know about Electromagnetic Fields,

   Electromagnetic Radiation, and Your Health. New York: Warner, 1995.

Raloff, Janet. "Electromagnetic Fields May Damage Hearts." Science News 155.3 (1999): 70.

---. "Electromagnetic Fields May Trigger Enzymes." Science News 153.8 (1998): 119.

---. "EMFs' Biological Influences." Science News 153.2 (1998): 29–31.

Sivitz, Laura B. "Cells Proliferate in Magnetic Fields." Science News 158.18 (2000): 196–97.

Stix, Gary. "Are Power Lines a Dead Issue?" Scientific American Mar. 1998: 33–34.

"Strong Electric Fields Implicated in Major Leukemia Risk for Workers." Microwave News XX.3

   (2000): 1–2. 15 Mar. 2007 <www.microwavenews.com>.   *[journal article posted online]*

Travis, R. C. "Melatonin and Breast Cancer: A Prospective Study" Journal of the National Cancer

   Institute 96.6 (2004): 889-89. Abstract. 22 April 2007: <www.ncbi.nim.nih.gov:80/entrez/

   query.fcgi?cmd=Retrieve&db=pubmed&dopt=Abstract&List_ulds=15026473>.

Taubes, Gary. "Fields of Fear." Atlantic Monthly Nov. 1994: 94–108.

United States Environmental Protection Agency. EMF in Your Environment. Washington: GPO, 1992.

Wartenberg, Daniel. "Solid Scientific Evidence Supporting an EMF-Childhood Leukemia

   Connection." Public Hearing, Connecticut Citing Council. Hartford. 9 Jan. 2007. Microwave

   News XXVII.1 (2007): 5-6. 10 April 2007 <www.microwavenews.com>.   *[transcript of testimony]*

13

14

FIGURE QG.4 *(Continued)*

APA Documentation Style

One popular alternative to MLA style appears in the *Publication Manual of the American Psychological Association,* 5th ed., Washington: American Psychological Association, 2001. APA style is useful when writers wish to emphasize the publication dates of their references. A parenthetical reference in the text briefly identifies the source, date, and page number(s):

Reference cited in the text

> In one study, mice continuously exposed to an electromagnetic
> field tended to die earlier than mice in the control group (de
> Jager & de Bruyn, 1994, p. 224).

The full citation then appears in the alphabetical listing of "References," at the report's end:

Full citation at document's end

> de Jager, L., & de Bruyn, L. (1994). Long-term effects of a 50 Hz
>   electric field on the life-expectancy of mice. *Review of
>   Environmental Health,* 10(3-4), 221-224.

Because it emphasizes the date, APA style (or some similar author-date style) is preferred in the sciences and social sciences, where information quickly becomes outdated.

APA Parenthetical References

How APA and MLA parenthetical references differ

APA's parenthetical references differ from MLA's (pages 640–41) as follows: The APA citation includes the publication date; a comma separates each item in the reference; and "p." or "pp." precedes the page number (which is optional in the APA system). When a subsequent reference to a work follows closely after the initial reference, the date need not be included. Here are specific guidelines:

- If your discussion names the author, do not repeat the name in your parenthetical reference; simply give the date and page numbers:

Author named in the text

> Researchers de Jager and de Bruyn explain that experimental mice
> exposed to an electromagnetic field tended to die earlier than mice
> in the control group (1994, p. 224).

When two authors of a work are named in the text, their names are connected by "and," but in a parenthetical reference, their names are connected by an ampersand, "&."

- If you cite two or more works in a single reference, list the authors in alphabetical order and separate the citations with semicolons:

Two or more works in a single reference

> (Jones, 2007; Gomez, 2005; Leduc, 2002)

- If you cite a work with three to five authors, try to name them in your text, to avoid an excessively long parenthetical reference.

A work with three
to five authors

> Franks, Oblesky, Ryan, Jablar, and Perkins (2003) studied the role
> of electromagnetic fields in tumor formation.

In any subsequent references to this work, name only the first author, followed by "et al." (Latin abbreviation for "and others").

- If you cite two or more works by the same author published in the same year, assign a different letter to each work:

Two or more works
by the same author
in the same year

> (Lamont, 2007a, p. 135)
>
> (Lamont, 2007b, pp. 67-68)

INDEX TO SAMPLE ENTRIES FOR APA REFERENCES

Books

1. Book, single author
2. Book, two to five authors
3. Book, six or more authors
4. Book, anonymous author
5. Multiple books, same author
6. Book, one to five editors
7. Book, indirect source
8. Anthology selection or book chapter

Periodicals

9. Article, magazine
10. Article, journal with new pagination each issue
11. Article, journal with continuous pagination
12. Article, newspaper

Other Sources

13. Encyclopedia, dictionary, alphabetical reference

14. Report
15. Conference presentation
16. Interview, personally conducted
17. Interview, published
18. Personal correspondence
19. Brochure or pamphlet
20. Lecture
21. Government document
22. Miscellaneous items

Electronic Sources

23. Online abstract
24. Print article posted online
25. Computer software or software manual
26. CD-ROM abstract
27. CD-ROM reference work
28. Personal email
29. Document from a university
30. Newsgroup, discussion list, online forum

Other examples of parenthetical references appear with their corresponding entries in the following discussion of the reference list entries.

APA Reference List Entries

How to space and
indent entries

The APA reference list includes each source you have cited in your document. In preparing the list of references, type the first line of each entry flush with the left margin. Indent the second and subsequent lines five character spaces (one-half inch). Skip one character space after any period, comma, or colon. Double-space within and between each entry.

Following are examples of complete citations as they would appear in the References section of your document. Shown immediately below each entry is its corresponding parenthetical reference as it would appear in the text. Note the capitalization, abbreviation, spacing, and punctuation in the sample entries.

What to include in an APA citation for a book

APA Entries for Books.   Any citation for a book should contain all applicable information in the following order: author, date, title, editor or translator, edition, volume number, and facts about publication (city and publisher).

1. Book, Single Author—APA

Kerzin-Fontana, J. B. (2007). *Technology management: A handbook*

(3rd ed.). Delmar, NY: American Management Association.

Parenthetical reference: (Kerzin-Fontana, 2007, pp. 3-4)

Use only initials for an author's first and middle name. Capitalize only the first word of a book's title and subtitle and any proper names. Identify a later edition in parentheses between the title and the period.

2. Book, Two to Five Authors—APA

Aronson, L., Katz, R., & Moustafa, C. (2007). *Toxic waste disposal*

methods. New Haven: Yale University Press.

Parenthetical reference: (Aronson, Katz, & Moustafa, 2007)

Use an ampersand (&) before the name of the final author listed in an entry. As an alternative parenthetical reference, name the authors in your text and include date (and page numbers, if appropriate) in parentheses.

Give the publisher's full name (as in "Yale University Press") but omit the words "Publisher," "Company," and "Inc."

3. Book, Six or More Authors—APA

Fogle, S. T., et al. (2006). *Hyperspace technology*. Boston: Little, Brown.

Parenthetical reference: (Fogle et al., 2006, p. 34)

"Et al." is the Latin abbreviation for "et alia," meaning "and others."

4. Book, Anonymous Author—APA

Structured programming. (2007). Boston: Meredith Press.

Parenthetical reference: (Structured Programming, 2007, p. 67)

In your list of references, place an anonymous work alphabetically by the first key word (not *The, A,* or *An*) in its title. In your parenthetical reference, capitalize all key words in a book, article, or journal title.

5. Multiple Books, Same Author—APA

```
Chang, J. W. (2005a). Biophysics. Boston: Little, Brown.

Chang, J. W. (2005b). MindQuest. Chicago: John Pressler.
```

Parenthetical references: (Chang, 2005a)

(Chang, 2005b)

Two or more works by the same author not published in the same year are distinguished by their respective dates alone, without the added letter.

6. Book, One to Five Editors—APA

```
Morris, A. J., & Pardin-Walker, L. B. (Eds.). (2007). Handbook of new
        information technology. New York: HarperCollins.
```

Parenthetical reference: (Morris & Pardin-Walker, 2007, p. 79)

For more than five editors, name only the first, followed by "et al."

7. Book, Indirect Source—APA

```
Stubbs, J. (2007). White-collar productivity. Miami: Harris.
```

Parenthetical reference: (cited in Stubbs, 2007, p. 47)

When your source (as in Stubbs, above) has cited another source, list only this second source in the References section, but name the original source in the text: "Kline's study (cited in Stubbs, 2007, p. 47) supports this conclusion."

8. Anthology Selection or Book Chapter—APA

```
Bowman, J. (1994). Electronic conferencing. In A. Williams (Ed.),
        Communication and technology: Today and tomorrow (pp. 123-142).
        Denton, TX: Association for Business Communication.
```

Parenthetical reference: (Bowman, 1994, p. 126)

The page numbers in the complete reference are for the selection cited from the anthology.

What to include in an APA citation for a periodical

APA Entries for Periodicals.   A citation for an article should give this information (as available), in order: author, publication date, article title (without quotation marks), volume or number (or both), and page numbers for the entire article—not just the page(s) cited.

9. Article, Magazine—APA

DesMarteau, K. (1994, October). Study links sewing machine use to
Alzheimer's disease. *Bobbin, 36,* 36-38.

Parenthetical reference: (DesMarteau, 1994, p. 36)

If no author is given, provide all other information. Capitalize the first word in an article's title and subtitle, and any proper nouns. Capitalize all key words in a periodical title. Italicize the periodical title, volume number, and commas (as shown above).

10. Article, Journal with New Pagination for Each Issue—APA

Thackman-White, J. R. (2006). Computer-assisted research. *American
Library Journal, 51*(1), 3-9.

Parenthetical reference: (Thackman-White, 2006, pp. 4-5)

Because each issue for a given year has page numbers that begin at "1," readers need the issue number (in this instance, "1"). The "51" denotes the volume number, which is italicized.

11. Article, Journal with Continuous Pagination—APA

Barnstead, M. H. (2007). The writing crisis. *Journal of Writing Theory,
12,* 415-433.

Parenthetical reference: (Barnstead, 2007, pp. 415-416)

The "12" denotes the volume number. When page numbers continue from issue to issue for the full year, readers won't need the issue number, because no other issue in that year repeats these same page numbers. (You can still include the issue number if you think it will help readers retrieve the article more easily.)

12. Article, Newspaper—APA

Baranski, V. H. (2006, January 15). Errors in technology assessment.
The Boston Times, p. B3.

Parenthetical reference: (Baranski, 2006, p. B3)

In addition to the year of publication, include the month and day. If the newspaper's name begins with "The," include it in your citation. Include "p." or "pp." before page numbers. For an article on nonconsecutive pages, list each page, separated by a comma.

What to include in
an APA citation for
a miscellaneous
source

APA Entries for Other Sources. Miscellaneous sources range from unsigned encyclopedia entries to conference presentations to government documents. A full citation should give this information (as available): author, publication date, work title (and report or series number), page numbers (if applicable), city, and publisher.

13. Encyclopedia, Dictionary, Alphabetical Reference—APA

Communication. (2007). In *The business reference book.* Boston: Business
    Resources Press.

Parenthetical reference: ("Communication," 2007)

For an entry that is signed, begin with the author's name and publication date.

14. Report—APA

Electrical Power Research Institute. (1994). *Epidemiologic studies of*
    electric utility employees (Report No. RP2964.5). Palo Alto, CA:
    Author.

Parenthetical reference: (Electrical Power Research Institute [EPRI],
1994, p. 12)

If authors are named, list them first, followed by the publication date. When citing a group author, as above, include the group's abbreviated name in your first parenthetical reference, and use only that abbreviation in any subsequent reference. When the agency (or organization) and publisher are the same, list "Author" in the publisher's slot.

15. Conference Presentation—APA

Smith, A. A. (2007, March). Radon concentrations in molded concrete. In
    A. Hodkins (Ed.), *First British Symposium on Environmental*
    Engineering (pp. 106-121). London: Harrison Press, 2007.

Parenthetical reference: (Smith, 2007, p. 109)

In parentheses is the date of the presentation. The name of the symposium is a proper name, and so is capitalized. Following the publisher's name is the date of publication.

For an unpublished presentation, include the presenter's name, year and month, title of the presentation (italicized), and all available information about the conference or meeting: "Symposium held at. . . ." Do not italicize this last information.

16. Interview, Personally Conducted—APA

Parenthetical reference: (G. Nasser, personal interview, April 2, 2007)

This material is considered a nonrecoverable source, and so is cited in the text only, as a parenthetical reference. If you name the respondent in text, do not repeat the name in the citation.

17. Interview, Published—APA

> Jable, C. K. (2006). The future of graphics [Interview with James
>> Lescault]. In K. Prell (Ed.), *Executive views of automation* (pp.
>> 216-231). Miami: Haber Press, 2007.

Parenthetical reference: (Jable, 2006, pp. 218-223)

Begin with the name of the interviewer, followed by the interview date and title (if available), the designation (in brackets), and the publication information, including the date.

18. Personal Correspondence—APA

Parenthetical reference: (L. Rogers, personal correspondence, May 15, 2007)

This material is considered nonrecoverable data, and so is cited in the text only, as a parenthetical reference. If you name the correspondent in your text, do not repeat the name in the citation.

19. Brochure or Pamphlet—APA

This material follows the citation format for a book entry (page 657). After the title of the work, include the designation "Brochure" in brackets.

20. Lecture—APA

> Dumont, R. A. (2006, January 15). *Managing natural gas.* Lecture
>> presented at the University of Massachusetts at Dartmouth.

Parenthetical reference: (Dumont, 2006)

If you name the lecturer in text, do not repeat the name in the citation.

21. Government Document—APA

> Virginia Highway Department. (2007). *Standards for bridge maintenance.*
>> Richmond: Author.

Parenthetical reference: (Virginia Highway Department, 2007, p. 49)

If the author is unknown, present the information in this order: name of the issuing agency, publication date, document title, place, and publisher. When the issuing agency is both author and publisher, list "Author" in the publisher's slot.

For any congressional document, identify the house of Congress (Senate or House of Representatives) before the date.

U.S. House Armed Services Committee. (2006). *Funding for the military*

academies. Washington, DC: U.S. Government Printing Office.

Parenthetical reference: (U.S. House, 2006, p. 41)

22. *Miscellaneous Items (Unpublished Manuscripts, Dissertations, and so on)— APA*

Author (if known). (Date of publication.) *Title of work*. Sponsoring

organization or publisher.

For any work that has group authorship (corporation, committee, and so on), cite the name of the group or agency in place of the author's name.

APA Entries for Electronic Sources.   When you cite sources in the References section of your document, identify the original source (printed or electronic) and give readers a path for retrieving the material. Provide all available information in the following order:

What to include in an APA citation for an electronic source

1. Author, editor, or creator of the electronic work.
2. Date the work was published or was created electronically. For magazines and newspapers, include the month and day as well as the year. If the date of an electronic publication is not available, use "n.d."
3. Publication information of the original printed version (as in the above entries), if such a version exists. Follow this by designating the electronic medium (as in "[CD-ROM]") or the type of work (as in "[Abstract]" or "[Editorial]" or the like).
4. The word "Retrieved" followed by the date (month, day, year) you accessed the source.
5. Information about the electronic publication, including the title of the site or reference database (as in "MEDLINE") and the date of the posting or the last update of the site. Name the sponsoring organization or provider of the CD-ROM (as in "ProQuest") or database service (as in "Dialog").
6. The full and accurate electronic address. For Internet sources, provide the complete URL (Uniform Resource Locator). For CD-ROM and database sources, give the document's retrieval number. If the electronic version is identical to the original printed version, omit the URL and give only the publication information of the print version followed by "[Electronic version]."

23. Online Abstract—APA

> Stevens, R. L. (2006). Cell phones and cancer rates [Abstract].
>> *Oncology Journal, 57*(2), 41-43. Retrieved April 10, 2007, from
>> Dialog database. (MEDLINE item: AY 24598).

Parenthetical reference: (Stevens, 2006)

The above entry ends with a period. Only entries that close with a URL (as in entry no. 24, below) have no period at the end of the URL.

NOTE   *If instead you are citing the entire article, retrieved from a full-text database, merely delete the "[Abstract]" from your citation.*

24. Print Article Posted Online—APA

> Alley, R. A. (2006, January). Ergonomic influences on worker
>> satisfaction. Industrial Psychology 5(12). Retrieved April 8,
>> 2007, from www.psycharchives/index/indpsy/2006_1.html

Parenthetical reference: (Alley, 2006)

If the page numbers of the printed original were posted on the online source and if you were confident that the document's electronic version and print version were identical, you could omit the URL and insert "[Electronic version]" between the end of the article title and the period.

25. Computer Software or Software Manual—APA

> Virtual collaboration [Computer software]. (2007). New York: Pearson.

Parenthetical reference: (Virtual, 2007)

For citing a manual, replace the "Computer software" designation in brackets with "Software manual."

26. CD-ROM Abstract—APA

> Cavanaugh, H. (1995). An EMF study: Good news and bad news [CD-ROM].
>> *Electrical World, 209*(2), 8. Abstract retrieved April 7, 2007,
>> from ProQuest File: ABI/INFORM database (62-1498).

Parenthetical reference: (Cavanaugh, 1995)

The "8" in the entry above denotes the page number of this one-page article.

27. CD-ROM Reference Work—APA

> `Ecoterrorism [CD-ROM] (2007).` *`Ecological encyclopedia.`* `Washington:`
> `Redwood.`

Parenthetical reference: `(Ecoterrorism, 2007)`

If the work on CD-ROM has a printed equivalent, APA currently prefers that it be cited in its printed form.

28. Personal Email—APA

Parenthetical reference: `Fred Flynn (personal communication, May 10, 2007)`
`provided these statistics.`

Instead of being included in the list of references, personal email is cited directly in the text.

29. Document from a University—APA

> `Owens, P. (2006). Internship guidelines. Retrieved June 12, 2007, from`
> `Clayton College, Department of Communication Web site:`
> `www.clayton.edu/comm/p-o.html`

Parenthetical reference: `(Owens, 2006)`

30. Newsgroup, discussion list, online forum—APA

> `LaBarge, V. S. (2006, October 20). A cure for computer viruses.`
> *`Firewall DiscussionList.`* `Retrieved December 15, 2007, from`
> `www.srb/forums/frwl/webZ/m2237.html`

Parenthetical reference: `(LaBarge, 2006).`

Although email is not included in the list of references, listserv, newsgroup, and forum postings are considered more retrievable.

APA Sample Reference List

APA's References section is an alphabetical listing (by author) equivalent to MLA's Works Cited section. Like Works Cited, the reference list includes only those works actually cited. (A bibliography usually would include background works or works consulted as well.) Unlike MLA style, APA style calls for only "recoverable" sources to appear in the reference list. Therefore, personal interviews, email messages, and other unpublished materials are cited in the text only.

The list of references in Figure QG.5 accompanies the report on a technical marketing career, pages 585–92. In the left margin, colored numbers denote elements of Figure QG.5 discussed below. Bracketed labels on the right identify different types of sources.

Discussion of Figure QG.5

1. Center the References title at the top of the page. Use one-inch margins. Number reference pages consecutively with text pages. Include only recoverable data (material that readers could retrieve for themselves); cite personal interviews, email, and other personal correspondence parenthetically in the text only. See also item 7 in this list.

2. Double-space entries and order them alphabetically by author's last name (excluding *A, An,* or *The*). List initials only for authors' first and middle names. Write out names of all months. In student papers, indent the second and subsequent lines of an entry five spaces. In papers submitted for publication in an APA journal, the first line is indented instead.

3. Do not enclose article titles in quotation marks. Italicize periodical titles. Capitalize the first word in article or book titles and subtitles, and any proper nouns. Capitalize all key words in magazine or journal titles.

4. For more than one author or editor, use ampersands instead of spelling out "and."

5. Use italics for a journal's name, volume number, and the comma. Give the issue number in parentheses only if each issue begins on page 1. Do not include "p." or "pp." before journal page numbers (only before page numbers from a newspaper).

6. Omit punctuation from the end of an electronic address.

7. Treat an unpublished conference presentation as a recoverable source; include it in your list of references instead of only citing it parenthetically in your text.

CSE and Other Numbered Documentation Styles

In the numbered documentation system, each work is assigned a number sequentially the first time it is cited. This same number is then used for any subsequent reference to that work. Numbered documentation is often used in the physical sciences (astronomy, chemistry, geology, physics) and in the applied sciences (mathematics, medicine, engineering, and computer science).

Particular disciplines have their own preferred documentation styles, described in manuals such as these:

A sampling of discipline-specific documentation manuals

- American Chemical Society, *The ACS Style Guide for Authors and Editors*
- American Institute for Physics, *AIP Style Guide*
- American Mathematical Society, *A Manual for Authors of Mathematical Papers*
- American Medical Association, *Manual of Style*

One widely consulted guide for numerical documentation is *Scientific Style and Format: The CSE Manual for Authors, Editors, and Publishers, 6th ed., 1994,* from the Council of Science Editors. (In addition to its citation-sequence system for documentation, CSE offers a name-year system that basically duplicates the APA system described previously.)

1

References

2

Anson, D. (2007, March 12). *Engineering graduates and the job market.* Lecture presented at
the University of Massachusetts at Dartmouth.   *[lecture]*

Bureau of Labor Statistics (2006a). *Occupation projections and training data:* 2006-07 Edition.
Washington, DC: Author. Retrieved April 23, 2007, from www.bls.gov/EMP/optd/optd.pdf

[online report]

Bureau of Labor Statistics (2006b). Sales engineers. *Occupational Outlook Handbook:*
2006-07 Edition. Retrieved April 21, 2007, from www.bls.gov/oco/ocos123.htm

[reference book online]

Bureau of Labor Statistics (2006c). Advertising and marketing managers.
Occupational Outlook Handbook: 2006-07 Edition. Retrieved April 21, 2007, from
ww.bls.gov/oco/pdf/ocos020.pdf

Cornelius, H., & Lewis, W. (1983). *Career guide for sales and marketing* (2nd ed.) New York:
Monarch Press.   *[book with two authors]*

Coy, P. (2004, March 22). The future of work. *Business Week,* 50–52.

3

Dolan, K.A. (2006, April 17). Offshoring the offshorers. *Forbes,* 74-76.   *[print article]*

4

Hira, R. & Hira, I. (2005). Outsourcing America: What's behind our national crisis and how we
can reclaim American jobs. New York: AMACOM.   *[book]*

Intel Corporation (n.d.). Programs: sales and marketing rotation. Retrieved April 20, 2007, from
www.intel.com/jobs/usa/students/programs/smrp.htm   *[web page]*

Jacobs, M.A. (2007, April 9). Tech workers, get ready for offshoring. *The Dallas Morning News.*
Retrieved April 12, 2007 from www.dallas.news.com/sharecontent/dws/
busindustries/techtelecom/stories   *[newspaper article online]*

5

Shelley, K. J. (1997, Fall). A portrait of the M.B.A. *Occupational Outlook Quarterly, 41*(3), 26–33.

[govt. periodical—author named]

6

Technology Marketing Group, Inc. (1998). *Services for clients.* Retrieved March 18, 2007, from
http://www.technology-marketing.com

7

Tolland, M. (2007, April). *Alternate careers in marketing.* Presentation at Electro '07 Conference
in Boston.   *[unpublished conference presentation]*

FIGURE QG.5 **A List of References (APA Style)**

CSE Numbered Citations

In the numbered version of CSE style, a citation in the text appears as a superscript number immediately following the source to which it refers:

Numbered citations in the text

> A recent study[1] indicates an elevated leukemia risk among children exposed to certain types of electromagnetic fields. Related studies[2-3] tend to confirm the EMF/cancer hypothesis.

When referring to two or more sources in a single note (as in "[2-3]" above) separate the numbers by a hyphen if they are in sequence and by commas but no space if they are not in sequence: ("[2,6,9]").

The full citation for each source then appears in the numerical listing of references at the end of the document.

REFERENCES

Full citations at document's end

1. Baron, KL, et al. The electromagnetic spectrum. New York: Pearson; 2007. 476 p.

2. Klingman, JM. Nematode infestation in boreal environments. J Entoymol 2006;54:475–8.

CSE Reference List Entries

CSE's References section lists each source in the order in which it was first cited. In preparing the list, which should be double-spaced, begin each entry on a new line. Type the number flush with the left margin, followed by a period and a space. Align subsequent lines directly under the first word of the first line.

Following are examples of complete citations as they would appear in the References section for your document.

INDEX TO SAMPLE CSE ENTRIES

1. Book, single author
2. Book, multiple authors
3. Book, anonymous author
4. Book, one or more editors
5. Anthology selection or book chapter
6. Article, magazine
7. Article, journal with new pagination each issue
8. Article, journal with continuous pagination
9. Article, newspaper
10. Article, online source

CSE Entries for Books. Any citation for a book should contain all available information in the following order: number assigned to the entry, author or editor, work title (and edition), facts about publication (place, publisher, date), and number of pages. Note the capitalization, abbreviation, spacing, and punctuation in the sample entries.

1. Book, Single Author—CSE

```
1. Kerzin-Fontana JB. Technology management: a handbook. 3rd ed.
       Delmar, NY: American Management Assn; 2007. 356p.
```

2. Book, Multiple Authors—CSE

```
2. Aronson L, Katz R, Moustafa C. Toxic waste disposal methods. New
       Haven: Yale Univ Pr; 2007. 316p.
```

3. Book, Anonymous Author—CSE

```
3. [Anonymous]. Structured programming. Boston: Meredith Pr; 2007.
       267p.
```

4. Book, One or More Editors—CSE

```
4. Morris AJ, Pardin-Walker LB, editors. Handbook of new information
       technology. New York: Harper; 2007. 345p.
```

5. Anthology Selection or Book Chapter—CSE

```
5. Bowman JP. Electronic conferencing. In: Williams A, editor:
       Communication and technology: today and tomorrow. Denton, TX:
       Assn for Business Communication; 1994. p 123-42.
```

CSE Entries for Periodicals. Any citation for an article should contain all available information in the following order: number assigned to the entry, author, article title, periodical title, date (year, month), volume and issue number, and inclusive page numbers for the article. Note the capitalization, abbreviation, spacing, and punctuation in the sample entries.

6. Article, Magazine—CSE

```
6. DesMarteau K. Study links sewing machine use to Alzheimer's
       disease. Bobbin 1994 Oct:36-8.
```

7. Article, Journal with New Pagination Each Issue—CSE

```
7. Thackman-White JR. Computer-assisted research. Am Library J
      2006;51(1):3-9.
```

8. Article, Journal with Continuous Pagination—CSE

```
8. Barnstead MH. The writing crisis. J of Writing Theory
      2007;12:415-33.
```

9. Article, Newspaper—CSE

```
9. Baranski VH. Errors in technology assessment. Boston Times 2006
      Jan 15;Sect B: 33(col 2).
```

10. Article, Online Source—CSE

```
10. Alley RA. Ergonomic influences on worker satisfaction.
       Industrial Psychology [serial online] 2006 Jan;5(11).
       Available from: ftp.pub/journals/industrialpsychology/2003 via
       the INTERNET. Accessed 2007 Feb 10.
```

Citation for an article published online follows a similar format, with these differences: write "[article online]" between article title and publication date; after "Available from," give the URL followed by a period and your access information.

For more guidelines and examples, consult the *CSE Manual* or go to these sites: <www.wisc.edu/writing/Handbook/DocCSE.html> and <www.lib.ohio-state.edu/guides/csegd.html>.

A Quick Guide to Grammar, Usage, and Mechanics

Common Sentence Errors

Effective Punctuation

Lists

Transitions Within and Between Paragraphs

Mechanics

The rear endsheet of this book displays editing and revision symbols and corresponding page references. When your instructor marks a symbol on your paper, turn to the appropriate section for explanations and examples.

Common Sentence Errors

The following common sentence errors are easy to repair.

Sentence Fragment

A grammatically complete sentence consists of at least one subject and verb and expresses a complete thought. Your sentence might contain several complete ideas, but it must contain at least one!

> [incomplete idea]   [complete idea]   [complete idea]
> Although Mary was injured, she grabbed the line, and she saved the boat.

Omitting some essential element (the subject, the verb, or another complete idea), leaves only a piece of a sentence—a *fragment*.

> Grabbed the line. [*a fragment because it lacks a subject*]
>
> Although Mary was injured. [*a fragment because—although it contains a subject and a verb—it needs to be joined with a complete idea to make sense*]
>
> Sam, an electronics technician.

This last statement leaves the reader asking, "What about Sam the electronics technician?" The verb—the word that makes action happen—is missing. Adding a verb changes this fragment to a complete sentence.

SIMPLE VERB	Sam **is** an electronics technician.
VERB PLUS ADVERB	Sam, an electronics technician, **works hard.**
DEPENDENT CLAUSE, VERB, AND SUBJECTIVE COMPLEMENT	**Although he is well paid,** Sam, an electronics technician, **is not happy.**

Do not, however, mistake the following statement—which seems to contain a verb—for a complete sentence:

> Sam being an electronics technician.

Such "-ing" forms do not function as verbs unless accompanied by other verbs such as **is, was,** and **will be.**

| **Sam,** being an electronics technician, **was responsible for checking the circuitry.**

Likewise, the "*to* + verb" form (infinitive) is not a verb.

FRAGMENT   To become an electronics technician.

COMPLETE   To become an electronics technician, **Sam had to complete a two-year apprenticeship.**

Sometimes we inadvertently create fragments by adding subordinating conjunctions (**because, since, it, although, while, unless, until, when, where,** and others) to an already complete sentence.

| **Although** Sam is an electronics technician.

Such words subordinate the words that follow them; that is, they make the statement dependent on an additional idea, which must itself have a subject and a verb and be a complete sentence. (See also "Subordination"—pages 676–77.) We can complete the subordinate statement by adding an independent clause.

| **Although** Sam is an electronics technician, **he hopes to become an electrical engineer.**

NOTE

Because the incomplete idea (dependent clause) depends on the complete idea (independent clause) for its meaning, you need only a pause (symbolized by a comma), not a break (symbolized by a semicolon).

Acceptable Fragments

Not all fragments are unacceptable in all circumstances. For example, a fragmented sentence is acceptable in commands or exclamations because the subject ("you") is understood.

ACCEPTABLE   Slow down.
FRAGMENTS   Give me a hand.
                  Look out!

Also, questions and answers are sometimes expressed as incomplete sentences.

ACCEPTABLE   How? By investing wisely.
FRAGMENTS   When? At three o'clock.
                  Who? Bill.

In general, however, avoid fragments unless you have good reason to use one for special tone or emphasis.

Comma Splice

In a comma splice, two complete ideas (independent clauses) that should be *separated* by a period or a semicolon are incorrectly *joined* by a comma:

| Sarah did a great job, she was promoted.

You can choose among several possibilities for repair:

1. Substitute a period followed by a capital letter:

    | Sarah did a great job. She was promoted.

2. Substitute a semicolon to signal a relationship between the two items:

    | Sarah did a great job; she was promoted.

3. Use a semicolon with a connecting (conjunctive) adverb (a transitional word):

    | Sarah did a great job; **consequently,** she was promoted.

4. Use a subordinating word to make the less important clause incomplete and thereby dependent on the other:

    | **Because** Sarah did a great job, she was promoted.

5. Add a connecting word after the comma:

    | Sarah did a great job, **and** she was promoted.

Your choice will depend on the specific meaning or tone you want to convey.

Run-On Sentence

A run-on sentence crams too many grammatically complete ideas together.

RUN-ON	The hourglass is more accurate than the waterclock for the water in a waterclock must always be at the same temperature in order to flow with the same speed since water evaporates it must be replenished at regular intervals thus not being as effective in measuring time as the hourglass.
REVISED	The hourglass is more accurate than the waterclock because water in a waterclock must always be at the same temperature to flow at the same speed. Also, water evaporates and must be replenished at regular intervals. These temperature and volume problems make the waterclock less effective than the hourglass in measuring time.

Faulty Agreement—Subject and Verb

The subject should agree in number with the verb. But when subject and verb are separated by other words, we sometimes lose track of the subject-verb relationship.

FAULTY   The lion's **share** of diesels **are** sold in Europe.

Although **diesels** is closest to the verb, the subject is **share**.

REVISED   The lion's **share** of diesels **is** sold in Europe.

A second problem in subject-verb agreement occurs with indefinite pronouns such as **each, anybody,** and **somebody.** They usually take a singular verb.

FAULTY   **Each** of the crew members **were** injured during the storm.
REVISED   **Each** of the crew members **was** injured during the storm.

FAULTY   **Everyone** in the group **have** practiced long hours.
REVISED   **Everyone** in the group **has** practiced long hours.

Collective nouns such as **herd, family, union, group, army, team, committee,** and **board** can call for a singular or plural verb, depending on your meaning. To denote the group as a whole, use a singular verb.

CORRECT   The **committee meets** weekly to discuss new business.
            The editorial **board** of this magazine **has** high standards.

To denote individual members of the group, use a plural verb.

CORRECT   The **committee disagree** on whether to hire Jim.
            The editorial **board are** all published authors.

When two subjects are joined by **either . . . or** or **neither . . . nor,** the verb is singular if both subjects are singular and plural if both subjects are plural. If one subject is plural and one is singular, the verb agrees with the one closer to the verb.

CORRECT   Neither **John** nor **Bill works** regularly.
            Either **apples** or **oranges are** good vitamin sources.
            Either **Felix** or his **friends are** crazy.
            Neither the **boys** nor their **father likes** the home team.

For two subjects (singular, plural, or mixed) joined by **both . . . and,** the verb is plural.

CORRECT   **Both** Joe **and** Bill **are** resigning.

A single **and** between any two subjects calls for a plural verb.

Faulty Agreement—Pronoun and Referent

A pronoun must refer to a specific noun (its referent or antecedent), with which it must agree in gender and number.

> CORRECT   **Jane** lost **her** manual.
>
> The **students** claimed that **they** had been ignored.

When an indefinite pronoun such as **each, everyone, anybody, someone,** or **none** is the referent, the pronoun is singular.

> CORRECT   **Anyone** can get **his** degree from that college.
>
> **Anyone** can get **his** or **her** degree from that college.
>
> **Each** candidate described **her** plans in detail.

Faulty Coordination

Give equal emphasis to ideas of equal importance by joining them with coordinating conjunctions: **and, but, or, nor, for, so,** and **yet.**

> This course is difficult **but** worthwhile.
>
> My horse is old **and** gray.
>
> We must decide to support **or** reject the dean's proposal.

But do not confound your meaning by coordinating excessively.

> EXCESSIVE COORDINATION   The climax in jogging comes after a few miles **and** I can no longer feel stride after stride **and** it seems as if I am floating **and** jogging becomes almost a reflex **and** my arms **and** legs continue to move **and** my mind no longer has to control their actions.
>
> REVISED   The climax in jogging comes after a few miles when I can no longer feel stride after stride. By then I am jogging almost by reflex, nearly floating, my arms and legs still moving, my mind no longer having to control their actions.

Notice how the meaning becomes clear when the less important ideas (**nearly floating, arms and legs still moving, my mind no longer having**) are shown as dependent on, rather than equal to, the most important idea (**jogging almost by reflex**)—the idea that contains the lesser ones.

Avoid coordinating two or more ideas that cannot be sensibly connected:

> FAULTY   John had a drinking problem **and** he dropped out of school.

> REVISED   John's drinking problem depressed him so much that he couldn't study, so he quit school.

Instead of *try and,* use *try to.*

> FAULTY   I will try and help you.
>
> REVISED   I will try to help you.

sub   ## Faulty Subordination

Proper subordination shows that a less important idea is dependent on a more important idea. A dependent (or subordinate) clause in a sentence is signaled by a subordinating conjunction: **because, so, if, unless, after, until, since, while, as,** and **although.** Consider these complete ideas:

> | Joe studies hard. He has severe math anxiety.

Because these ideas are expressed as simple sentences, they appear coordinate (equal in importance). But if you wanted to convey an opinion about Joe's chances of succeeding in math, you would need a third sentence: **His disability probably will prevent him from succeeding,** or **His willpower will help him succeed.** To communicate the intended meaning concisely, combine the two ideas. Subordinate the one that deserves less emphasis and place the idea you want emphasized in the independent (main) clause.

> | Despite his severe math anxiety (*subordinate idea*), Joe studies hard (*independent idea*).

This first version suggests that Joe will succeed. Below, the subordination suggests the opposite meaning:

> | Despite his diligent studying (*subordinate idea*), Joe has severe math anxiety (*independent idea*).

Do not coordinate when you should subordinate:

> WEAK   Television viewers can relate to an athlete they idolize and they feel obliged to buy the product endorsed by their hero.

Of the two ideas in the sentence above, one is the cause, the other the effect. Emphasize this relationship through subordination:

> REVISED   Because television viewers can relate to an athlete they idolize, they feel obliged to buy the product endorsed by their hero.

When combining several ideas within a sentence, decide which is most important, and subordinate the other ideas to it—do not merely coordinate:

> FAULTY   This employee is often late for work, and he writes illogical reports, and he is a poor manager, and he should be fired.
>
> REVISED   Because this employee is often late for work, writes illogical reports, and has poor management skills, **he should be fired.** (*The last clause is independent.*)

Faulty Pronoun Case

A pronoun's case (nominative, objective, or possessive) is determined by its role in the sentence: as subject, object, or indicator of possession.

If the pronoun serves as the subject of a sentence (**I, we, you, she, he, it, they, who**), its case is *nominative*.

> **She** completed her graduate program in record time.
>
> **Who** broke the chair?

When a pronoun follows a version of the verb **to be** (a linking verb), it explains (complements) the subject, and so its case is *nominative*.

> The killer was **she.**
>
> The professor who perfected our new distillation process is **he.**

If the pronoun serves as the object of a verb or a preposition (**me, us, you, her, him, it, them, whom**), its case is *objective*.

> OBJECT OF   The employees gave **her** a parting gift.
> THE VERB
>
> OBJECT OF   To **whom** do you wish to complain?
> THE PREPOSITION

If a pronoun indicates possession (**my, mine, our, ours, your, yours, his, her, hers, its, their, whose**), its case is *possessive*.

> The brown briefcase is **mine.**
>
> Her offer was accepted.
>
> **Whose** opinion do you value most?

Here are some frequent errors in pronoun case:

> FAULTY   **Whom** is responsible to **who?** [*The subject should be nominative and the object should be objective.*]

REVISED   **Who** is responsible to **whom?**

FAULTY   The debate was between Marsha and **I.** [*As object of the preposition, the pronoun should be objective.*]

REVISED   The debate was between Marsha and **me.**

mod   Faulty Modification

Modifiers explain, define, or add detail to other words or ideas. Prepositional phrases, for example, usually define or limit adjacent words:

> the foundation **with the cracked wall**
> the journey **to the moon**

So do phrases with "-ing" verb forms:

> the student **painting the portrait**
> **Opening the door,** we entered quietly.

Phrases with "*to* + verb" form limit:

> **To succeed,** one must work hard.

Some clauses also limit:

> the person **who came to dinner**

Problems with ambiguity occur when a modifying phrase has no word to modify.

DANGLING MODIFIER   **Dialing the phone,** the cat ran out the open door.

dgl   The cat obviously did not dial the phone, but because the modifier **Dialing the phone** has no word to modify, the noun beginning the main clause (*cat*) seems to name the one who dialed the phone. Without any word to join itself to, the modifier *dangles.* Inserting a subject repairs this absurd message.

CORRECT   As **Joe** dialed the phone, the cat ran out the open door.

A dangling modifier can also obscure your meaning.

DANGLING MODIFIER   **After completing the student financial aid application form,** the Financial Aid Office will forward it to the appropriate state agency.

Who completes the form—the student or the financial aid office? Here are other dangling modifiers that obscure the message:

DANGLING MODIFIER	**While walking,** a cold chill ran through my body.
CORRECT	While **I** walked, a cold chill ran through my body.
DANGLING MODIFIER	Impurities have entered our bodies **by eating chemically processed foods.**
CORRECT	Impurities have entered our bodies by **our** eating chemically processed foods.

The order of adjectives and adverbs also affects meaning.

> I **often** remind myself of the need to balance my checkbook.
>
> I remind myself of the need to balance my checkbook **often.**

Position modifiers to reflect your meaning.

MISPLACED MODIFIER	Joe typed another memo on our computer **that was useless.** (*Was the computer or the memo useless?*)
CORRECT	Joe typed another useless memo on our computer.
	or
	Joe typed another memo on our useless computer.
MISPLACED MODIFIER	Mary volunteered **immediately** to deliver the radioactive shipment. (*Volunteering immediately, or delivering immediately?*)
CORRECT	Mary immediately volunteered to deliver . . .
	or
	Mary volunteered to deliver immediately . . .

par | Faulty Parallelism

To reflect relationships among items of equal importance, express them in identical grammatical form:

CORRECT	We here highly resolve . . . that government **of the people, by the people, for the people** shall not perish from the earth.

Otherwise, the message would be garbled, like this:

FAULTY	We here highly resolve . . . that government **of the people, which the people created and maintain, serving the people** shall not perish from the earth.

If you begin the series with a noun, use nouns throughout the series; likewise for adjectives, adverbs, and specific types of clauses and phrases.

FAULTY	The new apprentice is **enthusiastic, skilled,** and **you can depend on her.**
CORRECT	The new apprentice is **enthusiastic, skilled,** and **dependable.** (*all subjective complements*)
FAULTY	In his new job, he felt **lonely** and **without a friend.**
CORRECT	In his new job, he felt **lonely** and **friendless.** (*both adjectives*)
FAULTY	She plans **to study** all this month and **on scoring well** in her licensing examination.
CORRECT	She plans **to study** all this month and **to score well** in her licensing examination. (*both infinitive phrases*)
FAULTY	She **sleeps** well and **jogs** daily, **as well as eating** high-protein foods.
CORRECT	She **sleeps** well, **jogs** daily, and **eats** high-protein foods. (*all verbs*)

shift Sentence Shifts

Shifts in point of view damage coherence. If you begin a sentence or paragraph with one subject or person, do not shift to another.

SHIFT IN PERSON	When **one** finishes such a great book, **you** will have a sense of achievement.
REVISED	When **you** finish such a great book, **you** will have a sense of achievement.
SHIFT IN NUMBER	**One** should sift the flour before **they** make the pie.
REVISED	**One** should sift the flour before **one** makes the pie. (*Or better: Sift the flour before making the pie.*)

Do not begin a sentence in the active voice and then shift to the passive voice.

SHIFT IN VOICE	**He** delivered the plans for the apartment complex, and the building site **was also inspected by him.**
REVISED	He **delivered** the plans for the apartment complex and also **inspected** the building site.

Do not shift tenses without good reason.

SHIFT IN TENSE	She **delivered** the blueprints, **inspected** the foundation, **wrote** her report, and **takes** the afternoon off.
REVISED	She **delivered** the blueprints, **inspected** the foundation, **wrote** her report, and **took** the afternoon off.

Do not shift from one verb mood to another (as from imperative to indicative mood in a set of instructions).

SHIFT IN MOOD	**Unscrew** the valve and then steel wool **should be used** to clean the fittings.
REVISED	**Unscrew** the valve and then **use** steel wool to clean the fittings.

Effective Punctuation

Punctuation marks are like road signs and traffic signals. They govern reading speed and provide clues for navigation through a network of ideas.

End Punctuation

The three marks of end punctuation—period, question mark, and exclamation point—work like a red traffic light by signaling a complete stop.

 Period. A period ends a sentence and is the final mark in some abbreviations.

> | Ms.   Assn.   Inc.

Periods serve as decimal points in numbers.

> | $15.95
> | 21.4%

Question Mark. A question mark follows a direct question.

> | Where is the essay that was due today**?**

Do not use a question mark to end an indirect question.

FAULTY	Professor Grim asked if all students had completed the essay**?**
REVISED	Professor Grim asked if all students had completed the essay.

or

Professor Grim asked, "Did all students complete the essay**?**"

Exclamation Point. Use an exclamation point only when expression of strong feeling is appropriate.

APPROPRIATE	Oh, no**!**
	Pay up**!**

Semicolon

Like a blinking red traffic light at an intersection, a semicolon signals a brief but definite stop.

Semicolons Separating Independent Clauses. Semicolons separate independent clauses (logically complete ideas) whose contents are closely related and that are not connected by a coordinating conjunction.

> The project was finally completed; we had done a good week's work.

The semicolon can replace the conjunction-comma combination that joins two independent ideas.

> The project was finally completed, and we were elated.
> The project was finally completed; we were elated.

The second version emphasizes the sense of elation.

Semicolons Used with Adverbs as Conjunctions and Other Transitional Expressions. Semicolons must accompany conjunctive adverbs like **besides, otherwise, still, however, furthermore, moreover, consequently, therefore, on the other hand, in contrast,** or **in fact.**

> The job is filled; **however**, we will keep your résumé on file.
> Your background is impressive; **in fact**, it is the best among our applicants.

Semicolons Separating Items in a Series.   When items in a series contain internal commas, semicolons provide clear separation between items.

> I am applying for summer jobs in Santa Fe, New Mexico; Albany, New York; Montgomery, Alabama; and Moscow, Idaho.
> Members of the survey crew were Juan Jimenez, a geologist; Hector Lightfoot, a surveyor; and Mary Shelley, a graduate student.

Colon

Like a flare in the road, a colon signals you to stop and then proceed, paying attention to the situation ahead. Usually a colon follows an introductory statement that requires a follow-up explanation.

> We need this equipment immediately: a voltmeter, a portable generator, and three pairs of insulated gloves.
> She is an ideal colleague: honest, reliable, and competent.

Except for salutations in formal correspondence (e.g., Dear Ms. Jones:) colons follow independent (logically and grammatically complete) statements.

> FAULTY   My plans include: finishing college, traveling for two years, and settling down in Sante Fe.

No punctuation should follow "include."
Colons can introduce quotations.

> | The supervisor's message was clear enough: "You're fired."

A colon can replace a semicolon between two related, complete statements when the second one explains or amplifies the first.

> | Pam's reason for accepting the lowest-paying job offer was simple: She had always wanted to live in the Northwest.

Comma

The comma is the most frequently used—and abused—punctuation mark. It works like a blinking yellow light, for which you slow down briefly without stopping. Never use a comma to signal a *break* between independent ideas.

Comma as a Pause Between Complete Ideas.   In a compound sentence in which a coordinating conjunction (**and, or, nor, for, but**) connects equal (independent) statements, a comma usually precedes the conjunction.

> | This is an excellent course, but the work is difficult.

Comma as a Pause Between an Incomplete and a Complete Idea.   A comma is usually placed between a complete and an incomplete statement in a complex sentence when the incomplete statement comes first.

> | **Because he is a fat cat,** Jack diets often.
> | **When he eats too much,** Jack gains weight.

When the order is reversed (complete idea followed by incomplete), the comma is usually omitted.

> | Jack diets often **because he is a fat cat.**
> | Jack gains weight **when he eats too much.**

Reading a sentence aloud should tell you whether to pause (and use a comma).

Commas Separating Items (Words, Phrases, or Clauses) in a Series.   Use commas after items in a series, including the next-to-last item.

> **Helen, Joe, Marsha,** and **John** are joining us on the term project.
>
> The new employee complained **that the hours were long, that the pay was low, that the work was boring, and that the supervisor was paranoid.**

Use no commas if **or** or **and** appears between all items in a series.

> She is willing to study in San Francisco or Seattle or even in Anchorage.

Commas Setting Off Introductory Phrases.   Infinitive, prepositional, or verbal phrases introducing a sentence are usually set off by commas, as are interjections.

INFINITIVE PHRASE	**To be or not to be,** that is the question.
PREPOSITIONAL PHRASE	**In Rome,** do as the Romans do.
PARTICIPIAL PHRASE	**Being fat,** Jack was slow at catching mice.
	Moving quickly, the army surrounded the enemy.
INTERJECTION	**Oh,** is that the verdict?

Commas Setting off Nonrestrictive Elements.   A *restrictive* phrase or clause modifies or defines the subject in such a way that deleting the modifier would change the meaning of the sentence.

> All students **who have work experience** will receive preference.

Without **who have work experience,** which *restricts* the subject by limiting the category **students,** the meaning would be entirely different: **All** students will receive preference. Because this phrase is essential to the sentence's meaning, it is *not* set off by commas.

A *nonrestrictive* phrase or clause could be deleted without changing the sentence's meaning and *is* set off by commas.

> Our new manager, **who has only six weeks' experience,** is highly competent.

MODIFIER DELETED	Our new manager is highly competent.

This house, **riddled with carpenter ants,** is falling apart.

MODIFIER DELETED	This house is falling apart.

Commas Setting Off Parenthetical Elements.   Items that interrupt the flow of a sentence (such as **of course, as a result, as I recall,** and **however**) are called parenthetical and are enclosed by commas. They may denote emphasis, afterthought, clarification, or transition.

EMPHASIS	This deluxe model, **of course,** is more expensive.
AFTERTHOUGHT	Your essay, **by the way,** was excellent.
CLARIFICATION	The loss of my job was, **in a way,** a blessing.
TRANSITION	Our warranty, **however,** does not cover tire damage.

Direct address is parenthetical.

> Listen, **my children,** and you shall hear . . . .

A parenthetical expression at the beginning or the end of a sentence is set off by a comma.

> **Naturally,** we will expect a full guarantee.
> **My friends,** I think we have a problem.
> You've done a good job, **Jim.**
> **Yes,** you may use my name in your advertisement.

Commas Setting Off Quoted Material.   Quoted items within a sentence are set off by commas.

> The customer said, **"I'll take it,"** as soon as he laid eyes on our new model.

Commas Setting Off Appositives.   An appositive, a word or words explaining a noun and placed immediately after it, is set off by commas when the appositive is nonrestrictive. (See page 684.)

> Martha Jones, **our new president,** is overhauling all personnel policies.
> Alpha waves, **the most prominent of the brain waves,** are typically recorded in a waking subject whose eyes are closed.
> Please make all checks payable to Sam Sawbuck, **school treasurer.**

Commas Used in Common Practice.   Commas set off the day of the month from the year, in a date.

> May 10, 1989

Commas set off numbers in three-digit intervals.

> 11,215
> 6,463,657

They also set off street, city, and state in an address.

> Mail the bill to J. B. Smith, 18 Sea Street, Albany, Iowa 51642.

When the address is written vertically, however, the commas that would otherwise occur at the end of each address line are omitted.

> J. B. Smith
> 18 Sea Street
> Albany, Iowa 51642

Commas set off an address or date in a sentence.

> Room 3C, Margate Complex, is my summer address.
> June 15, 2009, is my graduation date.

Commas set off degrees and titles from proper nouns.

> Roger P. Cayer, M.D.
> Gordon Browne, Jr.

Commas Used Incorrectly.   Avoid needless or inappropriate commas. Read a sentence aloud to identify inappropriate pauses.

FAULTY	The instructor told me, that I was late. [*separates the indirect from the direct object*]
	The most universal symptom of the suicide impulse, is depression. [*separates the subject from its verb*]
	This has been a long, difficult, semester. [*second comma separates the final adjective from its noun*]
	John, Bill, and Sally, are joining us on the trip home. [*third comma separates the final subject from its verb*]
	An employee, who expects rapid promotion, must quickly prove his or her worth. [*separates a modifier that should be restrictive*]
	I spoke by phone with John, and Marsha. [*separates two nouns, linked by a coordinating conjunction*]
	The room was, 18 feet long. [*separates the linking verb from the subjective complement*]
	We painted the room, red. [*separates the object from its complement*]

Apostrophe

Apostrophes indicate the possessive, a contraction, and the plural of numbers, letters, and figures.

Apostrophe Indicating the Possessive.   At the end of a singular word, or of a plural word that does not end in *s,* add an apostrophe plus *s* to indicate the possessive. Single-syllable nouns that end in *s* take the apostrophe before an added *s.*

> The **people's** candidate won.
> The chainsaw was **Emma's.**
> The **women's** locker room burned.
> I borrowed **Chris's** book.

Do not add *s* to words that already end in *s* and have more than one syllable; add an apostrophe only.

> Aristophanes' death

Do not use an apostrophe to indicate the possessive form of either singular or plural pronouns.

> The book was **hers.**
> **Ours** is the best school in the county.
> The fault was **theirs.**

At the end of a plural word that ends in *s,* add an apostrophe only.

> the **cows'** water supply
> the **Jacksons'** wine cellar

At the end of a compound noun, add an apostrophe plus *s.*

> my **father-in-law's** false teeth

At the end of the last word in nouns of joint possession, add an apostrophe plus *s* if both own one item.

> **Joe and Sam's** lakefront cottage

Add an apostrophe plus *s* to both nouns if each owns specific items.

> **Joe's** and **Sam's** passports

Apostrophe Indicating a Contraction.   An apostrophe shows that you have omitted one or more letters in a phrase that is usually a combination of a pronoun and a verb.

I'm	they're
he's	you'd
you're	who's

Don't confuse **they're** with **their** or **there.**

FAULTY	there books
	their now leaving
	living their
CORRECT	their books
	they're now leaving
	living there

Remember the distinction this way:

| Their friend knows they're there.

It's means "it is." **Its** is the possessive.

| It's watching its reflection in the pond.

Who's means "who is." **Whose** indicates the possessive.

| Who's interrupting whose work?

Other contractions are formed from the verb and the negative.

isn't	can't
don't	haven't
won't	wasn't

Apostrophe Indicating the Plural of Numbers, Letters, and Figures

| The **6's** on this new printer look like smudged **G's, 9's** are illegible, and the **%'s** are unclear.

Quotation Marks

Quotation marks set off the exact words borrowed from another speaker or writer. The period or comma at the end is placed within the quotation marks.

PERIODS AND COMMAS BELONG WITHIN QUOTATION MARKS	"Hurry up," Jack whispered. Jack told Felicia, "I'm depressed."

The colon or semicolon is always placed outside quotation marks.

COLONS AND SEMICOLONS BELONG OUTSIDE QUOTATION MARKS	Our student handbook clearly defines "core requirements"; however, it does not list all the courses that fulfill the requirements.

When a question mark or exclamation point is part of a quotation, it belongs within the quotation marks, replacing the comma or period.

SOME PUNCTUATION BELONGS WITHIN QUOTATION MARKS	"Help!" he screamed. Marsha asked John, "Can't we agree about anything?"

But if the question mark or exclamation point pertains to the attitude of the person quoting instead of the person being quoted, it is placed outside the quotation mark.

SOME PUNCTUATION BELONGS OUTSIDE QUOTATION MARKS	Why did Boris wink and whisper, "It's a big secret"?

Use quotation marks around titles of articles, paintings, book chapters, and poems.

CERTAIN TITLES BELONG WITHIN QUOTATION MARKS	The enclosed article, " *The Job Market for College Graduates,"* should provide some helpful insights.

But titles of books, journals, or newspapers should be underlined or italicized. Finally, use quotation marks (with restraint) to indicate irony.

QUOTATION MARKS TO INDICATE IRONY	She is some "friend"!

Ellipses

Three dots . . . indicate you have omitted material from a quotation. If the omitted words come at the end of the original sentence, a fourth dot indicates the period. (Also see page 636.)

> "Three dots . . . indicate . . . omitted . . . material. . . . A fourth dot indicates the period."

Italics

`ital`

Use italics or underlining for titles of books, periodicals, films, newspapers, and plays; for the names of ships; for foreign words or technical terms. Use italics *sparingly* for special emphasis.

> The *Oxford English Dictionary* is a handy reference tool.
>
> My only advice is *caveat emptor.*
>
> *Bacillus anthracis* is a highly virulent organism.
>
> *Do not* inhale these fumes under any circumstances!
>
> A *work-study student* is defined as one who works at least twenty hours weekly.

Parentheses

`()`

Use commas to set off parenthetical elements, dashes to give some emphasis to the material that is set off, and parentheses to enclose material that defines or explains the statement that precedes it.

> An anaerobic **(airless)** environment must be maintained for the cultivation of this organism.
>
> The cost of running our college has increased by 15 percent in one year **(see Appendix A for full cost breakdown).**
>
> This calculator **(made by Ilco Corporation)** is perfect for math students.

Material between parentheses, like all other parenthetical material discussed earlier, can be deleted without harming the logical and grammatical structure of the sentence.

Brackets

`[]`

Brackets in a quotation set off material that was not in the original quotation but is needed for clarification, such as an antecedent (or referent) for a pronoun.

> "She **[Amy]** was the outstanding candidate for the scholarship."

Brackets can enclose information taken from some other location within the context of the quotation.

> "It was in early spring **[April 2, to be exact]** that the tornado hit."

Use **sic** ("thus," or "so") when quoting an error from the original source.

| The assistant's comment was clear: "He don't **[sic]** want any."

Dashes

Dashes can be effective—if they are not overused. Parentheses deemphasize the enclosed material; dashes emphasize it.

| Have a good vacation—but watch out for sandfleas.
| Mary—a true friend—spent hours helping me rehearse.

Avoiding Ambiguous Punctuation

A missing hyphen, comma, or other punctuation mark can obscure meaning.

MISSING HYPHEN   Replace the trailer's inner wheel bearings. *(The inner-wheel bearings or the inner wheel-bearings?)*

MISSING COMMA   Police surrounded the crowd[,] attacking the strikers. *(Without the comma, the crowd appears to be attacking the strikers.)*

A missing colon after *kill* yields the headline "Moose Kill 200." A missing apostrophe after *Myers* creates this gem: "Myers Remains Buried in Portland."

Lists

Listed items can be presented in one of two ways: running in as part of the sentence (embedded lists) or displayed with each item on a new line (vertical lists).

Embedded Lists

An embedded list integrates a series of items into a sentence, as follows:

| In order to complete express check-in for your outpatient surgery, you must (1) go to the registration office, (2) sign in and obtain your registration number, (3) receive and wear your red armband, and (4) give your check-in slip to the volunteer, who will escort you to your room.

To number an embedded list, use parentheses around the numerals and either commas or semicolons between the items.

Vertical Lists

Embedded lists are appropriate for listing only a few short items. Vertical lists are preferable for multiple items. If the items belong in a particular sequence, use numerals or letters; if the sequence of items is unimportant, use bullets. The following examples illustrate how to introduce and punctuate vertical lists.

You can introduce a vertical list with a sentence that closes with "the following" or "as follows" and ends with a colon.

> All applicants for the design internship must submit **the following**:
> • Personal statement
> • Résumé
> • Three letters of reference
> • Portfolio

You can also introduce a vertical list with a sentence that closes with a noun and ends with a colon.

> All applicants for the design internship must submit **four items**:
> 1. Personal statement
> 2. Résumé
> 3. Three letters of reference
> 4. Portfolio

Finally, you can introduce a vertical list with a sentence that is not grammatically complete without the list items.

> To register as a new student:
> 1. Take the placement test at the Campus Test Center.
> 2. Attend a new student orientation.
> 3. Register for classes by Web or telephone.
> 4. Pay tuition and fees by the due date.

Do not use a colon to introduce a sentence that ends with a verb, a preposition, or an infinitive.

Incorrect because the introductory sentence ends with a verb:

> All applicants for the design internship **must submit**:
> • A personal statement
> • A résumé

> • Three letters of reference
> • A portfolio

Incorrect because the introductory sentence ends with a preposition:

> All applicants for the design internship need **to:**
> • Submit a personal statement and résumé
> • Forward three letters of reference
> • Provide a portfolio

Incorrect because the introductory sentence ends with an infinitive:

> All applicants for the design internship need **to submit:**
> • A personal statement
> • A résumé
> • Three letters of reference
> • A portfolio

If the sentence that introduces the list is followed by another sentence, use periods after both sentences. Do not use a colon to introduce the list.

> The next step is to configure the following fields. Consult Chapter 3 for more information on each field.
> • Serial port
> • Baud rate
> • Data bits
> • Stop bits

Note that some of the preceding examples use a period after each list item and some do not. As a general rule, use a period after each list item if any of the items contains a complete sentence. Do not use a period if none of the list items contains a complete sentence. Also note that items included in a list should be grammatically parallel. For more on parallelism, see page 679.

Transitions Within and Between Paragraphs

You can choose from three techniques to achieve smooth transitions within and between paragraphs.

1. **Use transitional expressions.** These are words such as *again, furthermore, in addition, meanwhile, however, also, although, for example, specifically, in particular,*

as a result, in other words, certainly, accordingly, because, and *therefore.* Such words serve as bridges between ideas. (See also page 682.)

2. **Repeat key words and phrases.** To help link ideas, repeat key words or phrases or rephrase them in different ways, as in this next paragraph (emphasis added):

> [1]**Whales are among the most intelligent of all mammals.** [2]Scientists rank whale **intelligence** with that of higher primates because of whales' **sophisticated** group behavior. [3]These **bright** creatures have been seen teaching and disciplining their young, helping their wounded comrades, engaging in elaborate courtship rituals, and playing in definite gamelike patterns. [4]They are able to coordinate such **complex cognitive activities** through their highly effective communication system of sonar clicks and pings. [5]Such **remarkable social organization** apparently stems from the **humanlike** devotion that whales seem to display toward one another.

The key word **intelligent** in the above topic statement reappears as **intelligence** in sentence 2. Synonyms describing intelligent behavior (**sophisticated, bright, humanlike**) reinforce and advance the main idea throughout.

3. **Use forecasting statements to tell the reader where you are going next.** The following list provides examples of forecasting statements.

> The next step is to further examine the costs of this plan.
>
> Of course, we can also consider other options.
>
> This plan should be reconsidered for several reasons.

If you encounter a situation where you think you need a better transition but none of these methods seems appropriate, you may need to delete or move some information.

Mechanics

The mechanical aspects of writing a document include abbreviation, hyphenation, capitalization, use of numbers, and spelling. (Keep in mind that not all of these rules are hard and fast; some may depend on style guides used in your field or your company.)

Abbreviations

The following should *always* be abbreviated:

- Titles such as *Ms., Mr., Dr.,* and *Jr.* when they are used before or after a proper name.
- Time designations that are specific (*400 BCE, 5:15 A.M.*).

The following should *never* be abbreviated:

- Military, religious, or political titles (*Reverend, President*).
- Time designations that are used without actual times (*Sarah arrived early in the morning*—not "early in the A.M.").

Avoid abbreviations whose meanings might not be clear to all readers. Units of measurement can be abbreviated if they appear frequently in your report. However, a unit of measurement should be spelled out the first time it is used. Avoid abbreviations in visual aids unless saving space is absolutely necessary.

Most dictionaries provide an alphabetical list of abbreviations. For abbreviations in documenting of research sources, see A Quick Guide to Documentation.

Hyphenation

Hyphens divide words at line breaks and join two or more words used as a single adjective if they precede the noun (but not if they follow it):

> Com-puter (*at a line break*)
> The rough-hewn wood
> An all-too-human error
> The wood was rough hewn.
> The error was all too human.

Other commonly hyphenated words include the following:

- Most words that begin with the prefix *self-* (*self-reliance, self-discipline*—see your dictionary for exceptions).
- Combinations that might be ambiguous (*re-creation* versus *recreation*).
- Words that begin with *ex* when *ex* means "past" (*ex-faculty member* but *excommunicate*).
- All fractions, along with ratios that are used as adjectives and that precede the noun, and compound numbers from twenty-one through ninety-nine (*a two-thirds majority, thirty-eight windows*).

Capitalization

Capitalize the first words of all sentences as well as titles of people, books, and chapters; languages; days of the week; months; holidays; names of organizations or groups; races and nationalities; historical events; important documents; and names of structures or vehicles. In titles of books, films, and the like, capitalize the first and last words and all others except articles, short prepositions, and coordinating conjunctions (*and, but, for, or, nor, yet*).

Do not capitalize the seasons (*spring, winter*) or general groups (*the younger generation, the leisure class*).

Capitalize adjectives derived from proper nouns (*Chaucerian English*).

Capitalize words such as *street, road, corporation, university,* and *college* only when they accompany a proper noun (*High Street, Rand Corporation, Bob Jones University*).

Capitalize *north, south, east,* and *west* when they denote specific regions (*the South, the Northwest*) but not when they are simply directions (*turn east at the light*).

Use of Numbers

Numbers expressed in one or two words can be written out or written as numerals. Use numerals to express larger numbers, decimals, fractions, precise technical figures, or any other exact measurements.

543	2,800,357
$3\frac{1}{4}$	15 pounds of pressure
50 kilowatts	4,000 rpm

Use numerals for dates, census figures, addresses, page numbers, exact units of measurement, percentages, times with A.M. or P.M. designations, and monetary and mileage figures.

page 14	1:15 P.M.
18.4 pounds	9 feet
12 gallons	$15

Do not begin a sentence with a numeral. If your figure needs more than two words, revise your word order.

Six hundred students applied for the 102 available jobs.
The 102 available jobs brought 780 applicants.

Do not use numerals to express approximate figures, time not designated as A.M. or P.M. or streets named by numbers less than 100.

about seven hundred fifty
four fifteen
108 East Forty-Second Street

In contracts and other documents in which precision is vital, a number can be stated both in numerals and in words:

> The tenant agrees to pay a rental fee of **three hundred seventy-five dollars ($375.00) monthly.**

sp Spelling

Always use the spell-check function in your word-processing software. However, don't rely on it exclusively. Take the time to use your dictionary for all writing assignments. And if you are a poor speller, ask someone else to proofread every document before you present it to your primary audience.

A Casebook: The Writing Process Illustrated

Critical Thinking in the Writing Process

Case 1—An Everyday Writing Situation: The Evolution of a Short Report

Case 2—Preparing a Personal Statement: For Internship, Medical School, or Law School Applications

Case 3—Documents for the Course Project: A Sequence Culminating in the Final Report

Every writing situation requires deliberate decisions for *working with the information* and for *planning, drafting,* and *revising* the document. Some of these decisions are illustrated in Figure CB.1. Each writer approaches the process through a sequence of decisions that works best for *that* person. No stage of decisions is complete until *all* stages are complete.

Critical Thinking in the Writing Process

The writing process is a *critical thinking* process: the writer makes a series of deliberate decisions in response to a situation. The actual "writing" (putting words on the page) is only a small part of the overall process—probably the least significant part.

In this section, we will follow one working writer through an everyday writing situation; we will see how he solves his unique information, persuasion, and ethics problems and how he collaborates to design a useful and efficient document.

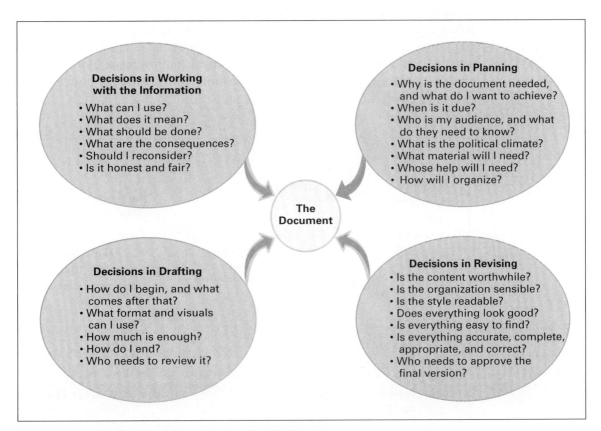

FIGURE CB.1 Typical Decisions During the Writing Process

Case 1—An Everyday Writing Situation: The Evolution of a Short Report

The company is Microbyte, developer of security software. The writer is Glenn Tarullo (BS, Management; Minor: Computer Science). Glenn has been on the job three months as Assistant Training Manager for Microbyte's Marketing and Customer Service Division.

For three years, Glenn's boss, Marvin Long, has periodically offered a training program for new managers. Long's program combines an introduction to the company with instruction in management skills (time management, motivation, communication). Long seems satisfied with his two-week program but has asked Glenn to evaluate it and write a report as part of a company move to upgrade training procedures.

Glenn knows his report will be read by Long's boss, George Hopkins (Assistant Vice President, Personnel), and Charlotte Black (Vice President, Marketing, the person who devised the upgrading plan). Copies will go to other division heads, to the division's chief executive, and to Long's personnel file.

Glenn spends two weeks (Monday, October 3 to Friday, October 14) sitting in and taking notes on Long's classes. On October 14, the trainees evaluate the program. After reading these evaluations and reviewing his notes, Glenn concludes that the program was successful but could stand improvement. How can he be candid without harming or offending anyone (instructors, his boss, or guest speakers)? Figure CB.2 depicts Glenn's problem.

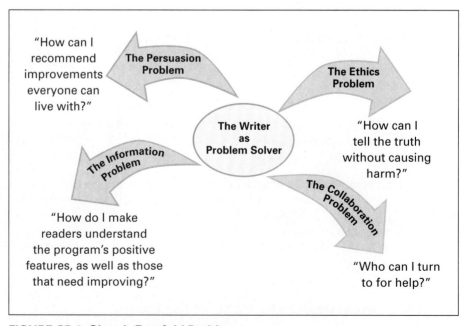

FIGURE CB.2 Glenn's Fourfold Problem

Glenn is scheduled to present his report in conference with Long, Black, and Hopkins on Wednesday, October 19. Right after the final class (1 P.M., Friday, the 14th), Glenn begins work on his report.

Working with the Information

Glenn spends half of Friday afternoon fretting over the details of his situation, the readers and other people involved, the political realities, constraints, and consequences. (He knows no love is lost between Long and Black, and he wants to steer clear of their ongoing conflict.) By 3 P.M., Glenn hasn't written a word. Desperate, he decides to write whatever comes to mind:

Glenn's first draft

> Although the October Management Training Session was deemed quite successful, several problems have emerged that require our immediate attention.
>
> • Too many of the instructors had poor presentation skills. A few never arrived on time. One didn't stick to the topic but rambled incessantly. Jones and Wells seemed poorly prepared. Instructors in general seemed to lack any clear objectives. Also, because too few visual aids were used, many presentations seemed colorless and apparently bored the trainees.
>
> • The trainees (all new people) were not at all cognizant of how the company was organized or functioned, so the majority of them often couldn't relate to what the speakers were talking about.
>
> • It is my impression that this was a weak session due to the fact that there were insufficient members (only five trainees). Such a small class makes the session a waste of time and money. For instance, Lester Beck, Senior Vice President of Personnel, came down to spend over one hour addressing only a handful of trainees. Another factor is that with fewer trainees in a class, less dialogue occurs, with people tending to just sit and get talked at.
>
> • Last but not least, executive speakers generally skirted the real issues, saying nothing about what it was really like to work here. They never really explained how to survive politically (e.g., never criticize your superior; never complain about the hard work or long hours; never tell anyone what you *really* think; never observe how few women are in executive or managerial positions, or how disorganized things seem to be). New employees shouldn't have to learn these things the hard way.
>
> In the final analysis, if these problems can be addressed immediately, it is my opinion we can look forward in the future to effectuating management training sessions of even higher quality than those we now have.

Glenn completes this draft at 5:10 P.M. Displeased with the results but not sure how to improve the piece, he asks an experienced colleague for advice and feedback. Blair Cordasco, a senior project manager, has collaborated with Glenn on several earlier projects. Cordasco agrees to study Glenn's draft over the weekend. Because of this document's sensitive nature, they decide to work on it face-to-face instead of transacting via email.

At 8:05 Monday morning, Cordasco reviews the document with Glenn. First, she points out obvious style problems: wordiness ("due to the fact that"), jargon ("effectuating"), triteness ("in the final analysis"), implied bias ("weak presentation," "skirted"), among others. Can you identify other style problems in Glenn's draft?

Cordasco points out other problems. The piece is disorganized, and even though Glenn is being honest, he isn't being particularly fair. The emphasis is too critical (making Glenn's boss look bad to his superiors), and the views are too subjective (no one is interested in hearing Glenn gripe about the company's political problems). Moreover, the report lacks persuasive force because it contains little useful advice for solving the problems he identifies. The tone is bossy and judgmental. Glenn is in no position to make this kind of *power connection* (see page 53). In this form, the report will only alienate people and harm Glenn's career. He needs to be more fair, diplomatic, and reasonable.

Planning the Document

Glenn realizes he needs to begin by focusing on his writing situation. His audience and use analysis goes like this[1]:

> I'd better decide *exactly* what my primary reader wants.
>
> Long requested the report, but only because Black developed the scheme for division-wide improvements. So I really have two primary readers: my boss and the big boss.
>
> My major question here: Am I including enough detail for all the bosses? The answer to this question will require answers to more specific questions:

ANTICIPATED READERS' QUESTIONS	What are we doing right, and how can we do it better?
	What are we doing wrong, and does it cost us money?
	Have we left anything out, and does it matter?
	How, specifically, can we improve the program, and
	how will those improvements help the company?

> Because all readers have participated in these sessions (as trainees, instructors, or guest speakers), they don't need background explanations.
>
> I should begin with the *positive* features of the last session. Then I can discuss the problems and make recommendations. Maybe I can eliminate the bossy and judgmental tone by *suggesting improvements* instead of *criticizing weaknesses*. Also, I could be more persuasive by describing the *benefits* of my suggestions.

Glenn realizes that if he wants successful future programs, he can't afford to alienate anyone. After all, he wants to be seen as a loyal member of the company,

---

[1]Throughout this section, Glenn's analysis will address *all* the areas illustrated in the audience and use profile sheet (page 35).

yet preserve his self-esteem and demonstrate he is capable of making objective recommendations.

Now, I have a clear enough sense of what to do.

STATEMENT OF PURPOSE	The purpose of my document is to provide my supervisor and interested executives with an evaluation of the workshop by describing its strengths, suggesting improvements, and explaining the benefits of these changes.

From this plan, I should be able to revise my first draft, but that first draft lacks important details. I should brainstorm to get *all* the details (including the *positive* ones) I want to include.

Glenn's Brainstorming List.   Glenn's first draft touched on several topics. Incorporating them into his brainstorming, he comes up with the following list.

1. better-prepared instructors and more visuals
2. on-the-job orientation *before* the training session
3. more members in training sessions
4. executive speakers should spell out qualities needed for success
5. beneficial emphasis on interpersonal communication
6. need follow-up evaluation (in six months?)
7. four types of training evaluations:
   a. trainees' reactions
   b. testing of classroom learning
   c. transference of skills to the job
   d. effect of training on the organization (high sales, more promotions, better-written reports)
8. videotaping and critiquing of trainee speeches worked well
9. acknowledge the positive features of the session
10. ongoing improvement ensures quality training
11. division of class topics into two areas was a good idea
12. additional trainees would increase classroom dialogue
13. the more trainees in a session, the less time and money wasted
14. instructors shouldn't drift from the topic
15. on-the-job training to give a broad view of the division
16. clear course objectives to increase audience interest and to measure the program's success
17. Marvin Long has done a great job with these sessions over the years

By 9:05 A.M., the office is hectic. Glenn puts his list aside to spend the day on work that has been piling up. Not until 4 P.M. does he return to his report.

Now what? I should delete whatever my audience already knows or doesn't need, or whatever seems unfair or insincere: 7 can go (this audience needs no lecture in training theory); 14 is too negative and critical—besides, the same idea is stated more positively in 4; 17 is obvious brown-nosing, and I'm in no position to make such grand judgments.

Maybe I can unscramble this list by arranging items within categories (strengths, suggested changes, and benefits) from my statement of purpose.

Glenn's Brainstorming List Rearranged.   Notice here how Glenn discovers additional *content* (see italic type) while he's deciding about *organization*.

Strengths of the Workshop

• division of class topics into two areas was useful

• emphasis on interpersonal communication

• videotaping of trainees' oral reports, followed by critiques

Well, that's one category done. Maybe I should combine *suggested changes* with *benefits,* since I'll want to cover them together in the report.

Suggested Changes/Benefits

• more members per session would increase dialogue and use resources more efficiently

• varied on-the-job experiences before the training sessions would give each member a broad view of the marketing division

• executive speakers should spell out qualities required for success and *future sessions should cover professional behavior, to provide trainees with a clear guide*

• follow-up evaluation in six months *by both supervisors and trainees would reveal the effectiveness of this training and suggest future improvements*

• clear course objectives and more visual aids would increase *instructor efficiency* and audience interest

Now that he has a fairly sensible arrangement, Glenn can get this list into report form, even though he will probably think of more material to add as he works. Since this is *internal* correspondence, he uses a memo format.

Drafting the Document

Glenn produces a usable draft—one containing just about everything he wants to cover. (Sentences are numbered for later reference.)

A later draft

[1]In my opinion, the Management Training Session for the month of October was somewhat successful. [2]This success was evidenced when most participants rated their training as "very good." [3]But improvements are still needed.

[4]First and foremost, a number of innovative aspects in this October session proved especially useful. [5]Class topics were divided into two distinct areas. [6]These topics created a general-to-specific focus. [7]An emphasis on interpersonal communication skills was the most dramatic innovation. [8]This helped class members develop a better attitude toward things in general. [9]Videotaping of trainees' oral reports, followed by critiques, helped clarify strengths and weaknesses.

[10]A detailed summary of the trainees' evaluations is attached. [11]Based on these and on my past observations, I have several suggestions.

- [12]All management training sessions should have a minimum of ten to fifteen members. [13]This would better utilize the larger number of managers involved and the time expended in the implementation of the training. [14]The quality of class interaction with the speakers would also be improved with a larger group.

- [15]There should be several brief on-the-job training experiences in different sales and service areas. [16]These should be developed prior to the training session. [17]This would provide each member with a broad view of the duties and responsibilities in all areas of the marketing division.

- [18]Executive speakers should take a few minutes to spell out the personal and professional qualities essential for success with our company. [19]This would provide trainees with a concrete guide to both general company and individual supervisors' expectations. [20]Additionally, by the next training session we should develop a presentation dealing with appropriate attitudes, manners, and behavior in the business environment.

- [21]Do a six-month follow-up. [22]Get feedback from supervisors as well as trainees. [23]Ask for any new recommendations. [24]This would provide a clear assessment of the long-range impact of this training on an individual's job performance.

- [25]We need to demand clearer course objectives. [26]Instructors should be required to use more visual aids and improve their course structure based on these objectives. [27]This would increase instructor quality and audience interest.

- [28]These changes are bound to help. [29]Please contact me if you have further questions.

Although now developed and organized, this version still is some way from the finished document. Glenn has to make further decisions about his style, content, arrangement, audience, and purpose.

Blair Cordasco offers to review the piece once again and to work with Glenn on a thorough edit.

Revising the Document

At 8:15 Tuesday morning, Cordasco and Glenn begin a sentence-by-sentence revision for worthwhile content, sensible organization, and readable style. Their discussion goes something like this:

Sentence 1 begins with a needless qualifier, has a redundant phrase, and sounds insulting ("somewhat successful"). Sentence 2 should be in the passive voice, to emphasize the training—not the participants. Also, 1 and 2 are choppy and repetitious, and should be combined.

ORIGINAL   In my opinion, the Management Training Session for the month of October was somewhat successful. This success was evidenced when most participants rated their training as "very good." (28 words)

REVISED   The October Management Training Session was successful, with training rated "very good" by most participants. (15 words)[2]

Sentence 3 is too blunt. An orienting sentence should forecast content diplomatically. This statement can be candid without being so negative.

ORIGINAL   But improvements are still needed.

REVISED   A few changes—beyond the recent innovations—should result in even greater training efficiency.[3]

In sentence 4, "First and foremost" is trite, "aspects" is a clutter word, and word order needs changing to improve the emphasis (on innovations) and to lead into the examples.

ORIGINAL   First and foremost, a number of innovative aspects in this October session proved especially useful.

REVISED   Several program innovations were especially useful in this session.

In collaboration with his colleague, Glenn continues this editing and revising process on his report. Wednesday morning, after much revising and proofreading, Glenn prints out the final draft, shown in Figure CB.3.

Glenn's final report is both informative and persuasive. But this document did not appear magically. Glenn made deliberate decisions about purpose, audience, content, organization, and style. He sought advice and feedback on every aspect of the document. Most importantly, he *spent time revising.*[4]

NOTE   *Writers work in different ways. Some begin by brainstorming. Some begin with an outline. Others simply write and rewrite. Some sketch a quick draft before thinking through their writing situation. Introductions and titles are often written last. Whether you write alone or collaborate in preparing a document, whether you are receiving feedback or providing it, no one step in the process is complete until the whole is complete. Notice, for instance, how Glenn sharpens his content and style while he organizes. Every document you write will require all these decisions, but you rarely will make them in the same sequence.*

---

[2] Notice throughout how careful revision sharpens the writer's meaning while cutting needless words.
[3] This revision has more words, but also much more concrete and specific detail (Figure CB.3). Completeness of information always takes priority over word count.
[4] A special thanks to Glenn Tarullo for his perseverance. I made his task doubly difficult by having him explain each of his decisions during this writing process.

⠿ MICRO**BYTE**

October 19, 20XX

To: Marvin Long
From: Glenn Tarullo *GT*
Subject: October Management Training Program: Evaluation
          and Recommendations

Begins on a positive note, and cites evidence

States his claim

The October Management Training Session was successful, with training rated as "very good" by most participants. A few changes, beyond the recent innovations, should result in even greater training efficiency.

Workshop Strengths

Especially useful in this session were several program innovations:

Gives clear examples of "innovations"

—Dividing class topics into two areas created a general-to-specific focus: The first week's coverage of company structure and functions created a context for the second week's coverage of management skills.

—Videotaping and critiquing trainees' oral reports clarified their speaking strengths and weaknesses.

—Emphasizing interpersonal communication skills (listening, showing empathy, and reading nonverbal feedback) created a sense of ease about the group, the training, and the company.

Innovations like these ensure high-quality training. And future sessions could provide other innovative ideas.

Suggested Changes/Benefits

Cites the basis for his recommendations

Based on the trainees' evaluation of the October session (summary attached) and my observations, I recommend these additional changes:

—We should develop several brief (one-day) on-the-job rotations in different sales and service areas before the training session. These rotations would give each member a real-life view of duties and responsibilities throughout the company.

FIGURE CB.3 Glenn's Final Draft

—All training sessions should have at least ten to fifteen members. Larger classes would make more efficient use of resources and improve class–speaker interaction.

Supports each recommendation with convincing reasons

—We should ask instructors to follow a standard format (based on definite course objectives) for their presentations, and to use visuals liberally. These enhancements would ensure the greatest possible instructor efficiency and audience interest.

—Executive speakers should spell out personal and professional traits that are essential to success in our company. Such advice would give trainees a concrete guide to both general company and individual supervisor expectations. Also, by the next training session, we should assemble a presentation dealing with appropriate attitudes, manners, and behavior in the business environment.

—We should do a six-month follow-up of trainees (with feedback from supervisors as well as ex-trainees) to gain long-term insights, to measure the influence of this training on job performance, and to help design advanced training.

Closes by appealing to shared goals (efficiency and profit)

Inexpensive and easy to implement, these changes should produce more efficient training.

Copies: B. Hull, C. Black, G. Hopkins, J. Capilona, P. Maxwell, R. Sanders, L. Hunter

FIGURE CB.3 *(Continued)*

NOTE *No matter what the sequence, revision is a fact of life. It is the one constant in the writing process. When you've finished a draft, you have in a sense only begun. Sometimes you will have more time to compose than Glenn did, sometimes much less. Whenever your deadline allows, leave time to revise.*

Case 2—Preparing a Personal Statement: For Internship, Medical School, or Law School Applications

Applications for jobs, grants, scholarships, and graduate school typically require a personal statement that addresses these basic questions:

What readers of a personal statement want to know

- *Why should we select you?*
- *Why do you want this?*
- *What will you bring to this experience?*
- *How, exactly, do you plan to use this opportunity?*
- *What do you hope to gain?*

In a short essay, the candidate presents her/his best argument for being selected. Statements that stand out are the ones that make the final cut.

In the situation that follows, Mike Duval, a junior in marine biology, is applying for a prestigious and highly competitive summer research internship at a leading oceanographic institute. Application requirements include a personal statement. Before writing a word, Mike wisely decides to analyze and anticipate what, exactly, his audience is looking for.

Audience Expectations in a Personal Statement

About Content

- a brief but specific proposal for a research project
- some new and *significant* ideas about the research topic
- a summary of the writer's qualifications to undertake this project
- neither too much nor too little information
- answers to questions about *what, why, how,* and *when*

About Organization

- a distinct line of reasoning and a clear, sensible plan, consistent with the best scientific methods
- an introduction that offers brief background and justifies the need for the project

- a body section that outlines the proposed scope, method, and sources
- a conclusion that describes the research benefits and elicits reader support

About Style

- a decisive tone with no hint of ambivalence
- at least a suggestion of enthusiasm
- an efficient style, in which nothing is wasted

Mike's technical writing instructor has invited him to bring in his best draft (shown in Figure CB.4) for review by the entire class.

Discussion of Mike's First Draft (Figure CB.4)

For the workshop on Mike's statement, the instructor asked the class to assume they were members of the committee screening fellowship applicants. Here is the summary of the class's critique:

1. An opening paragraph—especially in a competitive application—should grab the reader's attention and make the candidate stand out. Here, Mike opens with a self-evident observation followed by an unconvincing apology and then a rambling final sentence. Because the content is vague, readers have nothing concrete to *visualize*. Because the style is wordy, readers work harder than they should. Mike needs to paint a more vivid picture of who he is, why he is applying, and what he plans to do.
2. The second paragraph is where Mike should begin focusing on his proposed research topic, offering something new and significant. Instead, the content seems vague and abstract, lacking any real point or personality. Also the passive voice, excessive prepositions, and overall wordiness almost make the writer disappear. Mike needs to spell out his topic and show why it's important.
3. By this stage, Mike should be explaining what he can contribute to this fellowship experience instead of focusing only on the personal benefits he expects. In the audience's view, Mike's stated goal "to become a more marketable person" is hardly a persuasive reason. Mike needs to make a better case not only for what he hopes to gain but also for what he can offer—and he needs to project a likable *persona* (page 66) throughout.
4. The closing paragraph should leave readers with a clear and positive sense of this writer as a unique candidate who deserves to "make the cut." Instead, the paragraph continues the abstract theme about what the writer hopes to gain, then tells readers what they already know, and closes with a vague "this" statement that drowns the whole point of the essay. Mike needs to sum up his argument clearly and emphatically.

(See page 713 for discussion of Mike's Final Draft, Figure CB.5.)

Personal Statement

Michael C. Duval

1   I want to study marine science during the summer at Woods Hole Oceanographic Institute as I hope to add to my background and understanding of the marine environment. Presently, I have been unable to conduct any full-time research projects due to the time factor involved and the responsibilities of a full semester's course load. However, your program is an opportunity to study any aspect of the marine environment largely independent of that time factor, except for summer limitations.

2   Textbooks cannot develop techniques; they can only present concepts. Therefore, one has to develop these techniques himself by actually doing the thinking, the designing, the manipulating, and the interpreting. Once such skills are perfected, they can be carried on for further application in graduate studies or in job situations. And this is an important aspect of the summer program: mastering skills necessary in any kind of research, and developing that "research frame-of-mind." As I plan to further my education by attending graduate school, I think this program will prove invaluable to me.

3   However, I would like to work a year or so before entering a graduate program so that I can observe senior researchers and understand the requirements of various positions. In this way, and by completing graduate school, I can become a more marketable person.

4   My research at Woods Hole could lead to continued work as the topic of my graduate thesis. Presently, I am interested in marine microbes and their interactions with invertebrates such as mollusks or crustaceans. Since little is known about these interactions, much attention must be given to this subject. Recent studies have found that some human pathogens are part of the indigenous bacterial fauna of the oyster and other similar shellfish, and can be introduced into the gastrointestinal system via direct consumption. This increases the need to understand and thus control such vectors of human disease.

FIGURE CB.4 **Mike's Best Early Draft**

Personal Statement

Michael C. Duval

Tells who he is, why he's applying, and what he plans to do

Please consider my application for a summer research internship. I am a marine biology major at Southeastern Massachusetts University, interested in marine microbes and their interactions with mollusks and crustaceans. My plan is to attend graduate school, but I wish to work a year or so in the biological sciences before enrolling. In this way, I can recognize weak areas in my understanding of biology, and then take the appropriate graduate courses. After graduate studies, I plan to do research and advocate for the environment.

Describes his topic and explains its importance

I haven't yet had a chance to conduct full-time research; however, I am studying the indigenous bacterial fauna of the quahog (Mercenaria) as a semester project. I am particularly concerned with pathogenic interactions in shellfish, and their ultimate influence on public health through the transfer of dysentery and viral diseases such as herpes, hepatitis, and polio viruses.

Explains what he hopes to gain and what he can offer

Beyond the obvious prestige and resultant professional benefits of an internship at WHOI, I would anticipate more subtle and personal rewards. These include exposure to graduate-level work and practical applications of the research process—specifically the design, implementation, and interpretation of an experiment. My natural curiosity and determination to contribute to scientific understanding would, I think, be an asset to your program.

Mentions his work with a well-known professor

I enjoy working closely with my professors. For the past year, I have been working in a microbiological laboratory under Dr. Samuel Jennings. He, more than anyone, has helped me recognize my scientific abilities and deficiencies. I try to emulate his ways of thinking, incorporating that logic into my own problem solving. With his encouragement, I have learned to approach biology with the precision of a critical observer, the flexibility of an imaginative scientist, and the curiosity of a perennial student.

Sums up clearly and emphatically

I realize I have much to learn. Yet, I know enough to ask the kinds of questions that are socially and biologically significant. Are our methods of assessing microbial contamination in shellfish exacting enough? How can we approach a society that leans more toward reaction than prevention, and persuade its citizens that they must change their life-style in order to save their livelihood? A research internship at WHOI might prepare me to find answers to these questions.

FIGURE CB.5 **Mike's Final Draft**

Discussion of Mike's Final Draft (Figure CB.5)

After additional revisions and class workshops, Mike produced the final draft shown in Figure CB.5. This version is far more concise as well as more visual, offering concrete, persuasive support in a tone that is decisive. Mike's ideas are significant; his plan is clear and sensible; and his attitude is mature, realistic, and engaging. The persona suggests a writer who knows what he wants and how he can contribute.

Two Additional Examples for Analysis and Discussion

Examples of personal statements for Medical and Law School admissions appear in Figures CB.6 and CB.7, respectively. What are the specific qualities of content, organization, and style that make each of these personal statements effective? In preparing your analysis, refer to the "basic reader questions" and the sample audience analysis (page 709) and to relevant sections of Chapter 18, Employment Correspondence.

Tivon Sidorsky

Personal Statement

From seventy-five feet aloft all I see are endless crests of phosphorescent waves and the deck below. My task is to untangle the throat halyard, so we can drop the mainsail before the storm hits. With my legs wrapped around the end of the yardarm, I reach out for the snagged line, thrashing in the dark sky. Extending my torso parallel to the South Pacific, I am able to chase down the halyard. I call to my mates below and the sail is struck. As I descend the rigging I spot my silhouette painted on the foresail by the rising sun—my sense of self projected onto another amazing stage of life.

My passion for exploration and adventure has taken me through varied geographical, cultural, and academic landscapes, and has grounded my identity. I have pursued experiences that broaden my understanding of the world. My wish to pursue a medical career arises from the same passion. Through the process, I intend to translate a pluralistic perspective, liberal education, and medically related research into a humanitarian clinical practice.

For many years my father worked as a veterinarian on the Hopi Indian reservation in Arizona. Just like all other ten-day-old babies there, I was formally introduced to the sun, had my hair

FIGURE CB.6 **The Final Draft from a Medical School Applicant**

washed in yucca, and was given two Hopi names, one for each of the clans of my Hopi Godparents. Just two days earlier, I had been part of another ceremony known as a bris, a three-thousand-year-old ritual dating back to the time of Abraham. During this ceremony the baby receives its Hebrew name. Thus, I was simultaneously born into two separate cultures.

My parents eventually left Hopi to reestablish my father's veterinary practice in a small hill town. I soon was enrolled at an independent K–8 school where emphasis on social values paralleled the academic curriculum. Through the "responsive classroom," the Center School taught children compassion and caring, virtues that guide many of my decisions and objectives to this day.

I later attended a high school with a diverse international student body, and was elected to several leadership roles: as a Peer Educator, teaching and counseling students on issues of drugs and alcohol; as a member of Student Congress; and as a class officer. Needing to explore new territories by my third year, I developed an independent study program for myself. School administrators gave their go-ahead, enabling me to be the first junior to create and carry out an independent study abroad: as a deckhand/sailing instructor I sailed from the Dominican Republic to Grenada and back, teaching high school and college students how to sail and live on a tall ship. Later, after deferring entrance to college, I spent a postgraduate year sailing the South Pacific, skiing the Colorado Rockies, hiking through New Zealand and Hawaii, and visiting my Godmother on the Hopi reservation.

My liberal arts education has opened countless academic doors, and my travels have enriched and sculpted my worldview. However, my experiences in the health field have focused my desire to practice medicine. As a volunteer clinical research assistant, I assessed the effects of cognitive-behavioral interventions on quality of life, and physical and psychosocial health status, in African-American, Caribbean, and Hispanic women diagnosed with HIV/AIDS; I worked with elderly women who suffer from Alzheimer's or dementia and spent over four months researching treatments for depression, bipolar disorder, and schizophrenia. A summer internship in an adolescent psychiatric unit helped me appreciate the culture of a specialized hospital, some of the many roles physicians play, and the daily adventure that characterizes medical practice. I realized that a medical career is a perfect fit for my goals of working with individuals and communities to improve physical, mental, and social health.

From roping "moo cows" on the reservation, to assisting in the treatment of animals at my father's clinic, to negotiating squalls sailing through the Grenadines, to working with patients and families in the adolescent unit of New York-Presbyterian Hospital, I constantly seek experiences that will enrich and balance the way I approach each day. These experiences are the wind in my sails; they steer my aspirations towards a career where every day is a new, rewarding adventure, one in which I can make a difference. By gaining interdisciplinary perspective on the physical, mental, and social mechanisms that shape our lives, I hope to help my patients understand how to help themselves, as well as how to help others. A comprehensive medical education is the ideal next destination as I sail forward.

FIGURE CB.6   *(Continued)*

Daniel Lannon

Personal Statement

At eighteen I took a summer job with the Sierra Club primarily because I wanted to sleep late, and working hours began at noon. Two weeks later I was ready to change the world. Canvassing door-to-door for environmental groups taught me much about the complexities of confronting complete strangers. Each door that was answered with a smile and an open ear boosted my confidence as well as my resolve to make a difference. However, for every welcoming, open door, some twenty-five were routinely slammed in my face, reminding me that few people take grass-roots efforts seriously—at least not when an optimistic, young environmentalist knocks on their door at dinner time.

My first campaign was aimed at the "Filthy Five," a group of Massachusetts power plants that for decades had remained exempt from toxic emission regulations because of a grandfather clause approved by the legislature in the 1960's. My ignorance of the intricacies of such loopholes sparked my curiosity about our legal system and the mechanics of legislation. Also, I was frustrated by the notion that my peers and I had only the faintest voice: No matter how rational or articulate our cause, we had no direct influence on legislation. I realized that, beyond mere enthusiasm, effective advocacy requires intimate knowledge of the given system, that having a significant voice would mean working from inside the system rather than skirting the periphery. Law school became my logical choice.

In retrospect, my interest in persuasive discourse, in being heard clearly and taken seriously, actually dates back to my high-school days. I was one of six students elected to serve with six faculty members on the school's Judicial Committee. Students who faced expulsion or suspension would appear before this committee to present their final appeal. Our lengthy deliberations over a particular student's destiny often turned to heated debate. Through those long nights I learned how difficult it is—but also how vital—to analyze a situation accurately and thoroughly in light of the rules, to weigh opposing views, and to argue for a fair and reasonable course of action. At times, I had to concede my partiality and remove myself from a case involving a close friend.

In college, I remained involved in my immediate community. As Environmental Coordinator, I worked to strengthen the school's recycling program. As a member of House and Student Councils, I helped promote and expand alternative housing options. On Co-Sponsorship and Student Activity Committees I helped secure financing for the development and growth of special-interest groups on campus.

After college, I took a job in a family-practice law firm, for a first-hand look at legal practice. There, I've asked plenty of questions and have been exposed to many of the profession's ups-and-downs. I've seen the relief on an attorney's face after winning a trial. More often,

FIGURE CB.7 The Final Draft from a Law School Applicant

D. Lannon, Personal Statement, page 2

though, I've witnessed the harsher realities of law practice, such as dealing with a distraught family in the midst of a divorce or custody battle in which, no matter what the outcome, there are no real winners.

In short, my decision to attend law school has been carefully thought out, and is based on relevant background, work experience, and realistic guidance from insightful practitioners. While my initial intention may have been to "save the world," no longer am I that naive. Along the way, my experiences may have humbled my ambitions but they certainly have not laid them to rest. My father always told us kids to "leave the world a better place than you found it"; a law degree will help me manage to do that.

FIGURE CB.7   *(Continued)*

Case 3—Documents for the Course Project: A Sequence Culminating in the Final Report

Professionals in the workplace engage in one common and continual activity; they struggle with major decisions such as these:

- *Should we promote Jones to general manager, or should we bring in someone from outside the company?*
- *Why are we losing customers, and what can we do about it?*
- *How can we decrease work-related injuries?*
- *Should we encourage foreign investment in our corporation?*
- *Will this employee-monitoring program ultimately increase productivity or alienate our workers?*

Research projects routinely are undertaken to answer questions like those above—to provide decision makers the information they need.

A course research project, like any in the workplace, is designed to fill a specific information need: to answer a question, to solve a problem, to recommend a course of action. And so students of technical communication often spend much of the semester preparing a research project.

Virtually any major project in the workplace requires that all vital information at various stages (the plan, the action taken, the results) be recorded *in writing*.

The proposal/progress report/final report sequence keeps the audience informed at each stage of the project.

In the following course project, Mike Cabral, a communications major, works part-time as assistant to the production manager for *Megacrunch,* a computer magazine specializing in small-business applications.[5] (**Production** is the transforming of manuscripts into a published form.) Mike's writing instructor assigns the course project and encourages students to select topics from the workplace, when possible. Mike therefore asks *Megacrunch* production manager Marcia White to suggest a research topic that might be useful to the magazine.

White outlines a problem she thinks needs careful attention: Now six years old, *Megacrunch* has enjoyed steady growth in sales volume and advertising revenue—until recently. In the past year alone, *Megacrunch* has lost $250,000 in subscriptions and one advertising account worth $60,000. White knows that most of these losses are caused by increasing competition (three competing magazines have emerged in 18 months). In response to these pressures, White and the executive staff have been exploring ways of reinvigorating the magazine—through added coverage and "hot" features, more appealing layouts and page design, and creative marketing. But White is concerned about another problem that seems partially responsible for the fall in revenues: too many errors are appearing in recent issues.

When *Megacrunch* first hit the shelves, errors in grammar or accuracy seemed rare. But as the magazine grew in complexity, errors increased. Recent issues contain misspellings, inaccurate technical details, unintelligible sentences and paragraphs, and scrambled source code (in sample programs).

White asks Mike if he's interested in researching the error problem and looking into quality-control measures. She feels that his three years' experience with the magazine qualifies him for the task. Mike accepts the assignment.

White cautions Mike that this topic is politically sensitive, especially to the editorial staff and to the investors. She wants to be sure that Mike's investigation doesn't merely turn up a lot of dirty laundry. Above all, White wants to preserve investor confidence—not to mention the morale of the editorial staff, who do a good job in a tough environment, plagued by impossible deadlines and constant pressure. White knows that offending people—even unintentionally—can be disastrous.

She therefore insists that all project documents express a supportive rather than critical point of view: "What could we be doing better?" instead of "What are we doing wrong?" Before agreeing to release the information from company files (complaint letters, notes from irate phone calls, and so on), White asks Mike to submit a proposal, in which the intent of this project is made absolutely clear.

---

[5] In the interest of privacy, the names of all people, publications, companies, and products in Mike's documents have been changed.

The Project Documents

Three types of documents lend shape and sequence to the research project: the **proposal,** which spells out the plan; the **progress report,** which keeps track of the investigation; and the **final report,** which analyzes the findings. This presentation shows how these documents function together in Mike Cabral's reporting process.

The Proposal Stage

Proposals offer plans for meeting needs. A proposal's primary audience consists of those who will decide whether to approve, fund, or otherwise support the project. Reviewers of a research proposal usually begin with questions like these:

- *What, exactly, do you intend to find out?*
- *Why is the question worth answering, or the problem worth solving?*
- *What benefits can we expect from this project?*

Once reviewers agree that the project is worthwhile, they will want to know all about the plan:

- *How, exactly, do you plan to do it?*
- *Is the plan realistic?*
- *Is the plan acceptable?*

Besides these questions, reviewers may have others: *How much will it cost? How long will it take? What makes you qualified to do it?* and so on. See Chapter 23 for more discussion and examples.

Mike Cabral knows his proposal will have only Marcia White (and possibly some executive board members) as the primary audience. The secondary audience is Mike's writing instructor, who also must approve the topic. And at some point, Mike's documents could find their way to his coworkers.

White already knows the background and she needs no persuading that the project is worthwhile, but she does expect a realistic plan before she will approve the project. (For his instructor, Mike attaches a short appendix [not shown here] outlining the background and his qualifications.) Also, Mike concentrates on his emphasis: He wants the proposal to be positive rather than critical, so as not to offend anyone. He therefore focuses on achieving *greater accuracy* rather than *fewer errors.* So that his instructor can approve the project, Mike submits the proposal by the semester's fourth week (Figure CB.6).

The Progress Report Stage

The progress report keeps the audience up to date on the project's activities, new developments, accomplishments or setbacks, and timetable. Depending on the size and length of the particular project, the number of progress reports will vary. (Mike's course project will require only one.) The audience approaches any progress report with two big questions:

Rangeley Publishing Company

TO.:   Marcia White, Production Manager   September 26, 20XX
FROM: Mike Cabral, Production Assistant   *MC*
SUBJECT: Proposal for Studying Ways to Improve Quality Control at *Megacrunch*

Tells what the problem is, and what it means to the company

Introduction
The growing number of grammatical, informational, and technical errors in each monthly issue of *Megacrunch* is raising complaints from authors, advertisers, and readers. Beyond compromising the magazine's reputation for accurate and dependable information, these errors—almost all of which seem avoidable—endanger our subscription and advertising revenues.

Further defines the problem and its effects

Summary of the Problem
Authors are complaining of errors in published versions of their articles. Software developers assert that errors in reviews and misinformation about products have damaged reputations and sales. For example, Osco Scientific, Inc. claims to have lost $150,000 in software sales because of an erroneous review in *Megacrunch*.

Although we continue to receive a good deal of "fan mail," we also receive letters speculating about whether *Megacrunch* has lost its edge as a leading resource for small-business users.

Describes the project and tells who will carry it out

Proposed Study
I propose to examine the errors that most frequently recur in our publication, to analyze their causes, and to search for ways of improving quality.

Describes the research strategy

Methods and Sources
In addition to close examination of recent *Megacrunch* issues and competing magazines, my primary data sources will include correspondence and other feedback now on file from authors, developers, and readers. I also plan telephone interviews with some of the above sources. In addition, interviews with our editorial staff should yield valuable insights and suggestions. As secondary material, books and articles on editing and writing can provide sources of theory and technique.

Encourages audience support by telling why the project will be beneficial

Conclusion
We should not allow avoidable errors to eclipse the hard work that has made *Megacrunch* the leading Cosmo resource for small-business users. I hope my research will help eliminate many such errors. With your approval, I will begin immediately.

FIGURE CB.6 Mike's Proposal

- *Is the project moving ahead according to plan and schedule?*
- *If not, why not?*

The audience may have various subordinate questions as well. See pages 331–35 for more discussion and examples.

Mike designs his progress report for his boss *and* his instructor, and turns it in by the semester's tenth week (Figure CB.7).

Rangeley Publishing Company

TO: Marcia White, Production Manager   November 6, 20XX
FROM: Mike Cabral, Production Assistant   *MC*
SUBJECT: Report of Progress on My Research Project: A Study of Ways for
          Improving Quality Control at *Megacrunch* Magazine

Work Completed

My topic was approved on September 28, and I immediately began both primary and secondary research. I have since reviewed file letters from contributors and readers, along with notes from phone conversations with various clients and from interviews with *Megacrunch*'s editing staff. I have also surveyed the types and frequency of errors in recent issues. Books and articles on writing and editing round out my study. The project has moved ahead without complications. With my research virtually completed, I have begun to interpret the findings.

Preliminary Interpretation of Findings

From my primary research and my own editing experience, I am developing a focused idea of where some of the most avoidable problems lie and how they might be solved. My secondary sources offer support for the solutions I expect to recommend, and they suggest further ideas for implementing the recommendations. With a realistic and efficient plan, I think we can go a long way toward improving our accuracy.

Work Remaining

So far, the project is on schedule. I plan to complete the interpretation of all findings by the week of November 29, and then to organize, draft, and revise my final report in time for the December 14 submission deadline.

Margin notes:

Tells what has been done so far, and what is now being done

Tells what has been found so far, and what it seems to mean

Assesses the project schedule; describes work remaining and gives a completion date

FIGURE CB.7 Mike's Progress Report

The Final Report Stage

The final report presents the results of the research project: findings, interpretations, and recommendations. This document answers questions like these:

- *What did you find?*
- *What does it all mean?*
- *What should we do?*

Depending on the topic and situation, of course, the audience will have specific questions as well. See Chapter 24 for discussion and examples.

During his research, Mike Cabral discovered problems over and above the published errors he had been assigned to investigate. For instance, after looking at competing magazines he decided that *Megacrunch* needed improved page design, along with a higher quality stock (the paper the magazine is printed on). He also concluded that a monthly section on business applications would help. But despite their usefulness, none of these findings or ideas was part of Mike's *original* assignment. White expected him to focus on these questions, specifically:

- *Which errors recur most frequently in our publication?*
- *Where are these errors coming from?*
- *What can we do to prevent them?*

Mike therefore decides to focus exclusively on the error problem. (He might later discuss those other issues with White—if the opportunity arises. But if *this* report were to include material that exceeds the assignment *and* the reader's expectations, Mike could end up appearing arrogant or presumptuous.)

Mike tries to give White only what she requested. He analyzes the problem and the causes, and then recommends a solution. Mike adapts the general outline on page 571 to shape the three major sections of his report: *introduction, findings and conclusions,* and *recommendations.* For the user's convenience and orientation, he includes the report supplements discussed in Chapter 25: *front matter* (title page, transmittal letter, table of contents, and informative abstract) and *end matter* (a Works Cited page [MLA style] and appendices [not shown here]).

After several revisions, Mike submits copies of the report to his boss and to his instructor (Figure CB.8).

Virtually any long
report has a title
page

A forecasting title

Quality-Control Recommendations for *Megacrunch* Magazine

The primary user's
name, title, and
organization

Prepared for
Marcia S. White
Production Manager
Rangeley Publications

Author's name

by
Michael T. Cabral

Submission date

December 14, 20XX

FIGURE CB.8 Mike's Final Report

A letter of transmittal usually accompanies a long report

Addressed to the primary user

Identifies the report's subject and describes its scope

Maintains a confident tone throughout

Gives an overview of entire project and findings

Requests action

Invites follow-up

82 Stephens Road
Boca Grande, FL 08754
December 14, 20XX

Marcia S. White, Production Manager and Vice President
Rangeley Publications, Inc.
167 Dolphin Ave.
Englewood, FL 08567

Dear Ms. White:

Here is my report, recommending quality-control measures for *Megacrunch* magazine. The report briefly discusses the history of our quality-control problem, identifies the types of errors we are up against, analyzes possible causes, and recommends four realistic solutions.

My research confirmed exactly what you had feared. The problem is big and deeply rooted: our authors have legitimate complaints; our readers justifiably want information they can put to work; and developers and advertisers have the right to demand fair and complete representation. As a result of client dissatisfaction, competing magazines are gaining readers and authors at our expense.

To have an immediate effect on our quality-control problem, we should act now. Because of our limited budget, I have tried to recommend low-cost, high-return solutions. If you have other solutions in mind, I would be happy to research them for projected effectiveness and feasibility.

Sincerely,

Michael T. Cabral

Michael T. Cabral
Production Assistant
Rangeley Publications

FIGURE CB.8 *(Continued)*

Table of contents (reports with numerous visuals also have a table of figures)

Front matter (items that precede the report)

Heads and sub-heads from the report itself

All heads in the table of contents follow the exact phrasing of those in the report text

The various typefaces and indentations reflect the respective rank of various heads in the report

Each head listed in the table of contents is assigned a page number

End matter (items that follow the report)

iii

CONTENTS

LETTER OF TRANSMITTAL ii

INFORMATIVE ABSTRACT iv

INTRODUCTION 1

FINDINGS AND CONCLUSIONS 2

Elements of the Problem 2
    Errors in Grammar and Mechanics 2
    Errors in Information Accuracy and Access 3
    Technical Content Errors 3
    Distortions of the Author's Original Meaning 4

Causes of Our Editorial Inaccuracy 4
    Poor Initial Submissions from Contributors 5
    Lack of Structure in Our Editing Cycle 5
    Lack of Diversity in Our Editing Staff 6
    Lack of Communication with Authors and Advertisers 6

RECOMMENDATIONS 6

Expanded Author's Guide 6

Five-Stage Editing Cycle 6

A Checklist for Each Stage 7

Improved Communication with Contributors 7
    Author/Client Verification of Page Proofs 7
    Expanded Use of Our Electronic Mail Network 7
    Possible Use of Groupware 7

WORKS CITED 9

APPENDIXES A–F [Not shown here]

FIGURE CB.8 *(Continued)*

iv

INFORMATIVE ABSTRACT

The informative abstract (or summary) conveys the report's findings, conclusions, and recommendations. This is the one part of a long report read most often.

The summary stands alone in meaning—a kind of mini-report written for laypersons

Busy audiences need to know quickly what is important. A summary gives them enough information to decide whether they should read the whole report, parts of it, or none of it.

An investigation of the quality-control problem at *Megacrunch* magazine identifies the types of errors and their causes and recommends a solution.

Megacrunch suffers from the following avoidable errors:

- *Grammatical errors* are most frequent: misspellings, fragmented and jumbled sentences, misplaced punctuation, and so on.
- *Informational errors:* incorrect prices, products attributed to wrong companies, mismarked visuals, and so on.
- *Technical content errors* are less frequent, but the most dangerous: garbled source code, mismarked diagrams, misused technical terms, and so on.
- *Distortions of the author's original meaning:* introduced by editors who attempt to improve clarity and style.

The above errors seem to have the following causes:

- *Poor initial submissions from contributors* ignore basic rules of grammar, clarity, and organization.
- *Lack of structure in the editing cycle* allows for unrestrained and often excessive editing at all stages.
- *Lack of diversity in the editorial staff* leaves language specialists responsible for catching technical and informational errors.
- *Lack of communication with authors and advertisers* leaves the primary sources out of the production process.

On the basis of my findings, I offer four recommendations for improving quality control during the production process:

- *Expanded author's guide* that includes guidelines for effective use of active voice, visuals, direct address, audience analysis, and so on.
- *Five-stage editing cycle* that specifies everyone's duties at each stage. The cycle would require two additional staff members: a technical editor and a fact checker/typist for editorial changes.
- *A checklist for each stage,* to ensure consistent editing.
- *More communication with contributors* by exchanging galley proofs, increasing our use of the electronic network, and possibly using groupware.

FIGURE CB.8 *(Continued)*

1

INTRODUCTION

The reputation of *Megacrunch* magazine is jeopardized by grammatical, technical, and other errors appearing in each issue.

Megacrunch has begun to lose some long-time readers, advertisers, and authors. Although many readers continue to praise the usefulness of our information, complaints about errors are increasing and subscriptions are falling. Advertisers and authors increasingly point to articles or layouts in which excessive editing has been introduced, and some have taken their business and articles to competing magazines. One disgruntled subscriber sums up our problem by asking that we devote "more effort to publishing a magazine without the kinds of elementary errors that distract readers from the content" (Grendel). This kind of complaint is typical of the sample letters in Appendix A.

Granted, complaints are inevitable—as can be seen in a quick review of "Letters to the Editor" in virtually any publication. But if *Megacrunch* is to withstand the competition and uphold its reputation as the leading resource for Cosmo applications in small business, we must minimize such complaints.

Such negative reactions to errors in our magazine should not be surprising. Roughly two decades of research have verified this basic fact: errors in a business document —especially errors in grammar and usage—frustrate readers, and cause them to mistrust the quality of the writing in general.

As two noted communication researchers point out, "business readers tend to read rapidly, for meaning. A perceived error in the writing trips them up. They might not fall down—that is, misunderstand or even quit reading—but they are discomfited, distracted, and even annoyed" (Gilsdorf and Leonard 459).

This report identifies the major errors that recur in our magazine, and investigates their causes. My data is compiled from interviews with our editorial staff, a review of complaint letters from authors and readers, and a spot-check for errors in the magazine itself. Books and articles on writing and editing provide theory and technique. The report concludes by recommending a four-part solution to our error problem.

This section tells what the report is about, why it was written, and how much it covers

An overview of the problem and its effects on the magazine's revenues

The audience is referred to appendices for details that would interrupt the report flow

Request for action

Citing expert opinion lends immediate credibility to the report

Purpose and scope of report; overview of research methods and data sources

Because his primary audience knows the background, Mike keeps the intro-duction brief

FIGURE CB.8 *(Continued)*

This section tells what was found and what it means

The first sub-section analyzes the problem; the second will examine causes

Introduction to the problem, and a lead-in to the visual

A visual that illustrates parts of the problem

2

FINDINGS AND CONCLUSIONS

ELEMENTS OF THE PROBLEM

Errors in *Megacrunch* are limited to no single category. For example, some errors are tied to technical slip-ups, while others result from editors changing the author's intended meaning. My spot-check of *Megacrunch* 8.10, our most recent issue, revealed errors of the types listed in Table 1.

Table 1 Sample Errors

Spot-check of *Megacrunch* 8.10		
Error Type	**As Published**	**Corrected Version**
mechanical	varity of software	variety of software
technical	Xml	XML
informational	Deluxe Panel	DeluxePanel
grammatical	This will help	Editing will help
grammatical	. . . everyone helps for of a program's release date approaches. . . .	. . . everyone helps as a program's release date approaches. . . .
technical	ram	RAM
informational	cosmo	Cosmo
mechanical	We're back, now we will	We're back; now we will

My random analysis of only six pages identified errors in four categories: grammatical/mechanical, informational, technical, and distortions of meaning.

Discussion of the visual, and overview of the subsection

One part of the problem defined, with examples and effects

Citing authorities supports the author's position

Errors in Grammar and Mechanics

Basic correctness is a given—and a problem—for any publication. According to one editing expert, errors such as sentence fragments, confused punctuation, and poor spelling "serve as evidence of ignorance or sloppiness" (Samson 10). Even worse, as another expert points out, "if the writing is bad, readers will often question the accuracy of the content as well" (Johnson-Rew 16). These assertions are borne out by the sampling of reader complaints in Appendix A.

FIGURE CB.8 *(Continued)*

3

Although spelling and grammar checkers can eliminate many such errors, these electronic editing tools can't spot them all. For example, spelling checkers cannot detect words that are spelled correctly but used incorrectly (*it's* for *its, effect* for *affect, there* for *their,* and so on). Nor can they detect typos that create the wrong word that happens to be correctly spelled (*fort* for *port, risk* for *disk, the* for *then,* and so on). Grammar checkers often suggest revisions that are too simplistic or that distort the intended meaning and emphasis (such as the advice to use smaller words or shorter sentences). In fact, one survey found that professional writers consider electronic editing tools somewhat helpful—but no substitute for the human role in editing and proofreading (Johnson-Rew 3–4).

Errors in Information Accuracy and Access

Beyond basic errors, we have published some inaccurate information. For instance, we sometimes attribute products to the wrong companies or we list incorrect prices. Inaccuracies of this kind infuriate readers, product developers, and suppliers. And a retraction printed in the magazine's subsequent issue has little impact once the damage has been done.

Besides inaccurate information, *Megacrunch* too often presents inaccessible information. Mismarked visuals, misplaced headings, and misnumbered references to pages and figures make the magazine hard to follow and to use selectively.

Technical Content Errors

Technical content errors seem to be one of our biggest problems. While some readers might raise a proverbial eyebrow over grammatical errors or skim over informational errors, technical content errors are more frustrating and incapacitating. On a page of text, a misplaced comma or a missing bracket can be irritating, but in a program listing, these same errors can render the program useless. Even worse, a misnamed or misnumbered pin or socket in a hardware diagram might cause users to inadvertently destroy their data or damage their hardware.

Some technical slips in *Megacrunch* have veered close to disaster. Consider, for example, the flawed diagram in Figure 1, from our 7.12 issue:

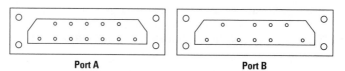

Port A　　　　　　　　　　　　Port B

To connect the SCSI cable, plug Cable Y into Port A

Figure 1　　Partial View of the Port Panel on the AXL 100

Margin notes (left column):

Request for action

Author refutes anticipated reader assumptions about a solution that would be overly simplistic

Another part of the problem defined

Examples

Effects of the problem

Other examples

Another part of the problem defined

Effects of the problem

Examples

A vivid example, as a visual

FIGURE CB.8 *(Continued)*

4

Discussion of the visual

Effects of the error

Interpretation—what it all means for the magazine

Our published diagram instructed users to plug a 9-pin SCSI cable into Port A, a 12-pin modem port; the correct connection was to Port B. Ron Catabia, author of the article and respected tech wizard, explained the flaw in our reproduction of his diagram: "Had any users followed the instructions as printed, the read/write head on their external drive could have suffered permanent damage." Our lengthy correction printed one month later was in no way a sufficient response to an error of this importance. Nor could we placate an enraged and discredited author.

Such errors do little to encourage readers' perception of *Megacrunch* as the serious user's resource for the latest technical information.

Distortions of the Author's Original Meaning

Another part of the problem defined

Example

Interpretation

Experts point out that editors are ethically obliged to "make only those changes that can be justified as assisting the reader while respecting the author's ownership of the work" (Allen and Voss 58). Most important in this regard is the need to preserve the meaning intended by the author. But our authors complain that, in our effort to increase clarity and readability, we distort their original, intended meaning. After reading the edited version of her article, one author insisted that "too often, edits changed what I had said to something I hadn't said—sometimes to the point of altering the facts" (Dimmersdale).

Another example

Editorial liberties inevitably alienate authors. Overzealous editors who set out to shorten a sentence or fine-tune a clause—while knowing nothing about the program being discussed—can distort the author's meaning.

The following excerpt typifies the distortions in recent issues of *Megacrunch*. Here, a seemingly minor edit (from "but" to "even") radically changes the meaning.

As submitted: A user can complete the Filibond program without ever having typed but a single command.

As published: A user can complete the Filibond program without ever having typed even a single command.

Effect of the error

As the irate author later pointed out, "My intent was to indicate that a single command must be typed during the program run" (Klause).

This type of wholesale editing (more examples of which are shown in Appendix B) is a disservice to all parties: author, reader, and magazine.

CAUSES OF OUR EDITORIAL INACCURACY

Second subsection

Justification for an analysis of causes

Before devising a plan for dealing with our editing difficulties, we have to answer questions such as these:

- Where are these errors coming from?
- Can they be prevented?

FIGURE CB.8 *(Continued)*

Scope of this sub-
section, so that
users know what
to expect

Interviews with our editing staff, along with analysis of our editing practices and review of letters on file, uncovered the following causes: (1) poor initial submissions from contributors, (2) lack of structure in our editing cycle, (3) lack of diversity in our editing staff, and (4) lack of communication with the authors and advertisers.

Poor Initial Submissions from Contributors

First cause
defined

Findings

Conclusion

Some contributors submit poorly written manuscripts. And so we edit heavily whenever "a submission otherwise deserves flat-out rejection," as one editor argues. Our editors claim that printing poor writing would be more damaging than the occasional editing excesses that now occur. Although editors can improve clarity and readability without in-depth knowledge of the subject, we often misinterpret the author's meaning. Clearer writing guidelines for authors would result in manuscripts needing less editing to begin with. Our single-page author's guide is inadequate.

Lack of Structure in Our Editing Cycle

Second cause
defined

In our current editing cycle, the most thorough editors see an article repeatedly, as often as time allows. Various editors are free to edit heavily at all stages. And these editors are entirely responsible for judgments about grammatical, informational, and technical accuracy.

Findings

Although "having your best give their best" throughout the cycle seems a good idea, this approach leads to inconsistent editing and/or overediting. Some editors do a light editing job, choosing to preserve the original writing. Others prefer to "overhaul" the original. With light-versus-heavy editing styles entering the cycle randomly, errors slip by. As one editor noted, "Sometimes an article doesn't get a tough edit until the third or fourth reading. At that point, we have no time to review these last-minute changes" (*Megacrunch* editorial staff).

Interpretation—
what it means

Any article heavily edited and rewritten in the final stages stands a chance of containing typographical and mechanical errors, some questionable sentence structures, inadvertent technical changes, and other problems that result from a "rough-and-tumble edit."

Findings

While some articles are edited inconsistently, others are overedited. Our editors tend to be vigilant in pursuit of clarity, conciseness, and tone. Unfortunately, they seem less vigilant about technical accuracy.

Interpretation

Conclusion

Instead of full-scale editing at all stages, we need a cycle that makes a manuscript progress from inadequate (or adequate) to excellent, through different levels of editorial attention. For example, a first edit should be thorough, but a final proofreading should be merely a fine-combing for typographical and mechanical errors.

FIGURE CB.8 *(Continued)*

6

Third cause defined and interpreted

Conclusion

Fourth cause defined and interpreted

Conclusion

This section tells what should be done

Scope of this section, so that users know what to expect

Lead-in to first recommendation

The recommendation

Lead-in to second recommendation

Lack of Diversity in Our Editing Staff

The variety of errors suggests that our present staff alone cannot spot all problems. Strong writing backgrounds have not prepared our editors to recognize a jumbled line of programming code or a misquoted price. To snag all errors, we must hire technical specialists. We need both a technical editor and a fact checker, to pick up where current editors leave off.

Lack of Communication with Authors and Advertisers

Some of our editing troubles emerge from a gap between the meaning intended by contributors and the interpretation by editors. In the present system, contributors submit manuscripts without seeing any editorial changes until the published version appears. Along with an expanded author's guide, regular communication throughout the editing process (and perhaps the writing process as well) would involve contributors in developing the published piece, and thus make authors more responsible for their work.

RECOMMENDATIONS

To eliminate published inaccuracies, I recommend: (1) an expanded author's guide, (2) a five-stage editing cycle, (3) a checklist for each stage, and (4) improved communication with contributors.

EXPANDED AUTHOR'S GUIDE

The obvious way to limit editing changes would be to accept only near-perfect submissions. But as a technical resource we cannot afford to reject poorly written articles that are nonetheless technically valuable.

To reduce editing required on submissions, I recommend we expand our author's guide to include topics like these: audience analysis, use of direct address and active voice, principles of outlining and formatting, and use of visuals.

FIVE-STAGE EDITING CYCLE

In place of haphazard editing, I propose a progressive, five-stage cycle: Stages one through three would refine grammar, clarity, and readability. Two additional staff members, a fact checker and a technical editor, would check facts and technical accuracy in the final two stages. Figure 2 outlines responsibilities at each stage.

FIGURE CB.8 *(Continued)*

A CHECKLIST FOR EACH STAGE

To ensure a consistent focus throughout the editing cycle, our staff should collaborate immediately to develop a detailed checklist for each stage (Hansen 15). As a guide for editors as well as for contributors, these checklists would enhance communication among all parties.

IMPROVED COMMUNICATION WITH CONTRIBUTORS

The following measures would reduce errors caused by misunderstandings between contributors and editors.

Author/Client Verification of Page Proofs

Two weeks before our deadline, we could send authors prepublication page proofs [which show the text as it will appear in published form]. Authors could check for technical errors or changes in meaning, and return proofs within five days.

Expanded Use of Our Electronic Network

We should require electronic versions of all submissions from authors, in either PDF format or as Word files that we can convert to PDF format. Instead of relying mainly on email communication among editors and authors, one expert suggests developing our own wiki-type blog (Hart 21). This would allow for real-time editing and discussion of a manuscript before we send it off for typesetting in page-proof format.

Possible Use of Groupware

For unified and efficient collaboration throughout the editing cycle, we should consider installing groupware such as *ForComment* or *XMetal Reviewer*. With *XMetal Reviewer*, for example, documents could be edited on-screen and copies of each stage of revision could be filed and accessed as needed. A record of all edits at all stages would be invaluable in helping us troubleshoot and refine our editing process.

As an economical alternative, we might explore the feasibility of open source groupware, which is becoming increasingly available for Windows and which can be downloaded directly from the Internet ("Open Source").

Taking these recommended steps will have an immediate impact on the quality of our magazine and on its prospects for long-term success in an increasingly competitive market.

Lead-in to final recommendation

First part of final recommendation

Second part of final recommendation

Third part of final recommendation

A closing call for action

FIGURE CB.8 *(Continued)*

The visual illustrates and summarizes the process being recommended

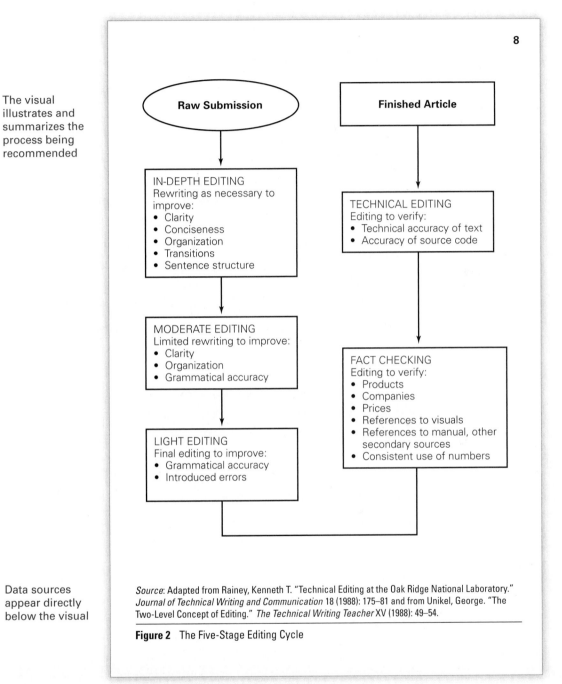

8

Raw Submission

Finished Article

IN-DEPTH EDITING
Rewriting as necessary to improve:
• Clarity
• Conciseness
• Organization
• Transitions
• Sentence structure

TECHNICAL EDITING
Editing to verify:
• Technical accuracy of text
• Accuracy of source code

MODERATE EDITING
Limited rewriting to improve:
• Clarity
• Organization
• Grammatical accuracy

FACT CHECKING
Editing to verify:
• Products
• Companies
• Prices
• References to visuals
• References to manual, other secondary sources
• Consistent use of numbers

LIGHT EDITING
Final editing to improve:
• Grammatical accuracy
• Introduced errors

Data sources appear directly below the visual

Source: Adapted from Rainey, Kenneth T. "Technical Editing at the Oak Ridge National Laboratory." *Journal of Technical Writing and Communication* 18 (1988): 175–81 and from Unikel, George. "The Two-Level Concept of Editing." *The Technical Writing Teacher* XV (1988): 49–54.

Figure 2   The Five-Stage Editing Cycle

FIGURE CB.8 *(Continued)*

This list of works cited clearly identifies each source cited in the report

9

WORKS CITED

Allen, Lori, and Dan Voss. "Ethics for Editors: An Analytical Decision-Making
    Process." IEEE Transactions on Professional Communication 41.1 (1998):
    58–65.

Catabia, Ronald. Notes from author Catabia's phone conversation with the
    Managing Editor. 10 Mar. 2007.

Dimmersdale, Olivia. Author's letter to the Managing Editor. 6 July 2007.

Gilsdorf, Jeanette, and Don Leonard. "Big Stuff, Little Stuff: A Dicennial
    Measurement of Executives' and Academics' Reactions to Questionable
    Usage Elements." The Journal of Business Communications 38.4 (2001):
    439–75.

Grendel, M. L. Subscriber's email to the Managing Editor. 14 May 2007.

Hansen, James B. "Editing Your Own Writing." Intercom Feb. 1997: 14–16.

Hart, Geoffrey S. "Designing an Effective Review Process." Intercom July-Aug.
    2006: 18-21.

Johnson-Rew, Lois. Editing for Writers. Upper Saddle River, NJ: Prentice, 1999.

Klause, M. Author's letter to the Managing Editor. 11 Nov. 2007.

Megacrunch editing staff. Interviews. 12–14 Nov. 2007.

"Open Source." Jan. 2007. Roseindia.net. 28 Nov. 2007 <www.roseindia.net/
    opensource/open-source-groupware.html>.

Samson, Donald C. Editing Technical Writing. New York: Oxford, 1993.

Specific names omitted from this citation, to protect in-house sources and to allow employees to speak candidly, without fear of reprisal

FIGURE CB.8 *(Continued)*

Is It Plagiarism?
Test Yourself on In-Text (Parenthetical) References

Read the excerpt marked "Original Source." Can you spot the plagiarism in the examples that follow?

Original source

> To begin with, language is a system of communication. I make this rather obvious point because to some people nowadays it isn't obvious: they see language as above all a means of "self-expression." Of course, language is one way that we express our personal feelings and thoughts—but so, if it comes to that, are dancing, cooking, and making music. Language does much more: it enables us to convey to others what we think, feel, and want. Language-as-communication is the prime means of organizing the cooperative activities that enable us to accomplish as groups things we could not possibly do as individuals. Some other species also engage in cooperative activities, but these are either quite simple (as among baboons and wolves) or exceedingly stereotyped (as among bees, ants, and termites). Not surprisingly, the communicative systems used by these animals are also simple or stereotypes. Language, our uniquely flexible and intricate system of communication, makes possible our equally flexible and intricate ways of coping with the world around us: In a very real sense, it is what makes us human (Claiborne 8).

Works Cited entry:

Claiborne, Robert. "Our Marvelous Native Tongue: The Life and Times of the English Language." New York: *New York Times*, 1983.

Plagiarism Example 1

> One commentator makes a distinction between language used as **a means of self-expression** and **language-as-communication.** It is the latter that distinguishes human interaction from that of other species and allows humans to work cooperatively on complex tasks (8).

What's wrong? The source's name is not given, and there are no quotation marks around words taken directly from the source (in **boldface** in the example).

Plagiarism Example 2

> Claiborne notes that language "is the prime means of organizing the cooperative activities." Without language, we would, consequently, not have civilization.

What's wrong? The page number of the source is missing. Parenthetical references should immediately follow the material being quoted, paraphrased, or summarized. You may omit a parenthetical reference only if the information that you have included in your attribution is sufficient to identify the source in your Works Cited list and no page number is needed.

Plagiarism Example 3

> Other animals also **engage in cooperative activities.** However, these actions are not very complex. Rather they are either the very **simple** activities of, for example, **baboons and wolves** or the **stereotyped** activities of animals such as **bees, ants, and termites** (Claiborne 8).

What's wrong? A paraphrase should capture a specific idea from a source but must not duplicate the writer's phrases and words (in **boldface** in the example). In the example, the wording and sentence structure follow the source too closely.

Works Cited

Abelman, Arthur F. "Legal Issues in Scholarly Publishing." *MLA Style Manual*. 2nd ed. New York: Modern Language Association, 1998: 30–57.

Adams, Gerald R., and Jay D. Schvaneveldt. *Understanding Research Methods*. New York: Longman, 1985.

Adler, Jerry. "For Humans, Evolution Ain't What It Used to Be." *Newsweek* 29 Sept. 1997: 17.

"Advertising and Marketing on the Internet." Sept. 2000. Online 8 pp. Federal Trade Commission. 17 Jan. 2001 <www.ftc.gov.bcp/conline/pubs/buspubs/ruleroad.htm>.

"Advisories on the Use of Medical Web Sites Issued." *Professional Ethics Report* [American Association for the Advancement of Science] XII.3 (Summer 1999): 2–3.

The Aldus Guide to Basic Design. Aldus Corporation, 1988.

American Psychological Association. *Publication Manual of the American Psychological Association*. 5th ed. Washington: Author, 2001.

"And the Winner of the Dubious-Study-of-Year Award Is . . . ." *University of California at Berkeley Wellness Letter* 14.6 (1998): 1+.

Anson, Chris M., and Robert A. Schwegler. *The Longman Handbook for Writers and Readers*, 2nd ed. New York: Longman, 2000.

"Any Alternative?" *The Economist* 1 Nov. 1997: 83–84.

Archee, Raymond K. "Online Intercultural Communication." *Intercom* Sept./Oct. 2003: 40–41.

"Are We in the Middle of a Cancer Epidemic?" *University of California at Berkeley Wellness Letter* 10.9 (1994): 4–5.

Armstrong, William H. "Learning to Listen." *American Educator* (Winter 1997–98): 24+.

Author's Guide. New York: Addison Wesley Longman, 1998.

Baker, Russ. "Surfer's Paradise." *Inc.* Nov. 1997: 57+.

Ball, Charles. "Figuring the Risks of Closer Runways." *Technology Review* Aug./Sept. 1996: 12–13.

Barbour, Ian. *Ethics in an Age of Technology*. New York: Harper, 1993.

Barnes, Shaleen. "Evaluating Sources Checklist." Information Literacy Project. 10 June 1997. Online. 23 June 1998 <www.2lib.umassd.edu/library2/INFOLIT/prop.html>.

Barnett, Arnold. "How Numbers Can Trick You." *Technology Review* Oct. 1994: 38–45.

Baumann, K. E., et al. "Three Mass Media Campaigns to Prevent Adolescent Cigarette Smoking." *Preventive Medicine* 17 (1988): 510–30.

Baumeister, Roy F. "Should Schools Try to Boost Self-Esteem?" *American Educator* (Summer 1996): 14+.

Bazerman, Max H., Kimberly P. Morgan, and George F. Loewenstein. "The Impossibility of Auditor Independence." *Sloan Management Review* 38.4 (Summer 1997): 89–94.

Beamer, Linda. "Learning Intercultural Communication Competence." *Journal of Business Communication* 29.3 (1992): 285–303.

Bedford, Marilyn S., and F. Cole Stearns. "The Technical Writer's Responsibility for Safety." *IEEE Transactions on Professional Communication* 30.3 (1987): 127–32.

Begley, Sharon. "Bad Days on the Lily Pad." *Newsweek* 13 July 1998: 67.

———. "Is Science Censored?" *Newsweek* 14 Sept. 1992: 63.

———. "Odds on the Greenhouse." *Newsweek* 1 Dec. 1997: 72.

Belkin, Lisa. "How Can We Save the Next Victim?" *New York Times Magazine* 15 June 1997: 28+.

Benson, Phillipa J. "Visual Design Consideration in Technical Publications." *Technical Communication* 32.4 (1985): 35–39.

Berry, Stephen R. "Scientific Information in the Electronic Era." *Professional Ethics Report* [American Association for the Advancement of Science] X.2 (Spring 1997): 1+.

Bjerklie, David. "E-Mail: The Boss Is Watching." *Technology Review* 14 Apr. 1993: 14–15.

Blaser, Martin J. "The Bacteria behind Ulcers." *Scientific American* Feb. 1996: 140+.

Blinder, Alan S., and Richard E. Quandt. "The Computer and the Economy." *Atlantic Monthly* Dec. 1997: 26–32.

Blum, Deborah. "Investigative Science Journalism." *Field Guide for Science Writers.* Eds. Deborah Blum and Mary Knudson. New York: Oxford, 1997. 86–93.

Bogert, Judith, and David Butt. "Opportunities Lost, Challenges Met: Understanding and Applying Group Dynamics in Writing Projects." *Bulletin of the Association for Business Communication* 53.2 (1990): 51–53.

Boiarsky, Carolyn. "Using Usability Testing to Teach Reader Response." *Technical Communication* 39.1 (1992): 100–02.

Bolles, Richard Nelson. *Job Hunting on the Internet.* 2nd ed. Berkeley, CA: Ten Speed, 1999.

Bosley, Deborah. "International Graphics: A Search for Neutral Territory." *INTERCOM* Aug./Sept. 1996: 4–7.

Boucher, Norman. "Back to the Everglades." *Technology Review* Aug./Sept. 1995: 24–35.

Branscum, Deborah. "bigbrother@the.office.com." *Newsweek* 27 Apr. 1998: 78.

Broad, William J. "NASA Budget Cuts Raise Concerns over Safety of Shuttle." *New York Times* 8 Mar. 1994, sec. B: 5+.

Brower, Vicki. "Ethics for Hire." *Technology Review* Mar./Apr. 1999: 25.

Brownell, Judi, and Michael Fitzgerald. "Teaching Ethics in Business Communication: The Effective/Ethical Balancing Scale." *Bulletin of the Association for Business Communication* 55.3 (1992): 15–18.

Bruhn, Mark J. "E-Mail's Conversational Value." *Business Communication Quarterly* 58.3 (1995): 43–44.

Bryan, John. "Down the Slippery Slope: Ethics and the Technical Writer as Marketer." *Technical Communication Quarterly* 1.1 (1992): 73–88.

Bureau of Labor Statistics. "Employee Tenure Summary." 19 Sept. 2002. *News.* 12 Feb. 2004 <http://stats.bls.gov/news.release/tenure.nr0.htm>.

Burger, Katrina. "Righteousness Pays." *Forbes* 22 Sept. 2000: 11.

Burghardt, M. David. *Introduction to the Engineering Profession.* New York: Harper, 1991.

Burnett, Rebecca E. "Substantive Conflict in a Cooperative Context: A Way to Improve the Collaborative Planning of Workplace Documents." *Technical Communication* 38.4 (1991): 532–39.

Busiel, Christopher, and Tom Maeglin. *Researching Online.* New York: Addison, 1998.

Byrd, Patricia, and Joy M. Reid. *Grammar in the Composition Classroom.* Boston: Heinle, 1998.

Caher, John M. "Technical Documentation and Legal Liability." *Journal of Technical Writing and Communication* 25.1 (1995): 5–10.

Carliner, Saul. "Demonstrating Effectiveness and Value: A Process for Evaluating Technical Communication Products and Services." *Technical Communication* 44.3 (1997): 252–65.

———. "Physical, Cognitive, and Affective: A Three-Part Framework for Information Design." *Technical Communication* 47.2 (2000): 561–76.

Caswell-Coward, Nancy. "Cross-Cultural Communication: Is It Greek to You?" *Technical Communication* 39.2 (1992): 264–66.

Chauncey, C. "The Art of Typography in the Information Age." *Technology Review* Feb./Mar. (1986): 26+.

Christians, C. G., et al. *Media Ethics: Cases and Moral Reasoning.* 2nd ed. White Plains, NY: Longman, 1978.

Cialdini, Robert B. "The Science of Persuasion." *Scientific American* Feb. 2001: 76–81.

Clark, Gregory. "Ethics in Technical Communication: A Rhetorical Perspective." *IEEE Transactions on Professional Communication* 30.3 (1987): 190–95.

Clark, Thomas. "Teaching Students to Enhance the Ecology of Small Group Meetings." *Business Communication Quarterly* 61.4 (Dec. 1998): 40–52.

———. "Teaching Students How to Write to Avoid Legal Liability." *Business Communication Quarterly* 60.3 (1997): 71–77.

Clement, David E. "Human Factors, Instructions and Warnings, and Product Liability." *IEEE Transactions on Professional Communication* 30.3 (1987): 149–56.

Cochran, Jeffrey K., et al. "Guidelines for Evaluating Graphical Designs." *Technical Communication* 36.1 (1989): 25–32.

Coe, Marlana. *Human Factors for Technical Communicators.* New York: Wiley, 1996.

———. "Writing for Other Cultures: Ten Problem Areas." *INTERCOM* Jan. 1997: 17–19.

Cohn, Victor. "Coping with Statistics." *A Field Guide for Science Writers.* Eds. Deborah Blum and Mary Knudson. New York: Oxford, 1997. 102–09.

Cole-Gomolski B. "Users Loathe to Share Their Know-How." *Computerworld* 17 Nov. 1997: 6.

Columbia Accident Investigation Board [NASA]. *Report,* Volume 1. Washington, DC: GPO, 2003.

Columbia Accident Investigation Board Press Briefing. August 26, 2003. Transcript. 7 May 2004. <http://www.caib.us/events/press_briefings/20030826/transcript.html>.

Communication Concepts, Inc. "Electronic Media Poses New Copyright Issues." *Writing Concepts* ©. Reprinted in *INTERCOM* Nov. 1995: 13+.

Congressional Research Report. Washington, DC: GPO, 1990.

Conlin, Michelle. "And Now, the Just-in-Time Employee." *Business Week* 28 Aug. 2000: 169–70.

"Consequences of Whistle Blowing in Scientific Misconduct Reported." *Professional Ethics Report* [American Association for the Advancement of Science] IX.4 (Winter 1996): 2.

Consumer Product Safety Commission. *Fact Sheet No. 65.* Washington: GPO, 1989.

Cooper, Lyn O. "Listening Competency in the Workplace: A Model for Training." *Business Communication Quarterly* 60.4 (Dec. 1997): 75–84.

"Copyright Protection and Fair Use of Printed Information." *Addison Wesley Longman Author's Guide.* New York: Longman, 2006.

Corbett, Edward P. J. *Classical Rhetoric for the Modern Student,* 3rd ed. New York: Oxford, 1990.

Cortese, Amy. "Automatic Web Downloads—without the Overload." *Business Week* 24 Nov. 1997: 152.

Cotton, Robert, ed. *The New Guide to Graphic Design.* Secaucus, NJ: Chartwell, 1990.

"Crime Spree." *Business Week* 9 Sept. 2002: 8.

Cronin, Mary J. "Knowing How Employees Use the Intranet Is Good Business." *Fortune* 21 July 1997: 103.

———. "Using the Web to Push Key Data to Decision Makers." *Fortune* 29 Sept. 1997: 254.

Crosby, Olivia. *Employment Interviewing.* Washington, DC: U.S. Department of Labor, 2000.

———. *Résumés, Applications, and Cover Letters.* Washington DC: U.S. Department of Labor, 1999.

Cross, Mary. "Aristotle and Business Writing: Why We Need to Teach Persuasion." *Bulletin of the Association for Business Communication* 54.1 (1991): 3–6.

Crossen, Cynthia. *Tainted Truth: The Manipulation of Fact in America.* New York: Simon, 1994.

Crumpton, Amy. "Secrecy in Science." *Professional Ethics Report* [American Association for the Advancement of Science] XII.1 (Winter 1999): 1+.

Curry, Jerome. "Trapping the Internet's Job Search Resources." *Business Communication Quarterly* 61.2 (1998): 100–06.

D'Aprix, Roger. "Related Thoughts." *Journal of Employee Communication Management* Nov./Dec. 1997: 66–70.

Daugherty, Shannon. "The Usability Evaluation: A Discount Approach to Usability Testing." *INTERCOM* Dec. 1997: 16–20.

Davenport, Thomas H. *Information Ecology.* New York: Oxford, 1997.

Debs, Mary Beth, "Collaborative Writing in Industry." In *Technical Writing: Theory and Practice.* Eds. Bertie E. Fearing and W. Keats Sparrow. New York: Modern Language Assn., 1989, 33–42.

———. "Recent Research on Collaborative Writing in Industry." *Technical Communication* 38.4 (1991): 476–85.

December, John. "An Information Development Methodology for the World Wide Web." *Technical Communication* 43.3 (1996): 369–75.

Desmond, Edward W. "How Your Data May Soon Seek You Out." *Fortune* 8 Sept. 1997: 149–50.

Detjen, Jim. "Environmental Writing." *A Field Guide for Science Writers.* Eds. Deborah Blum and Mary Knudson. New York: Oxford, 1997. 173–79.

Devlin, Keith. *Infosense: Turning Information into Knowledge.* New York: W. H. Freeman, 1999.

Dombrowski, Paul M. "*Challenger* and the Social Contingency of Meaning: Two Lessons for the Technical Communication Classroom." *Technical Communication Quarterly* 1.3 (1992): 73–86.

Dorner, Dietrich. *The Logic of Failure.* Reading, MA: Addison, 1996.

Dowd, Charles. "Conducting an Effective Journalistic Interview." *INTERCOM* May 1996: 12–14.

Doyle, Rodger. "Amphibians and Risk." *Scientific American* Aug. 1998: 27.

Dulude, Jennifer. "The Web Marketing Handbook." Thesis. University of Massachusetts Dartmouth, 1997.

Dumont, R. A., and J. M. Lannon, *Business Communications.* 3rd ed. Glenview, IL: Scott, 1990.

"Earthquake Hazard Analysis for Nuclear Power Plants." *Energy and Technology Review* June 1984: 8.

Easton, Thomas, and Stephan Herrara. "J&J's Dirty Little Secret." *Forbes* 12 Jan. 1998: 42–44.

Edelman, Rob. "Commentary on Prescription Drug Commercials." *Midday Magazine.* Albany, NY: WAMC Radio 5 Feb. 2001.

Elbow, Peter. *Writing without Teachers.* New York: Oxford, 1973.

"Electronic Mentors." *The Futurist* May 1992: 56.

Elias, Stephen. *Patent, Copyright, and Trademark.* Berkeley, CA: Nolo Press, 1997.

Elliot, Joel. "Evaluating Web Sites: Questions to Ask." 18 Feb. 1997. Online. List for Multimedia and New Technologies in Humanities Teaching. 9 Mar. 1997 <www.learnnc.org/documents/webeval.html>.

"Email Etiquette Revisited." *Manager's Legal Bulletin.* Ramsey, NJ: Alexander Hamilton Institute, 2000.

"Evaluating Internet-Based Information." May 1997. Online. Wolfgram Memorial Library, Widener University, PA. 17 Mar. 2001. <www.Ime.mankato.msus.edu/class/629/wid.html>.

Evans, James. "Legal Briefs." *Internet World* Feb. 1998: 22.

Extejt, Marian M. "Teaching Students to Correspond Effectively Electronically." *Business Communication Quarterly* 61.2 (1998): 57–67.

Fackelmann, Kathleen. "Science Safari in Cyberspace." *Science News* 152.50 (1997): 397–98.

Facts and Figures about Cancer. Boston: Dana-Farber Cancer Institute, 1995.

"Fair Use." 10 June 1993. Online. 2 pp. United States Copyright Office, Library of Congress. 10 June 2007 <http://www.loc.gov/copyright>.

Farnham, Alan. "How Safe Are Your Secrets?" *Fortune* 8 Sept. 1997: 114–120.

Fawcett, Heather. "*The New Oxford Dictionary* Project." *Technical Communication* 40.3 (1993): 379–82.

Felker, Daniel B., et al. *Guidelines for Document Designers.* Washington: American Institutes for Research, 1981.

Fineman, Howard, "The Power of Talk." *Newsweek* 8 Feb. 1993: 24–28.

Finkelstein, Leo, Jr. "The Social Implications of Computer Technology for the Technical Writer." *Technical Communication* 38.4 (1991): 466–73.

Fischman, Josh. "Who'll Pay for the Doc You Want?" *U.S. News & World Report* 18 Aug. 2003: 50.

Fisher, Anne. "Can I Stop Gay Bashing?" *Fortune* 7 July 1997: 205–06.

———. "I Didn't Spend Four Years in College to End Up as a Barista." *Fortune* May 12, 2003: 178.

———. "My Company Just Announced I May Be Laid Off. Now What?" *Fortune* 3 Mar. 2003.

———. "My Team Leader Is a Plagiarist." *Fortune* 27 Oct. 1997: 291–92.

———. "Truth and Consequences." *Fortune* 29 May 2000: 292.

Ford, Donna. "Phone Interviews: New Skills Required." *INTERCOM* April 2002: 18–19.

Foster, Edward. "Why Users Beef about Documentation." *INTERCOM* Nov. 1998: 10.

Fox, Justin, " A Startling Notion—The Whole Truth," *Fortune* 24 Nov. 1997: 303.

Franke, Earnest A. "The Value of the Retrievable Technical Memorandum System to the Engineering Company." *IEEE Transactions on Professional Communication* 32.1 (Mar. 1989): 12–16.

Freundlich, Naomi. "When the Cure May Make You Sicker." *Business Week* 16 Mar. 1998: 14.

Friedland, Andrew J., and Carol L. Folt. *Writing Successful Science Proposals.* New Haven, CT: Yale UP, 2000.

"From Mir to Mars." *PBS Online.* 11 Nov. 1998 <www.PBS.org>.

Fugate, Alice E. "Mastering Search Tools for the Internet." *INTERCOM* Jan. 1998: 40–41.

———. "Wowing Them with Your Web Site." *INTERCOM* Nov. 2000: 33–35.

"Full Responsibility." 3 Nov. 2000. Online. 3 Oct. 2001 <www.ABC News.com>.

Gallagher, Leigh. "Isn't That Special?" *Forbes* 9 Mar. 1998: 39.

Garfield, Eugene, "What Scientific Journals Can Tell Us about Scientific Journals." *IEEE Transactions on Professional Communication* 16.4 (1973): 200–02.

Garner, Rochelle. "IS Newbies: Eager, Motivated, Clueless." *Computerworld* 1 Dec. 1997: 85–86.

Gartaganis, Arthur. "Lasers." *Occupational Outlook Quarterly* Winter 1984: 22–26.

Gerstner, John. "Print Is Obsolete, but It Won't Go Away." *Journal of Employee Communication Management* Nov./Dec. 1997: 42–47.

Gesteland, Richard R. "Cross-Cultural Compromises." *Sky* May 1993: 20+.

Gibaldi, Joseph. *MLA Handbook for Writers of Research Papers.* 6th ed. New York: Modern Language Assn., 2003.

Gibaldi, Joseph, and Walter S. Achtert. *MLA Handbook for Writers of Research Papers.* 3rd ed. New York: Modern Language Assn., 1988.

Gibbs, W. Wayt. "Speech without Accountability." *Scientific American* Oct. 2000: 34+.

Gilbert, Nick, "1–800-ETHIC." *Financial World* 16 Aug. 1994: 20+.

Gilsdorf, Jeanette W. "Executives' and Academics' Perception of the Need for Instruction in Written Persuasion." *Journal of Business Communication* 23.4 (1986): 55–68.

———. "Write Me Your Best Case for . . ." *Bulletin of the Association for Business Communication* 54.1 (1991): 7–12.

Girill, T.R. "Technical Communication and Art." *Technical Communication* 31.2 (1984): 35.

———. "Technical Communication and Ethics." *Technical Communication* 34.3 (1987): 178–79.

———. "Technical Communication and Law." *Technical Communication* 32.3 (1985): 37.

Glassman, James K. "Dihydrogen Monoxide: It's a Killer." *Daily Hampshire Gazette* 22 Oct. 1997: 6.

Glidden, H. K. *Reports, Technical Writing and Specifications.* New York: McGraw, 1964.

Goby, Valerie P., and Lewis Justus Helen. "The Key Role of Listening in Business: A Study of the Singapore Insurance Industry." *Business Communication Quarterly* 63.2 (June 2000): 41–51.

Golen, Steven, et al. "How to Teach Ethics in a Basic Business Communications Class." *Journal of Business Communication* 22.1 (1985): 75–84.

Goodall, H. Lloyd, Jr., and Christopher L. Waagen. *The Persuasive Presentation.* New York: Harper, 1986.

Goodman, Danny. *Living at Light Speed.* New York: Random, 1994.

Goodman, Ellen. "Fear of Taxes Trumps Risk of Cancer." *Daily Hampshire Gazette* 24 June 1998: 6.

Grant, Linda. "Where Did the Snap, Crackle, & Pop Go?" *Fortune* 4 Aug. 1997: 223+.

Grassian, Esther. "Thinking Critically about World Wide Web Resources." 20 Aug. 1997. UCLA College Library. 25 Oct. 1997 <www.library.ucla.edu/libraries/college/instruct/critical.htm>.

Greenberg, Ilan. "Selling News Short." *Brill's Content* Mar. 2000: 64–65.

Gribbons, William M. "Organization by Design: Some Implications for Structuring Information." *Journal of Technical Writing and Communication* 22.1 (1992): 57–74.

Grice, Roger A. "Document Development in Industry." In *Technical Writing: Theory and Practice.* Eds. Bertie E. Fearing and W. Keats Sparrow. New York: Modern Language Assn., 1989, 27–32.

———. "Focus on Usability: Shazam!" *Technical Communication* 42.1 (1995): 131–33.

Griffin, Robert J. "Using Systematic Thinking to Choose and Evaluate Evidence." *Communicating Uncertainty: Media Coverage of New and Controversial Science.* Eds. Sharon Friedman, Sharon Dunwoody, and Carol Rogers. Mahwah, NJ: Erlbaum, 1999, 225–48.

Grimes, Brad. "Blazing a Paper Trail." *Fortune* 23 June 2003. [Advertising Supplement.]

Gross, Neil, "Between a Rock and a Hard Place." *Business Week* 20 Apr. 1998: 134+.

Gurak, Laura J., and John M. Lannon. *A Concise Guide to Technical Communication.* 3rd ed. New York: Pearson, 2007.

———. *A Concise Guide to Technical Communication.* 2nd ed. New York: Longman, 2004.

Hafner, Kate, "Have Your Agent Call My Agent." *Newsweek* 27 Feb. 1995: 76–77.

Hall, Judith G. "Medicine on the Web: Finding the Wheat, Leaving the Chaff." *Technology Review* Mar./Apr. 1998: 60–61.

Hamblen, Matt. "Volvo Taps AT&T for Global Net." *Computerworld* 1 Dec. 1997: 51+.

Hammett, Paula. "Evaluating Web Resources." 29 Mar. 1997. Ruben Salazar Library, Sonoma State University, 26 Oct. 1997 <www.libweb.sonoma.edu/resources/eval.html>.

"Handbooks." *The Employee Problem Solver.* Ramsey, NJ: Alexander Hamilton Institute, 2000.

Harcourt, Jules. "Teaching the Legal Aspects of Business Communication." *Bulletin of the Association for Business Communication* 53.3 (1990): 63–64.

Harris, Richard F. "Toxics and Risk Reporting." *A Field Guide for Science Writers.* Eds. Deborah Blum and Mary Knudson. New York: Oxford, 1997. 166–72.

Harris, Robert. "Evaluating Internet Research Sources." 17 Nov. 1997. Online, 23 June 1998 <www.sccu.edu/faculty/R_Harris/evalu8it.htm>.

Harrison, Bennett. "Don't Blame Technology This Time." *Technology Review* July 1997: 62.

Hart, Geoff. "Accentuate the Negative: Obtaining Effective Reviews through Focused Questions." *Technical Communication* 44.1 (1997): 52–57.

Hartley, James. *Designing Instructional Text.* 2nd ed. London: Kogan Page, 1985.

Haskin, David. "Meetings without Walls." *Internet World* Oct. 1997: 53–60.

———. "A Push in the Right Direction." *Internet World* Sept. 1997: 75+.

Hauser, Gerald. *Introduction to Rhetorical Theory.* New York: Harper, 1986.

Hayakawa, S. I. *Language in Thought and Action*. 3rd ed. New York: Harcourt, 1972.

Hays, Robert. "Political Realities in Reader/Situation Analysis." *Technical Communication* 31.1 (1984): 16–20.

Hein, Robert G. "Culture and Communication." *Technical Communication* 38.1 (1991): 125–26.

Herper, Matthew. "Why Oscar Winners Live Longer." *Forbes* 7 July 2003: 12.

Hill-Duin, Ann. "Terms and Tools: A Theory and Research-Based Approach to Collaborative Writing." *Bulletin of the Association for Business Communication* 53.2 (1990): 45–50.

Hilligoss, Susan. *Visual Communication: A Writer's Guide*. New York: Longman, 1999.

Hilts, Philip J. "Web Sites Inconsistent on Health, Study Finds." *New York Times* 23 May 2001. 8 July 2007 <www.nytimes.com/2001/05/23/health/23 NET.html>.

Hoger, Elizabeth, James J. Cappel, and Mark A. Myerscough. "Navigating the Web with a Typology of Corporate Uses." *Business Communication Quarterly* 61.2 (1998): 39–47.

Hogge, Robert. Unpublished review of *Technical Writing*. 2nd ed.

Holler, Paul F. "The Challenge of Writing for Multimedia." *INTERCOM* July/Aug. 1995: 25.

Hollowitz, John C., and Donna Pawlowski. "The Development of an Ethical Integrity Interview for Pre-Employment Screening." *The Journal of Business Communication* 34.2 (1997): 203–19.

Holyoak, K. J. "Symbolic Connectionism." *Toward Third-Generation Theories of Expertise: Prospects and Limits*. Eds. K. A. Ericsson and J. Smith. New York: Cambridge UP, 1991. 331–35.

Hopkins-Tanne, Janice. "Writing Science for Magazines." *A Field Guide for Science Writers*. Eds. Deborah Blum and Mary Knudson. New York: Oxford, 1997. 17–26.

Horgan, John. "Multicultural Studies." *Scientific American* Nov. 1996: 24+.

Horn, Robert E. *Visual Language: Global Communication for the 21st Century*. Bainbridge Island, WA: MacroVU, 1998.

Hornig-Priest, Susanna. "Popular Beliefs, Media, and Biotechnology." *Communicating Uncertainty: Media Coverage of New and Controversial Science*. Eds. Sharon Friedman, Sharon Dunwoody, and Carol Rogers. Mahwah, NJ: Erlbaum, 1999. 95–112.

Horton, William. "Is Hypertext the Best Way to Document Your Product?" *Technical Communication* 38.1 (1991): 20–30.

———. "Mix Media, Not Metaphors." *Technical Communication* 41.4 (1994): 781–83.

Howard, Tharon. "Property Issue in E-Mail Research." *Bulletin of the Association for Business Communication* 56.2 (1993): 40–41.

Huff, Darrell. *How to Lie with Statistics*. New York: Norton, 1954.

Hughes, Michael. "Rigor in Usability Testing." *Technical Communication* 46.4 (1999): 488–95.

Hulbert, Jack E. "Developing Collaborative Insights and Skills." *Bulletin of the Association for Business Communication* 57.2 (1994): 53–56.

———. "Overcoming Intercultural Communication Barriers." *Bulletin of the Association for Business Communication* 57.2 (1994): 41–44.

Humphreys, Donald S. "Making Your Hypertext Interface Usable." *Technical Communication* 40.4 (1993): 754–61.

Hunt, Kevin. "Establishing a Presence on the World Wide Web: A Rhetorical Approach." *Technical Communication* 46.4 (1996): 376–87.

IBM Corporation. "IBM Solutions." Advertisement, 1997.

Imperato, Gina. "35 Ways to Land a Job Online." *Fast Company* Aug. 1998: 192–98.

"International Copyright." July 2002. Online. United States Copyright Office, Library of Congress. 21 Mar. 2006 <www.loc.gov/copyright>.

Isaacs, Arlene B. "Tact Can Seal a Global Deal." *New York Times* 26 July 1997, sec. B: 43.

James-Catalano, P. "Fight for Privacy." *Internet World* Jan. 1997: 32+.

Jameson, Daphne A. "Using a Simulation to Teach Intercultural Communication in Business Communication Courses." *Bulletin of the Association for Business Communication* 56.1 (1993): 3–11.

Janis, Irving L. *Victims of Groupthink: A Psychological Study of Foreign Policy Decisions and Fiascos.* Boston: Houghton, 1972.

Johannesen, Richard L. *Ethics in Human Communication.* 2nd ed. Prospect Heights, IL: Waveland, 1983.

Jones, Barbara. "Giving Women the Business." *Harper's Magazine* Dec. 1997: 47–58.

Journet, Debra. Unpublished review of *Technical Writing.* 3rd ed.

Kahneman, Daniel, and Amos Tversky. "Choices, Values, and Frames." *American Psychologist* 39.4 (1984): 342–47.

Kane, Kate. "Can You Perform under Pressure?" *Fast Company* Oct./Nov. 1997: 54+.

Kapoun, Jim. "Questioning Web Authority." *On Campus* Feb. 2000: 4.

Karaim, Reed. "The Invasion of Privacy." *Civilization* Oct./Nov. 1996: 70–77.

Kawasaki, Guy. "Get Your Facts Here." *Forbes* 23 Mar. 1998: 156.

———. "The Rules of E-Mail." *MACWORLD* Oct. 1995: 286.

Kelley-Reardon, Kathleen. *They Don't Get It Do They? Communication in the Workplace—Closing the Gap between Women and Men.* Boston: Little, 1995.

Kelman, Herbert C. "Compliance, Identification, and Internalization: Three Processes of Attitude Change." *Journal of Conflict Resolution* 2 (1958): 51–60.

Kiely, Thomas. "The Idea Makers." *Technology Review* Jan. 1993: 33–40.

King, Ralph T. "Medical Journals Rarely Disclose Researchers' Ties." *Wall Street Journal* 2 Feb. 1999: B1+.

Kipnis, David, and Stuart Schmidt. "The Language of Persuasion." *Psychology Today* Apr. 1985: 40–46. Rpt. in Raymond S. Ross, *Understanding Persuasion.* 3rd ed. Englewood Cliffs: Prentice, 1990.

Kirsh, Lawrence. "Take It from the Top." *MACWORLD* Apr. 1986: 112–15.

Kleimann, Susan D. "The Complexity of Workplace Review." *Technical Communication* 38.4 (1991): 520–26.

Kohl, John R., et al. "The Impact of Language and Culture on Technical Communication in Japan." *Technical Communication* 40.1 (1993): 62–72.

Koretz, Gene. "The New World of Work." *Business Week* 10 Jan. 2000: 32.

Kotulak, Ronald. "Reporting on Biology of Behavior." *A Field Guide for Science Writers.* Eds. Deborah Blum and Mary Knudson. New York: Oxford, 1997. 142–51.

Koudsi, Suzanne. "Actually, It Is Like Brain Surgery." *Fortune* 20 Mar. 2000: 233–34.

Kraft, Stephanie. "Whistleblower Bill's Holiday Adventures." *The Valley Advocate* [Northampton, MA] 6 Jan. 1994: 5–6.

Kremers, Marshall, "Teaching Ethical Thinking in a Technical Writing Course." *IEEE Transactions on Professional Communication* 32.2 (1989): 58–61.

Lambe, Jennifer L. "Techniques for Successful SME Interviews." *INTERCOM* Mar. 2000: 30–32.

Lambert, Steve. *Presentation Graphics on the Apple® Macintosh.* Bellevue, WA: Microsoft, 1984.

Lang, Thomas A., and Michelle Secic. *How to Report Statistics in Medicine.* Philadelphia: American College of Physicians, 1997.

Larson, Charles U. *Persuasion: Perception and Responsibility.* 7th ed. Belmont, CA: Wadsworth: 1995.

Lavin, Michael R. *Business Information: How to Find it, How to Use It.* 2nd ed. Phoenix, AZ: Oryx, 1992.

Lederman, Douglas. "Colleges Report Rise in Violent Crime." *Chronicle of Higher Education* 3 Feb. 1995, sec. A: 5+.

Lee, Susan. "Death by Charcoal?" *Forbes* 25 Aug. 1997: 280.

Leki, Ilona. "The Technical Editor and the Non-native Speaker of English." *Technical Communication* 37.2 (1990): 148–52.

Lemonick, Michael. "The Evils of Milk?" *Times* 15 June 1998: 85.

Le Vie, Donald S. "Résumés: You Can't Escape." *INTERCOM* Apr. 2000: 8–11.

Lewis, Howard L. "Penetrating the Riddle of Heart Attack." *Technology Review* Aug./Sept. 1997: 39–44.

Lewis, Philip L., and N. L. Reinsch. "The Ethics of Business Communication." Proceedings of the American Business Communication Conference. Champaign, IL., 1981. In *Technical Communication and Ethics.* Eds. John R. Brockman and Fern Rook. Washington: Soc. for Technical Communication, 1989, 29–44.

Littlejohn, Stephen W., and David M. Jabusch. *Persuasive Transactions.* Glenview, IL: Scott, 1987.

Machlis, Sharon, "Surfing into a New Career as Webmaster." *Computerworld* 1 Dec. 1997: 45+.

MacKenzie, Nancy. Unpublished review of *Technical Writing.* 5th ed.

Mackin, John. "Surmounting the Barrier between Japanese and English Technical Documents." *Technical Communication* 36.4 (1989): 346–51.

Maeglin, Thomas. Unpublished review of *Technical Writing.* 7th ed.

Manning, Michael. "Hazard Communication 101." *INTERCOM* June 1998: 12–15.

Martin, Jeanette S., and Lillian H. Chaney. "Determination of Content for a Collegiate Course in Intercultural Business Communication by Three Delphi Panels." *Journal of Business Communication* 29.3 (1992): 267–83.

Martin, Justin. "Changing Jobs? Try the Net." *Fortune* 2 Mar. 1998: 205+.

———. "So, You Want to Work for the Best . . ." *Fortune* 12 Jan. 1998: 77–78.

Martin, Maurice, "Mars Needs Technical Communications." *INTERCOM* Jul./Aug. 2000: 3.

Matson, Eric. "(Search) Engines." *Fast Company* Oct./Nov. 1997: 249–52.

———. "The Seven Sins of Deadly Meetings." *Fast Company* Oct./Nov. 1997: 27–31.

Mayer, R. E. "When Less Is More: Meaningful Learning from Visual and Verbal Summaries of Science Textbook Lessons." *Journal of Educational Psychology* 88 (1996): 64–73.

McDonald, Kim A. "Covering Physics." *A Field Guide for Science Writers.* Eds. Deborah Blum and Mary Knudson. New York: Oxford, 1997. 188–95.

———. "Some Physicists Criticize Research Purporting to Show Links between Low-Level Electromagnetic Fields and Cancer." *Chronicle of Higher Education* 3 May 1991, sec. A: 5+.

McGuire, Gene. "Shared Minds: A Model of Collaboration." *Technical Communication* 39.3 (1992): 467–68.

Melymuka, Kathleen. "Not Another #$|&|$ Survey!" *Computerworld* 24 Nov. 1997: 82.

Menz, Mary. "Clip Art Comes of Age." *INTERCOM* May 1997: 4–8.

Merritt, Jennifer. "For MBAs, Soul-Searching 101." *Business Week* 16 Sept. 2002: 64–66.

———. "You Mean Cheating Is Wrong?" *Business Week* 9 Dec. 2002: 8.

Meyer, Benjamin D. "The ABCs of New-Look Publications." *Technical Communication* 33.1 (1986): 13–20.

Meyerson, Moe. "Grand Illusions." *Inc. Tech* 2 (1997): 35–36.

Microsoft Word User's Guide: Word Processing Program for the Macintosh, Version 5.0. Redmond, WA: Microsoft Corporation, 1992.

Miller, Julie. "Trade Journals." *A Handbook for Science Writers.* Eds. Deborah Blum and Mary Knudson. New York: Oxford, 1997. 27–30.

Mirel, Barbara, Susan Feinberg, and Leif Allmendinger. "Designing Manuals for Active Learning Styles." *Technical Communication* 38.1 (1991): 75–87.

Mirsky, Steve. "Wonderful Town." *Scientific American* July 1996: 29.

"Misconduct Scandal Shakes German Science." *Professional Ethics Report* [American Assoc. for the Advancement of Science] X3 (Summer 1997): 2.

Mokhiber, Russell. "Crime in the Suites." *Greenpeace* May 1989: 14–16.

Monastersky, Richard. "Courting Reliable Science." *Science News* 153.16 (1998): 249–51.

———. "Do Clouds Provide a Greenhouse Thermostat?" *Science News* 142.16 (1992): 69.

Monmonier, Mark. *Cartographies of Danger: Mapping Hazards in America.* Chicago: U of Chicago P, 1997.

Morgan, Meg. "Patterns of Composing: Connections between Classroom and Workplace Collaborations." *Technical Communication* 38.4 (1991): 540–42.

Morgenson, Gretchen. "Would Uncle Sam Lie to You?" *Worth* Nov. 1994: 53+.

Morse, June. "Hypertext—What Can We Expect?" *INTERCOM* Feb. 1992: 6–7.

Munger, David. Unpublished review of *Technical Writing.* 7th ed.

Munger, Roger H. "Finding Proposal Money for Nonprofits." *INTERCOM* June 2001: 28–30.

Munter, Mary. "Meeting Technology: From Low-Tech to High-Tech. *Business Communication Quarterly* 61.2 (1998): 80–87.

Murphy, Kate. "Separating Ballyhoo from Breakthrough." *Business Week* 13 July 1998: 143.

Nakache, Patricia. "Is It Time to Start Bragging about Yourself?" *Fortune* 27 Oct. 1997: 287–88.

Nantz, Karen S., and Cynthia L. Drexel. "Incorporating Electronic Mail with the Business Communication Course." *Business Communication Quarterly* 58.3 (1995): 45–51.

National Institutes of Health. "Study to Prove How Healthy Younger Adults Make Use of Genetic Tests." *NIH News.* 3 May 2007. Online. 4 May 2007 <www.nih.gov/news>.

Neergaard, Lauran. "U.S. Adults Face 'Health Literacy' Crisis." Associated Press Wire story. April 8, 2004 <http://www.miami.com/mid/miamiherald/living/health/8389092.htm7lc>.

Nielsen, Jakob. "Be Succinct! (Writing for the Web)." 15 Mar. 1997. Alertbox. 8 Aug. 1998 <www.useit.com/alertbox/9710.a.html>.

———. "Global Web: Driving the International Network Economy." Apr. 1998. Alertbox. 8 Aug. 1998 <www.useit.com/alertbox/9710a.html>.

———. "How Users Read on the Web." Oct. Alertbox. 8 Aug. 1998 <www.useit.com/alertbox/9710a.html>.

———. International Web Usability." Aug. 1996. Alertbox. 8 Aug. 1998 <www.useit.com/alertbox/9710a.html>.

———. "Inverted Pyramids in Cyberspace." June 1996. Alertbox. 8 Aug. 1998 <www.useit. com/alertbox/9710a.html>.

———. "Top Ten Web Design Mistakes of 2003." Alertbox. 12 May 2004 <www.uselt.com/alertbox/20031222.html>.

Nelson, Sandra J., and Douglas C. Smith. "Maximizing Cohesion and Minimizing Conflict in Collaborative Writing Groups." *Bulletin of the Association for Business Communication* 53.2 (1990): 59–62.

Nordenberg, Tamar. "Direct to You: TV Drug Ads That Make Sense." *FDA Consumer* Jan./Feb. 1998: 7–10.

Notkins, Abner L. "New Predictors of Disease." *Scientific American* March 2007: 72–79.

Nunberg, G. "The Trouble with PowerPoint." *Fortune* 20 Dec. 1999: 330–34.

Nydell, Margaret K. *Understanding Arabs: A Guide for Westerners.* New York: Logan, 1987.

Office of Technology Assessment. *Harmful Non-Indigenous Species in the United States.* Washington, DC: GPO, 1993.

"On Line." *Chronicle of Higher Education* 21 Sept. 1992, sec. A: 29.

"Online Health Companies Announce New Set of Ethics and Privacy Guidelines." *Professional Ethics Report* [American Association for the Advancement of Science] XIII.2 (Spring 2000): 3–4.

Ornatowski, Cezar M. "Between Efficiency and Politics: Rhetoric and Ethics in Technical Writing." *Technical Communication Quarterly* 1.1 (1992): 91–103.

Ostrander, Elaine L. "Usability Evaluations: Rationale, Methods, and Guidelines." *INTERCOM* June 1999: 18–21.

Oxfeld, Jesse. "Analyze This." *Brill's Content* Mar. 2000: 105–06.

Parrish, Deborah. "The Scientific Misconduct Definition and Falsification of Credentials." *Professional Ethics Report* [American Assoc. for the Advancement of Science] IX.4 (1996): 1+.

Parsons, Gerald M. Review of *Technical Writing.* 6th ed. *Journal of Technical Writing and Communication* 25.3 (1995): 322–24.

Pearce, C. Glenn, Iris W. Johnson, and Randolph T. Barker. "Enhancing the Student Listening Skills and Environment." *Business Communication Quarterly* 58.4 (Dec. 1995): 28–33.

"People, Performance, Profits." *Forbes* 20 Oct. 1997: 57.

"Performance Appraisal—Discrimination." *The Employee Problem Solver.* Ramsey, NJ: Alexander Hamilton Institute, 2000.

Perloff, Richard M. *The Dynamics of Persuasion.* Hillsdale, NJ: Erlbaum, 1993.

Peters, Tom. "The New Wired World of Work." *Business Week* 28 Aug. 2000: 172–74.

Petroski, Henry. *Invention by Design.* Cambridge, MA: Harvard UP, 1996.

Peyser, Marc, and Steve Rhodes. "When E-Mail Is Oops-Mail." *Newsweek* 16 Oct. 1995: 82.

Phillips, John I. *How to Think about Statistics.* New York: Freeman, 2000.

Pinelli, Thomas E., et al., "A Survey of Typography, Graphic Design, and Physical Media in Technical Reports." *Technical Communication* 32.2 (1986): 75–80.

Plumb, Carolyn, and Jan H. Spyridakis, "Survey Research in Technical Communication: Designing and Administering Questionnaires." *Technical Communication* 39.4 (1992): 625–38.

Pool, Robert. "When Failure Is Not an Option." *Technology Review* July 1997: 38–45.

Porter, James E. "Truth in Technical Advertising: A Case Study." *IEEE Transactions on Professional Communication* 33.3 (1987): 182–89.

Powell, Corey S. "Science in Court." *Scientific American* October 1997: 32+.

Publication Manual of the American Psychological Association, 5th ed. Washington, DC: American Psychological Association, 2001.

Pugliano, Fiore. Unpublished review of *Technical Writing*, 5th ed.

Raeburn, Paul. "Warning: Biotech Is Hurting Itself." *Business Week* 20 Dec. 1999: 78.

Raloff, Janet. "Chocolate Hearts: Yummy and Good Medicine?" *Science News* 157.12 (2000): 188–89.

Rao, Srikumar. "Diaper-Beer Syndrome." *Forbes* 9 Apr. 1998: 128.

Read Me First!: A Style Guide for the Computer Industry. Palo Alto, CA: Sun Microsystems Press, 2003.

Redish, Janice C., and David A. Schell. "Writing and Testing Instructions for Usability." *Technical Writing: Theory and Practice.* Eds. Bertie E. Fearing and W. Keats Sparrow. New York: Modern Language Assn., 1989. 61–71.

Redish, Janice C., et al. "Making Information Accessible to Readers." *Writing in Nonacademic Settings.* Eds. Lee Odell and Dixie Goswami. New York: Guilford, 1985.

Reichard, Kevin, "Web-Site Watchdogs." *Internet World* Dec. 1997: 106+.

Reinhardt, Andy. "From Gearhead to Grand High Poo-Bah." *Business Week* 28 Aug. 2000: 129–30.

Rensberger, Boyce. "Covering Science for Newspapers." *A Field Guide for Science Writers.* Eds. Deborah Blum and Mary Knudson. New York: Oxford, 1997. 7–16.

Research Triangle Institute. *Consequences of Whistleblowing for the Whistleblower in Misconduct in Science Cases.* (Report prepared for the Office of Research Integrity.) Washington: ORI, 1995.

Rifkin, William, and Brian Martin. "Negotiating Expert Status: Who Gets Taken Seriously." *IEEE Technology and Society Magazine* (Spring 1997): 30–39.

Riney, Larry A. *Technical Writing for Industry.* Englewood Cliffs: Prentice, 1989.

Ritzenthaler, Gary, and David H. Ostroff. "The Web and Corporate Communication: Potentials and Pitfalls." *IEEE Transactions on Professional Communication* 39.1 (1996): 16–20.

Robart, Kay. "Submitting Résumés via E-Mail." *INTERCOM* July/Aug. 1998: 13–14.

Robinson, Edward A. "Beware—Job Seekers Have No Secrets." *Fortune* 29 Dec. 1997: 285.

Rokeach, Milton. *The Nature of Human Values.* New York: Free, 1973.

Rosman, Katherine. "Finding Drug Ties at a Medical Mag." *Brill's Content* Mar. 2000: 100.

Ross, Philip E. "Enjoy It While It Lasts." *Forbes* 27 July 1998: 206.

———. "Lies, Damned Lies, and Medical Statistics." *Forbes* 14 Aug. 1995: 130–35.

Ross, Raymond S. *Understanding Persuasion*. 3rd ed. Englewood Cliffs: Prentice, 1990.

Ross-Flanigan, Nancy. "The Virtues (and Vices) of Virtual Collaboration." *Technology Review* Mar./Apr. 1998: 50–59.

Rottenberg, Annette T. *Elements of Argument*. 3rd ed. New York: St. Martin's, 1991.

Rowland, D. *Japanese Business Etiquette: A Practical Guide to Success with the Japanese*. New York: Warner, 1985.

Ruggiero, Vincent R. *The Art of Thinking*. 3rd ed. New York: Harper, 1991.

———. *The Art of Thinking*. 8th ed. New York: Longman, 2006.

Ruhs, Michael A. "Usability Testing: A Definition Analyzed." *Boston Broadside* [Newsletter of the Soc. for Technical Communication] May/June 1992: 8+.

Sabath, Ann Marie. *Business Etiquette: 101 Ways to Conduct Business with Charm and Savvy*. Franklin Lakes, NJ: Career Press, 1998.

Samuelson, Robert J. "The Endless Paper Chase." *Newsweek* 1 Dec. 1997: 53.

———. "Merchants of Mediocrity." *Newsweek* 1 Aug. 1994: 44.

Savan, Leslie. "Truth in Advertising?" *Brill's Content* March 2000: 62+.

Schafer, Sarah. "Is Your Data Safe?" *Inc.* Feb. 1997: 93–97.

Schein, Edgar H. "How Can Organizations Learn Faster? The Challenge of Entering the Green Room." *Strategies for Success: Core Capabilities for Today's Managers*. Boston: Sloan Management Review Assoc., 1996. 34–39.

Schenk, Margaret T., and James K. Webster. *Engineering Information Resources*. New York: Decker, 1984.

Schrage, Michael. "Time for Face Time." *Fast Company* Oct./Nov. 1997: 232.

Schwartz, Marilyn, et al. *Guidelines for Bias-Free Writing*. Bloomington: Indiana UP, 1995.

Scott, James C. "Dear ???—Understanding British Forms of Address." *Business Communication Quarterly* 61.3 (1998): 50–61.

Scott, James C., and Diana J. Green. "British Perspectives on Organizing Bad-News Letters: Organizational Patterns Used by Major U.K. Companies." *Bulletin of the Association for Business Communication* 55.1 (1992): 17–19.

Seglin, Jeffrey L. "Would You Lie to Save Your Company?" *Inc.* July 1998: 53+.

Seligman, Dan. "Gender Mender." *Forbes* 6 Apr. 1998: 72+.

Selzer, Jack. "Composing Processes for Technical Discourse." *Technical Writing: Theory and Practice*. Eds. Bertie E. Fearing and W. Keats Sparrow. New York: Modern Language Assn., 1989. 43–50.

Senge, Peter M. "The Leader's New York: Building Learning Organizations." *Sloan Management Review* 32.1 (Fall 1990): 1–17.

Seppa, Nathan. "Broken Arms Way Up." *Science News* 164.14 (2003): 221.

Shedroff, Nathan. "Information Interaction Design: A Unified Field Theory of Design." *Information Design*. Ed. Robert Jacobson. Cambridge, MA: MIT Press, 2000. 267–92.

Shenk, David. "Data Smog: Surviving the Information Glut." *Technology Review* May/June 1997: 18–26.

Sherblom, John C., Claire F. Sullivan, and Elizabeth C. Sherblom, "The What, the Whom, and the Hows of Survey Research," *Bulletin of the Association for Business Communication* 56:12 (1993): 58–64.

Sherif, Muzapher, et al. *Attitude and Attitude Change: The Social Judgment-Involvement Approach*. Philadelphia: Saunders, 1965.

Sittenfeld, Curtis. "Good Ways to Deliver Bad News." *Fast Company* Apr. 1999: 88+.

Sklaroff, Sara, and Michael Ash. "American Pie Charts." *Civilization* April/May 1997: 84–85.

Smart, Karl L., Matthew E. Whiting, and Kristen Bell DeTienne. "Assessing the Need for Printed and Online Documentation: A Study of Customer Preference and Use." *Journal of Business Communication* 38.3 (2001): 285–314.

Smith, Gary. "Eleven Commandments for Business Meeting Etiquette." *INTERCOM* Feb. 2000: 29.

Snyder, Joel. "Finding It on Your Own." *Internet World* June 1995: 89–90.

Sowell, Thomas. "Magic Numbers." *Forbes* 20 Oct. 1997: 120.

Spencer, SueAnn. "Use Self-Help to Improve Document Usability." *Technical Communication* 43.1 (1996): 73–77.

Spyridakis, Jan H. "Conducting Research in Technical Communication: The Application of True Experimental Design." *Technical Communication* 39.4 (1992): 607–24.

Spyridakis, Jan H., and Michael J. Wenger. "Writing for Human Performance: Relating Reading Research to Document Design." *Technical Communication* 39.2 (1992): 202–15.

St. Amant, Kirk R. "Resource and Strategies for Successful International Communication." *INTERCOM* Sept./Oct. 2000: 12–14.

Stanton, Mike. "Fiber Optics." *Occupational Outlook Quarterly* (Winter 1984): 27–30.

Stedman, Craig. "Data Mining for Fool's Gold." *Computerworld* 1 Dec. 1997: 1+.

Stemmer, John. "Citing Internet Sources." 4 Mar. 1997. Online. Political Science Research and Teaching List. 22 April 1997 <polpsrt@h—met.msu.edu>.

Stepanek, Marcia. "When in Beijing, Mum's the Word." *Business Week* 13 July 1998: 4.

Stevenson, Richard W. "Workers Who Turn in Bosses Use Law to Seek Big Rewards." *New York Times* 10 July 1989, sec. A: 7.

Stix, Gary. "Plant Matters: How Do You Regulate an Herb?" *Scientific American* Feb. 1998: 30+.

Stone, Peter H. "Forecast Cloudy: The Limits of Global Warming Models." *Technology Review* Feb./Mar. 1992: 32–40.

Stonecipher, Harry. *Editorial and Persuasive Writing.* New York: Hastings, 1979.

Sturges, David L. "Internationalizing the Business Communication Curriculum." *Bulletin of the Association for Business Communication* 55.1 (1992): 30–39.

"Sunday Sermons." *Scientific American* Feb. 2003: 26.

Task Force on High-Performance Work and Workers. *Spanning the Chasm: Corporate and Academic Preparation to Improve Work-Force Preparation.* Report. Washington, DC: Business-Higher Education Forum, Jan. 1997.

Taubes, Gary. "Telling Time by the Second Hand." *Technology Review* May/June 1998: 76–78.

Taylor, John R. *Introduction to Error Analysis.* 2nd ed. Sausalito, CA: University Science Books, 1997.

Teague, John H. "Marketing on the World Wide Web." *Technical Communication* 42.2 (1995): 236–42.

Templeton, Brad. "10 Big Myths about Copyright Explained." 29 Nov. 1994. Online. 6 May 1995 <www.law/copyright/FAQ/myths/part1>.

"Testing Your Documents." 16 Apr. 2001. Online. *Plain English Network.* 8 May 2007 <www.plainlanguage.gov/howto/test.htm>.

Thatcher, Barry. "Cultural and Rhetorical Adaptation for South American Audiences." *Technical Communication* 46.2 (1999): 177–95.

"The Art of the Online Résumé." *Business Week* 7 May 2007: 86.

"The Big Picture." *Business Week* 6 Nov. 2000: 14.

Thrush, Emily A. "Bridging the Gap: Technical Communication in an Intercultural and Multicultural Society." *Technical Communication Quarterly* 2.3 (1993): 271–83.

Timmerman, Peter D., and Wayne Harrison. "The Discretionary Use of Electronic Media: Four Considerations for Bad-News Bearers." *Journal of Business Communication* 42.4 (2005): 379–89.

Trafford, Abigail. "Critical Coverage of Public Health and Government." *A Field Guide for Science Writers.* Eds. Deborah Blum and Mary Knudson. New York: Oxford, 1997. 131–41.

Tufte, Edward R. *The Cognitive Style of PowerPoint.* Cheshire, CT: Graphics Press, 2003.

Turner, John R. "Online Use Raises New Ethical Issues." *INTERCOM* Sept. 1995: 5+.

Unger, Stephen H. *Controlling Technology: Ethics and the Responsible Engineer.* New York: Holt, 1982.

U.S. Air Force Academy. *Executive Writing Course.* Washington, DC: GPO, 1981.

U.S. Bureau of Land Management. *Plain Language.* 10 April 2004. Online. 7 May 2007 <www.blm.gov/nhp/NPR>.

U.S. Department of Commerce. *Statistical Abstract of the United States.* Washington, DC: GPO, 1994, 1997, 2000, 2003, 2007.

U.S. Department of Labor. *Tips for Finding the Right Job.* Washington, DC: GPO, 1993.

———. *Tomorrow's Jobs.* Washington, DC: GPO, 2000.

U.S. General Services Administration. *Your Rights to Federal Records.* Washington, DC: GPO, 1995.

"Using Icons as Communication." *Simply Stated* [Newsletter of the Document Design Center, American Institutes for Research] 75 (Sept./Oct. 1987): 1+.

van der Meij, Hans. "The ISTE Approach to Usability Testing." *IEEE Transactions on Professional Communication* 40.3 (1997): 209–23.

van der Meij, Hans, and John M. Carroll. "Principles and Heuristics for Designing Minimalist Instruction." *Technical Communication* 42.2 (1995): 243–61.

Van Pelt, William. Unpublished review of *Technical Writing.* 3rd ed.

Varchaver, Nicholas. "The Perils of E-mail." *Fortune* Feb. 17, 2003: 96–102.

Varner, Iris I., and Carson H. Varner. "Legal Issues in Business Communications." *Journal of the American Association for Business Communication* 46.3 (1983): 31–40.

Vaughan, David K. "Abstracts and Summaries: Some Clarifying Distinctions." *Technical Writing Teacher* 18:2 (1991): 132–41.

Velotta, Christopher. "How to Design and Implement a Questionnaire." *Technical Communication* 38.3 (1991): 387–92.

Victor, David A. *International Business Communication.* New York: Harper, 1992.

"Vital Signs." *Internet World* Jan. 1998: 18.

"Vitamin C under Attack." *University of California at Berkeley Wellness Letter* 14.10 (1998): 1.

"Walking to Health." *Harvard Men's Watch* 2.12 (1998): 3–4.

Wallich, Paul. "Not So Blind, After All." *Scientific American* May 1996: 20+.

Walter, Charles, and Thomas F. Marsteller. "Liability for the Dissemination of Defective Information." *IEEE Transactions on Professional Communication* 30.3 (1987): 164–67.

Wandycz, Katarzyna. "Damn Yankees." *Forbes* 10 March, 1997: 22–23.

Wang, Linda. "Veggies Prevent Cancer through Key Protein." *Science News* 159.12 (2001): 182.

Warshaw, Michael. "Have You Been House-Trained?" *Fast Company* Oct. 1998: 46+.

Weinstein, Edith K. Unpublished review of *Technical Writing*. 5th ed.

Weiss, Edmond H. *How to Write a Usable User Manual*. Philadelphia: ISI, 1985.

"Wellness Facts." *University of California at Berkeley Wellness Letter* 14.10 (1998): 1.

Weymouth, L. C. "Establishing Quality Standards and Trade Regulations for Technical Writing in World Trade." *Technical Communication* 37.2 (1990): 143–47.

White, Jan. *Color for the Electronic Age*. New York: Watson-Guptill, 1990.

———. *Editing by Design*. 2nd ed. New York: Bowker, 1982.

———. *Great Pages*. El Segundo, CA: Serif, 1990.

———. *Visual Design for the Electronic Age*. New York: Watson-Guptill, 1988.

Wickens, Christopher D. *Engineering Psychology and Human Performance*. 3rd ed. New York: Pearson, 1999.

Wiggins, Richard. "The Word Electric." *Internet World* Sept. 1995: 31–34.

Wight, Eleanor, "How Creativity Turns Facts into Usable Information." *Technical Communication* 32.1 (1985): 9–12.

Williams, Robert I. "Playing with Format, Style, and Reader Assumptions." *Technical Communication* 30.3 (1983): 11–13.

Wojahn, Patricia G. "Computer-Mediated Communication: The Great Equalizer between Men and Women?" *Technical Communication* 41.4 (1994): 747–51.

Woodhouse, E. J., and Dean Nieusma. "When Expert Advice Works and When It Does Not." *IEEE Technology and Society Magazine* Spring 1997: 23–29.

Wriston, Walter. *The Twilight of Sovereignty*. New York: Scribner's, 1992.

Writing User-Friendly Documents. Washington, DC: U.S. Bureau of Land Management, 2001.

Wurman, Richard Saul. *Information Anxiety*. New York: Doubleday, 1989.

Yen, Hope. "9/11 Panel: FAA Downplayed Suicide Hijacking." [Associated Press] *The Recorder* [Greenfield, MA] 28 Jan. 2004: 7.

Yoos, George. "A Revision of the Concept of Ethical Appeal." *Philosophy and Rhetoric* 12.4 (1979): 41–58.

Young, Patrick. "Writing Articles for Science Journals." *A Field Guide for Science Writers*. Eds. Deborah Blum and Mary Knudson. New York: Oxford, 1997. 110–16.

Zibell, Kristin J. "Usable Information through User-Centered Design." *INTERCOM* Dec. 1999: 12–14.

INDEX

Abbreviations, 694–695
Abstract terms, 238
Abstracts, 131. *See also* Summaries
　citation of, 645
　descriptive, 184
　documentation of, 565
　executive, 184–186, 603
　for formal report, 603–604
　informative, 183–184
Academic tone, 242
Accessibility
　audience needs in, 27–28
　elements of, 2–5
　features of, 5
　legal accountability and, 5
　in Web site usability, 427, 436–437
Accountability, legal, 5
Acronym use, 234, 444
Active listening, 103–105
Active voice, 218–221, 241, 503
Address, in business letter, 362
Adjustment letters, 381–384
Advertising
　deceptive, 86
　marketing literature, 482–485
Affirmative phrasing, for instructional documents, 505
Age-appropriate usage, 245
Aggregator, 353
Almanacs, 129
Alphanumeric notation, 198–199
Analysis
　causal, 562
　comparative, 562–563
　feasibility, 563–564, 566
　purpose of, 561–562
Analytical reports. *See also* Reports
　case study for, 583–592
　checklist for, 594–595
　conclusions and recommendations in, 567–569
　data amount in, 564–565, 567

defined, 327
elements of, 564–571
ethical implications, 561
feasibility reports, 338–341
goal identification in, 564
guidelines for, 593–594
justification reports, 341–345
legal implications, 561
outline for, 571–583
personal bias and, 567
recommendation reports, 341, 342–343
self-assessment and, 569, 571
supplements in, 583
visuals in, 567, 568
APA documentation style
　books, 657–658
　electronic sources, 662–664
　miscellaneous sources, 660–662
　parenthetical references, 655–656
　periodicals, 658–659
　sample reference list, 664–665
Apostrophes, 687–688
Appendices, 605–606
Applicant screening process, 409
Aptitude assessment, for job search, 389–390
Area graph, 267, 268
Arguable claims, 379–381
Arguments. *See also* Persuasion
　contradictory, of experts, 120
　defined, 50
　guidelines for, 66–67
　shaping, 67–70
Art brief, 278
Articles, index of, 130
Ascender, typeface, 310
ASCII résumés, 411
Assumptions, in research, 156–157
Attention line, 364

Audience
　assessment of needs of, 27–28
　communication constraints and, 59
　connecting with, 53–54
　differing expectations of, 26–27
　expectations of, 2
　feedback from, 42
　importance of knowing, 45
　multiple users in
　　document technicality for, 31–32
　　Web-based documents for, 33
　of oral presentations, 625
　in page design, 317
　of personal statement, 709–710
　persuasion of, 51–52
　predicting reaction of, 51
　primary and secondary, 31–32
　for proposals, 523–524, 534–535
　resistance of, 51–52
　for specifications, 479, 481
　technicality levels and, 28–32
　variation in standards of proof, 155–158
　in visuals selection, 257, 260, 291
　in Web site design, 432
Audience and use profile
　for analytical report, 583–584
　components of, 34–38
　example of, 39
　form for, 70
　for instructional document, 508
　for oral presentation, 610
　for process description, 476
　for proposal, 544–545
　for technical definitions, 449, 451
　for technical descriptions, 472
Authority, in acceptance of appeal, 60
Automated editing tools, 247
Averages, undefined, 162–163

Background checks, in employment process, 409
Bad news, conveying, 372–373
Band graph, 267, 268
Bar graphs, 260–266, 262–265
  guidelines for displaying, 265–266
  unethical distortion of, 289
  uses for, 255
Behavior
  emotional reaction to persuasion, 59–60
  listening, 104
  team conflict sources, 101–103
Bias
  in analytical report, 567
  in company literature, 146
  in direct observation, 146
  in meta-analysis, 165
  in online database content, 128
  personal, 157, 242–243, 567
  in questionnaires, 143
  of research sources, 117, 119
  of special-interest Web sites, 151
  underlying assumptions as, 156–157
Bibliographic databases
  hard copy, 128
  online, 127
Block diagrams, 276, 277, 278
Block format, 365, 367
Block pattern, 593–594
Blogs
  in electronic collaboration, 108
  external, 353
  internal, 352
  RSS feeds, 353, 354
  as source, 124–125
  vs. wikis, 352
Body, of document, 197, 508
  in analytical report, 572–581
  in proposal, 541–543
Boilerplate document, 301
Boldface type, 312
Book indexes, 130
Books, citation of
  APA style, 657–658
  CSE style, 668
  MLA style, 642–644
Brackets, 690–691

Brainstorming, 105, 703–704
Brainwriting, 106
Brochures
  instructional, 491, 492
  as technical communication, 6
  technical marketing, 482–484
Bulletin boards, Internet, 124
Business letters. *See* Letters

Capitalization, 311, 695–696
Card catalogs, 129
Causal analysis, 562
Causal relationships, 161
Causation
  defined, 164
  faulty reasoning on, 158–161
  vs. correlation, 164
Cause-effect relationships, 161, 593
Cause-to-effect sequence, 209
CD-ROM, 127, 320
Certainty levels, 156
Chalkboards, 618
Charts, 255, 269–274
Checklists
  for analytical reports, 594–595
  for email, 351
  for ethical communication, 90
  for instructional documents, 517
  for memo reports, 345–346
  for oral presentations, 631
  for page design, 321
  for persuasion, 71
  for proofreading, 22
  for proposals, 556
  for research process, 170
  for résumés, 422
  for style, 248
  for summaries, 187
  for technical definitions, 457
  for technical descriptions, 485
  for usability, 43
  for visuals, 293
Chronological sequence, 208, 469
Chunking, 211–212
Citation indexes, 130
Citations. *See* Documentation of sources
Claim letter, 377–381

Claims, 49
  exaggerating, 80
  in proposals, 535–536
  supporting, 60–63, 68–69
Clarity
  editing for, 217–222, 248
  vs. bluntness, 56
  vs. oversimplification, 5
Classification, in document organization, 195
Classroom, usability testing in, 514
Clichés, 234–235
Clinical trials, 167
Clip art, 283
Closed-ended questions, 142
Closing summary, 183
Clutter words, 228
Collaborative work
  active listening in, 103–105
  brainstorming in, 105
  brainwriting in, 106
  conducting meetings, 98, 101
  conflict management in, 103
  conflict sources in, 101–103
  creative thinking in, 105–106
  credit sharing in, 109
  design plan importance to, 38
  ethical abuses in, 109
  evaluation of members in, 99
  face-to-face vs. electronically mediated, 108–109
  group dynamics in, 78–79
  meeting minutes in, 337
  peer review and editing in, 107–108
  project management in, 97–98
  project planning form, 99
  in workplace communication, 15, 17–18
  writing process in, 110
Collaborative writing, 110
Colloquialisms, 246
Colon, 682–683
Color density chart, 288
Color use in visuals, 283–288
Comma splicing, 673
Commas, 683–686
Common knowledge, 639
Communication constraints, 56–59

Communication in the workplace
constraints on, 56–59
creative and critical thinking in,
18–21
due dates for, 38
ethical
checklist for, 90
constraints on, 58
guidelines for, 92
key tasks in, 15–18
legal guidelines on, 85–87
proofreading, 21–23
unethical
causes of, 77–79
examples of, 79–82
groupthink in, 78–79
recognizing, 76–77
usability issues in, 26–27
in "virtual" setting, 23
Communication styles
cultural differences in, 9–10
perception of American, 10
in team conflict, 102–103
usability and, 36
Community discussion groups,
Internet, 124
Compact discs, 127
Company style guides, 301–302
Comparative analysis, 562–563
Comparison-contrast, in technical
definitions, 447–448
Comparison-contrast sequence,
210–211
Complaint letter, 377–381
Complex table, 259
Complimentary closings, 363
Computer model fallibility, 165
Computer projection, 619
Computer scannable résumé, 410,
411, 412
Conciseness, editing for, 223–228,
248
Conclusion, 197, 508, 543,
581–582
Conclusive answer, vs. probable or
inconclusive answer, 156
Concrete terms, 238
Conference proceedings indexes,
131
Confidential sources, 639

Conflict management, 103
Conflicts of interest
in ethical judgment-making, 82
hiding, 80
Confounding factors, 164
Connection strategies, 53–54
Consistency, in acceptance of
appeal, 60
Constraints on communication,
56–59
Content
accessibility of, 5
in instructional documents,
495–496, 517
in proposals, 556
in summaries, 187
in technical definitions, 457
in technical descriptions, 485
usability checklist on, 43
in Web site usability, 427, 437
Contractions, 240, 688
Contributor citation, 538
Convergence, 6–7
Conversational delivery method,
612
Cookies, 435
Coordinating conjunctions,
675–676
Copyright
defined, 132
on electronic form information,
134
on email communication, 348
on hard copy information,
132–133
international, 133
workplace applications, 86
Corporate blogs, 352–354
Correlation
defined, 164
vs. causation, 164
Correspondence. *See* Employment
correspondence; Letters
Cover page, 598
Creative thinking
in collaborative teamwork,
105–106
defined, 18
in workplace communication,
18–21

Criteria, for ranking competing
items, 164
Critical thinking
about recommendations, 570
defined, 18
in research question development, 116
in workplace communication,
18–21
in writing process, 699
CSE documentation style
books, 668
discipline-specific manuals on,
665
numbered citations in, 667
periodicals, 668–669
Cultural factors. *See also* Interpersonal considerations
in acceptance of appeal, 60
analyzing, 64
communication style and, 9–10
in document organization, 200
in editing choices, 245–246
exploiting, in unethical communication, 81–82
generalization of, 65
in icon use, 283
imperative mood and, 504
oral presentations and, 629
in page design, 317
in persuasion style selection, 56,
63–65, 71
profile on users', 36
in salutation, 362
in standards of proof variation,
158
in team conflict, 102–103
in typeface selection, 309
usability checklist on, 43
in usability expectations, 26–27
in visuals use, 290, 292
in Web site design, 433
Cutaway diagrams, 256, 276, 277

Dangling modifier, 678–679
Dashes, 691
Data falsification, 80
Data mining, 164
Database networks, 128

Databases
  evaluation of, 151
  search of library, 125
  types of, 127–128
Deception, laws prohibiting, 85
Deceptive advertising laws, 86
Deceptive reporting, 167–168
Decimal notation, 199
Definitions. *See also* Technical
  definitions
  expanded, 442–443
  parenthetical, 441
  sentence, 442
Delivery method in oral presenta-
  tions, 611–612
Dependent clause, 676–677
Descender, typeface, 310
Description. *See* Technical descrip-
  tion
Descriptive abstract, 184
Design plan. *See also* Page design
  creation of, 38–41
  defined, 38
Desktop publishing, 301
Desktop publishing network, 23
Deviation bar graph, 263, 264
Deviation line graph, 267, 268
Diagrams, 256, 276–278
Dictionaries, 129
Digital format, vs. hard-copy,
  327
Digital whiteboard, 108
Direct address, 503
Direct organizing pattern
  in business letters, 371
  in memos, 330–331
Direct quotations, 636
Directories, 129
Distribution notation, 365
Document elements. *See also*
  specific document types
  abstract for, 603–604
  appendices, 605–606
  cover page, 598
  glossary, 604–605
  letter of transmittal, 598, 600,
    601
  table of contents, 601, 602, 603
  tables and figures list, 603
  title page, 598, 599

Document organization
  chunking, 211–212
  classification in, 195
  cultural factors in, 200
  outlining, 196–200
  overview of, 212–213
  paragraphing, 204–207
  partitions, 195
  report design worksheet, 200,
    201–202
  sequencing in, 207–211
  storyboarding, 200, 203
Documentation of sources, 87
  in abstracts, 565
  APA style
    books, 657–658
    electronic sources, 662–664
    miscellaneous sources,
      660–662
    parenthetical references,
      655–656
    periodicals, 658–659
    sample reference list, 664–665
  citation indexes and, 130
  common knowledge, 639
  confidential sources, 639
  CSE style
    books, 668
    discipline-specific manuals on,
      665
    numbered citations in, 667
    periodicals, 668–669
  decision making in, 638–639
  in formal reports, 606
  Internet, 126
  MLA style
    books, 642–644
    electronic sources, 648–651
    miscellaneous sources,
      645–448
    parenthetical references,
      640–641
    periodicals, 644–645
    sample works cited page,
      652–654
  paraphrases, 638
  in proposals, 538–539
  quotations, 636–638
  in research process, 635
Domain, Web site, 153

Dossier, for employment, 415
Downloadable images, 282–283
Due dates, 38

Economic Espionage Act (1996),
  86
Editing. *See also* Style
  active voice, 218–221
  automated tools for, 247
  for clarity, 217–222
  clutter words, 228
  in collaborative teamwork,
    107–108
  for conciseness, 223–228
  cultural context in, 245–246
  for exact words, 232–238
  for fluency, 228–232
  modifiers, 217–218
  nominalizations, 226–227
  overstuffed sentences, 222
  passive voice, 221–222
  of photographs, 281–282
  positive vs. negative expressions,
    227–228
  prepositions, 226
  pronouns, 217
  punctuation. *See* Punctuation
    marks
  qualifiers, 228–229
  revisions, 249
  sentence construction, 231–232
  sentence errors. *See* Sentence
    errors
  for tone, 238–244
  weak verbs, 225
  word order, 218–219
  wordiness, 223–225
Editing cycle, 733
Editing tools, 247
Effect-to-cause sequence, 208–209
Electronic communication. *See
  also* Email
  blogs and wikis, 352–354
  employee monitoring, 436
  instant messaging, 351–352
  as "new" media, 6–7
  unethical, 81
  vs. face-to-face, in collaborative
    teamwork, 108–109

Electronic information sources
  citation of
    APA style, 662–664
    MLA style, 648–651
  compact discs, 127
  copyright protection for, 134
  evaluation of, 151
  Internet-based, 123–127
  manual search of abstracts on, 123
  online retrieval services, 127–128
  pros and cons of, 123
Electronic Privacy Act (1986), 348
Electronic publishing, 301
Electronic theft laws, 86
Ellipses use, 636, 689
Email
  benefits of, 347–348
  checklist for, 351
  copyright and, 134, 348
  elements of, 347
  guidelines for, 349–350
  inquiries by, 377
  PDF files and, 320
  privacy issues, 348–349
  résumés submission by, 411
  in team collaboration, 108
  as technical communication, 5
  vs. alternative media, 350
Email lists, 125
Email résumés, 411
Embedded list, 307, 691
Emphasis
  color for, 287
  contractions and, 240
  highlighting for, 311–312
  positive vs. negative, 230–231
  short sentences for, 232
  visual distortion for, 290
  word order for, 218–219
Emphatic sentence, 209
Employees
  online monitoring of, 436
  privacy laws and, 86
  whistle-blowing by, 88–90
Employment and job search
  applicant screening process, 409
  background checks, 409

job interview guidelines, 418–420
job market research, 390
networking, 392–393
online searches, 390–392
portable skills in, 10
skill and aptitude assessment, 389–390
Employment correspondence
  dossier, 415
  follow-up letter, 420–421
  job application letter
    checklist for, 423
    guidelines for, 408
    solicited, 403–405
    unsolicited, 406–407
  letter of acceptance or refusal, 421
  portfolio, 415–416
  résumés
    checklist for, 422
    combined organization, 397, 401
    components of, 393–397
    electronic submission of, 409–415
    functional, 397, 400
    guidelines for, 398, 402
    organization of, 397
    references in, 395–397
    reverse chronological, 397, 399
    scannable, 410, 411, 412
Employment interview, 416–421
Enclosure notation, 364
Encyclopedias, 128
Engineers as audience, 26–27
Envelope selection, 369
Epidemiological studies, 167
Errors in reasoning, 158–166
Errors of interpretation
  anticipating, 38, 39
  consequences of, 44
Essential information in workplace communication, 15, 16
Ethical communication
  checklist for, 90
  constraints on, 58
  guidelines for, 92
Ethical dilemmas, 83
Ethical issues
  analytical reports and, 561
  blogs and, 353

collaborative project on, 24
complex tables and, 259
euphemisms, 235
hard choices about, 84–85
in job interviews, 418
legal guidelines in addressing, 85–87
memos and, 328
personal choices in, 88–90
plagiarism, 87
in research balance, 117
in summarizing information, 186–187
in team collaboration, 109
technical definitions and, 440, 457
technical descriptions and, 463
unethical communication
  causes of, 77–79
  examples of, 79–82
  groupthink in, 78–79
  recognizing, 76–77
usability checklist on, 43
in use of passive voice, 220
in visual use, 288–290
whistle-blowing, 88–90
in word choice, 246–247
in workplace communication, 15, 17
Ethical judgment criteria, 82–83
Etymology, 444
Euphemisms, 235
Evidence
  criteria for, 61
  defined, 154
  evaluation of, 154–155, 168–169
  hard, vs. soft, 155
  interpretation of, 155–158
  in persuasive appeal, 61–62
  standards of proof, 158
Exaggeration, 235–236
Examples, in persuasive appeal, 62
Exclamation points, 681
Executive abstract, 184–186
Executive summary, 183–184, 603–604
Executives
  as audience, 27
  standards of proofs for, 158
Expanded definition, 442–443, 452, 459

Experiments, as primary source, 146
Expert opinion
  evaluation of, 120
  in persuasive appeal, 62
  reliability of, 119–120
Exploded diagrams, 256, 276
Exploded pie chart, 270
Extemporaneous delivery method, 612
External blogs, 353
Extranet, 127
Eye contact, 628

Face saving, 64
Fact sheets
  as technical communication, 6
  technical marketing, 485, 487
Factual databases, 127
Factual statement, 61
Fair use, 132–133, 134
False advertising laws, 86
Falsification of data, 80
Faulty generalization, 158
Fear, in prevention of change, 59–60
Feasibility analysis, 563–564, 566, 585–592, 594
Feasibility reports. *See also* Feasibility analysis, 338–341
Federal False Claims Act, 89
Feedback
  audience, 42
  focus group, 512
Figures list, 603
Firewall software, 127
Flip charts, 618
Flowcharts, 255, 271, 272
Fluency, editing for, 228–232, 248
Flush right or left, 305
Focus groups, 512
Font, 308
Footers, 303
Forecasting phrase, 308, 694
Formal outline, 196, 198, 199–200
Formal reports, vs. informal, 327
Formal tone, 239
Format error proofing, 21, 22
Frame of reference, 155

Freedom of Information Act, 131, 146
Full-text databases, 127
Functional sequence, 467, 469
Funding proposal, 546–555

Gantt charts, 255, 272, 273, 274
Gender codes, in team conflict, 102–103
General terms, 238
Generalizations
  evaluation of, 169
  faulty, 158
Give-and-take, in persuasion, 55
Global communication, 9–10
Global search and replace function, 247
Glossary, 604–605
Goal statement, 564
Google, 123
Government publications
  access tools for, 131–132
  citation of
    APA style, 661–662
    MLA style, 647–648
  hard copy, 128
  indexes of, 130
  Web sites, 124
Grammar check, 247
Grant proposal, 530–532, 559
Graphic illustrations, 256
diagrams, 275–278
  downloadable, 282–283
  maps, 278, 279
  Graphics software, 282
Graphs. *See also* Visuals
  bar, 260–266
  line, 266–269
  unethical distortions of, 288–290, 289
  uses for, 255
  as visual Big Picture, 253, 254
Grid patterns, 303, 304
Group conflict
  cultural codes in, 102–103
  gender codes in, 102
  managing, 103
  sources of, 101–103
Groupthink, 78–79

Groupware, 108, 301
Guides to literature, 129

Handbooks, 129
Hard copy format, vs. digital, 327
Hard copy sources, 128–133
  abstracts, 131
  card catalogs, 129
  copyright of, 132–133
  guides to literature, 129
  indexes, 129–131
  manual search of, 123
  microforms, 132
  pros and cons of, 123
  reference works, 128–129
Hazard notices, 502–503
Headers, 303, 369
Headings
  format for, 313, 314
  guidelines for, 315
  lay out of, 312
  in letters, 360
  phrasing of, 315–316
  running, 316
  types of, 315
  in usable page design, 312–317
  visual consistency in, 316–317
Highlighting, 311–312
Highly technical documents, 28–29
Horizontal-bar graph, 262, 262
Horizontal grid pattern, 303, 304
Human exposure studies, 167
Human factor, in information exchange, 8–9
Hyperlinked pages
  in a searchable résumé, 411, 412, 413
  instructional, 492, 494
  as technical communication, 6
  in Web page design, 320
Hypertext markup language (HTML), 301, 426–427
Hyphenation, 695

Icons, 256
in visual presentations, 282–283
  vs. symbols, 282–283

Ideals, in ethical judgment-making, 83
Imperative mood, 503
Imprecise writing, 236–237
Impromptu delivery method, 611–612
Inconclusive answer, vs. probable or conclusive answer, 156
Independent clause, 230
Indirect organizing pattern
 in business letters, 371
 in memos, 330–331
Inferences, 158–159
Informal reports, vs. formal, 327
Informal tone, 239, 242
Information
 chunking, 211–212
 currency of, 150–151
 evaluation of
  cultural factors in, 158
  evidence, 154–155
  guidelines for, 168–169
  sources, 150–154
 hoarding of, in team collaboration, 109
 interpretation of, 150
  faulty reasoning in, 158–165
  findings, 155–158
  guidelines for, 168–169
 organization of. *See* Organization strategies
 qualitative, 257
 quantitative, 257
 questions in processing, 253
 summarized, 182–187
Information sources
 biases of, 117, 119
 copyright protection for, 86, 132–134
 deceptive reporting by, 167–168
 depth provided by, 117–118
 evaluation of, 150–154, 168
 government, 131–132
 hard copy, 128–133
 Internet, 123–128
 primary, 138–146
 in research balance, 117
Information technology, 8–9

Informational reports. *See also* Reports
 defined, 327
 meeting minutes, 337–338
 periodic activity reports, 335–336
 progress reports, 331–335
Informative abstract, 183–184
Informative interview, 138–140
Inoffensive usage guidelines, 244–245
Inquiry letters, 373–377
Instant messaging, 108, 351–352
Instructional documents
 affirmative phrasing in, 505
 background information in, 499
 checklist for, 517
 detail levels in, 496, 499–501, 500
 elements of, 495–507
 example of, 509–510
 faulty, 494–495
 formats for, 491–492
 guidelines for, 505–506
 legal liability and, 494–495
 notes and hazards notices in, 502–503
 online documentation, 510–512
 outline for, 507–508
 parallel phrasing in, 504–505
 purpose of, 491
 readability of, 503–505
 sentence structure in, 504
 as technical communication, 6
 title of, 495
 transitional expressions in, 505
 usability testing, 512–514
 visuals in, 496
 vs. procedural, 514–515, 516
Intellectual property
 electronic form copyright, 134
 hard copy form copyright, 132–133
 laws protecting, 86
 stealing, 80–81
Internal blogs, 352
International copyright, 133
International Standards Organization (ISO), 282

Internet and Internet resources, 123–128. *See also* Web-based documents
 blogs and wikis, 124–125
 bulletin boards, 124
 citation of, 126
 community discussion groups, 124
 corporate blogs, 352–354
 downloadable images, 283
 email lists, 125
 evaluation of, 151
 government sites, 124
 in job search, 390–392
 legal issues and, 129
 library chatrooms, 125
 library databases, 125
 online help screens, 492, 510–512
 online news and magazines, 123–124
 online retrieval services, 127–128
 plagiarism of, 87
 privacy issues and, 435–436
 research guidelines for, 126
 RSS feeds, 353, 354
Interpersonal considerations. *See also* Cultural factors
 conveying bad news, 372–373
 in letters, 369–371
 in memos, 328, 330
Interpersonal differences, 101–102
Interviews
 citation of
  APA style, 660–661
  MLA style, 646–647
 guidelines for, 138–140
 for job, 416–421
 sample of, 141
Intranet, 127
Introduction, 197, 507, 539, 572
It, as sentence opener, 224
Italic type, 312, 690

Jargon use, 233–234, 444
Job application letter
 checklist for, 423
 guidelines for, 408

Job application letter *(continued)*
   solicited, 403–405
   unsolicited, 406–407
Job interview, 416–421
Job market research, 390
Job search. *See* Employment and
   job search
Juror, standards of proof for, 158
Justification reports, 341–345
Justified text, 305

Key words
   in any sentence, 219
   as transitions, 694
   in topic sentence, 205
Keyword search, 126
Knowledge suppression, 79

Laboratory studies, 167
Latitude of acceptance, 56, 61
Lawyers, as audience, 27
Legal constraints on communication, 57–58
Legal guidelines on workplace
   communication, 85–87
Legal issues
   accountability, 5
   analytical reports and, 561
   blogs and, 353
   faulty instructions, 494–495
   Internet downloads, 126
   proposals and, 536
   specifications and, 479
   technical definitions and, 440,
      456
   usability checklist on, 43
   in Web site design, 434, 437
   whistle-blowing, 88–90
   in word choice, 246–247
Letter of transmittal, 598, 600, 601
Letterese, 370
Letters
   adjustment, 381–384
   body text, 362–263
   checklist for, 385
   claim or complaint, 377–381
   complimentary closing, 363
   conveying bad news in, 372–373

design features of, 365–369
direct vs. indirect patterns in,
   371
distribution notation, 365
elements of, 360–363, 361
enclosure notation, 364
of inquiry, 373–377
inside address, 362
interpersonal considerations in,
   369–371
of recommendation, 395–397
salutation, 362
signature, 363
specialized parts of, 364–365
as technical communication, 5
in technical marketing, 485
"you" perspective in, 369–370
Liability laws, 86
Libel laws, 85–86
Library chatrooms, 125
Library databases, 125
Lies, legal guidelines on, 85–87
Liking, in acceptance of appeal, 60
Line graphs, 255, 266–269
   unethical distortion of, 289
   Line length, 306
Line spacing, 306–307
Listening behavior, 103–105
Lists
   embedded, 307, 691
   in usable page design, 307–308
   vertical, 307–308, 692–693
Literature
   guides to, 129
   technical marketing, 482–485
Loaded questions, 138

Managers, as audience, 27
Manuals
   copyright of, 133
   instructional, 491
   as technical communication, 6
Maps, 256, 278, 279
Margin of error, 164
Margins, 305–306, 368
Marketing literature, 482–485
Markup languages, 301
Mean, 162–163
Measurement errors, 167

Mechanical error proofing, 21, 22
Median, 162–163
Meeting minutes, 337–338
Meetings, team
   conducting, 98
   face-to-face vs. electronically
      mediated, 108–109
   guidelines for running, 101
Memorized delivery method, 611
Memos. *See also* Reports
   analytical reports as
      feasibility reports, 338–341
      justification reports, 341–345
      recommendation reports, 341
   checklist for, 345–346
   direct vs. indirect patterns in,
      330–331
   elements of, 328, 329
   informational reports as
      meeting minutes, 337–338
      periodic activity reports,
         335–336
      progress reports, 331–335
   interpersonal considerations in,
      328, 330
   paper, 328
   persuasion styles in, 53–55
   purpose of, 328
   as technical communication, 5
Meta-analysis, bias in, 165
Microforms, 132
Mind-mapping, 106
Misleading euphemisms, 235
Misleading terminology, 165
MLA documentation style
   books, 642–644
   electronic sources, 648–651
   miscellaneous sources, 645–448
   parenthetical references,
      640–641
   periodicals, 644–645
   sample works cited page, 652,
      653–654
*MLA Handbook for Writers of
   Research Papers, 6th ed.,* 640
Mode, 162–163
Modem, 234
Modified block format, 365, 366
Modifiers, 217–218, 678–679
Multiline graph, 266, 267

Multiple-band graph, 269
Multiple bar graph, 260, 262, 262
Multiple users
    document technicality for, 31–32
    Web-based documents for, 33

Negative expressions, 227–228
Networked employee, 23
Networking, in job search,
    392–393
New media, 6
Newspaper indexes, 130
Nominalizations, 226–227
Nonprofit sector, 8, 525
Nonsexist usage guidelines,
    243–244
Nontechnical document, 30–31
Note-taking, 635
Notes, in instructional documents,
    502
Nouns, modifying, 218
Numbered documentation styles
    books, 668
    citations in text, 667
    discipline-specific manuals on,
        665
    periodicals, 668–669
Numbers use, 696–697
Numerical tables, 255, 257

Objective description, 463
Obligations, in ethical judgments,
    82
Offensive tone, 242
Offensive usage, 244–245
Ombudsperson, 90
100-percent bar graph, 263, 264
Online help screens, 320, 510–512
Online news and magazine
    sources, 123–128
Online newsfeeds, 6–7, 353, 354
Online privacy issues, 435–436
Online retrieval services, 126,
    127–128
Online submission of résumés,
    410, 411, 413, 414
Opaque projection, 619
Open-ended questions, 142

Optical scanners, 410–411
Oral presentations
    avoiding pitfalls in, 609–610
    checklist for, 631
    common mistakes in, 610
    cultural factors in, 629
    delivering, 625–629
    delivery methods in, 611–612, 613
    listener questions in, 628–629
    outlining, 614–615
    physical style in, 627–628
    planning for, 610–612
    preparation for, 612–623
    pros and cons of, 609
    software guidelines for, 623–624
    visuals in, 615–623, 626–627
Organization charts, 255, 271
Organization strategies
    accessibility and, 5
    color use in, 284–285
    for document
        chunking, 211–212
        classification in, 195
        cultural factors in, 200
        outlining, 196–200
        overview of, 212–213
        paragraphing, 204–207
        partitions, 195
        report design worksheet, 200,
            201–202
        sequencing in, 207–211
        storyboarding, 200, 203
    for instructional documents,
        517
    for memos, 330–331
    for summaries, 187
    usability checklist on, 43
    for Web site, 433
Organizational constraints on
    communication, 56–57
Organizational publications, 146
Outline view, 196
Outlines, 196–200
    alphanumeric notation in,
        198–199
    for analytical reports, 571–583
    decimal notation in, 199
    formal, 196, 198, 199–200
    for instructional documents,
        507–508

for oral presentations, 613–615
for process description, 475
for product description, 469–470
for proposals, 539–544
    sentence, 199
    topic, 205
Overhead projectors, 618
Oversimplification, 5
Overstatement, 235–236
Overview of document organiza-
    tion, 212–213

Page design
    accessibility and, 5
    audience considerations in, 317
    checklist for, 321
    defined, 298
    effective, 300
    flowchart for, 302
    headings in, 312–317
    highlighting guidelines, 311–312
    importance of, 298
    ineffective, 299
    in instructional documents,
        517
    list use in, 307–308
    margins, 305–306
    multicolumn, 506
    on-screen documents, 318–320
    of proposals, 556
    shaping the page, 303–308
    skills needed for, 301–302
    of technical definitions, 457
    of technical descriptions, 485
    typography in, 308–310
    usability checklist on, 43
    user profile in developing, 38
    in Web site usability, 427, 437
    of workplace letter, 361
Page numbers, 303
Pamphlets, 6
Paper communication, 7
Paper selection, 303
Paper trail, 328
Paperless office, 298
Paragraphs, 204–207
    in page design, 307
    transitions within and between,
        693–694

Parallel phrasing, for instructions, 504–505
Parallelism, faulty, 679–680
Paraphrases, 638–639
    citation of
        in APA style, 655–656
        in MLA style, 640–641
    plagiarism of, 638
Parentheses, 690
Parenthetical definition, 441
Partition, in document organization, 195
Parts, analysis of, 446
Passive voice, 220, 221–222
Patent indexes, 130
PDF files, 320
Peer review, in collaborative teamwork, 107–108
Percentage distortion, 163–164
Performance objectives, for document, 36–37, 40
Periodical indexes, 130
Periodicals, citation of
    APA style, 658–659
    CSE style, 668–669
    MLA style, 644–645
Periods, 681
Person-first language, 245
Personal bias, 157, 242–243, 567
Personal observation, as primary source, 146
Personal profile online, for protection of, 414–415
Personal pronouns, 240–241
Personal statement
    audience expectation in, 709–710
    final draft, 712, 713
    first draft, 710, 711
    two additional examples, 713–716
Personality tests, in employment process, 409
Persuasion
    audience and
        connecting with, 53–55
        reaction prediction, 51
        resistance and receptivity to, 51–52
    causal argument in, 161
    checklist for, 71

common goals and values in, 62–63
in conflict management, 103
constraints on, 56–59
cultural context in, 63–65
defined, 49
emotional reaction to, 59–60
give-and-take in, 55
goals in, 50–51
guidelines for, 65–67
in proposals, 523–524
reasonability in, 56
shaping argument in, 67–70
specificity in, 56
support of claims in, 60–63
in workplace communication, 15, 16–17
PERT charts, 274, 274
Photographs, 256, 279–282
Pictograms, 255, 274, 275
    unethical distortion of, 290
Pie charts, 255, 269–271, 270
Placement folder, 415
Plagiarism
    antiplagiarism tools, 636
    in editing process, 107, 735
    faulty paraphrasing as, 638
    in quoting the work of others, 636
    recognizing, 87
    in team collaboration, 109
    testing for, 735–736
    of Web-based documents, 87
Plain English use, 370
Planning proposal, 528–530
Point-by-point pattern, 593–594
Portable skills, 10
Portfolio, 415–416
Positive expressions, 227–228, 242, 505
Possessives, 687
Posters, 618
Postscripts, 365
Power connection, in persuasion, 53–54
PowerPoint, 620–623
Prefaces, 224–225
Prepositions, 226
Presentation software, 282, 620–623
Presentations. *See* Oral presentations

Primary audience, 31–32
Primary sources
    bias in, 146
    experiments as, 146
    informative interviews as, 138–140
    inquiry letters, phone calls, and email inquiries as, 143
    organizational publications as, 146
    personal observation as, 146
    public records as, 146
    surveys and questionnaires, 140–145
Privacy
    blogs and, 353
    electronic résumés and, 414
    email and, 348–349
    employee online monitoring, 435–436
Privacy laws, 86
Probable answer, vs. conclusive or inconclusive answer, 156
Probable causes, 160
Problem-causes-solution sequence, 209–210
Procedures, 514–516
Process description, 463, 465
    outline for, 475
    situation requiring, 476–478
Process visual, 468
Product description, 463, 464
    outline and model for, 469–472
    situation requiring, 472–474
Production vs. safety issues, 78
Professional organizations, in job search, 392
Progress reports, 331–335, 718, 720
Project management, collaborative, 97–98
Project management software, 108
Project planning form, 99
Pronouns, 217
    agreement with referent, 675
    faulty case, 677–678
    in headings, 315
Proofreading. *See also* Editing
    checklist for, 22
    common errors found by, 21

guidelines for, 21
in workplace communication,
    21–23
Proposal process, 524–526, 718
Proposals
    audience for, 523–524, 534–535
    benefits in, 535
    case study of, 544–545
    checklist for, 556
    claims in, 535–536
    detail levels in, 536
    documentation in, 538–539
    elements of, 534–539
    evaluation criteria for, 525
    funding, 546–555
    in nonprofit sector, 525
    outline for, 539–544
    paperless, 525–526
    persuasion in, 523–524
    planning, 528–530
    readability of, 537
    requests for proposals (RFPs), 6,
        525, 526, 527, 528
    research, 530–532
    sales, 532–534
    supplements in, 538
    as technical communication, 6
    title of, 534
    types of, 526–534
    visuals in, 537
    vs. reports, 523
Proprietary information
    laws protecting, 86
    stealing, 80–81
Prose tables, 255, 257, 258
Protocol analysis, 514
Psychological constraints on com-
    munication, 58–59
Public, as audience, 27
Public domain, 133
Public records, 146
Punctuation marks
    apostrophe, 687–688
    avoiding ambiguous, 691
    brackets, 690–691
    colon, 682–683
    comma, 683–686
    dashes, 691
    ellipses, 689
    end punctuation, 681

error proofing, 21, 22
    quotation marks, 688–689
    semicolon, 682

Qualifiers, 228–229
Qualitative information, 257
Qualitative testing, 512, 514
Quantitative information, 257
Quantitative testing, 514
Question headings, 315, 316
Question marks, 681
Questionnaire, 142–143, 144, 145
Questions
    in analytical report, 561
    in information processing, 253
    in informative interview,
        138–139, 141
    in job interview, 417–418
    loaded, 138
    in making human connection,
        370–371
    open-ended, 142
    in presentation preparation, 611
    in research, 115–116
    types of, 142
Quotation marks, 688–689
Quotations, citation of, 636–638

Ranking, distortions in, 164
Rational connection, in persua-
    sion, 53, 54–55
Reasonable criteria, in ethical
    judgments, 82
Reasoning
    causal, 159–161
    error avoidance in, 158–166
    generalizations, 159
    statistical, 162–167
    vs. rationalizing, 157
Reciprocation, 60
Recommendation reports, 341, 342
Recommendations, 567–569, 570,
    582
Redundancy, 223
Reference cards, 6, 492, 493
References, in résumé, 395–397
Relationship connection, in persu-
    ation, 53, 54

Relationships, color in showing, 285
Reliability, of research, 166
Repetition, needless vs. useful,
    223–224
Report design worksheet, 200,
    201–202
Report writing process case study
    brainstorming list, 703–704
    document planning, 702–704
    document revision, 704–706
    editing cycle in, 733
    final draft, 707–709
    first draft, 701–702
Reports
    abstract for, 603–604
    analytical
        case study for, 583–592
        checklist for, 594–595
        conclusions and recommenda-
            tions in, 567–569
        data amount in, 564–565, 567
        defined, 327
        elements of, 564–571
        ethical implications, 561
        feasibility reports, 338–341.
            See also Feasibility analysis
        goal identification in, 564
        guidelines for, 593–594
        justification reports, 341–345
        legal implications, 561
        outline for, 571–583
        personal bias and, 567
        recommendation reports, 341,
            342–343
        self-assessment and, 569, 571
        supplements in, 583
        visuals in, 567, 568
        appendices, 605–606
    causal reasoning in, 160
    citation of, 646
    cover page in, 598
    documentation in, 606
    executive summary of, 603–604
    formal vs. informal, 327
    glossary, 604–605
    informational
        defined, 327
        meeting minutes, 337–338
        periodic activity reports,
            335–336

Reports *(continued)*
  progress reports, 331–335
  vs. analytical, 327
  letter of transmittal for, 598, 600, 601
  in memo form. *See* Memos
  oral. *See* Oral presentations
  table of contents, 601, 602, 603
  tables and figures list, 603
  as technical communication, 6
  title page in, 598, 599
  vs. proposals, 523
Representational diagrams, 256
Requests for proposals (RFPs), 6, 525, 526, 527, 528
Research
  Bias in. *See* bias
  blogs and wikis in, 125
  defining questions in, 115–116
  depth of, 117–18
  electronic sources of, 127–128
  evaluation of, 119
    cultural factors in, 158
    evidence, 154–155
    guidelines for, 168–169
    sources, 150–154
  expert opinion in, 119–120
  government sources in, 131–132
  hard copy sources in, 128–133
  Internet sources in, 123–127
  interpretation of, 119, 150
    faulty reasoning in, 158–165
    findings in, 155–158
    guidelines for, 168–169
  for job interview, 417
  limits of, 166–168
  note-taking in, 635
  primary sources in, 138–146
  role of, 135
  sequence of, 115
  sources in. *See* Information sources
  strategic, 151
  underlying assumptions in, 156–157
Research process checklist, 170
Research proposal, 530–532, 559
Research report case study
  final report, 722–732
  final report stage, 721
  project documents, 718–720

Resistance, of audience, 51–52
Résumés. *See also* Employment correspondence
  checklist for, 422
  combined organization, 397, 401
  components of, 393–397
  electronic, 409–415
  functional, 397, 400
  guidelines for, 398, 402
  organization of, 397
  preferred forms of, by purpose, 414
  references in, 395–397
  reverse chronological, 397, 399
Revisions, 249
Routine claims, 377–379
RSS feeds, 353, 354
Run-on sentence, 673
Running heads and feet, 315, 316

Safety procedure, 515, 516
Safety vs. production issues, 78
Sales proposal, 532–534
Salutation, 362
Sample group, identification of, 140
Sans serif typeface, 308–309
Sarbanes-Oxley Act (2002), 89
Saving face, 64
Scannable résumés, 410, 411, 412
Scanners, optical, 410–411
Scarcity, persuasion and, 60
Schematic diagram, 256
Scientific Style and Format: The CSE Manual for Authors, Editors, and Publishers, 6th ed., 665
Scientists
  as audience, 26
  standards of proof for, 158
Scripted delivery method, 612
Searchable (hyperlinked) résumés, 411, 413, 414
Secondary audience, 31–32
Self-assessment, in preparing recommendations, 569, 571
Semicolons, 682
Semiformal tone, 239
Semitechnical document, 29–30

Sentence definition, 442
Sentence errors
  comma splicing, 673
  faulty agreement- pronoun and referent, 675
  faulty agreement- subject and verb, 674
  faulty coordination, 675–676
  faulty modification, 678–679
  faulty parallelism, 679–680
  faulty pronoun case, 677–678
  faulty subordination, 676–677
  proofreading for, 21, 22
  run-on sentence, 673
  sentence fragment, 671–672
  sentence shifts, 680–681
Sentence outline, 199
Sentences
  choppy, 229–231
  varying construction and length, 231–232
Sequencing of document, 207–211
Serif typeface, 308–309
Setting, for document use, 37, 39
Sexist usage, 243–244
Signature block, 363
Simple band graph, 268
Simple bar graph, 260, 262
Simple line graph, 266, 267
Simple pie chart, 270
Simplification, vs. clarity, 5
Skill assessment, 389–390
Slang, 246
Slide projection, 619
Social constraints on communication, 58–59
Social pressure, in unethical communication, 77–78
Social validation, in acceptance of appeal, 60
Software images, 282–283
Software theft laws, 86
Sound bytes, vs. clarity, 5
Sources. *See* Information sources
Spatial sequence, 207–208, 467
Special interest groups, research funded by, 151, 153
Specific terms, 238
Specification, 479–482

Specificity
  in persuasion, 56
  in word selection, 238
Spellcheck, 21, 247, 697
Spreadsheet software, 282
Stacked-bar graph, 262–263, 263
Standard Operating Procedure
    (SOP), 515
Standardized general markup lan-
    guage (SGML), 301
Standards of proof, 158
Statement headings, 315, 316
Stationery selection, 368
Statistical fallacies, 162–165
Statistics, as evidence, 61–62
Status, as expert, 119
Stealth marketing, 353
Storyboarding, 106, 200, 203, 615,
    616
Strategic research, 151
Style. *See also* Editing; Writing style
  checklist for, 248
  in instructional documents, 517
  in proposals, 556
  in technical definitions, 457
  of technical descriptions, 485
  of visuals, 293
Style sheets, 301–302
Subject and verb agreement, 674
Subject line, 364
Subjective description, 463
Subordinate clause, 676–677
Summaries, 174–191. *See also*
    Abstracts
  case study of, 176–182
  closing, 183
  defined, 174
  elements of, 175
  ethical considerations for,
    186–187
  executive, 183–184
  forms of, 182–186
  guidelines for, 175–176
  importance of, 188
  purpose of, 174–175
  technical, 183–184
  usability checklist for, 187
Supplements
  accessibility of, 5
  in analytical reports, 583

Support paragraph, 204–205
Suppressed information, 79
Surveys, 140–141, 166
Symbols, 256
  in visual presentations, 282–283
  vs. icons, 282–283
Synonyms, 236–237, 694

Table of contents, 601, 602, 603
Tables
  construction of, 261
  data in, 258
  prose, 257, 258
  uses for, 255, 257
Tables and figures, list of, 603
Task outline, in preparing a man-
    ual, 36–38
Teamwork. *See* Collaborative
    teamwork
Technical communication
  decimal notation in, 199
  defined, 2
  global audience of, 9
  need for, in all fields, 7–8
  purpose of, 34–36
  testing and revision of, 42
  types of, 5–7
Technical communicators
  career paths of, 7
  skills of, 7, 10
Technical definitions
  analysis of parts in, 446
  audience and use profiles for,
    449, 451
  background discussion in, 445
  checklist for, 457
  comparison and contrast in,
    447–448
  etymology in, 444
  examples in, 448–449
  expanded, 442–443, 452, 459
  expansion methods for, 444–449
  guidelines for, 456–457
  implications of, 440
  for layperson, 461
  levels of detail in, 441–443
  material requirements in, 448
  operating principle in, 445–446
  parenthetical, 441

  placement of, 454–456
  purpose of, 440–441
  sentence, 442
  situations requiring, 449–453
  visuals in, 447
Technical description
  case study, 472–475
  checklist for, 485
  chronological sequence in, 469
  descriptive sequence in, 467, 469
  detail levels in, 466–467
  elements of, 466–469
  functional sequence in, 467, 469
  high-information words in, 466
  in marketing literature, 482–485
  model for, 469–472
  objectivity in, 463–466
  process, 463, 465, 475
  product, 463
  purposes of, 463
  situations requiring, 472–474,
    476–478
  spatial sequence in, 467
  in specifications, 479–482
  types of, 463
  visuals in, 467
Technical marketing literature,
    482–485
Technical report indexes, 130
Technical summary, 183–184
Technicality of document
  high, 28–29
  for multiple users, 31–32
  nontechnical, 30–31
  semitechnical, 29–30
Telecommuter workplace, 23
Teleconferencing, 108
Telephone
  inquiries by, 377
  job interview by, 419–420
Terminology, misleading, 165
Testing and revision of document,
    42
There, as sentence opener, 224
Thinking process, writing as cen-
    tral to, 19
3-D bar graph, 263
Thumbnail sketch, 278
Time constraints on communica-
    tion, 58

Title
abbreviation of, 694–695
of instructional documents, 495
of persuasive proposal, 534
of technical description, 466
Title page, 598, 599
Tone, 238–244, 248
Topic headings, 315, 316
Topic sentence, 205
Topic statement, 205
Trade secrets laws, 86
Transitions, within and between
paragraphs, 693–694
Transmittal letter, 598, 600, 601
Tree chart, 255, 271, 273
Tree diagram, 106
Triteness, 234–235
Troubleshooting advice, 501–502
Truth, as level of certainty, 156
Typeface, 308, 309–311
Typist's initials, 364
Typographical error proofing, 21,
22
Typography, 308–310

Underlying assumptions, 156–157
Unethical communication
causes of, 77–79
examples of, 79–82
groupthink in, 78–79
recognizing, 76–77
word choice and, 246–247
Unjustified text, 305–306
U.S. government publications
access tools for, 131–132
citation of
APA style, 661–662
MLA style, 647–648
hard copy, 128
indexes of, 130
Web sites, 124
Usability
audience expectations and,
26–27
audience feedback on, 42
audience profiling for, 34–38
checklist for, 43
collaborative project on, 46–47
defined, 26

design plan and, 38–41
document technicality and,
28–32
of instructional documents,
512–514
purpose of, 26
of summaries, 187
testing of, 42, 512–514
of visuals, 293
of Web site, 427–428, 434
Usability survey, 513
Use and audience profile, 34–38,
39, 70
User-centered document, 2
User feedback, 42
Users. *See* Audience

Validity, of research, 166
Verbs
agreement with subject, 674
avoiding weak, 225
clarifying words preceding, 504
Vertical list, 307–308, 692–693
Videoconferencing, 108
Virtual workplace, 23
Visual noise, 293
Visualization, 256
Visuals
accessibility and, 5
in analytical reports, 567, 568
audience and selection of, 260
charts, 269–274
citation of, 648
color use in, 283–288
cultural considerations in use of,
290, 292
downloadable images, 282–283
essential features of, 254
ethical considerations in,
288–290
graphic illustrations
diagrams, 276–278
maps, 278, 279
graphs
bar, 260–266
line, 266–269
uses for, 255
as visual Big Picture, 253, 254
importance of, 253–254

in instructional documents, 496,
497
in mind-mapping, 106
in oral presentations, 615–623,
626–627
photographs, 279–282
planning sheet for, 291
PowerPoint, 620–623
in proposals, 537
selection of, 257
software, 282–283
in technical definitions, 447
in technical descriptions, 467
textual integration of, 292–293
types of, 255–256
in unethical communication, 80
usability checklist for, 293
in Web site usability, 428, 437
when to use, 254

Warning notices, in instructional
documents, 502–503
Web-based documents and sites.
See also Internet resources
checklist for, 436–437
color use in, 283–284
design of, 318–320
domain type, 153
elements of, 427–428
evaluating sources of, 153–154
FAQ format in, 448–449
government, 131–132
guidelines for creating, 432–434
library databases of, 125
markup languages for, 301
for multiple users, 33
online help screens, 320
online retrieval services for,
127–128
plagiarism of, 87
privacy issues and, 435–436
for professional organizations,
392
research guidelines for, 126
as research sources, 118
résumé posting on, 411–414
summary format of, 186
on technical marketing, 484
unethical, 81

Web browsers, 426
Web conferencing, 108
Webmaster, 153
Whistle-blowing, 88–90
White space, 303, 305
Whiteboards, 618
Wikis, 124–125, 352
Word choice, 248
Word order, 218–219
Word-processing software, 282
Word-processing templates, 365, 368
Word specificity, 238
Wordiness, 223

Works cited. *See* Documentation of sources
Writing process
    collaborative, 110
    creative and critical thinking in, 19, 699
    decision making in, 699
    stages in, 18–19
    in summarization, 175–176
Writing style. *See also* Editing
    accessibility and, 5
    elements of, 216
    ethical implications, 246–247
    inefficient, 216

legal implications, 246–247
mechanics of, 694–697
of summaries, 187
tone selection in, 238–244
transitions, 693–694
usability checklist on, 43
Written communication
    creative and critical thinking in, 18–19
    prevalence of, in all careers, 7–8
    types of, 11

"You" perspective, 369–370